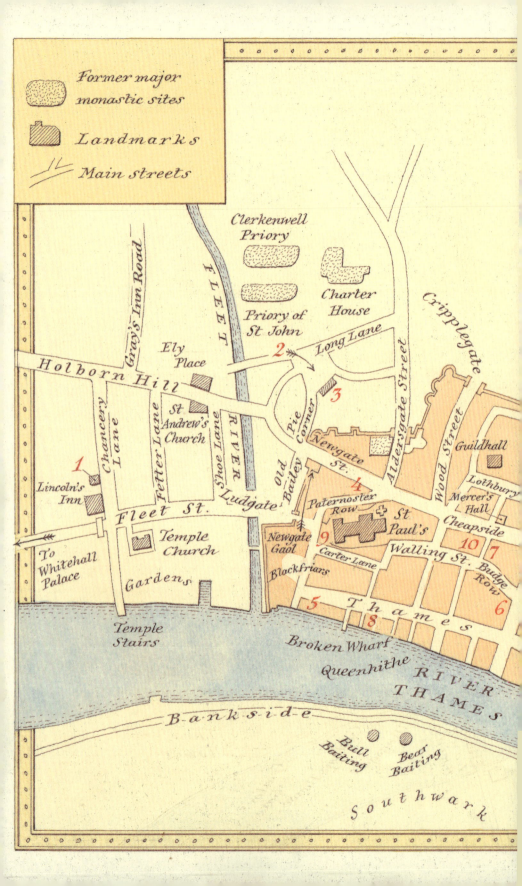

Former major
monastic sites

Landmarks

Main streets

Clerkenwell
Priory

Charter
House

Priory of
St John

Long Lane

Cripplegate

FLEET

Gray's Inn Road

Ely
Place

Holborn Hill

2

3

Aldersgate Street

Wood Street

Guildhall

Chancery Lane

St
Andrew's
Church

Fetter Lane

Shoe Lane

RIVER

Newgate St.

1

Lincoln's
Inn

Fleet St.

Ludgate

Old Bailey

Pie Corner

4

Paternoster Row

Lothbury

Mercer's
Hall

Cheapside

10

7

To
Whitehall
Palace

Temple
Church

Newgate
Gaol

9

St
Paul's

Walling St.

Budge Row

Gardens

Blackfriars

Carter Lane

5

Thames

6

Temple
Stairs

8

Broken Wharf

Queenhithe

RIVER
THAMES

B A N K S I D E

Bull
Baiting

Bear
Baiting

S o u t h w a r k

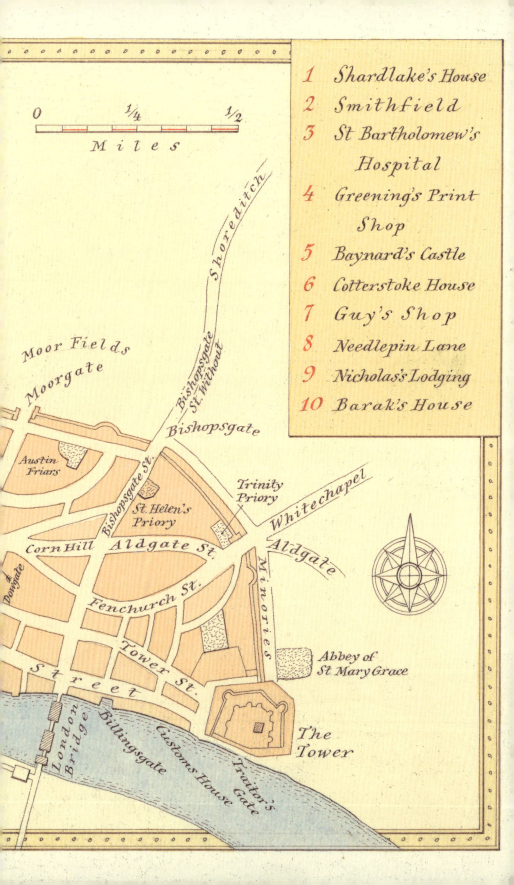

Praise for LAMENTATION

'Shardlake's back and better than ever . . . *Lamentation*, like its predecessors, is a triumph both as detective fiction and as a novel'
Independent on Sunday

'This gripping new novel by the inventive C. J. Sansom shows that, when it comes to intriguing Tudor-based narratives, Hilary Mantel has a serious rival'
Sunday Times

'Sansom is highly skilled at weaving together the threads of his plot with the real and riveting history . . . *Lamentation* is a wonderful, engaging read. The atmosphere of fear and suspicion is brilliantly rendered. Shardlake is always convincing, and he is endearingly battle-scarred and weary from his earlier adventures . . . spine-tingling'
The Times

'So engrossing . . . even when judged by the high standards of the earlier Shardlake novels, this one stands out . . . The orchestration of plot over 600 pages, and the final twist, is literary craft of a high order . . . Sansom has surely established himself as one of the best novelists around'
Spectator

'A terrific book . . . It is a convincing account of a cruel and fascinating period and a very exciting read'
Literary Review

'Sansom conjures the atmosphere, costumes and smells of Tudor London with vigour, from the gilded halls of Whitehall Palace to the dungeons of the Tower'
Observer

'Brilliantly conveys the uncertainty of the time when a frail young prince would ascend the throne with different factions fighting for regency . . . Sansom has the gift of plunging us into the different worlds of the period'
Independent

'A triumph of Tudor history and mystery . . . as bristling as its predecessors with outlandish deaths, suspicious behaviour, jeopardy and plots of fiendish deviousness . . . a rousing tour de force of period recreation'   *Sunday Times*

'The best novel in this richly entertaining series . . . History never seemed so real'   *New York Times*

'At once compulsively readable and highly satisfying . . . Sansom handles a large cast and a complex narrative with great skill and his set piece scenes . . . are simply stupendous. An entirely engrossing novel with an intriguing twist'   *Daily Express*

'Brings together a thrilling story, Tudor background and utterly believable characters . . . As ever with C. J. Sansom, the history is delineated with a masterly hand'   Antonia Fraser, *The Lady*

'Shardlake lives and breathes in an utterly convincing world, drawing the reader into the darker corners of history'   Philippa Gregory

'A great attraction of C. J. Sansom's series of novels set in the reign of Henry VIII lies not merely in the authentic background but in the personality of the main character – that persistent seeker after truth, Matthew Shardlake . . . Sansom brilliantly exploits the hindsight we bring to the historical novel, for we turn the pages with bated breath, waiting for the inevitable'   *Independent*

'Superb . . . terrific stuff, for both fans and newcomers to the series'
Laura Wilson, *Guardian*

'Hugely enjoyable . . . it is the rich characterization that really brings this series to life, none more so than Shardlake himself, a beguiling hero'   *Financial Times*

Praise for SOVEREIGN

'Don't open this book if you have anything urgent pending. Its grip is so compulsive that, until you reach its final page, you'll have to be almost physically prised away from it . . . Sansom's remarkable talents really blaze out'   *Sunday Times*

'Deeper, stronger and subtler than most novels in this genre (including Umberto Eco's *The Name of the Rose*) . . . This gripping and engaging series seems ominously prescient about the present, as well as genuinely enlightening about the past'   *Independent on Sunday*

'I was enthralled by *Sovereign* by C. J. Sansom, a novel combining detection with a brilliant description of Henry VIII's spectacular Progress to the North and it's terrifying aftermath'
P. D. James, *Sunday Telegraph*

'Sansom is excellent on contemporary horrors. This is a remorseless portrait of a violent, partly lawless country . . . You can lose yourself in this world'   *Independent*

'Historical crime fiction at its best'   *Sainsbury's Magazine*

'A brilliant evocation of tyranny in Tudor England'   *Literary Review*

'A fine setting for crime fiction and C. J. Sansom exploits it superbly . . . Never mind the crime: this is a terrific novel'
Times Literary Supplement

'I have enjoyed C. J. Sansom's series of historical novels set in Tudor England progressively more and more. *Sovereign* is the best so far . . . Sansom has the perfect mixture of novelistic passion and historical detail'   Antonia Fraser, *Sunday Telegraph*

'Both marvellously exciting to read and a totally convincing evocation of England in the reign of Henry VIII'   *Spectator*

Praise for DARK FIRE

'One of the author's greatest gifts is the immediacy of his descriptions, for he writes about the past as if it were the living present'
Colin Dexter

'Sansom's magnificent books set in the reign of Henry VIII bring to life the sounds and smells of Tudor England . . . *Dark Fire* is a creation of real brilliance, one of those rare pieces of crime fiction that deserves to be hailed as a novel in its own right'
Sunday Times

'I've discovered a new crime writer who's going to be a star. He's C. J. Sansom, whose just-published second novel, *Dark Fire*, is wonderful stuff, featuring a sort of Tudor Rebus who moves through the religious and political chaos of the 1540s with sinister élan'
James Naughtie, *Herald*

'Sansom gives us a broad view of politics – Tudor housing to rival Rachman, Dickensian prisons, a sewage-glutted Thames, beggars in gutters, conspiracies at court and a political system predicated on birth not merit, intrigue not intelligence . . . a strong and intelligent novel'
Guardian

'Spellbinding . . . Sansom's vivid portrayal of squalid, stinking, bustling London; the city's wealth and poverty; the brutality and righteousness of religious persecution; and the complexities of English law make this a suspenseful, colourful and compelling tale'
Publishers Weekly

Praise for DOMINION

'One of the thrills of *Dominion* is to see a writer whose previous talent has been for the captivating dramatization of real history creating an invented mid-twentieth century Britain that has the intricate detail and delineation of JRR Tolkien's Middle Earth . . . A tremendous novel that shakes historical preconceptions while also sending shivers down the spine'   Mark Lawson, *Guardian*

'Haunting, vividly imagined . . . There will be few better historical novels published this year, even if much of the history it uses never really happened'   *Sunday Times*

'Every detail of this nightmare Britain rings true . . . both as a historical novel and a thriller, *Dominion* is absorbing, mordant and written with a passionate persuasiveness'   *Independent on Sunday*

'Evocative, alarming and richly satisfying'   *Daily Express*

'The chase is exciting and the action thrilling, but the really absorbing part of this excellent book is the detailed creation of a society that could so easily have existed'   *Literary Review*

'Masterly . . . sketched with hallucinatory clarity . . . Sansom, whose Tudor mysteries showed his feeling for the plight of good people in a brutal, treacherous society, builds his nightmare Britain from the sooty bricks of truth'   *Independent*

'Absorbing, thoughtful . . . Part adventure, part espionage, all encompassed by terrific atmosphere and a well-argued "it might have been"'
                                                                    The Times

Lamentation

C. J. SANSOM was educated at Birmingham University,
where he took a BA and then a PhD in history. After working
in a variety of jobs, he retrained as a solicitor and practised in Sussex,
until becoming a full-time writer. Sansom is the bestselling author
of the critically acclaimed Shardlake series, as well as
Winter in Madrid and *Dominion*. He lives in Sussex.

Discover more at www.cjsansom.com

and facebook.com/CJSansomAuthor

C. J. SANSOM

Lamentation

§

MANTLE

First published 2014 by Mantle

This paperback edition published 2015 by Mantle
an imprint of Pan Macmillan, a division of Macmillan Publishers Limited
Pan Macmillan, 20 New Wharf Road, London N1 9RR
Basingstoke and Oxford
Associated companies throughout the world
www.panmacmillan.com

ISBN 978-0-230-74420-2

1 3 5 7 9 8 6 4 2

A CIP catalogue record for this book is available from the British Library.

Map artwork by Neil Gower
Typeset by Ellipsis Digital Limited, Glasgow
Printed and bound by CPI Group (UK) Ltd, Croydon, CR0 4YY

To Roz Brody, Mike Holmes, Jan King
and William Shaw, the stalwart writers' group,
for all their comments and suggestions for
Lamentation as for the last seven books.

AUTHOR'S NOTE

The details of religious differences in sixteenth-century England may seem unimportant today, but in the 1540s they were, literally, matters of life and death. Henry VIII had rejected the Pope's supremacy over the English Church in 1532–33, but for the rest of his reign he oscillated between keeping traditional Catholic practices and moving towards Protestant ones. Those who wanted to keep traditional ways – some of whom would have liked to return to Roman allegiance – were variously called conservatives, traditionalists, and even papists. Those who wanted to move to a Lutheran, and later Calvinist practice, were called radicals or Protestants. The terms conservative and radical did not then have their later connotations of social reform. There were many who shifted from one side to the other during the years 1532–58, either from genuine non-alignment or opportunism. Some, though not all, religious radicals thought the state should do more to alleviate poverty; but radicals and conservatives alike were horrified by the ideas of the Anabaptists. Very few in number but a bogey to the political elite, the Anabaptists believed that true Christianity meant sharing all goods in common.

The touchstone of acceptable belief in 1546 was adherence to the traditional Catholic doctrine of 'transubstantiation' – the belief that when the priest consecrated the bread and wine during Mass, they were transformed into the physical body and blood of Christ. That was a traditionalist belief from which Henry never deviated; under his 'Act of Six Articles' of 1539, to deny this was treason, punishable by burning at the stake. His other core belief was in the Royal Supremacy; that

God intended monarchs to be the supreme arbiters of doctrine in their territories, rather than the Pope.

☦

The political events in England in the summer of 1546 were dramatic and extraordinary. Anne Askew really was convicted of heresy, tortured, and burned at the stake, and she did leave an account of her sufferings. The celebrations to welcome Admiral d'Annebault to London did take place, and on the scale described. The story of Bertano is true. There was a plot by traditionalists to unseat Catherine Parr; and she did write *Lamentation of a Sinner*. It was not, though, so far as we know, stolen.

☦

Whitehall Palace, taken by Henry from Cardinal Wolsey and greatly expanded by him, occupied an area bounded roughly today by Scotland Yard, Downing Street, the Thames and the modern thoroughfare of Whitehall, with recreational buildings on the western side of the road. The whole palace was burned to the ground in two disastrous accidental fires in the 1690s; the only building to survive was the Banqueting House, which had not yet been built in Tudor times.

☦

Some words in Tudor English had a different meaning from today. The term 'Dutch' was used to refer to the inhabitants of modern Holland and Belgium. The term 'Scotch' was used to refer to Scots.

☦

The name 'Catherine' was spelt in several different ways – Catherine, Katharine, Katryn and Kateryn – it was the last spelling which the Queen used to sign her name. However, I have used the more common, modern Catherine.

Principal Dramatis Personae

and their places on the political–religious spectrum

In this novel there is an unusually large number of characters who actually lived, although, of course, the portrayal of their personalities is mine.

The royal family

King Henry VIII

Prince Edward, age 8, heir to the throne

The Lady Mary, age 30, strongly traditionalist

The Lady Elizabeth, age 12–13

Queen Catherine Parr

Family of Catherine Parr, all reformers (see Family Tree, pp. xx–xxi)

Lord William Parr, her uncle

Sir William Parr, her brother

Lady Anne Herbert, her sister

Sir William Herbert, her brother-in-law

Members of the King's Privy Council

John Dudley, Lord Lisle, reformer

Edward Seymour, Earl of Hertford, reformer

Thomas Cranmer, Archbishop of Canterbury, reformer

Thomas, Lord Wriothesley, Lord Chancellor, no firm alignment

Sir Richard Rich, no firm alignment

Sir William Paget, Chief Secretary, no firm alignment

Stephen Gardiner, Bishop of Winchester, traditionalist

Thomas Howard, Duke of Norfolk, traditionalist

Others

William Somers, the King's fool

Jane, fool to Queen Catherine and the Lady Mary

Mary Odell, the Queen's maid-in-waiting

William Cecil, later Chief Minister to Queen Elizabeth I

Sir Edmund Walsingham

John Bale

Anne Askew (Kyme)

Lamentation

CATHERINE PARR

Sir William
Parr

Maud
Green
(1492 ~ 1531)

═

Sir Thomas
Parr
(1478 ~ 1517)

m.
1509

①   (i)   (ii)   (iii)

CATHERINE
PARR
b. 1512

═

Edward
Borough
d. 1533

═

John Neville
Lord
Latimer
d. 1543

═

HENRY
VIII

m.
1529

m.
1534

m.
1543

ABBREVIATED FAMILY TREE

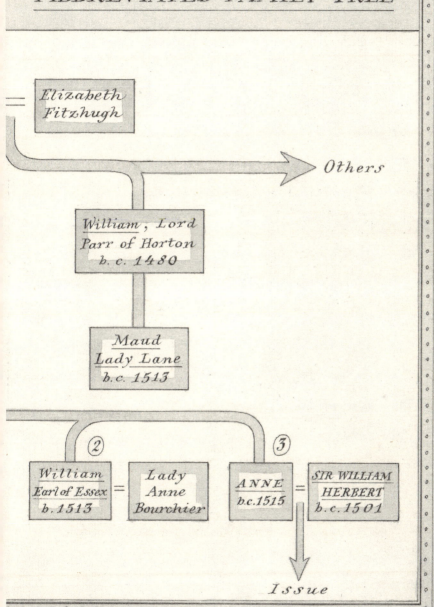

Elizabeth Fitzhugh

Others

William, Lord Parr of Horton
b. c. 1480

Maud Lady Lane
b. c. 1513

② William Earl of Essex b. 1513 = Lady Anne Bourchier

③ ANNE b.c. 1515 = SIR WILLIAM HERBERT b.c. 1501

Issue

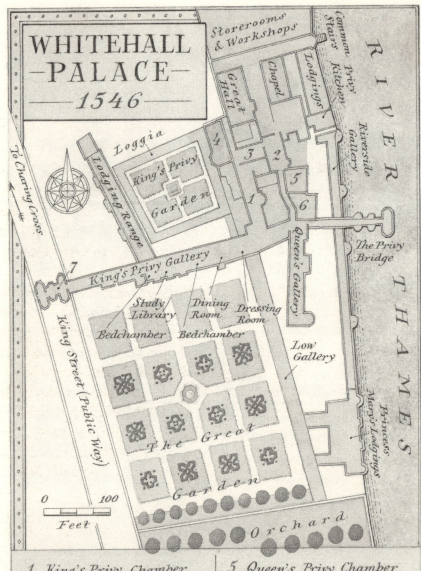

WHITEHALL
PALACE
1546

RIVER THAMES

To Charing Cross

Storerooms & Workshops

Common Privy Stairs

Privy Kitchen

Great Hall

Chapel

Lodgings

Riverside Gallery

Loggia

Lodging Range

King's Privy Garden

4

3

2

5

6

1

King's Privy Gallery

7

Queen's Gallery

The Privy Bridge

Study

Library

Dining Room

Dressing Room

Bedchamber

Bedchamber

Low Gallery

King Street (Public Way)

The Great Garden

Princess Mary's Lodgings

0   100
Feet

Orchard

1 King's Privy Chamber
2 Queen's Presence Chamber
3 King's Presence Chamber
4 King's Guard Chamber
   (Great Chamber above)

5 Queen's Privy Chamber
6 Queen's Bedchamber
7 Holbein Gate
   a.k.a. Great Gate
   (King's Secret Study above)

Chapter One

I DID NOT WANT to attend the burning. I have never liked even such things as the bearbaiting, and this was to be the burning alive at the stake of four living people, one a woman, for denying that the body and blood of Christ were present in the Host at Mass. Such was the pitch we had come to in England during the great heresy hunt of 1546.

I had been called from my chambers at Lincoln's Inn to see the Treasurer, Master Rowland. Despite my status as a serjeant, the most senior of barristers, Master Rowland disliked me. I think his pride had never recovered from the time three years before when I had been – justly – disrespectful to him. I crossed the Inn Square, the red brick-work mellow in the summer sunshine, exchanging greetings with other black-gowned lawyers going to and fro. I looked up at Stephen Bealknap's rooms; he was my old foe both in and out of court. The shutters at his windows were closed. He had been ill since early in the year and had not been seen outside for many weeks. Some said he was near death.

I went to the Treasurer's offices and knocked at his door. A sharp voice bade me enter. Rowland sat behind his desk in his spacious room, the walls lined with shelves of heavy legal books, a display of his status. He was old, past sixty, rail-thin but hard as oak, with a narrow, seamed, frowning face. He sported a white beard, grown long and forked in the current fashion, carefully combed and reaching half-way down his silken doublet. As I came in he looked up from cutting a new nib for his goose-feather quill. His fingers, like mine, were stained black from years of working with ink.

'God give you good morrow, Serjeant Shardlake,' he said in his sharp voice. He put down the knife.

I bowed. 'And you, Master Treasurer.'

He waved me to a stool and looked at me sternly.

'Your business goes well?' he asked. 'Many cases listed for the Michaelmas term?'

'A good enough number, sir.'

'I hear you no longer get work from the Queen's solicitor.' He spoke casually. 'Not for this year past.'

'I have plenty of other cases, sir. And my work at Common Pleas keeps me busy.'

He inclined his head. 'I hear some of Queen Catherine's officials have been questioned by the Privy Council. For heretical opinions.'

'So rumour says. But so many have been interrogated these last few months.'

'I have seen you more frequently at Mass at the Inn church recently.' Rowland smiled sardonically. 'Showing good conformity? A wise policy in these whirling days. Attend church, avoid the babble of controversy, follow the King's wishes.'

'Indeed, sir.'

He took his sharpened quill and spat to soften it, then rubbed it on a cloth. He looked up at me with a new keenness. 'You have heard that Mistress Anne Askew is sentenced to burn with three others a week on Friday? The sixteenth of July?'

'It is the talk of London. Some say she was tortured in the Tower after her sentence. A strange thing.'

Rowland shrugged. 'Street gossip. But the woman made a sensation at the wrong time. Abandoning her husband and coming to London to preach opinions clear contrary to the Act of Six Articles. Refusing to recant, arguing in public with her judges.' He shook his head, then leaned forward. 'The burning is to be a great spectacle. There has been nothing like it for years. The King wants it to be seen where heresy leads. Half the Privy Council will be there.'

'Not the King?' There had been rumours he might attend.

'No.'

I remembered Henry had been seriously ill in the spring; he had hardly been seen since.

'His majesty wants representatives from all the London guilds.' Rowland paused. 'And the Inns of Court. I have decided you should go to represent Lincoln's Inn.'

I stared at him. 'Me, sir?'

'You take on fewer social and ceremonial duties than you should, given your rank, Serjeant Shardlake. No one seems willing to volunteer for this, so I have had to decide. I think it time you took your turn.'

I sighed. 'I know I have been lax in such duties. I will do more, if you wish.' I took a deep breath. 'But not this, I would ask you. It will be a horrible thing. I have never seen a burning, and do not wish to.'

Rowland waved a hand dismissively. 'You are too squeamish. Strange in a farmer's son. You have seen executions, I know that. Lord Cromwell had you attend Anne Boleyn's beheading when you worked for him.'

'That was bad. This will be worse.'

He tapped a paper on his desk. 'This is the request for me to send someone to attend. Signed by the King's secretary, Paget himself. I must despatch the name to him tonight. I am sorry, Serjeant, but I have decided you will go.' He rose, indicating the interview was over. I stood and bowed again. 'Thank you for offering to become more involved with the Inn's duties,' Rowland said, his voice smooth once more. 'I will see what other – ' he hesitated – 'activities may be coming up.'

✟

ON THE DAY of the burning I woke early. It was set for midday but I felt in too heavy and mopish a frame of mind to go into chambers. Punctual as ever, my new steward Martin Brocket brought linen cloths and a ewer of hot water to my bedroom at seven, and after bidding me good morning laid out my shirt, doublet and summer robe. As ever, his manner was serious, quiet, deferential. Since he and his wife Agnes had come to me in the winter my household had been run like clockwork. Through the half-open door I could hear Agnes asking the boy Timothy to be sure and fetch some fresh water later, and the girl Josephine to hurry with her breakfast that my table might be made ready. Her tone was light, friendly.

'Another fine day, sir,' Martin ventured. He was in his forties, with thinning fair hair and bland, unremarkable features.

I had told none of my household about my attendance at the burning. 'It is, Martin,' I replied. 'I think I shall work in my study this morning, go in this afternoon.'

'Very good, sir. Your breakfast will be ready shortly.' He bowed and went out.

I got up, wincing at a spasm in my back. Fortunately I had fewer of those now, as I followed my doctor friend Guy's exercises faithfully. I wished I could feel comfortable with Martin, yet although I liked his wife there was something in his cool, stiff formality that I had never felt easy with. As I washed my face and donned a clean linen shirt scented with rosemary, I chid myself for my unreasonableness: as the master it was for me to initiate a less formal relationship.

I examined my face in the steel mirror. More lines, I thought. I had turned forty-four that spring. A lined face, greying hair and a hunched back. As there was such a fashion for beards now – my assistant Barak had recently grown a neat brown one – I had tried a short beard myself a couple of months before, but like my hair it had come out streaked with grey, which I thought unbecoming.

I looked out from the mullioned window onto my garden, where I had allowed Agnes to install some beehives and cultivate a herb garden. They improved its look, and the herbs were sweet-smelling as well as useful. The birds were singing and the bees buzzed round the flowers, everything bright and colourful. What a day for a young woman and three men to die horribly.

My eye turned to a letter on my bedside table. It was from Antwerp, in the Spanish Netherlands, where my nineteen-year-old ward, Hugh Curteys, lived, working for the English merchants there. Hugh was happy now. Originally planning to study in Germany, he had instead stayed in Antwerp and found an unexpected interest in the clothing trade, especially the finding and assessing of rare silks and new fabrics, such as the cotton that was coming in from the New World. Hugh's letters were full of pleasure in work, and in the intellectual and social freedom of the great city; the fairs, debates and readings at the Chambers of Rhetoric. Although Antwerp was part of the Holy Roman Empire, the Catholic Emperor Charles V did not interfere with the many Protestants who lived there – he did not dare imperil the Flanders banking trade, which financed his wars.

Hugh never spoke of the dark secret which we shared from the time of our meeting the year before; all his letters were cheerful in tone. In this one, though, was news of the arrival in Antwerp of a number of English refugees. *'They are in a piteous state, appealing to the merchants for succour. They are reformers and radicals, afraid they will be caught up in the net of persecution they say Bishop Gardiner has cast over England.'*

I sighed, donned my robe and went down to breakfast. I could delay no more; I must start this dreadful day.

✠

THE HUNT FOR heretics had begun in the spring. During the winter the tide of the King's fickle religious policy had seemed to turn towards the reformers; he had persuaded Parliament to grant him power to dissolve the chantries, where priests were paid under the wills of deceased donors to say Masses for their souls. But, like many, I suspected his motive had been not religious but financial – the need to cover the gigantic costs of the French war; the English still remained besieged in Boulogne. His debasement of the coinage continued, prices rising as they never had at any time before in man's memory. The newest 'silver' shillings were but a film of silver over copper; already wearing off at the highest point. The King had a new nickname: 'Old Coppernose'. The discount which traders demanded on these coins made them worth less than sixpence now, though wages were still paid at the coins' face value.

And then in March, Bishop Stephen Gardiner – the King's most conservative adviser where religion was concerned – returned from negotiating a new treaty with the Holy Roman Emperor. From April onwards there was word of people high and low being taken in for questioning about their views on the Mass, and the possession of forbidden books. The questioning had reached into both the King's household and the Queen's; among the many rumours circulating the streets was that Anne Askew, the best known of those sentenced to death for heresy, had connections within the Queen's court, and had preached and propagandized among her ladies. I had not seen Queen Catherine since involving her in a potentially dangerous matter the year before, and knew, much to my grief, that I was unlikely to see that sweet and noble lady again. But I had thought of her often and feared for her as the hunt for radicals intensified; last week a proclamation had been issued detailing a long list of books which it was forbidden to possess, and that very week the courtier George Blagge, a friend of the King's, had been sentenced to burn for heresy.

I no longer had sympathies with either side in the religious quarrel, and sometimes doubted God's very existence, but I had a history of association with reformers, and like most people this year I had kept my head down and my mouth shut.

I set out at eleven from my house, just up Chancery Lane from Lincoln's Inn. Timothy had brought my good horse Genesis round to the front door and set out the mounting block. Timothy was thirteen now, growing taller, thin and gawky. I had sent my former servant boy, Simon, to be an apprentice in the spring, to give him a chance in life, and planned to do the same for Timothy when he reached fourteen.

'Good morning, sir.' He smiled his shy, gap-toothed grin, pushing a tangle of black hair from his forehead.

'Good morning, lad. How goes it with you?'

'Well, sir.'

'You must be missing Simon.'

'Yes, sir.' He looked down, stirring a pebble with his foot. 'But I manage.'

'You manage well,' I answered encouragingly. 'But perhaps we should begin to think of an apprenticeship for you. Have you thought what you might wish to do in life?'

He stared at me, sudden alarm in his brown eyes. 'No, sir – I – I thought I would stay here.' He looked around, out at the roadway. He had always been a quiet boy, with none of Simon's confidence, and I realized the thought of going out into the world scared him.

'Well,' I said soothingly, 'there is no hurry.' He looked relieved. 'And now I must away – ' I sighed – 'to business.'

✝

I RODE UNDER Temple Bar then turned up Gifford Street, which led to the open space of Smithfield. Many people were travelling in the same direction along the dusty way, some on horseback, most on foot, rich and poor, men, women and even a few children. Some, especially those in the dark clothes favoured by religious radicals, looked serious, others' faces were blank, while some even wore the eager expression of people looking forward to a good entertainment. I had put on my white serjeant's coif under my black cap, and began to sweat in the heat. I remembered with irritation that in the afternoon I had an appointment with my most difficult client, Isabel Slanning, whose case – a dispute with her brother over their mother's Will – was among the silliest and costliest I had ever encountered.

I passed two young apprentices in their blue doublets and caps. 'Why must they have it at midday?' I overheard one grumble. 'There won't be any shade.'

'Don't know. Some rule, I suppose. The hotter for good Mistress Askew. She'll have a warm arse before the day's done, eh?'

✝

SMITHFIELD WAS crowded already. The open space where the twice-weekly cattle market was held was full of people, all facing a railed-off central area guarded by soldiers wearing metal helmets and white coats bearing the cross of St George. They carried halberds, their expressions stern. If there were any protests these would be dealt with sharply. I looked at the men sadly; whenever I saw soldiers now I thought of my friends who had died, as I nearly had myself, when the great ship *Mary Rose* foundered during the repelling of the attempted French invasion. A year, I thought, almost to the day. Last month news had come that the war was almost over, a settlement negotiated but for a few details, with France and Scotland, too. I remembered the soldiers' fresh young faces, the bodies crashing into the water, and closed my eyes. Peace had come too late for them.

Mounted on my horse I had a better view than most, better than I would have wished for, and close by the railings, for the crowd pressed those on horseback forward. In the centre of the railed-off area three oaken poles, seven feet tall, had been secured in the dusty earth. Each had metal hoops in the side through which London constables were sliding iron chains. They inserted padlocks in the links and checked the keys worked. Their air was calm and businesslike. A little way off more constables stood around an enormous pile of faggots – thick bunches of small branches. I was glad the weather had been dry; I had heard that if the wood was wet it took longer to burn, and the victims' suffering was horribly prolonged. Facing the stakes was a tall wooden lectern, painted white. Here, before the burning, there would be a preaching, a last appeal to the heretics to repent. The preacher was to be Nicholas Shaxton, the former Bishop of Salisbury, a radical reformer who had been sentenced to burn with the others but who had recanted to save his own life.

On the eastern side of the square I saw, behind a row of fine, brightly painted new houses, the high old tower of St Bartholomew's Church. When the monastery was dissolved seven years before, its lands had passed to the Privy Councillor, Sir Richard Rich, who had built these new houses. Their windows were crowded with people. A high wooden stage covered with a canopy in the royal colours of green and white had been erected in front of the old monastic gatehouse. A long bench was scattered with thick, brightly coloured cushions. This would be where the Lord Mayor and Privy Councillors would watch the burning. Among those on horseback in the crowd I recognized many city officials; I nodded to those I knew. A little way off a small group of middle-aged men stood together, looking solemn and disturbed. I heard a few words in a foreign tongue, identifying them as Flemish merchants.

There was a babble of voices all round me, as well as the sharp stink of a London crowd in summer.

'They say she was racked till the strings of her arms and legs perished – '

'They couldn't torture her legally after she was convicted – '

'And John Lassells is to be burned too. He was the one who told the King of Catherine Howard's dalliances – '

'They say Catherine Parr's in trouble as well. He could have a seventh wife before this is done – '

'Will they let them off if they recant?'

'Too late for that – '

There was a stir by the canopy, and heads turned as a group of men in silk robes and caps, many wearing thick gold chains around their necks, appeared from the gatehouse accompanied by soldiers. They slowly mounted the steps to the stage, the soldiers taking places in front of them, and sat in a long row, adjusting their caps and chains, staring over the crowd with set, stern expressions. I recognized many of them: Mayor Bowes of London in his red robes; the Duke of Norfolk, older and thinner than when I had encountered him six years before, an expression of contemptuous arrogance on his haughty, severe face. To Norfolk's side sat a cleric in a white silk cassock with a black alb over it, whom I did not recognize but I guessed must be Bishop Gardiner. He was around sixty, stocky and swarthy, with a proud beak of a nose and large, dark eyes that swivelled over the crowd. He leaned across and murmured to Norfolk, who nodded and smiled sardonically. These two, many said, would have England back under Rome if they could.

Next to them three men sat together. Each had risen under Thomas Cromwell but shifted towards the conservative faction on the

Privy Council when Cromwell fell, bending and twisting before the wind, ever with two faces under one hood. First I saw William Paget, the King's Secretary, who had sent the letter to Rowland. He had a wide, hard slab of a face above a bushy brown beard, his thin-lipped mouth turned down sharply at one corner, making a narrow slash. It was said Paget was closer to the King than anyone now; his nickname was 'The Master of Practices'.

Beside Paget sat Lord Chancellor Thomas Wriothesley, head of the legal profession, tall and thin with a jutting little russet beard. Finally Sir Richard Rich completed the trio, still a senior Privy Councillor despite accusations of corruption two years before, his name associated with all the nastiest pieces of business these last fifteen years, a murderer to my certain knowledge, and my old enemy. I was safe from him only because of the things I knew about him, and because I still had the Queen's protection – whatever, I wondered uneasily, that might be worth now. I looked at Rich. Despite the heat, he was wearing a green robe with a fur collar. To my surprise I read anxiety on his thin, neat features. The long hair under his jewelled cap was quite grey now. He fiddled with his gold chain. Then, looking over the crowd, he met my gaze. His face flushed and his lips set. He stared back at me a moment, then turned away as Wriothesley bent to speak to him. I shuddered. My anxiety communicated itself to Genesis, who stirred uneasily. I steadied him with a pat.

Near to me a soldier passed, carefully carrying a basket. 'Make way, make way! 'Tis the gunpowder!'

I was glad to hear the words. At least there would be some mercy. The sentence for heresy was burning to death, but sometimes the authorities allowed a packet of gunpowder to be placed around each victim's neck so that when the flames reached it, the packet would explode, bringing instantaneous death.

'Should let them burn to the end,' someone protested.

'Ay,' another agreed. 'The kiss of fire, so light and agonizing.' A horrible giggle.

I looked round as another horseman, dressed like me in a lawyer's silken summer robe and dark cap, made his way through the crowd and came to a halt beside me. He was a few years my junior, with a handsome though slightly stern face, a short dark beard and blue eyes that were penetratingly honest and direct.

'Good day, Serjeant Shardlake.'

'And to you, Brother Coleswyn.'

Philip Coleswyn was a barrister of Gray's Inn, and my opponent in the wretched case of the Slanning Will. He represented my client's brother, who was as cantankerous and difficult as his sister, but though, as their lawyers, we had had to cross swords I had found Coleswyn himself civil and honest, not one of those lawyers who will enthusiastically argue the worst of cases for enough silver. I guessed he found his client as irritating as I did mine. I had heard he was a reformer – gossip these days was usually about people's religion – though for myself I did not care a fig.

'Are you here to represent Lincoln's Inn?' Coleswyn asked.

'Ay. Have you been chosen for Gray's Inn?'

'I have. Not willingly.'

'Nor I.'

'It is a cruel business.' He looked at me directly.

'It is. Cruel and horrible.'

'Soon they will make it illegal to worship God.' He spoke with a slight tremor in his voice.

I replied, my words noncommittal but my tone sardonic, 'It is our duty to worship as King Henry decrees.'

'And here is his decree,' Coleswyn answered quietly. He shook his head, then said, 'I am sorry, Brother, I should watch my words.'

'Yes. In these days we must.'

The soldier had laid the basket of gunpowder down carefully in a corner of the railed-off area. He stepped over the rail and now stood with the other soldiers facing outwards at the crowd, quite close to us. Then I saw Wriothesley lean forwards and beckon the man with a finger. He ran across to the canopied stage and I saw Wriothesley gesture at the gunpowder basket. The soldier answered him and

Wriothesley sat back, apparently satisfied. The man returned to his position.

'What was that about?' I heard the soldier next to him say.

'He asked how much gunpowder there was. He was frightened that when it blew up it might send burning faggots flying towards the stage. I told him it'll be round their necks, well above the faggots.'

His fellow laughed. 'The radicals would love it if Gardiner and half the Privy Council ended up burning, too. John Bale could write one of his plays about it.'

I felt eyes on me. I saw, a little to my left, a black-robed lawyer standing with two young gentlemen in doublets bright with expensive dye, pearls in their caps. The lawyer was young, in his twenties, a short thin fellow with a narrow, clever face, protuberant eyes and a wispy beard. He had been staring at me hard. He met my gaze then looked away.

I turned to Coleswyn. 'Do you know that lawyer, standing with the two young popinjays?'

He shook his head. 'I think I've seen him round the courts once or twice, but I don't know him.'

'No matter.'

There was a fresh ripple of excitement through the crowd as a procession approached from Little Britain Street. More soldiers, surrounding three men dressed in long white shifts, one young and two middle-aged. All had set faces but wild, fearful eyes. And behind them, carried on a chair by two soldiers, an attractive, fair-haired young woman in her twenties. As the chair swayed slightly she gripped the sides, her face twitching with pain. So this was Anne Askew, who had left her husband in Lincolnshire to come and preach in London, and said the consecrated wafer was no more than a piece of bread, which would go mouldy like any other if left in a box.

'I had not known she was so young,' Coleswyn whispered.

Some of the constables ran to the faggots and piled several bundles round the stakes, a foot high. We watched as the three men were led there. The branches crunched under the constables' feet as they chained two of the men – back-to-back – to one stake, the third to another. There was a rattle as the chains were secured round their ankles, waists and necks. Then Anne Askew was carried in her chair to the third stake. The soldiers set her down and the constables chained her to the post by the neck and waist.

'So it's true,' Coleswyn said. 'She was racked in the Tower. See, she can no longer stand.'

'But why do that to the poor creature after she was convicted?'

'Jesu only knows.'

A soldier brought four brown bags, each the size of a large fist, from the basket and carefully tied one round the neck of each victim. They flinched instinctively. A constable came out of the old gatehouse carrying a lit torch and stood beside the railing, impassive. Everyone's eyes turned to the torch's flame. The crowd fell silent.

A man in clerical robes was mounting the steps to the lectern. He was elderly, white-haired and red-faced, trying to compose features distorted with fear. Nicholas Shaxton. But for his recantation he would have been tied to a stake as well. There were hostile murmurs from some in the crowd, then a shout of, 'Shame on you that would burn Christ's members!' There was a brief commotion and someone hit the man who had spoken; two soldiers hurried across to separate them.

Shaxton began to preach, a long disquisition justifying the ancient doctrine of the Mass. The three condemned men listened in silence, one trembling uncontrollably. Sweat formed on their faces and on their white shifts. Anne Askew, though, periodically interrupted Shaxton with cries of, 'He misses the point, and speaks without the Book!' Her face looked cheerful and composed now, almost as though she were enjoying the spectacle. I wondered if the poor woman was mad. Someone in the crowd called out, 'Get on with it! Light the fire!'

At length Shaxton finished. He slowly descended and was led back to the gatehouse. He started to go in but the soldiers seized his arms, forcing him to turn and stand in the doorway. He was to be made to watch.

More kindling was laid round the prisoners; it reached now to their thighs. Then the constable with the torch came over and, one by one, lit the faggots. There was a crackling, then a gasping that soon turned to screaming as the flames licked the victims' legs. One of the men yelled out, 'Christ receive me! Christ receive me!' over and over again. I heard a moaning wail from Anne Askew and closed my eyes. All around the crowd was silent, watching.

The screaming, and the crackling of the faggots, seemed to go on forever. Genesis stirred uneasily again and for a moment I experienced that awful feeling I had known frequently in the months since the *Mary Rose* sank, of everything swaying and tilting beneath me, and I had to open my eyes. Coleswyn was staring grimly, fixedly ahead, and I could not help but follow his gaze. The flames were rising fast, light and transparent in the bright July day. The three men were still yelling and writhing; the flames had reached their arms and lower bodies and burned the skin away; blood trickled down into the inferno. Two of the men were leaning forward in a frantic attempt to ignite the gunpowder, but the flames were not yet high enough. Anne Askew sat slumped in her chair; she seemed to have lost consciousness. I felt sick. I looked across at the row of faces under the canopy; all were set in stern, frowning expressions. Then I saw the thin young lawyer looking at me again from the crowd. I thought uneasily, Who is he? What does he want?

Coleswyn groaned suddenly and slumped in his saddle. I reached out a hand to steady him. He took a deep breath and sat upright. 'Courage, Brother,' I said gently.

He looked at me, his face pale and beaded with sweat. 'You realize any of us may come to this now?' he whispered.

I saw that some of the crowd had turned away; one or two children were crying, overcome by the horrific scene. I noticed that one of the Dutch merchants had pulled out a tiny prayer book and was holding it open in his hands, reciting quietly. But other people were laughing and joking. There was a smell of smoke round Smithfield now as well as the stink of the crowd, and something else, familiar from the kitchen: the smell of roasting meat. Against my will I looked again at the stakes. The flames had reached higher; the victims' lower bodies were blackened, white bone showing through here and there, their upper parts red with blood as the flames licked at them. I saw with horror that Anne Askew had regained consciousness; making piteous groans as her shift burned away.

She began to shout something but then the flames reached the gunpowder bag and her head exploded, blood and bone and brains flying and falling, hissing, into the fire.

Chapter Two

As soon as it was over, I rode away with Coleswyn. The three men at the stakes had taken longer than Anne Askew to die. They had been chained standing rather than sitting and it was another half-hour before the flames reached the bag of gunpowder round the last man's neck. I had shut my eyes for much of the time; if only I could have shut my ears.

We said little as we rode along Chick Lane, heading for the Inns of Court. Eventually Coleswyn broke the uneasy silence. 'I spoke too freely of my private thoughts, Brother Shardlake. I know one must be careful.'

'No matter,' I answered. 'Hard to keep one's counsel when watching such a thing.' I remembered his comment that any of us could come to this, and wondered whether he had links with the radicals. I changed the subject. 'I am seeing my client Mistress Slanning this afternoon. There will be much for both of us to do before the case comes on in September.'

Coleswyn gave an ironic bark of laughter. 'That there will.' He gave me a look which showed his view of the case to be the same as mine.

We had reached Saffron Hill, where our ways divided if he were to go to Gray's Inn and I to Lincoln's Inn. I did not feel ready to go back to work yet. I said, 'Will you come for a mug of beer, Brother?'

Coleswyn shook his head. 'Thank you, but I could not. I will return to the Inn, try to lose myself in some work. God give you good morrow.'

'And you, Brother.'

I watched him ride away, slumped a little over his horse. I rode down to Holborn, pulling off my cap and coif as I went.

☦

I FOUND A QUIET INN by St Andrew's Church; it would prob-ably fill up when the crowds left Smithfield, but for now only a few old men sat at the tables. I bought a mug of beer and found a secluded corner. The ale was poor, cloudy stuff, a husk floating on the surface.

My mind turned, as it often did, to the Queen. I remembered when I had first met her, when she was still Lady Latimer. My feelings for her had not diminished. I told myself it was ridiculous, foolish, fantasy; I should find myself a woman of my own status before I grew too old. I hoped she possessed none of the books on the new forbidden list. The list was long – Luther, Tyndale, Coverdale, and of course John Bale, whose scurrilous new book about the old monks and nuns, *Acts of the English Votaries*, was circulating widely among the London apprentices. I had old copies of Tyndale and Coverdale myself; an amnesty for surrendering them expired in three weeks. Safer to burn them quietly in the garden, I thought.

A little group of men came in. 'Glad to be out of that smell,' one said.

''Tis better than the stink of Lutheranism,' another growled.

'Luther's dead and buried, and Askew and the rest gone now too.'

'There's plenty more lurking in the shadows.'

'Come on, have a drink. Have they any pies?'

I decided it was time to leave. I drained my mug and went outside. I had missed lunch, but the thought of food revolted me.

☦

I RODE BACK under the Great Gatehouse of Lincoln's Inn, once again in my robe, coif and cap. I left Genesis at the stables and crossed to my chambers. To my surprise, there was a flurry of activity in the outer office. All three of my employees – my assistant Jack Barak, my clerk John Skelly, and my new pupil, Nicholas Overton – were searching frantically among the papers on the desks and shelves.

'God's pestilence!' Barak was shouting at Nicholas as he untied the ribbon from a brief and began riffling through the papers. 'Can't you even remember when you last saw it?'

Nicholas turned from searching through another pile of papers, the freckled face beneath his unruly light-red hair downcast. 'It was two days ago, maybe three. I've been given so many conveyances to look at.'

Skelly studied Nicholas through his glasses. It was a mild look but his voice was strained as he said, 'If you could just remember, Master Overton, it would narrow the search a bit.'

'What is going on?' I asked from the doorway. They had been so busy with their frantic search they had not seen me come in. Barak turned to me, his face an angry red above his new beard.

'Master Nicholas has lost the Carlingford conveyance! All the evidence that Carlingford owns his land, which needs to be presented in court on the first day of the term! Dozy beanpole,' he muttered. 'Bungling idiot!'

Nicholas's face reddened as he looked at me. 'I did not mean to.'

I sighed. I had taken Nicholas on two months before, at the request of a barrister friend to whom I owed a favour, and half-regretted it. Nicholas was the son of a gentry family in Lincolnshire, who at twenty-one had, apparently, failed to settle to anything, and agreed to spend a year or two at Lincoln's Inn, learning the ways of the law to help him run his father's estate. My friend had hinted that there had been some disagreement between Nicholas and his family, but insisted he was a good lad. Indeed he was good-natured, but irresponsible. Like most other such young gentlemen he spent much of his time exploring the fleshpots of London; already he had been in trouble for getting into a sword fight with another student over a prostitute. The King had closed the Southwark brothels that spring, with the result that more prostitutes had crossed over the river to the city. Most gentry lads learned sword fighting, and their status allowed them to wear swords in the city, but the taverns were not the place to show off such skills. And a sharp sword was the deadliest of weapons, especially in a careless hand.

I looked at his tall, rangy form, noticing that under his short stu-dent's robe he wore a green doublet slashed so the lining of fine yellow damask showed through, contrary to the Inn regulations that students must wear modest dress.

'Keep looking, but calm down, Nicholas,' I said. 'You did not take the conveyance out of this office?' I asked sharply.

'No, Master Shardlake. I know that is not permitted.' He had a cultivated voice with an undertone of a Lincolnshire burr. His face, long-nosed and round-chinned, was distressed.

'Nor is wearing a slashed silken doublet. Do you want to get into trouble with the Treasurer? When you have found the conveyance, go home and change it.'

'Yes, sir,' he answered humbly.

'And when Mistress Slanning comes this afternoon, I want you to sit in on the interview, and take notes.'

'Yes, sir.'

'And if that conveyance still isn't found, stay late to find it.'

'Is the burning over?' Skelly ventured hesitantly.

'Yes. But I do not want to talk about it.'

Barak looked up. 'I have a couple of pieces of news for you. Good news, but private.'

'I could do with some.'

'Thought you might,' he answered sympathetically.

'Come into the office.'

He followed me through to my private quarters, with its mul-lioned window overlooking Gatehouse Court. I threw off my robe and cap and sat behind my desk, Barak taking the chair opposite. I noticed there were odd flecks of grey in his dark-brown beard, though none yet in his hair. Barak was thirty-four now, a decade younger than me, his once lean features filling out.

He said, 'That arsehole young Overton will be the death of me. It's like trying to supervise a monkey.'

I smiled. 'Fie, he's not stupid. He did a good summary of the Bennett case papers for me last week. He just needs to get himself organized.'

Barak grunted. 'Glad you told him off about his clothes. Wish I could afford silk doublets these days.'

'He's young, a bit irresponsible.' I smiled wryly. 'As you were when first we met. At least Nicholas does not swear like a soldier.'

Barak grunted, then looked at me seriously. 'What was it like? The burning?'

'Horrible beyond description. But everyone played their part,' I added bitterly. 'The crowd, the city officials and Privy Councillors sitting on their stage. There was a little fight at one point, but the soldiers quelled it quickly. Those poor people died horribly, but well.'

Barak shook his head. 'Why couldn't they recant?'

'I suppose they thought recantation would damn them.' I sighed. 'Well, what are these pieces of good news?'

'Here's the first. It was delivered this morning.' Barak's hand went to the purse at his waist. He pulled out three bright, buttery gold sovereigns and laid them on the table, together with a folded piece of paper.

I looked at them. 'An overdue fee?'

'You could say that. Look at the note.'

I took the paper and opened it. Within was a scrawled message in a very shaky hand: '*Here is the money I owe you for my keep from the time I stayed at Mistress Elliard's. I am sore ill and would welcome a visit from you. Your brother in the law, Stephen Bealknap.*'

Barak smiled. 'Your mouth's fallen open. Not surprised, mine did too.'

I picked up the sovereigns and looked at them closely, lest this was some sort of jest. But they were good golden coins, from before the debasement, showing the young King on one side and the Tudor Rose on the other. It was almost beyond belief. Stephen Bealknap was famous not only as a man without scruples, personal or professional, but also as a miser who was said to have a fortune hidden in a chest in his chambers which he sat looking through at night. He had amassed his wealth through all manner of dirty dealings over the years, some against me, and also by making it a point of pride never to pay a debt if he could avoid it. It was three years since, in a fit of misplaced generosity, I had paid a friend to look after him when he was ill, and he had never reimbursed me.

'It's almost beyond belief.' I considered. 'And yet – remember, late last autumn and into the winter, before he became ill, he had behaved in an unexpectedly friendly manner for a while. He would come up to me in the courtyard and ask how I did, how my business was, as though he were a friend, or would become one.' I remembered him approaching me across the quadrangle one mellow autumn day, his black gown flapping round his thin form, a sickly ingratiating smile on his pinched face. His wiry fair hair stuck out, as usual, at angles from his cap. 'Master Shardlake, how do you fare?'

'I was always short with him,' I told Barak. 'I did not trust him an inch, of course, I was sure there was something behind his concern. I think he was looking for work; I remembered him saying he was not getting as much from an old client. And he never mentioned the money he owed. He got the message after a while, and went back to ignoring me.' I frowned. 'Even back then he looked tired, not well. Perhaps that was why he was losing business; his sharpness was going.'

'Maybe he's truly repenting his sins, if he is as ill as they say.'

'A growth in his guts, isn't it? He's been ill a couple months now, hasn't he? I haven't seen him outside. Who delivered the note?'

'An old woman. She said she's nursing him.'

'By Mary,' I said. 'Bealknap, paying a debt and asking for a visit?'

'Will you go and see him?'

'In charity, I suppose I must.' I shook my head in wonderment. 'What is your other piece of news? After this, were you to tell me frogs were flying over London I do not think it would surprise me.'

He smiled again, a happy smile that softened his features. 'Nay, this is a surprise but not a wonder. Tamasin is expecting again.'

I leaned over and grasped his hand. 'That is good news. I know you wanted another.'

'Yes. A little brother or sister for Georgie. January, we're told.'

'Wonderful, Jack; my congratulations. We must celebrate.'

'We're not telling the world just yet. But you're coming to the little gathering we're having for Georgie's first birthday, on the twenty-seventh? We'll announce it then. Will you ask the Old Moor to come? He looked after Tamasin well when she was expecting Georgie.'

'Guy is coming to dinner tonight. I shall ask him then.'

'Good.' Barak leaned back in his chair and folded his hands over his stomach, contentment on his face. His and Tamasin's first child had died, and I had feared the misery would tear them apart forever, but last year she had borne a healthy son. And expecting another child so soon. I thought how settled Barak was now, how different from the madding fellow, who carried out questionable missions for Thomas Cromwell, I had first met six years before. 'I feel cheered,' I said quietly. 'I think perhaps some good things may come in this world after all.'

'Are you to report back to Treasurer Rowland about the burnings?'

'Yes. I will reassure him my presence as representative of the Inn was noted.' I raised my eyebrows. 'By Richard Rich, among others.'

Barak also raised his eyebrows. 'That rogue was there?'

'Yes. I haven't seen him in a year. But he remembered me, of course. He gave me a nasty glance.'

'He can do no more. You have too much on him.'

'He had a worried look about him. I wonder why. I thought he was riding high these days, aligning himself with Gardiner and the conservatives.' I looked at Barak. 'Do you still keep in touch with your friends, from the days when you worked for Cromwell? Heard any gossip?'

'I go to the old taverns occasionally, when Tamasin lets me. But I hear little. And before you ask, nothing about the Queen.'

'Those rumours that Anne Askew was tortured in the Tower were true,' I said. 'She had to be carried to the stake on a chair.'

'Poor creature.' Barak stroked his beard thoughtfully. 'I wonder how that information got out. A radical sympathizer working in the Tower, it has to be. But all I hear from my old friends is that Bishop Gardiner has the King's ear now, and that's common knowledge. I don't suppose Archbishop Cranmer was at the burning?'

'No. He's keeping safely out of the way at Canterbury, I'd guess.' I shook my head. 'I wonder he has survived so long. By the by, there was a young lawyer at the burning, with some gentlemen, who kept staring at me. Small and thin, brown hair and a little beard. I wondered who he might be.'

'Probably someone who will be your opponent in a case next term, sizing up the opposition.'

'Maybe.' I fingered the coins on the desk.

'Don't keep thinking everyone's after you,' Barak said quietly.

'Ay, 'tis a fault. But is it any wonder, after these last few years?' I sighed. 'By the way, I met Brother Coleswyn at the burning, he was made to go and represent Gray's Inn. He's a decent fellow.'

'Unlike his client then, or yours. Serve that long lad Nicholas right to have to sit in with that old Slanning beldame this afternoon.'

I smiled. 'Yes, that was my thought, too. Well, go and see if he's found the conveyance yet.'

Barak rose. 'I'll kick his arse if he hasn't, gentleman or no . . .'

He left me fingering the coins. I looked at the note. I could not help but think, What is Bealknap up to now?

✝

MISTRESS ISABEL SLANNING arrived punctually at three. Nicholas, now in a more sober doublet of light black wool, sat beside me with a quill and paper. He had, fortunately for him, found the missing conveyance whilst I had been talking to Barak.

Skelly showed Mistress Slanning in, a little apprehensively. She was a tall, thin widow in her fifties, though with her lined face, thin pursed mouth and habitual frown she looked older. I had seen her brother, Edward Cotterstoke, at hearings in court last term, and it had amazed me how much he resembled her in form and face, apart from a little grey beard. Mistress Slanning wore a violet dress of fine wool with a fashionable turned-up collar enclosing her thin neck, and a box hood lined with little pearls. She was a wealthy woman; her late husband had been a successful haberdasher, and like many rich merchants' widows she adopted an air of authority that would have been thought unbefitting in a woman of lower rank. She greeted me coldly, ignoring Nicholas.

She was, as ever, straight to the point. 'Well, Master Shardlake, what news? I expect that wretch Edward is trying to delay the case again?' Her large brown eyes were accusing.

'No, madam, the matter is listed for King's Bench in September.' I bade her sit, wondering again why she and her brother hated each other so. They were themselves the children of a merchant, a prosperous corn chandler. He had died quite young and their mother had remarried, their stepfather taking over the business, although he himself died suddenly a year later, upon which old Mrs Deborah Cotterstoke had sold the chandlery and lived out the rest of her long life on the considerable proceeds. She had never remarried, and had died the previous year, aged eighty, after a paralytic seizure. A priest had made her Will for her on her deathbed. Most of it was straightforward: her money was split equally between her two children; the large house she lived in near Chandler's Hall was to be sold and the proceeds, again, divided equally. Edward, like Isabel, was moderately wealthy – he was a senior clerk at the Guildhall – and for both of them, their mother's estate would make them richer. The problem had arisen when the Will came to specify the disposition of the house's contents. All the furniture was to go to Edward. However, all wall hangings, tapestries and paintings, '*of all description within the house, of whatever nature and wheresoever they may be and however fixed*', were left to Isabel. It was an unusual wording, but I had taken a deposition from the priest who made the Will, and the two servants of the old lady

24

who witnessed it, and they had been definite that Mrs Cotterstoke, who though near death was still of sound mind, had insisted on those exact words.

They had led us to where we were now. Old Mrs Cotterstoke's first husband, the children's father, had had an interest in paintings and artworks, and the house was full of fine tapestries, several portraits and, best of all, a large wall painting in the dining room, painted directly onto the plaster. I had visited the house, empty now save for an old servant kept on as a watchman, and seen it. I appreciated painting – I had drawn and painted myself in my younger days – and this example was especially fine. Made nearly fifty years before, in the old King's reign, it depicted a family scene: a young Mrs Cotterstoke with her husband, who wore the robes of his trade and the high hat of the time, seated with Edward and Isabel, young children, in that very room. The faces of the sitters, like the summer flowers on the table, and the window with its view of the London street beyond, were exquisitely drawn; old Mrs Cotterstoke had kept it regularly maintained and the colours were as bright as ever. It would be an asset when the house was sold. As it was painted directly onto the wall, at law the painting was a fixture, but the peculiar wording of the old lady's Will had meant Isabel had argued that it was rightfully hers, and should be profession-ally removed, taking down the wall if need be – which, though it was not a supporting wall, would be almost impossible to do without damaging the painting. Edward had refused, insisting the picture was a fixture and must remain with the house. Disputes over bequests con-cerning land – and the house counted as land – were dealt with by the Court of King's Bench, but those concerning chattels – and Isabel argued the painting was a chattel – remained under the old ecclesi-astical jurisdiction and were heard by the Bishop's Court. Thus poor Coleswyn and I were in the middle of arguments about which court should have jurisdiction before we could even come to the issue of the Will. In the last few months the Bishop's Court had ruled that the painting was a chattel. Isabel had promptly instructed me to apply to King's Bench which, ever eager to assert its authority over the

ecclesiastical courts, had ruled that the matter came within its jurisdiction and set a separate hearing for the autumn. Thus the case was
batted to and fro like a tennis ball, with all the estate's assets tied up.

'That brother of mine will try to have the case delayed again, you
wait and see,' Isabel said, in her customary self-righteous tone. 'He's
trying to wear me down, but he won't. With that lawyer of his. He's a
tricky, deceitful one.' Her voice rose indignantly, as it usually did after
a couple of sentences.

'Master Coleswyn has behaved quite straightforwardly on this
matter,' I answered sharply. 'Yes, he has tried to have the matter post-
poned, but defendants' lawyers ever will. He must act on his client's
instructions, as I must on yours.' Next to me Nicholas scribbled away,
his long slim fingers moving fast over the page. At least he had had a
good education and wrote in a decent secretary hand.

Isabel bridled. 'That Coleswyn's a Protestant heretic, like my
brother. They both go to St Jude's, where all images are down and the
priest serves them at a bare table.' It was yet another bone of conten-
tion between the siblings that Isabel remained a proud traditionalist
while her brother was a reformer. 'That priest should be burned,' she
continued, 'like the Askew woman and her confederates.'

'Were you at the burning this morning, Mistress Slanning?' I
asked quietly. I had not seen her.

She wrinkled her nose. 'I would not go to such a spectacle. But
they deserved it.'

I saw Nicholas's lips set hard. He never spoke of religion; in that
regard at least he was a sensible lad. Changing the subject, I said,
'Mistress Slanning, when we go to court the outcome of the case is by
no means certain. This is a very unusual matter.'

She said firmly, 'Justice will prevail. And I know your skills,
Master Shardlake. That is why I employed a serjeant at law to represent me. I have always loved that picture.' A touch of emotion entered
her voice. 'It is the only memento I have of my dear father.'

'I would not be honest if I put your chances higher than fifty–fifty.
Much will depend on the testimony of the expert witnesses.' At the

last hearing it had been agreed that each side would instruct an expert, taken from a list of members of the Carpenters' Guild, who would report to the court on whether and how the painting could be removed. 'Have you looked at the list I gave you?'

She waved a dismissive hand. 'I know none of those people. You must recommend a man who will report the painting can easily be taken down. There must be someone who would do that for a high enough fee. Whatever it is, I will pay it.'

'A sword for hire,' I replied flatly. There were, of course, expert witnesses who would swear black was white for a high enough fee.

'Exactly.'

'The problem with such people, Mistress Slanning, is that the courts know the experts and would give little credibility to such a man. We would be much better off instructing someone whom the courts know as honest.'

'And what if he reports back to you against us?'

'Then, Mistress Slanning, we shall have to think again.'

Isabel frowned, her eyes turning to narrow little slits. 'If that happens, then we will instruct one of these "swords for hire", as that strange expression puts it.' She looked at me haughtily, as though it were I, not her, who had suggested deceiving the court.

I took my copy of the list from the desk. 'I would suggest instructing Master Jackaby. I have dealt with him before, he is well respected.'

'No,' she said. 'I have been consulting the list. There is a Master Adam here, he was Chairman of his Guild; if there is a way to get that painting off – which I am sure there is – he will find it.'

'I think Master Jackaby would be better. He has experience of litigation.'

'No,' she repeated decisively. 'I say Master Adam. I have prayed on the matter and believe he is the right man to get justice for me.'

I looked at her. *Prayed on it?* Did she think God concerned himself with malicious legal cases? But her haughty expression and the firm set of her mouth told me she would not be moved. 'Very well,' I said. She nodded imperiously. 'But remember, Mistress Slanning, he is your choice. I know nothing of him. I will arrange a date when the two experts can meet together at the house. As soon as possible.'

'Could they not visit separately?'

'The court would not like that.'

She frowned. 'The court, the court — it is my case that matters.' She took a deep breath. 'Well, if I lose in King's Bench I shall appeal to Chancery.'

'So, probably, will your brother if he loses.' I wondered again at the bitterness between them. It went back a long way, I knew that; they had not spoken in years. Isabel would refer contemptuously to how her brother could have been an alderman by now if he had made the effort. And I wondered again, why had the mother insisted on using that wording in her Will. It was almost as though she had wished to set her children against each other.

'You have seen my last bill of costs, Mistress Slanning?' I asked.

'And paid it at once, Serjeant Shardlake.' She tilted her chin proudly. It was true; she always settled immediately, without question. She was no Bealknap.

'I know, madam, and I am grateful. But if this matter goes on into next year, into Chancery, the costs will grow and grow.'

'Then you must make Edward pay them all.'

'Normally in probate matters costs are taken out of the estate. And remember, with the value of money falling, the house and your mother's money are going down in value too. Would it not be more sensible, more practical, to try and find some settlement now?'

She bridled. 'Sir, you are my lawyer. You should be advising me on how I can win, surely, not encouraging me to end the matter without a clear victory.' Her voice had risen again; I kept mine deliberately low.

'Many people settle when the outcome is uncertain and costly. As it is here. I have been thinking. Have you ever considered buying Edward's half-share of the house from him and selling your own residence? Then you could live in your mother's house and leave the wall painting intact, where it is.'

She gave a braying little laugh. 'Mother's house is far too big for me. I am a childless widow. I know she lived there alone but for her servants, but she was foolish; it is far too large for a woman by herself. Those great big rooms. No, I will have the painting down and in my hands. Removed by the best craftsmen in London. Whatever it costs. I shall make Edward pay in the end.'

I looked at her. I had had difficult, unreasonable clients in my time but Isabel Slanning's obstinacy and loathing of her brother were extraordinary. Yet she was an intelligent woman, no fool except to herself.

I had done my best. 'Very well,' I said. 'I think the next thing is to go over your most recent deposition. There are some things you say which I think would be better amended. We must show ourselves reasonable to the court. Calling your brother a pestilent knave will not help.'

'The court should know what he is like.'

'It will not help you.'

She shrugged, then nodded, adjusting her hood on her grey head. As I took out the deposition, Nicholas leaned forward and said, 'With your leave, sir, may I ask the good lady a question?'

I hesitated, but it was my duty to train him up. 'If you wish.'

He looked at Isabel. 'You said, madam, that your house is much smaller than your mother's.'

She nodded. 'It is. But it suffices for my needs.'

'With smaller rooms?'

'Yes, young man,' she answered tetchily. 'Smaller houses have smaller rooms. That is generally known.'

'But I understand the wall painting is in the largest room of your mother's house. So if you were able to remove the painting, where would you put it?'

Isabel's face reddened and she bridled. 'That is my business, boy,' she snapped. 'Yours is to take notes for your master.'

Nicholas blushed in turn and bent his head to his papers. But it had been a very good question.

✝

WE SPENT AN HOUR going over the documents, and I managed to persuade Isabel to take various abusive comments about her brother out of her deposition. By the time it was over, my head was swimming with tiredness. Nicholas gathered up his notes and left the room, bowing to Isabel. She rose, quite energetic still, but frowning; she had looked angry ever since Nicholas's question. I got up to escort her outside, where a serving-man waited to take her home. She stood facing me – she was a tall woman and those determined, staring eyes looked straight into mine. 'I confess, Master Shardlake, sometimes I wonder if your heart is in this case as it should be. And that insolent boy . . .' She shook her head angrily.

'Madam,' I replied. 'You can rest assured I will argue your case with all the vigour I can muster. But it is my duty to explore alter-natives with you, and warn you of the expense. Of course, if you are dissatisfied with me, and wish to transfer the case to another barrister—'

She shook her head grimly. 'No, sir, I shall stay with you, fear not.'

I had made the suggestion to her more than once before; but it was an odd fact that the most difficult and hostile clients were often the most reluctant to leave, as though they wanted to stay and plague you out of spite.

'Though . . .' She hesitated.

'Yes.'

'I think you do not truly understand my brother.' An expression I had not seen before crossed her face. Fear – there was no doubt about it, fear that twisted her face into new, different lines. For a second, Isabel was a frightened old woman.

'If you knew, sir,' she continued quietly. 'If you knew the terrible things my brother has done.'

'What do you mean?' I asked. 'Done to you?'

'And others.' A vicious hiss; the anger had returned.

'What things, madam?' I pressed.

But Isabel shook her head vigorously, as though trying to shake unpleasant thoughts out of it. She took a deep breath. 'It does not matter. They have no bearing on this case.' Then she turned and walked rapidly from the room, the linen tappets of her hood swishing angrily behind her.

Chapter Three

IT WAS PAST SIX when I returned home. My friend Guy was due for dinner at seven – a late meal, but like me he worked a long day. As usual, Martin had heard me enter and was waiting in the hall to take my robe and cap. I decided to go into the garden to enjoy a little of the evening air. I had recently had a small pavilion and some chairs set at the end of the garden, where I could sit and look over the flower beds.

The shadows were long, a few bees still buzzing round the hive. Wood pigeons cooed in the trees. I sat back. I realized that during my interview with Isabel Slanning I had not thought at all about the burning; such was the power of her personality. Young Nicholas had asked a clever question about where she would put the picture. Her answer had been further proof that, for Isabel, winning the quarrel mattered more than the picture, however genuine her attachment to it. I thought again of her strange remark at the end, about some terrible things her brother had done. During our interviews she usually liked nothing better than to abuse and belittle Edward, but that sudden spasm of fear had been different.

I pondered whether it might be worthwhile having a quiet word with Philip Coleswyn about our respective clients. But that would be unprofessional. My duty, like his, was to represent my client as strongly as I could.

My mind went back to the horror I had watched that morning. The great stage would have been taken down now, together with the charred stakes. I thought of Coleswyn's remark that any of us could come to the fate of those four; I wondered whether he himself had dangerous connections among the reformers. And I must get rid of my books before the amnesty expired. I looked towards the house; through the window of my dining room I saw that Martin had lit the beeswax candles in their sconces, and was setting the linen tablecloth with my best silver, meticulously, everything lined up.

I returned to the house and went into the kitchen. There, all was bustle. Timothy was turning a large chicken on the range. Josephine stood at one end of the table, arranging salads on plates in a pleasing design. At the other end, Agnes Brocket was putting the finishing touches to a fine marchpane of almonds and marzipan. They curtsied as I entered. Agnes was a plump woman in her forties, with nut-brown hair under her clean white coif, and a pleasant face. There was sadness there too, though. I knew that the Brockets had a grown son who for some reason they never saw; Martin had mentioned it at his interview, but nothing more.

'That looks like a dish fit for a feast,' I said, looking at the marchpane. 'It must have cost you much labour.'

Agnes smiled. 'I take pleasure in producing a fine dish, sir, as a sculptor may in perfecting a statue.'

'The fruits of his labours last longer. But perhaps yours bring more pleasure.'

'Thank you, sir,' she replied. Agnes appreciated compliments. 'Josephine helped, didn't you, dear?' Josephine nodded, giving me her nervous smile. I looked at her. Her cruel rogue of a father had been my previous steward, and when I had – literally – booted him out of the house a year before, Josephine had stayed with me. Her father had terrified and intimidated her for years, but with him gone she had gradually become less shy and frightened. She had begun to take care of her appearance, too; her unbound blonde hair had a clear lustre, and her face had rounded out, making her a pretty young woman. Following my look, Agnes smiled again.

'Josephine is looking forward to Sunday,' she said archly.

'Oh? And why is that?'

'A little bird tells me that after church she will be walking out again with young Master Brown, that works in one of the Lincoln's Inn households.'

I looked at Josephine. 'Which one?'

'That of Master Henning,' Josephine said, reddening. 'He lives in chambers.'

'Good, good. I know Master Henning, he is a fine lawyer.' I turned back to Agnes. 'I must go and wash before my guest comes.' Though goodhearted, Agnes could be a little tactless, and I did not want Josephine embarrassed further. But I was pleased; it was more than time Josephine had a young man.

As I left the kitchen, Martin returned. He bowed. 'The table is set, sir.'

'Good. Thank you.' Just for a second I caught Josephine glance at him with a look of dislike. I had noticed it once or twice before, and been puzzled by it, for Martin had always seemed a good master to the lower servants.

✝

GUY ARRIVED shortly after seven. My old friend was a physician, a Benedictine monk before the Dissolution of the Monasteries. He was of Moorish stock; past sixty now, his dark features lined and his curly hair white. As he entered I noticed he was developing the stoop that tall men sometimes do in their later years. He looked tired. A few months ago I had suggested that perhaps it was time for him to think of retiring, but he had replied that he was still quite fit, and besides, he would not know what to do with himself.

In the dining room we washed our hands at the ewer, put our napkins over our shoulders, and sat down. Guy looked admiringly over the table. 'Your silver has a merry gleam in the candlelight,' he said. 'Everything in your house looks well these days.'

Martin knocked at the door and came in, setting out the dishes of salad, with herbs and slices of fresh salmon from the Thames. When he had gone I said to Guy, 'You are right, he and Agnes were a find. His old employer gave him a good reference. But, you know, I am never at ease with him. He has such an impenetrable reserve.'

Guy smiled sadly. 'I remember when I was at the monastery at Malton, we had a steward such as that. But he was a fine fellow. Just brought up to believe he must never be presumptuous with his super-iors.'

'How are things at St Bartholomew's?' I asked. The old hospital, one of the few for the poor in London, had been closed when the King dissolved the monasteries, but a few volunteers had reopened it, to provide at least some service. Guy was one of the volunteers there. I recalled guiltily that when my friend Roger Elliard had died three years ago I promised his widow to continue his work to open a new hospital. But then the war came, everyone suffering from the taxes and fall in the value of money, which had continued ever since, and no one was willing to donate.

He spread his hands. 'One does what one can, though Jesu knows it is little enough. There is talk of the city authorities taking it over, with a grant of money from the King, but nothing ever seems to happen.'

'I see more driven into poverty in the city every day.'

'Poverty and illness both.'

We were silent a moment. Then, to raise our mood, I said, 'I have some good news. Tamasin is pregnant again. The baby is due in Janu-ary.'

He smiled broadly, a flash of good white teeth. 'Thanks be to God. Tell her I shall be delighted to attend her during her pregnancy again.'

'We are both invited to a celebration on George's first birthday. The twenty-seventh.'

'I shall be glad to go.' He looked at me. 'A week on Tuesday. And this coming Monday will be – ' he hesitated – 'the anniversary of . . .'

'The day the *Mary Rose* went down. When all those men died, and I so nearly with them.' I lowered my head, shook it sadly. 'It seems a peace treaty has been signed. At last.'

'Yes. They say the King will get to keep Boulogne, or what is left of it, for ten years.'

'Not much to show for all the lives lost, or the ruination of the coinage to pay for it.'

'I know,' Guy agreed. 'But what of you? Do you ever get that feeling of the ground shifting beneath you, that you had after the ship went down?'

I hesitated, remembering that moment at the burning. 'Very seldom now.' He looked at me sharply for a moment, then said, more cheerfully, 'Young George is a merry little imp. Having a new brother or sister may put his nose out of joint.'

I smiled wryly. 'Brothers and sisters,' I said. 'Yes, they do not always get on.' I told Guy, without naming names, something of the Slanning case. He listened intently, his dark eyes shining in the candlelight as the dusk deepened. I concluded, 'I have thought this woman actually takes pleasure in her hatred of her brother, but after what she said this afternoon I think there may be more to it.'

Guy looked sad. 'It sounds as though this quarrel goes back a very long way.'

'I think so. I have thought of talking quietly about it with my opponent – he is a reasonable man – see if we can work out some way to get them to settle. But that would be unprofessional.'

'And may do no good. Some quarrels go so deep they cannot be mended.' The sadness in Guy's face intensified. Martin and Agnes brought in the next course, platters of chicken and bacon and a variety of vegetables in bowls.

'You are not usually so pessimistic,' I said to Guy when we were alone again. 'Besides, only recently I was offered an olive branch by the last person I would expect to do such a thing.' I told him the story of Bealknap's note, and the money.

He looked at me sharply. 'Do you trust him? Think of all he has done in the past.'

'It seems he is dying. But – ' I shrugged my shoulders – 'no, I cannot bring myself to trust Bealknap, even now.'

'Even a dying animal may strike.'

'You are in a dark humour tonight.'

'Yes,' he said slowly. 'I am. I think of what happened at Smith-field this morning.'

I put down my knife. I had avoided discussing religion with Guy during these recent months of persecution, for I knew he had remained a Catholic. But after a moment's hesitation I said, 'I was there. They made a vast spectacle of it, Bishop Gardiner and half the Privy Coun-cil watching from a great covered stage. Treasurer Rowland made me go; Secretary Paget wanted a representative from each of the Inns. So I sat and watched four people burn in agony because they would not believe as King Henry said they should. At least they hung gun-powder round their necks; their heads were eventually blown off. And yes, when I was there, I felt the ground shift beneath me again, like the deck of that foundering ship.' I put a hand up to my brow, and found it was shaking slightly.

'May God have mercy on their souls,' Guy said quietly.

I looked up sharply. 'What does that mean, Guy? Do you think they need mercy, just for saying what they believed? That priests cannot make a piece of bread turn into the body of Christ?'

'Yes,' he said quietly. 'I believe they are wrong. They deny the Mystery of the Mass – the truth that God and the church has taught us for centuries. And that is dangerous to all our souls. And they are everywhere in London, hiding in their dog-holes: sacramentarians and, worse, Anabaptists, who not only deny the Mass but believe all society should be overthrown and men hold all goods in common.'

'There have only ever been a few Anabaptists in England, just some renegade Dutchmen. They have been raised up into a bogey.' I heard the impatience in my voice.

Guy answered sharply, 'Well, the Askew woman boasted herself that she was a sacramentarian. Askew was not even her name; her married name was Kyme and she left her husband and two little chil-dren to come and harangue the people of London. Is that a right thing for a woman to do?'

I stared at my old friend, whose greatest quality had always been his gentleness. He raised a hand. 'Matthew, that does not mean I think they should have been killed in that horrible way. I don't, I don't. But they were heretics, and they should have been – silenced. And if you want to talk of cruelty, think of what the radical side has done. Think what Cromwell did to those who refused to accept the Royal Supremacy ten years ago, the monks eviscerated alive at Tyburn.' His face was full of emotion now.

'Two wrongs do not make a right.'

'Indeed they do not. I hate the cruelties both sides have carried out as much as you. I wish I could see an end to it. But I cannot. That is what I meant when I said some quarrels go so deep they are impossible to mend.' He looked me in the eye. 'But I do not regret that the King has taken us halfway back to Rome and upholds the Mass. I wish he would take us all the way.' He continued, eagerly now. 'And the old abuses of the Catholic Church are being resolved; this Council of Trent which Pope Paul III has called will reform many things. There are those in the Vatican who would reach out to the Protestants, bring them back into the fold.' He sighed. 'And everyone says the King grows sick. Prince Edward is not yet nine. I believe it wrong that a monarch should make himself head of a Christian church and declare that he instead of the Pope is the voice of God in making church policy. But how can a little boy exercise that headship? Better that England take the opportunity to return to the Holy Church.'

'To the Church that burns people, in France, in Spain under the Inquisition? Many more than here. And besides, the Holy Roman Emperor Charles is making fresh war on his Protestant subjects.'

Guy said, 'You have turned radical again?'

'No!' My own voice rose. 'Once I hoped a new faith based on the Bible would clearly show God's Word to the people. I hate the babble of divisions that has followed; radicals using passages from the Bible like black-headed nails, as insistent they alone are right as any papist. But when I see a young woman taken to the stake, carried in a chair because she has been tortured, then burned alive in front of the great men of the realm, believe me I look with no longing for the old ways either. I remember Thomas More, that indomitable papist, the people he burned for heresy.'

'If only we could all find the essence of true godliness, which is piety, charity, unity,' Guy said sadly.

'As well wish for the moon,' I answered. 'Well, then, on one thing we agree: such divisions have been made in this country that I cannot see ever mending until one side bludgeons the other into defeat. And it made me sick this afternoon seeing men whom Thomas Cromwell raised up, believing they would further reform, now twisting back to further their ambition instead: Paget, Wriothesley, Richard Rich. Bishop Gardiner was there as well; he has a mighty thunderous look.' I laughed bitterly. 'I hear the radicals call him the Puffed-up Porkling of the Pope.'

'Perhaps we should not discuss these matters any more,' Guy said quietly.

'Perhaps. After all, it is not safe these days to speak freely, any more than to read freely.'

There was a quiet knock at the door. Martin would be bringing the marchpane. I had no appetite for it now. I hoped he had not heard our argument. 'Come in,' I said.

It was Martin, but he was not carrying a dish. His face, always so expressionless, looked a little perturbed. 'Master Shardlake, there is a visitor for you. A lawyer. He said he must speak with you urgently. I told him you were at dinner, but he insisted.'

'What is his name?'

'I am sorry, sir, he would not give it. He said he must speak with you alone. I left him in your study.'

I looked at Guy. He still seemed unhappy at our argument, picking at his plate, but he smiled and said, 'You should see this gentleman, Matthew. I can wait.'

'Very well. Thank you.' I rose from the table and went out. At least the interruption would allow my temper to cool.

It was full dark now. Who could be calling at such an hour?

Through the hall window I could see two link-boys, young fellows carrying torches to illuminate the way, who must have accompanied my visitor. There was another with them, a servant in dark clothes with a sword at his waist. Someone of status, then.

I opened the door to my study. To my astonishment I saw, standing within, the young man who had been watching me at the burning, still dressed soberly in his long robe. Though he was not handsome — his cheeks disfigured with moles — his face had a strength about it, despite his youth, and the protuberant grey eyes were keen and probing. He bowed to me. 'Serjeant Shardlake. God give you good evening. I apologize for disturbing you at dinner, but I fear the matter is most urgent.'

'What is it? One of my cases?'

'No, sir.' He coughed, a sudden sign of nervousness. 'I come from Whitehall Palace, from her majesty the Queen. She begs you to see her.'

'Begs?' I answered in surprise. Queens do not beg.

'Yes, sir. Her message is that she is in sore trouble, and pleads your help. She asked me to come; she did not wish to put her request in writing. I serve in a junior way on her majesty's Learned Council. My name is William Cecil. She needs you, sir.'

Chapter Four

I HAD TO SIT DOWN. I went to the chair behind my desk, motioning Cecil to a seat in front. I had brought in a candle, and I set it on the table between us. It illuminated the young man's face, the shadows emphasizing the line of three little moles on his right cheek.

I took a deep breath. 'I see you are a barrister.'

'Yes, of Gray's Inn.'

'Do you work with Warner, the Queen's solicitor?'

'Sometimes. But Master Warner was one of those questioned about heretical talk. He is – shall we say – keeping his head low. I am trusted by the Queen; she herself asked me to be her emissary.'

I spread my hands. 'I am nothing more than a lawyer practising in the courts. How can the Queen be in urgent need of my help?'

Cecil smiled, a little sadly I thought. 'I think we both know, Serjeant Shardlake, that your skills run further than that. But I am sorry; I may give you no more particulars tonight. If you consent to come, the Queen will see you at Whitehall Palace tomorrow at nine; there she can tell you more.'

I thought again, Queens do not beg or ask a subject to visit them; they order. Before her marriage to the King, Catherine Parr had prom-ised that while she would pass legal cases my way she would never involve me in matters of politics. This, clearly, was something big, something dangerous, and in wording her message thus she was offer-ing me a way out. I could, if I wished, say no to young Cecil.

'You can tell me nothing now?' I pressed.

'No, sir. I only ask, whether you choose to come or no, that you keep my visit entirely to yourself.'

Almost everything in me wanted to refuse. I remembered what I had witnessed that morning, the flames, the screams, the blood. And then I thought of Queen Catherine, her courage, her nobility, her gentleness and humour. The finest and most noble lady I had ever met, who had done me nothing but good. I took a deep, deep breath. 'I will come,' I said. I told myself, like a fool, that I could see the Queen and then, if I chose, still decline her request.

Cecil nodded. I got the sense he was not greatly impressed with me. Probably he saw a middle-aged hunchback lawyer deeply troubled by the possibility of being thrown into danger. If so, he was right.

He said, 'Come by road to the main gate of the palace at nine. I will be waiting there. I will take you inside, and then you will be conducted to the Queen's chambers. Wear your lawyer's robe but not your serjeant's coif. Better you attract as little notice as possible at this stage.' He stroked his wispy beard as he regarded me, thinking perhaps that, as a hunchback, I might attract some anyway.

I stood. 'Till nine tomorrow, then, Brother Cecil.'

He bowed. 'Till nine, Serjeant Shardlake. I must return now to the Queen. I know she will be glad to have your reply.'

☦

I SHOWED HIM OUT. Martin appeared from the dining room bearing another candle, opened the door for Cecil and bowed, always there to perform every last detail of a steward's duty. Cecil stepped onto the gravel drive, where his servant waited beside the link-boys with their torches to light him home, wherever that was. Martin closed the door.

'I took the liberty of serving the marchpane to Dr Malton,' he said.

'Thank you. Tell him I will be with him in a moment. But first send Timothy to my study.'

I went back into my room. My little refuge, my haven, where I kept my own small collection of law books, diaries and years of notes. I wondered, what would Barak think if he knew of this? He would say bluntly that I should cast aside my sentimental fantasy for the Queen and invent an urgent appointment tomorrow in Northumberland.

Timothy arrived and I scribbled a note for him to take round and leave at chambers, asking Barak to prepare a summary of one of my more important cases which I had intended to do tomorrow. 'No, pest on it! Barak has to chase up those papers at the Six Clerks' office . . .' I amended the note to ask Nicholas to do the job. Even if the boy came up with a jumble, it would be a starting point.

Timothy looked at me, his dark eyes serious. 'Are you all right, Master?' he asked.

'Yes, yes,' I replied irritably. 'Just harried by business. There is no peace under the sun.' Regretting my snappishness, I gave him a half-groat on his way out, before returning to the dining chamber, where Guy was picking at Agnes's fine marchpane.

'I am sorry, Guy, some urgent business.'

He smiled. 'I, too, have had my meals interrupted when a crisis overtakes some poor patient.'

'And I am sorry if I spoke roughly before. But what I saw this morning unmanned me.'

'I understand. But if you think all those who oppose reform – or those of us who, yes, would have England back in the bosom of the Roman family – support such things you do us great injustice.'

'All I know is that I hear thunder rolling all around the throne,' I said, paraphrasing Wyatt's poem. I then remembered again Philip Coleswyn's words at the burning and shuddered. Any of us may come to this now.

☩

EARLY NEXT MORNING Timothy saddled Genesis and I rode down to Chancery Lane. My horse was getting older; round in body, his head growing bony. It was another pleasant July day; hot but with a gentle cooling breeze stirring the green branches. I passed the Lincoln's Inn gatehouse and rode on to Fleet Street, moving to the side of the road as a flock of sheep was driven into London for slaughter at the Shambles.

Already the city was busy, the shops open and the owners' apprentices standing in doorways calling their wares. Peddlers with their trays thronged the dusty way, a rat-catcher in a wadmol smock walked nearby, stooped under the weight of two cages hung from a pole carried across his shoulders, each one full of sleek black rats. A woman with a basket on her head called out, 'Hot pudding pies!' I saw a sheet of paper pasted to a wall printed with the long list of books forbidden under the King's recent proclamation, which must be surrendered by the 9th of August. Someone had scrawled 'The word of God is the glory of Christ' across it.

As I reached the Strand the road became quieter. The way bent south towards Westminster, following the curve of the river. To the left stood the grand three- and four-storeyed houses of the wealthy; the facades brightly painted and decorated, liveried guards at the doorways. I passed the great stone Charing Cross, then turned down into the broad street of Whitehall. Already I could see the tall buildings of the palace ahead, turreted and battlemented, every pinnacle topped with lions and unicorns and the royal arms, gilded so they flashed in the sun like hundreds of mirrors, the brightness making me blink.

Whitehall Palace had originally been Cardinal Wolsey's London residence, York Place, and when he fell the King had taken it into his possession. He had steadily expanded it over the last fifteen years; it was said he wished it to be the most lavish and impressive palace in Europe. To the left of the broad Whitehall Road stood the main buildings, while to the right were the pleasure buildings, the tennis courts where the King had once disported, the great circular cockpit and the hunting ground of St James's Park. Spanning the street, beyond which became King Street, and connecting the two parts of the palace was the Great Gate designed by Holbein, an immense towered gatehouse four storeys high. Like the walls of the palace itself, it was tiled with black-and-white chequer-work, and decorated with great terracotta roundels depicting Roman emperors. The gateway at the bottom was dwarfed by the size of this edifice, yet wide enough to enable the biggest carts to pass two abreast.

A little before the Great Gate, the line of the palace walls was broken by a gatehouse, smaller, though still magnificent, which led to the palace buildings. Guards in green-and-white livery stood on duty there. I joined a short queue waiting to go in: behind me, a long cart pulled by four horses drew up. It was piled with scaffolding poles, no doubt for the new lodgings being constructed for the King's elder daughter, Lady Mary, by the riverside. Another cart, just being checked in, was laden with geese for the kitchens, while in front of me three young men sat on horses with richly decorated saddles, accompanied by a small group of servants. The young gentlemen wore doublets puffed and slashed at the shoulders to show a violet silk lining, caps with peacock feathers, and short cloaks slung across one shoulder in the new Spanish fashion. I heard one say, 'I'm not sure Wriothesley's even here today, let alone that he's read Marmaduke's petition.'

'But Marmaduke's man has got us on the list; that'll get us as far as the Presence Chamber. We can have a game of primero and who knows who might pass by once we're in.'

I realized these young men were aspiring courtiers, gentry most likely, with some peripheral connection to one of Sir Thomas Wriothesley's staff, some of the endless hangers-on who haunted the court in the hope of being granted some position, some sinecure. They had probably spent half a year's income on those clothes, hoping to catch the eye or ear of some great man – or even his manservant. I remembered the collective noun used for those who came here: a threat of courtiers.

My turn came. The guard had a list in his hand and a little stylus to prick off the names. I was about to give mine when, from an alcove within the gatehouse, young Cecil appeared. He spoke briefly to the guard, who marked his paper and waved me forward. As I rode under the gatehouse arch I heard the young men arguing with the guard. Apparently they were not on the list after all.

I dismounted beyond the gatehouse near some stables; Cecil spoke to an ostler, who took Genesis's reins. His voice businesslike, he said,

'I will escort you into the Guard Chamber. Someone is waiting there who will take you to see the Queen.' Cecil wore another lawyer's robe today, a badge sewn onto the chest showing the head and shoulders of a young woman crowned: the Queen's personal badge of St Catherine.

I nodded assent, looking round the cobbled outer courtyard. I had been there briefly before, in Lord Cromwell's time. To the right was the wall of the loggia surrounding the King's Privy Garden. The buildings on the other three sides were magnificent, the walls either chequered in black and white, or painted with fantastic beasts and plants in black relief to stand out more against white walls. Beyond the Privy Garden, to the south, I could see a long range of three-storey buildings reaching along to the Great Gate, which I remembered were the King's private apartments. Ahead of us was a building fronted with ornately decorated pillars. More guards stood at the door, which was ornamented with the royal arms. Behind soared the high roof of the chapel.

The courtyard was crowded, mostly with young men. Some were as richly dressed as the three at the gate, wearing slashed and brightly decorated doublets and hose in all colours, and huge exaggerated codpieces. Others wore the dark robes of senior officials, gold chains of office round their necks, attended by clerks carrying papers. Servants in the King's livery of green and white, HR embroidered on their doublets, mingled with the throng, while servants in workaday clothes from the kitchens or stables darted between them. A young woman accompanied by a group of female servants passed by. She wore a fashionable farthingale dress; the conical skirt, stitched with designs of flowers, was wide at the bottom but narrowed to an almost impossibly small waist. One or two of the would-be courtiers doffed their hats to her, seeking notice, but she ignored them. She looked preoccupied.

'That is Lady Maud Lane,' Cecil said. 'The Queen's cousin and chief gentlewoman.'

'She does not seem happy.'

'She has had much to preoccupy her of late,' he said sadly. Cecil looked at the courtiers. 'Place-hunters,' he said. 'Office-seekers, opportunists, even confidence tricksters.' He smiled wryly. 'But when I first qualified I, too, sought out high contacts. My father was a Yeoman of the Robes, so I started with connections, as one needs to.'

'You also seek to rise?' I asked him.

'Only on certain terms, certain principles.' His eyes locked with mine. 'Certain loyalties.' He was silent a moment, then said, 'Look. Master Secretary Paget.' I saw the man with heavy, slab-like features, brown beard and slit of a downturned mouth, who had been at the burning, traverse the courtyard. He was attended by several black-robed servants, one of whom read a paper to him as they walked, bending close to his ear.

'Mark him, Serjeant Shardlake,' Cecil said. 'He is closer to the King than anyone now.'

'I thought that was Bishop Gardiner.'

He smiled thinly. 'Gardiner whispers in his ear. But William Paget makes sure the administration works, discusses policy with the King, controls patronage.'

I looked at him. 'You make him sound like Cromwell.'

Cecil shook his head. 'Oh, no. Paget discusses policy with the King, but goes only so far as the King wishes, no further. He never tries to rule him. That was Cromwell's mistake, and Anne Boleyn's. It killed them both. The great ones of the realm have learned better now.' He sighed heavily. 'Or should have.'

He led me across the cobbles. Two burly men in the King's livery, each with a ragged boy in his grasp, passed us, went to the gate, and threw them outside with blows about the head. Cecil said disapprovingly, 'Such ragamuffins are always getting in, claiming to be the servant of a servant of some junior courtier. There aren't enough porters to throw them all out.'

'There's no security?' I asked in surprise.

'In the outer court, very little. But inside – that, you will see, is a different matter.'

He led me across to the door bearing the King's arms. Two

Yeomen of the Guard carrying long sharp halberds stood there in their distinctive red doublets decorated with golden Tudor roses. Cecil approached one and said, 'Master Cecil and lawyer for Lord Parr.' The yeoman marked his list, and we passed inside.

✝

WE ENTERED a large hall. Several men stood there on guard. Their clothes were even more magnificent than those of the yeomen; black silk gowns, and caps with large black feathers, their brims embroidered with gold. Round their necks each wore a large golden badge on a chain. All were tall, and powerfully built. They carried sharp poleaxes. This must be the King's personal guard, the Gentle-men Pensioners.

The walls were decorated with bright tapestries, painted wooden chests standing by the walls. And then I saw, covering the whole of one wall, a picture I had heard of, painted last year by one of the late Master Holbein's disciples: The King and His Family. It showed an inner room of the palace; in the centre, the King, solid, red-bearded and stern, sat on a throne under a richly patterned cloth of estate, wearing a broad-shouldered doublet in gold and black. He rested one hand on the shoulder of a little boy, Prince Edward, his only son. On his other side Edward's mother, Henry's long-dead third wife Jane Seymour, sat with hands folded demurely in her lap. Standing one on each side of the royal couple were a young lady and an adolescent girl: Lady Mary, Catherine of Aragon's daughter, and Lady Elizabeth, daughter of Anne Boleyn, both restored to the succession two years before. Behind each of the young women was an open doorway giving onto a garden. In the doorway behind Mary, a little woman with a vacant expression on her face was visible, while behind Elizabeth stood a short man with a hunched back, a monkey in doublet and cap on his shoulder. I stood for a second, enraptured by the magnificence of the painting, then Cecil touched my arm and I turned to follow him.

The next chamber, too, contained a fair number of richly dressed

young men, standing around or sitting on chests. There seemed no end
of them. One was arguing with a guard who stood before the only
inner door. 'There will be trouble, sir,' he said hotly, 'if I do not get to
see Lord Lisle's steward today. He wishes to see me.'

The guard looked back impassively. 'If he does, we'll be told. Till
then, you can stop cluttering up the King's Guard Chamber.'

We approached. The guard turned to us with relief. Cecil spoke
quietly: 'Lord Parr awaits us within.'

'I've been told.' The guard studied me briefly. 'No weapons?' he
asked. 'No dagger?'

'Certainly not,' I replied. I often carried a dagger, but I knew
weapons were forbidden within the royal palaces. Without another
word, the big man opened the door just wide enough for us to pass
through.

✝

AHEAD OF US WAS A broad flight of stairs, covered with thick
rush matting that deadened the sound of our footsteps as we ascended.
I marvelled at the decorations on the walls; everything a riot of colour
and intricate detail. There were brightly painted shields displaying the
Tudor arms and heraldic beasts, intertwined leaves of plants painted
on the walls between, and areas of linenfold panelling – wood intricately carved to resemble folded cloth – painted in various colours.
More Gentlemen Pensioners stood guard at intervals on the stairs,
staring impassively ahead. I knew we were approaching the Royal
Apartments on the first floor. We had passed out of the ordinary
world.

At the top of the stairs a man stood waiting for us, alone. He was
elderly, broad-shouldered, and carried a staff. He wore a black robe
bearing the Queen's badge and there was a gold chain of unusual
magnificence round his neck. The hair beneath his jewelled cap was
white, as was his little beard. His face was pale and lined. Cecil bowed
deeply and I followed. Cecil introduced us. 'Serjeant Shardlake: the
Queen's Lord Chancellor, her uncle Lord Parr of Horton.'

Lord Parr nodded to Cecil. 'Thank you, William.' Despite his age, his voice was deep and clear. Cecil bowed again and walked back down the stairs, a trim little figure amidst all the magnificence. A servant passed us, hurrying silently down the steps after him.

Lord Parr looked at me with sharp blue eyes. I knew that when the Queen's father died young, this man, his brother, had been a mainstay of support to his bereaved wife and children; he had been an associate of the King in his young days and had helped advance the Parr family at court. He must be near seventy now.

'Well,' he said at length. 'So you are the lawyer my niece praises so highly.'

'Her majesty is kind.'

'I know the great service you did her before she became Queen.' He looked at me seriously. 'Now she asks another,' he added. 'Has she your complete and unquestioning loyalty?'

'Total and entire,' I said.

'I warn you now, this is a dirty, secret and dangerous matter.' Lord Parr took a deep breath. 'You will learn things it is potentially fatal to know. The Queen has told me you prefer life as a private man, so let us have that out in the open now.' He looked at me for a long moment. 'Knowing that, will you still help her?'

My answer came immediately, without thought or hesitation. 'I will.'

'Why?' he asked. 'I know you are no man of religion, though you were once.' His voice became stern. 'You are, like so many in these days, a Laodicean, one who dissembles on matters of faith to keep quiet and safe.'

I took a deep breath. 'I will aid the Queen because she is the most good and honourable lady I have ever met, and has done naught but good to all.'

'Has she?' Lord Parr, unexpectedly, gave a sardonic smile. He looked at me for a long moment, then nodded decisively. 'Then let us go on, to the Queen's apartments.'

He led me down a narrow corridor, past a magnificent Venetian vase on a table covered with a red turkey-cloth. 'We must pass through the King's Presence Chamber, then the Queen's. There will be more young courtiers waiting to see the great ones of the realm,' he added wearily. Then, suddenly, he paused and raised a hand. We were by a small, narrow mullioned window, open against the heat of the day. Lord Parr looked quickly round to see if anyone was in the offing, then laid a hand on my arm and spoke, quietly and urgently. 'Now, quick, while we have the chance. You should see this, if you are to understand all that has happened. Look through the window from the side, he does not care to be seen thus. Quick now!'

I looked out and saw a little courtyard covered with flagstones. Two of the sturdy, black-robed Gentlemen Pensioners were helping an immense figure, clad in a billowing yellow silk caftan with a collar of light fur, to walk along, supporting him under the arms. I saw with a shock that it was the King. I had seen him close to twice before — during his Great Progress to York in 1541, when he had been a magnificent-looking figure; and again on his entry to Portsmouth last year. I had been shocked then at his deterioration; he had become hugely fat, and had looked worn with pain. But the man I saw now was the very wreck of a human being. His huge legs, made larger still by swathes of bandages, were splayed out like a gigantic child's as he took each slow and painful step. Every movement sent his immense body wobbling and juddering beneath the caftan. His face was a great mass of fat, the little mouth and tiny eyes almost hidden in its folds, the once beaky nose full and fleshy. He was bare-headed and, I saw, almost bald; his remaining hair, like his sparse beard, was quite grey. His face, though, was brick-red and sweating from the effort of walk-ing round the little courtyard. As I watched, the King suddenly thrust up his arms in an impatient gesture, making me jump back instinct-ively. Lord Parr frowned and put a finger to his lips. I glanced out again as the King spoke, in that strangely squeaky voice I remembered from York: 'Let me go! I can make my own way to the door, God rot you!' The guards stepped aside and the King took a few clumsy steps. Then he stopped, exclaiming, 'My leg! My ulcer! Hold me, you clods!' His face had gone ashen with pain. He gasped with relief as the men once again took him under the arms, supporting him.

Lord Parr stepped aside, gesturing me to follow. Quietly, in a strangely toneless voice, he said, 'There he is. The great Henry. I never thought the day would come when I would pity him.'

'Cannot he walk unaided at all?' I whispered.

'A mere few paces. A little more on a good day. His legs are a mass of ulcers and swollen veins. He rots as he goes. He has to be carried round the palace in a wheeled chair sometimes.'

'What do his doctors say?' I spoke nervously, remembering it was treason to foretell the death of the King.

'He was very ill in March, the doctors thought he would die, and yet, somehow, he survived. But they say another fever, or the closing of his large ulcer – ' Lord Parr looked round. 'The King is dying. His doctors know it. So does everyone at court. And so does he. Though of course he will not admit it.'

'Dear God.'

'He is in near-constant pain, his eyes are bad, and he will not moderate his appetite; he says he is always hungry. Eating is the only pleasure he has left.' He gave me a direct look. 'The only pleasure,' he repeated. 'It has been for some time. Apart from a little riding, and that grows more difficult.' Still speaking softly, and watching lest someone come, he said, 'And Prince Edward is not yet nine. The council think of only one thing – who will have the rule when the time comes? The kites are circling, Serjeant Shardlake. That you should know. Now come, before someone sees us by this window.'

He led me on, round a little bend to another guarded door. A low hubbub of voices could be heard from within. From behind, through that open window, I heard a little cry of pain.

Chapter Five

THE GUARD ON DUTY recognized Lord Parr and opened the door for him. I knew that the Royal Apartments were organized on the same principle in each palace: a series of chambers, with access to each more and more restricted as one approached the King's and Queen's personal rooms at the heart. The King's Presence Chamber was the most colourfully extravagant room yet in its decoration; one wall was covered with a tapestry of the Annunciation of the Virgin, in which all the figures were dressed in Roman costume, the colours so bright they almost hurt my eyes.

The room was full of young courtiers, as Parr had predicted. They stood talking in groups, leaning against the walls; some even sat at a trestle table playing cards. Having got this far through bribery or connections, they would probably stay all day. They looked up at us, their satin sleeves shimmering in the bright light from the windows. A little man dressed in a green hooded gown entered behind me and crossed the room. Small, sad-faced, and hunch-backed like me, I recognized the King's fool, Will Somers, from the painting in the Guard Chamber. His little monkey sat on his shoulder, picking nits from its master's brown hair. The courtiers watched as he walked confidently across to one of two inner doors and was allowed through.

'Sent for to cheer the King with his jests when he returns from that painful walk, no doubt,' Lord Parr said sadly. 'We go through the other door, to the Queen's Presence Chamber.'

One of the young men detached himself from the wall and approached us, removing his cap and bowing deeply. 'My Lord Parr,

I am related to the Queen's cousins, the Throckmortons. I wondered if there may be a place for my sister as a maid of honour—'

'Not now.' Lord Parr waved him away brusquely, as we approached the door to the Queen's Presence Chamber. Again the guard allowed us through with a bow.

We were in another, slightly smaller version of the Presence Chamber, a group of tapestries representing the birth of Christ decorating the walls. There were only a few young would-be courtiers here, and several Yeomen of the Guard, all wearing the Queen's badge. The supplicants turned eagerly when Lord Parr came in, but he frowned and shook his head.

He led me to a group of half a dozen richly dressed ladies playing cards at a table in a large window-bay, and we bowed to them. All were expensively made-up, their faces white with ceruse, red spots on their cheeks. All wore silken farthingales, the fronts open to show the brightly embroidered foreparts and huge detachable sleeves, richly embroidered in contrasting colours. Each gown would have cost hundreds of pounds in labour and material, and I considered how uncomfortable such attire must be on a hot summer's day. A spaniel wandered around, hoping for scraps from the dishes of sweetmeats on tables beside them as they conversed. I sensed tension in the air.

'Sir Thomas Seymour was at Whitehall the other day,' one of the ladies said. 'He looks more handsome than ever.'

'Did you hear how he routed those pirates in the Channel in May?' another asked.

A small, pretty woman in her thirties tapped the table to gain the dog's attention. 'Heel, Gardiner,' she called. It trotted over, panting at her expectantly. She looked at the other women and smiled roguishly. 'Now, little Gardiner, nothing for you today. Lie down and be quiet.' The dog was named for Bishop Gardiner, I realized; an act of mockery. The other women did not laugh, but rather looked anxious. One, older than the others, shook her head. 'Duchess Frances, is it meet to mock a man of the cloth so?'

'If he deserves it, Lady Carew.' I looked at the older woman.

This must be the wife of Admiral Carew, who had died with so many others on the *Mary Rose*. She had seen the ship go down while standing on shore with the King.

'But is it safe?' I saw the speaker was the Queen's cousin, Lady Lane, whom Cecil had pointed out to me in the courtyard.

'Well asked, daughter,' Lord Parr said brusquely.

One of the other ladies gave me a haughty look. She turned to Lord Parr. 'Is the Queen to have her own hunchback fool now, like his majesty? I thought she was content with Jane. Is this why we ladies have been sent out of the Privy Chamber?'

'Now, my Lady Hertford,' Lord Parr chided. He bowed to the ladies and led me towards the door the servant had passed through. 'Malaperts,' he muttered. 'Were it not for the loose tongues of the Queen's ladies we might not be in this trouble.' The guard stood to attention. Parr spoke to him in a low voice. 'No one else in the Queen's Privy Chamber till we finish our business.' The man bowed, opened the door and Lord Parr ushered me in.

Another magnificent room. A series of tapestries on the theme of the miracle of the loaves and fishes hung on the walls; there was more linenfold panelling, as well as vases of roses on several finely carved tables, an ornate chess set on another. There were only two people within. The Queen sat on a raised chair under a cloth of estate. She was dressed even more magnificently than her ladies, in a farthingale of crimson under a French gown in royal purple. The farthingale was covered with geometric designs; and as it caught the light I saw the intricacy of the needlework: hundreds of tiny circles and triangles and squares shot through with gold leaf. The bodice tapered to a narrow waist from which a gold pomander hung, and I caught the sharp-sweet smell of oranges. The bodice was low-cut; round the Queen's white powdered neck jewels hung on gold chains, among them a magnificent teardrop-shaped pearl. A French hood was set far back on her auburn hair. Yet beneath the magnificence, and the white ceruse covering her fine, intelligent features, I could see strain in Catherine Parr's face. She was thirty-four now, and for the first time since I had known her she looked her age. As I bowed deeply, I wondered what had happened to her, even as I asked myself what the other man, standing beside her, was doing here: Archbishop Thomas Cranmer, the man I had heard was keeping out of trouble down in Canterbury.

I raised myself. The Queen's eyes were downcast; she did not meet my gaze. Cranmer, however, had no such hesitation. He wore a silken cassock over a black doublet, a simple black cap over his grey hair. His large, expressive blue eyes were troubled.

'Serjeant Shardlake,' Cranmer said in his quiet voice. 'Why, it must be three years since we met.'

'And more, my Lord Archbishop.'

The Queen looked up, cast her sorrowful eyes over my face, and smiled tightly. 'Since the time you saved my life, Matthew.' She sighed, then blinked and turned to Lord Parr. 'Is Elizabeth gone to sit for her portrait?'

'Not without some swearing. She thinks it unseemly to be painted in her bedroom.'

'So long as she went. This portrait is important.' The Queen looked at me again, then said quietly, 'How have you fared this last year, Matthew?'

'Well enough, your majesty.' I smiled. 'I labour away at the law, as usual.'

'And young Hugh Curteys?'

'Well, too. Working for the clothiers in Antwerp.'

'Excellent. I am glad some good came out of that bad business.' She bit her lip, as though reluctant to continue.

There was a moment's silence, then Cranmer spoke. 'As the Queen remarked, once you saved her life.'

'It was my privilege.'

'Would you save it again?'

I looked at the Queen. Her eyes were cast down once more. This subdued figure was not the Catherine Parr I knew. I asked quietly, 'Has it come to that?'

'I fear it may,' Cranmer answered.

The Queen pressed her hands together. 'It is all my fault. My vanity, my forwardness—'

Lord Parr interrupted, his voice authoritative. 'I think it best we start at the beginning and tell Serjeant Shardlake all that has happened since the spring.'

The Queen nodded. 'Fetch chairs, all of you.' She sighed. 'It is no simple tale.'

We obeyed, sitting in a semi-circle before the throne. She turned to her uncle. 'Tell it all, tell it straight. Begin with what the King said in March.'

Lord Parr looked at me hard. 'You will be only the fifth person to know this story.'

I sat still, trying to keep my hands unclenched on my knees. I realized that I had truly launched myself into a deep well this time. The Queen was looking at me with a sort of desperation, toying with the pearl at her neck.

'The King was very ill in the spring,' Lord Parr began. 'He did not leave his rooms for many weeks. He would call the Queen to him for company; her presence much comforted him. The talk turned often to matters of religion, as it does with the King. At that time, though, Bishop Gardiner had just returned from abroad, in high feather from his success in negotiating his new treaty with the Holy Roman Emperor Charles.'

'And then I made my great mistake,' the Queen said, quietly and sadly. 'I have ridden high for three years, always careful in everything I have said. But I was overcome by the sin of vanity, and forgot I am a mere woman.' She looked down again, lifting the pearl on the end of its golden chain and staring at it. 'I argued with the King too forcefully, trying to persuade him to lift the ban on those of low rank reading the Bible. I told him that all need access to Christ's Word if they are to be saved . . .'

'Sadly,' Lord Parr said, 'her majesty went too far, and annoyed the King –'

The Queen calmed herself, letting the pearl drop. 'My greatest foolishness was to talk in such manner to the King once in the presence of Bishop Gardiner. After I left, the King told Gardiner – ' she hesitated – '"So women are become clerks, and I am to be lectured by my wife in my old days."' I saw tears prick the corners of her eyes.

Cranmer explained. 'We know this from one of the King's body-servants who was present. And we know that Gardiner, like the ravening wolf he is, told the King that the Queen and her ladies were heretics; they had had men to preach in the Queen's chambers during Lent who denied the bread and wine became the body and blood of Christ in the Mass, and who discussed forbidden books with them. Gardiner said such people were no better than Anabaptists, who would destroy royal rule.'

The Queen bowed her head. Lord Parr glanced at her, then continued. 'But the King was suspicious of Gardiner. Ever since Cromwell fell, he has been wary of those who would whisper in his ear about heretic plots. And despite his anger that night, he loves the Queen; the last thing he would want is to lose her. Hold fast to that, niece, hold fast.'

'But I have done dangerous things,' she said. I frowned. I had always known she was a radical in religion, and wondered with a chill whether she had indeed become a sacramentarian. For a second I smelled the smoke at Smithfield again.

'Your uncle is right,' Cranmer said reassuringly. 'The King loves you, for your goodness and the comfort you have brought him. Remember that, Kate, always.' I thought, Kate? I had not known the Queen and the Archbishop were so close.

Lord Parr continued. 'The King allowed Gardiner to search for evidence. And at the same time to order a general investigation into heresy throughout the country. He was worried already over the discontent caused by the price rises and the war – though, thanks be, God has led his majesty to see the sense of making peace.' He looked again at his niece. 'The Queen has loyal friends, and she was warned that searches were afoot. Any books that she or her ladies possessed, which Gardiner might twist as evidence to mean a supporter of heresy, were removed by me. And those who were questioned about discussions in the Queen's chamber stayed loyal and said nothing incriminating.' I wondered what those books had been. But any book with even a mildly Lutheran flavour could be used by Gardiner and his people.

The Queen spoke again. It was as though she had divined my thoughts. 'There were no books of a heretical nature, and nothing forbidden was said in the King's chambers. Though Gardiner set his dogs loose on my friends, my ladies, he came away empty-handed.' So that was why they had seemed brittle, and why Lady Carew had been anxious about Duchess Frances's mocking of Gardiner. 'Even though the place-seekers on the Privy Council became his willing tools. Lord Chancellor Wriothesley, and a man you know well, who would be glad to see me burn: Richard Rich.'

I shifted uncomfortably on my chair. 'It was through your protection of me last year that Rich became your enemy,' I said quietly.

Cranmer shook his head. 'No, Master Shardlake, Rich and Wriothesley saw the chance to rise in Bishop Gardiner's wake, and that of the Duke of Norfolk, who is hand in glove with Gardiner, and they both took it. As the senior peer of the realm, the Duke would like to be Regent for Prince Edward, should anything happen to the King. Though I pray daily for Our Lord to preserve him many years.' I remembered what I had seen from the window and saw from his face that Cranmer, man of faith as he was, had little hope those prayers would be answered.

Lord Parr took up the story again. 'You see, if Gardiner and his people could bring down the Queen and those of her ladies associated with radicalism, that would mean the end for their husbands, too: Lord Lisle, Sir Anthony Denny, the Earl of Hertford – whose wife made that unpleasant remark about you outside—'

The Queen looked up angrily. 'What has Anne Stanhope said now?'

I murmured, 'It was nothing, your majesty.'

Lord Parr said, 'She was discontented you sent the ladies out.'

'She may talk like a good Christian, but she has no charity. I will not have it!' For a moment the Queen sounded regal again, and I could not help but feel a little glow that it was mistreatment of me that had stirred her anger.

Lord Parr went on, 'So you see, Gardiner and his people sought to attack the reformers on the council through their wives. But when the investigations in the Queen's household found nothing, the King became angry; he divined that this was a deceitful plot to get him to change policy. And the rumours that Anne Askew had been tortured seemed to anger him, too.'

'No rumours,' I said. 'I was at the burning. She could not stand, she was put to death sitting in a chair.'

'We fear the torture was used to try and extract damaging information about the Queen. Though her majesty had never met the woman, Lady Hertford and Lady Denny had sent her money while she was in prison—'

'Lest she starve!' the Queen burst out. 'It was charity, charity. Mistress Askew—'

'Mistress Kyme,' Cranmer corrected gently.

'Mistress Kyme, then! That I may have been the cause of her torture . . .' Tears had appeared at the corners of the Queen's eyes again – she who had always been so self-controlled. I thought, what must it have been like for her these last months, knowing she was under investigation, but unable to say anything; all the time trying to behave normally with the King. I saw she was at the end of her tether, in no condition even to tell her story without help.

'We do not know that was the reason.' Lord Parr placed a gnarled hand on his niece's. 'But in any event, it seems the King has now had enough. He was angry, too, that his friend George Blagge was sentenced to burn; he has pardoned him.'

Cranmer nodded agreement. 'Gardiner's plot has failed. The King decided it was time to cry, "Enough!"' So that, I thought, explained Rich's worried look at Smithfield. Perhaps it explained, too, why Cranmer felt it safe to come back to court now. With a wry smile he added, 'And so he decided to teach the heresy hunters a lesson they would not forget.' He looked at the Queen. She closed her eyes.

The Archbishop took a deep breath. 'Three years ago, when Gardiner was after my head, hunting for heretics in my diocese, the King called me to see him. He said he had agreed that I should be examined by the Privy Council.' The Archbishop paused, and his face worked: a memory of fear. He took a deep breath. 'But his majesty told me the investigation into my diocese would be headed by me, and gave me his ring to present to the Privy Council to show I had his favour. Though not before he had frightened me by telling me he knew, now, who was the greatest heretic in Kent. Frightened me, warned me, but at the same time showed me I had his confidence.' He paused. 'And last week he used the same strategy with her majesty.' Cranmer looked pointedly at the Queen.

She lifted her head. 'I was called to the King's private chamber. Near two weeks ago, on the third. What he said astounded me. He said quite directly that Gardiner and his friends had tried to make him believe wicked lies about me, but now he knew better. He was unaware that I knew what had passed. Or perhaps he did know, but said nothing; he can be so – ' She broke off, fingering the pearl again, before resuming in strangely wooden tones. 'He said his love for me was undiminished, and asked for my help in teaching Gardiner and Wriothesley a lesson. He said he would have articles drawn up for my arrest, and tell Wriothesley to take me into custody. But we would pretend a copy of the articles had fallen into my hands by accident. I would be heard crying out in despair, and he would come to comfort me.' Her voice broke for a second and she swallowed hard. 'So that is what we did.' My heart beat hard with rage that the King should manipulate her so.

'Then the next evening I was to call on him in his chamber, and, in front of his gentlemen, apologize for going too far in discussing religion.' She closed her eyes. 'I was to say I knew a woman's duty is to be instructed by her husband, and that I was only seeking to distract him from the pain in his legs. I did as he asked, playing my part in the performance.' I discerned a note of bitterness, quickly suppressed, in her voice.

'The next day, I was to walk in the garden with him and my ladies. By prearrangement with the King, Wriothesley was to come and arrest me with fifty of the guard. Wriothesley thought he had won, but when he arrived the King tore the warrant from his hand, called him a beast and a knave in front of the men of the guard and my ladies, and ordered him from his presence.' She smiled sadly. 'Since then his majesty has been loving and attentive to me in front of all. I am to have new jewels; he knows I love bright jewels. I have ever had good measure of the sin of covetousness, as well as vanity.' She lowered her head.

'Then — then the crisis is over?' I said. 'That dreadful burning and the new proclamation on forbidden books — that was the last act? Wriothesley and the conservatives have been humiliated?'

'Would that it were the last act!' the Queen cried out. 'I have one book missing, the most dangerous of all, and it is my fault!'

Lord Parr put his hand over hers again. 'Calm, Kate, stay calm. You are doing well.'

Cranmer stood, walking to a window which looked out over a garden to the river, blue in the summer sunshine, dotted with the white sails of wherries and tilt-boats. Another world. There was a distant hammering from where the Lady Mary's new chambers were being built. The Archbishop said, 'I spoke of Bishop Gardiner negotiating a new treaty with the Empire. And Paget has succeeded in making peace with the French. Lord Lisle and the Earl of Hertford played their parts, too; both are abroad just now, but they will return next month, with feathers in their own caps, and the balance on the Privy Council will change in favour of the reformers. That, and the King's annoyance with Gardiner's faction, will help us. But something else is going on, Master Shardlake.' Cranmer turned and I felt the full force of those penetrating eyes. 'We do not know what it is, but we see the senior councillors in the conservative faction — Norfolk, Gardiner, and others like Paget – still smiling and talking in corners, when after their setback they should be cringing like whipped dogs. The other day, after the council, I heard Paget muttering to Norfolk about a visitor from abroad; they fell silent as I approached. Something else, something secret, is going on. They have another card still to play.'

'And I have given them a second,' the Queen said bleakly. 'Placed myself and all those I care for in jeopardy.'

This time neither her uncle nor the Archbishop sought to reassure her. The Queen smiled, not the gently humorous smile that in happier times was ever ready to appear on her face, but a sad, angry grimace. She said, 'It is time for you to know what I have done.'

Chapter Six

WE ALL LOOKED AT HER. She spoke quietly. 'Last winter, it seemed the King was moving in the direction of reform. He had made Parliament pass the bill that gave him control of the chantries; another bastion of popish ceremony had fallen. I had published my *Prayers and Meditations* that summer, and felt the time was safe for me to write another book, a declaration to the world of my beliefs, as Marguerite of Navarre has done. And so I wrote my little volume. I knew it might be – controversial – so I composed it in secret, in my bedroom. A confession – of my life; my sins, my salvation, my beliefs.' She looked at me intently; the light of conviction shone in her eyes now. 'It is called the *Lamentation of a Sinner*. I speak in it of how, when I was young, I was mired in superstition, full of vanity for the things of this world; of how God spoke to me but I denied His voice, until eventually I accepted His saving grace.' Her voice had risen with passion; she looked at Lord Parr and the Archbishop, but they had cast their eyes down. She continued, more quietly. 'It was God who brought me to realize it was my destiny to marry the King.' She cast her own head down, and I wondered if she was thinking of her old love for Thomas Seymour. 'In my *Lamentation* I speak in the most plain terms of my belief that salvation comes through faith and study of the Bible, not vain ceremonies.' I closed my eyes. I knew of books like this, confessions by radical Protestants of their sinfulness and salvation. Some had been seized by the authorities. The Queen had been foolish to write such a thing in these faction-ridden times, even in secret. She must have known it; but for once her emotions had overridden her political sense. And her hope that the times were shifting in favour of reform had again proved disastrously wrong.

'Who has seen the book, your majesty?' I asked quietly.

'Only my Lord Archbishop. I finished it in February, but then in March the trouble with Gardiner began. And so I hid it in my private coffer, telling nobody.' She added bitterly, 'You see, Matthew, I can still be sensible sometimes.' I saw that she was torn between conflicting emotions: her desire to spread her beliefs amongst the people, her acute awareness of the political dangers of doing so, and her fear for her own life. 'The book stayed locked in my coffer until last month, when I resolved to ask the Archbishop for his opinion. He came to me, here, and read it one evening with me.' She looked at Cranmer, smiling wistfully. 'We have spoken much on matters of faith, these last three years. Few know how much.'

The Archbishop looked uneasy for a moment, then said, his voice composed, 'That was on the ninth of June. A little over a month ago. And I advised her majesty that on no account should the book be circulated. It said nothing about the Mass, but the condemnation of dumb Roman ceremonies, the argument that prayer and the Bible are the only ways to salvation – those could be read, by our enemies, as Lutheran.'

'Where is the manuscript now?' I asked.

'That is our problem,' Lord Parr said heavily. 'It has been stolen.'

The Queen looked me in the eye. 'And if it finds its way to the King's hands, then likely I am dead and others, too.'

'But if it does not deny the Mass—'

'It is too radical for the King,' the Queen said. 'And that I should be its author, and have kept it secret from him . . .' Her voice faltered.

Cranmer spoke quietly. 'He would see that as disloyalty. And that is the most dangerous thing of all.'

'I can understand that,' the Queen said sadly. 'He would feel – wounded.'

My head reeled. I clasped my hands together in my lap to force my mind to focus, realizing the others were waiting for me to respond. 'How many copies are there?' I asked.

The Queen answered, 'Only one, in my own hand. I wrote it in my bedchamber, secretly, with my door locked.'

'How long is it?'

'Fifty pages of small writing. I kept it secure, in the strong chest in my bedchamber. I alone have the key and I keep it round my neck. Even when I sleep.' She put her hand to her bodice and lifted out a small key. Like the teardrop pearl, it was on the end of a fine chain.

Cranmer said bluntly, 'I advised her majesty to destroy the book. Its very existence was a danger.'

'And that was on the ninth of June?' I asked.

The Queen answered, 'Yes. I could not, of course, meet with the Archbishop in my bedchamber, so I brought it to this room. It was the only time it has left my bedchamber. I asked all the ladies and servants to leave so our discussion could be private.'

'And you told nobody about your meeting?'

'I did not.'

They were all looking at me now. I had slipped into the question-and-answer mode of the investigating lawyer. There was no pulling back from this. But I thought, if this goes wrong, it could be the fire for me as well as for them.

The Queen continued. 'My Lord Archbishop told me the book must be destroyed. And yet – I believed, and still believe, that such a work, written by a Queen of England, could bring people to right faith.' She looked at me pleadingly, as though to say: see, this is my soul, this is the truth I have learned, and you must listen. I was moved, but lowered my gaze. The Queen clasped her hands together, then looked between the three of us, her voice quietly sombre now. 'Very well, I know, I was wrong.' She added wearily, 'Such faith in my own powers is itself a token of vanity.'

I asked, 'Did you return the manuscript directly to your chest?'

'Yes. Almost every day I would look at it. For a full month. Many times I nearly called you, Uncle.'

'Would that you had,' Lord Parr said feelingly.

'Had it not been summer, had there been fires lit in the grate, once, twice, I would have burned it. But I hesitated, and days lengthened into weeks. And then, eleven days ago, the day after that scene with Wriothesley, I opened the chest and the book was gone. It was gone.' She shook her head. I realized what a shock that moment must have been to her.

'When had you last seen it?' I asked gently.

'That afternoon I looked over the manuscript again, wondering whether there were changes I might make that would render it safe to publish. Then, in the early evening, the King called me to his private chamber, and I was with him, talking and playing cards, till near ten. His legs were paining him; he needed distraction. Then, when I came to bed, I went to take it out, to look at it, to guide my prayers, and it was gone.'

'Was there any sign the lock had been tampered with?'

'No,' she answered. 'None at all.'

'What else was in the chest, your majesty?'

'Some of my jewels. Legacies from my second husband, and his daughter, dear Margaret Neville, who died this spring.' A spasm of sadness crossed her face.

Lord Parr said, 'All those jewels were of considerable value. But nothing apart from the manuscript was removed.'

I considered. 'And this was the day following the incident with Wriothesley?'

'Yes. The sixth of July. I have cause to remember recent days very well.'

Lord Parr said, 'My niece contacted me at once. I was horrified to learn of the existence of the book, and what had happened to it.'

I looked at the old man. 'I imagine the nature of the theft would make enquiries within the household – difficult.'

He shook his head. 'We dare tell nobody. But I checked with the guards who had been in and out of the Queen's bedchamber during those crucial hours. Nothing unusual: two pages to clean, a maid-in-waiting to prepare the Queen's bed. And Jane her fool, wandering in to see if the Queen was about. Jane Fool is allowed to go everywhere,' he added crossly. 'But she has not the wit to steal an apple.'

'Finding out who was seen to enter the chamber during those hours is important,' I said. 'But someone could have found out about the book earlier, and chosen the hours when her majesty was with the King to make the theft.'

'How could anyone have known,' the Queen asked, 'when I wrote it in secret, told no one, and kept it locked away?'

Lord Parr nodded agreement. 'We cannot see how this has been done – we have not known what to do. We have felt – paralysed.'

The Queen closed her eyes, clutching the pearl round her neck hard. We all watched her with concern. Finally she unclenched her hand. 'I am all right.'

'Are you sure?' Lord Parr asked.

'Yes. Yes. But you continue the story, Uncle.'

Lord Parr looked at me. 'It was then,' he said, 'that we heard of the murder by St Paul's.'

'Murder?' I asked sharply.

'Yes, there is murder in this, too. The book was stolen from the coffer sometime on the evening of the sixth of July. At dusk last Saturday, the tenth, a printer in a small way of business in Bowyer Road, hard by St Paul's, was murdered in his shop. You know how these little places have multiplied round the cathedral these last few years. Printers, booksellers, often just tiny businesses in ramshackle sheds.'

'I do, my Lord.' I knew, too, that many printers and booksellers were radicals, and that several had had their premises raided in recent months.

'The printer was a man called Armistead Greening,' Lord Parr continued. 'His shop was one of those little sheds, with only a single printing press. He had been in trouble before for publishing radical literature; he was investigated in the spring but nothing was found against him. Recently he had been printing schoolbooks. Last Saturday evening he was working in his shop. Several of the local printers were at work nearby; they toil away until the last of the light, to make the most use of their presses. Greening had an apprentice, who left at nine.'

'How do you know these details?'

'From the apprentice, but mainly from his neighbour, who owns a larger print-shop next door. Geoffrey Okedene. At around nine, Master Okedene was closing down his shop when he heard a great commotion, shouts and cries for help, from Greening's shed. He was a friend of Greening's and went to investigate. The door was locked, but it was a flimsy thing; he put his shoulder to it and broke it open. He caught a glimpse of two men running through the other door, at the side – these print-shops get so hot, and full of vile smells from the ink and other concoctions they use, that even small ones have two doors. Master Okedene did not pursue them, for an attempt had been made to set Greening's print-shop on fire. His stock of paper had been strewn around and set light to. Okedene was able to stamp it out – you may imagine that if such a place caught it would burn like a torch.'

'Yes.' I had seen these poorly erected wooden sheds that were built against the cathedral walls or in vacant plots nearby, and heard the loud rhythmic thumping that constantly resounded from them.

'Only when he had put out the fire did Okedene see poor Green-ing lying on the earthen floor, his head beaten in. And, clutched in Greening's hand, this . . .' Lord Parr reached into a pocket in his robe and carefully extracted a small strip of expensive paper covered in neat writing and dotted with the brown stains of dried blood. He passed it to me. I read:

The Lamentation of a Sinner, Made by Queen Catherine,
Bewailing the Ignorance of her Blind Life.

Most gentle and Christian reader, if matters should be rather confirmed
by their reporters than the reports warranted by the matters, I must justly
bewail our time, wherein evil deeds be well worded, and good acts evil
turned. But since truth is, that things be not good for their praises, but
praised for their goodness, I do not . . .

There the page ended, torn off. I looked at the Queen. 'This is your writing?'

She nodded. 'That is the opening of my book. *Lamentation of a Sinner.*'

Lord Parr said, 'Okedene read it and of course grasped its import from the heading. By God's mercy he is a good reformer. He brought it personally to the palace and arranged for it to be delivered into my hands. I interviewed him at once. Only then did he call the coroner. He has told him all he saw, except, at my instruction, about this piece of paper. Fortunately, the coroner is a sympathizer with reform, and has promised that if anything comes to light he will inform me. And he has been very well paid,' he added bluntly. 'With the promise of more to come.'

The Queen spoke then, an edge of desperation in her voice, 'But he has discovered nothing, nothing. And so I suggested we come to you, Matthew. You are the only one whom I know outside the court who could carry out such an investigation. But only if you will. I know the terrible dangers—'

'He has promised,' Lord Parr said.

I nodded. 'I have.'

'Then I thank you, Matthew, from the bottom of my heart.'

I looked at the torn paper. 'The obvious conclusion is that Green- ing was trying to keep the manuscript from the intruders, and whoever killed him snatched it out of his hands, but part of the top page tore away.'

'Yes,' said Lord Parr. 'And whoever killed him heard Master Okedene breaking down the door and fled. So desperate were they to avoid identification that they did not even pause to prise the piece of paper from the dead man's hands.'

'Or did not notice it at the time, more likely,' I said.

Lord Parr nodded. 'You should know that this was not the first attempt on Greening's life. He lived as well as worked in that hovel, in the most wretched poverty.' He wrinkled his nose in aristocratic dis- taste. 'As I mentioned, he has a young apprentice. Five days before, this boy arrived for work early in the morning and found two men trying to break into the shed. He called the alarm and they fled. From the apprentice's account they were different men from those who attacked and killed Greening shortly after.'

Cranmer said, 'Our first thought was that Greening had the manuscript given to him for printing. But that makes no sense. A Catholic might print it, so the book could be distributed around the streets, to the Queen's ruin, but no reformer.'

'Yes.' I considered. 'Surely if it fell into Greening's hands and his views were as you say, he would do exactly what Okedene did, return it. Could Greening have been a secret Catholic?'

Cranmer shook his head. 'I have had discreet enquiries made. Greening was a radical, a known man, all his life. And his parents before him.' He gave me a meaningful look.

A 'known man'. That meant Greening's family belonged to the old English sect of Lollardy. Over a hundred years before Luther, the Lollards had come to similar conclusions about the centrality of the Bible in the cause of salvation, and were known for their radical views about the Mass. Many of them had gravitated to the most extreme edges of Protestantism; with their long history of persecution, they had experience of being an underground community. They were as unlikely as any radicals to wish the Queen harm.

I asked, 'Is there anything else in the document that could identify it as the Queen's work?'

'It is all in the Queen's hand.'

'But the work as a whole would not be instantly identifiable, like that opening passage?'

'Even a superficial reading would identify the author.' Lord Parr looked at the Queen. 'It is, after all, a *personal* confession of sinfulness and salvation. It is obviously the Queen's work.' He shook his head. 'But we have no idea who has it now, or how it came into Greening's possession. The inquest was held two days ago; it returned a verdict of murder by persons unknown.'

The Queen looked at me. 'We have been waiting like rabbits

caught in a snare for something to happen, for the book to appear on the streets, but there has been nothing for eleven days save silence. We three have fretted day and night over what to do and decided the matter must be investigated, and not by someone closely associated with the court.' She held my gaze, her eyes full of appeal. 'And so Matthew, forgive me, my mind turned to you. But even now, I say again, I only *ask* if you will help me. I do not command; I will not. I have enough blood on my hands through my writing of that book; but for me, poor Greening would still be alive.' She added sadly, 'I meant only to do good, but truly the Bible says, "Vanity of vanities, all is vanity."' She sat back, exhausted.

I said – could only say, 'How would you have me proceed?'

Cranmer and Lord Parr exchanged a glance. Relief? Hope? Doubt as to the wisdom of placing this thing in my hands? Lord Parr stood abruptly and began pacing the room. 'We have a plan, though you must tell us if you see flaws in it. The matter is urgent and I think must be approached from both ends. So far as Greening's murder is concerned, agents of the Archbishop have spoken with his parents through their vicar. They know nothing of the book, of course, but want the murderer found. They live in the Chilterns, so cannot easily come to London.'

'The Chilterns, yes.' I knew the district had long been known for Lollardy.

'They have willingly given you a power of attorney on their behalf. So far as they are concerned, wealthy friends of their son wish to discover his murderer, nothing more. Now the inquest is over, investigations have been left in the hands of the local constable, a man called Fletcher, a plodder. You will know, Serjeant, that if a murderer is not found within forty-eight hours the constables lose interest, as the chances of finding the perpetrator are slim. I should think Fletcher will be glad if you take over the work from him. Speak to Greening's apprentice, his neighbours, his associates; look round the workshop. But say nothing about the book. Except to Okedene, who, thank God, is a man who knows how to keep his mouth shut. He is utterly loyal to reform and understands the importance of this.' Lord Parr looked at me with steely intensity.

'I will, my Lord.'

'The other aspect of the mission is to discover who stole the manuscript from here. It has to be someone with access to the Queen's chamber. You will have to be sworn in as an assistant on the Queen's Learned Council, as of this afternoon. You will be given a new robe with the Queen's badge sewn into it; wear the robe when you are making enquiries within the palace. Wear your ordinary robe when you are looking into the Greening murder – there you should not be visibly connected to the Queen.'

'Very well.'

Lord Parr nodded approvingly. Cranmer glanced at me, then quickly away; a look of pity, I thought, or perhaps doubt.

Lord Parr continued, 'So far as investigations at the palace are concerned, you are known to have worked for the Queen on legal cases before. The story we will put around is that a valuable jewel, a ring bequeathed to her by her stepdaughter, has been stolen from the Queen's coffer. Just to be sure, I have taken the ring and have it in safekeeping. It is worth a great deal. The Queen's closeness to Margaret Neville, too, is well known; everyone will understand her eagerness that it be found. You will have authority to question servants in the Queen's household about who might have gained access to that coffer. As it happens, some time ago a pageboy stole a jewel from one of the Queen's ladies and after an investigation was caught. At the Queen's insistence he was pardoned, because of his youth. People will remember that.' He looked at me. 'I would conduct the investigation myself, but for someone of my seniority to be seen taking this on personally would cause surprise. And in this place an outsider can often see things more clearly.' He sighed. 'The world of the court is an incestuous one. I am happier on my estates, I confess, but my duty lies here now.'

'I am known as an enemy to certain on the King's Council.' I spoke hesitantly. 'The Duke of Norfolk; above all, Richard Rich. And I once angered the King himself.'

Cranmer said, 'Those are old matters, Matthew. And your investigations will be confined to the Queen's household. If you uncover anything that seems to go wider, tell us and we will deal with it. I will not be returning to Canterbury until this is settled.'

'Forgive me, my Lord Archbishop,' I said, 'but word may still get to Norfolk or Rich. You spoke of spies reporting what Gardiner said to you from the King's Privy Chamber . . .'

'Sympathizers,' Cranmer replied reprovingly, 'not spies.'

'But may there not be those within the Queen's household who sympathize with the opponents of reform? The very fact the manuscript was stolen suggests as much.'

'That is the strange thing. We guard secrets very carefully in the Queen's household.' Cranmer looked at the Queen. 'Her majesty inspires great loyalty, which was tested during the heresy hunt. We can identify no one who could, or would, have done this.'

There was a moment's silence, then Lord Parr said, 'Begin now, Serjeant Shardlake; try to unravel the threads. Go to the printer's this afternoon. Come back this evening and I will swear you in, give you your robe and brief you further.'

I hesitated again. 'I am to work entirely on my own?'

'Young William Cecil may be useful, he has contacts among the radicals and is trusted by them. But he does not know of the *Lamentation*, and we will keep him out of it for now, I think.' He continued, in a lighter tone, 'Would you believe Cecil is already twice married, though only twenty-five? His first wife died in childbirth, and now he has a second. A woman with good connections. I think he will soon be a rising man.'

The Archbishop added, 'And where the printer's murder is concerned, you may employ your man Barak to help you. I understand he has been useful in the past.'

'But – ' Lord Parr raised a warning finger – 'he must know only that you are acting for the dead man's parents; make no mention of the Queen or the *Lamentation*.'

I hesitated. 'Barak is married now, with a child and another on the way. I would not put him in the way of even the possibility of danger. I have a student, Nicholas, but—'

Lord Parr interrupted. 'I will leave that to your discretion. Perhaps he can be employed in routine matters. So long as you tell him nothing of the *Lamentation.*' He looked at me intently again.

I nodded agreement, then turned to the Queen. She leaned forward and picked up the pearl on its chain round her neck. 'Do you know to whom this once belonged?' she asked quietly.

'No, your majesty. It is very fine.'

'Catherine Howard, who was Queen before me and who died on the block. A quicker death than burning.' She gave a long, desperate sigh. 'She, too, was foolish, though in a different way. All these rich things I wear, the cloth of gold and silken tissue and bright jewels, so many of them have been passed down from Queen to Queen. Always, you see, they are returned to the Department of the Queen's Wardrobe, to be preserved or altered. They are worth so much that they cannot be discarded, any more than the great tapestries.' She held up her richly embroidered sleeve. 'This was once worn with a dress of Anne Boleyn's. I have constant reminders of past events. I live in fear now, Matthew, great fear.'

'I will do all I can, put all other work aside. I swear.'

She smiled. 'Thank you. I knew you would succour me.'

Lord Parr inclined his head, indicating I should rise. I bowed to the Queen, who essayed another sad smile, and to Cranmer, who nodded. Lord Parr led me out, back to the window from which we had watched the King in the courtyard. The yard was empty now. I realized the window was in an angle of the corridor from which we could not be seen from either direction; ideal for private conversation. He said, 'Thank you, sir. Believe me, we do not underestimate the difficulties, or the dangers. Come with me now and I will give you more particulars of Greening, and the power of attorney from his parents.'

He looked out over the courtyard, hesitated, then leaned closer. 'You saw the physical state of the King. But as you will have realized from what we told you, his mind is still, mostly, sharp and clear. And it has always been full of anger and suspicion.'

Chapter Seven

IT WAS WITH A SENSE OF RELIEF that I rode out under the gate of the palace again. I made my way slowly towards Charing Cross. Genesis sneezed and shook his head at the dust from the Scotland Yard brickworks, which endlessly laboured to produce materials to embellish and improve Whitehall. The day was hot and the street stank. I decided I would take Nicholas with me to the printers' quarter. It would do no harm to have someone young and sizeable beside me.

At the steps of the great Charing Cross, dozens of beggars sat as usual. More and more of them these last two years, with the polling and nipping of poor men's wages caused by the collapsing value of the coinage. There were those who said that beggars were leeches, licking the sweat from hard-working labourers' brows, but most of the beggars had once been working men themselves. I glanced at them, men and women and children, wearing ancient dirty rags, faces red and harsh from constant exposure to the sun, some displaying their sores and weeping scabs to invoke pity from the passers-by. One man who sat with the stump of one leg exposed wore the tatters of a soldier's uniform; no doubt he had left his leg in Scotland or France during the last two years of war. But I averted my eyes, for it was well known that to catch the eye of one could bring a whole horde descending on you; and I had much to think on.

I was involved in a matter potentially more deadly than anything in my prior experience. It reached right into the heart of the royal court, at a time when the manoeuvring of various factions had never been more vicious. Recalling that spectacle of the King in the courtyard, I realized now that everything which had happened since the beginning of the year was part of a struggle to decide who would control the realm when Henry died and his throne passed to a child. In whose hands would the King leave the realm? Norfolk? Edward Seymour? Paget? The Queen?

I had let myself in for long days of fear and anxiety, as a harbourer of dangerous secrets which I did not want to possess. But a wise man knows he is a fool, and I was aware, of course, of my true motives. It was because I had long cast a fantasy of love around the Queen. It was an ageing man's hopeless foolishness, but that morning I realized how deeply I still felt.

And yet I knew I must see Queen Catherine clearly: her religious radicalism had led that most careful and diplomatic of women to risk all. She had called it her vanity but it was more like a loss of judge, ment. I wondered uneasily if she were verging towards fanaticism, like so many in these days. No, I thought, she had tried to draw back by submitting to the King and by asking for Cranmer's approval of the *Lamentation*; and yet her refusal to dispose of the book had led to potentially disastrous consequences.

The thought came to me, why not let the factions fight it out to the death? Why was the radical side any better than the conservative? But then I thought, the Queen would harm no man willingly. Nor, I believed, would Cranmer. I wondered, though, about Lord Parr. He was old and looked ill; but I had seen his devotion to his niece and sensed a ruthlessness about him, too – I was useful to him, but prob, ably dispensable as well.

Lord Parr had handed me the power of attorney from Greening's parents. I would go to the streets around St Paul's to talk to the con, stable, then to Greening's neighbour Okedene, and finally the dead man's apprentice, who had witnessed the earlier break,in. And I should try and find out who Greening's friends were.

Lord Parr wanted me back at the palace by seven. I was likely to be heavily involved with this for many days. Fortunately it was out of law term and the courts were not in session. I would have to ask Barak to do some extra preparation work on cases I had in hand, and super-vise Nicholas and Skelly. Uncomfortably I realized that I would have to lie to Barak and Nicholas; I could tell them I was involved in inves-tigating the printer's murder, but only on behalf of his family, and I must say nothing about the hunt for the Queen's missing book. I hated the thought of lying to Barak especially, but there was no obvious alternative I could see.

On impulse, I turned north, heading for the street of little houses where Barak lived with his wife, Tamasin. He would be at work but she would likely be at home this time of day. Like Barak, Tamasin was an old friend; the three of us had been through much together, and I had an urge to talk with someone ordinary, commonsensical, with no taste for intrigue; and to see my little godson. I wanted a moment of normality, perhaps the last I would be allowed for some time.

I tied Genesis to the post outside their house and knocked on the door. It was answered by their servant, Goodwife Marris, a formidable widow of middle age. She curtsied. 'Master Shardlake, we were not expecting you.'

'I was nearby, I came on impulse. Is Mistress Barak in?'

'Ay, and the master, too. He came home for lunch. I was about to clear the plates away.' I realized I had had nothing to eat. Goodwife Marris showed me into the little parlour overlooking Tamasin's small, immaculately kept garden. The shutters were open and the room was filled with the scent of summer flowers. Barak was sitting at the table with Tamasin, empty plates and mugs of beer before them. Jane began clearing the plates away. Tamasin looked well, her pretty face contented and happy. 'This is a welcome surprise, sir,' she said. 'But you have missed lunch.'

'I forgot about it.'

She clicked her tongue. 'That is not good for you.'

Barak looked at me. 'I came home to eat. I thought Skelly could keep an eye on young Nick for that long.'

'That is all right.' I smiled as a little figure in a white robe and a woollen cap tied in a bow came crawling out from under the table to see what was happening. He looked at me with Barak's brown eyes, smiled and said, 'Man!'

''Tis his new word,' Tamasin said proudly. 'See, he begins to speak.'

'He is well out of his swaddling clouts now,' I said, admiring George's progress as he crawled over to his father and then, furrowing his little brow with concentration, managed to stand for a moment before clutching at his father's hose. Smiling at his achievement, he lifted a foot and kicked at his father's ankle.

Barak lifted him up. 'Do you kick, sirrah?' he said with mock seriousness. 'In the presence of your godfather, too? Shameless imp.' George chuckled happily. I reached down and patted his head. A few curls, blond like Tamasin's and fine as silk, escaped from under his cap.

'He grows by the day,' I said wonderingly. 'Though I still cannot see whom he most resembles.'

'Impossible to say with that fat chubby face,' Barak said, tapping his son on his button nose.

'I hear you are to be congratulated, Tamasin.'

She blushed. 'Thank you, sir. Yes, George will have a little brother or sister next January, God willing. We both hope for a girl this time.'

'You feel well?'

'Apart from a little sickness in the mornings, yes. Now, let me fetch that bread and cheese. Jack, you have a pea in your beard. Please take it out. It looks disgusting.' Barak pulled the pea from where it had lodged, squashed it between his fingers, and gave it to a delighted George. 'I think I might grow one of those long forkbeards people have now. I could drop so much food in it I would have a nice snack always to hand.'

'You'd have to find a new house to eat it in,' Tamasin called from the kitchen.

I looked at Barak, sprawled comfortably in his chair, the little child playing at his feet. I was right to keep him out of this. 'Jack,' I said, 'I have a new piece of business which is likely to keep me out of the office a good deal for the next few days at least. Could I ask you to take charge, to supervise Nicholas and Skelly – though I may use Nicholas a little. I will see the more important clients if I can.'

'Like Mistress Slanning?' I knew Barak could not abide her.

'Yes, I will deal with her.'

He looked at me keenly. 'What is the business?'

'A printer murdered down by St Paul's. It is a week now, and no sign of catching the culprit. The coroner's office is lazy as usual. I have a power of attorney to investigate, from the printer's parents. They live in the Chilterns.'

'They gave you the case?'

I hesitated. 'It came through a third party.'

'You don't do jobs like that any more. Could be dangerous.'

'I felt a duty to take this on.'

'You look worried,' he said in his direct way.

'Please, Jack,' I answered, somewhat pettishly. 'There are some aspects to this I must keep confidential.'

Barak frowned. I had never left him out of such a matter before. 'Up to you,' he said with a touch of grumpiness.

George, meanwhile, left his father and toddled a couple of steps over to me. I picked him up, only to realize as he laid pudgy hands on my shirt that he had smeared the squashed pea all over it. I set him down again.

'That's a mess,' Barak said. 'Sorry. But you have to be careful picking him up.'

Tamasin came back with a plate of bread and cheese and a couple of wrinkled apples. 'Last year's,' she said, 'but they've been well stored.' She saw my shirt and took George. 'You muttonhead, Jack,' she scolded. 'You didn't give him that pea, did you? He could choke on it.'

'He hasn't eaten it, as you can see. Anyway, he tried to eat a slug from the garden last week, and it did the little squib no harm.'

'Fie, give him here.' Tamasin reached down and picked up her son, who gave her a puzzled look. 'You encourage him to trouble.'

'Sorry. Yes, it's best to keep out of trouble.' Barak looked at me meaningfully.

'If you can,' I answered. 'If you can.'

✝

I RODE HOME TO CHANGE my shirt before going down the street to Lincoln's Inn. I went into the kitchen. Josephine was standing there wearing a dress I had not seen before; of good wool, violet-coloured with a long white collar. Agnes knelt beside her, working at the skirt with pins. Agnes stood hurriedly and both women curtsied as I came in.

'What do you think of Josephine's new dress, sir?' Agnes asked. 'She got it for her walking out tomorrow. I helped choose it.'

Josephine, as ever, blushed. The dress became her. I could not, though, but reflect how the dye looked pale, washed-out, in comparison with the extraordinary bright colours that I had seen everywhere at Whitehall. But such clothes were all most people could afford.

'You look fine, Josephine,' I said. 'Master Brown cannot fail to be impressed.'

'Thank you, sir. Look, I have new shoes as well.' She lifted the dress a little to reveal square white shoes of good leather.

'A picture,' I said, smiling.

'And the dress is finest Kendal wool,' Agnes said. 'It will last you many a summer.'

'Where will you go walking?' I asked.

'Lincoln's Inn Fields. I hope it will be another fine afternoon.'

'The skies are clear. But now, I must hurry. Agnes, I need a new shirt.' I opened my robe to reveal a green smudge. 'My godson,' I said ruefully.

'What a mess! I will call Martin.'

'I can fetch one from the press,' I said, but Agnes had already called her husband's name. He appeared from the dining room, clad in an apron. He must have been cleaning the silver for his clothes smelled of vinegar.

'Could you get a new shirt for Master Shardlake, please, Martin?' As always when she spoke to her husband, Agnes's tone was deferential. 'His little godson has spoiled the one he has.' She smiled, but Martin only nodded. He seldom laughed or smiled; he seemed one of those men born without a sense of humour.

I went up to my room, and a couple of minutes later Martin appeared with my new shirt. He laid it on the bed and stood waiting. 'Thank you, Martin,' I said, 'but I can put on a shirt myself. I will leave the stained one on the bed.' Always he wanted to do everything. He looked a little put out, but bowed and left the room.

I changed the shirt and left my bedroom. At the foot of the stairs, I saw Josephine carrying a jug of hot water, held out carefully in front of her so as not to touch her new dress. She took it through the open door of the parlour to where Martin was still cleaning the silver.

'Put it on the table,' he said. 'On the cloth there.'

'Yes, Master Brocket.' She turned away, and I saw her give Martin's back a look of dislike, mingled with contempt, similar to the one she had given him yesterday. It puzzled me. Surely Martin's cold manner alone was not sufficient to evoke a look like that from someone as good-natured as Josephine.

✝

I LEFT GENESIS AT HOME and walked the short distance to Lincoln's Inn. Barak had not yet returned, but both Skelly and Nicholas were occupied at their desks. Skelly stood up and brought me a note, eyes shining with curiosity behind his wooden spectacles. 'This was just delivered for you, sir, by the woman who attends Master Bealknap.'

I took the note and broke the seal. Inside was another note, painfully scrawled. '*I am told I must soon prepare to meet my maker. Could you, as a kindness, visit me after church tomorrow? Stephen Bealknap.*'

I sighed. I had forgotten all about him. But I could not ignore this.

I scribbled a reply, saying I would be with him after church, and asked Skelly to run across with it. When he had gone I turned to Nicholas. He was dressed soberly today, in a short black robe, in accordance with the regulations. He handed me a sheaf of papers. 'My summary of the main points in that conveyance case, sir.'

I glanced through them quickly. The notes were scrawled, but seemed thought through and logically set out. Perhaps the boy was set-tling down after all. I looked up at him – he was six feet tall, I had no choice but to look up. His green eyes were clear and direct. 'I have a new case,' I said. 'It is a confidential matter, requiring discretion, and unfortunately for the next few days at least I will be much out of chambers and you will need to put in more hours. Are you willing to do that?'

'Yes, sir,' he answered, but I heard the unwillingness in his tone. It would mean fewer hours spent in the taverns with the other young gentlemen.

'Hopefully it will not be for long. I would also welcome your assistance with some aspects of this new case. I would like you to come with me now to interview some witnesses.' I hesitated, then said, 'It is a matter of murder, and at the request of the victim's parents I am helping the investigation. I am going to interview the constable, and then some witnesses.'

Nicholas immediately brightened up. 'To catch a villain, that is a worthy task.'

I answered seriously, 'If I take you with me on these enquiries, you must keep everything you hear entirely confidential. This is not a matter for discussion in the taverns. That could lead me, and you, into trouble.'

'I know that cases must be kept confidential, sir,' he answered a little stiffly. 'Any gentleman must respect that.'

'None more than this one. I have your promise?'

'Of course, sir,' he said in an injured tone.

'Very well. Then walk with me now to St Paul's. The murdered man was a printer. When I am asking people questions, listen hard, and if any questions occur to you, and you think them sensible, you may ask them. As you did with Mistress Slanning yesterday,' I added. 'You did well there.'

Nicholas brightened. 'I wondered if I had gone too far. Whether she might leave you.'

'That would be a tragedy,' I answered sardonically. 'And now, let us go.' A thought occurred to me. 'Did you bring your sword with you today?'

'Yes, sir.' Nicholas reddened. He liked to wear his sword when walking abroad, it was all part of his swagger.

I smiled. 'Since your father's being a landowner decrees you are a gentleman and gentlemen wear swords in public, we may as well turn the sumptuary laws to our advantage. It might impress the people we will be talking to.'

'Thank you.' Nicholas retrieved his sword, in its fine leather scabbard, tooled with a design of vine leaves. He buckled it on. 'I am ready,' he said.

Chapter Eight

W E WALKED ALONG the Strand, under Temple Bar and down Fleet Street. It was afternoon now, and I was glad of the bread and cheese Tamasin had given me earlier. Nicholas's natural walk was a fast lope, and I told him to slow down a little, reminding him that lawyers are men of dignity and should walk gravely. We crossed the Fleet Bridge, and I held my breath at the stink of the river. A rooting pig had fallen in and was thrashing about in the mud. Its owner stood knee-deep in the green, scummy water, trying to get it out.

We passed the Fleet Prison where, as always, the dirty hands of prisoners stretched through the bars seeking alms, for if no one brought them food, they starved. I thought of Anne Askew in New-gate, being brought money by the Queen's ladies. From there she had gone to the Tower to be tortured, and then to the stake. I shuddered.

We went under the city wall at Ludgate, the great edifice of St Paul's Cathedral ahead, its soaring wooden spire reaching five hun-dred feet into the blue sky. Nicholas looked at it with wonder. 'No building so fine in Lincolnshire, eh?' I said.

'Lincoln Cathedral is beautiful, but I have only seen it twice. My father's estate is down in the southwest of the county, near the Trent.' I caught a bite of anger in the boy's voice when he mentioned his father.

Beyond Ludgate, Bowyer Row was busy with trade. A butcher had set up a stall on which lay some stiff-looking, greenish meat. Prices were so high these days that stallholders could get away with selling rancid meat. To attract customers, he had set a live turkey in a cage at the end of his stall. People paused to stare at this extraordin-

86

ary bird from the New World, like a gigantic chicken, with enormous brightly coloured wattles.

An elderly peddler approached us, his tray full of pamphlets newly purchased from the printers. He leered at us. 'Buy my new-printed ballads, sirs. Full of naughty rhymes. *The Milkmaid and the Stallion Boy*, *The Cardinal's Maidservants*.' Nicholas laughed and I waved the man aside. Another peddler stood in a doorway, an old arrowbag full of canes over his shoulder. 'Buy my fine jemmies!' he called. 'Buy my London tartars! Well soaked in brine! Teach wives and sons obedience!'

A group of seven or eight little children, ragged shoeless urchins, ran towards us. I had glimpsed the sharp knife one boy was carrying. 'Cutpurses,' I murmured to Nicholas. 'Watch your money!'

'I saw them.' He had already clapped a hand to his purse, grasping his sword hilt with the other. We looked directly at the children and, realizing we had guessed their intent, they ran off to one side instead of crowding round us. One shouted, 'Crookback devil!', another, 'Carrot-head clerk!' At that Nicholas turned and took a step towards them. I put a hand on his arm. He shook his head and said sadly, 'People were right to warn me; London is a wild sea, full of dangerous rocks.'

'That it is. In more ways than one. When I first came to London I, too, had to learn things for myself. I am not sure I have ever got used to the city; I sometimes dream of retiring to the country, but distractions will keep coming.' I looked at him. 'One thing I should tell you. The murdered man and his friends were religious radicals. I take it dealing with such people will not be a problem for you.'

'I worship only as the King requires,' Nicholas said, repeating the formula of those who would be safe. He looked at me. 'In such matters I wish only to be left in peace.'

'Good,' I said. 'Now, turn up here, we are going to visit the constable first, in Ave Maria Lane.'

☦

AVE MARIA LANE was a long narrow street of three-storey buildings, a muddle of shops, houses and tenements, all with overhanging eaves. I noticed a couple of booksellers' shops, their publications laid out on a table in front, watched over by blue-coated apprentices with wooden clubs to deter thieves. Most of the books were aimed at the upper end of the market – Latin classics and French works – but among them there was also a copy of Becon's new *Christian State of Matrimony*, which urged women to quiet and obedience. Had it not been so expensive I might have bought a copy for Barak as a jest; Tamasin would throw it at his head. I wished I had not had to dissemble with him earlier.

'The constable is called Edward Fletcher,' I told Nicholas. 'He lives at the sign of the Red Dragon. Look, there it is. If he is not at home we shall have to try and find him about his business.'

The door was answered by a servant, who told us Master Fletcher was in and ushered us into a little parlour, with a desk and chairs all heaped with papers. Behind the desk sat a thin man of about fifty in the red doublet and cap of a city constable. He looked tired, on edge. I recognized him; he had been one of the constables who carried the faggots to the fires the day before.

'God give you good morrow, Master Fletcher,' I said.

'And you, sir.' He spoke deferentially, impressed no doubt by my robe. He stood and bowed. 'How may I help you?'

'I am here about the murder last week of Armistead Greening, God pardon his soul. I understand the coroner has put you in charge of the investigation.'

Fletcher sighed. 'He has.'

'I am Serjeant Matthew Shardlake, of Lincoln's Inn. My pupil, Master Overton. Master Greening's parents are sore grieved at his loss, and have asked me to assist in the investigations, with your permission. I have a power of attorney.' I passed the document to him.

'Please sit, sirs.' Fletcher removed papers from a couple of stools and laid them on the floor. When we were seated he regarded me seriously. 'You will know, sir, that if a murderer is not caught within the first two days, and his identity is unknown, the chances of finding him are small.'

'I know it well. I have been involved in such investigations before, and understand how difficult they are.' I glanced at the papers piled around. 'And I know how heavy the duties are for the city constables in these days.' I smiled sympathetically. 'Investigating a brutal murder must be yet one more burden.'

Fletcher nodded sadly. 'It is indeed.' He hesitated, then said, 'If you would take on the investigation I should be grateful.'

I nodded. I had read the man aright; many London constables were lazy and venal but Fletcher was conscientious and hopelessly overburdened. And affected, perhaps, by what he had had to do yesterday. The burning.

'I would keep you informed of any developments, of course,' I said. 'And you would be the one to report any discoveries to the coroner.' And take the credit, I implied.

He nodded.

'Perhaps I could begin by asking you what you know of the circumstances of the murder. My pupil will take notes, if you will permit.' Nicholas took quill and paper from his satchel. Fletcher gestured to him to help himself from his inkwell, then folded his arms and sat back.

'I was visited somewhat after nine on the evening of the tenth, just as the light was fading, by one of my watchmen. He told me that a printer of Paternoster Row, Armistead Greening, had been murdered, and also reported the hue and cry raised by his neighbour, Master Okedene, who discovered the body. I sent a message to the coroner and went across to Paternoster Row. Okedene was there, looking in a bad state. He said he had been working late in his print-shop with his assistant, using the last of the light, when he heard a loud cry for help from Greening's works next door, then bangs and shouts. Master Okedene is a man of some substance, but Greening was in a small way of business, his workshop little more than a wooden hut.'

'Not a very secure place, then?'

'No indeed. Master Okedene told me that when he ran to inves-tigate the door was locked, but he forced it open, just in time to see two men, big ragged-looking fellows, run out of the side door. Master Okedene's assistant, an old man, had stayed in the doorway of Okedene's shop, but saw the two men run out and climb over the wall behind the shed, into a garden. He gave a good description. Master Okedene would have pursued them, but he saw the print-shop had been set alight, a lamp dropped on a pile of paper.'

'They wanted to burn the place down?' Nicholas asked.

I said, 'If it burned down and a charred body were found in the ruins, Greening's death might have been attributed to his accidentally setting the place on fire.'

Fletcher nodded. 'That was my surmise. In any event, Master Okedene saw the fire and hurried to put it out before it reached more papers and the inks and other materials printers use. They are very flammable, a fire could have spread to his place.'

I nodded agreement. Fire in summer was one of the terrors of London, and probably a greater terror still among printers.

'Then he saw Master Greening lying in a pool of blood by his press, his head staved in.' The constable frowned. 'I was a little annoyed with Master Okedene, because after giving me his statement he went off and disappeared for several hours. At the inquest he said he had been so shocked by what had happened that he had had to get away and have a drink, and had wandered down to one of the taverns by the river that stay open after curfew.' The constable shrugged. 'Still, he told me all he knew before he left, and he is known as an honest man.' I reminded myself: during those hours, Okedene was actually at Whitehall Palace.

Fletcher hesitated, then continued, 'I should tell you, I was already under orders to keep a watch on Master Greening. He was known for having extreme views in religion, and radical friends. Three years ago he was closely questioned by Bishop Bonner about some books of John Bale, which were smuggled in from Flanders; there were reports that Greening was one of the distributors. But nothing was proved. It is a strange thing, though, that while his shop is small, with only one press and one apprentice, he has been able to keep the business going for some years, though you will know how risky the printing trade is.'

'Indeed. You need money to invest in the equipment. And once you have printed a book you must sell many copies to recoup any profit.'

Fletcher nodded agreement. 'And he was a young man, only thirty, and his parents I believe are not rich.'

'Small yeoman farmers only, I understand.'

The constable gave me a look of sudden suspicion. 'And yet they can afford to hire a serjeant at law.'

'They have connections to someone I owe a favour to.'

Fletcher studied me closely, then continued. 'Greening's known acquaintances were questioned, including some other radicals the Bishop has ordered us to keep an eye on. All had alibis, and no motive for killing him. He kept no money at the shop. He lived there, slept on a little truckle bed in a corner. There were several shillings in his purse, untouched. He was unmarried, and seems to have had no woman.'

I asked, 'What sort of radical was he?'

Fletcher shrugged his shoulders. 'He and his friends were thought to be sacramentarians, maybe other things. I have heard it said Greening's parents were Lollards from generations back. And old Lollards might be Anabaptists today. But no proof was ever found.' Fletcher gave me another suspicious look, perhaps wondering if I were a radical myself.

I said lightly, 'My pupil was just saying on the way here, it should suffice simply to worship as the King commands.'

'Yes,' Fletcher agreed. 'Safer that way, too.'

'What about his apprentice?'

'A hulking, insolent fellow, I wouldn't be surprised if he were another radical. But he was at home with his mother and sisters on the night of the murder, and all agree he got on well with his master. Master Okedene has taken on the boy now.'

'And the two men Master Okedene's assistant saw?'

'Vanished into thin air. From the descriptions they're not local men. I'd have taken it for a random attack by some beggars, hoping perhaps to steal some paper, which of course has some value – but for one thing . . .'

'What is that?'

The constable frowned. 'It was not the first attack on Greening.' I looked surprised, as though hearing the news for the first time. 'The apprentice, young Elias, told me that, some days before, he came to work early to find two men trying to break in, smash the lock. He shouted to waken Master Greening, who was asleep within, and called out, "Clubs!", which as you will know brings any apprentice within reach to aid one of his fellows. The two men fled at once. And according to young Elias's description, they were not the same men who killed Greening. He sticks to that.' Fletcher spread his arms. 'And that is all. The inquest returned its verdict of murder yesterday. I was asked to continue the investigation, but I have no further leads – nothing to investigate.'

'Do you have the names of the suspected radicals Greening associated with?'

'Yes. There were three.' Fletcher rummaged among his papers and wrote down the names and addresses of three men. We leaned over the desk as he pointed at each in turn. 'James McKendrick is Scotch; he works at the docks, used to be a soldier but turned into one of those radical preachers the Scotch have thrown out of their kingdom. Andres Vandersteyn is a cloth merchant from Antwerp; he trades between there and London – they say in forbidden books as well as cloth. The third, William Curdy, is a candlemaker, moderately prosperous. They all attend church regularly on Sunday and are careful what they say in public, but they were all friendly with Greening and sometimes used to meet together at his shop. And they were friends with other radicals of various sorts.'

'How do you know?' Nicholas asked.

'Informers, of course. Mine and the Bishop's. And I am told that these three have not been at their homes lately.' He raised his eyebrows. 'They may be keeping out of the way of officialdom.'

Nicholas said, 'A strange group to meet together. A Dutch merchant trading with the Low Countries would be of gentleman status, a candlemaker would be the middling sort, but a poor printer and a dockworker are from quite a different class.'

'Some radicals believe social divisions between men are wrong,' I replied. 'But meeting together is not an offence.'

'Nor being Dutch, nor a Scotch exile,' Fletcher said. 'More's the pity, for both groups are often radicals.' He sighed, shook his head at the restrictions that bound his work, then added, 'Nonetheless, the Bishop's men raided Greening's place back in April – '

'I did not know that,' I said, leaning forward.

'They raided several print-shops in search of some pamphlets by John Bale that had appeared in London. Printed somewhere in the city. Nothing was found anywhere.'

Yet somehow the most dangerous book in the kingdom had found its way into that shop. 'What do you think happened, Master Fletcher?' I asked.

'Greening obviously had enemies who were out to kill him. But no one seems to know of any. Perhaps there was a falling-out with another radical group; these people will turn from love of each other to hatred over the tiniest point of doctrine. The descriptions of the two sets of people who tried to break in tally with nobody known locally, and this is a close-knit district. You can see why the investigation is at a standstill.'

I nodded sympathetically. 'If you would not object, I would like to question Master Okedene and his assistant. And the apprentice. Perhaps these friends of Greening's. And I would like to look at Master Greening's shop, too. Is there a key?'

Fletcher produced a small key from his desk. 'I put a new padlock on. You may as well keep this for now. The shop is at the sign of the White Lion. I wish you well.' He waved his hands at the papers littered around. 'As you see, I am burdened with duties. This year I have had to hunt for heretics as well as criminals, though the hunt for the former seems to have died down now.' He looked me in the eye. 'I saw you at the burning yesterday, on your horse; your friend looked set to faint.'

'I saw you, too.'

'I have to carry out the duties the mayor gives me,' he said defensively, though for a moment his eyes looked haunted.

'I understand.'

He gave me a hard look. 'You will report anything you find in this case back to me, remember. I have jurisdiction under the coroner.'

'All and anything I discover,' I lied. 'By the way, what happened to the body?'

'It couldn't be kept lying around till his parents were able to get here from the Chilterns; not in summer. He was buried in the common pit.'

✝

WE WALKED UP Ave Maria Lane into Paternoster Row; a longer, wider street, which was the centre of England's small but growing printing trade. There were several more booksellers, some with printer's shops above, and a few smaller print-shops; as Fletcher had said, some were mere sheds fixed to the side of buildings, or erected on small plots of land leased from the owner. I thought of Greening's possible involvement with the printing of forbidden books by John Bale. Once a favourite of Lord Cromwell's, but now the most detested of radicals, Bale was hidden in exile somewhere in Flanders.

'What did you think of Fletcher?' I asked Nicholas.

'He was at the burning?'

'Yes. Doing his duty,' I added heavily.

'I would rather die than carry out such a duty.'

It was an easy thing for a young man of means to say. 'I do not think he liked it,' I observed.

'Perhaps. I noticed his fingernails were bitten to the quick.'

'Well spotted. I did not see that. Noticing things, that is the key in this business. We will make a lawyer of you yet. And what did you make of the murder?'

Nicholas shook his head. 'Two attacks, as Fletcher said; that sounds like Greening had enemies. Or perhaps he had something precious in his shop – something more than paper and ink.' I looked at the boy sharply; he had come a little too close to the mark for my comfort with that observation. 'Gold, perhaps,' Nicholas went on, 'that the thieves managed to take before they were interrupted.'

'If people have gold they spend it, or deposit it somewhere safe; only misers hoard it at home.'

'Like your friend Bealknap? I have heard he is such a one.'

'He is not my friend,' I answered shortly. Nicholas reddened, and I continued more civilly, 'Greening does not sound like such a man.'

'No, indeed.' Nicholas added, 'The constable looked over-worked.'

'Yes. In some ways London is a well-policed city. The constables and watchmen look out for violence, and violations of the curfew. If a few taverns open after hours they wink at it, so long as the inn keepers do not let customers get violent.' I looked at Nicholas and raised my eyebrows. His own tavern sword fight had become an item of gossip round Lincoln's Inn, to my discomfort. He reddened further.

I went on, 'The constables check that people obey the sumptuary laws regarding the clothes that may be worn by men of each station, though again they wink at minor infringements. And they run informers to report on crime and religious misdemeanours. But when it comes to investigating a murder requiring a long-term, detailed investigation, they have not the resources, as Fletcher said.'

'I confess I do not fully understand about the different types of radical,' Nicholas said. 'Sacramentarians and Lollards and Ana-baptists, what are the differences?'

'That is something it is as well to know in London. But lower your voice,' I said quietly. 'Open discussion of these matters is dangerous. Sacramentarians believe the bread and wine are not transformed into the body and blood of Christ during the Mass, which properly should be regarded only as a remembrance of Christ's sacrifice. By law, to express that belief is heresy. In most of Europe such opinion is new, but in England a man called John Wycliffe propounded similar doctrines more than a century ago. Those who followed him, the Lollards, were persecuted, but Lollardy has lived on here and there, in small secret groups. The Lollards were delighted, of course, by the King's break with Rome.'

'And the Anabaptists?'

They were one of the religious sects that sprang up in Germany twenty years ago. They believe in going back to the practices of the earliest Christians; they are sacramentarians, but they also believe that the baptism of children is invalid, that only adults who have come to knowledge of Christ can be baptized. Hence "Anabaptists". But also, and most dangerously, they share the belief of the earliest Christians that social distinctions between men should be abolished and all goods held in common.'

Nicholas looked astonished. 'Surely the early Christians did not believe that?'

I inclined my head. 'Looking at the Scriptures, there is a good argument they did.'

He frowned. 'I heard the Anabaptists took over a city in Germany and ran it according to their beliefs, and by the end blood was running in the streets.' He shook his head. 'Man cannot do without authority, which is why God has ordained princes to rule over him.'

'In fact, the Anabaptists were besieged in Münster, the Protestant Prince allying with Catholic forces to take the city. That was the real cause of the bloodshed. Though I have heard that yes, the Anabaptists' rule inside the city had become violent. But afterwards most of them renounced violence. They were run out of Germany and Flanders, too; a few from Flanders came here across the North Sea. The King burned those he could find.'

'But there could still be others?'

'So it is said. If they exist they have been forced underground as the Lollards were. Anyone with a Dutch name is looked at askance these days.'

'Like that friend of Greening's the constable mentioned? Vandersteyn?'

'Yes.'

Nicholas's brow furrowed. 'So the Anabaptists have renounced violence, but not the belief that rulers must be put down?'

'So it is said.'

'Then they remain a great danger,' he said seriously.

'They are a useful bogey.' I looked at Nicholas. 'Well, now you have seen what a murder enquiry begins to look like. It is seldom an easy thing to investigate, nor safe.'

He smiled. 'I am not afraid.'

I grunted. 'Fear keeps you on your toes. Remember that.'

✝

ALL THE SHOPS and printworks in Paternoster Row had little signs outside: an angel, a golden ball, a red cockerel. The sign of the White Lion, crudely painted on a board, hung outside a onestorey wooden building which was made to seem all the poorer by the finelooking house which stood next to it. That must be the neighbour, Okedene's. I used the key to open the padlock the constable had fixed to the splintered door, and pushed it open. It was dim within. There was a second door at the side of the shed, with a key in the lock, and I got Nicholas to open it. It gave onto a weedstrewn patch of ground. I looked round the shed. The single room was dominated by a large printing press in the centre, the press itself raised on its screw, the tray of paper empty. Nailed to the walls, cheap shelves held paper, ink and solutions in bottles, and blocks of type in boxes. A harsh smell permeated the place.

In one corner was a pile of printed pages, and others had been hung on lines to dry. I looked at the top page: *A Goodly French Primer.* I glanced at the pages hanging to dry: *Je suis un gentilhomme de l'Angleterre. J'habite à Londres . . .* I remembered such stuff from my schooldays. Greening had been printing a schoolbook for children. There was a straw bed in a corner, a blanket and pillow. Beside the bed was a knife and plate with some stale bread and mouldy cheese. Greening's last meal.

'Nicholas,' I said, 'would you look under the printing press and see if there is any type in the upper tray? I am not sure I could manage it.' If there was, I would have to get the boy to detach the tray somehow, so that I could see if it was the same type used in printing the French book, or something else; had Greening been planning to print the *Lamentation*?

Nicholas twisted his long body under the press and looked up with an easy suppleness I envied. 'No print in the tray, sir. It looks empty.'

'Good,' I said, relieved.

He rose and stood looking around. 'What a poor place. To have to live as well as work here, amidst this smell.'

'Many live in far worse conditions.' Yet Nicholas was right, a man who was able to keep a printer's business going should have been able to afford a home. Unless his business was failing; perhaps he had not been sharp enough for this competitive trade. Lord Parr had said Greening's parents were poor, so where had he got the capital to buy the press and other equipment to start the business? I saw, by the bed, a dark stain on the floor. Blood, from the injuries Greening had received. Poor fellow, not yet thirty, now rotting in the common graveyard.

There was a plain wooden coffer beside the bed. It was unlocked, and contained only a couple of stained leather aprons, some shirts and doublets of cheap linen, and a well-thumbed New Testament. No forbidden books; he had been careful.

Nicholas was bending over a little pile of half-burned papers on the floor. 'Here's where they tried to start the fire,' he said.

I joined him. 'Under the shelf of inks. If Okedene hadn't come the place would have gone up.' I picked out one of the half-burned pieces of paper '. . . *le chat est un animal méchant* . . .' 'Pages from the book he was printing,' I said.

Nicholas looked around the room. 'What will happen to all this?'

'It belongs to his parents now. The power of attorney gives me the right to take out probate on their behalf. Perhaps you and Barak could deal with that. The author will have paid Greening to print his book, that money will have to be repaid. Otherwise the materials will be sold and the proceeds given to his parents. The printing press will be worth something.'

I looked at the paper on the shelf. Not a large stock, but with nearly all paper in England imported, it had a market value, and as Fletcher had suggested, it would be worth stealing, as would the working type. But it hardly explained two attempted burglaries by separate parties.

I went to the side door and stepped outside, pleased to be away from the harsh fumes, and looked out. The little patch of weedy ground ended at a brick wall, seven feet high. I had a thought. I needed to speak to Okedene on his own, without Nicholas. Besides myself, Okedene was the only other person outside the palace walls who knew of the *Lamentation*.

'Nicholas,' I said, 'go and look over that wall.'

He did so, pulling himself up easily. 'A garden,' he said. 'In little better state than the ground this side.'

'Will you climb over, see where those men might have gone after they killed Greening, whether they left any traces? Then join me at Okedene's house.'

He looked worried. 'What if the owners see me poking about in their garden?'

'Make some excuse.' I smiled. 'A good lawyer should always be able to think on his feet.'

Chapter Nine

MASTER OKEDENE'S establishment was a three-storey house. The bottom floor was a bookshop, volumes displayed on a table outside. They were varied; from Eliot's *Castle of Health* to little books on astrology and herbs, and Latin classics. There were a couple of prayer books, approved ones, small volumes no larger than a man's hand, which one could carry as one walked. From the upper floors came a thumping, clacking sound: newly inked pages would be put under the press, it would be rapidly screwed down, the page taken out and a new one inserted. An old man stood in the doorway, guarding the bookshop; he was stringy and arthritic-looking, his hands knotted. He studied me warily; he would have seen Nicholas and me enter Greening's shed.

I smiled. 'God give you good morrow, goodman. I am a lawyer, representing the parents of the late Master Greening.'

He took off his cap, revealing a bald pate beneath. 'God pardon his soul.' He gave a wheezing cough.

'I have authority from Constable Fletcher to investigate the matter. Would you be Master Okedene's assistant, that saw the two men run from the building?'

'I am, sir,' he answered more cheerfully. 'John Huffkyn, at your service.'

'I am Master Shardlake. Would you tell me what happened?'

He nodded, clearly pleased to tell his story again. 'It was evening, I was helping Master Okedene run the press. He is printing a book on the voyages to the New World, with woodcuts showing the wondrous creatures there. A big contract. We were working till the light was done.' He sighed. 'Now that Master Okedene has taken on that lump Elias as apprentice, I am put to mind the shop during the day.' He paused. 'But thirty years in this business have worn my joints to shreds. And my chest—'

'That night . . .' I said, bringing him back to the point.

'Work had just finished, we were pinning up pages to dry over-night. The windows were open and we heard a commotion next door. Cries, then a loud shout for help. Master Okedene and I looked at each other. Master Greening could occasionally be heard in loud discussions with his friends, but these were sounds of violence. We ran downstairs. The master ran next door, but I stayed in the door-way. With my poor bent limbs and bad chest I could be of little assistance . . .' He looked ashamed.

'I understand,' I offered solicitously.

'From here I saw it all. Master Okedene battered the door in, and a second later I saw two men run out of there.' He pointed to Green-ing's side door. 'As I told them at the inquest, they were both in their twenties, dressed in dirty wadmol smocks. Vagrants, they seemed to me, masterless men.' He made a grimace. 'Both carried nasty-looking clubs. They were strongly built; one was tall and, young as he was, near bald. The other was fair-haired and had a big wart on his fore-head; it was visible even in the poor light. Both had raggedy beards.'

'You observed well.'

'My eyes at least are still sound. I would be glad to identify them, help see them hang. Master Greening was a good neighbour. I know he was a radical, but he was quiet, he wasn't one of those who button-holes people and starts preaching at them, putting them in danger of the law. He did no man harm – that I know of,' he added, looking at me sharply.

'I have heard no ill spoken of him.'

Huffkyn continued, 'When the two men had gone I went across to the shed, for I could smell burning. Master Okedene was putting out a fire, a heap of papers set alight on the floor, and poor Greening was lying there. A dreadful sight, the top of his head bashed in, blood and brains spilling out.' He shook his head.

'Thank you, Goodman Huffkyn.' I took out my purse and gave him a groat. 'And now, if I may, I would speak to your master. Can I go in?'

'Of course. He is at work with Elias, on the first floor.'

✝

I WALKED THROUGH the shop and went upstairs. The rhythmic thumping was louder now. The whole first floor had been knocked into one room, a larger equivalent of poor Greening's. Again there were shelves of paper and chemicals, printed pages in piles, more hung up on ropes stretched across the room, like linen on drying day. Although the shutters were open, the chamber was hot and smelled of heavy leaden dust; I felt sweat on my brow.

Two men were working at the press. Both wore stained leather aprons. A tall, clean-shaven, grey-haired man in his fifties was smoothing out a fresh piece of paper on the bottom tray. Holding the handle of the great screw above the upper tray, where the inked letters were set, was a large, strongly muscled boy of about eighteen, with a dumpish, heavy countenance. They looked round as I entered.

'I am Master Shardlake,' I said quietly. 'I have been sent to investigate poor Master Greening's murder.'

The older man nodded. 'Geoffrey Okedene,' he said. 'I had a message to expect you. Let us go to the book-binding room. Elias, we will be down in a while.'

The boy looked at me directly for the first time. His brown eyes were afire with anger. 'It was a wicked, godless thing,' he said. 'Good Christian people are no longer safe in these days.'

'Keep your place, boy.' Okedene frowned at him, then led me up to the top floor, where a middle-aged woman sat at a table, carefully sewing pages into a binding of thick paper. Okedene said, 'Could you go down to the kitchen for a few minutes, my dear? I need a private word with this gentleman of the law. It concerns the contract for the new book. Perhaps you could take Elias a jug of ale.'

'I heard you chide Elias just now. That boy needs a whipping for his insolent tongue.'

'He is strong and works hard, that is what matters, sweetheart. And the loss of his old master hit him hard.'

Mrs Okedene rose, curtsying to me before stepping out. The printer closed the door behind her. 'My wife knows nothing of this matter,' he said quietly. 'You have come from Lord Parr? He said he would send someone.'

'Yes. You acted well that night, Master Okedene.'

He sat at the table, looking at his work-roughened hands. He had a pleasant, honest face, but it held lines of worry. 'I had a note from Whitehall that a lawyer would be coming. They asked me to burn it, which I did.' He took a deep breath. 'When I saw the words on that page poor Greening held – I am no sacramentarian, but I have ever been a supporter of reform. I had work from Lord Cromwell in his time. When I saw the title page of that book, I knew it was a personal confession of sinfulness and coming to faith, such as radicals make these days, and could be dangerous to her majesty, whom all reformers revere for her faith and goodness.'

'How did you gain access to Whitehall Palace?'

'There is a young apprentice printer living on the street who is known as a fiery young radical. As is often the case with such young men, he has contact with other radicals among the servants at court. I went to him, told him I had hold of something the Queen's council-lors should know about. He told me of a servant I should approach at Whitehall, and thus I was led to Lord Parr himself.' He shook his head wonderingly.

'Is this boy friendly with Elias?'

'No. Elias tended to mix only with Master Greening and his circle.' Oakdene passed a hand across his brow. 'It is hard to find one-self suddenly inside Whitehall.'

I smiled sympathetically. 'It is.'

'It was – frightening.' He looked at me. 'But I must do what I can, for conscience's sake.'

'Yes. Lord Parr is grateful to you. He has asked me to take up the investigation into the murder, which the coroner has all but abandoned. I have told the constable and everyone else – including my own pupil, whom I have set to search the gardens behind Greening's shed – that I am acting on behalf of Greening's parents. I took the liberty of questioning Goodman Huffkyn, and I would like to speak to Elias as well. I understand he thwarted an earlier attempt to break in.'

'So he says, and Elias is truthful, if unruly.'

'You must not speak of that book to him or anybody else.'

He nodded emphatically. 'By our Lord, sir, I know how much discretion this matter demands. Sometimes good Christians must speak with the wisdom of the serpent as well as the innocence of the dove, is it not so?'

'In this matter, certainly. Now, would you tell me in your own words what happened that night?'

Okedene repeated what Huffkyn had told me about hearing a noise and rushing outside. 'As I ran up to the shed, I heard Master Greening call out to someone to leave him alone. I think he was fighting them. I tried the door and found it locked so I put my shoulder to it. It gave way at once.'

'It was locked from inside?'

'Yes, Master Greening lived there, as you know, and would lock the door at night. I can only guess the people who attacked him knocked at the door, pushed their way in when he answered, then locked the door behind them.'

'Huffkyn gave me a description of them.'

'Yes, I only caught the merest glimpse.'

'He seems a clever old man.'

'Poor fellow, he has a bad chest, as many of us in the trade do. I am afraid I took the chance, when poor Greening died, to take on Elias and put John Huffkyn to lighter work.'

'Probably a good arrangement for everyone.'

'I hope so.'

'When you entered, apart from that glimpse of the attackers, what did you see?'

'My eyes were drawn at once to the fire. I had to put it out.' He looked at me seriously. 'With all the paper and printing materials in this street, fire is a constant worry. Fortunately the pile of paper had only just started to burn, and I was able to stamp it out. Then I saw poor Greening – ' he took a long breath – 'on the floor. I hope never to see such a thing again. And then I saw the torn sheet of paper in his hand – the best quality paper on the market. I read it, and knew this was more than a matter of murder. I heard Huffkyn coming and stuffed the page into my pocket.'

'Do you think they killed him before they heard you trying to enter?'

He shook his head. 'When I first put my shoulder to the door Greening was still shouting. But then the noise stopped, save for a horrible crash – I think one of them clubbed him then, and he went down.'

'And they grabbed the book from his hands,' I mused, 'but left behind part of the title page. Probably failed to notice it in their hurry to get out; they set the fire and ran.'

'I think that might be how it was.' Okedene shook his head sadly. 'I wonder whether, had I not broken in just then, they might not have panicked and killed him.'

'I think they would have killed him in any case, in order to wrest that book from him.' He nodded sadly. 'How well did you know Armistead Greening?' I asked.

'He came to Paternoster Row five years ago. He said he had come from the Chilterns – he spoke with the accent of those parts – and wanted to set up as a printer. He had been married, he told me, but his wife died in childbirth and the baby, too, so he came to London to seek his fortune. Poor young man, he often had a sad cast of face. He leased that piece of land his shed stands on from the Court of Augmentations – it belonged to a little monastic house whose remains stand on the land behind the shed.' He smiled sardonically. 'Ironic, given his religious views. He built the shed himself with a couple of friends. I remember thinking I was glad he had found some friends in London. I did not know him well, he kept to himself, but – I heard and saw things, especially recently.' He hesitated.

'Nothing you tell me about him can harm him now. Goodman Huffkyn dropped some hints.'

'It might harm Elias. If it reached the ears of Gardiner and his wolves.'

'I report to no one but Lord Parr and the Queen.'

His eyes widened. 'The Queen herself?'

'Yes. I knew her when she was Lady Latimer,' I added, a note of pride in my voice.

'I think Greening was very radical.' Okedene looked at me seriously. 'A known man.'

I drew a sharp breath. The code for the old Lollards and, now, the Anabaptists. Okedene continued, 'Can you guarantee that nothing I tell you about Elias will get him into trouble?' He spoke quietly, intently, reminding me again how dangerous it was to discuss radical religion.

I hesitated. I knew Lord Parr, at least, would be quite ruthless if he thought it necessary to protect the Queen. And any mention of Anabaptism would be to shake a stick in a wasps' nest. 'Anything that might harm the apprentice I will speak of only to the Queen,' I answered. 'Her mercy and loyalty are well known.'

Okedene stood. He looked from the window at Greening's shed. 'The walls of that rickety place are thin. Armistead Greening had friends and visitors with whom he would have loud religious discussions. This summer especially, with everyone's windows open in the hot weather, I would sometimes hear them talking – arguing, rather – sometimes a little too loudly for safety. Mostly it was just a hubbub of voices I heard, the occasional phrase, though the phrases were enough to set my ears pricking. They were an odd mixture of people. Six or seven sometimes, but there were three constant regulars – a

Scotsman, a Dutchman and an Englishman, all known as local radicals.'

'McKendrick, Vandersteyn and Curdy.'

Okedene nodded. 'I think Master Curdy is quite a wealthy man. Master Greening told me he sent one of his assistants to help build that shed. The Scotsman helped as well; I remember seeing him. A big, strong fellow.'

'So Greening knew them almost from the time he came to London? Were you acquainted with them?'

'Only to nod to in the street. They kept themselves to themselves. I only really knew Armistead Greening as a neighbour and fellow printer. Sometimes we would discuss the state of business; once or twice we lent each other paper if we had a job in, and our stocks were running low.'

'What did you hear Master Greening and his friends arguing over?' I asked. 'The sacrament?'

He hesitated again. 'That, and whether we are predestined to heaven or hell. It is just as well, Master Shardlake, that I am no Catholic and John Huffkyn takes care to mind his own business.'

'They were careless.'

'They seemed much agitated this summer.' He set his lips. 'One evening I heard them arguing over whether people should only be baptized when they were adults, and whether all baptized Christians had the right to equality, to take the goods of the rich and hold them in common.'

'So Armistead Greening might have been an Anabaptist?'

Okedene shook his head, began walking to and fro. 'From the way he and his friends argued I think they had differing views. You know how the radicals disagree among themselves as much as with their opponents.'

'I do.' The last decade had been a time of shifting faiths, men moving from Catholicism to Lutheranism to radicalism and back again. But it was obvious that Greening and his friends were at least exploring the radical fringes. I wondered where those other three men were now: McKendrick, Vandersteyn and Curdy. Had they gone to ground?

Okedene said, 'I often used to wonder how Armistead made ends meet. I know some of the books he printed did not sell well, and sometimes he seemed to have no work at all. At other times he was busy. I wondered if he was involved in the trade in illegal books and pamphlets. I know a few years ago a large pile of books was delivered to him.'

'Books already printed?'

'Yes. Brought in from the Continent, illegally perhaps, for distribution. I saw them in his shed, in boxes, when I visited him to ask if he wanted to buy some surplus type I had. One box was open and he closed it quickly.'

'I wonder what those books were.'

'Who knows; works by Luther, perhaps, or this Calvin, who they say is making a new stir in Europe; or John Bale.' He bit his lip. 'He asked me not to tell anyone about these books, and I swore I would not. But he is dead now, it cannot hurt him.'

I said quietly, 'Thank you for trusting me, Master Okedene.'

He looked at me seriously. 'If I had reported what I heard to the wrong people, Armistead Greening and his friends could have ended up burning with Anne Askew yesterday.' His mouth twisted with sudden revulsion. 'That was a wicked, disgusting thing.'

'It was. I was made to go and watch, to represent my Inn. It was a horrible, evil act.'

'It is hard for me, Master Shardlake. My sympathies are with the reformers. I am no sacramentarian, still less an Anabaptist, but I would not throw my neighbours into Gardiner's fires.'

'Was Elias part of this radical group?' I asked quietly.

'Yes, I think he was. I heard his voice from Master Greening's shed this summer, more than once.'

'I must question him, but I will be careful.'

'Loutish as he is, he was devoted to his master. He wants the killers caught.'

'And he has one important piece of information for us. I understand he interrupted an earlier attack on the shop a few days before.'

'Yes. He is the only one who saw it, but he certainly raised the
alarm and brought other apprentices running.' He paused. 'One
strange thing I will tell you, for I doubt Elias will. A few days before
the first attack, Master Greening and his friends – Elias, too – were
holding one of their evening meetings. They were having a particularly loud argument. His windows were open and so were mine, a
passing watchman could have heard them from the street – though
even the watchmen are reformers round here.'

I knew that in many of London's parishes the people were increasingly grouping together into reformist and traditionalist districts. 'Is
everyone in this street of a reformist cast of mind? I know most printers are.'

'Yes. But the sort of talk I heard that evening would be dangerous
in any district. I was angry with them, for if they found themselves
arrested I would be questioned too, and I have a wife and three children to think about.' His voice trembled a little, and I realized how
much the thoughtless talk of his neighbours, to say nothing of finding
himself at Whitehall facing Lord Parr, had frightened him. 'I went
outside, intending to knock at the door and tell them they should have
regard for their safety and mine. But as I reached the door I heard the
Dutchman – he has a distinctive accent – saying a man was coming to
England who was an agent of the Antichrist himself, who could
bring down and destroy the realm, turn true religion to ashes. They
mentioned a name, a foreign name. I'm not sure I heard it aright.'

'What was it?'

'It sounded like "Jurony Bertano".'

'That sounds Spanish, or Italian.'

'That was all I heard. I banged on the door, called to them to
speak more quietly and shut their windows, lest they find themselves
in the Tower. They did not answer, but thank God they pulled the
window shut and lowered their voices.' He gave me a searching look.
'I tell you this only because of the danger to the Queen.'

'I am truly grateful.'

'But there is one thing that has puzzled me all along,' Okedene said. 'Why would radicals have stolen Queen Catherine's book and put her in danger?'

'That is something I wonder about, too.'

'Certainly I never overheard any mention of the Queen's name. But as I say, apart from that particular night when I heard that name Jurony Bertano, it was mostly just the occasional phrase I heard.' He sighed. 'But nowhere is safe in these days.'

Footsteps sounded outside. Someone had come up the stairs, quietly, and we had not heard. Okedene and I looked at each other in alarm. The door opened. Nicholas came in, looking pleased with himself. 'Could you not knock?' I said angrily. 'Master Okedene, this is my pupil, Nicholas Overton. I apologize for his manners.'

Nicholas looked hurt. He bowed to Okedene, then turned quickly back to me. 'I am sorry, sir, but I found something in the garden.'

I wished he had not blurted that out in front of Okedene. It was best for his safety that he knew as little as possible. But Nicholas went on. 'I climbed over the wall. The garden on the other side is very overgrown, with high grass and brambles. There was only a family of beggars there, taking shelter in the ruins of what looks like an abandoned monastic building.'

Okedene said, 'It was, boy, a little Franciscan friary. After the Dissolution, many of the stones were taken for building, and no one has bought the site yet. There is still a glut of land in London.'

Nicholas rattled on. 'I looked to see if there was still a trail through the long grass. There has been no rain, and I am a good tracker. I learned well when hunting at home. And there was a trail of flattened grass, as though people had run through it. And on a bramble bush, I found this.' He pulled a piece of cloth from his pocket, fine white silk embroidered with tiny loops and whorls of blackwork. I saw it was from a shirt cuff such as only a gentleman could have afforded. It looked quite new. Nicholas said proudly, 'My guess is that when the killers ran away one caught his shirt on the bramble thorns.'

Okedene looked at the scrap of cuff. 'A fine piece of work, best silk by the look of it. But you have it wrong, boy, my assistant saw the assailants clearly and they wore rough wadmol smocks. Someone else must have passed through the garden and torn his shirt.'

I turned the fabric over in my hand. 'But who would go wandering about an abandoned garden full of brambles wearing such finery?'

Nicholas said, 'Perhaps men who were not poor at all, but put rough clothes over their shirts so that people in the street would not notice them.'

'By Mary, Nicholas,' I said, 'you could have the right of it.' And whoever stole the *Lamentation* had access to the highest reaches of the court. 'Nicholas, did you speak to this beggar family?'

'Yes, sir. A cottager and his wife from Norfolk. Their piece of land was enclosed for sheep and they came to London. They are camping out in the one room that still has a roof. They were frightened of me; they thought someone had bought the land and sent a lawyer to throw them out.' He spoke of them scornfully; Okedene frowned disapprovingly. 'I asked if they had seen anything on the night of the murder. They said they were woken by the sound of men running through the garden. They saw two men with clubs, big young fellows; one was almost bald, they said. They escaped by climbing over the far wall.'

'So John Huffkyn saw aright.' Okedene looked at the piece of silk cuff. 'This worries me, sir. The killing could have been carried out by men of status.'

'Yes, it could. You have done well, Nicholas. Please, Master Okedene, keep this secret.'

He laughed bitterly. 'I can swear that, right readily.'

I put the scrap of lace in my pocket and took a deep breath. 'And now I must question young Elias.'

✝

THE APPRENTICE looked up from inking a tray of type. 'Master,' he said to Okedene as we entered, 'we will be falling behind — '

'We have a large order on hand,' Okedene explained. 'But Elias, these gentlemen are investigating Master Greening's killing, for his parents. We must help them.'

I put out a hand. 'I am Matthew Shardlake, of Lincoln's Inn.'

'Elias Rooke.' The boy's eyes narrowed. 'Master Greening told me his parents were poor folk. How can they can afford a lawyer?'

It was a brave question for a mere apprentice. 'Elias . . .' Okedene said warningly.

'I only want to find the truth of what happened, Elias, and bring Master Greening's killers to justice. I would like to ask you some questions.' The boy still looked at me suspiciously. I spoke encouragingly. 'I understand you were at home on the night of the murder.'

'With my mother and sisters. And a neighbour called in. I told them so at the inquest.'

'Yes. I understand you thwarted an earlier attack on Master Greening's premises.'

'I told them about that, too. I came to work early one morning – there was much to do – and two men were standing outside the shed, trying to pick the lock. They were very quiet, I think they knew Master Greening was within.'

'Not the same two who attacked him later?'

'No. Old Huffkyn described the men who killed my poor master as big and tall. These two were quite different. One was short and fat. The other was slim, with fair hair, and had half an ear missing. Looked like a slash from a sword, not the great hole you get from having your ear nailed to the pillory.'

'Were they carrying weapons?'

'They had daggers at their waists, but so do most men.'

'What were they wearing?'

'Old wadmol smocks.'

'Cheap garments, then?'

'Ay.' Elias relaxed a little, realizing I was just going over old ground. 'But those are all most folk can afford these days, with the rich land-grabbers and idle rout of nobles taking everything.'

Nicholas said, 'Do not be insolent to my master, churl.'

I raised a hand. I could put up with boyish insolence if it would get me information. And it seemed this boy held radical social views. 'When was this first attack?' I asked. 'I was told it was some days before the murder.'

'Just over a week. Monday, the fifth.'

I frowned, realizing that was the day before the *Lamentation* was stolen from the Queen. That made no sense. 'Are you sure of the date?'

Elias looked back at me directly. ''Tis my mother's birthday.'

'What did you do when you saw the men?'

'What any good apprentice would do. Shouted "Clubs!" to let the other lads in the street know there was trouble. A few came out, though they weren't quick — it was early, they were probably hardly awake. They will confirm the date if you doubt me. The two men were already gone, they went over the garden wall behind Master Greening's shed, the same way as the other two. Some fellows went in pursuit, but they lost them.' So these men, too, had probably surveyed Greening's place before attacking it, to find the best escape route. 'I stayed to knock up my master.'

'How did Master Greening react when you told him?'

'He was alarmed, what do you think?' Elias replied curtly. Nich- olas gave him a warning look, but he ignored it.

'Did your master have any idea who the men could have been?'

'Casual thieves, he thought. But they must be connected to the men who came later, and killed him. Mustn't they?'

I caught a slight tremor in his voice; under his bravado Elias was seriously afraid. I thought, if Greening had his premises attacked a week before his murder, why did he let the two killers in when they knocked? Had he perhaps been reassured by a request to enter from two men with cultivated accents; one with a silk shirt under his jerkin? I looked at Elias again. I thought, did he know about the book? If he did, he was in danger. Yet he had not gone to ground, as it seemed Greening's three friends had, and he had taken a job at the works next door. I asked, 'What do you know of your master's friends? I have the names McKendrick, Vandersteyn and Curdy.'

'I have met them.' The apprentice's eyes narrowed. 'Good, honest men.'

'They were all able to give account of their movements on that night,' I said with a reassuring smile. 'Though they have not been seen for some days.'

'I haven't seen them since the murder.'

'McKendrick is a Scotch name,' Nicholas said bluntly. 'Until just recently we were at war with them.'

Elias glared at him. 'The papists threw Master McKendrick out of Scotland for calling the soul of the Pope a stinking menstruous rag. As it is.'

Okedene snapped, 'Elias, I will not have such language in my shop!'

I raised a pacifying hand. 'Was there any woman Master Greening was close to? Your master was still a young man.'

'No. Since his poor wife died he devoted himself to his work and the service of God.'

I was considering how to broach the question of Elias's involvement in the religious discussions between his master and his friends, when Nicholas asked him suddenly, 'What about this Jurony Bertano that I heard my master mention as I came upstairs? Did your master know him?'

An expression of utter fear came over Elias's face, his ill-mannered surliness vanishing. He took a step back.

'How do you know that name?' he asked. He looked at Okedene. 'Master, these men are agents of Bishop Gardiner!' Before Okedene could reply, Elias shouted at me, his face red with fear and anger, 'You crawling crouchback papist!' And with that he punched me hard in the face, making me stagger. He threw himself on me, and with his size could have done me damage had not Nicholas put an arm around his throat and dragged him off. The boy twisted, grasped Nicholas, and the two fell grappling to the floor. Nicholas reached for his sword, but Elias threw him off and ran through the open door of the print-shop, his footsteps crashing down the stairs. I heard Okedene's wife call out, 'Elias!' The front door slammed.

Nicholas was on his feet in a second, running downstairs after him. Okedene and I looked from the window to see my pupil standing in the crowded street, looking up and down, but Elias had already disappeared. The boy would know these streets and alleys like the back of his hand.

Okedene stared at me in amazed horror. 'Why did that name cause him such terror? I never saw Elias react like that before.'

'I don't know,' I said quietly as I wiped blood from my cheek.

Nicholas came back upstairs. 'He's gone,' he said. 'Are you hurt, master?'

'No.'

Okedene's face darkened with anger. 'Elias was terrified. I doubt he will return.' He glared at Nicholas. 'Now I will have to find a new apprentice in the middle of a print run. All because you blurted out that name. Master Shardlake, I have done enough. I wish to have no more to do with this matter. I have a business, and am responsible for my wife and children.'

'Master Okedene, I am sorry.'

'So am I. Sorry, and sore afraid.' He looked out of the window again, breathing hard. 'And now, please go. And I beg you, involve me no more in this.'

'I will try to ensure you are not troubled again. But if Elias returns, can you send word to me at Lincoln's Inn?'

Okedene did not look round, but nodded wearily.

'Thank you,' I said again. 'I am sorry.' I turned to Nicholas. 'Come, you,' I snapped.

✝

I BEGAN WALKING fast down Paternoster Row. My cheek stung where Elias had struck it. I would have a nice bruise soon. 'We should go to the constable,' Nicholas said. 'For an apprentice to run away from his master is an offence.'

'We don't know that he's run away yet,' I answered. I was not going to involve the authorities in this without first consulting Lord Parr. I stopped and turned to Nicholas, 'What did you think you were doing, mentioning that name?'

'I heard you and Master Okedene discussing it as I came to the door. It seemed important. I thought it might be a good thing to scare that insolent boy into answering.'

'Could not you see that beneath his surliness was fear?'

'I saw only that he spoke to you as a lumpish apprentice should not to one of your rank.'

'Yes, Nicholas, you are full of your rank and class, and Elias annoyed you, so you thought to put him in his place. I was trying to soothe him, in order to gain his confidence. Do you not know the saying, never prick the stirring horse more than he needs? You have just lost us our most important witness.'

He looked crestfallen. 'You said I could ask questions.'

'Only after careful consideration. You didn't consider, you just reacted. The worst thing a lawyer can do.' I jabbed a finger on his doublet. 'Do not ever play the lusty-gallant gentleman again in my service.'

'I am sorry,' he said stiffly.

'So am I. So is poor Master Okedene.'

'It seems this murder touches the most delicate matters of religion,' he said quietly.

'All the more reason to be delicate ourselves,' I snapped back. 'Now, return to Lincoln's Inn and ask Barak what needs doing there. And do not say one word about where we have been. I think even you will realize the importance of confidentiality here. And now I will leave you. I have business elsewhere.'

I turned my back on him and walked away, down to the river, to get a boat to Whitehall.

Chapter Ten

WHEN I REACHED the Thames Street stairs there were plenty of boatmen waiting along the riverside, calling, 'Eastward Ho!' or 'Westward Ho!' to indicate whether they were going up- or downriver. I called to a man who was going upriver, and he pulled into the steps.

We rowed past Whitehall Palace; I had asked the boatman to take me to Westminster Stairs, just beyond. At the Whitehall Common Stairs servants were unloading great armfuls of firewood from a boat, presumably destined for the palace kitchens. I thought again of yesterday's burning, and shuddered. The boatman gave me an odd look. I lowered my eyes, watching him pull the oars in and out. He was a young man but his hands were already hard and knotted; I knew that older boatmen often got painful arthritis, the joints in their hands frozen into grasping claws. And all to take rich folk like me where they wanted to go.

We passed the King's Stairs: a wide covered gallery painted in green and white, jutting out fifty feet into the water, and ending in a broad, covered landing stage where the King's barge would pull up. Beyond, the long line of the palace facade was beautiful, the red brick-work mellow in the late afternoon sun, interspersed with projecting, richly glazed bastions, with tall glass windows, and at the south end the Lady Mary's new lodgings, covered in scaffolding. I paid the boat-man and walked back up the Whitehall Road, beside the west wall of the palace, to the Gatehouse. I was hot in my robe, dusty, tired and troubled.

This time there was no one to meet me, but my name was on the list and the guard at the gate allowed me in. I walked underneath the Gatehouse, across the courtyard, then up the stairs and into the King's Guard Chamber; my name checked at every door.

I went up to the King's Presence Chamber. A brown-robed servant carrying a silver ewer of water hurried past as I entered, almost colliding with me. I looked around. It was strange; already the effect of all the fantastic magnificence had worn off a little, though I was conscious of the Gentlemen Pensioners around the wall; their dress magnificently decorative. But they were big men, and carrying heavy poleaxes. Here I saw fewer young men come to fish for a name of fame standing around. My eye was drawn again to the picture of the royal family, the square solid frame of the King a total contrast to the grotesque, sad figure I had seen earlier that day.

Two of the would-be courtiers sat gambling with silver dice. One suddenly stood and shouted, 'You cheat! That is the third time you have thrown a five!'

The other stood up, moving his short Spanish cloak aside to free his arm. 'Dirt in your teeth! You insult me – '

Two of the Gentlemen Pensioners instantly moved forward, each grasping one of the popinjays by an arm. 'You forget where you are, churls!' one of them shouted. 'Do you dare think you can make a bray in this place, as though it were a common tavern? Get out! The King's Chamberlain will hear of this!' The two gamblers were marched to the door, now watched by everyone in the room.

I drew in my breath sharply at the sight of two men in black robes and gold chains, who had entered from the stairs and stood staring at the brawlers. I had seen both of them at the burning. One was Chief Secretary William Paget, his square face frowning above the bushy brown beard that framed his odd, downturned slash of a mouth. The other, his spare frame contrasting with Paget's solid build, and with a sardonic smile on his thin face, was Sir Richard Rich. They had not seen me; I moved quickly to the door leading to the Queen's Presence Chamber and whispered my name to the guard. He opened the door and I slipped through. On the other side another guard in the Queen's

livery looked at me interrogatively. 'Serjeant Shardlake,' I said breathlessly. 'Here to see Lord Parr.'

The Queen's uncle was already waiting for me in the chamber;
someone below must have told him I had arrived. Among all the mag-
nificent decoration, and the sumptuous clothes of a pair of courtiers,
Lord Parr made a sober figure in his black robe, the only colour the
Queen's badge on his chest and the heavy gold chain around his neck.
I bowed low. He said, 'Come to my private office, Master Shardlake.'

I followed him through another door. He led me on down a corridor, our footsteps making no sound on the thick rush matting that
covered the floors from wall to wall. Through an open door I glimpsed
the Queen's Presence Chamber, and caught sight of the Queen herself sitting sewing at a window, dressed in red, with some of the ladies
who had also been present earlier. Gardiner, the Duchess of Suffolk's
spaniel, sat on the floor, playing with a bone.

'We are passing on to the Queen's privy lodgings,' Lord Parr said.
'My office is there. The Queen likes me close to her since I was recalled
from the country in the spring.' He opened the door to a small, dark
office, with a window giving onto another courtyard, the papers on
chests and the little desk in neatly ordered piles. 'Here,' he said, taking
a lawyer's robe in fine silk from a chair and handing it to me. 'Change
into this.' The Queen's brightly coloured badge of St Catherine, I
saw, was sewn onto the breast. Before taking his place behind the desk
he went over and closed the window. Then he bade me sit.

'I prefer it open these summer days,' he said ruefully. 'But in this
place one never knows who may be listening from the next window.'
Lord Parr sighed. 'As you have probably realized, the court is a place
full of fear and hate; there is no real amity anywhere. Even among
families; the Seymours quarrel and scratch like cats. Only the Parr
family is united; we are loyal to each other.' He spoke with pride. 'It is
our strength.'

'You have been here only since the spring, my Lord?' I ventured.

'Yes. For much of the last few years I have delegated my duties
and stayed on my estates. I am old now, not always well. No longer the

man I was, when I served the King.' He smiled in reminiscence. 'As did my brother, the Queen's father; and the Queen's mother was lady-in-waiting to Catherine of Aragon. The Parrs have been a part of the court for a long time. The Queen's mother died just before the full storm of the King's Great Divorce broke. Well, she was spared that.' He looked up, eyes sharp again under the white brows. 'I have stood *in loco parentis* for my niece since then. I will do anything to protect her. When she asked me to come back to court, I did so at once.'

'I understand.'

'I should swear you in.' He took a Testament from a drawer, and I solemnly swore to serve the Queen loyally and honestly. Lord Parr nodded brusquely, returned the Testament to the drawer, and said, 'Well, what news?'

I took a deep breath. 'Not good, my Lord.' I told him that the first of the attacks on Greening had taken place before the *Lamentation* was stolen, that the authorities had given up on the case, that Greening's friends seemed to have gone to ground and might even be Anabaptists. Finally I explained how Elias had fled. I had promised to tell only the Queen of anything that might endanger the boy, but Lord Parr had to know of his plight. None of it made good hearing, and I had to mention Nicholas's careless use of the name Bertano, which had caused such distress to Elias, though I praised his discovery of the scrap of silk. I had brought it with me, and now laid it on the table. Lord Parr examined it.

'A fine piece of work, expensive,' he said. 'The blackwork decoration is distinctive.' He turned it over. 'The Queen's embroiderer, Hal Gullym, has worked all his life at the Queen's Wardrobe in Baynard's Castle; he knows all the fine shirt-makers in London. He might be able to find out who made this.'

'From a mere piece of sleeve?'

'Of this quality, possibly.' He frowned. 'The apprentice was certain that the first attack on Greening happened before the *Lamentation* vanished?'

'Certain. I am sorry he ran away. When that name Bertano was mentioned he became terrified.'

'I have never heard it before. And Okedene, he overheard them talking of this Bertano as one who would bring down the country, an agent of the Antichrist?'

'He is quite sure. And I believe Okedene is an honest man.' I added hesitantly, 'He asks that we leave him alone now; he fears for his family.'

'As I fear for mine,' Lord Parr answered bluntly. 'And yet – eleven days now since the book was stolen and not a word, nothing. Who could have taken it?'

'Not a religious radical, surely.'

'And yet if it was a papist, surely the book would be public knowledge by now, and God knows what would have happened to my niece. The King has a hard view of anything that smacks of disloyalty.' He bit his lip.

'We should find that apprentice,' I said.

He looked at me sternly. 'You should not have lost him.'

'I know, my Lord.'

'And those three associates of Greening's. Gone to ground?'

'It looks like it. Though they may just be keeping quiet for a while. The constable knows where they live. He has been keeping an eye on them this year, as suspected sacramentarians.'

Lord Parr frowned angrily, spots of colour forming on his pale cheeks. 'God's death, these extreme radicals with their mad ideas. They are a danger to those of us who know that reform must be sought through quieter means. They have no idea of the reality of politics. This Bertano, he may not even exist, may be some phantasm of their fevered minds!' He took a long breath, calming himself, then said, 'You must seek out these three friends of Greening's, talk to them, find what they know. Likely that apprentice has taken refuge with them.' He frowned again. 'And if you take your pupil this time, make sure he knows when to keep his mouth shut.'

'Rest assured, my Lord, I will.'

I thought, this meant even more work, and among people who could be dangerous to those they thought their enemies. I thought also of the work in chambers that I could not leave to my staff – the inspection of the wall painting in the Slanning case was coming up – and I had a moment's panic, felt the chair shifting under me. I grasped the arms hard.

'What is the matter?' Lord Parr asked sharply.

'I am sorry, my Lord, I – it has been a long day, and I was at the burning yesterday. Sometimes when I am tired I feel strange, the world seems to rock – '

I expected him to snap at me for being a mumping weakling, but to my surprise he spoke quietly. 'The Queen told me you were on the *Mary Rose* when she went down last year. That was a great tragedy. Though it is not permitted to speak of it at court, the King felt much humiliated by the foundering of his favourite ship.'

'I lost good friends, and nearly died myself. At times of strain – forgive me, my Lord.'

He grunted. 'I, too, am sometimes unwell. I have long suffered from fevers, and they grow more frequent. Sometimes I am so tired – ' He shrugged, then gave a tight smile. 'But we must go on. You know the Queen's motto?'

'To be useful in all I do.'

'And so must we be. I know this is a hard load, Serjeant Shardlake.'

'Thank you, my Lord, but is it really the best course for me to try to find and question these men? The radicals are suspicious of everybody. They will surely see me, as the apprentice did, as an inquisitive lawyer who may serve some master who would hurt them.'

Lord Parr smiled wryly. 'Yes, people are suspicious of your trade, they think all lawyers will serve any master for a fee.'

'Perhaps if someone else could approach these men initially, someone known as a sympathizer, who could reassure them that the lawyer who will be coming is not an enemy. No more than that need be said.'

The old man nodded. 'You are right. You met young William Cecil last night?'

'Yes.'

'He is known to have certain – contacts, shall we say. He is a very junior employee of the Queen's Learned Council, but I have already marked his cleverness, and his commitment to reform. As well as his ambition for himself, which is considerable.' He gave his sardonic smile again. 'Very well, I will send him to try and find these people, and reassure them that you merely wish to question them about the murder of Greening, but that you mean them no harm. That is all Master Cecil needs to be told. He does not know about the *Lamentation*, of course.'

'That may help our quest.'

Lord Parr stroked his beard. 'You say Greening was only printing some French primer when he was killed?'

'Yes. I checked the print-shop thoroughly.'

'The Queen, you may imagine, has no connection with such small-scale printers. Her *Prayers and Meditations* went to the King's Printer, John Berthelet.' He shook his head, then grasped the arms of his chair resolutely. 'And now,' he said, 'I would like you to question some servants of the household.'

'Yes, my Lord.'

'But first, look at this.'

He reached into his robe, and held up a little key on a gold chain. 'I have persuaded my niece to entrust this to me. It is the one she kept around her neck, that opens her private chest.'

I examined it, and saw it had several teeth of different sizes. 'It does not look like a key that would be easy to copy.'

'No. The chest itself I have removed to a place of safety, where it can be inspected.' Lord Parr replaced the key in the folds of his robe. 'Now, are you ready to question these servants?' He gave me a hard look.

'Yes, my Lord. Forgive me, I had but a weak moment.'

'Good.' He consulted a paper on his desk. 'I have checked the records and discovered who was on duty that evening. The Queen was in her chamber all that afternoon; she went to her bedchamber after lunch, looked at the book and thought again about disposing of it, then spent some time studying Spanish – she is working to increase her knowledge of languages, that she may be of most use in diplomatic functions.'

'She is often on her own during the afternoons?'

'No. But when an afternoon is free she does like to take the chance to be alone for a little – it is not always easy in this place,' he added feelingly. 'Then at six she was called to the King, as you know, and returned at ten of the evening. It was during those four hours that the *Lamentation* was stolen. According to the guards, the only people who came into the Queen's privy lodgings during that time were the two page boys whose duties are to clean the rooms and the Queen's Gallery, and feed Rig, the Queen's spaniel, and her birds. Also you will interview two women who have more or less free access – Mary Odell, a maid-in-waiting who has served the Queen for years, who makes sure her bed is ready and often sleeps with her in her chamber; and Jane, the fool she shares with the Lady Mary. Jane is much wanting in wit. Apparently she came into the Privy Chamber that evening, where some of the Queen's ladies were sitting, demanding to see my niece, saying she had something that would entertain her. She did not believe the ladies when they told her the Queen was with the King, and Jane can make a great fuss if she does not get her way – the Queen and the Lady Mary both overindulge her – so the guard let her into the Queen's privy lodgings to see for herself. She came out after a few minutes. And that is all.'

'How many rooms make up the Queen's privy lodgings?'

'Six. The bathroom, bedchamber, the closet for prayer, a study, and dining room. And beyond those the Queen's Privy Gallery, where she often walks. I have searched every inch of each chamber myself, by the way, in case the book was somehow secreted there. And found nothing.'

'Are two pages needed to clean each day?'

Lord Parr laughed scoffingly. 'Of course not. But this is the royal household, and a multitude of servants is a sign of the Queen's great status. There is another pair who come to clean in the morning. Only the King has more.'

'And the staff on duty vary?'

'Yes. There is a rota. I see what you are thinking. Another servant could somehow have discovered the book's existence earlier? But they could not have arranged in advance for the book to be taken on that day, as nobody knew the King would call the Queen to him that evening.'

'But he must do so fairly often?'

'Not every evening. And in recent days he has often had meetings in the evening with the councillors and ambassadors.'

'So, it seems the book must have been taken by one of these four servants, unless someone had secreted themselves in the Queen's Gallery.'

'Impossible. Nobody could. The guards at the doors to the Privy Chamber entrances check everyone who goes in and out. They are an absolute bar.'

I thought a moment. 'What about the guards themselves? Can they be trusted?'

'All selected by the Queen. On a rota, again, but if any guard left his post by one of the doors, it would be noticed instantly. Not least by would-be courtiers, who are ever eager to gain closer access to places they shouldn't. No, the only people who had entry when the Queen was absent were the two page boys, Mary Odell, and Jane Fool.'

'Four people only.'

'I have had both boys called in, and the two women. Using the pretext of the stolen ring, I want you to check the movements of each of them on that day. Present the jewel's loss as a matter of great sorrow to the Queen. She has given authority for you to see Mary Odell alone, but you will have to question Jane in her presence; Jane is so foolish she would be afraid if you were to question her alone, perhaps even defiant.' He frowned; he obviously thought her an unmitigated nuisance.

'Very well, my Lord.'

'Mary Odell is one of four chamberers. It is a junior post, but Mary is especially close to the Queen. She is her cousin once removed. There are many distant Parr relatives in the Queen's household now, just as once there were Boleyns and Seymours. As well as being her dependants, they all owe their posts to the Queen, so their loyalty can be counted on. But Mary Odell, particularly, is the Queen's close friend as well as her servant. Handle her gently. As for Jane Fool – ' he inclined his head – 'there are two types of fool: those skilled at gentle clowning, like the King's man, Will Somers, and natural fools like Jane. She has great licence. But she has a sharp wit as well.' Lord Parr looked at me closely. 'One never knows if fools are always so foolish as they seem,' he concluded darkly.

'And Jane serves as fool to the Lady Mary as well. So she has joint loyalties,' I ventured.

'I have considered that. It is ten years since the Lady Mary ended her defiance and agreed to the Royal Supremacy. She is conservative in religion, but has followed the King's wishes all this time. The Queen has tried to bring all three royal children together, but although Mary is fond of little Edward, she does not like the Lady Elizabeth.' He shrugged. 'Understandable, as Elizabeth's mother displaced hers. The Queen has done everything to befriend Mary. They are of an age, and often together.'

'But Mary is no reformer.'

'She has avoided all taint of plotting. She is safe. And now I will leave you.' Lord Parr stood. 'The pages will be sent in. It will attract less notice, as I told you, if the questioning is conducted by one of the Queen's Learned Council rather than myself. I will return later. The missing ring is plain gold with a large square ruby in the centre, and the initials of the Queen's late stepdaughter, MN, for Margaret Neville, on the inside of the band.' He stepped to the door. 'Watch the page Adrian Russell, he can be an insolent pup. Later I will show you the chest. By the way, I heard today the King is moving to Hampton Court next month. The rat-catchers have already been sent in. Everything and everybody in the Royal Apartments will be moved there by barge. So it is important that you see everything here as it was at the time of the theft, while you still can.'

✝

A GUARD SHOWED in the first page, a skinny fair-haired lad of about sixteen, with a haughty manner. He wore the Queen's red livery, her badge on his chest, and a black cap which he removed. I looked at him sternly, as though he were a hostile witness in court.

'You are Adrian Russell?'

'Yes, sir, of Kendal. My father is a distant relation of the Queen, and owns much property in Cumberland.' He spoke proudly.

'I am Serjeant Shardlake, of the Queen's Learned Council, set to investigate the matter of the ruby ring stolen from the coffer in the Queen's bedchamber. You have heard of the theft?'

'Yes, sir.'

'It was stolen while the Queen was with his majesty on the sixth of July, between six and ten in the evening. You were one of those on duty that night?'

Russell looked at me boldly. 'Yes, sir. Garet Lynley and I came in at six, to bring fresh candles, clean the rooms, and scent them with new herbs. I left at eight. Garet stayed. To attend to the bedchamber,' he added.

'Did you enter the Queen's bedchamber at all?' I asked sharply.

'No sir, only Garet Lynley. Only one page is allowed in there each evening, and it was not my turn that day.'

'Two pages carry out this work every day for two hours?'

'That is our assignment on the rota. We have to attend to the Queen's gallery, too, feed the birds there. And her dog.'

I did not like this lad's arrogant tone. I spoke coldly. 'Mayhap it does not always take two hours? Perhaps you sometimes sit down, rest?'

'All servants do, sir.'

'And boys are prone to meddle. A page stole something from the Queen before, you may remember. And he was sentenced to hang until the Queen pardoned him.'

Russell's eyes widened. He began to bluster. 'Sir, I would do nothing like that, I would steal nothing, I swear. I am of good family—'

'So you say. Did you see anyone else while you were there? Or anything unusual at all?'

'No, sir.'

'Think. Think hard. Perhaps the thief left something out of place, moved something?'

'No, sir. I swear, I would tell you if I had noticed anything out of place.' Young Russell was kneading his hands together with anxiety now, his childish arrogance gone. I could not see this callow lad being involved in the book's theft. In gentler tones, I got him to go over his exact movements, then told him he could go. He scurried from the room with relief.

The second page, Garet Lynley, was afraid from the outset; I could see that at once. He was the same age as Russell, tall and thin, his neatly combed brown hair worn long. I bade him sit and asked him about his duties in the Queen's bedchamber.

'I go in there, put new candles in the holders, lay out fresh linen on the coffer, then change the flowers and place fresh herbs and petals about the room. I feed the Queen's dog, Rig, if he is there, but he was not that night. I do not touch her majesty's bed or clothes, of course, that is for her chamberers. Mary Odell, I think it was, that day.'

I nodded. 'You put the linen on the chest. You know valuables are kept within?'

'I swear, sir, I did not touch it. I never do. I believe it is locked.'

'Have you ever tried the lock to find out?'

'Never,' he answered. 'I am loyal to her majesty — ' His voice rose in fear.

I made my tone friendlier. 'Did you notice anything unusual in the room that evening? About the chest, perhaps?'

'No, sir. It was dusk by then. I carried a lamp.' He frowned. 'But if anything had been amiss with the chest I think I would have seen. I placed the linen there every night that week.'

'Have you ever seen the stolen ring?'

'No. I am told the Queen wears it on her finger sometimes, but I always have to bow low each time she passes, so I have never seen it.'

'Very well.' I believed him, but Garet Lynley, I was sure, was frightened of something more than just my interrogation. 'Where are you from, boy?' I asked lightly. 'You have a northern cast of tongue.'

The question seemed to disturb him greatly; his eyes swivelled as he answered me. 'Lancashire, sir. My mother was once a maid-in-waiting in Catherine of Aragon's household. It was through her that my family were granted their lands. She knew the present Queen's mother, old Lady Parr.'

'And that was how you got this post? Through your family's connection with the Queen's mother?'

'Yes, sir. She wrote to Lord Parr as to whether there might be a place for me.' His breath was coming noticeably fast now.

'Are both your parents still alive?'

'Not my father, sir.' The boy hesitated. 'He was imprisoned in the Tower after the Northern Rebellion ten years ago, and died there.'

I considered carefully. A boy whose mother had served Catherine of Aragon and whose father had taken part in the Northern Rebellion. 'Your family history, then, might make people wonder about your religious sympathies,' I said slowly.

Garet's collapse was sudden, and total. Almost falling off his chair, he knelt on the floor, wringing his hands. 'It is not true! I swear I am no papist, I loyally follow the King's dispensations. I keep telling people, if only they would leave me alone — '

'Get up,' I said gently. I felt sorry to have unmanned him so. 'Take your chair again. Now, listen, I am not here to harm you. What people?'

He shook his head desperately. Tears were coursing down his cheeks now.

'Come, Garet. If you have done nothing wrong you will suffer no harm. If you have – and if you confess – the Queen will be merciful.'

The boy took a long, shuddering breath.

'I have done nothing, sir. But it is as you say, because of my family's past, people think I might be one who would spy against the reformers. Though Lord Parr and the Queen know my family wish only to live quietly and serve loyally. But since coming to the palace – ' He hesitated.

'Yes?'

'A man has approached me, twice, and asked if I would observe what I could about the Queen and report to those who would serve what he called true religion. I refused, I swear – ' He stared at me miserably, his face puffy with tears, and I realized suddenly what it must be like for an innocent boy to step into this gilded sewer-pit.

'Did you report this to your superiors? Lord Parr?'

'No, sir, I didn't dare. The man, he – frightened me.'

'When did this happen?'

'When I first came, last autumn. Then again in April, when the hunt for heretics began.'

'The same man approached you both times?'

'Yes. I did not know him. I told one of the other pages and he said it sometimes happens when you first come to court, an approach from one side or the other, and if you would keep your skin whole you should always say no. The approach is always by someone unknown at court, a servant of one of the great men, but from outside the palace.'

'What was his name?'

'He would not tell it. He approached me the first time in the street. The second occasion he was waiting for me outside an inn I frequent. There was something in his face that frightened me.' The boy looked down, ashamed of his weakness.

'Can you describe him?'

The boy looked up at me again. He realized it was all or nothing now. 'He was in his twenties, thin but wiry and strong. He wore cheap clothes but spoke like a gentleman. I remember he had half of one ear missing, like it had been cut off in a fight.' Garet shuddered.

Half an ear gone, like one of the men Elias had disturbed trying to break into the print-shop that first time. I tried not to let my excitement show. Garet continued, 'Both times he said that if I agreed to spy on the Queen I would earn the gratitude of a very great personage of the realm, who would reward me and advance my career at court.'

'Surely an enticing prospect,' I observed.

'No.' Garet shook his head fiercely. 'Now I only want to leave here as soon as possible.'

'You did the right thing in telling me,' I said soothingly. 'You have nothing to fear. Now, after you turned this man down for the second time, did you see him again?'

'Never. It is like that, I'm told, if they cannot turn you they give up. I wish I could go home to my family, sir,' he added in a small voice. 'Without disgrace.'

'I think that may be arranged.'

Garet wiped a satin sleeve across his face. I could not but sympathize with his weakness. If I had found myself in the same danger at his age my reaction would probably have been the same. I let him leave, and sat alone in Lord Parr's office. At last, I thought, a clue.

Chapter Eleven

MARY ODELL WAS a tall, plump woman in her early thirties, dressed in black silk livery, the Queen's badge fixed to the cap atop her fair hair. She had soft features, and something of a motherly air, although she wore no wedding ring. Her green eyes were keen and alert. I stood and bowed, inviting her to sit. She did so, folding her hands in her lap, looking at me with curiosity and, I thought, a touch of speculative amusement.

'I am Serjeant Matthew Shardlake.'

'I know, sir. The Queen has spoken of you. She believes you an honest and most clever man.'

I felt myself blush. 'I apologize for troubling you, Mistress Odell, but I must speak with everyone who was in the Queen's privy lodgings the night her ring was stolen.'

'Certainly. Her majesty asked me to do all I could to help you.'

'Lord Parr says you have been chamberer and friend to the Queen for some time.'

'We are related. I knew her majesty before she was Queen.' Mary Odell smiled slightly, with that hint of secret amusement the Queen herself had so often shown in happier days. 'Poor relations do well when a person reaches such exalted status.' She paused, and then continued, her voice serious now. 'But my loyalty to her majesty goes far deeper than gratitude for my post. She has favoured me with her trust and good friendship, and I tell you frankly I would die for her.' Mistress Odell took a deep breath. 'She has told me much of what has happened these last months. Her – troubles.'

'I see.' But not about the *Lamentation*. That would be too dangerous.

Mistress Odell looked at me quizzically. 'The Queen seems extraordinarily upset over the loss of her ring. She loved the good Margaret Neville, but even so seems somehow stricken very hard by the theft.' I could see this intelligent woman had guessed that more was involved here than a stolen jewel. But of course I could not comment.

'I understand you were on duty as chamberer that night. And that you – pray, excuse me – share the Queen's bed on occasion.'

'I do sometimes. For company, when my mistress is feeling lonely, or troubled.'

'Could you tell me everything that happened when you came to prepare the Queen's bedchamber the night the ring was stolen? Anything even slightly unusual that you saw or heard might help.'

She nodded, seeming to approve that I was getting down to business. 'I have two rooms in the lodgings by the gatehouse. That evening I left them perhaps ten minutes early, a little before nine; I was tired and wanted to get my duty done and out of the way. I crossed the courtyard to the Royal Apartments. The routine is that the pages clean the rooms, and then I go in to prepare the bed, make sure all is in order in the bedchamber, and lay out the Queen's nightgown and hairbrushes.'

'One of the pages always cleans the bedchamber first?'

'Yes.'

'Are the pages obedient? Boys are prone to mischief.'

'Once or twice I have caught them playing cards in the Queen's Gallery and reported them to the gentleman usher, but they would not dare to make any real trouble in the Queen's quarters. The boys on duty that evening had done a good enough job. One of the guards told me her majesty was with the King that evening. Sometimes when she returns she likes to talk with me, so as I went back to my lodgings I told the guard I would be there if she wanted me. I have to say, Serjeant Shardlake, it seemed a very ordinary evening. Nothing unusual, nothing out of place. Only – ' She wrinkled her nose. 'There was a slightly unpleasant smell in the bedchamber. So slight you could barely catch it.'

'What sort of smell?'

'Begging your pardon, of ordure. I thought perhaps it had come from the river, and closed the window. I looked round the room closely with my lamp as well, but could see nothing amiss. As I said, the smell was very faint.'

'And did you notice anything about the Queen's private chest? Where the ring was kept?'

'The page had laid the linen on top of it as usual. There was noth-ing untoward.' She paused. 'I wish I could help you more with this, sir, given the Queen's distress.' She spoke now with feeling. 'But there was nothing.'

'You will have seen inside the chest?'

'A few times. The Queen has sometimes taken out her jewels, or a half-finished letter in front of me; she always kept the key round her neck.' Her voice grew sad. 'But not these last few months. Recently her majesty has seemed reluctant to let me see inside it.'

I had to deflect her from this path, even if it meant lying. 'Some-times when a person has been under strain for a while, as I know the Queen has, some final event, such as the loss of a ring from a loved one, can unbalance their humours.'

She nodded. 'True.' But she looked at me keenly.

'You are quite sure, then, there was nothing unusual that night.'

She thought hard, then something seemed to occur to her. 'Apart from the smell, which soon vanished, there was only one thing, some-thing so small I hesitate to mention it.'

'What?' I leaned forward over Lord Parr's desk. 'Anything might help.'

'I told you I came over from my lodgings. You will have discov-ered how many guarded doors one must pass through in this place – at the entrance to the King's Guard Chamber, the Presence Chambers, the Privy Chamber, the privy lodgings . . . When I am on duty I am always on the list of people to be admitted. Sometimes a guard new to his duties will ask who I am, check that I am on the list and make a prick against my name with his pin. I do not complain, it is their duty. But in the Queen's apartments nearly all the guards know me; they just mark my name as I pass. That night the guard on the door to the privy lodgings was a man who has often been on duty there, named Zachary Gawger. To my surprise he stopped me and made a fuss about being unable to find my name on his list. I told him not to be foolish, but he insisted on checking the list twice before he finally found it and let me through. And he spoke in a loud, bullying tone, not fit for addressing a lady of my station.' She bridled slightly. 'I wondered if he might be drunk, but the guard captain always checks the guards are sober, and their equipment in order, before he allows them on duty.'

'It certainly sounds strange,' I agreed. 'I shall discuss it with Lord Parr.' I stood and bowed. 'I thank you for your time.'

Mistress Odell got up. 'I am asked to take you to the Queen's private prayer closet now. The Queen will meet you there. I understand you are to speak to Jane Fool.'

''Tis so.'

That touch of a humorous smile again, like Queen Catherine's. 'I wish you good luck with her, sir.'

She opened the door, and I followed her out.

✝

WE WALKED DOWN the hallway. A rich perfume of roses and lavender filled the air, the scent coming from petals laid alongside the wainscotting. Through an open door at the end of the hall I had a glimpse of an immensely long, brightly painted gallery with tall windows, and of caged songbirds within that made a pretty trilling. The Queen's Gallery, I surmised.

Mary Odell knocked on a side door and, receiving no reply, bade me enter. I found myself in a private closet, a room for prayer. The design was impeccably orthodox; richly painted like everywhere in the palace, with an altar covered with embroidered white linen and candles burning in niches. The Queen would make sure her private chapel presented no visible sign of reformism for her enemies to use against her.

Mary Odell turned in the doorway. 'The Queen and Jane should be here soon.'

'Thank you, Mistress Odell.'

She gave me a sudden winning smile. 'I know you will do all you can to help the Queen. God speed your efforts, Serjeant Shardlake.'

'You are kind.'

She went out with a rustle of silken skirts, leaving me alone. In the distance I could hear faint voices: the daily hubbub of the palace. At last, I thought, I gain a little ground. The man with half an ear who had been at the first attack on Greening was linked to someone at the top; Mary Odell's strange episode with the guard should be investigated, too. Even that odd smell should be considered further. And now I was about to see the Queen again. I looked at one of the red candles burning in the chapel, and for a moment felt an odd sense of contentment.

So thick was the rush matting that I did not hear approaching footsteps, and started as the door opened. Four women entered, but Queen Catherine was not among them. Two were young, dressed sumptuously in long-sleeved dresses. The two others, I realized with a shock, were familiar to me from the great portrait of the King and his family. One was the little round-faced woman who had been standing behind the Lady Mary in the doorway; the other was the Lady Mary herself. The little woman, who I realized must be Jane Fool, had with her, of all creatures, a fat white duck, which waddled beside her, a leathern collar and leash round its neck.

Jane was conspicuous in the comparative plainness of her dress, though her grey high-collared gown and white coif were of the best material. Her blue eyes darted around the chapel then fixed on me with a blank, frightened look. Beside her, scarcely taller, but magnificently dressed and with a bearing of regal authority, the Lady Mary studied me. I bowed almost to the floor, my heart thumping hard.

'Rise, master lawyer.' The voice was rich, surprisingly deep.

I looked at the King's eldest child. I knew Catherine of Aragon's daughter was much older than the Lady Elizabeth and Prince Edward; well into her twenties and, with her thin, narrow features, looking older still. She had auburn hair under a round French hood studded with diamonds, and a green gown decorated with pomegranates; a popular design but also the emblem of her long-dead, rejected mother. Small, shapely hands played with a golden pomander which she wore at her waist.

'Forgive me, my Lady,' I said. 'I did not know – '

She nodded and smiled pleasantly, though her dark eyes were coldly watchful. She struck me as someone who had been watchful all her life, despite her poised manner. She waved a hand. 'You were expecting the Queen, I know. But my father called on her to sit with him a little. Jane was with me when Mary Odell came to fetch her, and I said I would accompany her instead.' She looked at me quizzically. 'I believe you have been asked to investigate the Queen's stolen ring.'

'That is correct, my lady. By Lord Parr.'

Mary made a movement of her thin shoulders, a hint of a shrug. 'I had heard vaguely of it. But I have been much engaged these last few days observing the building of my new lodgings.' A touch of pride entered her voice. 'I have brought two of my ladies along, as you see, for propriety's sake.' She did not introduce them, but continued to address me. 'I am surprised poor Jane is to be questioned.'

She looked fondly at the little woman, who stared back at her appealingly and spoke, in a high voice. 'I haven't done aught amiss, my lady.'

I wondered, was Jane genuinely slow-witted and anxious, or was she acting? I could not tell; there was something oddly inscrutable about her moon face, either because her mind worked strangely or because she was a skilled actress. Perhaps it was both.

I said, 'The Queen wished it, because Jane – ' it seemed the custom to refer to her by her Christian name – 'was one of only four people who entered her majesty's bedchamber on the evening the ring was stolen.' I turned to Jane. 'You are not suspected of anything. It is rather a matter of whether you might have seen or noticed anything amiss—'

The Lady Mary's voice, suddenly sharp, interrupted me. 'I require that you address any questions to Jane through me, sir, as I am sure the Queen herself would wish, were she able to attend. I will not have her frightened.' She gave a slight frown, which the two ladies-in-waiting instantly copied. The duck pulled at its leash, keen to investigate a scattering of herbs lying in a corner of the prayer closet.

'Then may I request, my Lady, that you ask Jane where she went, and what she might have seen, from the time she entered the privy lodgings on the sixth of July?'

'Well, Jane?' the Lady Mary asked encouragingly. 'Do you remember anything?'

Jane Fool gave me a quick look before addressing her mistress. 'I wanted to show the Queen a new trick I have taught Ducky, to seek out herbs which I have hidden. But the ladies would not let me past the Privy Chamber, they said she was not in.' To my surprise Jane then stamped her foot like a child, and raised her voice. 'Often they try to keep me from the Queen, though I alone can divert her when she is sad. She has often been sad of late—'

Mary raised a hand, and Jane was instantly silent. 'Yes,' Mary said dryly. 'She has. And now such a fuss over a missing ring.' However hard the Queen might have tried to bring the King's children into amity with her and each other, it seemed that with Mary at least her success had been limited.

'It was of great sentimental value,' I murmured. 'My Lady, if Jane could say where she went – '

Mary turned back to Jane. She spoke patiently. 'When you went past the ladies into the privy lodgings, where did you go? Did you see anything strange?'

'I looked in all the rooms for the Queen,' Jane replied. 'And when I saw she was truly not there, I came out again into the Privy Chamber. Nobody was in her quarters, the pages had gone and Mary Odell not yet come.'

'Then all is well.' Mary spoke in a tone of finality and Jane Fool shot me a quick, triumphant look.

I persisted. 'Did she notice anything unusual in the Queen's bed-chamber? About her private chest, perhaps, where she kept the ring and other valuables?'

'No. Nothing,' Jane said – too quickly, I thought. 'The Queen never lets me near it. My Lady, this crookback frightens me.' I thought, you are lying. From the change in the Lady Mary's expression I realized she saw it too.

'Any information would be received most gratefully by the Queen,' I dared to venture.

The Lady Mary looked at Jane. 'Be calm, my dear. You know I can tell when you are playing games. Tell the gentleman anything you know, and I give you my word you will come to no harm.'

Jane Fool was red-faced now. Like a child, she pouted and stuck a finger in her mouth.

'Jane – ' A stern note had crept into the Lady Mary's voice.

'It's rude, it's naughty,' Jane blurted out.

'What is, Jane?'

There was a long moment of silence. Then she said, 'When I went into the bedchamber to see whether the Queen was there – '

I leaned forward. The Lady Mary said encouragingly, 'Yes – ?'

'I had Ducky with me, and – '

'Yes – ?'

'He shat on the floor.'

Whatever I had expected, it was not that. So that explained the smell. 'A little trail of shit on the matting,' Jane continued. 'I was afraid the gentleman ushers might have Ducky sent away. I took a cloth and cleaned it up, using water from the Queen's rosewater bowl. The scent of herbs in the room was so strong, I thought the smell might not be noticed. I went away at once, and told no one.' Suddenly she yanked the duck's leash, pulling it towards her with almost enough force to break its neck, then bent down and hugged it to her. It looked startled, as well it might. 'Don't let the hunchback tell, my Lady, I beg you. I love Ducky.'

'No one will tell, Jane,' the Lady Mary said. She looked at me then, her mouth twitching slightly, and I discerned she had a quality I had not guessed at before: a sense of humour.

'Does that satisfy you, master lawyer?' she asked.

'Of course, my Lady.'

'I will allow you to report the duck's misdemeanour to Lord Parr,' she said gravely. 'But only on condition Jane is not parted from it. I think the Queen would agree.'

'Of course, my Lady.'

'Then we will leave you to your business.'

One of the ladies-in-waiting helped Jane to her feet; the other opened the door for the Lady Mary. I bowed low again. They went out, the duck waddling after the group on its webbed yellow feet. As I rose, the Lady Mary turned, looked at me, and gave a sardonic little smile. The door closed. I stood there, shaken by the unexpected and ridiculous turn of events. Ridiculous? I could not help but wonder whether I had just been made the victim of an elaborate charade, and whether Jane Fool knew more than she had said. But if so, she was an accomplished actress. And I had no evidence, none at all. I thought of her childlike demeanour. Perhaps that was what had attracted the Queen and the Lady Mary to her, two mature women who were childless and likely to remain so. Perhaps she was a substitute child for them and nothing more. But there was something about Mary Tudor that made me afraid to think of the *Lamentation* ending in her hands.

☨

I STAYED IN the prayer closet, with the candles and incense. Half an hour passed, the light outside beginning to fade, before the door opened again and Lord Parr entered. He was frowning. 'I am told the Lady Mary accompanied Jane Fool to see you. You gave her no hint about the book?' He looked at me anxiously.

'None, my Lord.' I told him the absurd story about the duck, what I had gleaned from Garet Lynley about the man with half an ear missing, and Mary Odell's story of the guard.

He nodded. 'I will make discreet enquiries. A man with half an ear serving a great man of the realm . . .'

'The page said one of the great *personages* of the realm.'

He studied me closely. 'You mean the Lady Mary? That she might have sent Jane Fool to steal the book that evening after all?'

'We must make absolutely sure the Queen dropped no hint about the book to Jane.'

Lord Parr shook his head. 'Jane has always appeared a natural idiot.'

'Perhaps. Yet her speech, even though childish, is fluent. And sometimes one can be – indiscreet – before fools.'

He nodded, taking the point, but said, 'The Queen would not be. Not on this. And as I said before, the Lady Mary has stayed strictly orthodox for a decade. Nonetheless, I will speak to the Queen about Jane. Though even that theory begs the question of how someone managed to get the coffer open yet leave no signs of forced entry.' He sighed. 'Thank you, Master Shardlake, we may be starting to make progress. Now, the Queen is still with the King. A good time for us to take a look at the coffer. Come.'

✝

THE QUEEN'S BEDCHAMBER overlooked the river. It was a large, feminine room, richly scented, with flowers in vases and large embroidered cushions scattered on the floor where one might lie and read. A huge four-poster bed dominated the room. There was a desk, bare save for an ornate inkwell: here, at this desk, the Queen had written *Lamentation of a Sinner*. Next to the desk stood a solid wooden chest, two and a half feet high, a red-and-gold turkey carpet fixed to the top. On the front two carved nymphs flanked a Tudor rose. There was no bed linen on the chest; tonight's page had not arrived yet.

Lord Parr knelt down, with surprising suppleness for a man of his age, and I followed more slowly. He banged the side of the coffer, bringing forth a hollow echo.

'Firm, solid oak,' he said. 'All the Queen's valuables have been removed and placed elsewhere.'

I studied the lock. It was small but very solid, set firmly into the wood. I ran my fingers over it. 'No sign of scratches on the metal, nor the wood surrounding it. It was either opened with a key, or by a very skilled locksmith.'

'I have had the Queen's valuables taken elsewhere,' Lord Parr said, opening the chest carefully.

I looked at the empty interior, then bent carefully to study the lock from within. My back was hurting after this long day. No sign of scratches there, either. 'I have seen many chests and coffers for securing valuables,' I said. 'Mostly documents in my case. Often they have two or three locks, and complicated mechanisms inside.'

He nodded agreement. 'Yes. But this coffer was given to the Queen by her mother. She is very attached to it.'

I looked up at him. 'But the lock is surely new.'

'Yes indeed. When the hunt for heretics and the questioning of those within the royal household started this spring, the Queen had the locks on all her cupboards and coffers replaced. I asked if she wanted a more complex lock for this one, too, but she said it might damage the coffer. I remember her telling me, "If I have the only key and the new lock is strong, surely it is safe."' 'Of course,' he added, with a note of bitterness in his voice, 'I did not know then what lay within.'

'Who made the new lock?' I asked. 'They could have made another key.'

Lord Parr shook his head. 'You are right, it is an obvious point. But the Queen's own coffer-maker constructed this lock, as well as all the other new locks. He is well trusted. He has been the locksmith to successive Queens for twelve years, and you do not keep a man in such a post if he is not trustworthy.'

'Have you questioned him?'

'Not yet. Again, I thought it best to leave that to you. But I do not consider him a likely suspect.'

'Nonetheless, he is an obvious one.'

'He works down at Baynard's Castle. I thought perhaps on Monday you might go down there and question him. And talk to the embroiderer about that sleeve. Of course, they will not be there tomor-row, it being Sunday. That is a nuisance, but it will allow you a day of rest, and reflection.'

'Thank you.' I was grateful for the old man's consideration. But then he continued, 'What we really need is an expert on locks. Some-one from outside the palace.' He raised his eyebrows. 'Your assistant Jack Barak is known to have experience in such matters. From the days when he was employed by Lord Cromwell.'

I drew a deep breath. So Lord Parr had been making enquiries about Barak. My assistant's experience in such matters had indeed come in useful over the years, and yet – 'I would rather not involve him,' I said quietly.

'It would help the Queen,' Lord Parr pressed. 'Barak need not know what this is about – in fact must not know. We will keep to the story of the jewel. But now the chest is empty I can send it down to Baynard's Castle, and he can look at it when you are there on Monday.'

'He would not claim to be a great expert – '

Lord Parr looked at me hard. 'He knows locks. And has experi-ence of how the royal household works, the underside of it at least.'

I took a deep breath. 'I will speak to him tomorrow, see what he says – '

'Good.' Lord Parr spoke brusquely. 'Be at Baynard's Castle at nine on Monday. You can inspect the lock, speak to the cofferer and the embroiderer. I will arrange for William Cecil to be there, too; he can tell you what news he has of these religious makebates.' He rubbed his hands. 'We make a little progress.'

'And yet,' I said. 'Whoever has the book could still make it public at any moment.'

'I know that,' he answered testily. 'I have feared every day that someone will hand it to the King. Or that some papist printer is set-ting it into type in order to print it and distribute it in the streets. And it is not a long book, by now many copies could have been printed.' He shook his head. 'Yet day after day passes, and nothing happens. Someone is keeping it hidden. Why?' He looked suddenly old and tired. He stood up, his knees creaking. 'Tonight's page will be arriving soon, we should go. Take a good day of rest tomorrow, Master Shard-lake. We still have much to do.'

Chapter Twelve

THE LAWYERS AND THEIR wives progressed out of Lincoln's Inn chapel, slowly and soberly as always after service; the men in black robes and caps, the women in their best summer silks. I stepped into the July sunshine, fresher that morning for a thunderstorm that had broken in the night, waking me from an uneasy sleep. Some rain would help the crops. And now I had to keep my promise to visit Stephen Bealknap. As I walked down the side of the chapel, Treasurer Rowland came over to me, a hard smile on his narrow face.

'Good morrow, Serjeant Shardlake,' he said cheerfully. 'A fine service.'

'Yes, Master Treasurer. Yes, indeed.'

In fact I had scarcely heard any of it, even though tomorrow would be the anniversary of the sinking of the *Mary Rose*. I should have been praying for the souls of my friends and the hundreds of others who had died, although I was no longer sure there existed a God who would listen. But even on that of all Sundays, I could not get my mind away from thinking of the *Lamentation*.

Rowland inclined his head to one side like an inquisitive crow. 'I thought you looked a little strained during service. I hope it was not the effect of attending the burnings.'

'I have many matters on just now,' I answered brusquely.

'Well, the Inn notes with gratitude your representing us on Friday. And you may be called upon to represent us again next month, at a further public occasion.'

'Indeed,' I answered slowly, apprehensively.

'A celebration, though, not an execution.' Rowland smiled thinly.

'It is confidential still. But this will be a marvellous thing to see.' He nodded, bowed briefly, and was gone. I looked after him. Next month. Just now I could think no further ahead than tomorrow. I put his words from my mind.

✝

I WALKED SLOWLY on across the courtyard, ruminating. For all that I had found some leads yesterday, they were but threads in a great tangled skein. Why had the man with the damaged ear tried to break into poor Greening's premises *before* the Queen's book was stolen? How had someone managed to get into the coffer without leaving any marks, when the only key was around the Queen's neck? Could the locksmith have made a second key? And I wondered who this Jurony Bertano was, of whom Elias the apprentice was so terrified. The name sounded Spanish or Italian; I wondered if I dared ask Guy.

I almost tripped over a cobble which had become detached from its setting, and kicked it angrily away. I asked myself if I had done right to involve myself in a matter which could easily turn deadly. Images chased each other through my head: the weeping page, Garet Lynley, talking of the man with the slashed ear who would recruit him for a spy; Jane Fool, yanking at her duck's leash; Mary Tudor's severe face. I knew that if the *Lamentation* appeared in public I myself could be in danger, as would the Queen and Lord Parr. And that danger would extend to those who worked with me, like Nicholas: I had seen him standing on the far side of the chapel with the other clerks, a head taller than most of them, looking a little the worse for wear as he often did on Sundays.

The best protection I could give those who worked for me was to make sure they knew as little as possible of the true facts. But an order from Lord Parr was not to be denied. And so, before church that morning, I had gone round to Jack and Tamasin's house.

When I arrived at their house Jane Marris let me in, then went up to wake Barak and Tamasin from a late morning in bed. I had to sit uncomfortably in the parlour, listening as they clumped about getting dressed overhead, murmuring irritably. Jane brought George down. He was grizzling, and gave me a sad, tear-stained look. She took him to the kitchen, where I heard her starting to prepare breakfast.

Eventually Barak and Tamasin came down. I stood. 'I am sorry to disturb you so early.'

Tamasin smiled. 'It was time we were up. Will you have breakfast with us?'

'Thank you, I have eaten. How do you fare, Tamasin?'

'The sickness seems to have ended, praise be.'

'Good. I will not stay, I must get back to Lincoln's Inn, to church.'

'We don't bother any more than we have to,' Barak said. I knew both of them had had enough of religion for a lifetime.

'It's soon noticed if I stay away from the chapel too long,' I said. 'Besides, I have promised to see Bealknap.'

'You should leave him to rot, after all the harm he's done you,' Barak said. 'You're too soft.'

Tamasin nodded agreement. 'He is the worst of men.'

'Well, I confess I am curious to see what he has to say.'

'Curiosity killed the cat, sir,' Tamasin pressed.

I smiled sadly. 'Cats have nine lives, and perhaps mine are not all used yet. Jack, I wonder if I might have a quick word with you. It concerns — a work matter.'

Barak and Tamasin looked at each other knowingly. Perhaps they, like Rowland, could see the strain on my face. Tamasin said, 'I must see to Georgie. He is teething. He shall have a chicken bone to suck.'

Barak looked at me shrewdly as she left us. 'Young Nicholas was very subdued yesterday afternoon. He wouldn't say where you'd been, said you'd instructed him not to. I got the impression you'd told him off. Not that he doesn't need it sometimes.'

'I am sorry to have to leave so much to you.'

'We'll be all right for a few days. I've got Nicholas working hard. As I said, he seems quiet. Not his usual boisterous self.' Barak raised an eyebrow. He had guessed something serious was afoot.

I took a deep breath. 'Jack, I am afraid I have got myself involved in a piece of – delicate business. For Lord Parr, the Queen's Chamberlain.'

He frowned, then spoke with angry puzzlement. 'What is it that keeps drawing you back there? With all the rumours there have been about the Queen these last months, surely you should stay clear.'

'Too late now. The matter concerns a stolen jewel.' There, the lie was told.

Barak was silent a moment, then spoke quietly. 'You want my help? In times gone by, yes; but – ', he nodded at the doorway. Yes, I thought. Tamasin, George, the new baby.

I bit my lip. 'There is one small aspect where your expertise might be of help. I did not suggest it, the idea came from Lord Parr. I am sorry.'

'I still have a reputation in certain quarters?' His voice sounded surprised, but I detected some pleasure in it, too.

'So it seems. There is a chest at Whitehall Palace from which a valuable ring was stolen. Yet there is only one key, which the owner wore round her neck constantly, and there is no sign of forced entry.'

'You've seen this chest?'

'Yes. I spent much of yesterday at Whitehall Palace.'

'Whose is it?' he asked bluntly. 'The Queen's?'

'I must not say. It is being taken to the Queen's Wardrobe at Baynard's Castle for us to examine at nine tomorrow. Could you be there to look at it for me, see what you think?'

He gave me a long, hard stare. 'And that's all that is wanted of me?'

'Yes.'

'For myself, I wouldn't mind. But if Tamasin thought for a second that I was putting myself in peril again, she – ' he shook his head – 'she'd be furious. And she'd be right.' He sighed. 'But if it's an order from the Queen's Chamberlain – '

'It is. And I promise, I will keep you from further involvement.'

'I sensed trouble from your face when I came downstairs. So did

Tamasin. You spoke of a cat having nine lives. Well, you must be on number nine by now. So must I, come to that.'

'I am bounden to the Queen.'

'All over a stolen jewel?' He gave me a sidelong look. 'If you say so. Anyway, I'll come. I won't tell Tamasin, though I don't like misleading her.'

'No, this must be kept confidential.'

He nodded, then looked at me hard again. 'But remember. Only nine lives.'

✝

LIES, LIES, I thought, as I approached Bealknap's chambers, which stood more or less opposite to mine. Then I heard a voice behind me, calling my name. I turned round irritably; what now? To my surprise, I saw Philip Coleswyn, the lawyer acting for Isabel Slanning's brother, whom I had seen at the burning. I doffed my cap. 'Brother Coleswyn, God give you good morrow. You have not been at the Gray's Inn service?'

'I attend my local church,' he said a little stiffly. I thought, a church with a radically inclined vicar, no doubt. 'I came here after service, because I wished to speak with you.'

'Very well. Shall we go to my chambers? They are just at hand. Though I have another appointment . . .' I glanced up at Bealknap's shuttered window. 'I cannot tarry long.'

'It will take but little time.'

We walked to my chambers. I unlocked the door and led Coleswyn into my room, threw off my robe and invited him to sit. He was silent a moment, looking at me with his clear blue eyes. Then he said hesitantly, 'Occasionally, Serjeant Shardlake, a case comes up where it can be – useful – to talk to the other side's representative, in confidence.' He hesitated. 'If I think that, like me, the representative would wish to avoid an unnecessary degree of conflict.'

'The Cotterstoke Will case?'

'Yes. When we met two days ago, Serjeant Shardlake, at that

dreadful event at Smithfield – ' he blinked a couple of times – 'I thought, here is a man of probity.'

'I thank you, Brother. But strictly, probity means we must each represent our clients' interests, however troublesome they are. Their wishes must come first.'

'I know. But is it not a Christian thing to try to resolve conflicts where one can?'

'If it is possible.' I remembered Guy's assertion that some conflicts could never be resolved. I remembered, too, what Isabel had said: *If you knew the terrible things my brother has done.* 'I will hear what you have to say.' I added, 'And I promise it will go no further.'

'Thank you. We have the inspection of the wall painting on Wednesday. Your expert, of course, will be briefed to look for any ways in which the painting may be removed without damaging it.'

'While yours is likely to say it cannot be brought down.'

'My expert is an honest man,' Coleswyn said.

'So is mine.'

'I do not doubt it.'

I smiled. 'Yet both men are working to a brief, for a fee. I fear stalemate is the most likely outcome.'

'Yes,' Coleswyn agreed. 'It is in the nature of the system.' He sighed. 'And so the experts' charges will be added to the bills, and both the debt and the paperwork will grow.'

I replied wryly, 'What is the saying? "Long writing and small matter."'

'Yes.' And then Coleswyn laughed. I do not think he meant to; it was a release of tension. It made his hitherto serious face look quite boyish. I found myself laughing, too. We both stopped at the same moment, looking guiltily at each other.

'We cannot prevent them from fighting,' I said. 'Though I would happily be rid of this. Tell me, in confidence, does Master Cotterstoke hate Mistress Slanning as much as she does him?'

He nodded sadly. 'Edward Cotterstoke is never happier than when telling me what a wicked, vicious and evil-minded woman his sister is.

Oh, and he also says she is a traitor, a popish Catholic who observes the old ceremonies in secret. He was introduced to me through my church congregation; I have just come from him.' He raised his eyebrows. 'My appeals to his Christian charity go unheard.' I nodded sympathetically.

'And Mrs Slanning tells me her brother is a heretic whom she would happily see burned.' I paused, then added, 'And, I fear, you also.'

He frowned. 'They should both be careful with their tongues in these times.' He took a deep breath, then looked at me. 'Edward Cotterstoke will listen to no reason. I know his wife and children have tried to dissuade him from this battle with his sister. Without success.'

'Isabel is a childless widow, but even if she had family, I doubt they could move her either. Tell me, Master Coleswyn, have you any idea why they hate each other so?'

He stroked his short beard. 'No. Edward will only say that his sister has been a bad creature since they were children. And yet, though he enjoys abusing her – and we have both seen them standing in court glaring mightily at each other – I have a sense Edward is afraid of her in some way.' He paused. 'You look surprised, Brother.'

'Only because Mistress Slanning said some words that made me think *she* was afraid of *him*. How strange.' Though it was strictly a breach of confidence, I was sure of Coleswyn's honesty now, and I decided to tell him what Isabel had said about her brother – *the things he has done.*

When I had finished he shook his head. 'I cannot think what that might mean. Master Cotterstoke is very much the respectable citizen.'

'As is Mistress Slanning. Has it struck you how the wording of the old woman's Will was very odd? The specific reference to wall paintings.'

'Yes. It is almost as though old Mistress Cotterstoke wished to provoke a quarrel between her children, laugh at them from beyond the grave.' He shivered.

'She must have known they loathed each other. Perhaps there were not two members of this family hating each other because of Heaven knows what old grievance, but three. The mother, too,' I finished sadly.

'Possibly. But I know nothing of their early days. Only that their father, a Master Johnson, who can be seen in the picture, died not long after it was painted. And that their mother soon remarried, to Cot-terstoke, who took over her late husband's business. But he, too, soon died, leaving everything to his widow. There were no other children, and Edward and Isabel took their stepfather's name.'

'That tallies with what I know,' I answered. 'It does not sound as though there was an evil stepfather in the picture.'

'No.' Coleswyn stroked his beard again. 'If we could find what has brought them to this – '

'But how? Have you noticed that, though the two of them con-stantly abuse each other, it is always in general terms; nothing is ever specified.'

'Yes.' Coleswyn nodded slowly.

I heard the Inn clock strike twelve. 'Brother, I must go to my appointment. But I am glad you came. Let us each consider what we may do.' I stood and offered a hand. 'Thank you for speaking to me. So many lawyers would happily drive this witless matter on to Chan-cery, for the profits.' Bealknap would have, I thought, except that he would never have had the patience to deal with Isabel's carping and sniping. He had ever preferred some crooked land deal where every-thing was done in the dark.

Coleswyn smiled shyly. 'And to seal our little agreement, perhaps you would do me the honour of dining with my wife and me. Per-haps on Wednesday, after the inspection.'

The rules prevented barristers on opposing sides from discussing their clients behind their backs, but dining together was not prohib-ited. Otherwise, what would have become of our social lives? 'I would be glad to. Though I have a separate matter that is taking much time just now. May I take the liberty of agreeing subject to the possibility I may have to cancel at the last moment?'

'Certainly.'

I sighed. 'This other matter makes the Cotterstoke case look — trivial.'

'It *is* trivial.'

I smiled sadly. 'Yes. Though not to our clients, unfortunately.'

I showed him out, and through the window watched his trim stocky figure as he walked away to the gate. Then my eyes turned to Bealknap's shuttered chambers, and I took a deep breath.

Chapter Thirteen

I WENT ACROSS THE COURTYARD to the building that housed Bealknap's chambers, remembering his odd behaviour at the end of last year, those unexpected overtures of friendship, which I had rejected because he was not to be trusted. I knocked at the door and a porter answered. 'I have called to see Brother Bealknap.'

He looked at me gloomily. 'According to his nurse this may be the last day anyone will visit him. I will take you up.'

We climbed a long wooden staircase, passing other chambers, empty on the Sabbath. Very few barristers, save Bealknap, lived in chambers. I had not been inside his rooms for years; I remembered them only as untidy and dusty. He was rumoured to keep his great chest of gold there, running his fingers through the coins at night.

The porter knocked and the door was opened by an elderly woman in a clean apron, a short coif over her grey hair.

'I am Serjeant Matthew Shardlake.'

She curtsied. 'I am Mistress Warren. Master Bealknap has employed me to nurse him. He received your note.' She continued in the same cool, disinterested tone, 'He has a great growth in his stomach, the doctor says he has little time left now. The end will come in the next day or two.'

'Has he no family who might be summoned?'

'None he wished to contact. I think there was some falling-out, many years ago. When I asked him, he said he had not seen his family since the old King's time.'

I thought, that was near forty years past. Bealknap must have been only in his teens at the time. Another old family quarrel perhaps, such as the one I had just been discussing.

The old woman looked at me curiously. 'You are the only one he has asked to see. Other than the doctor and the builder, no one has been to visit.' *Builder?* I thought. 'Apart from the priest,' she added. 'Master Bealknap received the last rites this morning.' His death, then, was truly close. 'I will take you in,' Mistress Warren said, leading me along a dusty hallway. She lowered her voice. 'He refuses to have his shutters open, I do not know why. I warn you, his room smells bad.'

She spoke true. As she opened the door to a half-dark chamber a fusty smell of unwashed skin and diseased, rotten breath hit me like a blow. I followed her in. The room was poorly furnished, with a chest for clothes, a couple of wooden chairs, a bed and a crowded table filled with bottles and potions. The bed, at least, was large and comfortable-looking.

Bealknap had always been thin, but the figure under the covers was skeletal, the skin stretched tight over his skull, his ears and big nose prominent, the hands that lay on the sheet like white claws.

'I think he is asleep,' Mistress Warren said quietly. She bent over the dying man. 'Yes, asleep. Each time I think to find him gone, but he still breathes.' For the first time I heard a note of human sympathy in her voice. She shook Bealknap's shoulder gently. His eyes opened, those forget-me-not-blue eyes that had always roved around, never quite meeting yours. But today he stared right up at me, then smiled effortfully, showing his yellow teeth.

'Brother Shardlake.' His voice was scarce above a whisper. 'Ah, I knew if I sent you the gold, you would come.'

I brought one of the chairs over to the bed. Bealknap looked at the nurse. 'Go, Mary,' he said curtly. She curtsied and left.

'Is there anything I can get you?' I asked.

He shook his head wearily. 'No. I just wanted to see you one last time.'

'I am sorry to find you in this condition.'

'No,' he said softly. 'Let us speak the truth. You have always hated me, and I you.'

I did not reply. Bealknap's breath rasped painfully in his chest. Then he whispered, his breath in my face stinking, rotten, 'What is going to happen now?'

'None of us can know that for certain, Brother Bealknap,' I said uncomfortably. 'We must all hope for God's mercy on our souls – '

His eyes stayed fixed on mine. 'You and I know better than that. I think it is the one thing we agree on. We both know men have no souls, any more than cats or dogs. There is nothing afterwards, nothing. Only darkness and silence.'

I shook my head. 'I am not so sure as you. There is no way to know for certain. I do not know what or who God is, but – perhaps he exists.'

'No.' Bealknap sighed. 'I have had the rites, but only because that was necessary if my legacy is to be fulfilled.' He smiled again, and a dreamy quality came into his eyes. 'All my money, all my gold, is to go to the building of a great marble tomb in the Inn church, gilded and painted, with a stone image of me in my robes atop the tomb edged with gold so that all future generations of Lincoln's Inn lawyers will remember Brother Stephen Bealknap. I have been arranging the details with the man who will build it.' He laughed weakly. 'Treasurer Rowland took much persuading, but gold won the argument, as it wins them all.'

For a moment I could not think what to say. Bealknap must know how he was disliked. Was the commissioning of this memorial a last act of defiance? I thought sorrowfully, a lifetime's earnings put into such a thing. But something puzzled me. 'You said you are certain there is no afterlife, yet just now you asked what will happen now.'

He gave a throaty, painful laugh. 'I did not mean what will happen to *me*, Matthew Shardlake. I meant, what is going to happen to *you*?'

'I do not understand you.'

'I wanted to live to see what would happen to you.' He took a breath, winced with pain. 'Together with your good friend the Queen.'

My eyes widened. All the Inn knew that I had not worked for the Queen for a year. What could he know? 'What are you talking about?' I asked sharply, leaning over him. Bealknap gave me a look of satisfaction, then closed his eyes. I was angry now, realizing that he was playing games to the end. I shook him, but he had gone back to sleep and did not stir. I looked at him for a long moment. Then I could stand the terrible fug no longer; I was starting to feel sick. I went to the window and threw the shutters wide. The figure on the bed, now caught in full sunlight, lay white and wasted.

The door opened and the nurse came in. She went over to Bealknap, checked his breathing, then crossed to me, looking angry. 'Master, what are you doing? He wants the shutters closed. If he finds you have opened them he will complain fiercely when he wakes. Please.'

I let Mistress Warren close the shutters again. She looked at Bealknap. 'You must leave now, sir. Every effort tires him.'

'There is something I need to ask him.'

'Then return a little later. After lunch. Come now, please.' She took my arm, and I let her lead me to the door. From the bed I heard a grunt, then another. Bealknap was dreaming, and from those sounds, not of anything pleasant.

✟

I SAT IN MY ROOM in chambers, nursing a mug of small beer. I had been there for over an hour, trying to make sense of what Bealknap had said. Him, involved in all this? But how? He knew I once worked for the Queen, and must have heard the gossip that she was in trouble. But it was well known by everyone that I had stopped working for her a year ago. No, I thought, it is just that Bealknap knew that I had worked for Catherine Parr, knew she was in trouble as so many did, and hoped I might fall with her. I looked across the sunlit courtyard at the chamber where Bealknap lay. I would have to go over there again later, try to get more information from him. I shook my head. Vicious to the end. I thought of that great memorial Bealknap had planned; it would become a joke, a jest round Lincoln's Inn. But he would not foresee that. He had always been blind in so many ways.

I heard the outer door of my chambers open, then close again. I had locked it when I came back; it must be Barak come in for some-thing. I got up and opened the door. To my surprise I saw Nicholas taking papers from a table to his desk. His freckled face still looked tired, and there was a beer-stain on his robe. He stared at me.

'Nicholas? Here on a Sunday?'

He looked a little shamefaced. 'Some notes of cases came in yester-day from the Court of Requests, matters for the Michaelmas term. With your being busy, Barak asked me to summarize them. I was at the Inn for the service, and thought I might as well come in here and do some work.' To my amusement he looked embarrassed at being caught out coming in to work extra hours. It did not fit with the image he liked to convey.

'Nicholas,' I said. 'I was too sharp with you yesterday. You asked the apprentice Elias that question at the wrong time, and you must learn to judge more carefully. But — I should have made allowance for your youth, your inexperience. I apologize.'

He looked at me in surprise. 'Thank you, sir.'

'Are you getting a taste for the law?'

'I confess at first I found it — well — boring, but now — it seems less so. There are some matters I find interesting.'

'Most of all if a hunt for a murderer is involved, eh?'

He smiled. 'Does that not add some spice?'

'That is one way of putting it. The law is seldom so exciting, as you know. But it is necessary to see all aspects of it if you are to return to Lincolnshire and help manage your father's lands.'

The boy's face fell, the first time I had seen him look sad. 'I doubt I will go back, sir.'

I realized how little I knew of Nicholas; he had volunteered almost nothing about himself. 'How so?' I asked.

He looked at me with his dark green eyes. 'I was sent to law because my father disapproved of something I did.' He hesitated. 'Involving a proposed marriage.'

I nodded sympathetically. 'You wished to marry someone below your station?' I knew such cases were not uncommon.

Nicholas shook his head vigorously. 'No, sir. I am of age, I may marry where I like.' His eyes flashed with sudden anger, his chin jutting forward.

'Of course,' I soothed.

He hesitated. 'As my father's only son, the marriage I make is important. Our estates have suffered from the fall in money like so many, the value of our rents has fallen and the tenants can afford no more. A marriage to the wealthy daughter of a neighbouring estate would have brought a valuable dowry.'

'Yes. I know such arrangements can be – difficult. What is it they say of gentlefolk? Marry first and learn to love later.'

Nicholas's face brightened a little. 'You understand, sir. Well, a marriage was planned for me, with the daughter of a large estate near our manor at Codsall.'

'And you did not like her? Or she you?' I smiled sadly. 'Neither position is easy.'

His face set hard. 'We liked each other very much. But we did not love each other. I am no great catch, and nor in truth was she, so they thought we would go well together.' He spoke bitterly. 'So my father and mother put it to me. But Anys and I both desire, in God's good time, to marry for love. We have seen enough marriages of convenience that have ended in discord. So she and I made a pact, during one of the walks we were encouraged to take in my father's garden, as they watched us from the windows. We agreed to tell our parents we would not marry. My father was sore angry; he was already discontented with me for spending too much time hunting and hawking rather than helping on the estate, so he sent me here. As a sort of punishment, I think, though I was glad enough to leave the country and see London,' he added. 'Anys and I still write to each other, as friends.' He smiled ruefully. 'Well, sir, now you know me for a truly disobedient fellow.'

'It sounds as though you and Anys might have rubbed along together quite happily.'

'That is not enough.'

'No,' I said. 'Many would disagree, but I think like you, it is not.'

'The poor have it easier,' he said bitterly. 'They may marry for love.'

'Only when they can afford to, and that is often later than they would wish these days. As for the effects of the war, the taxation and the ruin of the coinage – well, your father still has his manor house, but his poor tenants will find it hard to pay the rent and eat.'

Nicholas shook his head firmly. 'Now the war is over, prosperity will surely return. And the security of everyone depends on people staying within the ranks to which they were born. Otherwise we would have the anarchy of the Anabaptists.'

That bogey again. I said, 'I confess that the more I see of mankind, the more I think we are all of one common clay.'

He considered for a moment, then said, 'My family have been gentlefolk by birth for centuries. Since before the Conquest, my father says; since the Norsemen settled Lincolnshire. It is our heritage to rule.'

'They became gentlefolk by conquest alone. The Norsemen took plenty from the English, as did the Normans. That is how most of our families become wealthy; I know, I am a property lawyer, I spend much time dabbling in ancient deeds.'

'Land may be taken honourably in warfare, sir.'

'As the Normans doubtless did from your Norse ancestors. You may have had more land once.'

'Too late to fight for it now, I suppose. A pity, perhaps.' He smiled.

I was starting to like Nicholas; he was showing signs of wit, and for all his upholding of gentlemanly conformity, he had himself defied convention. I said, 'Well, we shall have the chance to talk more of land and who owns it as the new law term approaches. But now I must go home for lunch.'

'Has there been any further progress on the murder of the printer?' Nicholas asked.

'No.' I raised a finger. 'And remember, do not speak of it.'

'You have my promise as a gentleman.'

'Good.' My eye was drawn to Bealknap's window. After lunch, I would lie down for an hour or two; I needed to rest. Then I would return.

☦

I WENT HOME. AS I walked up the path, Josephine appeared in the doorway in her new dress, a young man in a sober doublet at her side. Agnes Brocket held the door open, smiling at them, while Timothy stood at the corner of the house, looking on nosily. Josephine's companion was in his early twenties, slim, dark-haired and moderately handsome; this must be the young man she was walking out with. She blushed as I approached, and the boy doffed his cap and bowed.

'I am Edward Brown, sir. Servant to your brother-in-the-law, Master Peter Henning.'

'Ah, yes. A good man. I was sorry to hear his wife died – some months ago, was it not?'

'In December, sir. My master was much affected. He is thinking of retiring, going home to Norfolk.'

'I hope he will not,' Josephine ventured.

'I thank you for permitting me to take Josephine out walking,' Goodman Brown said.

I smiled at Josephine. 'I am glad to see her getting out and about. You are going to Lincoln's Inn Fields, I believe. It should be pleasant there today.'

'Watch you take good care of her,' Agnes said from the doorway.

'I will.'

I turned to Timothy. 'Did you need to speak to me, lad?'

'I – I just wanted to tell you Genesis will need some more hay.'

'Then get some tomorrow,' Agnes said. 'And for now, be off.'

Timothy scurried away. Josephine and young Brown looked at each other and smiled. Timothy had permission from me to buy new hay whenever it was needed; it was obvious he had come to have a look at Goodman Brown. That the young fellow seemed amused rather than annoyed was another mark in his favour.

I stood with Agnes and watched the two walk down the gravel path. Then I heard a sound, from up the road at Lincoln's Inn. The slow tolling of a bell. I felt a shiver down my spine. It was the dead-bell, sounded when an Inn member died: that must surely mean Bealknap. I would not now get the chance to question him again; even in death, he had cheated me.

'It is good to see Josephine so happy,' Agnes said.

I smiled at her. 'It is.'

She hesitated, then added, 'She has told me a little of her past. She owes you much.'

Martin appeared behind her from inside the house, moving quietly as usual. He looked down the path, where Josephine and Goodman Brown were just turning onto the roadway. A disapproving look. So the dislike between Martin and Josephine was mutual, I thought. I wondered what was behind it. Martin spoke sharply to his wife, 'Never mind them. Have you told Master Shardlake of his visitor?'

Agnes put a hand to her mouth. 'Oh, I am sorry—'

Her husband cut across her. 'The young lawyer gentleman who called two nights ago is come again. He still will not give his name.' Martin frowned at the breach of etiquette. 'I told him you would be back shortly for lunch. He is waiting in your study.'

'Thank you.' I went quickly inside. In the study, the slight figure of William Cecil sat in a chair, his thin face thoughtful and worried. He rose and bowed as I entered.

'I am sorry to disturb you on the Lord's Day, sir,' he said quickly, 'but there has been a serious development.'

'You visited Greening's friends? Lord Parr said you would.'

'I did. But all are fled from their lodgings. They have disappeared, all three. Nobody knows where.' He sighed heavily. 'But it is the apprentice, Elias, that we need to talk about.'

'Have you found him?'

Cecil took a deep breath, fixed his protuberant eyes on me. 'What is left of him. His mother found him last night, in the alley next to their house, beaten about the head and weltering in his own blood.' A spasm crossed his face.

'Jesu.'

'There was something he managed to say to her, a woman's name, just before he died.'

'What was it?' I dreaded to hear the Queen's name. But instead Cecil said, 'Anne Askew. He managed to say, "Killed for Anne Askew".'

Chapter Fourteen

ELIAS'S MOTHER LIVED IN one of the narrow lanes between Paternoster Row and St Paul's Cathedral, whose great shadow and giant steeple loomed over the poor tenements below. Cecil and I walked there from my house.

On the way, talking quietly, he told me what had happened. 'Lord Parr asked me to speak to Greening's three friends. He told me about Greening's murder, that there was no suspect yet, but there were delicate political ramifications and he wanted you to talk to them. I understand he has told you more.' He looked at me, and I saw a quick flash of curiosity in his large eyes.

'A little more. This must have been a busy day for you,' I concluded, sympathetically.

'It has. My wife was unhappy at me working on the Sabbath, but I told her needs must.'

'Did you know any of Greening's friends yourself?' I asked.

'No,' he answered, a little curtly. 'But a friend in my congregation knows Curdy, the candlemaker. It appears Curdy may be a sacramentarian, his family are certainly old Lollards, like Greening. He may even be an Anabaptist, though that is probably rumour.' He gave me a hard, unblinking look. 'Though be clear, Master Shardlake, I have never spoken for sacramentarianism, and I have nothing but loathing for these Anabaptists, who would overthrow all, interpreting the Bible after their own wild fantasies. The fact they may have played with such ideas does not mean Greening and his friends held them, of course.' For all his youth, Cecil spoke like an older, more experienced man.

'That is true.'

'All Greening's friends lived around Paternoster Row and the cathedral. I went out very early this morning; I thought it the best time to catch them, before church service. The exiled Scots preacher, McKendrick, lived in a cheap room he rented from Curdy, who was a widower. Curdy apparently was a friendly, jovial man, a journey-man, who worked with other candlemakers. McKendrick, on the other hand, had a reputation for surliness. And he is a big man, and an ex-soldier, so people tended not to get into quarrels with him.'

'These two friends of Greening's are very different people.'

'Which implies common religious affinities. In any event, when I arrived at Curdy's house both were gone. According to Curdy's housekeeper, they vanished overnight nearly a week ago, taking hardly anything with them.'

'Fled somewhere, then.'

'Unquestionably. The other friend of Greening's, the Dutchman Vandersteyn, is in the cloth trade, an intermediary for the Flanders wool buyers. He had a neat little house of his own, but when I got there his steward told me the same story; his master gone suddenly, taking only a few possessions.'

'Could they have been afraid of sharing Greening's fate?'

'Perhaps. Or if they were sacramentarians they might have feared the attentions of Bishop Gardiner's men. If that is the case, the Lord alone knows where they are.'

I remembered young Hugh's letter, the story of the refugees arriv-ing in the Low Countries, fearing persecution. And Vandersteyn hailed from Flanders.

Cecil continued, 'Then I decided to call on the apprentice Elias's mother, to see what news she had, or whether perhaps he had come home. I found her outside, on her knees, frantically washing blood off the wall of the alleyway.'

'Dear God.'

'She has two little daughters. Her husband died of quinsy last year.'

'Perhaps that was why Elias took another job rather than leaving the district as the others seem to have done.'

'Mayhap.' Cecil took a deep breath. 'Elias's mother told me that in the small hours of last night, she heard her son shouting for help outside. She rushed out, like a good mother.' He sighed again and shook his head. 'She saw him killed. Let her tell you the story herself. She has taken the body into the house. Jesu, the sight of it turned my stomach.'

'Has she told the authorities?'

'No. Because of what Elias said to her before he died.'

'The name Anne Askew?'

'Yes.' He lowered his voice. 'Quiet now, look there.'

We were passing along Paternoster Row. All the shops were shut for the Sabbath. However, a man in a black doublet was walking slowly along the sunlit street, peering into the shop windows. Cecil smiled sardonically. 'I know him. One of Bishop Gardiner's spies, trying to spot forbidden titles no doubt, or dubious-looking visitors to the printers.'

We walked past him. Looking back at him from a safe distance, I asked Cecil, 'Have you worked for the Queen's Learned Council for long?'

'Two years only. Lord Parr has been good enough to favour me.'

For Cecil's abilities, I thought; there was no doubting those. And for his reformist sympathies too, most likely. 'Where are you from?' I asked. 'I thought I caught a trace of Lincolnshire. My pupil is from there.'

'Well divined. My first wife came from there, too, like me, but sadly God took her to Him in childbirth, though He left me our son.'

I looked at him. His was an unremarkable face, but for those powerful, protuberant eyes which I had noticed seldom blinked, and that line of three moles running down one cheek. Yet he had been married, widowed and remarried, and become a confidant of the highest in the land, all by his mid-twenties. For all his ordinary looks and reserved manner, William Cecil was a man out of the common run. 'We turn down here,' he said abruptly.

We walked into a narrow alley, made darker by the shadow of the cathedral, onto which it backed. Chickens pecked in the dust. Cecil stopped in front of a door with flaking paint. Beside it, almost block‑ing the dusty alleyway, stood a cart, a tarpaulin slung over it. Cecil knocked gently at the door: two short raps then a long pause till the next, obviously a prearranged signal.

✝

THE DOOR WAS OPENED by a woman in her forties, as short and spare as Elias had been large and burly. She wore a shapeless grey dress and had not even put on a coif, her dark hair hastily knotted behind her head. Her eyes were wide with horror and fear. On her cuffs I saw flecks of red. She stared at me, then Cecil. 'Who's this?' she asked him fearfully.

'Master Shardlake. A lawyer. And, like me, one who would not have people persecuted for their opinions. May we come in, Goodwife Rooke?'

Her shoulders slumped helplessly, and she nodded. She led us into a poorly furnished parlour where two thin little girls of about eight and nine sat at table. The younger had her mother's small, birdlike features, the elder Elias's heaviness of face and body. Both stared at us in fear. I noticed a bucket and scrubbing brush on the floor, a dis‑carded apron, stained red, rolled into a ball beside it.

'Girls,' Goodwife Rooke said gently. 'Go and wait upstairs in our bedroom. But do not go in your brother's room. Do you swear?'

'I swear,' the elder girl said. She took her sister's hand and they sidled past us. Their footsteps sounded on a wooden staircase. Good‑wife Rooke sat down.

'It is no thing for his sisters to see,' she said. 'Nor a mother either,' she added, her voice breaking.

'Do the girls know?' Cecil asked gently.

'Only that Elias has been hurt, not that he is dead. I had a mighty job keeping them in our room last night, while I was heaving his body up the staircase. The noise made the girls call out to ask what was happening.' She rested her brow on a trembling hand for a moment, then looked at us desperately. 'I don't know what to *do*, sirs.'

Cecil said, 'We shall try to help you. Now, can you tell this gentleman what happened?'

'If it is not too much,' I added reassuringly.

'After seeing it, telling is little,' she answered starkly, and took a deep breath. 'My husband died last year. Elias, thankfully, had his job with Master Greening. But he spent too much of his spare time there, talking with Master Greening and his friends. Some of the things he said they discussed – ' her eyes flickered between us – 'they were dangerous.'

Cecil prompted, 'About faith and the Bible being the only keys to Grace, you told me, and questioning whether the social order was ordained by God.'

She nodded. 'I was angry with Elias for speaking of such things in front of his sisters. His father would have beaten him. Yet – ' her voice softened – 'my son was young, angry over the injustice in the world, full of newfound ideas. He was a good boy, he did not drink or roister, and his wages kept all of us.' She ran her hands through her hair. 'I do not know what will happen to us now. The girls – '

'I shall see what can be done,' Cecil said gently.

'What happened last night?' I asked after a moment.

She looked at me. 'It was around ten, the girls were in bed, thank God, and I was about to go up myself. I was worried, for Elias had not come home the night before. He had been surly, distracted, since poor Master Greening's murder. Then I heard his voice outside, shouting, "Help! Mother!"' She shook her head desperately. 'Almost the last words he ever said, and they were too late. I think he had been hanging around the house, checking to see whether it was safe to come home.' She swallowed. 'I threw open the door at once. Two men were running from the alleyway. One carried a cudgel. They ran past me, past that cart outside, and disappeared. I looked into the alley. There was my son. His head – ' she squeezed her eyes shut. 'There was blood, blood everywhere. Yet he was still just alive; he grasped my hand. He said, "Tell them, tell my friends, I was killed for Anne Askew." And then,' she added starkly, 'he died. I don't know how I found the strength but I dragged him indoors and upstairs and laid him in his room. I should have gone to the constable, I know, but after what he said – that name – ' Her voice fell to a whisper. 'Anne Askew. The one who was burned on Friday.' She looked at us. 'Elias wanted to go to the burning, shout cries of encouragement to the poor souls there. I think his friends persuaded him he would only end in the fire himself.' Her eyes grew angry. 'He would not be the first young apprentice to be burned these last few years.'

'No,' Cecil said. 'But they, and Elias, are safe now from the evils of this world, in Jesus' arms.' The words could have sounded trite, but he spoke them with quiet sincerity.

Goodwife Rooke pleaded again, desperately, 'What should I *do*, sirs?'

Cecil took a deep breath. 'Say nothing to the coroner, not yet. If people ask, say Elias never came back.'

'Lie to the officials?'

'Yes. For now. We have powerful friends, we can protect you from any trouble. Do not ask us more just now, but rest assured we shall hunt down Elias and Master Greening's murderers.'

I glanced at Cecil. 'They may be the same people. Could you describe them, Goodwife Rooke?'

She spoke in a dead tone. 'I could not see them clearly, it was dark. They were dressed roughly, like vagrants. Both young and strong. One, though, was near-bald. He looked at me for a second. A strange, wild look. It sore frightened me. He carried a club.' The poor woman put her face in her hands and shook violently. Then she seemed to col-lect herself; she glanced upstairs towards her daughters. 'Please,' she whispered, 'keep them safe.'

Cecil nodded.

I asked, 'That cart outside. Have you any idea who it belongs to?'

She shook her head. 'I never saw it before last night.'

I exchanged a glance with Cecil. Greening's killers – and it was obvious from Goodwife Rooke's description that it was they who had also killed Elias – might have learned that Elias had vanished, and been waiting around the alley lest he came home, a cart ready to remove the body. Had the boy not managed to shout out, he would never have been seen again.

Cecil said, 'I will arrange to have Elias's body taken away.'

For the first time, Goodwife Rooke looked hostile. 'Is my son to have no proper funeral?'

'It is safest, believe me. For you and your daughters.'

'And as we have told you,' I added, 'Elias's death will not go unpunished.'

She bowed her head.

'And now, might Master Shardlake look at Elias's body?' Cecil took her hand. 'We will say a prayer.'

She looked at me angrily. 'See what was done to my poor son.' She addressed Cecil. 'Was he killed for his beliefs? Was Master Greening?'

'As yet we do not know. But it may be.'

Goodwife Rooke was silent. She knew she was at our mercy. 'Come, Master Shardlake,' Cecil said quietly.

'Do not let my daughters see,' Goodwife Rooke called after us with sudden passion. 'If you hear them outside Elias's room, send them downstairs. They must not see that.'

✝

ELIAS LAY FACE UP on a straw bed in a tiny bedroom, the afternoon sun full on his bloodied face. He had been struck on the right cheekbone, hard enough to shatter it, for splintered shards of white bone showed through the dark mess of his face. He had also been struck on the top of the head, his hair a mess of gore. The shutters were open and blowflies had entered and settled on his head. In sudden anger I waved them away.

'Head wounds make much blood,' Cecil observed – calmly enough, though he stayed a couple of feet from the bed.

'He was killed the same way as Greening,' I said. 'Struck on the head. And that cart and tarpaulin were almost certainly arranged to take him away. They didn't want a great hue and cry.' I looked at the body again. I thought of Bealknap, lying in his bed. But he had been rotten with sickness, ready to die, whereas Elias had been but eighteen, full of young life. I turned to Cecil. 'Did you believe what you said, about Elias being safe in the arms of Jesus?'

The young lawyer looked stung. 'Of course. Do you wish to say a prayer with me now, as I told his mother we would?' he asked stiffly.

'No,' I answered, and asked bluntly, 'What do you plan to do with the corpse?'

'Lord Parr has some contacts. I should think he will arrange to have it buried out on the Lambeth marshes.'

I looked at him. 'Lord Cromwell used to do that, with inconvenient bodies. I remember.'

Cecil looked at me hard with those protuberant eyes. 'In high politics, Serjeant Shardlake, there are always people who work in the dark. You should know that. Do you want a commotion about the murder of two radical Protestant printworkers? Men with possible links to the Queen? There must be a link, mustn't there, or Lord Parr would not be involved?'

I nodded reluctantly, turning away from the sight of Elias's shattered head. 'What of Greening's three friends, Master Cecil? What if they are dead too?'

He shook his head. 'The evidence suggests they all fled their homes. They may have learned that the two men who killed Greening were about.'

I nodded agreement. That sounded right. 'I want something done for that poor woman.'

'As I said, I will ask Lord Parr.'

'It is what the Queen would wish. Send someone soon,' I added.

✝

WE LEFT GOODWIFE ROOKE sitting wearily at her table and went back outside. We examined the cart; it was just a cheap wooden

one, the tarpaulin old. But it was not valueless; it was unlikely someone would have just left it in these streets.

We walked slowly back to Paternoster Row. 'Why did Elias not
flee with those others?' Cecil asked.

'Because he had a mother and two sisters to support, and could
not just abandon them.'

He nodded agreement. 'I will report back to Lord Parr now. He
will probably want to talk to you when you go to the Queen's Wardrobe tomorrow morning. With your assistant, the one who used to
work with Lord Cromwell,' he added, looking at me curiously.

'Cromwell was a hard and ruthless man. But he had beliefs. If he
could see how those he promoted turned out – Paget, Rich, Wriothesley, helping Gardiner fight against everything he believed in.' I shook
my head.

'The balance on the Privy Council is about to change. Lord
Hertford and Lord Lisle return from France soon. With the peace
treaty well ensured. That will be a feather in their caps with the King.'

'Will the peace hold?'

'Oh, I think so. The coinage is so debased now that any English
money is distrusted in Europe. The German bankers who lent the
King so much to finance the war will allow him no more.' He smiled
sadly. 'England is bankrupt, you see.'

'Bankrupt indeed,' I said ruefully.

'But if we can solve this matter without trouble to the Queen the
reformists may begin to turn things round.' His manner was neutral,
detached, but I realized William Cecil knew a very great deal. He
fixed me again with those staring eyes, then raised his cap and bowed.
'God give you good evening, Master Shardlake.' He turned away,
heading for the river and a wherry to Whitehall.

Chapter Fifteen

I WALKED HOME THROUGH the quiet streets, thinking hard. Two men were dead now, three had fled, and I was no nearer to a solution to the problem of who had stolen the Queen's book, or why. I felt very alone. I had been unable to say too much to Cecil; he did not know about the missing book. The only ones I could talk to honestly were Lord Parr and the Queen.

When I reached Chancery Lane I turned into Lincoln's Inn; I had to confirm whether that tolling bell had been for Bealknap. The porter was sunning himself in the gatehouse doorway. He bowed. 'God give you good morrow, Serjeant Shardlake.'

'And you. I heard the chapel bell tolling earlier.'

He spoke in a pious voice. 'Master Stephen Bealknap has died, God's mercy on his soul. The woman who was nursing him has ordered the coffin already.' He inclined his head towards the courtyard. 'It's just been brought in. They'll take him to the coroner's till the funeral, as there's no family.'

'Yes.'

His eyes narrowed. 'I daresay you won't miss him that much.' The porter knew all the doings at the Inn, including my long enmity with Bealknap.

'We are all equal in death,' I replied. I thought, when news of Bealknap's planned monument got out, the porter would have a rich feast of gossip. I walked on to Bealknap's chambers. The shutters in his room were open now. There was a noise in the doorway as two men manhandled a cheap coffin outside.

'Light, ain't he?' one said.

'Just as well, on a hot day like this.'

They carried the coffin out of the gate. The sunlit quadrangle was quite empty. It was the custom that when a member of the Inn died his friends would stand outside as the coffin was taken out. But no one had come to mourn Bealknap.

I walked away, up to my house. I was hungry; I had missed lunch again. As I opened the door I heard Martin Brocket's voice, shouting from the kitchen. 'You obey *me*, young Josephine, not my wife. And you account to *me* for where you've been.'

I stood in the kitchen doorway. Martin was glaring at Josephine, his normally expressionless face red. I remembered how her father used to bully the girl, reduce her to trembling confusion, and was pleased to see Josephine was not intimidated; she stared back at Martin, making him redden further. Agnes stood by, wringing her hands, while Timothy was by the window, pretending to be invisible.

'No, Martin,' I said, sharply. 'Josephine answers to me. She is my servant, as you are.'

Martin looked at me. It was almost comical to watch him compose his face into its usual deferential expression. 'What makes you nip the girl so sharply?' I asked.

'My wife – ' he waved an arm at Agnes – 'gave the girl permission to walk out with that young man this afternoon without asking me. And she is late back. She told Agnes she would be back at three and it is nearly four.'

I shrugged. 'It is Josephine's day of rest. She can come back when she likes.'

'If she is seeing a young man, I should be informed.'

'You were. By your wife. And I saw you watch Josephine leave.'

'But for decorum's sake, she should be back when she said.' Martin was blustering now.

'She is an adult, she can return when she wishes. Mark this, Josephine. If you are seeing Goodman Brown on your free day, so long as you inform Martin, or Agnes, or me in advance, you may come back any time before curfew.'

Josephine curtsied. 'Thank you, sir.' Then she gave Martin a little triumphant look.

'And no more shouting,' I added. 'I will not have a brabble in my house. Josephine, perhaps you could get me some bread and cheese. I missed my lunch.'

I walked out. It was not done to support a junior servant against a steward in his presence, but Martin had annoyed me. I wished I understood what was the matter between him and Josephine. From the window, I saw Timothy leave the kitchen and cross the yard to the stables. On impulse, I followed him out.

✝

THE LAD WAS SITTING in his accustomed place, atop an upturned bucket beside Genesis. He was talking softly to my horse, as he often did. I could not hear the words. As my shadow fell across the doorway he looked up, flicking his black hair from his face.

I spoke casually. 'Master Brocket seemed much angered with Josephine just now.'

'Yes, sir,' he instantly agreed.

'Has he ever shouted at her like that before?'

'He – he likes to keep us in order.' His look was puzzled, as though to say that is the way of things.

'Do you know, is there some cause of enmity between them? Come, I know you are fond of Josephine. If there is a problem I would help her.'

He shook his head. 'They do seem to dislike each other, sir, but I do not know why. It was not bad at first, but these last few months she is always giving him unpleasant looks, and he never misses a chance to chide her.'

'Strange.' I frowned. 'Have you thought any further about what I said, about your maybe going for an apprenticeship?'

Timothy spoke with sudden vehemence. 'I would rather stay working here, sir. With Genesis. The streets outside – ' He shook his head.

I remembered how, until I found him, he had spent most of his early years as a penniless urchin. My home was the only place of safety he had ever known. But it was not right, a young boy knowing nobody his own age. 'It would not be like before you came here,' I said gently. 'I would ensure you had a good master, and you would learn a trade.' He stared back at me with large, frightened brown eyes, and I went on, a little testily, 'It does a lad your age no good to be alone so much.'

'I am only alone because Simon was sent away.' He spoke defensively.

'That was to ensure his future, as I would ensure yours. Not many lads get such a chance.'

'No, sir.' He bowed his head.

I sighed. 'We shall talk about it again.'

He did not answer.

☩

I WENT TO MY ROOM, where Josephine had left bread, cheese and bacon, and a mug of beer. I sat down to eat. Outside, the garden was green and sunny; at the far end my little summer pavilion was pleasantly shaded. A good place to go and set my tumbling thoughts in order.

I saw there was a new letter from Hugh Curteys on the table. I broke open the seal. Hugh had been promoted, I read, to a permanent position with one of the English trading houses, and was now thinking of a merchant's career. The letter went on to give the latest news of Antwerp:

In a tavern two days ago I met an Englishman, glad to find someone who spoke his language. He had been tutor to a Wiltshire family, well-connected folk, for some years. He is a radical in religion, and the family, though they had no complaint of him, feared that association with him might do them harm in these days. They gave him some money and arranged for a passage here. I marvel, sir, at what is happening in England. I never remember such times. I hope you are safe.

I wondered if Greening's three friends would also make for the Continent. Lord Parr should arrange for a watch to be kept at the docks, though I reflected gloomily that it might already be too late. I read the rest of Hugh's letter:

I was in the counting-house by the wharves yesterday, and a man was pointed out to me, standing with some others looking at the ships. He had a long grey beard and dark robe and a clever, watchful face, set in a scornful expression. I was told it was John Bale himself, the writer of plays against the Pope and much else; if King Henry got hold of him he would go to the fire. The Inquisition dare not interfere too much in Antwerp because of the trade, for all the Netherlands are under Spanish dominion, but I am told Bale does not parade himself publicly too often. Perhaps he was arranging the export of more forbidden books to England. I was glad to see him turn and leave.

I put the letter down. I thought, John Bale, Bilious Bale. Indeed he was a great thorn in the side of Gardiner and his people. As well for him that he was safe abroad.

I went into the garden, with pen, ink and paper and a flagon of wine, and sat in the shade of the pavilion. The shadows were lengthening but the air was still warm, and it would have been a pleasure to close my eyes. But I must get my thoughts in order.

I began by writing a chronology of recent events, beginning with the Queen's writing of the *Lamentation* during the winter. It had been in June, she said, that she had shown the completed manuscript to Archbishop Cranmer in her Privy Chamber, and argued with him when he said she should destroy it.

Then, on the 5th of July, came the first attack on Greening's premises, witnessed by Elias. By two roughly dressed men, one with half an ear sliced off. Then, on the 6th, the Queen discovered the manuscript was missing, stolen while she was with the King, at some time between six and ten that evening. Nobody would have known in advance that the King would call for her, which implied that someone had been waiting for their chance, with a duplicate key ready. I shuddered at the thought of someone in the Queen's household watching and waiting for an opportunity to betray her.

I turned my mind back to the key. The Queen had kept it round her neck at all times, so surely there *had* to be a duplicate. And that must have been made either by her locksmith, or somebody who had got hold of the original key before it was given to the Queen. Tomorrow's visit to Baynard's Castle would be important.

I leaned back, thinking of those I had questioned at Whitehall. I could not see either of the pages or Mary Odell taking the book. But I was not so sure of Jane Fool. I had a feeling she was less stupid than she pretended, though that in itself was not proof of guilt. And she served the Lady Mary as well as the Queen. I remembered Mary Odell's account of the strange behaviour of the guard on duty the night the manuscript was stolen. I must see what Lord Parr turned up there.

I looked up at the green branches of the large old elm beside the pavilion. The leaves moved in the faint breeze from the river, making a kaleidoscope of pretty patterns on the pavilion floor. I looked over at the house, shaking my head. For the most important question remained unanswered: how could anyone have learned that the *Lamentation* existed at all?

I wrote down the next important date. The 10th of July. The murder of Armistead Greening; the stolen manuscript of the *Lamentation* grabbed from his hand by two men who had come to kill him and hide the deed by setting his shed on fire. Different men from the earlier attack, on the 5th, though again young and roughly dressed. One of the earlier attackers seemed to have worn an embroidered sleeve, the mark of a gentleman. I remembered what Okedene's old servant had said about the man from the first group, who was missing half an ear. *It looked like a slash from a sword, not the great hole you get from having your ear nailed to the pillory.* So he had probably been in a sword fight; and the only people who were allowed to carry swords were those of gentlemen status, like Nicholas. I thought, what if *both* attacks were carried out by people of high status, dressed like commoners to escape notice? What if all four attackers were working for the same person? Yet that left unresolved the central problem that, at the time of the first attack, the *Lamentation* had not yet been stolen. Could both sets of attackers have been after something else and found the *Lamentation* by chance?

After Greening's murder, his associates had, except for Elias, fled. They had first been questioned by the constable, and all had alibis. Had they left because they were frightened of religious persecution, I wondered, or for some other reason? Only poor Elias had stayed because his mother and sisters needed him, and he had been killed by the same people who killed Greening.

And then there was that new mystery: Elias's dying words to his mother. *Killed for Anne Askew.* I wondered, had Greening's group had some association with her before her capture?

I thought more about Greening's group of friends. According to Okedene, apart from Greening himself and Elias, there had been one or two people who came from time to time, but the core of the little fellowship remained the three men who had vanished. I wrote down '*McKendrick, the Scottish soldier. Curdy, the candlemaker. Vandersteyn, the Dutch trader.*' Religious radicals, meeting for potentially dangerous discussions. Possibly sacramentarians, or even Anabaptists. And somehow, the *Lamentation* had come into Greening's hands.

The radical groups were well known to be disputatious, often falling out among themselves. Okedene had overheard them arguing loudly. I thought, what if *they* had somehow stolen the manuscript and planned to print it as proof that the Queen sympathized with religious radicalism? They might even have thought it would stir up the populace in support of their stance, so popular was the Queen. Of course, the notion was mad – the only result would be the Queen's death. But the religious radicals were often ignorant and naive when it came to actual political realities.

I stood up, pacing to and fro. This, I told myself, was pure speculation. And the person Okedene had heard them arguing over just before Greening's murder was not the Queen, but this mysterious

Jurony Bertano, that they called the 'agent of the Antichrist', who was soon to arrive, but about whom nobody at court appeared to know anything. I wrote the name down phonetically, as I was unsure of the spelling, and decided I would ask Guy about the possible nationality of its owner.

Then I wrote another, final name: *Bealknap*. What he had said was a complete mystery, and a worrying one. He had seemed certain that both the Queen and I had an ill fate in store. But I crossed out his name; his deathbed words had, surely, referred to the heresy hunt and his hope to live to see me and the Queen caught up in it.

I put down my pen, and stared over the garden, almost completely in shadow now. I thought of the Queen. That evangelism of hers, that desire to share her faith, had caused her to forget her habitual caution and common sense. She regretted it now, was full of guilt. The *Lamentation* itself might not be strictly heretical, but she had shown disloyalty to Henry by writing it in secret. That would not be easily forgiven. The King had not allowed her to be prosecuted without evidence, when Gardiner was after her, but if that manuscript were to be given to him — or, worse still, printed in public . . . I shook my head at the thought of what her fate might be then.

Chapter Sixteen

THE NEXT MORNING, Monday, Barak called at the house early. Like Genesis, his black mare, Sukey, was getting older, I noticed, as we rode out along Fleet Street, under the city wall. The sky had taken on that white milky colour that can portend summer rain.

'Bealknap died yesterday,' I said.

'There's one gone straight down to hell.'

'He told me he did not believe in an afterlife. And he was unpleasant to the last.'

'Told you so.'

'Yes, you did.'

'And this business. This chest. What's behind it?'

I saw Barak's curiosity had got the better of him. I hesitated, but realized I would have to give him something to satisfy that curiosity. 'A ring was stolen from it. Best you do not know more.'

We had just passed under Fleet Bridge, and the horses shied at a rattle of pots and pans. A middle-aged woman, dressed only in a shift, was seated backwards on a horse, facing the animal's tail and wearing a pointed cap with the letter S on it. Her head was bowed and she was crying. A man, his expression stern, led the horse along, while a little band of children ran alongside, banging sticks on pots and pans; several adults too.

'A scold being led to the stocks,' Barak said.

'Ay, Bishop Bonner's courts do not like women overstepping themselves.'

'No,' said Barak. 'And those folk will be her neighbours. How little excuse people need to turn on each other.'

✝

WE RODE DOWN to Thames Street, where Baynard's Castle stood by the river. It was an old building, renovated and expanded, like all the royal properties, by Henry. I had seen it from the river many times; its tall four-storey turrets rose straight from the Thames. Since Catherine of Aragon's time it had been the Queen's official residence, doubling as the Wardrobe, where her clothes and those of all her household were looked after and repaired. Catherine Parr's sister, Anne, resided there now with her husband, Sir William Herbert, a senior officer in the King's household. All the Parrs had found advancement in these last years; the Queen's brother, named William like his uncle, was on the Privy Council.

Baynard's Castle was reached from the street by a large gate, well guarded by men in the Queen's livery, for there was much of value inside. We dismounted, our names were checked off on the usual list, and our horses taken to the stables. The courtyard of Baynard's Castle seemed even more a place of business than Whitehall; two merchants were arguing loudly over a bolt of cloth they held between them, while several men unloaded heavy chests from a cart.

Those in the yard fell silent as a group on horseback clattered under the gate; two richly dressed men and a woman, accompanied by half a dozen mounted retainers. They rode towards an archway leading to an inner courtyard. I saw that the woman bore a strong resemblance to the Queen, and I realized it was Anne Herbert. The man riding beside her, in his forties, black-bearded with a military air, must be Sir William. The other man accompanying them was tall and slim, with a thin, hollow-cheeked face and a short auburn beard. His own resemblance to the Queen allowed me to recognize him as William Parr, Earl of Essex. They looked down at the people in the courtyard with haughty expressions – we had all doffed our caps as they passed. Yet all three were known as radicals, who would certainly fall if the Queen did.

A door in the main courtyard opened and Lord Parr stepped out. He wore his dark silk robe and cap, and his thick gold chain of office. Anne Herbert waved and hailed him from her horse. The little retinue halted as Lord Parr walked slowly over to them. He was leaning on a stick today. His nephew and niece greeted him and they exchanged a few words; I took the opportunity to open my satchel and take out my robe bearing the Queen's badge. Barak whistled quietly. 'So you're sworn to her household now?'

'Only while this investigation lasts.'

Lord Parr left his relatives, who rode on to the inner courtyard, and approached us.

'He doesn't look too well,' Barak whispered.

'No. He's near seventy and feeling the strain of the job, I think.'

'All over this stolen whatever-it-is,' Barak replied sceptically. I did not answer. We bowed deeply to Lord Parr.

'Serjeant Shardlake. You are on time,' he said approvingly. 'And this must be Goodman Barak, who knows about keys and locks.'

'I will assist in any way I can, my Lord.' Barak knew when to be deferential.

'Good. The chest is inside. I had it brought across, saying it needed repair. But first, Master Shardlake, a word in confidence.' He put his arm around my shoulder and led me a little away, leaving Barak looking put out.

'I heard from William Cecil what happened to the apprentice boy.' Lord Parr stroked his white beard, looking grave.

'I thought Cecil might be here today.'

Lord Parr shook his head. 'The fewer people seen to be making enquiries the better. Officially I am here to dine with my niece and nephew. So, what do you make of the apprentice's death?'

I told him about my reflections in the garden. 'Greening, Elias and the other three all had reason to fear danger. But I do not know whether any of them, other than Greening, had any connection with the *Lamentation*. I wonder, my Lord, whether Mistress Askew might have had any contact with the Queen, could have had knowledge of her book; whether she might not in fact have been tortured to try and find those things out.'

He shook his head. 'The Queen and Anne Askew never met. Mistress Askew had contacts on the fringes of the court, yes, and would have loved to preach at the Queen, but my niece and I were too careful to permit that. I made sure Anne Askew never came near her household.'

'Yet she must have been tortured for some reason. By the way, the news of that must have been leaked by someone inside the Tower. Is there any chance of finding out who that could have been?'

Lord Parr considered. 'When it became obvious at the burning that the street gossip about Askew's torture was true, I thought there would be a hue and cry in the Tower to find who set those rumours. Someone there, as you say, must have talked. But I have heard nothing.' He furrowed his brow. 'The Constable of the Tower, Sir Edmund Walsingham, was my predecessor as Queen's Chancellor and is a friend. I shall make enquiries. In the meantime I want you to come to the palace tomorrow to question the guard who was on duty the night the manuscript was stolen and who Mary Odell said behaved oddly. He comes back on duty in the morning.'

'Thank you, my Lord. And those three runaways: Curdy, McKendrick and the Dutchman. It is essential to interview them. I wonder whether they may even have taken the Queen's book in connection with some hare-brained scheme of their own. Perhaps even fallen out over it, so that one killed Greening and made off with the book.'

Lord Parr's face set hard. 'Then we are dealing with wild fools rather than an enemy at court.' He shook his head. 'But how could such people get hold of the book in the first place?'

'I do not know.'

'But nevertheless they should be found.'

'Yes.' I added, 'I was thinking about Okedene the printer, whether they might come after him now.'

'He has already told us what he knows.'

'Even so, his safety — '

Lord Parr looked irritable. 'I do not have a limitless supply of people I can employ on this matter; and none I would completely trust, apart from Cecil. I have no network of spies like your old Master Cromwell, or Secretary Paget,' he added caustically. 'I have asked Cecil to keep his ears and eyes open, which he will do. And I can arrange for him to bribe someone at the customs house. Cecil suggested that, to see whether anyone resembling these three men books passage on a ship. Perhaps he can bribe one of the dockers to keep a watch.'

I remembered Hugh's letter. 'Many radicals are going abroad these days,' I said.

Lord Parr grunted. 'And provided they are just little fish, the authorities wink at it. Glad to be rid of them.'

'Then they may already be gone. But if they are seen, would it be possible to detain them? Perhaps on suspicion of involvement in the theft of a missing jewel?'

'Yes, that may be a good idea. I will talk to Cecil.' Lord Parr raised a monitory finger. 'But remember, Master Shardlake, my powers are limited. And the Queen still has to watch every step.' He sighed deeply. 'For myself, I wish I were back in the country.' He shook his head. 'Nearly a fortnight since the *Lamentation* disappeared, and not a whisper of it.'

'And two men murdered.'

'I am hardly likely to forget. And I have still heard nothing about this man with half an ear sliced off, in the employ of someone at court.' All at once, beneath his finery, I saw a puzzled, frightened old man. 'We are in the midst of a deadly business. Surely the two attacks on Greening's premises must be connected. Yet the *Lamentation* had not yet been stolen when the first attack took place. Pox on it!' He spoke querulously, banging his stick on the cobbles. Then he collected himself, turned and looked at Barak. 'Will he be acting as your right-hand man in this?'

'No, my Lord. I'm sorry, but I fear his family commitments—'

Lord Parr grunted impatiently. 'Too much softness is not a good thing with those who work for you. It gets in the way of business. However, I am arranging for some money to be sent to the apprentice's mother when his body is taken away. Together with advice to leave London.'

'Thank you, my Lord.'

Another grunt. 'I would be in trouble with her majesty if I did not help the woman. And she is safer off the scene. Have you brought the piece of embroidery your boy found?'

'In my satchel.'

'Good. You will be taken to the embroiderer after seeing Master Barwic, the carpenter and locksmith. You can also tell the embroiderer the story of the stolen jewel. His name is Hal Gullym.'

'Has he been with the Queen long?'

'He is not an old retainer like Barwic, the cofferer. He was employed at court three years ago, when the Queen's household was set up. Like everyone at Baynard's Castle he is part of the *domus providenciae*, a servant, a craftsman. And he has a strong motive for loyalty and obedience. Working for the court takes you to the top of your profession. Every guildsman in London longs to work here.' He spoke patronizingly, I thought, an aristocrat talking dismissively of men who worked with their hands. 'So Hal Gullym will be happy to assist. Now – ' From his robes Lord Parr produced the Queen's key, still on its gold chain, and gave it to me. 'Handle that with great care.'

'I will.'

'The guard with a fair beard you see over at that door has been told you are coming to investigate a jewel theft; he will guide you, and wait while you examine the chest. Give the key to him afterwards to return to me; he can be trusted. Then he will take you to Barwic and then Gullym. If you find anything important, send word to Whitehall. Otherwise, attend me there at ten tomorrow morning.' Lord Parr turned and called to Barak. 'Over here, sirrah, your master has instructions.' Then he hobbled away to the inner courtyard to join the members of his family.

✝

THE INTERIOR OF THE BUILDING into which the guard led us was nothing like Whitehall, for all the fine tapestries adorning the walls. This part of Baynard's Castle was a clothing enterprise; embroiderers and dressmakers working at tables in the well-lit hall. The shimmer of silk was everywhere, the air rich with delightful perfumes from the garments. I thought of what the Queen had said, how the richest of these clothes had passed from Queen to Queen.

Barak shook his head at it all. 'All these people are working on the clothes of the Queen's household?'

'It has a staff of hundreds. Clothes, bedlinen, decorations, all have to be of the finest quality and kept in good repair.' I nodded to the guard, and with a bow he led us over to one of the many side doors. We were taken down a corridor to a large room where several clothes presses stood, bodices and skirts kept flat beneath them. The Queen's chest stood on a table; I recognized the distinctive red-and-gold fabric covering its top. It was oak, with strong iron brackets at each corner. Barak walked round it, felt the wood, looked at the lock, then lifted the lid and peered inside. It was a bare wooden box, empty except for the tills in the side where small valuables were kept.

'Good strong piece. You'd need an axe to break in. The chest is old, but the lock's new.' He leaned in and thumped the sides and bottom. 'No hidden compartments.'

'It is an old family heirloom.'

He looked at me sharply. 'Of the Queen's?'

'Yes. She had a new lock fitted in the spring, the other one was — old.'

He bent and peered closely at the lock, inside and out. Then he said, 'I'd better see the key. I saw Lord Parr give it to you.'

'Don't miss much, do you?'

'Wouldn't still be here if I did.'

I handed him the key. I wished he had not asked about the Queen. But if I limited his involvement to the chest, surely he would be safe. He studied the key's complicated teeth closely, then inserted it in the lock, opening and shutting the chest twice, very carefully. Finally he took a thin metal instrument from his purse and inserted it in the lock, twisting it to and fro, bending close to listen to the sounds it made. Finally he stood up.

'I'm not the greatest expert in England,' Barak said, 'but I would swear this lock has only ever been opened with a key. If someone had tried to break in using an instrument like mine, I doubt they'd have succeeded – the lock's stronger than it looks – and I'd expect marks, scratches.'

'The Queen says she kept this key always round her neck. So no one would have had the chance to make an impression in wax to construct another. I think there must be another key.'

'And the only person who could have made that is the locksmith, isn't it?' Barak said, raising his eyebrows.

'So it seems.'

He rubbed his hands, his old enthusiasm for the chase clearly visible. 'Well, let's go and see him.' He smiled at the guard, who looked back at us impassively.

✝

THE CARPENTER'S WORKSHOP was at the rear of the hall, a large, well-equipped room smelling of resin and sawdust. A short, powerfully built man with regular features only half-visible through a luxurious growth of reddish hair and beard was sawing a plank, while his young apprentice – like his master, wearing a white apron emblazoned with the Queen's badge – was planing another piece of wood at an adjacent table. They stopped working and bowed as we entered. At the back of the workshop I noticed a set of locksmith's tools on a bench.

'Master Barwic?' I asked.

'I am.' He looked a little apprehensive, I thought, at the sight of my lawyer's robe with its own Queen's badge. But then he would know of the theft, and that he might be under suspicion.

'I am Matthew Shardlake, Serjeant at Law. I am enquiring for Lord Parr into the loss of a jewel belonging to the Queen, which she values greatly.' I turned to the apprentice, who was small and thin, a complete contrast to poor Elias. 'Does this boy help you with lock-making?'

'No, sir.' He gave the boy an unfavourable look. 'I have enough trouble training him up on the carpentry side.'

I looked at the lad. 'You may leave us.' Barwic stood, hands on the table, frowning a little as the boy scurried from the room. 'I heard of the jewel's loss, sir. I think someone must have stolen the key.'

I shook my head. 'Impossible. The Queen wore the key round her neck at all times.' I saw his eyes widen; he had not known that. 'Come,' I said. 'I would like you to see the chest.'

'It is here?'

'In one of the rooms nearby.'

We led Barwic to the chamber, where he examined the chest care-fully. 'Yes, I made this lock, and fitted it to the chest, back in the spring.' I gave him the key and he studied it. 'Yes, this is it.'

'And you made no copies?' Barak asked.

Barwic frowned, obviously annoyed at being questioned by some-one junior. 'On the Queen's instructions,' he answered. 'It was unusual, but those were her majesty's orders. The chest was brought to my workshop. The lock was as old as the chest, though service-able enough. I made the new lock and key, tested them, then took the key and chest back to Whitehall myself, as instructed. I gave the key directly into the hands of Lord Parr.'

'Normally, though, you would make a spare key, in case the origin-al was lost?'

'Yes, and send both keys to the Chamberlain.' His calmness deserted him and his voice rose. 'I did as I was ordered, sir, simply that.'

'I have to question everyone connected with this chest,' I answered mildly.

'I am a senior craftsman.' Barwic rallied a little. 'I was Chairman of the Carpenters' Guild last year, responsible for its part in all the ceremonies and processions, and raising troops for the war.'

I nodded slowly. 'An honourable duty. Did you know what was kept in the chest?'

'They told me jewels and personal possessions. Sir, if you are accusing me—'

'I accuse you of nothing, good Master Barwic.'

'Ay, well, I am not used to being questioned like this.' He spread his hands. 'Perhaps someone was able to make an impression of the Queen's key. If so, they could open the lock, if the duplicate were made carefully enough. Someone in that great warren, the Queen's household. Surely she did not wear it all the time. I am a man of honest reputation, sir,' he added. 'Ask all who know me. A simple carpenter in his workshop.'

'Like Our Lord himself,' Barak said, straight-faced.

✝

BARAK ACCOMPANIED ME back out into the courtyard, the guard assigned us walking a little behind. 'Jesu,' Barak said. 'All that just to clothe a few women.'

'More than a few, I think. The ladies are granted the cloth, but pay for the work themselves.'

He stood rocking on his heels. 'That cofferer, he looked worried.'

'Yes. And he was Chairman of his guild last year. That's an expensive business, as he said.'

'He'll be well paid in this job.'

'It would be an expense, even so. And with the value of money falling, and all the taxes to pay for the war that are due this year, everyone has to be careful. He may have need of money.' I slowed. 'Could he have made a second copy for someone else? He did not know the Queen wore the only key constantly round her neck.' I considered. 'I think we'll let him sweat a little.'

'It would be a dangerous matter, stealing from the Queen. He'd hang if he was caught.'

'We both know the things people are capable of risking for the sake of money. Especially those who have gained status and wish to keep it.'

Barak looked at me askance. 'You said *we'll* let him sweat a little.'

'A slip of the tongue, I'm sorry. I told you, I just wanted your help with the chest and lock.'

He looked around the courtyard. Another cart was unloading. 'Jesu,' he said again, 'all this to keep fine clothes on the backs of great ladies. Just as well we didn't bring Tamasin. We'd never have got her out.'

'Remember she doesn't know you're here. And would be displeased if she did.'

'I won't forget. What do you want to see the embroiderer for?'

I sighed. He was interested now; he would not easily let it go. 'I'm only trying to trace a piece of fine silk sleeve Nicholas found, that may be connected to the case,' I answered. 'The embroiderer may be able to help me, perhaps suggest who might have made it.'

'If he gives you a name you may need someone to pay him a visit.'

'I think that might be a job for Nicholas. He found the sleeve, after all.'

Barak looked disappointed, then nodded. 'You're right, it's a job for a junior.'

'And now I have an appointment with the embroiderer.'

He fingered his beard, reluctant to leave, but I raised my eyebrows. 'All right,' he said, shrugging his shoulders, and quickly walked away to the gate.

✝

I NODDED TO THE GUARD and he took me back into the hall, knocking at another side door before entering. Within, a man was working at a desk set close by the window to get the best light. He was embroidering flowers on a piece of fabric, flowers so tiny he needed to look through a large magnifying glass on a stand. To my surprise, he was a big, black-bearded fellow, though I saw his fingers were long and delicate. He stood up at my entrance, wincing a little. For a man of his height, a life spent constantly hunched over was a recipe for a bad back.

'Master Gullym,' I asked, 'the Queen's head embroiderer?'

'I am.' His voice had a Welsh lilt.

'Matthew Shardlake. I am investigating the theft of a jewel from the Queen.'

'I'd heard something about a ring gone missing.' Gullym sounded curious, but unlike Barwic, unconcerned. But of course he was not under any suspicion. I took the piece of torn silk and laid it on the desk. 'We think this may belong to the thief. Is there any way of iden- tifying who made it?'

Gullym picked up the scrap of silk, wrinkling his features in dis- taste, for it was a little dirty now. 'Looks like an English design,' he said. 'Very fine, expensive. Someone in the embroiderers' guild made it, I'd warrant.' Carefully he slid the delicate silk he was working on from under the magnifying glass and replaced it with the piece of cuff. 'Yes, very well made indeed.'

'If the maker of this piece could tell me who commissioned it, it might help us. They would gain the favour of the Queen,' I added.

Gullym nodded. 'I can write you a list of names. Perhaps a dozen embroiderers in London could have made this. It was done recently, I would say, that design of little vines has only been popular this year.'

'Thank you.'

With slow, deliberate steps, Gullym crossed to a desk, wincing again as he moved. He took quill and paper and wrote out a list of names and addresses, then handed it to me. 'I think these are all the people who might help you.' He smiled complacently. 'I have been in the guild since I came to London thirty years ago, I know everyone.'

I looked at the list. Someone would have to visit all these London shops.

'Thank you, Master Gullym,' I said. 'By the way, I could not help but notice you have some problems with your back.'

'Goes with the job, sir.'

'I do, too, as perhaps you may imagine.'

Gullym nodded tactfully.

'There is a physician who has helped me much. He practises down at Bucklersbury, Dr Guy Malton.'

'I have been thinking I should see someone. It gets bad in the afternoons.'

'I can recommend Dr Malton. Tell him I sent you.'

Chapter Seventeen

THAT EVENING, AFTER DINNER, I rode down to Bucklers-bury to visit Guy. We had not parted on the best of terms three nights before, and I wanted to try and mend fences. I also hoped he might tell me about that name, Bertano.

The cloud had disappeared during the afternoon and the sun was out again, setting now, casting long shadows on the row of apothecar-ies' shops. Although Guy had come originally from Spain and qualified as a physician in the great French university of Louvain, his status as a foreigner – a Moor – and a former monk, had meant a long struggle for acceptance as a member of the College of Physicians. Before qualifying, he had practised as an apothecary and, although he now had a large practice and the status of an English denizen and could have moved to a good-sized house, he preferred to stay here; partly because of his old monkish vow of poverty, and because he was getting old and preferred the familiar.

As I dismounted and tied Genesis to the rail outside his house, I reflected that, apart from Guy, all my friends and contacts now were either reformers or people who preferred to keep out of the religious struggles. But I knew there were plenty in London, and many more in the countryside, who would welcome a return to the Catholic church.

Francis Sybrant, the plump, grey-haired man of sixty who served as Guy's general assistant these days, answered my knock. I liked Francis; he had worked for a neighbouring apothecary and when the man's business failed last year had come to work for Guy. He was grateful to have found a new berth at his age. A cheerful fellow, he was a good counter to Guy's habitual melancholy.

'Master Shardlake.' He bowed.

'God give you good evening, Francis. Is Master Guy at home?'

'In his study. Working with his books as usual of an evening.' He led me down the narrow hall, knocking gently on the door of Guy's study. Guy was sitting at his desk, reading his copy of Vesalius, with its gruesome anatomical diagrams, using the light of a candle to compare what was on the page with a human thigh bone he held up. He put it down carefully and stood. 'Matthew. This is a surprise.'

'I hope I am not interrupting you.'

'No. My eyes are getting tired.' He pinched the bridge of his nose. 'Francis says I should get spectacles, but I cannot face the thought somehow.'

'I am sorry I had to leave you so suddenly on Friday. After we – ' I hesitated – 'disagreed.'

He smiled sadly. 'That argument resounds all over England, does it not?'

'I was not myself that day.'

'I understand. You still look tired. A glass of hippocras?'

'That would be welcome. I have been working hard.'

Guy called to Francis, who fetched two mugs of warm spiced wine. I sat looking into mine then said, 'My old foe Stephen Bealknap is dead. A growth in his guts.'

Guy crossed himself. 'God pardon him.'

I smiled sadly. 'He did not want God's pardon. I was with him near the end, he said he had no faith. He has left all his money to build a great memorial to himself in Lincoln's Inn chapel.'

'Had he no family?'

'Nor friends. Nor God.'

'That is sad.'

'Yes.' I looked into my wine again, then pulled myself together. 'Guy, there is a piece of information I seek. About a foreign name. I have only my Latin and poor French, and with your experience of languages I hope you may be able to help me.'

'If I can.'

'In strict confidence.'

'Of course.'

'It has come up in the context of something I am working on. Reported second-hand. The name sounds foreign, and may be mis-pronounced, but I wondered if you could guess its origin.'

'What is the name?'

'Jurony Bertano. Could it be Spanish?'

He smiled. 'No. That is an Italian name. The first name is Gurone, spelt G-U-R-O-N-E.'

'Close enough then.'

'One of the Italian merchant community in London, perhaps?'

'Possibly.' I gave him a serious look. 'But I cannot discuss the matter.'

'I understand. The rules of confidentiality.'

I nodded unhappily. We were silent for a moment. Then I said, 'You know, on the way here I was thinking how few Catholic or traditionalist friends I have now. These last years most people have withdrawn into one circle or the other, have they not? Often without even thinking about it?'

'For safety, yes, sadly they have. I have few patients among the radicals or reformers. My practice began with people from – dare I say – my side, and they refer their friends to me, and so it goes on. It is probably much the same with you.'

'It is. Though, by the way, I have recommended you to someone else with back troubles. An embroiderer from the Queen's court.'

He smiled. 'A reformist sympathizer, then.'

'I have no idea.' I looked up at him. 'Do you ever doubt, Guy, that your view of God is the right one?'

'I have been prey to doubt all my life,' he said seriously. 'For a time, as once I told you, I doubted God's very existence. But I believe that if faith and doubt battle together within a human soul, that soul becomes the stronger and more honest for it.'

'Perhaps. Though I have far more doubt than faith these days.' I hesitated. 'You know, I have always considered that people who were unshakeable in their faith, on either side, to be the most dangerous sort of men. But just recently I wonder whether that is wrong, and rather it is those, like some of the highest at court – Wriothesley, or Rich – who shift from one side to the other to further their ambitions, who are truly the worst men.'

'What are you involved in now, Matthew?' Guy asked quietly.

I answered with sudden passion, 'Something I must protect my friends from knowing about.'

He sat silent for a moment before saying, 'If I can help, at any time – '

'You are a true friend.' Yet one whose conscience placed him on the other side of the divide from Catherine Parr, I thought. To change the subject, I said, 'Tell me what you are trying to learn from that old bone. Something far more useful to humanity than anything lawyers or Privy Councillors do, I'll warrant.'

✝

NEXT MORNING, I left home early to visit chambers before going on to Whitehall Palace. Everyone – Barak, Nicholas and Skelly – was already there and working. I felt grateful to them. John Skelly had always been a hard and loyal worker, and Nicholas, given a little trust, was responding well, while Barak was relishing being in charge. As I came in he was giving Nicholas a heap of case papers to be filed on the shelves. 'And don't lose any conveyances this time,' he said cheerfully.

I thanked them all for being in early. 'Nicholas,' I said, 'there is a particular job I would have you do for me.' I gave him the list the embroiderer Gullym had prepared the day before, together with the piece of silk, carefully wrapped in paper. I added some shillings from my purse, the copper already shining through the silver on the King's nose. 'I want you to visit the embroiderers on this list and see whether any of them can identify this work. It was likely made by one of them. Say that I have consulted with Master Gullym, who is one of the most important members of the Embroiderers' Guild. Do not reveal what it is about. Can you do that? Use your gentlemanly charm?'

Barak gave a snort of laughter. 'Charm? From that long lad?'

Nicholas ignored him. 'Certainly, Master Shardlake.'

'This morning, if you would.'

'At once.' Nicholas took the pile of work from his desk and dumped it back on Barak's. 'Afraid I'll have to leave you with these,' he said with a cheery smile.

✝

THIS TIME, I CAUGHT a wherry upriver to the Whitehall Palace Common Stairs, donning my robe with the Queen's badge as we approached. At the Common Stairs, watermen unloading goods for the palace mingled with servants and visitors. A guard checked my name as usual and directed me to the King's Guard Chamber. I walked along a corridor adjoining the Great Kitchens. Through open doors I glimpsed cooks and scullions preparing meals for the several hundred people entitled to dine in the Great Hall and lodgings. They wore no badges of office, only cheap linen clothes, and in the July heat some worked stripped to the waist. I passed on, through the Great Hall with its magnificent hammer-beam roof, and out into the court-yard.

It was dole day, and officials from the almonry stood at the main gate handing packets of food to a crowd of beggars, who were being closely watched by the guards. The remains of each palace meal, which consisted of far more than any one man could eat, were usually distributed daily to hospitals and charitable organizations, but twice a week the 'broken meats' were given out at the gate, a sign of the King's generosity.

Though most in the courtyard ignored the scene, going about their business as usual, I saw that two men were watching. I recognized both from the burning four days ago. One, in silken cassock and brown fur stole, was Bishop Stephen Gardiner. Close to, his dour countenance was truly formidable: heavy, frowning brows, bulbous nose and wide, broad-lipped mouth. Standing with him was the King's Secretary, William Paget. As usual, he wore a brown robe and cap; the robe had a long collar of miniver, thick snow-white fur with black spots. He ran the fingers of one square hand over it softly, as though stroking a pet.

I heard Gardiner say, 'Look at that woman, shamelessly pushing her way past the men, thrusting out her claws at the food. Did this city not have sufficient demonstration at Smithfield that women must keep their place?'

Paget said, 'We can show them again if need be.' They made no attempt to lower their voices, quite happy to be overheard. Gardiner continued frowning at the beggar crowd; that glowering disposition seemed to be how this man of God turned his face to the world. Paget, though, seemed only half-interested in the scene. As I passed them I heard him say, 'Thomas Seymour is back from the wars.'

'That man of proud conceit,' Gardiner replied contemptuously.

Paget smiled, a thin line of white teeth in his thick beard. 'He will get himself in trouble before he's done.'

I walked on. I remembered the ladies talking about Thomas Seymour in the Queen's Privy Chamber. Brother of the leading reformist councillor, Edward Seymour, now Lord Hertford, Catherine Parr would have married him after her second husband died, had not the King intervened. I knew the Queen and Seymour had been carefully kept apart since, with Seymour often sent on naval or diplomatic missions. I had had dealings with him before, not pleasant ones. Paget was right, he was a foolish and dangerous man, a drag on his ambitious brother. I wondered what the Queen would be feeling about his return.

Again I passed into the King's Guard Chamber, up the stairs, and through to the Presence Chamber. The magnificence everywhere still astounded me whenever I paused to let it. The intricacy, colour and variety of the decoration struck me afresh; the eye would rest for a moment on some design on a pillar, drawn to the intricate detail of the vine leaves painted on it, only to be at once distracted by a tapestry of a classical scene hung on a nearby wall, a riot of colour. My gaze was drawn again to the portrait of the King and his family; there was Mary, and behind her Jane Fool. I passed through, attracting no notice; a hunchback lawyer from the Queen's Learned Council, come no doubt to discuss a matter connected with her lands.

The guard checked me through into the Queen's Privy Chamber. Again a group of ladies sat sewing in the window. Once more Edward Seymour's wife, Lady Hertford, gave me a haughty look. The Duchess of Suffolk's spaniel saw me and gave a little bark. The Duchess scolded it. 'Quiet, foolish Gardiner! 'Tis only the strange-looking lawyer come again.'

The inner door opened, and Lord Parr beckoned me in.

☦

LORD PARR WENT to stand beside the Queen. She sat in her chair cushioned with crimson velvet, under her cloth of estate. Today she wore a dress in royal purple, with a low-cut bodice, the forepart decorated with hundreds of tiny Tudor roses. She was laughing at the antics of the third person in the room: dressed all in white, Jane Fool was executing a clumsy dance in front of her, waving a white wand. I exchanged a quick glance with Lord Parr. Jane ignored us, continuing with her steps, kicking up her legs. It amazed me that intelligent adults, let alone the highest in the land, could laugh at such a scene, but then it struck me that amid the formality of the court, with the endless careful watching of words and gestures, the antics of a fool could provide a welcome relief.

The Queen glanced at us and nodded to Jane. 'Enough for now, my dear. I have business with my uncle and this gentleman.'

'This gentleman,' Jane mimicked, giving me an exaggerated bow. 'This hunchback gentleman frightened me, he would have had Ducky taken away.'

I said nothing; I knew licence to insult and mock was part of a fool's role. Nonetheless the Queen frowned. 'That is enough, Jane.'

'May I not finish my dance?' The little woman pouted. 'One minute more, I beg your majesty.'

'Very well, but just a minute,' the Queen replied impatiently. Jane Fool continued the dance and then, with a skilled athleticism I would not have expected, bent over and performed a handstand, her dress falling down to reveal a linen undergarment and fat little legs. I frowned. Surely this was going too far.

I became conscious that someone else had entered the room through an inner door. I turned and found myself looking at the magnificently dressed figure of the Lady Elizabeth, the King's second daughter. Lord Parr bowed deeply to her and I followed suit. I had met Elizabeth the year before, in the company of the Queen, to whom she was close. She had grown since then; almost thirteen, she was tall and the outline of budding breasts could be seen under the bodice of her dress. It was a splendid concoction; crimson, decorated with flowers, the forepart and under-sleeves gold and white. A jewelled French hood was set on her light auburn hair.

Elizabeth's long, clever face had matured, too; despite her pale colouring I saw in her features a resemblance to her disgraced, long-dead mother, Anne Boleyn. She had acquired, too, an adult's poise, no longer displaying the gawkishness of a girl. She stood looking at Jane's antics with haughty disapproval.

The Queen seemed surprised to see her. 'My dear. I thought you were still with Master Scrots.'

Elizabeth turned to her stepmother. 'I have been standing still for hours on end,' she answered petulantly. 'I insisted upon a rest. Will the painting of this picture never end? Kat Ashley that is attending me fell asleep!'

'It is important you have your own portrait, child,' the Queen said gently. 'It helps establish your position, as we have discussed.'

Jane Fool sat down on the floor, pouting, clearly annoyed at the Lady Elizabeth for taking the attention of her audience. Elizabeth glanced at her, then turned to the Queen. 'Can you ask Jane Fool to go? She is unseemly, waving her great bottom in the air like that.'

Jane, quick as a flash, appealed to the Queen in a tone of injured innocence. 'Your majesty, will you let the Lady speak to me so, I that seek only to entertain you?'

Elizabeth's face darkened. 'God's death,' she snapped in sudden temper, 'you do not entertain me! Get out!'

'Leave now, Jane.' The Queen spoke hastily. Jane looked alarmed for a moment, then picked up her wand and left without another word.

The anger left the Lady Elizabeth's face, and she smiled at Lord Parr. 'My good Lord, it is a pleasure to see you.' She looked at me. I bowed deeply. When I rose, her dark eyes were puzzled for a moment but then her face cleared. 'This gentleman, too, I know. Yes, Master Shardlake, you and I once had an agreeable discussion about the law. I thought long on it.'

'I am greatly pleased it interested you, my Lady, though I am surprised you remember.'

'God has blessed me with a good memory.' Elizabeth smiled complacently. If she was half a woman in body now, she was more than half in mind and demeanour. Yet her remarkably long fingers fiddled nervously with the rope of pearls at her waist.

She said, 'You told me that lawyers acting even for wicked clients have a duty to find what justice there is in their case and bring it to court.'

'I did.'

'And that it is a virtuous undertaking.'

'Yes, my Lady.' I thought suddenly of the Slanning case. The inspection of the wall painting was due to take place tomorrow. Was fighting that case virtuous?

'But it seems to me,' Lady Elizabeth continued, 'for that to be so, there must be at least *some* virtue in the case.'

'Yes, my Lady, you are right.' And in the Slanning case, I realized there was no virtue on either side, only hatred. Young though she was, Elizabeth had nailed a central point.

'Elizabeth,' the Queen said gently, 'will you not go back to Master Scrots? You know the portrait is almost done. And there is business I must conduct here. Come back in an hour, perhaps.'

Elizabeth nodded and gave her stepmother an affectionate smile.

'Very well. And I am sorry for shouting at Jane Fool, but I fear that, unlike you and my sister, I do not find her amusing.' She gave me a brief nod. 'Master Shardlake. My Lord Parr.'

We bowed again as she left by the inner door. The Queen closed her eyes for a second. 'I am sorry for that scene. It appears I cannot even control the people in my own privy quarters.' I noticed the strain and tension writ large on her face.

Lord Parr addressed her. 'I told you what Master Shardlake said about Jane Fool. About her having been in your chambers that night, about her closeness to the Lady Mary.'

The Queen shook her head firmly. 'No. Jane Fool knew nothing of my book, and would not have had the wit to steal it.'

'Perhaps the Lady Mary would.'

'Never. Mary is my friend.' She frowned sadly, then said, 'Or at least not my enemy. The trouble over her mother, Catherine of Aragon, is long over.'

'Well, we may have some answers soon.' Lord Parr smiled at me, rubbing his thin hands together. 'The Captain of the Guard spoke to the man who was on duty guarding the Queen's lodgings on the night the book was stolen. And mark this, it was not Zachary Gawger, whose odd behaviour Mary Odell reported. It was another man entirely, called Michael Leeman. It seems there was a substitution. The captain has had Gawger placed in custody, though on my instructions has asked no questions of him yet. And Leeman was to be taken when he came on duty this morning. That was at six; he will have him under guard now. I ordered both to be held for you to question, Master Shardlake.' He smiled triumphantly at the Queen. 'I think we are about to find the answer.'

'I hope so.' But she spoke doubtfully. Lord Parr gave a quick frown of impatience. The Queen turned to me.

'First, Master Shardlake, may we go over the other developments? My uncle has told me, but I would like to hear first-hand from you.'

'Quickly,' her uncle murmured.

Rapidly, I summarized everything that had happened since we last met: Elias's murder, the disappearance of Greening's three friends, Bealknap's strange last words, my suspicion that all was not quite right with Barwic the carpenter. I added that the mysterious name Bertano was Italian in origin, and suggested that perhaps we could find out whether the name was known among the Italian merchants in the city.

'I will arrange that,' Lord Parr said. 'Discreetly. First, though, let us see what these guards have to say. And if after that there remains any question of the carpenter's involvement, I will come with you to Baynard's Castle and speak to the man myself.'

'But Lord Parr, I thought you wanted to keep your involvement in the enquiries to a minimum.'

'I do. But those at Baynard's Castle are household staff, responsible to me, and therefore frightened of me.' He smiled tightly. 'As for the docks, Cecil has persuaded one of the customs house officials to inform us if any of Greening's three friends are spotted and try to flee on a ship. All goods and persons entering or leaving the country have to go through there. And Cecil has also got one of the dockers to keep an eye on everything that happens on the waterfront. With a promise of a goodly sum in gold if these jewel thieves are captured.' He smiled wryly.

'That poor apprentice boy,' the Queen said. 'I cannot understand why he should say he was killed for Anne Askew. I made sure she and I never met.' She looked sadly at her uncle. 'At least there I was properly careful.'

Lord Parr nodded. 'I have spoken to my old friend Sir Edmund Walsingham,' he said. 'I am going to the Tower tomorrow. I have invented a piece of household business to justify the visit.' He turned to me. 'You will come too. We shall see what we can dig out about the news of Mistress Askew's torture being leaked. But now – the guard.'

The Queen, however, seemed reluctant to let me go. 'This man Bealknap?' she asked. 'Which side did he follow in religion?'

'Neither. But he was associated with Richard Rich.'

'Those words of his. Did they sound like a warning, or a threat?'

'Neither, your majesty. Merely a last gloating, a hope to see me charged with heresy, and you.'

Lord Parr said firmly, 'That's surely what it was.'

'Bealknap could not have been involved with the theft,' I said. 'He has been ill in his room for many weeks.'

'Then forget him,' Lord Parr said resolutely. He turned to the Queen. She swallowed, gripping the arms of her chair. Her uncle put his hand on hers. 'And now,' he said, looking at me, 'the Captain of the Guard, Master Mitchell, is waiting for you. With his prisoners. Question them. Alone, of course.'

Chapter Eighteen

THE GUARDROOM, I WAS TOLD, was on the other side of the Presence Chamber. As I crossed the chamber, a plump middle-aged man, sweating in a furred robe, stepped into my path, doffed a feathered cap and gave me an exaggerated bow. 'Good master lawyer,' he said in honeyed tones, 'I saw you come from the Queen's Privy Chamber. I regret interrupting you, but I am an old friend of the late Lord Latimer, visiting London. My son, a goodly lad, wishes to serve at court—'

'Such things are not my business,' I answered curtly. I left him clutching his cap disconsolately and made my way quickly towards the door to which I had been directed. 'Sent to Master Mitchell from Lord Parr,' I said to the yeoman standing with his halberd outside. He opened the door and led me into a small anteroom, where two black-robed guards sat playing dice. He crossed the room to another door and knocked. A deep voice called, 'Come in.' The guard bowed and I entered a cramped office.

A strongly built, fair-haired man in a black robe sat behind a desk, the Queen's badge set on his cap. My heart fell when he looked up; I could tell from his sombre expression that he had no good news.

'Serjeant Shardlake?' He waved a hand to a chair. 'Please sit. I am David Mitchell, Head of the Queen's Guard.'

'God give you good morrow. I believe Lord Parr has explained that I wish to question Michael Leeman, who was on duty the night the Queen's b—, I mean, ring – was stolen.' I cursed myself. I had nearly said 'book'. That one word, uttered to the wrong person, could bring everything crashing down.

Mitchell, for all that he was a big man, looked uncomfortable, somehow shrunken inside his uniform. He spoke quietly. 'I have Zachary Gawger in custody here. But I am afraid we do not have Michael Leeman.'

I sat bolt upright. 'What?'

Mitchell coughed awkwardly. 'I checked the rotas yesterday afternoon, when Lord Parr asked me to. Gawger and Leeman were both on the evening shift on the sixth of July, and it was Leeman that was assigned to stand guard at the door of the Queen's Privy Chamber. Yet according to Mary Odell it had actually been Gawger. Gawger was on duty last night and I had him immediately placed in custody. Leeman was supposed to be on duty at six, but he never arrived and when I sent for him, his chamber in the guards' lodgings was empty. His possessions had gone too.'

I closed my eyes. 'How did this happen?'

It was strange to see the Guard Captain, a military man of considerable authority, squirm in his chair. 'Apparently one of the other soldiers had seen Gawger taken into custody. He went to spread the news, and apparently Leeman was in the wardroom, heard the gossip. I was not quick enough. The sergeant I sent to arrest him must have arrived minutes after he left.' He looked at me. 'Lord Parr shall have my resignation this morning.'

'Is there any indication where Leeman may have gone?'

'He was checked out of the palace at eight last night. He said he was going into the city for the evening; he often did, it was not remarked upon, though the guard on duty noted he was carrying a large bag. Containing the Queen's lost ring, no doubt,' he added bitterly.

I stared up at the ceiling. A fourth man disappeared now. I turned back to Mitchell. There was no point in being angry with him. I little doubted Lord Parr would accept his resignation.

I said, 'I think the best thing will be for Gawger to tell me all he knows.'

'Yes.' He nodded at a door to the side of the office. 'He is in there.

Christ's mother!' he spat in sudden anger. 'It will be his last morning at Whitehall; tonight he will be in the Fleet Prison, the rogue.'

I looked at him. 'That is for Lord Parr to decide.'

Mitchell got up slowly, opened the door, and dragged a young man into the office. He was dressed only in undershirt and hose, his brown hair and short beard were bedraggled and there was a bruise on his cheek. He was tall and well-built, like all the guards, but he made a sorry figure now. Mitchell thrust him against the wall. Gawger sagged, looking at me fearfully.

'Tell the Queen's investigator all you told me,' Mitchell said. 'I shall be waiting outside.' He looked at the young man with angry disgust, then turned to me. 'I should tell you, Master Shardlake, that during the twelvemonth Gawger has worked here I have had cause to discipline him for drunkenness and gambling. He is one of those young fools from the country whose head has been turned by the court. I was already thinking of dismissing him. Would that I had.' He glared at Gawger. 'Spit out the whole story, churl!'

With that, Mitchell turned and left his office. The young man remained cowering against the wall. He took a deep breath, then gulped nervously.

'Well?' I asked. 'Best you tell the whole truth. If I have to tell Captain Mitchell I have doubts, he may be rough with you again.' It was no more than the truth.

Gawger took another deep breath. 'About three weeks ago, sir – it was at the start of the month – one of my fellow guards approached me in lodgings. Michael Leeman. I did not know him well – he had not made himself popular, he was one of the radicals, always telling us to amend our souls.'

'Really?' I leaned forward with interest.

'He said the palace soldiery were mired in sin and that when his term was done he would go to new friends he had, godly friends.'

'Do you know who they were?'

Gawger shook his head. 'I'm not sure. But they lived somewhere around St Paul's, I think. He was always off there during his free time.

But I steer clear of talk about religion. It's dangerous.' He stopped, breathing rapidly now, perhaps realizing that he was in deep danger. The rules governing the Queen's Guard were strict, and I had little doubt that what Gawger was about to confess to constituted treason. I took a deep breath.

He continued, a whining, desperate note in his voice now. 'I – I have had money troubles, sir. I have been playing cards with some of my fellows. I lost money. I thought I could win it back, but lost more. I appealed to my father; he has helped me before, but he said he had no more to spare. If I did not find the money soon I knew there would be a scandal, I would lose this post, have to return home in disgrace – ' Suddenly he laughed wildly. 'But that was nothing to what will happen now, is it sir? I gambled everything on this throw, and lost.'

'And exactly what was this throw Leeman wanted you to make?'

'He was in the middle of a fortnight's evening duty. He told me he had had a dalliance with one of the chamber servant women and had left a pair of monogrammed gloves, that could be traced to him, in the Queen's Long Gallery. He had taken this girl in there when no one else was around. If the gloves were discovered both of them would be dismissed.'

I raised my eyebrows. 'And him such a man of God?'

'I was surprised, sir, but men who lust fiercely after religion can often turn out to have strong lusts of the flesh as well, can they not?' He gulped again, then added, 'Leeman showed me a bag with ten sovereigns, old ones of pure gold.' The man's eyes lit up for a moment at the memory. 'He said it was mine if I would take his place as guard outside the door to the privy lodgings, just for a few minutes, while he fetched his gloves. We would both be on duty in the Presence Cham, ber for several days, and could change places when the Queen and her servants were absent. He said it needed to be done as soon as possible. But it was many days before we were able to do it.'

'So the switch happened on the sixth?'

'Yes, sir.'

I leaned back in my chair. It all fitted. Somehow Leeman had found out about the *Lamentation*, and had decided – why, I had no idea – to steal it. He had looked for an accomplice, found the wretched Gawger, and taken his opportunity when it came on the 6th of July. He was a religious radical. He had friends by St Paul's. Was he a member of Greening's group? I looked at Gawger. Such a young man as this could easily be won over with the promise of gold. And Leeman's story was plausible; even in July, carrying silk gloves of fine design was common round the court as yet another symbol of status. But how had Leeman learned of the book? Why had he stolen it? And how had he got a key to that chest?

I asked Gawger, 'How would Leeman know for sure when the Queen's lodgings were unoccupied?'

'Everything runs according to routine in this place, sir. In the evenings, the servants arrive and depart at fixed hours. If the Queen is called to the King, as she frequently is in the evenings, her personal attendants go with her and for a short time nobody is present in her apartments. I was on duty, but in reserve rather than at post. My arrangement with Leeman was that I would remain in the guardroom – the room you came through just now – and if the Queen was called away he would run across to tell me. Then I would take his place while he went inside for a few minutes. That would not be noted; there is always someone in reserve in case a guard is taken ill or has to relieve himself and cannot wait. And at that time of night, if the Queen was with the King, there was normally nobody in the Presence Chamber either. There wasn't that night.'

'Go on.'

Gawger took a deep breath. 'Just before nine, Leeman came into the Guard Chamber. I was the only one there. I remember how set his face was. He nodded to me, that was our signal. Then the two of us went back to the Presence Chamber and I took his position by the door while he slipped inside. I waited at the door – in a sweat, I may say.'

'Had you had a drink?' I asked.

'Just a little, sir, to give me courage. But I had only been there a minute when Mistress Odell arrived. I tried to delay her — '

'I know,' I said. 'You pretended her name was not on the list, and when she insisted on going in, as you opened the door you said loudly that everything must be done properly, no doubt to alert Leeman. She told me. It was that which first aroused my suspicions.'

Gawger lowered his head. 'Leeman must have hidden somewhere till Mary Odell had passed by him. Then he came out again.'

'Was he carrying anything?'

'Not that I could see.'

I thought, the manuscript was small, he could have concealed it under his voluminous cloak. Suddenly I felt angry. 'What if Leeman had been unbalanced? What if he had planned to murder the Queen, who you are sworn to protect? What then, master gambler?'

Gawger bowed his head again. 'I have no answer, sir,' he said miserably.

I went across to the door. Mitchell was waiting outside. I let him in and told him all that Gawger had told me; both, of course, thought that at issue was a stolen ring. 'It seems you have your answer, Serjeant Shardlake,' Mitchell said bleakly.

'I would rather have Leeman as well,' I answered curtly. 'Now I will report back to Lord Parr. Do not have this man publicly accused yet. Is there somewhere you can keep him?'

'Surely now he should be imprisoned and tried for conspiracy in this theft, and for endangering the Queen's person.'

'Lord Parr must say,' I answered firmly.

Mitchell stood up, grabbed the wretched guard, and thrust him back into the antechamber. He returned and sat behind his desk again, looking haggard. I said, 'I want this kept quiet till you receive further orders.'

'I place myself in the hands of the Queen. It is my responsibility Leeman is gone.' Mitchell shook his head. 'But it is hard sometimes, having to take on these young country gentlemen because their fathers have influence. And these last months have been terrible. All the rumours — I have served the Queen loyally these three years, but since the spring I have never known when I may be ordered to arrest her.'

I did not answer. I could feel no sympathy for him. However well organized, however disciplined a system of security might be, it only took one slip from a man in a crucial position for the line to be broken. 'Tell me more about Leeman,' I said eventually.

'His father is a landowner in Kent. He has some distant connection to the Parrs through their Throckmorton cousins, one of whom petitioned for a post for him. I interviewed young Leeman last year. I thought him suitable; as a gentleman, he was well trained in the arts of combat and he is a big, handsome young fellow, well set up. Though even then he struck me as a little serious. And godly; he said his main interest was the study of religion. Well, being a reformer was no hindrance then.' He sighed. 'And he was a good and loyal guard for two years. Never a hint of trouble, except that twice he had to be warned against evangelizing among his fellow guards. It annoyed them. I warned him early this year such talk was becoming dangerous.' Mitchell leaned forward. 'He is the last one I would have expected to have concocted a plot to steal one of the Queen's jewels. And Leeman is not rich, his family are poor and distant cousins of the Queen, delighted to have a son in such a post. How could he have come by such a huge sum as ten sovereigns to offer Gawger?'

'I do not know.'

Mitchell swallowed. 'I expect there will be a search for Leeman now.'

'It rests with the Queen and Lord Parr,' I said quietly, standing up. 'For now, keep Gawger close confined — and tell nobody.' I bowed and left him.

✝

I RETURNED TO the Queen's Privy Chamber. Lord Parr was pacing up and down, the Queen still sitting beneath her cloth of estate, playing with the pearl that once belonged to Catherine Howard. Her spaniel, Rig, lay at her feet.

I told them what had happened with Mitchell and Gawger.

'So,' Lord Parr said heavily. 'Thanks to you, we now know *who*, but not *how* or *why*. And thanks to that fool Mitchell, Leeman is gone.'

'As for the how, I think another word with the carpenter is called for. Especially now we know Leeman had money to wave before people. As to the why – I begin to wonder whether a whole group of radical Protestants may be involved in this, reaching from Leeman to the printer Greening. But that brings us back to the question of why. Why would they steal the book?'

'And how did they come to know of its existence in the first place?' Lord Parr asked.

Suddenly the Queen leaned forward, her silks rustling, and burst into tears: loud, racking sobs. Her uncle went and put a hand on her arm. 'Kate, Kate,' he said soothingly. 'We must be calm.'

She lifted her face. It was full of fear, tears smudging the white ceruse on her cheeks. The sight of her in such a state squeezed at my heart.

'Be calm!' she cried. 'How? When the theft has already caused two deaths! And whoever these people are who stole my book, it looks as though someone else was after them and has it now! All because of my sin of pride in not taking Archbishop Cranmer's advice and destroying the manuscript! *Lamentation*! Lamentation indeed!' She took a long, shuddering breath, then turned a face of misery upon us. 'Do you know what the worst thing is, for me who wrote a book urging people to forget the temptations of the world and seek salvation? That even now, with those poor men dead, it is not of them that I think, nor my family and friends in danger, but of myself, being put in the fire, like Anne Askew! I imagine myself chained to the stake, I hear the crackle as the faggots are lit, I smell the smoke and feel the flames.' Her voice rose, frantic now. 'I have feared it since the spring. After the King humiliated Wriothesley I thought it was over, but now – ' She pounded her dress with a fist. 'I am so selfish, selfish!

I, who thought the Lord had favoured me with grace – ' She was shouting now. The spaniel at her feet whined anxiously.

Lord Parr took her firmly by the shoulders, looking into her swollen face. 'Hold fast, Kate! You have managed it these last months, do not crumble now. And do not shout.' He inclined his head to the door. 'The guard may hear.'

The Queen nodded, and took a number of long, whooping breaths. Gradually, she brought herself under control, forcing her shaking body to be still. She looked at me, ventured a watery smile. 'I imagine you did not think to see your Queen like this, Matthew?' She patted her uncle's hand. 'There, good my lord. It is over. I am myself again. I must wash my face and get one of the maids to make it up again before I venture outside.'

'It sore grieves me to see you in such distress, your majesty,' I said quietly. But a thought had come to me. 'Lord Parr. You told her majesty that if she shouted the guard might hear?'

The Queen's eyes widened in alarm. Lord Parr patted her hand. 'I exaggerated, to calm her. These doors are thick, deliberately so that the Queen may have some privacy. The guard might make out a raised voice, but not each individual word.'

'What if it was a man who shouted?' I said. 'A man with a loud, deep voice, the voice of a preacher, trained to carry far?'

He frowned. 'No man would dare come here and shout at the Queen.'

But the Queen leaned forward, eyes wide, balling a handkerchief in her palm. 'Archbishop Cranmer,' she said. 'That evening when we argued over the *Lamentation*, and I resisted his arguments, I shouted and – yes – he shouted, too.' She gulped. 'We are good friends, we have discussed matters of faith together many times, and he was very afraid of what could happen if I let the *Lamentation* become public. How many times must he have feared the fire himself these last dozen years? And he was right, as I realize now.' She looked at me again. 'Yes, if the guard outside could have distinguished the words of anyone shouting in here, it would have been the Archbishop's. Telling me that if I tried to publish the *Lamentation* now, the King's anger might know no bounds.'

Lord Parr frowned. 'He had no right – '

I said, 'That was in early June, you told me?'

The Queen nodded. 'Yes.' She frowned. 'The ninth, I think.'

I turned to Lord Parr. 'My lord, do you know the evening duty hours?'

'Four till midnight.'

'It would be interesting to find out who was on duty outside on the night of the argument. Captain Mitchell will have the records.'

The Queen said, aghast, 'Then Leeman might have been outside when the Archbishop and I argued?'

I spoke with quiet intensity. 'And could have heard of the exist-ence of the book, and made his plans to steal it. So long as he was able to get a copy of the key. It all rests on that. My Lord, let us find out who was on duty then. And afterwards, I think we should question the carpenter again.'

✝

IT WAS LEEMAN on duty that night; Mitchell confirmed it. That made it almost certain: he had overheard Cranmer and learned of the existence of the *Lamentation*. Then he had planned, and waited, and bribed. But with what money, I wondered. I felt sure he was not acting alone.

Lord Parr and I left the distraught captain, and took the smaller of the Queen's two barges to Baynard's Castle, the rowmen in her livery sculling fast down the Thames, a herald with a trumpet signalling other craft to get out of the way. Mary Odell had been called to the Queen and would be with her in her private apartments now, making her fit to face the public again.

Lord Parr and I sat opposite each other under the canopy. In the sunlight he looked his age, with pale seamed skin and tired eyes. I ventured, 'My Lord, has her majesty often been – like that?'

He looked me in the eye for a moment, then leaned forward and

spoke quietly. 'A few times, these last months. You have little idea
of the control and composure she must have. It has always been one of
my niece's greatest qualities, that control. But underneath she is a
woman of powerful feeling, more so as her faith has grown stronger.
And since the spring – the questioning of those close to her, the persecutions, the knowledge that the King might turn on her – yes, she
has broken down before. In front of me, and Mary Odell, and her
sister. She is lucky to have those she can trust.' He paused and looked
at me hard.

'She can trust me, too, my Lord,' I said quietly.

He grimaced. 'For a commoner to see the Queen as you did – well,
let us say you are the first. And I pray the last.' He sat up straight,
looking over my shoulder. 'Here, the Baynard's Castle steps are close
ahead.'

✞

THE TWO OF US had agreed our approach, the words we would
use to bring a confession if Barwic was guilty. We had no time to
waste. Lord Parr strode through the courtyard and then the central
hall, looking stern, all the guards saluting the Queen's Chancellor in
turn. He came to the carpenter's door and flung it open. Barwic was
planing a length of oak – I noticed little pieces of sawdust in his russet
beard – while his assistant sanded another. They both looked up at our
entrance, the assistant in astonishment and Barwic, I saw, in fear.

Lord Parr slammed the door shut and stood with his arms folded.
He inclined his head to the apprentice. 'Go, boy,' he said bluntly, and
the lad fled with a quick bow. Barwic faced us.

'Michael Leeman, the thief, is discovered,' I said, bluntly. 'And his
confederate, Zachary Gawger.'

Barwic stood there for a second, his face expressionless, his wild
red hair and beard, flecked with sawdust, looking almost comical.
Then, like a puppet, he sank slowly to his knees, lowering his head
and clasping his work-roughened hands together. From this position
he looked up at the Queen's Chancellor, the clasped hands trembling.

'Forgive me, my Lord. At first I only made a copy of the key lest the original be lost. It is not a good thing for a chest containing valuables to have only one key.'

'So you made another secretly and kept it?' I asked. 'Where?'

'Safe, my Lord, safe. In a locked chest to which only I have the key.' All the while he did not shift his gaze from Lord Parr's face.

'Have you ever done this before?'

Barwic looked at me, then turned back to Lord Parr. 'Yes, my Lord, forgive me. If ever I am asked to make a lock with only one key, I make a second. I can show you the place I keep them all, show you the keys. It was for security only; security, I swear.'

'Then how did Leeman get hold of it?' I asked.

'Stand up when you answer, churl!' Lord Parr snapped. 'I will get a crick in my neck looking down at you.'

Barwic stood, still wringing his hands. 'He came to see me, near three weeks ago. I did not know him, but he wore the uniform of the Queen's Guard. He told me the key to the Queen's chest had been lost, said he had heard I might have another. I – I thought he came on behalf of the Queen, you see—'

Lord Parr brought his hand down on the bench with a bang, sending the plank of wood crashing to the floor. 'Don't lie to me, caitiff! You know well enough a member of the Queen's Guard would have no authority to demand a key. Especially when you kept the very existence of copies a secret!'

The wretched man swallowed nervously. 'I let it be known, to certain people, that I made extra copies of keys. Not officially, but you see – if a key was lost, I could provide a replacement for anyone who lost it.'

'At a price?'

Barwic nodded miserably.

'How long have you been doing this?'

'Since I first became the Queen's carpenter and locksmith twelve years ago. Perhaps half a dozen times I have provided a spare key to a chest or coffer, usually to a lady who has lost hers. But always to someone who is trusted, sir, and nothing has been stolen in all that time as a consequence. Nothing.'

Lord Parr shook his head. 'Dear God, the Queen's household has been lax.'

'Yes,' I agreed, 'and Michael Leeman, I would wager, ferreted out where the weak points were. How much did he pay you, Barwic?'

'Ten sovereigns, sir. I – I couldn't resist.' I thought, the same bribe as for Gawger. 'He told me the Queen had gone out and left the key with him for safekeeping and he accidentally dropped it through a gap in the floorboards. He did not want to have them taken up.'

'Did you believe him?' Lord Parr's voice was scornful.

'I was uncertain, my Lord. I told him to come back on the morrow. In the meantime I asked friends at Whitehall for information on Leeman – had he been there long, was he honest? I was told he was known as an honest man, godly. I wouldn't just hand out a key to anybody, sir, I swear.'

Lord Parr gave him a look of contempt. 'No. I imagine you would not, for fear of being hanged. But Michael Leeman *was* a thief. And you are deep in the mire.' He looked at me. 'I will have this man held close at my house for the moment. Come with us, Master Barwic. I'll put you in the charge of a guard, as a man suspected of conspiracy to rob the Queen. And you don't say a word about keys. Leeman, and his confederate, are discovered, but Leeman has escaped and you'll keep all this quiet till he is captured.'

Barwic sank to his knees again. His voice shook. 'Will – will I hang, sir? Please, would you ask the Queen to show mercy? I have a wife, children – it was all the expenses of being Guild Chairman, the taxes for the war – '

Lord Parr bent over him. 'You'll hang if I have any say,' he said brutally. 'Now, come.'

✟

BARWIC WAS PUT in the charge of a guard and led away, sobbing, across Baynard's Castle yard. Another man whose life now lay in ruins. Some men lifting bolts of silk from a cart turned to look at the weeping prisoner being taken away under guard.

'Well,' Lord Parr said quietly. 'You have taken us far, Serjeant Shardlake. We have the whole story of the theft, the how and the who. But still not the why. And who has the damned manuscript now? And why are they keeping quiet about it?'

'I do not know, my Lord. My young assistant is trying to trace the maker of that piece of torn sleeve he found near Greening's print-shop, but for now there are no other leads. We need to catch Greening's friends.'

He stirred the dust of the courtyard with his foot. 'I will send Cecil a detailed description of Leeman; I'll get it from Captain Mitchell. He can add it to those who are to be watched out for.'

'They will likely try to leave under false names.'

'Of course they will,' he said impatiently. 'But the customs house has the descriptions, and if any of them try to board a ship they will be arrested and held close till I can question them.' He shook his head. 'Though they may try to go via Bristol, or Ipswich.'

'That leaves our enquiries in the Tower,' I reflected. 'It may be possible we could find that it was another radical who leaked the truth about Anne Askew. Possibly someone linked to the others.'

He nodded slowly. 'I certainly smell some sort of radical conspiracy here. I wish I knew what it was about.'

'Whatever it was, that original group has been attacked and blown apart.' I looked at him. 'By internal dissension, or perhaps it could even be that someone in the group was a spy, maybe for someone in the conservative camp.'

His eyes widened. 'By God, you could be right. Secretary Paget has the main responsibility for employing spies to watch for internal dissension. But others could be doing the same, on their own account. Someone perhaps with a taste for plotting.'

He looked at me. 'Who are you thinking of?' I asked. 'Sir Richard Rich?'

'He has been assiduous in the heresy hunt.'

I paused, then said, 'My Lord, I am worried about Greening's neighbour, the printer Okedene.'

He inclined his head. 'I think we have got all the information we can out of him.'

'I was thinking of his safety. Two men have been killed already. I wondered if Okedene might also be at risk; whether our enemies, whoever they are, might try to stop his mouth for good.'

'He has told us all he knows. He has no further use.'

'All the same, much is owed to him. Could you not arrange some protection, perhaps a man to lodge in his house?'

'Do you not understand?' Lord Parr burst out. 'I've already told you, I do not have the resources! I cannot help him!' I did not answer, did not dare provoke him further, and he continued. 'Now, the Tower is next.'

'Yes, my Lord.'

'Until he retired recently, the Queen's Vice Chamberlain, my immediate junior in the Queen's household, was Sir Edmund Walsingham. He has also been Constable of the Tower of London for twenty-five years.'

'He combined both jobs?' I asked in surprise.

'Both are ceremonial rather than administrative roles. At the Tower the Constable, Sir Edmund, is a very old friend of mine; in fact he is almost as old as me.' He smiled wryly. 'Naturally he knows how everything works there. I have arranged to visit him tomorrow at eleven; I could not obtain an earlier appointment, though I tried.' He looked at me. 'Now, this is what we shall do. On the pretext that some information is needed for a legal case, we will see if you can get sight of the duty rosters that cover the period when Anne Askew was tortured. Between the twenty-eighth of June, when she was taken there, and the second of July when the rumours first began to fly around London. It will not be easy; I imagine the Tower authorities will be very reticent about what happened. My nephew William, Earl of Essex, tells me no investigation has been ordered by the Privy Council, which is strange. In any event, a good meal and good wine can loosen tongues between friends.'

Eleven o'clock. That would at least allow me time to carry out the Cotterstoke inspection early the next morning. I looked at Lord Parr; the old man's face had become quite animated at the prospect of progress. But I did not want to visit the Tower again. Five years before, thanks to a conspiracy between Rich and Bealknap, I had briefly been imprisoned there. I wondered whether Lord Parr knew about that. But, I reflected, he probably knew everything about me. He looked back at me quizzically. 'Is there a problem?'

'My Lord, forgive me, but the number who know that the Queen has suffered some sort of a theft is growing. News could reach the King. I cannot help wondering – well, whether the Queen might serve her interests best by going now and confessing all to him. He will surely be more merciful than if the book is hawked round the streets and he finds out then that she kept it secret from him.'

Lord Parr rounded on me. In the crowded courtyard he kept his voice low, but his tone was fierce as he spoke. 'You are not qualified to advise her majesty on such a matter. And remember, great danger still threatens her; it is common knowledge on the Privy Council that there is still something going on, secret talks are occurring between Paget and Gardiner and the King. My nephew William, the Queen's brother, like most of the Privy Council is outside the circle, but something is afoot that keeps Gardiner looking confident despite the failure of the persecution, that makes him look on with a secret smile when William passes him.'

'But the book is not heretical,' I said. 'And Sir Edward Seymour is expected soon at court, as, I heard, is Lord Lisle. Both are reformers, and in alliance with the Parrs they will be strong—'

'It is *not* safe for the Queen to tell the King.' The old man's voice shook with anger and I saw the strain on his face. 'You overstep the mark, sir, by God you do! The alliance between the Parr and Seymour families is none of your business. You know nothing of it, nor of the machinations at court.' He lowered his voice. 'But you should have come to realize, after all these years, that the one thing this King will not tolerate is any suspicion of disloyalty.'

'I only thought to help, my Lord.'

'Then keep your nose out of matters far above your station. And remember, Master Shardlake, you answer to me alone. Be at the Middle Tower gate at eleven tomorrow, with your horse, and wearing your robe.' And with that Lord Parr turned and limped away.

I watched him go, the hot sun beating down on my head. Stepping away, I tripped. I righted myself, yet still the ground seemed to rock under my feet, as it had when the *Mary Rose* foundered. I closed my eyes. The picture that came to my mind, though, was not the great ship turning over, nor the men falling into the sea, but Anne Askew on fire, Anne Askew's head exploding.

Chapter Nineteen

NEXT MORNING I SET OUT early again. The last four days had passed in a blur; but if the Queen's book was to be recovered, time was of the essence. The previous evening I had sent a note to Okedene; I was worried about him. I warned him that Greening's killers were still at large and urged him to make arrangements for his security. Lord Parr had not authorized me to write, but I felt it my duty nevertheless.

Downstairs, Josephine served my breakfast. I wondered again about her difficulties with Martin Brocket, but she seemed cheerful enough today.

Outside it was warm and sunny again. I remembered I was due for dinner at Coleswyn's that evening. I would be at the Tower later in the morning and I thought of cancelling the meal, but decided it might be good to have some ordinary human company after that particular visit.

First I called in at chambers. Barak and Skelly were there working already, doing my work as well as their own. Nicholas had left early, Barak said, to continue checking the embroiderers' shops, having had, apparently, no luck the previous day. His tone was slightly aggrieved; Barak really did not like being kept out of things. I said I was going to the painting inspection, and would also be out in the afternoon now.

'Why don't you just tell that Slanning creature to piss off and get another lawyer since you're so busy?'

'I can't, not without good cause,' I answered stubbornly. 'I've taken on the case, I have to see it through.'

'Even when you have this other thing on your mind?'

'Yes.'

I left him, feeling not a little uneasy.

✞

THE COTTERSTOKE HOUSE was at Dowgate, on the other side of the city, so I rode down Cheapside; the shops were just opening, market traders setting up their stalls. I remembered my last conversation with Coleswyn; our pact to try and bring this case to a decent resolution. It had crossed my mind to make discreet enquiries at the Haberdashers' Guild about the Cotterstoke family history, but that would be unprofessional, and besides I had no time.

Ahead of me I saw another black-robed lawyer riding along slowly, head bowed as though in thought, and realized it was Philip Coleswyn. I caught him up.

'God give you good morrow, Brother Coleswyn.'

'And you. Are you ready for the inspection?'

'My client will be there. And yours?'

'Master Cotterstoke. Oh, undoubtedly.' Coleswyn smiled ironically, then added, 'My wife looks forward to meeting you tonight. Around six, if that is not too late?'

'That would be convenient. I have business in the afternoon.'

We rode on. Coleswyn seemed preoccupied today and spoke little. Then we passed the mouth of an alleyway, where a commotion was taking place. A couple of burly men were bringing out furniture from a house in the alley: a truckle bed, a table, a couple of rickety chairs. They loaded them on a cart, while a woman in cheap wadmol clothing, several small children clinging to her skirts, stood by stony-faced. A middle-aged man was arguing loudly with a large fellow who had a club at his waist and was supervising the removal.

'We're only a month behind with the rent! We've been there twelve years! I can't help it trade's so bad!'

'Not my problem, goodman,' the big fellow answered unsympathetically. 'You're in arrears and you've got to go.'

'People don't want building repairs done this year, not with all the taxes there have been for the war! And the rise in prices – ' The man turned to a little crowd that was gathering. There were murmurs of agreement.

'An eviction,' Coleswyn observed quietly.

'There have been many of those this year.'

The builder's wife suddenly lunged forward and grasped a chest which the two men had brought from the alleyway. 'No!' she cried. 'That's my husband's tools!'

'Everything is to be taken to pay the arrears,' the big man said.

The builder joined his wife. His voice was almost frantic. 'I can't work without those! I'm allowed to keep my tools!'

'Leave that chest be!' A man who had joined the crowd shouted threateningly. The fellow with the club – the landlord's agent, presumably – looked round nervously; the number of spectators was growing.

We halted as Coleswyn called out, 'He's right! He can keep the tools of his trade! I'm a lawyer!'

The crowd turned to us; many of their faces were hostile, even though Coleswyn was trying to help. Lawyers are never popular. The man with the club, though, seemed relieved. 'All right!' he shouted. 'Leave that chest, if it's the law!' He could tell his employer later that a lawyer had interfered.

The men lowered the chest to the ground and the woman sat on it, gathering her children round her. 'You can go, pen-scratchers!' someone shouted at us. 'Salved your consciences, have you?'

We rode on. 'Poor men lie under great temptation to doubt God's providence,' Coleswyn said quietly. 'But one day, when we have the godly Commonwealth, there will be justice for men of all ranks.'

I shook my head sadly. 'So I used to believe, once. I thought the proceeds from the monasteries would be used to bring justice to the poor; that the King, as Head of the Church, would have a regard for them the old church did not. Yet all that money went on extending Whitehall and other palaces, or was thrown away on the war. No wonder some folk have gone down more radical paths.'

'Yet those people would bring naught but anarchy.' Coleswyn spoke with a desperate, quiet intensity. 'No, a decent, ordered, godly realm must come.'

✝

WE REACHED THE HOUSE. It was big, timber-framed like most London houses, fronting onto the busy street of Dowgate. An arch led to a stableyard at the back. We tied up the horses and stood in the summer sunshine, looking at the rear of the house. The windows were shuttered, and though the property was well-maintained, it had a sad, deserted air. Dry straw from the days when the Cotterstoke horses had been stabled here blew round the dusty yard on the light breeze.

'This place would fetch a good deal of money, even in these times,' Coleswyn observed.

'I agree. It is silly to leave it standing empty and unsold because of this dispute.' I shook my head. 'You know, the more I think of the strange wording of her Will, the more I believe that old woman intended to cause trouble between her children.'

'But why?'

I shook my head.

We walked round to the front and knocked. There were shuffling footsteps, and a small elderly man opened the door. I remembered him as Patrick Vowell, the servant who had been kept on to look after the place after old Mrs Cotterstoke died. He was fortunate. The other servants, including the witnesses to old Deborah Cotterstoke's Will, had been dismissed, as usually happened when the owner of the household died.

'Serjeant Shardlake with Master Coleswyn,' I said.

He had watery blue eyes, heavy dark pouches beneath, a sad look. 'Mistress Slanning is already here. She is in the parlour.'

He led us across a little hall where a large tapestry of the Last Supper hung, worth a good deal of money in its own right. The parlour, a well-appointed room, did not look to have been touched since my first visit, or indeed since old Mrs Cotterstoke died. The chairs and table were dusty and a piece of half-finished embroidery lay on a chair. The shutters on the window giving onto the street were open; through the glass we could see the bustle of the street. The light fell on Isabel Slanning, standing with her back to us before the beautiful painting that covered the entire far wall. I remembered Nicholas saying it would be hard to fit the painting into a smaller house. Not hard, I thought, impossible.

It was, indeed, extraordinarily lifelike: a dark-haired man in his thirties, wearing black robes and a tall, cylindrical hat, looked out at us with the proud expression of one who is getting on well in life. He sat to one side of the very window that now cast light on the painting, on another sunny day at the very start of the century. I had the strange feeling of looking into a mirror, but backwards in time. Opposite the man sat a young woman with a face of English-rose prettiness, though there was a sharpness to her expression. Beside her stood a boy and a girl, perhaps nine or ten; both resembled her strongly except for their prominent eyes, which were their father's. In the picture little Isabel and Edward Cotterstoke stood hand-in-hand; a contented, carefree pair of children.

Isabel turned her wrinkled face to us, the bottom of her blue silk dress swishing on the reed matting. Her expression was cold and set, and when she saw Coleswyn with me anger leapt into those pale, bulbous eyes. She had been fingering a rosary tied to her belt, something strongly frowned on these last few years. She let it fall with a clack of beads.

'Serjeant Shardlake.' She spoke accusingly. 'Did you travel here with our opponent?'

'We met on the road, Mistress Slanning,' I answered firmly. 'Are either of the experts here yet? Or your brother?'

'No. I saw my brother through the window a few minutes ago. He knocked at the door, but I instructed Vowell not to allow him in till you were here. I daresay he will return shortly.' She flashed a glare at Coleswyn. 'This man is our foe, yet you ride with him.'

'Madam,' Coleswyn said quietly, 'lawyers who are opponents in court are expected to observe the civilities of gentlemen outside it.'

This made Isabel even more angry. She turned to me, pointing a skinny finger at Coleswyn. 'This man should not be speaking to me; is it not the rule that he should communicate with me only through you, Master Shardlake?'

In fact she was right, and Coleswyn reddened. 'Gentleman, indeed!' She snorted. 'A heretic, I hear, like my brother.'

This was appalling behaviour, even by Isabel's standards. To imply that Coleswyn was not a gentleman was a bad enough insult but to call him a heretic was to accuse him of a capital crime. Coleswyn's lips set hard as he turned to me. 'Strictly your client is correct that I should not have direct converse with her. In any case, I would rather not. I shall wait in the hallway till the others arrive.' He walked out and shut the door. Isabel gave me a look of triumph. Her whole body seemed rigid with sheer malice.

'Heretics,' she snapped triumphantly. 'Well, they are getting their just deserts these days.' Seeing my expression, she scowled, perhaps wondering about my own loyalties, although knowing Isabel she would have been careful to ensure I was – at least – neutral in religious matters before appointing me.

A movement outside caught her eye. She looked through the window and seemed to shrink for a second before setting her face hard again. There was a knock at the door and a minute later Vowell showed Coleswyn back in, together with three other men. Two were middle-aged fellows whom I guessed were the experts; they were discussing the various methods by which small monastic houses could be converted into residences. The third was Isabel's brother, Edward Cotterstoke. I had seen him in court but, close to, the resemblance to his sister was even more striking: the same thin face with its hard lines of discontent and anger; the protuberant, glaring eyes, the tall, skinny body. Like the other men present he was dressed in a robe; in his case it was the dark green of a Guildhall employee, the badge of the City of London on his breast. He and Isabel exchanged a look of hatred, all the more intense somehow because it only lasted a second; then they both looked away.

The two experts, Masters Adam and Wulfsee, introduced themselves. Adam was a small, solidly plump man, with a ready smile. He
grinned cheerfully and grasped my hand. 'Well, sir,' he said, 'this is a
strange business.' He gave a little laugh. 'Interesting little set of papers
I read yesterday. Let's see if we can find some answers, eh?'

I could tell at once from his manner that Isabel had made the
wrong choice. Adam was clearly no sword-for-hire expert, but an
ordinary man, unaccustomed to testimony, who probably saw this
whole thing as an odd diversion from the daily grind. Wulfsee, however, Edward Cotterstoke's expert, was a tall man with a severe
manner and sharp eyes. I knew of him as a man who would argue a
technical point to death for his client, though he would never actually
lie.

Edward Cotterstoke looked at me, frowning, his back turned to
Isabel. 'Well, master lawyer,' he said in a dry, grating voice. 'Shall we
get this done? I have left my work at the Guildhall for this – nonsense.'
Isabel glared at his back, but did not speak.

The experts went over to the wall painting and looked it over with
professional interest. The servant, Vowell, had come in and stood
unobtrusively by the door, looking unhappily between Edward and
Isabel. It struck me that he probably knew as much of the family history as anyone.

The two men ran their practised hands gently over the painting
and the adjoining walls, talking quietly. Once, they nodded in agreement; this caused both Edward and Isabel to look anxious. Then
Adam, who had been bending to examine the flooring, got up,
brushed down his hose, then said, 'May we look at the room next
door?' Coleswyn and I exchanged a glance and nodded. The two men
went out. We heard the faint murmur of their voices from the next
room. In the parlour there was absolute silence, Isabel and Edward
still turned away from each other. Edward was looking at the wall
painting now, sadness in his eyes.

A few minutes later Wulfsee and Adam returned. 'We will prepare written reports, but I think Master Adam and I are in agreement,'

Wulfsee said, a triumphant glitter in his eye. 'This wall painting could not come down without irreparable damage to it. One can see from the room next door that the plaster in the wall has shrunk, leaving a distinct crack in the middle of the wall. It is barely visible from this side, though you can see it if you look closely. Were an attempt to be made to remove the wooden joists, the plaster would simply collapse. You agree, Master Adam?'

Adam looked at me, hesitated, then spread his hands apologetically. 'I do not see how anyone with knowledge of building work could think otherwise.' I heard a sharp indrawn breath from Isabel, and a nasty smirk appeared on Edward's face.

'See, we will show you,' Wulfsee said.

We all went through to the next room, where a fine crack was clearly visible on the wall. Going back to the parlour, looking very closely, we could see a faint line on this side too, under the paint. Edward smiled. 'There,' he said with satisfaction, 'the matter is settled.'

I looked again at the wall. Wulfsee, so far as I could tell, was right; an expert determined to make a fight of it might have blustered and prevaricated, but Adam was not like that. Coleswyn turned to me and said, 'It does seem so, Serjeant Shardlake. The wall painting was always intended to adorn the structure of the house, and can only exist as such. It must therefore be defined as a fixture.'

'I would like to peruse the experts' reports when they are prepared,' I said, to buy time. But I knew this was decisive. By insisting on an expert of her choice, Isabel had doomed her own case. Everyone, even Edward, looked at her. She stood like stone, gazing at the wall painting — so old and beautiful and fragile, that view across the years of her parents, her brother and herself. She had gone deathly pale with the news, but as I watched the colour rose until her normally papery face became scarlet. She pointed at poor Adam. 'What church do you attend?' she snapped.

He frowned, puzzled. 'I do not think that any of your business, madam.'

'Are you afraid to say?' Her voice was sharp as a file.

Edward intervened, throwing up a thin hand. 'Do not answer her, sir, she is not in her right wits.'

Isabel raised herself to her full height, still glaring at Adam. 'You do not answer, sir, but allow my brother to give you orders, though you are supposed to be acting for me. I have little doubt you are a heretic like my brother and his lawyer! You are all in league!'

Edward suddenly lost control. 'You are mad, Isabel!' he burst out. 'Truly mad! You have been since we were children, since you forced me—'

Vowell stepped quickly into the room, arms waving, so that everyone turned to look at him. 'Master! Mistress! Remember your mother and father – ' He was almost in tears. Edward stared at him, his mouth suddenly tight shut. Isabel, too, fell silent, taking long, deep breaths, but then continued, her tone quieter but still full of anger. 'I will find out, sir, I will discover whether you have associations with the heretics.' She pointed at Coleswyn. 'You and my brother are heretics; I know your priest has been under investigation by the Bishop, it is said he denied the body of Jesus Christ is present in the Mass!'

'Nothing was proven against him.' Coleswyn answered with dignity, though his voice shook with anger. 'I stand by all he has said.'

Edward gave Coleswyn an anxious glance. Isabel saw it and her eyes narrowed. 'I shall find out what he has said, mark that.'

Both Wulfsee and Adam were looking very uneasy at the turn the discussion had taken. Adam spoke, anxious now. 'I attend St Mary Aldgate, madam, and worship as the King commands. All know that.'

'You are an evil woman,' Edward Cotterstoke spat. 'You know what things I could say of you – '

Isabel looked at her brother fully in the face for the first time. 'And I of you,' she hissed. Brother and sister were glaring at each other now, eye to eye. Then Isabel turned and marched out of the house, slamming the door. I looked at the servant. Vowell stood clasping his hands, still near to tears.

Wulfsee and Adam bowed hastily to Coleswyn and me, then hastily followed Isabel out. I heard Master Adam say from the hall-way, 'By Mary, sir, I had no idea what I was getting into, coming here.'

Edward said, 'I shall leave too. Thank you, Master Coleswyn.' He looked troubled by his exchange with Isabel as he gave his lawyer a nod of thanks. He was shown out by Vowell, to whom neither he nor Isabel had spoken a word throughout. Coleswyn and I were left alone.

'I do not think you should have said what you did about your preacher,' I said quietly.

He looked shaken. 'I have never let someone provoke me like that before. Forgive me. It was unprofessional.'

'It was dangerous, sir. Your preacher, did he – ' I broke off as Vowell returned.

'Please, sirs,' the old servant said anxiously. 'I think it better you leave as well, if you would.'

He accompanied us to the door. I said, 'Thank you, Goodman Vowell.'

'And to think that this was once a happy house,' he replied, blink-ing tears from his eyes, then bowed and closed the door.

Coleswyn and I were left standing in the busy street, under the hot sun. He spoke quietly as we went round to the stables. 'My preacher has said nothing against the Mass.' He paused and added, 'In public.'

I did not ask, *And in private?* Instead I looked down at my feet, where two large black beetles were fighting in the dust, head to head. Philip said, 'How like our clients.'

'Yes,' I agreed. 'They snap at each other, but each is protected by a carapace.'

'But underneath there is softness, vulnerability, is there not? They are not hard right through.'

'Beetles, no. But some humans, I wonder.'

'After this morning, I would understand if you preferred not to come to dine tonight,' he said quietly.

'No, I will come.' To refuse the invitation now struck me as ungentlemanly, cowardly, especially after the insults he had borne from my client. Obstinacy, too, would not allow me to let that poisonous woman determine whom I saw socially. 'You said nothing actionable,' I added reassuringly. 'Only that you agreed with your preacher. Mistress Slanning was merely looking for a stick to beat you with.'

'Yes,' he said.

'I must return to chambers now.'

'And I have to visit a client near the river.'

As I rode away I could not help but wonder whether Coleswyn's preacher had said something dangerous to the wrong person, or whether Isabel was merely repeating gossip. I reminded myself the man had only been investigated, not prosecuted.

✝

I RODE BACK TO Lincoln's Inn. Genesis trotted along slowly. I thought how with his increasingly bony face and stiff whiskers he was starting to resemble a little old man, though mercifully a good-natured one. I remembered Isabel and Edward shouting about the things they could say about each other. What had they meant? I recalled again what Isabel had said to me in chambers: 'If you knew the terrible things my brother has done.' And Vowell, the servant whom they had otherwise ignored, intervening as though to stop them saying too much. Edward had said his sister was not in her right wits, and neither sibling had seemed entirely sane that morning. I hoped my client could now be made to accept that she could not win her case, but I doubted it.

I half expected her to be at chambers when I arrived, ready for a fight, but all was quiet. Barak was making notes on some new cases to be heard at the Court of Requests when the Michaelmas term began in September.

'What happened at the inspection?' he asked eagerly.

'The experts agreed that any attempt to remove the wall painting will make the plaster collapse.'

'That's it then? We'll never have to see that woman's sour face again?'

'Oh, I think we will. She stormed out in high dudgeon; but somehow I suspect she'll present herself here soon, probably today.'

Barak nodded to where Nicholas sat copying out a conveyance. 'He has some news for you. Won't tell me what it is. Been looking like the cat that got the cream.'

Nicholas stood. There was indeed a self-satisfied expression on the boy's freckled face. 'Come through,' I said. As Nicholas followed me to my office I saw Barak frown and Skelly smile quietly to himself. Barak indeed seemed jealous of my involving my pupil in a mission from which he himself was excluded. I felt a momentary annoyance. I was only protecting him; Tamasin would skin him alive if she suspected I had involved him in court politics again, as well he knew.

I closed the door. 'What is it?' I asked Nicholas. 'News of that sleeve?'

'It is, sir.' He removed the silk carefully from his pocket and laid it on the desk with his long, slim hands. 'The second embroiderer I visited today recognized it instantly. He sewed the shirt for a client. Mention of Master Gullym's name did the trick; the embroiderer knows him. He looked at his records. The shirt was made for a gentleman called Charles Stice. He gave me an address, down by Smithfield.'

'Well done,' I said.

'There's more. I noticed he wrinkled his nose when he spoke of Stice, so I asked what he was like. He said Stice was one of those young men who come into money or position and put on haughty airs.' Nicholas was finding it hard to keep the excitement from his voice. 'But here's the thing, sir. Charles Stice is a tall, brown-haired young man with half an ear missing. Looked like he got the injury from a knife or a sword in a fight, the man said.'

I looked again at the little, ragged piece of silk. Nicholas said, 'So this was left not by the men who killed Greening, but by those who fled into the garden after young Elias discovered them trying to break in earlier. They escaped the same way.'

I thought, and this Charles Stice was the man who had tried to suborn the Queen's page, young Garet. 'You have done well,

Nicholas. Very well.' I looked at him seriously. 'But leave the matter with me now. This man is dangerous.'

Nicholas looked disappointed. 'Will you arrange for him to be found?'

'This afternoon.' I must get the news to Lord Parr.

There was a gentle knock on the door, and Skelly entered. He spoke apologetically. 'A visitor, sir. Will not wait. Must see you immediately.'

I smiled wryly at Nicholas. 'Mistress Slanning?'

'No, sir. It is a man called Okedene. He says he is a printer, that he knows you, and that it is a matter of life and death.'

Chapter Twenty

S KELLY SHOWED OKEDENE IN. He wore a light wool doublet and his face was red and sweating, as though he had been running. As Skelly closed the door behind him I saw Barak looking in at us curiously. I stood. 'Master Okedene, what is it?' I wondered with a thrill of horror whether, as I had feared might happen, he or his family had been attacked.

The printer slowly regained his composure. The constant physical activity of his trade meant he had to be fit, but he was not young any more. 'Master Shardlake,' he said quickly, 'I've come to see you about that note you sent. To tell you I am leaving London. I am selling the business and putting the proceeds into my brother's farm, out in Norfolk. I have feared for my wife and children since the night poor Armistead was murdered.' He frowned at Nicholas, doubtless remembering his part in provoking Elias's flight. He did not know his former apprentice was dead.

'I am sorry,' I said. I saw how the lines of strain and worry on his face had deepened since we last met.

He raised a hand. 'Never mind that now,' he said. 'There is no time.'

'No time for what?' Nicholas asked.

'I stopped on the way here to buy a glass of beer – I was thirsty, it is a warm day. At the sign of Bacchus near St Paul's. It is a big inn – '

'I have been there,' I said.

'Inside, I saw two men sitting at a table by the window. I am sure it was the men who killed Armistead, even though they were wearing gentlemen's clothes today; the Bacchus is a respectable place.' He took another deep breath. 'I have never been able to get my old assistant Huffkyn's description of them out of my mind. Two young men, both big and tall, one fair and with a wart on his brow and the other near bald, young as he is. I have feared to see them ever since. Those murderers,' he added bitterly, 'sitting quietly supping beer in full view of everyone.' He looked from me to Nicholas, then squared his shoulders. 'I ran all the way here. The inn is less than fifteen minutes if we go fast.'

Nicholas said, 'The authorities—'

'There is no time, boy!' Okedene snapped. 'They must be taken before they leave. A citizen's arrest!' I saw he was eager to take the chance to capture Greening's killers himself, and perhaps to lift the cloud of worry from his family. 'Master Shardlake, have you any other people here who could help us?' he asked. 'Perhaps that bearded man in your outer office?'

I sighed. Okedene was right, this might be our only chance. But these were killers, young, fit men, experienced in violence. Nicholas might give a good account of himself but Okedene was no youngster, while I would be of little use in a fight. Nor would Skelly. That left Barak, whom I had sworn to involve no further. But here was a chance to take the killers, present them to Lord Parr myself. Nicholas and Okedene looked on impatiently as I considered. Then I crossed to the door and asked Barak to join us. He rose from his desk, an odd mixture of anticipation and reluctance flashing across his face.

I explained that Master Okedene had been a witness to the murder I was investigating, and he had just seen the killers at the Bacchus Inn. I said, 'These are dangerous fellows. I doubt we could take them without you. I've no right to ask you to come, and if you say no, I'll understand.'

Barak took a long, deep breath. 'Is this connected with the — other matter? With Baynard's Castle?'

I nodded slowly. 'This may be our one chance to settle both matters.'

Barak bit his lip. Through his shirt he fingered his father's old

Jewish mezuzah, which he wore round his neck as constantly as the Queen had worn the key round hers. Then he said, 'Have we weapons enough? Young Nick wore his sword into work today, showing off as usual. I have a good knife.'

'And I,' Okedene said.

'Mine is somewhere,' I said.

'Then let's go,' Barak said. 'I've been out of things a while, but I haven't forgotten how to fight.'

✝

AN ILL-ASSORTED quartet, we made our way along Fleet Street under a hot mid-morning sun, and under the city wall at Newgate. Skelly had stared as we left; Barak told him cheerfully that if Mistress Slanning called she was to be requested kindly to go and boil her head in a pot. Nicholas loped along, hand on his sword, eyes agleam, clearly looking forward to the fray. There was a reassurance in the presence of his weapon, which I knew Nicholas took pains to keep well-sharpened. But the men we would face were dangerous. I dreaded the thought of anything happening to Nicholas or to Barak, who was stepping along purposefully, his face set and watchful. Okedene and I had to hurry to keep up with them both.

'What's the layout of this place?' Barak asked Okedene.

'A door from the street, one big room with tables inside, a serving hatch with the kitchen behind. They serve food as well as drink. There's a door to a little garden at the rear, with more tables.'

'There'll be one to the kitchens too,' Barak said. 'Where are they sitting?'

'At a table in an alcove by the window.'

'Good,' Nicholas said. 'Then we can surround them, cut off any escape.'

Barak nodded approvingly. 'Well done, boy.'

'My swordsmanship teacher was a soldier in the French wars in the twenties. He always said, knowing the ground is essential in a fight.'

'He was right.'

Okedene looked at Barak curiously. 'You have much knowledge of such matters for a law clerk.'

Barak glanced at me. 'Wasn't always a law clerk, was I?'

We arrived at the Bacchus. It was one of the respectable London taverns where travellers stayed, and families of the middling sort sometimes went for weekend meals or celebrations. Through the open shutters we could see two men sitting at a big round table in the window, heads together, deep in conversation. As Okedene had said, they answered Huffkyn's description exactly. Both wore good clothes, slashed doublets and shirts, lace collars showing. Like Stice at the first attack on Greening, these two had pretended to be poor men when they went out set on murder.

It was a slack time of day, with only a few other people sitting at tables – tradesmen discussing business, by the look of them.

'Are you sure it's them?' I asked Okedene.

'Huffkyn's description is etched in my mind.'

Barak said, 'Did you notice if they have swords?'

'I didn't see. I didn't like to watch too long. They could have them under the table.'

'They're wearing gentlemen's clothes,' Nicholas said. 'They're entitled to carry swords.'

Barak looked at him seriously. 'Then you may need to use yours, Nicky boy. And these fellows may dress well now, but they won't act like young gentlemen in combat. You ready?'

'Ready and able,' he answered haughtily.

'I doubt the clientele will interfere,' Barak said. 'They'll all be scared shitless.'

I took a deep breath, fingering the knife at my belt. 'Come on, then.'

✞

WE STEPPED OVER THE THRESHOLD, into a smell of beer and pottage. One or two people glanced at my lawyer's robe, which I had kept on to lend our group an air of authority. We walked straight to the table where the two young men sat in the alcove, still talking intently. My heart pounded. Both, I saw, indeed had swords in their scabbards, lying on the benches beside them. As we approached I thought I heard the bald man mention the name Bertano.

The two broke off their talk and looked sharply up at us; hard, hostile faces. The bald one was in his late twenties, large, well-built and handsome, but with more than a touch of cruelty round the fleshy mouth. The fair one with the wart on his brow had narrow, greyhound-like features, and his expression held the same cold intensity as a hunting dog's.

Loudly enough for the other patrons to hear, I said, 'Gentlemen, we are making a citizen's arrest upon you, for the murder of Armistead Greening on the tenth of this month.'

The fair man tensed, his eyes narrowing to slits, but the bald fellow looked at us with large, unreadable brown eyes, and then laughed. 'Are you mad?' he asked.

'That we aren't,' Okedene said, raising his knife. 'You were seen running with a bloody club from Armistead Greening's workshop after killing him.'

There was a murmur of voices from the other tables. A couple got up hastily and left.

'You're not the authorities,' the fair man growled.

'We do not need to be,' Nicholas answered, putting his hand to his sword. 'Not for a citizen's arrest.'

The bald man laughed. 'What are you, a law student, by your little robe? Scratchy clerks come to arrest us?'

I said, 'I am Matthew Shardlake, Serjeant at Law, charged by the victim's family with investigating the murder under the coroner.'

The two glanced at each other, and I realized with a shiver that they had recognized my name. They looked over our little group more closely, weighing us up. The fair-haired man quietly slipped the hand furthest from us towards his sword, then jerked back as Nicholas swept his own sword from its scabbard and pointed it at the man's throat, a glint of sunlight on the razor-sharp edge. 'Don't dare move, churl,' he said, 'or I'll slit you. Hands on the table.' I had wondered whether, when it came to it, Nicholas's bravado would be matched by action. Now I knew.

The fair man sat stock-still. He looked at me, eyes boring into mine. 'You'd do best to let us go,' he said very quietly, 'or there'll be big trouble from those above us. You've no idea who you're dealing with, hunchback.'

'I can make a guess,' I said, thinking of Richard Rich. 'In any case, you're under arrest.'

Both men were looking at me now. With his right hand Barak reached swiftly under the table on the bald man's side, his left holding the knife on the table. 'I'll take your sword, matey,' he said.

Then, so quickly I could not follow with my eyes, the man pulled a knife from his belt and stabbed it straight through the muscle between the first two fingers of Barak's left hand, pinning it to the table. Barak yelled and dropped his knife with a clatter. Nicholas turned instinctively, and the narrow-faced man pushed his sword arm away with one hand, grabbing his own from under the bench with the other and slashing at Nicholas with it.

Both had moved with astonishing speed, and for a terrible second I thought Nicholas was lost, but he had raised his own sword in time to parry. Barak, meanwhile, reached for the knife pinning his hand to the table and, with another yell, managed to pull it out. Blood welled up. At the same moment the bald man reached for his sword, but Okedene, who had brought out his own knife, thrust it to the hilt into his shoulder. Quickly I pulled out my own weapon and held it to his throat. Barak could do no more than clutch at his hand.

For a moment I thought we had won, for Nicholas seemed to have the fair man at a disadvantage trying to fight from behind the table. But then with his free hand he reached down and grasped the table's underside. Despite his slim build he was strong, for he managed to tip the table right over on us, sending pewter tankards flying. Nicholas, staggering back, dropped his sword. The fair man slashed at him, catching him on the chest so that blood gushed out. Okedene, caught by the table, fell over with a yell. The fair-haired man jumped from the alcove. His companion, clutching at his shoulder, reached down with his free hand and took up Nicholas's sword.

Both made for the door, the fair man slashing at a potman who stood gaping at the scene; he jumped back frantically and a woman screamed. The two men turned in the doorway, menacing us with their swords for a moment, the face of the dark-haired man white with pain, Okedene's knife still in his shoulder. Then they turned and ran. I stood looking after them. There was nothing I could do alone. Barak and Nicholas were both hurt, though thank heaven not severely, and Okedene was only now stumbling to his feet, pale and groaning.

The innkeeper appeared with two assistants, each bearing a cudgel. 'What the hell's going on?' he asked angrily. 'Fighting and near murder in my inn. I'll have the constable on you!'

'Didn't you hear us say we were trying to arrest two murderers?' I shouted with sudden violence. I took a deep breath and swallowed, for what had happened must have terrified both staff and patrons. I took out my purse and produced a sovereign – one of those Bealknap had given me. I held it up.

'This should more than cover your trouble.'

The innkeeper looked at it hungrily.

I said, 'It's yours if you answer a couple of questions. Have these men been here before?'

'A few times these last weeks. They always sit talking in that corner after ordering something to eat. And I know their names; I remember because once a man came for them, a messenger from some-where. He asked if Master Daniels and Master Cardmaker were here. Said it was urgent. Then he saw them sitting in the alcove and went over to them. I didn't like the look of them. An innkeeper knows when people may be trouble. By Mary, I was right there,' he added bitterly, looking at the overturned table, the spilled beer on the floor, the deserted room. A few frightened faces peered in from the garden.

I took a deep breath. Learning their names like this was a great piece of luck, though it did not make up for the fact we had lost them, and that Barak and Nicholas had been hurt. I wondered, who had sent that messenger?

'Thank you,' I said. 'We'll go.' Barak was sitting down, his face white, wrapping his hand tightly with a handkerchief. Nicholas had undone his shirt, revealing a pale but muscular torso. To my relief he had suffered no more than a superficial cut. Colour was returning to Okedene's face.

'I must take you and Nicholas to Guy at once,' I told Barak.

'How the fuck am I going to explain *this* to Tammy?' he said thickly.

I helped him to the door. Outside I turned to Okedene. 'Sir, will you come with us?'

The printer shook his head. 'No, Master Shardlake, and I will have no more of this business. I should never have come to you. I will hasten with the sale of my printworks. Thank you for your care in sending that note, but please let us alone now.' He looked again at my injured companions, then walked slowly away.

Chapter Twenty-one

MERCIFULLY, GUY WAS AT HOME. His assistant, Francis, looked astonished when I appeared on the doorstep with two men who were both bleeding profusely. 'Robbers attacked us,' I lied. Francis hurried us through to Guy's consulting room, where he was mixing herbs. 'By Mary!' he cried. 'What has happened?'

I watched anxiously as he examined Nicholas and Barak. Nicholas's chest wound required only a couple of stitches, which he bore well, biting his tongue as Guy sewed. Then he carefully examined Barak's left hand. 'Thank heaven it was a narrow knife,' he said, 'and went through the fleshy part between the long bones of your fingers. But it will require stitching, and lavender and other oils to stop the wound becoming poisoned.'

Nicholas frowned. 'I thought wine was best to clear wounds.'

'Lavender is better. Though it stings. And a bandage.' Guy looked at Barak seriously. 'You will have to wear it for a week, and have it changed regularly. You are right-handed, aren't you?'

'Yes,' said Barak. 'God's wounds, it hurts.'

'It will. But with luck, there should be no damage save a little stiffness.'

Barak turned to Nicholas and me. 'You'll both be seeing Tamasin at George's birthday celebration in a few days. I'll make something up. We'll discuss the details later, to make sure everyone has them right. I'll tell her it was an accident at work. I don't want her catching you out.'

'Surely your wife will believe you?' Nicholas said, surprised.

'Don't bank on it, lad.'

Guy said, 'This is not the first time your master has brought Jack Barak here to be tidied up after – an incident of violence, shall we say. And Jack has brought your master, too.' Guy's tone was severe, but Nicholas looked at me with new respect.

I said, 'May I leave them with you, Guy? I am sorry, but I have an important appointment and I fear I will be late.' On the way I had seen the hand on a church clock showing near eleven.

He nodded agreement. 'A word, though, Matthew, if you please. I will see you out.' His mouth was set, his dark face troubled and angry.

Outside he spoke quietly. 'So, it was not a robbery.' He shook his head. 'Again you bring Jack to me after a dangerous encounter, married with a child and with Tamasin pregnant again. And this boy as well.'

'I am investigating a murder,' I answered. 'A pair of rogues who bludgeoned two innocent men to death. They were seen in a tavern, by a witness who brought the news to me at Lincoln's Inn. It was a chance, perhaps the only chance, to take them. Jack and Nicholas knew there was danger.'

'Did you take these killers?'

I shook my head angrily. 'No, they were experienced fighters. They got away.'

'Matthew,' Guy said, 'you ever follow danger. But now this boy, and Jack. Jack is no longer so young, and used to a quieter life now.'

I ran a hand across my brow. 'I know, I know. But it was my only chance to bring two murderers to justice.' I stared at my old friend defiantly. 'And perhaps stop them killing again.'

'You indicated when we last met that you were involved in something secret, the details of which it would be dangerous for others to know.'

'Yes.'

He inclined his head to the consulting room door. 'Have you made Jack and that boy aware of those details?'

I shook my head.

'Then you should not have involved them,' Guy said. 'I am sorry, but that is what I think.' He looked at me sharply. 'Is it something to do with the Queen?'

'What makes you ask that?'

'I see from your expression that it is. I know you have ever had an immoderate affection for her. I have seen your troubled looks these last months, worrying about her travails. But you should not let it place you in danger – and still less those who work for you.'

'Why?' I answered sharply. 'Because you think her a heretic?'

'No,' he snapped back. 'Because she is the Queen, and because, as you yourself said, thunder circles around thrones. Certainly this King's throne,' he added bitterly. I did not answer. 'Is this man Bertano you asked me about part of it?' he asked.

I remembered Daniels and Cardmaker mentioning his name back at the inn. I said seriously, 'Keep that name close, Guy, as you value your safety.'

He smiled wryly. 'See, you have even involved me in a small way. Think on my words, Matthew. I do not want to have to treat Barak or Nicholas again, and for something worse. Nor you,' he added in a gentler tone.

☩

I HURRIED TO THE TOWER, my mind full of conflict. Guy was right: it was my own feelings for the Queen that had set me on this path, trailing danger in my wake like the bad humours of an illness. But I could not just step aside now, even if I wanted to. Those two men at the inn had known my name.

Tower Hill rose ahead of me, where Lord Cromwell and so many others had died; and beyond, the Tower of London: the moat, the high white walls and there, the huge square bulk of the White Tower, where the conspiracy between Rich and Bealknap five years before had resulted in my briefly being held prisoner in its terrible dungeons.

I saw Lord Parr was already waiting outside the Middle Tower gate, on horseback. To my surprise young William Cecil sat on another horse beside him, two servants in Queen's livery holding the reins. Cecil was dressed in his lawyer's robe, and Lord Parr wore a light doublet, green and slashed at the shoulder to show the crimson silk lining. He sniffed at a pomander that hung by a gold chain from his neck, to ward off the stink from the moat.

'Matthew!' It was the first time he had greeted me by my Christian name, his tone much more civil than when we had last met. 'I brought Master Cecil with me, so that we might exchange news.'

'My Lord, I am sorry I am late, but I have just had an encounter with the men who killed Greening – '

He leaned forward in his saddle. 'Are they caught?' he asked eagerly.

'No, but Barak and my pupil were injured in the attempt. I had to get them medical attention.'

'Tell me what happened.'

I glanced at Cecil. 'William knows all,' Lord Parr said. 'Including about the *Lamentation*. The Queen and I agree he can be trusted, and he has already organized enquiries among the radicals, and agents at the docks.'

I looked at Cecil. Trusted indeed, I thought. I told them about our encounter with Daniels and Cardmaker, that the two seemed to know my name and had, I was sure, mentioned the name Bertano. I also told them Nicholas had identified the torn sleeve as belonging to one Charles Stice, who, from the description of his damaged ear, had been involved in the first attack on Greening, and the attempt to suborn the young page Garet.

Cecil said, 'I have made less progress, I fear. No sign of Greening's three vanished friends, nor the guard Leeman. And though all four have friends among the religious radicals, none are part of any known group. I think Greening and the rest set up their own little circle.'

'I think that may be right,' I agreed.

Lord Parr grunted. 'God knows there are enough of those springing up, even under Gardiner's nose. Maybe even Anabaptists. We know that one of the men is Dutch, and it is from there and from Germany that those wretched people come.'

'What about Bertano?' I asked Lord Parr.

'The name is not known in the Italian merchant community. They all have to be registered, and this name is not on the list.'

'He could have slipped into the country,' Cecil observed.

'Possibly.' Lord Parr shook his head. 'Or he may not be in England at all.' He looked across at the Tower. 'Well, Matthew, we must go in. They will take the horses at the gate. We are late enough already.' He turned to Cecil. 'There, William: Shardlake has another three names for you to investigate. Daniels, Cardmaker, Stice.' He inclined his head. 'But quietly.'

The young lawyer nodded gravely, then rode away. Lord Parr stroked his beard. 'There's a clever fellow,' he said quietly. 'And discreet.'

'You have told him everything?'

'Yes, the Queen approved it after meeting him. She took to him very much.' I felt an absurd pang of jealousy. Lord Parr watched Cecil's retreating figure. 'He is ambitious. If we succeed in this, it may be a stepping stone for him. Of course, there is religious principle involved for him as well. If we do not succeed, however,' he added bleakly, 'and the book is published for the King to see, all of us may be in dire straits.'

✠

THE GUARD AT THE Tower gate saluted Lord Parr. His horse was taken to the stable, and we walked across Tower Green.

'No word of the *Lamentation*, then?' I asked.

'No. More than two weeks now since it was taken. I tell the Queen that each passing day makes it less likely it will appear on the streets, but she does not believe it.' He gave a quick bark of laughter. 'Nor, in truth, do I. These men you encountered,' he continued. 'One said you did not know who you were dealing with. Implying it was somebody senior. And you said earlier you thought Sir Richard Rich might be involved?'

'Possibly.'

'There are so many possibilities: Norfolk, Gardiner, Paget, acting alone or in concert; perhaps someone else – ' He shook his head. 'But no, not Paget; he always works strictly to the King's orders.'

'Are you sure, my Lord? Wolsey and Cromwell did so at first, but later . . .'

He pursed his lips. 'You are right. We cannot be entirely sure of anything in these whirling days.'

'It still concerns me, my Lord, that when Jane Fool arrived to be questioned, the Lady Mary appeared with her.'

'That was just unfortunate.'

'I wondered whether it might be something more. Is Jane truly a woman of little wit, or could she be acting, concealing her true intelligence?'

Lord Parr shook his head. 'She is a mere idiot, of that I am sure. I cannot see her deceiving her mistress about that; you know how shrewd the Queen is. In any event she did not let Jane anywhere near that manuscript.'

'The Lady Elizabeth seemed not to like Jane Fool.'

He snorted. 'The Lady Elizabeth does not like a lot of people. Particularly anyone who upstages her with the Queen.'

✝

WE WERE APPROACHING the White Tower. Lord Parr had slowed down, and I noticed a faint sheen of perspiration on his forehead. I remembered his age, his remarks about his health. He looked at me, then said uncomfortably, 'I am sorry I was short with you when we last met. This business is a great strain.'

'I understand, my Lord. Thank you.' I realized it could not come easily to one of Lord Parr's rank and temperament to apologize to an underling.

He nodded brusquely, then looked towards the Tower. 'As I told you, Sir Edmund Walsingham used to be the Queen's Vice-Chancellor, and he is an old friend.' I thought, among the high ones of the realm everyone knows everyone, and they are either a friend or an enemy. 'I am going to tell him you have acted for my wife's family, and have a case coming up involving a witness who claims he was being questioned in the Tower sometime between – let us pick a broad range of dates – June the twentieth and July the fifth. We will say that you do not believe this man was in the Tower at all, that in fact he was up to mischief elsewhere.'

'I understand,' I said, uncomfortable at the thought of lying so blatantly to the Constable of the Tower.

'We will say that you wish to check the names of men imprisoned there between those dates,' Lord Parr continued. 'There have been plenty in and out these last few months and if I vouch for you I think Sir Edmund will let you see the records. Could you do that? Then try to find out who was on guard duty when Anne Askew was tortured. That was around June the thirtieth. The news of her torture was leaked the same day.'

'Very well.' The eviction which Coleswyn and I had witnessed that morning suddenly came back to mind. 'I could say the man concerned is trying to give himself an alibi for being part of a group of men who evicted a tenant without due process.'

'A landlord? Yes, you work at the Court of Requests, don't you?' he added, a little superciliously. 'Very well. But on no account mention Anne Askew. I do not wish to draw his mind to that.'

There was a sudden loud roar from the Tower menagerie, probably a lion. Lord Parr smiled. 'I hear they have a new creature there from Africa, an animal something like a horse but with an absurdly long and thin neck. I may ask Sir Edmund to let me see it.'

✝

WE ENTERED THE WHITE TOWER. A guard took us through the Great Hall, where as ever soldiers stood or sat talking and playing cards. At the far end, I recognized the door leading down to the dungeons.

We were led upstairs, along a corridor with rush matting that deadened the sound of our footsteps. We entered a spacious room where a man a little younger than Lord Parr, with white hair and a lined face ending in a long pointed beard, rose to receive us. There was another man standing by the desk, slightly younger, with grizzled hair and beard and a soldierly air. I bowed low to them, while Lord Parr shook hands.

'Sir Edmund,' Lord Parr said lightly. 'I have not seen you for months. And Sir Anthony Knevet, Master Lieutenant of the Tower, God give you good morrow.'

'And you, my Lord. If you will excuse me – ' the soldierly man tapped a folder of papers under his arm – 'I am due to present a report to Master Secretary Paget at Whitehall.'

'Then we will not detain you.' There was a note of annoyance in Walsingham's voice. The other man bowed and left.

Walsingham gestured for us to sit. Taking a chair, Lord Parr said, 'There are a couple of small matters from your time in charge of the Queen's household which I need to ask you about; I would have written, but thought to take the opportunity to visit you, now the Court is at Whitehall.'

'I am glad you have. This has been a busy few months at the Tower.' Walsingham raised his eyebrows knowingly.

'Does not Sir Anthony Knevet do most of the day-to-day work?'

'Yes, but the ultimate responsibility remains mine. And Sir Anthony has been sticking his nose into one or two places he should not have – ' Sir Edmund broke off, waved a hand dismissively, then changed the subject. 'How go things in her majesty's household?'

'Easier recently,' Lord Parr answered carefully. 'How is your family? Your clever nephew Francis?'

'He is at Cambridge now. Growing up fast,' Walsingham added sadly. 'Reminds me I grow old. I have felt my age these last months.'

'I too,' Lord Parr said feelingly. 'In time of age the humours alter and slow, do they not?' He continued casually, 'Sir Edmund, I crave a small favour. Serjeant Shardlake here is a barrister to the Court of Requests, who has also acted for my wife; he has a case coming on at Michaelmas where the Tower records may shed light on something.'

Walsingham looked at me. 'Oh?'

Lord Parr recounted the story of the fictional witness. Sir Edmund looked at me, his gaze keen from small tired eyes. 'Between June the twentieth and July the fifth, you say?' He grunted, looking at me. 'You know who was here then?'

I paused a moment, as though trying to remember. 'Anne Askew?'

'Just so. Not so many others, the heat was dying down by then.' He grimaced. 'Though not for her.' He looked at Lord Parr. 'You vouch for him?'

'I do.'

Walsingham turned back to me. 'Who was this witness?'

I spoke the first name that came to me. 'Cotterstoke. Edward Cotterstoke.'

Sir Edmund shook his head. 'I don't remember that name. But you can go down to the cells and look at the records, seeing as Lord Parr vouches for you.' He laughed abruptly. 'Don't look like that, master lawyer. I won't detain you down there.'

Lord Parr laughed too. 'Sir Edmund is doing you a favour, Matthew,' he said chidingly. 'Officially those documents are not for the public to see.'

'I am sorry, Sir Edmund. I am grateful.'

The Constable laughed scoffingly. 'Well, it shows the mere name of the Tower dungeons puts people in fear, which is partly what they're for.' He scribbled a quick note, then rang a bell on his desk. As a guard appeared, Sir Edmund said, 'Take this lawyer to the cells to see the record of prisoners between June the twentieth and July the fifth. See he writes nothing down.' He gave me a look of amused contempt. 'And bring him safely back here afterwards.'

✞

THE GUARD LED ME downstairs again, across the main hall. He was a big fellow in his thirties, with a heavy limp. Like Sir Edmund he seemed to take my apprehensive stare at the door as commonplace. 'Looking for a name, are you, sir?' he asked.

'Yes, a witness in a case who says he was questioned in the Tower.
I think he is lying.'

'A strange lie.'

'He probably thought I would be unable to make a check here.'

The guard winced. 'May I stop just a moment, sir? My leg pains
me.'

'Of course.'

'A Frenchie soldier ran it through with a half-pike in Boulogne
last year.'

'I am sorry. I know it was a fierce campaign.'

'They gave me this job afterwards. I won't be going soldiering
again. I'm all right to go on now, sir, thank you.'

The door was opened by a guard and we walked down that dreadful stone staircase, slick with green algae once we passed under the
level of the river. The light came now from torches, stinking with
smoke. At the bottom was a barred door which I remembered. My
escort called out and a hard, unshaven face appeared behind the bars.

'Yes, sir?'

'This gentleman has permission to look at the log.' Sir Edmund's
note was passed through the bars. The man on the other side looked at
it, then closely at me, before turning back to my escort.

'You're to wait and take him back?'

'Yes.'

There was a clank of keys, and the heavy door opened. I went
through, into a stink of damp, and entered a long vestibule with bare
ancient stone walls, a row of cells with barred windows along its
length. It was cold down here, even in high summer. I observed —
strange the things one notices at such times — that the layout of the
central vestibule had been changed: the desk which was its only furniture was larger than the one that had stood there five years ago, and
had been positioned against the wall to allow more space for people to
pass. It was covered in papers and a man sat behind it. I saw a large
open ledger.

The guard who had let me in looked me up and down. 'Your purpose, sir?' he asked in a voice which was quiet but not respectful.

'Matthew Shardlake, Serjeant at Law.' I told him the story of the dubious witness. Lying was not easy under his hard, watchful eyes.

'Well, if Sir Edmund agrees,' he said reluctantly. 'But you're to write nothing down, only look through quickly for the name you seek.'

'I understand.'

'My name is Ardengast. I am in charge here.'

Without further comment he led me to the desk. The man sitting behind it was a big, middle-aged fellow in a leather jacket, with an untidy straggling beard. He sat up straight as we approached. Ardengast said, 'This man is to see the logs from June the twentieth to July the fifth, Howitson. Looking for a witness in a case.'

The man in the leather jacket frowned. 'It's not to do with——?'

'No. Some law matter.' Ardengast waved dismissively. He glanced again at Walsingham's note. 'The name is Edward Cotterstoke. I don't remember him.'

'Nor I.'

'That is the point,' I said. 'I think he was lying about being here.'

Ardengast turned to me. 'I'll leave you with Howitson, I've got business.' He walked away, unlocked a door at the far end of the chamber, and passed through. From somewhere beyond I thought I heard a distant scream. I looked through the dark barred windows on the doors of the cells. They seemed empty, but who knew what pitiful souls and broken bodies lay within? I thought of Anne Askew alone and terrified in this place.

Howitson pulled the big ledger over to him. I saw there were two columns. One gave the times that prisoners arrived and left and their names, while the other, smaller column was for the signatures of the officers on duty. The writing was poor, scrawled, and I could not read it upside down. Howitson turned over several pages, pausing occasionally to lick his black-stained thumb. Then he leaned back in his chair.

'No one here called Cotterstoke, sir. I thought as much.' He looked up with a satisfied smile.

'Good,' I said. 'I suspected the witness was lying. However, I will have to see the book myself. The rules of court require me to testify to what I have seen personally. Simply to repeat what another has told me would be what is called hearsay, and thus inadmissible.'

Howitson frowned. 'I don't know about legal rules. But that book is confidential.'

'I know. And I will only testify that this particular name is *not* there, nothing else.' He still looked doubtful. 'It is the law,' I said. 'Sir Edmund said I could see the book.'

'We have our own laws down here, *sir*.' He smiled a little menacingly, an insolent emphasis on the last word.

'I understand, goodman. If you like I can ask Sir Edmund to be more specific, in writing, to satisfy you.'

Howitson grunted. 'All right, but be quick. No lingering over names. We've had enough rumours getting out of this place.'

'I understand.'

He turned the ledger round, going back a couple of pages. I ran my eyes quickly over the entries for late June; I was not interested in those. I noticed, however, that there were always two officers present to sign a prisoner in; one was usually Howitson, the other presumably whichever guard was on duty. From the 28th of June a signature more legible than the others began appearing during the afternoons. Thomas Myldmore. He was on duty when 'Mistress Anne Kyme', Anne Askew's married name, appeared on the record.

Howitson brought his big heavy hand down on the ledger. 'That's it, sir,' he said officiously.

'Thank you. I have seen all I need.'

I stepped away from the desk. As I did so the door at the end of the passage opened again and two men appeared. One was older, wearing an apron darkly stained with I knew not what. The other was young, small and thin, with dark blond hair and an oval face unsuited to the pointed beard he wore. I noticed his shoulders were slumped.

The older man began undoing the buckles on his apron, paying me no heed, but when the younger one saw me standing over the ledger his grey eyes widened a little. He came across. Howitson closed the book with a thump and gave the newcomer a glare.

'I'm going off duty now, Master Howitson,' the young man said in a surprisingly deep voice.

'Thank Sir Anthony Knevet you've still got a duty to be *going* off,' Howitson muttered. The young man looked at my lawyer's coif and robe. 'Is there a problem with the book?' he asked hesitantly.

'Nothing to concern you, Myldmore,' Howitson said. 'Don't recall anyone by the name of Cotterstoke, do you, being here late June or early July?'

'No, sir.'

'There you are then, sir,' Howitson said to me triumphantly.

'Then I thank you, sir,' I said with a little bow. I looked at Myldmore. His eyes were wide, burning yet frightened. 'Good day, fellow,' I said and headed for the door, where the veteran stood leaning against the wall outside, gently massaging his leg.

✝

THE GUARD LED ME back to Sir Edmund's room where he and Lord Parr were talking and laughing, drinking wine. I heard Sir Edmund say, 'The first time I saw a woman in one of these farthingales, I couldn't believe it. Waist braced with corsets so tight it looked like you could span it with your hands, and the wide skirt with those hoops underneath – '

'Ay, like barrels – ' Lord Parr looked round as I entered, instantly alert. 'Find your man, Shardlake?'

'His name was not there, my Lord, as I suspected. I thank you, Sir Edmund.'

Walsingham was in a relaxed mood now. 'Will you stay for some wine?'

'I fear I cannot. I have much to do. But I am most grateful to you.'

'Perhaps I should come with you, Shardlake,' Lord Parr said. He would want to know what I had found out.

Sir Edmund protested. 'No, no, my Lord, you have hardly got here – '

Lord Parr looked between us. Clearly he thought it might look suspicious if he left so soon. He said, 'One more drink, then, Edmund. Forgive me, though, I must go to the jakes. Master Shardlake, can you help me?' He made a show of finding it difficult to stand.

'You cannot take your wine any more, my Lord,' Sir Edmund called after him teasingly.

Once the door closed behind us, Lord Parr was instantly alert. 'Well?' he asked impatiently.

'The man who was most often on duty when Anne Askew was here is called Myldmore. I saw him; he looked anxious and seemed in bad odour with the fellow at the desk.'

Lord Parr smiled and nodded. 'Another name for Cecil to investigate. I wonder if he is connected with the others.' He clapped me on the shoulder. 'You are a good fellow, Master Shardlake, for all your long face and – well, never mind.' He spoke with sudden passion. 'We shall have them, end this game of hoodman blind, and unmask who is at the bottom of it all. I shall be in touch very soon. Good man.'

He went down the corridor, leaving me to walk, as fast as I could, towards the exit and the Tower gates.

Chapter Twenty-two

I WALKED SLOWLY home. It had been a long day, even by the standards of this last week. I was utterly weary. It was still afternoon, but the shadows were beginning to lengthen. Looking down a narrow street leading to the river, I saw a fisherman in a boat, casting a long net that turned the water silver as it splashed into the Thames, sending swans flying to the bank. Normality. I remembered Guy's words. Why did I keep walking into danger, taking others with me? My feelings for the Queen had led to my involvement in this case; yet it had been the same even before I met her. It went back to Thomas Cromwell, my association with him that first brought me into contact with the high ones of the realm who, like Cromwell himself, sought to use my skills and exploit my obstinate refusal to give up anything I had started. I thought, if I get through this, perhaps it is time to move out of London. Plenty did. I could practise in one of the provincial towns: Bristol, perhaps, or Lichfield, where I had been born and still had cousins. But I had not been there for years; it was a small place and not all of its associations were happy for me.

My musings reminded me of young Timothy and his reluctance to move on. I decided to speak to Josephine; she was fond of the boy. And I resolved, as well, to ask her directly what was the matter between her and Martin Brocket. My steward did not seem like a bully, but I did not see all that went on in my home. No master does.

I arrived home towards five. Martin opened the door to me, his expression deferential as always; I asked if there had been any messages and he told me none. I thought, perhaps I should visit Barak, then decided, better for him to establish a story first with Tamasin. Damn all the lies.

✝

JOSEPHINE WAS IN THE PARLOUR, dusting with her usual care. She rose and bowed as I entered. I looked longingly through the window to my little resting place in the garden, but as I had caught her alone I should take the chance to speak to her. I began in a friendly tone. 'I have had little chance to talk to you of late, Josephine. How go things with you?'

'Very well, sir,' she said.

'I wanted to speak to you about Timothy. You know I have suggested that when he turns fourteen he should go for an apprenticeship, as Simon did?'

'That would be a good thing, sir, I think.'

'And yet he is reluctant to go.'

Her face clouded. She said, 'He did not have a happy time before he came here.'

'I know. But that was three years since.'

She looked at me with her clear blue eyes. 'I think, sir, he sees this house as a refuge.' She blushed. 'As do I. But it is not good to cower from the world too long, perhaps.'

'I agree.' I paused. 'What do you think I should do, Josephine?'

She looked at me in surprise. 'You are asking me, sir?'

'Yes.'

She hesitated, then said, 'I should go carefully, sir. Slowly.'

'Yes. I think you are right.' I smiled. 'And you, Josephine, will you be seeing Goodman Brown again soon?'

She blushed. 'If you are agreeable, sir, he has asked me to walk with him again on Sunday.'

'If he is agreeable to you, so he is to me.'

'Thank you, sir.'

'If I remember, you met him at the May Day revels. At Lincoln's Inn Fields.'

'Yes. Agnes persuaded me to go with her, and to wear a little garland of flowers she had made. Master Brown was standing next to us, he said it was pretty. He asked where we worked, and when he found it was for a barrister he told us that he did, too.'

'The law was ever good for establishing friendships.' I thought of Philip Coleswyn. Was he a friend? Perhaps, I thought. I said to Josephine, gently, 'I think Master Brown is perhaps the first young man you have walked out with?'

She lowered her head. 'Yes, sir. Father, he did not want me — '

'I know.' There was an awkward silence, then I said, 'Make sure you behave in a ladylike way, Josephine, that is all I would say. I think you will not find that difficult.'

She smiled, showing white teeth. 'He asks nothing more, sir.' She added quickly, 'Your approval is important to me.'

We stood for a moment, both a little embarrassed. Then I said, 'You get on very well with Agnes.'

'Oh, yes,' she answered brightly. 'She advises me about clothes. No woman ever has before, you see.'

'She is a good woman. Martin, I suppose, did not come with you to the revels.'

She wrinkled her nose. 'No, sir. He regards such things as silly.'

'But he treats you well enough?'

'Yes, sir,' she answered hesitantly. 'Well enough.'

I pressed her, gently. 'Josephine, I have sensed an — unease — between you and Martin.'

She put the cloth down on the table. Then she took a deep breath and lifted her head. 'I have been meaning to speak to you, sir, yet I did not know if it was right — and Agnes Brocket has been so good to me — '

'Tell me, Josephine.'

She looked at me directly. 'Two months ago, I went into your study one day to dust, and found Martin Brocket going through the drawers of your desk. Agnes was out, perhaps he thought he was alone in the house. I know you keep your money in a locked drawer there, sir.'

I did, and my most important papers, too. Martin had keys to most places in the house, but not to that drawer, nor the chest in my bedroom where I kept my personal items. 'Go on,' I said.

'He snapped at me to get out, said that he was looking for some-thing for you. But Master Shardlake, he had the look of one uncovered in wrongdoing. I have been battling with my conscience ever since.'

I thought, thank heaven there was nothing in writing about the *Lamentation*; even the notes I had made in the garden I had destroyed. And, besides, two months ago it had not even been taken. But the news sent a chill down my spine, all the same. And how many times had Martin nosed around without Josephine seeing?

I said, 'I have never sent Martin to fetch anything from my desk. Thank you, Josephine, for telling me this. If you see him doing some-thing like that again, come to me.'

I had missed no money. But if not money, what had Brocket been looking for? 'You did right to tell me, Josephine. For now, let us keep it a secret.' I smiled uneasily. 'But remember, tell me if anything like this occurs again.'

'I did not like him from the start, sir, though Agnes has been such a friend, as I have said. Sometimes he speaks roughly to her.'

'Sadly husbands occasionally do.'

'And he was always asking about you when he first came, last winter. Who your friends were, your habits, your clients.'

'Well, a steward needs to find such things out.' It was true, but I felt uncomfortable nonetheless.

'Yes, sir, and it was only at first. Yet there has always been some-thing about him I did not trust.'

'Perhaps because he speaks roughly to Agnes, whom you like?'

Josephine shook her head. 'No, it is something more, though I am not sure what.'

I nodded. I felt the same.

She said, hesitant again, 'Sir, perhaps I should not ask — '

'Go on – '

'If I might say, this last week you have seemed – preoccupied, worried. Have you some trouble, sir?'

I was touched. 'Merely work worries, Josephine. But thank you for your concern.'

I felt uneasy. I thought of the books I possessed, forbidden by the recent proclamation. They were concealed in my chest, and under the amnesty I had another fortnight to turn them in; I thought, if I do that officially, my name will doubtless go on a list. Better to burn them discreetly in the garden. And I would keep a careful eye now on Master Martin Brocket, too.

✝

THAT EVENING I WAS due to visit Philip Coleswyn.

He lived on Little Britain Street, near Smithfield. I walked there by back lanes to avoid seeing Smithfield itself again. His house was in a pleasant row of old dwellings, with overhanging jettied roofs. Some peddlers and drovers in their smocks were pushing their carts back towards the city from the Smithfield market. They seemed to have many unsold goods; I wondered if the troubles caused by the King's debasement of the coinage would ever end. A small dog, a shaggy little mongrel, wandered up and down the street whining and looking at people. It had a collar – it must have come to Smithfield with one of the traders or customers, and got itself lost. Hopefully its owner would find it.

I knocked at the door of Coleswyn's residence, where, as he had told me, a griffin's head was engraved over the porch. He let me in himself. 'We have no servants at the moment,' he apologized. 'My wife will be doing the cooking tonight. We have a fine capon.'

'That sounds excellent,' I said, concealing my surprise that a man of his status should have no servants. He led me into a pleasant parlour, the early evening sunlight glinting on the fine gold and silver plate displayed on the buffet. An attractive woman in her early thirties was sitting with two children, a girl and boy of about seven and five, teaching them their letters. She looked tired.

'My wife, Ethelreda,' Coleswyn said. 'My children, Samuel and Laura.'

Ethelreda Coleswyn stood and curtsied, and the little boy gave a tiny bow. The girl turned to her mother and said seriously, 'I prefer the name Fear-God, Mamma.'

Her mother gave me a nervous look, then told the child, 'We want you to use your second name now, we have told you. Now go, both of you, up to bed. Adele is waiting.' She clapped her hands and the children went to their father, who bent to kiss them goodnight, then they left obediently.

'My sister has come from Hertfordshire to help with the children,' Coleswyn explained.

'I must see to the food.' Ethelreda got up. She left the room. Coleswyn poured me some wine and we sat at the table.

'That was quite a scene at the Cotterstoke house this morning,' he said.

'My client's behaviour towards you was insufferable. I apologize for her.'

'Her manners are not your responsibility, Brother Shardlake.' He hesitated, then added, 'Have you seen her again today?'

'No, I have not been back to chambers. If she called this afternoon, she was unlucky. No doubt there will be a message tomorrow.'

Coleswyn smiled wryly. 'I keep thinking of those two beetles we saw fighting in the stableyard. Why do Edward and Isabel need their carapaces, and what lies underneath?'

'God alone knows.'

He fingered the stem of his glass. 'Recently I met an old member of the Chandlers' Guild, Master Holtby. Retired now, over seventy. He remembered Isabel and Edward's father, Michael Johnson.'

I smiled. 'Met by chance, or design?'

'Not purely by chance.' He smiled wryly. 'In any event, he said that Michael Johnson was a coming man in his day. Shrewd, prosperous, a hard man in business but devoted to his family.'

'You can see all that in the painting.'

'Yes, indeed. He inherited the business from his own father and built it up. But he died way back in 1507; that was one of the years when the sweating sickness struck London.'

I remembered the sweating sickness. More contagious and deadly even than the plague, it could kill its victims in a day. Mercifully there had not been an outbreak for some years.

Coleswyn went on, 'The family were devastated, according to old Master Holtby. But a year later Mistress Johnson remarried, another chandler, a younger man called Peter Cotterstoke.'

'Common enough for a widow left alone to marry a new husband in the same trade. It is only sensible.'

'The children were about twelve, I think. Master Holtby did not remember any trouble between them and their stepfather. They took his name in place of their father's, and kept it. In any case, poor Cotterstoke also died, a year later.'

'How?'

'Drowned. He had been down at the docks on some business to do with a cargo, and fell in, God save his soul. But then to everyone's surprise, Mrs Cotterstoke sold the business soon afterwards, using the proceeds to live on for the rest of her life. Disinheriting her son, Edward, in effect. He would have started as an apprentice in the business in a year or so. Master Holtby told me there was no love lost between the mother and either of her children.'

'But why?'

'He didn't know. But he said old Mrs Cotterstoke was a strong, determined woman. He was surprised she sold the business; he would have expected her to run it herself, as some widows do. But no, she just lived on in that house, alone. Edward started work at the Guildhall soon after, and Isabel married, while she was still very young, I believe.'

I considered. 'So some quarrel divided all three of them. And old Mrs Cotterstoke – we agreed that the wording of the Will looks as though she wished to set her children against each other, taking revenge from beyond the grave.'

'But for what?'

I shook my head. 'These family disputes can start from something small and last till everyone involved dies.'

'Perhaps this one will end now, after today's inspection?' he said hesitantly.

I raised my eyebrows. Knowing Isabel, I doubted that. Coleswyn nodded agreement.

'Did you notice their servant?' I asked. 'The one left to look after the place.'

'He had a sad look,' Coleswyn said. 'And it was strange how he leapt in when Edward and Isabel began shouting of what each could tell about the other. He could probably tell some stories himself. But of course neither of us could question him without our client's authority.'

'Personally, I just want to be done with it. This is one mystery I do not need to solve.'

Coleswyn played with a piece of bread. 'By the way, I have told my wife nothing of what happened today. Those wild accusations of heresy would upset her. What Isabel Slanning said about our vicar being under investigation earlier this year was quite true.' His face darkened. 'My wife comes from Ipswich. She has a family connection to Roger Clarke.'

'I do not know the name.'

'He was burned in Ipswich a few months ago, for denying the Mass. My wife's brother was an associate of his. He was interrogated there but recanted, said he accepted the presence of Christ's body and blood in the Mass.' He gave a grimace of a smile. 'Turn rather than burn, as they say.' I remembered an old friend of mine from years ago: Godfrey, a barrister who had become a radical Protestant and left the law to go and preach on the streets. I had never heard from him again; if he had been prosecuted for heresy it would have been all round Lincoln's Inn, so he must have died on the road, or gone to Europe. But Godfrey had had no wife or children.

'Since then I know there have been eyes on me at Gray's Inn; Bishop Gardiner has his informers among the lawyers. And Ethelreda thinks this house is sometimes watched. But I am a lawyer. I know how to be careful. I have said nothing against the Mass, and will not.'

I was silent a moment. Then I said, 'The persecutions seem to be over. No one has been taken in recently.'

'It started out of the blue,' he said, the skin round one eye twitch-ing. 'And it may start again. That is why I dismissed our two servants. I was not sure I trusted them. But we must get another. Someone in my congregation has recommended a man. Not having servants is something that is noticed, too, among people of our class. And we thought it politic to make our daughter, who was christened Fear-God, use her second name, Laura.'

I shook my head. If the truth be told I did not know whether or not Christ's body and blood were present in the Mass, and now did not much care. But to bring ordinary people to such a state of fear was evil.

He continued quietly, 'When Parliament passed the act dissolving the chantries at the end of last year, our vicar thought the tide was turning his way and said some – well, I suppose, some careless things.' He looked at me with his clear blue eyes. 'He was questioned, and members of the congregation watched.' He took a deep breath. 'Has anyone asked you about me?'

'Nobody. I have heard nothing, apart from Isabel Slanning's rant-ings.'

He nodded. 'I am sorry to ask, but my wife is anxious. Ah – ' His voice became suddenly cheerful. 'Here she is. Now you will learn what a fine cook Ethelreda is.'

☦

I HAD EATEN BETTER MEALS; the capon was a little overdone, the vegetables mushy, but I made sure to praise the food to Ethelreda. Coleswyn and I tried to keep the conversation light, but his wife was preoccupied, smiling bravely at our jests about life at the Inns of Court, only picking at her food.

Coleswyn said, 'You have been a Serjeant at Law for some time. Perhaps you will be awarded a judgeship soon. It is the next step.'

'I have made too many enemies along the way for that, I think. And I have never been sufficiently conformist – in religion or aught else.'

'Would you like to be a judge? I think you would be a fair one.'

'No. I would either let people off or sentence them too severely. And seriously, I would not welcome having to waste time on all the flummery and ceremonial.'

'Some would give their right hands for a judgeship.'

I smiled. 'What is it the psalm says? "Vanity of vanities, saith the preacher. All is vanity."'

'And so it is,' Ethelreda said quietly.

Outside, the light began to fade. The noises from the street lessened as curfew approached; through the open shutters I heard the lost dog whine as it wandered up and down the street.

'This is the finest summer in some years,' I observed. 'Warm, but not too hot.'

'And just enough rain to keep the crops from drying out,' Coleswyn agreed. 'Remember the hailstorms last year? And all the men taken from work in the fields when we thought the French about to invade?'

'All too well.'

'Do you think this peace will last?'

'They are making much of it.'

'Peace,' Ethelreda said with a sort of flat despair. 'Peace with the French, perhaps. But what of peace at home?' She rubbed her hand across her brow. 'Philip says you are a man to be trusted, Serjeant Shardlake. Look at this realm. Last Christmas the King spoke in Parliament about how people call each other papist and traitor, how the word of God is jangled in alehouses. But from him there has been no constancy on religion these last dozen years. However the King's mind turns, we have to follow him. One year Lord Cromwell is bringing about true reform, the next he is executed. One month the

King dissolves the chantries for the empty papist ceremonial they are, the next Bishop Gardiner is set to find sacramentarians in every corner, including, some say, in the Queen's circle. Nowadays it is unsafe to hold any settled conviction. You cannot trust your neighbours, your servants – ' She broke off. 'Forgive me, you are our guest – '

Her husband reached across and put his hand on her arm.

'No, madam,' I said quietly. 'You speak true.'

She made her tone light. 'I have strawberries and sugared cream to come. Let me fetch them. A woman's place is to work, not lecture.'

When she had left, Philip turned to me apologetically. 'I am sorry. When it is unsafe to discuss certain things in general company, and one finds someone trustworthy, one talks of little else. It relieves the strain, perhaps. But we should not impose on you.'

'That is all right. I do not like these dinners where one fears to discuss aught but trivia.' I hesitated. 'By the way, do you think there are any Anabaptists in London these days?'

He frowned. 'Why do you ask?'

'The question has arisen in connection with a case. Their beliefs are very strange – that only adult baptism is valid, that Christ was not of human flesh – and, of course, that earthly powers should be overthrown and all men live in common.'

Coleswyn's mouth turned down in distaste. 'They are violent madmen. They brought blood and ruin in Germany.'

'I had heard that most of them, while holding to their social beliefs, have now renounced violence as a means of attaining them.' I thought, there are always other means, however misguided, including publishing a radical book by the Queen if they believed, however wrongly, that such an action would serve their political ends.

'Any that have been found have been burned,' Coleswyn replied. 'If there are any left they are keeping underground. Some I believe are old Lollards, and they had plenty of experience of living in hiding.'

'But perhaps Anabaptists, too, when in company, are tempted to talk unwisely,' I said thoughtfully. 'They are, after all, merely men like any other.'

He looked concerned. 'All the same, you do not want to meddle with such people.'

'No,' I answered feelingly. 'You are right.'

Ethelreda returned with the pudding, and we discussed politics no more. Master Coleswyn asked where I was from – he could not place my accent – and I told him about Lichfield: amusing stories of the poor monks' school where I received my early education. It grew dark and candles were lit in the sconces. Towards nine I became tired, suddenly finding it hard to keep my eyes open, and excused myself. Coleswyn showed me to the door. In the porch he shook my hand. 'Thank you for coming, Master Shardlake. Forgive my wife's anxiety, but the times – '

I smiled. 'I know.'

'Thank you for listening to us. I think in truth you are a godly man.'

'Many would disagree.'

'Study the Bible, pray.' He looked earnestly at me. 'That is the way, the only way, to salvation.'

'Perhaps. In any event, you and your good lady must come to dine at my house soon.' I sensed the Coleswyns had been isolating themselves with their worries. More than was good for them.

'That would be most pleasant.' He clasped my hand. 'God give you good night.'

'And you, Master Coleswyn.'

'Call me Philip.'

'Then you must call me Matthew.'

'I shall.'

He closed the door, leaving me to adjust my eyes to the darkness. The moon was up, but the overhanging eaves of the houses meant the sky was but a narrow strip. I began to walk towards the stables.

Ahead I saw a movement near the ground. I flinched, then realized it was nothing more than the lost dog, still wandering up and down the street in search of its owner. I had startled the poor creature, which ran into a doorway opposite.

There was a thud, a sudden yelp, then the dog flew out the doorway and landed at my feet, lifeless, its head at a horrible angle, its neck broken by a kick.

I jumped back, my hand going to my knife as I peered into the darkness of the doorway. Shadows moved within. I had been too careless. If this was Daniels and Cardmaker they could have me dead in an instant. But then, to my amazement, Isabel Slanning stepped out into the street. Two men in servants' dress followed her; one I recognized as the man she usually brought with her to consultations at Lincoln's Inn. She stood before me, staring right into my face, the moonlight making strange play with her features, those overlarge eyes glinting.

Her expression was triumphant. 'So, Master Shardlake,' she said, her voice a vicious hiss. 'I was right! You not only ride with Master Coleswyn, you dine with him. He calls you a godly man, you are his confederate –'

'Madam,' I said, aware that my voice was shaking with shock. 'I told you before, lawyers observe the courtesies with each other. They are not consumed with blind hatred as you are!' Behind her back, I caught a flash of white teeth as one of her servants smiled.

Isabel jerked her head back. 'I, Master Shardlake, am concerned with justice! A woman alone, faced with a confederacy of heretics! I am sure, now, that the so-called architect who came this morning to represent me is in league with my brother, too!'

'You picked him!'

'It is part of my brother's plot.' She waved a skinny finger in my face. 'But I have time, and will spare no energy in my search for justice! This is not the first time I have waited outside that man's house in the evening, to see who comes and goes. And tonight I see – you!' The last word was an accusing shout. It occurred to me again that Isabel Slanning was more than a little mad.

She smiled; I had never seen Isabel smile before and I had no wish to see it again – a wide grimace, splitting her face and exposing long yellow teeth. There was something savage in it. 'Well, *Serjeant* Shard-lake!' Her voice rose. 'You will represent me no more! I will find a lawyer who will prosecute my case honestly, without heretic conspir-acy! And I will write to the Lincoln's Inn authorities, telling them what you have done!'

I could have laughed. There could be no better news than that I was to be rid of Isabel. As for a complaint based on such evidence of wrongdoing as she possessed, it would have even Treasurer Rowland sniggering over his desk. I said, 'If your new lawyer will get in touch with me, mistress, I will happily give him the papers and answer any queries he has. And now I must get home.'

Philip's door opened. The noise had brought him and his terrified-looking wife to find out what was going on. He stared in amazement at Isabel. 'Brother Shardlake, what is happening?'

'No matter,' I said. 'Mistress Slanning has, I am delighted to say, just sacked me. Mistress Coleswyn, your husband said you thought someone was watching the house. It was this mad beldame.'

Isabel pointed at me again, her finger trembling. 'I will have you! I will have you all!' Then she turned and walked away, her servants following.

Ethelreda Coleswyn had started to cry. Philip said, 'All right, all right, my love, it was only that poor madwoman.'

'She will not be back,' I added reassuringly. Nonetheless, my eye was drawn to the poor dead dog. That must have been a vicious kick to break its neck like that, and Isabel had been standing in front of her servants in the doorway. It was she who had done it.

Chapter Twenty-three

THAT NIGHT I SLEPT DEEPLY, but woke early with a mind full of fears and discontents. I recalled Isabel Slanning's savage fury; I was sure she would like to serve me as she had that unfortunate dog.

There was a knock at the door and Martin entered, bearing towels and hot water, his face flatly expressionless as usual. 'God give you good morrow, Master,' he said. 'It is another fine, warm day.'

'Good morrow, Martin. Long may it continue.' I looked at his solid back as he laid the bowl on the table, wondering what went on inside that head of close-cropped fair hair. What had he been looking for in my desk that time? And Josephine said he had been constantly enquiring about my friends and contacts when he first came. Trying to nose into my life. Yet Martin, as I had reminded Josephine, needed to know all about me if he were to perform his duties as steward. His old master, another barrister, had given me a glowing reference; Martin and Agnes had been with the man for ten years, and were only leaving because he was retiring and moving to the country. I did not have a forwarding address, so could not get in touch with him.

Martin turned and gave me his tight little smile. 'Is there anything else, sir?'

'No, Martin. Not this morning.'

✞

AFTER BREAKFAST I WALKED up to Lincoln's Inn, wondering how Nicholas and Barak were, and whether they had come in. I thought, I should have visited them instead of going to Coleswyn's yesterday.

Barak was at his desk, working through some papers clumsily because of the heavy bandage on his left hand. Skelly looked at him curiously through his glasses. I could see no sign of Nicholas.

'Young Overton not in?' I asked with false jollity.

'Not yet,' Barak answered. 'He's late.'

Skelly looked up. 'Mistress Slanning called first thing this morning. She was in a – troubled state. She says she is going to a new lawyer.'

'Yes. I thought that might happen.'

'Should I send her a final bill?'

'Yes, we had better. If we don't she will take it as an admission of guilt or wrongdoing. With luck we shall not have to see her again.'

'She said she was going to take the case to Master Dyrick, whom you had dealings with last year.' Skelly looked at me curiously.

'Really? Well, if she wants someone to run a hopeless case with the maximum vigour, and charge her for the pleasure of it, she could not do better than Vincent Dyrick.' I turned to Barak. 'Come through, would you, Jack?'

He followed me into my office and I motioned him to sit. 'Dyrick again, eh? Well, they'll suit each other,' Barak said, managing a wry smile.

'I am only glad to be out of it. And I doubt Dyrick will encourage her to make trouble for me; remember, I know things about him.' I took a deep breath. 'Jack, I am more sorry than I can say for what happened yesterday.'

'I knew what I could be getting into.'

'I would have come round last night, but I thought you were best left to tell Tamasin – to tell her – '

'A pack of lies,' he finished heavily. 'Yes, you are right. So far as she is concerned I had an accident at the office. I was making a hole in a pile of papers with a knife, to thread a tag through, when my hand slipped. Tammy was full of sympathy, which makes it worse. Listen, when Nick gets in we need to meet to make sure we have the story straight between the three of us. You'll be seeing Tamasin next week at George's party. Please.'

'Yes, we will do that.' I closed my eyes a moment. 'Once again, I am sorry.'

He gave me his most piercing look. 'I just wish I knew what was going on.'

I shook my head. 'No. Safer not. How is your hand?'

'Sore as hell. But I have to play it down for Tamasin's sake, that's why I came in today. I'll survive,' he added.

'Any word from Nicholas?'

'He got but a flesh wound,' Barak said unsympathetically. 'By the way, there's a message for you, from Treasurer Rowland. He wants you to see him this morning. Before ten; he has a meeting then.'

'I'll go now. He did mention he had another task for me.' I got up. 'Dear God, I hope it's nothing like what he had me do last week.'

✝

ROWLAND WAS SEATED behind his desk again, writing. He raised his head, a cold look on his thin face. He had worn a similar expression when I had reported back to him after Anne Askew's burning, complimenting me on finding a place at Smithfield where my presence would be noted. I had, of course, not told him of Rich's glare at me. Looking at his white hair and long beard, I wished that, like Martin Brocket's old employer, he would retire. But he was the sort who savoured power, and would probably die at his desk.

'Serjeant Shardlake,' he said. 'Sit down.' He tapped the paper on his desk with a bony, inky finger. 'You knew the late Brother Bealknap, I believe. Had more than one passage of arms with him, I think.'

'Indeed I did.'

'I have just been composing a note to send round the Inn about his funeral. I am having to make the arrangements; his executor is not interested and there is no family. It will be in two days' time, the twenty-fourth, in the chapel. I doubt many will come.'

'No.' Certainly I would not, after Bealknap's piece of deathbed spite.

'You will appreciate this,' Rowland said. 'Bealknap left a vast sum of money to build what amounts to a mausoleum in the Inn chapel. With a marble image of himself, decorated and gilded and heaven knows what. He paid the Inn a good deal of money to agree to have it done.'

'So he told me. I saw him the day he died.'

Rowland raised his white eyebrows. 'Did you, by Mary?'

'He asked me to visit him.'

'A deathbed repentance?' Rowland's eyes narrowed with malicious curiosity.

'No.' I sighed. 'Not really.'

'You remember all the rumours that he had a great chest of gold in his chambers? Well, it was my duty to go and look for it. That chest did indeed exist, and contained several hundred sovereigns. But it wasn't at his chambers. Bealknap had had the sense to deposit it with one of the goldsmiths, for security. According to this goldsmith, Bealknap used to go there and sit with it of an evening.'

'He was a strange man.'

'There was certainly enough in the chest to pay for this mauso-leum. However, many of the benchers have objected. Bealknap was not, after all, a great credit to the Inn, and this thing is hardly in the chapel style. They are refusing point-blank to sanction it. As I sus-pected they would, at the time I made the bargain with Bealknap. He can lie under a marble slab in the chapel like a reasonable man.' Rowland gave that cynical smile of his, world-weary but also cruel; proud of his outwitting of a dying man.

I said, 'But if it is in his Will — '

Rowland spread his arms, black silk robe rustling. 'If the benchers will not agree, the legacy becomes impossible of execution.'

'Who is his executor?'

'Sir Richard Rich.' I looked at him sharply. 'It is an old Will. I know for a fact he hasn't worked cases for Rich for over a year. Rich stopped using him when he began to get ill.' I wondered, was that why Bealknap had come cosying up to me at the end of last year, in the hope that I could get him some work? I remember him saying he was not getting as much work from one of his clients. It must have been Rich. Rowland inclined his head. 'I keep an eye on which of the great ones of the realm give work to Lincoln's Inn barristers. As the Queen used to do with you. I have been in touch with Rich's secretary, and he said Sir Richard couldn't care less about the mausoleum.' He shrugged. 'And the Will specifically excludes members of his family from having a say. So, this thing will not be built, and all Bealknap's gold will be *bona vacantia*. So in the absence of anyone else, his fortune will go to – ?' He paused on a questioning note, as though I were a law student.

'The Crown,' I said.

'Exactly!' He gave his creaky laugh. 'Rich will be able to boast that he has garnered another few hundred pounds for the King to spend.' Now I really could not help feeling sorry for Bealknap. 'Talk-ing of the King and spending,' Rowland continued cheerfully, 'you remember you promised to undertake more duties for the Inn? Well, there is another big occasion coming up next month.' My face must have fallen, for he continued hurriedly, 'It is nothing like the burning. On the contrary, it will be the grandest celebration in London for years, some say since Anne Boleyn's coronation.'

'A celebration of what?' I asked, puzzled.

'The peace with France. A great chivalric display. I have had another letter from Secretary Paget. Apparently the very admiral who led the invasion fleet last year will bring a retinue of French ships up the Thames, including some that sailed against us. There will be a whole round of celebrations at the Tower and also at Hampton Court. Thousands will be present, royalty and nobility and repre-sentatives of the City Guilds and Inns of Court. They want a serjeant from Lincoln's Inn made available for the celebrations and I thought of you. As a sort of reward for that – less enjoyable occasion last week.'

I looked at him levelly. Rowland knew, of course, that I disliked ceremonial; again he was asserting his power. 'The King and Queen will be at many of the ceremonies,' he added, 'and I believe little Prince Edward is to be involved for the first time.'

I spoke quietly. 'There was a time, Master Treasurer, when the King was displeased with me. Perhaps it would be impolitic for me to attend.'

'Oh, the York business.' Rowland waved a dismissive hand. 'That was years ago. And all you'll be required to do is stand among many others in your best clothes and cheer when you're told to.'

I thought, cheer Admiral d'Annebault, who led the invasion fleet in the very battle during which the *Mary Rose* foundered. Chivalry, I thought, is a strange thing.

'I do not know the exact dates you will be required,' Rowland continued. 'But it will be during the last ten days in August, a month from now. I will keep you informed.'

There was no point in arguing. And I had other things to worry about. 'Very well, Treasurer,' I said quietly.

'The Lord alone knows how much it will all cost.' He laughed. 'Well, the King will have Bealknap's money to put towards it now.'

☩

I STEPPED OUT INTO the quadrangle. It had turned cloudy, that low, light summer cloud that seems to trap and thicken the heat. As I walked back to chambers I noticed a man loitering hesitantly nearby; young, well dressed in a dark doublet and wide green cap. I looked at him, then stared. It was a face I had seen only the day before, by the torchlight of the Tower dungeons. The gaoler Myldmore, who had appeared to be in trouble with his superior. He saw me and walked hesitantly across. His eyes were wide and frightened, as they had been at the Tower. 'Master Shardlake,' he said, a tremble in his voice, 'I must speak with you, in confidence. About – about a certain manuscript.'

Chapter Twenty-four

I TOOK MYLDMORE INTO my chambers. Barak and Skelly gave him curious looks as I led him into my room. I bade him sit. He did so, looking round uneasily. I spoke mildly, to try and put him at ease. 'Would you like a glass of beer?'

'No, sir, thank you.' He hesitated, pulling at his stringy little beard. He was an unimpressive-looking fellow; but as a Tower gaoler he would have seen — perhaps even done — some dreadful things. He spoke again suddenly. 'I believe you are investigating the murder of the printer Armistead Greening.'

'I am.'

'Officially?' His eyes turned on me with anxious intensity. 'They say it is on behalf of his parents.'

'Who says that?' I asked mildly.

'Friends. They told me a man they trust, called William Cecil, had been to see them and said it was safe to cooperate with you. Cecil is trying to trace three friends of Greening's who disappeared as well. His apprentice has vanished, too.' I looked at Myldmore closely. His eyes shifted, would not meet mine. If he knew all this he must have connections with the religious radicals. Suddenly he looked straight at me. 'Sir, why did you come to the Tower yesterday?'

I considered a moment, then said, 'I will answer you. But first let me reassure you that your friends are correct. I am not acting for any foe of the reformed cause.'

He looked at me narrowly. 'Is it believed there is a link between Greening's death and the — the Tower?'

'Rather that he had some connection with Anne Askew. Her

name has come up.' I could not mention Elias's dying message; Myld-more did not even know the apprentice was dead.

A bead of sweat appeared on the young gaoler's brow. He said, as much to himself as to me, 'I must trust you then. I cannot understand why they have not come for me. They would give me no mercy.' He shook his head. 'Not if they found out about the book.'

I gripped the arms of my chair, trying not to betray my feelings. In what I hoped was a casual manner, I asked, 'Did you know Master Greening?'

Myldmore clasped his skinny hands together. 'Yes. I was at some of the meetings at his print-shop. With those other men.' He took a deep breath, then said, his voice shaking, 'What I did in the Tower, for Anne Askew — pity and conscience moved me to it. But it is fear now that moves me to come to you.' He cast his head down.

'I think you have important matters to tell me, Goodman Myld-more, and I would give you time. I see you are troubled. Let me tell my assistant we are not to be disturbed.'

I got up. Myldmore nodded. He actually looked a little relieved now, as people sometimes will do when they have decided to confess an important secret. I went to the outer office. Still no sign of Nich-olas. I crossed to Barak's desk and swiftly scribbled a note to Lord Parr, telling him I had Myldmore in my chambers, and asking him to send some men to ensure that he, at least, did not get away. Barak looked puzzled, but I put a finger to my lips. I whispered, 'Can you take an urgent message to Whitehall Palace for me? To the Queen's Chamberlain?'

'Will they let me in?'

'Tell them I am working for the Queen's Learned Council, on urgent business for Lord Parr. Quick as you can.' I sealed the note and handed it to him. He gave me a sidelong look but got up and hurried out, making no noise as he closed the door. I ordered Skelly to tell any visitors I was absent, and went back to Myldmore. I was deceiving him, for my presence at the Tower had clearly made him believe, wrongly, that I was following a trail which had led to him. But as with so many others this past week, I had no alternative. This was, after all, a matter of a double murder.

☦

MYLDMORE WAS SLUMPED in his chair, gazing unseeingly through the window at the passing lawyers. I sat behind my desk. 'Now,' I said, 'we have as much time as we need.' I smiled and he nodded dully. I thought, start with the easy questions. 'What is your first name?'

'Thomas, sir.'

'How long have you worked at the Tower, Thomas?'

'Two years. My father was a gaoler there before me. He got me my position at the Tower. I was a guard outside first, and when Father died last year I was offered his place.' He looked at me directly, his eyes passionate. 'Though I did not like the work, especially as I had found God and was beginning to tread the path to salvation. And this year – the arrests of so many poor lambs of God – it put me in great turmoil.'

So he had started work as a gaoler last year. He had probably not wanted the job, but work was hard to come by and it would have kept him from being conscripted to the war. In the Tower that would have been a quiet time. The great ones of the realm were concentrating on winning the war, and the struggles between contesting factions and religious loyalties had been temporarily set aside. But in the spring, with the war over, it had all started again.

'I was sore troubled in conscience, sir.' Myldmore spoke as though I would understand; he obviously took me for another reformer. It was probably what Cecil had put around. 'It was through my church, our vicar, that I came to see that the only way to salvation is through Christ, and the only way to Him is through the Bible.' He continued, scarce above a whisper, 'I have doubted whether Our Lord's body is truly present in the Mass.' Now he did look at me anxiously, though he had not actually denied the Mass in what he had just said. I merely nodded sympathetically.

'My vicar said I was going too far — to deny the Mass is to go against the orders of the King, who is Head of the Church, appointed by God. But then, not long after, I met Master Curdy.'

'Greening's friend, who has vanished. The candlemaker.'

'Yes, sir. He knew my mother slightly. She died early this year. I spoke with him after the funeral, and he asked me to meet him for a drink. He turned the talk to religion. He is a learned man, self-taught, and a pleasant, engaging fellow; we met again and he told me he attended a discussion group of like-minded folk which I might find interesting.'

I looked at Myldmore's face, drawn and pale. A lonely, serious, conflicted young man, probably unpopular because of his job, just the sort who might be recruited to the radical cause. It struck me, too, that all the known members of the group were single, though Vandersteyn might have a wife back in Flanders. Otherwise, no wives or children to distract attention from the cause. 'And you went?'

'I attended my first group in April. They always met at Master Greening's print-shop. Only those invited could come, and we were asked not to tell anyone else about the meetings.' He broke off suddenly, biting his lip. 'And everyone I met there is gone now, vanished. Master Greening is dead and all the others have disappeared, I do not know whether of their own will. Elias the apprentice, Master Curdy, McKendrick the Scottish preacher, Vandersteyn the Dutchman, Michael Leeman that served the Queen at Whitehall — '

I sat up. 'Leeman was a member of your group?' I had wondered whether there might be a connection, and here was confirmation.

'He was.' Myldmore's eyes widened. 'Did you not know? What has happened to him?'

'I know only that he, too, has disappeared.' I drew a deep breath. So Leeman had taken the *Lamentation* and given it to Greening. That was clear now. And Myldmore had mentioned 'the manuscript', too. But I must tread carefully.

Myldmore was looking at me anxiously again. 'Please understand me, sir,' he said, 'I was never fully part of their group. They treated me with caution, asking me questions about my beliefs, always glancing at each other when I answered. It was as though — as though they were testing me.'

'Yes, I think I understand.' This was beginning to sound less like a group of radicals than a conspiracy.

Myldmore continued. 'They did not seem to like it that I was still uncertain about the Mass. Though they had strong arguments — about the Mass not being in the Bible — ' He broke off suddenly; he still did not quite trust me.

'We need not discuss that at all,' I said reassuringly. 'I promise, what anyone believes about the Mass is quite irrelevant to my enquiry.'

He looked relieved, and went on, 'Other things they said or hinted at I did not understand, or did not agree with. They were strong on the need for people to be baptized as adults, not as children, just as John the Baptist and the disciples had been. And when I said the King was appointed by God to be Head of the Church, that angered them; they said the forbidding of the Bible to poor folk was akin to plucking God's Word from the people, and thanked the Lord that John Bale and others were having works on the gospel sent from the Continent. Though they said Bale had no understanding of the need for the ruling powers to be thrown down.'

'They said that? Used those very words?'

'Yes, sir. And said the King's royal blood mattered not a jot, we were all descended from Adam our common father.' He shook his head vigorously. 'Such words are treason. I said it was not right.' He took a deep breath. 'Shortly after that, they told me there stood too much between us for me to remain a member of their group. And so I left, having sworn not to reveal their existence to anyone. I confess I was glad. I felt them more and more as a weight on me.'

'They were leading you into dangerous waters.'

'Perhaps. I do not know.' His manner had become evasive again, and he avoided my eye. Myldmore was young and callow but he was not stupid. He must have realized, as I had, that with their belief in adult baptism and their fierce criticism of the social order, he had found himself among a group which at least sympathized with the revolutionary Anabaptists. And if they themselves were Anabaptists, planning some extreme act, for them to gain a recruit in the Tower, having already secured one in the Queen's household, could be very useful.

'I am sure you did right,' I said, weighing my words carefully. I was desperate to get to the matter of the book, but must not push him too hard. And I must give Barak time to deliver the note and for Lord Parr to react. I said, 'It must have been sad, though, to break with these folk just as you were getting to know them.'

Myldmore sighed. 'They were not easy people. Curdy was a decent fellow; he would ask how I fared, alone in the world as I am now. And though I think he had succeeded in his business, and had money, he always dressed soberly. I think he supported the Scotchman with money, and Greening's business, too. From things Master Curdy said I think his people were Lollards from the old days, that used to read bibles secretly written in English. Well, he was generous, he practised what he preached about sharing.' Myldmore looked at me, and asked suddenly, 'Are they dead, sir?'

'I think not. But I need to find them. Not to harm them, but perhaps to prevent them from unwittingly doing something foolish.'

'They were not men of violence,' Myldmore said. 'They renounced it as wrong. Though they often spoke most hotly – ' He smiled sadly. 'Elias said that all rich men should be cast down and made to labour in the fields like common folk.'

I remembered Okedene saying that he had heard them arguing loudly with each other in Greening's shed, especially recently. 'Did they disagree much between themselves?'

Myldmore nodded. 'Often, though usually on points I found obscure, like whether someone baptized as a child needs a complete immersion when they are rebaptized as an adult.'

'What about matters concerning the social order? Did anyone disagree with Elias's remarks about throwing down the rich, for example?'

'No. No, they all agreed on that.'

I smiled back. 'People fierce in their righteousness?'

'Ay. Though Greening was a gentle and amiable man until you got him on to religion. The Dutchman was the worst; sometimes his accent was hard to understand, but that did not stop him calling you names like "blind simpleton" and "foolish sinner destined for Hell" if you disagreed with him. He was the one who spoke most often of John Bale.' I wondered, did Vandersteyn know the English exile? As a Dutchman involved in the cross-Channel trade it was not impossible.

Myldmore went on. 'The Scotchman, too, was an angry man, bitter, I think, at being thrown out of his own land. He could be frightening, big glowering man that he was. I think they treated him badly in his own country. I know he had a wife left behind there.'

'And Leeman?'

'The gentleman from Whitehall? I felt a brotherly spirit with him, for he was much worried, as I am, over the question of whether God had elected him for salvation. Like them all, Leeman was always talking about the coming of the End Time, as foretold in the Book of Revelation; how the Antichrist was about to come and we must be ready for judgement. I did not understand it all.'

The coming of the Antichrist prophesied in the Book of Revelation. It was another belief characteristic of the Anabaptists and other radical Protestants. Okedene had mentioned Bertano in that connection, and his name had been on the lips of Greening's killers at the inn yesterday. I asked, as casually as I could, 'Many have identified the Antichrist with a particular individual. Did the group ever mention a name?'

He looked genuinely puzzled. 'No, sir.'

'An Italian one, perhaps?'

'The Pope, you mean? They mentioned the Pope only to curse him.'

I realized that if the group had decided this Bertano was the Antichrist they would not mention his name to someone they did not fully trust. I said quietly, 'And this whole group has disappeared now. Why do you think that may be?'

A muscle in Myldmore's cheek twitched for a moment. Then he said, 'I think perhaps they have fled because of the book.'

I looked at his anguished, worried face. Then I took the plunge. 'You mean the book which Michael Leeman took?'

He stared at me blankly. 'Leeman? No, it was I who smuggled the book from the Tower and gave it to Greening. Anne Askew's account of her examinations.'

For a moment my head span. We stared at each other. As calmly as I was able, I said, 'Tell me about Anne Askew's book, Thomas.'

He frowned. 'Do you not know? I thought that was why you were at the Tower yesterday.' He shifted in his seat, and for a moment I feared he might panic and run.

'You are right,' I lied. 'I am concerned with Anne Askew's book. But I was misinformed about who gave it to Greening.' I continued calmly, 'You have told me much, Thomas. Best tell me the rest now. I swear to you, I am no enemy.'

He looked at me again, then bent his head. 'It seems I have no choice.'

I did not reply.

He took a deep breath, then he recounted the next part of his story in quiet, even tones, without looking up at me; his voice trembling occasionally so that I had to bend to catch his words.

Chapter Twenty-five

'I̲t was on the twenty-ninth of June, a Tuesday. Three weeks ago, though it seems a year. Anne Askew and those three men had been condemned to death for heresy at the Guildhall the day before. Everyone was talking of it. We expected she would lie in Newgate prison with the others till she was taken to be burned. That afternoon I was on duty in the Tower, checking on the prisoners in the dungeons and giving food to those allowed it. Afterwards I went to report on how they fared to Master Howitson – you met him yesterday.'

'Yes, I remember.'

'While I was with him at the desk I heard footsteps outside, several people coming down. The outer door opened and Master Ardengast, the senior guard, entered, accompanied by a couple of guards holding a young woman. She wore a blue dress of good quality, but to my astonishment she had a dirty sack over her head, so her face could not be seen. She was breathing hard, poor creature, very frightened. It was dreadful to see a woman treated so. Another couple of men followed, carrying a large trunk. Then Master Ardengast told Howitson and me this woman was to be lodged down here, and none of the other prisoners were to know of her presence. He said as we were on duty we must perform a double shift, for the fact she was here was to be known to as few as possible.'

Myldmore's voice fell to little more than a whisper. 'You would think one would protest at such a thing, but you get used to the worst in that place. And I am a weak, sinful creature. I only answered, "Yes, sir." The woman was led away, to a cell within, a place called the "special cell", better appointed than the others, for prisoners of gentle birth. But it is near the room where the rack and the other instruments of torture are kept.' He looked up at me. 'I have seen them.'

So have I, I thought, but did not say.

'After that, all the men left, leaving Howitson and me staring at each other. I began to ask who the woman was, but Howitson said we should not talk about it. So I went about my duties. Then, a couple of hours later, Master Ardengast returned. With him were the Lieutenant of the Tower, Sir Anthony Knevet, and two other men, in fine silk gowns with gold chains of office and jewelled caps. One I did not know, he was thin with a ruddy face and a little jutting red beard. The other I recognized, for I have seen him on business in the Tower before. The King's councillor, Sir Richard Rich.'

I stared at him hard. Rich, and by his description the other man was Lord Chancellor Wriothesley, who at the burning had been worried lest the gunpowder round the victims' necks send burning faggots flying at the councillors. And Knevet, who was in bad odour with his superior Walsingham. So, Richard Rich was deep in this business, as I had suspected.

Myldmore looked back at me now, his eyes frightened. 'Should I go on now, sir?'

I think he feared that at the mention of those names I might call on him to desist, and decide to get involved no further. But I said, 'No, continue.'

'They said nothing to me or Howitson, though Rich frowned when he saw that I recognized him. They passed on, through the door to where the woman was kept.'

'You still had no idea who she was?'

'No.' There was anger in his voice suddenly. 'But I knew Mistress Askew had been condemned, and that the law forbids torturing someone after sentence.'

'Yes, it does.'

Myldmore passed a hand over his brow. 'It was three hours before they all came out again. Rich and Wriothesley looked angry, and Rich had a sheen of sweat on his face, as though he had been at some hard labour. Sir Anthony Knevet looked worried. I remember Rich flexed his hands, little white hands they are, and winced as though he were in pain. They paused at the desk and Sir Anthony spoke to us roughly. "You two never saw these gentlemen, you understand? Remember your oath to the King." Then they all went out, back up the stairs. I heard Rich say angrily, "Another hour, Knevet, and I would have broken her yet."'

He paused. Outside in the quadrangle two barristers were talking, probably of some amusing incident in court, for both were laughing. Sunlight illuminated Myldmore's head, which he bent again as he continued. 'That evening it was again my duty to feed the prisoners. Howitson told me to take a bowl of pottage to the woman. So I went through to her cell. I knocked lest she was in a state of undress, and a voice bade me come in.

'The room had a table, chairs and a bed with a fine cover, as well as a chest. I recognized Anne Askew at once, for I had twice seen her preach in the streets, but now she sat awkwardly in a heap on the floor, her back against the wall and her legs spread out on the stone flags. It looked almost indecent.' Myldmore flushed, and I thought how young he was, how oddly innocent to be serving in that den of wolves.

'I noticed her dress was torn. She had cast off her coif and her fair hair hung down in rats-tails, bathed in sweat. Her face – a pretty face – was composed, but her eyes were staring, wide.' He shook his head, as though to try and clear it of that terrible image. 'Despite all this, when she spoke to me it was in pleasant, gentle tones. She asked, "Would you put the tray on the floor, please, goodman gaoler. I cannot rise."

'I know what racking does to people. God forgive me, I have seen it, the prisoner stretched out, arms above his head, fixed to the moving table with ropes tied to his wrists and ankles, and then the ropes wound so that the muscles and joints tear; and it came to me in a rush of horror that those men – Privy Councillors – had just racked this woman. I laid the plate and spoon on the floor beside her. She bent forward to pick the spoon up but gave a little cry of pain and leaned back, breathing hard.' Myldmore looked up at me, swallowing. 'In a man, it would have been bad enough. But to see a woman in that state – ' He shook his head. 'I think my expression must have betrayed me. She asked if I knew who she was. I answered, "Yes, Madam, I have seen you preach." Then I said, "What have they done to you?"

'She smiled in answer. "His majesty's noble councillors would have the Queen down, and her ladies and their husbands. They asked me what dealings I had had with them, the Countess of Hertford, Lady Denny, the Duchess of Suffolk. They wanted me to say they were all heretics who denied the Mass. But I said, truly, that I have never met any of them. So they racked me to get the answers they wanted. Sir Anthony Knevet refused to do it, so Rich and Wriothes-ley turned the rack." Her eyes seemed to burn into mine as she said, "I do not care who knows; I want the story spread abroad."'

Myldmore swallowed, looked at me. 'I was frightened, sir, I did not want to know this. But Mistress Askew continued, shifting her position as spasms of pain went through her. She said, "It was great agony, and there will be more when they burn me. But I know that this is all but a prelude to the bliss to come." And then she smiled again.' The young gaoler shook his head in wonder.

'I asked Mistress Askew, "Do you believe, then, that you are saved?" And she answered, "Truly, I believe I have God's grace in my heart." Her eyes were blue, bright as though from an inner light. It moved me to the heart, sir.' Myldmore's face worked a moment before he continued: 'I knelt before her and said, "You have endured, as Christ did. I wish I had your courage and certainty."' His eyes were wet now. 'And then she asked me to say the twenty-third Psalm with her. I did.' Myldmore whispered, softly, '*Yea though I walk through the valley of the shadow of death, I will fear no evil: for thou art with me . . .*' Then, as she could not feed herself, she asked me to spoon the broth into her mouth. She could scarce move without terrible pain.' He paused, then added quietly, 'I heard she was most brave at the end.'

'She was,' I answered. 'I was there.'

'Ah.' He nodded. 'You were one of the godly folk who went to comfort her.'

I did not contradict him. Myldmore took a deep breath. 'I left after feeding her. Howitson told me that the next day she was to be removed from the Tower to a house – I do not know whose – where she would be lodged to recover. He reminded me to keep my mouth shut. They hoped she would recover sufficiently to walk to the fire. I was angry, sir, more than ever before in my life.'

'Was it you who set the news afoot she had been tortured?'

'Yes.' He clenched his jaw with a new stubbornness. 'And they know it was. I was in such a fume of anger at what had been done, I told my landlady that same evening that Anne Askew had been tortured in the Tower. But I did not have the courage to name Wriothesley and Rich. My landlady is a good reformer, and also a great gossip. I wanted her to tell others. For that one evening, I did not think of my own safety. Next day it was the talk of the streets.' He said, sorrowfully, 'I confess when I heard the story jangled about everywhere, I began to be afraid again.'

He sighed, then continued, 'And soon enquiries were indeed made, by Master Ardengast. Only those who saw Anne Askew in the Tower, and those in the house to which she was taken, knew what had been done to her. I was questioned by Sir Anthony Knevet himself. I confessed at once. I was so afraid I wet my hose during the interview. Anne Askew did not wet herself,' he added quietly, in self-disgust.

'She was a rare creature,' I said.

'I was sure I would be arrested, but I was told only to keep my mouth shut. Which I have, until you came yesterday. I do not under-stand why I have not been arrested. But Sir Anthony was very mild with me, and there have been rumours in the Tower that he was so concerned at what Rich and Wriothesley had done, that he privately told the King. But I do not know.'

I considered. Perhaps nothing had happened to Myldmore because if he were put on trial for revealing Anne Askew's torture, that would involve admitting publicly that it had taken place.

'Did Sir Anthony Knevet enquire about your motives?' I asked. 'Your religious associations?'

'Yes. He asked about my church, my associates. But I did not tell him about Master Greening or his group. That would be the end of me because of − because of the book. And I had said nothing about that.'

'I think it is time to tell *me*, Master Myldmore.'

He looked down at his hands, then raised his head again. 'On the day I spoke with Mistress Askew, I was sent again, late in the evening, to take her supper, and to report on how she fared. When I went into the cell I found she was still on the floor, but had managed to drag herself half across the room. Jesu knows what that cost her. A candle had been brought in and she was sprawled next to her chest, which was open. She had managed to take out a bundle of papers, which lay on her lap, with an inkwell and a quill. She was writing, sweating and wincing with the effort. She looked up at me. There was silence for a moment, and then she said, in a strange tone of determined merri-ment, "Goodman gaoler! You have found me at my letters."

'I laid the bowl of pottage close beside her, and in so doing saw what she had written: "*. . . then the lieutenant caused me to be loosed from the rack. Incontinently I swooned, and then they recovered me again . . .*"

'I said, "That letter will not be allowed out, madam, it says too much."

'"A shame," she said. "It contains the whole truth."

'I asked her if she would like me to feed her again, and she said she would. She leaned back against the chest, like a helpless child, while I fed her and wiped her chin. She told me I was a good man, and a Christian. I said I wished I could be. She said then, "Will you report what I have been writing to Sir Anthony Knevet?" I did not reply and she stared at me, her eyes full of pain but somehow − unrelenting. Then she said, "This is a record, an account, of my examinations since my first arrest last year. I wrote that last piece this afternoon, though my arms sore pain me. It is strange, they have never searched among my clothes, where this testament has been hidden." She smiled again. "The King's councillors will tear the strings and joints of a gentlewoman's body, yet common gaolers hesitate to search her under-clothes."

'"It is rare for a woman to be imprisoned there," I said.

'Then she touched my hand and said, "They will search the chest soon, without doubt, and will find this. You are the first to have seen it, I had not the strength to put it away quickly when your key turned in the door. My fate is in your hands, sir, and if you feel you must take my journal to Sir Anthony Knevet, then you must." Those blue eyes, glinting in the candlelight, were fixed on mine. "But I ask you, as you seek salvation, to take my writings, now, and somehow get them pub-lished. That would make a mighty storm here. Do you think you can do that?"

'I thought at once of Greening. But I drew back. I said, "Madam, you ask me to risk my life. If I were caught – "

'"Your life, sir?" She gave a little smile and with an effort laid her hand on mine. "Life is fleeting, and beyond lies God's judgement and eternity." Then she asked my name. "To have the world know what is done in the King's name would be a mark of grace, Thomas, a great step to your salvation."'

I felt a sudden anger with Anne Askew. She had used the promise of salvation as a weapon against Myldmore, I thought, a sort of black-mail.

His eyes looked inward for a moment, then he gave me a fierce look. 'I said I would take the writings, her *"Examinations"*, as she called them. The document was not long. I hid it under my jerkin and took it from the cell that night. After speaking to my landlady I went straight to Master Greening's print-shop. He was alone there. He greeted me cautiously at first, but when I told him about the manu-script, and showed it to him, he was almost overcome with joy. "I can have this sent to Bale," he told me. "And five hundred copies smuggled back into England in a few months." I remember him saying, "This will make a mighty uproar."'

I did a quick calculation. 'That would have been – what – the twenty-ninth of June?'

He looked at me, surprised. 'Yes. I knew I must do it that night; already I could feel my courage beginning to fail. But I think the Lord gave me strength, he moved me to do it.'

I sat back. So there was not one book, but two. Myldmore had brought Anne Askew's *Examinations* to Greening, and later Leeman had brought the Queen's *Lamentation*. Because they knew Greening could get them smuggled out to Bale. A mighty uproar indeed. Yes, both books would certainly cause that. Perhaps these people thought, in their noddle-headed way, that the Queen's confession of faith, and Anne Askew's exposure of what had been done to her, would anger the populace sufficiently to overthrow their rulers in a great riot. They did not fully understand the strength and ruthlessness of those in power. Anne Askew was beyond harm now, but the publication of the *Lamentation* would place the Queen in great danger, and her fall would only advance the reformers' worst enemies.

'So what do you think has happened to them, sir?' Myldmore asked again. 'Greening's group? Why was he killed? Was it – was it because I brought them the book?'

'I do not know,' I answered honestly. 'But I think there was more to it than that.'

'What more? Sir, I have told you everything, I have trusted you. Yet I sense you know things that I do not.'

'I do, and may not tell you, as yet. But be assured, I mean you no harm.' I asked, 'What would you do now, go back to the Tower?'

'I am not on duty again until next Monday.' He shook his head. 'I tremble with fear every time I go to work. I feel them looking at me, waiting. I am terrified that sooner or later they will find out about the book – '

I heard several pairs of footsteps outside. Myldmore started up, then glanced at me, his eyes wide. The door opened and Barak came in with young William Cecil, who wore a stern look. There were two sturdy fellows at his side, each with a hand on a sword hilt. I thought

Myldmore might try to run but he just got up and stood meekly by his chair, shaking. He turned his eyes back to me and said, in tones of quiet horror, 'You have betrayed me.'

'No,' I said. 'To the contrary. You will be protected now.' I looked at Cecil, but his severe expression did not soften.

Chapter Twenty-six

LATE THAT AFTERNOON I stood again in Lord Parr's office at Whitehall Palace. With us were William Cecil and Archbishop Cranmer, whose white surplice made a contrast to the dark lawyer's robes Cecil and I wore. On the table was a large piece of paper covered with my writing, the fruit of much thinking that afternoon. We looked expectantly at the door, waiting.

We were to meet with Lord Parr at four o'clock, Cecil had informed me, when he and his men took Myldmore away from my chambers. He had told the terrified young gaoler only that he worked for people at court who were friends and would see him kept safe, housed somewhere quiet for now; a message would be sent to the Tower officials that he was ill, to buy some time.

Myldmore had been very frightened, pleading to be let go, but Cecil answered brusquely that Greening's killers were still at large and I had encountered them very recently, which I could only confirm. As he was led out, Myldmore looked at me over his shoulder; a look of sorrow and anger, for he had bared his soul to me, while all the time I had been preparing to have him seized. As I stood in Lord Parr's office I remembered that look. Yet Myldmore was safer hidden away somewhere – unless the Queen fell; in that case, he was just one more who would fall with the rest of us.

✝

FOR TWO HOURS AFTER they left I had remained in my office. I pulled the shutters closed, got out pen and paper, and sat thinking; about dates and individuals, and the disappearance, now, not of one

295

but of two crucially sensitive books. I tried to fit Myldmore's story into the rest of what I knew. It all came back to Greening and his group; who and what they were. I lost track of time; then the Inn clock sounded three, reminding me I should be on my way. I gathered up the paper on which I had written some crucial notes, and headed down to the river to catch a wherry to the Whitehall Stairs. Once again, I changed my robe in the boat; at the palace the guards were already beginning to recognize me; some nodded respectfully as they ticked my name off their lists. I was starting to become familiar with the layout of the palace, too; that tight-packed series of extraordinary buildings, all different, interspersed with little hidden courts that had seemed so hard to navigate at first. Even the brightness and beauty of the interiors was becoming almost commonplace to me now, and I could walk along the corridors without constantly wanting to stop and gaze in wonder at a statue, a painting, a tapestry.

I arrived at Lord Parr's office just before four; he arrived soon afterwards. Also in the room when I arrived was William Cecil and, to my surprise, Archbishop Cranmer, looking withdrawn and worried. I bowed deeply to him. Lord Parr told me the Queen would be attending us shortly. 'I have been trying to work out where this new development with Myldmore leaves us,' I said as we waited.

'And where is that, Matthew?' Cranmer pressed quietly.

'I think we are narrowing down the possible scenarios.'

There was a tap at Lord Parr's door and it opened. Lady Anne Herbert, the Queen's sister, whom I had seen at Baynard's Castle a few days ago, stood on the threshold. She bowed as the Queen herself entered, wearing a magnificent dress of gold silk, the forepart and sleeves white with a design of tiny golden unicorns. Her expression was calm and composed. Behind her stood Mary Odell. We all bowed low.

The Queen said, 'Mary, Anne, you may return to my chamber.' The ladies nodded to us briefly and left. She looked between the four of us and took a long breath; for a moment her composure slipped and she appeared haggard as she turned to address her uncle. 'Your message said there had been developments? Have you recovered my book?'

'No, Kate, but Master Shardlake has some news.' He nodded in my direction.

'Good?' she asked quickly, intently.

'Not bad, your majesty. Complicated,' he replied.

She sighed, then turned to Cranmer. 'Thank you for attending us, my Lord. I know my uncle has been keeping you informed of developments.'

'I was here for the meeting of the King's Council.'

'Now that Gardiner and his people are no longer on the offensive,' Lord Parr said. There was a touch of contempt in his voice, no doubt aimed at Cranmer's tendency to absent himself from the council when matters looked dangerous.

The Queen gave her uncle a severe look. 'We five,' she said, 'we are the only ones who know the *Lamentation* is gone. But first, my Lord Archbishop, what news from the council?'

'Most of the discussion was about the visit of the French admiral next month. The scale of the ceremonies will be huge. Wriothesley argued that with so many taxes falling due this year it may cause murmuring and grudging among the populace, but the King is determined on great celebrations, nevertheless.' He smiled. 'And you are to be at the forefront, your majesty.'

'I know. The King has told me of the new gowns and jewellery my ladies and I are to have. And all the time I deceive him,' she added, a tremble in her voice. I thought how if the *Lamentation* suddenly appeared in public all the new finery could vanish in an instant. I remembered Myldmore's description of Anne Askew in the Tower and suppressed a shudder.

The Archbishop continued, encouragingly, 'Your brother, as Earl of Essex, is to welcome the ambassador and ride with him through London. He will be at the forefront of the ceremonies, too. Gardiner and Norfolk remained quiet throughout the meeting. Their heretic hunt has ended in failure, madam, that is clearer every day.'

'Unless something brings it alive again.' The Queen turned to me.

'I have heard from my uncle that two of your employees were injured. I am sorry for it.'

'Neither was seriously hurt, your majesty.'

'And this man Myldmore, you have him somewhere safe?' she asked Lord Parr.

'Yes, together with the guard and the carpenter who helped Leeman.'

'Each could be open to a charge of treason,' Cecil observed.

Lord Parr shook his head. 'If this matter is settled we should ensure all three move quietly out of London, to somewhere far out in the provinces.'

I said, 'Myldmore can only pretend sickness for so long; eventually there will be enquiries made.'

'There is no connection to us. They'll think he's run away.'

'So many disappeared,' the Queen said quietly. 'And two dead. And all because of me.'

'Anne Askew played her part,' Lord Parr said gruffly. 'God rot her wild heresy.'

Cranmer bit his lip, looking troubled, then said, 'With your leave, your majesty, Master Shardlake would like to show us something he has worked out.' He gestured to the sheet of paper on his desk.

The Queen looked at me and nodded, and I bowed again.

Cecil produced chairs for the Archbishop and the Queen, then stood beside Lord Parr. In front of them was a list of names and dates:

Armistead Greening – *murdered 10th July*

James McKendrick – *vanished 11/12th July*

William Curdy – *vanished 11/12th July*

Andres Vandersteyn – *vanished 11th/12th July*

Elias Rooke – *fled 17th July, murdered 18th July*

Michael Leeman – *suborned carpenter Barwic and guard Gawger with money, almost certainly took* Lamentation of a Sinner *to Greening on 6th July. Fled Whitehall 19th July*

Thomas Myldmore – *took Anne Askew's writings to Greening on 29th June*

I said, 'These seven people constituted a radical group which met at Armistead Greening's house.'

Cranmer pointed to the paper. 'Why is Myldmore's name separated from the others?'

'Because he was never actually accepted into the group. There might also be others who were considered, but these first six are the core. Vandersteyn may have had links to the Anabaptists, while Curdy had the money and may have supplied the bribes which Leeman used to pay the locksmith Barwic and the guard Gawger. Greening himself almost certainly had links to John Bale in Antwerp, and likely imported forbidden books from Flanders. Myldmore's evidence makes clear that this was more than a discussion group; it shows the fervour of some sort of Anabaptist sect.' I looked round. 'I think the group was trying to recruit people with connections to positions of trust, in high or secret places – the guard Leeman and the Tower gaoler Myldmore being two examples. Myldmore, however, could not accept their views on social order, nor on the Mass, and they asked him to leave. But later, when he saw what happened to Anne Askew, he felt he must act. Greening was the obvious person for him to take the woman's book to. And he, in turn, planned to take it to John Bale.'

The others remained silent. The Queen nervously touched the pearl at her breast; Cranmer fixed me with a troubled stare. William Cecil nodded slowly. 'Then Greening was murdered,' I continued. 'As for the other five –' I ran my finger down the list of names – 'three immediately vanished: McKendrick, Curdy and the Dutchman. The guard Leeman remained in his place here at Whitehall. And Elias moved to work for his neighbour Okedene.'

'If the other three fled,' said Cecil, 'rather than being murdered, why did not Elias and Leeman go, too?'

'I have pondered that. It may be that Leeman thought, given he worked at Whitehall Palace, that he was safe. He has quarters there. He stayed till he found he was under investigation, and only then disappeared. As for the apprentice Elias, remember times are hard, and he provided the only income for his widowed mother and his sisters.' I sighed. 'He was obstinate, and probably rejected the advice of the others to join them in fleeing. He seemed, when I met him, to think Greening was the murderers' only target. And given his youth, and perhaps limited experience, it may well be that the others did not trust him with the knowledge that they had possession of the *Lamentation*. Though I believe he knew that Greening had been given Anne Askew's writings.'

Cecil said, 'Because he said "killed for Anne Askew" before he died.'

'Exactly.'

'The poor boy,' the Queen muttered. 'He stayed for the sake of his mother and sisters, and died for it.' She walked abruptly to the window and stood looking out over the little courtyard below, her head bowed.

Lord Parr said, 'So these other four? Are they still alive?'

'I do not know. The fact Elias was murdered, too, makes me think the killers were after the whole group. Whether they found them or not we do not know.'

Lord Parr stroked his white beard. 'And whoever killed Greening and Elias is likely to have both Anne Askew's writings and the Queen's.'

Cecil asked: 'Could someone powerful – Wriothesley or Gardiner, Rich or Paget – have an agent inside the group? One of the missing four? How else could anyone outside have come to know that Greening had the *Lamentation*?'

I said, 'Yes, someone within that group could have been working for an enemy. I think we can rule out Leeman – if he was acting for Gardiner, the last people he would take the *Lamentation* to is Greening's group. That leaves Curdy, Vandersteyn and McKendrick; three of them. But if one of them was a spy working for Gardiner or anyone else, and murdered Greening and took the *Lamentation*, Anne Askew's work too, why has nothing been heard of either book since? Anne Askew's work they might destroy, for it incriminates Wriothesley and Rich, but surely the spy, if there is one, would take the *Lamentation* straight to the King?'

Cranmer nodded. 'Yes. Norfolk and Gardiner knew that Lord Hertford and Lord Lisle are about to return to the Privy Council, and that the heresy hunt had failed. It has only been recently that I have felt it prudent to return to the council myself. The sensible thing for them would have been to act at once, so far as the *Lamentation* was concerned.'

I said, 'Yes, my Lord Archbishop, I agree.'

The Queen turned and looked at me, a spark of hope flashing in her eyes. 'So you think it may not be Gardiner's agents who killed Greening and took the *Lamentation*?'

'Possibly. Though Master Cecil's logic about an informer within the group is persuasive.'

She shook her head, mystified. 'Someone working against a group of the godly from within? Pretending to be one of them? How could anyone bear such a betrayal of their souls?'

Lord Parr spoke with sudden impatience. 'In God's name, niece, when will you realize not all are as pure in mind as you?'

The Queen stared back at him, then laughed bitterly. 'I am not pure. If I were, I would never have needed to write a book called *Lamentation of a Sinner* – nor failed, after my Lord Archbishop's good advice, to destroy it through my sinful pride, and hence caused all of this. And deceived my husband in the process,' she added bitterly.

I glanced at her. In other tones the words might have sounded self-pitying, but the Queen spoke with a sad, honest intensity. There was silence for a moment. Then Cecil turned to me. 'The way Greening and Elias were killed, and your description of the two killers – that speaks to me of the involvement of someone powerful, someone who can afford to hire experienced assassins.'

I looked at him. Cecil was young indeed to be included in a

council such as this, but his cleverness was as great as his calm. Lord Parr had chosen well. 'I agree,' I said. 'But that does not get round the problem of why the book is still kept hidden.' I shifted my stance, for I had been standing a long time and my back was hurting. 'Lord Parr, my Lord Archbishop, your majesty: with your leave I would show you what I have written on the reverse of this paper. It is a chronology, and may illustrate matters further.' The Queen nodded, touching Catherine Howard's pearl again. I had never seen her so subdued. But she leaned across the table with the others as I turned the paper over:

9th June	Leeman overhears the Queen and the Archbishop arguing over the *Lamentation*. He has his group plot to steal it.
29th June	Anne Askew brought to the tower and tortured.
29th June	Myldmore takes Anne Askew's writings to Greening.
5th July	Two men, one with half an ear missing (likely the same who earlier tried to recruit the Queen's page Garet) are disturbed by Elias trying to break into Greening's premises.
6th July	Leeman, having suborned the carpenter Barwic and the guard Gawger, steals the *Lamentation*. Logic suggests he took it to Greening.
10th July	Greening murdered by two men, different from those involved in the first attack, and the *Lamentation* (and perhaps Anne Askew's writings) stolen.
11th/12th July	McKendrick, Curdy and Vandersteyn disappear.
16th July	Anne Askew burned.
17th July	I question Elias, who flees at mention of the name Bertano (which according to Okedene was mentioned by the group in connection with the Antichrist).
18th July	Elias murdered.
19th July	Having got wind of my enquiries, the guard Leeman flees.
21st July	I encounter the two men who killed Greening (not the same as the men who tried to break into his house earlier). They know who I am and they mention Bertano.

They studied the chronology. I said, 'This timetable allows that there could be two different sets of people involved. One that was after Anne Askew's writings, and another that wanted the *Lamentation*.'

Cecil shook his head. 'But there can only have been one informer, surely. Is it not more likely the informer told Gardiner – or Norfolk, or Rich, or Wriothesley, or whoever – about Anne Askew's *Examinations* first, after Myldmore took them to Greening on the twenty-ninth of June, and agents were then sent to take it, but were interrupted by Elias? Then, on the sixth or seventh of July the *Lamentation* comes into Greening's hands, and two different men, also under the authority of whoever is behind this, are sent to kill him and seize both books – succeeding, apart from the torn page Greening held on to?'

'Possibly. But surely it would have been more sensible to send the original two men on the second visit?' I mused.

Lord Parr burst out, in sudden anger, 'When will we get *any* certainty?'

'Not yet, my Lord. And there is another possibility.' I took a deep breath before continuing. 'What if, after the first attempted attack, the group held divided opinions about what to do next? Perhaps some wanted to send the books abroad for publication, while others, more sensible, realized publication of the *Lamentation* could only damage the Queen? Remember that in terms of their understanding of politics, these people are very naive. What if the majority of the group decided not to publish the *Lamentation*, and those who attacked Greening that night were working for someone within the group who *did* want it published?'

Cranmer said, 'We know the extreme sects are ever prone to splitting and quarrelling with each other.'

'To the extent of murdering one another too?' Cecil asked.

'If enough were at stake,' Cranmer replied sadly. 'We should at least consider it as a possibility.'

The others were silent. Then the Queen nodded wearily. 'At least I know who the traitor within my own household was: the guard

Leeman.' She gave me a sad little smile. 'You were wrong, Matthew, to suspect Jane Fool and the Lady Mary.'

'I know, your majesty. But it was my duty to interview all the possible suspects.'

She nodded again.

'Where do we go now?' Cranmer asked.

I turned to Cecil. 'First, as I said, we cannot discount the possibility that one of the missing three men took the books, as part of a quarrel over strategy. If so, they may try to smuggle them out of the country. What sort of watch have you been able to put at the docks?'

'I have arranged discreetly at the customs house for outgoing cargoes to be searched thoroughly. Of course, the customs officials' main effort goes into searching goods coming *into* the country, particularly for forbidden literature. Books hidden in bales of cloth, tied in oilskin inside casks of wine—'

'And if they find them?' I cut in.

'They are to be delivered to me.' Cecil touched one of the moles on his face. 'Lord Parr has graciously allowed me much gold to grease those wheels.'

The Queen said, 'But what if the books go from Bristol, or Ipswich, or even on a small boat launched secretly from a creek?'

'Then there is nothing we can do,' Lord Parr answered flatly. He turned to me. 'I can see a radical group sending Anne Askew's writings abroad for Bale or someone like him to print and smuggle back to England. But the *Lamentation*? Surely it is obvious, with even a little thought, that printing and distributing it would do nothing but harm the Queen.'

'I have dealt with the outer fringes of fanaticism before,' I said. 'These people may have actively sought to recruit people in places where secret information could be had, precisely so it could be publicized. They may even realize that harm could come to her majesty, but not care if they had it in their heads that their actions could stir people to revolt.'

Again there was a silence in the room. I continued quietly, 'We still have two leads which have not been followed to the end, both crucial. Two people. Who is Stice, the man with the torn ear, and who is he working for? And who in God's name is Gurone Bertano?'

'Bertano's name is quite unknown,' Cranmer replied. 'Though, as you know, there is something, some initiative, going on involving only the religious traditionalists close to the King. Whether this man could be involved I have no idea. But it could be that Greening's group somehow got hold of a third secret, this man's name and purpose. But from whom?'

'The name certainly terrified Elias.'

'We dare not question too openly, my Lord Archbishop,' Lord Parr said. 'If this Bertano is involved in some secret machinations of the conservatives, and I come out with the name, they will demand to know where we heard it.'

Cecil said, 'The other man, the one with the torn ear. We know from the page that he works for someone at court, someone who was seeking information against the Queen, and who was involved in the first attempt on Greening.'

'If only he could be found, he might be the key to the whole conspiracy,' I said.

Lord Parr began pacing up and down, his body tensed with frustration. 'All the great men of the realm have large households, and spies.'

Cecil said, 'I still find it odd that Myldmore was not arrested directly after it was discovered he had spoken of Anne Askew's torture.'

The Queen spoke up, her voice strained. 'From what you told my uncle, Matthew, I understand Sir Anthony Knevet was unhappy about the illegality of that poor woman's torture, and said he would report it to the King?'

'Yes, your majesty.'

She took a deep breath. 'I remember dining with the King one evening, about three weeks ago. We were interrupted by a messenger telling him Sir Anthony begged to see him urgently, on a confidential matter. The King was angry, said he wanted to dine in peace, but the messenger insisted it was important. I left the room and Sir Anthony was shown in – the King was not fit to walk at all that night.' She took another calming breath. 'They were together some time and then he left and his majesty called me back. He said nothing about the meeting but he seemed – disturbed, a little upset.'

Lord Parr said, 'The dates certainly tally. And what else could Knevet have wished to discuss so urgently?'

The Queen continued, 'I can tell you this. If Rich and Wriothesley tortured Anne Askew on their own initiative, or on the orders of someone higher – Gardiner or Norfolk – if they had done such a brutal and illegal thing against a woman, the King's sense of honour would have been outraged. They would have smarted for it. Indeed, it was shortly after this that the King came up with his plan of false charges against me being brought by Wriothesley, so that he could humiliate him.'

She held herself stiffly, as though struggling to contain remembered fear. I had long known she looked on Henry with a loving, indulgent eye, though to me he was a monster of cruelty. Nonetheless, it was also known the King placed great store by traditional, chivalric values; such a mind could be shocked by a gentlewoman's torture, while seeing nothing amiss in burning her alive. 'That could explain why nothing has been done to Myldmore,' I said thoughtfully. 'And I remember Rich had a worried, preoccupied look at the burning.' I smiled wryly. 'Perhaps it was not only Wriothesley who felt the King's wrath.'

Lord Parr nodded agreement. 'Yes, my nephew's reports of Rich and Wriothesley being subdued at council meetings date from then. Though, as I say, they seem brighter now.'

Cecil asked, 'But would either of them then dare go on to murder the printer and steal those books?'

'Perhaps,' I said thoughtfully. 'If they had an informer in an Anabaptist sect and were told about the books. Recovering the *Lamentation* and presenting it to the King would then help enormously in restoring their position.'

They considered this theory. Then we all jumped at a sudden knock. We looked at each other nervously – perhaps it was not wise for us all to be seen together with the Queen. Lord Parr went to the door and opened it. One of the Queen's guards was outside. He bowed low to the Queen, then said, 'Master Secretary Paget is outside, my Lord. He would speak with you and her majesty.'

'Very well,' Lord Parr said. 'Give us a moment, then show him in.'

As the man closed the door Cranmer spoke quietly. 'It may be politic for me to leave. Perhaps go down to the Queen's Gallery.'

'Very well, my Lord Archbishop,' Lord Parr agreed.

The Archbishop opened the door and left swiftly. But immediately we heard a deep voice in the corridor. 'My Lord Archbishop. Visiting her majesty?'

'Indeed, Master Secretary.'

'Perhaps you could stay a moment. I have called to discuss arrangements for the French admiral's reception.'

Cranmer returned to the room, frowning a little. Then Secretary Paget entered, alone. He bowed to the Queen, then looked around at us with the confident stare of a man in charge of his surroundings. I remembered that square, hard face from the burning, the mouth a downturned slit between his long moustache and unruly forked beard. He wore a grey robe and cap today, no ostentation apart from his heavy gold chain of office, and carried a sheaf of papers under his arm. 'Meeting with men of the Queen's Learned Council, eh, my Lord?' he asked Lord Parr cheerfully. 'How would our lands ever be administered without lawyers dipping their quills in the ink, hey? Well, I, too, was a lawyer once. I hope you do not trouble her majesty too much?' he added maliciously, regarding Lord Parr with a flat, unblinking stare.

I glanced at the Queen; she had managed in an instant to compose her features. She now radiated quiet regality: a lift of the chin and shoulders, a slight stiffening of the body. 'My councillors simplify matters for my weak woman's wit,' she said cheerfully.

Paget bowed again. 'I fear I, too, must ask to indulge your well-known patience, but on a more congenial subject, I am sure. The King has given orders for new clothes for your ladies who will accompany you at the festivities for the French admiral. He wishes you to be very well attended.'

'His majesty is gracious as ever.'

'I know the festivities are a month away, but there is a great deal to organize. May we discuss the arrangements? Afterwards, my Lord Archbishop, perhaps we could talk about your role, which will also be important.'

Behind Paget's back, Lord Parr looked at Cecil and me, then curtly inclined his head to the door. Fortunately, we were too lowly to be introduced to Master Secretary. We bowed to the Queen and sidled out. Paget was saying, 'The finest cloth has been ordered, to be made up at Baynard's Castle . . .'

Cecil and I walked away up the corridor, saying nothing until we reached the discreetly positioned window overlooking the courtyard, where I had seen the King that first day. The courtyard was empty this afternoon apart from a couple of young courtiers lounging lazily against a wall. The afternoon shadows were lengthening.

I spoke quietly. 'Secretary Paget. I saw him at the burning.'

'Yes.'

'He is a traditionalist, is he not?'

'He was first brought to court under Bishop Gardiner's patronage, but he is not linked to him any more.'

'No?'

'He is the King's man now and nobody else's. With the King so physically weak, he puts more and more of the work in Paget's hands, but Paget never oversteps himself.'

'Yes, I heard he learned that lesson from Wolsey and Cromwell.'

Cecil nodded. 'Whichever way the wind blows, Paget will follow only the King's wishes. If he has any principles of his own they are well hidden away.'

'Bend with the wind rather than break.'

'Yes, indeed.'

'But – are we sure? If Paget is a traditionalist in religion, and on good terms with Rich and Wriothesley? It seems those two may have taken the initiative to torture Anne Askew without consulting the King; perhaps Paget, too, is capable of using his initiative. With the King so ill. And is the Secretary not responsible for all official spies and informers?'

'Official ones, certainly,' Cecil replied slowly. 'But as Lord Parr said earlier, all the great men run unofficial ones. As for the King's health, his body is breaking down, but, from all I hear, his mind and will are as sharp as ever.'

I looked at young Cecil: clever, always coolly in control, with more than a touch of unscrupulousness, I suspected. But nonetheless he had nailed his flag unhesitatingly to the Queen's mast. He gave a heavy sigh and I realized that he, too, must be feeling the strain of all this. I wondered whether he also felt afraid now when he smelled smoke. 'What happens next?' I asked him gently.

'It is in Lord Parr's hands, and mine, for now, I think. Watching the docks, trying to find this man with half an ear, and solving the mystery of Bertano.'

He touched my arm, an unexpected gesture. 'We are grateful to you, Master Shardlake. That talk clarified much – ' He broke off. 'Ah, see. Down there.'

I looked into the courtyard. Two men had entered and were walking across it, talking amiably. The two young layabouts who were already there stopped leaning on the wall and bowed deeply to them. One was the Queen's brother, William Parr, Earl of Essex, tall and thin with his gaunt face and trim auburn beard. The other was the man I had heard the Queen's ladies speaking of as being back in England, a man whom the Queen had once loved and whom I despised: Sir Thomas Seymour. He wore a short green robe, with white silk hose showing off his shapely legs, and a wide flat cap with a swan feather on his coppery head. With one hand he was stroking his dark auburn beard, which was long like Paget's, but combed to silky smoothness.

'The Parr–Seymour alliance in action,' Cecil whispered, with the keen interest of a connoisseur of politics. 'The two main reformist families meet.'

'Is not Sir Thomas too headstrong for a senior position?'

'Yes indeed. But for now his brother Lord Hertford is abroad, and Sir Thomas keeps the flag flying. Lord Hertford returns very soon, though. I have contacts in his household.' Cecil looked at me with a quick, vain little smile, then bowed. 'I will leave you now, sir. You will be summoned when there is further news. Thank you again.'

I watched him walk away down the corridor, with his quick, confident steps. That smile made me think: Cecil, too, would one day make a politician; already he had his foot on the first rung of the ladder. I wondered about the alliance between the Parrs and the Seymours. For now, they were united against the religious conservatives. But when the King died both families would have separate claims to govern the realm in the name of the boy Edward: the Parrs as the family of his stepmother, the Seymours as that of his dead true mother. And how long, then, would the alliance last?

Chapter Twenty-seven

A s I WALKED BACK ALONG the corridor towards the gilded
public chambers, I heard a strange sound. A creaking, clank,
ing noise from behind the wall, and what sounded like the rattle of
chains. I looked around, and saw a door in the corridor I had not
noticed previously. Unlike the others it did not have a magnificently
decorated surround but was set flush to the wall, with the same linen,
fold panelling as the walls on either side. There was a small keyhole,
but no handle. Overcome with curiosity, I pushed at it gently and to
my surprise it opened easily on oiled hinges.

Within was a wide, square platform, lit with torches bracketed to
the walls. The platform surrounded a staircase leading down to the
ground floor. To my astonishment, in one corner of the platform, four
men in the dark uniform of the King's Gentlemen Pensioners were
straining to turn the handles of a large winch, hauling something up
the stairwell from the ground floor. I heard a wheezy shout from
beneath, 'Careful, you dolts, keep me steady!' Then, as the men pulled
harder on the ropes, an immense figure rose into view, seated on a
heavy wheeled chair, secured by a leather belt round his immense
waist. I glimpsed a near,bald head, an immense, red, round face, folds
of thin,bearded flesh wobbling above the collar of a caftan. The
King's huge cheeks twitched in pain.

Another guard saw me and rushed over; a big, bearded fellow. He
clapped a hand over my mouth and pushed me through the door, back
into the corridor. He shut the door quietly, then grabbed the lapels of
my robe. 'Who are you?' he spat with quiet fierceness. 'How did you
get in there?'

'I – I heard strange noises behind the door. I pushed it and it opened easily – '

'God's death, it should always be locked from inside – I'll have Hardy's balls for this.' His expression suddenly changed, from anger to contempt. 'Who are you, crookback?' He glanced at my robe. 'I see you wear the Queen's badge.'

'I am new appointed to her majesty's Learned Council.'

He released me. 'Then learn, and quickly, that in Whitehall you go *only – where – you – are – allowed.*' He punctuated the last words with painful jabs to my chest with his finger, then glanced nervously over his shoulder. A heavy clunk from behind the door indicated the chair had been pulled in. He spoke hurriedly, 'Now go, and thank your stars he did not see you. You think his majesty likes to be watched like this, being winched upstairs? Be gone, now!' He turned and went back through the door. I scurried away as fast as possible. I knew the King could scarcely walk, but it had never occurred to me to wonder how he got to the Royal Apartments on the first floor. His immobility alone must be humiliating enough for that once famous athlete, but to be seen like that – I shuddered at my narrow escape. If he had glanced up momentarily and recognized me . . .

✝

AGAIN, THERE WAS A period of silence from Whitehall. I heard nothing for a day or so. I returned to work, but found it harder this time to settle or rest.

On Saturday morning, the 24th of July, I arrived at chambers late in the morning to find Nicholas absent.

'Perhaps he has had a late night in the taverns,' Skelly observed disapprovingly.

'He said yesterday his chest was hurting,' Barak observed. 'I'll go to his place at lunchtime if he hasn't come in, check he's all right.'

I nodded.

Skelly added reproachfully, 'That witness in that Common Pleas case called, as arranged, to have you take his deposition, and I had to say you had been called away on urgent business. Since I did not know where you were, sir,' he added pointedly.

'I am sorry,' I said, annoyed at having forgotten; things could not go on like this.

'And these notes were delivered for you.' Skelly handed me some papers.

'Thank you.'

I took them into my room and worked alone for the next few hours. Most were routine matters, but one was an official notification from Treasurer Rowland that a complaint had been made against me by my former client, Isabel Slanning. He asked me to call on him on Monday. I sighed. Well, that was not unexpected. There was nothing to it, but no doubt Rowland would enjoy trying to discomfit me.

I was a little worried about Nicholas. Barak had said he would visit him at lunchtime if he did not arrive at chambers. What if he found him ill, his wound infected perhaps, and needed to take him to Guy? But I knew Barak: if it was anything I should know, he would have sent a message. He might have gone home, as I had told him he could if he wished while Tamasin was expecting. I turned my atten-tion back to the work that was still upon my desk.

Shortly after, there was a knock at the door. I hoped it might be Barak returned, but Skelly came in. 'Master Dyrick has called to see you, sir, regarding the Slanning case.'

'Show him in.' I put down my quill, frowning. He must have come to collect the Slanning papers. They were on the table next to my desk. I would have expected him to send a clerk, though. We had had a passage of arms a year before, and I knew things about Vincent Dyrick that gave him an interest in not pushing me too far. Nonethe-less, he was a man who loved a fight. I could imagine Isabel looking for the most aggressive barrister available. Someone who did not mind acting for difficult clients with hopeless cases, so long as they paid well. That fitted Dyrick exactly. I knew from experience that he would be relentless in trying to make something of the case; probably even persuade himself that her cause was just.

Dyrick came in with his confident, athletic step, his green eyes sharp as ever in his thin, handsome face, strands of red hair showing under his coif. He bowed briefly and gave me his sardonic smile.

'God give you good morning, Brother Shardlake.'

'And you, Brother Dyrick. Please sit.'

He did so, folding his hands in his lap.

I continued, civil but unsmiling, 'So, you have taken Mistress Slanning's case? I have the papers ready.'

'Good. It is an interesting matter.'

'Hopeless, I think. But profitable.'

'Indeed, yes.' He smiled again. 'Brother Shardlake, I know that you and I have reason to keep apart, but – well – sometimes by chance we will find ourselves on opposing sides in a case.'

'My involvement in this one is over. Was it you who prompted her to complain to the Inn authorities?' I asked abruptly. 'The complaint is nonsense.'

He met my gaze. 'Actually, since you ask, no. I told her she should concentrate on the case. But she was insistent.'

'Mistress Slanning is certainly that.' I thought, he is telling the truth there. As far as the case was concerned, there was no advantage in making a complaint, and while Dyrick would like to make trouble for me, neither would he push matters too far.

'She is most displeased with your conduct of matters,' he said in a tone of mock reproof.

'I know.' I pushed the bundle of documents over to him. 'Here are the papers, and I wish you joy of them.'

He laid the bundle on his lap. 'A lot of meat on this chicken,' he said appreciatively. He switched his look to one of disapproval. 'Mistress Slanning tells me you conspired against her with her brother's lawyer, Master Coleswyn. You have been a guest at his house. Further, she claims that you guided her to an expert for an opinion on the wall painting at the centre of this case, who was unsympathetic. She says this man, Adam, was also in collusion with you and Coleswyn. It would help me in representing her if you could give me your response to those charges.'

For a brief moment I considered offering the sort of earthy response Barak might have made. Instead I spoke calmly. 'You will find she chose the expert herself, from the list I provided, without asking my advice.'

He inclined his head. 'Mistress Slanning also says that, like Coleswyn and her brother, you are an extreme religious radical. I fear she has insisted, despite my opposition, on raising that in court in September. I thought I should warn you.'

Dyrick fixed me with those cold green eyes. I answered, an edge in my voice, 'I am no extreme radical, as you well know.'

He shrugged. 'Well, it is nothing to me either way, but it is not the sort of accusation to have made in public these days. I should warn you, she has put that in her complaint to Lincoln's Inn as well.'

'You are right. It is not sensible to bandy around accusations of religious extremism in these days. For anyone.' There was a warning note in my voice. Dyrick possessed a reckless streak, a lack of sensible judgement, and enjoyed making trouble for trouble's sake.

He inclined his head again. 'I thought the heresy hunt was over.'

'One can never be sure.'

'Well, perhaps you know more of that than I. You have contacts at court, I remember.'

'Brother Dyrick,' I began, 'you must know this case is nonsense, the expert opinion clear and decisive. And my opponent Master Coleswyn, in case you are fishing for information about him, is a clever man, and a reasonable one. In my opinion both Isabel Slanning and Edward Cotterstoke have no aim other than to hurt each other. It would be in everyone's interest if the matter were settled quickly.'

He raised an eyebrow. 'I think you know as well as I, Brother Shardlake, that Mistress Slanning will never settle. Never.' He was right. A picture came into my mind of Isabel's face; lined, bitter, implacable.

Dyrick rose, slipping the file under his arm. He patted it smugly. 'As I said, there is a lot of meat on this chicken. I came to tell you, I will fight it hard; but I will not encourage Mistress Slanning in throwing around accusations of heresy. I am well aware how dangerous that is. As for her complaint to the Inn, I will have to leave you to deal with that.'

I nodded. I was glad he had some sense at least.

'I now look forward to doing battle with Brother Coleswyn.' Dyrick bowed and left the room.

☩

I SAT THERE AWHILE, more irritated than angry at having Vincent Dyrick back in my life. The notion of a religious conspiracy in the Slanning case was ludicrous. But it remained a worry to Philip Coleswyn – possibly even a threat – if Isabel continued making wild accusations. I would warn him.

Eventually, with a sigh, I returned to work. It was cooler now, the sun fading, and all was quiet outside in Gatehouse Court. Towards seven there was another knock at the door; I hoped again it might be Barak or Nicholas, but it was only Skelly come to bid me goodnight and hand me a note. 'This just came, sir. Someone slipped it under the door.' It was a folded paper addressed to me in scrawled capitals, sealed with a shapeless blob of wax.

When Skelly left I broke the seal and opened the note. It was unsigned, and like my address it was written in unidentifiable capitals:

MASTER SHARDLAKE,
    WE HAVE THE BOY NICHOLAS OVERTON. IF YOU WISH TO SEE HIM AGAIN CALL AT THE HOUSE WITH GREEN SHUTTERS TWO DOORS DOWN FROM THE SIGN OF THE FLAG IN NEEDLEPIN LANE, ALONE, AT NINE TONIGHT. TELL NO ONE AT THE PALACE; WE HAVE A SPY THERE. IF YOU DO NOT COME, WE WILL SEND YOU HIS HEAD.

Chapter Twenty-eight

I HALF-WALKED, HALF-RAN the few streets to Barak's house, earning curious stares from passers-by. My overwhelming fear was that he had found a similar note at Nicholas's rooms and had gone off on a hunt of his own. I told myself it was not like Barak to act impulsively, certainly not these days. But I was truly frightened now for both of them, and cursed myself anew for the trouble my involvement with the *Lamentation* had brought to all around me.

I was out of breath when I arrived, sweating and panting heavily as I knocked at the door. I realized I had become unfit these last months, doing little more than sitting at my work all day and eating Agnes Brocket's good food at home.

Jane Marris opened the door. She curtsied, then stared at me. 'Have you run here, Master Shardlake?'

'Half-run. From chambers.'

Unexpectedly, she smiled. 'All is well, sir. The mistress had a scare, but it turned out to be nothing. Dr Malton is with her.'

I frowned, not knowing what she meant, but followed her anxiously down the little hallway, breathing hard. In the neat little parlour Tamasin sat on cushions, looking pale. To my immense relief Barak sat on a chair beside her, his unbandaged hand in hers while Guy, in his long physician's robe, leaned over the table, mixing herbs in a dish. From upstairs I heard little George crying.

'Jane,' Tamasin said, 'will you go up to him? He knows there is something out of sorts.'

'What has happened?' I asked when Jane left the room.

Barak looked up. In the warm summer evening he wore only his shirt and hose, and I again glimpsed his father's ancient mezuzah on its gold chain round his neck. 'Tamasin had a pain in her stomach this morning. When I came home at lunchtime it was worse. She feared something was happening to the baby. I went round to Guy.'

Guy spoke soothingly, 'All is well, it was nothing more than wind.' Tamasin looked away, embarrassed.

'She had me worried,' Barak said. Tamasin lifted a hand and stroked his neat beard. He turned his head to look at me. 'Sorry I didn't come back to work. But it's Saturday. Paperwork day. How did you know I was here?'

'I – I didn't, for certain. But there was something I needed to discuss with you urgently, so I came round.'

'I am sorry I discommoded you,' Tamasin said.

''Tis you that needs the commode,' Barak answered with a wicked grin.

'Fie, Jack.' She reddened.

Guy stood up. 'Mix these herbs with some beer and take them with food,' he instructed. 'Sometimes the mixture can ease – what you have.' He smiled. 'There is nothing else to worry about.'

Tamasin took his hand. 'You are good to us,' she said. 'Only we worry, after – '

'I know,' Guy said. She was remembering their first, stillborn child.

'I'll see you out,' Barak said.

'Thank you.' I noticed there was still a reserve in Guy's voice when he addressed me. He gave me a formal little bow, which hurt me more than hard words would have done, and Barak showed him out. I was left with Tamasin. She leaned back on the cushions.

'I was worried,' she said to me quietly.

'I understand. In your condition any – upset – must make you fear some ill to the child.'

'Yes.' She looked wistful. 'I hope for a daughter this time. A little girl to dress in frocks and make rag dolls for.'

'Maybe it will be so.'

She smiled briefly at the thought, then said, 'Guy looked at Jack's hand. It is healing well. But it was unlike him to be so careless, and that is a nasty cut to get just from a paper knife.' Her eyes had narrowed slightly and I had to stop myself shifting uneasily; I knew how sharp Tamasin was.

'I am glad it is healing well,' I replied neutrally.

Barak returned. From the look of me he had guessed something serious was afoot. 'We'll go and talk up in the bedroom, Tammy,' he said. 'You won't want to hear a lot of legal business.'

'I don't mind.'

'Take Guy's advice, woman,' he said with mock severity, 'and get some rest.' He led me up the little staircase to their bedroom, where he sat on the bed, lowering his voice, for Jane Marris was still with George next door. He spoke quietly. 'What's happened?'

'Did you go round to Nicholas's lodgings today?'

'Yes. I promised I would. At lunchtime, before coming home. The other students he shares that pigsty with said he went out yesterday evening and didn't come back. They thought he'd probably found a whore to bed with.'

'He didn't, though. Read this.' I took out the note and handed it to him. 'It was pushed under the chambers door less than half an hour ago.'

After reading the message, Barak closed his eyes a moment before opening them and glaring at me furiously.

'All right,' he said, his voice still quiet. 'What in Christ's name is going on?'

'I can't tell you everything. I'm sworn to secrecy—'

'Fuck that!' His voice rose angrily. 'Something big's happening, isn't it? You've been using me and Nicholas to help with aspects of it. That stolen jewel of the Queen's down at Baynard's Castle, the murdered printer whose parents you're supposed to be acting for, those men who attacked us in that tavern; that scared-looking young man you questioned in chambers. They're all connected, aren't they? You send me with a note to the palace and then a whole troop of men come and take the poor arsehole away. He was terrified. And that young lawyer who came with them, the one with the warty face, he works for the Queen, doesn't he?'

'Yes.'

'I could tell by the manner, the cut of his robe, that he was a palace lawyer – I worked round people like that long enough. And I've known you six years; I know how jumpy and tetchy you get when something dangerous is on!' He stabbed a finger at me. 'The Queen's got you mixed up in something again, hasn't she? Someone's kid-napped Nick because of it, and you want me to help you get him back! Well, tell me everything first! Everything!'

I raised my hands. 'Lower your voice, or the women will hear.' I hesitated; if I told him all I would be breaking my oath and exposing him to dangerous secrets, but if I were to do anything for Nicholas I needed Barak's assistance now. So I told him the whole story: my first summons to the Queen, the missing *Lamentation*, the two men who had died and the others who had vanished, Myldmore's confession, Anne Askew's writings. I spoke softly, Barak asking a couple of questions now and again in an equally quiet voice.

At the end of my story he sat thinking, stroking his beard, but still looking angry. 'Can't you get the Queen's men to help you?'

'The note says they have a spy in the palace.'

'That could be bluff.'

'I daren't risk it.'

'Can't you get a personal note to the Queen herself – you who would do anything for her?' There was impatience in his voice.

I shook my head. 'There is no time. Nine tonight, remember. It's well past seven now.'

'If there *is* a spy at Whitehall Palace, they won't let you out of this house of theirs alive to tell of it. Let alone release Nick.'

I spoke quietly, 'I just want you to come to the house with me and hide nearby while I go in. You're good at that.' I took a deep breath.

'Then, if I don't come out in twenty minutes, try to get a message to the lawyer William Cecil. There is no danger to you in that.'

He shook his head, suddenly weary. 'You'd die for the Queen, wouldn't you?'

'Yes,' I answered simply.

He paced the room, then said, 'Shit. I'll come. Though I think Tamasin's already suspicious over my hand.'

'Thank you, Jack.' I spoke humbly. 'Thank you. I am more grateful than I can say.'

'So you fucking should be. Now wait here while I go and say goodbye to my wife, tell her some story about a witness that needs to be seen urgently. I don't want her seeing that drawn face of yours again. I'll call you down.'

'We've an hour and a half,' I said.

'Enough, then, to find a tavern, and think and plan properly.'

☨

WE WALKED INTO THE CITY, then down towards the river. Barak had donned an old leather jerkin over his shirt, and brought another for me, which I had placed over my doublet once we left the house. It would not be wise to stand out in the poorer areas for which we were headed. Greening's killers had known that.

'Have you any gold in your purse?' he asked.

'Yes. And some silver.'

'Gold's much better.'

We said little more as we walked along St Peter's Street and into Thames Street. To the south I could see the cranes on the wharves and the river beyond, white with sails. Over to the west the sun was setting. Barak never broke his stride; he had spent all his life in the city and knew every street and alley. Eventually he stopped. A respectable-looking tavern stood where Thames Street intersected with a lane of narrow, tumbledown houses that led down to the river, some of the buildings slanting at odd angles as they had settled, over the decades, into the Thames clay. A little way down the lane I saw a sign marking another, shabbier-looking tavern, painted with the red-and-white cross of St George. It was the Sign of the Flag mentioned in the note.

'Needlepin Lane,' Barak said. 'Mostly cheap lodging houses. Let's go in here to this tavern; sit by the window.'

The place was busy, mostly with shopkeepers and workers come for a drink at the end of the day. Barak got two mugs of beer and we took seats with a view of the lane; the shutters were wide open this hot evening, letting in the stifling dusty stink of the city. We had scarcely sat when Barak rose again. A solidly built man in a London constable's red uniform, staff over his shoulder and lamp in hand, was walking by. Later he would patrol the streets to enforce the curfew. Barak leaned over. 'Your purse. Quick!'

I handed it over. Barak darted outside and I saw him talking with the constable, their heads bent close. At one point the constable turned and stared at me for a moment, then he walked on down Thames Street. Barak returned to the tavern.

'Right,' he said, taking his stool. 'I've squared him.'

'I didn't see money pass.'

'He's good at passing coins unseen. So am I. I told him we're on official business about some stolen jewellery, and we're meeting an informant at the house two doors down at nine. Asked him to be ready to come to the house with anyone else he can muster, if I shout.'

'Well done.' I knew nobody better at such tasks; Barak's instincts were always extraordinary.

'I asked him if he knew who lived there. He said one or two men go there occasionally, but mostly it's empty. He thinks it might be where some gentleman takes a girl, though if so he hasn't seen her. You're four shillings poorer, but it's worth it.' He paused. 'It could well be a house belonging to some courtier, where people meet for unauthorized business. Lord Cromwell had such places; I expect the Queen's people are keeping that gaoler from the Tower in one.' He fell silent as a young boy set a candle on our table; outside it was getting dark. Barak took a draught of beer, then stood again. 'I'm going to take a quick walk up and down the street. See if there are any lights on in that house.' He left again, returning a few minutes later. 'The shutters are green, like the note said. They're closed but I could see a glimmer of light between the slats on the ground floor.' He raised his eyebrows and smiled. 'Nothing to do now but wait till the church clocks strike curfew.' Then he took a long gulp of beer.

'Thank you,' I said quietly. 'I would not have thought of any of that.'

He nodded. 'I quite enjoyed persuading the constable to back us up, spying out that house. And even that sword fight in the inn, if truth be told, for all it hurt my hand. Old habits die hard.' He frowned suddenly. 'But I've not the speed and energy I once had. I've a good wife, a good job, a child and another on the way.' He stared into space a moment, then said, 'Lord Cromwell pulled me out of the gutter when I was a boy. I enjoyed the work I did for him, too, the need for sharp wits and sometimes a sharp knife. But that's a job for the young, and those with little to lose.'

I quoted a biblical verse that came to my mind: '*When I was a child, I spake as a child, I understood as a child, I thought as a child; but when I became a man, I put away childish things.*'

'Never had much chance for childish things.' Barak took another swig of beer, and looked at me hard. 'The old ways – I still love that excitement of having to move, think, watch, quickly, on your feet. I've realized that again tonight.' He sat thinking, then looked at me and spoke quietly. 'I passed my mother in the street, you know, a few months back.'

I stared at him. I knew that after the death of his father, Barak's mother had quickly married another man, whom he detested; he had been out on the streets alone by the age of twelve. He said, 'She was old, bent, carrying a pile of twigs for the fire. I don't know what happened to *him*, maybe he's dead, with luck.'

'Did you speak to her?'

He shook his head. 'She was coming towards me, I recognized her at once. I stopped, I wasn't sure whether to speak to her or not. I felt sorry for her. But she walked straight past, didn't recognize *me*. So that was that. It's for the best.'

'How could you expect her to recognize you? You hadn't seen her in over twenty years.'

'A decent mother would know her own child,' he answered stubbornly.

'Did you tell Tamasin?'

He shook his head firmly. 'She'd press me to look for her. And I won't.' His jaw set hard.

'I'm sorry.'

'What's done is done.' He changed the subject. 'You realize Nick may not be at that house, if he's even still alive. These people want *you*, to find out what you know, and they won't be gentle. After that, they'll have no use for either of you.'

I met his gaze. 'I know. But if they are going to interrogate me, it will take time. That's why I need you to watch. If I don't come out in twenty minutes, call your new friend the constable. I was going to tell you to go to Whitehall, but this way's better and faster.'

'All right.' He fixed me with his hard brown eyes, and spoke seriously. 'You have to separate yourself from the Queen. Every time you go near that cesspit they call the Royal Court you end up in danger.'

'*She* is in danger.'

'Her own fault, by the sound of it.'

I lowered my voice to a whisper. 'The King is dying.'

'I've heard that rumour.'

'It's more than rumour. I've caught glimpses of him, twice. The state he is in – I don't see how he can last more than a few months.'

'And then?'

'Then, if the reformers are in the ascendant, the Queen may be one of those who governs for Prince Edward. She may even be made Regent, as she was when the King led his army to France two years ago. But that book in the wrong hands could kill her.'

Barak inclined his head. 'Even if she survives, and the reformers win, the Seymours will want to take over. And they're Prince Edward's blood relatives, after all. If they do, perhaps the Queen may marry again.' He looked at me narrowly. 'Another political marriage, probably, to someone powerful at Court.'

I smiled wryly. 'Jack, I have never had the remotest hopes for myself, if that's what is in your mind. Catherine Parr was far above me in status even before she married the King. I have always known that.'

'Then let this be the last time,' Barak said, with sudden fierceness.

✝

AT NINE THE CHURCH BELL sounding through the deepening dusk signalled curfew, and the tavern emptied. We went outside. I saw the constable on the corner, his lamp lit. A large, younger man stood beside him. 'Just about to start my patrol, sir,' he said meaningfully to Barak, who nodded. We left them and walked down Needlepin Lane as far as the Sign of the Flag, where again patrons were dispersing for the night. They were a younger, rougher crowd, several apprentices among them. Barak nodded at a doorway just beyond. 'I'll wait there,' he said. 'Just out of sight.'

I took a deep breath. 'Twenty minutes.'

'I'll count them off. Good luck.'

'Thank you.' I walked on, my legs trembling slightly. I passed a house where a ragged family could be seen through open shutters, eating a late supper by the light of a cheap candle; the next house was the one with the green shutters. Like Barak, I could see a light through the closed slats. Looking up at the upper storey, I glimpsed a faint light there too; someone was watching the street. But they could not have seen Barak from that angle.

I knocked at the wooden door. Immediately I heard heavy foot-steps within. The door opened and a short, heavyset man in a stained shirt stared at me. He had a candle in one hand, the other held over the dagger at his waist. Elias's descriptions of the men who had made the first attempt to break into Greening's shop had been vague, but this could have been one of them. He was in his late twenties and under bushy black hair his face was square, craggy, with an angry expression that spoke of temper.

'I am Master Shardlake,' I said. 'I received the note.'

He nodded curtly and stepped aside. I entered a room with rushes on the floor, the only furniture a trestle table bearing a large sconce of candles, with stools around. A rickety staircase led to the upper floor. On one of the stools sat Nicholas, his hands bound behind him and a gag in his mouth. He had a black eye, crusted blood on the gag and in his matted red hair. Behind him stood another young man; tall, in gentlemanly clothing – a good green doublet, with embroidery at the sleeves and neck of his shirt. He had keen, foxy features and a neatly trimmed fair beard. The outer half of his left ear was missing; at some point it had been sliced clean off, leaving only shiny scar tissue. He held a sword to Nicholas's throat; the boy stared at me with frantic eyes.

The man who had let me in closed the door. 'No sign of anyone else, Gower?' his companion with the damaged ear asked in cultivated tones.

'No, Master Stice. And he's watching above.' He cocked his head towards the staircase.

The other man nodded, his sword still held to Nicholas's throat. I thought, they've let me know both their names; that doesn't bode well for us. Stice looked at me then; his grey eyes were cool, appraising. He took the sword slowly away from Nicholas's throat and smiled.

'So, Master Shardlake, you came. We didn't think you would, but our master disagreed. He says you have courage and loyalty both.'

Gower stepped over, looking at me with his angry eyes. 'Perhaps you like the boy, eh, hunchback? Someone like you won't have much luck with women. Would have thought you could have done better than this beanpole, though.'

'Leave him alone, Gower,' Stice snapped impatiently. 'We've business to conduct, no time for jests.'

I looked at Stice contemptuously. 'What have you done to Nicholas?'

'We had to knock him out to get him here. And he wasn't very cooperative when he woke up. Gower had to give him a lesson in manners.'

'I have come as you asked. Release him.'

Stice nodded. 'You can have him, though Leonard here would have relished preparing his head to send you.' He glanced at Gower. 'Full of funny ideas is Leonard. He thinks you're a sodomite.' I would not have dared to mock the man like that, but he took it from Stice, who reached behind Nicholas and untied the gag, then used his sword to slice through his bonds. Gower went and stood beside Nicholas, hand held meaningfully on his knife, as the boy pulled the gag from his mouth. Eventually he spoke in a dry, hoarse voice. 'I'm so sorry, sir.'

'It is my fault,' I said quietly. 'I led you into danger.'

'I'd been to a tavern last night,' he croaked.' I was walking home when I was knocked out from behind. When I woke up I was here. Where are we?'

'A house near the river.' I turned to Stice. 'Well, are you going to let him go?'

He shook his head. 'Not yet. There's someone wants to talk to you, then if he's happy we'll let you both go. Leonard will take Nicky boy out back in the meantime.' Stice, sword still in hand, leaned against the wall, waiting.

Nicholas still sat. 'For mercy's sake,' he cried. 'May I have some water?' He swallowed uncomfortably and grimaced with pain.

'Poor baby,' Stice replied with a mocking laugh. 'Not much forbearance for a gentleman. Oh, get him some water from the barrel, Leonard.'

As Gower went through a door to the back of the house, Nicholas stood, shakily. I heard a creak from the floorboards above, and remembered there was another man in the house. Well, we had been here for five minutes; fifteen more and Barak and the constable would come with his men. In the meantime I would have to dissimulate well. Nicholas stood, stretching, and feeling his bruises. Stice still leaned against the wall, hand on his sword hilt, watching him with amusement.

Suddenly Nicholas launched himself at Stice, clearing the few feet between them with one leap, a hand closing on Stice's wrist before he could grasp his sword. Caught off guard, Stice let out a yell of anger as Nicholas grasped his other wrist and pinned him to the wall, then kneed him hard in the crotch. He cried out and bent over.

'Stop, Nicholas!' I shouted. A fight now was the last thing I wanted, and it was one we could not win. At that moment Gower came back with a pitcher of water. With a shout he dropped it on the floor and reached for his dagger, raising it high to bury it in Nicholas's back. I threw myself at him and knocked him off balance, but he did not fall, and turned on me with the dagger just as Stice managed to push Nicholas away from the wall and raised his sword. His face was white with anger.

Then rapid footsteps sounded on the stairs and a voice called out, 'Cease this mad brawling!' Not a loud voice, but sharp as a file; one I recognized. It was enough to stop Gower in his tracks, and make Stice pause, too. Confident footsteps walked into the room. I turned and beheld, dressed in sober black robe and cap, his thin face frowning mightily, his majesty's Privy Councillor, Sir Richard Rich.

Chapter Twenty-nine

Rich strode in, scowling. He was the smallest man in the room, but instantly commanded it. He pulled off his black cap and smacked Stice round the face with it. The young man's eyes flashed for a moment, but he lowered his sword. Rich snapped: 'I told you they were not to be harmed. You've already dealt with that boy more roughly than I wanted – '

'He went for me when he woke up—' Gower ventured.

'Quiet, churl!' Rich then turned to me, his voice quiet and serious. 'Shardlake, I want no violence. I took the boy because I knew it would bring you here, and I need to talk to you. I knew that if I made contact with you any other way you would go yowling straight to the Queen's people, and what I have to say needs to be kept secret. It may even be that this time we can be of use to each other.'

I stared at him. This was the anxious Richard Rich I had seen at Anne Askew's burning. His long grey hair was awry, the thin face with its neat little features stern, new lines around the mouth, and his normally cold, still grey eyes roamed around the room.

I said nothing, for the moment lost for words. Nicholas stared in astonishment at the Privy Councillor who had suddenly appeared in our midst. Rich's two men watched us closely. Then there was a knock at the door, making everyone jump except Rich, whose expression changed to a more characteristic, sly smile. 'Answer it, Gower,' he said. 'Our party is not yet quite complete.'

Gower opened the door. Outside stood the constable with his assistant. Between them, looking furious, was Barak. I saw the dagger was gone from his belt. They pushed him in. Rich nodded at Barak and addressed Stice and Gower. 'Watch that one, he's trouble. Master Barak, let me tell you that violence will not help you or your master.' Rich then walked over to the constable, who bowed deeply. 'There's no one else?' Rich asked.

'No, sir, only this one.'

'Good. You and your man will be rewarded. And remember, keep your mouths shut.'

'Yes, Sir Richard.'

The constable bowed again, and waved his assistant back outside. Rich shut the door on them and turned back to us. He shook his head, the sardonic smile on his face showing his straight little teeth. 'Barak, I would have expected better from you. Did you not consider that if I used a house I would bribe the local constable first? They can be bought, as you know, and I pay well.'

Barak did not answer. Rich shrugged. 'Sit at the table. You too, boy. I want a word with your master, and if it concludes well I will let you all go. Understood?'

Barak and Nicholas did not reply, but at a nod from me they allowed Stice and Gower to lead them to the table. They all sat. 'Watch Barak carefully,' Rich said. 'He's as full of tricks as a monkey.' He crossed to the staircase, crooking an imperious finger to indicate I should follow. 'Come up, Master Shardlake.'

I had no alternative. Once upstairs, Rich led me to a room which was as sparsely furnished as the rest of the house, containing only a desk with a sconce of lit candles, and a couple of chairs. He motioned me to sit, then regarded me silently, his expression serious again. In the candlelight it seemed to me his thin face had more lines and hollows now. His grey eyes were little points of light. I said nothing, waiting. He had said we might be of use to each other; let him say how. I wondered, did he know of the missing *Lamentation*? At all costs I must not be the first to mention that.

He said, 'You are working for the Queen again.' It was a statement, not a question. But it had been clear from his note that he knew that.

I said, 'Yes. And there will be more trouble for you if I disappear. Remember the things her majesty knows about you.' The 'more
trouble' had been a guess, but Rich's eyes narrowed. 'She will not be
pleased, for example, to learn that your man Stice once tried to suborn
one of her pages – as I know for a fact.' Rich frowned at that. Then I
asked, 'Is it really true, as you said in your note, that you have a spy in
her household?'

Rich shrugged. 'No. But I spotted you at Whitehall a few days
ago, in the Guard Chamber.'

'I did not think you saw me,' I replied, truly alarmed now.

He leaned forward. 'There is very little that I miss.' His tone was
both threatening and vain. 'You would hardly be coming to see the
King. I thought then, so he is working for her once more, after all
this time; I wonder why. And then right afterwards you began your
enquiries into the murder of a certain Armistead Greening, printer.'

'On behalf of his parents only.'

'Do not take me for a fool, Shardlake,' Rich said impatiently. 'You
are acting for the Queen on this.' I did not reply. He thought for a
moment, then said, 'Let me guess what you have found. Greening was
part of a little group of religious fanatics, probably Anabaptists. One
of their members, Vandersteyn, is a Dutch merchant, and we know
that Anabaptism still festers over there. And another is Curdy, a merchant from an old Lollard family – and we know how many of them
have been seduced by the Anabaptists in the past.' He raised a slim
hand and ticked off a series of names on the fingers of the other –
'Vandersteyn, Curdy, Elias Rooke, apprentice, McKendrick, a Scotch
soldier turned preacher, and – ' he leaned forward – 'Leeman, a
member of the Queen's guard, no less. And finally – ' he took a deep
breath – 'it seems, a gaoler from the Tower, called Myldmore. Six of
them, all vanished into thin air.'

I took a deep breath. He knew much, then, but not that Elias
had been murdered or that Lord Parr had Myldmore in custody.
There were four missing men, not six. I said, 'So you, too, are seeking
Greening's murderer?'

He leaned forward, linking his hands. 'No,' he said firmly. 'I am looking for a book. An important book to me, and perhaps to her majesty the Queen.'

A book. One book. But I had learned from Myldmore there were two – the *Lamentation* and the *Examinations of Anne Askew*. And the *Examinations* spoke of Rich's torture of her. What if he did not know about the *Lamentation*? 'A book by Anne Askew,' I ventured. 'About her time in the Tower?'

Rich leaned back. 'Good,' he said. 'We have it out in the open. Yes, the lies and ravings of that wretched woman. So you know about it. How?'

'I spoke to the apprentice Elias before he disappeared, and he told me Greening had it,' I lied. 'Tell me, was it because of that book that your men attempted to break into Greening's premises before he was murdered?'

Rich frowned. 'Where did you get that information from? Oh, the boy Elias, I would guess. Yes, those two were trying to break in and retrieve Askew's writings, but they were disturbed. And shortly after someone else killed Greening.'

'How did *you* know Greening had it, Sir Richard?'

'The gaoler Myldmore. Who has disappeared as well now. He knew certain things about Anne Askew's time in the Tower, never mind how, and I had him followed.'

'By Stice?' I asked.

'No, it was Gower. You wouldn't think it to look at him, but following people surreptitiously is something he excels at. And he reported back that Myldmore had called on Greening, with a small satchel on his shoulder that was full when he went in and empty when he came out.'

'I see.'

Rich shifted in his chair. 'I had Anne Askew questioned again – she was out of the Tower then, held in a private house under my watch until the day of her burning. She readily admitted she had written a scurrilous account of her time in the Tower, accusing me and

Wriothesley of torturing her, among other things, and had it smuggled out. She would not say how, or to whom it was delivered. But she did not need to; having Myldmore followed had given me the answer to that.' Rich frowned and a muscle in his jaw twitched. 'She laughed in my face, cackled triumphantly that she had got her writings out of the Tower.' His voice rasped angrily. 'Oh, Anne Askew loved nothing more than to be the one to have the last word. I wondered if she might say something awkward at the burning; there was a moment when I thought she might, but then – '

He paused, and I ended his sentence, 'The gunpowder exploded. I remember.'

'Yes, I saw you there.'

'What is it you fear she might have said, and written, Sir Richard?' I asked quietly.

'Things about me. And about another. All lies, but in these days of heretic propaganda – '

'If you knew Greening had those writings, why did you not have him arrested? And Myldmore?'

'It was better dealt with as a private matter,' Rich answered shortly. I thought, that is why he is frightened, the King is already angry with him for torturing Anne Askew to obtain information about the Queen, and he fears that if it becomes public knowledge it would be the end of his career. It was clear he knew nothing of the *Lamentation*, thank goodness.

Confidence returned to his voice again. 'Of course, just as I have concerns about Anne Askew's writings being discovered, so – since she employed you – must the Queen. Perhaps Anne Askew wrote something about her own connections with her majesty or her radical friends.' He waved a dismissive hand. 'But the Queen matters nothing to me now.'

'Sir Richard, I can hardly believe that. When you and Wriothesley have spent the last several months trying to entrap her, no doubt at the bidding of Bishop Gardiner.'

'Gardiner's plan failed,' Rich said bluntly. 'It depended on finding evidence against the Queen and none was discovered, as you no doubt know. The King warned us at the start that we must bring him firm evidence: he was annoyed with her for lecturing him, but he still loves the woman. Now he is angry with all those involved, and the Queen is back in favour. I have no more interest in whether she is a heretic or not.'

'So,' I began. 'It remains important to you to find Anne Askew's writings. You are interested in saving your own position. Perhaps even your skin.'

'Who does not want to do that?' A threatening tone had entered his voice. 'The Queen does, I am sure, and as you are involved, now my guess is that there are things in Askew's writings that could still endanger her.'

I did not answer. Rich sighed, then continued wearily. 'It is only the Askews and Gardiners of this world who would risk their lives over such questions as the nature of the Mass.' He pointed a finger at me. 'Working to preserve himself before all else is what any man endowed with reason does. You are right, Master Shardlake, I want to ensure I am safe, just as the Queen does. I have reached a dead end trying to find these missing people. I think you have, too. I have a spy at the docks, and from what he tells me, others are also there, watching for someone trying to get books out. Those people I suspect are work-ing for the Queen.' Again I did not answer. 'I have limited resources, as do you,' he went on in an irritated tone. 'My suggestion is that the Queen and I work together to recover Askew's book.' He gave a bitter little laugh. 'There have been stranger alliances these last fifteen years.'

'I cannot forget the outcome when last I made a bargain with you,' I said finally. 'You tried to kill me.'

He shrugged. 'Oh, I would like you dead, have no doubt. But larger matters are involved. I offer you limited cooperation for a spe-cific end. And you have the Queen's direct protection, of course.'

I sat back. 'I would need a little time to consider.' My feelings about Rich were violent; a mixture of disgust, loathing, and complete distrust. And yet I confess I also felt a certain pleasure sitting there dealing with him on equal terms for the first time, and pleasure, too, at the fact that I knew more than he did. And, in terms of reason, Rich was right. His proposition made sense. Furthermore, working with him would give me the opportunity to try and prevent the worst from happening – that he might get hold of the *Lamentation* as a by-product of retrieving Anne Askew's writings. For that was truly explosive material. This time, it would be me playing a double game with Rich.

He said, 'You mean, you need time to consult the Queen's people. Yes, I understand that.'

'You realize Anne Askew's book may already have been smuggled out of the country, to be printed abroad.' And the *Lamentation*, I thought, but did not say.

'I think not.' Rich leaned back again, interlacing his fingers. 'You know of John Bale? Currently residing in exile in Antwerp?'

'By reputation.'

'The main publisher of heretical books in English. A likely destination for this trash, you agree?'

'Yes.'

'John Bale has been watched, for some time, by agents of the King. Secretary Paget is in charge of that, but I am among the Privy Councillors who see the reports. We would have liked him arrested by the Emperor Charles's authorities and burned, as William Tyndale was a decade ago. But the Emperor's authority is weak in Antwerp now. We can only watch. And it is known that Bale is expecting a consignment. It is not there yet, or at least it was not two days ago, the date of the last report.'

'I see.' That tied in with what Hugh Curteys had told me, too. 'Where does Lord Chancellor Wriothesley fit into this?'

'He leaves the hard work to me. As people do.'

'Who leads your men? Is it Stice?'

'Yes. He has a distant family connection, one of those innumerable young gentlemen who seek a place at court. I watch for those with brains who do not mind getting their hands dirty, too. Gower is one of his lackeys.'

'Gower seems a little – unstable.'

'Stice assures me he is totally loyal to him, as he seems to be. And one must trust one's subordinates to some extent, or one would go mad, would one not?'

'True.'

'If we find Anne Askew's book, I want it agreed that it be destroyed unread.' He spoke slowly and clearly, as if to prevent any misunderstandings.

I nodded. 'I have no problem with that being agreed.' And there I had the advantage over Rich, knowing that there was nothing in it that implicated the Queen. I did not care what happened to it one way or the other. I had already decided I would recommend the Queen to make this temporary agreement with Rich. But I would watch him like a hawk. I was certain that, had I not kept this appointment, Rich would have killed Nicholas. And I would never have known who had done it.

'I will consider what you have said. With the Queen's people.'

He nodded. 'I thought you would.'

I smiled grimly. 'You have not done well these last few years, have you, Sir Richard? Those allegations of corruption when you were in charge of finance during the war? And now months of working for Gardiner and Wriothesley to help bring down the Queen, only for it to end in your total failure. I thought you did not seem your usual confident self at the burning.'

He had spoken civilly up to now, as one grown man negotiating with another, but now he glared and wagged a lean finger at me. 'The Queen may have ridden this storm, Shardlake, but do not be too confident all will go the reformers' way from now on. I offer cooperation on a specific issue, for a limited time. Tell that to your masters, and please remember when you speak to me in future that I am a Privy Councillor.' He frowned. Rich had lost his composure with me and I could see he regretted it. I thought, when he said the reformers should not be too confident, he can only have been referring to whatever new plot the traditionalists were hatching, the one Lord Parr said was afoot. The one plot in which Bertano – whoever he was – might be involved. But I dared not mention that.

I stood, making an ironic little bow. 'How do I get back in touch with you?'

'A note to this house will reach me. Stice will stay here for now, though he thinks the place beneath him.'

'One last thing, Sir Richard. You know that Stephen Bealknap is dead.'

'Yes. I am his executor.'

'His plans to have a monument erected to himself have been refused by Lincoln's Inn.'

He shrugged. 'I heard.'

'Sir Richard, did you ask Bealknap to try and get into my good graces? Last autumn?'

Rich looked genuinely puzzled. 'Why would I do that? Besides, I had ceased instructing Bealknap by then. His health was starting to become unreliable.'

I looked at him. He had appeared genuinely surprised. Whatever Bealknap had been doing, it did not seem to have involved Rich. Then again, Rich was a consummate liar.

'Reply to me tomorrow, please, Master Shardlake, we do not have much time.' He stood in turn. 'Now, you can go and collect that rogue Barak, and that long streak of piss, and get out.'

✝

STICE AND GOWER stood by as the three of us left the house. I knew that for Nicholas, and probably Barak, to leave thus meekly must feel like a defeat. I must get to Whitehall, I thought.

We walked along Thames Street, the city deserted after curfew. Windows were open this warm night, squares of candlelight flicker‑ing in the dark. A berobed city official walked past, his way along the dusty street lit by link‑boys carrying torches.

'That constable must have been offered a large bribe,' Barak said angrily. 'One that only someone like Rich could afford. Christ's bowels, if I ever find myself alone with that Stice I'll have his balls. He has a scoffing wit. He told me Lord Rich told him I once worked for Lord Cromwell; he asked was it true Cromwell picked all his men off the streets, instead of using proper gentlemen.'

'And that other churl,' Nicholas said, '*his* wits are awry. Some of the things he said – '

I looked at the boy, his face a mass of bruises. 'I am sorry,' I said quietly. 'I did not know we were dealing with Rich. He will stop at nothing.'

Nicholas looked at me. 'That was truly him? The Privy Councillor?'

'Ay,' Barak said angrily.

'I knew he had a bad reputation.'

'We've crossed swords with him before,' Barak said. 'He should have been hung a dozen times.' He turned to me, and burst out, 'What the fuck did he want you for?'

I laughed bitterly. 'To suggest we work together, believe it or not. Nicholas, I should not say more in front of you. It is not safe.'

'Am I to have my life threatened and simply accept it?' Nicholas answered hotly. 'To have no justice against those rogues?' I thought, he is foolhardy but, by God, he has courage to speak so, after what must have been a terrifying captivity.

'He has a point,' Barak muttered.

'I may not say any more, Nicholas, without breaking a promise and nor will I give you information which could be dangerous to you. I've already told Jack far more than I should.' I hesitated, then added, 'Did they hurt you much?'

'Apart from knocking me over the head? That Gower beat me when I tried to fight them after I awoke. But what manner of man in my position would not fight back? Then they said if I kept quiet and waited I would come to no harm. I had no option.' His voice trembled slightly, and I realized he had been more frightened than he would admit. 'Tell me this at least,' he asked. 'Did they use my life as a bargaining counter? Did they make you give them something in exchange for it?'

'No, please be reassured, Nicholas. Rich merely used you as bait to make me come to him. In fact, I got the best of that encounter.'

'I am glad of that at least.'

'How is the wound on your chest?'

'Healing well. But I should bathe these cuts.'

'Then go back to your lodgings directly.' I took a deep breath. 'Nicholas, when you came to work for me you did not expect to be attacked or to be held prisoner by murderous rogues. It might be better if I were to transfer you to another barrister. With the best of references, I promise.'

To my surprise he laughed. 'This is more interesting than the law!' I shook my head, remembering how some young gentlemen loved adventure, had been brought up to think it noble. Even his recent experiences had not knocked that out of him.

We parted at the head of Thames Street. 'So what happened?' Barak asked, when Nicholas had gone.

I told him. He stroked his beard. 'This is quite some game of hoodman blind we are playing. What will you do now?' he asked.

'Go to the palace, try to see Lord Parr, late as it is.'

'I would have thought you'd had enough for one day.'

'I must tell them about Rich immediately. What I said to Nicholas applies to you too, Jack,' I added. 'I think perhaps you should both walk away now.'

He shook his head. 'Not after this. My blood's up.'

'Your pride, rather. What about all you said earlier? What about Tamasin?'

He frowned. 'My wife doesn't rule me.'

'Jack — '

'I want to see this through. Besides,' he added more quietly, 'you need someone. You haven't anyone you can trust, none of those people at court cares what happens to you. What happens to my job if you get killed?'

'The Queen – ' I remonstrated.

'Her first loyalties are to her family,' he countered impatiently, 'and to the King, for all that she fears him. You need people you can really trust. I'm sure you can trust Nick, too, you know. And he's useful. Think about it.'

He turned and walked away homewards. There was a spring in his step now. He had been torn between his current life and his old ways, I realized, and the encounter had changed the balance for him. Barak's taste for adventure had won out, as it had so easily for Nicholas. I shook my head, and walked down to the river to find a wherry going upriver to Whitehall.

Chapter Thirty

I SAT IN LORD PARR'S OFFICE AGAIN. It was late, well past midnight. Whitehall Palace was dark and silent, everyone asleep apart from the guards ceaselessly patrolling the corridors. Lit only by dim candlelight, all the gorgeous decoration was in shadow, hidden.

Lord Parr was still working in his office when I arrived; his room brightly lit with fat buttermilk candles, the shutters closed. He had called for William Cecil, who arrived within minutes; he must have been staying at the palace. After I told them the story of my encounter with Rich, Lord Parr sent for the Queen; she had been with the King that evening but had returned to her own bedchamber. 'She must be consulted,' he insisted. 'This comes so near to her person.'

Sitting behind his desk while we waited, Lord Parr looked exhausted. 'Richard Rich, eh?' He shook his head and smiled wearily, the old courtier in him perhaps amused by this turn of the political screw.

'I thought Rich might be behind all of it,' I said. 'The murders and the taking of the book. But it seems not so, not this time.'

'But if he gets hold of the *Lamentation*—' Cecil began.

'Yes,' Lord Parr replied. 'He would use it. The campaign against the Queen could revive.' He looked between us. 'Well, you know the saying: keep your friends close and your enemies closer. Let us work with Rich, and keep him close.'

There was a gentle knock at the door. Mary Odell and the Queen's sister, Lady Herbert, stood in the doorway, bearing candles. They stepped aside to allow the Queen to walk into the room between them. Like the others she was dressed informally, in a gold-and-green caftan;

there had been no time for the long labour with pins and corsets necessary for her to be dressed fully. Her auburn hair was tied back under a
knitted hood. Under hastily applied whitelead, her face was tense. We
bowed to her, my back suddenly stiff after the long day. She dismissed
her ladies.

'What news?' she asked without preliminaries. 'Please, tell me my
book is found.'

'Not yet, niece,' Lord Parr said gently. 'But there has been another
development, a – complication. I am sorry to request your presence at
this time of night, but matters are urgent.'

He nodded to me, and again I told my story, though missing out
the part about Stice's threat to send me Nicholas's head. 'Rich knows
nothing of the *Lamentation*,' I concluded. 'He believes there may be
something in Anne Askew's writings which would compromise you
as well as him.'

'Rich doesn't know we have Myldmore,' Lord Parr added.
'Shardlake did well in foxing him.'

'The rogue, though.' The Queen walked past me to the shutters, a
rustle of silk and a waft of scent as she passed. She made to open
them. 'It is so hot—'

'Please, Kate,' Lord Parr said urgently. 'You never know who
may be watching.'

The Queen turned back to us, a bitter little smile playing on her
lips. 'Yes. For a moment I forgot, here one must guard one's every
movement.' She breathed deeply, then took a seat and looked at each
of us in turn. 'Must we cooperate with Rich?'

'We must at least pretend to,' Lord Parr answered. 'Work with his
people, but watch them every moment. More pairs of eyes at the docks
would be useful.' He turned to me. 'That information about Bale is
helpful, as well.'

'But who has the books?' Cecil asked. 'The four who have disappeared – McKendrick, Curdy, Vandersteyn, and that wretched guard,
Leeman? Or someone else entirely? We do not even know if the miss-

ing four are still alive. Who employed Greening's murderers? We know now it wasn't Rich.'

I said, 'I think the four missing men are radicals who want to get both books out of the country. We know from their actions in Germany what the Anabaptists are capable of, even if some have renounced violence now. Greening's killers could have been henchmen of theirs, employed after an internal falling out. I have said before, if it was the conservatives that took the *Lamentation*, all they would need to do is lay a copy before the King.' The Queen winced momentarily, but it had to be said. 'I think the answer lies with Curdy's people within the radical group.'

Lord Parr shook his head. 'We may know the limits of Rich's involvement, but someone else who bears the Queen ill will at the court could still be hiding the book, and could have employed one of the group as a spy.' He shook his head again. 'If so it would almost certainly be a member of the Privy Council, I am sure. But which one? And where is the book now?'

'We still have no idea,' Cecil said.

Lord Parr took a deep breath. 'All right. Shardlake, you liaise with Rich via this man Stice. You and Cecil can work with his people on trying to find the missing men, and keeping an eye on the docks.' He bent forward and scribbled on a piece of paper. 'These are our men at the customs house there. Give this to Stice, and get the names of their agents in return. Our men know only that we are look-ing for someone trying to smuggle out some writings.'

Cecil looked uneasy. 'There are murderers involved. There could be trouble. We may have to deal with the missing men if they try to escape, and if Stice calls on us we shall need help. We may have to deal with more of Rich's people, too, if the *Lamentation* is found. How many fit young men do you have?'

'There are four in my household whom I would trust with this,' Parr said. 'Though naturally I will tell them nothing about the *Lamentation*.'

The Queen said, 'I would have no violence.'

'There may be no alternative, niece,' Lord Parr answered sadly. 'Shardlake and Cecil may need to defend themselves, and should have help available.' He looked at me closely. 'How much does your man Barak know?'

'All of it now.' Lord Parr raised his eyebrows. 'I had to tell him,' I explained, 'when I asked him to watch for me at Needlepin Lane.'

He considered, then said, 'Then we can use him. And what of your pupil who was kidnapped?'

'He knows only a little. He has shown himself courageous, but he is very young. And Barak has responsibilities. I would not wish to put either into any further danger.'

'Do they want to help?'

I hesitated. 'Yes. They are good men.'

'Then we need them.'

Cecil asked, 'I know of Barak, but this boy, this –'

'Nicholas –'

'Is he truly fit to be trusted with this? To whom does he owe his loyalties?'

I considered. 'Nobody other than me, I think.'

'Would you vouch for him on that basis?'

'Yes, certainly.'

'What of his background? His religious loyalties?'

'He is of Lincolnshire gentry stock. He has no links to anyone at court. As for religion, he told me once he wishes only to worship as the King requires, and believes others should be allowed liberty of conscience.'

'Even papists?' There was a hint of disapproval in Cecil's voice now.

'He said only that. I do not see it as my place to interrogate my servants as to their religious views.'

Lord Parr fixed me with his eyes, bloodshot and tired now, but still keen. Then he came to a decision. 'Include the boy,' he said. 'Tell him the story. He has shown himself useful. But this is a new responsibility; make him swear that he will keep knowledge of the Queen's book secret. Barak as well.'

'This Nicholas sounds like a boy of little faith,' the Queen said sadly.

I replied with an unaccustomed boldness. 'As I said, your majesty, I have not sought to weigh his soul. I do not have the right. Nor, in fact,' I continued, 'do I have the right to involve him, or Barak, in more danger.'

She coloured slightly. Lord Parr frowned and opened his mouth to reprove me, but the Queen interrupted. 'No. Matthew has the right to speak. But – if he and Cecil are to do this, surely there is safety in numbers.' She looked at me. Slowly and reluctantly, I nodded agreement.

Lord Parr spoke brusquely. 'So. Rich knows the heresy hunt is over but believes the reformers have not yet won. The Queen's brother was at the Privy Council meeting today; he tells me that Gardiner and Wriothesley and Paget were whispering together again in corners. He heard them muttering about someone who was about to arrive in London.'

'This Bertano, whose name ever haunts us?' I asked keenly.

'We've no idea,' Lord Parr answered impatiently. 'But if Paget knows, the King knows. He turned to his niece. 'Did his majesty say anything to you tonight of this?'

The Queen frowned at her uncle. 'He spoke only of the preparation for Admiral d'Annebault's visit. Then we had the players in, and I sang to him. He was in much pain from his leg.' She looked away. The Queen hated reporting on what the King had said. But these last months she had needed allies.

Lord Parr stood. 'Very well, Shardlake. Get a message to Rich. Cecil will talk to our people at the customs house. And now I must go to bed.'

He bowed to the Queen. 'Thank you, Uncle,' she said quietly. 'And you, Master Cecil. Master Shardlake, stay. I would talk with you. We can walk a little in my gallery. Mary Odell can accompany us.' A bitter little smile. 'It is always safest for me to have a chaperone when I talk alone with any man not my relative.' Lord Parr gave me a sharp look; I knew he would rather any confidences went through him. Nonetheless he and Cecil left us, bowing deeply to the Queen. As he opened the door I saw Mary Odell and the Queen's sister still waiting outside. The Queen went out and spoke to them for a moment, leaving me alone in the room. Then she returned and said, 'Come with us.'

I stepped outside. Lady Herbert had gone but Mary Odell remained. The Queen spoke quietly. 'You remember Mary, Matthew. You asked her some questions last week.'

'Indeed. God give you good evening, mistress. Your information was most helpful.'

Mary Odell nodded. Her plump face was serious; those who served the Queen as closely as she would have divined that a new danger was afoot.

The Queen led us down the corridor, past her privy lodgings, through a door to a large vestibule where two or three guards stood at each of the four doors leading from it. They saluted the Queen as she walked to the door opposite. The guards opened it, and we passed through into a beautiful gallery, perhaps two hundred feet long, dark but for a view of the river from the long glass windows on one side. One guard took a torch from a bracket in the vestibule and at a signal from Mary Odell hurried down the gallery, lighting the sconces of candles standing at intervals on tables covered with colourful turkey-cloths. I looked around as the details of the gallery became dimly visible: the roof beautifully decorated in blue and gold, paintings of biblical and classical scenes lining the walls, occasional tapestries flashing with cloth-of-gold thread. At intervals large birdcages stood on poles, cloth over the cages for the night. The guard bowed and left. The Queen let out a long breath and visibly relaxed. She turned to Mary Odell.

'Walk a little behind us, Mary. There is something I would discuss with Master Shardlake.'

'Yes, your majesty.'

We walked slowly down the gallery. There were alcoves at intervals, each filled with rare treasures displayed on tables or stone columns: a box of gold and silver coins of strange design, stones and minerals in many colours, and several ornate clocks, their ticking an accompaniment to our progress. The Queen stopped at a desk where there was an open book and some sheets of paper with notes in her handwriting. I stared at it and she gave me a sad smile. 'Do not worry, Matthew. I am learning Spanish, it is a diversion, and useful for diplomatic meetings. These are only my notes.' She looked round the gallery. 'This is my favourite place in this palace. Where I can walk undisturbed, and rest my eyes on its treasures.'

'There is much beauty here.'

'The clocks remind me that however frantically courtiers plot and plan beyond these doors, time ticks by regardless.' She looked at me directly with her hazel eyes. 'Taking us to our judgement.'

Nearby a bird stirred and cheeped, woken by the noise. The Queen went over and lifted the cover of its cage; a pretty yellow canary-bird looked out at us between the bars. 'A shame to see it caged,' I dared to say.

The Queen looked at it. 'We are all caged, Matthew, in the prison of this earthly world.'

I did not answer. She said, 'I wish you would seek salvation, Matthew. I feel sure God must call to you.'

'I do not hear Him, your majesty.' I hesitated. 'I have recently become acquainted with another lawyer, a man called Philip. He is what would be called a radical. A good man. Yet in some ways – blinkered.'

'Is it blinkered to seek faith, to have faith?'

'Perhaps I am too cross-grained, too contrary, to know faith as you and he would understand it.' I asked quietly, 'Does that mean, do you think, that I am damned?'

Taken by surprise, she stood still, her face pale in the candlelight. Then she answered me softly. 'Only God can answer such questions

347

in the end. But He holds out the joys of true faith, for those who would take them.'

'Does He?' I asked. 'I cannot help but wonder.'

'Then why are you doing this for me? I ask more and more of you. It puts you and those you care for in great danger. I saw just now how concerned you are for those men who work for you.'

'I am. But Nicholas is young and adventurous, and Barak – ' I sighed. 'Well, he is no longer young, but he is still adventurous, despite himself.'

She looked at me closely. 'Are you doing all this because it is I who ask?'

'For you, and the loyalty I owe you,' I answered quietly. 'And because I hope that if your side wins people may be allowed some liberty of conscience and belief; that apprentices and young gentle-women and aged clerics will not be burned alive at the stake for their private beliefs, while men like Rich and Gardiner look on.'

She lowered her gaze. After a moment she whispered, 'You mean when my husband is dead?'

I answered, the words suddenly rushing from me, 'The people are sore afraid, your majesty. Afraid that any belief they hold may be approved one month, but the next may send them to the stake. It drives them to a careful, fearful orthodoxy which, whatever it is, is not faith. All fear the prison and the fire,' I added quietly.

'I fear it, too,' she replied. 'Sometimes these last months I have been so convulsed with terror I have scarce been able to rise from my bed, let alone converse and behave as the Queen must.' She shuddered.

I would have dearly liked to touch her then, to comfort her, but that I dared not do. We stood in silence for a moment, opposite a great ornate fireplace where carved heraldic beasts sported above the empty grate. A few yards off Mary Odell waited, hands held before her demurely.

At length the Queen drew a deep breath. 'My family hope that one day I may be Regent for Prince Edward,' she said quietly. 'If that happens there will be no burnings, no persecutions. The rules govern-

ing the church would change, and there would be no capital penalties.'
She smiled sardonically. 'But the Seymours, as the King's uncles,
believe they have a better claim. Although they too, I am sure, would
want to lighten the severity of the law. For the moment we stand
together against Gardiner and his people, but the future – it is in
God's hands.' She added, passion in her voice now, 'That is my comfort, that it is in His hands. Our duty is to be His handmaidens on this
poor sorry earth.' She lowered her head again. 'But it is a duty I failed
in when, out of pride, I kept that book despite the Archbishop's
advice.'

'And my duty is to recover a piece of property stolen from a most
noble lady, and bring a pair of murderers to book. That is all I can
promise, your majesty. I cannot promise to undertake a quest for faith.'

'It is more than most would do for me.' The Queen smiled, then
raised a hand impulsively, as though to touch my arm, but let it fall.
When she spoke again her tone was level, even a little formal. 'The
hour is very late, Matthew. Mary can arrange a room for you in the
outer lodgings, then you can leave tomorrow morning. I know you
have much to do.'

☦

I WAS FOUND A PLACE near the gate, in a large room with rush
matting and a comfortable bed. I slept well and woke late; the sun was
already high in the sky and I heard people talking in the wide courtyard outside. It was Sunday and church bells sounded both within the
palace grounds and beyond the precinct. I remembered that Bealknap's
funeral had taken place yesterday; I had forgotten about it. I wondered
if any mourners had gone. And as for Bealknap's strange deathbed
gloating, perhaps that mystery had died with him, too.

I dressed hurriedly – I had a message to get to Stice, and I also
wanted to talk to Nicholas. As I left the lodgings I saw people had
gathered round three sides of the courtyard, facing the King's Guard
Chamber. Servants, courtiers, officials, all seemed to be congregating

there. I saw William Cecil a little way off and shouldered my way through the crowd to greet him.

'Brother Shardlake?' he said. 'You have been here all night?'

'Yes. I was given lodgings as it was so late.'

'I often need to spend the night here, too. But I miss my wife and children.' He smiled sadly, then looked at me speculatively. 'You spoke with the Queen?'

'Yes. Mainly of religion.'

'She would have all see the light which she has seen.'

'Yes, indeed.' I changed the subject. 'It seems, Master Cecil, that we shall be working closely, perhaps even facing danger together.'

He nodded seriously. 'Yes. I did not know things would come so far as this.'

'Nor I.' I looked round curiously. 'Why is everyone gathered here?'

'Do you not know? When the King is in residence at Whitehall he always makes a public procession to the chapel on Sunday mornings.'

'The Queen too?'

'Yes. Observe.'

As I watched, a group of guards exited the ornate door of the King's Guard Chamber and took up places before it. Then another group, Gentlemen Pensioners in their black livery decorated with gold, marched out with their halberds. Then came the King. As he was on the side nearest to me, I could only catch a glimpse of the Queen on the other side of that vast bulk, a quick view of a brightly coloured dress. Those who wore caps took them off and then loud cheers erupted from the crowd.

I looked at Henry. Today he was dressed in formal finery: a long cream satin robe with broad padded shoulders furred with marten. He looked slightly less obese than when I had seen him last, and I wondered if he was corseted, as he was said to be when he went abroad in public. Those huge bandaged legs were covered with black hose. He walked very stiffly, leaning on a thick, gold-headed walking stick, his other arm through that of a Gentleman Pensioner.

The King walked round the courtyard and turned to smile at the crowd, at one point doffing his black cap embossed with little diamonds. I saw, though, how his lips were clenched together and sweat stood out on his red brow and cheeks. I could not help but admire his courage in still presenting himself to his public as a man who could walk. It must cost him great pain. He doffed his cap once more, his little eyes darting round the courtyard, and for a moment I thought they rested on me. He passed on slowly, down the other side of the courtyard and in through the doorway of the Great Hall. Senior officials and councillors followed: I saw the stern bearded face of Paget; thin-faced, red-bearded Wriothesley; the red-robed Duke of Norfolk in the procession.

'I thought he looked at me for a second,' I whispered to Cecil.

'I didn't see. I should think he was concentrating on keeping his feet. They'll put him in his wheeled chair as soon as he's out of sight.' He shook his head sadly.

'How long can he go on?' I asked.

Cecil frowned and leaned in close. 'Do not forget, Master Shardlake, it is treason to foretell the death of the King. In any way.'

✝

I AGREED WITH CECIL that I would contact him again as soon as I had spoken with Stice. Once more I took a wherry to Temple Stairs, envying those citizens who, church over, had taken a boat onto the river to enjoy the sunshine. I walked to the narrow lanes off Amen Corner where I knew Nicholas lodged.

A young man who looked like another student answered my knock. He seemed a little reluctant to take me to Nicholas. 'Are you his pupil-master?' he asked.

'I am.'

He said warily, 'Nick's been in a fight. He won't say what happened, but I'm sure it's not his fault — '

'I know about it. And no, it wasn't his fault.'

The student took me up a flight of stairs and knocked on a door. Nicholas answered. He was in his shirt, the strings untied, showing the line of the bandage across his chest. The bruises on his face had come out yellow and black. He made a sorry sight.

'How are you?' I asked.

'It looks worse than it is, sir. And my chest is healing well.'

I followed him into an untidy room thick with dust, unwashed plates on the table, law books scattered about. It took me back to my own student days a quarter-century before; though I had been tidier than this. Nicholas evidently lodged alone, as I had. But whereas my father had not been wealthy enough to send a servant with me, Nicholas's father had chosen not to; another sign, no doubt, of his disapproval. He invited me to take the only chair, while he sat on the unmade bed. I studied him thoughtfully. He had courage and intelligence, but also the reckless bravado of the young. But of his trustworthiness I felt certain now.

I said, 'Nicholas, you saw last night that the matter I am involved in concerns the highest in the land. The one I am working for is of even higher status than Rich.'

His eyes widened. 'The King himself?'

'No, not that high. Nicholas, you spoke to me once about the religious quarrels that ravage this country. You said you wish to steer clear of it all, to be left alone and have others left alone. That is my wish, too. But what I am working on now concerns a struggle at court. On the one side are those who would keep the Mass, and in some cases perhaps bring back the Pope. On the other, those who would end what Catholic ceremonies remain. Involvement in that struggle can end in torture, murder and burning. For some, it already has.'

He fell silent. I could see my words had impressed him. 'You still have not told me who you are working for,' he said at length.

'Nor can I, unless you swear an oath of secrecy.'

'Is Jack working with you?'

'Yes. He insists.'

'And you need more help?'

'Yes.'

He smiled sadly. 'Nobody has ever asked for my help before.'

'I say in all honesty, it may be better for you to stay out. Not because I doubt your courage or loyalty, but because of the danger. As I said last night, I can arrange for you to work for another barrister. Nicholas, you should not just think of yourself. Consider your parents, your inheritance, your future as a gentleman.' I smiled, thinking that would get through to him as nothing else could.

His reaction surprised me. He spoke with sudden, bitter anger. 'My parents! My inheritance! I told you, sir, why it was I came to London. My father – and my mother – would have had me marry someone I did not love. You know I refused – '

'Yes, and so were sent to London to learn the law. I am sure when your studies are finished your parents will have got over their anger, perhaps even come to respect you for what you have done.'

'That they never will,' he said bitterly. 'My father told me if I would not marry according to his wishes he would disinherit me. He sent me to learn law to get me out of his sight. My mother, too; she is even fiercer on the matter than he. She told me that in refusing to marry whom they chose I was no proper man, and not her son. So I have no inheritance.' He looked at me fiercely.

'That is very hard. But things said in anger – '

He shook his head. 'They meant it. I could see it in their faces when they spoke. I remember well the sinking feeling when I realized they did not love me.' There was a choking sound in his throat for a moment; he coughed. 'They have already hired lawyers to see what can be done about barring the estate to me. They would transfer it to a cousin of mine, a young popinjay who would marry a one-legged dwarf if she would bring enough money. No, Master Shardlake, they mean business.' He looked down, and smoothed the sheet on his unmade bed. 'I am their only child. That is a burden on me, as I am on them.'

'I, too, have no brothers and sisters. Yes, that can bring its burdens, though I never had such a hard one placed on me as you have.'

Nicholas looked around the untidy room at the law books. 'Sometimes I find interest in the law, though at others it all seems like rats fighting in a sack. The Slanning case – '

I smiled. 'Fortunately, cases such as that are rare. What matters do you find interest in?'

'Ones where one can sympathize with the client, where one sees an injustice to be righted.' He smiled. 'Exciting ones.'

'Exciting ones are dangerous ones. And as for the others, one cannot just act for those of whom one approves. However, in the autumn term perhaps you could assist with my cases in the Court of Requests.'

He made a face. 'Commoners suing the gentlemen who are their natural rulers?'

'Should everyone not have an equal right to go to law, just as they should have to their private religious views?'

He shrugged.

'Perhaps you would see matters differently if you were to work on the cases.'

'I do not know. For now, an active life, in pursuit of an honourable cause, that is what I want. Even if it means being kidnapped again.' He smiled then, his large green eyes shining.

'Something with meaning?'

He hesitated, then said, 'Yes. I need some – meaning.'

I realized now that Nicholas wanted a life of adventure partly to escape the memory of what his unworthy parents had done. I remembered the story I had heard of him getting into a sword fight over a prostitute. I thought, if he does not find the excitement he needs with me he may find it somewhere else, and end with a sword in the guts. And perhaps if he is with me I can guide him, check that self-destructive urge I detected in him. 'You think the cause I serve is just?' I asked.

He answered seriously, 'If it will bring an end to such persecution as I have seen since coming to London, then yes.'

'If I tell you for whom I am working, and the details of what this is about, you must first swear, on your oath as a gentleman, to tell nobody, nobody at all.'

'I have no bible here – '

'Your word will do.'

'Then I swear.'

'My employer is that honourable lady, her majesty Queen Catherine.'

His eyes widened. 'Skelly told me you used to do legal work for her.'

'I have known her since before she was Queen. She is a good lady.'

'Many say she has been in trouble.'

'She has. She is now. But she is no persecutor of anyone.'

'Then I will help you.'

'Thank you. And Nicholas, do as I tell you, with care; no heroics.'

He blushed under his bruises. 'I will.'

I took his hand. 'Then thank you.'

Chapter Thirty-one

I WALKED FROM NICHOLAS'S lodgings back to Needlepin Lane. In daylight it looked even more dingy, the plasterwork crumbling on the old houses, the lane a narrow track with a stinking piss-channel in the middle. Though it was Sunday, men were standing outside the Flag Tavern, quaffing beer from wooden mugs in the sunshine. Among them I saw a couple of girls in bright make-up and low-cut dresses. The King had ordered the Southwark brothels closed that spring, but although prostitution was already illegal in the city and conviction could bring a whipping, many whores had come north of the river. One girl, well in her cups, caught my glance and shouted out, 'Don't glower at me like that, crookback, I'm a respectable lady!' People stared at me, and some laughed. I ignored them and knocked on the door of the house with the green shutters. Stice opened it immediately.

'You're back soon.'

'I have a message for your master.' I nodded over my shoulder. 'I'd best come in; I've attracted notice from the people outside the tavern.'

'Common churls, they're always shouting at passers-by.' He stood aside, and I walked into the bare room. My hand closed instinctively on my knife as he shut the door and went over to the table. He sat down, smiling insolently. The sword with which he had nearly killed Nicholas the night before lay there; he had been polishing it. The sun glinted on its razor-sharp edge. There was a jug of beer and some pewter mugs on the table, too. 'No hard feelings, eh, Master Shardlake?' Stice said. 'We each serve those to whom we are pledged.' Then, with an edge to his voice, 'You have an answer for my master?'

'Yes. Those I work for agree to our collaborating to try and locate these missing people, and Anne Askew's writings. I will liaise with you. We have another man, a lawyer named William Cecil, who has been keeping an eye on the docks. These are the people he has paid to look for writings being smuggled out.' I handed him a copy of Cecil's list. Stice looked it over and nodded. 'Well, between us,' he said, 'I think we have the docks and the custom house covered.'

'How many men do you have there?'

'In our pay, two officials.' He wrote two names on the bottom of the sheet of paper, tore it off and gave it to me.

'Sir Richard said that Bale is expecting a consignment. Let us hope we are in time.'

'Amen to that.'

'One important condition, Master Stice. If either party has word of the cargo, they warn the other at once.'

'Of course.' Stice smiled and spread his arms. 'By the way, if there's any fighting to be done – say with what's left of Greening's people, if they turn up – how many men can you bring to bear?'

'Two for certain. Probably two or three more.'

'Are the first two Barak and the boy?'

'Yes.'

Stice nodded appreciatively. 'They're both handy.'

'Cecil will likely be able to call on more.'

'And I have three on hand, including Gower, whom you met yesterday. He's down keeping an eye on the docks now. I'm sure my master will agree those terms.' He laughed. 'Who would have thought, when you came in last night, we'd end by working together? Come, sit, let's share a beer.'

Reluctantly, I dropped into a chair opposite him. The more I could learn about these people the better: I had no doubt that if they got hold of the *Lamentation* Rich would betray us in an instant.

Stice poured me a beer, then lounged back in his chair. He was, I reckoned, about twenty-five. He dressed well – again the silk cuff of his shirt was visible below the sleeve of his doublet, like the one he had torn on his aborted raid on Greening's premises. His face was good-looking in a hard way, though that lopped ear was a disfigurement. I wondered that he did not wear his hair long to hide it.

Stice saw me looking and put his hand to the ear. 'Can't miss it, eh? People's eyes get drawn to it, as I daresay they do to your back. I'm not ashamed of it, I came by it in an honest duel, with a mangehound who impugned my ancestry. And in the sort of business Master Rich sometimes has me on, it shows people I'm not to be treated lightly.'

'How long have you worked for Rich?'

'Two years. I come from Essex, where Sir Richard has many properties. My father's land adjoins his, and he sent me to court to try my luck. Sir Richard was looking for young gentlemen with no ties and a taste for adventure.' He smiled again.

I thought, another young gentleman, like Nicholas, in search of excitement. Yet Stice, I guessed, would stoop to anything, including murder, for the sake of rising in Rich's service. That, no doubt, was why Rich had chosen him.

He laughed. 'By Mary, sir, you have a grim look. Sir Richard said you had the manner of a canting Lutheran, though not the religion.'

I did not answer directly. 'You hope to advance under Rich?' I asked.

'I do. Sir Richard is loyal to those who serve him. It is well known.'

I laughed. 'Loyalty is not the word that comes to my mind.'

Stice waved a dismissive hand. 'You speak of his dealings at the King's court. None of the great men is truly loyal to any other. But Sir Richard is known to stick by those who serve him, and reward them well.' His eyes narrowed over his mug. 'I hope the same can be said of the Queen and her people. Who is it you work for? Sir Richard told me it was probably Lord Parr, her uncle.'

I was not going to be drawn. I put down my mug and stood abruptly. 'I will let you know if I have news of any developments. And you can contact me at my house. It is in Chancery Lane.'

He raised his mug in a mocking gesture. 'I know where it is.'

✝

I HAD DECIDED to warn Philip Coleswyn of the latest turn in the Slanning case, but I thought that was best done after I had discussed Isabel Slanning's complaint with Treasurer Rowland on the morrow. I went home; I had what remained of Sunday to myself, and there were two other things I needed to do.

First I went to my study and wrote a letter to Hugh. I wrote of the general news, and my part in the coming ceremonies to welcome Admiral d'Annebault. Then I advised him that John Bale was a dangerous man, that he was to be avoided, and warned Hugh not to write to me of him again. There, I thought: at least I have not drawn Hugh into this. I sealed the letter and put it in my satchel to be posted from Lincoln's Inn tomorrow.

I went downstairs. The house was silent. As agreed, Josephine had gone walking with her young man again, so I knew she was not at home. There was nobody in the kitchen; a tallow candle was burning on the table there, in order that there should be fire ready for cooking later. I went out to the stables, where Timothy was energetically mucking out the stable, a pile of old straw and horse dung already by the door.

'God give you good morrow, master,' he said.

'And you, Timothy. Remember to keep the horse-dung for Mistress Brocket's vegetable patch.'

'Ay. She gives me a farthing for a good load.'

'Have you thought any more about going for an apprenticeship? I could speak to the Lincoln's Inn stablemaster about what places may be available among the farriers.'

A shadow crossed his face. 'I would still rather stay here.'

'Well, I would like you to give it some more careful thought.'

'Yes, sir,' he replied, but unenthusiastically, his head cast down.

I sighed. 'Do you know where Master and Mistress Brocket are?'

'They went for a walk. Mistress Brocket asked me to keep an eye on the candle in the kitchen, light another from it if it got too low.'

'Good.' So the house was empty. There was nothing illegal in what I planned to do next, but I did not want to be seen by anyone.

'They had a letter delivered this morning, by messenger,' Timothy added. 'I was in the kitchen with them. I don't know who the letter came from but they both looked upset. They ordered me from the kitchen and a little after they said they were going for a walk. Master Brocket looked grim, and I think poor Mistress Brocket had been crying.'

I frowned, wondering what that was about. I said, 'Timothy, there is a job of work I have to do. Can you make sure I am undisturbed for an hour? If anyone comes to the door, say I am out.'

'Yes, sir.'

'Thank you.'

I went upstairs, and unlocked the chest in my bedroom. My heart was heavy as I looked at the books within; several were on the new forbidden list and must be handed in to the city authorities at the Guildhall by the 9th of August. After that date, possession of any of the books would attract severe penalties. With a heavy heart I lifted out my copies of Tyndale's translation of the New Testament, and some old commentaries on Luther dating from twenty years before. These books had been my friends in my old reformist days; one of them had been given me by Thomas Cromwell himself. But given my current employment with the Queen, to say nothing of the trouble with Isabel Slanning, I had decided it was definitely better to burn them privately than hand them in and risk my name appearing on a list of those who had owned forbidden books.

I took them downstairs, lighting another candle from the one in the kitchen, then went out to Agnes's neatly tended vegetable patch behind the house. There was a large iron brazier there, used for burn-ing weeds and other garden rubbish. It was half-full, the contents brown and dry after all the recent sun. I took a dry twig from the bra-zier, lit it with the candle and dropped it in. The fire flared up quickly, crackling. I looked around to ensure I was unobserved, then, with a sigh, I took the first of my books and began tearing out pages and dropping them on the fire, watching the black Gothic script I had once read so carefully curling up. I remembered Anne Askew, her skin shrivelling in the flames, and shuddered.

✝

NEXT MORNING, MONDAY, I went into chambers early and caught up with some work. When Barak arrived I told him of my talk with Nicholas, and my meeting with Stice. I said there was nothing to do for now but wait for news from him or Cecil.

'How is Tamasin?' I asked.

'Does nothing but talk of tomorrow's party. All our neighbours are coming. You know what women are like.' He looked at me shrewdly. 'I think she's forgotten any suspicions she had about what I might be doing. Let's hope she goes on forgetting, eh?' He raised his hand and I saw the bandage was off and the stitches out. 'I'm ready for action,' he said.

✝

LATER THAT MORNING I crossed the sunlit Gatehouse Court to visit Treasurer Rowland. The old man was as usual seated behind his desk, his office shutters half-closed, and he greeted me with a curt nod.

'I looked for you at Bealknap's funeral on Saturday. I wondered if you would come.'

'Actually, I forgot about it.'

'So did everyone else. There were only me and the preacher there. Well, Brother Bealknap lies in the chapel now, under a flagstone like any other, with his name and dates of birth and death inscribed upon it. He merited no mausoleum.'

'Poor Bealknap,' I said.

'Oh no,' Rowland said. '*Rich* Bealknap. Much good it did him in the end.' I did not reply, and he turned to the pile of papers on his desk. 'Secretary Paget's people have sent me more details about the French admiral's visit next month. It is going to be an even bigger event than I thought. I'll show you the correspondence. But first,' his voice deepened, 'I've got to waste my time on this nonsense.' He pulled a letter from the pile on his desk and threw it across to me: Isabel's complaint, two pages covered in her neat, tiny writing. As expected, it accused me, along with Philip Coleswyn, her brother and the expert Master Adam, of collusion to defeat her case, 'out of wicked spite', as she was of honest religion while we were all heretics.

'It's all nonsense,' I said. 'She chose that architect herself.'

'Is he a radical?'

'No. The accusations of heresy she sent flying around at the inspection scared him out of his wits. As I said, it's all nonsense.'

Rowland gave his laugh, a sound as though rusty hinges were opening and closing in his throat. 'I believe you, Brother Shardlake. It is years since you associated with the radicals; we spoke not long ago of how you have been careful. Though you did not attend Mass yester-day.'

'Urgent business. I will be there next weekend.'

He leaned back in his chair and regarded me closely, stroking his long white beard with fingers stained black from a lifetime's work-ing with ink, as mine were. 'You seem to attract trouble, Serjeant Shardlake, despite yourself. How did you end up working for this madwoman?'

'Ill luck. Every barrister has such clients.'

'True. I am glad I am out of such nonsense. What of this Coleswyn, is he a radical?'

'He has a reputation as a reformer.'

Rowland looked at me sharply. 'Mistress Slanning says you went to dinner at his house.'

'Once. We became friendly because we were both frustrated by our clients' behaviour. Mistress Slanning's brother is as much a vex-atious litigant as she is. And Mistress Slanning found out about my visit because she sometimes passes the evening spying on Coleswyn's house. That gives you a flavour of the woman.'

'She says her brother met Coleswyn because they both attend the same radical church.'

'It is a common enough way for lawyers to meet clients.'

He nodded agreement, then made a steeple of his fingers. 'Who represents her now? Do we know?'

'Vincent Dyrick of Gray's Inn. He called to get the papers last week.'

Rowland frowned. 'He has a vicious reputation. He'll make something of this conspiracy theory in court. Probably instigated the complaint.'

'He said he did not, it was all Isabel's idea. Actually, I believe him there. But he won't be able to stop her from making her allegations in court.'

'Do you think she might complain to Gray's Inn about Coleswyn?'

'She'd have no right. He is not acting for her.'

Rowland considered. 'Very well. I will try to make this go away. I will write to Mistress Slanning saying she has no evidence to back her complaints, and to warn her about the laws of defamation. That should frighten her off.' He spoke complacently, though I feared such a letter would only anger Isabel further. 'And you, Master Shardlake,' Rowland continued, his voice full of angry irritation, 'stay out of this case from now on. I don't want you mixed up in any religious quarrels when you are to represent the Inn at the celebrations next month.'

'I will step down from attending the ceremonies if you wish,' I answered mildly.

Rowland gave his unpleasant half-smile and shook his head. 'Oh no, Brother Shardlake, you will do your duty. I have already given in your name. Now, see this.' He passed me another sheaf of papers. 'Details of the peace celebrations.'

I looked them over, remembering what Paget and the Queen had said about the jewels ordered for her, the new clothes for the Queen's ladies. Even so, my eyes widened at the scale of what was planned. The admiral was to sail up the Thames on the 20th of August with a dozen galleys. The King's ships, which had met those galleys in battle exactly a year before, were to be lined up along the Thames from Gravesend to Deptford to welcome him. He would be received by the King at Greenwich, then next day go upriver to the Tower of

London, before riding through the streets of the city. During this procession the London aldermen and guildsmen — and others including
senior lawyers from the Inns of Court — would line the streets to cheer
him, all in their best robes. I closed my eyes for a moment and remembered standing on the deck of the *Mary Rose* a year before, watching
as those same French galleys fired at our fleet.

'Quite something, is it not?' Rowland said. Even he sounded a
little awed.

'It is, Master Treasurer.'

I read on. The admiral would stay in London two days, riding to
Hampton Court on the 23rd. On the way to Hampton Court he
would be welcomed by Prince Edward, lords and gentlemen and a
thousand horses. Next day he would dine with the King and Queen
and there would be enormous festivities at Hampton Court. Again
my presence would be required, as one of the hundreds in the background.

I put down the papers. 'It is all about impressing him, I see.'

'Great ceremonial was ever the King's way. All you will be
required to do is stand around like scenery, richly garbed. Have you a
gold chain for such ceremonies?'

'No.'

'Then get one, before they are all sold out.'

'I will be ready.'

'Good,' Rowland said. 'And I will write to Mistress Slanning.'
He made a note, then looked up at me and spoke wearily. 'Try to keep
out of trouble, Serjeant Shardlake.'

✝

DESPITE ROWLAND'S WARNING, that afternoon I fetched
Genesis from my house, rode up to Gray's Inn and asked for Philip
Coleswyn's chambers. His outer office, which he shared with another
barrister, was neatly organized — it made me realize that my own
chambers were starting to look a mess. I was shown into Coleswyn's

office, which again was immaculate, all the papers filed neatly in pigeonholes. He laid down his quill and stood to greet me.

'Brother Shardlake. This is an unexpected pleasure. So Mistress Slanning has dismissed you. I had a note this morning from her new representative, Brother Vincent Dyrick.'

'Yes.' I raised my eyebrows. 'I know Dyrick.'

'So do I, by repute.' He sighed. 'His letter said Mistress Slanning plans to raise in court the nonsense about us and her brother conspiring with Master Adam, because we are all heretics. He said she has also made a complaint about you to Lincoln's Inn.'

'I had a meeting with the Treasurer this morning about that. I came to reassure you he recognizes the complaint for the foolery it is. But also to warn you about Dyrick: he is persistent, and unscrupulous.'

'I think perhaps Brother Dyrick hopes that by airing these allegations of a heretic conspiracy he will frighten me, and perhaps Master Cotterstoke, into coming to a settlement.' Philip shook his head. 'But we both know nothing on this earth will bring those two to settle.'

'Treasurer Rowland ordered me to steer clear of the business, particularly since I am to play a small part in the ceremonial welcoming the French admiral next month.'

'Then I thank you all the more for coming to see me. I spoke to Edward Cotterstoke about these latest allegations yesterday. He will not shift an inch. In fact he lost his temper when I told him of his sister's latest ploy. He said a strange thing: that if the worst came to the worst, he knew things that could destroy her.'

'What did he mean?'

'Heaven knows. He said it in anger, and refused to elaborate. Insisted it was nothing to do with the case and quickly changed the subject.'

'And Isabel once said her brother had done terrible things. What is it with those two, that they hate each other so?'

'I do not know,' Coleswyn said. He shook his head again.

'You remember the old family servant, Vowell, who became upset by their behaviour at the inspection. Is he still taking care of the house?'

'Yes. But Master Shardlake, you should do as your Treasurer advises, and leave the matter alone now.'

'But I will still be involved, if this conspiracy allegation comes up in court. I am named.'

'You are not a radical reformer. You have nothing to fear.'

'Do you?' I asked bluntly.

He did not answer, and I continued. 'Isabel Slanning will make whatever trouble she can. What if she asks you, through Dyrick, to swear in court that the Mass transforms the bread and wine into the body and blood of Christ?'

'I doubt the court would allow it.'

'But if they do?'

Coleswyn bit his lip. 'I am not sure I could do that.'

'That is what I feared,' I said quietly. 'I beg you to think carefully, Philip. That would be an admission of heresy. Think what could happen not just to you, but to your wife and children. To all those associated with you. Even me.'

His face worked. 'Do you think I have not already considered that, agonized over it? I pray constantly, trying to seek out God's will for me.'

I looked at his honest, troubled face. I realized that Philip Coleswyn was a man who, despite his qualities, might put others at risk to save – as he saw it – his soul. I spoke quietly, 'Think what God's will may be for the rest of us as well.'

☩

I HEARD NOTHING FURTHER from Stice that day, nor the one following. Little George's party was early that evening. The weather had changed; it was cooler and clouds were coming slowly in from the west. The farmers could do with the rain as harvest approached, but I knew Tamasin hoped to have the party in her garden.

I arrived shortly after four. It was still dry, but the sky was growing slowly darker. The little house was spotless, the table in the parlour covered in a white linen cloth on which stood flagons of beer and, I saw, some wine. Pewter mugs had been laid out. Outside in the tidy little garden another table was set with sweetmeats. About fifteen men and women, mostly in their thirties, stood there talking, all in their best finery; neighbours and clerks and solicitors from Lincoln's Inn and their wives. Sadly, no family was present, for Tamasin's father had abandoned her as a child and her mother was dead. And I remembered what Barak had told me about meeting his own mother in the street; he had not mentioned it again. I saw Guy, standing a little apart nursing a mug of beer.

Barak and Jane Marris were waiting on the guests, taking flagons to and fro to ensure mugs were kept full, Barak looking a little uneasy in this unfamiliar role. Nicholas was there in his best bright doublet, his fading bruises attracting looks from some of the guests. Tamasin stood with George in her arms, the baby in a white robe and bonnet, holding him out for guests to come and admire. They congratulated her, too, on her pregnancy, which had evidently already been announced. She herself wore her best dress of yellow silk. I filled a mug with beer and went outside. Tamasin smiled at me and held out a welcoming hand.

'Master Shardlake.' She addressed me formally. 'My friends,' she said proudly, 'this is my husband's master, a serjeant of the King's courts.' I reddened as everyone looked at me. Fond as I was of Tamasin, the touch of snobbery in her nature could be embarrassing. Behind her I saw Barak nudge Nicholas and wink. I bent low over George, who stared at me with blank eyes. 'A happy birthday, little fellow.' I touched his plump cheek.

'Thank you for coming,' Tamasin said quietly. 'And for all you have done for us over the years.'

'How are you now?' I asked. 'Feeling better?'

'Yes. In good health and spirits.' She looked round, smiling contentedly. 'Our little party goes well.' My conscience pricked at the thought of how Barak and I were deceiving her. I said, 'I should go and speak to Guy, he is on his own.'

'A good idea.'

I went over to my old friend. 'Well, Matthew.' I noted the neutrality of his tone.

'Tamasin says she is feeling better.'

'Yes, everything is going as it should. And how are things with you?' His look was sharp.

'Well enough.'

'Jack's hand is healed. And the boy's chest wound. As well they did not get infected.'

'I know.'

He asked quietly, 'That business which led to their injuries. Is it settled?' I hesitated. I did not want to lie to him. 'I guessed as much,' he said quietly. 'Something in Jack's manner. I have been observing people carefully for forty years, it is part of my trade. I think Tamasin suspected something when he was hurt, though she appears settled now. But she is expecting a child, Matthew, and lost one before. If anything should happen to Jack—'

'Guy,' I spoke with sudden heat, 'sometimes one takes on duties, swears oaths, and sometimes, to do what one is sworn to, one needs – help.'

'Matthew, I know of only one loyalty you have which would let you place yourself – and others – in danger. I thought the Queen had manoeuvred herself out of the trouble she got herself into earlier, but perhaps I am wrong. Well, hers is not my cause. I agree, one must fulfil a debt of honour. But when others are dragged in, one should think also of them.'

'Guy – '

'I worry for my patient.'

I felt something on my hand, and looked down to see a fat splash of water. More heavy drops were falling from the grey sky. Barak said, 'Indoors, everybody. Come, wife, get George inside.'

We all went in as the rain turned to a downpour, some of the women helping Jane rescue the sweetmeats before they got soaked. When we were in the parlour I looked around for Guy, but he had gone.

Chapter Thirty-two

I STAYED ONLY A LITTLE LONGER. Outside, the rain pattered down relentlessly, then the thunder came. Guy's departure had been noted. I told Tamasin he had said he was feeling unwell. I left myself a short while later. The thunderstorm had ended, and as I walked home the air smelt damp and oddly fresh, though a nasty brown sludge of sewage and offal squelched under my feet.

When I got home I heard a woman weeping in the kitchen. Josephine's young man, Edward Brown, stood in the hall. He looked embarrassed, twisting his cap in his hands.

'What's going on?' I asked sharply. I had thought him a decent young man. If he had done something to upset her –

'It is Goodwife Brocket, sir,' Brown said hastily. 'I came back with Josephine and we found her distraught in the kitchen. Forgive me waiting in your hallway, sir, but Josephine sent me out.'

'Very well.' I went to join the women. Agnes Brocket sat at the table, her coif removed, her head in her hands. Josephine sat beside her. Agnes looked up as I entered, wisps of nut-brown hair falling over her face.

'What is amiss?' I asked.

Josephine answered. 'Mistress Brocket has had some upsetting family news, sir. I found her crying when Edward and I got back. She will be all right, I will take care of her.'

Agnes looked up. 'Forgive me, I am but a silly woman – '

'Where is Martin?'

'Gone into town, sir.' Agnes made an effort to pull herself together, taking out a handkerchief and dabbing her eyes. 'He's not happy with the bread delivered by Master Dove, he has gone to complain. Please don't tell him you saw me thus, Master Shardlake.'

'I would like to know what is amiss, Agnes.'

She took a deep breath and turned to Josephine, who looked uncertain. Then she answered me quietly, 'We have a son, sir. John. Our only child, and he is in deep trouble. Some business matters went wrong, and he is in the debtors' prison in Leicester.'

'I am sorry to hear that.'

She shook her head. 'He was such a handsome, charming boy. He had such plans to rise in the world.'

I sat down opposite her. 'Nothing so wrong in that.'

For the first time since I had known her, Agnes frowned. 'Martin does not think so. He believes everyone should keep to their appointed place in the social order. He was always severe with John; I think that was why the boy left home early.' She looked up quickly. 'But I do not mean to speak ill of my husband, sir. Despite his severity he has always doted on John.'

'How did your son end in prison, Agnes? Perhaps, as a lawyer, I may be able to assist you.'

She shook her head sadly. 'It is too late for that, sir. John managed to persuade some investors in Leicester to lend him money to buy up some of the land belonging to the old monasteries. He planned to hold on to it until land prices rose.'

'They lent money without security?' I said in surprise.

Agnes smiled sadly. 'John can charm the birds out of the trees when he wants.' Then her face fell. 'But the price of land continued to fall, they sued for debt and for the last year he has sat in Leicester gaol, where he will remain until the debt is paid. Martin and I send him money – if you cannot provide food and clothing for yourself, you are left to starve in that dreadful place. And he tries to pay off his debts, little by little. But it is twenty pounds. Now John has written saying what we send does not cover the interest, and his creditors say the balance is larger than ever.' She shook her head. 'I fear he will die in the prison now. Last winter he had a congestion in his lungs, and another winter in there . . .' Her voice tailed off for a moment. 'Please do not tell Martin I have spoken with you, sir. It is shameful, and he is so proud, and does not like others knowing our trouble – '

I raised a hand. 'If you wish, Agnes. But perhaps I may be able to do something – '

'No, sir, please. We have already consulted a lawyer, he said there was nothing to be done. Do not tell Martin,' she pleaded urgently. 'He will be – distressed.'

'Very well. But consider what I said. I will help if I can.'

'Thank you, sir.' But her tone told me she would say nothing to her husband.

✝

I WENT INTO CHAMBERS early next morning, for there was work to catch up on. The weather was hot and sunny again. Martin Brocket attended me as usual on rising, no sign on his face of anything unusual, and I guessed Agnes had not told him of our conversation.

As I was leaving, Josephine asked to speak to me. I took her into the parlour. 'Agnes Brocket asked me to thank you for your kindness yesterday. She asked me to speak for her as she is – well, ashamed.'

'It is not her shame.'

'She thinks it is. And Martin would be angry if anyone else knew. It would hurt his pride,' she added, a note of contempt in her voice.

'I have been thinking how seldom the Brockets go out, except for walks.'

'And Agnes never buys clothes.'

'All their money must be going to their son. And, Josephine, that makes me think again about the time you found Martin going through the drawers of my desk. I wonder whether, in a moment of desperation, he considered turning to theft.'

'I wondered the same thing yesterday, sir.'

'It would be an explanation. But I have found nothing missing, and you do not think he has done such a thing again.'

'No, sir, I don't. And I have been watching him.' She gave a slight smile. 'I think he knows that. I think that is why he dislikes me.'

'Well, if it was a moment of madness, then no harm done – but it must not happen again. Go on keeping an eye open, will you? I have other matters on my mind just now, but when I have a little more time I will have to decide what is best to do about him.'

Josephine smiled, pleased at the responsibility. 'You can rely on me, sir.'

☦

IN CHAMBERS I FOUND everyone already at work; Barak and Skelly at their desks, Nicholas doing some much-needed filing. Apart from the disapproving looks Skelly cast at Nicholas's puffy face, it was like any normal day, spent working with my staff on preparing cases for the new court term in September.

The quiet did not last long. At noon Barak came in and closed the door to my office behind him, his expression serious. 'Stice has turned up.'

I laid down my quill. 'Here?'

'Yes. Says he has news. Shall I bring him in?'

'Yes. Fetch Nicholas as well.'

Stice walked confidently into the room. He was well dressed as ever, sword at his hip, every inch the young gentleman. I did not invite him to sit and he surveyed the three of us with a cynical grin.

'All together again, hey?' He looked at Nicholas. 'That's a fine pair of shiners you have.'

'They're fading. At least in a few days my face will look normal, which yours never will.'

Stice laughed, but put a hand to his ear. 'Well, I am keeping my part of the bargain,' he said to me. 'There's news from the customs house. I think some birds may be about to fly into our trap.'

'The missing men?' I could not keep the eagerness from my voice.

'Four of them, at least,' Stice said. I exchanged a look with Barak.

There were only four survivors of Greening's group, but Stice did not know that.

He continued, 'A balinger arrived yesterday from Antwerp, with a cargo of silks for the peace celebrations. A Dutch crew. They're load⁄ing up a cargo of wool now to take back tomorrow, spending the night moored at Somers Key Wharf. Meanwhile my man at the cus⁄toms house says four men presented themselves there this morning, claiming they had business in Antwerp, and had passage booked on that ship. One Dutch, one Scotch, and two English. He sent word to me. The four answer the descriptions of Vandersteyn, McKendrick, Curdy and Leeman from the Queen's household.' Stice's thin face lit up with excitement. 'Though they gave false names, of course. No sign of Myldmore or that apprentice. They've been told they can go aboard at ten this evening.' He smiled. 'So, we beat your associate Cecil to the quarry.'

'It's not a competition,' I answered calmly. 'If the coming of these four has been recorded at the customs house I have no doubt the news will get to our people today.'

'Isn't ten at night an unusual hour to go aboard?' Nicholas asked.

Stice looked pleased with himself. 'I'd told my man at the customs house to say it would take till ten to process the papers. It'll be dark then, easier to take them. All we need to do is wait at Somers Key Wharf tonight. It'll be quiet, work will have finished for the day. With luck we'll take them all. And hopefully Askew's confession will be in their luggage, or more likely about the person of one of them.' And the *Lamentation* too, I thought. My heart quickened.

'Why tell us?' Barak asked Stice. 'You could have taken them yourselves.'

'Because Sir Richard keeps his word, fellow.' Stice smiled, then shrugged. 'And as you said, your people will likely get wind of it today, in any case. Besides, if we take them on the wharf there may be trouble. I've told the customs people to keep out of it, that this is private business of Sir Richard, but the crew of that Dutch ship may not like us seizing their passengers, particularly if they're all heretics.'

'The crew will probably be getting drunk in the city,' Barak said.

'There will be a couple of men left on board at least,' Stice replied. 'To keep watch, and help the passengers aboard. And these four may bring their own protection with them, of course.'

I had to agree. 'Yes, there is still the question of those two men who murdered the printer.'

'If there is a fight at the wharf, won't that attract people?' Nicholas asked.

'It could do,' Barak agreed. 'But if swords are being waved around, and a good number of men are involved, people are unlikely to intervene.'

'I agree,' Stice said. 'I can bring another two men tonight besides me and Gower. Can you three come?'

Nicholas and Barak nodded, Nicholas looking Stice in the eye. I said, 'And I will send a note to Cecil, to see if he can provide anybody, too.'

Stice thought a moment. I wondered if he was considering, if Cecil brought some more men, whether his own party would be outnumbered if it came to trouble between us. Then he smiled again. 'Wear dark clothes. We can look forward to an exciting evening.'

'My instructions are to see these people are taken alive,' I said. It had occurred to me that Rich might prefer that anyone with knowledge of Anne Askew's writings be put permanently out of the way.

'Of course. Sir Richard and your friend Cecil will doubtless want to question them all. Unless they decide to act the hero and fight back. They're fanatics, remember.' Stice looked serious now.

'Yes,' I agreed. 'Unless they fight back.'

'Nine o'clock then, at Somers Key Wharf. I've been down there and paid the wharfmaster to ensure a big stack of empty barrels is moved to a place opposite the Dutch ship. We wait behind them; it's an ideal arrangement to take them by surprise. We'll meet first at Needlepin Lane at eight, get to the wharf by nine and hide ourselves. There's no moon tonight, it'll be dark. When they come they won't know what's hit them.'

'You have organized everything very well,' I said grudgingly.

Stice gave an exaggerated bow and looked round at the three of us again. Barak met his gaze stonily, Nicholas angrily. 'Come, sir,' Stice said chidingly to him. 'No ill feelings, as I said to Master Shardlake earlier. You gave a good account of yourself, for all you're a lad just up from the country.'

'In an even fight, Master Stice, one on one, I may do even better.'

'Who knows? But we're on the same side now.'

'For the moment,' Nicholas said quietly.

✝

THAT EVENING Barak and I met Nicholas at his lodgings, and the three of us walked into town. It was a beautiful evening, the sun setting slowly, light white clouds in a sky of darkening blue. A cooling breeze had risen from the west. I looked at my companions. Barak's expression was keen and alert, Nicholas's coldly determined. I spoke quietly to him. 'No bravado tonight. Do not let yourself be roused by Stice, and do not put yourself at risk unnecessarily.'

'I will not let you down, sir.' He paused, then added, 'I know how dangerous this is. And that we must watch our allies as carefully as our enemies.'

'If enemies they are. We are not even sure they have the *Lamentation*. But we must find out.'

'Tonight we will.'

I nodded. I was more glad of his and Barak's company than I could say; I did not fancy my prospects were I to be caught on my own between a group of religious fanatics and a clutch of Rich's men. I had received a reply from Cecil to say he would be joining us at Stice's house, with two strong men from Lord Parr's household. I guessed Cecil would be as little use in a fight as myself, so Stice's party and ours would have four fighting men each.

We turned into Needlepin Lane, past the tavern where once again patrons were gathered outside, and knocked on the door of Stice's house. He let us in. The big man Gower was sitting at the table. Two other men sat with him, large young fellows with swords. They looked, as Barak would have said, useful.

Stice was cheerful and animated. He introduced us to his two new men with a mock bow. 'Here is Serjeant Shardlake, representing the interest of a certain personage who also has an interest in seeing the scribbles of Mistress Askew destroyed. And his men Barak and Master Overton. Overton and Gower had a row a few days ago, as you can see from the state of young Overton's face.'

Nicholas gave him a blank look. 'I get bored with your baiting, sir. This is no time for silly games.'

'Quite right,' I agreed.

Stice shrugged. 'Just a little sport.'

There was another knock at the door. Stice opened it again and William Cecil entered, with two heavyset men, a little older than the two Stice had brought. Like all of us they were dressed in dark clothes. Cecil took a deep breath, looking round the gathering with the sort of cool stare he might have given to an assembly of fellow lawyers. Stice grinned at him. 'Young Master Cecil! I had you pointed out to me a little while ago as a rising man in the service of a certain person.'

Cecil's reply was cold and clear. 'You are Stice, I take it, Sir Richard's man. I was told your appearance was – distinctive.'

Stice scowled but nodded, then Cecil asked, 'We are all to go down to Somers Key Wharf?'

'Yes.' Stice looked out of the window. 'It's pretty dark already. We get there by nine, hide behind the barrels, and wait. When they come, we rush them and bring them, and any baggage they have, back here. It's likely the writing we're looking for will be on their persons rather than in their luggage. I've another man waiting near the wharf with a horse and a big cart with a tarpaulin; we'll bind and gag them to keep them quiet on the way back here, knock them out if we have to.'

'We shall have to act quickly, and all together,' Barak said.

'Agreed. And if any watchmen question us about what we're doing, I have Sir Richard's seal.' Stice looked at Cecil. 'But if they fight back, and someone gets killed, that's not our fault. And if the printer's murderers arrive, too, and they get killed, you agree that's no loss?'

'Agreed,' Cecil answered coldly. He pointed to the empty grate. 'And any writings we find on them, we destroy immediately in that fire. That is also agreed?'

Stice hesitated, but Cecil continued smoothly. 'I think your master would prefer that nobody look at anything we find. In case it incriminates him.' He met Stice's eye. I admired his cool judgement. Rich would not want even his own men to see any record of his and Wriothesley's torture of Anne Askew. No doubt Rich would have liked to find something damaging to the Queen among Anne Askew's writings, and I had let him believe that such incriminating statements might exist; but as he had told me, that was not his priority now. Cecil's hope was doubtless that we would be able to quickly burn all writings we found, including the *Lamentation*, if the survivors of Greening's group turned out to have it. And as Greening had torn off the title page when he was attacked, I was hoping it might not be clear, from the face of the manuscript, who had written it.

'Ready then?' Barak asked.

'Yes,' Stice agreed.

'Then let us go.'

Chapter Thirty-three

W E WALKED DOWN THAMES STREET; ten of us, all in dark clothes, most carrying swords. It was just past curfew, and the few people on the streets gave our intimidating-looking group a wide berth. A watchman did step out to ask what we were about, a little nervously, but Stice answered peremptorily, 'Business of Sir Richard Rich, Privy Councillor,' and produced a gold seal. The watchman held up his lantern to look at it, then bowed us on our way.

We walked past London Bridge; candles were being lit in the four-storey houses built along its length. The tide was full, just starting to ebb; we could hear the roar of the waters as they rushed under the broad stone piers of the bridge. It was dangerous for boats to 'shoot the bridge' and for that reason the wharves dealing with foreign trade were sited immediately downriver. They ran along the waterfront between the bridge and the Tower of London; a line of masts near a quarter of a mile long when trade was busy, as it was now. Behind the waterfront stood a long row of warehouses. I saw the tall, skeleton-like arms of the cranes at Billingsgate Wharf outlined against the near-dark sky; beyond the wharves, the Tower appeared a strange phantom grey in the last of the light.

We turned down Botolph Lane to the waterfront, walking quietly, stumbling occasionally, for we had no lamps. From several buildings came the sound of revelry, even though it was past curfew – illegal ale-houses and brothels, serving sailors ashore for the night, which the authorities tended to leave alone.

We reached the waterfront and the long line of ships. It was quiet here after the noise of the surrounding streets. For a moment I thought

I heard something, like a foot striking a stone, from the mouth of the lane from which we had just emerged. I looked back quickly but saw only the black empty passageway. I exchanged a glance with Barak; he had heard it, too.

Stice led the way onto the cobbled wharf, keeping close to the warehouse buildings. Beyond it the ships bobbed gently on the tide; low, heavy, one- and two-masted trading vessels lined stern to prow, secured by heavy ropes to big stone bollards, sails tightly furled. From a few cabins came the dim flicker of candlelight. With the re-opening of French and Scottish trade, and the import of luxury goods for the admiral's visit, the wharves must be busy indeed during the day. Out on the river itself pinpricks of light, the lanterns of wherries, glinted on the water.

Nearby stood a long pile of barrels, three high, secured with ropes. 'No talking now,' Stice said in a whisper. 'Get in behind them.'

One by one we slipped into the dark space. I crouched next to Cecil and Stice, peering between two of the barrels, which smelled strongly of wine. Opposite us a two-masted crayer was berthed, a squat heavy vessel for North Sea carriage of perhaps thirty tons, *Antwerpen* painted on the side. There was a little deck-house, the windows unshuttered; two men in linen shirts sat inside, playing cards by the light of the lamp. They were middle-aged, but strong-looking.

Next to me Cecil's face was quietly intent. I thought, this is not his usual form of business, and wondered whether underneath his coolness he feared the prospect of violence. I whispered to him, 'I thought I heard something, at the mouth of that lane, just as we came onto the docks. Like someone dislodging a stone.'

He turned to me, his face anxious now. 'You mean we have been followed?'

'I don't know. Barak heard it too. I had a strange feeling.'

Stice, on my other side, turned to Barak who had taken a position beside him. 'Did you?'

He nodded yes.

Stice's eyes glittered in the dark. 'Once or twice I've felt the house in Needlepin Lane is being watched. But I've not been able to catch anybody at it.'

'We've never known for sure that Greening's murderers were connected with these Anabaptists,' Cecil said. 'What if there's a third party involved, someone we don't know about?'

'Then perhaps tonight we'll find out,' Stice answered. 'Now be quiet, stop talking, just watch.'

We crouched there for the best part of an hour. My back and knees hurt; I had to keep shifting position. Once, we tensed at the sound of footsteps and voices, and hands reached for swords and daggers, but it was only a couple of sailors, weaving drunkenly along the dockside. They climbed aboard a ship some way off. Apart from an occasional distant shouting from the taverns, all was quiet save for the sound of water lapping round the ships.

Then I heard more footsteps, quiet and steady this time, and from another narrow lane to our left I saw the bobbing yellow glow of a lantern. A whisper passed along our row of men. 'Four of them,' Stice said into my ear. 'Looks like our people. Right, you and Master Cecil stay at the rear, leave it to us fighting men.' And then, with a patter of feet and the distinctive *whish* of swords being pulled from their scabbards, the others ran out from behind the barrels. Cecil and I followed, our daggers at the ready.

The men were taken totally by surprise. The lantern was raised to show four astonished faces. They matched the descriptions I had committed to memory: the tall, powerfully built square-faced man in his thirties must be the Scotch cleric McKendrick, the plump middle-aged man the merchant Curdy, and the rangy fair-haired fellow the Dutchman Vandersteyn. The fourth man, in his twenties, tall, strongly built and dark-haired, had to be Leeman, the Queen's guard who had deserted. He would be trained as a fighting man, and I also remembered that McKendrick had formerly been a soldier. Apart from Curdy, who had the round flabbiness of a prosperous merchant, each looked as if they could give good account of themselves.

All four rallied in an instant, bringing up swords of their own.

They were going to make a fight of it. Apart from Curdy, who had been holding the lamp and now laid it down, only the fair-haired man had been encumbered by luggage, a large bag which he let drop to the cobbles. But Stice and his crew, Cecil's two men, and Barak and Nicholas, made eight against them. They fanned out in a circle, surrounding the smaller group, who cast glances, as did I, at the ship from Antwerp. The two crewmen had now left the cabin and stood at the rail, staring at what was happening. Then another man climbed up from below to join them.

Stice called out, 'Lower your swords. You're outnumbered. You are under arrest for the attempted export of seditious literature!'

The fair-haired man shouted something in Dutch to the men at the ship's rail. One of Stice's men lunged at him with his sword but he parried immediately, just as the three men from the boat jumped nimbly over the ship's rail onto the wharf, each carrying a sword. My heart sank; the number of fighting men was almost even now.

One of Cecil's men turned and raised his weapon, but in doing so he turned his back on the blond Dutchman, who thrust his own sword swiftly through his body. The man cried out, his sword clattering onto the cobbles. Then Vandersteyn turned to face the rest of us and, with his three compatriots, began retreating slowly to the boat. I looked at the fallen man; there was no doubt now that we were not dealing with some amateurish group of fanatics but with serious, dangerous people.

'Cut them off!' Stice yelled. A moment later there was a melee of swordplay, blades flashing in the light of the lamp. I stepped forward, but felt Cecil's hand restraining my arm. 'No! We must stay alive; we have to get hold of the book.'

There was a battle royal now going on beside the ship, blades flashing noisily. Watchmen came out to the rails of nearby ships and stood gawping. Curdy, the weakest of the fugitives, lunged clumsily at Gower, who, ignoring our agreement to take these men alive if possible, sliced at his neck with his sword, nearly severing his head. Curdy thumped down on the cobbles, dead, in a spray of blood.

From what I could see of the melee, the surviving fugitives were effectively parrying blows from our side, backing slowly and deliberately towards the *Antwerpen*. We must not let these people get aboard. I stepped closer, though in the feeble lamplight I could see little more than rapidly moving shapes, white faces and the quick flash of metal. Stice received a glancing blow to his forehead but carried on, blood streaming down his face, felling one of the sailors with a thrust to the stomach. I stepped forward, but again Cecil pulled me back. 'We'd only be in the way!' I looked at him; his face was still coldly set, but the rigidity of his stance told me he was frightened. He looked at Lord Parr's dead servant, face down on the cobbles, blood pooling around him.

Nicholas and Barak had their hands full with the guard Leeman, who was indeed a fierce fighter. He was trying to edge them away from the centre of the fight, towards the little lane we had come down.

'At least I can get this!' I said, darting over to Vandersteyn's bag, which lay disregarded on the ground. I picked it up, thrusting it into Cecil's arms. 'Here! Look after this!' And with that I pulled out my dagger and ran to where Leeman, wielding his sword with great skill, continued to lead Barak and Nicholas back towards the alley, thrusting mightily and parrying their every blow, years of training making it look easy. His aim was clearly to separate them from the others, to allow McKendrick and Vandersteyn to get on board the ship. Beside the *Antwerpen* the fighting continued, steel ringing on steel.

I raised my dagger to plunge it into Leeman's shoulder from behind. He heard me coming and half-turned; Nicholas brought his sword down on his forearm in a glancing blow as Barak reversed his sword and gave him a heavy blow to the back of the head. He went down like a sack of turnips in the entrance to the lane. Barak and Nicholas ran back to the main fight.

It was now seven against five − Vandersteyn and McKendrick and the three surviving Dutch sailors. I hoped the other members of the crew were all in the taverns getting drunk. But suddenly one of the sailors managed to jump back on board the ship. He held out an arm and Vandersteyn, despite having been wounded in the leg, jumped after him, leaving only one sailor and the Scotchman behind.

On deck, Vandersteyn and the crewman used their swords to sever the ropes securing the ship to the wharf. The sailor snatched up a long pole and pushed off. The *Antwerpen* moved clumsily away from the wharf, instantly caught in the current. Vandersteyn shouted to the two men left behind, 'I'm sorry, brothers! Trust in God!'

'Stop them!' Stice yelled. But it was too late, the *Antwerpen* was out on the river. The current carried her rapidly downstream, bobbing wildly, the two men on board struggling to control her, almost over-turning a wherry which just managed to row out of the way in time. A stream of curses sounded across the water as the boat headed for the middle of the river. I saw a sail unfurl.

The remaining Dutchman and McKendrick had their backs to the river now. Realizing it was hopeless, they lowered their swords. 'Drop them on the ground!' Stice shouted. They obeyed, metal ring-ing on the cobbles, and Stice waved his men to lower their own weapons. I looked at the four prone bodies on the wharf: the Dutch sailor, Curdy, Cecil's man and, a little distance away, Leeman, lying on his front in the entrance to the alley. 'He's dead,' Barak said loudly.

On neighbouring boats watchmen still stood staring, talking ani-matedly in foreign tongues, but Barak had been right; they had not wanted to get mixed up in a sword fight involving a dozen men. One man shouted something at us in Spanish, but we ignored him. More men, though, might appear from the taverns. I looked at the Dutch-man and McKendrick. Returning my look, the Dutchman spoke in heavily accented English. 'Citizen of Flanders. Not subject to your laws. You must let us go.'

'Pox on that!' Stice shouted. 'Your bodies will go in the river tonight!' His head and shoulders were covered with blood from his wound; in the light of the lamp he looked like some demon from a mystery play.

The Dutch sailor seemed shaken, but McKendrick spoke boldly, in the ringing tones of a preacher, his Scotch accent strong: 'Ye've lost!

We know Mynheer Vandersteyn had a book, by Anne Askew. Carried on his person, not in that bag. That's why we got him aboard. Ye've lost!' he repeated triumphantly.

Stice turned wildly to Cecil. 'We have to get that boat intercepted!'

'On what grounds?' Cecil said, his voice sharp and authoritative now. 'Exporting heretical literature? The book would be public knowledge in a day. And intercepting a foreign trading vessel could cause diplomatic trouble; that's the last thing we need just now.'

Stice wiped his face with a bloody sleeve, then looked at the bag which Cecil still held. 'Maybe they're lying! Maybe it's in there!' He grasped it from Cecil's arms and upturned it on the ground, dragging the lantern across to examine the contents. I helped him go through them; nothing but spare clothing, a Dutch bible and a purse of coins. He threw the purse down and stood cursing.

'Search those men!' he shouted, pointing to McKendrick and the Dutchman. Two of Stice's men grabbed them and searched them roughly, watched carefully by Cecil and me, then turned back to their master, holding out a couple of purses. 'Nothing but these!'

'Examine them!'

The two men opened the drawstrings and bent to look inside. Seizing his moment, the Scotchman suddenly jumped forward and grabbed his sword. Gower was next to him. Taking the big man by surprise, McKendrick lunged at him, thrusting his sword deep into his stomach. With a cry, Gower staggered back into the man next to him, unbalancing him, and the Scot, with an astounding turn of speed for such a big man, ran for the lane, jumping over Leeman's prone body. Stice's men ran after him, disappearing into the darkness.

'By God's body sacred!' Cecil shouted out. It was the first outbreak of temper I had seen from him. 'We've lost them all!' He approached the Dutchman and, to my surprise, addressed him in Flemish. A brief exchange followed before Cecil turned away. 'He knows nothing,' he said fiercely. 'They all belonged to some heretic congregation in Antwerp, came over knowing their friend Vandersteyn had an important book to bring back. This one says there are two more crewmen who will be back from the tavern soon. And we *can't* have a diplomatic incident over this.' He spoke desperately, look, ing at the four bodies and at Gower, who had fallen to his knees and was gasping as he clutched the wound in his stomach, blood trickling down between his fingers.

The two who had run after McKendrick returned empty-handed. 'He got away from us, those lanes are pitch-black. The devil knows where he is now.'

'No!' We all turned to the Dutchman, who spoke in heavily accented English. '*God* knows where he is. He is God's servant, unlike you shavelings of the Pope.' Stice and his men looked at him threaten, ingly; they would have given him a beating, but Cecil called them off sharply. 'Let him go,' he said. He looked at the sailor. 'Run, you, while you can!'

The Dutchman disappeared into the lanes. 'Search Leeman and Curdy's bodies,' Cecil said. 'Quick, there's little time.'

'What for?' Stice asked. He had taken out a handkerchief and was dabbing at his face.

Cecil nodded at the direction in which the Dutchman had fled. 'In case he's lying and one of them has the book on his person.'

Barak and Nicholas went over and searched Leeman's body, while one of Stice's men searched Curdy's, Cecil and I standing over him in case a manuscript should be found. But there was nothing on either man, save more purses full of coins for the men's new life on the Con, tinent. I sighed. Gower had collapsed to the ground now, coughing; Stice went over and knelt beside him. 'We'll get you seen to,' he said in a surprisingly gentle tone.

I turned to the body of Cecil's man. 'Had he family?' I asked.

Cecil shook his head. 'I don't know. The poor fellow was in Lord Parr's household.' He turned to the other man who had come with him. 'Did you know him?'

'Only slightly, sir. But he had a wife.'

'What do we do with the bodies?' Nicholas asked quietly.

'Put them in the river,' Stice answered, standing up. 'There's nothing to identify them, and with luck they'll be carried far downstream before they surface. When the crew return they'll find the ship gone and they'll learn about the fight from the one we let go, who'll be running to them now. But they'll say nothing, their business was illegal and there's nothing to lead anyone to us. Get them in the water, now.'

'Not my man,' Cecil answered firmly. 'You heard, he had a wife. My other man and I will have him taken back to Whitehall in a wherry. We owe him that. We can say he was robbed.'

Stice took a deep breath. 'We've got to get Gower to a doctor. He'll take some carrying to the cart.'

On the next ship the sailor was calling to us in Spanish again – asking questions, by the tone of his voice. Stice turned and shouted, 'Fuck off!'

'All right, Stice,' Barak said briskly. 'We'll dispose of these other two; you're right, if they're left lying here there'll be questions.'

Stice nodded agreement. He turned to me, braced his shoulders and said, 'We have failed, Master Shardlake. Sir Richard Rich will want an accounting for this.'

'He is not the only one,' Cecil said.

Stice left his two remaining men carrying the wounded Gower between them. Barak shook his head. 'Stomach wound like that, doubt he'll make it.'

'No,' I said. 'Well done, Nicholas, for battling with Leeman. He was a powerful fighter.'

Barak smiled. 'Not was. Is. Come and look. Bring the lamp.'

Puzzled, Cecil and Nicholas and I followed him over to where Leeman lay prone. Nicholas turned him over. The wound on his arm had stopped bleeding. Barak put a hand to the man's nostrils. 'There, he's breathing. I only knocked him out.' He looked between me and Cecil and smiled.

Nicholas said, 'You told me he was dead!'

'There's an art to where you hit a man on the head. I thought it a good idea to pretend he was dead. Now that Stice has gone we can take him in to question him alone.' He allowed himself a smile. 'I was scared he might come to and moan, but he's still out cold.'

Nicholas looked at Barak with a new respect. Cecil bent over Leeman dubiously. 'Are you sure he's all right?'

'Pretty sure. He'll come round soon.'

I looked at the young guard's still face. 'It seems Anne Askew's writings have gone, but as for the *Lamentation*, if anyone knows what's happened to it, it's him.'

Cecil smiled with relief. 'Yes. You did well, Barak.'

'He may not want to talk,' Nicholas muttered.

Cecil looked at the boy, his large eyes set hard now. 'One way or another, he will.' He looked round. People were still watching us from the boats, but nobody had come yet from the taverns. 'All right,' he said. 'Get those bodies in the river. Quick!'

Chapter Thirty-four

I QUICKLY BOUND LEEMAN's injured arm with my handkerchief. Fortunately the blow Nicholas had struck him, though a
long gash, was not deep. Cecil and Lord Parr's surviving man stood
watching. Meanwhile Barak and Nicholas rolled the bodies of Curdy
and the Dutch sailor into the Thames, watched in horror by the Span-
iard on the neighbouring boat. I cringed when I heard the splashes.
Beside me, Leeman remained unconscious. I feared Barak had hit
him too hard and that the business of the Queen's book would
bring yet another death after all. *Lamentation* indeed, I thought bitterly
as Barak and Nicholas walked back to us, Barak looking grimly
determined and Nicholas slightly shocked. In the water I saw a body
rolling over as the current carried it rapidly downriver – Curdy's, I
thought, from its round shape.

Barak knelt and examined Leeman. 'We have to get him away
somewhere, question him when he comes round.'

'Where?' I asked.

'We cannot take him to Whitehall.' Cecil spoke firmly.

'My lodgings are not far,' Nicholas said. 'And I know my fellow
students are out. A friend's birthday celebration. It'll go on till very
late, they may not be back at all tonight.'

'You left the party to join us?' Barak said. 'We're honoured.'

'Yes, we are,' I said seriously. 'Your help was important. And that
was a grim task.'

Nicholas gave a strange, halting laugh. 'I have never seen anyone
killed before.'

When Cecil spoke his voice was cool but his large eyes held a shocked look: 'Take Leeman to the boy's place.'

'We could carry him between us,' Barak said, 'pretend he's a drunk friend that's passed out, if we're asked.'

Cecil looked down at the body of Lord Parr's man. 'And we will take this poor fellow straight on to Whitehall and rouse Lord Parr. What is your address, boy? We will send some men there later, to pick up Leeman. It may take a few hours, though. Keep him safe.'

'We must be careful,' I said. 'I had a sense we were followed here. I'm sure I heard someone accidentally kick a stone in that alley.'

'I thought so, too,' Barak said. 'Watch out for us. Nick boy, keep your hand near your sword.'

Barak and Nicholas heaved Leeman up, putting his limp arms over their shoulders. Cecil looked on, his eyes wide. Barak gave him a grim smile. 'Don't worry, he'll come round in a while.' Cecil shook his head, as though wondering whether all this could actually have happened, then motioned Lord Parr's second man to help him lift the dead man's body.

✝

WE REACHED Nicholas's lodgings without incident, taking the conspirators' discarded lamp to light our way. I kept a keen ear out for anyone following us through the dark streets, but heard nothing. Leeman was still unconscious when we reached Nicholas's lodgings. Barak and Nicholas laid him on the bed, which needed a change of sheets. I coughed at the dust in the room. 'Don't you have someone in to clean?' I asked.

'We had a woman, but Stephen next door tried it on with her once too often. We haven't found anyone else yet.'

I looked at Nicholas's bookshelf, noting that along with some legal tomes and a New Testament which seemed suspiciously pristine, there were a couple of volumes on gentlemanly conduct and the *Book of the Hunt.*

'I'm hungry,' Nicholas said. 'I have some pork dripping and bread. I think the dripping's still all right.' Under the fading bruises his face was pale. Barak, too, looked tired and grim. We were all exhausted. I studied Leeman, lying prone on the bed. He was young, tall and strongly built, with dark hair, a neatly trimmed beard and a handsome face with a proud Roman nose. He wore a jerkin of ordinary fustian, a far cry from the finery of the Queen's court. I felt gently round the back of his head; there was a large swelling there.

Barak and Nicholas had sat down at the table, and were hungrily devouring the bread and dripping which Nicholas had brought from a cupboard. 'Here,' Barak said to me. 'Have some food. We could be here a while.'

I joined them, but continued to check on Leeman. I had some time, at least, to question him before Lord Parr's men arrived. I sensed that, like Myldmore, this man might be willing to speak if we could convince him that we were working for the reformist side. It was worth a try. I remembered what I had said to Nicholas that time Elias had fled. Never prick a stirring horse more than he needs. I was desperate to find out what Leeman knew but a soft touch might work here. I remembered Cecil's remark that he would talk in the end, and had a momentary vision of fists thudding in a darkened room.

After a while, Leeman groaned and began to stir. Barak took some water from a bucket and squeezed a cloth over his face. Leeman coughed, then sat up, clutching his head. Grimacing with pain, he looked down at his bound arm.

'I did that,' Nicholas said. ''Tis but a flesh wound.'

Leeman's pale face darkened suddenly. 'Where am I?' he asked. He sounded angry but I detected an undertone of fear there, too.

I stood up. 'You are held, Master Leeman, if not by friends then not by the enemies you may think, either.'

Leeman looked round the room, gradually taking in the student messiness. 'This is not a prison,' he stuttered, confusion on his face.

'No,' I replied gently. 'You are not under arrest, not yet. Though others will be coming here for you in a while. I am Matthew Shard lake, a lawyer. It would certainly be better for you to talk to me first. I may be able to do something to help you, if you help us.'

Leeman only glared at me. 'You are the agents of Bertano, emissary of the Antichrist.'

'That name again,' Nicholas said.

I pulled a stool over to the bed and sat face to face with Leeman. 'We have heard that name many times recently, Master Leeman,' I said. 'But I swear to you I do not know who Bertano is. Perhaps you could tell me.' I considered a moment. 'By the Antichrist I take it you mean the Pope.'

'The Beast of Rome,' Leeman confirmed, watching carefully for our reaction.

I smiled. 'Nobody here is a friend of the Pope, I assure you.'

'Then who do you work for?'

I took out the Queen's seal which I had been given on the day of my appointment and held it up for him to see. 'For her majesty. Privately. I am trying to find out what happened to a certain book.'

Leeman frowned, then said, 'Lawyer or courtier, 'tis all the same. You all steal bread from the mouths of the poor.'

'Actually I am an advocate at the Court of Requests, and most of my work is done on behalf of the poor.' His look in response was contemptuous; no doubt he despised the charitable doings of the rich. But I persisted. 'Tonight we were looking for a manuscript which we believe you and your friends were trying to smuggle abroad. I also seek, by the way, the murderers of Armistead Greening.'

'Who is now safe in heaven,' Leeman said, looking at me defiantly.

'There is another manuscript, also missing, by the late Mistress Askew, who was cruelly burned at Smithfield.'

'It is gone.' There was a note of triumph in Leeman's voice now. 'Vandersteyn had it with him.' He paused. His face paled. 'Curdy — your people killed him. Good McKendrick, I saw him run. Did you catch and kill him, too?'

'He escaped. And it was not us who killed Curdy, but some

others we have been forced to work with. They are concerned with finding Anne Askew's writings, but we are not.' I spoke slowly and carefully: I saw I had his attention. 'I am interested only in the other manuscript, which they do not know about. The one stolen from the Queen.' I leaned forward. 'A book which, if published, could do great damage to the Reformist cause. Just when her majesty's troubles appeared to be over, and the tide beginning to swing against Bishop Gardiner, you steal it. Why, Master Leeman?'

He did not reply, but looked at me through narrowed eyes, calculating. A slight blush appeared on his pale cheeks and I wondered if he was remembering his oath to the Queen, which he had broken. I continued quietly. 'I traced you through the guard Gawger, whom you bribed, and the carpenter who gave you the substitute key for the Queen's chest.'

'You have learned much.'

'Not enough. Where is the book now?'

'I do not know. Greening had it. Whoever killed him took it.'

'And who was that?' He did not answer, but I sensed he knew more. He looked at me, then surprised me by saying, in a scoffing tone, 'You think the danger to the Queen is ended, if the book I took is recovered?'

'So it has seemed. I have lately been at court, Master Leeman.'

He answered, weariness and scorn mingling in his voice: 'It is not over. How did you learn the name Bertano, if you do not know who he is?'

'Greening's neighbour, Okedene, heard you arguing loudly in Greening's shop, shortly before Greening was killed. He heard the name Bertano mentioned as an emissary of the Antichrist.'

Leeman nodded slowly. 'Yes. The Queen may be a good woman, and perhaps in her heart she recognizes the Mass as a blasphemous ceremony, but because of Bertano she is doomed anyway. The King is about to receive a secret emissary from Rome. That can only mean he is going to return to papal servitude. Many would fall then, Catherine

Parr chief among them.' And then I felt a chill as I understood. 'Bertano is the *official* emissary of the Pope,' I breathed.

'Whether that is true or not,' Nicholas said angrily, 'you broke your oath to guard and protect her.'

'In the end she is no more than another of the idle rout of nobles and princes, the refuse of mankind.' Leeman spoke so fiercely, I wondered again whether his conscience pricked him.

Nicholas frowned. 'God's death, he *is* an Anabaptist. That mad company of schismatics. He'd have all gentlemen murdered and their property given to the rabble.'

I turned round and gave him a warning look. 'I am in your hands,' Leeman said fiercely. 'And know that I will soon be killed.' He swallowed hard. His angry tones held the defiance of a martyr, but his voice also trembled slightly. Yes, I thought, he is afraid; like all men he fears the flames.

'Indeed,' he continued. 'I am what your boy calls an Anabaptist. I understand baptism may only be allowed once one has come to true knowledge of God. And that just as the Pope is the Antichrist, seducing men's hearts while living in pomp and magnificence, so earthly princes and their elbowhangers are likewise thieves and must be overthrown if Christians are to live as the Bible commands!' His voice rose. 'With all goods held in common, in true charity, recognizing we are all of the same weak clay, and that our only true allegiance is to Our Lord Jesus Christ.' He leaned back, breathing hard, staring at us defiantly.

'That's some lecture,' Barak said sardonically.

'So,' I began quietly, 'you would overthrow the King, who is said to be, by God's decree, Supreme Head of the Church in England?'

'Yes!' he shouted. 'And I know I have just committed treason with those words, and could be hanged and drawn and quartered at Tyburn. As well as burned for heresy for what I said about the Mass.' He took a deep, shuddering breath. 'Best to get it all out now. I can only die once. It is what I believe, and because of that I will be received in Heaven when you kill me.'

'I told you earlier, Leeman, that we are not necessarily your enemies. If you can help guide us to the Queen's book, I may be able to help you.' I looked at him closely before continuing. 'You come from the gentle classes. You must do, to have been appointed to the position of status and trust you held. So what brought you to your present beliefs?'

'You would have me incriminate others?' Leeman took another breath. 'That I will not do.'

'You have no need to. Master Myldmore has already told us all about your group. We have him safe. We know the names – the three who came with you tonight: Curdy who was killed, Vandersteyn who got away in the boat, and McKendrick who fled. And Master Green-ing and the apprentice Elias, both of whom were murdered.'

A look of astonishment crossed his face. 'Elias, too, is dead?'

'Yes, and by the description and methods of the killers, by the same hands that murdered Greening.'

'But we thought – ' He checked himself and whispered, 'Then Elias is in heaven, by God's mercy.'

I pressed on. 'We also know, through Myldmore, how Anne Askew's *Examinations* came into the hands of your group. And my enquiries at court led me to you as the man who stole the Queen's book.'

Leeman slumped back on the bed. 'Myldmore,' he said despair-ingly. 'We knew he could not be trusted. That man had been seduced by Mammon.'

'And had residual doubts about the Royal Supremacy.'

Leeman said, 'Yes. We could not let him into our secrets. Master Greening was firm on that.' He shook his head. 'Greening brought me to the truth, he and the others. God rest him.'

I said, 'We would like to find his killers. Please help us.'

Leeman lay quietly, thinking. I burned to know all, but I was sure that, as with Myldmore, gentle persuasion was the best tactic, though Leeman seemed a much tougher and more intelligent man. Finally he spoke again, in more subdued tones. 'You know so much, it will do no harm to tell you the rest. As for me, yes, I was born and raised a gentleman. In Tetbury, in the Cotswolds. It is sheep country, and my father owned many flocks. He had grown fat on the cloth trade, and by his connections he was able to get me a position at court as one of the Queen's guard.' He smiled sadly. 'My father, landowner though he is, at least embraced the new faith, as did I as I grew up. Though the King himself has moved steadily back to the old ways. And would now go further.'

'Back to Rome, you think?' Barak fingered his beard thoughtfully.

'Yes. My father warned me that when I came to London I would see things I would not like, but in order to advance myself I must hold my tongue and wait for better times. Concentrate on advancement, always advancement.' He clenched a hand into a fist. 'Towards riches and power, not towards God. That is all that fills the hollow hearts at court. My father could not see that,' he added sadly. 'He saw only part of what Christ demands of us. As through a glass, darkly.' He turned to me. 'You have seen Whitehall, Master Shardlake?'

'I have.'

'It is magnificent, is it not? And still a-building. Getting grander by the day.'

'Some say the King wishes it to be the greatest palace in Europe.'

Leeman gave a hollow laugh. 'It is designed to reduce those who come to a state of awe. Every stone speaks of the King's power and wealth, every stone cries out: "Look, and fear and wonder." While within,' he added bitterly, 'the dirty game is played called kingly craft, wherein no man is safe.'

'I agree with you,' I said. 'Certainly about kingly craft.'

Leeman looked at me hard, surprised by my reaction – I think he had intended to provoke me into defending the King and his court. He went on: 'I hate it. The great palace, every stone built with the sweat of poor men, the stench and poverty and misery just beyond its walls. My vicar in Tetbury was a man who had come to see the emptiness of the Mass, and he put me in touch with friends in London, men of faith.' Leeman paused, his eyes seeming to look inward for a

moment. 'It is as well that he did, for royal service offers many temptations – debauchery of the flesh, vanity in dress and manner, fine
clothes and jewels – oh, they are tempting, as the Queen herself says in
her book.'

'You have read it?'

'Yes, when it was in Master Greening's possession.'

The thought of him reading the stolen manuscript made me suddenly angry, but I forced myself to keep my expression open and
amiable as he continued. 'Through friends outside I progressed further
towards God, and the right understanding of our wicked society.' He
looked me in the eye again. 'One discussion group led me to others as
my faith deepened, and last year I was introduced to Master Greening.'

I could see how it had happened: a sensitive young man, with a
conscience and radical inclinations, tempted by the magnificence of
the court but aware of the evil within. His beliefs had deepened as he
moved into more radical circles, eventually coming into Greening's
orbit. I ventured, 'So, you were accepted into Greening's little group,
unlike Master Myldmore. Who also had access to secrets,' I added
meaningfully.

Leeman laughed. 'I guessed you had made that connection.
Master Vandersteyn had connections, too; not here, but in the courts
of France and Flanders, with men who would tell him things. It was
his idea to build a similar group here, of true believers who were in a
position to find out secrets that might harm both papists and princes,
help stir the population to rebel against both.'

'I see.' So Vandersteyn, now heading out into the North Sea, had
been the key.

'He met Master Greening on a business trip to London two years
ago, and so our little group was born. McKendrick had already come
to see the truth. Then the papists came sniffing at his heels and he had
to flee Scotland. He had held a junior position at the Scotch court of
the child Mary and knew all the schemings and bitings among the
rival lords there.'

'And Master Curdy? He does not seem to have been a man of connections.'

'No. But he was a man of faith, with an instinct for truly sniffing out who might be trusted and who might not.'

'So,' Barak said flatly. 'A little cell of Anabaptist spies, rooting for secrets to disclose.'

Leeman looked at him defiantly. 'And we found them. Even Myldmore, whom we had rejected because he had not reached true faith, came back to us when Anne Askew entrusted him with her writings. We knew that if her story of illegal torture by two council-lors of state were published abroad and smuggled back into England it would rouse the populace. English printers are too closely watched for it to be done safely here. And it will be published,' he said defiantly. 'The government has agents in Flanders, but Master Vander-steyn's people are adept at avoiding them.'

'I see.' I took a long breath. 'Well, I told you, I do not care about Anne Askew's book. Others did, and it was necessary for me to work with them for a while.'

'Richard Rich?' Leeman asked. 'There is a villain.'

I inclined my head. 'As for you, you overheard the Queen and Archbishop Cranmer disputing loudly one night when you were on duty, and learned of the existence of the *Lamentation*.'

He groaned, wincing at a spasm of pain. 'By my faith, sir, you are a clever man.'

I took another deep breath. 'And I guess you told your group about the Queen's book, and it was decided you would steal the *Lam-entation*, even though publication could seal the Queen's fate. Because you believed her fate was already sealed and publication would at least show that she held radical beliefs before she was toppled. And you knew her fate was sealed because of Bertano?'

'Yes. I argued within the group that it was better to expose Bertano publicly, that knowledge of his coming would truly rouse the popu-lace. But others argued against, saying we would not be believed and it was too late to prevent his coming.'

'Who argued that position?'

'Master Curdy and Captain McKendrick both.'

'And how did you find out about Bertano?'

'I told you, Vandersteyn has informants on the Continent. In-cluding a junior official at the French court. Suffice to say that his responsibilities involved accommodation for foreign visitors, which gave him the opportunity, like me, to overhear conversations. Such as the arrival in France of Gurone Bertano, a papal ambassador who once lived in England and was being sent to seek an agreement between the Pope and King Henry. At the King's invitation.'

Barak shook his head firmly. 'The King would never surrender his authority back to Rome.'

'Yes,' Leeman agreed. 'Master Vandersteyn was mightily shocked when his emissary from Flanders brought him the news.' He looked at me, his dark eyes hard. 'But his people can always be trusted. Bertano is now at the French court, and he will arrive here within a few days. It has been done secretly, only a few men at court know, and nobody with any sympathy for reform. Certainly not the Queen.'

I glanced at Barak, who sat stroking his beard, frowning hard. It was an outlandish, extraordinary story, yet it fitted what Lord Parr had told me – that despite their failure to destroy the Queen and those around her, the conservative faction were not downcast, were rather comporting themselves as though they had something else up their sleeves. If this was their trump card, the stakes could not be higher.

'When did the news about Bertano come?' I asked.

'Just after I told our group about overhearing the Queen's argu-ment with Cranmer over the *Lamentation*. And we all agreed: if the King decides to go back to Rome, it surely follows that the Queen must be replaced. The Pope would insist on it. But if the *Lamentation* were published, the populace would see the King had executed a good and true woman.'

I got up and walked to the window. I was horrified. If what Leeman said about Bertano was true, the Queen was in deadly danger from another source, too, and was a dispensable pawn in a far bigger game. It was hard to take in. But at least it seemed Greening's group had made a majority decision not to publish the *Lamentation* before the Queen fell, but only to keep it in Greening's shop. Safe, they supposed.

Barak spoke bluntly to Leeman. 'Making public that the King was about to receive a secret emissary from the Pope would surely have roused popular anger, perhaps prevented the visit taking place at all.'

'Ay,' Nicholas nodded agreement. 'The outrage among reformers would be tremendous.'

Leeman replied, 'That is what I said when we discussed Bertano in the group. We argued over it for days.'

I came back to him and sat down again. 'But Curdy and McKendrick opposed it? I ask, Master Leeman, because I think one of your group might have been a spy in the pay of a third party, I know not who. I am fairly certain, by the way, that we were followed to the docks tonight, and that events there were watched.'

He nodded sadly. 'That is what we also came to think, after Master Greening was murdered and the *Lamentation* disappeared. That is why we all fled. Vandersteyn had Anne Askew's writings, ready to take abroad, so at least the killers would not get them. Afterwards, we realized there must have been a spy, for nobody else knew what we were doing.' He shook his head. 'But we thought it was Elias, as he was the only one that refused to leave the country.'

'He had not been told about the *Lamentation*, he was too young for such a secret but he could have . . .'

'He could have overheard. That is what we thought, afterwards. And he needed money, with his family to support.' Leeman shook his head. 'Poor Elias.'

'If there was a spy, it wasn't him.' I thought quickly; that left only Curdy, who was dead, Vandersteyn, who was gone, and McKendrick. And I could not see it being Vandersteyn; he had too long a history as a radical and had been at the very centre of the conspiracy. That left Curdy and McKendrick, who had lived in the same house and had both been against exposing Bertano before his arrival. I asked, 'What was Curdy's and McKendrick's argument against making Bertano's visit known immediately?'

'Curdy said we had no clear evidence, and if we set the story abroad it would simply be denied, and the negotiations would take place anyway. McKendrick agreed, he said stronger evidence was needed, perhaps more detail of where the negotiations were to take place, and with whom. He said he knew from experience in Scotland how rumours can fly, only to be quickly quelled if there is no evidence. He suggested Vandersteyn try to get more information from the Continent, and then break the news in detail, when Bertano was actually here. We knew only that he was coming around the start of August. In the end we agreed to wait, and Vandersteyn sent letters to his associates abroad, in code, to try to get more information.'

'Was there any reply?'

'No.' He sighed. 'Vandersteyn's agents could discover no more. And then came Master Greening's murder; we fled, hid in secret in the houses of good friends, keeping separate, moving from place to place while Master Vandersteyn arranged for a ship to come over and take us to Flanders. We knew we were being hunted. One of the households which sheltered Master McKendrick was attacked by ruffians just after he left.' He looked at me. 'None of that was arranged by you or your confederates?'

'No.'

'How did you know we would be at the docks tonight?'

'It was not difficult to work out that you would try to get yourselves, and perhaps both books, abroad. Spies were placed at the docks. You were too confident, going through the customs house. You should have smuggled yourselves on board the ship.'

Leeman bit his lip.

'Let's get this clear,' Barak said. 'Your little group were Anabaptists, who want to overthrow not just the whole of established religion, but society itself——'

'As we one day will! It is clear in the Bible—'

Barak cut in. 'A group which was put together by the Dutchman Vandersteyn, who is part of a similar circle on the Continent, and whose particular goal was to obtain information that could incite the people to rebellion.'

'Ay. The people are deceived by the lies of popes and princes. But believers such as ourselves are the leaven in the yeast.' Leeman spoke as though chanting a prayer.

'But,' I said, angry now, 'because you did not realize there was a spy in your group, someone — almost certainly working for a leading figure on the conservative side — has the Queen's book in their posses-sion, ready to give to the King at any moment, with the intention of making him angry with the Queen again just as this papal emissary arrives!' Leeman lowered his head. I went on, 'You needed money for bribes and materials in order to steal and publish the Queen's book. Substantial sums. Where did you get them?'

'Master Curdy has money. From his business.' A spark appeared in Leeman's eyes again. 'You see, Master Shardlake, we practise what we preach, the holding of all goods in common.'

I sighed, and turned to Barak and Nicholas. 'Both of you, a word in private. Nicholas, can you bring the candle?' I turned to Leeman. 'Do not even think of running, we will be near. Lie here and think on what you have brought about with your foolishness.'

We went out, leaving him in darkness.

Chapter Thirty-five

WE WALKED DOWNSTAIRS TO the dusty little entrance hall. I set the candle in its holder on the wall. Noises from the street came to us faintly. I had lost track of time – it must be far past midnight. I wondered when Lord Parr's people would arrive.

'Well,' I asked Barak, 'what do you think? The Bertano story first.'

Barak stroked his beard. '*If* it's true, and the news got out, then Leeman is right, there would be unrest in the streets. I don't mean a revolution, but trouble certainly. You have to hand it to them, their tactic of placing spies in sensitive places paid off. But – ' he looked intently between us – 'if you're going to have a tightly controlled group, with secret knowledge, you have to be sure everyone in it can be completely trusted. But with some of the wilder radicals – ' he shrugged – 'duping them is easy. Provided the person concerned continually parrots the right phrases, I imagine they're all too ready to believe they're genuine.'

'Yes,' I agreed. 'But you said, *if* it's true about Bertano.'

Barak grunted. 'Remember I've been out of politics for six years. But don't forget that after Anne Boleyn was killed, there was no longer any impediment to the King's going back to Rome. But he didn't.' He gave a cynical laugh. 'He enjoys his power as Head of the Church too much, to say nothing of the money he got from the monasteries. But there's something else.' He furrowed his brows, making shadows on his face in the dim candlelight. 'I know Lord Cromwell thought the key to understanding the King was to remember that he truly believes God has appointed him to be Head of the Church in England. That is why every time he changes his mind on the matter of doctrine, the country has to follow – or else.' He shook his head firmly. 'He wouldn't hand all that power back to the Pope easily – not when he believes God himself has chosen him to exercise it.'

'And when Henry dies?' Nicholas asked quietly.

I thought of the shambling wreck I had seen in Whitehall Palace, the groaning figure winched upstairs. 'The Supreme Headship must pass to his son.'

Barak agreed. 'Nothing would ever shake Henry on his right – his duty, as he would see it – to bequeath the Supreme Headship to Prince Edward.'

Nicholas asked, 'But how can a little boy, below the age of judgement, decide the correct path in religion?'

I answered, 'They'll have a Regent, or a Regency Council, until Edward comes of age. Probably the King will decide in his Will who will rule.' And, I thought, it will not be the Parrs, if the Queen has fallen. 'The council will exercise judgement on matters of religion on Edward's behalf, I suppose, till he reaches his eighteenth year. It's theological nonsense, of course, but that's what they'll do. No, Barak is right, if this Bertano is truly coming over, he won't return with a sworn allegiance from Henry in his pocket.' I considered. 'But I have heard all sorts of things are happening in Europe. It is said the Pope is attempting a dialogue with some of the Protestants through his new Council of Trent. I wonder if Henry thinks some sort of compromise is on the cards.'

'What sort of compromise?' Barak asked impatiently. 'Either the headship of the Church lies with the King or with the Pope. There's no halfway house in between. If there was, someone would have proposed it years ago.'

Nicholas shook his head. 'But perhaps the King thinks there *may* be some way to compromise, short of accepting papal allegiance. Perhaps Bertano has been sent to explore that? After all, the King has been keen this year to try and make peace everywhere . . .'

Yes, I thought, because he knows he is dying. I nodded. 'You could be right, Nicholas. A good point.'

'It'll never happen,' Barak said scoffingly.

'But who was the spy in their group?' I asked. 'And who was he reporting to?'

'It certainly wasn't Leeman,' Barak said. 'He's a true believer if ever there was one. Nor Myldmore; he knew nothing of Bertano or the Queen's book. Greening and Elias were murdered. Vandersteyn – I doubt it, he's crossed the Channel in triumph with Anne Askew's manuscript. That leaves Curdy, who's beyond questioning, and the Scotchman McKendrick, who's still out there somewhere.'

'And McKendrick was Curdy's lodger.' Nicholas knitted his brows. 'It has to be one of them, or perhaps both.'

'If it's McKendrick,' Barak said, 'he'll be running to his master at court by now. Whoever that is.'

'Someone who's working with the conservative faction,' I said. 'But who? Secretary Paget runs the official spy network. But each of the courtiers has their own network: the Duke of Norfolk, Rich and Wriothesley who have hitched themselves to Gardiner's wagon.'

Nicholas asked, 'You think Rich could have been involved with the theft of the *Lamentation*?'

I sighed. 'Rich was after Anne Askew's book, and he didn't seem to know anything about the *Lamentation*. But you can never trust that snake.'

Barak said, 'Whoever is holding it may indeed be ready to reveal it to the King when Bertano comes. For maximum impact. That could explain why it hasn't already been made public.'

I shook my head. 'I am sure these men would have done it already, to bend the King's mind further against the reformers and towards making an arrangement with Bertano when he arrives. Use it to turn the wind against the reformers again as soon as possible.'

'Then where is it?' Barak asked angrily. 'Who has it?'

'God's death, I don't know!' I passed a hand over my brow.

'Could McKendrick have it?' Nicholas said thoughtfully. 'If he was the spy, and was given the book by the thieves, then maybe – if he's been on the run with the others – he hasn't had time to hand it over to whoever he's working for?'

'But it's been nearly a month,' Barak answered.

I said, 'It's unlikely. But anything is possible. I'll have to discuss it all with Lord Parr.'

'Or . . .' Nicholas said.

'What?'

'What if the spy was playing both ends? What if McKendrick — assuming it is him — was indeed working to some master at court, but kept his own beliefs, and made sure the *Lamentation* did not fall into the wrong hands? Perhaps he had it stolen, but kept it himself?'

'It's far-fetched, but it's possible. Thank you, Nicholas.' The boy looked pleased.

'Now, Jack, it is late. Nicholas and I will wait here, but you must get back to Tamasin. Where did you tell her you were going tonight?'

'Only that I was meeting old friends for a drink.'

'But the taverns are long closed. She will be worried. And on your way back,' I added, 'remember those two killers are still out there, and that we were watched tonight. Be careful. Nicholas, will you stay here with me to guard Leeman until Lord Parr's people return?'

'You can trust me.' He shook his head. 'Leeman's nothing but a rogue and a villain.'

I sighed. 'He was doing what he believed was right.'

'And that justifies all he has done?' Nicholas answered hotly. 'The betrayal, the bribery, this — chaos? The threat brought to the Queen by stealing her book?'

Barak turned to him, his tone indulgent. 'He gets soft, Nick, it's his way.' He looked up to the top of the stairs. 'But better have God's true representative bound and gagged in case he starts shouting if the students come back. I'll help you.'

Nicholas said with a sort of appalled admiration, 'That Dutchman, Vandersteyn. He already has informers working on the Continent who found the information about Bertano. Meanwhile he is over here, recruiting fanatics who might be able to spy on those in high places in London.'

Barak said, 'He knew the atmosphere here was seething with plots and religious discontent. Decided to come over and further his revolution in England, no doubt.'

'And found Leeman, then Myldmore. Men with access to two sets of writings that could cause great stir.' He shook his head. 'He must truly think God is working through him.'

Barak snorted. 'He got lucky. Twice. But not *really* lucky: it sounds as if what Anne Askew wrote would be damaging only to Wriothesley and Rich, and they're not the top players. And releasing the *Lamentation* would do the radical cause more harm than good. But some in his group were too bone-headed to see that. If they'd found evidence that Gardiner had been in bed with a choirboy, say, that would've been real luck.'

I said, 'Vandersteyn has probably been running schemes like this on the Continent for years. He was skilful in weeding out those among the radicals who might be of use to him.'

'Not skilful enough to notice he had a spy in his midst,' Barak said.

I nodded agreement. 'No.'

✝

LEEMAN WAS SITTING ON the side of the bed. He blinked in the light. 'Are they here for me yet?' he asked in a quiet voice, with a slight tremor. Being left alone in the darkness had given his fear time to grow.

'No,' I answered.

'What will they do with me?'

'You will be taken somewhere safe for now. I will tell them you have cooperated fully.'

He looked at me keenly. 'Do you know, lawyer, I think perhaps you have it in you to see the light.'

'Do you?' I replied heavily.

'Perhaps. Like me, you were brought up on lies and I think you see that. Read the New Testament, read Revelation. These are the last days before Christ's return. It is foreordained.'

'The Book of Revelation, is it? You and your people have found the key to that text?' Anger spilled out of me. 'You should know, Leeman, I once uncovered a killer who slaughtered several innocent people, who believed himself inspired by Revelation! I wish you could see the trail of blood and torture he left.'

Leeman did not answer. After a moment he asked, 'Will you tell the Queen's officials about Bertano?'

'Yes.'

'Then at least they will be warned.'

I looked at him. 'They will undoubtedly want to question you further.'

He swallowed. 'They will torture me, then kill me. I suppose I must prepare myself.'

'You broke an oath to the Queen. Nonetheless, I shall plead with her for your sorry life. I am not even sure why.'

'We'll keep you with Nick to guard you for now, matey,' Barak added in a matter-of-fact way. 'I'm going to bind your hands together, so stretch them out. No trouble, or we'll do it by force.'

Leeman put out his arms. Barak bound them tight with strips torn from Leeman's own shirt. 'Have to gag you as well, matey, though I know you love to gabble on. Nicholas's fellow lodgers may be back sometime.'

'Can I go to the jakes first?' Leeman's face reddened with embarrassment. 'My guts trouble me.'

Barak looked at me. 'Might as well,' I said. Barak raised his eyebrows. I snapped impatiently, 'We don't want a mess in here. Where's your jakes, Nicholas?'

'Out the back, in the yard. But watch it's not a trick. No noise, or I'll knock you out again.'

'We'll all go, bring him back, then Jack will go home, while you and I – ' I took a deep breath as I looked at Nicholas – 'will wait with him for Lord Parr's people.'

✝

WE WENT BACK DOWNSTAIRS, Barak and Nicholas holding
Leeman between them. He was almost as tall as Nicholas and broader,
the build of a royal guard. But he gave no trouble. As we descended,
a church clock somewhere struck one. 'No sign of your friends,' I said
to Nicholas, relieved.

'They probably won't be back at all now; they'll have fallen drunk
in a corner.'

'I remember those student birthday celebrations. A bit rowdy for
me.'

'There's a surprise,' Barak said warmly.

We opened a creaking door to the little backyard, where a ramshackle wooden shed stood in a corner of an untended garden, against
a stone wall separating the students' garden from the one next door. By
the smell, the cesspit beneath badly needed emptying. Nicholas opened
the wooden door, and we all stepped back at the stink from within.
Barak said to Leeman, 'Get in, then.'

He hesitated on the threshold, so powerful was the stench.

That hesitation killed him. There was a thunderous noise from the
neighbouring garden, and a brief flash of light. In the second before
Leeman crashed to the ground I saw, by the light of the lamp, that he
had lost half his head. We stood there, shocked for a few seconds, then
Nicholas threw me to the ground, just as there was a second flash and
a bang, and the smell of smoke. Glancing aside I saw that Barak had
also thrown himself down. He kicked over the lamp he had been
holding and it went out, leaving us in almost total darkness. I smelled
gunpowder in the air.

'Quick!' Barak whispered. 'Back inside. Before he has time to
reload. Nick, you know the way in the dark!'

Nicholas scrambled to his feet and, with his long body bent over,
made for the back of the building, which was visible only as a slightly
deeper darkness. Barak followed, and then I, biting my lip as a muscle
in my back went. There was another bang, another flash, and something hit the wall ahead of us. Then I heard the door creak open, and
Nicholas pushed me unceremoniously inside. Barak followed, kicking

the door shut behind him. Outside dogs had begun to bark and someone in a neighbouring house, woken by the noise, shouted, 'Hey! What's going on?'

Nicholas led us to the front of the house and the shelter of the stairs. We stood in the darkness, breathing hard. I said, 'What in hell – ?'

'A gun,' he answered. 'An arquebus. I've seen them used in hunting. They're deadly, but take an age to reload. Leeman – ?'

'Dead,' Barak answered flatly. 'It took his head off. So we were followed here, by someone who brought an arquebus. Clever idea to post the assassin in next door's garden; we were bound to come out to the jakes sooner or later. Great way of killing a person from a distance. There may be more of them out the front.' He walked cautiously to the front door and peered through the keyhole. 'Can't see anyone. I'd guess it was Leeman they were after. To stop him talking to us.'

'At least they failed there,' Nicholas said defiantly.

'Come on, back upstairs. Thank God we kept the window of your room shuttered.'

We returned to Nicholas's room. 'Sir,' he said urgently, 'it would be dangerous for Jack to go out now. There may be more of them waiting in the streets.'

Barak shook his head. 'I should think they've run, now we're safe indoors. But you're right. We should all wait here till Lord Parr's men come from Whitehall.'

'But why didn't they follow us in when we first arrived?' Nicholas asked me.

'Perhaps because they thought the house might be full of students, and they'd have a fight on their hands.'

'Tamasin will be in a state,' Barak said, 'but it can't be helped – ' He broke off, staring at my neck. I put my hand to it. My fingers came away covered in sticky red-and-grey slime. At first I thought I had been hit, then I realized what it was: I was looking at Leeman's brains.

Chapter Thirty-six

I WALKED WITH LORD PARR through the Great Garden of Whitehall Palace. It was the next morning, the sun high in a cloudless sky. The brightness of the white gravel on the paths hurt my tired eyes, and I turned to look over the broad squares of lawn, the flowerbeds at their centre, each ablaze with its own variety of summer bloom. Gardeners in smocks laboured endlessly, weeding and trimming. Heraldic beasts stood on poles at the corners of each path, and the water in the great fountain at the centre of the garden made a relaxing plashing sound. Men, and a few women, strolled along the paths in their finery. The Great Garden was where courtiers and senior servants came to walk, but it was also a sort of enormous outdoor waiting room for would-be courtiers who were not, or not yet, allowed access to the King's Privy Gallery. Here they strolled, and waited, and hoped it did not rain. To the south, work continued on the new quarters for the Lady Mary, the constant banging and hammering a strange counterpoint to the sound of the fountain. On the north side the garden was bounded by the King's Privy Gallery and private lodgings; I glanced up at them nervously.

'He could be watching us,' I said uneasily.

Lord Parr smiled reassuringly. 'I doubt the King even knows of your presence on the Queen's Learned Council, nor your hunt for this elusive jewel. And I have made sure that within the Queen's Court it is known only as a minor matter.' He, too, glanced towards the three-storey Privy Gallery, the black-and-white chequerwork facade easily a hundred yards long. It ended at the Holbein Gate, which was twice as high as the gallery itself and spanned the public road, connecting the King's quarters with the recreational wing of the palace on the western side. In earlier years the King would have crossed through the gate to play tennis, or joust, but that was long over now. 'Besides,' Lord Parr added, 'I heard his majesty was working in his study in the Holbein Gate this morning. He likes looking down on his subjects passing along the street as he works.'

'I did not know he did that.' That, too, gave me an uneasy feeling.

'As for the real issues, while we may be seen here, we have the advantage that we cannot be heard.'

He stopped at a corner under a pillar painted in stripes of Tudor green and white. A golden lion on top held an English flag, fluttering in the river breeze that also played with Lord Parr's white beard. He leaned heavily on his stick. In the morning light his thin face was pale, dark bags visible under the eyes. He had been wakened by Cecil, who had arrived at the palace near midnight. Since my own arrival with Leeman's body, at three o'clock, he had been busy. After I had told him all that had happened he arranged a room for me in the lodgings again to snatch a few hours' sleep, though hard thoughts kept me awake. Four more men killed last night, including one of Lord Parr's own servants, and a new threat to the Queen divulged, if the story about Bertano were true. At nine in the morning Lord Parr had sent for me and suggested a walk in the Great Garden.

He closed his eyes, breathing in the scent of the herbs planted alongside the path. 'I could lie down and fall asleep here right now,' he said quietly. 'As could you, from your looks.'

I winced at a spasm in my back. I had pulled a muscle when Nicholas pushed me to the ground last night, but his act had saved my life. Lord Parr continued, 'It is a great pity Leeman was killed.' He raised a hand. 'No, sir, I do not blame you. But I would have liked to question the villain myself.' He clutched the silver handle of his stick hard. 'An Anabaptist, those pestilent scum.'

'They were a small group. In Europe too, I understand, there are but few left.'

'They are like rats, a few in the sewers of the common streets may breed and at a time of hardship or discontent become thousands. They can bring fire and death to us all.' He waved his free hand in a gesture of anger. 'They should be extirpated.'

'Have you told her majesty what Leeman said?' I asked.

'Yes. I wakened the Queen early to tell her the latest news. I thought it best. She wept and trembled, she is much afraid. She is worried that the book remains unfound, and now even more about Bertano. But – ' he paused to look me in the eye – 'she is brave, and well-practised in assuming a composed and regal manner, whatever she feels inside.'

He fell silent as a couple of black-robed officials wearing the King's badge passed. They bowed to us. I had sent for my robe after arriving at Whitehall; Timothy had brought it round and I wore it now. Such things mattered greatly here. The two walked on, stopping briefly to admire a peacock with its huge multicoloured tail as it crossed the lawn. 'I have one servant less,' Lord Parr continued soberly. 'Poor Dunmore, who died last night, was a good and useful man.'

'I never even learned his name.'

'Who *is* it?' Lord Parr banged the white gravel with his stick. 'Who masterminded the theft of her book, employed those two men – of whom we can find no trace – to kill everyone in that Anabaptist group? I do not believe the theory that whoever took the book from Greening would intend to wait until Bertano was about to arrive before revealing it. Not if they know the King. They would show it to him immediately, let his anger against the Queen and the reformers burst out at once, make him more receptive to whatever proposals this wretched emissary of the Pope brings.'

'Would it be so bad as that?'

He spoke quietly. 'The King still loves the Queen, of that I am sure. But that would only make him even angrier at her disloyalty. And hurt. And when he feels hurt – ' Lord Parr shook his head. 'The existence of the book itself is a lesser matter; Cranmer says it is not heretical, though it sails close to the wind.'

I did not reply. I had never heard Lord Parr talk so openly of the

King before. 'His majesty has always been suggestible, vain. He listens to the endless whispers in his ear, especially when they concern the loyalty of someone important to him. And once he has made his mind up he has been betrayed, then – '

'How is his health?' I asked.

'A little worse each week.' He fell silent for a moment, perhaps reflecting that he had said more than was wise, then burst out angrily, 'Why keep it for near a month, Shardlake? I cannot work it out, and nor can Cecil.'

'I cannot either, my Lord. You know far more of the court than I.'

'We have to find that Scotchman, God rot him—'

I placed a hand on the arm of his silk robe to quiet him. He frowned at my presumption, but I had seen what his aged eyes had not: two slim figures with long beards approaching us. Edward Seymour, Lord Hertford, Prince Edward's uncle and a leading figure among the reformers on the Privy Council; and his younger brother, Sir Thomas, who had been the Queen's suitor before her marriage to the King. So, I thought, Lord Hertford is back in England.

The brothers halted before us. They had been arguing with quiet intensity as they approached, but now Sir Thomas's large brown eyes fastened on mine. We had crossed swords in the past.

I had seen them together years before, and reflected anew how alike they were, yet how different. Above his light brown beard Lord Hertford's oval face was pale, and not handsome, with slightly knitted brows that gave him an air of half-suppressed impatient anger. He exuded power, but not authority, or not enough. As a politician he was formidable, but they said he was henpecked and embarrassed by his wife. He wore a long brown robe with a fur collar, and a splendid gold chain round his neck befitting his status as a senior Privy Councillor. Sir Thomas Seymour was more sturdily built, his face another oval, but with regular features and compelling brown eyes above that long coppery beard. While Lord Hertford wore a plain robe, Sir

413

Thomas sported a green doublet of finest silk, slashed at the shoulders and sleeves to show a rich orange lining. He too wore a gold chain, though a smaller one.

The two men removed their jewelled caps and bowed, the links of their chains clinking. We bowed in turn.

'Master Shardlake,' Sir Thomas said, a mocking note in his rich deep voice. 'I hear you are sworn to her majesty's Learned Council now.'

'I am, sir.'

Lord Hertford cut across him, addressing Lord Parr. 'I trust the Queen is in good health, my Lord.'

'Indeed. She is viewing the Lady Elizabeth's new portrait this morning, before it is shown to the King. Master Scrots has painted a good likeness.'

'Excellent. Lady Elizabeth should have a portrait, it is fitting for her high estate.' He inclined his head meaningfully to where Mary's new quarters were being built. 'I am sure the portrait will be a pleasure to his majesty.'

'Indeed. He loves both his daughters, of course, but now Eliza-beth is growing, she needs more – exposure.'

I recognized the coded exchange for what it was. Lord Parr and Lord Hertford were both on the reforming side, and Elizabeth, her father's least favourite child, was being brought up a reformer, unlike the traditionalist Mary, who had been raised a Catholic before the break with Rome.

Sir Thomas looked bored. He turned to me again. 'I see, Shard-lake, you are on the list of those attending on Admiral d'Annebault.'

'Indeed, Sir Thomas.'

'I have a large role on the committee organizing the ceremonies,' he said self-importantly. 'There is much to be done. The admiral is bringing a thousand men with him.' He smiled. 'It will be a mag-nificent chivalric celebration of reconciliation after honest combat between soldiers.'

I did not reply. I thought again of my soldier friends who had gone down with the *Mary Rose* and all the others killed in that failed, unnecessary war.

Seymour raised his eyebrows. 'Do you not agree? Well — ' he laughed and squared his broad shoulders — 'some of us are built and fitted for war, while others are not.' He glanced ostentatiously at my back.

It was an appalling insult. But Sir Thomas was in a position to make it, and I did not reply. His brother, though, looked at Sir Thomas fiercely as he now turned to Lord Parr and said mockingly, 'Beware of Master Shardlake, my Lord, he is too clever for his own good. He will be after your job.'

'I hardly think so, Sir Thomas.' Lord Parr glared at him.

Hertford snapped, 'You are ever ready with your nips and quips, Thomas. You will nip yourself into trouble one day.'

Sir Thomas's face darkened. Lord Parr gave him a sardonic smile, then turned to his brother.'

'Is there much foreign business now on the Privy Council, my Lord? My nephew William says the French and Spanish treaties are settled.'

Hertford nodded seriously. 'Indeed, though it has been a mighty labour these last months.' He looked across at the Holbein Gate. 'Well, I am due to attend the King in his study. I must not be late.' He gave me an awkward nod, bowed to us both, and walked on with his brother. Lord Parr watched them go.

'Thomas Seymour is a fool and a bully,' he said. 'But Lord Hertford is our ally. His return, and Lord Lisle's, have shifted the balance of the council towards the reformers. And Cranmer is seen more these days.'

'And Sir Thomas?' I added. 'What role does he play?'

He gave me a considering look. 'I know from my niece that you and he worked together once, and dislike each other. I am not surprised, Thomas Seymour is as full of bluster and empty display as that peacock over there. He did not distinguish himself in the positions he held in the war. Sitting on a committee to organize this ceremonial will test the limits of his ability.' He gave a bitter laugh. 'When he returned in the spring he made great play of how he'd escaped some pirates in the Channel. Made himself a laughing stock by telling the story over endlessly.' He smiled sardonically. 'He wants the power his older brother has on the Privy Council. He feels that, as he is also Jane Seymour's brother and Prince Edward's uncle, he should have equal authority. But he lacks judgement and intelligence, with him all is empty show and bluster. The King knows it. He only ever chooses men of ability for the council. Thomas is a drag on his brother.'

'What is Sir Thomas's position on reform?'

Lord Parr shrugged. 'I do not think he has any religion. Some even say he is an atheist. It is extraordinary that the Queen loved him once, they are such opposites in nature.'

'Extraordinary indeed.'

He shook his head. 'I would never have thought Kate was one to be taken in by such a creature; but we have seen how – emotional – she can be. It is the way of women,' he concluded with a sigh.

I spoke suddenly. 'I suppose there is no motive for anyone on the reformist side of the council to steal the *Lamentation*?'

He shook his head. 'None. The reformist group at court, like every faction, is an alliance of family interests – between the Parrs, the Seymours and the Dudleys, whose foremost figure is John Dudley, Lord Lisle. When, in course of time – ' he stressed those words care-fully – 'his majesty is gathered to God, the various family interests may find themselves in conflict. But for the present we are united by our common faith. If Henry does agree to take England back under the authority of the Pope, we shall all be in danger, and must run and fetch our rosaries or face a grim death.' He sighed with unexpected emotion. 'When I think of that, I thank God I am a sick old man.'

We stood in silence for a moment. Then I said thoughtfully, 'But if Sir Thomas is one of those who has no religion, and seeks only power, he might see an advantage in taking the *Lamentation* to the King – '

Lord Parr looked at me, frowning. 'Why? From ambition?'

'That, and perhaps because he courted the Queen before her marriage, and was rejected. Proud men harbour thoughts of revenge. And finding the *Lamentation* could give him the status in the King's eyes that he longs for.'

Lord Parr considered for a moment. 'Earlier in the summer, though few know of it, there were attempts to unite the reformist and traditionalist factions through a marriage between the Duke of Norfolk's daughter and Thomas Seymour. The negotiations came to nothing, partly because the Duke's daughter did not want him.'

'That surely proves he will bend any way to gain power.'

Lord Parr shook his head decisively. 'No. Thomas Seymour does not have the intelligence, nor the resources, to send spies into the radical groups. I think your dislike of him, Master Shardlake, justified though it may be, is colouring your judgement.'

'Possibly,' I admitted reluctantly. 'But who in court *would* have motive and money to do that?'

'Paget, of course, as Master Secretary. But if he had a spy in the Anabaptist camp, whether Curdy or McKendrick or both of them, that would have been in an official capacity, and as soon as they had taken Askew's book, or the Queen's, he would have had to arrest everyone in the group and report to the King. And I am sure Paget has no loyalty to either faction. He survives, the Master of Practices, by taking orders only from the King. But the other courtiers – Gardiner and his hirelings Wriothesley and Rich – yes, if they got wind of an Anabaptist group, they have the resources to infiltrate it. It is just the sort of business Rich would be good at. But how would they get wind of it? It seems Rich got lucky only in finding that the gaoler Myldmore had Askew's book. Unless Rich was lying,' he added slowly, turning to me.

'I still think Rich knows nothing of the *Lamentation*.'

'We must find that Scotchman,' he said again emphatically. 'It is very likely he was the spy.'

I considered. 'My assistant suggested there could have been some sort of double agent, working for a master at court while keeping his

Anabaptist beliefs. In that case, it is likely he would seek to keep the *Lamentation* safe.'

'Anything is possible. Only finding McKendrick will solve that mystery.'

'Thinking of Rich, if his only interest was Anne Askew's book, since that is now gone I do not think he would put any more resources into finding McKendrick.'

'No. That would indeed be shutting the stable door after the horse has bolted.'

I looked at him. 'But if he *is* interested in finding the Scotchman, that would indicate he is interested in something more – the *Lamentation*, perhaps.'

Lord Parr considered, then nodded. 'Yes, that makes sense.' He smiled wryly. 'Either way, Rich will be sweating in his shoes, dreading the day Anne Askew's words appear in print in London, smuggled back from Flanders.'

'Yes, he will be.' I could not help but feel satisfaction.

'Go and see Rich now,' Lord Parr said. 'Find out how the land lies. I must go to the Queen, see how she fares.' He bowed and then turned, in his abrupt way, and walked slowly back towards the Queen's chambers, leaning on his stick. I took a deep breath. A little way off I heard laughter and saw a couple of ladies throwing seed to the peacock.

✝

LATER THAT DAY I went again to the house in Needlepin Lane to see Stice. I asked Nicholas to attend me. As we walked down Thames Street I thanked him for saving my life. 'I shall not forget it,' I told him.

He replied with unaccustomed seriousness. 'I am glad to have saved a life, sir, when so many have been lost in this business. Leeman – I felt hot with anger against him last night, with his mad beliefs. I was starting to say too much, wasn't I?'

'Yes. He needed to be gentled along.'

'And I remember I was the cause of Elias fleeing,' he said quietly. 'And then later he, too, was murdered. That has been on my conscience ever since.'

'It need not be. We have all made mistakes in this business.'

He shook his head. 'I knew London was a place of violence and murder, but this — '

'It is not my normal trade, though over the years certain people high in the realm have made it seem so.'

He hesitated, then asked, 'Her majesty?'

I hesitated. 'Yes. And others before her. Cranmer and Cromwell, too.'

He looked impressed. 'You have truly known the great ones of England.'

'That can have its disadvantages.'

'Those names are all on one side of the religious divide,' he said hesitantly.

'I was once myself on that side, and as the realm has divided so my contacts have remained there. But my religious loyalties — ' I shrugged — 'they are gone.'

'Surely it is enough just to believe.'

I looked at him. 'Do you believe, Nicholas?'

He laughed uneasily. 'Just about. I know that at heart I want to save life, not destroy it. Yours was a life I am glad to have saved,' he added, his face reddening.

'Thank you, Nicholas.' Now I was embarrassed, too. Such words from pupil to barrister could have been sycophantic, but Nicholas had none of that sort of guile in him. I said gruffly, 'Let's see if these villains are at home.'

☩

STICE OPENED THE DOOR. He wore a bandage round his forehead. 'You.' He looked at us with displeasure. 'Come to discuss the mess you made last night?'

'We all failed.'

'My master's here.' He lowered his voice. 'He's not pleased.'

'How is Gower?'

'Like to die.'

'I am sorry.'

'My shitten arse you are.'

He led the way upstairs. Sir Richard Rich was sitting behind his desk. The shutters were drawn, making the room stifling. No doubt he did not want people in the street to see him here. He glowered at us. 'Bowels of Judas! You made a fine butcher's shambles of last night's business!'

'They were good fighters. We could not stop Vandersteyn getting away.'

'We did our best, sir,' Stice added. 'Everyone did.'

'Shut your mouth, mangehound! You were all as much use as a rabble of women! And the physician says I will have to deal with Gower's poxy corpse soon!' He glared at Stice. 'God's death, it would have been better if you had lost your whole head in that duel, rather than half an ear.' He pointed at Stice's disfigurement. 'A fine ornament for a gentleman.' Stice's mouth set hard, but he did not reply.

Rich turned his baleful gaze on me. 'I expect you've been to Whitehall, to tell the Queen's minions that Askew's book is gone. Halfway across the North Sea by now, I imagine.' His little grey eyes bored into mine. 'Well, I can expect the lies Askew told about me to surface in due course.' He spoke with self-pity, though he could hardly imagine I would care.

'The Scotchman remains out there,' I said.

'That canting Anabaptist madman. I hope he gets caught and burned.' Rich gave a long, angry sigh. 'Our alliance is over, Shardlake. How could I have ever thought a hunchbacked scratching clerk could be of use to me?' He waved a slim, beringed hand. 'Begone!'

I looked at him. I had told Lord Parr that if Rich showed no interest in McKendrick it would be an indication that he had been concerned only with Anne Askew's book. Yet there was a blustering, half-theatrical quality to his fury that made me wonder. Then again, perhaps it was just anger and fear that what he had done would soon be exposed. He could still pursue McKendrick on his own, of course. Bluff and counter-bluff, everywhere.

'Will you keep this house on?' I asked.

'Mind your own business!' His face darkened. 'Go, or I'll have Stice give that boy some new bruises, and you a few as well.' He banged his fist on the desk. 'Get out! Never let me see you again!'

Chapter Thirty-seven

L ATER THAT DAY I REPORTED back to Lord Parr. Cecil was with him in his study. The young lawyer looked strained, and there were large bags under his eyes. He could not have experi-enced anything like that battle at the wharf before. I told them what had happened with Rich, and that while I doubted he knew of the *Lamentation*'s existence I could not be sure. Lord Parr told me he was arranging for people from his household to look for McKendrick around the London streets. By now he might be reduced to begging, but equally he could have fled the city entirely. Where the Bertano story was concerned, Lord Parr had learned only that members of the King's own guard had been posted outside a house near the Charing Cross, which was kept for diplomatic visitors. An ominous sign, but there was nothing to do now but wait.

✝

A WEEK PASSED . . . July turned to August, with two days of rain before the hot weather returned, and the first week of the month went by with no further news from Whitehall. I feared every day to hear that some new arrangement with the Pope had been struck, and the Queen and her radical associates arrested. However, I forced myself to give attention to my work. Nicholas's bruises faded; he seemed a little restless but nonetheless set himself to work well enough. He spoke with pleasurable anticipation of the forthcoming ceremonies to welcome the French admiral; apparently additional cannon were being brought to the Tower for a great welcoming cannonade when d'Annebault arrived. I had told Nicholas I would be involved; he envied me, though I told him I would gladly have avoided the task. Meanwhile Barak's hand had healed completely and he, I sensed, was not sorry to return to a normal life.

At home I kept a continued eye on Brocket, but he did not put a foot wrong and Josephine had nothing further to report to me. Brocket and Agnes seemed more cheerful and I wondered whether there had been better news from their son, though I did not ask. Josephine also seemed happy; she was seeing her young man regularly and had a new confidence about her; sometimes I even heard her singing around the house. I smiled at the sound; it was good to reflect, among my troubles, that I had given Josephine a home and a future. Timothy, though, seemed to avoid conversation with me, perhaps afraid I would raise the subject of his apprenticeship again.

I made sure I had all the appropriate finery ready for the admiral's visit, buying a new black doublet and a shirt with elaborate embroidery at the wrists and collar. I would not, however, go to the expense of a gold chain; my purse had suffered enough from the taxes required to pay for the war.

On the 5th of August, I had a letter from Hugh. For the most part it contained only the usual news of business and entertainment in Antwerp. Hugh did mention, though, that a small cargo ship was recently arrived from England, and a certain Englishman had been at the wharf to welcome the owner, a merchant of Antwerp. I checked the date: the ship, I was sure, was the *Antwerpen*, with Vandersteyn on board; and the Englishman who had met it John Bale. So he would have Anne Askew's writings now, for printing. Well, so much the worse for Rich.

✝

ON FRIDAY THE 6TH I had been busy with paperwork all morning – I had almost caught up at last – and after lunching by myself in a refectory almost deserted in the heart of the summer vacation, I decided to take some much-needed air. I had a case coming on in the next law term involving the boundaries of some properties in

Gloucestershire: the barrister representing the other side, a member of
Gray's Inn, had the coloured map which always accompanied the
deeds, delineating the boundaries. In accordance with convention I
was allowed to make a copy. Normally that was clerks' work, but
while neither Barak nor Nicholas had a good hand for drawing, I did,
and took pleasure in it. I decided I would do the job myself, though I
could only charge a clerk's rate for it.

Thinking of Gray's Inn reminded me of Philip Coleswyn. I had
not seen him since warning him about Isabel's complaint – about
which I had heard no more from Treasurer Rowland. I walked the
short distance to my house and fetched Genesis, reflecting that he, too,
needed some air. Young Timothy was with him in the stable, reading
something, which at my entry he shoved hastily up his shirt, turning
bright red. I had insisted Timothy go to school to learn to write, so he
knew his letters at least. Some pamphlet of lewd rhymes, no doubt;
what wonders the printed word had brought to the world, I thought
sardonically, as I set the boy to saddling the horse.

It was peaceful riding up the lanes, between the hedges where bees
droned, the cattle fat and sleek in the fields. It was one of those hot
August days when the countryside can seem almost drugged with
heat, cattle and sheep grazing lazily, a faint shimmer rising from the
dusty highway. I looked forward to my map-work; earlier, while
sorting through the little bottles of coloured ink I would need, I
remembered the days when I used to paint. Why had I allowed that
gentle pastime to slip from me?

I left Genesis with the Gray's Inn porter and crossed the central
square. The trees had a dusty look. I was still thinking about my
painting days when, turning a corner, I walked straight into the last
two people I wished to see: Vincent Dyrick, in robe and cap, his handsome aquiline face a little red from the sun; and Isabel Slanning, in a
dark blue summer dress and gable hood, her thin features gaunt, her
expression sour as always. Dyrick was frowning and I wondered
whether, experienced though he was with difficult clients, perhaps
Isabel was too much even for him.

We all stood still a moment, taken aback. Then I removed my cap and bowed. 'God give you good afternoon, Brother Dyrick. Mistress Slanning.'

Dyrick bowed in return and spoke with unexpected civility. 'And you, Master Shardlake.' I moved to pass them, but Isabel, standing rigidly in front of me, fixed me with her steely gaze.

'Master Shardlake, have you been visiting Master Coleswyn to discuss my complaint, or perhaps to conspire with him against another honest believer who cleaves to the miracle of the Mass?' Her voice was loud and shrill, reminding me of the night she had confronted me outside Coleswyn's house.

To my surprise Dyrick took her by the arm. 'Come, mistress,' he said quietly. 'Let me accompany you to the gate.'

She shook off his arm, still fixing me with that steely look, and pointed a skinny finger at me. 'Remember, Master Shardlake, I know all about the conspiracy: you, and my brother, and that Coleswyn. You will all pay the highest price. Just wait.' She bared her teeth – good teeth for a woman of her age – in a smile of undiluted malice. 'Master Dyrick would spare you, but I will not,' she ended triumph- antly, nodding at Dyrick, who looked uncomfortable.

With that, she turned, allowing Dyrick to lead her round the corner. I stared after them. Isabel's behaviour had been absurd, almost unbalanced. But Dyrick had seemed worried, and I could not help but wonder anxiously what she had meant.

✞

I SPENT AN HOUR making a copy of the map in the chambers of my opponent on the case. I found it hard to concentrate, though, for the bizarre encounter with Isabel still preyed on my mind. I decided to see if Coleswyn was in his chambers.

His clerk said he was, and once more I entered his neat, tidy office. He held out a welcoming hand. He was more at ease than I had ever seen him, relaxed and welcoming. 'Matthew, how go things with you?'

'A busy summer. And you, Philip?'

'My wife and I feel happier now the heresy hunt is over.' He shook his head sadly. 'I took some books in yesterday, under the amnesty, good books written by men of true faith, but now forbidden. I have delayed doing it, for I was much attached to them, but the amnesty expires on Monday.'

'I had some, too. I burned them, as I preferred not to have my name appear on a list.'

'The amnesty is public, and many people have brought in books. Perhaps even some from Whitehall.' He laughed uneasily. 'If they prosecuted those who took advantage of the amnesty, that would be a great breach of faith, and illegal.' He smiled sadly, looking out of the window at the quadrangle. 'My books are a big loss to me, but our vicar says we must wait, for better times may be coming.'

I was glad he did not know about Bertano. I said, 'I am visiting Gray's Inn on other business this afternoon, but I have just had a strange encounter with Isabel Slanning and Brother Dyrick. I thought I should tell you.'

His face became serious. 'What now? Dyrick has been pestering and bothering me about the depositions and other aspects of the case, trying to bully me in his usual manner. But he has not mentioned this nonsense about conspiracy again. I had hoped he was discouraging Isabel from going down that path. I would, if I were him. The courts will not welcome it.'

'I think he may be trying to. When I ran into them just now, Dyrick was civil enough for once, and tried to hustle Isabel away. But she told me again she knew all about you, me and her brother conspiring together, and that we would pay, as she put it, the highest price.'

'Dyrick did not back her up?'

'Far from it, which is unusual for him. I begin to think Isabel is seriously unhinged. But Dyrick looked worried, and I cannot but wonder what she may have planned.'

Philip's cheerful manner was gone. 'Is there further word concerning her complaint about you to Lincoln's Inn?' he asked anxiously.

'None. But Treasurer Rowland was going to write her a sharp

letter. I should have expected a copy but I have heard nothing yet. I will call on him.'

Coleswyn considered a moment, then said, 'I have discovered something else.' He took a deep breath. 'A few days ago, I was dining in hall when I saw a friend of mine from another chambers, who knows I have the Cotterstoke case – Dyrick's cases are always a source of gossip round Gray's Inn. He introduced me to a retired barrister, now over seventy, but of good memory. When he was young – this is over forty years ago – he acted for Edward and Isabel's mother.'

I looked up with interest. 'Oh?'

He hesitated. 'Strictly, even though old Deborah Cotterstoke is dead, his duty of confidentiality remains. But you know how old fellows like to gossip. And I cannot help but be interested in anything concerning that family.' He frowned. 'I should not tell you, I suppose.'

I smiled gently. Coleswyn's integrity was one of the things I admired in him. 'I no longer represent Isabel. And I promise it will go no further.' I inclined my head. 'And if a former client threatens a barrister, as Isabel did this afternoon, I think he is entitled to seek out anything which might throw light on the circumstances. I take it the old man's story does that, Philip?'

He grunted acknowledgement. 'Not directly. But you and I have both wondered whence came the mutual hatred, and perhaps fear, in which Edward Cotterstoke and Isabel Slanning hold each other.'

'Yes. It is surely something out of the ordinary.'

'We know from the old merchant I spoke to before that Edward and Isabel's father died young, their mother married again, but her second husband also died. And the merchant said that ever after she and both children seemed at odds with each other.' Coleswyn leaned forward in his chair. 'This old barrister I spoke to was consulted in 1507, back in the old King's time. By Mrs Deborah Johnson, as she then was. At the time she was an attractive widow in her thirties with two children.'

'Edward and Isabel.'

'Yes. Deborah's first husband, Master Johnson, had just died. Of the sweating sickness, you remember, which was raging in the city that summer.'

I remembered the confident-looking young father in the painting, with his tall hat, and the pretty wife and two little children. How easily even a rising man could be suddenly cut down.

'Isabel and Edward's mother had inherited his business. She was quite rich. There had recently been a case in Chancery over whether a woman could inherit and run a business and be a member of a Guild. The old barrister was able to reassure her that she could. He remembered her as a formidable woman.'

'I recall her face in the painting. Pretty, but with a sharpness, a hardness to it. Like her daughter's.'

'Yes. A year later, Mistress Johnson consulted him once more. She was minded to marry again, a man in the same trade as her, Peter Cotterstoke, but she was concerned her rights in the business would pass to her new husband on marriage.'

'As they would. Automatically.'

Philip nodded. 'And so she was advised. She said her son and daughter, who were around eleven and twelve then, were worried they would lose their inheritance. But she was set on marrying Master Cotterstoke. And she did. But Cotterstoke proved an honourable man. Deborah Cotterstoke, as she now was, came back to the lawyer a third time, some months later, together with her new husband, and Master Cotterstoke made a Will stating that if he should die before Deborah, the combined business – his own and the late Master Johnson's – would pass to her. He sealed the matter by formally adopting Edward and Isabel; therefore even if Deborah were to die first they would still inherit their share. Deborah, apparently, was visibly pregnant at the time, and the couple thought it best to formalize arrangements.'

I scratched my cheek. 'So Cotterstoke was a good stepfather to the children. And they kept his name, which they surely would not have done if they disliked him. Did this old fellow know anything of a quarrel within the family?'

'Nothing,' Coleswyn replied. 'Only that shortly after, poor Master Cotterstoke drowned. That we knew, but I decided to look out for the coroner's report.' I sat up. 'Apparently one Sunday, shortly after the children were adopted and the Will made, Master Cotterstoke walked from their home just beyond Aldgate, through the city and down to the docks, where a ship had just come in with some goods he had purchased abroad. He took the two children with him, and he also had two servants in attendance, a normal thing for a gentleman walking out. One was Patrick Vowell, which is the name of the old man who is taking care of the house now.'

'Indeed?' I asked, my interest growing.

'Both servants testified that Master Cotterstoke seemed perfectly happy that day, as did the two children. He was looking forward to the arrival of his new child. The servants left him at the customs house; Master Cotterstoke said he did not know how long he would be and they should wait outside. The children went on to the docks with him.

'It was quiet at the docks, being Sunday. A little time later, a labourer heard shouting and crying from the water. He thought it was gulls at first but it came again and he realized it was a human cry. He ran to the water and saw a man floating there. The tide was full and anyone who fell off the wharfside would plunge into deep water. He called for some of his colleagues to help him get the body ashore but it was too late. It was Master Cotterstoke, and his lungs were found to be full of water; he certainly drowned. And apparently it was a misty day in autumn; someone walking near the edge could easily make a mis-step.'

'True.'

'Both children gave evidence at the inquest. They said their step-father had visited the ship, and then said he wanted to take a walk to see what goods might be available on other ships that had come in, and they should go back to the servants, which they did. Not uncommon for a merchant to do on a Sunday, though apparently the wharves were not busy that day.'

'Was this lawyer you met involved in the inquest?'

'No. But he met Deborah Cotterstoke once more afterwards, when he visited the house to help with formalizing the documentation for probate after the funeral. He said he remembered her as being in a piteous state of grief, which was unsurprising in a woman who had lost two husbands in little over two years, and the children also appeared shocked and stunned.'

'Did she ever come back to see him?'

Coleswyn shook his head. 'He wrote to her asking if she wished to make a new Will, but she did not reply. He heard a little later that she had lost the child she had been carrying at that time, again not surprising, given her sad circumstances.' Philip sighed. 'He remembered seeing her and the children in the streets from time to time. Then she sold the business and her son, my client Edward, decided to seek a different trade.'

'And she never married again?'

'No. Apparently she made a point of wearing sober clothes for the rest of her life.'

I considered. 'Are you saying a third party may have been involved in Master Cotterstoke's death?' I caught my breath. 'Or even one of the children? The coroner would only have their word that their stepfather was alive when they returned to the servants.' I frowned. 'Or that old Mistress Cotterstoke held them both responsible for her husband's death? All the evidence indicates she came to dislike both her children; we have said before that the wording of the Will looks like an attempt to set them against each other.' I looked at Philip. 'These are horrible thoughts.'

'They are. But given the Will their stepfather made, the children and his wife Deborah had no reason to dislike or distrust him.' He looked at me seriously. 'But I have been struggling with my conscience as to whether I should go and speak to the old servant, Goodman Vowell. I have no authority from my client, but . . .'

I smiled sadly. 'You would pluck up the roots of this madness.'

'I wonder if their stepfather's death has something to do with this carapace of hatred between them. And each has said they could do great damage to the other.'

'I remember how old Vowell seemed distraught at Edward and Isabel's quarrel at the inspection,' I said. 'He was obviously upset by their behaviour.'

'But I do not see that I have the right to go and question him.'

'You looked out the coroner's report. And if Isabel's behaviour now involves some possible threat to us both – ' I raised my eyebrows.

'A madwoman's bluster.' He sighed heavily. 'Let me consider this further, Matthew. Let me pray on it.'

I would rather that he had gone to the Cotterstoke house at once and taken me with him. But I was not in a position to insist. I rose from my stool.

'When you decide, let me know. And let us keep each other informed of anything else concerning this case that may affect us – personally.'

He looked up, fixing me with his clear blue eyes. 'Yes. I promise.'

Chapter Thirty-eight

LATER THAT DAY I called in at Treasurer Rowland's office, only to be told he was in a meeting. On Monday I called again and this time the clerk said he was out, though passing his window on the way in I was sure I had caught sight of his long, black-robed figure leaning over his desk through the half-open shutters. When I went out again the shutters were closed. I wondered uneasily whether Rowland was avoiding me.

That day in the refectory I dined with another barrister I knew slightly; he planned to hire a wherry on the morrow and take his family on a trip down beyond Greenwich. As Rowland had told me last month, virtually all the King's ships, fifty or so, were coming to the Thames to form a line from Gravesend to Deptford, past which the admiral's ships would sail, and they were starting to arrive. 'They say the *Great Harry* is already moored at Deptford,' my colleague said. 'All those ships that were at Portsmouth last year, and saw off the French.'

'The *Mary Rose* will not be there.'

'Casualty of war, Brother Shardlake,' he said portentously. 'Casualty of war.'

✝

ON TUESDAY, the 10th, at the end of the working day, I invited Barak and Nicholas to take a mug of beer with me in the outer office. Skelly had gone home. Thoughts about the missing *Lamentation* still constantly buzzed in my head, and I thought a talk with them might give me some perspective. Barak asked if I had heard any more from the palace.

'Not for over a week now.'

He shook his head. 'Someone's still holding on to that book. But who, and whyever not reveal it to the King, if they wish to harm the reformers?'

'I wish I knew.'

'And this Bertano,' Nicholas added. 'He must be here, if what Leeman said was true. We are well into August now.' He sighed and his green eyes looked inward for a moment. Lord Parr had had Leeman's body removed by the men he had sent to fetch me to the palace on the night of the shooting; fortunately, the students had not returned until the morning. I was sure that, like me, Nicholas would never forget Leeman's face, suddenly destroyed in front of us.

I said, 'We know now that the Anabaptists had the book. And Leeman was right, one of them was a spy; nobody else knew about the *Lamentation*. It must have been either Curdy, who is dead, or McKendrick who escaped. Or both. And whoever it was, they were working for someone at court, they must have been.'

'One of the big men,' Barak agreed. 'But there's still the question of *who* – and why have they not yet shown their hand?' He looked at me quizzically. 'Do you still rule out Rich?'

'I'd never rule out Rich. But whoever it is, it's dangerous for them to wait. As soon as that book came into anyone's possession it was their duty to take it to the King. And if whoever stole it wants to anger Henry, and thus help the negotiations with Bertano to succeed, the best plan would have been to give it to him as soon as possible.'

'If Bertano exists,' Barak said. 'We're not even certain of that. And if he does, I'm still convinced the King would never surrender the Royal Supremacy.'

'Lord Parr thinks the arrival of someone such as this Bertano fits with the comportment of certain councillors recently. And we know there is a house reserved for diplomats at Charing Cross, which apparently is being guarded by the King's men.'

'In that case,' said Nicholas, 'the best moment to reveal the book has surely passed, as you say. And I hear the Queen is to feature prominently at the ceremonies to welcome the French admiral. That must be a sign she is back in favour.'

Barak grunted. 'Thomas Cromwell was at the height of his power when he fell. He was made Earl of Essex, then a few weeks later suddenly hauled off to the Tower and executed.'

Nicholas shook his head. 'What sort of mind does the King have?' He asked the question in a low voice, despite the safety of my office.

'A good question,' I answered. 'Lord Parr and I have spoken on it. He is impressionable, suspicious, and if he turns against someone, ruthless and relentless. A man who thinks he is always right, and who believes what he wants to believe. He would see the Queen's hiding the book and concealing its theft from him as a betrayal, almost certainly. And yet – he still loves her, has never wanted to lose her. He made Gardiner's people pay when they called her a heretic without the evidence for it.'

'None of this helps us with the question of who has the book, though,' Barak said.

'No,' I agreed. 'It doesn't.'

'What about my idea of a double agent?' Nicholas asked. 'Someone who told his masters about the book but then, before it could be taken, got it for himself, killing Greening in the process?'

'To what end?' Barak asked.

'Perhaps to smuggle it safely abroad.'

I said, 'If so, the only one who could have it now is McKendrick. Wherever he is.'

A sudden knock at the door made us all jump. The relief in the room was palpable when, in answer to my call to enter, Tamasin came in.

We all stood. After the business of bows and curtsies Tamasin smiled at us. 'So this is how you fathom out the secrets of the law.' Barak and I laughed, though Nicholas frowned a little at the latitude she allowed herself. But she and I were old friends, and Tamasin had never been a shrinking violet.

Barak said mock severely, 'We allow ourselves a little relaxation at the end of a hard day; a fine thing when women squirrel their way in to chide us for it.'

'Perhaps it is needed. Seriously, Jack, if you are finished I wondered if you would come with me to Eastcheap Market, to see if there are any apples in.'

''Tis late. And you know there are none ripe yet; only the dregs of last year's poor harvest, expensive for all they are shrunk and wrinkled.'

'I have such a craving for them.' She gave Nicholas an embarrassed glance. 'There may be some from France, now we are trading again.'

'God help my purse,' Barak said. But he put down his mug.

'I should leave too,' I said. 'There are some papers in my office I should take home. Wait while I get them, then I can lock up.'

'Thank you,' Tamasin said. She turned to my pupil. 'And how are you, Master Nicholas?'

'Well enough, Mistress Barak.'

'Jack tells me you do not lose papers and knock things over the way you used to,' she said mischievously.

'I never did,' Nicholas answered a little stiffly. 'Not much, at least.'

In the office I sorted out the papers I wanted. When I opened the door to the outer office again Nicholas had left, and Tamasin had seated herself on Barak's desk. He was gently winding a strand of blonde hair that had escaped from the side of her coif round his finger, saying quietly, 'We shall scour the market. But the craving will cease gnawing soon; it did last time.'

I coughed. We all went out. As I watched them set off into the late summer afternoon, bickering amiably as usual, that moment of intimacy between them, caught thus unexpectedly, clutched somehow at my heart. I felt sadly aware of the lack of anything like it in my own life.

Except casting a fantasy at the Queen of England, like the most callow boy courtier at Whitehall.

☦

I HAD A QUIET DINNER on my own, good food cooked by Agnes and Josephine and served by Martin with his usual quiet efficiency. I looked at his neat profile. What had he been doing that day Josephine saw him going through my desk? The uncomfortable thought came to me that Josephine was heavy-footed, and it would not be difficult for Martin to ensure she was not near before doing something illicit again. But I thought, more likely he had simply yielded to a momentary temptation, to see if he could find some money for his son. Temptation which, in any case, he had resisted, for I had carefully gone over my accounts and no money had ever gone missing.

Afterwards, it still being light, I took the papers I had brought home out to my little pavilion in the garden. They concerned a Court of Requests case for the autumn, a dispute between a cottager and his landowner over the cottager's right to take fruit from certain trees. As with all these cases the landlord was rich, the cottager penniless, the Court of Requests his only recourse. I looked up to see Martin approaching across the lawn, his footsteps soundless on the grass, a paper in his hand.

He bowed. 'This has just come for you, sir. Brought by a boy.'

He handed me a scrap of paper, folded but unsealed. 'Thank you, Martin,' I said. My name was drawn in capitals. I remembered uneasily the note telling me of Nicholas's kidnap.

'Can I fetch you some beer, sir?'

'Not now,' I answered shortly. I waited till he had turned his back before opening the paper. I was surprised but relieved to see that it was written in Guy's small spiky hand.

Matthew,

I write in haste from St Bartholomew's Hospital, where I do voluntary work. A man, a Scotchman, was brought in two days ago suffering from bad

knife wounds, and is like to die. He is delirious, and has spoken all manner
of strange things. Among them he has mentioned your name. Could you
come, as soon as you get this note?

    Guy

This had to be McKendrick, the only one of the Anabaptist
group to escape the fight at the wharf. He must have been attacked after
his flight, and very recently by the sound of it. I stood up at once, then
as I walked to the stable, realized that Guy had simply signed his
name, not prefixed it with the customary farewell of good fellowship,
Your loving friend.

✝

I FETCHED GENESIS and rode up to Smithfield. I had not been
there since Anne Askew's burning over three weeks before. I remembered noticing then how what was left of the old monastic precinct of
St Bartholomew's was hidden by the new houses built by Rich.

It had been market day at Smithfield, and the cattle-pens were
being taken away, boys with brooms clearing cow dung from the open
space. Farmers and traders stood in the doorways of the taverns, enjoying the evening breeze. Ragged children milled around; they always
gathered at the market to try and earn a penny here or there. The awful
scene I had witnessed last month had taken place right here. One
might have thought some echo would remain, a glimpse of flame in
the air, the ghost of an agonized scream. But there was, of course,
nothing.

I had never been to the hospital, which gave directly onto the open
ground of Smithfield. I tied Genesis at the rail outside, paying one of
the barefoot urchins a penny to watch him, and went inside. The large
old building was in a dilapidated state, paint and plaster flaking – it
was seven years now since the dissolution of the monastic hospital. I
asked a fellow who had lost half a leg and was practising walking on
crutches where Dr Malton might be. He directed me to the main
ward, a large chamber with perhaps twenty beds in two long rows, all

occupied by patients. I walked to the far end, where Guy in his physician's robe was attending to a patient. Beside him was his assistant, plump old Francis Sybrant.

They looked up as I approached. The patient in the bed was a girl in her teens, who whimpered as Guy wound a bandage round her calf, her leg held up carefully by Francis. Two wooden splints had already been bound to the leg.

'Thank you for coming, Matthew,' Guy said quietly. 'I will be with you in a moment.' I watched as he completed winding the bandage. Francis lowered the girl's leg slowly down onto the bed, and Guy said to her quietly, 'There, you must not move it now.'

'It pains me, sir.'

'I know, Susan, but for the bone to knit you must keep it still. I will call again tomorrow.'

'Thank you, sir. May I have my rosary, to pass the time – ?' She broke off, looking at me anxiously.

'Master Francis will give it to you,' Guy replied. He turned to his assistant. 'Give her some more of the drink I prescribed later. It will ease her pains.'

'I will, Dr Malton.'

Guy stepped away. 'I have put the man I wrote of in a private room.'

I followed him down the ward. 'What happened to the girl?'

'She assists at the cattle market for a few pennies. A frightened cow pressed her against the side of an enclosure. It broke her leg.'

'Will it mend?'

'It may, if she is careful. The bone did not come through the skin, so the leg will not go bad. I would be grateful if you would forget that she asked for a rosary. There are those who think this hospital still stinks of the old religion. Francis was once a monk here, by the way. He helps here still, through Christian charity.'

I looked at Guy in surprise. But there was no reason why his assistant should not be an ex-monk; there were thousands in England now.

I replied, frowning, 'You know I would never do such a thing as mention that child's rosary to anyone.'

'It does no harm to put you in remembrance that it is not just radicals who have to be careful these days in what they do, and what they say.'

'I do *not* forget it.'

He gave me a hard look. 'And for myself, I take no note of words spoken by patients who sound impiously radical. As you will shortly see.' I took a deep breath. There was no give in my old friend nowadays.

✝

HE LED ME INTO A SIDE WARD. Like the main chamber it was but poorly equipped, a little room with a small window containing only a truckle bed with an old thin blanket and a stool. The window was open to let in air; the sound of voices drifted faintly in from Smithfield.

I recognized the man within at once: McKendrick, whom I had last seen running from the wharfside. He had been a physically powerful man, and had proved himself to be a fierce fighter. He looked utterly different now. His square face was covered with sweat, white as paper, and his cheeks were sunken. He tossed uneasily on the bed, making it creak, his lips moving in delirious muttering. Guy closed the door and spoke quietly. 'He was fetched in the day before yesterday. It is a strange story: a group of apprentices were hanging about outside one of the taverns near Cripplegate, around curfew, when all of a sudden a man rushed out of an alley into their midst. He was covered in blood and they caught a glimpse of two men pursuing him. Whoever they were, they turned tail when they saw the crowd of apprentices. They brought him here. It is a miracle he lived at all: he had been stabbed, thrice. He must have fought his pursuers and managed to run away. But the wounds have gone bad. He cannot live long; I think he will die tonight.' Guy gently lifted the blanket and under the man's shift I saw three wide wounds on his chest and abdomen. They had been stitched, but around two of the wounds the skin was swollen and red, and the third had a yellowish hue.

'Dear God,' I said.

Guy replaced the blanket gently, but the movement disturbed McKendrick, who began muttering aloud. 'Bertano . . . Antichrist . . . Pope's incubus . . .'

Guy looked at me sternly. 'When I heard some of the things he was saying, I put him in here. Safest for him, and perhaps for others.'

'And he has mentioned my name?'

'Yes. And others. Including, as you just heard, that name Bertano which you asked me about. Generally what he says in his delirium is nonsense, but I have heard him mention Queen Catherine herself. Disconnected talk, about spies and traitors at the English court. Mostly it makes no sense, and his Scotch accent is unfamiliar to me. But I have understood enough to realize he knows dangerous things, and is a religious radical. Once he cursed the Mass, saying it was no more than the bleating of a cow. Another time he spoke of overthrow, ing all princes.' Guy hesitated, then added, 'I see you know him.'

'I saw him only once, though I have been seeking him for weeks.'

'Who is he?'

I looked him in the eye. 'I cannot say, Guy, for your safety. I beg you, continue to keep him apart from the other patients; he knows dangerous things. Did he have anything on him when he was brought in?' I asked urgently. 'Perhaps – a book?'

'He had a copy of Tyndale's forbidden New Testament with his name inside, and a purse with a few coins.'

'Nothing else?'

'Nothing.'

I looked at McKendrick, quiet now, his breathing shallow. 'I would have prevented this, Guy, I hope you believe me.'

'Yes,' Guy answered, 'I believe that. But you are still involved in something deeply dangerous, are you not?'

'Yes.' I looked again at McKendrick. 'May I question him?'

'His mind is in a fever most of the time.'

'Would you leave me to try? The only reason I ask you not to stay is in case you hear something that might imperil your safety. I would not drag you into this bog as well.'

Guy hesitated, then nodded. 'I will leave you for a little. But do not tax him.' He went out, closing the door gently. There was a stool in the room, and I dragged it across to McKendrick's bed. It was getting dark, the sound of voices quieter as Smithfield emptied. I shook him gently. His eyes opened; they were unfocused, feverish.

'Master McKendrick?' I asked.

'Dominie McKendrick,' he whispered. 'I am Dominie. Teacher, preacher.'

'Dominie, who did this to you?'

I was not sure he had heard my question, but then he said wearily, closing his eyes tight, 'There were two o' them, two. They took me by surprise, though I'm careful. Jumped out of the doorway an' stabbed me. Two o' them. I got one o' them in the shoulder, managed to run.' He smiled sadly. 'Escaped in the alleys. Got to know the London alleys these last years. Same as the ones in Stirling, always running, running from the lackeys of popes and princes. But I weakened, loss o' blood.' He sighed. 'Running, always running.'

I bent my head close. 'Did you know your attackers, Dominie?'

He shook his head wearily.

'Were they two tall young men, one fair, with a wart on his face, the other almost bald?'

'Ay, that was them.' He looked at me, his eyes focusing properly for the first time. 'Who are you?'

'One who would punish those who attacked you.' Daniels and Cardmaker had underestimated the ex-soldier's strength and speed, and he had managed to run into the crowd of apprentices. But too late, it seemed, to save his life.

He reached a hand out from under the blankets, grasping mine. His was hard and callused, the hand of a man who had worked and soldiered, but hot and clammy. 'Did they kill Master Greening?' he asked.

'Yes, and his apprentice, Elias.'

His grip tightened and his eyes opened wider, blue and clear. He stared at me. 'Elias? We thought he was the traitor.'

'No, it was not him.' Nor you either, I thought.

McKendrick released my hand and leaned back on the bed with a groan. 'Then it can only have been Curdy, William Curdy we all thought such a true soul.' Yes, I thought, and Curdy is dead, unable to say who his master was. Killed by one of Richard Rich's men.

He looked at me. 'Are you one of us?' he asked.

'One of who?'

'The brethren. The believers in a new heaven and a new earth. Those our enemies call Anabaptists?'

'No. I am not.'

The dying man's shoulders slumped. Then he looked at me fiercely. 'I see it, among these dreams I have here. The greater vision, a future Commonwealth where all share equally in the bounty of nature, and worship the one Christ in peace. No princes, no warring countries, all men living in harmony. Is it a dream, do you think, or do I see Heaven?'

'I think it a dream, Dominie,' I answered sadly. 'But I do not know.'

A few moments later McKendrick slid back into unconsciousness, his breathing shallow. I stood, my knees creaking. I had learned what I needed to know and returned slowly to the main room, where Guy was writing notes at a desk at the back of the ward.

'He is unconscious again,' I sighed. 'Or perhaps in a sleep of wondrous dreams. There is nothing to be done for him?'

He shook his head. 'We doctors know the signs of coming death.'

'Yes.' I remembered Cecil telling me about the King's doctors saying he could not last long now. 'Thank you for summoning me, Guy. One thing more. When – when he dies, it would be safer for the hospital if he were buried under a different name. He is wanted in connection with possible treason.'

Guy looked at me, then spoke with quiet passion. 'I pray every night that whatever terrible thing you are involved in, it may end soon.'

'Thank you.'

I left the hospital. At home I sent a note to Lord Parr, telling him the Scotchman was found, and that he was not the spy. Very early next morning, Brocket woke me with two notes that had arrived with the dawn: one on expensive paper with the seal of the Queen in red wax, the other a second folded scrap from Guy. The first told me that I was required at Whitehall Palace again that morning, the second that McKendrick had died in the night. Again, Guy had signed his note only with his name.

Chapter Thirty-nine

A ND SO I TOOK A BOAT to Whitehall Palace. I had no more
information to bring Lord Parr about what might have happened to the Queen's book; and I realized that, with all Greening's
group gone, its fate might remain unknown.

On the way to Temple Stairs I called in at chambers to tell Barak
I would be away that day, I did not know for how long. He was alone
– Nicholas and Skelly had not yet come in – and I summoned him to
my room.

'Whitehall?' he asked.

'Yes. I found McKendrick last night.' I told him what had happened at the hospital.

'So the late Master Curdy was the spy.'

'So it seems.' I sighed. 'I have reached a dead end.'

'Then leave it to the politicians now,' he said roughly. 'You've
done all you can.'

'I cannot but feel I have failed the Queen.'

'You've done all you can,' he repeated impatiently. 'Risked your
life.'

'I know. And yours, and Nicholas's.'

'Then have done with it. If Queen Catherine falls, it will be
through her own foolishness.'

✝

I ENTERED THE PALACE by the Common Stairs again, the
wherry jostling for space at the pier along with boats carrying newly
slaughtered swans for the royal table and bolts of fine silk. The pier

ran a long way out into the water, so that unloading could take place even at low tide. The tide was almost full now, though, just starting to ebb. Dirty grey water washed round the lowest of the stone steps. I thought for a moment of poor Peter Cotterstoke, tumbling into the river on a cold autumn day. As I left the boat, gathering my robe around me and straightening my cap, I looked upriver to the Royal Stairs. There, a narrow, brightly painted building two storeys high jutted out of the long redbrick facade of the palace. It ended at a magnificent stone boathouse, built over the water. A barge was heading towards it, oarsmen pulling hard against the tide. A man in a dark robe and cap sat in the stern. I recognized the slab face and forked beard: Secretary Paget, master of spies, and one of those who knew whether an emissary of the Pope called Bertano was truly in London.

I went into the maze of buildings, tight-packed around their little inner courts. Some of the guards recognized me by sight now, though as always at strategic points my name had to be checked against a list. All the magnificence within had become familiar, almost routine. I was accustomed now to avoid looking at all the great works of art and statuary as I passed along, lest they delay me. I saw two stonemasons creating a new and elaborate cornice in a corridor, and remembered Leeman saying how every stone in the palace was built on common people's sweat. I recalled that craftsmen were paid a lower rate for royal work, justified by the status that accrued from working for the King.

I was admitted again at the Queen's Presence Chamber. A young man, one of the endless petitioners, stood arguing with a bored-looking guard in his black-and-gold livery. 'But my father has sent to Lord Parr saying I was arriving from Cambridge today. I have a degree in canon law. I know there is a position on the Queen's Learned Council come vacant.'

'You are not on the list,' the guard answered stolidly. I thought, who was leaving? Was it me, now my work was done?

In the bay window overlooking the river some of the Queen's ladies sat as usual, needlework on their laps, watching a dance performed with surprising skill by Jane Fool. I saw Mary Odell sitting with the highborn ladies despite her lack of rank. The pretty young Duchess of Suffolk, her lapdog Gardiner on her knee, sat between her and the Queen's sister Lady Anne Herbert, whom I had seen at Baynard's Castle. A tall thin young man with a narrow, beaky face and wispy beard stood behind them, watching with a supercilious expression.

Jane came to a halt in front of the gentleman and bowed. 'There, my Lord of Surrey,' she said to the man. 'Am I not fit to be your part-ner at the dancing at Hampton Court for the admiral?' So this was Surrey, the Duke of Norfolk's oldest son, but reportedly a reformer, said to be a skilled poet, who last winter had been in trouble for lead-ing a drunken spree in the city.

He answered curtly, 'I dance only with ladies of rank, Mistress Fool. And now you must excuse me. I have to meet my father.'

'Do not be harsh with Jane,' the Duchess of Suffolk said reprov-ingly; for the fool's moon face had reddened. But then Jane saw me standing a little way off, and pointed at me. 'There is the reason the Queen has gone to Lord Parr's chamber! The lawyer has come again to bother her with business! See, he has a back as hunched as Will Somers'!'

The company turned to look at me as she continued. 'He would have had Ducky taken from me. But the Lady Mary would not let him! She knows who her true friends are!' There was a glimmer in her eyes that told me Jane was indeed no halfwit; all this nonsense was deliberate, to humiliate me.

Mary Odell stood up hastily and came to my side. 'Her majesty and Lord Parr are waiting for you, Master Shardlake.'

I was glad to walk away with her to the Queen's inner sanctum.

✝

AGAIN THE QUEEN was seated on a high chair under her red cloth of estate; today she wore a bright green dress on which flowers, leaves, even peapods on a bush, were sewn to scale. Under her French hood I thought I caught the glint of grey strands in her auburn hair. Lord Parr stood to one side of her in his usual black robe and gold chain, and Archbishop Cranmer on the other, in his white cassock. As I bowed deeply I saw the Queen's chess set on a table nearby and thought: a black piece and a white.

All three had been studying a life-size portrait set before them on an easel, the newly painted colours so bright they drew the eye even amid the magnificence of Whitehall Palace. The background showed the dark red curtains of a four-poster bed, the foreground an open bible on a lectern and next to it the Lady Elizabeth, whom I recognized at once. She was wearing the same red dress as the day I saw her, when she had complained at having to stand so long, and being painted beside her bed.

Her trouble had been worthwhile, for the portrait was truly lifelike. Elizabeth's budding breasts contrasted with the vulnerability of her thin, childlike shoulders. She held a small book in her hands and her expression was composed, with a sense of watchful authority despite her youth. I read the meaning of the painting: here was a girl on the brink of womanhood, scholarly, serious, regal, and in the background the bed as a reminder of her coming marriageability.

The Queen, who had been looking at the portrait intently, sat back in her chair. 'It is excellent,' she said.

'It says everything that is needed,' Cranmer agreed. He turned to me. 'I have heard your latest news, Matthew,' he said quietly. 'That there *was* a spy in this group, and he is dead. His master is likely someone senior, a Privy Councillor, but we do not know who.'

'Yes, my Lord,' I added. 'I am sorry.'

'You did all you could,' he said, echoing Barak. I glanced at the Queen. She looked troubled now, her body held with that air of slight stiffness I had come to recognize as denoting strain. She did not speak.

'At least this group of Anabaptists is gone,' Lord Parr said. 'I'd have seen them burned!'

Cranmer said firmly, 'The guard who Leeman suborned at the palace, and the gaoler Myldmore, must be sent abroad. For all our safety.'

'You would have had them burned too, my Lord Archbishop,' Lord Parr growled, 'were moving them not necessary.'

'Only if earnest preaching could not bring them from their heresy,' Cranmer said, anger in his voice. 'I wish no man burned.'

'You have helped us greatly, Matthew,' the Queen said gently, 'with Leeman's information about Bertano.'

I asked, 'It is true, then, about him?'

Lord Parr glanced at Cranmer and then the Queen, who nodded. He spoke sternly. 'This is for your ears only, Shardlake, and we tell you only because you first brought us that name and would welcome your view. Only we four know about Bertano. We have not even told the Queen's brother or sister. And that man and boy who work for you must say nothing,' he added in a threatening tone.

'We know you have absolute trust in them,' Cranmer said mildly.

'Tell him, niece,' Lord Parr said.

The Queen spoke: heavily, reluctantly. 'A week ago, his majesty had a visitor brought to his privy quarters during the day. All the servants in the Privy Chamber were cleared out. Normally he tells me if a visitor from abroad is coming,' she added, 'but the night before this visit he said that it was for him alone to know about, and I was to stay on my side of the palace.' She lowered her eyes.

Her uncle prompted her gently, 'And then?'

'I know the meeting did not go well. His majesty sent for me to play music for him afterwards, as he does sometimes when he is sad and low in spirits. He was in an angry humour, he even hit his fool Will Somers on the pate and told him to get out; he had no patience for idle jest. I dared to look at him questioningly, for poor Somers had done nothing to warrant being struck. The King said, "Someone wants the powers granted me by God, Kate, and dares send to ask for them. I have sent back such answer as he deserves." Then he struck the arm of his chair so fiercely with his fist that it jarred his whole body and caused a fearful pain in his leg.' The Queen took a deep breath. 'He did not make me swear to keep his words confidential. So, though strictly it goes against the honour due my husband, because of the dire straits we have all found ourselves in, I confided in my uncle and the Archbishop.'

'And now we have told you,' Lord Parr said brusquely. 'What do you make of it?'

'It adds weight to the suspicion that what Vandersteyn learned on the Continent was true. Someone asking the King for the powers granted him by God. That can only mean the Supreme Headship, and only the Pope would demand that.'

He nodded agreement. 'That is what we think. If Bertano was an emissary from the Pope it sounds as though the price for a reconciliation was the King's renunciation of his Headship of the Church in England.'

'And from all the King said, a message was to be sent back to the Pope?'

Cranmer answered. 'I think it has already gone. And if it has, it would be through Paget.' He smiled humourlessly. 'And yesterday Paget told the Privy Council that after d'Annebault's visit, the King and Queen will be going on a short Progress – only as far as Guildford – and announced those of the council he has chosen to accompany him, all sympathizers with reform. Gardiner, Norfolk, Rich, all our enemies, remain in London, kicking their heels and keeping the wheels of government turning. Those who will be about the King's person, and have his ear, will be our allies.'

Lord Parr raised his hands. 'The pieces all fit.'

Cranmer smiled, more warmly this time. 'Those left behind did not look pleased to hear the news at the council table. I think Bertano's mission has failed at the start.' There was satisfaction in his voice, relief too.

I said, 'But there remains the *Lamentation*.'

'There is nothing more to be done about that,' Lord Parr said bluntly. 'Except hope that whoever stole it realizes they have squandered their chance, that the Catholic cause is lost, and – forgive me, Kate – that they dispose of it.' He added, 'The King will not turn his policy again.'

Cranmer shook his head emphatically. 'With the King, that can never be ruled out. But I agree, the trail on the book is quite cold.'

I looked at the Queen. 'Believe me, your majesty, I wish I had been able to recover it. I am sorry.'

'God's wounds,' Lord Parr said abruptly. 'You did your best, even if it wasn't good enough. And now, all that remains is for you to keep quiet.'

'I swear I will, my Lord.'

Cranmer said, 'Your efforts to serve her majesty will not be forgotten.'

It was a dismissal. I adjusted my posture a little, so I could bow to them without pain, for I was still suffering from when Nicholas had thrown me to the ground, to save me from the man with the gun. But the Queen rose from her chair. 'Matthew, before you go I would talk a little with you again. Come, you have seen my Privy Gallery, but not by daylight. Let us walk there. Mary Odell can accompany us.' She nodded to Cranmer and Lord Parr, who bowed low. I followed the Queen as she walked to the door, silk skirts rustling.

✝

WITH DAYLIGHT COMING in through the high windows, showing the gorgeous colours to full effect, the Queen's Privy Gallery was magnificent. The little birds in their cages hopped and sang. The Queen walked slowly along; I kept a respectful pace or two away, while Mary Odell, summoned from the gallery, brought up the rear. The expression on her plump face was neutral, but her eyes were watchful, I saw, as I glanced back.

The Queen halted before an alcove in which a jewelled box was set atop a marble pillar. Within were coins of gold and silver, showing portraits of long-dead kings and emperors. Some were worn almost smooth, others bright as though new-minted. She stirred them with a long finger. 'Ancient coins have always interested me. They remind us we are but specks of dust amid the ages.' Carefully, she picked up a gold coin. 'The Emperor Constantine, who brought Christianity to the Roman Empire. It was found near Bristol some years ago.' She lifted her head and looked out of the window; it gave on to the Thames bank below the palace, exposed now as the tide ebbed. I followed her gaze, my eye drawn to a heap of rubbish from the palace that had been thrown onto the mud: discarded vegetable leaves, bones, a pig's head. Gulls swooped over it, pecking and screaming. The Queen turned away. 'Let us try the view on the other side,' she said.

We crossed the gallery. The opposite window looked down on another of the small lawned courtyards between the buildings. Two men I recognized were walking and talking there. One was Bishop Gardiner, solidly built, red-faced, dressed again in a white silk cassock. The other, younger man was sturdy, dark-bearded, saturnine: John Dudley, Lord Lisle, who had commanded the King's naval forces at Portsmouth last year. His defensive strategy had done much to ward off invasion. So the other senior councillor who favoured the radicals was back from his mission abroad. All the chess pieces were in place now. Gardiner, I saw, was talking animatedly, his heavy face for once wearing a civil expression. Something in their postures suggested Gardiner was on the defensive. Lord Lisle inclined his head. This, I thought, was how the real power-play went: conversations in corners and gardens, nods, shrugs, inclinations of the head. But nothing in writing.

The Queen joined me. An expression of distaste and fear, quickly suppressed, crossed her face at the sight of Gardiner.

'Lord Lisle is back,' I observed.

'Yes. Another ally. I wonder what they are discussing.' She sighed and stepped away from the window, then looked at me and spoke seriously. 'I wanted you to know, Matthew, the depth of my gratitude for the help you have given. I sense it has cost you much. And my uncle can be – less than appreciative. But all he does is for my interest.'

'I know.'

'It looks as though my book will never be found. It saddens me to think it may be on some rubbish tip, for all it may be safer there. It was my confession of faith, you see, my acknowledgement that I am a sinner, like everyone, but through prayer in the Bible I found my way to Christ.' She sighed. 'Though even my faith has not protected me from terrible fear these last months.' She bit her lip, hesitated, then said, 'Perhaps you thought me disloyal, earlier, for repeating words spoken to me by the King. But — we needed to know what this visit from abroad signifies.'

I ventured a smile. 'Mayhap a turn in fortune for you, your majesty, if the meeting went badly.'

'Perhaps.' She was silent again, then said with sudden intensity, 'The King — you do not know how he suffers. He is in constant pain, sometimes he near swoons with it, yet always, always, he must keep up the facade.'

I dared to say, 'As must you, your majesty.'

'Yes. Despite my fear.' She swallowed nervously.

I remembered what Lord Parr had said about how the King might react to disloyalty. For all that the Queen revered her husband, her fear of him over these last months must have been an unimagin-able burden. I felt a clutch at my heart that she so valued me as to unburden herself thus. I said, 'I can only imagine how hard it must have been for you, your majesty.'

She frowned. 'And always, always there are people ready to whis-per poison in the King's ear — '

Mary Odell, perhaps concerned the Queen was saying too much, approached us. 'Your majesty,' she said. 'You asked me to remind you to take these to the King when you see him. They were found down the side of a chair in his Privy Chamber.' She had produced a pair of wood-framed spectacles from the folds of her dress, and held them out to the Queen.

'Ah yes,' she said. 'Thank you, Mary.' The Queen turned to me. 'The King needs glasses now to read. He is always losing them.' She tucked the spectacles away, then began walking down the gallery again. 'The court will be moving from Whitehall next week,' she said, more brightly. 'The French admiral is to be received first at Greenwich and then at Hampton Court, so everything is to be moved.' She waved a hand. 'All this packed up, transported by boat, set out again in a new place. The Privy Council meeting in a new chamber. With Lisle and Hertford both present,' she added with a note of satisfaction.

I ventured, 'I saw Lord Hertford with his brother Sir Thomas Seymour at the palace last time I came.'

'Yes. Thomas is back, too.' She looked me in the eye. 'You do not like him, I know.'

'I fear his impulsiveness, your majesty.'

She waved a dismissive hand. 'He is not impulsive, just a man of strong feeling.'

I did not reply. There was a brief, awkward silence, then she changed the subject. 'You have knowledge of portraiture, Matthew. What was your opinion of the picture of my stepdaughter?'

'Very fine. It shows the coming substance of her character.'

She nodded. 'Yes. Prince Edward, too, is a child, well advanced for his years. There are those in my family who hope that one day I may be appointed Regent when he comes to the throne, as I was when the King went to France two years ago. If so, I would try to do well by all.'

'I am sure of it.' But the Seymours as well as the traditionalists would oppose her there, I knew.

She came to a halt. 'Soon the French admiral will come, and afterwards the King and I go on Progress, as you heard.' She looked at me seriously. 'You and I may not have another opportunity to talk.'

I answered quietly, 'A young courtier waiting outside said there is a vacancy on your Learned Council. Do you wish me to resign my position?'

'The vacant post is not yours but Master Cecil's. He asked to go. What he experienced at the docks was too much for him, not that he is a coward, but he fears if anything happened to him his wife and children would be left alone. And Lord Hertford has asked him to become one of his advisers. I consented; Cecil is a man of great loyalty and will say nothing of the *Lamentation*. As for you, Matthew, I wonder if it might be best for all if you were to leave as well.'

'Yes. After all, I was supposedly appointed only to find a missing jewel.' I smiled. 'And sadly, it indeed seems there is no chance of finding your book. Perhaps it would be – politic – for me to leave now.'

'So my uncle thinks, and I agree.' She smiled tiredly. 'Though I would still rather have your counsel.'

'If you need to call on me again – '

'Thank you.' She looked at me, hesitated, then spoke with quick intensity. 'One thing more, Matthew. Your lack of faith still troubles me. It will eat away at you from the inside, until only a shell is left.'

I thought sadly: was the real purpose of our talk for her to make another essay at bringing me to faith? I answered truthfully, 'I have wished for God, but I cannot find him in either Christian faction today.'

'I pray that may change. Think on what I said, I beg you.' She looked into my eyes.

'I always do, your majesty.'

A sad little smile, then she nodded and turned to Mary Odell. 'We should go back, sit with the ladies awhile. They will think we are neglecting them.'

We walked back up the gallery. Near the door she paused at a table on which stood a magnificent gold clock a foot high, ticking softly. 'Time,' the Queen said softly. 'Another reminder we are but grains of sand in eternity.'

Mary Odell went in front of us and knocked at the door. A guard opened it from the other side and we stepped through into the heavily guarded vestibule, with its doors leading to the Queen's rooms, the King's, and the Royal Stairs. At the same moment another guard opened the doors leading to the King's chambers, and two men stepped out. One was the red-bearded Lord Chancellor Wriothesley, the other Secretary Paget, a leather folder thick with papers under his arm. They had probably just come from seeing the King.

Seeing the Queen, they bowed deeply. I bowed to them in turn, and rose to see both staring at me, this hunchbacked lawyer wearing the Queen's badge, who had been walking with her in her gallery. Wriothesley stared with particular intensity, his gaze only relaxing a little when he saw Mary Odell standing by the door: her presence showed the Queen had not been walking alone with a man who was not a relative.

The Queen's face immediately assumed an expression of regal composure; still, quiet, a little superior. She said, 'This is Serjeant Shardlake, of my Learned Council.'

Wriothesley's stare intensified again. Paget's large brown eyes held mine with a forceful, unblinking look. Then, turning to the Queen, he lowered his eyes and spoke smoothly. 'Ah yes, the man appointed to help you seek your stolen jewel.'

'You have heard of that incident, Master Secretary?'

'Indeed. I was grieved to hear of its loss. A present from your late stepdaughter Margaret Neville, I believe, God save her.'

'It was.'

'I see Serjeant Shardlake's name has been added to the list of those on your Learned Council. And I see young William Cecil has moved to Lord Hertford's service. He will be a loss, your majesty, he is marked down as a young man of ability.' I thought, yes, Paget would know of all the changes in the royal household; he would inspect all the lists and ensure nothing of interest passed him by. He would have learned that trick from Thomas Cromwell, his old master and mine.

The Queen said, 'Serjeant Shardlake is also leaving my council. My jewel has not been discovered, despite his best efforts. There seems little chance of finding it now.'

Paget looked at me again, that stony unblinking stare, and ran a hand down his long forked beard. 'A great pity the thief could not be caught, and hanged,' he said, a note of reproof in his voice. He patted his thick leather folder. 'If you would excuse us, your majesty, the King has just signed some important letters, and they should be immediately dispatched.'

'Of course.' She waved a hand in dismissal. Wriothesley and Paget bowed low, then passed through a small door leading into the labyrinthine depths of the palace. The Queen, Mary Odell and I were left standing with the impassive-faced guards. In their presence the Queen's face remained regally expressionless, giving away nothing of how she had felt at thus encountering Wriothesley and Paget. She knew that Wriothesley, at least, would have had her in the fire.

With a formal smile she said, 'Farewell, then, Matthew. I thank you again.'

I bowed low, touched her hand briefly with my lips; a scent of violets. In accordance with the rules of etiquette I remained bowed until she and Mary Odell had walked back into her quarters and the doors closed behind her. Then, painfully, I straightened up.

I left my robe bearing the Queen's badge with one of the guards before I quitted Whitehall, my relief tinged with sadness.

Chapter Forty

ARLY NEXT MORNING I SAT at breakfast, morosely studying a printed circular from Paget's office, which had been sent to me by Rowland's clerk. It detailed the duties of those who were to wait in the streets to welcome Admiral d'Annebault's party when it paraded through London. Representatives of the Inns of Court were to take positions with the city dignitaries beside St Paul's Cathedral, and cheer as the French party passed. We would be present again at the reception of the admiral given by Prince Edward near Hampton Court Palace two days later, and at the great banquet fixed for the day after. I was not looking forward to any of it, and was still in a sad humour after leaving the Queen, my mission unfulfilled. I had been terse with Martin as he served me that morning, snapping because the butter was on the turn. As usual he reacted with a deferential lack of emotion, apologized, and went to fetch some more.

He returned, laying a fresh dish on the table. I said, 'I am sorry I spoke roughly just now, Martin.'

'You were right, sir,' he answered smoothly. 'I should have checked the butter. Although Josephine set it out.' I frowned; he could not resist the chance to criticize her. 'A visitor has called to see you,' he said then. 'Master Coleswyn, of Gray's Inn.'

'Philip? Ask him to wait. I will be with him in a moment.'

Martin bowed and left. I wondered if this meant Philip had reconsidered investigating the story of Isabel and Edward's stepfather. I wiped my lips with my napkin and went through to the parlour. Philip, his handsome features thoughtful, was looking through the window at the garden, bright in the August sunshine. He turned and bowed.

'Matthew, forgive this early visit. God give you good morrow.'

'And you. I am glad to see you.'

'You have a beautiful garden.'

'Yes, my steward's wife has done much to improve it. How is your family?'

'They are well. Much relieved that matters of state have – settled · down.'

I invited him to sit. He placed his palms together, then spoke seriously. 'Since our talk last week, I have struggled mightily with my conscience over what to do about Edward Cotterstoke. Considered my duty to God.'

'Yes?' I said encouragingly.

'I decided I could not let the matter rest. If there is any question of my client being involved with his stepfather's death, that would be a crime against God and man. Not only could I no longer represent him, I would be obliged at the very least to tell our vicar, who ministers to both our souls.' He took a deep breath. 'Last Sunday, after church, I spoke to Edward. I explained I had been told the story of his stepfather's death, and wondered whether that tragic event was in any way connected with his feelings towards Isabel.'

'How did he react?'

'Most angrily. He said the old barrister I spoke to had no right to divulge information about matters on which his mother had instructed him, however many decades ago, and that I should not be listening to such tattle.'

'Strictly he is right.'

Philip leaned forward, his expression urgent. 'Yes. But the fierce manner in which Edward reacted – you should have seen it. He was angry, but also perturbed. There is something hidden here, Matthew, something serious.'

'So I came to think when Isabel was my client.' I paused, then asked, 'Well, what next?'

'I believe now that I should talk to the old servant Vowell. Doing so without Edward's instruction is a breach of the rules, but nonetheless I believe it is my duty.' He set his lips tight. 'I will go to him today.'

'May I come also?'

He hesitated, then nodded agreement, giving a rare slantwise smile. 'Yes. I would welcome your presence, and if I am to break the rules by taking my ex-opponent with me, I might as well be hung for a sheep as a lamb.' He took a deep breath. 'Let us go now. I came by horse. We can ride there.'

I got Timothy to saddle Genesis, then sent him to chambers with a note saying I would be in late.

✝

IT WAS STILL EARLY, the city just coming to life, as we rode to the Cotterstoke house at Dowgate. I glanced round periodically; it had become habit since the night of the fight on the wharf. But if I were still being followed, which I doubted, it was by someone very skilled. And perhaps now that all in Greening's group were dead, or in Vandersteyn's case fled, there was no longer a need for me to be watched.

We passed a thin, ragged old woman going from house to house calling out, 'Any kitchen stuff, maids?' She was one of those who collected kitchen rubbish to sell for a few pence, for use as compost in the vegetable gardens round London. She was old for such a heavy, dirty task. As I looked at her blackened face I remembered Barak talking of seeing his mother in the street. This old woman could even be her. Family quarrels, they were hard things.

We passed the Great Conduit in Eastcheap, maids and goodwives lined up with their pails to fetch water. Some of the beggars who always haunted the conduit left off troubling the women and ran to us, one coming almost under the nose of Philip's horse, making it shy. 'Take care, fellow!' Philip shouted, straining to bring his mount under control. 'He'll kick you if you're not careful!' As we rode on he said,

'By Heaven, that fellow stank. Could he not wash himself, seeing as he is lounging by the conduit?'

'Hard to keep yourself clean if you're begging in summer.'

He nodded slowly. 'You are right to reprove me. We must have charity for those who have suffered ill fortune. It is a Christian thing.'

'Of course. But perhaps we should not give them charge of the realm,' I added, half-mockingly. 'As the Anabaptists would wish?'

He looked annoyed. 'You know I do not approve those heresies.' He sighed. 'It is a common enough thing for papists to accuse reformers of being Anabaptists, but I am surprised you give credence to such nonsense.'

'I do not. I am sorry.'

'The Anabaptists are not of the Elect,' he continued severely.

'Do you believe people are divided between the Elect and the damned?' I asked seriously.

'Yes.' He spoke with certainty. 'Some are predestined by God for salvation, while those without faith burn forever. Read St Paul.'

'I have always thought that a harsh doctrine.'

'The justice of God may be beyond our comprehension, but it is inviolable.' Philip looked at me seriously. 'Coming to faith, Matthew, may confirm one's place in Heaven.'

'And show one the way to right living; such as working to uncover whether one's client may be a murderer.'

He looked at me hard. 'That possibility is in both our minds.'

I nodded agreement. 'Yes. Let us find out.'

☦

THE COTTERSTOKE HOUSE was unchanged since the inspection, shuttered and silent, the stableyard to the rear again empty and bare in the sultry morning; it was hard to remember we were in the centre of the great city. Old Mrs Cotterstoke, I thought, lived here over fifty years. We tied up the horses. As we stepped into the sunshine, Philip, once more the practical lawyer, said, 'They should get the house sold. The value of money keeps falling. But neither of them will take a single step till this dispute is resolved.'

We walked back under the stableyard arch into the street, and knocked at the door. Shuffling footsteps sounded within and the old man Vowell opened the door. His watery blue eyes widened with surprise at the sight of us, standing there in our robes. He bowed quickly. 'Masters, I did not know you were coming, I have had no instructions. Is there to be another inspection?'

I realized from his words that he was unaware that I no longer represented Isabel. Philip replied amiably, 'No, goodman, but there are some questions you might help us with.'

Vowell shook his head, obviously reluctant. 'I do not know how I can help you. I was the late Mistress Cotterstoke's servant all her life, but I knew nothing of her affairs. My only duty is to keep the house safe.'

I said, 'We have both been eager to see whether there may be a way to resolve this dispute before it comes to court.'

'Little chance of that,' Vowell said sadly. 'But come in, sirs.'

He led us to the parlour. I noticed the old lady's half-finished embroidery still lay on its chair, facing the wall painting, and wondered if anything at all had been moved since she died. I looked at the picture. 'That is a very fine piece of work. Were you here when it was painted?'

'Yes, sir. I was little more than a boy then, but I remember thinking how lifelike it was. My late mistress, her first husband, and the two little children; all just as they were then. It saddens me to see it now, my mistress dead and the children at such odds.' He looked at us, something wary in his eyes now.

'I heard a story of the death of their stepfather,' Philip said. 'A sad tale.' Philip related the old barrister's story. As he spoke, the old servant's posture seemed to droop and tears came to his eyes. At the end he said, 'May I sit, sirs?'

'Of course,' Philip said.

Vowell took a stool. 'So you have learned that old story. I thought, with this new quarrel, it must come out sooner or later.' He clenched his fists, looking down at the matting on the floor, then seemed to come to a decision.

'Master Edward was eleven then, Mistress Isabel twelve. As children they were — not close. Both had proud natures, wanted their own way, and they often quarrelled. Their mother was often sharp with them too, I have to say. Though she was a good enough mistress, and she has provided for me in her Will — '

'Though the Will must be proved first,' I said. Vowell would not get his legacy till then.

The old servant nodded and continued, 'The children loved their father. When he died they were both so sad. I remember coming across them, crying in each other's arms. It was the only time I saw that.' He looked up at us. 'Since my mistress died and this argument over the painting began, I have not known what to do or say. It has been a burden, sirs — '

'Then let us help you,' Philip said quietly.

Vowell sighed deeply. 'Mistress Johnson, as she was then, perhaps remarried too soon, only a year after Master Johnson died. But it was hard for her to keep the business going on her own, some people didn't like trading with a woman, and the children were too young to help. But her new husband, Master Cotterstoke, he was a good man. My mistress knew that. The children, though — '

I spoke quietly, remembering Barak and his mother. 'Perhaps they thought it a betrayal?'

He looked up. 'Yes. It was not — nice — to see them then. They would sit giggling and whispering together in corners, saying and doing — ' he hesitated — 'bad things.'

'What sort of things?' Philip asked.

'Master Cotterstoke had a fine book of Roman poems, beautifully written and decorated — it was all done by hand; most books then were not these blocky printed things we have nowadays — and it disappeared. All the servants were set to look for it, but no one found it. And I remember the children watching us as we searched, smiling at each other. Other things of the master's would go missing, too. I think the children were responsible. Yet Master Cotterstoke and especially the mistress thought it was us, careless servants. We always get the blame,' he added bitterly.

'The mistress and Master Cotterstoke were much preoccupied with each other then; the mistress had become pregnant. They barely noticed the children.' He shook his head. 'That angered them even more. I think Edward and Isabel had become much closer, united in their anger. Once I overheard them talking together on the stairs. Master Edward was saying they would be disinherited, everything would go to the new baby, their mother scarcely looked at them any more . . . And then – '

'Go on,' I urged gently.

'Sometimes Master Cotterstoke worked at home in the afternoon, going over his accounts. 'He liked a bowl of pottage mid-afternoon. The cook would prepare it in the kitchen and take it up to him. One day after eating it he was violently sick, and very poorly for several days after. The physician thought he had eaten something bad. He recovered. But one of my jobs then was keeping down vermin, and there was a little bag of poison bought from a peddler that was good for killing mice. I remember just after Master Cotterstoke was ill, getting the bag from the outhouse to put a measure down in the stables and noticing that some had been taken – it had been almost full.'

'You mean the children tried to poison him?' Philip asked, horrified.

'I don't know that, I don't know. But when I spoke to the cook she said the children had been round the kitchen that day.'

Philip's voice was stern. 'You should have spoken up.'

Vowell was looking at us anxiously now. 'There was no evidence, sir. The children were often round the kitchen. Master Cotterstoke recovered. And I was just a poor servant; making an accusation like that could have cost me my post.'

'How did the children react to Master Cotterstoke's illness?' I asked.

'They went quiet. I remember after that, their mother looked at them in a new way, as though she, too, suspected something. And I thought, if she is suspicious of them, she will look out for her husband, there is little point in my saying anything. Yet it pricked my conscience, that I had not spoken.' He added sadly, 'Especially after – what happened next.' He hunched forward again, looking at his feet.

I said, 'The drowning?'

'The coroner found it was an accident.'

'But you doubted it?' Philip said sternly.

Vowell looked up at that. 'The coroner investigated everything, it is not for a servant to contradict him.' I heard a touch of anger in his voice now. 'There were enough unemployed servants trailing the road even back then.'

I spoke soothingly. 'We have not come to criticize you, only to try and discover what caused the quarrel. We understand Master Cotterstoke went down to the docks on business that day, and you and another servant accompanied him and the children. And then after a while the children came back, saying they had been told to wait with you beside the customs house till he returned.'

'Ay, that is what happened, as I told the coroner.'

'How did the children seem when they returned?'

'A little quiet. They said their stepfather wanted to look over some goods on a ship newly come in.'

I thought again, there was only the children's word for that. Anything could have happened when they and Cotterstoke were alone. The children could have pushed their stepfather into the water. They would have been fourteen and thirteen then.

I asked Vowell, 'Was Master Cotterstoke a big man?'

'No, he was short and slim. One of those fast-thinking, energetic little men. Not like my first master.' He stared up at the wall painting, where Edward and Isabel's father, in his smart robes and tall hat, looked out on us with patrician confidence.

'What were things like in the family after the drowning?' Philip asked.

'Things changed. They were told of their stepfather's dispositions, I imagine. That he had left his estate to his wife, and to all his children equally if she died first. In any event, Edward and Isabel seemed to alter. They had become close while Master Cotterstoke was in the house. They didn't go back to quarrelling like before, but they – avoided each other. And oh, the fierce looks they would give one another. Mistress Cotterstoke's attitude to them seemed to change as well, even before she lost the baby she was carrying. She had been sharp with them before, but now she almost ignored them. She sold the business, and arranged for Edward to start clerking at the Guild-hall, which meant he had to live out. That was just a few months later.'

'So he did not inherit the business after all.'

'No. And though Isabel was only fifteen her mother seemed keen to marry her off; she was always inviting potential suitors to the house. But Mistress Isabel, as ever, would not be brought to do something against her will.' Vowell smiled sadly, then shook his grey head. 'There was a horrible atmosphere in this house, until at length Isabel agreed to marry Master Slanning and left. Afterwards Mistress Cotter-stoke seemed to – I don't know – retreat inside herself. She didn't often go out.' He looked over at her empty chair. 'She spent much of her time sitting there, sewing, always sewing. Kept a strict house, though, kept us servants on our toes.' He sighed deeply, then looked up at us. 'Strange, is it not, with all the sad things that happened here, that she never moved, even when she was alone, the house far too big for her.'

I looked at the wall painting. 'Perhaps she remembered she had once been happy here. I notice her chair faces the picture.'

'Yes. She was sitting there when she had her seizure. Edward and Isabel seldom visited, you know, and never together. And the mistress didn't encourage them. It saddened me to see how they were with each other when they came here for the inspection. And that strange Will – ' He shook his head. 'Perhaps I should not have told you all this. What good can it do? It was so many years ago. Whatever hap-pened, it cannot be mended.'

Philip stood pondering, fingering his bearded chin. Vowell gave a despairing little laugh. 'What will happen, sir? Shall I remain as care-taker of this empty house till I die? I don't like being here alone.' He added in a rush, 'At night sometimes, when the wood creaks – '

I felt sorry for the old man. I looked at Philip. 'I think we have learned all we need, Brother Coleswyn.'

'Yes, we have.' Philip looked at Vowell. 'You should have spoken before.'

I said, 'He is right that it can do no good to rake it all up now. Not a matter of a possible murder, so many decades ago, with no evidence to reopen the case.'

Philip stood silent, thinking.

'What will you do, sir?' Vowell asked him tremulously.

He shook his head. 'I do not know.'

✝

WE STOOD OUTSIDE in the stables, with the horses. I said, 'It may be that the children, or one of them, put Master Cotterstoke into the water. Clearly Goodman Vowell thinks so.'

'And their mother. It seems clear now: she made that Will to start a new quarrel. It was revenge.'

'But there is still no new evidence to overturn the coroner's ver-dict.'

'I think that is what happened, though.'

'So do I. Two children, grieving for the father, believing they might be disinherited by their mother's new husband – '

'Quite wrongly,' Philip said severely.

'They did not know that. Perhaps it started with little tricks, then they encouraged each other to go further, and as they spoke constantly of the rejection and betrayal each felt, maybe they drove each other to – a sort of madness.'

'Who put him in the water?'

I shook my head. 'I don't know.'

'Whoever did it was a murderer.'

'This all remains speculation,' I said emphatically. 'Likely, but not certain. Master Cotterstoke's drowning could still have been an accident. And the old man is right. Who could benefit from this being exposed, after forty years? And remember, you have a duty of confidentiality to your client. You can only break it if you think he is about to commit a crime, and that is hardly likely.'

Philip set his mouth hard. 'It is a matter of justice. I shall question Edward directly. And if he cannot satisfy my doubts, I shall cease acting for him and report the circumstances to our vicar. You are right about the lack of evidence, but if it is true he must still be brought to see the state of his soul. How could a man who had done such a thing ever be one of the Elect? Our vicar must know.'

'And Isabel? There is no point taking this tale to Dyrick. He wouldn't care. I know him.'

Philip looked at me. 'You would have me let sleeping dogs lie?'

I thought for a moment, then said, 'I think so. In this case.'

Philip shook his head decisively. 'No. Murder cannot go unpunished.'

Chapter Forty-one

NEXT DAY I WENT AGAIN to ask Treasurer Rowland for a copy of his letter to Isabel Slanning, and to see whether she had replied. I had done much thinking about what old Vowell had told Philip and me. It seemed all too possible that, forty years before, Isabel or Edward, or both, had killed their stepfather. Again I remembered Isabel's words to me, weeks ago, about her brother: *If you knew the terrible things my brother has done.* But what could be achieved by confronting them now, without new evidence? I knew Philip would be seeing Edward, perhaps had done so already. I had an uneasy feeling that the consequences of that old tragedy might ripple out anew.

My uneasiness was not assuaged when Rowland's clerk told me the Treasurer would not be available for appointments until Monday. It struck me that there was something a little furtive in the clerk's manner. I made an appointment for that day; it was three days hence, but it was at least a firm commitment.

✝

LATER THAT MORNING I was working in chambers, researching a precedent in a yearbook so that when the new term started next month I should have everything prepared. There was a knock at the door and John Skelly entered. His eyes behind his thick spectacles had a reproachful look, as often this last month. Not only had I frequently been out of the office, leaving the work to fall behind, but I knew he was conscious that Barak and Nicholas and I shared some secret he knew nothing about. It was better he did not, and safer for him, a married man with three children. But I knew he must feel excluded. I must talk to him, thank him for the extra work he had done for me, give him a bonus.

I smiled. 'What is it, John?'

'There is a visitor for you, sir. Master Okedene. The printer who came before.'

I laid down my book. 'What does he want?' I asked a little apprehensively, remembering how his last visit had led us to the tavern and the fight with Daniels and Cardmaker.

'He says he has come to say goodbye.'

I told him to show Okedene in. He looked older, thinner, as though his strong solid frame was being eaten away by worry. I invited him to sit.

'My clerk says you are come to bid me farewell.'

He looked at me sadly. 'Yes, sir. I have sold the business and we are moving in with my brother, at his farm in East Anglia.'

'That will be a great change in your life.'

'It will. But my family have never been at ease since Armistead Greening's murder and Elias's disappearance. I hear Elias has never been found, nor those others who used to meet with Master Greening.'

I hesitated before replying, 'No.'

He looked at me sharply, guessing I knew more than I was saying. I wondered what rumours were circulating among the radicals. Okedene sat, rubbing his brow with a strong square hand, before speaking again. 'I have not told my family of our encounter with Armistead's killers in that tavern, but knowing those people are still out there only makes me feel more strongly than ever that we are not safe. We must think of our children. Every time I see the ruin of Master Greening's workshop it reminds me, as it does my wife.'

'Ruin? What do you mean?' I sat up.

'You do not know, sir? The print-shop took fire, two weeks ago, in the night. A young couple, workless beggars, had got in there, and one of them knocked over a candle. You remember the building was all wooden; it burned quickly. Poor Armistead's press, the only thing of value he had, destroyed; his trays of type no more than lumps of useless lead. If we and the other neighbours had not rushed out with water to quench the flames, it could easily have spread to my house. And others.'

Okedene had spoken before of the printers' fear of fire. I knew how quickly it could spread in the city in summer. Londoners were careful of candles in a hot dry season such as this.

Okedene added, 'And those two killers are still in London. The fair one and the dark.'

I sat up. 'Daniels and Cardmaker? You have seen them?'

'Yes. I hoped they might have left the city, but I saw them both, in a tavern out near Cripplegate last week. I was passing; it was market day and very busy, they did not see me. But I would never forget those faces. I thought of coming to you then, but after what happened last time I felt myself best out of the business.'

'I understand. I have heard nothing more of them since the day of the fight.' I thought again of the feeling I had had of being followed at the wharf, the chink of a footstep on stone.

'All is settled,' Okedene said firmly. 'We go next week. We have sold the works to another printer. But I thought I would come to tell you I had seen those men. And to ask whether there has been any progress in finding who was responsible for killing Armistead Greening? Those two thugs were employed by someone else, were they not?' His eyes fixed on mine. 'Someone important? Someone who, perhaps, is still protecting them, for they still dare to show their faces in the taverns.'

I bit my lip. I had learned much since first meeting Okedene: who Bertano was, how the Queen's book had been stolen, what had happened to the others in Greening's group. But not the answer to the most important question, the one he had just asked. Who was behind it all?

'I think you are right,' I answered. 'I think Daniels and Cardmaker were employed by someone important, but whoever it was has covered his tracks utterly.'

His eyes fixed on mine. 'And that book? The one called *Lamentation of a Sinner*?'

'It has not been found, though — ' I hesitated — 'at least it has not been used to damage the Queen.'

Okedene shook his head. 'It is all terrible, terrible.' I felt a stab of guilt, for I had scarcely thought of him recently. An ordinary man whose life had been turned upside down by all this. 'I fear more troubled times may be coming,' he added, 'for all the heresy hunt has ended. People say the King may not last long, and who knows what will happen then?'

I smiled wryly. 'One must be careful what one says about that. Forecasting the King's death is treason.'

'What is not treason these days?' Okedene spoke with sudden fierce anger. 'No, my family is better out in the country. The profit we will make on our crops may be little, with the coinage worth less every month, but at least we can feed ourselves.'

'I am sorry my enquiries brought such trouble to you,' I said quietly.

Okedene shook his head. 'No, the fault lies with those who killed my poor friend.' He stood up and bowed. 'Thank you, sir, and good-bye.' He went to the doorway, then turned back and said, 'I thought I might have had some word, perhaps some thanks, from Lord Parr, for going to tell him privately what had happened that night.'

'He is not best known for gratitude,' I said sadly.

✝

LATER THAT MORNING my work was disturbed again, un-expectedly. From the outer office I heard Nicholas's voice call out, 'No!' followed by a tinkling sound.

I hurried out. I found Barak and Skelly staring in astonishment at him. He stood red-faced, his long body trembling, staring at a letter in his hand. On the floor at my feet I saw a golden coin, a half-sovereign: others were scattered around the room.

'What has happened?' I asked.

'He has just had a letter delivered,' Skelly said.

Nicholas stared at me then swallowed, crumpling the letter in his hand. Skelly stepped out from behind his desk and began going round the room, picking up the scattered coins.

Nicholas spoke coldly. 'Leave them, please, John. Or put them in the Inn chapel poor-box. I will not take them.'

'Nicholas,' I said, 'come into my office.'

He hesitated, but followed me in slowly, his movements strange and stiff. I gestured him to a chair and he sat down. I took my place on the other side of my desk. He looked at me with unseeing eyes. His face, which had been red, turned slowly white. The boy had suffered a shock. 'What has happened?'

He slowly focused on me, then said, 'It is over. They have dis-inherited me.' He looked at the letter, which he still held. His face worked, and I thought he might break down, but he took a deep breath and set his features stiff, hard. I reached out a tentative hand to the letter, but he clutched it all the tighter. I said again, 'What has happened? Why did you throw those coins away?'

He answered coldly, 'I am sorry for my outburst. It will not happen again.'

'Nicholas,' I said, 'do not treat me like this. You know I will help you if I can.'

His face worked again for a moment. 'Yes. I am sorry.' He fell silent, staring out of the window at the quadrangle, then, his head still turned away, said, 'I told you my parents had threatened to disinherit me in favour of my cousin, because I would not marry a woman I did not love.'

'That is a hard thing to do.'

'My mother and father are hard people. They — they could not bend me to their will, so they found someone more amenable.' He gave a sad half-smile. 'The duel was the last straw; I did not tell you about that.' He turned and looked me in the face, his expression half-fierce, half-desperate.

'What duel?'

He gave a harsh little laugh. 'When my father was trying to get me to marry this poor girl against both our wishes, I made the mistake of confiding in a friend who lived nearby. Or friend I thought he was; certainly a gentleman.' He spoke the word, which signified so much to him, with sudden bitterness. 'But he had been overspending and his family had put him on short commons. He said if I did not give him two sovereigns he would tell my father that I did not intend to marry her. '

'What did you do?'

Nicholas spoke with a sort of bleak pride. 'Challenged the churl to a duel, of course. We fought with swords, and I cut him in the arm.' He clutched the letter again. 'Wish I'd taken half his ear off, like that rogue Stice. His parents saw he had been injured and came complaining to mine. When they confronted me I told them why we had fought, and that I would not marry.' He took a deep breath, and ran a hand down his face. 'It was then they decided to send me to law, and threatened to disinherit me. I did not think they would go through with it, but they have.'

'What does the letter say? May I see it?'

'No,' he answered quietly. 'I shall keep it, though, as a reminder of what parents can be. My father calls me undutiful, uncontrollable. The duel and my refusal to accept their choice of wife have undermined their position locally, my father says. Neither he nor my mother want to see me again. He sent this letter by special messenger, with five pounds. He says he will send me the same sum every year.' He fell silent again, then said, very definitely, 'I think it cruel, and wrong.' A fierce look came onto his face. 'Who do you think, sir, has done the greater wrong here?'

'They have.' I answered without hesitation. 'When you first told me about the girl I, too, thought that perhaps they would get over their anger. But it seems not.'

I knew that Nicholas would have liked to rage and shout, but he kept himself under control. He took more deep breaths, and I was glad to see colour returning to his face. 'I already have in my possession barely enough to pay for my pupillage with you, sir,' he said, his voice sad. 'I think I must leave.'

'No,' I said. 'You have learned almost enough now to earn your keep.' He looked at me and I could see he knew that was not true: he was still learning, and for a while at least I would spend as much time teaching and correcting him as benefiting from his labours. 'Or at least you will soon, if you continue to work hard, as you have during these last difficult weeks.' I smiled. 'And you have helped me in much more important ways.'

'I will not be a burden,' he burst out angrily. 'I will fend for myself from now on.'

I smiled sadly. 'The Bible tells us, Nicholas, that pride goes before a fall, and a haughty spirit before destruction. Do not leave me – us – because of pride, do not make that mistake.'

He looked down at the crumpled letter. I had an uneasy feeling that if he did follow his pride and anger he would end badly, for there was a self-destructive element to his nature. There was silence for several seconds. Then a knock, and the door opened. Barak entered, not with a flourish but quietly. He, too, held something in his hand. He came up to the desk and laid a neat little stack of half-sovereigns on it. Nicholas looked at him.

'Done it, then, have they?' Barak asked roughly. 'Your parents?'

Nicholas answered thickly, with a dark look, 'Yes.'

'I feared they might. They – can do bad things, parents.' Nicholas did not answer. Barak said, 'I know all about it. But I know another thing, too. Money is money, wherever it's from. There's as much here as five poor men would earn in a year. Take it, spend it, put two fingers up to them.'

Nicholas met his gaze. Then slowly he nodded and reached out his hand to the money.

I said, 'You will stay?'

'For now, sir, while I think.'

Barak clapped him on the shoulder. 'That's a good lad. Come on then, work to do.' He gave Nicholas a weary, worldly grin, which, after a moment, the boy returned.

✝

ON SATURDAY, I HAD the first good news in some time, though even that was not unmixed. I was sitting in the parlour, pondering whether to invite Guy for dinner the following week. I had been heartened by the small steps towards reconciliation we had taken at the hospital, but still worried that he might refuse. There was a knock at the door and Agnes Brocket entered. She seemed full of suppressed excitement. I wondered if there had been better news of her son. But she said, 'Sir, Goodman Brown, Josephine's young man, has called. He asked if he might talk to you.'

I laid down my pen. 'Do you know about what?'

She took a step closer, clasping her hands. 'Sir, perhaps I should not say, but I always think it well for people not to be taken by surprise in important things. So – in confidence – he wishes to ask your approval to marry Josephine.'

I stared at her. I liked Brown; I was glad Josephine had found a swain, it had made her happier and more confident. But this was unexpected. I said, 'This is sudden. Josephine is not—'

She flushed with embarrassment. 'Oh no, sir, no, it is nothing like that.'

'But they have not been seeing each other long, have they?'

'Nearly four months now, sir.'

'Is it so long? I had forgot.'

'They have no plans for a hasty marriage,' Agnes said, a trifle reproachfully. 'But I believe they are truly in love, and wish to be betrothed.'

I smiled. 'Then show Master Brown in.'

The young man was nervous, but reassured me that he intended a six months' engagement. He said that his master would be glad to take Josephine into his home; currently he had no female servant. But then he added, 'He is retiring at the end of the year, sir. Moving his household to his family property in Norwich. He would like us to go with them.'

'I see.' So after Christmas I would probably not see Josephine again. I would miss her. I took a deep breath, then said, 'You have always struck me, Brown, as a sober young man. I know Josephine is very fond of you.'

'As I am of her.'

I looked at him seriously. 'You know her history?'

He returned my look. 'Yes, when I asked if she would marry me she told me all. I knew her father was a bullying brute, but not that he had stolen her from her family during one of the King's invasions of France.'

'He was a hard, brutal man.'

'She is very grateful to you for ridding her of him, and giving her a home.'

'Josephine needs gentleness, Master Brown, above all. I think she always will.'

'That I know, sir. And as you have been a kind master to her this last year, so I shall be a kind husband.' His face was full of sincerity.

'Yes, I think you will.' I stood and extended my hand. 'I give my consent, Goodman Brown.' As he shook my hand I felt a mixture of pleasure that Josephine's future was thus assured, coupled with sadness at the thought that she would be leaving. I remembered how her clumsiness and nervousness had irritated me when first she had come to my household. But I had seen that she was troubled, recognized her essential good nature, and determined to be kind.

Young Brown's face flushed with pleasure. 'May I go and tell her, sir? She is waiting in the kitchen.'

'Yes, give her the good news now.'

☦

LATER I JOINED the two of them in the kitchen, together with the Brockets and Timothy, to drink their health. Timothy looked astonished, and also distressed. How that boy hated change. It worried me.

Agnes acted as hostess, dispensing wine which I had asked her to bring up from the cellar for the occasion. Even Martin unbent so far as to kiss Josephine on the cheek, though I think he noticed, as I did, her tiny flinch, and while the rest of us made merry conversation he stood a little apart. Josephine wept, and young Brown drew her to him. She wiped her eyes and smiled. 'I will try not to be one of those wives who weep at every excitement.'

'I know you will be the best and most obedient of wives,' her fiancé said quietly. 'And I shall try to be the best of husbands.'

I smiled; I knew Josephine was no Tamasin, whose strong nature demanded a relationship of equality with her husband, sometimes to the disapproval of others. Josephine had been brought up only to obey, and I suspected sadly that she would find anything other than a sub-ordinate role in life frightening. I had a sense, though, that she would be a good mother, and that that might give her strength. I raised my glass. 'May your union be happy, and blessed with children.'

As the others raised their glasses to toast the couple, Josephine gave me a look of happiness and gratitude. I decided that I would, after all, write to Guy.

✝

THEY CAME FOR ME at dawn, as they often do. I was still abed, but wakened by a mighty crashing at the door. I got up and, still in my nightshirt, went out. I was not frightened but angry: how dare anyone bang so loudly on the door at this hour? As I came out onto the landing I saw Martin was already at the door, like me still in his nightclothes, pulling back the bolts. 'I'm coming,' he shouted irritably. 'Stop that banging, you'll wake the house—'

He broke off as, opening the door, he saw Henry Leach, the local constable, a solidly built fellow in his forties. Two assistants with clubs stood at his side, silhouetted against the summer dawn. As I walked downstairs my anger turned to fear, and my legs began to tremble. The constable held a paper in his hand. Leach had always been prop-erly deferential before, bowing when I passed him on the street, but now he frowned solemnly as he held the paper up for me to see. It bore a bright red seal, but not the Queen's. This time it was the King's.

'Master Matthew Shardlake,' Leach intoned gravely, as though I were a stranger.

'What is it?' I was vaguely aware of Agnes and Josephine behind me, likewise roused from bed, and then Timothy ran round the side of the house into view; he must have been up attending the horses. He skidded to a halt when one of the constable's men gave him a threatening look. I took a deep breath of air, the clean fresh air of a bright summer morning.

Leach said, 'I am ordered by the Privy Council to arrest you on a charge of heresy. You are to appear before them tomorrow, and until then to be lodged in the Tower.'

Chapter Forty-two

L EACH TOLD ME TO GO AND DRESS. 'I have been asked to search your house for forbidden books. I have a warrant,' he added and held up a second document.

'I have none.'

'It has been ordered.'

His assistant had grasped Timothy by the collar and, quite unexpectedly, the boy slipped out of his grip and ran at the constable, grabbing at the warrant. 'No! No! It is false! My master is a good man!'

Leach held the paper above his head, easily beyond Timothy's reach, while his assistant took the boy by the collar again, lifting him up in the air. He made a choking sound. The man set him on the ground, keeping a firm hold on his arm. 'Don't try anything like that again, lad, or I'll throttle you!'

I glanced at my other servants. Agnes and Josephine stood wide-eyed, clutching each other. 'I thought this hunting people out of their homes was over,' Agnes whispered. Martin looked on impassively.

Leach said to me, 'I will conduct the search while you dress.' His tone remained level, official, disapproving, though I sensed he was enjoying the opportunity to humble someone of my status. He did not meet my eye.

I let him in. On that score at least I had nothing to fear; I had burned all my newly forbidden books and there was nothing concerning the hunt for the *Lamentation* in the house. He sent one of his men upstairs with me to watch me as I dressed; my fingers trembled as I secured buttons and aiglets. I tried to calm myself and think. Who had done this, and why? Was this part of some new plot against Queen Catherine? When I had been imprisoned in the Tower of London five years before, on treason charges manufactured by Richard Rich, Archbishop Cranmer had rescued me; could the Queen save me now? I put on my summer robe, laid out as usual last night by Martin, and stepped to the door.

My servants were still standing in the hall, Josephine with her arm round a weeping Timothy. It was to her, not my steward, that I instinctively turned. I grasped her hand and said urgently, 'Go at once to Jack Barak's house and tell him what has happened. You remember where it is? You have taken messages there.'

Though her own hands were shaking she composed herself. 'I will, sir, at once.'

'Thank you.' I turned to the constable, trying to muster a shred of dignity. 'Then let us start, fellow. I take it we are to walk.'

'Yes.' Leach spoke severely, as though I were already convicted.

Martin Brocket spoke up then, in reproving tones. 'Master Shard-lake should be allowed to ride. A gentleman should not be led through the streets of London like a common fellow. It is not fitting.' He seemed far more concerned by the breach of etiquette than the arrest itself.

'Our instructions are to bring him on foot.'

'There is no help for it, Martin,' I said mildly. I turned to Leach. 'Let us go.'

We walked through the streets; thankfully few people were out and about yet, though a few stared fearfully at us as we passed, Leach in his constable's uniform in front, a bulky armed fellow each side of me. The arrest of a gentleman, a senior lawyer, was a rare thing; it did no harm for it to be seen in public, a reminder that everyone, regardless of rank and status, was subservient to the King.

✚

WE ENTERED THE TOWER by the main gate. The constable left me with a pair of red-uniformed Tower guards, the edges of their

halberds honed to razor sharpness, the rising sun glinting on the polished steel of their helmets. I remembered the twist of fear I had felt
when I entered here a few weeks ago with Lord Parr, to see Walsingham. Now the fate dreaded by all, being brought here a prisoner, had
befallen me again. The ground seemed to sway under my feet as they
led me across the manicured lawn of the inner courtyard towards the
White Tower. Far off I heard a roaring and yelping from the Tower
menagerie; the animals were being fed.

I pulled myself together and turned to the nearest guard, an
enormously tall, well-built young fellow with fair hair under his steel
helmet. 'What is to happen now?' I asked.

'Sir Edmund wishes to see you.'

I felt a little hope. Walsingham was a friend of Lord Parr; perhaps
I could get a message to him.

I was marched through the Great Hall, then upstairs. Sir Edmund
was engaged and I had to wait nearly an hour in a locked anteroom
overlooking the summer lawn, sitting on a hard bench trying to gather
my scattered wits. Then another guard appeared, saying brusquely
that Sir Edmund was ready.

The elderly Constable of the Tower sat behind his desk. He
looked at me sternly, fingering the ends of his white beard.

'I am sorry to see you again in such circumstances, Master Shardlake,' he said.

'Sir Edmund,' I answered, 'I am no heretic. I do not know what
is happening, but I must inform Lord Parr that I am here.'

He spoke impatiently. 'Lord Parr cannot interfere in this, nor
anyone else. You are brought by the authority of the King's Privy
Council, to answer questions from them. Lord Parr is not a member
of the council.'

I said desperately, 'The Queen's brother, the Earl of Essex, is.
And I was with the Queen but four days ago. I am innocent of all
wrongdoing.'

Sir Edmund sighed and shook his head. 'I had you brought
here to me first as a matter of courtesy, to tell you where you will be

spending today and tonight, not to listen to your pleas. Leave those for the council. My authority comes from them, under the seal of Secretary Paget.'

I shut my eyes for a second. Walsingham added, in gentler tones, 'Best to compose yourself, prepare for the council's questions tomorrow. As for tonight, you will be held in a comfortable cell, together with the others who will answer accusations with you.'

I looked at him blankly. 'What others? Who?'

He glanced at the paper on his desk. 'Philip Coleswyn, lawyer, and Edward Cotterstoke, merchant.'

So, I thought, this is Isabel's doing. But her harebrained ravings were surely not enough to have us brought before the council. Then I remembered Philip's fears that he was already under suspicion, and that Edward Cotterstoke was also a radical. Walsingham continued, 'You may have food and drink brought. Is there anyone you wish to send for?'

'I have already sent word to my assistant that I am – taken.'

'Very well,' he said neutrally. 'I hope for your sake that you acquit yourself satisfactorily tomorrow.' He nodded to the guard and made a note on his paper, and I was led away.

✝

THEY TOOK ME BACK through the Great Hall, then again downstairs, to those dank underground chambers. The same loud clink of heavy keys, the same heavily barred door creaking open, and I was led by the arm into the central vestibule, where Howitson, the big man with the untidy straggling beard, sat behind his overlarge desk. The guards gave him my name and left me in his care. He looked at me, raising his eyebrows in puzzlement for a moment at the sight of a recent visitor returned as a prisoner, before quickly adopting the blank mask of authority again. I thought of the guard Myldmore, who from what Lord Parr had said would soon be smuggled out of the country. I wondered what Howitson made of his employee's disappearance.

He called for a couple of guards and two more men appeared from the direction of the cells. 'Master Shardlake, to be kept till tomorrow, to go before the council. Put him with the others in the special cell for prisoners of rank.'

I knew who had occupied that cell recently; Myldmore had told me. Anne Askew.

✝

I WAS LED DOWN a short, stone-flagged corridor. One of the guards opened the barred door of the cell, the other led me inside. The cell was as Myldmore had described it, with a table and two chairs, but this time there were three decent beds with woollen coverlets, not one – they must have put in the other two when they heard three were to be brought in. The chamber, though, held the clammy, damp stink of the dungeons, and was lit only by a high barred window. I looked at the bare flagstones and thought how Mistress Askew had lain there in agony after her torture.

Two men lay silent on the beds. Philip Coleswyn got up at once. He was in his robe; the shirt collar above his doublet untied, his normally neat brown hair and beard untidy. Edward Cotterstoke turned to look at me but did not rise. At the inspection of the painting I had marked his resemblance to his sister, not only physically but in his haughty, angry manner. Today, though, he looked frightened, and more than that, haunted. He was dressed only in his shirt and hose. From those protuberant blue eyes, so like Isabel's, he regarded me with a lost, hopeless stare. Behind me the door slammed shut and a key turned.

Philip said, 'Dear Heaven, Matthew! I heard you were being brought in. Isabel Slanning must have done this – '

'What have they told you?'

'Only that we are to appear before the Privy Council tomorrow, on heresy charges. I was taken by the constable at dawn, as was Master Cotterstoke.'

'So was I. It makes no sense. I am no heretic.'

Philip sat on the bed, wiping his brow. 'I know. Yet I – ' he lowered his voice – 'I have had reason to fear. But I have been careful not to speak heresy in public. Edward, too.'

'And your vicar? Has he spoken carelessly?'

'Not to my knowledge. If he had, surely he would have been arrested, too.'

I nodded at the sense of this. 'The only thing that connects the three of us is that wretched case.'

Edward, from his bed, spoke softly. 'Isabel has undone us all.' Then to my surprise he curled up his legs and lay hunched on the bed, like a child. It was a strange thing to see in a grown man.

Philip shook his head. 'I fear you have been caught up in this because of suspicions against me and Edward.'

'But Isabel's conspiracy charge is ridiculous, easily disproved! Surely we would not be hauled before the council on Isabel's word alone. Unless,' I took a deep breath, 'unless her complaint is being used by someone else, someone who wishes to see me undone.'

Philip frowned. 'Who?'

'I do not know. But Philip, I have been involved, perhaps against my better judgement, in matters of state. I could have enemies on the Privy Council. But friends, too, powerful friends. Why would I be attacked now?' My mind was in a whirl. Could this be the moment after all when whoever was the holder of the *Lamentation* had decided to expose it? And question me about the hunt to find it? I had never spoken with the Queen or Lord Parr about what we would do with the *Lamentation* should we recover it; but I knew Lord Parr would almost certainly have the book destroyed. To ensure the King never saw it.

'Listen.' I grasped his arm. 'Have you ever specifically denied the Real Presence of Christ's body and blood in the Mass to someone who might have reported it?' I spoke quietly, lest a guard be listening at the door.

Philip spread his arms wide. 'Given what has happened this summer? Of course not.'

'And you, sir – ' I turned to Edward, still curled up on his bed –

'have you said anything that could be dangerous? Have you kept forbidden books?'

He looked at me. 'I have spoken no heresy, and I handed in my books last month.' He spoke wearily, as though it did not matter.

I turned to Philip. 'Then we must cleave to that, and tell the council the accusations against us are false. If someone is trying to use Isabel's accusations to get at me, we must show them up as nonsense.' I remembered, my heart sinking, how Treasurer Rowland had avoided making an early appointment with me to discuss Isabel's accusations further. Had someone got to him?

Edward sat up, and with great weariness, as though his body were made of lead, leaned back against the stone-flagged wall. He said, 'This is the vengeance of the Lord. Isabel is his instrument. It was all foreordained. Given what I have done, I cannot be saved. I am damned. All my life has been a fraud. I have lived in pride and ignorance – '

I looked at Philip. 'What does he mean?'

Philip spoke quietly, 'Two days ago I confronted him with what the servant Vowell told us. He thinks this is a judgement on him. He told me that he did indeed kill his father.'

'So it was true.'

Philip nodded despairingly.

Then we all jumped at the sound of keys in the door. The guard held it open. I was overjoyed to see Barak step inside. Beside him, carrying a large bundle, was Josephine. She looked terrified. With them came Coleswyn's wife, Ethelreda, with whom I had dined that fateful evening when Isabel surprised us. She, too, was clutching a bundle. Her face looked ghastly, her hood askew. 'Ten minutes,' the guard said, and slammed the door on us.

Barak spoke, his gruff tone belying the worry on his face. 'So, you've landed yourself here again. Josephine insisted on coming. Nicholas wanted to come too, but I wouldn't let him. State he's been in, he'd probably break down and start crying like a big girl.'

'He'd come at you with his sword if he heard that,' I said. In the midst of this horror, Barak had made me laugh for a second. I turned to Josephine. 'Thank you for coming, my dear.'

She gulped. 'I – I wanted to.'

'I am grateful.'

'She insisted,' Barak said. 'Brought a great pile of food for you.'

'Does Tamasin know what has happened?'

'In her condition? You must be fucking joking. Thank God when Josephine came to the house she had the sense to ask to speak to me on her own; Tammy thinks there's some crisis on at chambers. What the hell's happening?'

'I don't know. Isabel – '

I broke off at the sound of an angry voice. Ethelreda was leaning over Edward Cotterstoke, berating him angrily. 'Answer me, sir. Why did you tell the Tower authorities your wife and children were not to be admitted under any circumstances? I have had your good lady at my house; she weeps and weeps, it is cruel.'

Edward answered in a miserable voice. 'It is best my wife and the children never see me again. I am an unclean thing.'

Ethelreda stared at him, then at her husband. 'Has he gone mad?'

Philip looked at his client sorrowfully. 'Leave him, my love.' He sat on the bed and pulled her down to sit beside him. They clung together.

I spoke to Barak, urgently. 'Listen, I want you to go to Whitehall Palace, get a message to Lord Parr.'

He answered impatiently, 'I've just come from there. I got a wherry as soon as Josephine brought the news. I knew that was what you'd want. But they wouldn't let me in. It's chaos at the Common Stairs, stuff being moved out by the boatload, to Greenwich for when the King meets the admiral, and to Hampton Court where they're all moving afterwards. They wouldn't even tell me whether Lord Parr was there.'

'The Queen – '

'I tried that one, too. The guards didn't want to know. All I got was, "The Queen is not here. The Queen is going to Hampton

Court.''' He took a deep breath. 'It strikes me your friends in high places have abandoned you.'

'No!' I answered fiercely. 'Lord Parr perhaps, but never the Queen. Besides, this matter could have implications for them. There's no rumour of anything having happened to the Queen, is there?' I asked anxiously.

'No.'

'Listen, I will write a message. Get it to the Queen's servant, Mary Odell.' I spoke feverishly. 'Find out whether she is at Whitehall still or Hampton Court, and get it to her. Tell the guards they will be in trouble with the Queen if the message does not reach her.'

Barak had brought quill and ink, anticipating my request. I scribbled a note explaining what had happened and addressed it to Mary Odell. 'Seal it at chambers,' I told Barak. 'They like a seal. But for God's sake, hurry.'

'I'll try,' he said, but his tone was not hopeful.

The guard opened the door again. 'Time's up,' he said brusquely. Barak and Josephine went out with Ethelreda; she was weeping, and Josephine, though trembling herself, supported her. The door slammed shut again.

✝

I SAT BESIDE PHILIP on his bed and looked at Edward. I feared the state he was in, what he might blurt out when brought before the council. He was sitting up now, his head bowed. I whispered to Philip, 'He told you he killed his stepfather?'

Philip nodded sadly. Edward had heard me, despite my lowered voice, and looked up, still with that expression of despair. 'Yes, I killed him, a man who was guilty of nothing, and I must answer to God for it. I have hidden the truth from myself and the world for forty years, blamed Isabel for everything, but now the secret is discovered I must answer for it along with her. Somewhere in my heart I always knew this time would come.'

'What happened, Master Cotterstoke, all those years ago?' I needed to try and reach this shocked and devastated man.

He was silent a moment, then said quietly, 'Our father was a good man. Isabel and I were always quarrelling, but though it merely annoyed our mother, our dear father would always settle things between us, bring us round. He was our rock. When he died, the sorrow, for Isabel and me — ' He shook his head, fell silent.

'And then your mother married again?' I prompted.

'When our father had not been in his grave a year.' I heard a touch of the old anger in his voice now. 'Another few months and her belly was swelling with a new child. She fawned on Peter Cotterstoke, ignoring Isabel and me. How we hated him.' He looked at me. 'Have you brothers or sisters, sir?'

'No, but I have seen families broken by hatreds before. Too many times.'

Edward shook his head sadly. 'Children — their minds can encompass such wickedness, such depravity. We were sure Peter Cotterstoke would give everything to his new child and disinherit us. Though we had no evidence.' He shook his head. 'We started by doing little things, stealing possessions of his and destroying them. Sometimes the idea was mine, more often Isabel's.' He shook his head. 'We got bolder; we burnt a book he valued — in a field, dancing round the little fire we made, tossing in the illuminated pages one by one. We were wicked, wicked.'

'You were but children,' I said.

He looked back at me bleakly. 'We tried to poison him. Not to kill him, not then; just to make him sick. But he was ill, very ill. We thought we would be discovered, but he never suspected us.' He shook his head sorrowfully. But your mother did, I thought, and watched for her husband. But not close enough.

Edward went on in that flat, toneless voice. 'Always Isabel and I kept a mask of loving childishness before him, and he did not see through it. We used to giggle at his innocence. And then Isabel had the idea of killing him. To secure that inheritance, and gain vengeance. For depriving us — as we had persuaded ourselves — of our inheritance.' He closed his eyes. 'And for not being our dear father, whose place no man could take.' A tear coursed down Edward's lined cheek. In that house, I thought, there was no reminder of their real father save that wall painting, no one left whom they trusted, whom they could talk to. Some children make friends among the servants, but I guessed neither Edward nor Isabel had been that sort of child. They had driven each other slowly but steadily into a kind of madness.

Edward continued, 'We talked of all sorts of plans to kill him secretly, but could not think of one that might work. I truly believe I never intended to match the word to the deed, though perhaps Isabel did. Then that day on the wharf — Peter Cotterstoke looking out over the river, right on the edge of the wharf; Isabel whispering in my ear that now was our chance. The tide was full and the water cold, he would not be able to climb out. It took only one push from behind, and I was a big boy, tall for my age.' He lowered his head. 'Strange, it was only afterwards that we realized what we had done. Murder. Isabel took charge, decided we must say we had left our stepfather at the wharf.'

Philip said, 'And no one could prove otherwise.'

'And then — then we learned he had not planned to disinherit us at all.' Edward hid his face in his hands, his voice scarcely audible. 'Mother suspected, somehow. Afterwards she could not stand the sight of us, got both of us out of the house as soon as she could. She had no interest in my family, her grandchildren. And that Will she made — ' He broke off.

I said, 'Her revenge.'

He shook his head. 'Yes. I see it now. I never thought Vowell had guessed, even on the day of the inspection when he was so upset. I have been blind, blind for so long.' He made a fist of his hand and banged it against his forehead.

I said quietly, 'All these years, you and Isabel have blamed each other, because it was easier than facing the truth.'

Edward nodded dumbly. 'A truth too terrible to bear.'

'In a way, all this time you have still been conspiring together, each determined to avoid your share of the blame.' It was a strange, turn-about thought.

'After it was done, I blamed her for pressing me to do it, while she said she never intended me to actually push him, it was just play-acting. We ceased speaking. But, in truth, it was both our sin. Though I hid it even from the sight of the Lord when I came to true faith. But He knew, and now He has His just vengeance.'

I did not reply. At law, both Edward and Isabel were guilty of murder. An open confession from either would see both hang, even now. I thought of their mother, suspecting all these years what her children had done, unable to prove anything but hating them. I took a deep breath. 'What will you do now, Master Cotterstoke?'

He shook his head. 'I will confess. That is what the Lord commands.'

I spoke carefully. 'You understand that your being brought before the Privy Council has nothing to do with your stepfather. It is about heresy. If you have not spoken heresy, it may be that you and Brother Coleswyn are being used to get at me.'

He stared at me with genuine puzzlement. 'I thought this arrest was concerned somehow with — with what we did. Though, yes, they did say heresy. But I could not understand why we were brought here, why the Privy Council should be involved.' He frowned. 'Why would the Privy Council have an interest in you, sir?' I noted with relief that he looked attentive as well as puzzled. I had brought him back to the real world, at least for now.

'Because I have been involved in — political matters,' I said carefully. 'I may have made enemies on the traditionalist side.'

'Those rogues! Lost and condemned by God I may be now, but I am not so far fallen that I do not still revile those enemies of faith.' A look of angry pride appeared on his face.

'Then for all our sakes, Master Cotterstoke, when they ask you at the council tomorrow whether you have ever publicly condemned the Mass, tell them the truth, that you have not.'

'In my heart, I have.'

'It is what you *say* that could burn you. Keep your beliefs locked in your heart, I beg you.'

Philip nodded. 'Yes, Edward, he is right.'

'But what we did, Isabel and I – '

'Leave that until after, Edward. After.'

Edward's face worked as he thought. But then he said, 'If I am asked about my stepfather's murder, I must tell the truth. But if I am not, I will say nothing.' He looked hard at Philip. 'Afterwards, though, I must pay for my sins.' I thought, he is a strong man, hard and tough like his sister. And indeed it must have taken a strange, perverted strength of mind for him and Isabel to each blame every-thing on the other, for forty years.

✝

AFTER THAT THE HOURS hung heavy. Philip persuaded Edward to pray with him, and they spent a long time murmuring in the corner, asking God for strength, and afterwards talking of the pos-sibility of salvation in the next world for Edward if he publicly confessed his crime. At one point they discussed Isabel's cleaving to the old ways in religion, and I heard Edward's voice rise again, calling her an obstinate woman with a cankered heart, in those cadences of self-righteousness and self-pity so familiar to me from the time I had spent with his sister. I thought, if Edward confesses, Isabel, too, is undone.

The barred window above us allowed a square of sunlight into the room, and I watched it travel slowly across the walls, marking the pas-sage of the afternoon. Edward and Philip ended their talk, and Philip insisted we eat some of the food that our visitors had brought.

Evening was come and the square of light fading fast when the guard returned with a note for me. I opened it eagerly, watched by Philip and Edward. It was from Barak.

I returned to Whitehall, and managed to persuade the guard to admit me to the Queen's Presence Chamber. The Queen has left for Hampton Court, with most of her servants, Mistress Odell, too, it seems. Workmen were removing the tapestries, watched by some sort of female fool or jester with a duck on a leash; when the guard asked if she knew where Mistress Odell was she said Hampton Court, and when he said I brought a message from you she turned and made childish faces at me. I got the guard to ensure the note is forwarded. I am sorry, I could do no more.

Jane Fool, I thought, who had taken against me so fiercely. I put down the note. 'No news. But my message has been forwarded to – an important person.'

Edward looked at me with incomprehension, as though this were all happening to someone else; he had retreated inside himself again. Philip said nothing and lowered his head.

☦

IT WAS A LONG, LONG NIGHT. I slept fitfully, waking several times, tormented by fleas and lice that had been drawn from the bedding. I think Philip slept badly too; once I woke to hear him praying softly, too quietly for me to make out the words. As for Edward, the first time I woke he was snoring, but the next time I saw the glint of his open eyes, staring despairingly into the dark.

Chapter Forty-three

THEY SAT IN A LONG ROW behind a table covered with green velvet, six members of the King's Privy Council, the supreme body answerable to him for the administration of the realm. All wore the finest robes, gold chains and jewelled caps. Philip Coleswyn and Edward Cotterstoke and I were given seats facing them, the three Tower guards who had brought us in taking places behind us. My heart pounded as I thought, this was where Anne Askew had sat, and many others as well these last few months, to answer the same charge of heresy.

Sir Thomas Wriothesley, Lord Chancellor of England, waved a beringed hand in front of his face. 'God's death, they stink of the Tower gaol. I've said before, can people not be washed before they are brought here?' I looked at him, remembering his fear at Anne Askew's burning that the gunpowder round the necks of the condemned might hurt the great men of the realm when it exploded. Nor did I forget that he had tortured Anne Askew together with Rich. He caught me looking at him and glared at my presumption, fixing me with cold green little pebble eyes.

All the councillors had documents before them, but Sir William Paget, sitting at the centre of the table in his usual dark silken robe, had a veritable mound of paperwork. The square pale face above the long dark beard was cold, the thin-lipped mouth severe.

On Paget's left sat Wriothesley, then Richard Rich. Rich's face was expressionless. He had made a steeple of his slim white fingers and looked down, his grey eyes hooded. Next to him Bishop Stephen Gardiner, in cassock and stole, made a complete contrast. With his heavy build and powerful features, he was all force and aggression. He laid broad, hairy hands on the table and leaned forward, inspecting us with fierce, deep-set eyes. The council's leading traditionalist, with his supporters Wriothesley and Rich beside him. I wondered if he had known of Anne Askew's torture.

Two other councillors sat to Paget's right. One I hoped was a friend: Edward Seymour, Lord Hertford, tall and slim, his face and body all sharp angles. He was sitting upright. I sensed a watchful anger in him and I hoped that if it emerged it would be to our advantage. Beside him sat a slim man, lightly bearded, with auburn hair and a prominent nose. I recognized the Queen's brother, William Parr, Earl of Essex, from my visit to Baynard's Castle. My heart rose a little on seeing him: he owed his place at the council table to his sister. Surely if she were in trouble today he would not be here. His presence made up a little for the absence of the figure I had hoped most of all to see – Archbishop Cranmer, counterweight to Gardiner. But Cranmer, whose attendance at the council was said always to be motivated by strategy, had stayed away.

Paget picked up the first paper on his pile. He ran his hard eyes over us, the slab face still expressionless, then intoned, 'Let us begin.'

✝

WE HAD BEEN BROUGHT to Whitehall Palace by boat. The Privy Council followed the King as he moved between his palaces, and I had thought we might be taken on to Hampton Court, but apparently the council was still meeting at Whitehall. First thing that morning the three of us, red-eyed, tousled and, as Wriothesley noted, smelly, were led to a boat and rowed upriver.

At the Common Stairs there had been a great bustle, as Barak had described; servants were moving everything out. A little procession of laden boats was already sculling upriver to Hampton Court. I saw huge pots and vats from the royal kitchen being carried to one boat and thrown in with a clanging that reverberated across the water. Meanwhile a long tapestry wound in cloth was being lifted carefully into another waiting boat by half a dozen servants. A black-robed clerk stood at the end of the pier, ticking everything off on papers fixed to a little portable desk hung round his neck.

One of our guards said to the boatman, 'Go in by the Royal Stairs. It's too busy here.'

I looked at my companions. Philip sat composed, hands on his lap. He caught my eye. 'Courage, Brother,' he said with a quick smile. It was what I had said to him when he grew faint at Anne Askew's burning. I nodded in acknowledgement. Edward Cotterstoke stared vacantly at the great facade of polished windows, his face like chalk. It was as though the full seriousness of his position had only just sunk in.

The boat halted at the long pavilion at the end of the Royal Stairs, green-and-white Tudor flags fluttering on the roof. We climbed stone steps thick with the dirty green moss of the river, then a door in the pavilion was opened by a guard and we were led into the long gallery connecting the boathouse to the palace, fitted out with tapestries of river scenes. We were hustled along the full length of the pavilion, past more servants carrying household goods, then into the palace itself. We found ourselves in a place I recognized, the vestibule which formed the juncture of the Royal Stairs with three other sets of double doors, all guarded. I remembered that one led to the Queen's Gallery, the second to the Queen's privy lodgings and the third to the King's. It was the third door which was now opened to us by the guards. A servant carrying a decorated vase almost as large as himself nearly collided with me as he emerged, and one of our guards cursed him. We were marched quickly to a small door, the lintel decorated with elaborate scrollwork, and told we would wait inside until the council was ready. It was a bare little chamber stripped of furniture, but with a magnificent view of the gardens. A few minutes later an inner door opened and we were called into the council chamber itself.

✝

PAGET BEGAN BY GETTING each of us to confirm our names and swear on a Testament to tell the truth before God, as though we were in court. They had that power. Then he said, with a note of heavy reproval which, I suspected from long dealings with judges, was intended to intimidate us, 'You are all charged with heresy, denial of the Real Presence of the body and blood of Christ in the Mass, under the Act of 1539. What do you say?'

'Sirs,' I said, surprised by the strength in my own voice, 'I am no heretic.'

Philip answered with a lawyer's care, 'I have never breached the Act.'

Edward Cotterstoke closed his eyes and I wondered if he might collapse. But he opened them again, looked straight at Paget, and said quietly, 'Nor I.'

Bishop Gardiner leaned across the table, pointing a stubby finger at me. 'Master Shardlake uses words similar to those his former master Cromwell employed when he was arrested at this very table. I remember.' He gave a contemptuous laugh. 'Parliament found differently. And so may the City of London court, if we decide to send them there!'

Paget glanced at Gardiner, raising a hand. The Bishop sat back, scowling, and Paget said, more mildly, 'We have a couple of questions which apply only to you, Master Shardlake.'

He nodded to Wriothesley, who leaned forward, his little red beard jutting forward aggressively. 'I understand you were recently sworn to the Queen's Learned Council.'

'Yes, Lord Chancellor. Temporarily.'

'Why?'

I took a deep breath. 'To investigate the theft of a most precious ring from the Queen's chambers. Bequeathed to her majesty by her late stepdaughter, Margaret Neville.' I was horribly aware that I was lying through my teeth. But to do otherwise meant revealing what I had actually been looking for and causing grave danger to others. I glanced at Lord Hertford and William Parr. Neither returned my look. I swallowed and my heart quickened. I had feared the floor might seem to tremble and shake beneath me but it had not, yet.

'A rare and precious object,' Wriothesley said, a note of mockery in his voice. 'But you have not found it?'

'No, my lord. And so I have resigned my position.'

Wriothesley nodded, the little red beard bobbing up and down. 'I understand there have been several sudden vacancies in the Queen's household. Two senior guards, a carpenter, Master Cecil who now serves the Earl of Hertford. Most mysterious.' He shrugged. I wondered whether he was fishing or had just noted these changes and wondered if they were more than coincidence.

Then Richard Rich spoke, looking not at me but down at his clasped hands. 'Lord Chancellor, these domestic matters are not part of the accusations. Master Shardlake has advised the Queen on legal matters for several years.' Rich turned to look at Wriothesley. I realized with relief that his own involvement in my investigations meant it was in his interests to help me. Wriothesley looked puzzled by his intervention.

Gardiner knitted his thick black brows further, glowering at Rich. 'If this man – ' he waved at me – 'and his confederates are under a charge of heresy, any links to her majesty must surely concern this council.'

Lord Hertford spoke up suddenly, sharply. 'Should we not first find whether they are guilty of anything? Before turning to subjects the King wishes closed.' He emphasized his words by leaning over and returning Gardiner's fierce stare.

The Bishop looked set to argue, but Paget raised a hand. 'Lord Hertford is right. In the discussions over whether this matter should be included in today's agenda, we agreed only to ask these men whether they had breached the Act. The evidence before us relates solely to that question.'

'Flimsy as it is,' William Parr said. 'I do not understand why this case has been brought before us at all.'

I looked between them. Someone had wanted the charge of heresy against us to be put on the council agenda. But who? And why? To frighten me, assess me, to see me condemned? To try and get at the Queen through me? Which of them was accusing me of heresy? Gardiner was the most obvious candidate, but I knew how complicated the web of enmities and alliances around this table had become. I glanced quickly at my companions. Philip remained composed, though pale. Edward sat upright and attentive now, some colour back in his cheeks. Mention of the Queen had probably brought back to him what I had told him in the Tower, that this interrogation might concern the religious factions on the council. In this regard at least, whatever his dreadful turmoil of mind, Edward would try to serve the radical cause.

'Then let us get straight to the point,' Gardiner said reluctantly. 'First, have any of you possessed books forbidden under the King's proclamation? Philip Coleswyn?'

Philip returned his gaze. 'Yes, my Lord, but all were handed in under the terms of his majesty's gracious amnesty.'

'You, Edward Cotterstoke?'

He answered quietly, 'The same.'

Gardiner turned to me. 'But you, Master Shardlake, I believe you did not hand in any books.' So I had been right: they kept a list.

I said evenly, 'I had none. A search was made of my house when I was arrested yesterday morning, and nothing can have been found, because I had nothing.'

Gardiner gave a nasty little half-smile, and I wondered for a dreadful moment whether a forbidden book had been planted in the house; such things were not unknown. But he said only, 'Did you ever possess books forbidden under the Proclamation?'

'Yes, my Lord Bishop. I destroyed them before the amnesty expired.'

'So,' Gardiner said triumphantly, 'he admits he had heretical books that were not handed in. I know, Master Shardlake, that you were seen burning books in your garden.'

I stared at him. That was a shock. Only Timothy had been at the house that day, and he had been in the stables. Moreover he would never have reported it. I remembered his frantic anger when they had come to arrest me the day before. I answered quietly, 'I preferred to destroy them. The proclamation declared only that it was illegal to keep books from the list after the amnesty expired. And I have had none since before that date.'

Wriothesley looked at me. 'Burning books rather than handing them in surely indicates reluctance to draw your opinions to the attention of the authorities.'

'That is pure supposition. It was never said that a list would be kept.'

Paget gave a tight smile; he was a lawyer too, and appreciated this point, though Gardiner said scoffingly, 'Lawyer's quibble,' and glowered at me. I wondered, why this ferocious aggression? Did it betray his desperation to find a heretic linked to the Queen?

Lord Hertford leaned forward again. 'No, my Lord, it is not a quibble. It is the law.'

William Parr nodded agreement vigorously. 'The law.'

I looked along the row: enemies to the left of Paget; friends, I hoped, to the right. Paget himself remained inscrutable as he said, 'Master Shardlake has the right of it, I think. It is time we turned to the main matter.' He reached into his pile and pulled out some more papers, handing three sheets to each of us in turn across the table, his hard unblinking eyes briefly meeting mine. 'Members of the council have copies of these letters. They concern a complaint by a former client of Master Shardlake, Mistress Isabel Slanning, sister of Master Cotterstoke here. We have called her as a witness today.' He turned to one of the guards. 'Bring her in.'

One of the guards left. Edward's face twisted briefly; a horrible, tortured look. Gardiner, taking it for guilt, exchanged a wolfish smile with Wriothesley.

I looked at the papers. Copies of three letters. Isabel's original complaint to Rowland, accusing me of conspiring with Edward and Philip to defeat her case. A reply from Rowland, short and sharp as I had expected, saying there was no evidence whatever of collusion, and pointing out that unsupported accusations of heresy were seriously defamatory.

It was the third letter, Isabel's reply, that was dangerous. It was dated a week before and was, by her standards, short.

> Master Treasurer,
> I have received your letter saying that my allegations of collusion between Master Shardlake, Master Coleswyn, and my brother, to defeat my just claims, are unsubstantiated. On the contrary, they are just, and the heresy of these men clear and patent. Master Shardlake, taking farewell of Master Coleswyn after going to his house for dinner, said in my hearing that the way to salvation is through prayer and the Bible, not the Mass. I am sending a copy of this letter to his majesty's Privy Council, so the heresy of these men may be investigated.

So that was why Rowland had been avoiding me: he wanted no association with matters of heresy if they became official. I had been concerned that Isabel had overheard Coleswyn's words on the night of the dinner. Yet she had misremembered or falsified what happened: that evening Philip had adjured me to pray and study the Bible, as the only sure path to salvation. I had made no reply. And neither of us had mentioned the Mass. What Philip had said marked him as a radical reformer but not a heretic; just as, from what I had been told was contained in the *Lamentation*, the Queen's views marked her. They were risky views to express, but not illegal. I frowned. Paget's office must receive a dozen such letters a week, written from malice by quarrelling family members, former lovers, business enemies. At most, the accuser would be questioned by an official from the council. Why indeed had such nonsense been brought here?

Another door opened and Isabel, dressed in her finery as usual, entered. Behind her came the tall, black-robed figure of Vincent Dyrick. He looked uneasy.

Edward stared at his sister, a long, unfathomable look. Isabel, whose expression a moment before had been haughty as always, seemed to quail a little at the sight of these great men. She glanced quickly at her brother, who only stared back at her stonily. Then she curtsied. Dyrick bowed, rising to look at the men behind the table, his eyes scared, calculating slits.

Hertford said bluntly, 'It is not customary for those brought before the Privy Council to be allowed lawyers.'

Paget answered firmly, 'Two of the accused are lawyers themselves. In the circumstances it is reasonable to allow the witness her legal representative.'

I looked at the Secretary, the King's Master of Practices; it was still impossible to discern whose side he was on. But someone had made a miscalculation if he thought Vincent Dyrick would help Isabel. He was obviously here under pressure; he was not a man who would willingly appear before such a powerful group to plead a pack of nonsense.

Paget addressed Dyrick. 'We have been discussing the correspondence. You have copies?'

'We do. And Mistress Slanning knows them by heart.' That I could imagine.

Paget grunted, and looked at Isabel. 'You say there was a conspiracy between these three men to cheat you, motivated by their being heretics?'

Isabel turned to Dyrick. 'You must answer yourself, mistress,' he said quietly.

She swallowed, then replied, hesitantly at first but with growing confidence. 'Master Coleswyn and my brother attend the same church, where the preacher is known to be radical. Coleswyn and Master Shardlake dine together, and once I heard them speaking heresy afterwards. And Master Shardlake knowingly chose an expert who would look at my painting and undermine my case.' She was speaking rapidly now. I wondered, could she actually believe what she was saying? I knew from experience how people could twist facts to suit what they wanted to believe, but this was a very dangerous forum for such self-delusion. She continued, 'Edward will do anything to thwart my case, he is wicked, wicked – '

Edward answered, quietly, 'No more than you.'

Paget glanced at him sharply. 'What is that supposed to mean?'

Philip spoke up. 'Only that the conflict between my client and his sister goes back to events when they were children.' Isabel's face took on an expression of fear as she realized that Philip had just referred obliquely to what she and Edward had done near half a century before – and that he might refer to it openly now. Her face paled, the wrinkled flesh seeming to sink. She looked terrified.

'And this expert?' Paget looked at Dyrick.

'His name is Master Simon Adam, an expert on house construction. My client says there are – rumours – that he may have radical sympathies.'

'More than rumours,' Isabel said boldly. 'A friend told me her servant knew the family – '

'That is third-hand hearsay,' I said flatly.

Isabel turned to Dyrick for support. He was silent. Edward Seymour said, 'Master Shardlake advised you to pick this Master Adam?'

Isabel hesitated, then said, with obvious reluctance, 'No. But I asked him for a list of experts. This man's name was first on the list. He put it first so I should pick it, I am sure.'

'Mistress Slanning insisted on my providing a list of experts, and chose Master Adam against my advice.' Could she really be misremembering what had happened to this extent? Looking at her, I realized she could.

And then William Parr, Earl of Essex, did something which shifted the whole balance of the interrogation. He laughed. 'Sound choice,' he said. 'Nobody comes before Adam, not since the world began.'

Hertford and Rich laughed too, and a wintry smile lifted the corner of Paget's mouth. Isabel's face was like chalk. Gardiner, however, banged his fist on the table. 'This is no matter for levity. What of the heresy spoken among these men?'

Philip said, clear and steady, 'My Lords, there was no heresy. And it was not Master Shardlake who spoke the words referred to in Mistress Slanning's letter. It was I, as I took farewell of him at my door.' I gave him a glance of gratitude. 'And I did not mention, let alone argue against, the Real Presence.'

'Well, madam? Is that right?' Edward Seymour asked sharply.

Isabel looked genuinely confused. 'I thought – I thought it was Master Shardlake who spoke about the Bible, but it may have been Master Coleswyn. Yes, yes, I think it was.' For a second she looked embarrassed, but rallied. 'Either way, those were the words.'

'And the Mass?' Paget asked.

'I – I thought they said that. I am sure – I thought – ' Flustered, she turned to Dyrick, but he said flatly, 'You were there, madam, not me.' Isabel looked at him, helpless for once in her life. She began to tremble. It was known that Dyrick would take on anyone as a client, the more blindly aggressive the better. But Isabel Slanning had proved too wild a card even for him.

Then Rich said, his voice contemptuous, 'This woman is wasting our time.'

Gardiner glared at him again, then said to Philip, 'But you did speak those words about faith coming through study of the Bible, and prayer?'

'Yes. But that is no heresy.'

Blustering now, Gardiner went on, 'All know the King mislikes this endless talking over religion. As he said in his speech to Parliament last Christmas, though the Word of God in English is allowed, it is only to be used for men to inform their consciences.'

'And that is what Master Shardlake and I were doing, informing our consciences.' Philip looked at Isabel. 'Rather it is Mistress Slanning who makes light use of God's Word, to further her personal quarrels.'

He had spoken well, and left a silence behind him. After a moment Wriothesley said to him, 'You swear neither of you denied the Real Presence when you met?'

'I did not,' I answered.

'Nor I,' Philip said.

Paget looked at Isabel. 'What were you doing at Master Cole-swyn's house that evening, Mistress Slanning? You were not at the dinner?'

She swallowed. 'I see it as my duty, when I suspect heresy, to watch and wait for it. That I may inform the authorities.'

'You spied on them,' Lord Hertford said flatly.

Paget leaned forward, his voice hard. 'Yet you did not see fit to inform the authorities of this alleged collaboration between heretics until the Lincoln's Inn Treasurer rejected your accusations.'

'I – I did not think at first. I was so angry at my brother's lawyer conspiring with mine – ' She looked at Edward, who stared at her strangely, his expression blank yet intense.

William Parr said, 'Is it not manifestly clear to all that this woman's claims are those of an ill-natured litigant – unfounded, motivated by mere spite – and that these men are guilty of nothing?'

Lord Paget looked between us, then inclined his head. 'Yes. I think it is. Mistress Slanning, you are a vicious and vexatious creature. You have wasted our time.' Isabel gasped, fighting now to control her emotions. Paget turned to us. 'Gentlemen, we will discuss this a little further between ourselves. All of you wait outside until council business is finished.' He made a signal to the guards and we were led away.

✝

WE WERE RETURNED to the room where we had waited before. As soon as the door was closed I spoke to Philip in heartfelt tones. 'Well done, and thank you. You answered well.'

He replied sorrowfully, 'One must speak more with the wisdom of the serpent than the innocence of the dove, where matters of faith are concerned. Jesus Christ said so.' He looked at me. 'Do you think we will be released now?'

'I have every hope. Isabel made a fool of herself. We are lucky I have friends on the council, and Rich has his own reasons not to see me brought down. Paget, too, seemed won over to our side.'

'Yes.' He frowned. 'Gardiner and Wriothesley would have taken the chance to examine us further about our beliefs, which for me at least would have been – a concern.'

Edward had sat down on the windowsill, his back to the magnificent view of the river, and put his head in his hands. I said to him, 'You did well too, sir.'

He looked up. It was as though all the energy had drained from him once more; he seemed again the exhausted, tormented figure of the day before. He spoke quietly, 'You told me I must stand firm, lest they use these allegations to build a case against the Queen's friends. But now it is over – the other matter remains: what Isabel and I did.' He looked at Philip. 'And I know I must pay.'

Before Philip could answer, the door opened. Richard Rich entered. He looked at Philip and Edward, who stood hastily. 'You two,' he snapped, 'outside. Wait in the corridor with the guards. I want to talk to Shardlake.'

Philip and Edward did as he ordered. Rich pushed the door shut and turned to me. His face wore a strange expression, half-admiring, half-angry. 'Well, Master Shardlake, you got out of that one. With my help. It was a strange thing to give it, sitting between Wriothesley and Gardiner, who, knowing our history, thought I would be glad to see you burned.' He laughed mirthlessly. 'A strange feeling.'

I looked back at him. He deserved no thanks, for like Dyrick he had sought only to protect his own skin. I kept my voice low. 'Who wanted that matter brought before the Council, Sir Richard? Normally such a silly accusation would surely not have gone there? And why? Was it to do with the Queen? Gardiner said—'

Rich waved a hand dismissively. 'Gardiner seizes every chance that comes his way to take a tilt at the Queen. He's wasting his time; he should realize by now that ship has sailed.' Rich took off his cap, revealing his thick grey hair. 'But you are right about it being silly, and I have been trying to find out who pressed for it to be included on the council agenda. I was not consulted. Paget decides, on the basis of advice from many quarters. I dare not press the matter too closely.' His thin face was momentarily pinched with worry, reminding me how he had looked at Anne Askew's burning. How he must dread her book appearing on the streets.

'So it could have been anybody?'

'Gardiner, Wriothesley, the Duke of Norfolk, though he was not present today – anyone – ' His voice rose angrily. 'Lord Hertford, for all I know. He and his brother Thomas were with Paget yesterday, and shouting was heard, I know that.'

'But Hertford is on the reformist side. He helped me.'

'He seemed to, I grant you. But on the council people may take one line in public and another in private.' Rich's voice lowered to an angry whisper. 'The Parrs and Seymours would both like the Regency of little Edward when the King dies, and Seymour and his brother quarrel constantly. Sir Thomas Seymour thinks he should have a place on the Privy Council, but the King knows he has not the ability. More knives are sharpened every week.' He gave me a look of hatred. 'And as for my private feelings, do not think I will help you again, crook-back. Unless it is in my own interest. I *would* gladly see you burned. And watch with pleasure.'

I smiled wryly. 'I have never doubted that, Sir Richard.'

'Then we understand each other.' He bit off the words. 'Now, the council says you can go, the guards will take you out.' Then, with those grey eyes burning, he said, 'You have been lucky. If you have any sense left you will keep well away from here. Do not think the time of crisis is over.' Then, in an undertone – more to himself than me – he added, 'Of late sometimes I have wished I, too, could run like a rabbit.'

Chapter Forty-four

W E WERE LED TO THE Common Stairs. The guards got into their boat, leaving us in the midst of all the removals. As a large, ornate cabinet was heaved out of the door by four men a drawer fell open and a little mouse jumped out onto the landing stage. It stood for a moment in the forest of legs, not knowing where to run, till someone saw it and kicked it into the river.

I managed to hail a passing wherry. We sculled downriver, away from Whitehall; I hoped for ever. The three of us sat in silence, still recovering from our ordeal. I noticed a tear on Edward's cheeks: he was weeping, silently. The boatman looked between us curiously.

I spoke quietly to Philip. 'Can you look after him?'

'I will take him to my home, do what I can.' He looked sadly at his client. 'Will you come with me, Edward?'

Edward looked at him. 'Yes,' he whispered. 'I know what must be done now.' He shook his head in anguish. 'The disgrace, the disgrace to my wife and children.'

'We can talk about that later. When you are rested. About what God requires of you.'

He shook his head violently. 'I shall never rest again. I do not deserve it.'

I said to Philip, 'I must go to my house.' I needed to speak to Timothy; I could not imagine that he had betrayed me, but I must know.

We rounded the bend in the river. In the distance, past the riverside houses and the docks, the square solid shape of the Tower was visible. I turned away.

✝

I FOUND TIMOTHY AT his accustomed place in the stables, sitting on an upturned pail eating bread and cheese. He jumped up as I entered, astonishment and relief on his face. 'Sir! Thank the Lord you are back! We thought you—' He broke off.

I stood, weary and dishevelled, looking down at him. 'I am released,' I said quietly.

'We none of us knew why – '

'I have been questioned by the King's Privy Council. Do you know how serious that is?'

'All know that,' he answered quietly.

'It was, among other things, about an allegation that I owned forbidden books.'

Timothy stepped backwards, his eyes widening, and my heart sank as I began to believe that, after all, he had given me up. But I kept my voice low. 'Do you remember an afternoon, about three weeks ago, when Martin and Agnes and Josephine were out? I told you to turn visitors away, as there was something I needed to do.'

He backed away another step, up against the wall. He looked frail and thin, his arms and legs like twigs. Genesis looked round, sensing something strange between us. I asked, 'Did you watch me that afternoon, Timothy? Did you see what I did in the garden?'

The boy nodded, misery on his face. 'You burned some books, sir. I came into the house and watched you, from a window. I know I shouldn't have, but I – I wondered what was so secret, sir.'

'There is a surfeit of secrets in this world,' I said, angrily now. 'And stable-boys spying on their masters can cause grave trouble. Had you heard of the King's proclamation?'

He looked frightened. 'What proclamation, sir? I know only that all must obey his commands.'

'He recently made a proclamation forbidding ownership of certain books. I had some, and that was what I burned. In the garden, that day.'

'I – I didn't know they were forbidden, sir.'

Standing there, the boy looked pathetic. And the thought came to me, he is but thirteen, and thirteen-year-olds are nosy. I asked, very quietly, 'Who did you tell, Timothy?'

He hung his head. 'Nobody, sir, nobody. Only when Master and Mistress Brocket came back, Mistress Brocket said something had been burned in her vegetable garden, it looked like papers. Master Brocket went and stirred them round, brought back a few unburned pieces. I was in the kitchen. I saw him. He knew I had been alone here that afternoon, sir, and he asked who had been burning papers. He said he would strike me if I lied, so I told him it was you.'

'Martin,' I said heavily. So, Josephine had been right about him all along. And he was not just a thief, he meant to do me harm. 'You let me down, Timothy,' I said sternly. 'I shall talk with you again. But first,' I added grimly, 'I must speak to Martin.'

He called after me, 'I didn't mean for anything to happen to you, sir, I swear. If I had known you might be arrested – ' His voice rose to a howl behind me as I walked away to the house.

☩

MARTIN BROCKET was in the dining room, polishing the silver, running a cloth round a large dish which had belonged to my father. He regarded me, as usual, with cold eyes and a humble smile. 'God give you good afternoon, sir.' Evidently he had decided, with deferential tact, not to refer to my arrest at all.

'Put that down, Martin,' I said coldly. The shadow of an emotion, perhaps fear, crossed his face as he laid the silver dish back on the table. 'I have been talking to Timothy. Apparently the boy told you he saw me burning books in the garden.'

I discerned only the slightest hesitation, then Martin answered smoothly, 'Yes, sir. Agnes saw the burned papers and I asked Timothy about it. I thought he might have been up to mischief.'

'Somebody has,' I answered flatly. 'I was questioned about those burned books at the Privy Council this morning.'

He stood stock-still, the cloth still in his hands. I continued, 'Nobody knew what I had done, save the friend who was questioned with me.' Still Martin stood like a statue. He had no answer. 'Who did you tell?' I asked sharply. 'Who did you betray me to? And why?'

He laid the cloth on the buffet with a hand that had suddenly begun to tremble. His face had paled. He asked, 'May I sit down?'

'Yes,' I answered curtly.

'I have always been a faithful servant to my employers,' he said quietly. 'Stewardship is an honourable calling. But my son – ' his face worked for a moment – 'he is in gaol.'

'I know that. I found Agnes crying one day.' He frowned at that, but I pressed him. 'What has that to do with what you did?'

He took a deep breath. 'Rogue though I know my son John is, I feared he might die for lack of food and care in that gaol if I did not send him money, and I could only get him out of it by paying off his debtors.' His eyes were suddenly bright with anguish and fear.

'Go on.'

'It was in early April, not very long after Agnes and I came to work for you. John had had a fever of the lungs in that vile place last winter, and nearly died. We were at our wits' end.'

'You could have come to me.'

'It is for me to care for Agnes and John – me!' Martin's voice rose unexpectedly, on a note of angry pride. 'I would not go running to you, my master, soft though I saw you were with Josephine and the boy.' There was a note of contempt in his voice now. There, I thought, that was why he disliked me. He had an iron view of the place and responsibilities of servants and masters. It had led him to betray me rather than ask for help.

He pulled himself together, lowering his voice again. 'I had arranged to have what money I could scrape together delivered to John in prison by a merchant of Leicester who travels between there and London, and who knew my story.' He took a long breath. 'One day, as I was leaving his London office, a man accosted me. A gentleman, a fair-haired young fellow wearing expensive clothes.'

I stared at him. 'Was he missing half an ear by chance?'

Martin looked startled. 'You know him?'

'Unfortunately I do. What name did he give?'

'Crabtree.'

'That is not his real name. What did he say?'

'That he was an acquaintance of the merchant, had heard of my son's trouble and might be in a position to help. I was puzzled. I know there are many tricksters in the city, but he was well-dressed and well-spoken, a gentleman. He took me to a tavern. Then he said he represented someone who would pay well for information about you.'

'Go on.' Martin closed his eyes, and I shouted, 'Tell me!'

'He wanted me to report your movements generally, but especially if you had any contact with the Queen's household. Or any radical reformers.' He bowed his head.

I persisted. 'And this was in April?'

'Yes. I remember the day well,' he added bitterly. For the first time he looked ashamed.

I ran my hands through my hair. Stice, the servant of Richard Rich who I had reluctantly worked with, had been spying on me since the spring. But as I thought it through, it began to make sense. April was when the hunt for heretics linked to the Queen was getting going. Rich knew I had worked for her; if he was able to link me to religious radicals, he might be able to incriminate her by association. This could have been a small part of his and Gardiner's campaign to destroy her. But of course he would have found nothing. Then, after the campaign against the Queen failed in July, and Rich found me hunting for Greening's murderers – and, as he thought, Anne Askew's book – he could easily have switched from spying on me to using me.

Yet it did not add up: I had not burned my books till the end of July, when Stice and I were already working together, and if it was actually Rich who brought that matter to the Privy Council, then why had he helped me today, when it was likely to bring him into bad odour with Gardiner? But the paths Rich followed were so sinuous, it could all still be part of some larger plan. I had thought him sincere this morning, but Rich could never, ever be trusted. I had to talk this through with Barak.

Martin was looking at me now, a twitch at the corner of his mouth. 'Crabtree gave me the money I needed to start to pay down the debts. But only little by little, and all the while the interest was mount/ing. Agnes, she was at the end of her tether.'

'I know.'

'And Crabtree kept demanding information.' Brocket looked at me in a sort of desperate appeal. 'I was bound to him, he could expose what I had done, if he chose.'

'That is the problem with being a spy. Where did you meet?'

'In a house, a poor place, barely furnished. I think it was used for business.'

'In Needlepin Lane?'

He shook his head. 'No, sir, it was at Smithfield, hard by St Bar/tholomew's Hospital.'

'Exactly where?'

'In a little lane off Griffin Street. Third house down, with a blue door and a Tudor rose above the porch.'

It did not surprise me that Rich kept more than one place for secret meetings. He owned half the houses round St Bartholomew's.

'I suppose Agnes and I must go now, sir,' Martin said quietly.

'I take it she knows nothing of this.'

'No, sir. She would not have let me do it. She would have argued, it would have upset her mightily – women, they do not understand the hard necessities men can be driven to.' He attempted a quick half/smile, man to man, as though we could at least agree on the vagaries of women. I stared back at him coldly. Though he recognized how dishonourably he had behaved, he had still not apologized. And he had disliked me from the beginning, as I disliked him. That made the next thing I said easier.

'You will not leave yet, Martin. The game is not quite played out. A game involving the highest in the realm, which your betrayal has involved you in. When did you last meet Crabtree?'

He began to look worried. 'Last Wednesday. I meet him once a week at the house near St Bartholomew's, to give him what informa/

tion I have. If there is urgent intelligence I am to leave a message that I wish to see him at a tavern nearby. I did that when I learned you had been burning books.' He had the grace to lower his head as he said that.

'For now you will say and do nothing. We shall go on apparently as before. I may need you to go to the tavern with a message, I do not know yet.'

He looked seriously worried now. 'Could Agnes and I not just leave now?'

'No. And if you go before I say you can, I will ensure you never work again. Now, I have to send a message to Hampton Court.'

Martin looked frightened. He must have realized Stice was connected to the heresy hunt, that politics was involved, but he had doubtless preferred not to think about it. 'Is that understood?' I asked sternly.

'Yes, sir. I will do as you command.' He took a deep breath, and before my eyes his face composed itself into its normal expressionless mask. He rose from his chair, a little shakily, and took up the silver bowl.

✝

MY APPOINTMENT WITH ROWLAND was for two o'clock, and it was almost that now. My stomach rumbling with hunger, I left the house and walked down to Lincoln's Inn. When I was shown into his chamber the Treasurer was sitting behind his desk as usual. He smiled at me, quite unashamed. 'So the Privy Council let you go, Brother Shardlake?'

'Yes. They recognized Mistress Slanning's accusations for the rubbish they were.'

He inclined his beaky head, stroking the ends of his long beard. 'Good. Then the matter is over, with no disgrace to Lincoln's Inn. Secretary Paget sent a message asking me not to see you before today.' He smiled. 'They like to do that, ensure that the people to be brought before them have no advance warning.' My anger must have shown in my face, for he added, 'Take care what you say next, Brother Shard-lake. Do not abuse me as you did once before: remember who I am.'

I replied quietly, 'I know exactly who you are, Master Treasurer.' He glared at me with his flinty eyes. 'As the Slanning matter is over,' I continued, 'I take it there is nothing more to discuss. Except that, in light of my arrest, I presume someone else will attend the ceremonies to welcome the admiral later this week.'

Rowland shook his head. 'You do presume, Brother Shardlake. The message from Secretary Paget was that if your appearance before the council led to your arrest for heresy I should find a substitute, but if you were released you should still attend. They want someone of serjeant rank and you are the only one in town, except old Serjeant Wells, who is entering his dotage and would probably turn up on the wrong day. So you will attend as planned, starting with the parade through the city on Friday. I take it you have the requisite robes and chain.'

'The robes, no chain. Who can afford a gold chain these days?'

He frowned. 'Then get one, Serjeant, in the name of Lincoln's Inn, which you will be representing.'

I could not resist one piece of insolence. 'Perhaps the Inn could provide me with one. After all, it has recently acquired the late Brother Bealknap's estate. You will have his chain, surely.'

'Gone to the Tower mint to be melted down like the rest of his gold,' Rowland snapped. He waved a hand. 'Now, that is enough, Brother.' He pointed a skinny, inky finger at me. 'Get a chain. And a shave as well. You look a mess.'

✝

I NEEDED TO GET THE NEWS about Brocket to Lord Parr as fast as possible, but I was hungry, and exhausted already. As I crossed the square to the refectory I realized both my hands were clenched tight into fists. Timothy's stupidity, Brocket's betrayal and Rowland's insou-ciant rudeness had left me in a state of fury.

Feeling a little better for my meal, I went into chambers and asked

Barak and Nicholas to come to my room. From the expression on Nicholas's face Barak had told him about my arrest. When the door was closed behind us Barak said, 'Thank God you're out.'

'No reply to the message you took?'

'Nothing.'

I sat looking at him. It hurt that those I had served seemed to have abandoned me. The Queen most of all. I said, 'Well, I must get another message to Hampton Court now. Something else has happened. It had best go direct to Lord Parr.'

'Perhaps it might be better for me to take this one,' Nicholas said. 'The guards there may have instructions to hold Jack off; another messenger may get through more easily.'

I looked at him; the boy seemed himself again, after the dreadful hurt his father's letter had caused. Yet I sensed a new sadness and seriousness in him.

Barak nodded agreement. 'God's blood, Nick boy, you're learning the ways of politics fast.' He gave him a mocking look. 'So long as it's not just a chance to see all the ladies inside Hampton Court.'

He answered quietly. 'On my oath, after what has just happened to Master Shardlake, I have no wish to step into a royal palace.'

'Thank you, Nicholas,' I said. There was still loyalty in chambers at least, and my spirits rose a little.

'But what happened at the council?' Barak asked.

I told them about my appearance there, Rich's unexpected help, and Martin's disloyalty, concluding with my encounter with Rowland. I asked ruefully, 'Has either of you a spare gold chain you don't need?'

'Rowland's an arsehole,' Barak said. 'The way he cheated Bealknap, it almost makes me feel sorry for the old rogue.' He looked at Nicholas. 'If you make a career in the law, be sure you don't turn out like either of them.'

Nicholas did not reply. I studied him. What would he do when his period with me came to an end in a few months? Run for the hills, if he was wise. But I hoped he would not.

'So you still have to go to the ceremonials?' Barak said. 'I'm going with Tamasin to see the admiral arriving at Greenwich on Friday. She insisted.'

'I should like to see that,' Nicholas said.

'I wish it were all over, these ceremonies that I must attend.' I looked at him. 'Try all you can to get the message through that I am about to write. It may be possible, now, to set up a meeting between Brocket and Stice at the house and then grab Stice. We may be able to find out exactly what Rich has been doing.'

Barak raised his eyebrows. 'How? He won't willingly betray his master. He's not some youngster who got himself involved with crazy Anabaptists, like Myldmore and Leeman.'

'I'll leave that to Lord Parr,' I answered grimly.

He looked at me askance. 'I quite agree; but that's a bit ruthless for you, isn't it?'

'I have had enough.'

'What is Rich up to? We all thought he'd changed tack after the heresy hunt ended and Anne Askew's book was taken. That he was helping you. But it was him, through Stice and Brocket, who reported your burning those books.'

'Rich can never be trusted. And yet I can't see either why he would report my burning the books to the council now. It was risky, I could have spilled the truth about Anne Askew.'

'Rich always turns with the political wind, doesn't he?'

'Yes. He started as Cromwell's man.'

'What if this was a double-bluff? Rich gets the matter onto the council agenda along with the Slanning complaints because he knew that your burning the books wasn't illegal, and that the Slanning charges were all shit?'

'Why would he do that?' Nicholas asked.

'Because he is turning with the tide towards the reformers,' Barak answered excitedly. 'The whole performance could have been intended to show a shift of loyalty on his part, by siding with Lord Hertford and the Queen's brother.'

'That sounds too devious to be credible,' Nicholas said doubtfully.

'Nothing is too devious for those courtiers,' I replied vigorously. 'But the problem with that idea is that Rich knew nothing of the Slanning case. He didn't know Isabel would have no evidence and make a fool of herself as she did. And he seemed genuinely worried afterwards.' I sighed. 'Only Lord Parr can help to sort this out. And he ought to be told about it.'

Barak said, 'The Queen's brother will have told him.'

'Not the whole story.'

'What role is Secretary Paget playing in all this?' Nicholas asked. 'They say he is the King's closest adviser.'

'No: his closest *servant*. There is a difference. He is the King's eyes and ears, the ringmaster, if you like. From all I understand, he never challenges the King over policy. He remembers Wolsey and Cromwell too well.' I smiled wryly. 'He is the Master of Practices, not Policy.'

'He must have an eye to the future; when the King is no longer here.'

'Well said,' Barak agreed. 'He'll be looking out for his own interest; he'll no doubt jump to whichever faction is most likely to win.'

'He is like all of them,' I said angrily. 'He will do anything to anybody. And people like me are the pawns, useful in the game but dispensable. And now, Nick, smarten yourself up a little, while I write this letter.'

✝

I DID NO WORK FOR the remainder of that afternoon. After sending Nicholas with the message, I went out and sat in the shade on a bench under an old beech tree, occasionally nodding to colleagues who passed by. Nobody, thank God, knew I had been in the Tower a second time, though doubtless the news would get out, as it always did. Exhausted, I closed my eyes and dozed. After a time I heard something fall onto the bench beside me and, opening my eyes, saw it was a leaf, dry and yellow-tinged. Autumn would soon be here.

I turned at the sound of someone calling my name. John Skelly was running towards me. I stood. It was too early for a reply from Hampton Court. 'Master Coleswyn has called to see you, sir,' he said as he came up. 'He seems agitated.'

I sighed. 'I will come.'

'I thought you no longer represented Mistress Slanning, sir. I thought your involvement in that case was over.'

I said with feeling, 'I wonder, John, if that case will ever end.'

But it was about to, and for ever.

Chapter Forty-five

P HILIP WAS WAITING IN MY OFFICE. He looked haggard. 'What has happened?' I asked breathlessly. 'Not more accus-ations?'

It was more a tremor than a shake of the head. 'No, not that.' He swallowed. 'Edward Cotterstoke is dead.'

I thought of the desperate figure in the boat that morning. Edward was not young, and the last few days had turned his world upside down. 'How?'

Philip took a deep breath, then started to sob. He put a clenched fist to his mouth, fought to bring himself under control. 'By his own hand. I took him home, fed him and put him to bed, for he seemed at his last gasp. He must have taken the knife from the kitchen. A sharp one.' He shuddered, his whole solid frame trembling. 'I went to see how he was, two hours ago, and he had slit his throat, from ear to ear. It must have taken great force.' He shook his head. 'There is blood everywhere, but that is the least of it. His soul, his soul. He was in great torment, but such a sin . . .' He shook his head in despair.

I remembered Cotterstoke's words on the boat, talking of the dis-grace that confessing to his stepfather's murder would bring his family. He had said he knew what had to be done. I said, 'He felt he deserved death for what he did, and believed he was damned anyway; he did not want his family to suffer.'

Philip laughed savagely. 'They will suffer now.'

I answered quietly, 'Suicide is a terrible disgrace, but less than murder. His family will not see him hang, nor will his goods be dis-trained to the King.'

'There could have been some other way; we could have talked about it, talked with our vicar. This is — is not — sane.'

'After what had just happened to him, anyone might lose their reason. Perhaps God will take account of that.'

✝

A REPLY FROM Hampton Court arrived just as I was going to bed. Martin brought it up, his expression a deferential mask as usual. I examined the Queen's seal carefully in the privacy of my room, to ensure it was unbroken, before opening it. The letter was from Lord Parr:

> *Matthew,*
>
> *Forgive my not replying to your earlier messages: there has been much to do, with the move to Hampton Court and the arrangements for the admiral's coming, and also I have been ill. Furthermore, Jane Fool told the guard your first message was not urgent; out of spite against you, I think. I have seen that she is well punished for it, despite the Queen and the Lady Mary's softness towards her.*
>
> *Neither I nor the Queen knew you were to appear before the Privy Council; Paget kept that to himself, though the Queen's brother told me afterwards. We do not know who pressed to have the matter brought there; thank heaven the Slanning woman made a fool of herself, and Rich had motive to speak on your behalf.*
>
> *Regarding your faithless steward, yes, keep him on for now. But other than that, do nothing. I will have the house you mentioned watched.*
>
> *I will write further, and we may see each other at the ceremonies.*
>
> *By the way, your boy, the messenger, did well. He was gentlemanly and polite, which is not always true of your other man.*

I felt relieved as I laid down the letter. Lord Parr's tone was friendly; the observation about Barak made me smile. The Queen and her uncle had not, after all, abandoned me. The story about Jane Fool rang true. I wondered, not for the first time, whether she was a fool of any sort at all, or merely a woman who had found a profitable role in pretending it.

☦

NEXT DAY WAS the 17th, only three days before the admiral's arrival at Greenwich, and I still needed a gold chain. I went to a shop in the goldsmith's quarter, one of the smaller ones, guarded outside by a large man ostentatiously bearing a club. Barak accompanied me. Asking around on my behalf, he had discovered the service this shop provided.

Inside, another man was posted beside an inner door. The owner, a stout elderly fellow, came over and gave me a deep bow. 'God give you good morrow, sir.'

'And to you. I require a gold chain; I have to be at the ceremony welcoming the French admiral on Saturday.'

'Ah yes, his progress through the city. It has brought some good business.' He looked me over professionally. 'A lawyer, sir? Is that a serjeant's coif you wear?'

'Well observed.'

'It is the nature of my business, to judge who people are. You should buy a good long chain, with thick links.' He smiled unctuously.

'I look only to rent one, for a week.'

The man stared. 'Rent?' He shook his head. 'People are expected to wear their own chains on such an occasion, of a size in accordance with their status. To rent one − ' he shook his head sadly − 'that might be thought shameful among your colleagues, if it got out.'

'So it would,' I agreed. 'That is why I asked my clerk here to find a goldsmith who rented chains discreetly.'

'Best look one out and save time,' Barak told the goldsmith cheerfully. 'I know you rent them for a good price.'

That got the goldsmith moving: he went into the back room and returned with a heavy chain with large, solid links. It was a little dirty, but gold is easily cleaned. I wrote a note confirming receipt, paid over a half-sovereign as deposit, and asked Barak to put the chain in his knapsack.

'Don't you want to wear it?' he asked mockingly.

'Not till I have to.'

✝

I HAD AGREED to go down to Greenwich with Barak, Tamasin and Nicholas on Friday, to watch Admiral d'Annebault's arrival. He would be welcomed by the King and stay the night at Greenwich Palace before his procession through London on Saturday. Going to see this would help me get used to it all, before playing my, mercifully small, part later.

The four of us met at Temple Stairs. There were many people waiting for wherries and tilt-boats to take them downriver; mostly family groups in their best clothes, for the day had been declared a public holiday. One young man stood alone, his expression grave; he had only one leg and stood on crutches. I wondered if he had been a soldier in the war.

Our turn came and a tilt-boat, with a white canopy to shield us from the sun, took us down the busy river. Even the boatman was dressed cheerfully, a garland of flowers in his cap. Tamasin sat under the canopy with Barak, Nicholas and me on the bench opposite, Nicholas wearing a broad hat against the sun. I had on my robe, but no chain.

Tamasin looked cheerfully out over the brown water. 'I wonder if we shall get close enough to see the King. They distributed a leaflet giving the details. He will be on the royal barge just below Green-wich, and the admiral's barge will pull up beside it for the King to welcome him aboard.'

I looked at her. Her time of sickness was over and she was bloom-ing. She wore the dress she had worn at George's birthday, yellow, with a bonnet, a little ruby brooch at her breast. She met my gaze and leaned over, putting her hand on mine. 'I know this will be hard for you, sir, after last year. Forgive my enthusiasm, but I do not see much spectacle.'

'While I see too much. But no, Tamasin, enjoy the day.'

The river turned south, past the Isle of Dogs. The path winding around it was filled with people of the poorer classes, walking down to watch the admiral's arrival. Beyond the muddy path was marshy woodland dotted with vegetable gardens that cottagers had set up, their shacks in the middle. Guard dogs tied to posts barked furiously at all the passers-by.

Greenwich Palace, built by the King's father as a symbol of the new Tudor dynasty, came into view, with its splendid facade and pointed towers. Boats were pulling into the bank on both sides of the river, passengers disembarking and walking on to get as close as possible to the palace. Our boat pulled in to the left-hand bank. Beside the palace I saw a great barge at anchor, brightly painted in Tudor green and white, an enormous English flag flying from the prow. A dozen liveried oarsmen sat on each side, now and then sculling with their oars to keep the craft steady. The barge had a long cabin gilded with gold and silver. Purple curtains had been pulled back to show those within, but they were too far away to make out. Tamasin leaned over the edge of the crowded path to see better, risking a fall into the mud below, and Barak pulled her back. 'Control yourself, woman.'

For a while nothing happened. We stood amid the watching, murmuring crowd. Beyond the barge a long row of mighty warships was moored along the south shore. The King's great ships, which I had seen last year at Portsmouth. Streamers in many colours, some a hundred feet long, were hung from the masts and swung gently in the light river breeze. The ships themselves I remembered: enormous, magnificent, their upper decks brightly painted. One, though, was absent: the King's favourite warship, the *Mary Rose*, now sunk at the bottom of the Solent.

There was a crash as gunports opened along the sides of the ships. Cannon appeared and fired volleys; no actual cannonballs, of course, but emitting thick clouds of smoke and making enough noise to shake the pathway. People shouted and cheered. Nicholas joined in enthusi-astically, waving his hat in the air. Some women whooped at the noise, though Tamasin glanced at me with a sombre face.

Then they appeared, coming fast upriver; first a French warship, guns firing on both sides, then over a dozen French galleys, long and narrow: sleek, fast vessels of war. They were brightly painted, each in a different colour, and their cannon, set in the prows, fired off blasts in reply to ours. The largest galley, covered from prow to stern in a white canopy decorated in gold fleur-de-lys, pulled alongside the King's barge.

It was too much for me. The sight of those galleys, which I had last seen firing at the *Mary Rose*; the smoke; the gunfire that shook the ground. I touched Barak on the shoulder. 'I have to go.'

He looked at me with concern. 'God's blood, you look sick. You shouldn't go alone. Nick, get a boat.'

'No!' I answered stubbornly. 'I'll be all right, you stay here.'

Nicholas and Tamasin were also staring. Tamasin took my hand. 'Are you sure? I could see you were troubled earlier.'

'I will be all right.' I felt ashamed of my weakness.

'Nick,' Barak said peremptorily, 'go back with him.'

The boy stepped forward. I opened my mouth to protest, then shrugged.

'Call on us later,' Tamasin said.

I nodded. 'I will.'

I walked away, fast as I could through the crowds, Nicholas for once having to lengthen his long stride to keep up with me. The end-less crash of cannon suddenly ceased; the admiral must have boarded the King's barge at last.

'Watch out there!' a man called out as I nearly fell into him. Nicholas grasped my arm.

'He's drunk, sodden old hunchback,' another man observed. And in truth it was as though I were drunk, the ground like a ship's deck, seeming to shift and slide beneath my feet.

✝

WE GOT A BOAT TO the Steelyard stairs. When we stepped off I felt strange, light-headed. Nicholas said, 'Shall I walk you home?' He was embarrassed, and had hardly spoken during the journey.

'No. We'll walk to chambers.'

Today being a holiday and so many people down at Greenwich, the city was quiet, as though it were a Sunday. I was walking steadily again now, but thought with renewed grief of my friends who had died on the *Mary Rose*. Their faces came before me. And then I found myself saying an inward goodbye to them all, and something lifted in my heart.

'Did you say something, sir?' Nicholas asked.

I must have murmured aloud. 'No. No, nothing.' Looking round, I realized we were at Lothbury. 'We are close to the Cotterstoke house,' I said. 'Where that painting is.'

'What will happen to it now?'

'Edward's half of his mother's estate will go to his family. In these circumstances I imagine his wife will want to get rid of the house as soon as possible, painting or no painting.'

'Then Mistress Slanning may get her way.'

'Yes. I suppose she may.'

He hesitated, then asked, 'Will Master Coleswyn tell Edward Cotterstoke's wife why her husband took his life? That old murder?'

'No. I am sure not.'

I realized the old servant, Vowell, would know nothing of Edward's death. Perhaps I should tell him, and make sure he kept his mouth shut.

✝

THE OLD HOUSE was quiet as ever. Nearby a barber had opened his shop, but there was little custom and he stood leaning disconso-lately against a wall under his striped pole. I remembered Rowland saying I needed to shave before taking my place for d'Annebault's progress through London tomorrow; I would do so after visiting Vowell. I knocked at the door.

He opened it at once. He looked agitated, his eyes wide. He stared at us in surprise, then leaned forward and spoke quietly, his voice shaking. 'Oh, sir, it is you. I sent for Master Dyrick.' He frowned. 'I didn't think he would send you in his place. Sir, it may not be safe for you.'

I lowered my voice in turn. 'What do you mean, fellow? I have not come from Dyrick.' I took a deep breath. 'I came to tell you poor Edward Cotterstoke is dead.'

Vowell wrung his hands. 'I know, and by his own hand. One of his servants told someone who knows me. Wretched gossiping women, everybody knows already. Mistress Slanning—'

'Isabel knows?'

'Knows, sir, and is here.' He cast a backward glance at the gloomy hall. 'In such a state as I have never seen anyone. She insisted I let her in. She has a knife, sir, a big knife she took from the kitchen. I fear she may do as her brother did—'

I raised a hand; the frightened old man's voice was rising. 'Where is she?'

'In the parlour, sir. She just stands looking at the painting – she will not move, nor answer me – holding that knife.'

I looked at Nicholas. 'Will you come with me?' I whispered.

'Yes.'

We stepped inside, past Vowell. The door to the parlour was open. I walked in quietly, Nicholas just behind. There, with her back to me, stood Isabel. She wore one of her fine satin dresses, light brown today, but had cast her hood on the floor. It left her head bare, long silvery-grey tresses cascading down her shoulders. She was staring at the wall painting, quite motionless, and as Vowell had said, a broad, long-bladed knife was clutched in her right hand, so tightly that each bony white knuckle stood out. The image of her mother and father, of little Edward and her own young self, stared back at her, appearing more real than ever to me at that terrifying moment.

She did not even seem to be aware that we had come in. Vowell stayed outside; I heard him breathing hard in the corridor.

Nicholas stepped quietly forward, but I put up a hand to restrain him. I said softly, 'Mistress Slanning.' Strange, even in that extremity, I could not allow myself the presumption of calling her by her first name.

I would not have thought her body could have tensed any further but it did, becoming quite rigid. Then, slowly, she turned her head to look at me. Those blue eyes, so like her brother's, were wild and staring. Her brows drew together in a frown.

'Master Shardlake?' she said in a quiet, puzzled voice. 'Why are you here?'

'I came to speak to Vowell. To tell him your brother is dead.' I moved my right hand a little. 'Mistress Slanning, please let me have that knife.' She did not reply; her breath came in short pants, as though she were trying to hold it in, to stop breathing. 'Please,' I implored. 'I wish only to help you.'

'Why would you help me? I tried to destroy you, and Edward and that lawyer Coleswyn. I called you heretics. As you are.' Her grip on the knife tightened, and she lifted the blade slightly.

'I think you were not yourself. Please, mistress, give me the knife.' I took half a step forward, stretching out my hand.

She slowly lifted the knife towards her throat.

'No!' Nicholas cried out, with such force and passion that Isabel paused, the blade almost at her neck, where the arteries pulsed under the wrinkled white skin.

'It's not worth it!' he said passionately. 'Whatever you did, madam, whatever your family did, it's not worth that!'

She stared at him for a moment. Then she lowered the knife, but held it pointing outwards. I raised my arm to protect myself, fearing she would attack: Isabel was a thin, ageing woman, but desperation gives strength to the weakest. But it was not us she attacked; instead she turned round again and thrust the knife into her beloved picture, stabbing at it with long, powerful slashes, so hard that a piece of plaster broke off beside the crack in the wall that the experts had noticed. She went on and on, making desperate grunting sounds, as more of the paint and plaster crumbled. Then her hand slipped and the knife gashed her other arm, blood spurting through the fabric of her dress. She winced at the unexpected pain and dropped the knife. Clutching her arm, Isabel crumpled in a heap on the floor, and began to cry. She lay there, sobbing desperately with the grief and guilt of a lifetime.

Nicholas stepped forward quickly, picked up the knife and took it outside to Vowell. The old servant stared at Isabel in horror through the doorway. The painting was now scored with innumerable slashes, spaces where pieces of plaster had fallen revealing the lath behind. A tiny stream of plaster dust trickled down. I saw that the section of the painting she had attacked most fiercely, now almost entirely obliterated, was her mother's face.

I looked at Nicholas, who was pale and breathing hard. Then I knelt beside Isabel. 'Mistress Slanning?' I touched her shoulder lightly. She flinched, huddling further away from me, as though she would squeeze herself into the floor, clutching at her injured arm.

'Mistress Slanning,' I said gently. 'You have cut yourself, your arm needs binding.'

The sobbing ceased and she turned her head to look at her arm. Her expression was bereft, her hair wild. She looked utterly pitiful. Lifting her eyes, she met mine briefly before shuddering and turning her face away. 'Do not look at me, please.' She spoke in an imploring whisper. 'No one should look at me now.' She took a deep, sobbing breath. 'He was innocent, our stepfather, a good man. But we did not see it, Edward and I, till it was too late. Our mother was cruel, she left that Will so we would quarrel, I understand it now. It was because both Edward and I loved the painting so. Mother never wanted us to visit her, but I would come sometimes, to see the painting. To see our father again.'

I looked at their mother's empty chair, facing what was left of the painting, the embroidery still lying on the seat.

'He died so suddenly, our father. Why did he leave us? Why?' She wept again, the tears of a lost child. 'Oh, Edward! I drove him to that unclean act. All these years I could have confessed; the old faith allows that if you repent and confess your sins it is enough, you are forgiven. His faith did not allow even that. But I – ' her voice fell to a whisper – 'my hardened heart would not allow me to confess. But it was both of us together did that thing, both of us!'

I jumped at the sound of a sharp knock at the door. I heard Vowell and another voice, and then Vincent Dyrick strode into the room, gown billowing theatrically behind him, his lean hawk face furious. He looked at Nicholas and me, at Isabel weeping on the floor, then gaped at the wrecked painting.

'Shardlake! What have you done? Why is my client in this state?'

I rose slowly to my feet, my knees cracking and my back protesting in pain. Isabel was looking at Dyrick; it was the same puzzled, otherworldly look Edward had worn in the Tower, as though she barely understood who he was.

'Ask her,' I answered heavily.

Dyrick was staring again at the painting. Perhaps he saw the prospect of endless fees from this case trickling away like the plaster dust still falling from the ruined wall. 'Who did this?'

'Isabel, I fear.'

'Christ's wounds!' Dyrick looked down at his client. Isabel was still hunched over, so ashamed she could not meet our eyes. 'See her condition – ' He pointed at me. 'I cannot be held responsible for anything she has done! It was she who insisted on sending a copy of that complaint to the Privy Council. I tried to dissuade her!'

'I know. And I may tell you, since Isabel is your client and you must keep it confidential, that Edward and Isabel conspired to murder their stepfather the best part of half a century ago. Edward has killed himself, and Isabel might have done the same had we not come in time.' I looked again at the painting. 'This is a tragedy, Dyrick. One made worse by the tangles of litigation, as their mother intended. My efforts with Brother Coleswyn to find a settlement only uncovered a horror,' I added sadly.

I stepped wearily to the door. Dyrick looked down at Isabel.

'Wait!' he said, turning. 'You cannot leave me alone with her, in this state – '

'Vowell will help you bind her wound. Then, if you will take my honest advice, you should send for her priest. Make sure it is him, she is of the old religion and it matters to her. He may be able to help her, I do not know.' I turned to Nicholas. He was looking at the face of Isabel's father, still staring out from the wreckage with his benevolent, confident, patrician air. 'Come, lad,' I said. We walked past Dyrick, past old Vowell, out into the street.

There, in the August sunshine, I turned to Nicholas. 'You saved her.'

'She came to this, even with a good and loving father,' he said quietly. And I realized with a chill that his parents' letter had brought thoughts of suicide to Nicholas as well. But he had rejected them, and that was why he had been so passionate with Isabel. 'What will happen to her?' he asked.

'I do not know.'

'Perhaps it is too late for that poor woman now.' Nicholas took a deep breath and stared at me, his green eyes hard and serious. 'But not for me.'

☩

EARLY THE FOLLOWING AFTERNOON I stood at the front of a great concourse outside the church of St Michael le Querne, which gave onto the open space at the west end of Cheapside. More crowds lined the length of Cheapside, along which Admiral d'Annebault would shortly progress. Mayor Bowes, whom I had last seen at Anne Askew's burning, stood alone on a little platform. I waited in a line with the aldermen and other leading citizens of London, all wearing our gold chains. As at the burnings, a white-robed cleric stood at a makeshift lectern, but on this occasion he was to deliver an oration in French, welcoming the admiral to the city. There was a steady murmur of voices, while water tinkled in the conduit by the church.

The admiral had come by boat from Greenwich to the Tower that morning, all his galleys following. The previous evening I had taken Nicholas with me to visit Barak and Tamasin, and had spent a quiet night playing cards. I had not told them what had happened to Isabel – it was no thing for Tamasin to hear in her condition. Then I had gone home and slept late, to be woken by the crash of guns from the Tower welcoming the admiral. Even out at Chancery Lane the noise rattled the windows. From the Tower d'Annebault would progress through the city, finishing at St Michael's Church, accompanied by the Queen's brother, William Parr, the other great men of the realm following.

Martin helped dress me in my very best. I put on the gold chain which I had set him to cleaning last night. Neither of us said a word. Then I walked down to the church. As I left I saw Timothy peering through the half-open door of the stable, looking disconsolate. I knew I must speak to him about Martin's betrayal; but for now Lord Parr had sworn me to secrecy and I gave the boy only a severe look. Too severe, perhaps, but I was still sore troubled by what he had done, and by my experiences of recent days.

A royal official lined us up, peremptorily ordering the mayor and aldermen into position like children. The sun beat down, making our heads hot under our caps and coifs. The golden links of our chains sparkled. Streamers and poles bearing the English flag beside the fleur-de-lys of France fluttered in the breeze, and bright cloths, too, had been hung from the upper windows of houses and shops. I remembered how only a year before I had seen dummies wearing the fleur-de-lys used in target practice by new recruits to the army – hundreds of men who had marched to Portsmouth from London to resist the threatened invasion.

Next to me Serjeant Blower of the Inner Temple stood proudly, his fat belly sucked in and his chest thrust out. He was in his fifties, with a short, neatly trimmed beard. I knew him slightly; he was too full of himself for my taste. It was said that Wriothesley was considering appointing him a judge. 'We have a fine day to greet the admiral,' he said. 'I cannot remember such ceremonial since Anne Boleyn's coronation.'

I raised my eyebrows, remembering how that much-acclaimed marriage had ended.

'Are you going to be present when Prince Edward meets the admiral tomorrow?' Blower asked. 'And at the Hampton Court celebrations?'

'Yes, representing Lincoln's Inn.'

'I too,' he said proudly. He looked askance at my chain. 'Have you had that long? By the smell of vinegar you have just had it cleaned.'

'I only wear it on the most special occasions.'

'Really? It looks somewhat scratched.' Blower glanced proudly down at the broad, bright links of his own chain. Then he leaned closer and said quietly, 'Could you not find time to shave, brother? We were instructed to. It is a pity your hair is dark, your stubble shows.'

'No, Brother Blower. I fear I have been very busy.'

'In the vacation?'

'I have had some hard cases.'

'Ah.' He nodded, then quoted the old legal saying, 'Hard cases make bad law.'

'They do indeed.'

He gave me a sidelong look. I wondered if news of my appearance before the council had filtered out. Servants would speak to servants at Whitehall, the city and the Inns of Court. A rousing cheer sounded from Cheapside. People had been told to cry a welcome as d'Annebault passed. Blower pulled his fat stomach in further. 'Here he comes,' he said eagerly, and shouted a loud 'Hurrah!'

Chapter Forty-six

AFTER THE CEREMONY I went home. I was exhausted, and with another one to face on Monday, and a third the day after. For all his poor conduct at the Battle of the Solent last year, Admiral Claude d'Annebault had cut an impressive figure riding up to St Michael's: a large, handsome man of fifty, on a magnificent charger, the Earl of Essex riding beside him. I was glad to see the Queen's brother so prominent; another sign the Parr family was secure.

After the welcoming address the mayor had presented the admiral with great silver flagons of hippocras, and marchpane and wafers to refresh him after his journey. My back hurt from standing so long, and I slipped away as soon as possible, wanting only to spend the remainder of the day quietly by myself. I walked home. As I entered the house I heard Josephine and Agnes talking cheerfully in the kitchen about the wedding, fixed now for January. I thought, poor Agnes, she knows nothing of what her husband has done. Soon she will be leaving with him.

Martin came out of the dining room, a letter in his hand, his manner deferential as usual. 'This came while you were out, sir.'

'Thank you.' I recognized Hugh Curteys's handwriting. Martin said quietly, 'Sir, is there any more news concerning — that matter? About my going to that house?' Though his face remained expressionless, I saw the signs of strain about his narrowed mouth and eyes.

'No, Martin,' I replied coldly. 'I will let you know as soon as I have instructions.'

'Will it be soon?'

'I hope so. I do not know. I will tell you as soon as I do. You brought this on yourself,' I added.

☩

In my room I read Hugh's letter. Apparently Emperor Charles had decided to curb the independence of the Flanders cities: '*There have been arrests of many reformist citizens here, and in other places in Flanders, and there are like to be imprisonments and burnings. Certain English and other foreigners have crossed into Germany.*' I wondered if Bale was among them, Anne Askew's book hidden in his luggage. Probably; he must have become used to moving quickly since he fled England after the fall of his patron Cromwell. This would surely delay the publication of Anne Askew's writings now.

The letter continued: '*Many in the English merchant community are worried, and I fear if the atmosphere in the city changes for the worse I, too, may consider going to Germany.*'

I sighed; I thought my ward had found a safe haven, but it seemed not. I remembered that it was over Hugh's wardship case that I had first crossed swords with Vincent Dyrick. Thoughts of Dyrick led me to Isabel; what would happen to her, now that the whole weight of what she had done – and Edward's death – lay upon her? I remembered her frantic, deranged slashing at the painting she had fought for so single-mindedly. On an impulse, I sat down, took up quill and ink, and wrote a note to Guy:

I have not seen you since I visited that poor man at St Bartholomew's, but you have been in my thoughts. There is a woman I represented in a case – a sad family matter – who is now in great travail of soul. She is of the old faith, and I asked her lawyer to arrange for her priest to see her, but I am anxious how she fares. If you have time, perhaps you might visit her. I think perhaps you could comfort her.

I added Isabel's name and address, signed the note 'your loving friend', and sanded and sealed it. There, I thought, he will see I do not cavil at religious counselling being offered to one of the old beliefs, and he might even be able to do something for Isabel, though I feared her mind was broken now.

☦

ON THE MORNING of Monday 23rd I dressed in my finery again and went down to the stables. Today's ceremony was to welcome d'Annebault to Hampton Court. It was to take place three miles from the palace, beside the river, and the admiral was to be greeted by little Prince Edward. It was the boy's first public occasion. Those of us coming from the city had to ride out there, but it was some consolation to me that during the occasion we would remain on horseback. I had gone to be shaved yesterday and my cheeks were smooth: Blower would not be able to make remarks at my stubble today.

I had asked Martin to tell Timothy to ensure Genesis was well rubbed down, and his mane tied in plaits. When I entered the stable I was pleased to see the boy had done a good job. He did not look me in the eye as he placed the mounting block beside the horse. As I slid my feet into the stirrups, though, he looked up and smiled nervously, showing the gap where his two front teeth had been punched out when he was still an orphaned urchin, before I took him in.

'Master,' he said nervously. 'You said you would talk to me again about – about the burned books.'

'Yes, Timothy. But not now. I am due at an important occasion.'

He grasped the reins. 'Only – sir, it must have been Martin who told people about the books; I wouldn't have, yet Martin is still in his place, and he was sharp as ever with me last night.' He reddened and his voice rose a little. 'Sir, it isn't fair, I meant no harm.'

I took a deep breath, then said, 'I have kept Martin on for my own private reasons.' Then I burst out, 'And what he did pains me less than your spying. I trusted you, Timothy, and you let me down.' Tears filled the boy's eyes and I spoke more calmly. 'I will speak to you tomorrow, Timothy. Tomorrow.'

☦

A BROAD HEATH by the river had been chosen as the site for the ceremony. When I arrived almost everyone was there. Near a thousand yeomen had been commandeered for the day, dressed in brand new livery with the King's colours. City officials and we representatives from the Inns were again shepherded to places in the front rank, facing the roadway. A little way off, with a guard of soldiers, the great men of the realm waited on their horses. All those I had seen at the Privy Council were present: Gardiner, his solid frame settled on a broad-backed horse; Rich and Wriothesley side by side; Paget stroking his long forked beard, a little colour in those flat cheeks today, surveying those around him with his usual cool eye. The Earl of Hertford looked stern and solemn, while beside him Thomas Seymour, with his coppery beard combed and no doubt perfumed, wore a happy smile on his handsome face. Others too: Lord Lisle, who had proved a better commander than d'Annebault at Portsmouth last year, and other lords in their finery, the feathers in their caps stirring in the river breeze. The water was blue and sparkling, reflecting the bright sky.

And at their head, on a smaller horse, sat the boy, not yet nine, who was King Henry's heir, the control of whom after the King died was the focus of all the plotting by the men behind him. In a broad-shouldered crimson doublet with slashed sleeves, a black cap set with diamonds on his head, Prince Edward was a tiny figure beside the adults. He sat firmly upright on his horse, though. He was tall for his age, his thin little face stiffly composed. His serious expression and small chin reminded me of his long-dead mother, Jane Seymour, whose likeness I had seen in the great wall painting at Whitehall. I pitied him for the weight that must soon fall on him. Then I thought of Timothy: I had been too hard with him; one should not hold a grudge against children. I would speak to him when I returned.

Once again my allotted place was next to Blower. The big Ser-jeant nodded to me but said little; he kept leaning forward, looking towards the party behind Prince Edward, trying to catch the eye of Lord Chancellor Wriothesley, who might give him his coveted judge-ship. Wriothesley did see him, but in answer to his nod and smile gave only a little frown as though to say, 'Not here.' I remembered the old saying, big fleas have little fleas to bite them.

At length we saw d'Annebault's party approach slowly along the riverbank. There must have been three hundred of them; I knew d'Annebault had brought two hundred men over from France. From the English party heralds stepped forward, blowing trumpets. The admiral, accompanied again by the Earl of Essex, rode up to Prince Edward and bowed to the little boy from the saddle. The Prince began delivering, in a high childish voice, an address of welcome; he spoke without pause, in perfect French. At the end the admiral's horse was led forward and he and Prince Edward embraced.

✠

THE ADDRESS OVER, the French party and the bulk of the English lords rode away to Hampton Court, the Prince and the admiral leading the way, a tall soldier holding the reins of Prince Edward's horse. Those of us left behind, as usual on such occasions, relaxed immediately, everyone swinging their shoulders and drawing deep breaths, pausing to talk with friends before riding back to London. I supposed that for civility's sake I would have to ride back with the disgruntled-looking Blower, but as I was about to speak to him I felt a touch at my arm. I turned to see Lord Parr standing at my elbow, accompanied by two serving men, one holding his horse.

'My Lord,' I said. 'I did not see you with the Prince's party.'

'No, the Queen's household is not involved in this. But I came, and would speak with you.'

'Of course.' I looked at the old man; in his note he had said he had been ill, and indeed he looked frail, leaning hard on his stick. He nodded to his men and one helped me dismount while the other took Genesis's reins. Blower looked at Lord Parr with surprise, not knowing that I had acquaintance with such a senior figure. He bowed to Lord Parr and rode off, looking more put out than ever.

Lord Parr led me away a little, to stand beside the river. 'You had my letter?'

'I did. I have spoken to my steward Brocket and he stands ready, though very reluctantly.'

'I am still trying to discover who put that item on the council agenda. But I make no progress, and Paget is as close-mouthed as any man can be.'

'He was fair at the council,' I observed. 'He seemed genuinely concerned to find the truth or otherwise of the allegations.'

'Ay, perhaps.' Lord Parr sighed deeply. 'I am getting too tired for all this. After the admiral leaves next week the King and Queen are going on a short Progress to Guildford, so I must move these old bones yet again.' He looked out over the river for a moment, then spoke quietly. 'The King is taking none of the traditionalist councillors with him, not Gardiner, nor Wriothesley, nor Norfolk. Lord Hertford and Lord Lisle, though, will be accompanying him.' He looked at me, a keenness now in his bloodshot eyes. 'The tide is shifting fast in our favour. The King has not seen Bertano again; he is cooling his heels somewhere in London. Rumours are beginning to spread of a papal emissary here. And if I can prove that Rich has been playing some double game, perhaps seeking to damage the Queen through you, it will anger the King, and help the Queen. And the Parr family,' he added. 'But before I do anything with that man Stice, I must know more. No sign of those others, I take it, the men who killed Greening?'

'Daniels and Cardmaker? No, the printer Okedene saw them about the town, but I have not.'

'Who did they take the Queen's book for? Not Rich, I am sure, he would have used the *Lamentation* at once.'

'Could its release still harm the Queen?'

'I think so.' He paused, then made a fist with his bony hand. He shook his head. 'It is her hiding the book from him that would anger him most, I know.'

'The disloyalty, rather than the *Lamentation*'s theology?'

'Exactly. Though her stress on salvation by faith alone would hardly help. And the King's illness makes him all the more unpredictable. One never knows how he may turn, or in what direction.' For a second Lord Parr seemed to sway, and I put out a hand. But he righted himself, taking a deep breath. 'Give me a few days, Master Shardlake, to try and worm out some more information. And I will have a watch set on that house where Stice meets your steward.' He turned, and we walked back to our horses.

'I will contact you soon,' Lord Parr said after we had mounted. 'Keep that steward safe. Is he well frightened?'

'I think so.'

'Good.' As I turned away he said, 'I almost forgot. The Queen sends you her best wishes.'

☩

I RODE SLOWLY BACK to the city. I had not gone far, though, when another horseman pulled up beside me. To my surprise I saw it was young William Cecil, his face serious as usual.

'Brother Cecil. I had not thought to see you again so soon.' I allowed a note of reproach to enter my voice. He had been of great help earlier, but now Lord Parr must feel his absence greatly.

'Brother Shardlake.' His thin lips set slightly at my tone.

'How goes your service with Lord Hertford?'

'Well, thank you.' He hesitated. 'His secretary retires soon, it is possible I will take his place.'

I inclined my head. 'You made a good move, then.'

He pulled his horse to a halt, and I, too, stopped. The young lawyer looked at me squarely, fixing me with those large, keen blue eyes. 'Brother Shardlake, I was sorry to leave the Queen's service. But an offer of serious advancement came and I had to take it.'

'As men do.'

'Also, I confess, after that turmoil on the wharf, I did some serious thinking. About what I am – and am not – capable of. I am not a fighting man, and I have a young family to consider. My talents, such as they are, are best put to use behind a desk. Where,' he added, 'I can serve the cause of reform. Believe me, I am sincere in that, as in my continued love and respect for the Queen.'

I dared to say, 'But your first loyalty now is to the Seymours, not the Parrs.'

'Both families serve reform. And I followed you today, Brother Shardlake, to tell you something I thought you should know. Lord Parr's health is failing. I did not know how ill he was when I left, but my purpose now is to tell you that if your involvement in the Queen's matters continues – and I know you have appeared before the Privy Council – you must rely on your own judgement as well as his.' He looked at me earnestly.

'I saw just now that he was not well,' I said quietly.

'And under pressure, with all this – ' Cecil cast an arm behind him at the disappearing cavalcade. 'He has much to do at Hampton Court, the Queen is to play a prominent role at the ceremonies there.'

'I know. I will be attending tomorrow.'

There was no need for him to have ridden up to me to tell me this. 'Thank you, Brother Cecil,' I said.

'If I hear anything that may be of use to you or the Queen, I will tell you.'

'What do you think has happened to the Queen's book?'

'Lord Parr thinks it destroyed,' Cecil said.

'Do you?'

'I do not know. Only that the moment for the conservatives to use it to maximum advantage has passed. The wind is blowing fast in the other direction now. Perhaps whoever took it realized that and destroyed it.' He shook his head. 'But likely we shall never know.'

We rode on, talking of the ceremonies and the autumn Progress that was to begin afterwards, apparently going only to Guildford for a couple of weeks because of the King's health. We parted at the foot of Chancery Lane. 'This mystery is not yet unravelled,' I said. 'If you do hear anything, please inform me.'

'I will, I swear.'

As I rode down Chancery Lane I thought, yes, you will, but only so long as it serves the Seymours as well as the Parrs.

Chapter Forty-seven

I TURNED INTO MY HOUSE, aware of the sweat stiffening on my forehead under my coif, and rode round to the stable. Now I would speak to Timothy. But the boy was not there; Martin or Agnes must have set him some task around the house. I dismounted wearily, removed my cap and coif, and went indoors.

Immediately I heard the sound of a woman crying in the kitchen; desperate, racked sobbing. I realized it was Agnes Brocket. Josephine murmured something and I heard Martin say in loud, angry tones, 'God's bones, girl, will you leave us alone! Don't stare at me with those cow eyes, you stupid creature! Get out!'

Josephine stepped into the hall, her cheeks burning. I said quietly, 'What is happening?'

'Oh, sir, Master and Mistress Brocket – ' She broke off as Martin stepped out, having heard my voice. His square face was angry. But he pulled himself together and asked quietly, 'May I speak with you, sir?'

I nodded. 'Come to the parlour.'

When the door was closed I said, 'What is it, Martin? You have not told Agnes about your spying?'

'No! No!' He shook his head impatiently, then said more quietly, 'It is our son.'

'John?'

'We have had a letter from the gaoler at Leicester. John has another sickness of the lungs, a congestion. They called a doctor and he said he is like to die. Sir, we must go to him. Agnes insists we leave today.'

I looked at him. I realized from the desperation in his eyes that, whatever the consequences, Agnes would go to her son. And Martin,

541

who for all his faults loved his wife, would go, too. 'When was the letter sent?' I asked.

'Three days ago.' Brocket shook his head despairingly. 'It may be too late already. That would kill Agnes.' When I did not reply he said, suddenly defiant, 'You cannot stop us. You may do what you like. Give me bad references, spread the word round London about what I did. Tell the Queen's people. It makes no difference, we are going today.'

I said, 'I am sorry this has happened to you.'

He did not reply, just continued staring at me with that desperate look. I considered, then said quietly, 'I will make a bargain with you, Martin Brocket. Take one more message to that tavern, now, saying you have important news and will be at the house in Smithfield at nine tomorrow night.'

He took a deep breath. 'We go today,' he repeated, an edge to his voice now.

'I do not expect you to keep the appointment. Others will do that. But to set the wheels in motion you must deliver the message, in your writing, in person.'

'And in return?' he asked, suddenly bold.

'In return, I will give you a reference praising your household skills and diligence. But I will not say you are a trustworthy man, for you are not.'

'I was honest all my life,' Martin replied, a tremble in his voice, 'until John's actions brought me to this.' Then he added spitefully, 'I might not even have agreed to play the spy but for the fact I never respected you, Master Hunch — ' He broke off, realizing he was about to go too far.

I answered quietly, 'Nor did I respect you, Martin, proud, narrow man that you are. With a wife too good for him.'

He clenched his fists. 'At least I have one.'

In the silence that followed I heard Agnes sobbing uncontrollably again. Martin winced. I spoke quietly. 'Come to my study. Write me

that note and deliver it. While you are gone I will compose a reference. I will give it to you when you return. Then you can get out.'

✝

IN THE STUDY I THOUGHT, what is sure to bring Stice, and
perhaps Rich, to that house? I told Martin to write '*I have urgent news
concerning the visit of an Italian gentleman*'. There, that would do: Lord
Parr had told me that rumours of Bertano's presence were starting to
leak out. Rich would be keenly interested. I had Martin add: '*Please
make sure we are alone. It is all most confidential.*'

When the note was written and I had gone over it, Martin left
for the tavern; I wrote out a reference for him in ill conscience. I wondered whether he might throw the note away and not deliver it, but
before he left I warned him again that very senior people were involved
in this, and oddly I also felt that his pride would ensure that he
honoured this last promise. Josephine took Agnes upstairs to pack.
I stood at my parlour window, looking out on the sunny lawn, full of
sad thoughts. A wife. I would have wished the Queen for a wife.
I wondered whether perhaps I was a little mad, like poor Isabel.

There was a knock at the door. Agnes Brocket entered, her face
weary and tear-stained. 'Martin has told you our news, sir?'

'About John? Yes. I am sorry.'

'Thank you for letting us go, sir. We will return as soon as we can.
Martin has gone out on a last piece of business.' She smiled wanly.

So Martin had not told his wife they would not be returning. No
doubt he would make up some story later. Poor Agnes, so honest and
hard-working, so full of goodwill. Her son in prison, her husband's
deceits kept from her. I said gently, 'I have been looking out at my
garden. You have done much good work there, and in the house.'

'Thank you, sir.' She took a deep breath, then said, 'My husband,
I know he is not always easy, but it is I who insisted we must go to
John today – the fault is all mine.'

'No fault to want to see your son.' I reached for my purse which I
had put on the desk. 'Here, take some money, you will need it on the

journey.' I gave her a half-sovereign. She clutched it tightly and lowered her head. Then, with a desperate effort at her old cheerfulness, she said, 'Make sure Timothy and Josephine stay out of mischief, sir.'

I waited till Martin returned and confirmed he had delivered the message. I gave him the reference. I did not want to watch them leave, so I left the house again and walked to Lincoln's Inn. I needed to speak to Barak and Nicholas and take their counsel.

☦

I TOOK THEM BOTH INTO my office and told them what had just happened. I said, 'This means Stice must be dealt with tomorrow.'

'What grounds are there to lift him?' Barak asked. 'He hasn't done anything illegal, and Rich won't be pleased.'

'That's a matter for Lord Parr. I will look for him at this great banquet at Hampton Court tomorrow afternoon. My last assignment for Treasurer Rowland. From what I gleaned from the instructions, it will be just a matter of standing round with hundreds of others,' I said bitterly, 'showing d'Annebault how many prosperous Englishmen with gold chains there are. Though most are struggling with the taxes to pay for the war, while many thousands more that he will not see struggle simply to exist.'

Barak raised his eyebrows. 'You sound like one of the extreme radicals.'

I shrugged. 'Anyway, I should be able to find Lord Parr then.'

'What if you don't? Among all that throng?'

'I will.' Then all the anger that had been building in me in these last few days burst out and I banged a fist on my desk, making the glass inkpot jump and spill ink. 'I'll find what Rich and Stice have been up to. Damn them, spying on me for months, kidnapping Nicholas, cozening me into working for them. I'll have no more of it! I'm tired to death of being used, used, used!'

It was seldom I lost my temper, and Barak and Nicholas looked at each other. Nicholas said tentatively, 'Might it not be better to leave the matter where it is, sir? Your faithless steward is gone. Anne Askew's book is taken abroad, the Queen's book vanished. And it was taken by different men, not Stice. There is now no trace of the men who killed Greening and those others in his group.'

'And no evidence at all they are connected to Rich,' Barak agreed. 'Quite the opposite.'

'There has always been some — some third force out there, someone who employed those two murderers,' I said. 'But we have never been able to find out who. Whatever Rich and Stice's reason for spying on me — as they have been since well before the book was stolen — it may be nothing to do with the *Lamentation*; but it *is* to do with the Queen. Brocket said he was told particularly to watch for any contact between us. For her sake I have to resolve this. And, yes, for mine!'

Nicholas looked at me seriously. 'Do you want me to come to the house tomorrow?'

Barak nodded at him. 'There is no guarantee Stice will be alone tomorrow.'

'Lord Parr has sent a man to watch the house, he'll know who's coming and going.'

'You should still have somebody with you, sir,' Nicholas persisted. I looked at him; the expression on his freckled face was sincere, though I did not doubt that his youthful taste for adventure had been stirred again.

Barak said, 'Well, if he goes, I'd better go too, to keep an eye on you both.'

I hesitated. 'No, you have both done enough. I'm sure I can persuade Lord Parr to send some men.'

'But if you can't — ' Barak raised his eyebrows.

I looked at them. I realized that from the moment I had sent Brocket with the message I had wanted them to offer to come. And both of them had made their offer mainly from loyalty to me. My throat felt suddenly tight. 'We will see,' I said.

Nicholas shook his head. 'I wish we could have discovered who was behind those men who stole the Queen's book.'

Barak laughed. 'You're doing a lot of wishing, long lad. It doesn't look like Rich but it's not impossible. Or it could be Wriothesley, or either of them acting on Bishop Gardiner's orders.'

'Yes,' I agreed. 'But I don't know. The Lady Mary could even be involved, with that so-called fool Jane; though I doubt that now. Or even the Seymours, working against the Parrs.'

Barak raised an imaginary glass. 'Here's to the King and all his family, and all his grand councillors, and the great Admiral d'Annebault. To the whole bloody lot of them.'

✝

I RETURNED HOME TIRED, and with a guilty conscience. It was my feeling of being used that had caused me to lose my temper, but what was I myself doing if not using Barak and Nicholas?

The house was quiet, the late afternoon sun glinting on the window panes. A rich man's house; in many ways I was lucky. I thought of Martin Brocket and poor Agnes, now no doubt riding hard northwards, kerchiefs round their mouths against the dust. At least the money I had given Agnes should ensure them decent mounts. I would have to rely on Josephine and Timothy until I could find a new steward.

Josephine was in the kitchen, preparing the evening meal. 'They are gone?' I asked.

'Yes, sir.' I could see she had been crying. She added, a little hesitantly, 'Sir, before he left, Master Brocket went to the stable, to take leave of Timothy.' I frowned. Martin had never had any time for the boy before, thinking I spoiled him. 'I don't know what he said, but I saw Timothy afterwards and he was upset, he was crying and wouldn't say what about. Then he ran back to the stable. He will be sad that Agnes is gone. He has – not been himself of late.'

'I have had – well – cause to be displeased with Timothy. I meant to speak to him today. I will do it now.'

She looked relieved. 'I think that a good idea, sir – if I may say,' she added hastily.

I smiled at her. 'You may, Josephine. You are in charge of the household now.' Her eyes widened with a mixture of pleasure and apprehension.

I went to the stable. I could hear Genesis moving inside. I took a deep breath as I opened the door. 'Timothy,' I said quietly, 'I think we should have that talk – '

But there was nobody there, only my horse in its stall. Then I saw, on the upturned bucket where the boy habitually sat, a scrawled note addressed to *Master Shardlake*. I picked it up. I unfolded the note apprehensively.

I am sorry for what I did, my spying on you that day. I was bad. I never meant harm to you, sir. I swear to Lord Jesus. Master Brocket says he and Mistress Agnes are leaving and it is all my fault, it is because of what I did. I do not deserve to stay in your house so I go on the road, a sinner in lammentation.

A sinner in lamentation. The misspelt word jolted me. But its use was common now, in a land where more and more believed they had great sins to lament before God. I put the note down, realizing that my terseness with the boy had done more damage than I could have imagined. Martin had delivered the note to the tavern for me, I was sure, but then he had taken his anger and bitterness out on a child. The foul churl.

I crumpled the note in my fist. Then I ran back to the house, calling to Josephine. 'He is gone! Timothy. We must find him!'

Chapter Forty-eight

JOSEPHINE WENT TO FETCH her fiancé, young Brown. He was happy to help look for Timothy and he and Josephine went one way, I another, to search all the surrounding streets, up beyond New-gate. But although Timothy could not have been gone more than an hour, we found no trace of him. Only when it grew dark did I aban-don the search, returning to a deserted house where I lit a candle and sat staring dismally at the kitchen table. I cursed Brocket, who had deliberately humiliated the boy. I realized that I had come to think of Timothy almost as my own son, just as I had come to see Josephine, in a way, as a daughter. Perhaps that was why I had been so hurt by what Timothy did, and had in turn hurt him, by letting my anger fester. Foolish, foolish, I. It would have been better for us all had I looked on them only as servants.

As I sat there, hoping Josephine and Brown would return with Timothy, Bealknap's words as he lay dying came back to me: *What will happen to you?* Almost as though he had foreseen the disasters that would come.

Then I drew a deep breath. I remembered again how, last autumn, Bealknap had made those uncharacteristic overtures of friendship; for a while seeming to be always hovering nearby, as if wishing to engage me. And then he had fallen badly ill – in the first months of the year, that would have been; at just about the time I took Martin on. I had thought Martin's spying was connected with the heresy hunt. But what if Bealknap, too, had been trying to spy on me? Perhaps Stice had first recruited him and then, when Bealknap's efforts to worm his way into my confidence failed, and he fell ill, Stice had gone looking for another spy and found that my new steward had money worries.

I ran a shaking hand through my hair. If Bealknap had been spying on me, that would explain his deathbed words. But who could have had an interest in me as long ago as last autumn? The heresy hunt had not yet begun and I was not even working for the Queen then.

My reverie was interrupted by the sound of a key turning in the kitchen door. Josephine and Brown entered, looking exhausted. Brown shook his head as Josephine slumped at the table opposite me. 'We can't find him, sir,' he said. 'We asked people, went into all the shops before they closed.'

Josephine looked at me. 'Timothy – he has good clothes, and surely anybody who saw that gap in his teeth would remember it.'

Young Brown put a hand on her shoulder. 'There are many tooth-less children on the streets.'

'Not with Timothy's smile.' Josephine burst into tears.

I stood up. 'Thank you for your help, both of you. I am going to Jack Barak's house now. He may have some ideas.' He would, I was sure; he had been a child on the streets himself once. 'With your employer's permission, Goodman Brown, we shall resume the search at first light tomorrow.'

✝

'OFFER A REWARD.' That was Barak's first suggestion. I sat with him and Tamasin in their parlour, nursing a jug of beer. As always, it was a cosy domestic scene: baby George abed upstairs; Barak mending a wooden doll the child had broken; Tamasin sewing quietly by candle-light, her belly just beginning to swell with the coming child.

'I'll do that. When we go out tomorrow. Offer five pounds.'

Barak raised his eyebrows. 'Five pounds! You'll have every lost urchin in London brought to your door.'

'I don't care.'

He shook his head. Tamasin said, 'What is Josephine's fiancé's first name? You always speak of him just as Brown.'

'Edward, it's Edward. Though I seem to think of him as just young Brown.'

She smiled. 'Perhaps because he is taking Josephine away from you.'

'No, no, he is a fine lad.' I thought of his uncomplaining willing, ness to help tonight, his obvious love for Josephine. She could not have done better. Yet perhaps there was some truth in what Tamasin said.

She said, 'I will go out tomorrow with Goodwife Marris. I'll come to your house in the morning and we can divide the city into sections.'

'No, you won't,' Barak interjected. 'Going up and down the streets and stinking lanes. No.' He put down the doll. 'I'll talk to some people; plenty of the small solicitors and their servants would be happy to look for the boy for five pounds.' There was still amazement in his voice at the size of the sum I was prepared to lay out. 'Have you paid the latest instalment of your taxes?' he asked me.

'Not yet. But remember I got four pounds from Stephen Bealknap.' I frowned slightly, thinking again of his deathbed words.

'Make sure you find him,' Tamasin told her husband. 'Or I will be out looking the next day.' She asked me, 'Is tomorrow not the day you go to Hampton Court?'

'Yes. But I do not have to be there till five in the afternoon. I'll search for Timothy till I have to leave.'

✟

NEXT MORNING, while Barak was busy rousing people to join the hunt, Josephine and Goodman Brown and I went out again. They took the road eastward, to see if the boy had left London; if he had, he would be impossible to find. But he had spent all his life in the city, he must surely be here somewhere.

There was a little crowd in Fleet Street, for today was hanging day and people always gathered to watch the cart that carried the con, demned to the great gibbet at Tyburn, its occupants standing with nooses round their necks. Some of the crowd shouted insults, others encouraged the condemned to die bravely. Though I shuddered as always at this spectacle, I stopped and asked people if they had seen Timothy. But none had.

I went along Cheapside, calling in all the shops. I had dressed in my robe and coif, to impress the shopkeepers, but perhaps some thought I was mad as I asked each a set of questions which soon became a chant: 'I am looking for a lost stable-boy . . . ran away yesterday afternoon . . . thirteen, medium height, untidy brown hair, his two front teeth missing . . . Yes, five pounds . . . no, he hasn't stolen anything . . . yes, I know I could get another . . .'

I asked among the beggars at the great Cheapside conduit. At the sight of a rich gentleman they crowded round me, their stink overpowering. There were children among them, filthy, some covered in sores, eyes feral as cats'. Women as well, too broken or mad even to be whores, in no more than rags, and men missing limbs who had been in accidents, or the wars. They were all blistered by the sun, with cracked lips and dry, matted hair.

More than one said they had seen Timothy, holding out a hand for a reward. I gave each a farthing to whet their appetites and told them the extraordinary sum of five pounds awaited if they produced the boy – the *right* boy, I added emphatically. One lad of about twelve offered himself in Timothy's stead, and bared a skinny arse to show what he meant. One of the women waiting for water at the conduit called out 'Shame!' But I did not care what they thought, so long as Timothy was found.

✝

THERE WAS ONE further resource I had not tapped. Guy had met Timothy several times at my house, and the boy liked him. What was more, if something happened to him, he might turn up at St Bartholomew's. Despite the distance that had come between us, I needed Guy's help.

His assistant Francis Sybrant opened the door and told me his master was at home. He looked at me curiously, for I was dusty from the streets. I waited in Guy's consulting room, with its pleasant per-fume of sandalwood and lavender, and its strange charts of the human body marked with the names of its parts. He came in; I noticed he was starting to walk with an old man's shuffle, but the expression on his scholarly brown face under the thinning grey curls was welcoming.

'Matthew. I was going to write you today, about Mistress Slanning. I am glad you told me about her.'

'How does she fare?'

'Not well. Her priest has spoken with her, but she told him what she and her brother did, and allowed him to tell me, but then broke down again badly. I have prescribed her a sleeping draught; she has a good household steward, he will keep her from doing what her brother did, so far as anyone can. Perhaps in a little while she may confess fully, and receive absolution.'

'Do you think confession would rest her mind?'

He shook his head sadly. 'I think it will never rest again. But it would ease her.'

'Guy, I need your advice on another matter – nothing to do with the great ones of the realm,' I added as his expression became wary. I told him Timothy was missing, and he readily offered to look out for him at the hospital. But he added sadly, 'There are thousands of homeless children in London, more every week, orphans and those cast out from their homes, or coming in from the countryside. Many do not live long.'

'I know. And Timothy – it is partly my fault.'

'Do not think of that. I am sure you are right, he is still in the city, and your offer of a reward may find him.' He put a comforting hand on my arm.

✝

I RETURNED TO THE HOUSE shortly before lunchtime. Barak was there, and said he had half a dozen people out looking. He had told those who had joined the hunt to recruit others, on the promise that each would get a portion of the reward if they found the boy.

'Contracting the job out,' he said with a grin. 'I've got Nick out look‚ ing too, we've more than caught up with the work at chambers.'

'Thank you,' I said, grateful as ever for his practicality.

'I think you should stay here now, to hand over the reward if someone finds him. What time must you be at the banquet?'

'Five. I must leave by three.'

'I'll take over here then.' He stroked his beard. It was tidy as usual, Tamasin kept it well trimmed. 'You'll look for Lord Parr?'

'I'll make sure I find him,' I answered grimly.

'Remember, Nick and I are available tonight, if we're needed.'

'Tamasin — '

'Will be all right. You'd be mad to go there alone.'

'Yes. I hope Lord Parr will supply some men, but bring Nicholas back here after the search for Timothy, and wait for me. Just in case. Thank you,' I added, inadequately.

Chapter Forty-nine

B Y THREE O'CLOCK, several ragged boys had come or been brought to my door, but none was Timothy. I left Barak and took a wherry upriver to Hampton Court. I had done my best to clean the London dust from my robe before I left. I carried the rented gold chain in a bag; wearing it in the city would be a sore temptation to street robbers. I was tired, my back hurt, and I would have liked to lie down rather than be forced to sit on the hard bench of the boat.

'Going to the celebrations to welcome the French admiral, sir?' the boatman asked.

'That's right.'

'They enlisted me last year, sent me to Hampshire. Our company didn't go on the King's ships, though. We came home after the French fleet sailed away. I lost a lot of money through being taken from my trade.'

'At least you came back with your life.'

'Ay. Not all did. And now we've to welcome that Frenchie like a hero.' He turned and spat in the river as the high brick chimneys of Hampton Court came into view in the distance.

✝

ONE OF THE MANY GUARDS posted at the landing stage led me into the Great Court fronting the palace. The wide lawned court backed on to high walls, and in the centre was the Great Gate leading to the inner court and the main buildings, whose red-brick facade looked mellow in the sunlight. Hampton Court was a complex of wide interlocking spaces, a complete contrast to the cramped turrets and tiny courts of Whitehall – less colourful, but more splendid.

In the Great Court I saw two large temporary banqueting houses, skilfully painted to look like brickwork, with the flags of England and France flying from pennants above. Even the smaller of the two structures looked as though it could seat a hundred people. Some of the royal tents had also been put up, their bright varied colours making a vivid picture. Hundreds of people, mostly men, but a goodly number of women too, stood conversing in the wide courtyard, all in their finest clothes. Servants bustled to and fro, handing out silver mugs of wine and offering sweetmeats from trays. There was a steady hum of conversation.

An usher marked my name on a list – there was a list, of course, and anyone who did not turn up would hear about it – and told me that at six o'clock the King and Queen would walk with Admiral d'Annebault and their households from the Great Gate, cross the Great Court and enter the banqueting halls. Later there would be music and dancing. All of us were to cheer loudly when the trumpets sounded. Until then I was told I should mingle, just mingle.

I took a mug of wine from a servant and made my way through the throng, looking for Lord Parr. I could not see him, though there were many other faces I recognized. The old Duke of Norfolk, in a scarlet robe with white fur trim despite the heat, stood with his son the Earl of Surrey, whom I had seen with the ladies in the Queen's Presence Chamber at Whitehall. Both looked over the crowd with aristocratic disdain. In one corner Bishop Gardiner in his white surplice was talking earnestly to Lord Chancellor Wriothesley. Both looked angry. Edward Seymour, Lord Hertford, peregrinated across the court, looking over the crowd of city dignitaries and gentry courtiers with confident, calculating eyes. On his arm was a thin woman in a green farthingale and feathered hat. I recognized her from my first visit to Whitehall Palace to see the Queen; she had asked if I was another hunchback fool. It had annoyed the Queen. Only five weeks ago; it seemed like an age. Many said that Hertford's wife,

Anne, was a shrew who ruled him in private, for all his success as soldier and politician. She certainly had a sour, vinegary face.

The wine was very strong. That and the hubbub made me feel a little light-headed. I saw Sir William Paget in his usual dark robe, walking with a woman who despite her finery had a pleasant, homely countenance. He turned to her as she said something, his hard face softening unexpectedly.

I recalled the boatman spitting in the river. All this splendour for d'Annebault, ambassador of France. I wondered where Bertano, the Pope's emissary, was. Not here, for sure: his mission was still a secret. Perhaps he had already left England. As I walked slowly around, trying to spot Lord Parr, I began to find the gold chain heavy and the sun hot. I halted for a moment under the shade of one of the broad oak trees beside the outer wall.

I felt a tap on my shoulder and I turned: Sir Thomas Seymour, in a silver doublet, with a short yellow cloak over his shoulder and a matching cap worn at a jaunty angle. 'Master Shardlake again,' he said mockingly. 'Are you here as a member of the Queen's Learned Council?'

'No, Sir Thomas. As a serjeant of Lincoln's Inn. I no longer serve the Queen.'

He raised his eyebrows. 'Indeed? Not out of favour with her majesty, I hope?'

'No, Sir Thomas. The task she set me came to an end.'

'Ah, that missing jewel. Wicked, that some servant should steal an object of such great value to the Queen and get away with it. He should have been found and hanged.' His brown eyes narrowed. 'It *was* a jewel, wasn't it?'

'It was.'

Seymour nodded slowly, fingering that long, shiny, coppery beard. 'Strange, strange. Well, I must find my brother. We shall be sitting at the King's table at the banquet.' He smiled again, with preening self-satisfaction. You vain, stupid man, I thought. No wonder not even your brother wants you on the Privy Council.

My feelings must have shown on my face, for Seymour frowned. 'A pity you will not be dining. Only the highest in the land will be seated at the banquet. It must be uncomfortable for you, standing about here. See, even now you shift from foot to foot.'

I knew Thomas Seymour would never part without an insult. I did not reply as he leaned close. 'Watch your step, Master Shardlake. Things are changing, things are changing.' He nodded, smiled maliciously, and walked away.

I looked at his back, and that ridiculous cloak, wondering what he meant. Then, a little way off, I spied Mary Odell, in a dress of deep blue, the Queen's badge on her cap, talking to a young man in an orange doublet. She looked bored. I crossed to her, removed my cap and bowed. The gold links of my chain tinkled.

'Master Shardlake,' she said, relief in her voice.

The young man, handsome but with calculating eyes, looked slightly offended. He twirled the stem of his silver goblet. I said, 'Forgive me, sir, but I must speak with Mistress Odell on a matter of business.'

He bowed stiffly and walked away. 'Thank you, Master Shardlake.' Mistress Odell spoke with that agreeable touch of humour I remembered. 'That young fellow is another would-be courtier, keen to talk with someone close to the Queen.' She grimaced.

'I am glad to have served,' I answered with a smile. Then, more earnestly, 'I need to speak with Lord Parr urgently. I hoped to see him here.'

She glanced back at the Great Gate behind us. 'He is in the Palace Court, with the Queen and her ladies, waiting for the King to come out with the admiral.'

'Could you fetch him? I am sorry to ask, but it is very urgent. He is expecting to talk to me today.'

Her face grew serious. 'I know you would not ask on a trivial matter. Wait, I will try to find him.'

She walked away, her dress swishing on the cobbles, and was allowed by the guards to pass through the Great Gate. I took some more wine and a comfit from a waiter. Looking over the crowd, I saw Serjeant Blower with a couple of aldermen, laughing heartily at some joke. William Cecil passed with an attractive young woman who must be his wife. He nodded to me but did not come over. Then, a little way off, I saw that Wriothesley was now talking to Sir Richard Rich, their heads together. I looked back at the gate. The feather plumes on the guards' steel helmets stirred in a cooling breeze from the river. The sun was low now.

Lord Parr appeared at the Great Gate, looking out at the throng. He craned his neck, trying to find me in the crowd. He looked tired. I walked over to him.

'Master Shardlake,' he said, irritation in his voice. 'I am needed inside. The King and Queen and the admiral will be out in ten minutes.'

'I am sorry, my Lord. I would not interrupt, but we must act against Stice tonight. He will be at the house near St Bartholomew's at nine. Have you heard any more? Has anyone been to the house?'

The old man shifted his weight a little uneasily. 'My man says Stice came briefly yesterday, but soon left again.'

'Alone?'

'Yes.'

I spoke urgently, 'Then if you could spare a couple of men to go tonight, I will go too. Stice must be questioned. Even if we have no cause — '

Then Lord Parr said firmly, 'No.'

'My Lord?'

'Things have changed, Master Shardlake. Charles Stice must be left alone.'

'But — why?'

He leaned in. 'This is confidential, Shardlake. I have had a direct approach from Richard Rich. He is in bad odour with Gardiner, for several reasons; his speaking up for you at the Privy Council did not help. He has offered to aid the Seymours and Parrs against Norfolk and Gardiner. He has changed sides, following the wind again.'

I looked at him in amazement. 'The Queen will work with Rich now? But she loathes him.'

'She will,' Lord Parr answered firmly. 'For the sake of the Parr family, and the cause of reform. Rich is on the council, he is important, the King respects his skills, if not the man. As do I.'

'But — why has he been spying on me? And may he not have information about the *Lamentation*?'

Lord Parr shook his head firmly. 'Rich will do nothing to harm the reformers now. Even if he had the book, which I do not believe he ever did.'

'If he is your ally now should you not ask him?'

Irritation entered the old man's voice. 'Our agreement involves my drawing a veil over all his activities this spring and summer. Those are not to be discussed. That includes what he did to Anne Askew, and everything else. As for his spying on you,' he added more civilly, 'in due course, when the time is right, I will ask him.'

Stunned, I continued to stare at Lord Parr. He flushed, then burst out with sudden impatience, 'God's death, man, do not stand there with your mouth open like a fish. These are the necessities of politics. Rich and his people are to be left alone.'

And with that, the Queen's Chamberlain turned away, back to the Great Gate.

†

I STEPPED BACK, feeling as though I had been punched in the stomach. So Rich was finally turning his coat. And, I thought wearily, Lord Parr was right; these were the necessities of politics. Why should it matter to any of them what Rich had done to me? I looked across to where he stood talking to Wriothesley; Wriothesley's face was red, they were arguing. The alliance between them, which had led to the torture of Anne Askew, was over now.

A trumpet blew, then another. The guards at the Great Gate stood to attention and everyone ceased talking and looked towards it in silence. Then the King appeared in the gateway, Admiral d'Annebault at his side. The King was dressed more magnificently than I had ever seen before, in a yellow coat with padded shoulders and fur collar, a cream-coloured doublet set with jewels, and a broad white feathered cap on his head. He was smiling widely. One arm rested on his jewelled stick, the other round the shoulder of Archbishop Cranmer. No doubt he needed Cranmer to hold him up. Fortunately it was but a short walk to the banqueting houses. On d'Annebault's other side, her arm through the admiral's, was the Queen. She wore a dress in Tudor green and white, her auburn hair bright under a green cap, a light smile on her face. She looked radiant: knowing her inner turmoil, I marvelled again at her composure.

The royal party was followed by the men from the King's household, and women from the Queen's ladies in their bright new livery, led by Lord Parr. The crowd in the Great Court parted to let them walk through to the larger of the two banqueting houses. I joined the others in raising my cup. There were claps and shouts of 'God save the King!'

Now the junior members of the households halted and turned towards the second, smaller banqueting house. Guards opened the doors of both and I glimpsed cloth-covered tables on which candles in gold sconces were already lit against the coming dusk. The leading men of the realm – Norfolk and Gardiner and Paget, the Seymour brothers and others – left the crowd and followed the King, Queen and d'Annebault into the larger banqueting house. From within I heard lutes starting to play.

The Lady Mary had now appeared through the gateway, followed by her own retinue. Jane Fool was there, and began dancing and frolicking round Mary, who laughed and bade her cease. They, too, passed into the royal banqueting house.

The crowd outside relaxed, as a fresh column of servants came through the Great Gate carrying large trays of food from the Hampton Court kitchens. They were followed by a group of guards bearing torches, which they slotted into brackets set into the walls of the Great Court and on the trunks of trees. As the servants handed round cold meats and more wine, I saw some people were getting drunk; in Serjeant Blower's party, one or two were swaying slightly. Son of a drunkard myself, the sight revolted me.

I looked over all these rich men and women and thought of Timothy, somewhere alone out on the streets. The notion came to me that perhaps the Anabaptists had something after all: a world where the gulf between the few rich and the many poor did not exist, a world where preening peacocks like Thomas Seymour and Serjeant Blower wore wadmol and cheap leather, might not be so bad a place after all.

I waved away a waiter carrying plates in one hand and a silver dish of swan's meat in the other. I was shocked by what Lord Parr had said. It was dusk and the breeze felt suddenly cold. My back hurt. My mission was over. I should go and tell Barak and Nicolas they would not be needed.

I saw that Rich and Wriothesley were still engrossed in their argument, whatever it was. They would be in trouble if they did not soon make their way to their appointed places in the royal banqueting hall. Then I saw somebody else I recognized. Stice. I stepped back into the deepening shadows of the tree. He wore an expensive grey doublet, with 'RR' embossed on the chest, and as he passed at a little distance a torch picked out the shiny scar tissue of his damaged ear. The way he was moving puzzled me; he walked stealthily as he moved towards the royal banqueting house, constantly seeking cover, slipping behind those who stood between him and his master. There could be no doubt, I realized suddenly: Stice was avoiding Rich, not seeking him. Rich and Wriothesley were still arguing fiercely; Rich waved a waiter aside so violently that the man dropped a tray filled with goblets of wine. People laughed as the waiter bent to pick them up, Rich berating him angrily as though it were the waiter's fault. Stice took the opportunity to move swiftly to the guards at the doors of the banqueting house. A steel-helmeted soldier put out a hand to stop him.

Stice pulled something from the purse at his belt and showed it to the guard. I could not make it out but it looked like a seal, that of one of the great men of the realm, no doubt. Not Rich, who still stood with Wriothesley, glowering at the unfortunate waiter, for Stice would have pointed to him. As the guard examined the seal, Stice cast a quick glance over his shoulder at Rich. Then the soldier nodded to him, and Stice entered the tent.

I stood there, my heart thudding. For I realized now that Stice, like Curdy the spy, had more than one loyalty. A man in Richard Rich's employment had outmanoeuvred his master. Stice had used that seal to get himself into the royal banquet, and his purpose in hurrying there now must be to tell his other master, whoever that was, about the note retrieved from the tavern where Brocket had left it, the note mentioning the 'Italian gentleman'. But who, among those leading men, was Stice's other master? Whoever it was, he had ordered Stice to spy on me, for many months. Rich had been telling the truth, after all. I stared intently at the open doors, but I could only vaguely make out the bright-clad courtiers moving to take their seats.

Rich and Wriothesley realized they were late. They began walking towards the banqueting house with long strides, not speaking. The guards let them through. Would Rich see Stice now?

No. For a moment later Stice walked briskly along the outside wall of the banqueting house, ducking as he passed a window; he must have left through a rear entrance. Keeping close to the tree, I watched as he stepped rapidly away to the river steps, and disappeared.

A group of minstrels walked into the centre of the Great Court, strumming their instruments for the crowd. People cheered, and as I watched a space was cleared. Men and women began dancing, robes and skirts whirling. I thought for a moment, Lord Parr should be told about Stice, especially if Rich was on his side now. But he was inside the main banqueting house. I had seen how difficult it had been for Stice to gain entrance; and I no longer had the Queen's seal to show anyone, for I had returned it along with the robe with her badge on it.

Stice must already be on his way back to London by boat, to go to what he thought was a rendezvous with Brocket. I clenched my fists. Obstinacy and anger rose in me. Well, it would be me and Barak and Nicholas whom Stice would be meeting. Three of us against one, we would take him easily, and we would finally have some answers.

Chapter Fifty

BARAK AND NICHOLAS WERE waiting for me at home, drinking beer in the kitchen. I had hailed a boat quickly at the
Hampton Court stairs; a long line of wherrymen was waiting to bring
people back to London once the festivities ended, and I was leaving
early. I asked the boatman whether I was the first to depart; he replied
that one of his fellows had picked up another customer a few minutes
before. As we pulled downriver I saw another boat a little ahead of us,
a man in grey doublet and cap sitting in the stern. I told the boatman
to slow a little so I might enjoy the cool airs of evening; in fact it was
to let Stice get out of view. It was peaceful out there on the river, the
boatman's oars making ripples that glinted in the setting sun, insects
buzzing over the water. I asked myself: is this right, what I am doing?
And I answered yes, for surely Stice's true master was the one who had
ordered the murder of the Anabaptists and taken the *Lamentation*.
There might be a chance of recovering the Queen's book after all.

✝

BACK HOME, there was no news of Timothy. Barak, who had
remained at the house all afternoon, had had several visitors who
said they knew where the boy was but wanted the reward first. Barak
had dealt with them bluntly. Nicholas had also returned. I thanked
them for their efforts, telling myself that for the next few hours I must
put Timothy's fate from my mind.

Looking at Barak and Nicholas, I considered again whether what
I was doing was right. This was for the Queen and the murdered men,
but I knew also for myself, because I wanted answers. Barak and

Nicholas had come equipped for danger; Nicholas's sword was at his belt and Barak had one, too. Both knew well how to use them.

I told them about seeing Stice at Hampton Court, and what Lord Parr had said. When I had finished I asked them once more, 'Are you sure you wish to do this?'

'All the more, now,' Barak said. 'With Brocket gone it's our last chance.'

'What did you tell Tamasin?'

He looked uncomfortable. 'That we were going to continue searching for Timothy this evening.'

'I'm glad of the chance to get back at that churl who kidnapped me,' Nicholas said. 'But sir, if we catch him, what do we do with him? We can't take him back to my lodgings as we did with Leeman, my fellow students are there.'

'I've thought of that. We'll keep him in that house until morning; question him ourselves, then take him to Lord Parr.'

'I'll get answers out of him.' Barak spoke coldly. 'He wouldn't be the first.' I thought, no, there are things you did when you worked for Cromwell that we have always drawn a veil over. I did not dissent.

'Can we be sure Stice will be alone?' Nicholas asked.

'I got Brocket to ask him to come alone as always. And Lord Parr's man who is watching the house says Stice only came there once, and by himself.'

Barak said, 'I got one of the men helping me on the search for Timothy to walk up and down that street this afternoon and report back to me. I didn't want to go myself as Stice knows me. It's a lane of small, newly built houses, much better places than on Needlepin Lane. Most of the houses have porches, quite deep. We could hide in one and watch until just before nine. We might even see Stice arrive.'

'Very well.' I looked out of the window. It was quite dark now. I thought, at Hampton Court they would be dancing by torchlight in the courtyard, sounds of loud revelry coming from the King's banqueting house. Several more banquets, as well as hunts, were planned for the next few days. The Queen would be at all of them. Then I thought of Timothy, alone on the dangerous streets for a second night. I collected myself. 'Let us go now,' I said. 'But remember, Stice is a man who will stop at nothing.'

'Fortune favours those with justice and honour on their side,' Nicholas said.

Barak responded, 'If only.'

✟

THE STREETS WERE QUIET as we walked up to Smithfield. Fortunately it was not a market day and the big open space was silent and deserted. We went down Little Britain Street, following the wall of St Bartholomew's Hospital, then turned into a broad lane, a reput-able row of newly built two-storey houses, most with glass windows rather than shutters, and little porches, too. Candles flickered behind most of the windows but at a house that was in darkness Barak waved us into the porch. I hoped the owner would not return expectedly; he would think himself about to be robbed.

Barak pointed to a house on the opposite side of the lane, a little further down. 'That's the one. There's a big Tudor rose on the arch above the porch, as Brocket mentioned. You can just see it.'

I followed his gaze. The house's shutters were drawn and all was silent.

We stood, waiting and watching. A serving woman came out of a nearby house with a bucket of dirty water and poured it into the channel in the centre of the road. We tensed as the light of a torch appeared at the top of the lane, and voices sounded. It was, however, only a link-boy, leading the way for a small family party who were chattering happily, returning from some visit. They disappeared into one of the houses further down the lane.

'What time is it?' Nicholas asked quietly. 'It must be near nine.'

'I think it is,' Barak said. 'But it doesn't look like Stice is here yet.'

'He could already be inside,' I whispered. 'At the rear of the house, perhaps.'

Barak's eyes narrowed. 'All right, let's wait till the clocks chime.

Stice wouldn't be late for this one, not if he's been all the way to Hampton Court and back to consult his master.'

We waited. When the bells rang out the hour, Barak took a deep breath. 'Let's go,' he breathed. 'Rush him as soon as the door opens.'

✝

WE HALF-RAN ACROSS THE STREET. I glanced up at the Tudor rose on the lintel of the porch, as Barak hammered on the door. He and Nicholas both had their hands on their sword hilts, and I grasped my knife.

I heard quick footsteps, sounding indeed as though they were coming from the rear of the house. There was the glimmer of a candle between the shutters. As soon as we heard the handle turn on the inner side of the door Barak put his shoulder to it, and crashed inside. The interior was dim, just a couple of candles in a holder on the table. By their light I saw Charles Stice stagger back, hand reaching to the sword at his waist. But Barak and Nicholas already had their blades pointed at his body.

'Got you,' Nicholas said triumphantly.

Then, at the edge of my vision, I saw rapid movement as the men who had been waiting on either side of the door stepped quickly out. Two more swords flashed. Barak and Nicholas turned rapidly as two well-built young men ran at them from behind. I recognized them by the candlelight: one fair with a wart on his brow, the other almost bald. Greening's killers, Daniels and Cardmaker.

Barak and Nicholas were both quick, managing to parry the blows. Meanwhile, drawing my knife, I lunged forward, ready to plunge it into the neck of the bald man, but he was faster than me. Though still fighting against Nicholas, he managed to half-turn and elbow me in the face with his free arm. I staggered back against the wall. The distraction, however, was enough to allow Nicholas to gain the advantage, and begin to force him back.

Barak, meanwhile, was facing not only the other man in front but Stice behind. And before he could turn, step aside and face both of them, Stice raised his newly drawn sword and slashed at Barak's sword-arm. To my horror the razor-sharp weapon, with the full force of Stice's arm behind it, slashed down into Barak's wrist just above his sword. Into it and through it, and I cried out at a sight I shall never forget: Barak's severed hand, still holding his sword, flying through the air and hitting the ground.

He screamed, turned and grasped his arm, which was spraying blood. Then Stice stabbed him in the back with his sword. Barak looked at me. His face was a mask of astonishment, his eyes somehow questioning, as though he wanted me to explain what had just happened. Then his legs gave way and he crashed to the floor. He lay on his face, unmoving, blood pumping from the stump of his wrist.

In a fury, I flew at Stice, knife raised. My move was unexpected and he did not have time to block my path with his sword. I aimed for his throat but he ducked and the knife slashed his face instead, from mouth to ear. He cried out but did not drop his sword, instead raising it to my throat and forcing me backwards, pinning me against the wall.

'Stop now!' he shouted. 'You can't win!'

Glancing to the side, I saw the other two had Nicholas. The bald man shouted, 'Drop the sword, boy!' Nicholas gritted his teeth, but obeyed. His weapon clattered to the floor. He looked in horror at Barak, face down on the floor. Stice withdrew his sword from my throat. He reached into his pocket and pulled out a handkerchief to staunch the blood welling from his cheek. I caught a glimpse of white bone.

Barak made a sound, a little moan. He was still alive, just. He tried to raise his head but it dropped back to the floor with a crack and he lay unmoving again. Blood still poured from his wrist, and more from the wound in his back, making a dark patch on his shirt.

'He's still alive,' the bald man said with professional interest.

'Not for long,' Stice replied. 'He'll bleed out soon if nothing else.' Blood dripped down the hand holding the kerchief to his face. 'He was once known as a fighter,' he added, with sudden pride.

I looked at Stice, and spoke savagely, through bruised lips. 'At least you'll have a scar on your face to match that ear.'

He looked at me coldly, then laughed. 'So, you caught Brocket out, did you?'

'It was me who sent the message.'

Stice smiled. 'Brocket seemed to have found out something big. I thought it time to bring him in person to my master, so I arranged help to secure him.'

'So all of you were working together, all the time?'

'That's right. All part of the same merry band, working for the same master.'

The fair-haired man, his sword still pointed at Nicholas's throat, said, 'He'll be pleased then? We've caught a big fish, as well as this long minnow?'

Stice sat on the edge of the table. 'Yes. He'll be keen to find out why he mentioned an Italian.' He winced at the pain from his face. 'God's wounds, I'll have to get this stitched. But we must take Shardlake to him first. The boy as well. Bind their hands; we'll ride. I'll get treatment at Whitehall. He's waiting there.'

Whitehall? I thought. But the royal family and high councillors had all moved to Hampton Court.

'It's past curfew,' the fair-haired man said. 'What if the constables see us?'

'With my seal, they won't challenge us. Not when they see who we are taking them to.'

There was a sudden bang on the wall separating the house from its neighbour. A man's voice shouted, 'What's going on?' The voice was cultured and angry, but frightened too. 'What's all this noise?'

Stice called out, 'We're having a party! Fuck off!' His confederates laughed. There was silence from the next house. I looked down at Barak, quite still now, blood still flowing from his severed wrist, though less freely. I glanced at his severed hand, lying a foot away on the floor, still holding his sword. 'Right,' Stice said decisively. 'Time to go.'

I said, 'Who is your master? It's not Richard Rich, is it? I was at Hampton Court, and saw how you avoided him. Who are you really working for?'

Stice frowned. 'You'll find out soon, Master Hunchback.'

The bald man nodded at the prone Barak. 'What about him?'

'Leave him to bleed out,' Stice replied.

I said desperately, 'Leave him to die here? Leave a body in this house to be found? That neighbour is already worried. He'll be looking in the windows tomorrow. Then there'll be a coroner's enquiry – in public – and they'll do a search to find out who owns the house.' I continued rapidly, for I knew this was my last dim hope of saving Barak's life, if indeed he was not already dead. 'It's known that Jack Barak works with me. Whatever you have planned for me, this is murder and it won't be allowed to rest. Not when the Queen hears – she won't let it.'

'Our master could soon stop a coroner's enquiry,' the bald man said scoffingly. Stice frowned, though. He looked down at Barak; his face, from what I could see, was still and ashen against his brown beard. He could be dead already. I thought of Tamasin, pregnant. I had brought him here.

'The hunchback could be right,' Daniels said uneasily.

'All right,' Stice agreed. 'Our master would wish us to be careful. Here, one of you make a tourniquet with your handkerchiefs, or he'll bleed all over us as well as the floor.'

'I know where we can put him.' The bald man gave a little giggle. 'I came here round the back ways. There's an empty building lot the people round here have turned into a rubbish heap. Two streets away.'

'All right,' Stice agreed. 'Bind those two now.'

Cardmaker produced a length of rope from the bag at his belt, which he must have brought for Brocket. He cut it in two with his knife, then approached us. 'Hands behind your backs.'

We could do nothing else. I looked desperately at Barak's prone form as they bound our hands behind us. Meanwhile Stice bound Barak's arm tightly with a handkerchief, making a tourniquet to lessen the flow of blood, and tied another securely round the stump. Bright red blood immediately began to seep through. Then Stice said, 'Daniels, throw him across your horse. We'll put these two on the horse we brought for Brocket, tie their legs together under the horse's belly. If we're stopped on the way to Whitehall, say they're traitors and we've arrested them.' He looked at Barak's severed hand lying on the floor in a pool of blood, still gripping his sword. 'God's teeth, what a mess. We'll have to come back and clean this up after. Our master often uses this house.'

They took us out to the back, where there was a stable, three horses waiting. It was horrible to see Barak unconscious, being lifted up under the arms by Cardmaker and dumped over the back of one of the horses as though he were a sack of cabbages. From what I could see, the bleeding was much less, though a few drips still fell to the ground. But I knew enough to understand that even if Barak still lived, he did not have long, perhaps fifteen minutes, before he bled out.

Stice looked at me over his handkerchief, his eyes bright with savage pleasure. 'It'll be up to my master whether the two of you live. He'll get a surprise; he was only expecting one frightened steward.'

Chapter Fifty-one

W E RODE DOWN THE LANE behind the stables. Nicholas and
I had been placed, hands bound, on one of the horses, Nicholas in front. It was a moonlit night, though the narrow track between
the garden fences of the new houses was hard to see. Then we turned
into a second lane, running down the back of another row of houses.
Halfway down the lane there was a square plot where for some reason
no building had been put up. As Cardmaker had said, it was a rubbish heap. I saw an old bed frame, broken stools, household refuse and
a huge heap of grass clippings where servants had been scything the
gardens. It had mulched down into a soft green compost. The rubbish
heap stank.

We halted. Stice's men dismounted and Barak was lifted from his
horse and tipped, head first, into the compost. I seldom prayed nowadays — even if God existed, I was sure that he was deaf. Now,
though, I prayed hopelessly that somehow my friend might live.

We rode back to the main road. It was hard merely to keep my
balance. My face throbbed from where I had been elbowed. Stice's
confederates walked one on either side of us; Stice, leading the horse
which had carried Barak, rode in front, still dabbing at his face with
his handkerchief. We came out onto Smithfield and passed the front
door of the hospital. I wondered if Guy was working within.

We were stopped at Newgate by a constable. Lifting his lamp
and seeing our bound hands and Stice's bloody face, he asked Stice
sharply what was happening. But Stice took out a seal, thrusting it into
the man's face. 'Official business,' he snapped. 'Two traitors to go to

Whitehall for questioning. As you'll see from my face, they made a fight of it.'

The London constables knew the different seals of all the great men, it was part of their training. The man not only withdrew, but bowed to Stice as he did so.

☩

WE RODE ON through the quiet streets, past Charing Cross and down to Whitehall. I wondered why we were being taken there rather than to Hampton Court. Surely, apart from the guards, there would be only a few servants left to maintain the place? Yet such consider-ations hardly mattered in comparison to what had happened to Barak. I was sitting tied up on the horse, my back was excruciatingly painful and my face throbbed. A wave of exhaustion washed over me, and my head slumped forward onto Nicholas's back. He took the weight, saying over his shoulder, 'Stay awake, sir, or you will fall.'

'Just let me rest against you a little.' Then I said, 'I am sorry, sorry.' He did not reply. Whatever happened now, I must try to save Nicholas at least.

☩

AS EXPECTED, Whitehall Palace was dark and deserted, only a few dim lights visible within. But the guard at the gatehouse had obvi-ously been told to expect Stice, for as we rode up he stepped forward. Stice bent to speak to him; there were some murmured words and then I heard the guard say, 'He's waiting in the Privy Council Chamber. Rode here from the Hampton Court celebrations half an hour ago.'

Two more guards came out of the gatehouse. Stice dismounted and quickly scribbled a note, and the first guard ran into the building with it. No doubt it was to inform Stice's master that he had come back not with Brocket, but with me.

The two guards accompanied us across the courtyard, the horses' hooves clattering loudly on the cobbles. We came up to the wide doors of the King's Guard Chamber. Stice dismounted and cut the ropes binding us. Nicholas helped me to dismount, and I stood a little shakily at the bottom of the steps. Stice, bloodied handkerchief still held to his face, turned to Daniels and Cardmaker. 'Thank you, goodmen, for your work these last two months. Your money is in the gatehouse. Leave London for a while, find some alehouses and brothels in another town to spend your wages. But keep in contact, in case you are needed again.'

The two murderers bowed, then turned away without another glance at us. I watched them go, the men who had killed Greening and Elias and those others. Hired murderers, strolling cheerfully to collect their reward. I looked at Stice, who glared back at me. 'I will leave you as well now, Master Shardlake. I need to get your handiwork on my face seen to. I doubt you will leave here alive, which is a comfort. If you do, watch out for me.' Then he followed his henchmen back to the palace gatehouse. Nicholas and I were left with the two guards. One inclined his halberd towards the doorway of the Guard Chamber. 'In,' he said brusquely.

I looked at Nicholas, who swallowed hard. Then we mounted the steps, one guard ahead of us, one behind.

✠

THE MAGNIFICENT STAIRCASE leading up to the King's Guard Chamber was quiet and barely lit, only two men posted at the top; the torches in their niches showing empty spaces on the wall where paintings had been removed to Hampton Court. One of the guards at the top said we were to be taken to the Privy Council Chamber, where I had stood and sweated the week before. 'He's not ready yet, you can wait in the Privy Chamber. It's empty as the King's not in residence here.'

We were led through a series of dim rooms until we reached a large chamber. The walls were almost bare here too, everything no doubt removed to the Privy Chamber at Hampton Court. We were ordered to stand and wait, a guard staying with us. I looked at the opposite wall, and saw that it was covered from floor to ceiling by a magnificent wall painting, irremovable, for it was painted directly onto the plaster just like the Cotterstoke family portrait. I had heard of Holbein's great mural, and now, in the dim flickering candlelight, I looked at it. The other large wall painting I had seen at Whitehall had shown the present King and his family; this one, however, was a magnificent display of dynastic power. The centrepiece was a square stone monument, covered in Latin words which I could not make out from where I stood. The old King, Henry VII, stood on a pedestal with one lean arm resting on the monument, his sharp foxy face staring out. Opposite him was a plump woman with arms folded, no doubt the King's mother. Below her, on a lower step, stood Queen Jane Seymour. I thought again how Prince Edward resembled his mother. But it was the present King, standing below his father, who dominated the mural: the King as he had been perhaps half a dozen years ago: broad-shouldered, burly but not fat, his hand on his hip and his bull-like legs planted firmly apart, with an exaggerated cod-piece jutting from the skirts of his doublet.

This image of the King had been reproduced many times and hung in countless official buildings and private halls, but the original had a life and power no copyist could imitate. It was the hard, staring, angry little blue eyes which dominated the painting, whose back-ground was in sombre colours. Perhaps that was the whole point of the mural, to make those who were waiting to see the King feel as if he were already watching and judging them.

Nicholas stared open-mouthed at the mural and then whispered, 'It is like looking at living people.'

Another guard came in then and spoke to the first. We were taken roughly by the arm, and led out, through a second and then a third magnificent chamber, before we reached a corridor I recognized; the Privy Council Chamber. We came up to the door. The guard stand-ing before it said, 'Not the boy. He says to put him somewhere till he knows whether he needs to question him.'

'Come on, you.' The first guard pulled Nicholas's arm, leading him away. 'Courage, Master Shardlake,' Nicholas called back to me.

Then the remaining guard knocked at the door, and a sharp voice I recognized called, 'Enter.'

I was pulled inside. The guard left, shutting the door behind me. There was only one man in the long chamber, sitting on a chair at the centre of the table, a sconce of candles beside him. He looked at me with hard eyes set in a slab face above a forked beard. Master Secretary Paget.

'Master Shardlake.' He sighed wearily. 'How much work and effort you have made for me.' He shook his head. 'When there is so much else to do.'

I looked at him. 'So you were behind it all,' I said quietly. My voice sounded thick and muffled, my face swelling now where I had been struck.

His expression did not change. 'All what?'

Recklessly, far beyond deference now, I answered, 'The murder of those Anabaptists. The theft of the – the manuscript. Spying on me for the last year, I know not why. Nor care.' I gulped a breath, my voice breaking as a picture came into my head once more of Barak dumped on that rubbish heap.

Paget stared back at me. He had the gift of sitting still, focused, like a cat watching its prey. '*Murder?*' His tone was admonitory, accusing. 'Those men were heretics, and traitors too, who would gladly have killed me, or the King, or you for that matter, to advance their perverted notions. They had easier deaths than they deserved, they should have been burned. They were stupid, though. When my spies among the radicals warned me of a nest of Anabaptists in London, my man Curdy infiltrated it with ease. Now *there* was a loyal servant, and he *was* murdered.' Paget drew his heavy eyebrows together in a frown.

'He was killed in a fight.'

'Yes. By one of Richard Rich's men.' He waved a hand contemptuously. 'Rich was after what Anne Askew wrote before she was burned, I know that. I believe John Bale has it now.' For the first time Paget laughed, a flash of surprisingly white teeth amid the coarse brown of his beard. 'That may come back to haunt Sir Richard yet.'

'You suborned Rich's servant,' I said.

Paget shifted a little, settling more comfortably in his chair. 'I keep my eye on those who work for the great men of the realm, and sometimes I find men among them of such ambition they can be persuaded to work for me and earn two incomes. Though organizing a watch to be kept on you, Shardlake, that was a nuisance, a waste of Stice's talents, I thought. And there was nothing to find. Until – ' he leaned forward, frowning now, his voice threatening – 'until last month.' He paused, then spoke slowly and deliberately. 'A moment ago you mentioned a manuscript.'

I did not reply. I should not have spoken of it. I must keep my control. I waited for Paget to question me further, but he only smiled cynically. 'The *Lamentation of a Sinner*,' he said, 'by her majesty, the Queen Catherine.'

My mouth fell open. 'Yes, Master Shardlake,' he went on, 'it was me who arranged for that book to be taken from the heretic printer Greening, as soon as Curdy told me it had been brought to his group by that wretched guard.'

I closed my eyes for a moment. Then, having nothing left to lose, I said, 'No doubt you took it to further your own ends in the power struggle. Have you been waiting, like Rich, to see which way the wind will blow, whether the Queen would fall and Bertano's mission succeed, keeping the *Lamentation* in reserve? Be careful, Master Secretary, that the King does not find you have kept it from him.'

I was speaking recklessly, dangerously. 'Mind your words with me, master lawyer,' Paget snapped. 'Remember who I am and where you are.' I stared back at him, breathing heavily. He inclined his head. 'You are right that the King was gracious enough to receive an emissary from the Bishop of Rome, but it seems that as a condition of peace His Holiness, as he styles himself, demands that the King surrender the Headship of the Church in England – the Headship to which God has appointed him. Bertano is still here, but I think it is time now he took himself back to his master. How did you know of his presence?' he asked sharply.

'The Anabaptists were overheard,' I said quietly. 'You rogue, that cut such a swathe of murder through ordinary folk to serve your ambition.'

'My ambition, eh?' Paget asked coldly.

'Yes.'

And then, to my surprise, he laughed grimly, and stood up. 'I think it is time for you to see what you never guessed, master clever lawyer. Even Stice did not know anything of this.' He picked up the sconce of candles and walked past me to the door. 'Follow me,' he said with an imperious sweep of the arm, throwing the door open wide.

I got up slowly. He said to the guard outside, 'Accompany us.'

The guard took a position beside me as Paget opened a door opposite. I found myself in a darkened gallery filled with beautiful scents, like the Queen's gallery, though wider and twice the length. As we walked along, our footsteps silent on the rush matting, the sconce of candles in Paget's hand showed glimpses of tapestries and paintings more magnificent than any I had seen elsewhere in the palace, before we passed marble columns and platforms on which rested gigantic vases, beautiful models of ships, jewelled chests with who knew what within. I realized this must be the King's Privy Gallery, and wondered why the contents had not been taken to Hampton Court. We passed an enormous military standard, the flag decorated with fleur-de-lys; no doubt a French standard seized when Henry took Boulogne. It was covered in dark spots. Blood, I realized, and remembered again Barak's severed hand flying through the air. I jumped at something small running along the wainscoting. A rat. Paget frowned and barked at the guard. 'Get that seen to! Bring one of the ratcatchers back from Hampton Court!'

At length we reached the end of the gallery, where two further guards stood beside a large double door. Glancing through a nearby window I saw we were directly above the palace wall, on the other side of which I could see the broad way of King Street. A group of young gentlemen were walking past, link-boys with torches lighting their way.

'Master Secretary.' One of the guards at the door bowed to Paget, and opened it. I blinked at the brightness of the light on the other side, then followed Paget in.

It was a wide chamber, beautifully furnished, and brightly lit by a host of fat buttermilk candles in silver sconces. The walls were lined with shelves of beautiful and ancient books. In the spaces between the shelves, splendid paintings hung, mostly depicting classical scenes. A window looked out directly over the street. I realized we must be inside the Holbein Gate. Under the window was a wide desk littered with papers and a dish of comfits beside a golden flagon of wine. A pair of spectacles lay atop the papers, glinting in the candlelight.

The King's fool, little hunchbacked Will Somers, stood beside the desk, his monkey perched on the shoulder of his particoloured doub-let. And sitting beside him, in an enormous chair, staring at me with blue eyes as hard and savage as those in Holbein's portrait, for all that they were now tiny slits in a pale face thick with fat, was the King.

Chapter Fifty-two

INSTANTLY, I BOWED AS LOW AS I COULD. After what had happened to Barak I had given Paget none of the deference due to him, but faced with the King I abased myself instinctively. I had time to take in only that he wore a long caftan, as on the day Lord Parr showed him to me from the window, and that his head with its grey wispy hair was bare.

There was a moment's silence. The blood rushed to my head and I thought I might faint. But no one was permitted to rise and look the King in the face until he addressed them. I heard him laugh. It was a laboured, creaking sound, oddly reminiscent of Treasurer Rowland. Then he spoke, in that same unexpectedly high voice I remembered from my brief encounter with him at York, though underlain with a new, throaty creakiness. 'So, Paget, my Master of Practices, he found you out. Someone has punched him in the face.' That creaky laugh again.

'There was a fight, I believe, your majesty, before Stice took him,' Paget said.

'Have you told him anything?'

'Nothing, your majesty. You said you wished to do that.'

The King continued in the same quiet voice, though I discerned a threatening edge to it now. 'Very well, Serjeant Matthew Shardlake, stand.'

I did so, my bruised face throbbing, and looked slowly up at the King. The pale bloated face was lined, full of pain and weariness. His grey beard, like his hair, was thin and wispy. His huge bulk strained against the satin arms of his chair, and his legs stuck out, swathed in thick bandages. But grotesque and even pitiable as he now was, Henry's gaze remained terrifying. In the portrait outside it was the eyes which seemed most chilling, but in the living man it was the tight little mouth, straight and hard as a blade between the great jowls; angry, merciless. Looking at him my head swam for a second; it was as though none of this were real, and I was in some nightmare. I felt oddly disconnected, dizzy, and again I thought I might faint. Then in my mind's eye I saw Barak's hand fly through the air in a spray of blood, and I jerked convulsively.

The King held my gaze another moment, then turned and waved at Somers and the guard. 'Will, top up my goblet, then take the guard and begone. One crookback at a time is enough.'

Somers poured wine from the flagon, the monkey clinging to his shoulder with practised ease. The King lifted the goblet to his mouth and I caught a glimpse of grey teeth. 'God's death,' he murmured, 'this endless thirst.'

Somers and the guard went out, closing the door quietly behind them. I gave Paget a quick glance; he looked back with that flat, empty gaze of his. The King, his eyes locking on mine again, spoke in a voice full of quiet menace. 'So, Master Shardlake, I hear you have been spending time with my wife.'

'No, your majesty, no!' I heard the edge of panic in my own voice as I answered. 'I have merely been helping her to search for, for — '

'For this?' With difficulty the King reached behind him to the desk, his surprisingly delicate fingers clutching at a sheaf of papers. He heaved himself round again, holding it up. I saw the Queen's writing, the first page torn in half where Greening had grasped it as he died. The *Lamentation of a Sinner*.

I felt the ground shift beneath me; again I almost fainted. I took deep breaths. The King stared at me, waiting for an answer, the little mouth tightening. Then, from beside me, Paget said, 'Naturally, Master Shardlake, when I learned from my spy in that Anabaptist group that they had stolen a book written by the Queen, I told his majesty at once. He ordered the book brought to him, and the sect extirpated. It has been in his possession all this time.'

I stared foolishly at the manuscript. All this – all the weeks of anxiety and fear, the terrible thing that had happened to Barak tonight – and the *Lamentation* had been in the King's possession all along. I should have been furious, but in the King's presence there was no room for any emotion but fear. He pointed a finger at me, his voice rasping with anger. 'Last year, Master Shardlake, when the Queen and I were at Portsmouth, I saw you at the front of the crowd as I entered the city.' I looked up in surprise. 'Yes, and I remembered you, as I do all those I have had cause to look on unfavourably. You failed once before to discover a stolen manuscript. At York, five years ago. Did you not?'

I swallowed hard. The King had insulted me in public, then. Yet he would have done far worse had he known that I had succeeded in discovering that particular cache of papers and had destroyed them on account of their incendiary contents. I looked back at him, fearing irrationally that those probing eyes could see into my very mind, that they could see what I had truly done at York, and even my treacherous thoughts this very afternoon about the Anabaptists' creed.

The angry edge in the King's voice deepened. 'God's blood, churl, answer your King!'

'I – I was sorry to have displeased you, your majesty.' It sounded craven, pathetic.

'So you should have been. And when I saw you last year at Portsmouth, when you had no reason to be there, I had Paget make enquiry, and learned you had visited my wife at Portchester Castle. And that you did lawyer's work for her. I allowed that, Master Shardlake, for I know that once, before our marriage, you saved her life.' He nodded slowly. 'Oh yes, Cranmer told me about that, later.' His voice had softened momentarily, and I saw that, indeed, he still loved Catherine Parr. And yet he had used her as a tool in his political machinations all these months, had allowed her to go in fear of her life.

His voice hardened again. 'I do not like my wife receiving visitors unsanctioned by me, so when I returned from Portsmouth I arranged to have you watched.' He laughed wheezily. 'Not that I would suspect my Kate of dalliance with an ugly brokebacked thing like you, but these days I watch all those who might take too great an interest in those I love. I have been betrayed by women before,' he added bitterly. 'My wife does not know that I watch certain of her male associates. Paget is good at employing discreet men to observe and spy. Eh, Sir William?' The King half-turned and gave Paget a blow on the arm which made him stagger slightly; he blinked but did not flinch. The movement meanwhile set the King's whole vast body, uncorseted under the caftan, wobbling and juddering.

I swallowed hard. 'Your majesty, I hold the Queen in great esteem, but only as her employee, and as a subject admiring of her kindness, her learning—'

'Her religion?' the King asked, suddenly and sharply.

I took a deep breath. 'It is not a matter her majesty and I have discussed at length.' But I remembered those conversations in the gallery. I was lying, plain and simple, because terrifying as the King was, to reveal the truth might still endanger the Queen. My heart thumped in my chest, and it was hard to keep my voice from shaking as I continued. 'And when I spoke with her, in London and at Portsmouth – someone was always present, one of the ladies, Mary Odell or another –' I was almost stammering, my words tumbling over each other.

Paget looked at me contemptuously and said, 'Stice's spies, the lawyer Bealknap and afterwards the steward Brocket, reported no dealings between you and the Queen or her court for a year. But then last month, out of the blue, you were sworn to the Queen's Learned Council. With the mission, people were told, of finding a missing jewel. But as the steward Brocket overheard you saying to Lord Parr's man Cecil, it was actually the *Lamentation of a Sinner* you sought. A search that led you to join Richard Rich in his hunt for Anne Askew's ravings.'

I remembered when Cecil had visited me after Elias was murdered.

The *Lamentation* had been mentioned then. That rogue Brocket must have been listening at the door. If they know all this, I thought, there is no point telling lies about a stolen jewel. With horror, I realized the depth of the trouble I was in, and felt my bruised face twitch.

The King spoke again, in a strangely quiet voice. 'Anne Askew. I did not mean her to be tortured. I only gave Wriothesley permission to use strong measures.' He wriggled slightly in his chair, but then added sternly, 'That is his fault, and Rich's. Let them suffer if her writings are published.' Then the King looked at me again, and spoke with biting coldness. 'But the Queen should have told *me* this manuscript existed, and that it was stolen, not set forth a search under cover of lies about a missing jewel. What say you to that, lawyer?'

I swallowed hard. And I decided that whatever I said must be calculated to protect the Queen, to deflect any possible charge of disloyalty from her. Otherwise, truly, it would all have been for nothing. I took a deep breath. 'When Lord Parr consulted me, just after the book was stolen, the Queen was quite distracted, frightened, too, after – recent events.' I knew that with what I planned to say next I could be signing my own death warrant: 'It was I who asked her to let me try and find the book secretly, using the story of the stolen jewel.'

'I will be questioning Lord Parr tomorrow,' Paget said quietly.

I felt relief at that. I knew the Queen's uncle, whatever his faults, would also do his best to deflect responsibility from the Queen to himself. And to make sure our stories tallied I said, 'Lord Parr did agree that we should try to find the book secretly.'

'Who else knew?' the King asked sharply.

'Only Archbishop Cranmer. The Queen knew the book might be considered too radical, after she wrote it. She sought his opinion, and he said the manuscript should not be published. But before it could be destroyed, it disappeared. Stolen by that guard,' I dared to say. 'So she did not deceive you, your majesty, she intended to destroy the book at once lest it anger you.'

The King was silent, his brow puckered. He shifted his legs, wincing. When he looked at me again the expression in his eyes had changed. 'The Queen was afraid?' he asked quietly.

'Yes, your majesty. When she discovered its disappearance she was astonished, confused – '

'She would have been. Coming after all these months of Gardiner and his minions trying to turn me against her.' His voice rose angrily, but I was – for the moment – no longer the object of his fury. 'Gardiner told me she was a heretic that denied the Mass; they would have broken my heart again!' He leaned back in his chair. 'But I knew their ways, I knew my Kate was faithful and true, the only one since Jane. So I told them I would do nothing without strict proof. And they brought none, none!' His face was red now, sweating. 'Those rogues, that would have had me turn against Kate, and take me back to Rome! I have seen through them, they will pay—'

The diatribe ended in a bout of painful coughing which turned the King's face puce. The *Lamentation*, which he had been holding on his lap, began to slide to the floor. I leaned forward instinctively, but Paget, with a quick frown at me, returned it to the King before taking his goblet, hastily refilling it, and handing it back to him. Henry drank deeply, then sat back in his chair, gasping. Paget murmured, 'Your majesty, perhaps too much should not be said in front of this man—'

'No,' the King said. 'This he should know.' He looked at me. 'When the manuscript was brought to me, I feared what it might hold. But I have studied it.' Then, quite unexpectedly, he gave a prim little smile. 'Its sentiments are a little thoughtless, but – ' he waved a hand dismissively – 'the Queen is but a woman, and emotional. Nothing is said here against the Mass. The book is not heretical.' His tone now was pompous, judgemental, as befitted one authorized by God Himself to decide such matters, as Henry truly believed he was. 'Kate fears too much,' he concluded. I thought, how fast his emotions change, and how he wears them on his sleeve. At least when he chooses to. For the last few months had shown, too, how coldly secretive he could be. Yet his last words gave me hope for the Queen.

'May now be the time to tell her you have it?' Paget asked him, hesitantly.

'No,' the King answered sharply, the edge back in his voice. 'In these days the more things I keep safe in my own hands the better.' I realized he had kept the manuscript to himself because, until Bertano's mission failed, there remained at least the possibility that he might still decide against the reformist faction. Then a Protestant Queen would be a liability, and the *Lamentation* could still be a weapon. He loved the Queen, yes, but ultimately, like everyone in the realm, she was only a pawn on his chessboard. He would have killed her if he thought he had to, little as he wished it. And it would, of course, all have been someone else's fault.

He studied me again. 'So, it was you that inclined the Queen to keep its loss a secret?' A query in his voice now. I remembered Lord Parr telling me how suggestible the King was, how he believed what he wanted to believe, and also that to him disloyalty was the greatest of sins. Now, I was sure, he wanted to believe Queen Catherine had not taken the initiative in hiding the theft of the *Lamentation* from him. He would rather the blame fell on me, whom he despised and who, politically, counted for nothing at all. Perhaps he had already chosen me as a scapegoat, perhaps that was why he had told me so much. But after what had happened tonight, I no longer cared. 'Yes, your maj-esty,' I answered, perhaps signing my death warrant a second time.

He considered a moment, then he said petulantly, 'But Kate still deceived me — '

I took a deep breath. Somehow I was fluent again, fluent as at the climax of a court hearing. 'No, your majesty. It was I who hunted for the *Lamentation* behind your back.'

With a struggle, the King managed to sit more upright in his chair. He was silent a moment, trying to decide just what the role of his wife had been in all this. Then he seemed to reach a conclusion. He leaned forward, eyes and mouth set mercilessly now. 'You are an insolent, base-born, bent-backed common churl.' He spoke the words quietly, but I could feel his rage. 'Men like you are the curse of this land, daring to say they answer only to themselves on religion and the safety of the realm, when their loyalties are to *me*!' His voice rose again. 'Me, their King! I call it treason, treason!' He looked at me in such a vengeful way that, involuntarily, I took half a step back.

'Do not dare move unless I give you liberty!' he snapped.

'I am sorry, your majesty.'

Seeing my abject fear seemed to change his mood again. He turned to Paget and spoke scornfully. 'How could I ever think such a poor reed of a creature could be any sort of threat to me, hey?'

'I do not think he is,' the Secretary answered quietly.

The King considered a moment. 'You say one of the two men working for Shardlake is dead.'

'By now, yes.' Paget's tone was completely indifferent.

'And the other, that was brought here with him?'

'Little more than a boy.' Paget ventured a smile. 'A tall young fellow, with red hair, as your majesty was in his youth, though I believe this churl is nothing like so well-looking.'

The King smiled at the flattery. And I realized that Paget was trying to soften the King's anger, and I wondered why. There was a moment of silence as the King considered further, but then shook his head. 'This man suborned the Queen to keep secrets from me. That is treason.' He looked at me again, those little blue eyes buried in their wrinkles still hard and merciless. 'And I would be rid of him, he is a pestilential nuisance.'

I bowed my head. I felt cold, my racing heart had slowed. Treason, I thought. I would be dragged to Tyburn at the tail of a horse, hanged until almost dead, cut down, and then the executioner would cut out my innards. And naked, I thought strangely, quite naked. Then finally I would be beheaded. I thought, can I face that, can I act with courage as some have? I doubted it. And when I was dead, would I go then to hell? Would I burn for lack of faith, as Philip Coleswyn would believe? I stood there, in the King's study, quite still. The image of Barak, thrown on that rubbish heap, came to me again.

Beside me, Paget drew a deep breath. He spoke slowly. 'Your majesty, a trial for treason before a jury would make the recent problems concerning the Queen public. And also the deaths of those Anabaptists. We do not want that getting out. Not at this time.'

'He can be condemned by Parliament, through an Act of Attainder.'

'That would make it all the more public.'

Henry waved a hand, as though this were a trifle, but I could see from his expression that he realized it was not. Paget took another deep breath, before pressing home his point. 'Even if Shardlake were put quietly out of the way, it would become known, and some might see it as a move against the Protestant side. The new political balance is still very delicate. We do not want to upset it unnecessarily.'

He fell silent; Henry was glowering at him now. It was a scene I imagined Henry playing out with anxious chief advisers repeatedly over these last thirty-seven years; the King angry, demanding ferocious measures, his councillors trying to warn him of the possible damaging consequences.

The King sat, considering. At length he grunted, a strange sound like a pig's squeal, full of frustration. He gave me a savage look. 'But surely we could do him quietly to death.'

'I have no affection for this man, your majesty, believe me. But still I do not think that a wise move. The Parrs, in particular, would be concerned if he disappeared.'

The King sighed. 'You give me straight advice, Paget, you always have. Even though I may dislike to hear it.'

'Thank you, your majesty.'

Henry gave him a sharp look. 'And you know on which side your bread is buttered, eh? Always you act to further my will, never go down your own road, like Wolsey and Cromwell?'

Paget bowed deeply. 'I serve only to implement your majesty's chosen policies.'

'Yet I would be rid of this man,' the King repeated. He gave me a long stare, unblinking as a snake's. I knew my life, and Nicholas's, hung in the balance. An eternity seemed to pass before he spoke again. 'Paget is right. You are a serjeant and it is known that you have been working for the Queen. Your disappearance would make a stir.' He took a deep breath. 'I will let you go, Master Shardlake, you and your boy. For policy reasons alone. But take note of this.' He leaned forward, his voice rising again. 'You will never, ever, again come anywhere near the Queen, or any royal palace, or do anything that might, even possibly, bring you to my notice. Do you understand? I do not wish to hear of you, still less see you, ever again. And if I do see you, it will not be your bent back I see, but only – your – head!' The last words were accompanied by the King banging on the arms of his chair. He leaned back, breathing hard. 'Now, Paget, get him out of here. And send in Will Somers, I need distraction.'

Master Secretary bowed and then, beckoning me, walked backwards to the door; it was forbidden to turn one's back on the King. I followed, dreading to hear the King summon me again. Paget knocked on the door, it was opened from outside by a guard, and we backed through safely. Will Somers, the monkey still perched on his shoulder, stood outside with the guards. Paget inclined his head sharply to the door. Somers and the guard who had been with the King slipped back in. The sound of the door closing brought me an overwhelming rush of relief.

Paget led me back up the corridor. Then I felt the floor sway and slide under me again and had to lean against the wall, breathing hard. Paget looked at me, his face expressionless. 'A narrow escape, I think,' he said, his voice hard. 'You were lucky, Master Shardlake.'

I felt steadier now. 'Will he – could he – call me back?'

'No. He has made up his mind now. You spoke very well, all things considered,' he added reluctantly. He inclined his head. 'Was it truly you that persuaded the Queen to let you search for the book?'

I did not answer. Paget gave a little smile. 'Well,' he said. 'It does not matter now.'

I looked at him gratefully, despite myself. Given all that had happened, it was a strange paradox that it was Paget who had saved me at the end, for without his intervention I knew I would already be on my way to the Tower, Nicholas as well: he would not be the first innocent caught in the King's net. I took a deep breath. 'Did the King come all the way from Hampton Court for this?'

Paget gave a quiet, mocking laugh. 'You flatter yourself, lawyer. No, he and Admiral d'Annebault are going hunting in St James's Park tomorrow. He came here unofficially to spend the evening in peace. He is tired, he had to do much standing today, he wanted a little time away from them all.' Paget looked out of the window, down at King Street, deserted at this hour. 'His study is always kept ready for him. Here he can rest, work, watch the doings of his realm from the window.' He added quietly, 'It is not easy, being a King.'

I dared not answer, and Paget continued in a strangely dispassion-ate tone. 'I think, you know, your search for the *Lamentation* these last few weeks may have saved the Queen.'

I stared at him. 'Do you?'

He stroked his long forked beard. 'Yes. When I first brought him that book, Bertano had not yet arrived. The King indeed found no evidence of heresy in the *Lamentation* — it sails close to the wind in places, but as he said, it does not deny the Mass. But the Queen had hidden its existence from him and that rankled seriously.'

'Disloyalty,' I murmured.

'Quite so. The Queen could have been in trouble there and then. For several days he considered arresting her. But then your hunt for the book, and Rich's for Anne Askew's writings, caught his attention and he ordered me to let the matter play itself out, although of course those Anabaptists had to die.'

'Curdy was your spy.'

'Yes. And when the allegations from that Slanning woman came before me, I decided you should be brought before the Privy Council, so I could see for myself whether there might indeed be a chance you were a heretic.'

'So we were all moved like puppets,' I said bitterly.

'Be grateful that you were. That allowed time for Bertano's mission to fail, and the King's mind to turn finally and decisively against the conservatives.'

I looked at his slab of a face and thought, you enjoy all this; you would side with radicals or conservatives alike to keep your position. Another of those great men in the middle, bending with the wind.

Paget spoke again, his voice stern now. 'Of course, you will forget everything that was said in there, not least what the King let slip about authorizing strong measures against Anne Askew.'

I took a deep breath. 'Of course, Master Secretary.'

His eyes narrowed. 'And you heard what the King said. Make sure he has no more trouble from you. Do not cross me again, either. And now, fetch your boy; then get out of here. And, as the King said, never, ever, return.'

Chapter Fifty-three

P AGET BECKONED A GUARD, then without further word led the
way back through the King's Gallery, then to the Presence
Chamber. He crossed the room to speak briefly with one of the guards
standing there. I looked again at the Holbein mural, the King in his
prime; the swagger, the square hard face, the ferocious little eyes and
mouth. The candlelight caught Jane Seymour's face, too: demure,
placid. Paget returned with the guard. 'Take him to the boy, then get
them both out of the palace. Quickly.' And then Master Secretary
turned and walked away, without so much as a nod or a backward
glance, his long black robe swishing round his legs. He was done with
me. The mind of the King's Master of Practices had probably already
returned to its coils of conspiracy.

Nicholas was crouched in the corner of a small, bare receiving
room, his long arms folded round his bent knees. When he stood I saw
spots of blood on his doublet. Barak's blood. 'Come, Nicholas,' I said
quietly. 'We are free, but we must go quickly.'

The guard led us along the dark corridors to the Guard Chamber,
then down the stairs again, across the cobbled court, and through the
gates. As soon as we were out in the street Nicholas said, 'I thought
we were undone.'

'I, too. But I think we are safe, so long as we never come here
again.' I looked upwards at the Holbein Gate and its windows, wondering if the King were watching. I turned away hastily; it was
dangerous now even to glance in that direction.

'Stice and his men, are they — ?'

'Free as air,' I answered bitterly, looking at him. His face looked haunted. 'But do not ask me to tell you more, ever.'

He ran a hand through his red hair, then gave a little choking laugh. 'I was told before I came to London how magnificent the royal palaces were. And I have seen for myself, it is true. And yet – fear and death stalk there, even more than in the rest of the world.'

I smiled with desperate sadness. 'I see you are beginning to learn.'

'In there – I felt it.' He gulped. 'What now? What of – Jack?'

'We must go back to get him at once,' I said, though I was terrified of what we would find there.

✝

WE REACHED THE LANE near an hour later, the clocks striking one shortly before we arrived. It was easy to find the place. I halfran to the rubbish heap, full of dread at what I might see, then drew up abruptly. Barak's body was gone.

'Where is he?' Nicholas asked in astonishment. 'He couldn't have – got up?'

'That would have been impossible. Someone has taken him.' I looked frantically round the darkness of the lane, but there was nothing to be seen.

'But where?'

I thought hard. 'If someone found him, they might have taken him to St Bartholomew's. It is hard by. Come, we will go there first.'

We arrived at the hospital ten minutes later: Nicholas had had not only to accommodate his long stride to my own, but almost to run. The doors were closed, but a porter answered our knock, holding up a lamp. I spoke urgently. 'We wish to ask whether a man was brought here tonight. He had a sword wound to the body and – he had lost his hand.'

The man's eyes narrowed. 'Was it you that left him there? A man so wounded, left on a dungheap?'

'No, it was not us, we are his friends.'

'Old Francis Sybrant found him, and brought him in.'

The porter still looked at us dubiously. 'Please,' Nicholas asked. 'Does he live?'

'Just, but he's as near death as a man can be. He has been unconscious since he came.'

'Has the doctor been sent for? Dr Malton?'

The man shook his head. 'A doctor only comes once a day.'

'Well, send for Dr Malton now,' Nicholas said. 'He is a friend of my master here, and also of the man brought in by Francis Sybrant.'

I looked at Nicholas's face in the lamplight. I would swear new lines had appeared on it since this afternoon. I reached for my purse and thrust two shillings at the porter. 'Here. Get someone to fetch Dr Malton, then take us to Barak.'

The porter stared at the coins in his palm, then back at me. 'Who's Barak?'

'The man who was brought in. Please, hurry.'

He scurried away, leaving us in the vestibule. Nicholas smiled wryly. 'With all the money you're giving away, sir, you'll have none left.'

I thought, insolence, the boy becomes more confident. Then I thought of Timothy, and wondered whether he was lost to me as well. Between the fight at the house, and my ordeal at Whitehall, I had forgotten him.

The porter returned, his manner obsequious now. 'I will take you to your friend. Sybrant is with him. He is in a chamber we keep for those who may need the last rites.'

☦

BARAK LAY IN THE SAME ROOM where the Anabaptist McKendrick had died, in the same bed, a cheap candle on a chair beside it. His clothing had been removed and the blankets covered only his lower body; his strong scarred torso was as pale as though he were dead already. He lay on his side, a bloodstained bandage covering the place on his back where he had received the sword-thrust. His right arm, the stump of the wrist thickly bandaged, lay on a pillow. I put a hand to my mouth.

The door of the little room opened and a man with a lamp entered. I recognized Guy's assistant, Francis Sybrant. His brow furrowed when he saw me.

'You, sir? You were here before – to see that other man who was attacked – '

'The porter said you brought Barak in. How – ?'

'I was coming on duty earlier this evening. I come by the back ways, always. Often one finds sick beggars, sometimes people who have been injured and abandoned, though never like this.' He looked at us accusingly. 'You left him there?'

'No! We were prisoners, we could do nothing. Dear God, you must have come on him just in time.' I thought, perhaps my prayers had been answered after all. 'Please, this man is a good friend, can you tell us – ' my voice faltered – 'will he live?'

Sybrant looked at us dubiously. 'That wound in his back – it was made by a sword?'

'Yes.'

'It has damaged no vital organs that I can see, but between that and what was done to his hand – he has lost much blood. Too much for him to survive, I fear.'

'He is a strong man.'

Sybrant shook his head. 'He would need to be exceptionally so to survive this. Has he family?'

I exchanged an anguished look with Nicholas. I had put thoughts of Tamasin from my mind. 'Yes,' I answered haltingly. 'And a child. His wife is expecting another.'

Nicholas said, 'Perhaps it may be better if she is not told till the doctor comes.'

Sybrant said, 'Dr Malton has been sent for.'

'You are right, Nicholas,' I said. 'I will wait for Guy.'

Nicholas turned to Sybrant. 'Is there anything we can do?'

The old man looked at the ashen figure on the bed. 'Only pray, sirs, pray.'

✝

GUY ARRIVED SOON AFTER, a heavy bag over his shoulder. He appeared shocked, haggard, for he had known Barak and Tamasin almost as long as I. He looked at us, then at Barak lying on the bed. He drew in his breath sharply. 'What happened to him?'

'There was a sword fight; he was stabbed in the back and his hand sliced off.'

'Dear Jesus!' Guy looked angry. 'Was this sword fight part of this mission of yours?'

I lowered my eyes. 'Yes.'

'Were you there?'

'Yes. But we were taken prisoner. We have only just been released.'

Guy moved across to the bed. 'Does Tamasin know?'

'I thought it better to wait for you.'

He did not reply, but knelt over Barak, gently removing the bandages from the wound on his back and examining it closely, then uncovering that dreadful stump, still oozing blood, white bones visible against the torn flesh. I closed my eyes. Gently, Guy replaced the bandages. He looked at me again, his face as sombre as I had ever seen it. 'The wounds show no sign of infection – yet. They must be cleaned, properly. But he has lost enough blood to kill most men.' He stood up briskly. 'I must get fluid into him.'

'Will he live?'

'He is far more like to die,' Guy answered starkly. I realized how hard it must be for him, having to treat a critically injured patient who was also a friend. 'I knew something like this would happen, I knew it! Are there going to be any more men brought to me dead and crippled through whatever it is you are doing?' His voice was full of rage.

'No,' I answered quietly. 'It is over. It ended tonight.'

He looked at me, his face hard as stone. 'Was it worth it, Matthew?' There was an angry tremor in his voice. 'Was it?'

'I think one person was saved – a woman.'

'Who? No, I think I can guess.' He raised a hand. 'Tell me nothing more.'

'My master did not wish it to end like this,' Nicholas said.

'I do not doubt that,' Guy answered in gentler tones. 'Now, Master Nicholas, would you ride to Mistress Barak's house, and fetch her here?'

I protested, 'But in her condition – '

'Jack will probably die tonight,' Guy said quietly. 'What do you think Tamasin would say if she were denied the chance to be with him at the end?'

'Then let me be the one to tell her.'

'The boy will be quicker. I would rather have you here. And I may need your help if Francis is called away to other patients.' He turned to Nicholas. 'Tell Mistress Barak only that there has been an accident. Say I am in attendance.'

He nodded sombrely. 'I will.'

'Hurry now. Use my horse, it is outside. And tell Francis to come in and assist me.'

Nicholas looked at me. I nodded, and he hurried from the room. When he was gone Guy said quietly, 'Can you face her?'

'I must.'

He bent and opened his bag. Barak lay unmoving.

✝

IT WAS NEAR AN HOUR before Nicholas returned with Tamasin. Guy had been working to clean Barak's wounds the whole time, moving deftly and quietly. I sat in the chair next to the bed, so exhausted that, despite the appalling circumstances, I had dozed off, waking with a start when I almost tumbled from the chair. By the light of a lamp which Sybrant held up I saw Guy re-bandaging Barak's wrist, a concentrated expression on his dark face, suppressing God knew what emotions. He paused to glance across at me. 'You slept near half an hour.'

I looked at Barak. His breathing was ragged, irregular. Guy said, 'I tried to make him drink something, poured some apple juice into his mouth. It made him gag, and waken for just a second.'

'Is that a hopeful sign?'

'He did not swallow. I have to get some nourishment into him, so his body can make more blood to replace all he has lost.'

Then I heard footsteps outside. Nicholas's fast, heavy tread, lighter steps behind. The door opened; Nicholas held it as Tamasin came in, her eyes wide, breathing hard and fast. When she saw the state of her husband I thought she might scream or faint but she only looked at Guy. 'Is he dead?' she asked in a trembling voice.

'No, Tamasin, but he is very badly hurt.'

I stood up and indicated the chair. 'Tamasin, please sit down.'

She did so, but without looking at me, brushing aside some strands of blonde hair which had escaped from her coif. She held her stomach with her free hand, as though to protect the baby within from the sight on the bed. She spoke to Guy again. 'Nicholas said Jack was badly injured. He would not say why, but I pressed him and he said there was a sword fight. He said Jack had lost a hand. Dear God, I see now that it is true.' Her voice still trembled but she made a fist of her hand, willing herself not to break down.

Nicholas said, 'She insisted I tell her, Dr Malton – '

Guy nodded. 'Yes, there was a fight.'

Tamasin turned her face to me, full of fury. 'Why? Why was there? Why did you get Jack to lie to me about where he was tonight?'

I said, 'I needed help. He gave it, as he always does.'

She shook her head angrily. 'I thought he was past all that now, I've suspected there was something going on for weeks but I told myself he would never endanger himself again, nor you lead him into trouble.' She cried, 'Well, it is for the last time. He cannot do your dirty work any more now, can he? Even if he lives? And if he does, he will not work for you again, not ever. I shall see to that!'

'Tamasin, I am sorry, more than I can say. You are right. It was my fault. But if – when he recovers – he can come back to work for me, in the office – '

Tamasin answered savagely, 'How? What can he do? When he will no longer even be able to write?'

'I will arrange something – I will make sure you do not lose – where money is concerned – I will take care of you – '

She stood up, fists bunched at her side. 'I see how you have taken care of my husband! You will leave us alone, never come near us again!' Nicholas reached out a hand to steady her, but she slapped it aside. 'Get off me, you!' She turned back to me. 'Now, get out! Get out!' She put her face in her hands and sat down, sobbing.

Guy said, 'You should go, Matthew. And you, boy. Please, go.'

I hesitated, then walked to the door. Nicholas joined me. Just as we reached it we heard a sound like a groan from the bed. Whether from all the commotion or from hearing his wife's voice, Barak appeared to be waking. I glanced back at Tamasin; she reached out to her husband. I took a step back into the room but she cast me such a look that without further ado I let Nicholas lead me out.

✝

HE TOOK ME HOME, carrying a lamp the porter gave him. He could see I was nearly spent. He had the sense not to speak, only to take my arm when I stumbled a couple of times. I asked him once, 'Do you think, now he is awake, Jack may live?'

'Yes, I'm sure.' He spoke with a confidence which, I could tell from his voice, he did not feel.

He walked me up the path to my door. As we approached, it opened and Josephine stood in the doorway. The only one of my household left now. As I came up to her I saw she was smiling. She said, 'We found him. Edward and I. At that pond on Coney Garth where he goes to fish sometimes. He was there, trying to catch something to eat.' Then she saw my face and her eyes widened. 'Sir, what has happened?'

I walked past her into the kitchen. Timothy, filthy dirty, sat at the table with Edward Brown. As I came in the boy essayed a nervous smile, showing the wide gap in his teeth. He said tremulously, 'Josephine said you were not angry any more, sir.'

I said, my voice breaking, 'No, Timothy, I was wrong to hold a grudge so long. And what Martin Brocket told you was untrue. His leaving was not your fault. Are you safe?'

'Yes, sir.' He looked at me, then at Nicholas standing in the doorway behind. 'But sir, has something happened to you?'

'It is nothing.' I laid my hand on Timothy's, small and thin and dirty. I thought, at least I did not lose him. Of all those whose lives had been uprooted by the trap the King and Paget had set, he was the least important – to them, though not to me, not to me.

Epilogue

FEBRUARY 1547, SIX MONTHS LATER

THE CROWDS STOOD SIX DEEP outside Whitehall Palace. They lined both sides of the roadway, up past Charing Cross and along Cockspur Street. Some said people were standing all the way to Windsor. Everyone was huddled in their warmest clothes; the sky was blue but there was an iron-hard frost in the air, the puddles grey and frozen, a bitter wind from the east. Some from the poorer classes, in leather jerkins or threadbare coats, were shivering and hunched in the cold. But they stayed, determined to see the spectacle.

I wore my heavily furred winter robe, but no gold chain. That had been returned to the goldsmith back at the end of August. For on this royal occasion there was no great central figure to impress. King Henry VIII was dead, and his funeral procession about to begin.

✝

THE KING, IT WAS KNOWN, had fallen gravely ill again during the short royal Progress to Guildford in September, and never fully recovered. He worsened again in December and at the end of January he had died. The gossips at the Inns of Court had had much to chew over in recent months. It was, as ever, hard to distinguish truth from rumour, but most agreed that during the autumn the reli-gious radicals had utterly triumphed; Bishop Gardiner had been publicly struck in the face by Lord Lisle in the Privy Council, and the King had refused to see him in the weeks before he died. It made sense to me: the conservative faction had bet everything on the Queen being found guilty of heresy, and on the success of Bertano's mission. Both gambits had failed and the King, knowing he was dying, had turned to those who would ensure that the Royal Supremacy over the Church was preserved for his son.

In December the Duke of Norfolk and his son the Earl of Surrey had been suddenly arrested, the Earl accused of illegally quartering the royal arms with his own. Parliament had passed an Act of Attainder convicting both of treason; the young Earl had been executed in January, and Norfolk, the arch-conservative, would have followed him to the block had not the King died the night before the execution. It sounded to me like a put-up job – the King had used such methods before, to rid himself of Anne Boleyn and Thomas Cromwell. For now the old Duke remained alive, in the Tower.

It was said that as he lay dying at Whitehall the King had called for Archbishop Cranmer, but by the time he arrived Henry was past speech. And when the prelate asked him to give a sign that he died in the faith of Christ, he had been able only to clutch Cranmer's hand. No confession then for Henry, no last rites. His death – perhaps by accident – had been one which Protestants could approve. And yet, extraordinarily, the King in his Will had ordered traditional requiem Masses to be said over his body. Henry, in death, was as inconstant as he had been in life.

☦

'VIVE LE ROI EDWARD THE SIXTH!' So the heralds proclaimed the new King, that thin, straight-backed little boy. The new Council which the old King had appointed by his Will made shortly before his death, to govern England during Edward's minority, was dominated by those identified with the Protestant cause. Lord Lisle and the Earl of Essex, Catherine Parr's brother, had places. So, too, did those in the middle, who would bend with the wind: Paget remained Master Secretary, Wriothesley was still in place on the Council, and Rich. All had bent to the King's final change of path.

But not Bishop Gardiner; he was left seething impotently on the side-lines. It was said that radical religious reform would soon be coming.

Within the reforming camp, the Seymours had won out over the Parrs. There was to be no Regency for Catherine Parr, despite her hopes. She was now merely Queen Dowager, while the council had immediately appointed Edward Seymour, Lord Hertford, as Protector of the young King. He it was who sat now at the head of the Council table, to which he had also appointed his brother Thomas.

All sorts of stories were flying around that the King's Will had been doctored after his death, Hertford conspiring with the careerists to insert a clause concerning 'unfulfilled gifts' from the King which allowed the new council to award them titles, setting their loyalty in stone. Certainly there was a great crop of new peers: Richard Rich, for instance, was now Lord Rich of Lees in Essex. But exactly what had happened in the days just after the King died, nobody knew for sure; perhaps no one ever would.

✝

ATTENDANCE AT the funeral procession was officially encouraged, but not compulsory. Most of the great crowd, like me, had come, I think, to witness the passing of an epoch. The younger people pres-ent would have known no other ruler, and I could only dimly recall, when I was seven, my dear mother telling me that King Henry VII was dead and a second Tudor had ascended the throne.

I shook myself and rubbed my gloved hands together. Opposite, Whitehall Palace was silent and empty; the procession was to begin at the chapel of Westminster Palace, further south. Next to me, Philip Coleswyn said, 'Ay, a chill day, but perhaps there now begin the days of true religion.'

Nicholas, on my other side, murmured, 'Days of snow, from the feel of that wind.' His Lincolnshire accent lengthened the vowels of his words.

'Ay,' I agreed, 'I think you are right.'

The boy had been a rock to me these last months. In chambers he had worked with a new energy and intelligence, taking over much that Barak had formerly done. Though he needed supervising, and could be too haughty in manner for some of Barak's more lowly friends among the clerks and solicitors, he was learning fast. He still made mistakes and, as those promoted rapidly often will, had taken on a certain insolence that needed gentle correction. But I had come to see that under his bravado and flippancy there was a core of steel in Nicholas Overton. I did not know how long he would stay with me, or even why he was so loyal: perhaps he needed to root himself some-where after the quarrel with his family. Whatever the reason, I was grateful, and had invited him to accompany me to the funeral proces-sion today.

When the two of us reached Whitehall I saw a large crowd of lawyers, their status ensuring them places at the front of the crowd, just north of the great Holbein Gate. They were all in their black robes and most had their hoods up against the cold; for a moment they reminded me of a crowd of monks. Heads turned as we approached; as I had anticipated, news of my arrest and appearance before the council had got out and was soon an item of gossip, as was the fact that Barak, known round Lincoln's Inn for his wit and disrespectful-ness, was gone. I nodded to people I knew with formal politeness. Treasurer Rowland, his long nose red with cold, looked at me disap-provingly. Vincent Dyrick, a woman and three children at his side, gave me a quick glance before turning away. And right at the front, William Cecil raised a hand in greeting, and gave me a nod. I returned it, thinking how well Cecil had done; Secretary now to the Earl of Hertford, already this young man was becoming a power in the land.

A familiar figure shouldered his way through the lawyers and called a greeting. I had not seen Philip Coleswyn since the summer, but took his hand gladly as he led Nicholas and me to stand beside him in the front row. I asked after his family and he said all were well. He looked relaxed and content, his terrible anxieties over the summer long gone. When he asked after my health I said merely that I was well. Even though I wore my coif, and had the hood of my robe up against the cold like everyone else, Philip glanced at my head. Perhaps someone had told him that after that night in August my hair had turned completely white; first just at the roots, giving me the aspect of a badger, but growing out until only white was left. I had got used to it.

✟

'They're late,' Nicholas observed, stamping his feet.

'There is much to organize at Westminster,' Philip said. 'There are near two thousand men going to Windsor, on horse and foot. Everyone will have to be in their correct place.'

'And it is nothing to them if common folk are kept waiting,' I snapped. Philip looked at me, struck by my bitter tone. I thought, I must be careful, people will be taking me for an Anabaptist soon, and that creed of equality would have no more of a place under the new regime than it had under the old, however radical the religious changes which might come. I looked up at the windows above the wide arches of the Holbein Gate. There was the King's study, to which he had called me on that dreadful night. He would never watch his people from his window again. All at once, I felt free.

Philip asked, 'I do not suppose you have heard how Mistress Slanning fares?'

'I have, in fact.' Guy had kept me informed. He had been furious with me that night in August, and rightly so, but in the weeks that followed, when I was subject to blacker moods than ever in my life, he helped take care of me, counselled me. His compassion won out over his anger, for which I was eternally grateful. I looked at Philip, wondering how he would take what I had to say: 'She is gone to France, as people may since the peace. She has returned to the Catholic faith and entered a nunnery, somewhere out in the French countryside.'

'A nunnery?' He sounded shocked.

'I do not know if she has taken any vows yet. There is a long preparation.' I wondered if Isabel had, at last, made her confession. 'I think it is best for her, she would find it hard now to face the world. She has given her worldly goods to the nuns. Edward's share of that house will pass to his family, for she had none left living.'

Philip inclined his head disapprovingly. 'However comfortable a refuge the papists may provide, she has lost any chance of salvation.'

Nicholas looked at him narrowly. 'Then you believe that when she dies she will burn, sir, as Mistress Anne Askew did, but in her case for all eternity?'

'God's laws are beyond human understanding, boy,' Philip answered firmly.

I spoke quietly, 'If such are his laws, then indeed they are.' I thought of Hugh Curteys, my ward. As the persecution of Protestants had intensified in Antwerp the previous autumn, Hugh had moved to Hamburg, and worked now with the German Hanse merchants. This great struggle between Protestants and Catholics all across Europe could now make anyone a refugee, a prisoner, or worse.

✝

STILL THE PROCESSION did not come, though officials had begun scurrying to and fro around the Holbein Gate, under which the procession would pass, one of them shivering in a clerical cassock. I remembered how the vicar had been late at the infinitely smaller ceremony a month before, when Josephine married Edward Brown. The wedding had been celebrated in the little parish church Edward attended; his family and friends from the Inn had come, together with Edward's master. Josephine had no family and I had given her away; I had been proud to do so, though I would miss her greatly. They had moved to Norwich last week. I had hired an old fellow called Blaby, a grumbling creature, to look after my house until I found a new steward; apart from him, the household now consisted only of Timothy and myself. Gently, very gently, I was nudging the boy towards an apprenticeship with the Lincoln's Inn farrier when he turned fourteen, which I would finance to give him a chance in life.

Then I saw them, for the first time in six months, near the front of the crowd a little way off. Barak and Tamasin. Tamasin wore a thick coat with a hood, but looked pale; I knew from Guy that, a fortnight before, on the night the King died, she had given birth to a healthy daughter. She should not be out in this cold so soon, but I imagined she had insisted.

Barak, beside her, still looked sick. There was a heavy puffiness to his features now, and he had put on weight. I saw, with a clutch of sorrow at my heart, how the right sleeve of his coat trailed empty. He glanced up and his eyes met mine. Tamasin looked up too; when she saw me her face stiffened.

'They're coming!' Murmurs and an excited shuffling in the crowd, heads craning to look towards the Holbein Gate. From beyond, the sound of sung prayers in the clear cold air. But then, for another minute, nothing happened. People shuffled and stamped their feet, some beginning to mutter and grumble a little in the bitter cold.

A movement nearby. I turned to see Barak sidling through the crowd towards us. Tamasin stayed behind, glaring at me, fierce as ever.

Barak took Nicholas by the arm with his remaining hand. 'How are you, Nick boy? I haven't seen you since that night. Are you all right?'

'Yes – yes. And you?' Nicholas sounded surprised, as indeed he might, for when he had gone to visit Barak one night in October, Tamasin had slammed the door in his face. Money which I had sent to her via Guy had been returned without a word.

'How's he treating you?' Barak asked, inclining his head towards me. 'Keeping you busy?'

'Yes – yes. We miss you at chambers.'

Barak turned to me. 'How goes it with you?' His eyes, like his puffy face, were still full of pain and shock.

'Well enough. But I have wished for news of you –'

'Listen,' he said quietly. 'I'll have to be quick. Tammy doesn' want me talking to you. I just wanted to say, I'm all right. When I'm a bit better I've an offer from a group of solicitors to work with them interviewing clients, finding witnesses, that sort of thing. Work where you don't need two hands. So don't worry.'

'I am desperately sorry, Jack, desperately,' I said. 'Tamasin is right to think it was all my fault.'

'Balls!' Barak answered with something of his old vigour. 'It was me decided to get involved with all that, me that told her lies about what I was doing. Am I not still a man with responsibility for my own decisions?' A spasm of anger crossed his face and I realized that, in his own eyes, he was not fully a man any more. I did not reply.

'How does the new baby fare?' Nicholas asked. 'We heard you have a daughter.'

Barak spoke with a touch of his old humour. 'Can't keep anything quiet within a mile of Lincoln's Inn, can you? Yes, she's lusty and healthy, lungs on her like her mother. We're going to call her Matilda.'

'Congratulations, Jack,' I said quietly.

He glanced over his shoulder at Tamasin. 'I'd better get back. Listen, I'll be in touch when I'm working again. And this – ' he gestured to his empty sleeve – 'Guy's making me some sort of attachment now the stump's healed. It won't be anything like a hand but I suppose it'll be better than nothing. As for Tammy, give her time. I'm working on her. Easier for her to blame you than me, I suppose.'

There was some truth in that. Yet she had every reason to blame me for Barak's maiming, as I blamed myself. He gave me a nod, then walked back to his wife. Tamasin had seen him speaking to me; the look she gave me now had in it something despairing, defeated, that cut me to the heart. I turned away.

The murmuring had ceased, the crowd fallen silent again. Beyond the Holbein Gate the singing of prayers was growing louder as it approached. People bared their heads. I lowered my own hood, feeling the icy air against my coif. Two officials on horseback rode under the main arch, looking up the roadway to ensure the way was clear. Then beneath the wide arches walked the choir and priests of the Chapel Royal, still singing. There followed perhaps three hundred men in new black coats, carrying torches. The poor men who, by tradition, headed the funeral processions of the great. Well, there were plenty of poor men in England now, more than ever there had been.

The men who came next, on horseback, dozens of them bearing standards and banners, were certainly not poor: the great ones of the realm, flanked by Yeomen of the Guard. I glimpsed faces I recognized – Cranmer, Wriothesley, Paget. I lowered my head in a pretence of mourning.

Eventually they all passed, and the great hearse approached. A lawyer behind me leaned round Nicholas, saying impatiently, 'Aside, beanpole, let me see!'

The hearse was drawn by eight great horses draped in black, each ridden by a little boy, the children of honour, carrying banners. It was richly gilded, with a cloth-of-gold canopy covering the huge coffin, on top of which lay a wax effigy of King Henry, startlingly lifelike, though looking not as I had seen him last summer but as he was in the Holbein mural: in his prime, hair and beard red, body solidly power- ful. The effigy was fully dressed in jewelled velvet, a black nightcap on its head. The face wore an expression of peace and repose such as I doubted Henry had ever worn in life.

Bells began to toll. People lowered their heads, and I even heard a few groans. I looked at the effigy as it passed and thought, what did he really achieve, what did his extraordinary reign really bring? I remem- bered all that I had seen these last ten years: ancient monasteries destroyed, monks pensioned off and servants put out on the road; persecutions and burnings – I shuddered at the memory of Anne Askew's head exploding; a great war that had achieved nothing and impoverished the country – and if that impoverishment continued to deepen, there would be trouble: the common people could only stand so much. And always, always under Henry, the shadow of the axe. I thought of those who had perished by it, and in particular of one I had long ago known well, and still remembered: Thomas Cromwell.

Beside me Philip said softly, 'And so it ends.'

✝

IT WAS A FORTNIGHT later that the horseman brought the note to chambers, riding from Chelsea through the heavy snow that had lain for days. Henry was buried now, and little King Edward crowned. There was a tale that while lying overnight on the way to Windsor, Henry's body had exploded, that stinking matter had dripped out and attracted the attention of a dog, fulfilling an old friar's prophecy that the dogs should lick Henry's blood as they had Ahab's in the Bible. But that sounded too neat, and I doubted it had happened.

I was working in my room when the messenger arrived, while outside Skelly prepared a case for court and Nicholas laboured, inky-fingered, over a deposition. I recognized the seal at once. That of the Queen; the Queen Dowager, as she was now. I opened the letter, bright light from the snow-covered square outside making the copper-plate lettering stand out on the white paper. It was brief, from a secretary, asking me to attend her the following afternoon at Chelsea Palace.

I laid it down. I had not expected to hear from Catherine Parr again; after that confrontation with the King, I had tried, so far as I could, to put her from my mind. But the King's edict against my coming near had died with him. I had been sorry that Catherine Parr had not, as she had hoped, been appointed Regent, though glad when people said the King had been generous in his Will to her, as well as to the Ladies Mary and Elizabeth; each now had great wealth and status of their own. People said Catherine Parr might marry again, in time, and the name Thomas Seymour was mentioned.

✝

I RODE TO Chelsea alone. Genesis plodded his way out of London slowly, for the roadway was covered with compacted snow and ice. Chelsea Palace, on the riverbank, was a fine new mansion of red brick, set in wide gardens which would be beautiful when spring came; I estimated it could easily house a staff of two hundred. The guards at the gate still wore the Queen's livery. I was admitted, a steward taking me to the house. Inside, servants passed quietly to and fro, but there were no guards on the doors as at Whitehall, no sidling politicians. He led me to a door at the rear of the mansion, and knocked. A familiar voice bade him enter.

I followed the steward into a large room. I recognized some of the items displayed there from the Queen's Gallery: an ornate clock, her box of coins which lay on the table beside a chess set. The Queen Dowager herself stood with her back to a large bay window, her black mourning clothes and gable hood contrasting with the snow-covered lawns outside. I bowed low. She dismissed the steward.

'Matthew,' she said. 'It has been many months.'

'Yes, your majesty.'

Her pale face was as attractive and composed as ever. In her stance I discerned a new relaxation, a new authority. Gently, she said, 'I am sorry that your efforts to help me ended – badly. I know now who had the *Lamentation*. And what happened to you – and your poor servant.'

I wondered, did she know that I had lied to the King for her? I could not tell from looking at her, and I must not ask. 'The book has been returned to you?'

'Yes. By the Protector.' I discerned a little bite in her voice at mention of the man who had taken the position she had hoped for. She added, 'I plan to publish it later this year.'

I looked at her, surprised. 'Is that – safe, your majesty?'

'Quite safe, now. Master Cecil has offered to write a preface. He thinks, like me, that the *Lamentation of a Sinner* may help some suffering souls to salvation. He remains a good friend.'

'I am glad. He is a young man of great talent.'

'And you shall have a copy, signed by me.'

'I – thank you.'

She came a step closer. 'But I say again, I know what the search for it cost you.' Her hazel eyes looked into mine and I thought suddenly, yes, she knows I told the King a lie: that I had been responsible for the decision to search for the book rather than telling him it was missing. Along with her uncle, whom I remembered Paget was to question the next day, and who must also have taken a share of the responsibility.

She said, 'I will be grateful to you, unto death.'

'Thank you, your majesty.' There was an awkward pause, then I asked, 'How fares Lord Parr?'

'He has gone back to the country,' she answered sadly. 'To die, I fear. His great service to me last year was too much for him, ill as he is.'

'I am sorry to hear it.'

She looked at me earnestly. 'If he was ever rough with you, it was only through love for me.'

I smiled. 'I always understood that.'

She moved over to the chess set. The pieces were laid out for a new game, and I wondered for a moment whether she might ask me to play. But she only picked up a pawn and set it down again. 'It is because I owe you so much that I have sent for you.' She smiled. 'To offer you some employment, if you wish to take it.'

I did not reply. Not politics – I would say no to that, even to her.

The Queen Dowager pressed her palms together. 'My circum-stances are much changed now. I am a widow, free to remarry. In a little time, I may.' She coloured then, and looked quickly down, as though knowing that I and many others would disapprove. I thought, so the rumours are true, it is Thomas Seymour. My heart sank and I thought: what a waste.

I think the expression on my face gave me away, for she took a deep breath, and said, 'If and when that time comes, I am afraid I should not be able to employ you, or see you again.' Yes, I thought, it is Sey-mour, who detests me as I do him. But then, what had she meant by employment?

She continued, 'You will know about the – promotions – that have taken place since the late King's death.'

'Only the gossip,' I answered cautiously.

She smiled sadly. 'Do not worry, Matthew. I am going to tell you something which should be kept confidential for now, but only because it is in your interest to know.'

I spoke quietly, 'Forgive me, your majesty, but I wish to know no more secrets. Ever.'

'It concerns Richard Rich,' she said, her eyes on mine. 'Baron Rich, as we must now call him.'

I bit my lip, did not answer. The Queen Dowager looked down at the chessboard. 'Rich shifted his allegiances just in time. He has been promoted, and I fear he is about to be promoted further.' She looked at me intently. 'Thomas Wriothesley is a peer now, too, but strangely he of all people has had an attack of conscience, and is raising diffi-culties regarding some of the powers Lord Hertford is taking to himself. Wriothesley will not long remain Lord Chancellor. That is the word I have, and I trust my source.' Thomas Seymour, I thought, the Protector's brother. 'His successor will be Rich.'

I took a deep breath. 'It is what he has lusted after for years.'

'Anne Askew's book has already been smuggled in from the Continent. Its revelations regarding Rich will soon be public. The Protector already knows them.' She frowned, then bent to the chess-board and moved a knight forward. 'But he wants Rich for Lord Chancellor – he is a clever and experienced lawyer, he knows the ways of politics intimately, and – ' she sighed – 'people fear him.'

'Rich, Chancellor, head of the legal profession. He will be able to destroy my career.' I shook my head. Well, I thought, perhaps now was the time to retire. I had been thinking of it last summer, before the trouble began. But then I thought, stubbornly, I do not want to be forced out. I like my work, and I have responsibilities: Timothy, Nicholas and, yes, Barak. And I thought, too, where would I go? What would I do?

'I am sorry, Matthew.' The Queen Dowager raised an arm as though to take mine, then dropped it. 'I fear your position as serjeant at the Court of Requests may soon be given to another.'

'Yes. Rich would do that to me, and worse. Perhaps another accu-sation of misconduct; which this time will not be dropped. I am sure Treasurer Rowland would not be sorry to cooperate with him.'

She nodded sadly. 'That is possible.' Then she continued, her voice serious. 'But not if you also have a secure position with someone of high enough status.'

I looked at her, puzzled. 'But your majesty, you just said that you – '

'I do not mean me.'

'Then who?'

She smiled. 'You will not know yet, but I have been given the guardianship of the Lady Elizabeth. She is to reside with me here, along with her tutor and her staff. She has been left numerous proper-ties by her father. She is a young lady of great wealth now. As is the Lady Mary, who if she accommodates herself to the religious changes that are coming, may marry. As for our young King – ' her smile widen-ed – 'he is a fine boy, healthy and clever. If he lives even so long as his father he could reign near half a century.' I saw her happiness that her side had won, even if her own family had not reached the pinnacle.

'The Lady Elizabeth is far from the throne. In due time no doubt she will marry into the senior nobility. For now, she is but thirteen, and under my guidance. A council must be appointed to deal with her estates, and in the nature of things there will be much legal business to be done. To begin with, her new properties must be conveyed into her name.' She took a deep breath, smiled again. 'I would like you to take on all the legal work connected with her properties. It will be regular employment. You would report not to me but to her Treasurer, Sir Thomas Parry. He will instruct you when legal advice is needed. He will be based near the law courts rather than here.' She added, 'I have spoken to the Lady Elizabeth. She remembers her meetings with you, and readily agreed to my suggestion.'

I stood, thinking hard. Elizabeth might be the least important of the King's children, but an assured place working for her household would provide ample protection against unwarranted persecution by Rich. And my official appointment to the Court of Requests was indeed all too likely to go. This new appointment would bring a steady flow of legal work, in the field of property law too, my specialist area.

The Queen Dowager said, 'A new start, Matthew, for us both.' She gave a hesitant smile, with something of apology in it.

I looked at her and thought again, how could this sophisticated, beautiful and profoundly moral woman marry a creature like Thomas Seymour? But perhaps Catherine Parr, after so many years of duty, felt the right to her own choice. And Seymour had good looks, if nothing else.

'You will take the post?' she asked.

I looked at her, and nodded. 'I will.'

'The Lady Elizabeth is not here at present, she is down at Rich-mond Palace. I would like you to go there now, take your oath to her. I sent a message you might come today. My barge is ready.'

I said, smiling, 'You knew I would accept.'

'I knew you would let me do this for you.'

I nodded, slowly, in acknowledgement. 'Thank you.'

She regarded me seriously. 'Elizabeth is not yet fourteen, yet already she has the will and intelligence of an adult. There is one thing she asked me to say to all those appointed to work for her. From another girl her age it might be childish boasting, but not Elizabeth.'

'What is that?'

The Queen Dowager smiled ruefully. 'My dogs will wear my collars.'

'Yes,' I answered quietly. 'I can imagine her saying that, and meaning it.'

She stepped forward, and now she did take my hand and pressed it tightly. 'Goodbye, Matthew. I shall never forget all you have done. Or the true regard in which you hold me. Believe me, I understand that, and value it.'

She looked me in the eyes, then stepped away. I was too choked with emotion to reply, as I think she saw, for she rang a bell for the steward to come and take me down to her barge. There were tears in my eyes, which I tried to hide with the depth of my bow.

Outside the steward said, respectfully, that he would ensure Genesis was taken safely back to Chancery Lane for me. He led me outdoors, and I huddled into my coat as we walked down the path between the snow-covered lawns to the river. He helped me into the barge waiting at the landing stage, where two liveried oarsmen sat. They pulled slowly out into the slate-grey Thames. I glanced back once at Chelsea Palace, then turned to face the oarsmen. They carried me downriver, to Elizabeth.

Acknowledgements

As well as my friends in the writing group, many thanks to Maria Rejt, Liz Cowen, Sophie Orme, Antony Topping, Chris Wellbelove and Wes Miller. Thanks once again to Graham Brown of Fullerton's for meeting my ceaseless stationery demands.

I would also like to thank Dr Stephen Parish for advice on Henry VIII's medical symptoms. My interpretation of what happened to Henry during the last months of his life is of course entirely my own.

My last Shardlake novel, *Heartstone*, centred on the sinking of the King's warship *Mary Rose* during the battle of the Solent in July 1545. Since its publication the new Mary Rose Museum has opened in Portsmouth, showing the surviving half of the ship with, as a mirror image, the widest ranging and most beautifully presented collection of Tudor artefacts anywhere in the world. It is truly an extraordinary place, which I have been privileged to be associated with, and I am again grateful to the museum, the staff and especially Rear-Admiral John Lippiett, for continued insights into the vanished world of the 1540s.

Many works were invaluable for my research. Catherine Parr has received some deserved attention in recent years. Janel Mueller's (ed.) *Katherine Parr: Complete Works and Correspondence* (Chicago, 2011) is a work of fine scholarship, as well as an exhaustive compendium, which includes the text of *Lamentation of a Sinner*. Anthony Martinssen trod the biographical ground a generation ago with *Queen Katherine Parr* (New York, 1971). Two excellent recent biographies are those by Susan James, *Catherine Parr* (Stroud, 2008) and Linda Porter, *Katherine the Queen* (London, 2010). For other characters, Dairmaid MacCulloch's biography, *Cranmer* (London, 1996), was yet again an invaluable resource.

Samuel Rhea Gammon's *Statesman and Schemer: William, First Lord Paget – Tudor Minister* (Devon, 1973) is an excellent biography of this unshowy, and therefore perhaps neglected, Tudor politician. Along with McCulloch, he gives the remarkable Bertano affair the attention it deserves. Glyn Redworth's *In Defence of the Church Catholic: The Life of Stephen Gardiner* (Oxford, 1990) was very helpful, though it failed to convince me that Gardiner did not play a leading role in the events of 1546. Stephen Alford's *Burghley: William Cecil at the Court of Elizabeth I* (Yale, 2008) was helpful on Cecil's early career and first steps on the political ladder.

Dakota L. Hamilton's *The Household of Queen Katherine Parr* (unpublished PhD thesis, Oxford, 1992) was a treasure trove on the structure of the Queen's Court. Simon Thurley's *Whitehall Palace, The Official Illustrated History* (London, 2008), *Whitehall Palace, An Architectural History of the Royal Apartments 1240–1690* (London, 1999) and his *The Royal Palaces of Tudor England* (Yale, 1993) brought the vanished palace back to life, although a good deal of my reconstruction had of course to be imaginative. David Loades's *The Tudor Court* (London, 1996) and Maria Hayward's *Dress at the Court of King Henry VIII* (London, 2007) were also of great help.

For the wider London world, Liza Picard's *Elizabeth's London* (London, 2005) was once again invaluable and, as with MacCulloch's *Cranmer*, never far from my side. James Raven, *The Business of Books* (Yale, 2007) was especially helpful on the early printing trade. Susan Brigden's *London and the Reformation* was another book which, again, was always near to hand. Irvin Buckwalter Horst's *The Radical Brethren: Anabaptism and the English Reformation to 1548* (Holland, 1972) was a mine of information on the early Anabaptists.

My description of Henry's funeral is based on the account in Robert Hutchinson, *The Last Days of Henry VIII* (London, 2005).

Thanks also to Amanda Epstein for discussing the legal aspects of the Cotterstoke Will case with me, and to Jeanette Howlett for taking me to Sudeley Castle, where Catherine Parr lived during her sad fourth marriage, and where some beautiful examples of her clothing and possessions survive, as does her tomb, where I left some flowers in memory of Henry's last, and to me most sympathetic, Queen.

HISTORICAL NOTE

THE LAST YEAR OF Henry VIII's life saw some of the most tumultuous political events of his entire reign: a major heresy hunt, an attack
on the Queen, radical changes in foreign policy, an attempt at reconciliation with the Pope and, at the end of 1546, a switch in control of the
Privy Council from religious traditionalists to radicals, who were left in
charge of England upon Henry's death. Unfortunately the sources are
very thin, which leaves events open to a wide variety of interpretations.
The historian Glyn Redworth has said, rightly, that 'all accounts are
obliged to be in the nature of interpretative essays'.*

My own attempt at interpreting the events of 1546 forms the background to the story of *Lamentation* (except of course for the fact that
Catherine Parr's *Lamentation of a Sinner* was not, in the real world,
stolen). So I will start with those elements of the story where the facts are
clearer, before moving on, for those who may be interested, to my own
venture at an 'interpretative essay' on what happened in the tumultuous
last months of Henry's life.

☥

IN 1546, ENGLAND'S ruling elite, as well as the common people in
London especially, were split between those sympathetic and those hostile
to religious reform. It was a matter of degree, and many people either
kept their heads down to avoid trouble, or, among the ruling classes, bent
with the wind for political advantage. And the wind blew very fiercely
in the mid-Tudor period, as Henry VIII, following the split with Rome

* Redworth, G., *In Defence of the Church Catholic: The Life of Stephen Gardiner* (1990)

in 1532–3, lurched between traditional and radical religious policies for a decade and a half.

Most of those in the reforming camp were not social radicals, except for one group, which became a bogey for the traditionalists: the Anabaptists. In Holland and Germany various sects had grown out of Luther's Reformation, and the Anabaptists (or adult Baptists) believed in returning to the practices of early Christianity. These beliefs included holding goods in common, which meant overthrowing the feudal ruling classes – although they seem to have been more ambivalent about the rising merchant classes. When they took over the German city of Münster in 1534, the local Protestant rulers joined with Catholics to exterminate them, but the Anabaptists continued as a persecuted minority in north-western Europe. A very small number fled to England, where they may have made contact with the survivors of the fifteenth-century Lollards, but were quickly caught and burned. In England they were very few; but a Dutch Anabaptist coming to London in 1546 and forming a small group there would have been possible.

Of course, like the group in *Lamentation*, these men would have been vulnerable to infiltration by official spies, of which there were plenty. The slowly emerging world of London printing (at this period most books were imported from the Continent) was watched by the authorities, with printers often being reformers, and some having contacts with exiled English polemicists in Germany and the Netherlands, of whom John Bale (a religious, though not a social, radical) was the most feared. And Anne Askew, hiding in London in 1546, was captured by informers – and later tortured in the Tower by Wriothesley and Rich. She was one of many brought before the Privy Council for questioning during the 1546 heresy hunt; although, as Shardlake observes in my novel, it would have been very unusual for an accusation as weak as Isabel Slanning's in the story to go that high.

✝

LONDON IN 1546 was a tumultuous, violent, sectarian and impoverished place. It was only a year since the country had faced a serious threat of invasion. The King's French war had, literally, bankrupted England – Continental bankers were refusing to lend Henry any more money – and the debasement of the coinage continued apace, to the impoverishment of the lower classes especially. The harvest of 1546 seems to have been a good one, which was probably just as well for the elite; bad harvests later in the decade contributed to large-scale rebellions.

✝

WHITEHALL PALACE, located on the fringes of the city, was an utterly different world. The palace, seized by Henry VIII from Cardinal Wolsey, was extensively expanded and enriched by the King, although its development was restricted as it was bounded on the east by the Thames, and on the west by the great thoroughfares of Whitehall and King Street, leading from London to Westminster. The problem was solved by building the recreational side of the palace on the western side of the roadway, and bridging the road with the magnificent Holbein Gate, where Henry had his private study. The two great paintings mentioned in the book – one showing Henry and Jane Seymour with the King's father Henry VII and his Queen, and the other showing Henry and Jane Seymour (by that time long dead) with Henry's three children, and two figures in the background who are believed to have been the royal fools Will Somers and Jane – were highlights of the magnificent decoration of the palace. Scrots's portrait of the young Princess Elizabeth was painted at this time, and can be seen in the National Portrait Gallery in London. Baynard's Castle, which like Whitehall Palace no longer exists, was home in 1546 to the Queen's wardrobe as well as to her sister Anne and brother-in-law William Herbert.

✝

THE ELITE GOVERNING ENGLAND at the end of Henry VIII's reign was divided by religion, but it was also divided into family blocs. Catherine Parr, like all Henry's queens, placed family members in positions of importance within her household, such as Lord Parr and Mary Odell, while her brother-in-law William Herbert was an important member of the King's private chamber, and her brother William Parr took a place on the Privy Council, the King's executive council, as well as the earldom of Essex.

This would now be called nepotism, but the Tudor view was entirely different – people were expected to advance members of their own family networks. So far as the royal court was concerned, this led inevitably to distant relatives and family hangers-on making their way to court in the hope of a place in royal service, as described in the book.

The Parrs were all on the reformist side, and their family loyalties seem to have been exceptionally tight; more so than their reformist allies and potential political rivals, the Seymours, the family of Prince Edward's mother Jane Seymour. Thomas Seymour was a drag on his brother Edward, now Lord Hertford. Nonetheless Lord Hertford was close to Henry and had considerable political ability, although when he actually rose to the top after Henry's death he proved inadequate for the job. Meanwhile, during 1546 William Paget, the King's Secretary, appears to have moved from being a protégé of Bishop Gardiner's to an ally of Lord Hertford.

☩

AT THE SAME TIME a young man named William Cecil was beginning to make his career on the fringes of politics. I have invented his position on Queen Catherine's Learned Council, although he was certainly a friend of the Queen, and moreover wrote the preface to *Lamentation of a Sinner* when it was published in 1547. During that year he first appears on the record as Edward Seymour's secretary, beginning the meteoric rise which was to culminate, in 1558, when he became chief adviser to Elizabeth I. Edmund Walsingham, meanwhile, was the uncle of Elizabeth's famous future spymaster, Thomas Walsingham.

☩

THE FACT THAT all these people knew each other is indicative of just how tiny the Tudor elite was – essentially a group of titled country landowners, though increasingly open to men from the gentry and merchant

classes, who sought positions at court to amass wealth and, like Rich and
Paget, went on to create their own great estates. Paget and Rich were
both lawyers of undistinguished lineage but great ability, who were first
chosen for service by Thomas Cromwell – as Shardlake observes, six
years after his death much of the political elite still consisted of men
whom Cromwell had advanced. 'Gentleman' status, meanwhile, was
everything for young men like Nicholas Overton, who guarded it jeal-
ously; allowed to wear swords and colourful clothes of rich material
forbidden to the common populace, they were brought up to see themselves as quite different from the common run.

✞

FOR THE VISIT of Admiral d'Annebault in August 1546 I have
followed closely the short account in Charles Wriothesley's *Chronicle*. As
one traces the ceremonies, one realizes their huge scale. Henry played a
prominent role, but this was to be his last hurrah. Five months later he
was dead. Greeting the admiral near Hampton Court was also Prince
Edward's first public appearance.

✞

Catherine Parr and the Politics of Henry VIII's Last Months – An Interpretative Essay

Historians have long puzzled over the huge upheavals in English politics
during the last months of Henry VIII's life. The source material is fragmentary, mainly scattered correspondence and ambassadors' reports, and
the reliability of one major source regarding Catherine Parr, John Foxe's
Book of Martyrs, has been called into question. Historians are divided over
Foxe; he was a radical Protestant who wrote, highly polemically, about the
sufferings of Protestant martyrs in the years before Elizabeth I ascended the
throne. Some have said that Foxe is too biased to be credible, adding that
where Catherine Parr is concerned he was writing seventeen years after the
event he described. Others respond that Foxe was meticulous about trying

to get his facts right, whatever gloss he put on them. I tend to agree with those who say that Foxe was an honest and assiduous gatherer of witness testimony, while also agreeing with pretty much everyone that his chronology was notoriously unreliable — of which more below.

If one looks at a timeline of political events in 1546, two things stand out. The first is that during the spring a major heresy hunt was ordered from within the court, targeting people who had denied the truth of transubstantiation. Transubstantiation is the doctrine which claims that during the ceremony of the Mass, the bread and wine are physically transformed into the actual blood and body of Christ; many Protestants, however, disagreed. It was over this point that, in 1539, Henry VIII drew a firm line. Under the 'Act of Six Articles' of that year, denial of transubstantiation, or 'sacramentarianism', was defined as heresy. One recantation was allowed; a refusal to recant, or a second offence, was punishable by burning alive.

In the 1546 heresy hunt the net spread widely, and those questioned by the council included the younger son of the Duke of Norfolk — who was interrogated about his presence at potentially subversive 'preachings in the Queen's chamber' in Lent — and Henry's courtier and friend George Blagge. The Queen was clearly under threat herself, as we shall see. The heresy hunt climaxed with the burning of Anne Askew and three others at Smithfield on the 16th of July. (The description of this in this book is based on the account by Foxe.) Meanwhile, though few even in Henry's circle knew this, plans were being made for a papal emissary, Gurone Bertano, to be received by the King in London in August, to explore whether a rapprochement with Rome, after thirteen years of separation, was a possibility.

One gets the impression from this timeline that the ship of state which, steered by Henry, had for years veered wildly between support of traditional Catholic practice — but without the Pope — and a more thoroughgoing reform, set a firm course during the early months of 1546. With increasing speed it sailed towards the extirpation of Protestant heresy and the victory of those who favoured a traditionalist position — and possibly some agreement with the Pope.

Then suddenly, around the end of July, the ship of state turns round and steers, even faster, in exactly the opposite direction. The heresy hunt stopped dead in July, and some who had been convicted were quietly released, George Blagge being pardoned personally by the King.

In early August, Bertano arrived. He had his first and only meeting with the King on the 3rd. We do not know what was said, but the meeting was clearly unsuccessful. Afterwards, Henry wrote a letter to the Pope to which the Pontiff never replied. Bertano remained in a 'safe house' until late September, not seeing the King again, until word of his presence began to get out and he was ordered to go home.

☩

DURING THE AUTUMN months Henry steered the metaphorical ship of state ever faster in a Protestant direction. He went on a Progress to Guildford, which was intended to be brief but was lengthened, probably because he fell seriously ill, and for over a month he stayed at Windsor on the way back. During this period, as was normal during Progresses, the Privy Council was split into two: those attending the King and those left in charge of business in London. Access to the King, as ever, was all-important, and the councillors Henry chose to be with him until he returned to London at the end of October were all either radical sympathizers or those who would bend to the wind, whichever way it blew.

☩

IN NOVEMBER, BISHOP GARDINER, the leading conservative, found himself marginalized and denied access to the King. Then, in December, the other leading traditionalist, the Duke of Norfolk, and his son, the Earl of Surrey, were suddenly arrested and charged with treason. By now Henry's health was deteriorating fast. He shut himself up at Whitehall Palace with his closest advisers, and in late December wrote a last Will, which appointed a council of sixteen to govern England until his nine-year-old son reached his majority. All the council members were either Protestants or centrists.

✝

SPRING 1546 SAW, as well as the start of the heresy hunt, a complete about-turn in foreign policy. The two-year war against France had been a disastrous and costly failure. The English occupied Boulogne, but were besieged there, supplied by boat across the Channel, strongly opposed by French ships, at enormous cost. Despite his advisers' entreaties during the winter of 1545–6, Henry refused to end the war.

Meantime, relations were uncertain with the Holy Roman Empire, which was at odds with its own Protestant subjects. England remained formally at war with Scotland, and the Pope continued to be an implacable foe. In March 1546 the ever warlike Henry finally accepted that this dreadful mess would have to be sorted out. Peace negotiations began with France, and a settlement was reached in June. Admiral d'Annebault, who had led the French fleet against England the year before, was invited to come to England as ambassador in August, and enormous celebrations were planned. This was surely a signal of Henry's intent to make a lasting peace.

At the same time Henry negotiated a new treaty of peace with the other major Catholic power in Europe, the Holy Roman Empire. Peace with Scotland, too, was encompassed in the French treaty.

✝

MOST ASTONISHING OF ALL was the arrival, via France, of the papal emissary Bertano. The previous year Pope Paul III had convened the Council of Trent, part of whose purpose was to see whether the Protestant powers could somehow be reconciled with the Holy See. This, I think, is the context for Bertano's visit – to establish whether some arrangement could be made between England and the Pope, some formula to allow Henry to keep his Supreme Headship of the Church, which he genuinely believed had been awarded him by God, while making some friendly arrangement with the Pope. Theologically, however, the Royal Supremacy and the papal function were irreconcilable, and on this diplomatic front at least, Henry failed.

✝

IF, AS THE TIMELINE SUGGESTS, March 1546 was the crucial date for changes in both domestic and foreign policy, what happened during that month? I think the answer lies in a development often over-looked – the collapse of Henry's health.

It is impossible at this distance to be clear what was wrong exactly with Henry by the 1540s, but some things can be said confidently. The old idea that the King suffered from syphilis is long discredited – there is no evidence for this, and much against. At the core of Henry's problems seems to have been lack of mobility. David Starkey has suggested in his *Six Wives: The Queens of Henry VIII* (2004) that in Henry's jousting accident in 1528 he broke his left leg; it healed but left a piece of detached bone in his calf, which decayed and formed a large and painful ulcer. In any event, Henry gradually had to give up his former regime of very active exercise and, as the years passed, he became increasingly immobile. His portraits show growing obesity, especially in the period 1537 to 1540, during his late forties, between his marriages to Jane Seymour and Anne of Cleves.

By 1544, measurements for his armour showed a waistline of 54 inches; even a modest further weight gain might give a waistline of around 58 inches by 1546; even for a man of 6'2", this puts Henry at the outside edge of gross, morbid obesity. Why did a man who had so prided himself on his appearance allow this to happen? The most likely explan-ation is that his initial weight gain and immobility, especially given the Tudor elite's diet of meat and sweetstuffs, would have made likely the development of type 2 diabetes, a disease not understood at the time. If this happened it would have added another element to the vicious cycle of immobility and weight gain, for Henry would have been constantly hungry and thirsty.

By 1546 it seems that walking any distance was difficult and painful for the King. He already sometimes used a 'tram' (a type of wheelchair) to get around the palaces, and had a 'device' to get him up and down stairs. And his gross obesity and immobility would have made him prone to yet another problem, deep-vein thrombosis in his legs, both of which were now described as ulcerated (a condition consistent with diabetes). Blood clots would form in the legs, then could become detached and travel to the lungs (to trigger a pulmonary embolism). If the clot can dissolve, a patient can survive, but otherwise dies. The descriptions of Henry's medical crises from 1541 seem consistent with a series of pulmon-ary embolisms, the last of which killed him in January 1547, although he would also be liable to strokes or heart attacks – all his organs would have been under tremendous strain.

If Henry did become diabetic as well as morbidly obese around 1540, he could also have become impotent. He had no problems in making his first three wives pregnant, but none of his last three conceived. Catherine Parr was in some ways an odd choice for a sixth wife; she was past thirty and had already had two childless marriages (neither, as in popular myth, to men too old to sire a child). Henry badly needed a second male heir. Prince Edward (again contrary to popular myth) was not a sickly child, but child mortality in Tudor England was high and, if he died, Henry would be back where he had started, without a male heir. Yet in 1543 he married a woman who was a most unlikely candidate to bear a child. Catherine Parr did not fall pregnant during her three-and-a-half-year marriage to Henry, but she conceived during her subsequent marriage to Thomas Seymour. So Catherine was not incapable of bearing chil dren; but Henry by now may well have been.

None of this, of course, was the King's fault. If what I suggest i right, Henry was trapped in a dreadful cycle of pain, immobility and consuming hunger. He seems to have suffered no major health crises in 1544 or 1545, but in March 1546 he did fall very ill, perhaps with an embolism, and his life was feared for, although he recovered after som weeks of convalescence. His next health crisis did not come until Sep tember, although it was then followed by a whole series of illnesses whic culminated in his death in January 1547. I suggest, though, that th March 1546 crisis was bad enough for Henry's doctors (who, while the may not have been very good at preserving life, would have known well the signs of impending death), his councillors, and Henry himself to realize that he probably did not have long to live, and preparations needed to be made for Prince Edward's succession. Some final choice between the radical and conservative factions on the council now had to be made, and the crises in foreign policy had to be resolved. The frantic round of diplomatic and political activity that began then and continued for the rest of the year stemmed, I think, from Henry's March illness.

✟

AND SO TO MY ATTEMPT at an interpretation of the plot against Catherine Parr (I think there was only one, not two as has sometimes been suggested, and it spanned several months). Recent historical work – by Susan James, Linda Porter and Janel Mueller – has given us a much clearer picture of Catherine. She was an attractive, sophisticated woman who had spent her life on the fringes of the court (the Parr family were minor players in the royal household during her childhood) and would have known the King for years. After the death of her second husband, Lord Latimer, she herself later wrote to Thomas Seymour that she had wished to marry him, but the King had set his sights on her. Thus, she believed, she was called by God to marry Henry, and she meant to, surely, in order to influence his religious policy so far as she could. Her letter indicates she was already a reformist sympathizer when she married Henry.

Catherine, who had great style, was an extremely successful and sophisticated performer of the visible and ceremonial aspects of Queen Consort, including the entertainment of foreign ambassadors. She was also, it seems, a very sympathetic personality; loyal and trustworthy and, one detects, with a sense of humour.

Unlike most Tudor women, Catherine had received a good education from her mother, Lady Maud Parr. She learned Latin as a girl; it became rusty, but she picked it up again when she became Queen. She also studied other languages – in the last months of Henry's reign she was learning Spanish, a useful language then for diplomacy. She had a wide range of interests, collecting clocks and coins, and was clearly drawn to scholarship. Her intelligence, while very considerable, seems to have been broad rather than of great depth and focus – in that, she resembled Henry.

Religious influences on Catherine before her marriage to the King in 1543 were contradictory; her brother, Sir William Parr, her uncle Lord William Parr (following the early death of her father, the principal male influence on the family), and her sister and brother-in-law Anne and Sir William Herbert, were all reformist sympathizers. Her mother Lady Maud Parr, however, had been a lady-in-waiting and friend to Catherine of Aragon, but she died in 1529 before Henry expelled his first wife from the royal household. The Boroughs, the family of Catherine's first husband, were reformist sympathizers, but her second husband, Lord Latimer (her marriage to whom appears to have been happy), was a traditionalist. However, her later letter to Thomas Seymour seems to me to indicate she was already travelling a reformist path by 1543. She was to journey further.

✝

CATHERINE PARR WAS NOT, nor would she have claimed to be, a serious theologian. Her little book *Prayers and Meditations*, published in 1545, is quite orthodox. The *Lamentation of a Sinner*, however, probably written over the winter of 1545–6, shows a writer passionate about salvation, which could only be found through reading the Bible and ultimately through faith in Christ. Confessional writings in this vein were common at the time, though not from an English Queen.

Catherine tells of how her own love of the world's pleasures blinded her for a long time to God's grace, before she succumbed to Him. She writes with the fiercely self-critical religiosity of similar contemporary 'confessions' and 'lamentations'. There is enough in the *Lamentation* to ground suspicion of her among traditionalists, because of her belief in salvation coming through a personal relationship with Christ, and study of the Bible, rather than through the practices of the official church. However – and this is vital – the *Lamentation* says nothing at all about, or against, the Mass.

Writing it at all was risky, although in the winter of 1545–6 Henry had taken a new and radical step against the old religion in appropriating the chantries, where Masses were said for the dead, although this move was probably motivated primarily by his desire to get hold of some much-needed money – their endowments were large. But in the early months of 1546 Catherine's caution seems to have quite deserted her in her public association with reformers and, according to Foxe, in openly arguing religion with the King.

✝

ACCORDING TO FOXE, *'In the time of his sickness, he (Henry) had left his accustomed manner of coming, and visiting his Queen: and therefore she would come to visit him, either after dinner or after supper.'* This surely dates this part of the story to March–April 1546 (though most authorities put it months later); as this was the only period before the autumn when Henry was so seriously indisposed. Foxe tells us that Catherine took to lecturing the King on religion, and one night was careless enough to do so in the presence of Bishop Stephen Gardiner, the leading conservative, who, again in that crucial month of March, had returned from a long foreign embassy and quickly gained the King's ear. Gardiner, according to Foxe, subsequently told the King:

> . . . *how dangerous and perilous a matter it is, and ever hath been, for a Prince to suffer such insolent words at his subjects' hands: the religion by the Queen, so stiffly maintained, did not only disallow and dissolve the policy and politic government of Princes, but also taught the people that all things ought to be in common; so that what colour soever they pretended, their opinions were indeed so odious, and to the Princes estates so perilous* . . . (that they) *by law deserved death.*

Then, according to Foxe, Gardiner persuaded the King to begin an investigation into radical religion, in the Queen's household as well as elsewhere – having frightened Henry, among other things, with the mention of people who wished to hold all goods in common, in other words the Anabaptist creed, although Catherine's (and indeed Foxe's) beliefs were very far from Anabaptism.

If I am right and this happened in March–April when the King was convalescing, that fits with the records of arrests and enquiries which began in April and went on till July. But why, some have asked, should the religious conservatives focus on Queen Catherine Parr? It seems to me that she was the obvious target – she was the centre of a group of high-born ladies who, certainly during Lent in 1546, met together to hear sermons and discuss religion. They included her sister Anne (wife of Sir William Herbert), Lady Denny (wife of the chief gentleman of Henry's household, Sir Anthony Denny) and potentially most important of all, Anne Stanhope, wife of Lord Hertford. If heresy was proved against Catherine, not only would Henry's sense of betrayal by a woman he still loved be terrible (there is no evidence at all that he *wanted* rid of Catherine Parr in 1546, rather the reverse), but likely all the women in her circle would fall too, and with them, crucially, their husbands. Catherine Parr, therefore, was the keystone in the arch; knock her out and the whole reformist edifice faced total collapse.

The heresy hunt went on for three months. The spring and early summer of 1546 must have been a desperate time for Catherine, but she seems to have maintained her composure and behaved calmly throughout. Everyone in her circle seems to have stuck loyally together; though this is hardly surprising – if one fell, all fell. It is possible that searches took place within the Queen's household, and certainly she gave some books (which may have included *Lamentation of a Sinner*) to her uncle Lord Parr for safekeeping in April.

By July nothing had been found against her. By then the questioning of suspects seems to have been largely over. No evidence had been discovered against anyone within the circle of the court except for Henry's courtier and friend George Blagge, and nobody from within the Queen's circle. If Thomas Wriothesley and Richard Rich were actively seeking out heretics on behalf of Bishop Gardiner (and possibly, behind the scenes, the Duke of Norfolk), by July they must have been getting desperate.

✠

THEN, IN LATE JUNE and early July came the extraordinary and gruesome story of Anne Askew, whose memoir, the *Examinations of Anne*

Askew, was smuggled out to Flanders, and published the next year by John Bale. Anne Askew, or to use her married name, Anne Kyme, was the wife of a Lincolnshire gentleman. She was aged around 25. By the standards of the time, her behaviour was extraordinary. A radical Protestant who had openly denied the Real Presence in the Mass, she left her husband, a religious conservative, and their two children to come to London and preach in 1545. She had relatives there, certainly a cousin, and distant connections to low-ranking courtiers. Soon she was brought before the Common Council of London, where she denied she was a heretic. Nonetheless, a year later she was back, and this time, although her initial technique in argument was to hedge, she eventually admitted enough to be found guilty of heresy. She refused to recant, and having been brought before the Privy Council and questioned by Gardiner, among others, she was convicted at the end of June and sentenced to be publicly burned, along with three men, on the 16th of July.

There is no evidence that Catherine Parr and Anne Askew ever met or corresponded. They may have had acquaintances in common, but again that is not surprising given the small size of the Tudor elite. Once condemned, according to law, Anne should have been held in prison until her execution. However, at the beginning of July she was sent to the Tower, where, according to her memoir, she was questioned again by Rich and Wriothesley; this time specifically about her links to women in Catherine Parr's household. Not only was she questioned, she was tortured by Rich and Wriothesley personally, to the horror of the Lieutenant of the Tower, who was present. Asked specifically about her links to ladies in Queen Catherine's circle, Anne admitted she had had gifts of money from men who claimed to be servants of the Duchess of Suffolk and Lady Hertford, but denied any direct links to them or the Queen. It was not illegal to bring prisoners money to buy food; in fact these donations were necessary to keep them alive.

There seems no reason to doubt Anne Askew's story; Rich and Wriothesley's behaviour has all the hallmarks of a last, desperate effort by the religious conservatives to find some evidence damaging to the Queen. Desperate indeed, for torture of a person already convicted –

and a woman from the gentlemanly classes – was not only illegal but scandalous; even more so when Wriothesley – as Lord Chancellor, the most senior law officer in England – had himself turned the rack. It was too extreme for the Tower Lieutenant, who promptly went off and told the King, who was horrified. It has been suggested the King himself may have secretly ordered the torture, but there is no evidence to support this accusation one way or the other. It seems more likely to me that Henry was genuinely angered at this attempt to torture someone into providing accusations against the Queen when months of enquiry had failed to find anything credible.

Henry was, by now, already angry with the conservatives. He said that in arresting the courtier George Blagge they had come 'too close to his person' and Blagge was pardoned. Given this move, the scale of the King's anger at those who had tried to torture Anne Askew into providing something harmful to the Queen can only be imagined.

✝

IN FOXE'S ACCOUNT, there was a second plot against Catherine, involving a warrant being issued for the Queen's arrest, a copy of which, however, was conveniently dropped where it would fall into her hands. This event has been convincingly dated by Dakota Hamilton and others to July 1546. According to Foxe, Catherine's response was to rush to the King and persuade him that she had never intended to lecture him on religion, only to engage his mind to distract him from the pain in his legs. Again according to Foxe, the gambit succeeded. Henry accepted Catherine's submission, and Lord Chancellor Wriothesley, when he arrived with the warrant to arrest the Queen the next day, was insulted and beaten about the head by Henry and ordered from his presence – in other words, completely and publicly humiliated.

This has, to me, the flavour of a deliberate ruse by the King, rather than a spontaneous sequence of events as reported to Foxe by two survivors from Catherine's ladies (though it may have looked genuine to them). To begin with, it is hard to guess the legal grounds on which Catherine could have been arrested in July, since extensive enquiries about her and her ladies had revealed nothing at all. If Henry had actually wanted to dispose of her, he could easily have manufactured something, as he did when he wanted to rid himself of Anne Boleyn and Thomas Cromwell, and was soon to do again with the Duke of Norfolk.

It is worth noting in this context that three years before, when Archbishop Cranmer had been the subject of accusations of heresy by Gardiner, the King had turned the tables on the conservatives in a very similar manner, agreeing that Cranmer should be called before the Privy Council, but giving him his ring beforehand to show to the council as proof he still had the King's support. The outcome was that a commission to investigate Cranmer was appointed, but headed by Cranmer himself! This tactic had the benefit of humiliating one party (in both cases the religious conservatives) while reminding the other (first Cranmer, then Catherine) very firmly who was in charge. Given the failure of the heresy hunt, it would have been quite characteristic of Henry to humiliate Wriothesley in this way, while forcing Catherine, like Cranmer earlier, to play a part in the deception – and in Catherine's case, publicly to admit that as a woman it was her place to learn from, and not lecture, her husband.

I think, therefore, that the arrest warrant was nothing more or less than a put-up job, designed to humiliate Wriothesley and also to signal that the heresy hunt was over and the Queen still in Henry's favour. Catherine herself was likely ordered to be involved, and the whole thing stage-managed by Henry himself.

By the end of July, when new jewellery was ordered for her for the forthcoming visit of Admiral d'Annebault, Catherine Parr was clearly and visibly once more high in the King's favour. Her brother, as Earl of Essex, rode at the admiral's side on his procession through London in August. And in October, crucially, Catherine's brother-in-law Lord Herbert was promoted to Deputy Chamberlain, a position which was to be of critical influence in the King's last days. The Parrs had successfully weathered the storm.

✝

THERE REMAINED BERTANO'S visit, but as noted previously, it was a failure. When the papal emissary arrived early in August, hopes of some sort of accommodation with the Pope seem to have been immediately dashed. And from now on the King began to move, steadily, back towards the reformers. He may well have feared that if Gardiner and Norfolk were left in charge of the realm during his son's minority, they would take England back to Rome. And Henry's first priority was always to ensure that the Royal Supremacy passed to his son. Such a fear on the King's part was not unrealistic; a decade later Gardiner was to be key lieutenant to Henry's daughter, Mary I, when she returned England, briefly, to papal allegiance.

✝

AFTER THE FAILURE of Bertano's mission, the focus turned back to relations with France, and much attention was devoted to the preparations to welcome Admiral d'Annebault to London at the end of the month. The sheer scale of the celebrations, in a country financially ruined by Henry's war, has, I think, been rather ignored. There had been no such celebrations to welcome a foreigner, at least not since the arrival of the ill-fated Anne of Cleves in 1539. Archbishop Cranmer's secretary, Ralph Morice, later recounted how Henry stood at one of the Hampton Court banquets for d'Annebault, with one arm round the admiral's shoulder and the other round Cranmer's (a sign of favour to both, although Henry by now may have found it difficult to stand unsupported) and, according to Morice, made the astounding statement that he and the French king would soon abolish the Mass and establish a common Communion. This was never remotely possible, of course (Francis I of France remained firmly Catholic), but for the King to say such a thing even in jest could only be a sign of radical intention, quite unthinkable even a few weeks before.

✝

THE BALANCE OF POWER on the Privy Council had shifted back towards the reformers with the return from abroad of the Earl o

Hertford and Lord Lisle, and it was mainly reformers who accompanied Henry on his Progress at the beginning of September. This Progress was intended to be unusually brief, lasting only a couple of weeks and going only so far as Guildford, but Henry fell ill again during this time and moved from Guildford only to Windsor, where, halfway back, he stayed until the end of October. During most of that time the conservatives on the Privy Council remained in London dealing with routine business, while the radicals were with Henry. As was Catherine Parr.

Henry may well have spent these autumn months plotting his final decisive moves; perhaps his latest bout of severe illness gave him further intimations of mortality. In November and December Gardiner was sidelined, at one point struck in the face at a council meeting by Lord Lisle – without consequences for Lisle, though it was a serious offence – and repeatedly denied an audience with the King. Then, in December, Norfolk and Surrey were arrested, found guilty of treason and sentenced to death. The ostensible cause was Surrey's quartering of the royal arms with his own, but the whole affair smacks of a manufactured attempt to get rid of Norfolk. As the senior peer in England, he thought he should have control of Henry's successor, the young Edward; as noted already, Henry had used far-fetched accusations of treason before to dispose of Anne Boleyn and Thomas Cromwell. Surrey was executed in January 1547; Norfolk himself was due to follow his son to the block on the 28th, but the King's death in the early hours of that morning saved him; he languished instead in the Tower of London for the next six and a half years.

In early December, Henry was seriously ill again and seems never to have recovered fully. The last two months of his life appear to have been passed entirely at Whitehall. Some historians have seen the fact that Henry was apart from the Queen during the last month of his life as politically significant. Certainly Catherine did not get the Regency she had hoped for. However, though she spent Christmas at Richmond Palace, away from the King, her chambers were prepared for her at Whitehall in mid-January, although it is not known whether she actually took up residence, before Henry fell ill for the final time, just afterwards.

But the point is not that Henry did not see the Queen during these last weeks of his life, but that he saw hardly *anyone* except Secretary Paget, and – significantly – the two chief gentlemen of his bedchamber.

Always in Henry's reign, the gentlemen of the bedchamber, chosen by him and with the closest access to his person, wielded serious political power. His two chief gentlemen during most of 1546 were Anthony Denny, a radical sympathizer, and his deputy William Browne, a conservative. In October, Browne was moved and his replacement was none other than William Herbert, the Queen's brother-in-law and a reformer. This surely puts paid to any idea that the Parrs were out of favour following the heresy hunt.

Henry also, inevitably, saw much of his doctors. His long-standing chief physician, the reformer William Butts, had died in 1545 and was succeeded by his deputy, Thomas Wendy, another radical who also served as chief physician to the Queen. Indeed, it has been suggested that he was the man who got a copy of her arrest warrant to the Queen in July, either secretly or, as I think more likely, acting as go-between in Henry's scheme to humiliate Wriothesley.

✝

WITH THESE MEN in close attendance, the King wrote his last Will at the end of December. The Will has caused much controversy. For the last few years of Henry's life, with so many documents to be signed and the King in poor health, use had been made of a 'dry stamp', a stamp with a facsimile of the King's signature. When Henry approved a document, it was stamped and the King's signature inked in, most often by Paget. One would have expected the King to sign his own Will, but the dry stamp was used. The Will, too, was not entered on the register of court documents until a month after its signature, by which time Henry was dead.

Without venturing too far into this area of controversy, the provision that during Edward VI's minority the realm was to be governed by a council of sixteen persons, with a strongly radical balance, almost certainly reflects Henry's intention in December. However, it is quite possible that the clause giving Secretary Paget the power to make 'unful, filled gifts', the details of which Paget said the King had confided to him personally, was a forgery. After the King's death on the 28th of January 1547, Paget and Edward Seymour quickly seized the initiative; peerages and gifts of money were handed out liberally to members of the council as 'unfulfilled gifts', and the council made Lord Hertford Protector.

✝

HERTFORD BECAME, for a while, something like a dictator. A new religious policy of Protestant radicalism began. The Mass was abolished, church interiors whitewashed, a new Prayer Book installed. Whether Henry VIII wished for any of this is very doubtful, but he had secured his main aim – the preservation of the Royal Supremacy for the young Edward VI. By the time Edward reached fifteen, in late 1552, his own personality as a radical and rather severe reformer was emerging. Had he lived as long as his father, which no one saw any reason to doubt, a Protestant revolution, as thoroughgoing as that which took place in 1560s Scotland, would probably have become firmly established. But by one of history's ironies, Edward died from tuberculosis in 1553, a few months short of his sixteenth birthday.

The throne then passed to the King's elder daughter Mary, who reversed course all the way back to papal allegiance, renounced the Royal Supremacy, re-established monasticism and married the Catholic Prince (later King) Philip of Spain. But in 1558, after only five years' rule, Mary too died, probably of cancer, and the throne passed to Elizabeth, who re-established Protestantism, albeit of a distinctly moderate kind.

It has often been suggested that the 'Protestant' and 'Catholic' fac, ions at Henry's court were motivated more by desire for power than any religious conviction, and indeed many councillors – Paget, Rich, Cecil and others – managed to survive and hold office under both Edward and Mary, the younger councillors continuing to serve Elizabeth. But Edward's senior councillors, who implemented radical Protestantism, were mainly former Henrician radicals, while Mary's were mainly former Henrician conservatives. This reminds us that while many clerics and councillors were motivated by the desire for power and wealth, it is a mistake to think the Tudor ruling classes took religion lightly.

☩

THE STORY OF the last two years of Catherine Parr's life is tragic. To her disappointment, she did not become Regent. Then this most capable and usually astute woman decided to follow her heart rather than her head, and quickly married her old love, the Protector's brother Thomas Seymour. The result was disastrous. She moved with him (and the teenage Elizabeth) to Seymour's castle at Sudeley. There, at thirty-five, Catherine fell pregnant for the first time. Thomas Seymour, who had probably married Catherine because of her status as Queen Dowager, diverted himself during his wife's pregnancy with sexual abuse of the fourteen-year-old Elizabeth. When Catherine found out, Elizabeth was sent away from the household of the stepmother she had been close to for four years.

In September 1548 Catherine gave birth to a daughter, but like so many Tudor women, she died shortly afterwards from an infection of the womb. In the delirium of her last days she accused her husband of mocking and betraying her.

Seymour, who seems by now to have been hardly sane, then launched a crack-brained plot, in February 1549, to seize his young nephew Edward VI, and perhaps make himself Protector in his brother's place. He had no support whatever, was immediately arrested and executed for treason in March 1549. Elizabeth, hearing of his execution, is said to have remarked, 'Today died a man of much wit and little judgement.' As so often, she summed things up exactly.

Catherine's baby, the now orphaned Mary Seymour, passed into the care of Catherine's friend the Dowager Duchess of Suffolk, but disappears from the records after 1550, and must have died in infancy like so many Tudor children. It was the saddest of endings to the story of Catherine Parr.

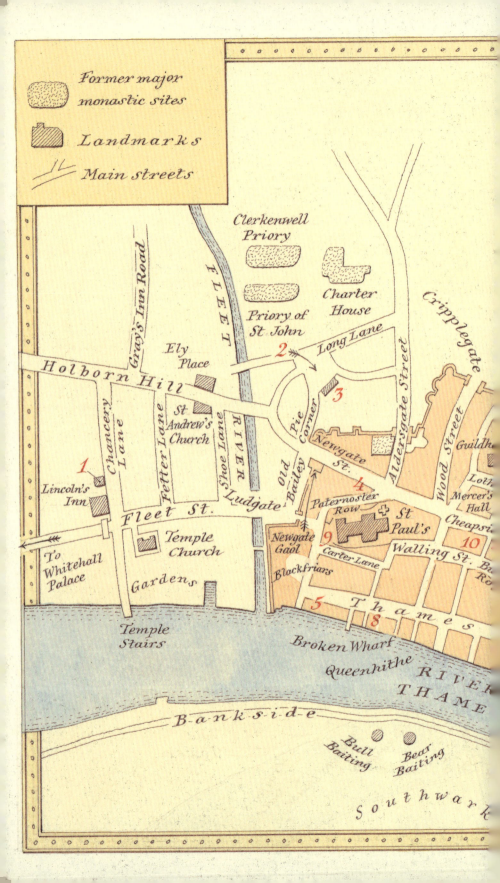

Former major monastic sites

Landmarks

Main streets

Clerkenwell Priory

Charter House

Priory of St John

Gray's Inn Road

FLEET

Long Lane

Cripplegate

Ely Place

2

Holborn Hill

3

Aldersgate Street

Wood Street

Guildh

Chancery Lane

St Andrew's Church

Shoe Lane

Pie Corner

Newgate St.

1

Fetter Lane

RIVER

Old Bailey

4

Loth
Mercer's
Hall

Lincoln's Inn

Ludgate

Paternoster Row

St Paul's

Cheapsi

Fleet St.

9

10

To Whitehall Palace

Temple Church

Newgate Gaol

Carter Lane

Walling St.

Bu
Ro

Gardens

Blackfriars

5

Thames

Temple Stairs

8

Broken Wharf

Queenhithe

RIVER
THAME

B a n k s i d e

Bull
Baiting

Bear
Baiting

S o u t h w a r k

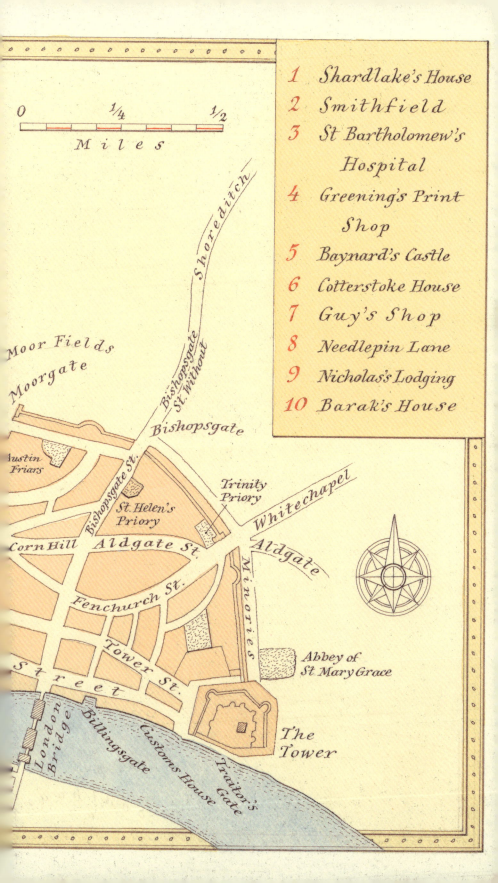

Lady of the Butterflies

FIONA MOUNTAIN

preface

Published by Preface 2009

10 9 8 7 6 5 4 3 2 1

First published in Great Britain in 2009 by Preface Publishing
1 Queen Anne's Gate
London SW1H 9BT

An imprint of The Random House Group Limited

www.rbooks.co.uk
www.prefacepublishing.co.uk

Addresses for companies within The Random House Group Limited can be found at:
www.randomhouse.co.uk

The Random House Group Limited Reg. No. 954009

A CIP catalogue record for this book is available from the British Library

ISBN 9781848091641

The Random House Group Limited supports The Forest Stewardship Council (FSC).
the leading international forest certification organisation. All our titles that are printed
on Greenpeace approved FSC certified paper carry the FSC logo. Our paper procurement
policy can be found at www.rbooks.co.uk/environment

Mixed Sources
Product group from well-managed
forests and other controlled sources
www.fsc.org Cert no. TT-COC-2139
© 1996 Forest Stewardship Council
FSC

Typeset in Fournier MT by Palimpsest Book Production Limited,
Grangemouth, Stirlingshire

Printed and bound in Great Britain by Clays Ltd, St Ives plc

For Tim, Daniel, James, Gabriel and Kezia

Also in memory of my mother,
Muriel Swinburn

'You ask what is the use of butterflies? I reply to adorn the world and delight the eyes of men; to brighten the countryside like so many golden jewels. To contemplate their exquisite beauty and variety is to experience the truest pleasure. To gaze enquiringly at such elegance of colour and form devised by the ingenuity of nature and painted by her artist's pencil, is to acknowledge and adore the imprint of the art of God.'

John Ray, *History of Insects*, 1704

'If a man will begin with certainties, he shall end in doubts; but if he will be content to begin with doubts he shall end in certainties.'

Sir Francis Bacon, author, courtier and philosopher (1561–1656)

November 1695

They say I am mad and perhaps it's true.

Look, can't you see? There are butterflies, bright orange butterflies, even though it's night, even though it's November. The black sky is filled with them. They are reflected in the dark floodwaters that lie over the wetlands. But, no, I realise in an instant that I am mistaken, of course. It is nothing but the glowing ashes of the Gunpowder Treason Night bonfire, flitting upwards in the smoke and the mist.

I hug my arms around myself inside my cloak. I try not to scream.

At the very time when I need all my wits about me, it is frightening to think I can't even depend upon myself, that my own mind, my own eyes, might betray me, even for a moment. This turbulent century that is nearly at an end has seen brother turn against brother and fathers take up arms against their own sons, but for my little family the treachery goes on.

I walk towards the end of the cobbled causeway that stretches straight and unhindered across the floodwater, all the way to Nailsea. The ground is sodden. The mud sucks at me and the sodden hem of my gown grabs and slaps at my ankles. My feet are so cold and wet I can hardly feel them. But there are far worse troubles than cold toes.

At first no one dares to meet my eyes. They regard me with superstitious fear, as if I were a will-o'-the-wisp. Tenant farmers, eelers, fishermen, wildfowlers and sedge-cutters, they are all gathered here with their kin at the edge of the flooded fields, their faces ghoulish in the flickering flames. No one misses this annual festival of hatred, but in Tickenham this year it feels as if much of the hatred is turned upon me. My heart is beating too fast and my legs feel weak as reeds. But I keep my head held high. I keep on walking. Though I may only be slight, I am much stronger than people always assume. None shall see that I am afraid.

Fingers reach out to clutch at my cloak, others claw at my arm, at a windblown wisp of my hair. Alice Walker, once my little cookmaid, is the first to throw a rotten apple. It hits my shoulder and splatters. Surprisingly hard they are, apples, when turned into missiles. There is a dull pain and the sudden cloying smell of decay. Someone else spits and the disgusting gob lands on my cheek. I wipe it away with the palm of my hand and pretend not to care. These people were once my neighbours, servants and friends, my family, but now, instead of warm greetings, I hear only their insults, their whispered accusations:

'Papist!'

'Whore!'

'Witch!'

'Lunatic!'

I am none of those things, am I? How could a passion for small, bright-winged creatures have led to this? Just as it led me to James Petiver, the dearest friend any person could hope to have.

But it was another man who set passion burning within me more fiercely than all the fires that flame across England this night, who consumed me until I am nothing but a husk blowing on the wind. It is Richard Glanville, beautiful as a girl with his black curls and blue eyes, who brought me light in the darkness and warmth in the cold, in a way that no winter bonfire ever can. In my memory his caress is like the brush of a butterfly's wing upon my skin, upon my breasts and the secret places beneath my shift, but all such memories have turned to dust in the glare of what I have discovered.

What have you done, Richard? What have you done? Is it the flames of Hellfire that you conjured? My own Judas, did you betray me with a kiss?

Why?

I began keeping a journal to record my work. Though I don't presume it amounts to much, is of any great significance to the world of natural philosophy, James told me it was the best way to record my observations and to learn. I'm glad now that I've done it, for reasons I'd never have considered.

The time is coming when my voice may be silenced for good. God in

Heaven, how has it come to this? It is well known that lust brings madness and desperation and ruin. But upon my oath, I never meant any harm.

All I ever wanted was to be happy, to love and to be loved, and for my life to count for something.

That is not madness, is it?

Part I

Winter 1662

Thirty-three years earlier

I was woken in darkness by the joyful pealing of church bells. The church stood not a hundred yards from my chamber window, just across the barton wall, so the room was filled with the merry and insistent clamour. My head was filled with it, and my heart. It was the loveliest sound. I stuck out my hand to part the heavy crewel drapes that were drawn around the great bed-frame to keep out the icy winter draughts, but it was bright silvery moonlight that shone through the chink in the curtains at the window. Why ever were the bells ringing with such jubilation in the middle of the night? Then I remembered. It was Christmas morning. The bells were calling everyone to the pre-dawn Christmas service, everyone except my father and me. Christmas was to be celebrated across the whole of England again this year, in practically every household, except for a few of the staunchest Puritan ones, such as ours, where it was still forbidden, as it had been under Oliver Cromwell.

I dropped back against the pillows, fighting tears. I was nine years old, not a baby any more. I was too old to cry just because I could not have what I wanted. I knew that in any case, crying was a waste of time, would make no difference at all. With a little sigh I pulled the blankets up to my chin, wriggled down beneath them seeking non-existent warmth, and stared up at the dark outline of the bed-canopy. I should be counting my blessings rather than feeling sorry for myself. I was very privileged, after all. I lived in the manor house of Tickenham Court, with its medieval solar wing and dairy, its ancient cider orchards and teeming fishponds. My father owned all the land for miles around, over a thousand acres of furze and heath and fen meadow, or moors as they were called in Tickenham. I was far more fortunate than the village children, wasn't I? The children who at this very moment were clutching excitedly at their mothers' hands as they left their holly-bedecked cottages to make their way in their little boats over the flooded fields to church, with the prospect of a day of feasting on plum pottage and mince pies and music and games before them.

I laid my hand on my flat belly as it rumbled its own protest. In rejection of what my father saw as the evil gluttony of Christmas, I was to be made to fast all day. All day, and already I was hungry. If I were really lucky, there'd be a dish of eel stew tomorrow, bland and unspiced, according to Puritan preferences.

The bells chimed on, ringing out their tumult in the darkness, the high tinkling of the treble bell and the low boom of the tenor, and round again in a circle. It was as if they were summoning me, had an urgent message to impart. Oh, I did so want to go. We had a merry king on the throne of England now, a king who had thrown open the doors of the theatres again and restored the maypoles, much to my father's disgust. But I did so want to know what it was to be merry, to dance and sing and laugh and wear bright, pretty gowns and ribbons. Even just to see the candlelit church would be something. What harm could it do just to look? If God had gifted me with my irrepressible curiosity, surely He would forgive me for giving in to it now. Wouldn't He?

I pushed back the blankets, exhaling mist, bracing myself for the rush of icy air through my linen shift. But it was not the cold that made my fingers shake as I crouched by the stone fireplace to light a candle from the dying embers. I was afraid of going out in the dark on my own, wary too of the reception I would receive from the villagers. The serving girl had warned me that, since we shunned all their celebrations, my appearance at one might well be regarded with animosity, mistrust. But inquisitiveness eclipsed all else, as it always did for me. I was too impatient to put on my woollen dress and left my hair in its long, thick golden night-plait. Bare-footed I crept down the narrow spiral stone stairs that led from the solar to the great hall. I put on my mud-stained shoes and my hooded riding cloak. It was made from the thick red West Country cloth that was so traditional in Somersetshire that even my father did not balk at its bright colour.

My heart hammering fit to burst with a mixture of excitement and terror, I slipped out of the door and through the gate in the barton wall that led into the misty moonlit churchyard, stole silent as a ghost through the silvery lichen-encrusted gravestones, past those of my little sister and of my mother, both dead over a year now. I breathed deep of the cool air and listened to the honking and trilling of the swans and marsh birds feeding out on the floodplains, the beating of hundreds upon hundreds of wings. An owl hooted and the air was redolent with the familiar tang of marsh and peat and mist. Out on the vast dark water there was a straggling line of bobbing lanterns from the rowing boats carrying the worshippers to the service. They seemed to me like small stars travelling through the night to join with the great illumination that emanated from the wide-open door of the church of St Quiricus and Juliet, a holy golden light that blazed a welcome.

I peered tentatively round the carved oak doorway, not quite daring to let my feet cross the threshold, and gasped wide-eyed at the beauty and colour of it. There must have been a hundred candles or more, all around the altar and the pulpit and lining the nave and pews. There were garlands of rosemary and holly and fresh scented rushes strewn on the floor, and wicker baskets of marchpane sweets and sugarplums set out for the children. The fiddlers and drummers were waiting to begin the music and the players were already assembled at the front of the church, the kings with beautiful velvet cloaks trimmed with real ermine, the shepherds accompanied by real sheep. Two cows had been brought in, too, and a placid-looking donkey.

I felt a light tap on my shoulder and nearly jumped out of my skin. It was Thomas Knight, the dark-haired, dark-eyed son of a sedge-cutter. He was over a foot taller than me and three years older, twelve years to my nine, and for some reason I had never been able to fathom, he hated me. I wanted Thomas to like me, as all children want people to like them, I think, and I had made a consistent effort to be friendly and polite to him, even when sometimes what I really wanted to do was stick out my tongue at him. But it seemed to make no difference what I did. Except that now, there was the definite curve of a smile softening his long, swarthy face. I returned it gladly, but warily. 'Hello, Thomas,' I said.

'Merry Christmas, Miss Eleanor,' he said, with what I took, delightedly, to be complicity, acceptance.

'Merry Christmas to you too,' I replied. The forbidden greeting felt peculiar on my lips, beneficent as a charm, not like a sin at all.

'D'you think it so very evil then?' He nodded towards the gilded interior of the church.

'Oh, Thomas. I've never seen anything so lovely.'

'Here. I've got something for you.' People were walking towards the porch now and Thomas grabbed hold of my arm and pulled me round the side into the dark. I was not frightened, only surprised and very interested to see what it was that he had. He uncurled the palm of his big hand to reveal a little marchpane sweet, delicate as a rosebud, incongruous against his chapped and cold-reddened skin. My mouth watered, but even if it hadn't looked so delicious and appealing, I'd have wanted to take it, just because Thomas had been so kind and generous as to think to offer it to me. I hated to think how I might hurt his feelings if I rejected his gift.

He thrust the sweet impatiently towards my face. 'Well, go on then,' he said gruffly. 'What are you waiting for?'

Still I hesitated, then gave a small shake of my head. 'I thank you, Thomas. But I had better not.'

His expression suddenly changed. His deep-set dark eyes narrowed and there was a glint of challenge, of a slow-burning resentment. 'Not good enough for you, taking food from the hand of a sedge-cutter's son, is that it?'

I was mortified. 'Oh, Thomas, please don't think that. Please don't be offended. I am grateful, really I am.' With a child's fear of being seen to be different, I was almost ashamed to admit the real reason, yet it was preferable to having him think me haughty. 'It's just that I'm not supposed to eat anything at all today.'

'Who's going to know?' He said it in such a conniving, nasty way that all of a sudden I was no longer so concerned about upsetting him. I didn't like the feeling that I was being forced to do something against my will. I didn't want the sweet at all now anyway. 'Leave me be, Thomas,' I said quietly.

Susan Hort, one of the tenants' daughters, stepped out from behind a gravestone where she'd obviously been hiding and watching. 'Told you,' she scoffed. 'Told you you'd not get her to touch it. She's stubborn as a little ox, that one.'

Thomas shoved the sweet right up under my nose. 'Just one bite,' he said. 'You know you want to.' He glowered at me threateningly so that I felt a twinge of panic, but I would not give him the satisfaction of seeing it. 'Let me alone, Thomas,' I said with as much confidence as I could summon. 'I said I don't want it.'

I took a step back, but out of the corner of my eye I saw Susan Hort move behind me as if to trap me. Thomas thrust out his arm and forced the sweet against my mouth as though he were going to ram it through my closed lips. With a rush of rage and humiliation I batted his hand away so that the sweet went flying. Almost before I knew what was happening, Susan had grabbed my plaited hair and jerked me back, had me by the waist, trapping my arms at my sides. She was a sturdy country girl and easily tall enough to lift my feet off the ground. I twisted and squirmed but she held me all the tighter so I struck back with my boots at her shins.

'You vicious little rat!' She threw me to the ground where I fell, sprawled on the soggy grass. I saw the marchpane lying by a clump of sedges right beside my hand. Thomas saw it too and snatched it, and before I could get up he had sat himself down on top of my chest, turning me over and pinning me flat on my back on the damp, chill earth, the crushing weight of him making it hard for me to breathe. He gripped my jaw tightly between his roughened forefinger and thumb, and squeezed.

'Get up. Right now. Leave that child alone.' It was Mary Burges, the new rector's wife, and at the sound of her firm command Thomas reluctantly released me and scrambled to his feet as Susan fell back.

Mary was not much past twenty, but she had had five younger brothers and sisters, so she knew very well how to manage scrapping. She was bustling and plump and maternal, with a soft, round face and eyes as sweet as honey. I was always glad to see her, though never so much as now.

She offered her hand to help me up. 'Are you hurt, Eleanor?' she asked, concerned, bending to draw my cloak around me.

I shook my head, blushing. Bar a few scratches, it was only my pride that was wounded. I stood up straight and tried to be dignified, though there was mud on my shift and I could feel a wet smear of it on my cheek. Tendrils of my hair had sprung free and were falling down around my face. I smoothed them away, rubbed at my dirty cheek. I felt very foolish and embarrassed to be the cause of such a scuffle and over something as trifling as a sweetmeat.

'What do you think you were doing, the pair of you?' Mary said sternly to Thomas and Susan. 'And on Our Lord's birthday, a time of good will and peace.'

Thomas turned his sullen eyes on her and did not answer.

I licked at my lips and tasted the faintest trace of almond sweetness. 'It was nothing, Mistress Burges,' I said, wanting it over and done with now. 'Just a silly game.'

Mary glanced at me appreciatively. 'It seems little Eleanor here has enough good will for all three of you.' She fixed Thomas with a reproachful look, as if she knew him to be the main culprit. 'It didn't look like a game to me, but if you both apologise and run and take your seat in the pews, we'll say no more of it.'

Thomas glowered menacingly at me while he and Susan mumbled an apology of sorts and slunk away. I watched them scurry together into the bright church, where the fiddlers and drummers were starting to play. Only now did I realise that I was trembling.

'We'd better get you back to the house,' Mary said kindly. 'Before your father finds you're missing. Look at you, child. You're not even properly dressed.'

Someone came to close the church door and the emission of lovely, gilded light was abruptly shut off, leaving only the darkness and the cold moonlight. 'Why does Thomas hate me?' I asked. 'Is it just because we are Puritans?'

'That is no doubt part of it.' Mary put her hands on my shoulders and looked down into my face. 'But I expect it is not only that.'

'What, then?'

She smiled. 'Well, it does not help that you are such an unusual child. When people see you down on the moor, climbing trees for birds' eggs, pond-dipping and hunting under rocks for beetles and whatnot, they do not understand why a little girl should take such an interest in such things – a little girl who will one day be their Lady of the Manor at that. Most people are very fond of you, for all your strange ways, on account of your sweet nature and kind heart. But that does not mean that gossip does not get passed around and exaggerated. One of the first things the kitchen boy told me when we came here was that you have a collection of animal skulls and bones in a little casket in your chamber.'

'Oh, but I do,' I admitted, my disappointment suddenly forgotten in a rush of enthusiasm. 'It is amazing what you find in owl pellets. I think the bones must belong to water voles or mice since they are the right size and owls hunt them. I have a dead grass snake and damselfly too, and all kinds of shells and feathers and fossils.'

'I am sure they would look very well in a curio cabinet,' Mary said. 'But in a little girl's bedchamber?'

'If I were a boy nobody would think it so strange, would they?'

She did not deny that. 'The trouble is that people fear what they do not understand, and all too often that kind of fear makes them hostile.'

My eyes widened. 'Thomas Knight and Susan are afraid of me?'

'A little, perhaps.'

It seemed extraordinary, unlikely, but not altogether unpleasing. I had never considered that I could be capable of frightening anyone. Then I remembered the flinty resentment in Thomas's eyes and I shuddered. 'No,' I said. 'There is more to it that that, some other reason he does not like me. I'm sure of it.'

'Well, it's not a problem you'll have with many lads in a few years' time,' Mary said, smiling down at me. 'No boy with eyes in his head will be able to do anything but fall in love with you then, since you are already so uncommonly pretty.' She stroked my cheek with the back of one finger. 'Even with dirt on your face.'

'Thank you,' I said politely as we started walking together, but I was sure she was only trying to cheer me. My father's wish to protect me from the depravity of the world had not stopped me glimpsing the tall and curvaceous Digby girls from Clevedon Court or the Smythe sisters from Ashton Court. I saw them riding out to suppers at their fathers' mansions and sometimes to Bristol, in their ringlets and ribbons and gowns of satin and brocade. Though I did not possess a single looking glass, I'd seen my reflection in the water and in windowpanes plenty of times. I knew that my hair was thick and fair and my eyes were large and wide-set and blue as cornflowers, but my skin was not marble white like those other girls'. It was honey-coloured from being so much outside, and rather than having a long straight nose to look down, mine was small and turned up very slightly at the end, like an infant's. And there was something else. 'I am so small,' I said to Mary despondently.

'You are indeed,' she agreed. 'You are as delicately delightful as a pixie.'

I pulled a face, not at all sure of the appeal of that.

Mary laughed. 'You are a dear child and I am glad you are so humble.' She fell silent for a moment, then went on in a less confident tone, 'Your father strives after humility above all else, and so far it has served him well. He commands respect and affection, despite being such a zealot. But I do fear for him, and for you, if ever he gives in to the pressure he is under to drain these wetlands. If the people are hostile to you now, a move like that will stir up no end of trouble.'

'Oh, he'll not do it,' I said confidently. 'Tickenham Court was my mother's. He'd want it to stay just the way she left it.'

'I'd not be so sure about that.'

One thing I was entirely sure of was that I would not escape the severest punishment if my father found out where I'd been. I had intended to be back long before he woke for morning prayers and so drew back into Mary's shadow when I saw him waiting for me in the gloom by the cavernous stone fireplace in the great hall, beneath the impressive display of armoury. I trembled a little as he came to loom over me in the flickering torchlight, taking in my muddy cloak and state of undress in one scornful glance. His frugal suppers of a single egg and draught of small beer had always kept him lean but now grief for my mother and my sister, coupled with long bouts of penitence and fasting for the punishment of their deaths, had made him gaunt. His craggy face, with its long, aquiline nose and strong jaw, had lost nothing of its power and authority, though. In his black coat with starched square white collar worn over it he was imposing as ever. He was every inch Major William Goodricke of the Parliamentarian army, Cromwell's formidable warrior.

But he was all I had in the world now and I loved him above anything. I was truly sorry for displeasing him, knew that what I had done was wrong. It was just that it had not felt so wrong, and in my heart I could not regret it. Life could be so confusing sometimes.

'You should be ashamed of yourself, Eleanor,' he said.

I hung my head only half in repentance, but also so that he would not see the lack of contrition in my eyes

Mary Burges tightened her arm protectively around my shoulders and drew me into her skirts. 'On the contrary, you should be very proud of your little daughter, sir. She showed great courage and strength of will this day.'

I stole a glance at my father and relaxed a bit as I caught his expression of faint relief and pleasure.

'I am glad to hear it,' he said, as if he would have expected no less from me.

'Some of the village children had dared each other to make her eat marchpane,' Mary explained. 'But Eleanor refused so much as to touch it, even when they had her pinioned on the ground. There's not many a child would not give in to such taunting and temptation.'

My father harrumphed as he addressed me. 'Who was it?'

'Thomas and Susan, Papa. But they said they were sorry,' I added quickly. 'They didn't mean anything by it.'

I desperately didn't want my father to cause more trouble with their families. Puritans could be as harsh and unforgiving as their God sometimes, and after what I had seen, and what Mary had told me, I wasn't at all sure we could afford to be.

The Somersetshire nobility, along with most of the people hereabouts, had been Royalist during the Civil War and now Anglicanism was increasingly the religion of the gentry, so for one reason or another our own class had largely disowned us. And every member of our household, every one of our neighbours and servants who were made to attend the secret Puritan prayer meetings in our great hall, saw their lord's empty pew during church services, knew that my father's deliberate absence from church branded him a recusant, still a capital crime. It would take only one person to denounce him to the court or the bishop to render him liable for fines and penalties, to send him to gaol, or worse. So far his fairness and the esteem in which he was held locally had secured his safety, my safety, and enabled him to continue to stay true to his conscience and practise his beliefs in private. I did not want him to demand that Thomas Knight be punished. We had already set ourselves far enough apart from the rest of this little community. There seemed nothing to be gained from drawing more attention to the fact that we were different.

My father reached out and took me by the arm. 'I thank you for bringing her back,' he said brusquely, dismissively.

Mary gave me an encouraging smile as she turned to leave.

'I only went to watch, Papa,' I said when we were alone. 'I just wanted to see what it was like.'

'And did you like what you saw?'

I hesitated, not wanting to appear defiant but feeling too passionate to lie, even if it might spare me much trouble. 'I liked it very much,' I said. 'Oh, Papa, it was so lovely, and so holy. Not sinful at all. If you would only go and see for yourself then I know you'd . . .'

'I am going nowhere, child,' he said stonily. 'And neither are you for a good while. It is not those village children who need to be taught a lesson, I think, but you.'

He took me by the arm and led me back up the narrow stone stairs to my chamber. Fear tightened my throat when he put his hand in his pocket and produced a large key. I'd have preferred to have my hands or backside whipped, really I would. Anything was better than being locked up. I hated being inside for any length of time. I needed open air and space and the sky above me and freedom to roam. Even in the winter, when I had to go everywhere by boat and there were weeks and weeks of rain and mist and ice, I loved to be outside, lived to be outside. I had a strange terror of doors and walls, of locks and keys. Of being confined.

'You'll stay in this room until this day is done,' my father said. 'And if you have any sense, you will spend much of that time on your knees praying for forgiveness for your disobedience.' He turned to go, his hand on the door latch.

'Why is it so wrong to celebrate the birth of Jesus?' I asked quickly.

My father turned back to me, as I had known he would. 'You should not need me to tell you, child,' he said, exasperated but patient, always ready to answer my questions and explain. 'The Bible does not tell us to observe Christ's birthday. Christmas is just an excuse for debauchery, a commemoration of the Catholic idol of the Mass.' He took a deep breath and I saw the dangerous glint of fanaticism in his eyes. 'We must be on ever more constant guard now the King has placed a Catholic Queen on the throne of England. The danger from Rome is present now more than ever. The hand of the Jesuit is still too much amongst us.'

The questions were pushing against my lips and I had no choice but to ask them. 'Most Puritan ministers call themselves Protestants now,' I persisted, my mouth drying at my own audacity. 'Why can't we be Protestants?

Why must we always be different, always excluded?' I gulped in a breath. 'What's the harm in lighting up midwinter with a church full of candles?'

I braced myself for my father's rage but instead he regarded me with deep sorrow, as if I was the greatest disappointment to him. More than that even – as if he feared that all the time he had spent answering my questions and explaining his doctrines had been wasted. He looked at me as if he feared for my immortal soul. I was appalled to see there were tears in his eyes. I had never seen my father cry, not even when my mother and my sister died.

I ran to him and threw my arms around his legs. 'Oh, Papa, I'm sorry. Please don't be upset. I'll try to be good from now on, I promise.'

He uncoiled my arms and held me gently away from him. 'Little one,' he said with great weariness. 'Will you never learn? The only light we need is the light of the Lord.'

With that he turned away, picked up the candle and left me, closing the low, studded door behind him. I heard the key turn with a grating click in the rusty lock. My chest tightened. I felt as if I couldn't breathe, as if all the air was being pressed out of my lungs and I was sure that I was going to faint. I forced myself to resist the urge to rush at the door and hammer on it until my fists were bruised and bleeding. I knew it would do no good, only make matters worse. I was expected to accept my punishment meekly and with penitence, no matter how frightening it was, no matter how unjust I believed it to be. What was the use in trying to be virtuous? I might as well have eaten that marchpane, since I was being punished anyway.

I went to sit quietly on the edge of the high bed, picked up my poppet doll and hugged it. I took deep breaths, tried to think calm thoughts, to imagine myself somewhere else. It was a trick I had practised ever since my mother's death, to take myself back in time to another place, a happier, better place. If I concentrated hard I could see her kind and radiant smile quite clearly, as if she was still with me. Almost.

Dawn had only just broken but it would be a short day, would be pitch dark again in just a few hours, and I had no candle. I had always been petrified of the dark, no matter how much I tried to rationalise the terror away. Eleanor Goodricke, I told myself very sternly now, how can you ever hope to be a natural philosopher if you are prey to such superstitious fears? But I did not dare turn my head towards the far corners of the chamber where strange-shaped shadows already lurked. If only I had a candle. But I knew there was no use calling for that either.

The only light we need is the light of the Lord.

I bit my lips against blasphemy but still my heart cried out: It is not enough for me.

January 1664

Two years later

Thomas Knight's sister, Bess, was my new maid, and despite her brother's dislike of me, she and I had become fast friends.

'Hold still now,' she commanded, giving me an apple-cheeked smile that revealed the wide gap between her two top front teeth. 'Or the gentlemen visitors will take you for a little vagabond.'

I was so excited by the prospect of visitors that I didn't mind having to stand still for an age while Bess brushed and brushed at the hem of my plain, dark dress to rid it of the worst of the ever-present rim of mud stains. Made of wool, it could never be washed or it would shrink. I didn't mind either that Bess combed and combed at my long fair hair until it crackled with life and sparkled like spun gold, only for the great mass of it to be pinned and braided and tightly fastened away beneath a lace cap that was starched as crisp and white as my square collar.

I went to kneel up on the seat in the oriel window, my nose practically pressed against the uneven panes of leaded glass, keeping a look out over the ghostly waterland patterned with droves and causeways that rose above the submerged world. I was determined to be the first to see our guests, though the drifting mist had rendered even the nearby stables indistinct. It had been raining all night, was raining still, and the floodwaters were lapping at the barton wall now. We were half-marooned, accessible from the south only by the main causeway or by boat.

As my father chose to shield me from the world and all that was worldly, he allowed me to mix with only the most restricted society. I seldom saw a new face, seldom saw anyone but the servants who made up our wider family. I had hardly ever travelled beyond the confines of the estate, beyond the isolated village of Tickenham, had never even been to Bristol.

I didn't mind much, because I didn't know any different, but also because I loved Tickenham so that I could not in all honesty imagine myself away from it. Tickenham was a part of me, was who I was. I was Eleanor Goodricke of Tickenham Court. Since the day I was born I had imbibed the water from the springs and the cider from the apples in the orchard along with my mother's milk. What little flesh there was on my limbs was nourished by the fish from the rivers and the wildfowl from the wetlands. And Tickenham's moods, its spirit, reflected my own. The isolation and secrecy caused by the winter floods and mist echoed my own unusual need for seclusion, for time to myself, whilst the profusion and lushness of summer on the moor satisfied my deep and unquenchable yearning for colour and sunshine. Tickenham for me was the world and I did not want to be anywhere else. Though that did not mean I did not relish the chance to meet outsiders.

William Merrick, a Bristol merchant, had visited several times recently to talk to my father, about financial matters mostly, but never before had he brought anyone else with him. Eventually I saw them riding along the causeway. Mr Merrick was a barrel-chested and bulbous-nosed man who took great pains to hide his lack of refinement beneath immaculate clothes. He was a Puritan, supposedly, yet he could not help displaying his considerable wealth in a flash of silk brocade waistcoat, in subtle but obviously expensive rings, in the finest silk stockings. He sat, square-shouldered and square-jawed, on his dun mare as it trotted up the miry path past the rectory. Even the way he rode was brash. But it was the rider on a roan gelding who interested me, the tall, straight-backed gentleman from Suffolk.

I ran round to the cobbled stable yard then held back, suddenly struck by shyness as I watched them dismount amidst a scattering of chickens. They were both wearing long black cloaks and tall hats which shadowed their faces. Rain was dripping from the brims, I saw, by the time they'd walked the short distance to the door beneath the oriel.

With a look of distaste on his florid features, Mr Merrick wiped his highly polished beribboned shoes with a clump of straw. He lived in a smart new street in Bristol, by the docks, where the marshland had been nicely tamed, so he had little patience with mud and damp, or with anything with even the slightest tendency to disorderliness, such as me.

He wasted no time in introducing Edmund Ashfield, who shook my father's hand. It was an odd greeting, only used by true Parliamentarians. Then he turned to me and bowed, removing his hat. As he came up again, he smiled at me and my eyes widened in wonder. It was as if the mist had cleared to reveal a burst of sun, or else his entrance had been announced with a fanfare of trumpets. His short-cut hair was thick and wavy, and of the brightest copper colour I'd ever seen. When he straightened, I took in just how very tall and broad-shouldered he was. He had clear grey eyes, an open, ready smile, and his nose and cheeks were sprinkled with pale gold freckles. He was as different from the rustic Tickenham boys as it was possible to be. He shone. He lit up the austere stone-walled hall like a sunbeam, and seemed to me like a knight in gleaming armour who had stepped straight from the pages of a romance.

Still beaming warmly at my father and me, he clutched his hat in front of him in both hands and turned it round like spinning top. 'I beg your pardon for our late arrival. We had a slight skirmish with an uprooted tree on the high road and daren't venture round it on to the flooded fields, lest we be washed away or sink up to our waists in the bog. It's mightily hostile out there, I tell you. But this is a delightful place in which to wait out the siege.'

I wasn't in the least disheartened to hear that his manner of speech was not as unusual as his appearance. Overuse of military language was common amongst my father's few visitors, an inevitable consequence of the years when the chief topics of conversation had been Civil War and armoury and battle strategy. Just like me, Mr Ashfield must have a father who had fought for Cromwell.

'Didn't I tell you Major Goodricke had a pretty little daughter?' Mr Merrick interposed. He had never paid me even the scantest compliment before and it did not sound very sincere now. But I barely wondered at it. I barely noticed his cold and calculating smile, and for once did not pause to consider what he, ever the merchant, might be looking to trade this time. I did not think of him at all.

'I've been looking forward very much to coming here,' Edmund Ashfield said, with sincerity enough for both of them.

I silently cursed myself for being so tongue-tied. For what must be the first time in my life, I could think of absolutely nothing to say.

'Are you staying in Bristol for the winter, Mr Ashfield?' my father inquired.

'Oh, no, sir. I'm on my way home from the Twelfth Night celebrations in London.'

My eyes flew anxiously towards my father and I saw his bushy grey brows knit in a tight, disapproving scowl. My need to cover his displeasure and make Mr Ashfield feel entirely comfortable was so great that it helped me to find my voice at last. 'Have you been to London before, sir?' I asked.

He turned to me and gave me his full attention. 'I have, miss. Several times.'

I felt myself blush in the full warmth of his glorious smile, now miraculously directed solely at me. 'And is it very foul and wicked and full of thieves and cut-throats?' I asked.

'And many more things besides. Not all bad.' His eyes shone with such amusement that I could not help but smile back. I thought I had never seen a face so full of laughter. He looked like a person who was always happy, would never have a care in the world. A person who could never look dour or severe or Puritanical. He seemed made for Twelfth Night festivities, for capering and merrymaking, and, for me, the knowledge that he had come direct from such forbidden entertainments, from the great and wicked capital city, only served to add to his appeal.

'Have you seen the lions in the Tower?' I asked. 'What do they feed them?'

'Nosy little girls, I shouldn't wonder,' Mr Merrick said disapprovingly.

Mr Ashfield ignored that remark completely. 'I am afraid I have not been there at feeding time,' he answered, finding my question worthy of a considered reply. 'I shall make an effort to do so and report back, since it interests you.'

'Thank you, sir.'

'You are most welcome.'

I wondered who had been lucky enough to enjoy the Twelfth Night festivities in his company. 'Do you have family in London, Mr Ashfield?'

'Do hush, Eleanor,' my father chided. 'You mustn't interrogate our guest before he has even taken some refreshment.' He apologised on my behalf. 'My daughter is renowned for her curiosity.'

'I was there with a very good friend of mine,' Mr Ashfield said to me, and my heart melted because once again he'd taken the trouble to answer me. 'Another lad from Suffolk. Name of Richard Glanville.'

I saw my father tense.

'Ah, that young blade again,' Mr Merrick snorted. 'You mustn't judge a man by his friends,' he added hastily, with a glance at my father that was, astonishingly, almost nervous. 'Edmund's a very respectable fellow, aren't you? For all that you choose to mix with Cavaliers.'

My mouth fell open. I gaped at Edmund Ashfield whose allure had suddenly multiplied beyond all imagining with this new revelation. He actually knew a Cavalier! Was friends with a Cavalier! He might as well have admitted to supping with the King himself, or rather with the Devil. Which, in my father's eyes, amounted to exactly the same thing.

'Richard has never been anywhere near Whitehall Palace and he was born during the Commonwealth,' Edmund said very amiably. 'After the war was over.'

'Makes no difference,' Mr Merrick said, with another fawning glance at my father. 'He's the son of defiantly Royalist parents who mixed with the court in exile, which makes him as Cavalier as Rupert of the Rhine.'

'I'm surprised that an upstanding gentleman such as yourself would choose to fraternise with men of pleasure,' my father said critically.

'They are not half as debauched as we've been led to believe, you know.' Mr Ashfield smiled, his cordiality still totally unruffled.

'Come now,' my father said. 'You'll not tell me that the news of lewdness and perversion that reached us from Europe was all fabrication? The depravity of the public and private morals of Charles Stuart and his band was the scandal of the country – still is, now they've brought their vile wickedness to Whitehall. It was well reported how they abandoned themselves to their lusts, and drank and gambled, fornicated and committed adultery. How they committed these blackest of sins and saw none of them as any sin at all. These are men in contempt of all decency and religious observation. Or would you deny that they are a crowd of short-tempered quarrellers, violent heavy drinkers and murderous ruffians, who would brawl and duel to the death over so little as a game of tennis?'

Carried away by his own fervour, my father seemed entirely to have forgotten that I was standing there in wide-eyed enthralment, listening raptly to every word. Oh, I was used to hearing him rail against Cavaliers.

In many ways they stirred up his moral indignation even more than did Catholics. But never before had he been so specific, and I was caught between utter fascination and an acute embarrassment that made me half wish I could fall into a hole and hide. I felt so dreadfully sorry for poor Mr Ashfield, though he did not appear at all affronted.

'I can't speak for all Royalists,' he said good-naturedly. 'But I assure you that Richard Glanville is possessed of great wit and courage and is one of the most cultured and charming young men I have ever had the pleasure to socialise with.'

'Cultured?' my father snorted. 'It is a culture of monstrous indulgence, drunken gaiety and sensual excess that our monarch and his circle cultivate and would wish to impose on this country. The sooner they all rot and decay in their own filth, the better. God forbid it brings us all to moral ruin first.'

There was an excruciating silence. 'I heard young Richard swims as though he were a fish, not a boy,' Mr Merrick interjected rather desperately. 'He'll have his pick of the new drainage channels and widened rivers next time he visits Ashfield land, eh?'

Fen drainage was Mr Merrick's favourite topic of conversation, one he unfailingly managed to bring up at every visit. It might have made me uneasy, after my conversation with Mary Burges, but I didn't much mind what the three of them talked about so long as they were not insulting poor Mr Ashfield and his friend. So long as I could listen to him and watch him and stay near him.

But it was not to be. 'I suggest we move into the parlour for some coffee,' my father said brusquely, remembering his manners at last. 'Eleanor,' he said to me, 'find Bess, would you, and ask her to send a pot through to us.'

I wished I knew why Mr Merrick was honoured with the great luxury of coffee every time he visited, but I was very glad Mr Ashfield was to be given the best that we had, would not begrudge him anything at all.

He went with the others towards the oak-panelled parlour, and when I took a step to follow, my father halted me with one of his sharp looks. I actually shivered, as if, deprived of the nearness of Edmund Ashfield's bright hair and sunny smile, I was being cast back out into shadows and darkness. I lingered like a little phantom beneath the vaulted roof in the empty hall as he took the seat of honour in a carved oak chair that was drawn up beside the fire, while the wind boomed outside like distant cannon-fire and the rain peppered the windowpanes like tiny arrows. The flames behind him were pale in comparison, only served to make him appear all the more burnished and gleaming. He had all the glorious grandeur of autumn, a blaze of red and gold that defied the closeness of winter.

He was talking of the windmills that were used in his home county to drive back the water. 'There's clearly a great advantage to be gained from combating the floods and claiming the territory for lush meadows in their stead,' he said mildly.

'You tell him, Edmund my boy,' William Merrick said heartily. 'For he'll not listen to me.'

'On the contrary, William,' my father replied. 'I listen to you very carefully.'

'Yet you do not heed my advice. Even when it seems you have little choice.'

'There is always a choice.' My father added gravely, 'If we trust in God to provide.'

'And what if His way of provision is by way of reclaiming land from water?'

My father hesitated, as if to consider, and I held my breath as I waited for his reply. 'You know I have the gravest reservations about that, William. Your gentlemen adventurers are playing God, tampering with His creation, and not only is that wrong, it is also highly dangerous.'

The mist and rain had cleared when I stood with my father and watched our visitors ride on to Bristol beneath a glorious winter sunset that shimmered on the surrounding sheets of water. In the dusky light I could see, both inside and out, the translucence of my face reflected in the panes of grey-green leaded glass, and beyond the lapwings and redshanks and curlews wading in the shallows and the great herds of swans and wild geese out on the lake, gliding between the rows of half-submerged pollarded willows that were always an eerie sight, no matter how familiar.

Had Mary Burges been telling the truth when she said I was pretty? I wondered. Never had it seemed to matter so much before. But I wanted to be pretty enough to make a man like Edmund Ashfield fall in love with me when I grew up. Bess constantly complimented my gold hair and blue eyes, but it was their liveliness and brightness she said she liked, and I was not sure that gentlemen would like that at all. Ladies were supposed to be demure and docile and saintly, and I was none of those things.

'Will Mr Ashfield come here again?' I asked, making a great effort not to sound as forlorn as I felt.

'He'd not be unwelcome,' my father said, surprising me. 'An extremely likeable young fellow. I shall pray for him, that he is not ruined by his objectionable associations.'

'Do you even know Richard Glanville, Papa?' I asked, feeling a strange need to defend this man whom I had never met.

'I know of his family.' My father scowled. 'I know his type.'

'Men of pleasure.' I whispered it like a creed. At the age of eleven, my naive notion of pleasure extended not much beyond music and dancing and feasting, all that was forbidden to me and therefore infinitely fascinating and desirable. Was Edmund Ashfield a man of pleasure despite being a Parliamentarian? He must be, a little, to have such a friend.

'Young Edmund was probably not as persuasive as William Merrick had hoped he would be,' my father added. 'So maybe he'll be brought back again for another try, since it seems Merrick will use any ploy to try to convince me that we are sitting on a fortune and that our drained fields could become the richest pastureland in all of England.'

I loved it when my father talked to me as if I was an adult rather than a child, as he had taken to doing more and more recently. But I remembered Mr Merrick's opportunistic smile, predatory as a vulture, and even the small surge of joy I'd experienced at the prospect of seeing Edmund Ashfield again was marred by the notion of it being for Mr Merrick's benefit.

He had even turned being a Puritan dissenter to his own advantage. Barred from the professions, he'd made a great fortune as a merchant trading in tobacco and sugar. My father saw it as a sign of God's supreme approval that Mr Merrick's business ventures had flourished, and as a result generally relied whole-heartedly on his financial acumen and shrewdness. Seemingly not in this one instance, though.

'You disagree with him totally about drainage then, Papa?'

'If I had a shilling for all the failed schemes to drain Somersetshire, I'd have had no need to take out a mortgage with him, or even consider letting him act as my agent to embark on some such risky scheme here. But I can't deny that it's tempting . . . even making a small fortune would be useful to us now.' He stroked my hair. 'Don't look so alarmed, my little one. We're not facing ruin just yet.'

I was about to ask him what a mortgage was but I didn't get the chance.

'It's the war, of course,' he ran on. 'We're still suffering for maintaining a troop of horse rather than our land, and we've still not recouped the revenue that was forfeit to the new King for his pardon. But we will, given time, and at least our house is not a burnt-out shell like so many others. At least our fields do not lie abandoned and overgrown with weeds, even if they are underwater for half the year.'

'If we drained them, would we become very rich, then?'

Rich to me meant satin and silk and ribbons a-plenty. It meant diamonds and rubies. Although not for rich Puritans, of course.

'If only it was as easy as that,' my father sighed. 'What William Merrick conveniently omits to mention is the disorder and violence that erupted when attempts were made to drain the Fens, the mobs and riots led by Fenlanders who feared the destruction of their way of life. I would think long and hard before stirring up that kind of strife here. I have lived through enough years of war and discord to value being at peace with our neighbours.'

I knew better than to remind him that some of them, Bess's brother Thomas for one, were not so peaceably disposed towards us even now. He still looked at me with disdain and contempt whenever I met him on the moor.

My father smoothed a stray lock of hair off my brow, rested his big hand on top of my head, and I looked up into his craggy, kindly face which was dearer to me than any other. 'Running this estate is the gravest responsibility,' he said. 'It is your birthright, precious to us as the crown jewels to a royal heir. Tickenham Court has been in your mother's family for generations. I want to do what is right in her memory, and to safeguard it for you and your children. I am only a custodian here after all. This house is your future, your children's future.'

My mother gave birth to my sister and me late in life, so I had grown up knowing that there would be no sons to follow, and that one day the manor of Tickenham Court would be mine. I used to dream of being a grand and gracious lady of a grand and gracious mansion. But now I fully understood that what had to happen for me to attain this position was the last thing I wanted. I moved closer to my father and slipped my hand into his as if to hold on to him. 'Don't speak of it, Papa,' I said quietly. 'I don't want you to die.'

He gave my hand a little squeeze. 'I'm afraid there's no avoiding that, Eleanor. We may live in an age when physicians are constantly making new discoveries about the workings of the body, but not even they can shy away from the one inevitability of life: death. You must be ever mindful of that, living your life in such a way as to prepare yourself for entry into the Kingdom of Heaven.'

God help me and my rebellious heart, but I felt a sudden surge of defiance then that was like anger, like desperation. I did not want to listen to him any more, did not want to be dragged down into melancholy with him. I did not want to be mindful of death. I was eleven years old and I did not want to prepare myself for Heaven.

My sister had died of ague not a month after my mother, and to think of her now gave me such a dreadful sense of my own mortality, of death's nearness and its inevitability. I thought of all the delights of this life that little Margaret would never have the chance to experience, some of which I was not sure that even my mother ever experienced. Music and dancing. Singing and pretty clothes. Beauty and colour. Christmas and feasting. Love. I could not, would not, die until I had had a taste of those things. I had such a powerful yearning to taste them, such a yearning to be happy, that it made me feel like a chick trapped inside an egg. I knew that all that separated me from light and from life was the thinnest shell. If I could only shore up enough strength to break through and find my way out . . . Well, one day I would. Oh, I would. I felt the strength growing inside me all the time, a tough, unshakeable determination. For my sister's sake as well as my own, I was not going to die until I had truly lived.

Summer 1665

A warm spring had turned into the most sweltering summer anyone could remember and today was yet another day of achingly bright blue skies. Knowing how I preferred to be outside, my father suggested that rather than have morning lessons in the parlour, we should have them out on the moors. 'We shall see what wonders of nature we can find to study,' he said, tucking my hand into the crook of his arm.

The moors always had a profound tranquillity in summer, but in the uncommon heat the pace of life there seemed to have grown even more restful. The air was heavy with the scent of meadowsweet and the meadows were a riot of colour, with orchids and yellow iris lining the ditches and silvery water-filled rhynes, and knapweed like exploding bright pink fireworks. Lazy Shorthorn cattle nibbled at the river's edge where mallards bobbed their heads beneath the surface. Even the Yeo flowed more sluggishly, dotted with water violets, parts of it growing stagnant with weeds.

We watched pond skaters and mayflies and water boatmen. I caught a stickleback and found the conical shell of a limpet to add to my collection. When my father, usually so hale and fit, had to pause to catch his breath, I assumed it was on account of the cloying humidity. 'Shall we go to the woods now and look for fungi, Papa?' I suggested. 'It will be cooler.'

'That is thoughtful of you, Eleanor. But I am not suffering from the heat,' he said. 'Not at all.'

We were by a bend in the riverbank, just upstream of where Susan Hort's father, John, was inspecting his wicker eel traps. I kicked off my shoes and went to dip my toes in the gurgling Yeo. A heron stood with a fish in its beak and I smiled to see an otter slip out of the reed bed and go for a swim. 'The river won't dry up completely, will it, Papa?' I asked.

He smacked his cheek where the gnats were biting again and I saw that his wrist was ringed with raised and angry-looking sores. 'Even if it does, there's always the spring water.'

Springs gushed up through the peat all across the land and it was thanks to them that, instead of remaining an island in the midst of a lake, our little estate was now a lush haven in a desert. The pastures were red-brown in places, not from dust and drought like elsewhere in the country, but from sorrel and herbs.

'We can count on the springs to water our beasts and crops,' my father added. 'We'll have eggs and fowl, beef, cheese and vegetables. Nobody will starve. We must thank the Lord that even if it does not rain for months yet, we will be spared here.'

'You said the same thing when we heard there was plague in London, sir,' John Hort grunted over his shoulder, then turned to face us with a slippery eel writhing in his huge hands. 'Those first two cases in St Giles . . . are you still so sure we're safe? They say it's spreading towards the City. What stops it from spreading west?'

My father clutched his leather jerkin tighter around his shoulders and I realised with a stab of alarm that he'd been wearing it all morning, despite the sweltering heat, despite its being the hottest month anyone could remember. I noticed also that his hand shook slightly, and it sent tremors reverberating through my own body.

It was my turn now to fend off the mosquitoes. I slapped them away as if I could slap away the threat of disease. There was nothing at all to fear, was there? London was miles and miles away. As we walked back towards the garden, scores of butterflies criss-crossing our path, it might have been another world. I turned a cartwheel in the grass, skipped off determinedly through the long sedges, the activity and the prettiness of the bright wings helping me to forget the trembling of my father's hand. My own brushed the top of the long grass stems and a little multi-coloured cloud of butter-flies swirled around my dark skirts and my head, like living flowers broken free from their stems.

In the walled garden I stopped to watch two of sulphur yellow playing together over the flowerbeds, fresh and rich as new-churned butter. Butter-flies indeed.

I felt my father's eyes move approvingly to my upturned face. 'It is the duty of everyone, women as well as men, to admire our creator in all the works of His creation,' he said. 'Butterflies are an overlooked though beautiful part of that creation, and surely the most wondrous of all. Wait here. I'll show you something.'

He strode off towards the kitchen garden, and I watched, delighted and astonished, as he crouched down and started rummaging about examining the underside of the cabbage leaves, his jerkin trailing in the peaty soil. I was filled with warmth and love for him then. How fortunate I was to have for a father someone scholarly who was always looking to inspire and stimulate, who delighted in teaching me and wanted to share his knowledge with me. Daily lessons had followed morning prayers ever since I was old enough to hold a quill, and they weren't confined to a girl's usual lot but extended to the fascinating subjects generally reserved for boys: botany, geography, astronomy.

'Hold out your hand,' my father instructed me when he eventually came back, for all the world as if he was going to cane me out there in the garden. There was a fervent sparkle in his brown eyes that I had only ever seen before when he was at his devotions.

I did as he bade and he placed a little worm on my palm. It was the same colour as a cabbage, green with a hint of blue. It wriggled and arched its segmented back, straightened, arched again, crawled towards my thumb. I giggled. 'It tickles me.'

'Consider this, Eleanor,' my father said. 'Just as raindrops yield frogs and rotten meat births worms, so this little creature has been spontaneously generated from the leaves of those cabbages over there. And it will eat those leaves that birthed it until it grows rather fatter than it is now. Then it will weave a tiny silken coffin around itself and inside that coffin a transformation will take place that is truly miraculous. The coffin will open and the humble worm will have turned into a beautiful butterfly.'

I gazed at the squirming maggot. The idea of a grub springing forth from a leaf and then growing bright wings was too fantastical. We were supposed to be living in an age that was throwing aside all belief in magic. But I had not quite lost my childish belief that my father was as omniscient as God, that there was nothing he did not know, and so how could I not believe it? 'Where do they build their coffins? How do they do it? Can I see one of them now?'

'I've never even seen one myself.' He patted my head. 'I know you always want to see proof of a thing with your own eyes, my little one, but the only way to acquire great knowledge is to read and build on the knowledge of those who have gone before.'

By which he meant dusty, ancient texts, the pens of Pliny and Aristotle and others who were long dead, could not be called to account.

'Why do you think God made butterflies?' he asked.

I thought for a moment, wanting to give the right answer, or a considered one at least. 'To make the world beautiful?'

'In part, no doubt. But as far back as the Ancient Greeks, it has been believed that butterflies represent the souls of the dead. They are a token, Eleanor, a promise. A caterpillar begins as a greedy worm, which surely represents the baseness of our life on earth. Then they are entombed, just as we are entombed in the grave. They emerge on glorious wings, just as the bodies of the dead will rise at the sound of the last trumpet on the final Judgement Day. God put butterflies on this earth to remind us of paradise, of his promise of eternal life. To give us hope.'

I looked from the caterpillar to the bright yellow butterflies, dancing so joyfully in the bright sunshine over the flowers, and I was filled with hope. God must love beauty and colour to create such beautiful and colourful things. It was not wrong to want to be happy, to want all the things I so badly wanted.

I decided that if I could not see a butterfly coffin, I could at least try to observe spontaneous generation. So next morning I went off to the scullery where Jack Jennings, the kitchen boy, was peeling a mound of carrots. When I thought he wasn't looking I sneaked past him to the coolness of the larder, where hung a row of dead, plucked ducks. Bunching my skirt out of the way, I clambered on to a cupboard and hooked down the one that looked the freshest. Its skin wasn't particularly nice to touch, all pimply and cold, as you'd imagine the skin of a grass snake might feel, though actually they don't feel like that at all. Snakeskin is quite pleasant to touch. But I'd never been remotely squeamish and I didn't even grimace at the dead duck. I hid it behind my back, dangling it by its scraggy neck, peeked out into the kitchen and, when Jack and Mistress Keene, the cook, were busy at last with the various pots simmering over the great hearth, I stepped across the drainage channel and was out of the door.

Since I didn't want the numerous household dogs or cats to maul the duck, the only safe place to take it was my chamber. The chambermaid had done her tidying for the day and it wouldn't be immediately obvious, since I'd have to cover it up to prove the maggots didn't get at it from the air. I set it down by the window, reasoning that as not much was born in winter, warmth and sun were likely contributing factors to birth. There was something quite disturbing about the bird's lifeless beady eyes, so I wrapped it quickly in a thick blanket. Content as it always made me to be caught up in the thrill of discovery and experiment, I ran off gaily to learn of far-flung lands; Mexico and Suriname and the Americas.

I'd never have imagined one dead duck could cause such a rumpus. It took Mistress Keene until the following morning to discover that it was missing from the larder. But as soon as she did she came in a fluster to the parlour, where my father was hearing me recite a passage in Latin. Mistress Keene was as round as she was tall and had a permanently red face and bright beady eyes like a blackbird. 'I beg your pardon for interrupting, sir,' she said with a glance at me, as I stood demurely with the leather-bound book open in my hands. 'But I'm afraid I have to report that we've been robbed of a duck. Fresh caught and plucked just the other day.'

My father bade her wait until I had finished my recitation, which I achieved, somehow, with only the faintest faltering in my voice.

'Well done, Eleanor,' he said, indicating I might close the tome. 'That was a pleasure to listen to.' He condemned the reciting of Latin in church and advocated the Bible being written in English for all to understand, but he accepted that Latin was still the gateway to science, the language in which all the most interesting books were written, and he was very keen for me to be fluent. 'Nobody who hears you as I do could go along with the common belief that one tongue is enough for any woman.'

Pride leapt inside me like a hare in springtime. But one glance at Mrs Keene and I feared my happiness was going to be very short-lived. I didn't want my father to be angry with me, didn't want to let him down. Nor did I want to be locked in my chamber again, especially on such a lovely sunny day. But I did not see how it was to be avoided.

My father had returned his attention to Mistress Keene. 'Now, just one duck, you say? Nothing else? None of the cheeses or butter or cider?'

'Not that I am aware of, sir. But a duck is a duck.'

'Indeed,' my father agreed.

'I know how insistent you are on honesty, sir,' Mistress Keene added obsequiously, wiping her hands on her apron. 'I'd hate you to blame me or little Jack.'

I clasped my hands behind my back guiltily, as if I could hide what I'd done. I'd concealed the duck under my bed away from Bess and the other maids, but now they had finished upstairs it was back by the window again, plain as day.

'I am not blaming anybody,' my father was saying patiently. 'Now, did you see anything suspicious? Anyone lurking around in the kitchen the other day who shouldn't have been there?'

'Well, sir . . .' another glance at me that was enough to tell me she suspected exactly where the duck might be '. . . I don't like to say.'

'Out with it, Mistress Keene.'

She didn't get a chance to come out with anything for just then Jack Jennings came bursting in through the parlour door, holding the duck up by its neck so its body swung back and forth.

'It is found,' he proclaimed, as triumphant as if it was a cache of silver that had been recovered. He threw an odd look at me, his eyes wide. 'You'll never guess where.'

'I don't have time for puzzles, Jack,' my father said.

Mistress Keene had gone over to the boy to relieve him of the dead bird. 'Poof!' she said rather melodramatically, grasping her nose with one hand while holding the bird at arms length with the other. 'It reeks to high heaven. It surely can't be the same bird you plucked just the other day, to have gone bad so quick.'

'It was laid beside the window in Miss Eleanor's chamber.' Jack announced it with a mixture of scandalmonger's glee and horrified awe. 'Swaddled tight in a good blanket it was, laying in the sunshine, just like a small babe that needed to be kept warm and snug.'

All eyes were on me now, sickened and appalled. My heart had started hammering and I gripped my hands together very tight.

'Surely you knew it was dead, miss?' Mistress Keene asked me patronisingly, as if I was two years old or a simpleton. 'Surely you've lived on this moor long enough to know a dead duck when you see one and not to let it upset you?'

34

'Of course I knew it was dead,' I said quietly. 'I wasn't upset. I wasn't trying to keep it warm either.'

'Then what were you doing, wrapping it up and keeping it in your chamber, child?'

'Seeing if maggots would grow in it.'

My father make a noise in his throat, a mixture of suppressed laughter and groaning. Mistress Keene gave a sharp intake of breath and her hand flew to her throat. Jack Jennings flinched away. The two of them looked at me as if, instead of seeing a slight young girl with fair hair and blue eyes and wearing a long plain black wool gown, they saw a freak, a grotesque hunchback, or a child with two heads. They looked at me as if the Devil himself had come to sit upon my shoulder. Tears pricked my eyes and my belly fluttered with fear. Why did they look at me like that? I remembered what Mary Burges said about people being afraid and aggressive towards what they did not understand, and had a sense then that I might make life very difficult for myself if I did not curb this passion I had for discovery and observation. And yet I did not want to curb it, did not think it was even possible. Nor, in truth, did I see why I should.

'I thank you, Mistress Keene, Jack,' my father said quickly. 'That will be all. You may go back to your work.'

Mistress Keene gathered herself as if she was about to faint away with terror and revulsion. 'What would you have me do with the bird, sir?'

My father waved his hand impatiently then went to take it from her. 'Best to leave it with me.' I was alarmed to see that his hand was shaking again, more noticeably than it had done on the moor.

He turned to me with the duck held aloft as the servants scurried out of the room, casting furtive backward glances at me. By the look on my father's face I guessed that whatever amusement he had felt when I first mentioned maggots was long gone. It was at such times that I understood how, with a powerful combination of praise and chastisement, he had won the fierce loyalty of all the soldiers who had served under him in the Roundhead Army. Why every man there had willingly followed him into the most bloody of battles, would have lain down their lives for him, why every man had loved him and feared him in equal measure.

Above all else I wanted him to love me, to be proud of me and pleased with me.

He tossed the stinking bird on the floor and pinched the bridge of his nose. 'In pity's name, Eleanor, but what were you thinking of?'

'Spontaneous generation, sir.'

His eyes softened. He coughed into his hand, rubbed his chin. 'And what do you suppose the servants will make of that?'

A tendril of my hair had come free from the braids and pins again, had drifted down over my cheek. I smoothed it away, gave a small shrug, shifted my feet. 'Probably that I am a little odder than they already thought?'

'It would have been a good deal better if you had let them go on thinking that you had grown overly sentimental, had formed an attachment to a dead duck and wanted to coddle it like a poppet.'

'That's macabre!'

'Indeed it is.' His mouth was twitching with a smile, which made mine do the same. 'But not quite so macabre as keeping dead meat in your room just to see if you can breed maggots from its rotting flesh. It is all well and good to be curious,' he said. 'You are a persistent little thing, and also, it appears, somewhat ingenious, and I would not have you any other way. Nor would I have you conform simply in order to placate narrow minds. I blame myself for encouraging your curiosity.' He sighed. 'But have a care. Folk are used to seeing you with jars of water beetles and shrimps. They doubtless think it odd but let it pass as a harmless enough activity for a child, but this tale of maggots and rotting flesh will inspire nothing but fear. Jack and Cook will add the grisly story to the pot and who knows what will come of it? What they will all think of you? They are still burning witches in Somersetshire,' he added, deadly serious now. 'Have a care, Eleanor.'

'I will, Papa.' I took a breath. 'May I have my duck back, please?'

He looked at me as if he couldn't believe he had heard me correctly. 'No, child. You may not have your duck back. Have you listened to one single word I have said?'

'I just want to see if there are any maggots yet.'

'Fortunately, there are not. Otherwise the poor little kitchen boy might never have recovered from the shock.'

'I'm sorry, Papa. I didn't mean any harm.'

'I know that, little one.'

'Please don't send me to my chamber.'

'Now why ever would I do that? Surely you know I'd never punish you for this kind of inquisitiveness? It is different altogether from running off to the church on Christmas morning.' He held out his hand to me and I tried so hard to ignore how terribly cold it was, and how pale was his face, but my skill for forcing out unwanted thoughts completely failed me for a moment. His hand felt just as my mother's had done a few days before she died. It felt just like my little sister's before she started to shiver uncontrollably.

My father said I was to come with him to the far corner of the parlour where he kept his ever-expanding case of books behind a dusty brocade curtain. 'I'll show you something very special, arrived not more than a week ago from London,' he said. 'I think you'll find it of great interest.'

I hadn't noticed the book box on top of the settle. As my father moved it in order to sit, I came to sit next to him. He lifted out a large folio and rested it on his lap, running his fingers over the embossed lettering on the glossy tooled calf binding which read: *Robert Hook, Micrographia.*

I nestled closer to him, inhaling the comforting leathery, smoky scent of my father as he moved the book so that it lay companionably between us. I rested my hand on his arm as he lifted the front cover and turned a few of the thick creamy leaves, past pages of lavish illustrations, then folded out one of the plates. It was breathtakingly strange and beautiful, even more astounding when I realised what I was looking at.

'A louse!' I exclaimed. 'But, Papa, it can't be.'

We both had a sudden urge to scratch our heads, which made me giggle. Lice had always seemed to me mightily troublesome for something no larger than the head of a pin, but this one was bigger than my foot, and it had eyes not unlike my own, and hairs on its legs. He turned another page and there was part of the leaf of a stinging nettle, such as I had never seen a stinging nettle before, with barbs as big as claws.

'He's a brilliant man, isn't he?' my father commented, clearly both delighted and surprised by the intensity of my interest. 'He uses a microscope, an instrument such as is used to study the heavens. But instead of looking upwards it's used to look down, at all manner of nature's miniature marvels, and see them as if they were a hundred times their real size. It's the latest fashionable device, so I'm told, though very expensive.'

If only I could make some such discoveries one day, see something that nobody else had ever really seen before, see it in a way it had never before been seen. Imagine seeing a dragonfly wing through a microscope, or a leaf of watercress. 'Papa, could we . . . ?' I wanted a microscope so badly but I knew there was no point in asking. It was further out of my reach than the stars.

'Educating a girl with books is one thing.' My father tweaked my nose. 'If people found you with your big blue eyes pressed up against a microscope, dabbling in the male domain of experimentation, they'd think I'd been infecting you with the wrong ideas for sure.'

'There's a far worse contamination to fear from that book, sir.'

Shocked, we looked up to see Mary's husband, the Reverend John Burges, framed in the doorway. A sandy-bearded, neat-featured and surprisingly hesitant and unassuming young man, given his calling, I'd never heard him speak with the gravity he had used just now, not even when delivering a sermon.

My father was just as bewildered. 'Reverend, whatever do you mean?'

'The plague has reached the City of London. It is far worse than the usual summer outbreaks. Nearly a thousand died there last week.'

At the mention of that dreaded word, the heavy book slid from my father's fingers and crashed to the floor. I didn't need him or John Burges to explain the reference to contamination. The book over which we'd been poring, so newly arrived from London, could carry the seeds of plague with it.

The Reverend was wringing his hands, seeming even more anxious and uncertain than he usually did. 'Poor Mary is beside herself with worry,' he said, coming towards us. I remembered then that her entire family, her mother, father, brothers and sisters, all worked in the textile trade and lived in Southwark. 'I confess, I don't know what to do.'

Reverend Burges never looked sure enough of anything, not even of his own fitness to be God's voice on earth. But that was probably at least partly because he was so awkward in my father's presence, could never feel entirely welcome.

He and Mary had come to Tickenham four years ago, after the Act of Uniformity had come down like a brutal sword of retribution against Puritans for beheading a king, forcing my father's closest friend, the previous minister, out of the Anglican church and from Tickenham. Reverend Burges's arrival was an insult to everything my father had striven and fought for. Ordained by a bishop, rejecting the solemnly sworn Covenant, Reverend Burges accepted Prayer Book rubrics, including the wearing of Popish surplices and the idolatrous kneeling to receive the sacrament. He had even brought with him a pair of silver candlesticks for the altar.

But Reverend Burges had much sympathy for my father and for all dissenters. He allied himself with the Latitudinarians who thought the Act too harsh and wanted to see it relaxed. He overlooked the heresy of our absence from his church services, was even willing to act as chaplain and lead our morning prayer meetings here. Toleration was not enough for my father though. He was convinced that Puritans belonged to the English Church, were indeed the body of it, and could not come to terms with schism. For him, being a dissenter was akin to being cast into the wilderness like the Children of Israel. It was a very uneasy situation, but one we all had no choice but to accept since our house, our minister's house and God's stood in such close proximity, in each other's shadow, isolated together from the rest of the straggling village, on a little mound of higher ground.

I knew that my father was concerned that Reverend Burges's willingness to quote from Puritan tracts and to stress the weekly cycle of the Lord's day in the privacy of our parlour, whilst also abiding by the new decrees of the Church for the benefit of his parishioners and in order to retain his living, signified a dangerous lack of conviction.

'We must trust in God to keep us all safe,' my father said now, with enough conviction for ten men.

'Amen to that,' John Burges agreed.

'Amen,' I whispered fervently.

'Mary's sister says there is panic throughout the whole of London,' John Burges continued. 'Her letter is filled with unimaginable horror. She writes of bodies and coffins piled high in the churchyards and of death carts rumbling through the streets at night with cries to bring out the dead. They are slaughtering dogs and cats to try to stop the contagion. The whole city stinks of rotting flesh. The King has moved to Hampton Court Palace, the nobility have all fled for their country estates, followed by the merchants and lawyers and anyone else who is able. Even the physicians have abandoned the sick.' He dragged on his beard. 'I don't know what to do for the best. If they were to come here to us, do we risk the plague coming with them? I'm afraid it may already be too late. There's talk of the Lord Mayor closing the gates to anyone who hasn't a certificate of health.'

'Then we can be sure the forgers will be the only ones who stand to benefit,' my father said.

I waited for him to say more, since he'd long predicted a terrible calamity would befall London to punish its people for their wickedness and depravity. The plight of Mary's relatives would not normally cause him to miss such an ideal opportunity to illustrate the mortal danger of sin. But he remained gravely silent and I knew it was because he feared the plague may already have come to our godly house in the pages of a lovely book.

He laid it in the grate and sent for the tinder box to set it alight. A shiver ran through me too when I looked at his creased, pale face as he suggested Reverend Burges should lead us in a short prayer to call upon God to show mercy to the people of England's great capital.

John Burges bowed his head and, as usual, talked to God not as a mighty unseen being set on high, but as if He was his dearest and most trusted friend. I clasped my hands as tight as I could and squeezed my eyes shut, as if that might make my prayer stronger, all the more likely to be heard and answered. As John spoke of suffering on earth for a far greater reward in Heaven, my stomach clenched too, clenched with dread, and I prayed for those that I loved. For Bess and for Mary and John. For myself and my father. But even as I prayed, I imagined the plague wind blowing and the deadly miasma drifting inexorably westward like smoke, so noxious that no amount of sweet-scented flowers could ward it off.

'How does slaughtering dogs and cats stop the plague from spreading?' I asked when the prayer was done.

John Burges shook his head in despair. 'It is believed the animals are the plague carriers.'

'How do they carry it?'

'This is no time for your questions, Eleanor,' my father admonished me gently.

I kept my mouth shut but it seemed to me that it was very much the time. I though of the giant flea in the beautiful book that must now be burned and it seemed that we knew so little still about nature and the world we lived in, so little about disease. Except, as my father constantly warned, that death had a thousand ways to guide us to the grave.

Next morning my father was late for prayers. John and Mary Burges arrived before first light as usual and I joined the rest of the household who'd fallen to their knees on the hard stone floor in the great hall, in readiness for the candlelit routine with which we all began each day. It was unknown for my father not to be the first there and cold fear gripped my heart. I tried to hide it, as my father would expect me to do, but I knew by the way Bess looked at me that I had failed.

Please God, I prayed silently, do not let there be plague in this house, do not let my father be ill. Don't let him have survived the Royalist muskets and cannons and bayonets to be struck down now. Don't let him die. Oh, I know he must one day. But do not let it be for a very long time. You already have Mama and Margaret. Please let me keep my papa for a little while longer.

I told myself my father was robust and straight as a pikestaff from his regular exercise on horseback. He was far stronger than my mother and my sister. Wasn't he?

There was much tittering while we all waited. Fear was in the air and would ignite like kindling at the slightest spark. Even those who couldn't read the news sheets had heard of how disease was laying waste to London, had decimated whole streets, whole districts, claiming thousands. Everyone was afraid that it might spread west. Bess told me that her mother had made her wear three spiders in her shoes for protection. Everyone was ill at ease.

It made little difference when Papa sent the chambermaid down with word that he was suffering from a chill and had decided to remain in bed. I knew it would take more than a chill to keep him from prayers. I knew that, in any case, chills and fevers were cause for the greatest concern, that the first sign of one in the morning could herald death by night. 'I'll see if he needs anything,' I said, rising to my feet on legs as unsteady as my voice.

'I'll go, Eleanor,' John Burges said swiftly. 'He'll want a blessing.'

More waiting. People were standing now, rubbing their sore, cramped knees. I did not want them to act as if my father would not be coming to join us any minute, that the day would not go on as normal. And then at last I heard John Burges come back down the stairs from the solar. 'How is he, sir?' I asked.

'I am no surgeon, Eleanor,' he said carefully. 'But the stable boy will fetch one.'

'It's not . . . ?'

'I doubt it very much but we will know soon enough, child. We will know soon enough.'

'Is he shivering?' I persisted quietly. 'Does he have a headache? Has he vomited?'

A single nod.

Mary instantly enfolded me in her arms, pressed my head against her chest. She must have seen my terror, everyone must have seen it. But they would not have known its cause. I didn't either, not for sure. I didn't know which I feared the most: the plague, that most dreaded disease, or ague which had already killed the rest of my family.

Shivering, aching muscles, nausea . . . the same symptoms for both diseases.

Plague.

Ague.

They both sounded the same to me.

They both sounded like death.

I wasn't allowed near my father until Dr Duckett had made his diagnosis.

I should have been relieved to see the Tickenham surgeon and yet I wasn't, not at all. He was a tall, thin man, not unlike a heron in his gaunt, grey watchfulness, and I could not help but shiver at the mere sight of him. In my mind his presence on our land, in our lives, was so closely connected to sickness and loss that I could only view him as a prophet of doom. I so wanted to put my trust in him, to believe he had the power to heal the sick, but so far, in my experience, he had always failed. Even with all the hope in Heaven, I could not summon any confidence in him now.

We didn't have to wait long for him to deliver his verdict. Soon, too soon, we heard his ponderous footsteps descending the stone stairs to the great hall where Mary was waiting with me, her arm around me as I clutched the worn poppet doll I had discarded as a babyish plaything years ago but had now resurrected, finding I had a sudden need of it again.

Dr Duckett spoke. 'I am pleased to be able to tell you that there are no signs of swellings under the arm or in the groin, no marks upon the skin. Which means . . .'

'He doesn't have the plague.'

Dr Duckett looked both very startled and intensely annoyed by my interruption. 'That is my considered opinion,' he admitted tersely.

'So it is ague that sickens him.' My voice was a cracked whisper.

His look of grudging acknowledgement proved my deduction was correct. 'I believe so,' he said through pursed lips.

I was small for my age, had a small child's wide eyes and was wearing a little lace cap and clutching a poppet, so I could hardly blame him for taking me for several years younger than I was, but did he not remember that I had been here before? Twice? Did he think me a fool not to remember the symptoms that had preceded the deaths of Margaret and our mother?

'I have made a thorough examination of Major Goodricke's urine,' he pronounced. 'It is of good colour and taste, but his body is filled with noxious matter which must be released. I have lanced his leg and the cut must be kept open with a seton. If that doesn't work, I will try a cantharide and pierce the blisters to let more matter out.'

I remembered the agony my mother had suffered from the cantharides and the blisters they had caused, needless agony, since it had not saved her.

'I have consulted the stars,' Dr Duckett added. 'Jupiter is in the ascendant, which is not at all good. Its qualities are hot and moist, which leads me to predict fever and sweats.'

'Forgive me, sir, but if my father has tertian ague, you don't need the charts to predict fever and sweats,' I said evenly. 'There is always a cycle of shaking and heat and sweats.'

'Eleanor,' Mary chided gently, 'Dr Duckett is only trying to help.'

I had not meant to be rude, it was just that I was not used to being treated as a child, or a fool, and I did not take very kindly to either. I was going to lose my father. My father was going to die, and there was nobody to help him.

'I wonder that you sent for me at all,' the surgeon said snidely. 'When you have such a knowledgeable young physician already in situ. Perhaps the little lady would like to prescribe an appropriate treatment?'

Mary laid a restraining hand on my arm, as if she was worried I might actually put forward a suggestion. If I had done, it would only be to say that I would be sure not to give my father anything that would cause him more distress. 'Please tell us what we must do for Major Goodricke to help speed his recovery,' she said.

'The patient is to have feverfew and sage mixed with half a pennyworth of pepper, one little spoonful of chimney soot and the white of an egg, all laid together on the wrist.'

'And if that doesn't do any good?' I whispered, trying not to despair.

'I have every confidence . . .'

'It didn't help my mother or my sister.'

'You can also try a spider bruised in a cloth, spread upon linen and applied to the patient's forehead. Or dead pigeons placed at his feet to draw down the fever.' He glanced round the great hall with distaste as he left us. 'It's living for so long in this place that's the problem. It is not healthy to live in such proximity to bogs and marshes and unhealthy damp vapours. You only need to meet a few of the local inhabitants to see how it twists the body and subdues the spirit.'

So why was it that ague struck most often in the heat of summer? The physicians said it was bad air that caused it, and who was I, a mere child – a girl child at that – to question them? And yet question them I did. The fact remained: my sister and mother had both fallen ill and died, not in the dankness of winter but on beautiful sunny days both. And now my father was dying in the hottest summer for decades.

My poor father's body was subjected first to convulsive shivering and then to raging fever, followed by another punishing bout of quaking and shuddering two days after the onset of the first. Propped up on pillows, he no longer looked like the man who'd distinguished himself at the Battle of Langport, the battle that had heralded the beginning of the end for the Royalists in this county. He had not been defeated then but even I had to admit that he looked defeated now, or rather as if he had willingly surrendered, as if there was no fight left to be won. The seton on his leg had turned smelly and nasty and his skin had become a waxy yellow, but I recoiled from the prospect of recalling Dr Duckett for more of his purges.

'Can we not send for the London physician?' I beseeched Mary as she met me, coming out of my father's chamber with an untouched dish of toast soaked in small beer.

It was Ned Tucker, when he took our pike and eels to market, who'd heard that Thomas Sydenham, the West Country gentleman said to be the most eminent physician in all of England, had fled his practice in Pall Mall to escape the plague and had come with his wife and sons to stay with relations near Bristol.

'Some kind of physician he must be,' Mary said, a judgmental tone to her voice that I'd never heard from her before, 'if he can abandon the dying to save his own skin. I guarantee he won't set foot outside his front door for less than five guineas either.'

'I don't care what it costs,' I said. 'We will pay him whatever he wants.'

She cupped my face in her hands and looked down into my eyes that were shadowed with worry and the exhaustion of caring for my father. Mary and Bess had both offered to sit up with him through the night but I had insisted upon doing the bulk of it, needed to do it.

'Send for the physician, by all means,' she said with a smile. 'So long as I don't have to be civil to him.'

I smiled back ruefully. 'Shall you be as uncivil to him as I was to Dr Duckett?'

She laughed, stroked my hair. 'Maybe not quite.'

We sent to Mr Merrick, begging him to use his connections to find the physician, and later that day he escorted him to us on horseback, and for once looked shabby and insignificant in comparison. Dr Sydenham was dressed in a dark grey cloth riding suit with a wide collar trimmed with lace. He wore no wig and his own light brown hair, parted at the centre, fell gently to his shoulders with threads of silver at the temples. He rode his enormous bay hunter as if he and the beast were one. Gait prancing, muscles rippling, his powerful steed was docile as a lamb under its reins. Dr Sydenham was the kind of man even diseases would obey, I decided, still hoping.

Ned had been sweeping the stable yard and Bess had been fetching water from the pump, but as the physician dismounted a hush descended upon everyone. He was like a king riding into our cobbled yard, yet didn't seem in the least perturbed to find himself amidst manure and warm straw, still steaming with horse piss.

'I thank you for coming so quickly, sir,' I said shyly, as he gave a low bow.

He held up his hand to stem my words of gratitude. 'Please take me to your father, child.'

I glanced at him as I led him up to the bedchamber, taking quick, long strides to keep abreast with him. Despite his eminence there was something about him that put me instantly at ease. 'Have you treated many patients with ague before, sir? Forgive me for asking, but I wondered if Londoners suffered from it as much as we do in Tickenham.'

'I've seen enough cases of the disease to call myself something of a specialist,' he replied conversationally. 'I am presently writing a classification of the fevers which I hope to publish next year. But your comment about marsh-dwellers being most at risk is very pertinent. I've observed for myself how particular dispositions of the atmosphere do cause a particular fever to predominate. And around marshland and stagnant rivers, for whatever reason, it is intermittent fever that prevails. An effervescence of the blood.'

'My mother died of ague. And my sister.'

'I am most sorry to hear that.'

I ushered him into the stiflingly hot chamber that was dimly lit with candles, all the drapes closed and a fire banked high in the hearth despite the hot day. As the physician approached my father's bedside, I made to leave.

'Please stay, Miss Goodricke. I shall need to ask you some questions.'

My father had stirred at the sound of a strange voice.

'Ah, remember me, do you, Goodricke, my good fellow?'

'Sydenham,' Papa murmured with surprise. 'Cromwell's Captain of Cavalry.'

I was in even greater awe of him now than before and took great heart from the fact that he was a staunch Parliamentarian, that he and my father had fought battles together before, and won.

'I'm a physician now, not a soldier,' Dr Sydenham said. 'I'd rather try to cure than kill.'

He began his examination by asking me for a full history of my father's illness. He took out a small notebook and a lead pencil with which he recorded the physical signs and symptoms, paying great attention to everything I said, as if I was an esteemed colleague and not just a young girl.

I watched, impressed and inspired by his attention to detail and patient analysis. He must have seen hundreds of fevers before, and yet he approached my father's case as if it was the first and most intriguing instance he had ever come across, as if he could learn more at this bedside than he could from books and was privileged to have been asked to attend. He took my father's pulse and listened to his breathing.

I asked him if he wanted to examine my father's water but he dismissed this as 'piss-pot science for quacks', which made me giggle for the first time in days.

'Ah, that is better.' He smiled. 'See, Goodricke, I have wrought one important cure already. Your lovely daughter here had the most tragic, woebegone little face when I arrived, and such enormous wistful eyes as would break any man's heart. Now she is smiling – and such a vivacious and dimpled smile at that, it gladdens me to see it.'

My father gave a weak smile before his eyes slid closed again.

The physician gently took hold of my elbow and drew me away from the bed to speak to me. 'His humours are putrefied and need rebalancing,' he said confidentially, and I listened intently, feeling very proud to think he trusted me to carry out his instructions. 'It must not be achieved by any interventionist methods. The most important thing is to do nothing to hinder the removal of froth through the pores of the skin.'

'You mean, let him sweat, sir?'

'Just so. Just so. But don't force it, try to cool him rather than let him overheat. Put that fire out, open the windows, cover him with light bedclothes and make sure he has plenty of rest. Let nature do its work.'

'Yes. I will. Oh, I will.' I clasped his hand. I wanted to throw my arms around him and kiss him. 'I don't know how to thank you, Doctor.'

He looked at me as if my exuberant appreciation pained him. 'No thanks are due, child,' he said in a sorrowful tone. 'I can't promise that any of what I tell you will do any good. I guarantee it won't do any harm, but it may not be enough.'

'Dr Sydenham, is my father going to get well again?' I saw there was a practised reply already on his lips. 'Please tell me the truth, sir. I want to know. Is he going to die?'

He looked at me almost in wonder. 'That is a very courageous question to ask, child. In all my years as a physician, I am hardly ever asked it so directly. But I am afraid that, in this instance, I honestly do not know the answer.'

'I don't want my father to die, sir.'

'I don't want him to die either, Miss Goodricke. I would save him for you if it were in my power to do so. But I am not God. Unlike some in my profession, I don't pretend to hold dominion over life and death.'

'There must be something more you can do.'

He stood back as if to make a proper study of me. 'What a singular child you are. Tell me, are you always so determined?'

I smiled faintly. 'I am told that I am.'

He looked thoughtful for a moment then gave my arm a quick tap. 'As a matter of fact, there is something.' He was a wonderfully kind and caring man, I decided, even if he had deserted the plague victims. I was sure now he must have had a perfectly valid reason for it. He glanced towards the bed then stepped even further away from it, motioned me to come with him and lowered his voice to the faintest whisper. I leaned slightly towards him, tilting my head, amused by such clandestine behaviour, which seemed entirely unnecessary but rather fun. It was almost as if we were playing a game. 'There's a new remedy for ague,' he murmured, 'heralded as a miracle cure. But I did not suggest it before because I guarantee your father will not want to touch it.'

'Why not, sir?' I whispered, turning to look at the still figure in the bed. 'What is it?'

'Powdered tree bark, brought from Peru to Spain and just this year made readily available in this country.' He dropped his voice still lower. 'It is commonly known as Jesuits' Powder, on account of the fact that it was discovered by Jesuit missionaries.' He saw that I understood instantly. This was no longer a game. Anything connected to that most despised order was highly suspect in my father's eyes. 'He will know that Oliver Cromwell himself allegedly refused the powder,' Dr Sydenham explained quietly, 'and died as a result, I believe. He will also know that it was given to an important London alderman during the last major outbreak of ague in the city seven years ago. The alderman died and Protestants all across England, no doubt your father amongst them, scented a Jesuit plot. They believed the bark to be an insidious poison which the Jesuits had brought to Europe for the express purpose of exterminating all those who have thrown off their allegiance to Rome.'

I blinked, then fixed my eyes on him. 'But you do not believe that, sir?'

'I do not. However, I've not had the opportunity to conduct proper trials of the powder, though I hope to soon, but I've heard from numerous other sources that it is very effective.' He looked across at my father, his expression a great deal less impartial now. 'If we could only get him to take it, I believe it would be worth a try.'

'What is?' my father mumbled, his eyes still closed. 'What's all this whispering?' When neither of us answered, his eyes snapped open. Somehow he guessed what we had been discussing and I swear his yellow skin turned white. 'I'll tell you now, I'll not touch that new-fangled potion pedalled by Jesuit priests. I'll not be Jesuited to death.'

'Please, Papa.' I tried not to sound desperate.

'It has been used in Peru and Italy with remarkable results,' Dr Sydenham put in persuasively.

'Bah!' My father exploded into a coughing fit that turned his face puce. 'The work of the Devil. How could you, Sydenham? You who matriculated at the very centre of Oxford Puritanism?'

'You'll not die for Puritan intolerance, I trust, Goodricke?'

My father had marched into war beneath a banner proclaiming 'Down with the Papists'. He'd risked fines and imprisonment and the plundering of his property rather than renounce his principles and his faith. He was a zealot.

Of course he would die for Puritan intolerance. And there was nothing I or anyone else could do about it.

Mr Merrick had been closeted with my father, the chamber door firmly shut, since after dinner. Whatever it was they were discussing at such length, I only hoped it was not tiring Papa too much.

I wandered out into the garden but there was no escaping the sombre tolling of the church bell that announced the approach of death and called everyone to his bedside to pay their last respects. I wanted to run from it, to put my hands over my ears to try to block it out, but it would have been a pathetically childish thing to do and I knew, already, that I was leaving childhood behind me forever. I went down on to the moor, watched the dragonflies and damselflies flashing azure wings, listened to the willow warblers, the booming of a fat little bittern in the reed beds, the joyous call of lapwings and the low soft whistle of a widgeon. Life was going on all around, heartlessly, even whilst my father's life was ending.

When finally Mr Merrick emerged he looked like a cat with a dish of cream. He said that my father was asking for me so that he could give me his special blessing. I walked into the darkened chamber feeling much older than eleven. During the fever I had done as Dr Sydenham suggested and opened the drapes and the windows, but now that my father was close to death he had wanted them all closed again. If I were dying, I thought, I'd demand to be taken outside, into the brightest sunshine.

'You must not grieve too hard, child,' my father said quietly, seeing my stricken face. 'You must not grudge Him for taking me when it is my time. I just pray that I can make a good death.'

How could there be such a thing?

I knelt on the plaited rush mat by the bed and took his hand. I felt him place the other upon my lace cap. 'My little Eleanor, may your father in Heaven bless you and keep you. May He watch over you when I can do it no longer.'

I was so determined not to disappoint him now, to appear brave and composed and accepting as he would want me to be, but the effort of holding back tears was making my head hurt terribly. Like a sea wall holding back a great weight of water, the pressure was building up inside it. There was a pain in my throat as harsh as if I had tried to swallow a rock.

I sat on a low stool, holding his large hand in both of mine. It was neither cold nor hot now, but somehow desiccated. 'I wish I could make up for all the times I've ever displeased you, Papa,' I said in a faltering voice, lifting his hand to my lips and kissing it, before holding it to my cheek. 'I am sorry . . . so sorry.'

'You are a good girl,' he said, then gave me a wan smile. 'For the most part. Just try to live the rest of your life as you know I would want you to live it.' His once commanding voice was now so feeble that I had to lean closer to hear him. 'John Burges has given me his word that he will tutor you as best he can, but he will not have as much time to devote to it as I have done, nor the inclination to teach you the things I did. You must continue those studies in private. Promise me that you will?'

'I promise,' I said waveringly, fighting for control. 'I promise.'

'Don't be sad for me, little one. None should fear death for it sets us free. It is better than birth, for we are born mortal but die immortal. Remember the butterflies. Remember how they rise from their coffins on shining wings.'

'Papa, do you swear to me that is true?'

'As God is my witness, it is my firmest belief that it is.'

'I keep thinking . . . I'm worried . . .'

'What are you worried about, my little darling?'

'All the thousands of people dying of plague and all the millions of people who have ever lived and died. How can there be room in Heaven for them all?'

'I am a great advocate of scientific exploration, but Heaven forbid it ever takes such precedence that nobody believes in anything unless they can fully explain or understand it.' He pointed to his cup then and I held his head, tilted the cup to his lips and helped him drink some water, guessing he was girding himself for a final sermon. How bitterly I regretted the times I had inwardly groaned when he had begun one before. Now I was determined to listen closely to every precious word he spoke. It was the last guidance I would ever have from him and I must take good note so that it could sustain me for the rest of my life. Oh, but there was so much I wanted to ask him, would never now have the chance to ask.

'The whole purpose of studying nature is to bring us closer to God through a better understanding of His creation,' he said, with a heart-rending echo of his previous fervour. 'It is not to cast doubt over His works and throw His very existence into question.' He grimaced then continued, his voice weakening again. 'Science must not lead us into a godless world. We may strive to learn but we must never take a bite from the Tree of Knowledge.' He laid his head back on the pillow then, exhausted from his short speech.

I knew I should urge him to rest but did not want to, wishing only to prolong this last conversation I was ever to have with him. There was so much still to be said.

'If only you had been a boy,' he sighed.

I straightened my spine on hearing that, assuming that now the time had come for the most important conversation of any landowner's life, he regretted not being able to have it with a son, regretted not having a boy to carry on his name and to whom he could bequeath Tickenham Court. Which hurt me sorely. 'I can care for this estate as well as any man,' I said spiritedly.

'Oh, I do not doubt that for a moment.' He gasped for breath. 'How I would have welcomed men with your courage and fortitude to march beside me against the Cavaliers. But you are not a man, Eleanor. One day you will marry, and the man who seeks to win your hand in marriage will first and foremost seek to gain land and a fortune – to win Tickenham Court. You have a loving nature, a trusting nature, and no guardian or trustee will watch over your interests the way a father would. To make matters worse, you are growing to be a little beauty. There is a radiance about you that will attract men like bees to nectar, the worst kind of men, the type I fear you will find all too appealing.' He was struggling now to talk and breathe at the same time, which only lent extra weight to his words, since it cost him such effort to voice each one. 'On every count you will be susceptible to all manner of philanderers and ne'er-do-wells. May the Lord help you, but you will be prey to every unscrupulous Cavalier who happens by.'

'Do not worry, Papa,' I said reassuringly. 'When the time comes I will choose a husband wisely.'

'Ah, my child, the heart is seldom wise.'

'I swear to you, Papa, I will ensure the man I marry will be a good lord for Tickenham Court.' Like Edmund Ashfield, I thought. My father had liked Edmund.

'You can speak dispassionately now,' Papa sighed, 'but you are just a child still. When you do marry you will be a woman, with a woman's baser nature, a woman's low passions and greater temptations.' I was shocked at his sudden severity, especially when the woman he had known most intimately had been my mother whom I considered as unblemished as the Virgin Mary. He took another laboured breath. 'Never forget, Eleanor, that you carry the stain of Eve's sin upon your soul. Never forget that Eden was lost to her because of that sin.'

Those were the very last words he spoke, to me or anyone else.

We gathered round his bed and watched life slowly leaving him. He grew gradually whiter and colder but the end when it came was quiet, very gentle. A breath and then no breath. A heartbeat and then no heartbeat. A little trail of spittle had dribbled from the corner of his mouth and when I wiped it away he looked as if he was only sleeping still. His hand around mine was still warm and I did not ever want to let it go. I wanted to hear his voice again, for him to say something else to me. Anything. I laid my head on his arm, where I used to nestle when I was tired of walking and he carried me home from the moor. It felt so familiar and safe, even now. I twisted my face round to look up at his. One of his eyelids had opened slightly and I saw there was no life at all behind his eyes.

I let go of him and bolted, his last words ringing inside my head, louder and more ominous than the death knell.

I fled down the stairs and out through the garden, running until there was a pain in my side as if I had been stabbed. Only when I reached the moor did I stop.

It was dusk and a little cooler now, the air fragrant with the heady scents of summer, but all the colours of the wildflowers in the meadows were muted, fading to grey.

Mary found me in my favourite place, down by the hump-backed bridge. She put her arm around my shoulders. 'Let me tell you something,' she said, as we watched bats flit over the fields and listened to the strange triple call of the whimbrel. 'When John and I first came here, what immediately impressed me was how, in a land as flat as this, the sky is such an overwhelming presence. I told John that it was a good place for us to be, a place where the border between earth and Heaven has been blurred and weakened. Nobody who crosses it is ever very far away when you view it from here'

'At least Papa will be with my mother now,' I whispered. 'He has missed her so much.' I realised with distress that I could no longer picture her face. My father's insistence on modesty meant I had not so much as a rough charcoal sketch to remind me of it. 'I can't even remember what she looked like,' I cried to Mary in distress. 'I can't even see my mama's face any more.'

Mary took me into her arms and rocked me like a baby against her soft breasts, stroking my hair as tears poured down my face and soaked the front of her dress. 'Yes you can,' she said. 'Think hard enough and you can.'

I felt her own breath turn ragged then and looked up to see that she was crying too. I forced my own anguish aside. 'Mary, have you news from London?'

'A letter from my cousin,' she said quietly. 'She went to call at my family's house and found fires burning outside the door and a fearful red cross daubed upon it. The doors and windows were all nailed shut until the contagaion passes or all inside have succumbed to it. She saw the children's little faces at the locked window. Now I see them too. I cannot get them from my mind.'

Bess and Mary washed my father's body, wrapped him in a white linen winding sheet and laid him on the long oak table in the great hall.

In all other respects William Merrick assumed control the minute my father was gone and nobody questioned his right to do so. I'd been judged too young to take a turn watching over my mother's body but, when I asked, Mr Merrick said I might do it this time. Or rather, he said that I could do whatsoever I pleased. Nobody had ever said that to me before but, dismayingly, it gave me little pleasure. Even if I could do anything, there was nothing I particularly wanted to do. It was beyond me even to decide if I wanted a cup of small beer or not. Perversely, without my father there to rebel against, I could see little joy to be had from being free to wear ribbons or eat a whole plate full of marchpane. There was no point in anything. No pleasure in being good and clever either, if there was no one to praise and be proud of me. But that felt dangerously close to self-pity, and I would not give in to self-pity.

My situation was not uncommon, I reminded myself. Mine was by no means the only family to suffer such loss. Almost every child my age had some close experience of death, had lost a parent or sibling. People died all the time, every day, every hour, every minute. Remember Mary's family. Remember them, and the thousands of others dying of plague. The grave-yard across the barton wall and the crypt beneath the church were filled with the dead. Death was perfectly normal and natural. Yet it didn't feel normal or natural to me at all.

'Won't you be very afraid?' Bess whispered, her brown almond-shaped eyes clouded with alarm as she glanced at my father's shrouded corpse. Her hands pecked worriedly at her homespun apron. 'What if his soul's not quite detached, is still hovering nearby? It can happen, you know.'

Her simple but powerful country superstitions did not touch me. Despite my small stature I felt as if I looked down at her from a great height, or as if a great distance separated her from me, this girl who would soon go home to her brother and both her parents. I stared down at my father's face, the skin already waxen and sinking against the bones to reveal the shape of his skull. I had no mother and no father any more. The two people who'd given me life were dead. I was no longer anybody's little girl.

I hardly noticed Bess quietly leave the hall, eager for escape. But there were no ghosts here. It was only Mr Merrick who hovered like a spectre by the oriel. He came silently across the floor and moved a lighted taper off the table to the court cupboard in the corner of the room. 'There must be no candles near the body, no question of Popish practices,' he muttered, taking up another candle and standing in its flickering light with the stick in his hand. 'Your father entrusted me with his last wishes, as he entrusted me with so much else.' I felt his eyes resting on me, wished he would just go. 'Now is perhaps not the time, but you may as well know — he has appointed me as your guardian.'

I stared at my father's beloved face in consternation. Too late now to ask him why.

I knew anyway. Wardships were bought and sold just like anything else, and since part of the estate of Tickenham Court was mortgaged to Mr Merrick, my father would have had little choice but to sell the rest of the guardianship to him. He cared for me but it was more important that the estate was left in safe hands. Tickenham Court, my family's past and its future. I was just a passing encumbrance, part of the package.

'Why must it be done in the dark?' I asked Mary, as the wooden bier, draped with black mortuary cloth, was brought from the church after dusk.

She stroked my hair. 'It was your father's wish that the burial be conducted at night, in the latest Puritan fashion, to keep the vulgar at bay.'

There were to be no rings or gloves for the visitors, no feasting or distribution of alms and dole of bread. Biscuits and burnt wine were to suffice. With her customary frankness, Bess had told me how peeved everyone was to be denied a spectacle, though they'd expected nothing more.

I wore a black taffeta cloak and hood and Mr Merrick and the other men had black silk weepers falling from their hats down their backs, but true to my father's last wishes, neither the house nor the church was hung with mourning drapery. Mr Merrick headed the pallbearers who carried the oak, lead-lined coffin the short distance to the churchyard. The bells gave one short peal as the procession, lit by links and flaming torches, moved with silent dignity through the dark. Reverend Burges met us at the church stile and the coffin was taken into the church and set to rest on two trestles near the pulpit, where just a few candles burned, flickering wildly in the draughts and casting an eerie sepulchral glow.

My father had naturally wished to forgo all ceremony but at the final hour Reverend Burges lost the courage entirely to abandon standardised Anglican practice. He began with a touching eulogy praising my father's virtues, followed by a sermon designed to draw attention to our mortality.

The coffin was then taken to a prominent position beside my mother's burial place on the south side of the graveyard. Reverend Burges read from the Order of the Burial of the Dead: '*Ashes to ashes, dust to dust, in sure and certain hope of the Resurrection.*'

My father had surely been certain of it. Was I? I did not know.

I stared down into the dark pit of the grave. It was supposed to be six foot deep but was not nearly that much because of the water level and the soft black peat which flowed back to fill any hole or ditch as quickly as they were dug. Even in the worst drought the country had known, our land was still waterlogged at its very heart. Water had disappeared from the surface but was still there, had merely retreated to its subterranean depths. It was glimmering now, in the torchlight, as at the bottom of a well.

The coffin was lowered and I heard a faint plashing as the wood slapped against the water, like a little boat being put to sea.

'Ironic, isn't it?' Mr Merrick was standing at my shoulder and spoke in a hushed voice, for my ears alone. 'Duckett and Thomas Sydenham were both of the opinion that it was living in such close proximity to marsh and floodwater that killed him, and now in death the water is receiving him into its depths.'

'He need not have died.' Tears stung my eyes, blurred my vision, so that I was only vaguely aware of everyone staring at me. 'He could have been cured.'

I had a sudden disturbing realisation that my father was not infallible; he was not incapable of making a mistake, of being foolish and stubborn. He was just a man, a normal man, with weaknesses and failings just like everyone else.

I was standing suddenly on sand, with the waves sucking it away beneath my feet. Everything I believed in, everything my father had told and taught me, the very foundations of my life, were all stripped away from beneath me, cast into doubt. I did not know if butterflies rose up from tiny coffins as he had said they did. I did not know if death was the beginning or the end. I knew only one thing for sure. It was not bad air that had taken my father from me, nor ague. It was Puritan fanaticism and prejudice that had killed him.

I turned and ran through the churchyard, crashed through the gate in the barton wall and all the way into the darkened hall of the house. I climbed on to a bench and reached up to the sword that hung on the wall. It was heavy, nearly as tall as me, but I had good strong muscles from climbing trees and wielded it like an avenging angel. I was already halfway up the winding stone stairs before I saw torches coming through the dark garden.

I flung the sword on the bed and ripped off my black dress. Holding it at arm's length, standing like a ghost in the darkness in just my shift, I slashed at the black material with the sword, slashed and slashed with all my might, until my dress was torn to shreds, a mass of black ribbons. Black for mourning. Black for Puritanism. Black for despair.

I threw it on the floor and dragged my other identical dress from the chest. I hacked at that too, stuck in the sword and twisted it to gouge great holes. When I was satisfied with the damage I'd caused, I cast the ruined garment on to the pile of rags and stamped on it, the tears streaming down my face now. Then I stood there in my shift in the silence, the ripped dresses an unidentifiable black mass, like a formless shadow at my feet.

But it wasn't totally silent. Something was tapping lightly on the glass, like ghostly fingers. I stood perfectly still and listened, my heart pounding, a sudden flood of guilt convincing me that my father had come back from the dead to punish me for what I had just done.

I made myself creep over to the window. I lifted my hand and tentatively moved the drapes aside, gasping at what I saw. A white butterfly, luminous in the dark, trapped behind the heavy crewelwork, was trying to escape. I remembered what my father had said about butterflies symbolising the souls of the dead and a shiver ran down my spine. I flung open the window to set the little creature free. It fluttered out instantly and, as I watched it disappear into the warm dark sky, my heart soared with it.

My father's hand had been so dry after the fever but I tried to see his entry into the watery grave not as a final sinking but as a second baptism. I tried to picture the water seeping into him, replenishing his body, making it whole so that one day it would rise again, just as he had described, as if on white shimmering wings.

Find a way to believe in that, Eleanor, find a way to believe in it.

Part II

Spring 1673

Eight years later

Crisp March sunlight streamed in at the window of the smart Bristol tailor's shop where I stood amidst bright bolts of satin and silk. I turned around slowly, making the sky blue silk skirt of my lovely new gown swish and sway around my ankles. The gown was full-sleeved, with a low, broad neckline and tightly boned, pointed bodice. This was set over a full overskirt, drawn back to reveal a petticoat heavily decorated with silvery braid and cascades of frothy white Italian lace.

'It's been smuggled into the country,' the fashionably-dressed young tailor informed me proudly. 'Much finer than regulation English lace.'

'It's beautiful,' I murmured, rubbing it gently between my thumb and forefinger. 'Like a cobweb.'

He raised an eyebrow. 'You're the first girl I've ever met who's referred to a cobweb as a thing of beauty. Most ladies find them rather ghastly.'

'Oh, but they are beautiful, sir,' I exclaimed, looking up at him with a smile. 'Every bit as beautiful and intricate as this lace. With the frost or the dew sparkling on them first thing in the morning, they are more lovely even than a necklace of diamonds. There is nothing in the world more lovely. Spiders are amazing creatures, don't you think, to be able to create such things?'

'You're a quaint one, all right.'

'You must have seen silkworms at work?' I asked. 'Since you work with the material all the time.'

He laughed at that. 'I've no interest whatsoever in the worms themselves or how they do what they do. Just so long as they keep on doing it, that's all I ask.'

'Did you know, a single cocoon is made of one unbroken thread of raw silk over three thousand feet long?'

'Is it now?'

'Don't you think that's astonishing?'

'I suppose it is.'

I stroked the material of my beautiful new gown. Well, I at least was very grateful to the little worms that had spent so much time and energy spinning it for me to wear.

'D'you like it then, miss?'

'Oh, yes. Very much. Thank you.'

He smiled at my unrestrained gratitude. 'A beautiful girl like you was born to wear a gown like this.' His words sounded genuine, for all that they were probably a practised trick of his trade.

Under his appraising eyes I felt myself flush and glanced away, surreptitiously, to the tall mirror on the far wall. I was still so unaccustomed to seeing my own image clearly that it utterly fascinated me, but I cast a critical glance over the stranger I saw reflected back at me, a girl in a shimmering blue silk gown, with eyes of the same colour framed by long sooty lashes. They were still as wide as a child's, those eyes, but they were a woman's eyes now, and they were far too direct, too animated and vivid, not at all docile and modest as all definitions of feminine beauty dictated. Even after a long winter, this girl's skin was creamy rather than alabaster, the impression of vitality enhanced by the brightness of her curls. She was like the watermeadows in springtime, bursting forth with an abundance of life, too much life to be contained in such a slight body. Was she really me? And was she beautiful? I was not at all sure many respectable gentlemen would think so.

There was only one gentleman whose opinion mattered to me, though, and I would know soon enough what it was.

'Hold still now,' the tailor said, 'while I adjust the hem.' He removed a pin from where it was gripped between his teeth and stuck it into the fabric. 'I'll need to take up another inch. How old did you say you are?'

'Almost twenty.' I smiled proudly, as if confessing to a very great age indeed.

He looked at me as if he didn't quite believe me. But it was true. I was under five feet tall, a good three or four inches shorter than most girls my age, but I didn't have any more growing to do.

'For a special occasion, is it, the gown?' the tailor asked. 'Sweetheart paying you a visit, is he?'

My blush deepened. 'Oh, I don't have a sweetheart.'

He glanced up at my pink cheeks, and winked at me. 'Ah, but there is someone you like, I think?'

I had not seen Edmund Ashfield since I was eleven. Nine whole years had passed since then. I knew for a fact that my guardian had long favoured a match between us and he had surely invited Edmund to visit to determine if he too was in favour of it. Why else was I to have a lovely new gown for the occasion? Edmund was arriving from Suffolk on Friday, and for so many reasons I was half in dread of seeing him again. What if he had changed? It was surely impossible for him to be as wondrous as I remembered him. As I had grown from child to woman, all my fantasies of falling in love had centred on him. And how could any man possibly live up to them, live up to my most cherished memory of a gleaming knight striding in out of the rain and lighting up my life?

What if he did not want me?

To help pass the time until Edmund's arrival, I went to tend the bulbs beneath my mother's walnut tree. It stood on the stretch of grass bordered by the cow byre and the rectory. She had planted it herself but never lived to see its first blossom. Soon it would be a mass of white petals and fresh green leaves and, despite its smallness, it already hinted at the majesty it would one day possess.

I was kneeling down on a jute sack, pulling weeds from the black peaty earth, when Mr Merrick came strutting across the soggy ground with his stiff lacquered cane and – never before seen, this – a book in his hands. I wrenched out a particularly tenacious dandelion by its roots, showering my skirt with particles of soil in the process, then stood, as was expected of me in my guardian's presence, not that I was favoured with it very often. He was too busy attending to his business interests in Bristol. My aged Aunt Elizabeth from Ribston had been installed in the house to watch over me. Supposedly. She was kind but she had suffered an apoplexy a year ago and barely moved from her chamber now.

I wiped my dirty hands hastily on the jute and then smoothed away the lock of hair that had broken free from its pins as usual and tumbled down over my brow.

'Why must you be forever fussing with that blessed shrub?' Mr Merrick snapped.

I judged that question unworthy of a reply, seeing that the dignity and splendour of the little tree didn't touch him at all. Though doubtless he'd be quick to calculate how much its wood would be worth in a few years to cabinet-makers and gunsmiths.

'I was wondering when the walnuts will come, since they're such a delicacy,' he said. 'No doubt you can tell me precisely, given that you have an answer for everything.'

I shaped my mouth to say October, but he didn't wait to hear. 'I had a most interesting conversation with the tailor when I went to settle the bill for your gown,' he said acidly. 'You made quite an impression him.'

'Did I, sir?'

'He's not accustomed to having conversations with ladies about insects while he's doing his measuring.'

'Isn't he?'

'You know damned well he's not, girl.' His small nondescript eyes had all but vanished, they were so narrowed in his reddened face, and he puffed up his pigeon chest and glowered at me. 'I blame John Burges for this entirely,' he exploded. 'I left him and his wife in charge of your welfare and only now do I find that they have been utterly negligent.'

'That's not true,' I said indignantly. 'John and Mary have cared for me very well.'

'Evidently,' he spat. 'They have taught you that it is acceptable for a young lady to quarrel with and contradict her guardian. And instead of ensuring you are proficient in embroidery and drawing and dancing, as well as balancing budgets and managing a household, you have been learning about worms.'

I could have told Mr Merrick that if he had taken any interest in me whatsoever over the past years, he would have discovered that though I had no liking for embroidery I loved to dance, had a whole sketchbook filled with studies of butterflies and orchids and watersnails, and had paid great attention to the lessons I had been given on how to balance budgets since I wanted to manage the estate competently as I had promised my father I would do. Admittedly I had given just as much attention and care to the books in the library and to my own natural observations. If

Mr Merrick had ever bothered himself about my welfare before now, he would have known that those books had become my constant companions, that I loved them so well I had practically memorised every page. I had taught Reverend Burges as much about God's natural creation, about the behaviour of grass snakes and damselflies, as ever he had taught me about algebra and Latin and geography. 'John made a pledge to my father that he would make sure I continued my studies,' I said quietly. 'I made a pledge to him too.'

'Well, then, you will have to break it,' Mr Merrick rounded on me spitefully. 'You will continue these absurd studies no more. From now on you will receive instruction *only* in dancing and music and drawing and housewifery, like a proper young lady. You have had your final lesson with the Reverend Burges, or he will find he has preached his final sermon in this parish. Do I make myself clear?'

For John and Mary's sake, I nodded submissively, even as I clenched my hands into fists behind the folds of my skirt.

'I have already removed all of your father's books from the house.'

'No! Please, sir, anything but . . .'

'They will be returned to you when you come into your inheritance and are no longer my concern. Your father made the gravest mistake, teaching you to take an interest in masculine concerns,' he added superciliously. 'The weaker sex may have fruitful wombs but they've barren brains. Learning only makes them impertinent and vain and cunning as foxes. I fear I shall never get you off my hands, even if you do come with a fine manor and a good income. I caution you to mind your tongue when you meet Mr Ashfield again.' He smirked nastily, as if he knew very well that what he was about to say would cut me to the quick. 'No gentleman wants to marry an educated girl.'

'I understand your own wife is very competent in business, sir,' I said, voicing what I had always taken for proof that women could have a role beyond homemaking. 'She is a trusted partner in most of your ventures, I gather.'

'She is a city wife.'

He did not need to elaborate. City merchants were happy to have wives who were helpmeets, whereas gentry marriages were bound by an entirely different set of rules. What gentry husbands looked for were meek and dutiful wives. What a man like Edmund Ashfield would be looking for was a meek and dutiful wife, not a know-it-all.

Not me.

'Your father chose me as your guardian because he knew I would make a good guardian for Tickenham Court,' Mr Merrick continued. 'You have me and the trustees to thank for the fact that you shall have an income of six hundred pounds a year.' He touched the bedraggled hem of my dress with the toe of his highly polished buckled shoe. 'Enough to keep you in pretty gowns, no matter how many you'll undoubtedly ruin by wandering around like a Romany. But pretty gowns do not come cheap and I want to see a return on my investment. I'd like to see you betrothed and off my hands as soon as possible.' He glanced at the book he had been holding, drumming his stubby beringed fingers on the cover. 'This is the only book you will be reading from now on, and since you are so keen on study, I urge you to study this particularly well.'

He held it out to me and I took it reluctantly, glanced at the cover.

'It's a conduct book, in case you are wondering. For most gentry girls it is as important as the Bible. It instructs you on how to behave. The skills you will need in order to secure a husband and then fulfil your wifely duties.'

Stubbornly, I knelt back down on the ground. I laid the conduct book to one side on the grass and attacked another dandelion. But as soon as Mr Merrick had gone, I picked up the book and flicked through its pages.

Edmund Ashfield arrived at Tickenham Court in the early evening while Bess was dressing me in my new gown. He and Mr Merrick immediately shut themselves away in the parlour so I did not get to see him until supper, when my guardian seated himself beside our guest at the polished oak refectory table.

I took the place directly opposite Edmund and tried not to gaze at him or act the mute ninny I had been before. It was not easy. For he was just as I had remembered him after all, and more. He had filled out in the intervening years, lost any trace of boyish lankiness, so that he seemed even taller and broader-shouldered and more imposing than ever. But his grey eyes were just as merry, and in the light from the candles in the wall sconces his wavy copper hair rippled and shone luxuriantly. If I touched it, I wondered, would it be soft as a kitten's fur or as prickly as a bulrush?

66

As he helped himself to a slice of cold beef off the pewter platter, I stared at the flurry of pale freckles and red-gold hairs scattered across the back of his hand. I reached out for a slice of meat and my fingers brushed against his, making every fibre of my body start to tingle. Solicitously, he moved the platter nearer to me but I found that I was not in the least hungry, despite the fact that I had been too excited to eat all day. I did not think I could manage one bite. There was no room in my belly anyway. With the corset laced up tight, there was barely room left to draw air into my lungs, not that I was complaining. With my hair piled on my head and ringlets coiling down to my shoulders, I had never felt so grown-up or so elegant.

I watched Edmund cut his meat as if I had never seen a person use a knife before. Then he stopped cutting and his hands were quite still. I looked up and our eyes met. He gave me one of his gloriously sunlit smiles and my heart skipped.

'Eat up, girl,' Mr Merrick scolded. 'What's the matter with you today?'

'Yes, do eat, Miss Goodricke,' Edmund said, and the little apple in his neck bobbed up and down as he swallowed. 'I have never tasted beef this good.'

'We've killed the fatted calf for you, my boy,' Mr Merrick said heartily. 'Mind you, if this land were to be drained and reclaimed like your father's, we'd have no end of fatted cows. These pastures would breed the fattest most succulent cattle in all of England, isn't that so?'

So that was why he was so keen to marry me off to Edmund, I realised with sickening dismay. I should have guessed. I should have known. If I tried to eat the beef now, I thought, I might very well choke on it.

Edmund must have been looking at me closely enough to notice the colour drain from my face. 'Reclaimed land may breed fat cattle, but wetlands draw and breed good fat wild geese,' he said supportively. Astonishingly he must even have noticed the faintest flicker of disagreement in my eyes, for he added quietly: 'Or don't you think so, Miss Goodricke?'

I parted my lips to speak, hesitated.

'Please, do go on,' he said, encouragingly. 'You had something to say, I think.'

'The girl always has something to say,' my guardian said through gritted teeth, his eyes like daggers intending to pierce my tongue and hold it still.

I gave a small shake of my head, eyes downcast. 'It was nothing.'

'But I should like to hear it all the same,' Edmund persisted gently.

I set down my knife and fork as if throwing down armour and relinquishing weapons. I looked up defiantly. It was absurd to try to pretend to be what I was not, especially since every thought I had seemed to show on my face. If Edmund Ashfield did not like the fact that I was educated, that I took an interest in the natural world and so-called masculine concerns, then so be it. I might as well know sooner rather than later. I had always been proud of my learning, too proud maybe, but I could not, would not, consider it a shameful thing that must be concealed. I had not read the conduct book Mr Merrick had given to me, nor had I any intention of ever doing so, but I had glanced at sufficient pages to know that I could never be the kind of modest and maidenly girl it set out to create. I would never be content with a life of needlework and gossip. If Edmund wanted such a girl, then I would never be happy with him, did not want him at all, no matter how handsome he was, no matter how his smile made me feel all warm inside and aware of my body in a way I never had been before.

I gulped down my wine, swallowed, handed the glass to Jack Jennings to be refilled. Edmund was still looking at me expectantly.

'It is just that . . . well, the wild geese never breed here,' I said.

Mr Merrick snorted derisively. 'Miss Goodricke is a proper little know-it-all, I am afraid,' he said grimly. 'Though I imagine much of what she says is nonsense. How can anyone possibly know a thing like that?'

I flushed hotly with embarrassment and anger. 'All the wild geese have flown away by spring,' I countered with quiet confidence. 'Long before the mallard ducklings and the heron chicks are born. I have watched them.' Overcome suddenly with a need to make mischief, I turned my head slightly, flickering my eyes sideways at Edmund as I had seen Bess do to Ned, the stable boy, whom she had married a year ago. 'I've never once seen wild geese climbing on each other's backs like the cock does to the hens.'

Mr Merrick spluttered as if the succulent beef was poisoned. This was followed by a deathly hush. I hardly dared even glance at Edmund Ashfield. But when I did I saw with enormous relief that he was grinning from ear to ear as if I had said the most amusing and delightful thing he had ever heard. I could not help but grin back at him. I had not meant to test him, not really, and yet it had been a kind of a test and my heart sang at how completely he had passed it.

'This is not a conversation for the supper table,' Mr Merrick said when he had recovered. 'Indeed it is hardly fit conversation for a young lady in any situation.'

'My father taught me that it is a godly duty to take a keen interest in the world,' I said with a pert smile.

'You take rather too keen an interest in worldly things,' Mr Merrick grunted. 'I ask you! How the deuce do you even know that the behaviour you so eagerly describe results in the begetting of offspring?'

'Oh, I've thought about it a lot,' I said, so happy and so emboldened by how much Edmund Ashfield seemed to be enjoying the conversation that I felt almost invincible. 'You couldn't live amongst livestock for long and not work it out.'

'It's true, Merrick,' Edmund said supportively. 'You merchants and town-dwellers are shielded from the basic facts of life in a way that those of us who work the land and live in proximity to beasts and birds can never be. I'd say there was nothing at all amiss with having an earthy approach to life.'

'You may be nineteen years old, Eleanor,' Mr Merrick said, 'but I've a mind to send you to your chamber at once, supper or no. You are too forward by half.'

I hated my guardian then. I hated him for making me appear like a child when I was trying so very hard not to be one. But again Edmund Ashfield leapt to my rescue.

'Oh, don't send her away, William,' he said in his affable tone. 'I beg of you. She's such delightful company and we would be so dull without her. And I have to say, I don't think she's too forward at all.'

Actually, until that day, I'd considered myself rather backward when it came to the intriguing subject of mating. Though when I thought of Edmund while I was out riding it made me shift restlessly in the saddle, I'd been quite disturbed at the idea of men and women doing together what I had watched the bull doing to the cows. But now I did not think I should mind it so very much at all, so long as it could be Edmund Ashfield who was doing it to me.

'Are you on your way back from London?' I asked him. 'As you were when last you came to Tickenham?'

'Fancy you remembering that after all this time,' he said.

I blushed, feeling I had given away the secrets of my heart too freely and he would know now that I had been half in love with him since I had been a little girl. That might perhaps be a grave mistake. But then I saw the way he was looking at me, almost wonderingly, and knew I need not be concerned. He would never use such knowledge against me, never do anything to hurt me. He seemed very straightforward, not the kind of person to appreciate dissembling at all. I did not care if I had inadvertently declared my feelings. In fact, I was glad that I had.

He looked at me as if he could hardly believe I had been that little girl in the drab dress he had first met all those years ago. 'I am on my way to rather than from London this time,' he replied.

'And are you going to meet your friend again?' I asked.

'Richard Glanville, yes.'

'I wonder, does young Glanville ever spend any time at Elmsett?' Mr Merrick asked disparagingly.

'He doesn't like to,' Edmund said with a glance down the table at the other man. For just a moment the merriment dimmed in his eyes. 'You can surely sympathise with him on that score, sir.'

'Or is it just that he prefers the attractions of London?' Mr Merrick blundered on. 'The theatres and coffee houses?'

'The taverns more like.' Edmund smiled with such fondness and familiarity that I was almost jealous of his friend, for the fact that Edmund clearly had such affection for him. 'Though he loves horses and weapons every bit as much as he does canary wine and tobacco. He is an extraordinary young horseman and swordsman.'

'And does he still like to swim?' Mr Merrick asked.

'Oh, aye. He's set on teaching me, did his utmost to get me into the Thames with him.'

'Would it be safe for you to learn to swim in the Thames, sir?' I was dismayed by the depth of fear I felt for him, the fact that already he meant so much to me the idea of him coming to harm was intolerable. That too must have been written all over my face, but I saw that it delighted Edmund to know that I was so concerned for him.

'I promise you, I will take good care of myself,' he said.

When it was time for the gentlemen to go to the parlour to drink their port and smoke their clay pipes, I went to my chamber where the candles and the fire had been lit and waited impatiently for Bess to come to get me ready for bed. I rushed at her and grabbed her hands as soon as she came into the room. 'Bess, tell me honestly, do you not think Edmund Ashfield very pleasing?'

'Passable,' she said wryly, taking the candle from the stand and holding it up to examine my excited face by its light. Her almond eyes missed nothing. She sighed and smiled, revealing the large gap between her two front teeth. 'Oh, my, here we go. It is my guess that you still find Mr Ashfield just as pleasing as you did when you were a child. And I know what you're like when you fix on a thing. You can never do anything by half measures, can you? So I suppose that's all I'm going to hear from now on . . . Edmund . . . Edmund . . . Edmund. But at least it makes a change from butterflies and caterpillars I suppose. Or – what was it before? – tadpoles.'

'Bess, he's the finest gentleman I've ever met.'

'Not that that is saying much. I can count the number of gentlemen you've had contact with on the fingers of my one hand. Or is it just the one finger? It's no wonder you're in such a stew, poor lamb.'

'I feel as if I'm floating.'

'Well, how about floating into your nightshift?' I lifted my arms obediently and she slipped the cool linen over my head, fastened the ties under my chin then pressed me on to a stool beside the fire. 'Now sit down and I'll brush your hair.'

Bess took out the pins, let my hair tumble down my back and started work with the ivory comb, long luxuriant strokes that normally made me feel pleasantly drowsy, but not this time. 'I shall never be able to sleep,' I sighed. 'I couldn't eat my supper.'

'Well, that'll not do you much good. There's nothing of you as it is, and if you don't eat you'll disappear entirely and he'll not even notice you.'

'He noticed me tonight, I think.'

'Oh, he most certainly did.' When I swivelled round to face her, nearly jerking the comb from her hand, she gave me a knowing look. 'I happened to hear him.'

Bess was as inquisitive about people as I was about the natural world, and her friendliness and fondness for chatter meant that she received the confidences of all the servants. There was not much she didn't happen to hear, either through their ears or her own. 'What did he say?' I asked, not entirely sure I wanted to know.

'He was talking about you when I went to knock on the parlour door to take in the Bristol Cream. I felt obliged to wait until he'd done before entering.'

'But what did he *say*, Bess?'

She shrugged nonchalantly. 'Oh, just some nonsensical prattle about you not being nearly so bold as Mr Merrick suggested, but how there was a refreshing sweetness and honesty about you that had brightened his day.'

'Did he really say I'd brightened his day?'

'I'd be hardly likely to invent such silly mooning, now would I?'

'I can't believe he'd talk like that about me to Mr Merrick, of all people.'

'Oh, your guardian seemed more than pleased to encourage the praise.'

I turned away. 'I do not doubt it,' I said with a stab of unease that I did my best to ignore.

'So what was it that you liked so much about *him* anyway?' Bess continued cheerfully.

'Oh, every part of him.' I closed my eyes and tilted my head back as the strokes of the comb sent delicious tingles down my spine. 'His hair,' I began. 'And his smile. His hands, his lips.'

'His lips!'

'I wanted them to kiss me.'

'Just what do you know about kissing?'

'I know what it is to feel desire now.'

'Desire! You're practically a child still.'

'I am not. I've been having my courses every month for six years,' I reminded her.

'Seems like only last week that I warned you about them.' Bess chuckled to herself. 'You were that shocked!'

'Is it any wonder? How can it not come as a shock, to hear suddenly that you're going to bleed, once a month, from between your legs?'

'You scolded me for lying to you, as I do recall.'

'I was sure you must be. Until you told me that when it happened it meant I had become a woman, that my body was readying itself to make and to carry a child.'

'You've always loved to talk about babies,' Bess said softly, no doubt thinking of her own little Sam who had been born almost a year ago, after she had allowed Ned Tucker to take her to the hayloft for a fondle. I had been allowed to keep Bess on as my maid after her hasty marriage because I could not bear to part with her, and Sam was cared for by his doting grandmother. 'You always wanted to know all about them,' Bess said. 'About making them and tending them and everything.'

'I remember I asked you if it hurt . . . the bleeding, I mean . . . if it was like when you cut your finger? You told me it was just an ache inside. Oh, Bess, I have such an ache inside me now,' I said plaintively. I looked down at my hands as they rested lightly in my lap, my hair falling over my shoulders in a cascade of glossy new-combed gold curls. 'He's leaving in the morning and I don't know when he'll come back.'

'But you know that he will. If Mr Merrick wants to see you wed to him, then wedded you will be.'

'I suppose so.' Again that confusing prickle of disquiet. Because I knew why Mr Merrick wanted me wed to Edmund. And though I wanted very much to be wedded to him, I did not want what must come with it. Perhaps I was wrong. Perhaps I could talk to Edmund and explain. Perhaps there was a way around the problem.

'When you do have a baby,' Bess said, 'I suppose you've got it into your head that it must be Edmund Ashfield's baby?'

'I'd like to bear him a little son to carry on his name.' I smiled dreamily. 'And a little girl, too, with hair as red as his.'

Bess tutted. 'I'm tired of him already. I think I prefer your fondness for butterflies after all.'

'A little boy with freckles over his nose,' I ran on, 'and a smile as sunny as his father's. Oh, just imagine, Bess! A son of Edmund's would be so placid. He would never cry and I would love him so much. Edmund would teach him to ride and I would make sure he learned all about the world and we would all be so happy . . .'

'You'll doubtless make some gentleman ecstatically happy one day,' Bess said salaciously. 'There's not a man I know who doesn't want a hot and passionate lover. Every gentleman wants the joy of a whore in his bed even as he is expected to have a docile little miss on his arm in the parlour.' Then, more seriously: 'All men want to be adored and I don't think you're capable of doing any less than throwing your whole heart into a thing. It is a big heart you have, for such a small person. Only, be warned – there's many folk think it unnatural to see such passion in a lady as they have always seen in you.'

I did not sleep at all. I did not even feel tired and I longed to be outside, to clear my head with fresh air and exercise. Heedless of draughts, I opened the hangings a little way at one side of the bed so that I could see out of the window and watch for the first blue tinge of dawn to creep into the sky. As soon as it did, I dressed myself in my grey wool gown, my boots and cloak. It seemed odd to be clothed for the day and have my hair all plaited still for bed, so I undid it and left it free. It was much more comfortable like this than with the pins and tight braids that pulled and scraped my scalp and always made my head ache by the end of the day. I liked to feel the weight and sway of it, tumbling over the hood of my cloak and down to my hips like a thick gold mantle. What did it matter that it was improper? Who was going to see me at this hour?

I wandered down towards the edge of the flooded moor, my feet squelching through the mud, the cold water lapping against my ankles, enjoying the special magic of dawn breaking over the wetlands. I breathed in the clean cool air and listened to the piping of the waders and the sombre beating of swans' wings. There was no wind and the water was mirror calm. Ethereal wraiths of mist turned the flooded meadows into a land of great mystery, wreathing the pollarded willows so that only the tops of the trees were visible. The lone mound of Cadbury Camp floated above the greyness like a galleon, the only easily distinguishable natural feature for miles.

I untethered the flat-bottomed boat that was moored by the hump-backed bridge and set the lantern down in the bottom, away from the bilge. I clambered aboard and took up the oars.

The water could flood up to six feet deep in places in the winter, quite enough to drown a girl as small as me. The thought of it always made me afraid and exhilarated at the same time. It was the closest I ever came to an adventure.

I tried to imagine what kind of person could swim like a fish, as Edmund's friend could apparently do. What an advantage it would be in a waterland such as this, to be able to slip away beneath the surface of the lake, to a world that none but the fishes ever saw.

74

Richard Glanville. The Cavalier. The fine horseman and swordsman.

His name had always held a fascination for me but I tried to push him out of my mind. He was just a phantasm. It was Edmund Ashfield to whom my heart belonged. Yet I was intrigued by the idea of his friend Richard. He must be very fearless, very strong, very strange. We were not made to swim any more than we were made to fly, or surely God would have given us gills and fins. I looked down at the dark water and almost imagined I saw a lithe body moving through it, a face looking back at me, ghostly through the ripples, a cloud of long black Cavalier curls.

So powerful was the vision that I was almost afraid to turn around in case he had climbed soundlessly aboard my boat and was sitting right behind me. He could grab hold of me with cold hands and drag me over the side, take me down with him, into the depths of the lake where the drowned grass of summer still grew but was no longer green. I would not be able to breathe down there, but he would put his mouth to mine and breathe air and life into my lungs.

I took a deep breath to clear my head of such fanciful, romantic nonsense.

But when I looked up I saw a solitary light moving ahead in the mist, where the water gave way to bog and marsh, and I froze in real fear. There was no doubting this was real, as unearthly as it appeared, a wandering marsh light, a will-o'-the-wisp, a creature of the Devil. Well, it served me right. I'd always yearned for colour and brightness, silk and ribbons and Christmas candles, and here I finally had my wish, in the form of an evil apparition come to seek me out. It was growing brighter still and there was a long shadow moving beside it, gaining in substance as it drew closer, the disembodied head and shoulders of a cloaked figure, drifting above the mist.

My grip tightened on the oars but as I kept on watching I saw that there was nothing unearthly about the light at all. It came from an ordinary lantern, carried by Edmund Ashfield. I rowed back to the bridge, my heart beating far faster than ever it had done from fear.

'You worry about me swimming in the Thames and yet you come out here all by yourself?' There was a touch of admiration and respect in Edmund's voice.

'I know what I am doing, sir.'

'I can see that you do. May I join you nonetheless?'

'Gladly.'

He climbed into the boat, sending it rocking wildly and dipping lower in the water. I moved to the facing bench so he could take the oars. There was not very much room for the two of us and we had no choice but to sit with our knees pressed tightly together. Not that I minded that at all.

I watched his large hands, tilling expertly back and forth, his big, powerful shoulders flexing in a smooth, easy rhythm. I was about to warn him to steer away from a clump of rushes poking just above the water, indicating where we would run aground, but he had judged for himself, was already resting the right oar in the rowlock and we were turning. He drew a deep, appreciative breath. 'As a boy I spent all my free hours in a boat just like this,' he explained. 'Now our land is drained we never have cause to use one.'

I was instantly on my guard. 'Mr Merrick sent you to talk to me, didn't he?'

He glanced away awkwardly so that I knew I was right. 'I would have come anyway,' he said quietly. 'I wanted to see you.'

'I am well aware that Mr Merrick was always trying to influence my father to drain Tickenham,' I said. 'As heir to this estate, it is I who must now be influenced and I am afraid, sir, that he means to use you to do it. I may as well tell you now that I am against it.'

He laughed. 'And I do pity any poor soul who hopes to urge you against your wishes.' His eyes sparkled with kindly and disarming humour. 'I give you my word,' he said earnestly, 'I would never try to convince you to do something I did not consider to be in your best interests. Do you believe that?'

I considered him. 'I do,' I answered quite truthfully.

'So do think you could trust me, even a little?'

'Yes,' I said without hesitation. I was sure that I could trust him more than a little, could trust him completely.

'You are very young to be worrying about land management,' he commented after a while. 'It is a great weight to carry on such small shoulders.'

I gave those shoulders a quick shrug. 'There has been nobody else to do it.'

'I have never met anyone like you before,' he said. 'You are not at all like other girls.'

'Is that a good thing or bad?' I asked lightly, but with trepidation.

'Most girls do not run around at dawn with their hair trailing down their back. They do not know about the behaviour of wild geese and chickens.'

'Don't they?' I noted that he had neatly sidestepped my question.

'They can be very tiresome,' he added. 'With their polished manners and their practised coquetry and their perfectly painted faces.' He gave his easy laugh. 'I confess I am terrified of most of them. I have no sisters, you see, so the ways of young women are a mystery to me. But you, I think, are as plainspoken and courageous as a boy. I like that. I feel I know where I am with you. You must call me Edmund, by the way.'

I had called him by that that name in my head for so long that I was itching to speak it out loud to him, even though for a moment I could think of nothing else to say. 'Edmund,' I said simply.

He smiled expansively. 'Eleanor.'

If we were married, we should both have the same initials. Edmund Ashfield. Eleanor Ashfield. When I had sat at my little writing desk aged about fourteen, allegedly transcribing a passage in Greek, I had played at writing the name that I would have if I became Edmund's wife, and it had seemed an impossible and lovely dream. It still did, and yet he was here with me now, wasn't he? When I was fourteen that would have seemed just as unlikely. Which was probably why I expected to wake up any minute and find that I had indeed been dreaming, that I had never come down to the lake, but was still alone in my great bed.

'What is it like, having William Merrick for a guardian?' Edmund asked affably. 'Don't worry, he's no particular friend of mine. And I promise not to repeat one word of what you say.'

'Oh, I hardly ever see him,' I said, determined to be gracious. I glanced at Edmund's open face and instantly lost my resolve. 'To be honest, that is a most blessed relief.'

'I can imagine,' he said, making me giggle.

'He's always in Bristol. Except when he leaves his wife to mind his interests so he can come here for a day or two, but even then he is usually too busy with the estate to pay any attention at all to me, except for when he wants something. Have you ever met his wife?'

'Once.'

'What's she like?'

'Not nearly so friendly or forthright as you.' He smiled. 'For all her city sociability she's like William in many ways, shrewd and shrewish. She likes everything immaculate and gleaming, new as their wealth. Their mansion is not so luxurious as to be unbefitting to the Puritan, mind, but I swear not one item in it is more than a decade old. I can't imagine she'd feel much inclination to care for an orphan girl.' He glanced at me with sudden pity. 'You must have been lonely.'

'I don't know what it is to be lonely,' I said frankly. 'I am used to being on my own. I like it, in fact. Though sometimes,' I smiled at him a little shyly, 'it is good to have company. Depending on who the company is, of course.'

Nevertheless I could not help thinking how lovely it would be to be part of a real family again, to make a new family of my own, here on this land that I loved, with a husband I loved and who loved me.

'So who said your prayers with you at night?' asked Edmund as if it genuinely concerned him. 'Who was it who comforted you when you were hurt?'

'Our minister John Burges and his wife Mary have cared for me very well,' I said gratefully. 'John made sure I said my prayers. He used to play skittles with me, too, and he rides with me as far as Clevedon when he has time. I had Mary to put salves on my knees when I grazed them, and she always came to kiss me goodnight. And my maid Bess was always ready to play leapfrog with me and fly kites.' I did not add that all that had been missing, all I had needed, and increasingly so, was somebody to love. One person on whom I could lavish all the love that seemed to be filling my heart until it was ready to burst. 'So, you see, all Mr Merrick had to do was manage the estate,' I finished.

'Even so, I for one will be forever grateful to him,' Edmund said quietly. 'Why is that?'

His cheeks had turned a soft pink beneath the pale freckles. 'For introducing me to you.' His smile was bashful, as if he was not accustomed to having such conversations, and it made me like him even more than I already did, if that was possible.

'I am thankful for that too,' I said quietly. And then: 'Why are you blushing?'

He smiled with mild surprise, as if nobody had ever asked him such a personal question before, then raised his hand and touched his head. 'It is the hair,' he said diffidently. 'All redheads blush annoyingly easily.'

'Oh.' I grinned. 'I can see that must be a great nuisance.'

'It is.' He drew in the oars and took hold of my hands, held them inside both of his as we drifted. His hands were very warm from all the rowing and his eyes were just as warm as he gazed into mine, making my heart race. 'May I come and see you again, Eleanor?'

'Isn't it my guardian's permission you should be seeking?'

'I am conscious that your guardian would willingly arrange a match between us, but I shall not court you unless you are happy for me to do so.'

I smiled at him. 'I am happy.'

He smiled back with relief. 'May I come again soon then?'

'Soon.'

'And may I kiss you?' he asked with aching politeness.

I did not think gentlemen asked ladies if they could kiss them. I thought they just did it. 'You may,' I said, my heart pounding.

He leaned forward in the boat and made it rock. I closed my eyes and waited. I felt his lips lightly brush my own.

'I should like to help you carry the burden of running this estate, and all others you may have,' he said soberly. 'If you would let me.'

I stood at the great oriel window and watched Edmund ride away along the causeway, the surface of the water that lay all around him ruffled by a brisk breeze. I did not know how to feel, caught halfway between misery and joy. He was leaving, but he had kissed me and told me he wanted to come back.

In such a flat land, when the mist had lifted, it took a long time for people to disappear completely from view. They just grew smaller and smaller until they were no more than a speck on the wide horizon. But I stayed at the window until Edmund and his horse had vanished beyond it. I did not know what else to do with myself. I would find no solace on the moor as I usually did, for I was sure the little boat would seem utterly desolate now without him in it.

'Why look so melancholy?' Mr Merrick asked in an unusually genial tone that would have made me very wary had I not been so preoccupied.

He had come to stand by my side but I did not even acknowledge him. 'Extraordinary as it may seem, Edmund Ashfield appears to be bewitched enough by your pretty little face and blue eyes to overlook completely the initial peculiarities he cannot have failed to notice in your character. I expect he is charmed by your quaintness, views you as something of a curiosity.' He paused. 'He wishes to enter into a courtship with you. He knows of course that his own family would approve fully of such an advantageous match. As a second son, it is most desirable for him to form an alliance with an heiress of some means.'

Something in his self-satisfied tone alerted me. 'An advantageous match?' I repeated slowly, turning to face him. 'Advantageous to whom, sir?'

'To all concerned.'

'The alliance would benefit you too, wouldn't it? My father's will forbade you to use your guardianship of me and this estate to advance a drainage scheme, but if I marry Edmund, you are counting on him doing it for you, aren't you?'

Smugly, he dusted an invisible fleck of dust off the shiny brass buttons of his embroidered saffron silk waistcoat, neither agreeing nor disagreeing.

'I know all about coverture,' I said.

'I do not doubt it.'

'I know that a husband and wife become one person when they marry, and that legally that one person is the husband. I know that, as a wife, I must relinquish all my rights, my identity, my belongings. Upon our marriage Tickenham Court would belong solely to Edmund, every acre of it, his to do with as he saw fit. And if he, like you, saw fit to drain it, there is nothing I could do to stop it.'

The prospect of marriage had seemed so distant that I had not fully considered what it would mean until now, and it dragged at my heart to realise that in order for Edmund Ashfield to be mine, Tickenham Court would no longer be. And yet at that precise moment I'd have given anything just to see him again.

Mr Merrick gave a swift tug on his waistcoat, his grin sly. 'Hard as it is for you, you must accept that coverture is an unavoidable consequence of marriage.'

'But I do not have to accept Edmund's hand. He only wants me if I want him. He told me so. He will not allow you to force me into marriage with him against my will.'

'Ah, but you want to be his wife, do you not?'

I was being trapped. Gain Edmund. Lose Tickenham Court to drainage. It was a trade, a bargain. Mr Merrick bargained with everyone and every-thing. Why should he not bargain with my heart?

'You also have to accept that drainage will happen sooner or later,' he said. 'If not in your generation then in the next. This land is in a deplorable condition and eventually must be reclaimed, like the rest of the wetlands in the Fens and at King's Sedgemoor.'

I said nothing. Instinctively, with every ounce of my being, I resisted the very idea of this land that I loved being dug up and dredged and destroyed. For what? For profit primarily, as I saw it. It seemed a heresy, a sacrilege. I loved bright satin and ribbons and Christmas celebrations, but there seemed something very treacherous in rejecting this ardent belief of my father's, one he had so cared about he'd had it written into his will, one not born from bigotry but surely from common sense. So steeped was I in my respect for God's creation, that even to consider tampering with it, to countenance the idea that we could attempt to control the elements, seemed an arrogant and hazardous thing to do.

'I urge you not to waste too much time deliberating,' Mr Merrick warned. 'Edmund's father is pressing him to make a match before his third of a century which is not long off. Are you prepared to see him promised to someone else?' I failed to hide my misery at this prospect and he smirked. 'No. I thought not.'

I was in the habit of taking a slice of apple pie and custard and a glass of Bristol Cream up to my Great Aunt Elizabeth in the afternoon, of sitting with her and keeping her company while she ate. She liked to hear of the servants and doings in the village, of how I was progressing with my dancing and music lessons.

I was her only real contact with the outside world. Since the mild attack of apoplexy had left her left side slightly weakened, she was permanently ensconced in the small lime-washed guest chamber, where she spent most of the day in a high-backed oak chair drawn up to the window, her violet-veined hands still stiffly busy with a needle. She seemed ancient to me, but she did not seem to feel the cold and kept the small leaded casement window open no matter how thick the fog that curled up off the river. She still had the noble bearing of the girl who had been presented at King James's court as the daughter of a baronet, and a complexion as pale as the ornate square lace collar she always wore over her black gown. She had wispy silver hair like moonlit mist and she was most profoundly deaf. But her kindly grey-blue eyes more than compensated for it. With their aid she missed not a thing.

She set down her crewelwork as soon as she saw me. 'You come and tell me what's troubling you, my dear,' she said in her clipped, aristocratic voice. 'And don't say it's nothing because I won't believe it. You've had such a wistful look in those lovely eyes of yours these past days. Now I've had quite enough of seeing you moping about, all lost and lovelorn.'

I brought round a small tapestry-draped table, removed the covering and put down the plate and glass, finding that I wanted nothing more than to tell my aunt exactly what had been troubling me.

I sat at her feet, took hold of her hands and looked up into her handsome, wise face so she could read the words on my lips even if she could not hear them. As soon as I started I wanted to pour it all out, but I made myself speak carefully and calmly so that she could catch every word. I told her everything: how I was in love with Edmund and was sure he had feelings for me, but that if I married him it seemed inevitable that he would push for Tickenham land to be drained. 'My father did not want that to happen,' I said. 'And yet he did approve of Edmund, I know it. He said he was very likeable.'

'And since people always want most what they cannot easily have – you especially, I think – I am quite sure that he seems a lot more than likeable to you now.'

'I love him,' I said mournfully.

'Are you quite sure about that, my dear?'

'Oh, what does it matter?' I sighed, my shoulders drooping.

My aunt laughed. 'You have your father's Yorkshire cussedness combined with a wetlander's tenacity – what a combination! You'd not even consider drainage on principle, would you? Just because William Merrick wishes it. Not even if you knew it to be for the best.'

'Do you think it is for the best, Aunt Elizabeth?'

'There's plenty that do.'

'My father was not one of them,' I said grimly. But this land had belonged to someone else before it belonged to him, hadn't it? 'You knew my mother,' I pleaded. 'What would she have had me do?'

'Well, now.' My aunt sat back a little in her chair. 'Your Uncle Henry, my son, the Baronet of Ribston, was very fond of both your parents and they of him. He spent a lot of time here after they were first married. Somersetshire is as different from Yorkshire as it is possible to be, as low and flat as Yorkshire is high and hilly, yet your mother taught him to love Tickenham as she did, precisely for these differences. My Henry told me how she loved this land, but most of all she loved its people. She was the first person the village women called on if they went into labour and the midwife was busy. There are dozens of your neighbours and servants who were brought into the world by her.'

'I never knew.'

'Well, now you do. She would be very proud of you. You want to do what is right, and you are prepared to sacrifice your own happiness in order to do so. There could be nothing nobler than that. The question is, what is the right thing? Your mother's overriding concern was the good of the people of Tickenham, so if you want to know what she would have done, what she would think was right, it would be whatever is best for them. I cannot tell you what that is. But if anyone can work it out for themselves, it is you.'

I kissed the old lady's parchment hand. 'Thank you, Aunt.'

'I've not done anything, child.'

'Oh, you have,' I said. 'You've given me hope.'

'Hope?' She smiled. 'You usually have a way of finding a little of that for yourself, I think. May you always.' She took my face in her hands, tilted it towards hers.

'Perhaps it is your hopefulness that makes your eyes and your smile so bright. You are such a pretty girl. You know, once in a while, in the middle of an ordinary life, love gives us a tale straight from the pages of a romance. And if ever there was a girl made for such a tale it is you. But I fear you want it so badly you're at risk of running headlong in the wrong direction.'

'What do you mean?'

She allowed herself a short silence then continued, 'I hope Edmund

Ashfield is the great love of your life, child. Not everyone has a great love, but you, I think, must have one, or it will be the most dreadful waste.'

I thought about what my aunt had said about my mother as I accompanied Mary on her rounds of the poor thatched cottages straggling along the line of the road that ran parallel to the course of the River Yeo. The position was not high enough for them to escape the winter floods which forced their inhabitants to cook and sleep in a single room upstairs for months, and I began to think that surely anything was better than that. Even when the floodwaters finally diminished, leaving the rivers gurgling and pools of bright water glinting in the ditches all across the moor, it left the lower earthen floors of the cottages thick with viscous mud which no amount of rushes could properly soak up.

When Bess told me her father had a persistent and hacking cough, I helped mix up salad oil and aqua vitae and took it to the Knights' little hovel myself. Bess's mother was crippled with rheumatism, hobbling about around the table where they'd just finished eating their pottage. Bess's little boy, Sam, toddled after her with mud smeared up to his knobbly knees. There was a smoky fire burning in the grate but it had made little impression on the damp wattle walls, and yet the dark little room felt surprisingly warm and homely, a well-loved and cared for place. There was a bunch of marsh marigolds in a jug in the middle of the scrubbed table, and a battered but polished copper pot still simmering over the fire.

'If you're stopping you'd better sit down,' Mistress Knight said in a friendly way when I made no move to leave. She had a deeply wrinkled face, a gruff almost manly voice, but her eyes were kind. She plonked a wooden spoon and bowl of curds and whey on the table together with a pot of small beer. 'There. You eat up now.'

'Thank you,' I smiled, taking a rickety stool beside Mr Knight and only cursorily tucking up my skirts to stop them trailing in the sludge, not really caring if they did. Mr Knight looked at me with genuine pleasure and surprise, as if he had not expected me to want to sit and stay, but was glad I did. He had spent so many years on the moor cutting sedges that he was almost as much a feature of the landscape as the birches and willows. He seemed at one with the sky and the water, and yet he did not look out of place in this small, smoky room but quite comfortable and content. He was tall and lean as a withy, with short and thinning brown hair and eyes as dark brown as coffee beans. I wondered how the two of them had fathered a son as disagreeable as Thomas, who was thankfully nowhere to be seen.

I handed over the cough mixture. 'I hope it helps, Mr Knight.'

He was a typical marsh-man. To foreigners we are strange people living in a strange land. Isolation and dependence on soggy marshes, which only those born here know how to survive, breed a spirit that is taciturn, obstinate and determined. Yet as Mr Knight took the remedy he seemed to wish he could shrug off his habitual uncommunicativeness and say much more to me than thank you. 'You could have sent it with Bess, you know,' he said. 'You needn't have come all this way.'

'It is no trouble. I wanted to come.'

'You're a good girl, miss, despite what some folk say about you.'

I laughed. 'Thank you – I think. My Aunt Elizabeth told me how well my mother cared for the people of Tickenham,' I added.

'Oh, aye, she cared for us all right.' Mrs Knight gave an ironic laugh, shuffled over to give the fire a sharp stabbing poke. 'Some of us, at least.' Her husband cast her an equally sharp glance as if to silence her. I was left feeling that I had inadvertently made a terrible blunder, but since I did not know how, or why, was at a loss as to how even to begin to make amends.

Sam presented me with a crudely carved little horse. 'Thank you, Sam.' I smiled gratefully, lifting him into my lap, heedless of his little muddy feet.

Mr Knight sipped his pot of ale awkwardly. I noticed that his nails were broken and dirty, the skin around them cracked and sore from constant exposure to cold and wet. They were outdoor hands, but the fingers were as long and slender as the fronds of sedges he spent his life cutting, though the knuckles on his right hand looked so stiff and sore it was a wonder he could do his job at all. 'I'll bring a rub for your joints next time,' I told him.

'We'll have no need of rubs soon,' Mistress Knight retorted. 'His joints won't trouble him, nor mine me, soon as we get some warm dry days.'

It was not the best moment to ask, but ask I did. 'Mr Knight, don't you sometimes wish you could live somewhere that was dry all year round?'

The affection was suddenly gone from his eyes to be replaced by an expression of extreme truculence. 'I'm a sedge-cutter,' he said almost aggressively. 'I've cut sedges all my life. I've reared my son to be a sedge-cutter. And as you know full well, Mistress Goodricke, sedges don't grow where it's dry. They only grow in marshland.'

I stood before my guardian's desk, my feet together and my hands lightly laced in front of me as he pored over his great ledger, his fleshy features knitted in concentration. I drew a deep steadying breath. 'Please invite Edmund Ashfield to come and visit again,' I requested.

Mr Merrick set aside his quill-pen and looked up with a victorious smile that did not quite reach his small eyes. 'I am glad to hear that you've come to your senses. By God, it has taken long enough.'

I had rehearsed what I was going to say a dozen times. Why had I not accounted for him leaping to such a conclusion? I let my hands fall to my sides, flexed my fingers, knowing that what I was about to say now would anger him beyond all reason, but there was nothing for it but to plough on. 'I have not yet reached a decision on whether I will consent to his seeking my hand, sir. I need to ask him some questions first, about drainage, in order that I might do so.'

Mr Merrick slammed his fist against the desk, making the quills and the silver inkpot bounce. 'You and your damned questions! Out with them. I'll answer them myself and be done with it.'

I felt a bead of sweat trickle down my back but I was not going to be intimidated. 'With respect, sir, you do not understand drainage as Mr Ashfield understands it. As you said yourself, he has first-hand experience. I have none, and cannot be expected to make such an important decision in ignorance. I want to ask him what it will be like, what it will entail, what it will mean for everyone living here.'

'What kind of fool do you take me for?' roared my guardian.

But I was my father's daughter. I knew how to stand my ground. 'Mr Ashfield is in favour of drainage, is he not? So talking to him about it can only persuade me I that it is a good thing, surely?'

There was no rejoinder to that. Mr Merrick banged the ledger shut with a puff of dust and an expression on his face that made me flinch. But inside I was smiling, for I knew that I had won. This first battle at least.

'Very well,' he growled. 'I will send for Ashfield.'

* * *

I ran as fast as I could through the tangle of reeds and sedges, for no other reason than the sheer joy of feeling the sun on my face. I stretched out my arms to either side like wings. If only I could run just a little faster I really might take off. On days like this we lived in a cloudland; the ground was insignificant, there was only the wide dome of the sky, and I wanted to be as much a part of it as were the birds.

The faint sounds of pipes and drums reached me from across the fen meadows.

Spring had arrived early this year and already it felt like summer. The moor was teeming with life, ablaze with colour. Frogs croaked and otters slipped in between the bulrushes while above me skylarks sang as they climbed higher and higher in the heavenly blue sky. Against the emerald of the rushes blazed purple loosestrife and yellow rattle, while the ditches and riverbanks were flushed pink with orchids. In my long, plain cloth dress, I was the only point of darkness in the wide, flat wasteland. It was hardly the thing to wear to the May Day celebrations but Mr Merrick had been left strict instructions by my father not to condone my attendance of pagan celebrations, and had confiscated my blue silk gown. But today I did not care. Edmund Ashfield was coming to visit again. Winter was over. And at least the gold of my hair could not be dulled, Bess had said as she'd combed it earlier, braiding it tightly upon my head while whispering naughtily about how she'd be wearing hers loose with flowers in it for the festivities.

It didn't look to be too far to the edge of Horse Ground meadow where the revels were taking place, but the moor was deceptive. It took a long time to cross the shortest distance because of the continuous obstructions from rivers that were too wide to jump, stretches of open water and ponds and bog. I crossed the Boundry Rhyne by Causeway Bridge and beyond it was a little grove of alder, willow and birch that formed a natural screen. The silver-blue pointed leaves of the willows seemed to be swaying and quivering to the music that sounded much louder now. I saw flashes of colour and frantic movement beyond the trees.

The May King and his Queen presided over everything in their flower-decked arbour, the dancers were merry in their red and white girdles and embroidered jackets, bells jingling and handkerchiefs swinging. The Devil's Dance, my father had called it. And maybe it was, for it took tight hold of me. There was nothing in the world I could do then to stop my hips from swaying, my cold, wet toes from tapping along to the rhythm.

'Very bawdy and lewd, is it not?' Bess's voice in my ear made me leap an inch in the air. She gave a voluptuous trill of laughter, cupped her hand round her mouth and bent her chestnut head closer to whisper to me again. 'Not half as bawdy and lewd as the way I've been dancing with my Ned, mind.'

I pulled her back into the trees. 'Did you love Ned on your first sight of him, Bess?'

'What? Up to his elbows in horse dung? Can't remember exactly when I realised I loved him, nor a time when I didn't.' There was a saucy gleam in her eyes. 'But I have a mind to take him into the bushes and let him love me back right now.' She tilted her head alluringly. Her round cheeks were flushed and she had a crown of foliage set askew on her head. 'D'you think he'll be able to resist?'

'Oh, definitely not.' I looked at her seriously. 'Am I irresistible, do you think?'

For a moment I thought she would tease me, but instead she gave me a quick, tight hug. 'Of course you are, little lamb.'

'You're not to flatter me, Bess. I need to know. Am I pretty? Tell me, honestly?'

'You are sweet as a sugarplum.'

'I was up at dawn this morning collecting May dew,' I told her. 'So my skin will be beautiful when I see Edmund again. He won't have changed his mind, will he? He will still like me?'

'How could he not? But there's plenty more gentlemen in the world besides Edmund Ashfield, you know.'

'But he's the only one I want.'

'He's the only one you've met, you mean.' She peered at me. 'Never mind about May dew. Your skin is soft as a rose petal. A cowslip wash on your nose would not go amiss, mind. I do believe you've got the beginnings of sunspots already. If you're not careful they'll turn into freckles.'

'I don't mind if they do. I have changed my mind about freckles entirely. I think they are very attractive and desirable. I don't mind at all if I grow a whole speckling of them.'

Bess rolled her eyes. 'Is he really all you can think about?'

'Weren't you the same with Ned? Didn't you think about him all the time?'

'Not likely.' She gave me a hug, kissed my cheek. 'But then I'm not you. You're like those blue birds diving for fish. When your mind's set on a thing, that's all you see.'

She linked her arm through mine and took me back through the trees. 'Stop pining now. Look at that.'

The throng parted and I had a proper view of the slender tower of the maypole, covered with herbs and garlands of hawthorn and pinks, with streamers and flags flying.

'"The hated heathen idol."' Bess quoted the Puritans with a ribald smile. '"Encouragement to wantonness and lust." Not that some people need much encouragement.'

As if to prove her point, Ned Tucker came up behind her and seized Bess round her shapely waist. 'I was beginning to think you'd gone and left me for good, bonny Bessie.'

'Would I ever?' She twisted round in his arms and he trickled a few drops of ale from his tankard down the top of her dress then tried to lick it off. She writhed and screeched and slapped him away until he fumbled her for a kiss.

Ned was a hefty sandy-haired lad with a pleasant round ruddy face and I watched, giggling at them, thinking that I very much wanted to be kissed myself.

'Stop it, Ned,' Bess laughed. 'Miss Eleanor will have me for a common strumpet.'

Ned winked at me and then flung Bess away towards the dancing, swiping a pie from a long table as he passed by. With no contribution from the Lord of the Manor, the spread today was simple fare but no less mouthwatering for that: rye bread and curds, custards and cakes, hogsheads of ale and cider. Our dining table in the great hall never looked half so laden and my belly felt empty as usual.

I stepped towards the table, about to help myself to a jam tart, when I saw something that made me lose my appetite in an instant. Thomas Knight was standing sullenly watching the merriment, hands stuffed into the pockets of his breeches.

He turned and stared right at me with his insolent black eyes and I shrank back into the shadows. I looked for Bess but could not see her.

I retreated into the trees, almost wishing I had not come. It was cool and damp in the wood, almost primeval, the floor blanketed with huge ferns and moss and fungi. A nightingale was singing, and there was the hollow rap-tap of a woodpecker at work. A shimmer of brightness flashed past my nose. A crimson and gold butterfly. My eyes darted after it but at first I couldn't see where it had gone. There it was again. It fluttered its gilded wings, dipped, drew a little figure in the air, a gliding aerial dance of more beauty and colour than any I'd just watched. A tiny, bright-winged creature, it reminded me of the fairies Bess swore lived in these trees.

But it was gone again. Where? I was struck with disappointment, as if I'd been handed a precious gift only to have it snatched away.

A glittering, fleeting little presence. There it was! I ran forward. It was playing a game with me, leading me on, flickering over the low vegetation. It alighted on a thistle. I stopped. It flittered off. I followed. It finally settled on a water dock, folding its wings coyly, revealing an underside of orange and white and blue.

I crept as near as I could.

The wings suddenly flipped open, magnificent golden-red wings with snowy fringes and inky black spots, I thought it prettier even than the maypole. I cupped my hands, lifted them slowly, trapped the butterfly in a single downward swoop.

In that instant I felt a sharp pain in the small of my back, heard feet smashing through the sedges right behind me, and spun round.

'Well, if it isn't the Lady of the Manor, little Miss Eleanor Goodricke.' Thomas Knight's voice was thick and slurred with drink. 'What were you up to then? Chasing after fairies, were you?' He sniggered. 'I knew you were soft in the head. Not got your full wits about you.'

He was red-faced and dazed-looking, his shirtsleeves rolled up to show brown and brawny arms. He had a nasty smirk on his thick lips and another jagged stone in his hand, much larger than the one that had already hit me. He rubbed his bleary black eyes, flexed his arm. I squared my shoulders and lifted my chin, telling myself that he must not see I was afraid. I tightened my cupped hands and felt the butterfly's wings frantically beating against the cage of my palms, so strong for such a small, fragile-looking thing, a peculiar echo of the feeling inside my belly.

'So much for quality folk having better brains than us,' Thomas sneered. 'You're obviously missing half yours. Your father educated you like a son, so maybe that's what's turned you soft-headed, eh? Maybe that's what makes you think you're better than the rest of us, that you know what's best for us all, that you've got the right to steal what's ours. As if you've not stolen enough from me already.'

I frowned. 'I don't understand, Thomas. What are you talking about? What have I stolen from you?'

He lowered his spiteful eyes to my breasts, lurched forward. 'Maybe I'll take something from you, to make it even. Maybe I'll teach you a few things myself.'

I pressed my hands against my chest, my arms shielding my body. The butterfly had quietened, as if it was waiting, its wings trembling against my palms. 'Don't you dare touch me,' I threatened. 'Don't you dare come any closer.'

'Or what? Tell Merrick, will you?' He stepped up to me. 'Bet he doesn't know you're here. Bet nobody knows it, do they? Mary Burges will not be coming to rescue you this time, will she?' He looked me up and down with his leering eyes. I could smell the acrid sweat from his armpits; it reminded me that he was a grown man now and this was no childish scrap. We were no longer children. He was a man and I was a woman and this time it would be much more than a marchpane sweet he would try to force upon me.

'I'll scream . . . I swear I will.'

'Nobody can hear you scream out here,' he jeered. 'And even if they do, they'll just think you're enjoying yourself.'

He took a step nearer. 'Tiny and light as a fairy yourself, aren't you?' He smirked. 'Let's see if you have a little pair of wings hidden away somewhere.' He lunged at me, thrusting his hand down my bodice.

I ducked away, jerking free from his grasp, and ran as fast as I could.

Drink may have made him too unsteady on his feet to pursue me but it hadn't damaged his aim much. I felt the stone graze the side of my head. Bright lights spun in front of my eyes and hot liquid trickled down my brow. I kept running. I ran all the way back across the moor, up the winding stone stairs to my bedchamber. I kicked the door shut and rested my back against it, my chest heaving and my head throbbing.

I carefully uncurled my fingers. The butterfly lay at an angle against my palm, wings firmly closed and crumpled at the top. I gave the little creature a prod. It didn't move. I touched its brown furry body. Nothing.

The poor little thing was dead. It must have been the shock, or else I'd held it too tight, squeezed the life out of it. I felt sad for a moment but then realised that at least I could keep it now, could look at it whenever I wanted. It was bright and beautiful and it was mine. Gently, I picked it up by its folded wings, its threadlike legs dangling, its feet briefly sticking to my skin. Gently, I prised open the wings.

I lifted my great King James Bible from beneath my pillow and carefully smoothed the butterfly between the pages of the Gospel of St John, beside the meadow flowers I'd collected with my mother.

I closed the book, turned my hand palm up and saw that it was stained with the finest sparkling of golden powder, which looked for all the world like fairy-dust, as if marking me out as someone under an enchantment, someone chosen, someone to whom special things might happen.

In the afternoon I was in the parlour with my father's pair of globes, one of the earth and one of the heavens. I rested my finger on the terrestrial globe and spun, waiting to see where it would come to land. The Atlantic Ocean. I spun again. Continents whirled past dizzyingly.

But it wasn't only that which was making me dizzy. There was a scab as well as a bruise on my temple, and it hurt when I moved my eyes. I shut them for just a moment, opening them to see Mr Merrick scrutinising me with thunder in his gaze.

'What's wrong with you, girl?'

'Nothing, sir. I've a headache, that's all.'

'That is not what I meant and you know it. Tell me, how did you enjoy the Maying?'

Any number of tenants could have told him they had seen me there, but I didn't understand why he was so angry about it. I knew for a fact, from what Bess had overheard, that he was holding a supper for his merchant friends tonight in Bristol. Though not exactly a traditional May celebration, it happened to be taking place on the very same day.

'It was . . . interesting,' I said, picking the right word carefully. 'I can't see what's so wrong with letting the villagers dance and enjoy themselves.'

'According to your father, it is what it invariably leads to that's so wrong.

Can you tell me there wasn't all manner of wanton and ungodly behaviour on display?'

That I could not. My cheeks flared as I remembered my encounter with Thomas Knight.

'What happened?'

'Nothing.'

He repeated: 'Name of God, what happened?'

'Thomas teased me for chasing after a butterfly.'

Mr Merrick's arms were hanging down at his sides and I saw him clench and unclench his fists. 'What exactly did he say to you?'

'That I must be soft in the head.'

A mirthless laugh of agreement. 'Is that all he did?'

I was too ashamed to tell him, did not want to tell a blatant lie either, so I said nothing.

He seized me by my shoulders and in doing so disordered my carefully arranged hair, revealing the bruise and crusted scab.

'He threw a stone at me,' I said quickly.

The corded veins thickened in Mr Merrick's broad neck. I did not see why his anger was directed at me rather than at Thomas Knight, as if it was I who had done the greater wrong.

'You are a little fool,' he hissed, thrusting me from him, 'who deserves to have stones thrown at you. You are a little fool to think you can ask the likes of the Knights to pass comment on the fate of this land. Now every damned commoner and tenant knows what is afoot. I've already had half a dozen of them marching up here demanding to know what is going on.'

'Why shouldn't they know what you are considering? Why should they not have their say? They are accustomed to using the common. Why shouldn't they have an opinion on what is to happen to it?'

'Why? Why? Why? Why don't you realise there are some questions you just do not ask?'

'Why not?'

'Because . . .' Spittle showered from his mouth as he shouted and flexed his knuckles and punched his clenched fist against his own palm, as if it was me he really wanted to hit, and hard. 'Because the Levellers and the Diggers were crushed before you were born, and their foolish radical ideals with them. All men are not freeborn. They do not have natural right.

Commoners have no right to an opinion. They do not have a natural God-given right to the land. That is the way of it. And that is the way it will always be. Whether you like it or not. Do you understand?'

I did not. But I knew better than to say so.

I could not bear to wait around inside for Edmund's arrival so I asked the kitchen to make me up a parcel of white manchet bread and cheese and apple chutney, and went down to the moor to watch for him. Irises and purple orchids were in flower along the riverbank and the radiance of their petals matched my mood of optimism. Once Edmund was here, once I could talk to him, all would be well.

When at long last I saw him, wearing no hat, his cropped copper hair bright in the sun and ruffled by the soft breeze as his horse cantered along the cause-way, I abandoned all pretence of modesty. My blue silk dress had been returned to me for his visit but neither the whalebone corset clamping my lungs nor my full petticoat with its tiers of lace stopped me from picking up my skirts and running to him as fast as my legs would go, tresses of hair tumbling about my cheeks. He saw me, and his face relaxed into one of his wide, open smiles. If I wasn't completely in love with him before, I thought I was then.

He reined in and dismounted. We stood looking at each other as I caught my breath.

'I waited and waited for an invitation until I was sure I must have offended you in some way. Please tell me I did not?'

'You didn't. Of course you didn't.'

'Well, I am here now. That is all that counts,' he said with his unwavering and infectious good humour.

'So you did want to see me again?' I asked, shyly flirtatious.

'You need not ask that, surely? You must know I wanted it more than anything else.'

Edmund took my hand in his, leading his horse by the reins, and we started to walk back to where I had left the food beneath a willow. He shouted a cheery good day to the fishermen nearby. 'Fortunate fellows,' he commented to me. 'Having such a delightful place as this to wait for their catch.'

'Will it be as delightful after drainage?'

'Ah, William warned me that you had questions to ask me.' He grinned at me. 'It wasn't just a ruse to bring me here?'

'Partly. Edmund, the tenants and commoners . . . everyone who lives here . . . all seem totally opposed to the very idea of draining the land.'

'Of course they are,' he said mildly.

'They seem entirely content with the state of the moors, are willing to tolerate them being inundated for half the year and waterlogged for a good time longer. They would rather that than have their way of life changed.'

'Of course they would. Life on the wetlands is all they have ever known.'

'It is all I have ever known.'

'But they do not have your intelligence and imagination. They are simple people and lack the foresight to appreciate the benefits that drainage will bring. But benefits a-plenty there are. Fertile pastures all year round to grow crops and graze livestock. Dry cottages to live in.'

'But what about the people whose livelihoods depend on eeling and fishing and fowling? It would seem like robbery to them. I am not so sure it is not.'

'They will still have the rivers after drainage,' he said kindly. 'Wider ones, deeper ones, and a whole network of drainage ditches too. There will still be fish and eels to catch. I grant the sedges will be lost with the draining of the marsh, but fertile agricultural land yields other crops. There'll be hemp, flax, woad and mustard, and opportunities for new, more wholesome labour than wading up to the knee in a bog all day.'

'But they will lose the common for grazing their cattle, won't they?'

'The majority will be apportioned other land. An acre per beast lease, which should satisfy.'

'You make it all sound so straightforward.'

'Then I mislead you, which I hope you know I would never wish to do. Make no mistake, what we are contemplating here is a process fraught with difficulty and opposition, not straightforward at all, but when it is all complete the problems will be quickly forgotten and few will want to go back to the way it was before.'

'You have absolutely no doubts that it is for the best?'

'No doubts whatsoever.'

'My father was wrong then?' I asked thoughtfully.

'No,' Edmund said. 'He was a man of a different time, that is all. In recent years practically every lowland area has seen some attempt at reclamation.'

He halted while his horse bent its head to drink from a pool of water. He squeezed my hand, lifted it to his mouth in a very courtly gesture, kissed it. 'Dear Eleanor, let us talk no more of this now. Drainage or no, Tickenham is the most delightful place to me because you are here. There is nowhere I'd rather be, and no one I'd rather be with.'

I leaned in closer to him and laid my cheek against his arm. 'That is the loveliest thing anyone has ever said to me.'

'Is it? Well, it's fortunate for me that you've seen so little of the world, or you would realise that I am really very poor at this kind of thing.'

'I have seen enough of the world to know that, for me, you are the centre of it,' I said with girlish impetuosity.

Edmund looked touched if a little overwhelmed by my declaration. 'I could not hope for more than that.'

Just then a large copper-gold butterfly came flying swiftly at us, the sunlight glinting on its magnificent shiny wings. It swooped and glided right in front of my eyes, as if it was taunting me. I itched to catch it to stow away in my Bible along with the other one, as if I really had fallen under an enchantment. When it danced away I held on to Edmund's hand just a little tighter, to stop myself from hitching my skirts up to my knees there and then and chasing after it.

Edmund looped his horse's reins round a branch and spread out his riding cloak for us to sit on while we ate the food that I had brought. But I did not sit. I waited and watched to see what plant the butterfly chose to land on. A water dock, I noted with interest.

When I did sit down and broke off a piece of the crusty bread, my mind was still elsewhere.

Edmund tickled me under the chin with a grass stalk. 'What are you thinking about now?'

I smiled at him. 'Oh, nothing really.' Determined as I was that he should love me for myself, I feared he might think me completely crack-brained if I said I was wondering what it was about water docks that made them appealing to copper-coloured butterflies.

Did it really matter anyway? Perhaps, for Edmund, I would not mind so much becoming like every other good wife. Perhaps if I were his wife I would be perfectly content with embroidering my sampler with great bumbling caterpillars and brilliant giant butterflies. It would not really matter that they could never be as beautiful as the real thing, no matter how many minute seed pearls I painstakingly stitched on to their wings.

'You like butterflies,' Edmund observed idly, relaxing back on one elbow.

'What girl could not? They are very pretty.'

'Not half as pretty as you.'

I turned to look at his handsome face beneath its cap of copper hair, and all thoughts of the copper butterfly flew from my head.

Edmund sucked a reed between his teeth. 'D'you like them too?' he asked, with a nod towards the dragonflies and damselflies which were busy about the tall reeds, their diaphanous wings all a-whir.

I considered this for a moment. 'Not so much,' I said. 'They are all too frenzied, too agitated. They lack the playful joy of butterflies.'

'You have clearly given it much thought,' he said in amusement.

I broke off a piece of bread, threw it to one of the mallards that had come waddling out of the river, and was instantly surrounded by two dozen of its greedy, quacking, flapping companions, all threatening to peck the rest of the bread from my hands and take my fingers with it. I jumped to my feet and Edmund followed suit, laughing to see me ambushed by the sudden commotion of ducks. He threw a piece of his own bread over-arm so that it travelled some distance, luring the whole flock away to search for it in the long grass. Then he looked at me as if he had just realised something.

I cocked my head to one side. 'What?'

'I think, dear Eleanor, that you are playful and joyful as a butterfly yourself. For such a staid fellow, I do seem to be drawn to people who like to enjoy themselves.'

'You are not staid at all,' I said passionately.

'Richard says I am. He thinks me far too settled in my habits.'

'He is not then?' I said, bending down to pick a little white mallow.

Edmund laughed. 'Oh, no.'

I twirled the flower between my fingers. 'He does not have a sweet-heart?'

'He's had a good many. But they tend not to last very long.'

'Why not?'

'Hard to say. Except that he's entirely driven by emotion, which makes him rather impulsive. That is part of his appeal, I suppose, but it also makes him a difficult person to be with for too long. Though most ladies like to try. When you see him you'll understand immediately why he leaves a string of broken hearts behind him. He's damnably attractive, curse him, if you like pretty boys.'

I added that to my list. Cavalier. Swimmer. Fine horseman and swordsman. Breaker of hearts.

'You are very fond of him, aren't you?'

'It is impossible not to be. Richard can charm the birds right out of the sky. I am sure he will charm you too.' He took the little mallow from my hand, leaned towards me and tucked it in my hair, behind my ear. 'But not too much, I trust.'

I smiled into his handsome, sunny face. 'I have already been charmed.'

He looked lovingly into my eyes. 'I promise you this, dearest Eleanor. Your heart is quite safe with me. I shall never break it.'

Summer 1675

Bess poured warm water into the small bowl on the three legged table and I washed my face with Castile soap, put salt on my fingers to scrub my teeth, stripped off my shift so that I could rub my body, under my arms and between my legs, with a linen cloth wrung in water perfumed with herbs and essences.

'I must say, I can't see why you insist on going through all this rigmarole every time Mr Ashfield is due a visit,' Bess grumbled. 'He's been coming to see you every fortnight for two years and the pair of you do no more than hold hands and coo at one another. What's the point of having your privates smelling sweet as roses if he's not going to have a sniff of 'em?'

'Bess!' I exclaimed with laughter. 'You are disgraceful.'

'I do know what it is to want a man and to want to make him wild for me,' she retaliated, as she started removing the curl papers from my hair. 'I just can't say I'd ever be prepared to go to half as much trouble as you gentry ladies do.'

'It's hardly any great chore to be clean and to wear ringlets and ribbons and lace,' I said, smiling.

'I meant the dancing lessons and the drawing,' she sniffed.

'That's not for Edmund. Well, not just for him. I have always wanted to dance, and it would be wonderful to be a competent enough artist to be able to capture the set of a butterfly's wing or the clouds at sunset, not that I have any talent for drawing at all. But my dancing master says dancing comes as naturally to me as breathing,' I added proudly. 'He said only yesterday that he's never seen a girl who is so light on her feet.'

'That you are, lamb,' Bess agreed, unravelling another curl. 'But you should try dancing barefoot round a bonfire. Or with a fiddler in the fields at harvest time. I dare say you'd find it more to your liking than balancing precariously on your toes and bobbing back and forth, as stiff as a bobbin on a loom.'

'Gliding to a rhythm of eight, you mean?' I looked at her out of the corner or my eyes. 'D'you think Edmund would like to see me dancing round a fire?'

Bess grinned with satisfaction as she took up my new lemon-coloured gown from where it was spread out on the bed. 'That's my girl.'

I giggled. 'You really shouldn't talk to me like that, you know,' I teased, my nose held in the air. 'You must be more respectful or I shall have to consider hiring a French maid.'

Bess was too busy now to rise to my teasing. She had been shown how to help me dress by a very affected French maid loaned to us by one of Mr Merrick's Bristol neighbours, but it was a complicated business that still required her utmost concentration.

'If I were really doing all I could to convince Edmund I'd make a good wife for him, I'd make sure I was fluent in French rather than Latin,' I said thoughtfully as I leant forward against the bedpost while Bess wrestled with the laces of my corset. 'And I'd make sure I was as practised in the art of carving at table as I am at naming all the continents and constellations.'

'I'd have thought any man might consider himself very fortunate to be loved by a lady who spoke the language of goddesses and could find her way amongst the stars.'

I could tell from the sound of her voice that Bess wasn't fooling any more, was entirely sincere, and I twisted round to look at her, as surprised by her vehemence as by her eloquence and very touched by both. 'I thank you, Bess,' I said, sincerely. 'That was very nicely put.'

'You're welcome. And, to think, all my Ned expects of me is that I know how to please him in bed, an' he's happy enough to teach me that himself!'

I laughed, pressing my hand against my corseted midriff.

'Stop it or I'll never manage it,' Bess chided, trying to straighten her own face as she pulled the laces tighter round my ribs. 'Suck your breath in harder.'

Much as I'd longed to wear fine clothes, I did not like the feeling that I might die in them for lack of air. With the great piece of whalebone thrust down the middle of my stomacher, I could barely breathe or eat, let alone laugh. I certainly couldn't skip about on the moor and play leapfrog and turn cartwheels on the grass any more. I did sometimes wonder, just for a moment, why I had been so keen to wear such silly garments. It seemed to me they must have been invented by men, expressly to hamper women and keep us in our place.

When Bess had done trussing me she finished dressing my hair in a knot on top of my head, from which cascaded a mass of long, shiny golden ringlets fastened with gold ribbon.

Finally she stood in front of me to admire her work. 'Don't let him find you in amongst the trees or he'll take you for a nymph.'

'I feel like one.' When I moved, the lemon silk sounded like a breeze rustling through leaves.

I fastened on some delicate topaz drop earrings and a matching necklace which Edmund had given to me last Valentine's Day.

'Pity you don't have any rouge to put some colour in your cheeks.' Bess reached out and gave both of them a pinch with her fingers. 'Try that just before he sees you.' She tutted. 'I do believe you have a touch of the green sickness. You are in the most dire need of bedding.'

'Oh, I am,' I giggled. 'I am.'

'Bite your lips too, like this.' She demonstrated. 'It'll make them look so red with lust he'll have to push his tongue between them, even if he can't get his cock between your legs.'

'Bess!' I gaped at her then burst out laughing. 'Here.' I grabbed the damp cloth and threw it at her, showering us both with droplets of water. 'You are far more in need of a wash than me. I've never heard such filthy talk! As you well know, Mr Ashfield's tongue has never been near my mouth. Nor even his lips, for more than one fleeting moment, more's the pity.' Amidst a great billow of skirts, I sighed and threw myself backwards on to the high bed where, earlier, I'd been examining my collection of love tokens for the hundredth time. 'Maybe he's read that conduct book Mr Merrick thrust upon me. It is very clear that mutual liking and respect is all that is called for between a man and a woman who vow before God to share their lives. Amorous love is a contemptible disease. But I want to be loved,' I breathed, staring up at the faded crewelwork canopy. 'I want Edmund to love me.' I snatched up a pair of salmon pink gloves he'd sent to me and clutched them to my heart. 'Liking will never be enough for me.'

'I do wonder if Mr Ashfield will ever be enough for you,' Bess said coming to perch beside me and clucking. 'Or, rather, that you will be altogether too much for him.' Her dancing, almond-shaped eyes grew uncommonly serious then, their expression almost protective, and as I sat up beside her on the edge of the bed, she kissed my cheek. 'I just hope he is capable of loving you even half as much as you love him.'

I unfolded the letter from Edmund that had arrived days ago.

'You've read it so often it's in tatters already.' Bess smiled. 'Shame he hasn't written you a few more.'

'I don't mind,' I said, quick to defend him. 'He told me not to be offended or think badly of him for not writing more often. He doesn't have an easy way with written words.'

'Let's see then.' Bess scrambled up behind me and tucked her chin on to my shoulder. '"My best beloved . . ."' She knew that bit by heart. '"O-u-r-p-a-r-l-e-y-i-s-n-e-a-r-i-n-g . . ."' She broke off.

With the help of a little bone tablet I was trying to teach her to read, but she never concentrated for long enough and we were having great trouble progressing past isolated letter sounds.

'Oh, it's too hard,' she huffed. 'You do it.'

I shuffled back further on to the bed and read aloud: '"Our parley is nearing an end. Now I have stormed the cherry bulwarks of your sweet mouth, I am convinced I may gain your surrender. But if I must lay siege to your heart to secure my final victory then I shall do so willingly." He goes on to describe another week he's spent in London with Richard Glanville. They've visited the playhouse a dozen times and marvelled at the novelty of seeing females on stage, but Edmund said none of the actresses was as enchanting as me.'

'How does he end it?'

'"I shall be making advances in your direction again very soon. I beg of you, Eleanor, remove all fortifications against me or I am crushed."'

Bess chortled. 'You have to admit, he uses some very peculiar words to woo a girl. I just hope he can do better than that when he gets you between the sheets or his weaponry might prove woefully inadequate!'

'Oh, stop it,' I giggled, giving her a gentle shove that toppled her. 'I think his letter is very charming. And he doesn't talk the way he writes, or at least he only does when he is unsure of himself. Besides,' I sighed, 'it's entirely appropriate. After all, gentry love is very like the waging of war. Allies are sought to make approaches, concessions are bargained over. The reason I'm certain Edmund is about to propose now is because I know very well he's been in negotiation with Mr Merrick for weeks and they've finally reached an agreement.'

All Bess did was raise her eyebrows. As well she might.

Edmund tucked my hand into the crook of his arm and we went to walk in the garden, where the light was so thick and golden that it gilded everything it touched.

'I feel as if I have drunk a barrel full of this sunshine,' I told him. 'Or else I cannot imagine how it is that I feel so happy and warm inside.'

'You're sure it's not Somersetshire cider you've been drinking?' Edmund quipped. 'It tends to have that effect on me.' He grinned down at me again. 'As does the sweetness of your face.'

'Oh, Edmund. I do like it when you talk to me like that. Say something else.'

'I'm not sure that I can pay compliments on command.' His brow creased as he tried to think of another all the same.

I did not have to try at all. 'I can't decide if it is the sunshine or having you here that has made the colours of all the flowers seem so much brighter,' I said, quite truthfully.

'Oh, it is me, most definitely.' Edmund looked down at me and I looked up at him and neither of us took another step, so that for one wild and wonderful moment I thought he was going to kiss me properly, finally, amidst the beds of pink hollyhocks.

Instead he let his arm drop to his side, took hold of my hand and carried on walking. He talked about his journey and how his horse had lost a shoe. 'I've saved it for you so you can hang it on your door to bring you good luck.'

I did not tell him that we were living in an age that was supposed to be casting aside such talismans, to be moving from the dark age of superstition into an enlightened age of science, because I would be glad to have a horseshoe on my door if it had belonged to Edmund's horse and he had given it to me. Besides, I was too busy trying to think of a way I could contrive to get him to take me in his arms and kiss me.

'Let's play Barley Break,' I said suddenly.

'Barley Break?'

'Yes. Oh, you must have played it. It's very simple. I run away and you have to chase me.'

'I'm not sure I like the sound of that at all,' he said with a grin. 'I don't think I want to have to catch you. I like having you right here, by my side, at all times.'

'Oh, but this is far more exciting.' I let go of his arm and slipped away from him across the scythed lawn, my gold curls bouncing and my yellow silk skirt swishing out behind me. Even my laughter sounded gilded and bell-like in the still afternoon. I had forgotten that I could not run very fast in a corset and petticoats, but it did not matter since the only point in running was to be caught and as soon as possible. I glanced over my shoulder, saw Edmund coming after me but not very fast, as if he didn't want to spoil the game for me. Just as he turned the corner by the stone bench I hid behind a rosebush, hoping he'd spied the edge of my skirt as I disappeared. I peeped round the bush to watch him then scampered off when he was almost upon me, giggling deliciously at the prospect of my imminent capture.

I let him catch me by the arbour entwined with honeysuckle. He grabbed my hand and I pretended to take a little stumble so that he had to grasp me properly around my tightly laced waist. I twisted round in his arms and he held me close to him for a moment as we both caught our breath. I felt a hardness between his legs, pushing against my stomacher, secret and surprising. He bent his head and placed a swift kiss on my lips, but it was over in an instant, leaving me yearning for more.

He plucked a blossoming honeysuckle off its stem and held it under my nose for me to smell its sweet fragrance, and I didn't know whether to laugh or cry with frustration when I remembered what Bess had said about the fact that I smelled of roses but that Edmund would never get close enough to me to find out.

Why did he have to be so maddeningly respectful? It would all change when he was my husband and was permitted by law and by God to love me, wouldn't it? But I did not know how I was going to wait that long. I touched his flame-red hair and imagined him inflamed with desire, running his tongue all over my skin as Bess said Ned did to her. I was sure that when the time came Edmund would be a very passionate husband.

'Edmund, there is something I have to ask you.'

We had gone inside for glasses of cider in the parlour and Edmund was sitting facing me in the window embrasure.

'Ask and I shall grant it,' he said, setting his glass down on the sidetable.

'Will you take me to the Fens? So that I may see for myself what has been done there?'

'It would be my pleasure.' He took a deep breath and looked very sombre all of a sudden. 'It would be the prefect opportunity to introduce you to my father and brother. They are longing to meet you.' He paused. 'Actually, there is something I have to ask you too.' He took my hands in his, looking more earnest than ever, so that I thought I knew exactly what he was about to ask me. Even though I was expecting it, my heart started fluttering frantically.

'It's such a beautiful day,' I said impetuously, jumping to my feet without letting go of his hand. 'Let us go back into the garden and you can ask me there.' I would treasure the memory of my betrothal forever, and it would be so much more memorable if it was done under a blue sky, surrounded by flowers and butterflies and serenaded by bird song, instead of in this sombre, oak-panelled room. He stood too and I tried to lead him but he stayed as rooted to the spot as a tree. Apparently he needed formal surroundings for such a formal event. It was so like Edmund to want to do everything just right.

I sat down again. He sat down. He cleared his throat. 'Difficult manoeuvre,' he said, his face turning a little pink. 'I'm not sure where to begin. I don't suppose Merrick has said anything to you?'

'About what?' I asked, all innocence.

'About my . . . my intentions. No. Of course. Not up to him. Not the occasion to mount a joint ambush.'

I waited, smiling encouragingly, wondering how I might help him along. It was touching that he was so nervous, though I did not know why he should be.

'We'd do well against the world, you and I, if we joined forces, don't you think?'

'I do.'

'So you'll be my wife?'

This was it then, the most important decision I'd ever make. I was about to enter a binding contract to change my life, something that would determine my entire future, and now that it came to it, I hesitated. As Edmund himself had just jested, I had seen so little of the world, so very little of men. In accordance with my father's last and very strict wishes, I'd still only been to a few sedate local gatherings at Ashton Court. No dances or dinners. I had not mixed in society like most girls of my age. All I really had to measure Edmund against were heroes from romances and ballads. He was kind and infinitely patient and very fine-looking, and from the moment I first saw him, I'd believed we were meant to be together, but how could I be certain he was the man to whom I wanted to be yoked forever? At the very back of my mind was a very troubling doubt, a notion that somewhere out there, someone else was waiting for me.

'Do you love me, Edmund?' I asked him, very quietly, realising he had never actually said that he did.

He blushed. 'I hope to have the chance to grow to love you more each day.'

'And would you love me if I were not the heiress of Tickenham Court?'

'Dear Eleanor,' he said, looking flustered, 'what questions you do ask.' I thought he was going to say that of course he would love me, whatever my circumstances. But that was not what he said at all. 'You look at me with those great searching eyes of yours that demand an answer, demand the truth, but how can I answer such a thing truthfully without hurting you? For you *are* the heiress of Tickenham Court. And if you were not, you would not be as you are.'

'Oh,' I said despondently, but I saw that what he said was entirely true. And I knew I should consider myself very fortunate even so, since so many courtships between gentry couples were conducted for financial reasons alone. I realised also that Edmund had answered my question bravely, for it would have been much easier for him to reassure me with false platitudes.

'Be frank with *me* now,' he said gently. 'Would you have allowed yourself to fall in love with me if I were a chandler or an inn-keeper, for instance, if I were not the son of a landed family, born to a life of squiring an estate like Tickenham Court?' He quickly put his finger across my lips. 'No need to answer,' he said with a dazzling smile. 'I ask only so that you do not think less of me for the answer I gave you.'

I experienced such a rush of love for him then, coupled with a powerful sense of romantic sacrifice, that suddenly the prospect of losing control of my home mattered to me not at all. I would give it up, gladly. In fact, I loved Edmund so very much that I was pleased I had something so valuable to offer to him.

Perhaps from dismay that it was taking me such a long time to answer his proposal, Edmund sank down on one knee at my feet. 'Say you will marry me, Eleanor, please?'

I was presented with a view of the top of his head. The sun had appeared from behind a cloud and a long golden ray slanted in through the window, lighting the spot where he knelt, waiting for me to say yes to him. It lit up his copper hair, surrounding him in a dazzling golden corona. I couldn't have been sent a more potent sign. It was my beacon, guiding me forward to a bright new future. I reached down to stroke the copper waves, almost expecting them to be flame-hot or for something like lightning to crackle up through my fingers.

'Oh, Edmund my love, I will marry you. Gladly.'

He scrambled to his feet then and hugged me with relief. He couldn't really have doubted me. I couldn't really have doubted myself.

Mr Merrick suddenly burst through the door so that I knew he had been listening outside.

'Blessings to you both,' he said as he kissed me and shook Edmund's hand.

Edmund dug his hand in his pocket and brought out a twenty-shilling piece, put it between his teeth and bit the thin coin in two, handing me half. 'Proof of our promise.'

I reached out and closed my fingers over it, the sliver of broken metal that sealed my fate. The ceremony in church would be just a formality now our contract was legally witnessed.

'When will we do it?' I asked. 'When shall we be married?'

'Next spring, I thought,' Edmund replied.

'Oh, yes,' I said delightedly. A May wedding, with music and dancing and a feast in the meadow. I could hardly wait. I should be a May Queen after all.

'I'll purchase an ecclesiastical licence so that we can marry quietly and privately,' he said. 'Without the banns being read and our affairs declared to the whole world.'

The sun seemed to disappear behind the clouds again. 'But I want the whole world to know . . .'

'Surely you don't want all the neighbours gawking and hundreds of noisy, drunken guests?'

Oh, but I do, I do.

'Practically all gentry marriages are by licence now,' he asserted. 'It's quite the custom to marry without any fanfare on a weekday morning, with just two witnesses and the minister and sexton in attendance. I'd like our marriage to begin as it should go on, in quietness and tranquillity. In such troubled times as we were born into, that's all I've ever hankered after.'

'But, Edmund, I've always dreamed of a merry wedding.'

'A licence means we can marry in a parish away from home,' he said with a puzzled but patient smile. 'I know how much you want to see London. I thought we would marry there.'

'London?' I felt a stir of excitement, even if was hard to adjust to the idea of not marrying in Tickenham.

'I shall have to go to London just as soon as I've been to Suffolk to give the news to my father and brother,' Edmund said happily. 'I can't break it to Richard in a letter that I am betrothed. Oh-ho, he will be vexed to learn that I have found a bride before him!'

William Merrick was so gleeful that I half expected him to break into a jig. 'Come the next floods, a survey will be conducted to ascertain exactly what extra channels are required to draw off the water,' he explained with unbridled enthusiasm. 'We also need to know what quantities of wood and stone will be needed.'

'Then what happens?' I asked.

'We draw up the documents to petition the Court of Sewers and state our case.'

'And how long does that take?'

'Impossible to say,' Edmund answered.

I knew very well that at Congresbury it had taken years, with the local commissioners delaying making any decision to task the area with drainage because they were not sure of their power to order new channels. Eventually the petitioners had had to obtain an Act of Parliament, which had taken another age to obtain. The process here might be equally as protracted.

'You can leave it all to me and my partners,' William Merrick said to Edmund. 'We will act as your agents, arrange all the financial and legal matters, instruct the surveyors and then the engineers. The Court of Sewers will supervise all the works and future maintenance. You yourself will have to do nothing.'

'Except grant you a significant acreage of the drained land,' I said wryly.

'A fair price for our labours,' Mr Merrick intoned. 'We will be investing considerable sums in this project ourselves and that is the only reasonable way we can be recompensed. As we discussed, to keep all the newly drained land for yourself and the commoners, and reward us with payment out of the rent, is too slow a process to commend itself to any prospective investor.'

'Rest assured, William,' Edmund said mildly, 'you will have your land.'

Autumn 1675

I had hoped Edmund would take me back with him to Suffolk, but though Mr Merrick had initially been in complete agreement to my wish to see the reclaimed Fens, he inexplicably changed his mind, forcing me to remain behind.

Edmund ended up staying in Suffolk for more than three months to tend his father who was suffering so severely from gout in both feet that he could barely walk. I missed him very much, the more so because, though I sat at my little desk and composed long, impassioned letters to him almost daily, the sporadic replies he sent continued to be stilted and a little awkward. I almost began to fear he did not miss me at all, until he wrote promising to return to Tickenham before travelling on to London, saying he could not go so long without seeing me.

Even so, he did not come back until the swans started flying in for the winter, until the rivers had burst, and the three men from Bristol had already been to conduct their surveys. On the day of Edmund's return, after we had spent not an hour alone over a dinner of roast duck, Mr Merrick arrived with charts of the proposed drainage works.

He rolled out the parchment on the long refectory table in the parlour and the three of us gathered round. I looked down at a carefully drawn map of the moor, the place I knew so intimately and loved best in the world. There were the existing pastures, Cut Bush and Church Moor and Court Leaze; the little hump-backed bridge where the boat was moored in winter. There were the boundary rhynes and tributaries that flowed from Cadbury Camp and on into the Yeo and Middle Yeo, towards the clay belt and out to sea.

'The course of the river will need to be widened and straightened, here and here.' Mr Merrick pointed a finger with a clean, carefully trimmed nail to the beautiful natural curve in the Middle Yeo that would be bypassed. 'The end of the old course may need to be dammed with stones. The banks will need to be strengthened, a new bridge built, and droves for the cattle. The earth thrown up for the cuts will be used to make embankments. The old drainage channels will be deepened and reoriented, and new ones will be dug that will link up to the existing drains. Here, here and here.' He pointed again, at the places where the moor would be carved up by a network of new ditches. 'We will need to explore the possibility of erecting a tidal sluice, the strengthening of the sea walls at Clevedon.'

'It's a very ambitious plan,' I said quietly.

'Well, what did you expect? There's no point going to all this effort just to turn common grazing pastures into meadows that produce an occasional hay crop. We might as well drain the land so thoroughly it can be properly cultivated. It could be worth up to fifteen shillings per acre – eight at least.'

I hadn't noticed Bess come into the room with coffee. She set the tray down on the table without a word, with only a glance at the parchment. But I knew her well enough to know she would have overheard and seen everything and felt like a conspirator, a traitor.

'Thank you, Bess.' I touched the sleeve of her dress as she busied herself by my side arranging the cups. She paused and looked at my hand on her arm as if a pigeon had dropped its excrement on her. I removed it and she didn't so much as acknowledge me as she turned to go.

'This may be about how many shillings we can make per acre for you, sir,' I said to Mr Merrick when I was sure Bess was safely up the stairs. 'For me it is more about improving local living conditions.' I straightened myself to my full, if still insufficient, height. 'You propose destroying the thickets that families have used for generations, for wood to build their houses and to burn on their fires.'

He shrugged. 'Unavoidable, I am afraid.'

'They have always been able to gather brushwood and firewood by the boatload. What right have we to take even that from them?'

He gave an indifferent wave of his hand. 'That is for the courts to decide.'

Edmund tried to mollify me. 'Eleanor, it is the surveyor's opinion that the moors of Tickenham, Nailsea and Kenn are in a lamentable condition compared with the rest of the county . . . the rest of the country, for that matter. They are the areas most badly affected by flooding but where the least has been done. Half measures are no good here. What they are proposing is no more than was begun by the monastery at Glastonbury before the Dissolution. We are trying to ensure these moors are neglected no longer.'

'There must be some reason they've been neglected?' I asked pointedly. 'Why have speculators avoided Tickenham until now?'

'Peat lands are the hardest to drain,' William Merrick explained nonchalantly. 'Dig wet peat and it flows back to fill the pits. Build anything on it, sluices or walls, and come wet weather the foundations are rendered unstable. But with modern engineering methods these difficulties can be overcome.'

'Just like that?'

'They are not insurmountable problems,' Edmund soothed me.

I looked at him with dread weighing heavy in my chest. 'Perhaps those difficulties can be solved, but they may be the least of our concerns.' I ran my fingers across the plans. 'Once all this gets underway, I am not so confident that the problem of the commoners and freeholders can be so easily overcome.'

And if we could not overcome them . . . I heard an echo of my father's warning again. I did not want to forfeit the good will of my neighbours. I did not want to stir up discord and live amongst people I had turned into my enemies.

I went to find Bess in my chamber where she was brushing the dried mud off the hem of one of my gowns, a relentless task given that we lived in a world of mud.

'Bess, please stop what you're doing for a moment. I need to talk to you.'

She set the brush down, obediently but not willingly, waiting with belligerent eyes for me to speak. I took a deep breath. 'You know this has to happen sooner or later?' I realised I was echoing Mr Merrick's argument and hated myself for it.

'I never thought I'd see it. I never thought *you'd* do it.'

Edmund's argument then: 'Everyone stands to gain.'

'That's a lie, and you know it! We'll be left with a paltry share of land,

and the meanest, wettest share at that. My father keeps four cows and if we no longer have the common he will not be able to keep so much as a goose, and you ask me what we *lose* by it?'

'Bess, can't you see what Edmund is trying to do? Can't you see how drainage will transform Tickenham, how our land will become dry and warm and solid and full of fruit, with well-fed oxen and the fattest sheep? It will be like summer all year long.' I picked up the teasel she'd been using and waved it at her temptingly. 'No more mud?'

'Nothing wrong with mud.'

She held out her hand for the tool. I gave it to her with a sigh and she went back to her work. I had always told her everything, we had always shared our innermost thoughts. She was as dear to me as a sister. And yet she believed I had betrayed her.

Winter 1675

Spears of icicles still hung outside the window, frost flowers clung to the leaded panes. The floodwaters had turned to ice that extended all the way to Yatton.

I had been sitting by the window for days, for an eternity it seemed, my face white as the snow with fear. I had watched the ice whiten and thicken, blessedly changing from the thinner, deadly kind that was strong enough to hinder the passage of boats and yet not able to bear the weight of a man. Bess had brought a brazier of hot coals from the kitchen but I felt as frozen as the earth and the water. Still I vowed to keep my vigil until Edmund appeared.

Today the icicles were dripping, the frost flowers fading. The deadly ice would return. He should have been here by now; he should have been back from London days ago. He was no doubt waiting out the big freeze in some wayside inn, but I knew how perilous the rutted countryside tracks could be when they flooded and iced over. Horses frequently sank right up to their bellies in them. I was terrified in case he was lying frozen in an icy ditch somewhere, with his leg broken or his neck. I was terrified in case death should snatch him from me before my wedding day. I had worn the colours of mourning all my childhood. I did not want to feel like a widow before I had the chance to be a bride.

But now, at last, there were two dark shapes moving closer along the silver ribbon of causeway. Not one horse and rider but two. Just like the first time he had come to Tickenham.

Almost weeping with relief, I flung on my red riding cloak and raced outside as they came cantering into the yard, with their swords glinting like icicles at their sides.

Riding beside Edmund on an ebony Spanish stallion was a slim, black-haired boy, about twenty years of age. He was dressed in a long elaborate coat and breeches of jade silk, with flounces of elegant white lace at collar and cuffs. He wore knee-high riding boots and a shallow, wide-brimmed hat that danced with exotic green ostrich plumes. In the sparkling, white, winter world, he looked like a prince. His hair was glossy black as the King's, loosely curled and worn long enough to reach his shoulders. Framed by those black curls was the most exquisitely beautiful face: the face of an angel. His mouth was soft and sensitive with the slightest pout to his upper lip and little indentations at the corners, like dimples. His eyes were heavy-lidded, long-lashed, and of a sparkling blue, deeper and brighter than my own.

Seated on his impressive mount, his slender fingers resting lightly on the tooled saddle, he affected the elegant, heroic pose that distinguished the Cavaliers I'd been brought up to so scorn and to fear, but which had therefore always held for me a glamorous allure. Everything about him marked him out as just the type of young man my father had warned me against. It almost felt that simply by admitting him on to this land I was doing something dangerous and forbidden, something which could only end in trouble.

Except that he was smiling at me, a smile of gentle charm, the loveliest smile I had ever seen.

I had the strangest feeling that I was falling. I had completely forgotten my anxiety of moments before. I had completely forgotten who I was, a girl betrothed to be married. I could barely tear my eyes away from this beautiful stranger who seemed no stranger to me at all, but like someone whose image I had carried forever in my heart, held in my imagination like a promise of something more, something better, of escape, of the essence of life itself. The very idea of him spoke of colour and richness, of gaiety and beauty, in a life that had felt so drained of those things. And now at last he was here, he had come, and nothing could ever be the same for me again.

Edmund dismounted, bowed courteously and kissed my cheeks.

'I'm so glad you are safe, Edmund,' I said. 'I have been so worried.'

'We would not have been here now if I'd had my way,' he said. 'We almost turned back. But Richard was adamant we keep going.'

'Richard?' My lips shaped his name and I turned to him again as he removed his hat and swept it low. He bowed, his horse did a little prance and he pulled back smoothly on the reins.

'I'm pleased to meet you, sir,' I said. 'Edmund did not say that you were to come with him. What brings you to Somersetshire?'

He gazed searchingly into my face for a moment, said in an unusually soft-spoken voice: 'You do.'

The odd thing was that I was not at all surprised to hear it.

'As soon as I told Richard we were to be married, he insisted on coming to see you for himself,' Edmund explained cheerily.

His friend swung down from the saddle, his silver, star-shaped spurs jangling in the crisp air. He was tall, though not as tall as Edmund, his shoulders and chest not as broad, tapering to narrow hips and long legs.

'I congratulate you on an excellent choice, Edmund my friend,' he said warmly, his eyes never leaving my face. 'But even your glowing description did not do her justice. She is a dainty little maid for sure. I do fear, great ginger bear of a man that you are, you will crush her.'

Edmund smiled, not seeming at all put out by such an overt reference to bedsport, and any embarrassment I might have felt at this sally was outweighed by a mild sense of indignation. 'I assure you, sir,' I said. 'I am much stronger than I look.'

Richard laughed, but kindly. 'We shall soon see.'

He turned back to his horse and unstrapped from the saddle a small portmanteau inside which was a wooden box, elegantly wrapped in silver tissue and ribbons. He presented it to me, his blue eyes twinkling. 'A Twelfth Night gift for the bride-to-be, but since I am returning to London for the festivities, you may open it early.'

'Thank you,' I said, suddenly shy. 'That was very thoughtful of you.'

'Oh, you will find Richard a master of the grand gesture,' Edmund quipped.

I could not think what the box might contain. Too large and heavy by far to be the jewellery or gloves that Edmund always gave to me. Books perhaps.

Edmund came forward and pecked my cheek. 'I'll leave you in my friend's good care. The fire beckons and my toes need to thaw.'

I was nonplussed. 'We may as well all go inside.'

'You need to open your present out here,' Richard said. 'Don't worry, Edmund,' he added, turning his head slowly towards his friend but letting his eyes linger on mine, 'I shall not let anything happen to her. I promise to take very good care of her.'

'That is just what gives me cause for worry,' Edmund joked in parting. 'But even though I know what's in that box, I guarantee Eleanor will not fall at your feet like the rest of them. She's very different from other ladies.'

'I can see that,' Richard said quietly.

I untied the ribbon around the box and lifted off the lid. In the bottom lay two strips of metal attached to leather straps.

'You fasten them to your shoes,' Richard explained. 'They're for skating on the ice. They are all the fashion in the Fens since the Dutch brought the idea over. I had them forged 'specially,' he added quietly. 'I trust they're the right size? Edmund told me you had tiny feet.'

'They look to be a perfect fit. Thank you,' I said again, touched that he would have gone to so much trouble for a person he had never even met. I found that I could not look him in the face.

'Don't be shy with me,' he said very gently. 'I want to be your friend, if you will let me.'

I raised my eyes, a strange feeling in my belly that was like excitement but much nicer.

'Shall we be friends, do you think?' he asked, as if it mattered to him very much.

'Surely,' I said briskly, trying to hide my mounting confusion.

I moved quickly over to rest against the mounting block, trying to work out how to put the skates on. It would never have occurred to me to ask for directions. But my fingers were numb with cold, which didn't help.

'Ouch! Damn.' I dropped one of the skates on to the frozen yard and it rang out like the echo of the blacksmith's hammer that had beat it into shape. A bead of dark red blood had sprung up on the pad of my thumb.

'Be careful, they're very sharp.'

'You could have told me that before.'

'I didn't know you'd be so impatient.'

I glanced up, prepared to glare at him, but he was smiling at me again, a tender smile, with neat white teeth softly biting his lower lip and his dark eyebrows drawn up together in a little quizzical peak.

'Do you think you could help me?' I asked him.

'With the greatest pleasure.'

He sauntered over and took hold of my wrist with slender fingers that were partially covered by the intricately patterned lace at his cuffs. 'You are hurt,' he said. 'Let me see.'

The ruby bead of blood on my thumb had grown into a large droplet that was threatening to brim over and snake down my arm. Without preamble he lifted my hand and pushed my thumb into his beautiful mouth, and almost before I knew what was happening I felt his lips close around it, felt the hard, moist heat of his tongue slide round and over. He withdrew my thumb, looking with some amusement at my stunned expression: 'All better now, I think.'

My gaze shifted sideways in search of Edmund, not in appeal for help, but for guidance as to how I should manage this friend of his, with whom I now felt entirely out of my depth. But Edmund had gone which, oddly, helped put me at my ease. He knew what his friend was like; had no doubt seen him behave this way countless times. He would have known that such flirtation meant nothing at all. I reminded myself that Richard Glanville came from another world, a morally corrupt and licentious world that my father despised, a world that was entirely different from and far more sophisticated and complex than my own. This was evidently how people behaved in that world. The very last thing I wanted was to appear gauche or prudish, so I should just have to do my best to play along.

Richard had gone down on one knee at my feet to help me with the skates, but it did look for all the world as if he was going to ask me to be his wife.

'I am afraid you are too late, sir,' I said teasingly. 'I am already taken.'

He carried on adjusting a strap on the skate and, without fully lifting his head, smiled again, flicked up his sapphire eyes to look at me though his lashes, lowered them again to check what he was doing, raised them once more so swiftly that they sparkled. It was an extraordinarily coquettish gesture that left my bones feeling as if they had been turned to water. 'Maybe Edmund and I shall fight a duel over you,' he said. 'Would you like that?'

What was it my father had said about Cavaliers being murderous ruffians who would duel over a game of tennis? 'I should not like either of you to be wounded, or worse, for my sake.'

He lifted my right foot and placed it on his thigh. 'Already you care for me so much you don't want me to be hurt?'

'Not before you have taught me how to skate, at least. I should like to learn to swim too. You are very good at it, I hear.'

'You'd have to undress for me to teach you that.' He half raised the hem of my skirt. 'May I?'

It took me half a moment to realise he only needed to see what he was doing with the skate, was not seeking permission to strip me naked there and then. He was just a boy, but he seemed so cocksure, so well versed in the ways of men, that it was I, a betrothed woman, who was made to feel young and naive. I smiled down at this angel-faced, dark-haired boy who would seduce me away from his friend, and said, 'Please do.'

He tucked my skirt out of the way, cupping his hand around my heel. One of his fingers slipped over the top of my shoe and caressed my silk stocking. I wanted to snatch my foot away and yet I did not, could not. I clutched at the mounting block for support, sure that my legs would give way beneath me as shivers of sensation shot all the way up the insides of my thighs and carried on deep inside me until it felt as if the ice was cracking and splintering all around me and I was melting from the inside out.

He deftly secured the straps across first one foot and then the other. 'Have you never worn pattens?'

'No.'

'You don't know what they are, do you?'

'Please don't mock me, sir.'

'I would never mock you,' he replied seriously. 'Ladies in London strap pattens under their shoes,' he explained. 'So that they don't get spoiled in the filth.'

I laughed out loud at the very idea. 'London filth could never be so bad as living on a marsh! Here we just grow used to having dirty wet feet.'

He stood up, dusting down his green breeches. 'You deserve much better. Desire it too, I think.'

'Do you now?' I stood up and immediately wobbled over.

'Whoa! Steady.' He caught both my hands in his, held them for a moment longer than was necessary, blue eyes locked with mine, a strange expression in them now that was almost like sadness. He rested me back against the mounting block again. 'Wait for me.'

There was a small voice speaking inside my head. I refused to listen to it but it whispered: I have been waiting for you all of my life.

Richard had quickly strapped skates to his own boots. 'Ready?'

I nodded, not trusting myself to speak and then, gripping his arm for support, I hobbled with him across to the edge of the ice.

He let go of me and strode gracefully out on to it with total mastery and control. 'One step at a time,' he cautioned, spinning round to face me with a hiss of blades cutting ice. 'I suspect it is completely against your nature, but you need to go slowly at first.'

It couldn't be as hard as all that, could it? I stepped out determinedly and immediately felt my foot slip away alarmingly beneath me. I tightened my muscles and froze.

'Not as easy as you thought?' Richard's eyes sparkled as bright as sunlight on water. He offered me his hand and I took it. I was glad of the tightness of his grip as he slid forward, pulling me with him. I wobbled once but didn't fall.

He slipped his hand beneath my cloak and around my waist, and I felt the hard strength of his young body against mine as he held me steady at his side.

'Right, left, march,' he commanded. I had just enough time to think how, spoken in his softly melodious voice, military language was powerful and compelling, rather than friendly but formal as it had sounded to me on Edmund's lips. 'Hold tight on to me.'

We shot forward with dizzying speed. I was gliding beside him, not daring to take my eyes off my feet, appearing and disappearing beneath my skirt, following his lead. It was more like dancing than marching, a mysterious, forceful kind of dance, and I could feel the muscles of Richard's strong legs working as they pressed against mine, feel his arm encircling me tight, our skates slicing parallel lines with a swishing sound, like a sword being drawn or the noise a comet or a falling star might make if only you could hear it.

And then I looked up and realised how fast we were going, a dizzying, magnificent speed such as I had never thought possible. Faster than a galloping stallion, faster than the wind.

He glanced at me, smiling with pleasure at my obvious delight.

'Let me go,' I said. 'I can do it now.'

'Are you sure?'

'Yes.'

Suddenly I was on my own, racing forward. I pushed my legs into the glide, harder and harder, until I picked up even more speed. I screamed with glee but the wind snatched away my voice, my very breath. I cut an arc towards the causeway, the sunken trees whizzing past, the clouds wheeling overhead.

I lifted my arms to each side of me like wings, as I liked to do when I was running. This time I was really soaring. My cloak flew out behind me. At last I really did have wings, like the swans and the butterflies. I was no longer earthbound. For the first time in my life I felt utterly free. I was flying.

I skated right into Richard Glanville's arms. He caught me as I skidded to an abrupt halt and I was thrown against the hardness of his chest, wind-blown, laughing, my face aglow. 'You never told me how to stop.'

'I never expected you to go so fast.'

I was motionless but the world carried on spinning around me faster than ever, the trees and clouds whipped up like a storm. I clung on to him as if he was the still centre of my orbit. I couldn't let go of him or I was sure I would fall. He had taught me how to fly. Like an eagle, he had seized me and carried me up with him into the infinite sky, and if he released me I should come crashing down again and be shattered.

'That was extraordinary.'

'It is you who are extraordinary, Eleanor Goodricke.' There was not a hint of flirtation in his voice any more. He had slipped his hands inside my cloak again, to either side of my narrow corseted waist, and though I was perfectly balanced now, he had not let go of me. 'You are utterly fearless,' he said. 'A little force of nature.' Wisps of hair had blown free across my face. He brushed them away with the tip of one finger. 'A little Viking. Golden flames without signifying golden flames within, I wonder?'

I slipped backwards away from him, like a boat casting off from the shore. 'That is for my husband to find out.'

He held on to my extended arms until only our fingertips were touching.

As Edmund had once been a beacon of light in the dark hall so now was this boy, in rich green velvet, a single point of colour in a white wilderness, as glamorous and gleaming and as rare and precious as an emerald.

He must not be. Could never be. I loved Edmund. I had always loved

Edmund. I must not let myself be attracted to this man. He was no more than a boy in any case, a dangerous, raffish boy, and I was promised to another. I was promised to his friend.

I twirled round as if I was in the tailor's shop once more, trying on my first gown. With a swirl of my crimson cloak I skated off in a wide sweep, into the sparkling white world.

'You learn very quickly,' Richard called.

I shouted back to him over my shoulder, 'You'll never keep up with me now.'

His voice came to me on the icy wind. 'I shall enjoy trying.'

The next day was one of unremittingly bright sunshine, of surprising warmth and strength for the time of year, and it raised the temperature well above freezing. By mid-morning it was slowly but surely thawing the ice, laying upon it a shimmering sheen of treacherous water, ruining any hopes I'd had of being able to go skating again and practically confining all three of us to the house, since conditions were not fit for riding either.

'How about a game of dicing?' Edmund suggested when he had finished his small beer and cheese. 'Or cards perhaps?'

'I'd rather chess,' Richard said amiably.

'I'm sure you would.' Edmund grinned. 'But at least I have half a chance of beating you if some luck is involved.' He glanced at me considerately. 'Besides, only two can play chess.'

'Oh, please don't worry on my account,' I said, reaching for Edmund's hand and giving it a quick pat. 'I'll read.'

'Maybe Eleanor should play against you, Richard,' Edmund suggested. 'She beats me more often than not.'

'No,' I said quickly, picking up a travelogue that had just arrived from the bookseller. 'You two play.'

Bess brought a tray of hot, spiced cider and I made myself comfortable by the fireside as Richard and Edmund drew up chairs to the little table by the window and perused the chessboard.

I read a little, sipped the cider, watched as Richard reached across to pick up a black marble knight, the trailing lace at his cuff almost upending Edmund's castle. I went back to the story of a sailing ship battling the storms of Cape Horn and had read a dozen or so pages, become quite lost in the adventure, when, with that strange sixth sense that tells us we are being observed, I looked up to find Richard's eyes resting on me. Edmund was deciding on his next move, totally absorbed in his pawns and knights, and I wondered how long his friend had been studying me. As our eyes met he gave me a lovely, enigmatic smile. There was a fragility about it, as if despite the physical strength that made him such a good rider, swimmer and skater, there was within him a part that was not so strong, could easily be damaged, had perhaps been damaged already, and it stirred in me an unexpected protectiveness. He seemed so different today from the boy I had skated with, not nearly so self-assured, and I was intrigued by the change in him. Had something shaken his confidence, or was that confidence just a disguise, a mask that easily slipped?

I smiled back at him and his blue eyes seemed to light up, illuminating his whole face. I was struck afresh by his beauty, the almost feminine prettiness which contrasted so starkly with his long, lean legs, stretched out in front of him, booted ankles crossed, in a way that was utterly, powerfully male.

Edmund made his move and Richard languidly picked up his cider, drank, turned back to the chess pieces. He moved his black queen without appearing to give it any thought at all.

'Hah.' Edmund gave his castle a triumphant nudge. 'Checkmate.'

Richard lounged back in the chair. 'So it is,' he said with an air of indifference.

'Well, well,' Edmund chortled. 'When was the last time I won against you at chess?'

'I can't remember, it was so long ago,' Richard smiled very charmingly.

'You've not been concentrating, lad,' Edmund replied. 'You've not had your mind on the game at all.'

The evening was marked by the most magnificent winter sunset. Badly needing to escape the house, I walked down to the bridge the better to enjoy it. The vast sky was streaked with crimson and bright orange, soft pink and mauve, and it was reflected in the wide sheets of icy water. It was as if I hung suspended in a shimmering world of radiant colour.

As if from nowhere the sky was filled with swarms of chattering starlings, a black mass against the inflamed sky, swirling and spilling down in unbroken ribbons to fill the branches of the bare trees then swirling up again as if blown by unseen winds, the whole throng plunging, turning in on itself, sucked upwards in a spiralling current and then sweeping out again horizontally. How did they do it? How did they all know which way to go? It was an awesome sight and I was struck with an almost desperate desire to preserve the magic and the wildness of this place for my children, and for theirs. Suddenly it seemed the greatest tragedy and folly that it would be lost.

Or maybe it would not be, I thought, ever hopeful.

What made William Merrick and his partners so sure they would succeed where more grandiose schemes had failed, where even the agents of the Crown had failed? King James himself had been thwarted in his repeated efforts to drain the peat lands of Kings Sedgemoor. Cornelius Vermuyden, the greatest drainage engineer there was, under a commission from Cromwell, as Lord Protector, had had his bill rejected because the tenants and freeholders did not consent. His skills as a drainage engineer, his owner-ship of a third of the land and his position of influence, could not prevail against the opposition of the commoners.

And there was similar opposition in Tickenham. I sensed it now: when-ever I went up to the village with Mary, or in my daily dealings with the servants. Talks with local families were underway, to untangle and settle the complicated claims for common rights, to establish the validity of the claims and allot land in proportion, but resentment seethed not far beneath the surface. It expressed itself in surliness; small acts of defiance that became increasingly annoying and disturbing. Ink spilled on one of my father's books that nobody admitted was their fault, general refusal to pay rents on time, my little mare lamed by a rusted iron nail that had mysteriously been driven into her hoof. It could have been an accident but I suspected it was not.

It was not just the local commoners who were implicated but uplands farmers and freeholders and tenants who had enjoyed unlimited grazing rights here and had taken cattle in for fattening from other areas for a fee.

I didn't like to think what would happen if these near and far-flung neighbours of mine were to rise up and act together to try to put a stop to what we had determined to do. It had happened in the Fens: mobs and gangs destroying the work of the engineers, ripping out the sluices, filling in the drains as quickly as they were dug. I could imagine all too easily how such violence could rip apart this little community – after all, it had happened in the Civil War.

I felt the lightest touch in the small of my back and turned to see that it was Richard, not Edmund, who had come to find me. My heart gave an odd little flutter.

'There will still be sunsets even when the water is gone, you know,' he said perceptively.

'But they won't look like that.'

He raised his eyes skyward, making them seem bigger and bluer and more beautiful than ever. 'No,' he admitted softly, lowering them slowly again to look out over the lake, and then at me. 'They won't.'

The colours were changing, deepening to shades of luminous rose-pink. Like this, with the sky lit with the most wondrous shades and the swans and wild geese like silhouettes sailing on a bright sea, it was impossible to see it as a dark or unwholesome place. It was surely the loveliest place on earth. Even when the colour faded and the mist swirled in, it brought with it a mysterious sense of peace, a special haunting beauty that I realised now I would miss dreadfully. I listened to the wild bugle call of the swans, the sepulchral clap of their great white wings, and felt such a sense of loss it was almost overwhelming.

'You feel bound to this place,' Richard said, not as a question but a statement of fact. 'And it to you. For as long as you live. You do not want it to change, to be lost. It will be like losing a part of yourself that you can never get back.'

I turned to him, startled. 'Yes.' I might have said more, but he looked almost grief-stricken and I was afraid of treading too close to the source of whatever was causing him such hurt.

'Edmund is so keen for it to happen,' I said.

'But what about you? What do you want?'

'Oh, nobody really stopped to ask me.'

'I am asking you now.'

'Edmund is so certain that what we are doing is for the good of all,' I said after a moment. 'I wish I shared that certainty.'

'Better that you do not.'

'Is it?'

'It means you care,' he said. 'You care about what it will mean to the people who live here.'

I should have been astounded that this man who rode Spanish stallions and was dressed now in a velvet cloak and the finest lace should spare even a thought for commoners and tenants. And yet I was not at all.

'It is not only their land and their rights they are losing,' he said with fierce empathy. 'It is their independence, the ability to provide the basic necessities of life for their families, that is at stake. And pride. There is pride in being able to put bread into your children's mouths, in seeing them grow strong on milk from your own cow and eggs from your own hens. Edmund has no comprehension – how could he be expected to have? How could you? And yet you do, don't you? You think about such things.'

I smiled. 'Sometimes too much, perhaps.' I paused, glanced at him. 'You too, I think.'

'Since time began, men have been prepared to fight and die to defend their land,' he said. 'It makes no difference if that land is a miserable strip, good for nothing but a few vegetables, or a thousand acres of fields and meadows.' It was as if he had ceased talking about the commoners now, nameless people he did not know, but was speaking from some direct personal experience, and I was sure then that his must have been one of the Royalist families who had suffered from the sequestration of their estates under Cromwell – except that he was surely too young to remember it, to feel it so deeply. So deeply that I felt entirely prevented from asking him about it.

I shivered and, seeing that I was cold, he wordlessly took off his cloak, draped it around my shoulders. Heat drawn from his body still clung to the fabric of it and I pulled it closer about me than I needed to for warmth alone. The collar felt very soft against my cheek.

Richard cupped his hands round his mouth, blew on his fingers.

'Now I am warm and you are cold.' I smiled. 'We should go back.'

'Not yet,' he said. 'It is so lovely here, and I shall be leaving for London in the morning.'

'You are very welcome to stay,' I said, the words coming unbidden. 'For as long as you like.'

'That is kind of you,' he said, his tone strangely tight. 'But I cannot.'

As we walked back to the house I wondered what he had meant, wondered at the sadness behind his beautiful eyes, but as we were approaching the yard something else broke into my thoughts. My nostrils twitched and I inhaled, like a wild creature alert to the first sign of danger. A smell of smoke. The air over the stables was thick with a grey pall that was not mist. I almost heard the crackle of the flames before I saw them, bright and luminous as the sunset had been. I heard the panicked whinnying and snorting of the horses, the frantic thudding of their hooves against the stable door. The whole of the building was ablaze.

I ran, shouting for someone to come, for someone to help.

Ned was already running from the kitchen garden.

'The horses!' I yelled. 'Help me get them out.'

'I'll go,' Richard said to me. 'You stay here.'

But I was already inside the burning stable. The smoke was so thick and billowing that I couldn't see where I was going, couldn't breathe. I choked and covered my mouth with the edge of my cloak. My eyes stung as if scorched and the heat was a solid barrier in front of me, pressing me back, tongues of fire leaping and writhing. I bent my arm up over my face, pushed forward through flames that were licking through straw and bedding, leaping from the roof and the hayloft and from the bubbling, cracking walls. I smelt the bitter stench of singed horsehair.

The horses were bucking, their eyes rolling in terror. With my hand on the halter and using the most soothing words I could marshal, I dragged out Edmund's hunter, let him bolt for the safety in the direction of the church-yard where Richard's stallion was already heading. I dived back in for my little grey mare and her foal, not able to find my way to their stall. The walls of the stable were sheets of fire now, the roaring sound like an angry mob. A length of timber crashed to the ground in front of me in an eruption of crimson sparks which stung like demonic gnats from Hell. I couldn't see where I was, which way I had come and which was the way out. Then I felt a hand grasp mine, pull me back just in time as another beam came smashing down on the place where I had been standing a second before.

'This way!' Richard shouted.

I could barely see him. He was just a hand to hold on to in the fiery darkness and I gripped it tight, let him lead me to safety.

'They're all out, miss,' Ned shouted, leading a cob in one hand and the carthorse in the other.

I bent double and coughed, rubbed my sore, stinging eyes.

'Here, drink this.' From somewhere Richard had produced a cup of water and I tipped it gratefully down my dry throat. 'Are you all right?' he asked.

'Yes. Thank you. Are you?'

He nodded, raised his arm and turned his head into it to wipe the smuts and sweat off his brow.

Bess and Mistress Keene and Jane the cookmaid were all running back and forth across the yard with water buckets, doing their best to douse the flames. I ran to Jane and took the other side of a handle, helping her carry a heavy bucket, to lift it up and throw the contents over the fire. I was about to run and fetch some more when someone stopped me.

'It's no use, Eleanor.' It was Edmund who held me back as the flames leapt towards the sky. 'It's no use.'

I pulled away from him in a fury. The flames were licking round the whole of the building, fanned by the breeze that was blowing off the moor, towards the cow byre . . . towards the house. 'We can't just give up, damn it! We must at least try to contain it, make sure it doesn't spread. Please God,' I heard myself say, 'don't let it spread to the house.'

'It won't,' Richard said.

I stopped fighting against Edmund for a moment and looked to his friend, his face still smeared with soot just as mine must be and his eyes full of compassion, as if he felt my anxiety in his very core and wanted only to ease it. 'It is raining,' he said, with an upward glance at the darkening sky. 'The rain will put the fire out.'

Rain was by no means a rare occurrence in Somersetshire in September, but this felt like a miracle. It was just a fine drizzle, so fine that I had not immediately felt it, but in minutes it had turned into a typical autumn deluge of heavy, fat raindrops which poured down from the darkening sky and did for us the work of a hundred men and buckets.

I let it lash me, soak me, saw it washing the soot in black streaks from my skin. I turned my face to the rain as I usually would to the sun, letting it pour down upon me, over me, cleanse and cool me. I had never been so glad of rain in all my life. I opened my lips and drank it in, letting it rid me of the foul, choking taste of soot. The taste of the water on my tongue was sweet as wine.

In hardly any time the stable had been reduced to a smoking ruin, a blackened skeleton. It was still hissing angrily like a snake, would smoulder for a long time yet.

'What could have started it?' Edmund asked.

'I don't know.'

There was straw and hay aplenty in the stable, and when Ned had slept there, before he married Bess, there would have been tallow candles with naked flames. But Ned had not slept above the horses for years. Nobody did now.

Richard bent down, picked up something that had been discarded or dropped in haste on the ground. He held it out in his hand and looked at me. It was a battered liquor flask, an empty liquor flask, and no words were necessary. *Since time began men have been prepared to fight and die to defend their land*. The fire was no accident. It was no coincidence that as the day when the drainage project would start grew ever closer, a fire had been started. Discontent had ignited something dangerous and sinister.

I was kneeling on the rush-strewn church floor by the altar, helping Mary arrange branches of greenery to decorate it for Christmas. The whole place was filled with the warm spicy scent of the rosemary and bay that adorned the pews. We'd lit a dozen candles and the light of them gleamed on the gilded candlesticks and dark oak.

We were keeping the front of the aisle clear for the musicians and theatre troupe to perform the nativity play. Afterwards there would be fiddlers and drummers and a wassail procession, dancing and feasting and Blind Man's Buff. If I were to be denied a grand wedding celebration, I would at least enjoy the Christmas festivities to the full. I was determined to find the charm in the cake and be Queen For a Day.

'It will be wonderful to be married in London, even quietly,' Mary said, knowing where my thoughts often strayed these days.

I handed her another bough of holly. 'You must come with us. Please say you will?'

She was expertly twisting ivy around the holly and didn't take her eyes off her task. 'We shall already be there.'

I assumed she meant she'd be visiting her mother and younger brother, the only members of her family who had survived the plague and who still lived in Southwark.

She stopped what she was doing and glanced at me. 'I've been meaning to tell you, Eleanor, John and I are leaving Tickenham. We're returning to live in London.'

I felt as if I had suddenly lost my way in a dark wood. 'Leaving?'

'I promised your father that I would take care of you, but you are grown now and about to be a wife. It's my mother and my brother Johnnie who need looking after.'

She came to put her arms around me, as if I was still the orphan child I felt myself to be, not the girl who disguised herself in the colourful gowns of a lady and hid behind a pretence of self-possession and poise. 'Come now, it's not so bad. You can visit whenever you like.'

I thought I might cry. 'But I shall miss you so much.'

'I shall miss you too.' Mary was past thirty but still looked young, her waist and breasts only slightly more plump. 'You have been my blessing, Eleanor. Each time another month passed and still I bled, I thanked God for the little girl he had already given to me. That though the cradle was empty, my arms were always full.'

'Oh, Mary.'

'It is you who showed me my vocation, with your love of learning and constant quest for knowledge. You were our first little pupil, and always the most special. John and I are going to run a boarding school.'

I grasped both of her hands. 'You will be excellent tutors, both of you. There could be none better. Oh, I wish I could come, Mary. I wish I could come with you and help you with your school.'

Her smile hid a hint of concern. 'Your life now is with your new husband, with Edmund.' She peered into my face. 'Eleanor, you do still want to marry him?'

I glanced away. 'Of course.'

I could not tell her that my most precious possessions were now the little skates Richard Glanville had given to me, could not tell her of the strange, secret vice I did not seem able to give up. Every night before I went to sleep I took the skates out of their box and stroked them, ran my finger along the blade, dangerously close to the sharp edge, risking a cut, almost wanting a cut, wanting to feel that sharp sting of pain so I could better remember the warmth of his mouth as he had sucked my pain away.

I was no wiser about the source of his own pain, afraid that if I tried to talk to Edmund about him, if I so much as allowed Richard's name to touch my lips, I would give myself away.

'You've been so good to me, Mary.'

'It is kind of you to say so, but I'm not so sure your father would agree. I fear he'd be of the opinion I'd led you a long way off the path of righteousness.'

'No, he wouldn't.'

She looked at me, considering her words before she spoke. 'Do you remember the prayers we used to say, Eleanor? How we came here when the church was empty, like it is now, and lit candles for all those we loved who were no longer with us: your sister and mother and father, and my father and brothers and sisters, who had all perished in the plague year? Do you remember that we asked that they be safe and happy in Heaven?'

I nodded.

'Eleanor, you do know it's only Catholics who say prayers for the souls of the dead?'

There had seemed nothing wrong in it at the time. It had seemed a fitting thing to do.

'In my heart, I converted to Catholicism a long time ago,' Mary continued, keeping her voice as quiet as if the ancient stones of the church might be listening.

I stared at her in utter disbelief. 'You are Catholic?'

'I would never have practised while I had you to mind. It would have felt like the most dreadful betrayal of your father. Now our work here is done and we are leaving, I am free to follow my own conscience.'

I had grown up so steeped in anti-Catholicism that I couldn't help but look at her with a mixture of dismay and horror. I turned away, towards the simple altar. Once so carefully divested of crucifixes, gilded cloths or other obvious Catholic trappings, it looked almost Papist now, festooned with greenery and ablaze with candles.

'And is John a Catholic too? But how can he be? When he delivered his sermon on Gunpowder Treason Night he thanked God for delivering England from the hellish plots of the papists.'

Mary smiled. 'John is a follower, not a leader. As you are well aware, he is easily influenced. He can see all sides and goes wherever the wind blows him, so long as he believes it to be God's wind. He would like nothing more than for England to be a haven of religious pluralism. He was a Puritan while ever Puritans were shouting the loudest, until the new laws meant he would have lost his pulpit if he'd clung to such ideology. He was happy to be called a Protestant then, though your father could still bring out the Puritan in him. Now I am to become a Catholic, he'll convert with me. I can help him see the reason in it.'

I was suddenly consumed with terror for her and gripped her arm. 'But, Mary, it's so dangerous. If only you could hear the things Mr Merrick and his Bristol friends discuss over their claret. The Duke of York's declaration of his conversion to Rome, and the Test Act that has expelled Catholics from public office . . . they have made fear of Popery greater than ever. It is worse for Catholics even than it was when everyone blamed the Great Fire on the treachery and malice of a Papist plot. There have been Pope burnings all across London and even here in Somersetshire, in Bridgwater.'

'It's almost as if the Civil War has never ended,' Mary agreed quietly. 'There's no safe side to be on. One moment our enemy is the Papists, the next the Dutch, then it's the French or even our own neighbours. Intolerance and suspicion are as rife as they ever were when the Roundheads and Cavaliers were slaughtering each other in their beds. Effigies of the Pope are burned on bonfires. I'd not even be surprised to see Thomas Knight cry witchcraft when he sees you chasing after butterflies. It's not safe to be different, but different you are. And so am I. And what is the good of living if we must live a lie, if we cannot be true to ourselves?'

I stared at the candlelit altar, lovely and glittering and, to be quite honest, far more appealing to me now than it ever was under my father's direction. Just as the maypole had once looked lovely to me too, even though I knew it to be evil and Popish. But was it truly? I was back beside my father's grave again, in my black taffeta funeral cape, and the ground was falling away beneath my feet. Was nothing I had grown up believing in actually true?

I looked at Mary, the first Catholic I had ever known. There were so many questions buzzing in my head, I did not know where to begin. 'I was taught to despise Catholics. I was taught that they are hell-spawn, the Anti-Christ.'

'Except that you do not despise me, do you?'

'Never.'

She smiled. 'Do I appear any different to you now at all? Do I look evil to you?'

I looked deep into her soft brown eyes and slowly shook my head. 'Of course you do not.'

I realised I was no better than the commoners who had always been prejudiced against me, for being a Puritan and a girl with an interest in science.

'You are not your father,' Mary said gently. 'You do not have to hate Catholics because he did. Your mind is your own.'

'What if I do not always know my mind?'

'That means it is an open one like John's, a good one.'

Was it? I thought of Richard, the most beautiful, intriguing boy, a person my father would have reviled.

I realised I had not even asked the reason for her conversion. 'Why, Mary?'

'My namesake, for one,' she replied simply. 'Far better for womanhood to have saintly, motherly Mary as their guide than to be left with only wicked Grandmother Eve, don't you think?'

I could not disagree with her.

'The Catholics have women for saints, too.' She let me ponder that for a moment. 'I believe, in time, women will accomplish much in this world as well, by example from the next.'

The week after Christmas Edmund received a letter from his brother, telling of a severe flood in the Fens that had caused much damage: washed away whole cottages, uprooted ancient trees, torn down bridges, ripped up gravestones, made ancient droves and trackways vanish as if they had never been.

'But I thought there could be no more floods now the land had been reclaimed?' It felt as though my heart had come up into my throat and I swallowed hard, as if to force it down.

'So did I. So did we all.' Edmund stared at the letter in disbelief then concentrated on folding it very slowly, as if it was important to replicated the original creases exactly. 'It seems the dried out peat is shrinking. And as the surface of the land dries, crumbs of soil are picked up and carried away by the Fen winds. The rivers are now running higher than the fields around them.'

I was horrified by the image of such an upside down, unnatural world. It seemed the stuff of nightmares. My father's nightmares. 'That's why Mr Merrick didn't want me to go to Suffolk with you, isn't it? He didn't want me to see what was happening.'

'My brother says the fear is that serious floods will become commonplace.'

'So Papa was right about that after all,' I said tremulously. 'We are fools to think we can tamper with God's creation.'

'No,' Edmund said firmly. 'We learn by our mistakes. What the engineers are trying to accomplish is a monumental feat. There will inevitably be setbacks.'

'But we must call a halt to the plans for Tickenham,' I said resolutely. 'Edmund, you do see that? We cannot proceed until we know how to avoid these same problems here.'

'I doubt even William Merrick and his associates would argue with the prudence of that.'

So, a reprieve.

Spring 1676

The next time Richard Glanville visited Tickenham Court, he came riding up the lane past the rectory in sharp spring sunshine and apple-blossom scented air, with an invitation from our most illustrious neighbour George Digby no less, to attend a banquet and dancing at Clevedon Court that very same evening. I had been gathering marsh orchids to take to Bess's mother, whose rheumatism was troubling her so much she wasn't able to venture far to pick any for herself.

'We're all three of us invited,' Richard said, leaning forward, arms lightly crossed and resting on the pommel as he smiled very gallantly down at me from the elegantly tooled saddle of a powerful Barbary bay. His dark curls were tumbling to his shoulders – in a way my father would have considered a sure sign of a debauched and decadent character, I swiftly reminded myself. He was more modestly dressed today than before, though the riding suit of smooth brown wool that he was wearing did not detract from the beauty of his face but, rather, threw it into relief, like a lovely and perfect pearl set upon a bed of homespun. 'Digby's welcome extends to me, to you and to Edmund,' he said, then glanced towards the house. 'I take it he's here?'

'He is.' It was Edmund's last visit before he became my husband and this house his permanent home. Before Tickenham became his.

Richard swung down from his horse and stood before me, making a cursory examination of the bouquet of purple and white flowers in my hand. 'You look as delighted by my news as a little maid who's never been dancing before,' he said, with gentle amusement. 'Or is it that you are just pleased to see me?'

He had the most expressive brows, I noticed. Silky, dark and high-arched, the way they had of drawing together at a slightly oblique slant when he smiled was very endearing and highlighted the humour in his eyes.

'As a matter of fact, I haven't ever been to a dance before,' I said, a little defensively. 'But I do know all the steps.'

'Then, since it is I who brought your first invitation, I hope you will reward me by allowing me to have the first dance with you?'

There was invitation to much more than a dance in those lovely twinkling blue eyes of his, but I was wise to his flirtation now and met them boldly. 'I would be honoured to dance with you,' I said. 'So long as Edmund does not mind.'

He looked so discouraged and unhappy at this that it made me feel as if I had been unnecessarily cruel, and I was struck again by a strangely compelling need to reassure him in some way.

'However did you manage it?' I asked brightly. 'I've lived but four miles away from Clevedon Court all my life and not once have I been past the gatehouse.'

Richard gave a nonchalant shrug. 'I met one of the Digby girls and her father out riding just now, and introduced myself.'

I laughed. 'You just rode up and introduced yourself to the Earl of Bristol?'

His confidence was apparently entirely restored, I was glad to see, and he smiled at me as if to say, What of it?

George Digby, Earl of Bristol, was one of the most striking figures of our time, a great orator in the House of Commons and a remarkably handsome person of irrepressible good spirits. He had assumed a great mystique for me because of the staunch disapproval he had earned from my father for his role as advisor to the first King Charles. The Digby family had suffered dispossession at the hands of Oliver Cromwell's army, and only recently had Clevedon Court been restored to them.

Richard turned his head and flashed a smile at Edmund who came hurrying over, face lit with pleasure at the sight of his friend. He trapped him in a rough hug that Richard returned with as much affection.

'I cannot wait for a banquet before I eat,' Edmund said, after they had discussed the invitation. 'I'm ravenous.'

'When are you not?' Richard said laughingly. 'Shall we go and catch something fresh for an early supper then?'

He rode off with Edmund over the moor with their fishing rods and I went inside to fetch a book. My father's library had been returned to me in its entirety after my betrothal and I chose a volume, going to sit on the sunny grass by the walnut tree to read. I found I could not settle but kept reading the same line over and over again without taking it in. All I saw before me was Richard Glanville's face, his smile, as if it had been burned on to my brain.

The shadows were lengthening when Edmund came back with a brace of gleaming pike.

'Well done,' I said as I stood up and he kissed my cheek, handing over his catch with pride. 'We shall have them baked with almonds. Where's Richard?'

'Oh, he wanted to stay by the river a while longer.'

Richard rode up not long after, his own catch slung over his shoulder. He had taken off his coat and his frilled white linen shirt was undone, revealing a scattering of fine, dark chest hairs. I clasped my hands together, as if I did not trust myself not to slip my fingers inside his shirt and stroke them.

'We'd go hungry if it was left to Edmund here,' he said to me sweetly, producing not a brace but half a dozen larger fish, their translucent tails almost as wide as the span of his hand. He stuck his tongue into the side of his cheek. 'The rivers here are very bountiful, if only you know what you are about.'

Edmund was shaking his head in affectionate disbelief. 'How the devil did you manage to land all those?' He chuckled softly. 'I should have known you'd not be outdone, especially when there is a pretty lady to impress. Eleanor, you must look suitably amazed by this plenitude or the effort will all have been in vain.'

'It is an excellent catch,' I said offhandedly, keeping my eyes very firmly fixed on the fish rather than the person who had caught them.

I was thankful that I had a new gown to wear to Clevedon Court. It was made of sea-green silk with a beaded stomacher and a long, tight, off-the-shoulder bodice. Bess arranged my hair, so that long elaborate curls framed my face, and decorated it with tiny pearls. I wore an emerald necklace and eardrops that Edmund had given me.

Richard was waiting in the great hall. As I descended the stairs from the solar, he turned and fastened his eyes on me.

'You look beautiful,' he said, almost bleakly.

'Thank you.'

Standing alone in the gloomy, cavernous hall, he looked very young, troubled, a little lost. He wore a heavy pewter ring on the middle finger of his left hand, and was twisting it back and forth in a way that must chafe at his skin. I wanted to put my hand over his and hold his fingers still. Wanted at least to ask him if he was all right.

But Edmund came up behind me then and wrapped me in a dark green velvet cloak that had once belonged to my Aunt Elizabeth, who had passed quietly and peacefully from this world the winter before he and I were betrothed. 'Time to go,' he said.

It was a clear night, almost a full moon, and the wide, wild, featureless landscape was flooded with a milk-white light. Edmund wore a topaz brocade vest and coat, and Richard was very elegant in a coat of burgundy silk, so that as we rode out three abreast at dusk, I felt like a princess with her handsome young courtiers trotting to either side, swords at their hips.

As we made our way up the Tickenham Road to Clevedon, we were joined by a stream of fine coaches. More were already drawn up outside the house where flaming torches had been lit. Clevedon Court was a medieval manor on a much grander scale than Tickenham, with a massive thirteenth century tower and great hall twice the size and a hundred years older than Tickenham Court's.

Tonight it was lit up even brighter than a church at Christmastime. Candlelight gleamed on the oak-panelled walls and long polished tables laid with silver platters and engraved glasses. Musicians were playing: a lute, viola, cello, oboe and bassoon.

We were introduced to George Digby, Earl of Bristol, resplendent in crimson and gold, but I was so overawed just to be in his presence in such magnificent surroundings that I barely noticed what he said, except that it was something about how he hoped I could set aside my father's prejudices, so that we might be strangers no longer. We ate a feast of roast gull and lark, stuffed swan and Carbonado, drank claret and sack, then had sweet-meats in the parlour while we waited for the tables to be cleared away.

'Are you enjoying yourself?' Richard asked me.

'Never more.' I smiled at him 'I hope you are too.'

'You would not look at me when I came back from the river this after-noon,' he said quietly. 'Why? What did I do?'

I was stunned. 'You didn't do anything.' I said, wondering what in the world had happened to him to make him so sensitive. 'I'm sorry if I offended you.'

Everyone was moving back into the hall.

'Dance with me,' he urged, and before I had a chance to ask for Edmund's blessing, he had led me away into a courant. At first I was so busy concen-trating on counting the vigorous beats that I did not even notice the feel of his hand pressing warmly against my boned waist, as it had done when we skated.

Then his soft black curls tickled my face as he leaned in towards me, his cheek against mine, to whisper something in my ear. 'Look at me,' he murmured. 'Not at your feet.'

I turned my eyes up to his, his face still so close to mine that I could feel the warmth of his breath. The irises of his eyes were intricate and delicate as flower petals.

'I'll not let you make a mistake,' he said, as if referring to far more than dance steps, but I had no time to consider his meaning because I was so determined not to put a foot wrong.

One, two, three. Pause, hop, glide, turn. I quickly found, though, that I did not need him to guide me at all. As my dance master had said, dancing came to me as easily as walking. I stopped concentrating and let my body move as it had always yearned to do. I let myself be swept up in the glorious swish and rustle of silk clothes, the tap and drag of leather-soled shoes.

'I knew you would dance as gracefully as you skate,' Richard murmured to me.

'So do you,' I replied, wishing to God that he would stop looking at me like that, as if he wanted to eat me.

The music changed to the sarabande, a slow and halting Spanish dance. I had never been held so close by a man before. It was an extraordinary sensa-tion to feel the heat of his body close to mine, to feel the muscles in his chest and arms and legs, the sway of his slim hips as we moved to the alien rhythm. I knew that, for the rest of my life, whenever I heard the sarabande I would be back in this room, with Richard. It was like a wonderful dream, the sounds and sights so piercingly bright and colourful that I was spellbound.

'So if you have never been to a ball, Edmund has never danced with you?' he enquired.

I shook my head.

Richard seemed inordinately pleased by that news. 'Shame on him. He does not know what he is missing.'

Except that, seemingly, he did. On the edge of my vision I glimpsed Edmund coming towards us as the music faded and felt a stab of shame for having abandoned him for so long. I smiled across at him and immediately made to excuse myself from Richard. But he held on to my hand as tightly as if he was trying to stop me from sliding over the side of a boat into a floodtide, or as if he himself was slipping away.

I tried surreptitiously to tug myself free, but when it was clearly no use, and as Edmund came closer, I pulled our still interlocked hands behind me in a vain attempt to hide them in the folds of my skirts.

'My turn now, I think,' Edmund said amiably. 'You'll have to let her go, I'm afraid, my friend. She's to be my bride, after all.'

Richard slipped his fingers through mine, weaving us together, and drew me imperceptibly but firmly closer to him, away from Edmund. 'One more dance,' he bargained. His tone was mischievous and yet it was underlaid with a challenge that was entirely serious, so that I was caught between feeling touched, amused, embarrassed and annoyed.

Edmund was merely annoyed. 'Damn it, lad,' he hissed under his breath, the first time I had ever seen him riled, 'you go too far. Unhand her.' The trumpets sounded for Lord Monk's March and Edmund stepped between us. 'Now.'

Richard's eyes darkened to indigo and anger flared in them, as sudden and as bright as quicksilver. But he had no alternative but to release me or else cause a spectacle. He relaxed his hold on my hand and I took it from his, feeling suddenly deprived. He stood for a moment longer where he was as we moved away, then turned and made for the side of the dance floor.

'I'm sorry,' I said to Edmund a little breathlessly, not quite sure exactly what I was apologising for, not really quite sure even what had just happened.

'Oh, you're not to blame, my dear,' he said in a tone of fond amusement. He planted a kiss on my cheek and smiled as we started marching together. 'It is just that he finds it insufferable to see me with the most beautiful girl in the hall.'

I glanced back quickly to where Richard stood leaning back against the dark carved wainscoting, beneath a flaming wall sconce. He was surrounded by people, yet seemed totally alone. 'Were you jealous to see him dancing with me?'

Edmund looked at me as if he did not know the meaning of the word. 'Jealous? No. I trust him and I trust you,' he said simply. 'Because you are to be my wife and he is my friend. It's a sorry affair if we cannot trust our friends and our spouses.'

He clearly did not possess one jealous bone in his body. Unless it was just that he did not love me enough to be jealous.

'You are very tolerant of him. I wonder that you are such good friends.'

'I swear I have no idea what goes on in the lad's head half the time,' Edmund said. 'Except that everything is a competition with him. He can't help himself. And since he has no brother to compete against, I am his natural opponent.'

'You don't mind?' But I saw that, on the contrary, Edmund enjoyed the challenge. 'You were right when you said he is not an easy person. He seems rather . . .' I searched for the word. '. . . erratic.'

'He is inclined to brood. Has had a great deal to brood upon.' The dance formation parted us so, for a moment, Edmund could say no more. As soon as we were marching side by side again, he quietly explained. 'He never speaks of it, or at least not to me, would far rather suffer in silence. But I do know, from what I have gleaned from those who knew him as a child, that he has endured the most dreadful hardship, deprivation and unhappiness in his young life.'

I felt a pain somewhere beneath my ribs. 'Has he?'

We parted, came together again. The music switched to the Longways country dance.

'He was born into exile and spent his entire childhood as a fugitive, shifting from place to place, in constant and severe want of both friends and funds. As I understand it, he came close to perishing for lack of bread and clothing. His brother did not survive the ordeal. Nor his mother. She was of Irish descent, had relations who were massacred by Cromwell's New Model Army at Drogheda and others who were amongst the Royalists who were deported to Barbados. The death of one son proved too much for her. Richard was left in a state of abject destitution with his embittered father who treated him harshly, from what I can gather.'

I turned my eyes back to the side of the hall where Richard had been standing. I needed to look upon him again in the light of this new knowledge I had of him. But he was gone. I scanned the room, suddenly desperate to seek him out amidst the blur of silk and smiling candlelit faces. And then he was there again, by my side, as the music faded. It started up again with the gavotte and Richard cupped his hand beneath my elbow, his eyes locked on mine. 'Please, Edmund,' he said in a low voice. 'You have had your turn. Do not keep her all to yourself.'

'Time enough together when we are wed, I suppose,' Edmund said, graciously stepping aside.

We danced the whole of the gavotte in silence, then the music slowed into a piece that required partners to kiss twice on the turn and I felt such longing and need in Richard's brief kiss on my cheek, in the way that he held me, it made tears start to my eyes.

'What's the matter?' he asked anxiously. 'Why are you crying?'

'I'm not crying.' I blinked, and a single tear spilled down my cheek and rolled to the corner of my mouth.

'It is my fault for . . .'

'No.' I shook my head. 'No.'

There were two little vertical furrows between his brows, just above his nose. They gave him an expression that was softly pained, and I had the most powerful urge to put my fingers to them and smooth them away.

When he stepped up to kiss me again, he turned his head slightly and instead of kissing my cheek he aimed for the tear, his lips brushing gently against the corner of mine, kissing it away. It was a surprising and tender thing to do, and yet he managed to imbue it with a delicate eroticism.

As the lines of dancers parted, I stared at him over the divide.

I held out my hands to him as the other dancers held out their hands for their partners. Richard took told of my fingers with the lightest touch, a tingling, magnetic touch, and I was drawn back to him as the needle of a compass is drawn to its true north.

But I had no compass to guide me through this strange and alien territory I had stumbled blindly into, a dangerous and dark place where I could seemingly care for two different men at the same time. I did not know which way to turn, who to run to and who to run from. I was utterly lost.

As soon as the ball was over, Richard made his farewells to the Earl as was polite but did not seem able to get away fast enough. Outside in the crisp moonlit night, he thrust his boot into the groom's cupped hands and threw himself up into the saddle, spurring the flanks of his horse as if he was riding into battle.

Edmund and I caught up with him on the open Tickenham Road.

'A race, Edmund?' Richard suggested with fevered enthusiasm. 'Across the moors?'

I turned to Edmund and to my amazement, saw that rather than dismiss this for the extraordinarily foolhardy idea it so obviously was, he nodded almost as eagerly.

I looked quickly from one of them to the other, then back again. 'Are you quite mad, the pair of you?'

The horses seemed to sense their riders' excitement and were already tossing their heads, prancing and snorting and champing at their bits, as the coaches clattered past.

'It is folly,' I argued. 'It is past midnight. The moor is covered in marsh and bog. You'll not even see the river.'

'We'll jump the damned river,' Richard exclaimed.

'And break your necks.'

'The moonlight is bright enough to see by,' Edmund placated me. 'And we'll stop before the mill. Agreed, Richard?'

He gave an agitated nod but the dangerous glint of recklessness in his eyes made me lean over and grab the rein of Edmund's horse. 'Please, I beg of you, use your sense. I know these moors, every inch of them, and would not do what you are about to do. I know how dangerous they can be. Don't do this.'

He glanced across at Richard. 'I don't have much choice,' he said grimly. 'I've not seen him quite like this before, but when this sort of mood is on him he needs some release. Believe me, a midnight gallop is far safer than the clash of swords, or much else he might try.' Edmund leaned across, grabbed my hand and delivered a firm, swift kiss to it. I could see that what he had said was just an excuse. He was itching for the thrill of the race every bit as much as his friend was.

Richard was the first to dig his spurs into his horse's flanks. With a whoop and a clatter of hooves they were off.

This is my doing, I thought despairingly. If anything happens to either of them, I will be to blame. Except that I did not know quite what I had done wrong, or what I could have done differently that might have prevented it.

I watched the two riders streak away across the moonlit moor, expecting at any moment to see a foreleg buckle, snap like wicker, for horse and rider to go down. But it did not happen. Their cloaks billowed out behind them like black sails as they splashed headlong though an area of marsh, the spray flashing in the moonlight as silvery bright as their swords. I could not bear just to trot along on my own far behind them, so I urged my own little mare into an easy gallop that soon had me splattered with clods of mud and droplets of icy water. I felt my hair tear free from its pins and whip away behind my back and yelped with the thrill of it, understanding exactly why Richard had suggested this wild, starlit chase. Not reckless-ness at all but high spirits and a zest for life, and there was nothing wrong with that, nothing wrong with it at all.

Edmund had been out in front at first by a head, but now it seemed that Richard had edged closer to take the lead. Both riders leaned lower over their horses' straining necks but Edmund looked to be gaining ground again. They were careering towards the mill house now and just beyond that was the Yeo. Neither horse showed any sign of slowing. Richard was ahead and I knew with a sickening certainty that he, at least, was going to try to jump the river. I knew also that it was too wide to jump and that he would fail to clear the bank. If Edmund tried to follow him, they might both be dead or fatally wounded or drowned, in a matter of minutes.

'Stop!' I called at the top of my voice, galloping full pelt at them now. 'Edmund! Richard! For Christ's sake, stop.'

Edmund reined in at the moment that Richard's stallion sat back on its hocks and launched itself over the river. For a moment both horse and rider seemed to hang suspended over the water, then both crashed down just short of the far bank. With an almighty splash, the horse landed awkwardly with its hind legs in the river and its forelegs floundering and thrashing halfway out. Propelled by its momentum, Richard was thrown headfirst over the horse's neck on to the bank, one of his legs for a moment tangled messily in the stirrup.

As I galloped on towards them Edmund had already abandoned his mount and was wading chest-deep through the fast-flowing river. Richard could swim, Edmund could not, but I thanked God that he was tall and strong, that the sluice would be down and there had been no heavy rainfall to speed the flow of the millrace.

Richard, I could see, was lying very still on his back on the ground. As the horse flailed to try and gain a footing, he was in serious danger of being crushed or trampled to death. If he was not dead already.

Edmund had reached the far bank now and, at no small risk to himself from the thrashing hooves, was grappling with the stallion's reins, to try and haul it to its feet and lead it safely away.

One glance at the surging water and I knew I would stand no chance in it. I hauled on the reins, spun my horse around, blinded for a moment as the wind whipped my hair across my face, then tossed my head to shake it free. I galloped along the bank to the bridge that crossed by Church Lane. It seemed to take forever to reach it. I made a promise to myself that night that, if Richard survived, I would damn well make him teach me how to swim.

Edmund had tethered Richard's horse to a tree and was now crouched beside his friend, speaking to him, urgently trying to solicit a response. 'Richard! Can you hear me?'

He gave no sign that he could. His eyes were closed. Against the black of his hair and lashes his skin seemed bloodless, white as chalk in the moonlight.

'Move back, Edmund,' I ordered, surprised by how authoritative I sounded when inside I was sick with dread. Edmund did move, immediately, seemingly relieved to have someone take charge, someone who appeared to know what to do: not that I did at all, but I had at least the common sense to crouch down by Richard and lay my ear against his chest. I felt it rise and fall, heard his heart beating, fast and uneven, but strong. I had never heard such a welcome sound. 'He's alive, at any rate.'

I wanted to shake him, make him wake up, clasp him to me. Idiot man, what had he thought he was doing?

'There's no blood,' Edmund said. 'I can't see any blood.'

'It doesn't mean he's not bleeding somewhere inside.' I quickly unfastened my cloak and laid it over his prostrate body. 'Stay with him,' I said to Edmund, getting to my feet. 'I'll fetch Ned and the cart.'

Just then Richard groaned and opened his eyes. Groggily, he looked from Edmund to me.

'Thank God.' I knelt back down beside him and took hold of his hand in both of mine. 'Richard, do you have any pain?' I asked him gently.

He looked at me pathetically, gave a small shake of his head.

'Can you move your legs, do you think?' I looked the length of them and saw his boots twitch.

He was wet from the waist down, shivering now, and there was a cold wind that I felt keenly through the thin silk of my dress. All I wanted to do was to gather him into my arms and wrap him up warm and hold him. 'I'm going to fetch the cart. I'll be back soon,' I explained to him softly, but as I moved away he clutched at my arm with surprising strength and almost pulled me down on top of him. 'Don't leave me,' he said. 'Let Edmund go.' And, in an afterthought: 'He'll be faster.'

I looked over at Edmund who nodded at the logic of that and quickly went to mount my horse.

'Take Richard's,' I said.

He shook his head. 'Too skittish. Yours will carry me. It's not far.'

He rode off at a gallop and then there was just the profound and soothing peace of the moonlit moor. An owl hooted, hunting low over the reed beds, and the slight breeze rushing through the reeds was like a deep sigh.

Richard's eyes were open and he was looking up at me, lips slightly parted.

'Are you still cold?' I asked him.

He nodded.

I moved closer to him, positioned myself with my legs out in front of me. 'Here.' I gently lifted his head and cradled it in my lap, tucking my cloak around him more snugly. 'Is that better?'

'Much.'

I held him tighter and my hair fell down around us both like a pale shroud. 'You're still trembling,' I said anxiously. 'It is the shock.'

He lifted his hand and stroked a tendril of hair back off my face. 'I do not think it is that.'

'Do you always take such risks, Richard?'

He did not reply, but looked at me almost as if he did not understand the question.

'You do remember what happened?' I asked fearfully.

'I am forever doing and saying things I later live to regret. I cannot seem to help it. But I could never regret this. Even if I had broken both my legs, it would have been entirely worth it.'

I sucked in a breath. 'You don't mean . . . ?'

He gave a brief grin. 'I am far too good a horseman to have misjudged that jump so badly. Though I had intended a softer landing in the water.'

I was incredulous. 'You could have been killed.'

'I do not think so.'

He looked up at me with eyes that were fathomless in the silvery darkness. There was a graze on his temple and I wanted so much to put my lips to it.

'We only have one life,' he said. 'And to love and be loved, that is all there is.'

'Hush.' I could not resist stroking his black curls, glossy with river water. 'You must not say such things to me. You must not. You know I am promised to Edmund. You know we are to be married within a sennight.'

'I know it. And it makes me wish I had broken my neck just now.'

'Never say that. Don't even think it.'

'I can't help it.'

'Richard, you hardly know me.'

'I know you well enough to understand that Edmund is not the man for you.'

I smiled. 'If you had not just fallen from your horse, I would scold you for being so presumptuous.'

'It is not presumption. You forget how well I know him. And I know he is the most solid, steadfast, even-tempered man I have ever met.'

'Most women would think themselves fortunate indeed to find a steadfast and even-tempered husband.'

'But you are not most women, Eleanor. You have a heart that is all on fire.'

I felt it hammering so hard now it was like a throbbing pain in my chest, and I was sure he must feel it, must see the tremors.

'You have an energy and a passion for life,' he said softly. 'A capacity for love that a man like Edmund could never understand. That he can never match.'

'Oh, and you could, I suppose?'

'Yes,' he said levelly. 'I could.'

'You judge Edmund unfairly. He is a good man.'

'Meaning that I am not?'

I said, half smiling, 'I don't think you can be. If you were a good man, you would not be having this conversation with your friend's betrothed, especially after that friend has just saved your life.'

'It takes two to make a conversation,' he said softly. 'I was not aware that I had been talking to myself. You like talking to me, I think.'

'You are being presumptuous again.' Except that I understood the reticence in his smile now, understood that the confidence and swagger he so often displayed was just a shield. His glamour and vulnerability were two sides of the same coin and, to me at least, made him utterly irresistible. 'I do like talking to you,' I admitted gently. 'Very much. Of course I do. And I hope we shall still talk to one another after I am married to Edmund.'

'I love you, Eleanor,' he said desperately. 'I think about you all the time. I cannot sleep for wanting you. I don't know what to do.'

And I did not know what to say, but my soul was singing with the overwhelming joy of being so needed and loved.

'I think I loved you before I even met you,' he said. 'When Edmund told me how he had found you in a little rowing boat, in the mist, at dawn. I pictured you like a water sprite, with your gold hair trailing down your back and only the swans for company. When I met you, when I saw you skating, I saw that wildness in you and I was captivated. I knew you were the only person I should ever love. That you had ruined me for anyone else.'

'Don't.'

'You love me too, don't you? I can see that you do.'

I gave a small shake of my head. 'No.' I did not mean that I did not love him, only that I could not. 'I love Edmund.'

He suddenly heaved himself on to his side, winced and clutched his arm around his ribs, pain evident on his face as it had not been before, almost as if it was what I had said that had wounded him. I took hold of him to make him be still. 'Don't try to get up. Wait for the cart.'

'I cannot wait.' He pressed determinedly down with his hand on my legs and struggled to sit, grimacing with pain.

'Where does it hurt?'

He touched his hand to his right side.

'Let me see.'

I knelt by him, undid his coat with shaky fingers, pulled his shirt free from his breeches and pushed it up. Even by the light of the moon, the red-purple welt that ran along his ribcage was clearly visible. I touched the edge of it with my fingertips and he jerked away from me. 'For the love of God, stop!' He dragged down his shirt, as if the touch of my fingers on his bare skin was too much for him to bear.

'I'm sorry.'

He drew up his knees, then supporting himself with his hand on my shoulder, struggled to his feet. I stood with him, let him lean on me for a moment. He staggered and I tried to take hold of his arm. He gave a grunt of pain.

'Your arm is hurt too?'

'My shoulder,' he said carelessly. 'I expect it will mend.' He shook me off and walked unsteadily to where his horse was waiting peacefully now, tethered to a willow.

'Where are you going?'

He unhooked the reins and turned to me. 'I shall go back to your house, unless you have any objection to that. I do not think I am fit enough to ride back to London tonight.'

'Of course, I didn't mean . . .'

'I know you didn't.' He put his boot in the stirrup and with a grunt, clutching his arm around his ribs, managed to heave himself into the saddle. 'I would offer to let you ride back with me,' he said, taking up the reins. 'But I don't think it would be wise. If I had you close to me for one more minute, I am not sure that I could answer for my actions.' He walked the horse up to where I stood and looked down at my upturned face. 'I'll try not to cause you further embarrassment. I shall leave at first light. Please don't come to bid me farewell. I do not think that I could bear it.'

I did not think that I could bear it either. But I must. What other choice did I have?

Edmund and I left for London three days later in a smart blue post coach which he had hired, and as it rocked over the uneven road that linked the straggled cottages of Tickenham, I had leaned my beribboned, ringleted head out past the canvas screens for one last glimpse of my home while it was still mine. My last glimpse of it as an unwedded and unbedded girl.

Everything was golden, a burst of shining yellow. In the watermeadows celandines and dandelions gleamed like small suns, whilst the rivers were edged with yellow flag irises. For a moment I thought I saw one of the first yellow butterflies of the spring, dancing in the churchyard, but it was just the bright bloom of a kingcup.

As we passed on to the Fosse Way that would take us east, our guide told us it would take three days to reach London. I couldn't imagine being on the road so long. Near Winchester we were stuck in the mire for six hours without food or water. We arrived at an inn by torchlight when it was too late for supper and next morning were woken to get back into the coach before dawn to make up time. We were jolted and shaken mercilessly, and before we reached Guildford had crashed headlong into a great pothole that caused the leather straps to break, sending the coach careering off its wheels and entailing another long wait for it to be mended. I felt battered and bruised and weary. It was by no means a smooth and painless journey to the altar for me, but today would mark the end of that journey and the start of another one, from which there was no turning back. Today was my wedding day.

I rested my head against the velvet seat of the swaying carriage and thought of my father's fantastical story of transformation, tiny caterpillars weaving their own mythical little coffins. Today it was I who was to be transformed, about to enter holy wedlock, to pass from one state to another. Dressed in my gown of cherry silk with scarlet and silver brocade and gold lace, I was as bright as any butterfly and this carriage might as well be my coffin. I would emerge from it to take my nuptial vows, after which I would not be as I was before. I would have a different name. I would be expected to adhere to a high standard of virtue. My good name, and that of my husband, would depend upon my housewifely accomplishments and modesty.

I had no mother to tell me how to be a good wife but I was thankful that at least I had had Bess, married for years now and twice as experienced as me in the arts of love. She had instructed me on how to fulfil my marriage duties and make my husband happy on his wedding night. I smiled to myself as I remembered the advice she'd given me the previous night when we'd lain awake in bed together, talking beneath the sloping roof of the inn.

'Every man knows that we women have much stronger carnal appetites than them,' Bess said, 'since they can only reach the peak of pleasure once at a time but we can do it over and over again. So he'll expect you to look as if you're enjoying yourself. You will, eventually, but you might not the first time because it'll hurt. Just pretend it hurts much more than it actually does. Moan and sigh as though you are in the most dreadful agony and he will think you are in an ecstasy of pleasure. Before you know it, he will be moaning and groaning too.'

It seemed very comical, not to mention complicated, but I'd do my best. I slid my eyes across for a peek at Edmund. The sprig of willow I'd tucked into the scarlet ribbon of his hat was nodding and jigging to the movement of the carriage.

Bess was sitting opposite me in the carriage, beside Mr Merrick. She and my guardian, together with Mary and John Burges and Edmund's brother, were to be our only guests, unless Richard came too, which I very much doubted. He had been invited, of course he had, and had not sent word that he would not attend, but somehow I knew that he would not be there and was doing my very best not to think how I felt about that, not to think about him at all.

Edmund's father still suffered badly from gout and was unable to travel any distance so it would be a quiet wedding, but I didn't mind so much now. I was on an adventure, the furthest I had ever travelled in my life.

'Are we nearly there now?' I asked Edmund, for what must have been the tenth time.

'Your nose will tell you,' Mr Merrick instructed me. 'You smell London long before you see it.'

'There'll be nothing but fresh countryside smells in Marylebone,' Edmund reassured me. 'Though it's on the outskirts of London, it's in truth a small rural village, entirely distinct and separate, divided from the metropolis by acres of green fields.'

I was crestfallen. 'You mean we shan't even see the river and the Palace of Whitehall and the lions in the Tower?'

He patted my arm as if I was a small child, and I suppose I was behaving rather like one. 'We can take a drive to see the sights tomorrow, if you'd like.'

I sighed and stared out at the woods and rivers and fields. The countryside was not as flat as Somersetshire, but somehow less interesting for it, and I felt suddenly very homesick. I slid up closer to Edmund and whispered in his ear, 'Let me see my ring?'

'Certainly not.'

'At least tell me what it's like. Does it sparkle?'

'It does.'

'You mean, it has diamonds?'

'Wait and see.'

'Do you know where diamonds come from? Do you know how they are made?'

He smiled his broad, jovial smile. 'Can't say I've ever thought about it.'

I retreated back into my corner as if I was travelling in a stagecoach with only strangers for companions. While the potholes grew more numerous the nearer we got to London, and the coach jolted on, the questions started up inside my head again, clamouring to be heard. What was the point of living if it was not to learn? There were things I wanted to know, that I couldn't live without knowing, couldn't die not knowing, or not at least without trying to find out. I did not think that, as my husband, Edmund would try to stop me, but nor did I think he would encourage it. And I would have liked to have been able to have discussions with him.

We were passing a great park at the edge of which stood a gabled brick mansion as sumptuous as a royal palace, but which Edmund told me was the Manor House of Marylebone. It made the little Manor of Tickenham look no more than a cottage. We carried on past it and I waited to see how similarly grand would be the church where I was to be married.

Presently I saw a humble chapel, built of stone and flint, standing entirely alone in a field except for the crooked gravestones that surrounded it. It looked hundreds of years old, as if it had been there since before the Reformation. It had small arched windows and a little pinnacled tower on top of which was a weathercock. We were approaching it up an ancient, narrow, winding track and had to stop twice to let a horse and cart pass and then a farmer driving a herd of cattle. As we came nearer I saw that it stood on the banks of a little burbling brook that ran down from the slopes of undulating hills to the north.

Surely that could not be it?

'St Marylebone,' Edmund announced.

It was a somewhat unpromising start to what I'd hoped would be my bright and colourful future.

There was no sign of Richard, and I told myself I was relieved rather than disappointed. Edmund acted as if he was totally unsurprised. 'He is the son of a Cavalier after all,' he said flippantly, as though that should be explanation enough. 'We all know there's only one thing upon which you can utterly rely in a Cavalier – and that is that he will be utterly unreliable. He'll probably turn up halfway through the service, or more likely sometime next week. I did write to him twice to give him the details but he has no notion of time, no concern at all for instructions, or for duty and responsibility for that matter, especially if he can wash it all away with a bottle or two of sack.'

That seemed a little harsh, so that I knew Edmund was more disappointed than he was admitting, but I was very glad to learn that Richard could be unreliable. Even if he did not give that impression, or at least not to me, it was exactly what I needed to hear. For what would life be like married to such a man? Even the most adorable, fascinating man. I had promised my father I would choose my husband well. And what kind of lord would Richard Glanville have made for Tickenham?

I hoped for Edmund's sake that Richard's absence did not mar his enjoyment of the day, but all my own disappointment in the unprepossessing church vanished as soon as I saw Mary and John Burges, waiting round the side with a gentleman who, despite his much paler ginger hair, could be none other than Edmund's elder brother.

'You look so beautiful,' Mary said admiringly, as she kissed me and pressed into my hands a little aromatic posy of rosemary and myrtle and daisies. 'Did you know the great Sir Francis Bacon was married here?' she chatted on, linking her arm through mine. 'In an extravagant purple suit, and his bride in a gown of cloth of silver that cost half her dowry.'

'Dear Mary, how is it you always know exactly what to say to cheer me?' I felt wholly better now. It seemed an extraordinary coincidence. My father had always commented on my inability to accept anything without evidence, and now here I was, about to be married in the very same church as Sir Francis Bacon, my hero, remembered as the inventor of the 'Scientific Method' of testing a theory by controlled experiment. 'If this church is good enough for Sir Francis, it must surely be good enough for me,' I said to her.

Edmund must surely be good enough for me too. Until I had met Richard Glanville, I had wanted nothing more than him.

'Are you happy?' Mary asked.

'Yes,' I said, glancing at Edmund who did look very grand and handsome as he strode ahead with his brother. 'I am.' If I had never met Richard, I would have been blissfully happy this day. But I had managed to find happiness in far less favourable circumstances, had resisted unhappiness all my life.

Mary was looking as radiant as a new bride herself. 'City air's obviously good for you,' I told her.

'Hackney's far from the city. But it's home to me now.'

I thought with a pang of Tickenham, which I had left behind for the first time and which in a matter of minutes would be mine no longer. 'Have you any pupils for your boarding school yet?'

'Two keen girls.'

I stopped walking, looked at her. 'Girls!'

'Of course,' she said, pulling me on. 'What do I know about boys? We're not the first. There are two Quaker establishments and a fine girls' school in Chelsea that's already quite famous.'

'Am I too old to go?'

She laughed. 'In a few minutes, you'll be a wife.'

'And wives, of course, can never pursue their education, Heaven forefend.' I do not know if I sounded resentful, did not mean to but it did feel for a tiny moment as if my life, in a way, was ending instead of beginning.

Mary relinquished me to Mr Merrick, who took my arm as we all walked into the chapel. The heavy doors swung closed behind us with a resounding clang. The interior smelled musty and damp and was very dim after the brightness of the spring sunshine, so that for a few seconds, until my eyes adjusted, I couldn't see where on earth I was going. I walked slowly past the boxes of locked pews towards the altar as one who is blind, my footsteps ringing down the stone nave.

Eventually I could see enough to make out that the little church was in a very poor state of repair. The banners and escutcheons were dusty and faded. The monumental slabs we walked upon were crumbling. The Apostles' Creed was marked with damp and there was a dusty spider's web over the poor box. Not a particularly auspicious start to my marriage at all. I saw also that the stone Commandments upon the wall were riven with a great diagonal crack and it made me shudder in premonition.

The plain little altar had at least been adorned with bays, but I yearned again for Tickenham. I thought of the golden morning on which we had left it and wished with all my heart that we were marrying in the familiar surroundings of the Church of St Quiricus and Juliet, sharing this day with our neighbours and household family: with Mistress Keene from the kitchen, with Bess's parents. I even found myself thinking quite fondly of Thomas Knight and Susan Hort. I should like to have had Reverend Burges officiating, or even the new young curate, John Foskett, and blessings and psalms of rejoicing and a procession of pipers to lead the way and make the occasion feel festive and joyous, instead of rather furtive and solemn, as it did now.

The minister was waiting with his service book already open, two worn hassocks placed at his feet in readiness for us. He looked extraordinarily old and as worn as his church, his hair wispy and white and his eyes almost lost in the deep wrinkles and furrows on his face. He spoke in a hushed voice more suited to a funeral than a wedding.

But the marriage service is a grave and sombre affair, though beautiful and dignified nonetheless, for all that it comes from the notorious *Book of Common Prayer.*

"*Not to be entered into unadvisedly, lightly or wantonly . . . those whom God hath joined together let no man put asunder.*"

With a monumental effort I pushed away the thought that it should be someone else standing by my side at this altar.

The minister read the part about 'accustomed duty' and Edmund dutifully fished in his pocket for a five-shilling piece which he placed on the minister's service book to pay him for marrying us. Then came the ring, and Edmund found it in another pocket and placed that, too, upon the pages of the open book, a band of gold set with many jewels. Considerate of my background, he'd asked me if I would find the ritual of the ring offensive, as did scores of Puritans who saw its part in the marriage ceremony as a relic of Papistry.

He could not have been more wrong. I had secretly dreamed of the day when the man I loved would place a ring upon my finger, from which it was said a certain vessel ran direct to the heart.

I looked at it, gleaming with jewels in the dim light. The symbol of my transformation, its placing upon my hand as powerful as the placing of a crown upon the head of a new queen. The ring. Token and symbol of constancy, of a love that has no end but death, a heart that is sealed from even the thought of another man.

But as I held out my hand for Edmund to slip the ring on to my finger, I suddenly remembered how it had felt when Richard Glanville encircled my thumb with his lips. I remembered the caress of his tongue upon my skin as he tasted my blood. However was I to vanquish such thoughts?

As I made my vows, I turned my head from the ominous tablet of stone upon which were engraved God's Ten Commandments. I did not want to see how the sacred edict had been broken, split asunder as if by a wrathful bolt of lightening.

We went directly from the church to the Rose of Normandy public house on Marylebone Lane, the oldest building in the parish or so we were told by the landlord, set inside a brick-walled garden with fruit trees and broad walks and a square central bowling green, edged with quickset hedges.

Our small wedding party was served a good dinner of rabbit fricassée and started to work its way merrily through several flagons of claret and ale.

I sat on the bench beside my new husband in the pale, smoky rushlight and we held hands beneath the table. Though I convinced myself I had to be happy, I seemed bent on self-destruction, oblivion, on blotting out all thought. I must have drunk more wine in that night than I usually drank in a month. As the evening wore on, I felt my cheeks grow very pink, and when the room started to spin around me I tilted my head against Edmund's broad shoulder.

'You make a pretty sight.' Mary smiled. 'It puts me in mind of my own wedding night.'

'Oh, do tell,' I giggled, and then hiccupped behind my hand. Which made me giggle all the more.

'Perhaps it is time to show a little restraint, Eleanor,' Mr Merrick suggested reproachfully.

I giggled again. Hiccupped more loudly and didn't even try to be polite and conceal it. 'I'm afraid I don't know the meaning of the word, sir.'

'Neither do I,' Bess said, taking it literally. 'You should though, miss. You read enough books.' Her hand flew to her mouth. 'Beg pardon. Is that supposed to be a secret now?'

'Restraint means moderation and self-control, my dear,' Mr Merrick answered patronisingly.

'How dull,' I replied. Hooking my foot around Edmund's ankle, I let my satin brocade slipper slide off and wiggled my toes against his silk stockings. He gave a little jerk of surprise and then smiled at me, rather drowsy-eyed. 'I do not believe in moderation,' I whispered to him. 'Or self-control. Especially not on my wedding night.' I clapped the palm of my hand against the table. 'Now, all of you be quiet and let Mary tell us about hers.'

The look Mary gave John was so loving and devoted that it pierced through my fuzzy brain. 'I was very gauche and green,' she remembered softly, her eyes lowered. 'I was marrying a man of the cloth, so I assumed we'd be very chaste and only be able to kiss and touch in the dark. You can imagine my surprise when I went to sit beside my husband in an inn much like this and he pulled me down into his lap and fondled me all evening.'

'Dearest John,' I said gushingly. 'God bless you. I do believe you are blushing as pink as Edmund.'

I was overcome with a rush of affection and wanted to fling my arms around both John and Mary and hug them. But I saw that they only had eyes for each other. So I sprang to my rather wobbly feet and promptly flopped down again in a puff of petticoats on Edmund's lap, much to his surprise and everyone's amusement.

'That's it, Eleanor.' Bess clapped. 'You lead the way. I was starting to worry the pair of you were just going to hold hands all night long.'

'That's all you and Ned did after your nuptials, I'm sure?'

'He wanted me to hold a lot more of him than just his hand, I can tell you.' She winked at me and burped very loudly. 'I was more than happy to oblige.'

Uninhibited with wine, I lunged across the bench, nearly upsetting a glass, and smacked a kiss on her cheek. 'Bess, you are so perfectly coarse and shocking.' I gave another loud hiccup. 'Have I ever told you how much I love you for it?'

'You love everyone tonight, I think, Ma'am. But best you save some of it for your new husband.' She smiled at me warmly as I twined my arms around Edmund's neck. 'Mind, you do have more of it to give out than most people I know. I hope Mr Ashfield appreciates that.'

Drunk as I was, I was concerned for a moment that he would disapprove of a maid speaking so out of turn, but I should not have worried at all. As I felt his arms go around my waist, he looked at Bess and a playful gleam came into his clear grey eyes. 'Tell me, Bess, is my wife wearing a garter?'

'Certainly, sir. I helped her put it on myself.' She grinned at me, then at him. 'Now I'd say it's high time it came off, wouldn't you agree?' She made a grab at my skirts. 'Come on, Mistress Burges, lend me a hand. It's about time we brought these two to bed, don't you think?'

I giggled and squirmed and kicked on Edmund's lap and he did not help me at all, but only laughed delightedly as they started pulling at my laces and ribbons and the silk sashes tied below my knees.

Bess started singing a bawdy song and Edmund's brother joined in. Then they all grabbed my hands and Edmund's and dragged us both, still giggling and protesting, to our small sloping-roofed room at the top of the inn.

Mary and Bess had conspired to make our own Hymen's revels to compensate for my wedding being so quiet. They had bedecked our half-tester bed with ribbons, scented it with essence of jasmine and strewn it with violets. Mary had even gone so far as to ask the landlady to make up a sack posset for us to drink and I swigged it down, barely savouring the delicious combination of wine and cinnamon and egg.

Bess took charge of flinging the garter and John helped Edmund undo his buttons and stumble out of his breeches.

'Time to leave you in peace now,' Mary said, kissing my forehead.

'I hope neither of you has any peace at all,' Bess tittered, with another wink. 'Go to it, the pair of you. Heaven knows, you've waited long enough.'

Edmund's brother slapped him between the shoulder blades. 'Time to let your little wife see your goods,' he guffawed.

Then they were gone. And there we were, with a single candle and clothes scattered around the floor and the smell of jasmine entirely vanished, replaced by the acrid stink from the tallow candle. Edmund was still in his knee length drawers and I in my voluminous shift.

We lay on our backs, side by side, like the marble statues of a knight and his lady upon their tomb. The room seemed to be rocking slightly, as if we were in a boat. But apart from that I felt exactly the same, as if being married made no difference at all. I flicked my eyes sideways to see what Edmund was doing. I wished he would make some move, make of our two bodies one flesh, make us truly man and wife.

The sheets smelt faintly of damp and tobacco and unwashed bodies. There was a draught coming from a gap in the ill-fitting window. I missed my own bed, my home, and wished Edmund would at least hold me. He had his eyes closed and I feared he'd drunk so much he might soon fall asleep. It was my wedding night and I totally refused to feel miserable and homesick. I reached out and touched Edmund's freckled cheek, which was prickly with a fresh crop of coppery whiskers. He gave a mock drowsy smile, so I knew he'd been teasing me by pretending to have dozed off.

I bounced up on to my knees, gold curls tumbling down around my face. 'Don't you dare, Edmund.'

He reached out his arms and pulled me into them, then rolled me on to my back and heaved himself on top of me, smiling down into my face. 'How do you do, Mistress Ashfield?'

I giggled. 'How do you do, Mr Ashfield?'

'Very well indeed. Pistol's loaded and ready for its first husbandly foray.'

'Oh! Ouch!'

He was a big man, in every way, I was alarmed to discover. He was squashing me and I could feel his cock, hard and hot, pressing into my pubic bone. I'd hardly taken a proper breath before he was fumbling with my shift, dragging it up. I closed my eyes as he rubbed himself up and down against me and poked and prodded about as if he was tending a fire, rather than inflamed with passion.

Then, suddenly, he stopped.

I opened my eyes.

'I'm afraid of hurting you. You will say if I am?'

I wrapped my arms around his broad back and pulled him closer. 'Oh, Edmund, I think you must hurt me. Bess said it would hurt, the first time. I shan't mind.'

He looked at me doubtfully and I wriggled underneath him.

Alarmingly, he reared up as if he had been stabbed in the back, let out a groan and impaled me with one single thrust. The hot, piercing pain made me think how very aptly pricks are named, for my insides were most definitely being jabbed, his cock indeed a burning poker. He thrust again and I banged my head on the bedpost. He flopped down on me, heavy and leaden as a bag of grain.

'Sorry,' he mumbled against my shoulder.

'It's all right.'

We lay there for a minute or two.

'Edmund?'

He moaned contentedly and didn't reply, so I knew, this time, he really was asleep.

I put my hands against his shoulders and, with some effort, managed to push him off.

He lay stretched out beside me, his red-gold head on my shoulder.

I lifted up the sheets. There was a spot of blood, token of my lost maidenhead. I tried so hard not to think of what else I had lost. Most of all I tried not to think how it had felt when Richard Glanville's tongue had licked away a drop of my blood. But, vexingly, the very act of trying not to think brought him more swiftly and powerfully to mind.

An hour later Edmund stirred, stroked me a little and entered me again, very gently this time. It did not hurt so much, and it might have been all I could ever have imagined wanting, if only I did not have something else with which to compare it. I might have been quite happy and satisfied, had I not been secretly hoping to experience again what I had felt when Richard had touched the tips of my fingers as we danced. Edmund gazed down at my face lovingly, but not even on our wedding night did he look at me as intensely as Richard did every time he saw me.

I lay on my back and hot tears slid out of the corners of my eyes and tricked into my hair.

I glanced across at my now softly snoring husband and stroked his head, thought sadly of how all was not gold that glistened. I was terribly, bleakly afraid that I had married the wrong man, and I knew also, bewilderingly, that I did love Edmund and that he deserved much, much better. I vowed there and then that I would never hurt him. I could not control how I felt, but I could control what I did about it. I would make the very best of my marriage, would honour my wedding vows. Somehow I would find a way to banish Richard Glanville forever from my head and from my heart.

Banishing him from my head was going to be much the easier of the two, I decided. I should start with that. And I thought I knew just the way to do it. Fill it up with something else.

I waited for dawn to lighten the sky before I crept out of bed. My head throbbed, my mouth was dry and there was a hollow, nauseous feeling in my belly, but I draped a green morning gown and cloak over my arm, found a lead pencil and scribbled a brief note, telling Edmund that I'd woken early and didn't want to disturb him, so had gone for a drive into London.

I dropped a kiss on his brow, tucked the sheet back around him and left the letter beside him on the pillow. I softly opened the door and tiptoed down the dark corridor to the first door on the right.

Bess was snoring soundly, huddled down beneath the sheets on her little truckle bed. I gave her a firm shake, putting my hand over her mouth to stop her squealing. 'Help me get dressed, Bess, quick as you can.'

She sat bolt upright. 'You're not running away, are you? It wasn't that bad, surely?'

'Of course I am not running away, silly.'

She put her hand to her head. 'Ugh, I don't feel very well.'

'Nor do I.'

'Then why are you sneaking about in my room? Why aren't you enjoying your new husband and your marriage bed?'

'Hurry.' I pushed her shoes at her. 'I don't want Edmund to hear us and decide to come along too.'

'So you have had enough of him? Poor fellow.'

'There is no need to feel sorry for him, Bess,' I said tetchily. 'Really.'

'How was it then?' she asked, circumspect, as she slipped on her shoes, fastened my gown for me.

'I'll tell you later.' Impatient, I turned to go.

She caught my arm. 'I'm not going anywhere unless you tell me all, right now.'

'It is private.'

'That is so unfair,' she wailed. 'I tell you everything. We promised always to tell each other everything.'

It was true. But I did not want to be disloyal to Edmund. Nor could I lie to Bess. She would see straight through it anyway. 'You said that I might still be left wanting more,' I said. 'So I am sure it was perfectly normal.' I reached for the door-latch.

She held on tighter. 'Normal? That's hardly the word to describe your wedding night.'

I looked at her. 'We women are ruled by insatiable lust. We are driven by stronger sexual desires and much lower passions than are men, is that not so?'

'So the preachers are always telling us, yes.'

'Men are allegedly governed instead by reason and intellect.'

She smirked. 'Now that, I'm not so sure of.'

I laughed. 'Well, I think it must be just so. And I think I have married an extremely reasonable and intelligent man.'

Bess gave me a sceptical frown.

'Now, please, can we go!'

'As you wish, miss . . . I mean, Ma'am.'

Downstairs the maid was already about, sweeping grates and fetching pails of water. The door to the yard was unlocked.

It was a dull, grey morning, very different from yesterday. Bess shouted up to our coachman, who was sleeping in a loft above the stable, and told him to make the coach ready.

'Where to, Ma'am?' he asked.

'Pall Mall.'

Bess looked at me. 'I thought you wanted to see the river and the lions?'

'But first I want to find Dr Sydenham, the physician who came to treat my father. There's something very important I have to ask him.'

As we came to the fashionable squares and myriad streets of Soho, London assailed my senses. Bess was all for putting up the canvas screens, but I didn't want to miss a thing, not even the stench. It wasn't the countryside stink of dung but a much less wholesome combination of what I could see all around: decaying refuse that littered dirty cobbled streets, and alleys running with filthy open sewers. I clasped my scented handkerchief to my nose but almost retched at the reek of rotten eggs which came from the sulphurous smoke belching out of the mass of crooked chimneys and darkening the air with a yellow choking smog as thick as any mist that descended over the Tickenham moors. But this fog was not accompanied by an unearthly peace, as it was in Somersetshire.

On the contrary, horses neighed, and the deafening clatter of iron-bound carriage wheels competed with the shouts of drivers of drays and wagons and the apprentices who bellowed from open shops. I had never seen so many vehicles and animals and people all crammed together. Sailors and mountebanks rubbed shoulders with women carrying baskets of fruit on their heads, grandees in velvet-lined coaches, and sedan chairs escorted by liveried servants and black slave boys.

The mess and chaos of London diverted me for a while from the mess and chaos I had seemingly already managed to make of my young life, just married to one man and already hopelessly in love with another. But Bess wasn't enjoying the experience at all. 'This question you have to ask Dr Sydenham, it had better be important, worth going to all this trouble for,' she muttered.

I let the screen drop over the window and leaned back, clasping my hands in my lap. 'It's as important as can be. It's a matter of life and death.'

Bess stared at me, white-faced.

I laughed to see her expression of panic. 'Oh Bess, I'm sorry.' I grabbed her hand. 'I'm not ill.' Unless, of course, Galen was right to treat love as a disease. 'It's just that I'm afraid I might die of longing for something I can never, ever have.'

She looked bemused. 'Dr Sydenham has a cure for longing?'

'I believe he might. I pray he might. If only we can find him.'

I knew Bess was waiting for me to tell her what it was that I longed for, but I did not want to. For once, this was something I did not want to share. I did not want to have these powerful, delicate, confusing emotions held up to her scrutiny, picked over and belittled. I wanted to keep them close and safe, a secret, even as I sought to dispel them. Whatever Bess saw in my face then, it was enough to stop her from enquiring any further.

On to Pall Mall, a fine, paved thoroughfare, lined with a row of shady elm trees behind which were grand mansions. I leaned my head and shoulders rather precariously out of the window, and searched up and down the street. We were passing a red-brick mansion with wings and pediments which looked far too impressive even for such an eminent physician.

'Be sure you have the right place or you could find yourself calling on the King's mistresses,' Bess said. 'Mary told me Lady Castlemaine has a residence here, and Nell Gwynn.'

I remembered dimly something else Mary had told me, from the time of the plague, when London was a place of death. I had listened as always to any details about it with a morbid fascination. I shouted for the carriage to stop outside the sign of the feathers, the only place where you could buy the Countess of Kent's Powder Virtues, allegedly believed by all the physicians of Christendom to guard against malignant distempers.

I walked into the dark little shop where a wizened old man in a long apron was busy behind the counter, dusting bottles of potions. He told me that Dr Sydenham lived over near the pheasantry.

I set off towards a small grove of chestnut trees and did my best not to gape at two ladies who were walking down the wide pavement carrying vizards which they held up to their faces on short sticks, beneath which it was possible to glimpse the tiny black leather patches in moon and star shapes that they wore stuck to their cheeks. Even in my fine silk morning gown I looked like a country girl who didn't belong here, much as I might wish I did.

I tried to appear serene and sophisticated, glancing up at the house I was passing.

And there I saw him, a face I recognised, despite the luxuriant periwig he wore upon his head, despite the passage of over ten years. He was sitting by the open sash window, deep in thought as he smoked a clay pipe, with a silver tankard set before him on the table.

My step faltered. I almost carried on walking. All at once I felt extremely foolish. What in the world did I think I was doing? What was I going to say? Well, it was too late now to turn back. I would be very annoyed with myself later if I did not go through with it, now I had come so far.

I told Bess to wait on the pavement and made myself climb the stone steps to the door. He saw me and came to open it himself, giving me a bow.

'Dr Sydenham, sir, I am sorry to trouble you, but we met when I was just a child, in Somersetshire.'

'Ah, of course. I remember you very well. Miss Goodricke, isn't it?'

I was astonished. 'I'm Mistress Ashfield now.'

He held open the door. 'Won't you come inside, Mistress Ashfield?'

I stepped into a regular and well-proportioned hall, from which tall white painted double doors led into an equally sumptuous room lit by the light flooding in through enormous sash windows. The high ceilings were adorned with elaborate swags of plaster, the walls covered in flocked paper decorated with curlicues of flowers.

There was a huge gilded mirror on the opposite wall that completely diverted me from my purpose. It was so strange to see myself reflected within something so ornate and extravagant, and the gold frame reminded me of the gold dust that had once stained my palm, like a mark of destiny.

I turned to face him. 'I'm surprised you remember me, sir,' I said. 'It was such a long time ago.'

'You made a great impression on me,' Dr Sydenham said genially. 'Such a brave little girl. I never felt my limitations as a man of medicine more strongly than I did then, not even when I ran from the plague because I knew I was powerless against it. I was very sorry I was no help to you either.'

'I need your help now, sir. You are the most learned gentleman I know . . . the only learned gentleman I know, in fact . . . so there is nobody else I can ask. I wonder, do you know how I might learn more about the study of butterflies?'

His looked at me for a moment as if I'd dumbfounded him. Then the skin around his eyes creased and he bellowed with laughter. 'Forgive me, my Mistress Ashfield,' he said when he recovered himself and saw my puzzled smile. 'I don't mean to offend. It's just that I have all manner of callers at my door making all manner of strange requests. But I do believe that is the most original inquiry that has ever been put to me. You were the most enchanting and unusual child and I am delighted to see you have grown into a most enchanting and unusual young lady. You will join me in drinking some coffee?'

'I wish I could, sir. But I was married only yesterday and I have left my husband asleep at an inn in Marylebone. I mustn't abandon him for too long.'

His eyes widened with renewed amusement. 'I'd have thought any man would gladly wait a lifetime for such a remarkable person,' he replied. 'Even if she did flit off immediately he had ensnared her.'

'Oh, I don't know about that, sir.'

'Spare me the time to tell me this at least – why butterflies?'

I couldn't very well tell him that I had come for the sake of my marriage. That I needed a distraction to stop me from lusting after another man, who happened to be my husband's closest friend. Maybe I should have asked him for a cure for love-sickess too. But I doubted that the standard remedies would work nearly so well for me as the study of butterflies.

'I want very much to learn more about them,' I told him, 'I find them . . . irresistible. And I'm sure I'm not as original as you suggest, sir. Surely there are others who are as interested in them as I?'

'Indeed there are whole hosts of dusty natural philosophers who devote hours to the careful study of insects and sit around in coffee house societies discussing their finds. But I'm afraid they'd not admit a woman, not even one of your intelligence, and in any case, I'd hesitate to introduce you to them, in case their earnestness caused you to lose your spark.'

'Can you at least tell me how I might contact them, perhaps obtain their scientific papers?'

He reflected for a moment. 'There's an apothecary who lives on this street, a smart young man by the name of Thomas Malthus, from a very intelligent family who are good friends of mine. Young Thomas is a member of the Society of Apothecaries, naturally, and has mentioned an associate of his, James Petiver, who sounds like just the type of eccentric and enthusiastic young person you'd get along with very well.'

I smiled. 'How might I find James Petiver?'

'Easily. I hear he all but lives at the apothecaries' new Physic Garden in Chelsea, supposedly herbalising and botanising but not in fact studying the plants at all, only the butterflies that are attracted to them. The best way to get there is by river.'

I took a step towards the door. 'Thank you, sir. You've given me exactly what I wanted.'

'I'm glad to see you still know what you want and pursue it single-mindedly, Ma'am.'

I thought of Edmund then and how I had dreamt for more than a decade of marrying him. 'I'm very afraid that I do, sir, and it will probably prove to be my undoing.'

Bess was hungry, so we bought game pies from a cookshop and made our way towards the Thames. Our first sight of London Bridge with its tall houses and archways of elaborate shops was marred by the shock of seeing the stakes impaled with the rotting heads of traitors, blackened gargoyles with rictus grins and holes where their eyes and noses once were.

I shuddered and looked down at the torrent of water surging with terrifying force beneath the stone piers. The tide was at low ebb. We made our way over stinking mud to the slippery pier, to hire a tilt boat to take us upstream.

The Yeo in full gushing winter flood was nothing to the sheer expanse of London's river. Bess cowered behind the narrow skiff's canopy as we rocked alarmingly from side to side. I held on tight to the shallow sides, sure the swell and suck and power of the currents would capsize us or drag us under.

We negotiated a throng of pleasure boats and sailing ships, their masts as thick as a forest, and presently the air cleared and the river quietened and widened into a fine reach. Our oarsman said it was called Hyde Park on the Thames, on account of the fact that it was a fashionable rendezvous, where even the King himself came to bathe in the calm, clean water.

So His Majesty King Charles, like Richard Glanville, also knew how to swim. With his rich velvet suit and sword at his side, Richard could easily be a royal courtier, my own sweet, dark prince. Except that he was not mine, and never would be. Somehow I must find a way to school myself not to think of him as anything other than my husband's friend.

The busy wharves had given way to open fields and a large mulberry garden, and then a country village with a terrace of red brick houses that faced out over the water. Upstream from the riverside Swan Tavern was a small bay with steps leading up to a landing pier that our oarsman was steering us towards. 'This is the place, madam.'

I could see now that the land that lay behind the pier, open to the river, had been transformed into a garden. It was laid out in regular beds outlined with neat hedges of box, straight rows of plants and narrow avenues created between them. But it smelled like no ordinary garden. It smelled like

Christmas, like Maytime, it smelled like the wedding day of my dreams. The air was filled with the scent of bay, rosemary, lavender and thyme.

In the centre, where all the avenues converged, was a sundial. In the bed nearest to it a man bent low over one of the shrubs, plucking leaves and placing them into a wide-mouthed glass jar. Two bewigged gentlemen were standing about smoking pipes by an ornate boathouse. I drew myself up to my full height, such as it was, and walked towards them. I asked where I might find James Petiver, the young apothecary who studied butterflies.

One of the gentlemen nodded towards a secluded area of the garden behind some fruit trees. 'Expect that's who you mean.'

I told Bess to wait on a nearby stone bench and went on alone.

The first thing I saw was a little cloud of yellow butterflies, a whole throng of them. Then I saw that they were massing around the head and shoulders of a boy. He had a pleasant, clever face and corn-fair hair, two shades darker than my own. He was perhaps four or more years younger than I. His shirtsleeves were rolled up to his elbows and he was dressed in the blue apron of an apprentice. As many as a dozen butterflies were fussing and flitting around him, brushing him with their wings. He had one of them poised on the tip of his finger and, miraculously, it stayed there, perfectly still, as he lifted it until it was on a level with his nose, at which point it obligingly unfolded its wings as if for his sole admiration.

I stood and stared until he noticed me watching him. He crouched down and placed his finger next to a white flower. The yellow butterfly dutifully hopped off.

'How do you make them do that?' I said in wonder.

He stood. '*Vin rose*. You sprinkle it on your hands and they come and drink it.'

'Could I try?'

'If you like.' His smile was friendly but doubtful, as if he couldn't quite believe I was interested, couldn't quite believe I was even real.

I walked closer and offered him my hand and he sprinkled some pinkish liquid from a glass vial on to my skin. The butterflies started swirling around me. I stood very still. One settled on my shoulder, another in my hair and one on my hand. They were tame as kittens. I felt curled antennae probe my skin, quick and fleeting as a grass snake.

'See, they think you're a flower.'

I laughed. 'I wonder what kind?'

'Something rare and pretty,' he said, matter-of-factly.

I raised my eyes but I could hardly see the sky, all I could see were butterflies. 'I'm Eleanor. Eleanor Goodri— I mean, Ashfield.'

He didn't seem perturbed by the fact I appeared not even to know who I was.

'James Petiver.' He gave me a quick bow, like a country boy from Tickenham would do, and I found it enormously refreshing in the midst of London polish and sophistication. I felt as if I had come home.

'I understand you're interested in butterflies,' I said. 'Well, I can see very well that you are.' Now both of us had them in our hair. 'So am I, and I want very much to learn more about them. I hoped that perhaps you could help me.'

He looked at me keenly, through the fluttering wings. 'What is it that you want to know?'

'Oh, everything.'

'That'll take a long time.' He smiled but not in a derisive way. 'But if everyone learns as much as they can and shares that knowledge, then we shall make a good start. I'll gladly help you.'

'You will?'

'Of course. Butterflies are such a neglected, though beautiful part of God's creation, but I hope in time that will change.'

I noticed some intricate drawings carelessly scattered on the ground at his feet and bent down to pick one up. It depicted a red and black butterfly, and beside it a thistle. 'Did you do these?'

'Yes.'

'They're beautiful.'

'Thank you. They're not as accurate as I'd like, but I do my best.'

'I'm not very good at drawing at all.'

'No matter. You can make accurate descriptions instead.'

'I caught one of these,' I said, leafing through more drawings and recognising the red and orange markings and the orange tips on the antennae.

'You have a Large Copper?' James Petiver's eyes had opened wide. 'They are most prized amongst butterfly collectors.'

I could hardly see why, when they were so abundant on the moor. 'Do you collect butterflies too?'

'You can't study a creature from a sketch.'

'Mine are pressed between the pages of a book, but they're damaged so easily.'

'That's not such a bad way. Adam Buddle and Leonard Plukenet preserve their specimens like flowers too. But butterflies have mealy wings so the colours get rubbed off. I place mine between sheets of mica, or sometimes in frames, like lantern slides. I'll send you some mica, if you like.'

'Thank you.'

His enthusiasm and directness were a little overwhelming. Already my head was spinning with all this new information, but I was hungry for more. 'And is there a way of catching them without damaging them?'

'Ah, what you need is one of these.' He produced a strange contraption that had been lying on a bench behind him. 'It's a clap net or butterfly trap.' It was a strip of muslin held between two poles. He held them out to demonstrate. 'You clap them together to trap the butterfly, see? The poles are of hazel.'

I imagined willow withies would do just as well. 'Now why didn't I think of that?'

'It's not my idea either. It's the only useful piece of information I learned at school. One of the masters collected butterflies for his curio cabinet.'

'Didn't you care for school?' I'd known him only a few minutes yet we were talking as if we'd known each other for years. I felt I could ask James anything.

'I was born in Warwickshire. My father was a haberdasher. My grandfather had high ambitions for me and wanted me to have an education. He paid for me to go to Rugby but I've learned a lot more since I left.'

'We're the same then.' I grinned. 'I don't much like being told what to do, or what to believe.'

We were alike in so many ways. For a start, it was unusual for me to be able to have a conversation with a person eye-to-eye, rather having to look up at them. His eyes, I noticed, were impossible to describe. They were hazel, flecked with green and gold and blue, as if they had absorbed something of the grass and the trees and the sunshine and the sky, and there was an extraordinary warmth and intelligence in them that was reflected in his smile. The butterflies still encircled and flickered around us, as if drawing us together, and I felt a bond forming between us, something strong and simple, not at all like my girlish infatuation with my husband, nothing like my disturbing desire for his friend. I thought of the dangerous rush of the Thames and of how this would be better than being able to swim, would be something to hold on to if my new life turned out to contain such undercurrents. I knew I had found a friend and had a strange sense that we were meant to find each other.

James was just a boy. He was the same height as me, lean as a withy, and his shoulders beneath his white shirt were bony still. He looked as if he had plenty of growing left to do but would never be particularly sturdy.

'How old are you?' I enquired.

I smiled to see him do what I so often did and straighten up to make himself appear taller. 'I became bound apprentice to St Bart's three years ago,' he said, with all the touching pride of a boy trying to be a man. I thought how frightening it must be to leave home and come down alone from the country to live in a strange city. 'I'm supposed to be here studying plants, but everyone is doing that. I want to show that insects are equally worthy of our effort, for the ultimate benefit of mankind.'

'How?'

'There are two reasons to collect and cultivate plants – taxonomy and nomenclature.' When he saw that I didn't understand he added quickly: 'So we can classify and name them according to their shared characteristics, as well as keep a record of their medical and commercial uses.'

'You think butterflies could be similarly useful?'

'I'm sure of it. They can teach us much about the processes that have generated the diversity of life on earth. Their transformation seems to hold the key to the origins of life itself.'

'My father told me it held the key to life after death.'

'He is far from alone in that belief. Metamorphosis is the source of much speculation, particularly in the Netherlands. A painter there claims to have kept caterpillars in jars and observed the entire cycle. In his book he compares it to Resurrection, the rebirth of the soul after death.'

I was elated. 'There are others, in the Netherlands, who have seen this happen?'

'Jan Swammerdam has written a *Natural History of Insects* which categorises them by type of metamorphosis. He is certain worms come from eggs rather than being born from dew or cabbages, though I don't believe he has seen an egg or even a pupa. And he also says that Adam and Eve contained all the humans that came after them, which seems a rather wild notion.'

Now I was confused.

'It's just a matter of time,' James said brightly, as if he understood my bemusement. 'There is still much to be discovered, about metamorphosis and everything else. But all is possible from the close observation of nature. If we study birds and butterflies, I believe even people will be able to take to the skies one day.'

Human flight seemed such an impossible but splendid fantasy, I'd thought it was mine alone. 'Do you, honestly?'

He shrugged. 'Why not?'

'Your grandfather must be very proud of you.'

'He was, I think. He died in January.'

'I'm sorry for that. Both my parents are dead.'

'I'm sorry too.' He looked at me speculatively, then put his hand in his pocket and offered me a hard-boiled egg. I thanked him, peeled it, took a bite and then he handed me a hipflask. I took a long swig and molten fire ran down my throat. My eyes watered and I screwed up my face, laughing. 'What in the Devil's name is that?'

'Whisky.' Grinning, he took the flask back, swallowed a nip himself and secured the top. 'I want to help to encourage a free exchange of specimens and opinions,' he said. 'To build a community of scholars, with everyone contributing. If nobody communicates properly, progress will be very slow and fragmented, with nobody knowing what anyone else is doing or has discovered. To avoid duplication of effort, and in the broader interest of science, I believe very strongly that correspondence with like-minded people in other countries is as important as private study and experiment.'

'"Many shall pass to and fro and knowledge will increase,"' I said, quoting Francis Bacon, feeling almost as if the Father of Science was watching over me, guiding me.

'Exactly,' James said. 'Ships' surgeons constantly visit apothecaries to provision their chests of medicines before a voyage. It is my plan to enlist their help. If I can send them off with instructions for collecting, they will spread an interest in insects across the seas at the same time as they bring specimens back. There are butterflies in the New World that nobody here has ever seen, that we will never see in England, but this way we have access to them all.'

I could hardly believe my luck in finding this boy. He was a genius, a visionary. He made everything seem possible. My own ambitions at once seemed very limited, yet I had never felt so inspired.

'I could write to you?' he offered.

'I'd like that.'

'And will you write to me?'

'I will.' I agreed with all the wholehearted solemnity and sweet joy of a wedding vow.

We were home. It was pitch dark with no moon and it was raining, a fine windswept spring rain that brushed my face like cobwebs as Edmund handed me down from the carriage and I breathed in the familiar peaty tang of the marshes. I was tired and I was hungry and it was so good to be home.

I knew this house, with its long-standing absence of mirrors, far better than I knew my own face. It called to me, spoke to me in a way that nowhere else ever could. I knew the sound of the great hinges and the bolts of the studded oak door as well as the sound of my own voice. The cracks in the flagstones were as familiar to me as the lines in the palm of my own hands. My feet directed me without the need to think. I knew how many worn stairs to climb up to my bedchamber, how many paces took me from the parlour to the great hall. I had been on a long journey but here I was again, back where I belonged. Though Tickenham Court was now entirely Edmund's, had passed from my father to him as if I did not count, I did not feel disorientated or displaced by that, as I had expected to. I had an unaccountable feeling that I had not really lost it at all.

Edmund looked very comfortable at the head of the long table, in the great carved chair with arms that had been polished by the repeated touch of my father's hands. I was in the smaller carved chair, my mother's chair, and had a very strong sense of the generations of Ladies of the Manor who had sat before me in this very hall. Edmund and I would eat our supper here, more of a late dinner really since it was hot, and then we would go up the stone stairs to the bedchamber which generations of Tickenham Court ladies had shared with their lords. We would sleep together in the sturdy oaken matrimonial bed, the very same one in which my mother and father had spent their first nights as newlyweds. There was a reassuring continuity in it all, though I felt and understood, as if for the first time, the weight of responsibility my father had always spoken of.

Edmund smiled benignly at me down the table then went back to enjoying his meal, chewing with relish, as if he had not a care in the world, as if nothing troubled him or indeed ever would.

There was one small thing that marred my pleasure in being home. I set my fork down on the pewter plate, pushed it away, leaned back against the unyielding carved wood of the chair and folded my arms. 'D'you know, I hate eel pie. I have always hated eel pie.'

Edmund glanced up at me, his mouth full. 'Can't think why. It's delicious.'

I smiled. 'Not when you've had to eat it at least three times a week for your entire life, it's not. I hate eels in whatever way they are served. Salted, cured, smoked, stewed.'

'So tell the cook what you'd like prepared instead,' Edmund said, forking up another generous helping. 'You have governance of the kitchen now, of the entire household. This is like our own little Commonwealth.'

'Didn't you know? The days of Commonwealths are over. Thanks be to God. Just because you are sitting in my father's chair, there is no need to start talking like him.'

He grinned back at me. 'You sit in your mother's chair, yet I see you do not intend to emulate her at all. Pity. I have heard exceptional reports of her from William Merrick. It is my understanding that she was chaste and loyal as well as meek and modest. The best things a wife can be.'

I was sure he must be teasing, but still I stiffened.

Edmund did not appear to notice, or else chose not to. 'My own father always advised me of the benefits of marrying a young girl,' he added. 'One not yet spotted or sullied, one I could shape and mould into the wife I wanted her to be. There's no need to look at me like that.' He smiled. 'I mention it only because I should like you to know that I am very content with your shape, just as it is.'

The tension left my shoulders.

He stood up and walked the length of the long table, taking my hands in his and raising me to my feet, kissing my fingers with his soft lips. 'We have never had a falling out, have we?' he said. 'And I do not ever want us to have one.'

That seemed a rather daunting aim, though maybe not for someone as mild-mannered as my husband. 'We are bound to have misunderstandings, I think, aren't we? At least at first,' I ventured. 'There is so much we still do not know about each other.'

'We have plenty of time to learn. We have our whole lives ahead of us. Our whole lives to spend together.'

'Dearest Edmund.' I looked at his open handsome face and much of the emotional turmoil of the past few days drained away like the winter floods in spring. I just needed a little time to adjust to my new situation, that was all.

'We shall be happy here,' he said. 'This is a beautiful house.' He kissed the tip of my nose, then my forehead. 'It is our house now. Our home.'

I looked around the gloomy hall and an idea glinted at the back of my mind, like a solitary jewel swept beneath the floorboards. I could make Tickenham Court truly ours. I could make it beautiful, transform its Puritan austerity with brightness and comfort.

'We can hang printed calico or striped muslin at the windows,' I whispered, tentative at first and then growing bolder as fresh plans rushed at me. 'We can replace all the dark oak with rosewood and walnut. We can light the rooms with great candelabra. And we can have mirrors, and padded armchairs upholstered in striped silk, and replace the rush matting with oriental carpets. And we can buy pepper and ginger and cinnamon, too, so we can eat food that doesn't taste of marsh and peat.' I was grinning now, thinking that I could and would do it. I would work very hard to make a success of this marriage. Edmund was good and kind and I did love him. What I felt for Richard was surely just desire and lust, not love at all. And I didn't need desire and lust to make me happy, did I? I would make Edmund happy too. 'The very first thing we shall have,' I said, 'is a silk quilt for our bed, stitched with all the colours of the rainbow.'

Edmund was looking concerned. 'I doubt we can afford quite all that.'

'But of course we can, we're wealthy landowners. Mr Merrick has always said so.'

'We've lived through enough dire and changeable times to learn that we can never know what's waiting round the corner,' he said judiciously.

'The King might make a levy on us tomorrow, for horses or arms for another war with the Dutch.'

'Then we may as well spend it first.'

'We should invest and save. We mustn't be reckless.'

The rain had turned heavier, beating at the windows, and it was blowing a gale. It would only take a high spring tide to pile up the waters in the estuary and block the outflow of the already swollen rivers. They would burst their banks, inundate the fields and drown all the fresh grass and the bright spring flowers in their first bloom. Suddenly, I knew just how that felt. 'Surely buying a few new furnishings for our marital home is not reckless?' I rested my palms against his chest and felt how steady his heartbeat still was. I picked at a thread in his waistcoat, tweaking the stitched cloth gently between my fingers. 'Besides, I'd like to be reckless, just a little. I'd like to know what it feels like. For a short while, at least.'

'I know how much you liked the trinkets I sent you before we were betrothed,' Edmund said. 'I realised then you had a rather worrisome liking for material possessions. But we don't need such folderols. We have each other. We have this lovely house and a comfortable income. We already have everything we could possibly need.' He smiled at me, a little shyly. 'And if, with God's grace, we were to have a child, I should have everything I could ever want.'

I slipped my arms around his back and rested my cheek against the bumpy brocade of his waistcoat. 'Oh, Edmund, so would I. I want a baby too. I want your baby. Lots of your babies.'

He dropped a kiss on the top of my head. 'The household accounts are in your charge now,' he encouraged me brightly, as if he was presenting me with the key to a castle. 'The monthly housekeeping is yours to spend as you see fit. I daresay there's enough to buy some spices at least.'

Next morning, I struggled with the practicalities of adjusting to my new position and duties. Mary and John were gone, Mr Merrick had handed over all the great ledgers and account books and receipts and bills of fare, which were my responsibility now. I sat at my mother's small writing desk, in her tiny green panelled closet, as if I might feel her guiding presence. I felt nothing but claustrophobia, and mounting frustration and inadequacy. The ledger had been open at the same page for what seemed hours. I rubbed the tips of my fingers against the closed lids of my eyes. When I opened them again the neat rows and columns of figures swam before me worse than before.

Bess bustled past the open door with an armful of linen. 'Still there, miss? I mean, Ma'am?'

'Bess, I am not a nincompoop, am I?'

'You're the cleverest person I've ever met,' she said, coming to stand in the doorway.

I smiled appreciatively at her loyalty. 'Bless you for that, Bess. Oh, I should be able to do this easily,' I said determinedly. 'There is nothing especially difficult about it. A simple case of balancing profits from rents and the fisheries against outgoings on wages and expenses.'

'That all sounds quite difficult to me.'

I propped my chin on my hand and frowned at the ledger. I knew what to do in principle, but the practice was rather different. The real trouble was that I wasn't overly interested, never had been, never would be, I suspected. But this was my life now. 'It looks as if it does balance. We do have a small fortune, but it seems to cost as much to run this estate. And it's up to me now to see that the larder and pantry are amply stocked with provisions, to make arrangements for meals, to make sure you and the other maids are paid.'

'Keeping house can't be as hard as learning to read a whole book in Latin,' she said helpfully.

'It can, Bess. It is bewildering.'

'Your mother was good at it, by all accounts.'

'I know it. You don't need to tell me again.' The servants and villagers had told me a hundred times how her gentleness had hidden formidable organisational skills. 'I know she ordered the kitchen garden and the dairy and the fishery, with patience and grace. I know she was always willing to roll up her sleeves and lend a skilled hand with the cookery and fruit preserving.'

'You are gentle and graceful, Ma'am, and willing and hardworking. And I am sure you can learn to be ordered.'

I laughed. 'Well, right now, I can't even calculate if we can afford a new carpet.'

'Your father taught you arithmetic, didn't he?'

'He did, but he did not rear me to be a housekeeper.'

And yet he entrusted this house into my keeping. He taught me that it was first and foremost my obligation to be a diligent custodian of my birthright, of my children's inheritance, but at the same time had encouraged my interests in a world beyond mere accounts-keeping.

'You could ask Mr Merrick to help you,' Bess suggested, tentatively.

'I could, yes. If I could put up with the I-told-you-so look on his face. I don't need him to remind me that much good geography has done me, when what I really needed to be paying attention to was how many loaves of bread are needed to feed a houseful of servants.'

'I'd best leave you to work on it then,' Bess quipped. 'Unless I want to go hungry.'

She left me gazing longingly out of the tiny closet window, absently brushing the quill feather against my cheek. The rain of the previous night had passed, and with the typically capricious nature of spring, the sun was shining enticingly. A buzzard wheeled higher and higher in the milky blue sky. For my father this house had represented my security. To me just then, much as I loved, it, it felt more like a kind of imprisonment, the one thing that frightened me above all else. I groaned and laid my head down on the table, folding my arms up around it as if I feared the roof of this grand and ancient manor might fall down and crush me.

'It can't be that bleak,' Edmund said breezily, as well he might when he'd been out riding all morning. 'Mr Merrick assured me all was in good order.'

I sat up, saw him and stared, aghast. 'Good God!' Then I laughed.

'Don't you like it?' he asked chirpily. 'It's very fashionable.'

He was wearing the most vile brown periwig.

'It just arrived with the carrier from Bristol. I ordered it last time I was there. Thought, now I am a husband, I'd better have one, so I look more distinguished.'

'Take it off,' I pleaded. 'Edmund, I mean it. Take it off right now, please.'

'Why?'

I stood up and swiped the horrid thing off his head myself. My hands flew to my mouth. 'Edmund! What have you done?

To accommodate the wig, he had shaved off every lock of his own lovely copper hair.

I sank back into my chair. Ridiculously, I looked from Edmund's shaved head to the ledger in front of me and a tear slid down my cheek. It splashed on to the page, instantly blurring the neat, inked figures. I made to wipe it away but Edmund whipped the book from under my fingers.

'You'll only smudge it and make it worse,' he said, with no hint of reproof, handing me a neatly laundered cloth as he sat the ghastly wig back on his bald head. 'I'll grow my hair back if it really means so much to you. Please don't cry about it. For heaven's sake, it is nothing to cry about.'

'I know it's not,' I said, hurriedly wiping the tears away. 'I'm sorry. I don't know what's the matter with me.'

Edmund handed the accounts back to me.

'I don't know what to do with them,' I admitted.

'You'll soon learn,' he said. 'You'll be a prudent and frugal housekeeper before you know it. Here's something to cheer you anyway.' He produced a flat, square parcel from behind his back.

'Oh, Edmund! A present!'

'It's not from me. The carrier brought it as well. From the bookseller, I assume.'

I hadn't ordered any books, and if it was a book, it was a decidedly thin one. But it was definitely addressed to me: Eleanor Ashfield, Tickenham Court, Somersetshire. The writing was small and crabbed. It was the first time I had seen my new name in writing and it gave me a strange feeling, made me feel like a small tributary that flows down from Cadbury Camp and loses itself in the Yeo, as it is swept onwards towards the sea.

Edmund had walked away, not at all curious to see what was inside the parcel.

I slipped my finger beneath the brown paper wrapping. It was not a book at all but a sheaf of papers bound in vellum. I caught my breath as I carefully turned over the leaves. It was a collection of original, coloured drawings of butterflies, rich with yellows, orange, reds, blues. Beside each illustration were notes on the location of sightings, on flight patterns and preferred foodplants. It was like looking through a rich illuminated manuscript, like the ones John Burges had shown me once.

There was an inscription on the covering page, in the same untidy, almost childish hand as had penned the address.

There are no books in existence that are solely devoted to butterflies, so I have made one for you. Your friend, James Petiver.

There were tears in my eyes again but for a totally different reason. I dashed them away before they had time to fall and spoil the lovely paintings. I was stunned by such thoughtfulness and generosity. It must have taken him hours, days, to copy out all his drawings and notes for me. I might know nothing of the cost of a bottle of claret, or of running a household, but I knew that what I had here was worth more than money could buy. This gift was more precious than any silk or silverware, more precious than any trinkets or lace. I knew, somehow, that this gift, this friendship, would be my salvation.

Summer 1676

I held my breath. Some distance away but unmistakable, flying power-fully over the sedges, was the magnificent lemon and black butterfly with scalloped, sickle-shaped wings, like the Gothic arches in a church or a swallow's tail. It was larger than any other butterfly and so stunning it seemed almost unreal. It was my most burning ambition to see one up close. I'd learned their favourite haunts, knew they seemed to like milk parsley, but so far they were proving extraordinarily elusive.

I walked forward slowly, at the ready, remembering how kittens learned to wait for the right moment to pounce. I whispered a quick prayer that this specimen would drift within my reach. Miraculously, it alighted on a thistle and I crept as close as I dared, then sprang forward, my hands cupped. I tripped and landed flat on my face, while the butterfly danced off, gaily evading capture, much to Edmund's amusement and the other fishermen's undisguised and total mystification.

'It seems rather cruel, anyway,' my husband said, having set down his fishing rod on the riverbank to watch me. 'How can you like butterflies and also quite happily kill them?'

'This from the person who likes nothing better than a plate of eels fried alive for his dinner? James says it is the only way to study them properly.'

Edmund was no more jealous of my correspondence with James Petiver than he had been of Richard's attentions to me. 'I can't see any point what-soever in catching what you cannot eat,' he added indulgently. 'But if it makes you happy, then so be it.'

It did make me happy and I was sure that I could remain so, could be quite content with this life, if only Richard did not come to visit, as he soon must, to upset my equilibrium again.

I turned my mind determinedly to the problem of the elusive specimen. I needed a net like James Petiver's.

I had written to James to thank him for the drawings and enclosed one of the copper-coloured butterflies he so valued. In little more than a week, almost no time at all, I had had a reply to my letter.

I did not open it at once, did not want household distractions to ruin my concentration or enjoyment, so I waited until I could take it down to the moor. Then, leaning against a willow trunk by the Yeo's curved bank, I broke the seal.

It was a long letter, scrawled in his untidy, hurried, boyish writing that was rather a struggle to read, but which pleased me because it suggested that the author had far more important matters with which to concern himself than the forming of neat curves and hooks. Just the sight of his handwriting made me feel unaccountably, uncomplicatedly happy, and I smiled to myself as I read, imagining him bent over a little desk, scribbling away with ink-stained fingers, all the things he wanted to tell me coming into his head faster than he could write them down.

Besides asking me how I did, the letter contained directions on how to study, preserve and log butterflies. He emphasised the importance of keeping an observation book, to note down exactly where and when I had found each specimen, and to record colours in case they faded. He had drawn a little diagram of a clap net, in case I'd forgotten how it looked, and explained how I might make one for myself.

Over the next days I set about hacking off withies and cut up two perfectly fine muslin kerchiefs. With a notebook and lead pencil, I spent hours amidst the lilac haze of lady's smock and cuckoo flowers on the moor. I wrote to tell James the net was a miraculous invention that let me swipe butterflies from the air, of how amazed I was each time I trapped one, saw its fine legs poking through the tiny holes.

I found that cataloguing and preserving butterflies in the mica James had sent to me seemed to give me extra enthusiasm for other tasks. With Edmund's patient help, I mastered the accounts, and though I'd never find my vocation as a bookkeeper, butterfly collecting brought out a method-ical side to my nature which, when applied to the household finances, made them start to make sense. It gave me great satisfaction to see neat rows of figures in my own sloping hand and to realise that I could make a success of running this house. If I felt Edmund was shaping me slowly and very subtly into a good housewife, for all that he had said he would not want to, then I told myself that it was not such a bad thing and I did not really mind so much after all.

I did not even mind overseeing the beating of the bed-hangings or the ordering of the linen cupboard because, surprisingly, there were other aspects of housewifery that I found interesting, and which even offered me opportunity for experiment and observation. From Bess I learned that pewter was best burnished with marestail, brass cleaned with charcoal, and silver with salt and vinegar. Ned Tucker's sister, Lizzie, who worked in the ciderhouse and stillroom, taught me all about the process of fermentation. I pored over the book of herbal remedies, used by my mother and Mary Burges, and made up poultices and ointments, as and when they were needed.

'You like being Lady of the Manor, I think?' Edmund said to me one evening, as we shared a supper of cold beef and talked about our day, in the manner that had quickly become routine for us. Usually, the conversation centred around impersonal matters: boundary disputes between the tenants, the hiring of labourers to tend the orchard for the harvest, the incompetence of the dairymaid who had let the milk sour. It was rare for him to express an interest in my likes and dislikes, in what I wanted from life, and I welcomed the opportunity to talk to him about what was closest to my heart.

I reached for the fruit bowl and took a bite from a juicy purple plum. 'I like walking up to the cottages and drinking dishes of cold cream and sympathising over toothaches and boils and fractious babies,' I said. 'I like feeling needed and appreciated.'

'I shall always need you and appreciate you,' Edmund smiled fondly at me. 'But the villagers certainly seem to have taken you to their hearts.'

It pleased me perhaps more than anything that the people of Tickenham seemed to have accepted me as mistress of the manor so readily. I had brought them a new lord who was far more lenient than their previous one, and was proving to be a good wife to him, in their eyes. And, as they saw it, I had called a halt to the drainage plans. True, Thomas Knight and Susan Hort did whisper aside together when they saw me with my strange butterfly trap, but I did not let that trouble me.

'I like rocking the babies best of all,' I said. 'I could do that for hours.'

Edmund's eyes softened. 'You will be an expert mother.'

'I hope I can be one very soon. If only so I don't have to pretend not to see the women's knowing glances at my belly and answer their constant enquiries after my own health.' I chuckled. 'When I tell them I am well, they are so disappointed. They'd rejoice if I said I was nauseous and exhausted. As would I.'

'I too,' Edmund agreed.

'I do pray every night and every morning that God will let me be fruitful.'

'My dear, I am certain He will. If only you were more patient and at ease about it.'

'That is easier said than done.'

'Aye, for you, most certainly.'

'It is only that I cannot think of a punishment much worse than barrenness.'

'My wife, why ever should you be punished? What have you ever done that is so wrong?'

There was a moment of silence which I hurried to fill. 'I was raised a strict Puritan, remember? I live in constant fear of punishment.'

'It is, of course, a Puritan's duty to multiply,' he said with levity. 'Your bounden duty as a wife.'

I licked the plum juice from my fingers. 'My bounden duty and my most passionate wish,' I said seductively, but he looked almost alarmed as I took his hand and pulled him towards the stone stairs leading to our bedchamber.

Autumn 1676

Five months later, still in my nightshift, I drew my knees up on the oriel windowseat and hugged them as I waited for Bess to come and help me dress. I turned my head and rested my cheek against my folded legs and gazed out of the window. The sky was colourless, an even blanket of thick cloud, and a low ground-mist hung over the rivers and flat fields.

'What's the matter?' Bess asked.

'My courses have started again,' I said, twisting my head round to face her. 'Bess, why aren't I with child yet?'

She put her arm around me and sat herself down beside me in the embrasure. 'Have you been doing it with your husband regularly?' she asked, coming straight to the heart of it as usual.

I stared at my bare toes, twiddled them. 'Is every other night regular enough?'

'Not every night? Not several times a night?'

'He's very considerate,' I said quickly, not wanting her to think less of Edmund.

She gave me a look that was almost pitying. 'Does he not like it if you try to lead him, lamb?'

I tucked a loose lock of hair behind my ear, shook my head.

Bess tutted. 'Does the man not accept you have needs of your own?'

I smiled. 'Oh, I think he'd be most disconcerted by the very idea of that.'

'Doesn't sound very considerate to me then.' She sniffed. 'Does he at least take longer over it than he did at first?'

'Does that make a difference?'

'Well, it most certainly would to me.'

I could not help but laugh. 'I mean, surely it doesn't make any difference to whether you can make a baby or not? So long as his seed is inside me, surely that's all that counts?'

'Pumping seed is probably all it takes to make a baby, but if you ask me, it's most definitely not all it takes to make a husband.'

I laughed again, even as I drew my knees tighter as if to banish and deny the dull ache in my abdomen. 'Is it true that a woman has to experience real pleasure in bed, for the seed to take root?'

'Absolutely vital. I thought everyone knew that. So has he found your little mound of pleasure yet? Do you still have to pretend?'

I didn't answer immediately. We had always talked like this, Bess and I, and there had seemed nothing wrong in it until now. I knew Edmund would be so hurt if he knew I had discussed the most intimate details of our lovemaking, and found him wanting. And yet I needed somebody to talk to, to confide in.

'Maybe I'll never have a baby then,' was all I said.

Winter 1677

I had woken up hungry in the middle of the night and was in the pantry helping myself, by the light of a single candle, to cheese and rye bread. My breath was misty and I shivered in my nightshift. It was not much warmer when I took my little feast through to the kitchen, where the glowing embers of yesterday's great cooking fire had been covered over with a brass dome, waiting for the bellows to breathe life back into them come the morning.

I set the round of crumbly Cheddar on the long scrubbed table and cut off a chunk. I had just put it in my mouth, when I heard a soft tap at the door in the great hall. It was still completely dark outside and I was sure I'd misheard. But there it came again. Firmer this time, more urgent, a definite rap against the thick studded oak. I hesitated, uncertain what to do. There were no servants about yet, nobody else to answer it except me, and I was hardly dressed to receive a visitor. Yet I couldn't ignore it. Nobody would call at this hour unless it was an emergency.

I took up my candlestick, shielded its guttering flame with my hand as I made my way through the draughty cross passage and across the great hall, bracing myself to find a distressed commoner who'd not been able to rouse the midwife, or had news, God forbid, of a breach in the sea wall. I drew back the bolts and swung open the door. Froze.

'Richard!'

'Eleanor,' he echoed, with almost as much surprise. 'Not a butler or a serving girl, but the little lady herself. How very fortunate.' He slid one leg forward, swept his feathered hat off his black hair, bowed low and came up again gracefully, the white lace ruffles of his shirt luminous in the dark.

'Is something the matter?' I asked him. 'What are you doing here at this hour?'

His eyes twinkled with mischief. 'I might have hoped for a warmer welcome. When I've ridden all through the night, and a bitterly cold night at that, just to be sure I was the first person to see you this St Valentine's Day morning, just to be sure I was in time to take you as my own Valentine.'

'In time to . . . as your . . . what?'

'Your Valentine,' he repeated with a smile, his teeth biting softly on his bottom lip and his eyebrows slanting rakishly. 'Or had you forgotten it's February the fourteenth? The feast of St Valentine? The one day in the calendar when even a wedded girl is free to kiss whosoever claims her first.'

There was not a trace now of the vulnerability he had revealed when he had lain wounded with his head in my lap. I did not know which of these different sides of his personality was the more devastating. One moment he had all the sweetness of an angel, the next all the charm of a devil. The very way he swung between the two left me feeling breathless and strangely exhilarated.

'Aren't you going to let me in?' he asked. 'Before I catch my death of cold.'

I moved aside and he stepped through the door, pushing it closed with his foot.

I was acutely aware of the contours of my body, silhouetted inside my fine linen shift, my breasts and nipples, hardened by the cold and by a desire that descended on me like the mist over the moor, occluding my senses, blocking out all else save his beautiful face, his black curls, the swirling folds of his riding cloak and the soft, velvety richness of his voice. 'Since I've explained why I'm here,' he said, 'why don't you tell me what you're doing, wandering around a dark house at night all alone?'

'I was hungry.'

'I can see hunger in those pretty eyes of yours well enough. But I doubt very much that it's the kind of hunger anything in your larder can satisfy.'

'Richard, stop it. Please.'

He removed the candleholder from my hand, set it on a little table. He moved closer to me and I took a step back. He followed, as if we were conducting some strange, silent dance. Then he reached out one finger and traced the line of my cheek, making me quiver with a pleasure so intense it was almost like pain. 'Please,' I said again. 'You have to leave.'

'Not before I have claimed my Valentine's kiss.'

My eyes moved to his mouth, the lips slightly parted. It was the most fascinating mouth, as beautiful as the rest of him. Small and neat and with a slight pout, there was an almost childish sweetness about it. His upper lip curved like a bow. It was a mouth made to kiss and be kissed.

I swallowed. 'You aren't the first to see me this morning, at all,' I argued lamely. 'Edmund and I share a bed, naturally. So he was the first person I saw when I woke. I am not for the claiming.'

'I assume he was sleeping. He didn't see you. It does not count.'

'I've never heard that before.' I half smiled. 'You can't just make up your own rules, you know.'

'If I can't make them, I'm quite prepared to discard them if they stand in my way.'

'What would you have done if I had not been awake, had not heard you at the door?'

'I'd have broken in and woken you with a kiss.'

'And what if one of the servants had been about to open the door to you?'

'I'd have told them I had a most urgent and private message to give to you and I'd have sent them to fetch you to me.'

'You had an elaborate plan.'

'But I didn't need it. You were here yourself, waiting for me, as if you knew I was coming. As if this was meant to be.'

'It is not meant to be, Richard,' I said slowly. 'You know that.'

He cupped my face in his hand, his expression suddenly desolate. 'Little Nell, I know nothing any more.'

I struggled for something to say, anything that might anchor me in some normality. 'Nobody has ever called me Nell.'

He stroked his thumb firmly along my cheekbone. 'D'you like it?'

'Yes,' I said, laying my hand over the back of his, as if to remove it, though instead I just held it closer, tilted my head into his touch. 'Yes.'

'Nell,' he said again, making it sound like the sweetest endearment. 'You must let nobody but me ever call you by that name.'

'I don't really think you can take such possession of another man's wife.'

He let his hand slip away and fall to his side, leaving my cheek feeling suddenly cold and exposed. 'I am sorry that I missed your wedding.'

'Edmund did say you are dependably undependable.'

He did not return my brief smile. 'You know the reason I did not come.'

'It was very quiet anyway. We had only a few guests.'

'If you were my bride I should want to celebrate it before everyone, with a feast that went on for twelve days.'

'I never can be your bride, Richard.'

He did not answer. There was for an instant an awareness for both of us that what I had said was not wholly true, but that there was only one eventuality that would leave me free to marry again. For one wild beat of my heart I was afraid of what he was capable of and of what he might do. I looked into those capricious, quicksilver eyes of his and for one chilling, insane half-beat of time, it wasn't so very hard to see him as amoral and corrupt, like the worst picture my father had ever painted of Cavaliers, a murderous dueller, the kind of man who'd stop at nothing to have what he wanted.

'I love my husband,' I said firmly. 'I love Edmund.'

'I love Edmund too,' he echoed savagely. 'I've known him all my life. His father and my father knew each other all their lives. Do not think I am not tortured by guilt for this, for how I feel about you. But I cannot help myself. I cannot help it that for these past months I have tossed and turned in my bed every night from longing for Edmund's little wife. Nell, I have never wanted a woman as I want you.'

When I said nothing he slid his hand around my waist, drew me closer to him. Then his hand moved around my back as he held me. 'You know what it is like to be driven by an obsession, I think,' he whispered. 'You know what it is to want something and to strive after it, and to desire it all the more the harder it is to catch, the more unattainable it is.' He fixed me with a melting blue gaze. 'I saw Edmund when he was last in Suffolk. He told me how you have a favourite butterfly that is yellow and black but you can never catch one of them. He made me look for them with him, but he wouldn't look as you look, as if your life itself depended on finding one, as if your whole being was caught up in pursuit of it, in possessing it and having it to keep with you forever. Edmund doesn't know the power of such an obsession. He is not passionate. He does not know the force of a desire that overrules all reason, a hunger that can never be satisfied yet demands to be satisfied.'

I had forgotten how to breathe. 'That sounds like madness.' Except that I understood exactly what he was talking about, saw that he understood me, as if he had seen into my soul.

'If it is madness, little Nell, then it is you who have driven me mad,' he said. 'And I must have my kiss, or I cannot account for what I might do.'

'Very well,' I said quietly, feeling my lips already softening to receive his. 'A Valentine kiss. That is all it is.'

Almost before I knew what was happening he bent his head and pressed his mouth against mine, so softly at first, slow and tender, and then harder, deeper, more insistent. Sensation rippled down through my body, through every limb, to the ends of my fingers and the tips of my toes, to an agonisingly sweet peak of sensation between my legs. I felt the firm, warm moistness of his tongue as it slipped inside my mouth and sought my own, tasting and exploring. I raised my hand in a half-hearted attempt to push him off, but he caught my wrist and held it, poised in mid-air, as if time itself had stopped, as if the night would never end and the sun would never rise. For once I didn't mind, didn't long for morning, for light, only for this, only for him.

He clasped me to him, his fingers splayed against the small of my back, pressing me urgently against his groin. I could feel the shaft of his arousal through my shift, against my belly. I did not move away but found myself pressing back. With his other hand he was caressing my breast, stroking and kneading. Entirely of their own accord, as if driven by instinct alone, my own hands had slipped up inside his shirt, were travelling up the warm nakedness of his back to his smooth shoulders, round again on to his taut belly, brushing against the fastenings of his breeches. He trembled at my touch, his eyes closed, long-lashes shadowing his cheek. He moaned softly. I tipped my head back as his tongue travelled from my lips and down my throat. He held me tighter, pushed his leg between mine.

'No!' I broke free and shoved at him with both palms against his chest. 'No. I cannot.'

His eyes opened and they were full of hurt, of rejection, shadowed now by the agony of frustrated desire that matched my own.

'Go!' I said hoarsely, feeling faint, wanting to weep with desire for him. 'You've had your kiss. You've got what you came for. Please, just go!'

'I have had what I came for, but I find it wasn't nearly enough,' he said. 'It can never be enough.'

I could not sleep. I felt ill. So that I thought love must indeed be a sickness. I was lovesick. I must be suffering with what the physicians called erotic melancholy, the dangerous, infectious malady that was caused by excessive passion and unfulfilled desire. A physical disease that inflamed the body, boiled the blood, took possession of the mind, caused the humours to combust and consumed the liver. A rage of love, that could, it was said, actually burn the sufferer's heart so that, upon examination after death, the organ resembled a charred timber.

I did manage to doze, eventually, but when I woke later in the morning I gagged the instant I sat up. I reached for the ewer and was violently sick, sicker than I had ever been since I was a child and my mother stroked my brow and murmured to me that she was there.

Now it was good, kind Edmund who sat with me on the edge of the bed and stroked the hair off my face and I was swamped by intolerable, crippling guilt. I thought I had never felt so wretched, but fully deserved to feel much worse. Wanted to feel much worse. I spewed into the basin again and when I had done, Edmund handed me his own cup of warm ale, holding it for me while I sipped.

'Eleanor, my love, can it be . . . ?'

My lips still felt bruised by Richard's kiss, my cheeks still scratched by his stubble. I could still taste him, could feel his body imprinted against my own. I could not bear to look at Edmund's trusting, expectant face. I hardly dared to hope myself. It was preferable to lovesickness at any rate. It could be true. I was hungry in the night, sick in the morning. I was with child?

'Maybe,' I said hesitantly.

Edmund kissed my hand, in that formal, chivalrous gesture of his, but his kindly, freckled face was radiant with such pure joy that it made him look saintly, and beside him I felt like the very blackest and most wicked of sinners.

'Oh, Eleanor, that's wonderful news, the best news.' He kissed the side of my head. 'And I almost forgot, it is St Valentine's Day.'

I had been taught to be observant of signs and portents, but did not wholly believe in them and for that I was very glad. For if I saw this pregnancy as a sign that my marriage had been blessed, that the sin I had committed would go unpunished, there soon followed more ominous signs that the blessing might be taken away.

The sickness worsened around the forty-fifth day, the time when it is said that a baby's soul is born. I felt nauseous as soon as I sat upright and could barely keep down a morsel of food. The constant retching left me limp as a wet leaf, but I believed I deserved no less, welcomed it, bore it like a penance.

Edmund was as thoughtful as he had sworn always to be. He touched me cautiously as if I was made of porcelain and refused to lie with me at all for risk of dislodging the baby. He took over the household management, so I wouldn't tire too much, and took me on outings to Bath, where the waters were said to be beneficial for women who were with child. His concern and his love for me and for our baby were almost unbearable. The kinder he was to me, the more wretched I felt.

When he came to find me one morning, I was sitting on the chamber floor in my cambric chemise, my hair lank and loose, my back against the wall and my legs outspread before me like a rag doll as I cradled a basin in my lap.

'What is it about being with child that causes a woman to vomit?' I wondered apathetically, trying to be objective in the hope it might help a little. 'Maybe it's the growing womb pressing on my insides, but surely that would be worse at the end of term rather than at the start?'

Edmund, not at all interested, took the basin off me and helped me to my feet. 'Darling, this cannot go on.'

'I'm sure it will ease soon.'

'You've been saying that for weeks.'

I grabbed the basin off him again, tossed my hair over my shoulder, doubled over and heaved, until it felt like my guts were being torn from within me. The retching was dry. There was nothing left inside my belly but a baby, and I was increasingly afraid that if this went on much longer that baby must be ripped from me too.

And if it was not . . . It is well known that the womb is absorbent, that womb children are in danger from corruption, are susceptible to bad external influences, and I had exposed this little soul to so much wickedness. Richard had caressed my body wherein, unbeknownst to me, there had been planted my husband's seed. My body had been shaken to its core with a sinful passion for a man who was not the father of the child it carried. I was sure there could be no greater carnal sin. If my baby was not shaken from me, I feared it would be marked with the most baleful influences for the rest of its life.

Edmund must have seen fear in my face. 'That's it,' he decided. 'I'm sending for Dr Duckett.'

'No.'

'Eleanor, be sensible. We must.'

'I will not see that charlatan, no matter how ill I am.'

'He could bring you some physic,' Edmund reasoned. 'He could make you well.'

'I have never seen Dr Duckett make anyone well. All he has ever brought to this house is suffering and death.'

Edmund looked at me, uncomprehending. 'You are being absurd,' he said helplessly.

I saw myself for a moment as he must see me, long fair hair in tangles, eyes enormous in a face that was drawn and pale with sickness, and I almost agreed to do as he wanted, just to make him happy, even if it did me no good at all. But I could not. 'I have so longed for this baby,' I said as I rested my hand on my still flat belly. 'Already I love him so much.'

'Him?' Edmund smiled questioningly.

'I am sure we shall have a boy,' I said. 'I feel it. I cannot bear to think that anything will go wrong.'

I let Edmund take me into his arms. 'Eleanor, it is so unlike you to be gloomy,' he said stroking my back. 'Be of good cheer. Have faith.'

I could not tell him that it was faith that made me gloomy. I had thought I had thrown off much of the indoctrination of my Puritan upbringing, but in the empty void of guilt it had rushed back with a vengeance. How could I forget the Puritan God who was always watching, waiting to reward good deeds and punish the bad? How could I ever forget the Puritan code which deemed that ill-fortune followed wrongdoing just as night followed day? How could I ever forget years of teaching about how carnal lust was the way only to madness and ruin? Puritan law had once made adultery a capital crime, but it made no difference that it was no longer enforced, made no difference that Richard and I had not actually lain together. By

God's law, I had committed adultery almost nightly ever since the day I learned to skate. I had no need of Dr Duckett and his purges. It felt as if my own body was trying to purge itself of my longed for little child. The worst punishment I could imagine.

'Lie still and rest, at least,' my husband said.

But I knew that what I needed was not rest but reparation.

Alone in my chamber, I went down on my knees, clasped my hands and begged God for forgiveness, for allowing myself to be led into sin and temptation. I read the Bible and I murmured the Catechism I had learned as a child. 'My duty towards my neighbour is to do to all men as I would they should do unto me . . . to bear no malice nor hatred in my heart . . . to do my duty unto God, to keep my body in soberness and chastity.'

I had learned to repeat those words before I even knew their meaning. I could say them backwards, in my sleep. I did want to live by and be all those things. I did want to be sober and chaste. But, oh, it was so much easier to say than to do.

Autumn 1677

The nausea did abate, to be replaced by ravenous hunger. My stomach gnawed me as if there was a hole growing there, not an infant, but I delighted in piling my plate with odd combinations of cheese and fruit, pastries and meats, thinking that my baby had a fine appetite, must be growing strong and healthy after all. I had been forgiven, even if I could not forgive myself.

When I wrote to tell James I was expecting a child and that Edmund would not risk having me go chasing after butterflies, James sent me one small wing, iridescent purple-blue, from a butterfly he'd caught on an expedition to the fields that lay around King Henry VIII's great Hampton Court Palace. I wondered what had happened to the other half of the butterfly. It was an odd thing to send me, when we were usually so concerned with pristine specimens, but it was very pretty nonetheless, like a little petal or a fragment of sky, and I stored it away in the back of my Bible.

The bigger and less mobile I grew, the more I looked forward to receiving James's letters and the more I enjoyed replying to them. He said he and his friends had been butterfly hunting in Greenwhich, too, beside the new observatory, and on Primrose Hill, in the Mitcham lavender fields and in Fulham Palace Gardens. I would have been envious of this like-minded group of men, for whom a passion for butterflies was a social pursuit, who could visit such romantic sounding places and share their discoveries, but for once I was glad to be a woman, for only a woman could know the joy of feeling a child move inside her own body.

James told me to drink sage ale to strengthen my womb, said that lilies and roses, cyclamen, or sowbread and columbine would nourish my unborn child and procure an easy and speedy delivery for me. I was very touched by his concern and told him what a skilled apothecary he was going to become.

He wrote, too, of the debate raging amongst his naturalist friends, one faction questioning spontaneous generation as a relic of ancient times, while another was arguing that if a caterpillar could become a butterfly inside a pupa, why could a leaf not transmute into a caterpillar? All sides were calling for further investigation.

Preoccupied as I was by the changes in my own body, I tried to describe to him how the subject of metamorphosis had a strange resonance for me at this time. My swelling womb was just like a tightly wrapped pupa, ripening with the promise of new life. A new life that kicked and squirmed inside me, with tiny limbs forming and fluttering beneath my taut skin, just like wings. As I wrote the words, it occurred to me that I had never tried to describe the experience to Edmund because he had never shown any real interest, considering it women's work. It was to James that I told my eagerness to meet my baby. To James that I explained how the promise of holding the little thing in my arms even helped ease my utter dread of banishment to a darkened lying-in chamber for weeks on end.

'Is that really all you are afraid of?' Bess said in disbelief, as I sat on a stool and let her release my corset and rub my aching back. 'Do you really fear the banishment more than the pain and peril of childbirth itself?'

'I was doing my best not to think of that until you kindly brought it up.' I grinned.

'Ned lived for the whole nine months in terror of my being taken from him for good, and I was petrified myself, I won't pretend otherwise. Any more than I can pretend that your danger is not great and the pains will not be grievous.'

I laughed. 'I thank you for your honesty, Bess. I can always rely on you to tell it to me as it is.'

I wondered. Was Edmund afraid as Ned had been? If he was, he had not shared it with me at all. But then, when he came into the chamber one night as I lay half asleep, I felt the mattress dip to his weight as he sat down beside me. He laid his hand very gently upon my head, and I heard his whispered private prayer. 'Lord, look upon my dear wife as she is great with child, give her strength and a gracious delivery from these perils.'

It sounded very much like the prayers Puritans still said on Gunpowder

Treason Night, to thank God for delivering us from the deadly plot of the Papists.

I awoke to a dull pain in my lower back which sent out aching tentacles all the way round to my belly. It eased. I listened to the rain pit-pattering on the window. Then came another twinge, which also passed. The next one was more severe but it, too, subsided. So it went on for hours, with the spasms growing sharper as the downpour became more and more torrential, windswept and battering the glass, so that when I finally cried out for Edmund, for Bess, sleeping nearby, I was not sure they would hear me above the clatter.

For weeks I had been confined to this room. The bed had been draped with hangings and drawn close to the fire, the windows and doors kept closed and covered, and I had a sudden need just to open the curtains and see daybreak, even if it was only a dank and murky one. I rolled clumsily to the edge of the mattress, pushed open the bedcurtains. Bess woke and ran to the bed just as I stood up, and a huge gush of water poured out of me, dousing my feet and the floor, as if I had lived on the wetlands so long even my body had been flooded.

'Get back in bed,' she ordered, almost pushing me under the blankets as Edmund rushed in, still in his nightshirt, tousle-haired and blurry-eyed and carrying a candle.

I drew up my knees against another wave of pain. 'It's started, Edmund,' I grunted. 'The baby is coming.'

He was by my side in an instant. 'Are you sure?' he asked, his voice ringing with panic.

'Don't sound so shocked. It is not as if we have not been expecting it to happen these past nine months.'

'I'll send for the midwife, and the gossips.'

'The midwife first,' I urged.

'Yes, yes. Of course. The midwife.' He was rushing to the door fast as a scalded cat but I called him back.

'Would you open the curtains for me before you go, Edmund?'

He hesitated. 'But the manuals are very strict.'

'I do not want this baby to be born into darkness,' I said firmly. 'Please, do as I ask.'

Reluctantly, he went to the widow as I screwed a ball of blanket in my hand while another wave reached its peak.

He came back to my side and watched my face twist with pain. 'I would be so much happier if you were attended by a surgeon.'

'If the parish midwife is good enough for the yeomen's wives, she is good enough for me,' I said when the spasm abated. 'Mother Wall may not be able to write her own name, but her knowledge of childbirth is the best there can be. It comes from the experience of her own eyes and ears and hands, and from the scores of babies she has safely delivered before.'

He nodded. 'I will fetch her for you.' He left the room, hurtled back to give me a kiss, rushed off again. As Bess went to fetch the linen and I listened to a horse galloping off from the stables, I looked at the oak canopied rocking cradle that had been moved over from the corner of the room to the side of my bed. 'Please God,' I whispered, 'let me rock my baby in his crib. Have compassion for me through the torture that's coming. Preserve my life and the life of my little child.'

I felt much safer when Mother Wall arrived, with her stool and her knife, followed by more than a dozen gossips: Ann Smythe from Ashton Court; Bess and her mother; Mistress Keene, our cook; Jane Jennings, the former kitchenmaid, with her baby daughter in her arms; Mistress Bennett, wife of a wildfowler; Mistress Walker from the Mill; and lastly Mistress Hort.

Between eating pasties and caraway comfits from the kitchen, they drew up stools around the bed and kept up a constant flow of chatter about their own labours and childbeds, their numerous children and their households. I was not expected to join in but it was comforting to listen to them, enjoying being all together, and to have their support, companionship and recollected experience as the crushing pains grew stronger and closer together, until I gripped Bess's fingers hard enough to break them and screamed that I couldn't bear it any longer. 'Something must be wrong,' I yelled though gritted teeth. My shift clung to my body, soaked in perspiration, and my hair hung below my waist in sweaty rat's tails. 'This cannot . . . cannot be normal.'

'It is normal, child,' Mistress Bennett soothed. 'More's the pity. Now you stop worrying about it and let nature do its work.'

'Why is it never like this for cows in calf?'

'We have Grandmother Eve to thank for that,' Mistress Keene said.

'Thank her!' I grunted. 'I'd like to strangle her.'

Bess chuckled.

The pain subsided once more and I took consolation from watching Mother Wall issuing confident instructions for the fire to be got ready, the candles kept lit. She could have been forty or she could have been a hundred. Her hair was silvery, her back stooped, but her fingers, with their neatly trimmed nails, were soft and remarkably supple for a marsh dweller. She anointed my womb and her own hands with oil of lilies, rubbed soothing salves and liniments into my skin, and gave me cups of caudles and herbal infusions. I did not ask her what was in them, for once I was content just to obey without question.

She probed me gently to see how the birth progressed and how the baby lay, and all the while she talked to me in her soothing country burr, telling me to move about and not lie still on the bed, to stand and lean against the bed posts, as the great waves of pain rose ever higher, so that I was sure they would rip me apart.

She patted my hand as I bore down and pushed with all my might. 'You are doing very well, Ma'am,' she said. 'You screech all you want. We are nearly there now.'

'You'll meet your little one soon enough,' Mistress Knight soothed, and the thought of that made it more bearable, reminded me what lay at the end of my labour.

'How much longer?' I gasped.

'The babe will come in its own good time,' Mother Wall said.

That turned out to be just before midnight. I squatted over a pile of rushes, with Bess supporting me under my arm on one side and her mother on the other, while Mother Wall knelt below me and peered up between my legs. 'Its head is crowned,' she said, as if he were a little prince.

And then in one fiery eruption of ripping, gushing, hot, wet agony, my baby boy came slithering out like a fish between my knees, into the waiting arms of Mother Wall who caught him like a child catches a football. She flipped him over and slapped him on the back and he howled in protest, his little balled fists punching the air, his face red and contorted with anger.

I sat where I was on the floor and tears of joy and relief spilled down my hot cheeks. I had a child. A healthy, living child, and I had survived to see him born. He was so perfect. I held out my arms. 'Let me hold him,' I said. 'I want to hold my baby.'

I did not need anyone to tell me to use my hand to support his fragile little skull. Holding him was for me as natural and instinctive as his first breath. I held him in my left arm, close to my heart, and with my other hand I carefully wiped the blood and stickiness off his tiny head with the edge of my shift. I noted that he had the blackest hair. Where Edmund was red-headed and I was fair, our son had hair as black as peat, and for a while at least he also had soft blue eyes. I kissed him and rocked him, stroked him and crooned over him, could not take my eyes off him. I was filled with love, a protective and pure love that was so powerful it was overwhelming.

'Thanks be to God,' Bess's mother said. 'You are delivered of your first-born son.'

Everyone crowded round with blessings for us both, examined him and pronounced him very well made. I was struck by an enormous sense of affection and kinship with these women who had been with me though my travail. They were my sisters now and it was a joy to be a woman, to be in the exclusive company of women. I felt exalted. With God's help, and with some help from my husband, admittedly, I had created life inside me. I had brought life forth. And I had survived to see a miracle. If death had seemed an everyday tragedy, so birth was an everyday wonder.

The midwife took my son back into her expert hands and I watched as she took her knife to cut the navel string. She dressed it with frankincense, then, as I was put to bed, she took the baby to the basin of warm water and sweet butter to bathe him.

'So, I have a son.'

I tore my eyes away from the perfect little bundle and saw that Edmund had come into the birthing room. Poor Edmund. He looked so exhausted and so happy and so alarmed amidst the carnage, that all at once my heart went out to him.

I held out my hand and he came and took it and bent down to kiss my damp forehead. 'Eleanor darling, I heard your screams and was sure you were dying.'

'You were not the only one.' I smiled across at our baby as he was being swaddled by the midwife. 'But it was worth the pain. I've almost forgotten it already.'

He kissed me again. 'I'm so proud of you. You were so brave.'

The midwife handed our son to Edmund, who took him tenderly but awkwardly. 'Father, see, there is your child. God give you much joy with him.'

Much joy indeed. I felt a sweet elation that I had never felt before. I didn't even feel tired. Edmund placed the baby back in my arms and I kissed the top of his downy head, his sticky ebony hair.

'I feel as if it is I who have been born,' I said. 'Born again this day as a mother.'

We called him Forest. It was my choice and I was adamant that he must have his own name. He was to be Forest Edmund but would be known as Forest. He was a child born to inherit this land and I wanted him to have a name taken from nature.

Edmund acquiesced, no doubt thinking the name rather whimsical, but despite agreeing to that, for all he said he never wanted us to have fallings out, we did have an almighty disagreement about Forest's baptism.

Edmund was determined it should be just like our wedding, quietly and privately done, removed from public view, with only a select gathering present. He wanted it to take place in the evening, in the chamber where Forest was born. He wanted to present his son himself, with witnesses rather than sponsors, without the font or the Sign of the Cross.

'The Roundhead kind of christening, you mean,' I said disapprovingly, leaning back wearily against the angled pillows. 'The kind of christening my father gave me and my sister.'

'Surely you would prefer it to be done in your presence?' Edmund reasoned. 'Rather than have him taken away from you? Surely you'd prefer to be there to see our little one become a Christian soul?' He looked down at our baby as he slept peacefully in the crib at the side of the bed. 'You have not been parted from him since he was born. I can't believe you'd consider letting him go to the church without you. I'd have thought that nothing would induce you to send him away.'

I shifted to a more comfortable position, wriggled my feet under the blankets to get some feeling in them. I was sure I'd have forgotten how to use them by the time I was allowed out of this room again. 'Of course I would rather be with him. But since I am not permitted to leave my chamber so soon after I have given birth, it is not possible.'

'Then have it done here, in the chamber. It is more comfortable and more convenient, after all, and healthier too, to have the minister come to us rather than risk infection by taking someone so tiny out in the cold and the wet.'

'The church is hardly very far.' But I knew everything Edmund said was right, and did not blame him for thinking me very contrary. My fingers idly pleated the woven blanket. 'Of course I would like to be at my son's baptism, but it is more important to me that it be a joyous celebration. What matters to me more than anything is that Forest should have the most joyous start to his life.'

I may have submitted to the prescribed three days in the dark to give me time to recover from the birth, with the help of restorative drinks and dressings and doses of burnt wine. But I would not allow them to move my baby's cradle into a dark and shadowy corner, no matter that the manuals said not to let the beams of the sun or moon dart upon him as he slept. I didn't care what the manuals said, any more than I cared if mothers were supposed to play no part in the arranging of a baptism. I could not let Edmund do it his way.

'I want it to be a grand celebration,' I said. 'I know if it's done in church it means I can't come, but so be it. You can tell me all about it afterwards. I shall be content just to imagine the benches adorned with arras and cloth of gold and the font framed by heraldic banners, and our little boy, mantled in silk lawn and wool, carried proudly at the front of the procession in the arms of Mother Wall.'

Edmund harrumphed. 'Your father will turn in his grave.'

It was undoubtedly true. For him the font was an enchanted holy relic, or an abomination left over from popery, and the Sign of the Cross was akin to Devil worship, the mark of the beast. It was no wonder we were arguing about it. After all, friction over fonts had helped spark the Civil War. Baptism was an issue that had split families, communities and congregations.

'My father made his choices and I'm making mine,' I said. 'I cannot agree that our baby might just as well be baptised in a pail. When I was born, the font was being used as a trough for the cattle to drink from, but

John Burges later saw to it that it was gilded again and reinstalled. It is fit for use now and I want us to use it. I want our baby baptised in it.'

'John Burges can no more call himself a Puritan than can you,' Edmund said, rather pompously.

'I don't call myself a Puritan.'

'Except in one respect.' Forest had started wailing again and I had reached over and lifted him gently to my breast to give him suck. 'And for that, I can forgive you much,' Edmund said gently, watching us.

I settled the baby and gazed down as he guzzled contentedly, kneading my breast with his little dimpled hand. 'Yes, I suppose I am Puritan in this, at least. How could I not agree with the Puritan ministers who claim nursing is a godly responsibility? Even if it is so exhausting and unrelenting.'

Forest was uncommonly greedy, seemed to be constantly hungry, impossible to satisfy. He fed at all hours, all through the day and all through the night. But such was my infatuation with him that I couldn't bear to leave him to cry even for five minutes. I wanted to hold him and touch him and gaze at him all the time. My nipples were sore and cracked, so that when he latched on to them with his surprisingly sharp little gums, the pain sometimes made my toes curl. But I wouldn't have missed even that. 'I could no more give him to a wet nurse than I could cut off my own hand.'

Edmund handed me a cup of small beer, anticipating the raging thirst that hit me as soon as I started feeding. I drank and then Forest let go of me and drew up his legs and started to squawk again. I lifted him on to my shoulder and patted his back. 'There, there, my little man. Do you have a pain? I'll soon make it go away.' I bent my head to him and kissed the crown of his head.

'How many times a day do you kiss him and tell him he is handsome and how much you cherish him?' Edmund asked me softly.

I kissed Forest again and smiled. 'Not nearly often enough.'

'We will do as you wish,' my husband said, bending to drop a kiss on my own head.

I caught hold of his fingers as he moved away. 'Thank you, Edmund.'

He turned to me at the door. 'I shall ask Richard to be Forest's sponsor.'

'Richard?' His name shattered the peace of the chamber like a clap of thunder on a sultry summer day.

'Richard,' Edmund repeated, with what passed for harshness in his mild-mannered nature. 'Or do you have objections to that too? Since it's your wish that our baby have a grand baptism, with cloth of gold and holy water and sponsors and whatnot, at least allow me to have my say over who those sponsors should be.'

Because we had already had such a lengthy disagreement, I had to agree to this, wrong and twisted as it felt.

'I shall write to Richard now and ask him to come as soon as he can. I am sure he will accept. He is very fond of you, you know.'

How could he be so trusting, so oblivious?

They'd all gone to the church and as I waited alone, the chamber desolate without Forest in it, I tried very hard to concentrate on imagining my little son being anointed, John Foskett, the curate, saying the words of the baptism over him. How we were born in sin, entered this wicked world bathed in blood, and were born again, through water. I prayed that the Holy Ghost would descend upon my boy and live within him, would give him grace and goodness, such as it seemed I did not have. For I had heard Richard Glanville's soft-spoken voice in the garden as the party returned to begin the evening of festive drinking, and my heart had tuned to its cadence as my ears strained only to hear him again.

I listened to the noisy merriment downstairs and for once I didn't long to join in. I clung to the seclusion and safety of my chamber like a startled rabbit will hide in the woodpile when a fox is about.

Now they'd all raised a glass or three of canary wine and enjoyed the christening supper in the hall. They'd had their fill of oysters and anchovies and wafers and caraways and christening cake, and the other guests had all been brought to my bedside to congratulate me and see the gifts of silver spoons and gilt bowls on formal display in the chamber.

'God bless your little one and grant you as much comfort as every mother had of a child,' said Mary Burges, the other sponsor.

Edmund had given the midwife her ten shillings, the nurse her five, and every gossip had her sweetmeats to carry away in her handkerchief.

Still I had not seen Richard. And I would not let his name touch my lips to ask after him, told myself that it would be for the best if he did not come to see me.

Surely he must come.

The Smythe girls, Florence and Arabella from Ashton Court, crowded round Forest adoringly, kissed me and him and wished me much joy in my new little Christian. One of the boys from Clevedon Court poked his head between the beribboned heads of the sisters and looked at them cheekily in turn out of the corner of his eyes. 'There's just as much joy to be had in begetting a babe as there is in cooing over one,' he said, setting the girls blushing and giggling.

'At this rate, this one christening will beget a hundred,' Mr Merrick complained to me as he kissed my hand. 'You look well. Motherhood suits you.'

'It certainly does.' The voice had come from the other side of the room.

I looked up to see Richard framed in the doorway, standing at the entrance to my bedchamber with an anxious look in his beautiful blue eyes, as if he was not certain he would be welcome.

I smiled at him, and as soon as I did he smiled back, strode confidently towards the high bed as if there was nobody else in the room but the two of us, as if he would throw aside the blankets and climb in beside me, would gather me into his arms, with the drapes drawn to shut out the rest of the world.

'Motherhood does suit her indeed,' he whispered tenderly, as if in response to the earlier comment, but speaking to me alone. 'She has never looked more lovely.'

'I thank you, sir,' I said, as if there had been nothing more to it than a regular compliment. Only the hammering of my heart and a slight trembling of his hands told otherwise.

'It must be sweet torture for her husband,' he added with feeling. 'He must be in torment, knowing the joy of her but being barred from her bed, not being able to touch her. When she lies there half-dressed like a goddess of fertility, with her rosy cheeks and golden hair and her ripe breasts.'

I was sure that everyone must hear the torment in his own voice, must see the need in his eyes. But not one eyebrow was even raised at this lewd exchange. Of course it was not. It was, after all, entirely in order at baptisms to spice the talk with plenty of bawdiness. Only I guessed it was spoken with a real emotion. And I did not know how to manage it. I heard little Forest stir and called for them to bring him to me, even though he hadn't yet worked himself up to a proper cry. I clutched him before me as a knight might hold up a shield.

Richard seemed quite unable to stop his eyes wandering from my face to the fullness of my breasts, so that I hesitated before opening my shift in front of him. But Forest could smell the milk and began to nuzzle and root with his open mouth for my nipple, then to wail with impatience.

Richard looked down at him with a sudden sweet smile. 'I never thought Edmund had it in him to father such a lusty child.'

I thought with utter dismay how I was as lusty and greedy as my son. Richard had kissed me, and even if he had made love to me, I knew it would never sate my longing for him, not at all, but would only make me want him all the more. I had prayed for forgiveness and believed my prayers had been granted, but, oh, how terrifyingly easy it would be to fall again. Was it always to be like this, every time I saw him? Was there to be no peace at all for either of us?

I bent my head low over my baby, my cheeks burning with a mixture of shame and longing and utter panic. 'Our marriage has been blessed,' I whispered.

'Edmund is a fortunate man. I would think myself the most fortunate man alive had I found such a pretty little mother for my son.' The others had moved tactfully away from the bed to allow Forest's sponsor to get a better look at him. Richard leaned closer and with one slender finger pushed back the blanket as if better to study my baby's face. The lace cuff of his shirt brushed against the inside of my wrist like a caress. 'What would a son of ours be like, I wonder?' he whispered, so quietly that nobody but me could hear, his eyes seeking mine. 'Would his hair be black as night like this one, or golden as the sun like yours?'

'We shall never know.'

'Is that a note of regret I detect in your voice, Nell?'

I should have come back instantly with a retort to let him know he was in danger of overstepping the limit of permissible baptism banter, but I could not do it to him. There was a quiet desperation about him, as if he was barely holding himself together. One small push and he would fall to pieces. It seemed to make him revel in the risk he was taking, talking to me this way in a crowded room, and I felt the safest thing for me to do was to play along. Or, at least, that is what I pretended to myself I was doing. 'You can never get a son on me, but you can at least kiss me,' I murmured lightly. 'That is what is done at these occasions, after all. Everyone here has kissed me and so far you are the only one who has not. It would be entirely in order.'

'Forgive me,' he said a little harshly, as if he did not want to be flirted with. 'This is a new experience for me. I have not attended many baptisms. Indeed I have seldom been with a lady in her bedchamber without covering her skin with kisses.'

I felt my own skin tingle, as if it had been sprinkled all over with icy water. It was with a stab of torment of my own now that I imagined those other ladies who had lain naked with him, who had tasted what I could never taste.

'I'm curious,' he said abruptly. 'How long must you remain abed?'

'One month. Until I am churched.'

He smiled, bit his lip. 'Until then, you are still impure?'

'I am not a Jewess, Richard. I don't need cleansing. Only to give thanks.'

As he moved closer to me still, as his lips brushed against my hair, I breathed in the scent that emanated from his clothes and black curls, a faint mix of masculine sweat and horses, overlaid with sweet cologne. I felt his breath on the nape of my neck, on the soft lobe of my ear. If ever there was a woman in need of cleansing it was me.

I tilted my head closer, towards his mouth.

He drew back.

I had to bite my own lips to stop a little moan escaping from my throat.

'I shall not kiss you again,' he said quietly, and it felt as if the world had suddenly gone very dark, so dark that if it had not been for my little son, I might as well have closed my eyes and never opened them again.

My month of privilege after bearing my child was at an end. But when it came to the matter of how it should end, to whether or not I should be churched, Edmund had me all wrong yet again.

'I see that, now you are mistress of this house, you choose to reject every principle and value upon which you were reared. Surely then a progressive little spirit like you wouldn't want anything to do with such a ritual?

Surely you can't go along with the view of childbed taint, that there's something loathsome in the natural birthing of a child? My father was not the radical yours was, but even he saw churching as heretical, Popish foolery that mocked God.'

'Oh, Edmund.' I groaned in exasperation, pulled a pillow round to the front of me, clasped it as I threw myself back against the rest. Then I glanced at him out of the corner of my eye as he stood beside the bed with his mug of small ale. I did not want to argue again. 'D'you know, for someone so seemingly even-tempered and set on harmony, you can be mighty quarrelsome and opinionated?'

'You'd like a husband you could lead like a bull by the nose, a man with no mind of his own?'

'No. Not at all.' I cuffed him playfully with the pillow. 'I like a good debate very much. I am progressive, as you say. Which is why I want a churching.'

He reached down and took the pillow off me, carefully set it aside. 'You're all for discarding the old and embracing the new. But there's nothing new about churching, you know. It was restored to the churches with the King's restoration to the throne. Restored not invented, mark.'

'Resistance to it was one of the surest signs of Puritan feeling before Cromwell . . . before the war,' I added. 'I know all that very well. I don't need a lesson in history, thank you very much. But I am too young to have known the time before the war, as are you. It may not be new and different to the world, but it's new and different for me. I'm ready to walk out into our bright new age, but all the time I'm held back in the shadows. First by my father and now by you.'

'I am sorry you feel that way.'

'I just want to be like everyone else, for once.'

He laughed. 'You have a damnably odd way of showing it.'

'In some things, at least,' I demurred. 'It's the current law and custom to be churched and for once I want to go along with that. That's all.' I took Edmund's hand, drew him down to sit on the bed beside me. 'I don't see it as a blasphemous ritual but a joyous occasion, a time for thanksgiving.' I held his hand against my heart. 'We have so much to give thanks for, Edmund,' I said. 'I was so very afraid, so very sure that I would never get to hold our son in my arms, that he would be taken from us.' I said it as an affirmation, to remind myself. 'I want to celebrate Forest's life.' I glanced across at his crib. 'I want to celebrate being alive, being a mother. Being your wife.'

'You are my wife, but why is it we want such different things?' Edmund said wearily. 'I had hoped we would pull together, that we were yoked as close as two oxen at the plough, but so often these days you pull one way and I pull t'other.'

I lowered my eyes so that he would not see that, though it saddened me, I knew it to be true. But it need not be, it must not be. I looked back at him suggestively. 'Once the churching is over, you need no longer be excluded from my bed,' I said.

'Won't it sour your milk if I lie with you?'

'Oh, I don't believe that nonsense. And I don't believe Forest would care too much anyway. He's far too greedy to be so particular.' I let my eyes linger on Edmund's kind face. 'I shall be as a virgin again, your bride again. It will be like our wedding night.'

'You mean, when you ran away from me, while I was sleeping, as if you couldn't bear to face me in the cold light of day?'

'Dear Edmund, that is not how it was and it's not how it will be this time.'

He waved his hand in a resigned gesture of capitulation. 'I lack the will to stand against you. It's far too tiring. Your victory again.'

'There's no battle between us, Edmund.'

He stood, kissed my nose end. 'Aye, only because I always surrender.'

I smiled. 'That's how you used to talk before we were married, remember? When you were shy with me I think.' I quoted from the letter he once sent me. '"Now I have stormed the cherry bulwarks of your sweet mouth, I am convinced I may gain your surrender."'

'You ridicule me?'

'No! No, not at all, you silly goose. It's just that I read your letter so often I learned every word of it by heart. I treasured it and I've still not forgotten it.'

'You are not so very different from your father, you know,' he said thoughtfully. 'You are a little fighter. You fight for what you believe in until the very end, don't you?'

'Is nothing worth the fight to you?'

'I would fight for my family,' he said with all the touchingly protective pride of a new father. 'I would do anything for my son, and for you.'

I cocked my head. 'Anything?'

He gave me a wry smile. 'If it is what you really want, I'll send for Mother Wall right away.'

I caught his hand as he stood. 'Edmund, tell me you don't really mind if we do this?'

He beamed at me. 'I don't really mind.' He kissed my hand. 'You are a rebel, Eleanor Ashfield. I am not, and so I do admire you for it.'

As my midwife, Mother Wall organised my churching and, when the day came, it was she who escorted me to the church. I wore a new gown of creamy silk with a stomacher decorated with seed pearls, and we were followed by a gaggle of wives and mothers, all wearing their most fashionable outfits. We walked arm-in-arm and giggled and chatted and were truly as bawdy as wives at a gossiping.

In view of the whole congregation I was led by my attendants through to the main body of the church, to the most prominent benches covered with the kersey churching cloth. As I knelt at the altar, to be sprinkled with holy water, and as I let the droplets fall upon me, I bowed my head and closed my hands in prayer. I prayed silently that the blessed water from Tickenham's springs would cleanse me, not from the stain of childbirth but from all shameful desires and impure thoughts. I prayed with all my heart that I could be a good mother to Forest and a good wife to his father.

The minister recited the psalms and spoke of my deliverance from the peril of childbirth.

Oh, it was so lovely to be out of seclusion at last, to return to normal life, and it was nice to be the centre of attention with all eyes upon me. I felt special, that this was a very special day. As my wedding day should have been. It was a new beginning, this baby our pledge of love.

I looked across at my husband, who rocked our son in his arms, shushing to quieten him when he wriggled and whimpered and started to look for yet more food and root around against Edmund's brown brocade waist-coat, little head bobbing and mouth opened like a baby chick. Edmund stuck his little finger into it just as I had shown him how to, and Forest started to suck. They made a pretty picture and it occurred to me that

Richard might not have made such a devoted father to my children. I vowed before God to try very hard to be as good to Edmund as he was to me. We had all been spared and I would strive harder to show my gratitude.

When we'd all gone back to the house and eaten our venison pasties, I left the women's room and went to seek out the gentlemen in theirs. Bawdiness was as much in order at churchings as it was at baptisms and this time I would turn that practice to good use. In my heart I was as brazen as an orange girl waiting for custom outside the doors of the theatre, but with my eyes lowered to the ground and my quiet step, I sought to appear chaste as an angel, come to steal a soul in its sleep.

Inhaling an intoxicating fug of pipe smoke and brandy fumes, I walked straight through the men without once looking at any of them. I ignored their ribald comments as I went up to Edmund and took hold of his hand. 'Excuse me, gentlemen,' I said, looking only at Edmund. 'But I have missed my husband. I have more need of him this night than do you.'

Edmund appeared shocked, a little embarrassed, but I could tell he was also aroused by my boldness. I drew him gently towards me and then I turned and, still holding him by the hand, led him back through the lewd laughter and cheering of his friends.

Mr Merrick clapped him on the back. 'I do believe you're blushing, dear fellow.'

I imagined that was true, since Edmund still blushed remarkably easily, but I didn't look back to see. I didn't look at him until I had him in the chamber, with his back against the limed wall.

'My wife, what has come over you?' he whispered thickly. 'You are so thankful for being a mother that you want me to make another child on you tonight?'

I stood up on my tiptoes as I always had to do if I wanted to kiss him, and he bent his head so that we met halfway. I slid my hand up under his shirt and walked my fingers up his smooth chest, let my palm rest flat against his hot, damp skin. For once his heart was racing much faster than mine. 'If you do,' I said, 'I promise that this time I will still be close beside you when you wake.'

Summer 1678

The sunlight was sweet and golden as the best cider and it was the time of year when every lovely day was a bonus that could not be wasted. The air already smelled of wood fires and of distant rain. Humming a happy tune to myself and to Forest, I carried him down on to the moor straddled across my hip, butterfly net over my shoulder. My black lead pencil and notebook were tucked inside my corset, along with a little *Book of Psalms*. I didn't have enough hands to bring a cushion of pins and a deal collecting box, so I had reverted to my original method of pressing specimens between the pages of a book. Since my Bible was also too big and too heavy, the *Psalms* would have to do.

At nine months, Forest was growing heavier by the day, but I'd always had strong arms and legs and lungs from rowing and walking and riding and it was no great effort to carry him, even on such a warm day. Edmund had gone on a visit to his father and brother in Suffolk and I had stayed behind, hoping to have some time to please myself. I hadn't quite accepted that now I had a baby there was no such thing unless I entrusted him to someone else's care, which I could not bear to do, not even for a little while.

On the far side of the moor was a little group of roe deer, half-concealed in the long grass, and I stood and watched them grazing, glad to be given a glimpse into their private and secret lives.

Forest wriggled and I set him down amidst the buttercups and sat beside him. There was no point going all the way to the river. All summer I had been trying to show him the otters, but he was never quiet or still for two seconds and they understandably kept well out of our way.

I laid him on his back so he could look up at the kestrels and sparrow hawks soaring above him, but he was instantly squirming to roll over on to his belly and, before I knew it, he'd be trying to chew the grass, no matter how much I told him babies weren't supposed to eat grass. Though maybe it would be a good thing if this one did. Maybe it would help to satisfy him, since nothing else seemed to.

I sat cross-legged and scooped him up on to my lap, dandling him up and down, making him gurgle with delight. I dropped a kiss on his fat little cheek, rubbed our noses together, and he suddenly grabbed at my hair and pulled very hard.

'Ouch, little whelp! That hurts.'

He blew bubbles at me with his mouth and pulled all the harder, so that I had to prise open his grasping fist and unwind my hair from it.

'I'll always love you, no matter how you hurt me,' I said.

With eyes that were turning from blue now to a brown so dark it was almost black, he regarded me as if he understood every word I spoke. Then his whole body suddenly went rigid and he arched his back to free himself and be off again, so I put him back down on the grass.

I slid my arms out behind me and turned my face up to the sun. The movement of grass snakes nearby sounded like the rustle of dead leaves and already there was the scent of autumn in the air. Where had the summer gone? I hadn't caught a single butterfly since Forest was born. I'd not even made one entry in my observation book. Though James still wrote to me it was with less regularity, his letters growing shorter. I'd only managed a few brief replies.

Now Forest was tearing at a buttercup. Pity any butterfly that came near while I had this tiny destroyer with me. Why had I even bothered to bring my net along?

'We might as well pay a visit to Mistress Knight,' I sighed. 'She'd love to see how you've grown into such a pudding.'

We were nearly at the Knights' cottage when I saw it, not too far away, in an open area of sedge and reed where the milk parsley grew. It was flying, slowly and powerfully, a spectacular sweep of yellow and red and blue. I gently deposited Forest in a soft patch of grass. 'I'll be right back, poppet,' I whispered.

I bunched up my petticoats, kicked off my slippers and ran, slowing as the butterfly came drifting down towards me. It hovered, not quite settling, its wings a flutter, as it sucked the juice from the milk parsley. It was a fine example, the colours still luminously vivid in the bright sunshine, wings perfectly unragged. Almost before I knew what had happened it was there, unbelievably, imprisoned like a rare jewel beneath the veil of my muslin trap.

I pinched its black and yellow abdomen carefully and swiftly between my finger and thumb, just below its head. Wings and antennae quivered a moment, then were still, outspread and undamaged, not a single pearly scale missing. A yellow stain appeared on my palm. I suffered an instant of remorse at the loss of a little life, that it would no longer flutter innocently in the sunshine. But it was outweighed by the satisfaction of having a pristine swallowtail specimen to add to my collection, at last. I stared in wonder at its glorious Gothic-sculpted wings, the magnificent markings, and thought of how I would describe in a letter the thick dusting of lemon meal that gave it its predominant colour. I thought of how I couldn't wait to tell James about my find.

I laid it carefully inside the *Psalms* and closed the little book, reverential as a Puritan girl should be, tying a ribbon round it to keep it shut tight.

'What kind of unnatural, unfeeling mother are you?' Mistress Knight, Bess's mother, was standing right behind me, clutching Forest to her in her gnarled old hands as if she had snatched him out of the jaws of death itself. 'Tom heard your child wailing from yards away, even if you did not. You are not fit to care for a babe if you leave it crying in a marsh, amidst a herd of cattle, to go gadding after butterflies.'

It made no difference to Mistress Knight that I was Lady of the Manor now. She had known me as a little girl, one she had felt quite entitled to chastise if need be. That Forest had been wailing I doubted very much. He looked perfectly content. And since I heard his every snuffle from the depths of my sleep, I would surely not have failed to hear him crying. There were indeed a great number of cattle on the moor, not just those of the commoners but the beasts of others they grazed for a fee, but they were all so far off as to be almost invisible. Not so Thomas Knight. He was loitering by the bend in the river, hands stuffed in his pockets and a pile of cut sedges at his feet.

Annoyed, but doing my utmost not to show it, I quickly pushed the *Psalms* back inside my gown, took Forest into my arms, cradled his head in the crook of my neck. 'I was only gone a moment, Mistress Knight.'

'A moment is all it takes for a cow to trample him, or for him to roll into the bog or ditch, or eat a poison plant that will make him vomit for a week, or worse,' she said gruffly. 'The wild swans and geese tend their chicks better than you tend yours.'

I knew she cared very much for my little son whose birth she had witnessed. She had supported me as he was being born, and walked behind me and laughed with me at my churching. 'I thank you for your concern,' I said evenly. 'But Forest was perfectly safe, I assure you. I know very well which are the poison plants and there were none near him. He was nowhere near any bogs or ditches either.'

'This is no place for a child.'

'I came down here every day when I was one.'

'Aye, and look how you've turned out.'

'I will ignore that comment. We were on our way to see you,' I said shortly. 'But I think we had better go back to the house instead.'

'And I think you had better stay there, out of harm's way, until your husband is returned.' She cast a strange, longing glance at Forest, as if she wanted to run off with him and rear him herself. 'Your father should have shown you a stiffer hand. He should have known you'd grow to be as wild and wayward as your mother.'

I was astounded. 'What do you mean?'

'I mean nothing,' she said, flustered. 'Now be off with you, before I say more than is wise.'

'I think you had better say it, Mistress Knight.'

'I think I had better not.' She flicked her rheumy eyes towards Thomas.

He was still standing there, watching us. For some reason that I was no closer to understanding, he hated me still. He was my enemy, and an increasingly dangerous, insidious and underhand one, who would use whatever weapons he could muster against me. He would make sure that this dispute was round the village like wildfire, spread by scandalmongers and gossips, exaggerated and distorted. Everyone would hear of it. Edmund would hear of it.

'I once clouted my boy for calling you whimsy-headed, for putting it about that you must be cracked to go chasing after fairies,' Mistress Knight went on. 'But now I think he was maybe not so wrong.'

'You've been a good friend to me and to my family,' I said carefully. 'But I'll ask you to mind your tongue. I would never put my baby in any danger.'

'So you say.' She turned and hobbled off on arthritic legs towards her son.

I held my own son very close, in the middle of the milk parsley, and stroked his broad little back. 'You weren't upset at all, were you, my little cherub? You know I'll always look after you.'

I couldn't face going inside yet, so I took him into the orchard and sat with him under an apple tree. 'If she could see us now, she'd likely criticise me for endangering your life from falling apples,' I jested.

Forest was sleepy after so much sun and fresh air, so I rested him against my shoulder and rocked him gently. Instead of singing to him, I told him about a letter I had written to him before he was born.

'I wrote it in case I died giving birth to you,' I whispered into his pink shell of an ear. 'I wrote down all my hopes for you, in case I wasn't there to bring you up and tell you them myself. It's very important, even though I am still here, so please listen very carefully.

'I want you grow to be a good man, like your father and your grand-father. Above all else, I hope that you are just and wise and honest in all that you do. I pray you take an interest in the world around you and find some worthy occupation that pleases you and is of some service to God and to mankind. For then, you will be sure to be happy and fulfilled.' I paused and slipped my hand between my waist and his dangling legs. 'Find yourself a pretty and kind girl and be good to her, and be good to any little brothers and sisters you may have. Take care of them, protect them and be someone they look to for counsel and guidance. I always wished I'd had an older brother. Be the brother I would have wanted. Be a son to make me proud.' I nuzzled his warm neck, kissed it. 'Oh, and most important of all, always be good to your mother.'

He'd grown even heavier so I knew that he was asleep, a puzzling phenom-enon I could not even begin to comprehend since surely a sleeping child did not in actual fact gain extra pounds, to be lost again the moment he woke. So why did it feel as if that was exactly what happened? I tilted him over to cradle him and look down into his peaceful sleeping face. He had pushed his thumb in his mouth and now and then his little lips puckered with sucking movements that seemed to comfort him as once only my breast or finger had done. Something about this tiny show of independence tore at my heart. He was already growing away from me. Day by day, he needed me less.

I opened my *Book of Psalms*. The beautiful yellow butterfly with curved wings, the first I had ever caught, was broken in two. No matter. I would give one of the wings to James. He would like that. In his most recent letter to me he had enclosed another of his strange little broken gifts, the single brilliant emerald and black wing of a large tropical butterfly that had been sent back to him from a ship's surgeon who had sailed to Brazil. James was sticking to his plan, his life's task of building a worldwide community of natural scientists.

Maybe that was why my walk on the moor today hadn't been the balm to me it usually was. The wide wetland horizon just drew attention to how vast was the world and how little of it I would ever see, how far I would never travel.

I had been a small part of something important which had mattered to me more than anything else. Now I had my baby, he mattered more than life itself. So I was torn, for it felt as if all time borrowed from my child was misspent, but also that when I was not studying butterflies, I was somehow missing out on what I was supposed to do.

I closed the *Psalms*. If I wanted to be a good mother, I could not be a good scientist. If I wanted to be a good scientist, I could not be a good mother.

I wanted so very much to be able to be both, to be good at being both.

Autumn 1678

The autumn rains returned before Edmund did; steady, incessant rain. Accustomed to it as I was, it was still alarming to watch a deluge of water pouring down from the sky as more water rose up the riverbanks and the rhynes, came gushing up through the very earth to meet it, quickly turning the moors into a desolate, wild morass of bog and marsh and wide lagoons.

I sat on the window seat in the parlour and traced the raindrops with my finger as they raced haphazardly down the small panes, like animated versions of the tiny air bubbles trapped within the glass. I was Persephone of the Greek myths, abducted by Hades, the King of the Underworld. I was a child of Somersetshire: land of the summer people, fated to live out half of each year in darkness.

Though it was London, now, that was gripped by a great ague epidemic. The latest gazette lay on the table, filled with news of how the King himself had contracted the disease and demanded the services of an Essex man, Robert Talbor, a self-styled feverologist whom the College of Physicians had dubbed a quack. No one knew his secret and he refused to reveal it, but he had seemingly cured the King and was to be knighted for his services.

Jesuits' Powder? I wondered. Was that his secret cure? It would certainly explain why he'd be so desperate to hide the truth now, at the very time Jesuits were being accused of plotting to assassinate the King and put his Catholic brother on the throne. The gazette reported that all of London was hysterical with terror at a clergyman's claim that thousands of Jesuits were crouching in cellars, ready at the signal to leap out and slaughter all Protestants in England. They were, apparently, conspiring to poison the whole world by means of the so-called medicine commonly known as the Jesuits' Powder.

I was expecting Edmund to be home today before dark, in plenty of time for supper, and I couldn't sit here any longer. Forest was sleeping, with luck would sleep for another hour, and Bess would listen out for him. I snatched my red, hooded riding cloak and set out for the causeway.

The rain had eased, but the cobbles were slick and slippery and I walked carefully to avoid twisting my ankle. There was a stiff south-westerly wind and I clutched my cloak tight, pulling up the hood.

The heavy sky was the colour of pewter and the willows were delicately pencilled in the mist. The watermeadows were shimmering with pools of silver while flocks of little dunlins skimmed the air, their flight rapid and direct, all abruptly changing direction at once, like a wave breaking in the air as they flashed their dark backs and then white undersides.

I'd gone about half a mile before I heard the faintest sound of a horse's hooves above the wild and lonely call of the curlews. Like a beast from the legends of King Arthur, Edmund's chestnut gelding came splashing across the causeway, with only the head and shoulders of his rider visible above the mists, a rider with copper hair which shone warm as the welcoming light of a distant inn to a lone traveller.

He reined in beside me. 'Eleanor, what are you doing out here? What's wrong? Little Forest . . . ?'

'Is fast asleep in his crib. Nothing's wrong.' I held on to the horse's bridle as the animal snorted and tossed its head, the bit jangling, and smiled up at my husband, my hood falling back from my face. 'I've been lonely without you. That's all.'

'Have you? Have you really?' He beamed down at me, like he had the first time I ever saw him, the first time he'd come to Tickenham, on a day not unlike today.

'You're going to tell me I'm foolish,' I said. 'That you've not been gone very long.'

He reached out his hand to pull me up into the saddle in front of him, settled his arms around me. I rested my hands on the reins between his as he gave them a jerk.

'As a matter of fact, I've been lonely without you too,' he said. 'I'm very glad to be home.'

'Do you still think of your father's house as home, too?'

'My father barely recognises it himself. Drainage doesn't just alter the landscape, it creates a whole new society, a whole new economy. But, tell me, how does my little boy? Is he talking yet? Has he missed me too, do you think?'

'He is greedier than ever,' I said fondly. 'He's probably doubled in size since last you saw him.' I paused and then my confession came tumbling out of my mouth, like the river over a weir.

As I told him about the swallowtailed butterfly and Mistress Knight's accusations, Edmund's hold on the reins remained light and his arms around me didn't tense or recoil.

'I wanted you to hear it from me, rather than through village scandal-mongers,' I finished. 'I know Forest was perfectly safe and yet I am annoyed with myself. He is still waking twice in the night and I'm so tired that, it's true, I probably wasn't as alert as I should be. But I would never neglect him. Never.'

'I know you wouldn't. You are a wonderful mother. And he's thriving, as you said yourself. That's all that matters.' Edmund kissed the top of my head and then tucked it under his chin. 'What's done is done, and there's no use worrying about what might or might not have been.'

How much easier life would be if I was as unruffled as Edmund, if I could skim along as he did and not look too closely or delve too far beneath the surface of things, if I didn't have to question from every angle and worry about what might never be. It was good that I had him to act as my counterbalance. And maybe, once I'd been married to him for a few more years, I'd become a little more like him.

'So, did you catch your prize?'

'I did.'

'I'm glad. I know how much you wanted one.'

That surprised me. But I remembered then how Richard had said Edmund had once made him look for one.

'Do you find them all over the country? Does your butterfly friend in London see them there?' My husband sounded genuinely interested.

'No. He's seen dead ones others have collected, but he has never seen one on the wing.' I nestled up closer to Edmund's shoulder and almost drew back a little on the reins. The steady clop and gait of the horse was as pleasant and easy as our conversation. I didn't even feel the cold and the rain, was warm and cosy as if we were curled up together beneath the blankets in bed, with a fire glowing in the brazier. 'Since when were you so interested in butterflies anyway?'

'Since I saw that they interested you.'

'Oh.'

'Whatever matters to you, matters to me too.'

I put my small hands over Edmund's much larger ones, slipped my fingers down so they were meshed with his. I knew, clearer than I could see the summit of Cadbury Camp on a sunny day, that though he had been prompted at least in part to marry me because I was the heiress of Tickenham Court, and though he may not love me as I wanted to be loved, he loved me with all that he had. And I valued that love more than ever.

'William is keen to press on with the drainage again here now,' he said presently.

I felt my muscles tauten. 'Must we?'

'There's a fresh move across the whole of the country for agricultural improvement. William has watched a hundred acres being successfully recovered at Wick St Lawrence, not so very far away, and it's renewed his enthusiasm for land reclamation here. But we are under no obligation now, since that first scheme was abandoned. It is not William's decision.'

I didn't want to ruin the closeness between us with another disagreement, so I chose my words carefully. 'You don't sound as if you share his enthusiasm so much any more.'

'It's not that I can't still see the benefits. But for all that, I would rather leave well alone for as long as is possible.'

'You would? Why?'

'I am growing soft and sentimental in my old age, that's why.' I heard the trace of humour in his voice. 'I can't say for sure. All I *can* say is this. If we drained the moor, you'd have seen the last of your swallowtails here. When I was a boy, they were as abundant in the Fens as they are in Tickenham. But now the water has gone, the swallowtails have gone with it.'

'They can't have!'

'They have.'

'Are you certain?' Dry meadows should mean more butterflies, not less, surely?

'Believe me, Eleanor, I looked. I looked last summer and I looked again this time. Knowing how much you love them, I looked hard. But I didn't see a single one.'

I was still coming to terms with the fact that he even knew what a swallowtail was.

'It's the same with the orange ones you once told me are so prized amongst collectors. They were plentiful too, as they are here, but now, in the Fens, they have totally vanished.'

I would have felt a jolt of dismay at this discovery, except that I was so delighted it was Edmund who had made it. That he had made it because of me. 'I can't believe you noticed.'

'You notice, so I notice.'

I twisted my head sideways against his shoulder, felt his bristly copper whiskers snag my hair. We carried on in silence but my mind was not at all quiet, was whirring busily as ideas crystallised inside me. 'It must mean they can live only on marshes, that there is something about marshland necessary for their life.'

'That seems a fair conclusion.'

'So if all the wetlands in England are to be drained, will swallowtail and large copper butterflies disappear completely? The specimens in the collections of butterfly hunters might be all that is left to prove they ever existed.' There was something portentous in that. 'If drainage causes a little creature at the bottom of the great Chain of Being to die out, then could it have some effect upon those further up – on people? Could land unable to sustain a tiny butterfly ever sustain us?'

'I am afraid you are losing me,' Edmund laughed.

It seemed too dramatic and too abstract a theory to dwell upon now. What mattered far more right at this moment was that I was having a proper conversation with my husband, at last. I had thought that I might grow more like Edmund. Instead it seemed he was growing more like me. That was probably not a wholly good thing, but I liked the idea all the same. I liked being able to talk to him about things I cared about. I liked this new feeling of closeness very much.

We had reached the stable. Edmund released the reins to dismount, but something prompted me to hold on to his hands. Maybe it was because of the ominous disappearance of the butterflies, but I didn't want him to let go of me. I had the alarming sense that, though he was here with me now, I was losing him, just as he had jokingly said I was during our conversation. But to what, I did not know.

He swung to the ground, turned around to help me down.

I slid into his arms and held him tight, standing on tiptoe to kiss him, as always.

The mist seemed to close in around us.

Bess told me that Forest was awake and had just that moment started to bawl for food, or attention, or both. I told her I would go to him. He was lying on his back, kicking his sturdy little legs, and I lifted him out, surprised afresh by how solid and strong he was growing. 'Come here, little fellow. Your papa's home and wants to see you.' I swung him, still kicking, on to my hip and he quietened as we made our way down the stairs to the parlour where I handed him over to Edmund, who promptly tossed him the air and caught him, much to Forest's delight.

'Do you think he's changed while you've been away?' I asked.

'You make it sound as if I've been gone months.'

Forest was playing with the brass buttons on Edmund's waistcoat.

'He's changing all the time, can't you see it? His legs are a fraction longer, his eyes darker. His cheeks just a bit more plump.'

Edmund looked bemused. 'All to the good, surely. Why look so sad about it?'

'Oh, I don't know. I'm being foolish. But I do wish I were a better artist. I'd draw him every day so I could hold on to each moment. I want to see him walk and hear him speak proper words to me, yet I hate the thought of him even being old enough to be breeched. I want him to stay a baby forever.'

'Ah, but then he'd not grow to be a fine young lord for Tickenham Court. That is what I want to see, above all else. I do realise, of course, that he cannot actually take the seat until I have vacated it,' my husband added jocularly, 'but I shall enjoy rearing him to sit in it well.'

Forest promptly stuffed the lace-trimmed edge of Edmund's square white collar into his little gummy mouth.

'So you have a taste for finery, do you, my little lad?' Edmund said. 'Just like your godfather. Richard sends you his love by the way, Eleanor, promises to come and visit very soon.'

'You have seen him?' I asked, as casually as I could.

'Aye, rather ironically he asked if he could come to the Fens to escape the ague outbreak, not to mention the outbreak of mass hysteria at this Popish Plot.'

'They are still claiming that we are all to be poisoned?'

'Would you believe, a facsimile of Jesuits' Powder has been paraded through the city streets, with great signs warning of exactly that.'

'But what if Jesuits' Powder really does hold the cure for ague? Thousands who fear it might die needlessly, just like my father.' It seemed to me that the world had gone totally mad.

'That man who cured the King swears he does not use it, that he has seen most dangerous effects follow the taking of it.'

'But he has to say that, Edmund, doesn't he?'

Bess had been in to light the candles in the wall sconces but I felt a sudden, powerful need to light some more. I went and stuck a candle into the fire and went round lighting all the others in the candelabra on the table and the buffet, one by one, until the shadows retreated and the room was shimmering with light.

'You are an extravagant little wench,' Edmund told me, smiling nevertheless.

But still it did not seem enough to hold the darkness at bay.

Winter 1679

I studied Richard's pensive profile as he leaned against the parlour doorway, watching Edmund capering with Forest and a puppy in front of the fire. It was well past the time that the child should have been in his cot, but Edmund, so bent on routine in all other matters, constantly chose to forgo this one, in order to enjoy a few extra minutes of play with our little boy.

The sound of sleet slapping the windows made the room seem cosy and warm and the supper we had all just eaten, finished off with furmenty and baked apple tart, had left me feeling pleasantly drowsy as I took up a botany book and sat in the chair beside my little family.

But the feeling of content vanished when I happened to glance up from my reading and saw Richard lingering by the threshold, as if he felt unable or unwilling to intrude on our little scene of happy domesticity. As Edmund held the pup for Forest to fondle its floppy brown ears, there was envy and jealousy plain to see in Richard's eyes. What I could not tell was whom he most envied, of what he was most jealous. Edmund, for having a son and a wife? Or Forest, for robbing him almost totally of Edmund's attention, for enjoying a privileged childhood and having a happy and hearty young father, when, according to Edmund, Richard had seen his own father embittered and demoralised in exile. Either way, I could not bear to watch any longer.

I put down my book, went to my husband and quietly held out my hands for him to give Forest to me. 'Time for sleep,' I said.

'Since when has your mother ever been governed by time?' Edmund smiled, picking Forest up and handing him over to me, thereby eliciting a squeal of protest. 'I think the puppy needs its bed too,' he said firmly. Doting as Edmund was, he never gave in to Forest's tantrums. Forest knew it and the squawks soon turned to mewling.

'Why don't you ride into Bristol tonight with Richard?' I suggested to Edmund.

He stood, stroked Forest's sleek little head. 'What for?'

'I don't know.' I shrugged. 'Go to a tavern or the coffee house,' I suggested rather exasperatedly. 'Whatever the pair of you used to do together in London.'

Edmund looked as abashed as a mischievous lad caught under a table, trying to sneak a look up ladies' skirts. 'That'd not do at all,' he blushed. 'Not now I have a wife.'

He had never spoken of women he had known before me, but I had the impression there had not been a great many. I did know that now he was wed there would be no more. I trusted him in this, as in all things, trusted him absolutely, and so I let the comment pass. 'Go to Bath then,' I sought to persuade him. 'There's time if you leave now. Give Richard a taste of the waters to refresh him, before he goes back to the city.'

'Why are you so keen to be rid of me all of a sudden?' my husband asked.

'Oh, you know it's not that. I think it would do you good. You used to enjoy gallivanting together, did you not?'

'That was before,' Edmund said affectionately. 'Before I had a wife and a family. Now I've no wish to seek entertainment elsewhere. Now every-thing I need and want is right here in this house. And here,' he added gently, laying his palm against the small curve of my three-month pregnant belly.

I gave him a grateful smile, glanced at Richard and saw his disappoint-ment as he turned and absently picked up my lute. He slouched down into a chair, one long booted leg hooked over the carved arm, and started idly plucking a remarkably pretty and competent melody. For a moment I watched his fingers on the lute strings, the wistful expressions that crossed his face as he played, but I tore my gaze back to Edmund, leaned in closer to him over our son's little head. 'I think Richard would like you to go to Bristol with him.'

'Aye, he's restless as a tomcat.' Edmund smirked. 'The lad needs to find himself a wife.'

'Yes,' I said quietly. 'But for now he does not have one. And you are his friend.'

Edmund deposited a kiss on my forehead. 'You would be friend and mother to all waifs and strays. And I do treasure you for that.'

I squeezed his arm affectionately. 'Good. Then listen to what I am saying, why don't you?'

'All right, but I'll settle Forest in the nursery first.'

Forest went very willingly back into his father's arms and Edmund hoisted him up on to his shoulders and away.

I drew up a chair opposite Richard. He tilted his head slightly, looked back at me out of the corners of his eyes as he continued to play.

'It is very pretty,' I said. 'What's it called?'

'*L'Amour Médecin*,' he replied, perfectly accented.

I laughed. 'The Love Doctor?' I was glad that my French studies had proven useful at last.

'It is a comedy by Moliéré.'

'What's it about?' I thought, even as I spoke, that I might well regret asking.

Richard kept his head lowered over the lute, raising his eyes to look at me in a way that made them seem darker, smouldering. I'd always thought blue was either a cold colour, of ice and of water, or at most only as gently warm as a summer sky. I'd never have imagined that blue eyes could burn with the slow gentle heat that his did now. Yet his voice was strangely flat. 'Lucinde is depressed,' he related tonelessly. 'Desperate to cheer her, Sganarelle offers her whatever she wishes. When she declares that she wants to be married to Clitandre, Sganarelle becomes angry, refuses to grant her desire.' The music stopped. His fingers were still. 'He admits that his reason for refusing her request is that he cannot stand the thought of her with another man.'

I was out of the chair in an instant, on my way straight out of that room.

He cast the lute aside with a discordant sound, swung his legs to the floor and sprang to his feet. He caught my hand, the momentum of my flight swinging me back round so I was flung against him.

'That was unfair of me,' he said.

Our bodies were touching down their entire length. 'Yes,' I breathed, standing back from him. 'It was.'

He let go of me with obvious reluctance, held on to me only with the intensity of his gaze, a hold more powerful then ever his hand had been on my arm. 'You did ask.' He smiled at me then.

I smiled back. 'I did, and I knew it to be a bad idea.' I picked up the lute, handed it back to him. 'Would you play some more?'

I sat again, as did he, but he looked at the instrument for a moment as if he had forgotten what to do with it, or as if it had entirely lost its appeal for him. Then he turned his eyes to me meditatively. 'Being with you is like listening to a Lully ballet,' he said. 'It is music that is filled with vitality and stirs the deepest sentiment. That is how you make me feel, Nell, how you have always made me feel. I have tried and tried to understand what it is about you. But look at you. With your golden hair and honey skin, you are a Rubens painting come alive, that's what you are. All exuberance and emotion and depth of colour and sensuality. And, as if you really were a painting, I must content myself with just looking at you.'

Nobody had ever talked to me the way he did. But I could have listened to his voice forever, no matter what he spoke of.

'I cannot disagree with you,' I said. 'Since I have never seen a Rubens painting or heard a Lully ballet.' I imagined that even in poverty he must have been exposed to all kinds of new experiences during his years of exile in Europe and felt again that restless desire to see more of the world myself, to make of my life more than it was. 'It must be wonderful to compose a piece of music, or paint a picture that will last for all time,' I said. 'So that your name is forever linked to something beautiful.'

'Is that what you want to do?' he asked me gently. 'To be like Rubens or Lully?'

I smiled. 'I have no particular talent for art or music, but since I was a child I have wanted to discover something, to do something of lasting significance. I should like to be remembered.' I realised I had never confided that to anyone before, not even to James Petiver. 'That doesn't sound very humble, does it?'

'I think it is a fine ambition.' He gave me a little meaningful smile. 'I too should like to have my name linked to something beautiful.'

I would have loved to have asked him more about Rubens and Lully, about art and ballet, but Edmund came back into the room and so they went off to Bristol, and whatever they found to do there kept them occupied until the early hours of the next morning.

I was tending to Forest when I heard them crash and stumble through the door, spurs and swords jangling. Edmund, in particular, was talking and laughing loud enough to rouse the dead.

I settled Forest in his crib and went back to bed. Later, I heard one set of footsteps mount the stairs, the quiet tap of expensive leather-soled boots in the passage. They paused outside my door. And then there was a light tap on the wood.

No, Eleanor. Do not go to him. If you know what's good for you, ignore it, pretend you are sleeping. If you open that door to him, you are undone.

I threw on a loose gown, padded in bare feet across the cold oak boards.

'I hope I did not wake you,' Richard said softly.

I shook my head, clutched the neck of my gown and held on to the door, fooling myself that I was entirely capable of closing it at any moment in his beautiful face.

He was still wearing his long cloak but had removed his hat and unbuckled his sword. His eyes were sparkling like a moonlit sea and I could detect the warm scent of brandy on his breath, although he seemed entirely sober.

'I wondered where I might find some spare blankets,' he said.

'Blankets?' I felt mildly annoyed, was in no mood now to bandy innuendo with him. 'You were not warm enough last night?'

He gave me a wry smile. 'Nell, if that were so, I would have spoken to your maid about it earlier. I would not trouble you with my discomfort in bed, whatever its cause.'

I felt my cheeks flush, not sure if it was from my blunder or the intimate inference.

'I'm afraid poor Edmund can't hold his drink the way he used to,' Richard explained. 'He's sound asleep in a chair in the parlour and I'll never manage to get him up all these stairs to bed. We are in for snow tonight, I think. I don't want him to catch cold.'

'There are plenty of rugs in the linen cupboard. I'll fetch some for you.'

He gestured with his hand. 'I'll get them,' he said quietly. 'Go back to bed. I am sorry for disturbing you.'

I could have told him that his very presence in this house disturbed me constantly. But I didn't want him to go now, wanted to keep him with me for as long as I could, just to talk to him again. 'Did you have a good evening?'

'We did. Thank you. It was thoughtful of you to suggest it. Edmund will probably not thank either of us for it in the morning, mind.'

I smiled at him, found my eyes were irresistibly drawn to the loose black curl that shaped itself around his ear and lay so softly coiled against his neck, brushing his left shoulder. I wanted to touch it, was ridiculously envious of it. I wanted to rest my head on his shoulder the way it did, wanted to nuzzle into his neck, to put my lips against that tender skin where a little pulse was beating.

I pulled my plait of hair over my shoulder, toyed with the end of it. 'Were you very wild, the pair of you, when you were in London?' I asked him.

'Come now, Nell, you can hardly expect me to answer that.'

'No. I suppose not.' For just a second I had forgotten that his companion in these exploits had been my own husband.

'Well, goodnight then.'

'Goodnight.'

He paused, half turned to go, turned back. 'London is a bed of vice and sin,' he said. 'As I am sure your father warned you. And Bristol is not so different, if you know where to look. It would be very easy for me to sow a seed of doubt that would despoil your contented marriage. For me to tell you that your husband is not nearly so upstanding as you think him. I could easily tell you how you do wrong to trust Edmund so implicitly, as you so clearly do trust him. I could tell you how, under the influence of drink and bad company, he did not deserve your trust, did not behave honourably towards you this night.' His look was reflective. 'But none of it would be true. Oh, I don't deny that Edmund has enjoyed a dalliance from time to time, with society beauties and strumpets alike, as have we all, but not once has he ever behaved with less honour than you would expect of him. And tonight, amidst the myriad temptations of Bristol, all he did was talk and talk about your son and the new baby. And about you. Not that I need him to tell me how wonderful you are and how very fortunate he is to have you. There is not one day goes by that I do not brood upon it.'

He sounded so terribly sad and lonely, I wished I could think of something to say to make it better. Felt also an intense irritation with Edmund for his lack of sensitivity and tact, for bragging about his own happiness when anyone with half a heart could surely see that Richard was unhappy.

'Nell, do you ever wish that you were married to me instead of Edmund?' He shot his hand out to hold the door open as if he expected me to slam it shut on him. 'Please,' he said quickly. 'I think it would help me to know.'

When I did not answer, his eyes flickered over my face, reading it, as seemingly he could do all too easily. He let his arm slide down the door, sighed disconsolately. I do not know what he had seen. Indecision? Alarm? Denial? Whatever it was, it plainly did not help him at all, and I so wanted it to.

I reached down, touched the back of his hand with my fingertips, said very quietly: 'I wish.'

His answering smile was very sweet and uncertain. It made the little crescent-shaped dimples appear at either side of his mouth. I almost laughed out loud at myself. I could write a whole book on this man's features and expressions, so carefully did I note each one, so carefully did I store them all up in my heart, like so many treasures.

'What is so amusing?' he asked me.

I wanted to tell him. I wanted just to say to him: You are so very beloved to me, that I could describe your face well enough for an artist to paint a perfect portrait, without ever once having seen you.

If I had not known it before, I knew it then. It was not lust I felt for him, not just desire, but love. And how could such a love be a sin? It did not feel like a sin at all, but something pure and special, something to be cherished. I had kissed him once, just once, and there could never be more between us than that. I could never have him, but nothing would ever stop me loving him. I loved him, would always, always love him even if I could not be with him, even if I never saw him again. There it was, and there was no use in denying it or fighting it any more. Nor could I regret it. How could I ever have regretted that kiss? How could I regret having known, even just once, for such a short time, the feel of his sweet, beautiful mouth upon mine? If I had a heart that was all on fire, as he had told me I had, it was love for him that had set it blazing. Until then, it had been more like a little barrel of gunpowder, waiting for the spark that would make it explode into life. And if he had not lit it, I would have spent my whole existence not knowing what it felt like to have a furnace inside my soul, would never have known that such a dark, wild, sweet passion could exist. Better by far to experience that passion, even if it brought more grief than joy, than to die not knowing it was even possible.

'What happened to you?' I asked him very quietly, suddenly needing to know more than I had ever needed to know anything else. 'In the war. Can you tell me?'

Instantly I cursed myself and my confounded curiosity. Never had I seen those little indentations above his nose appear so defined. He looked to be in actual bodily pain, a pain that I felt as if it were my own.

I laid my hand on his wrist. 'Forgive me. I should not be so inquisitive.'

'It is all right,' he said very softly. 'I want to tell you.'

I wished we could go somewhere else to talk, wished I could pour a glass of wine for him, and for myself, but it was so late and I could not invite him into my chamber, did not want to go downstairs to where Edmund was sleeping, and so I leaned against the door and Richard did the same.

'When the Parliamentarians drove away all my family's cattle and pillaged just about everything else, Edmund's family saw to it that mine did not starve,' he began, almost shyly. 'But when victory came for Cromwell and for the Ashfields, our estate was confiscated and that, together with punitive fines, deprived my family of any means of existence. Not that my father's pride would ever have permitted him to sign engagements of loyalty to the Commonwealth, to submit to the authority of those he always called rebels and regicides. And so he fled from this country as from a place infected with plague.' He took a breath, fixed his eyes on my face, as if he needed something to hold on to. 'My brother went with him, and my mother, sick and big with a child who turned out to be me. They were accompanied by two servants but had nothing else but the poor riding suits they stood up in. They took ship for Bruges but I was born in Antwerp, after they had endured months of grinding hardship. I do not know exactly how my brother perished but apparently he had never been strong, and the rough sea passage and harsh conditions proved too much for him. And for my mother, who died in a miserable charity hospital. They said she had an ulcer in the gut, but I think it must have been terrible homesickness and unhappiness that did for her. She was half-Irish and had lost so many people she had loved and cared for. So many.'

His eyes had grown distant as the horizon, as if he had withdrawn into himself, into this painful past. I wanted to reach for him and bring him back but I was almost afraid to, sensed that it would be more damaging to stop him talking, now that at last he had begun. The kindest thing I could do was just to let him talk and listen to him.

'My earliest memories are of travelling,' he said. 'Always travelling.

Calais, Boulogne, Rotterdam, Normandy, Brussels, Amsterdam. But wherever we were, always it was the same, always huddling in miserable lodgings and hiding from creditors. We were entirely dependent on the willingness of innkeepers and tradesmen and the keepers of lodgings to extend indefinite credit, and doomed to wander from place to place, in search of ever-cheaper rooms and more generous hosts. We lived destitute of friends, begging our daily bread of God and fearing every meal would be our last. I seemed always to be hungry and cold for want of clothes and fuel for a fire. I still have dreams where I am cold, so cold I can never get warm. My father felt his powerlessness to relieve our distress acutely. He refused to admit that the royal cause had been defeated, but he kept away from the bitter feuding and factions, the quarrelling and duelling, the endless failed conspiracies that made his unrealistic hopes swing to the deepest depths of despair. It was loss of pride and respect that upset him as much as anything, I think. He admitted to me once that for three months he had had not a crown, that he owed for all the meat and bread we had eaten the past weeks to a poor woman who was no longer able to trust him. It was that lack of trust he found insufferable.' He broke off as if something had jolted him back to the present. He reached out to my face and wiped away tears from my cheek with his hand. 'Oh, Nell, don't cry for me. Please don't cry. I didn't mean to make you cry.'

'I thought I had it so hard,' I sobbed with self-loathing. 'I used to feel so sorry for myself. Because my father forbade Christmas and would not let me wear ribbons in my hair. And you . . . you . . .'

'There is nothing wrong with wanting ribbons and Christmas,' he said very tenderly. 'To my mind it is cruelty to deprive a little girl of such things, especially one as pretty as you. But then, I have ever been of the opinion that Parliament men were rather cruel. When I came to England at last, it was to a once beautiful moated manor house that had been sacked and plundered and was little more than a burnt-out ruin. Parliament men seemed to me more hateful than Hell, fully deserving of the royalist vow to seek revenge by cutting a passage to the throne through their traitorous blood.'

I was not at all shocked by the apparent malice of his words since there was none whatsoever in his voice, nothing but a weary irony that was almost indifference.

He gave me the ghost of a smile. 'And yet here I am, having spent a very pleasant evening with my good friend, the son of a staunch Parliamentarian, about to sleep under the roof of a house that belonged to a Roundhead major, tarrying late at night with his lovely daughter.'

I sniffed, then smiled. 'Something convinced you that Cromwell's supporters were not to be so despised?'

He ran his fingers through his black curls. 'One day, when I was about ten years old, I saw an older boy flying a kite on a watermeadow, very like your watermeadows here. I did not see the son of my father's one time friend. Nor did I see the son of a Parliamentarian. All I saw was a friendly, laughing face, and bright copper-gold hair, and a kite made of red silk that soared in the wind. The boy offered to let me have a turn, without even knowing my name, let alone my father's allegiances, and then he offered to share his bread and cheese, just as later he offered to share his fishing pole, and even his new dappled pony. For years, Edmund Ashfield had everything and I had nothing.' He broke off and his eyes met mine, held them. 'And still it is just the same.'

I saw that if I could find solace in knowing that I loved him, even when I could not have him, it was intolerable for him when he had already been deprived of so much. 'It is not true that you have nothing now,' I said. 'You have . . .'

'Oh, yes, thanks to a small grant paid to my father by our grateful new King, I have enough to indulge in the best clothes, the best horses and the best wine. But still, Edmund has the only thing that really matters, the only thing I really want.'

I forced myself to say it, even if I could not bear to think of it, selfish as that was. 'You will find someone else, Richard.'

'I shall need to take a wife, but I shall not love her. Which will make me no different from many a husband, of course. Except that I shall not be able to find ease in the arms of a mistress as such husbands are wont to do, unless I close my eyes and do not look upon her face.'

I held his gaze, as if somehow I could tell him without words that it was the same for me, just the same. But I wanted to give him so much more. I could not help the cold, hungry and friendless little boy he had been, but I wanted to comfort the man he had become, find a way to mend the wounds that had gone so deep within that little boy that they had never stopped hurting. When I was miserable after the death of my mother and sister, I had retreated into happier memories, but Richard had no such consolation, he had nowhere to go, and I wished only to give him somewhere now, a safe, warm place that he need never leave.

'You would look well in Europe, Nell,' he said to me. 'The buildings are as elaborate and theatrical as the paintings and music we were talking about earlier. There are churches filled with columns and curves, with painted rays of golden light and angels streaming to the clouds of Heaven. You would like it, I think.'

But only if I could see it all with you. Only if you were there to show it to me. And that can never be.

'Do not misjudge me,' he said. 'Just because Edmund shared everything with me when we were boys, I did not expect him to share his wife. Doubtless you think me the most abominable cur for trying to seduce you, but I swear I cannot help it. I despise myself for it. I am tortured by guilt for it. Yet I cannot even promise I will never attempt it again.'

'I could never think of you as a cur.'

'I am trying to be good.' He gave me the most gentle, heart-breaking, contrite smile. 'But it is not easy.'

'No,' I said. 'It is not.'

For a moment neither of us spoke. Then he said: 'I shall at least take that blanket to my friend before he gets cold, and I promise you I will not try to take advantage of the fact that his pretty wife is left all alone in her bed. For tonight, at least, you are quite safe.'

God help me, but I did not want to be safe from him. As he turned to go, I almost grabbed his hand. I almost begged him to kiss me again, to take me, to make me his. No matter my good intentions of a few minutes ago, I did not think I could go on living without knowing what it was to be loved by him. But I let him go. I did what was right, not what my heart and my body demanded. I went alone to bed, let him go to his own down the passageway. I wrapped my arms around the bolster, wanting to go to him, aching to go to him. I buried my face in the hard pillow, so that none but me should know that I had cried myself to sleep with love and longing for him.

And when I went downstairs in the morning, Edmund was still fast asleep in the parlour chair, just as Richard had left him. The blankets were tucked around him as carefully and caringly as I would have wrapped little Forest.

So I could not understand how Edmund seemed still to have caught a chill which kept him huddled by the brazier all day as the snow fell softly and silently all around.

The night before Richard was due to leave, I dreamed of the first time I had carried a child inside me and had been kissed by him in the dark kitchen. I woke in the eerie blue light of fresh fallen snow and my body was damp with sweat, on flame with desire, or so I thought when I kicked off the blankets and felt the shock of the icy air on my burning skin. I thought it was the lustfulness of my dreams that had caused me to overheat, until I realised that the sweat on my body was not my sweat, that the heat I felt was not heat from my own body. I was so hot because Edmund had curled himself around me and, though he was trembling still, his body was as fiery as a blacksmith's furnace. The chill had passed, and it had been replaced by a raging fever. I touched his scorching brow and recoiled in horror, as if my fingers were scalded.

'Edmund!' I shook him, gripped by a blind panic. 'Edmund, wake up!'

He looked dazedly at me through his delirium, as if he didn't even know who I was. His lids slipped shut again as a low moan escaped his parched lips.

I backed away from the bed, the drapes falling closed between us like a final curtain, as one word clanged its death knell inside my head.

Ague. Ague. Ague.

Why now? Why again? It hardly ever struck in winter. I would not let it claim Edmund too. I would save him. I would not let him die. I would not.

I turned and fled from the room and down the corridor, to the room where Richard was sleeping. I burst through the door without seeking permission to enter and ran to his bed, throwing back the hangings. He was sprawled on his stomach atop the blankets, still half-dressed in shirt and breeches, with his head turned to the side, one arm flung up over his head and one knee crooked. I put my hands on his shoulders and shook him harder than I had shaken Edmund. 'Richard, help me! Edmund is sick.'

He sat up, regarded me with sleepy eyes for a moment, as if I was a visiting seraph.

'You have to ride to London right away,' I said frantically. 'As fast as you can.' I grabbed his cloak off the trunk and thrust it at him, followed by my pocketbook. 'Take this. You will probably need it.'

'What for?'

'It is very expensive.'

'What is?' He looked at me now as if I was a jabbering loon. He took firm hold of my shoulders and looked into my eyes. 'Nell, you are not making any sense at all. What's wrong with Edmund?'

'A fever,' I said. 'He has a fever. I am sure it is ague.'

'Tell me exactly what it is that you want me to do.'

'Find Robert Talbor,' I said more calmly. 'The man who cured the King of it.'

'How do I find him?'

'Go to Dr Sydenham on Pall Mall. He is sure to know.'

He nodded, releasing me to push his arms through the sleeves of his coat and his feet into his boots. He stood and threw his cloak over his shoulders, handed me back my pocketbook from where it lay on the bed. 'I have money, Nell.'

'You may not have enough.'

'I am sure that I do.'

A dusting of snow lay on the ground and still came down in flurries, but I followed him out to the stables in just my shift and with no shoes on my feet, and barely felt the bite of the wind or the coldness between my bare toes. As Ned hurriedly bridled and saddled Richard's horse, he glanced askance at me, as if to say that even in the direst distress he'd have expected me to make some pretence at respectability.

Richard put his right boot in Ned's cupped hands and vaulted into the saddle.

'Ride as fast as you can,' I pleaded.

'You can be sure of it,' he said. 'Do not worry, Nell.' He dropped his feathered hat on to his head with gravitas, as if a part of him relished this chance to do me this service, had been waiting for a reason to ride to my aid. 'I will be back within four days, I promise you.'

I was so grateful to him I could have wept. I clutched at his hand for a last moment. 'Godspeed, Richard. Go safely.'

I watched him gallop away through the snow towards the church, with all my hopes and prayers resting on him, and felt quite reassured.

This was not like before. Edmund might have sat in my father's chair and taken his position as the head of Tickenham Court, but he was not my father. He would not refuse the Jesuits' Powder, if that was what Robert Talbor used. Richard would fetch the miracle remedy and Edmund would take it and be cured. My father had been past his prime when he'd died, weary and disillusioned from the wars, crushed by grieving. Edmund was different. Edmund was young and strong. He had a small son and another baby expected. He had a wife who loved him. Who did truly love him. He'd said it himself: he had everything he could ever want. He had everything to live for. He had to live.

I willed my husband to live. I held on to his palsied hand as if I could stop him slipping away from me, but the feel of it set my own hand shaking in fear. It was so icily cold it hardly felt like a hand at all, felt as if he had died already, and his teeth rattled so hard in his head that he could not speak to me.

I slept in a wooden chair by his bed, if I slept at all. I watched over him constantly, trying to understand his incoherent ramblings and mumbles and anticipate his every need, so he would not have to exert himself. When he was shivering with cold I kept him warm, brought rugs and blankets and made sure the fire was kept banked high. As soon as the chill passed and the heat started again, I soaked cloths and sponged his scarlet face. When his parched tongue licked at the moisture, I reached for the cider cup and trickled some into his mouth, glad just for the opportunity to have something to do. His hand, when I held it, was burning now. The sweat poured off him in waves and I brought dry sheets when the ones beneath him became quickly drenched.

'Edmund, I cannot bear to see you suffer,' I said, turning the damp compress over to the cool side and placing it back on his scarlet brow.

Even ravaged and weakened by disease, he had lost none of his placid acceptance. Even in such misery he did his best to smile through it. 'I don't feel so bad now, really I don't.'

'I know that is not true. I wish you would complain. You are allowed to, you know. I know I would in your place.'

He squeezed my hand as his smile remained. 'No, you would not. You would be magnificently strong and brave. Just as you always are. As you are now.'

'But you have to fight this,' I pleaded. 'You once told me you would fight for me and for our son. You need to fight for us now. You have to hold on, do you hear me?' I stroked his damp hair which had turned the colour of wet rust. 'Just hold on. Richard will be here soon.'

'Oh, aye, so long as he's not waylaid by some pretty harlot with a fair face and fairer bosom. Or else by a not-so-fair bottle of wine that will make him forget entirely where he is going, or what he is going there for.'

'He won't,' I said firmly. 'You'll see. He knows how important it is that you have the Powder. He promised to be back in four days.'

'I'm sure he did. Well intentioned he may be, diligent he is not.'

Judged against Edmund's steadfastness, all would be found wanting, me included. 'Richard will be diligent if it matters enough,' I said. 'He will.'

'So how long has it been now?'

'Nearly five days.'

'So already he has broken his promise.' My husband smiled wanly. 'To think, my life now depends on a most undependable person.'

But next morning, just after daybreak, I heard the blessed sound of hooves clattering on the slushy cobbles and I rushed to the window. 'He is here!' I shouted. 'Edmund, Richard is back.'

Edmund was dozing fitfully, his face still flushed with fever, and did not appear to hear me.

I ran down the stairs and outside to see Richard's black Spanish stallion steaming in the glittering white light of sun reflected on snow. Flecks of froth were dripping from the bit.

'How is he?' Richard asked.

'Weakening,' I said, more harshly than I'd intended. 'What took you so long?'

He slid slowly from the saddle with a wince of pain.

'Are you all right?'

He nodded grimly as he handed the reins to Ned. 'Besides a few saddle sores, I've never been better.'

I took in the dark stubble that covered his cheeks and noted the signs of hard riding: his ragged curls, dry lips, the dust that coated his clothes and the shadows of exhaustion beneath his eyes. 'Forgive me,' I said.

'I've ridden without stopping, except to change horses, for two days and two nights,' he said. 'I'd have got back in half the time, if you'd not sent me on some damned wild goose chase.'

'You did find Robert Talbor?'

'I found his shop all right, but he was not there. His butler told me he was called to France to tend the Dauphin and the King. He sent me to Mr Lords, a barber in St Swithin's Lane, but I didn't trust the look of him at all. So I went back to Pall Mall, to Dr Sydenham, had to wait around all day for him until he came back from his visits. He swore that Talbor's secret cure is Jesuits' Powder and gave me directions to an apothecary who receives the bark directly from the Jesuit college at St Omers in Belgium, guaranteeing the highest quality . . .'

I was barely listening. 'You do have it?'

'I said I would get it for you, Nell, and I have.'

Considering what he had told me, it was a wonder he had managed to be back so quickly. With hands that trembled with fatigue, he took the precious little brown-paper package out of his pocket and held it out to me.

'Thank you, Richard.'

'You do not need to thank me.'

I turned to go back to the house, but when he started to walk with me I saw that he was almost bow-legged from so many hours spent on horseback. He was all but stumbling in his tiredness and looked to be in considerable pain from the saddle sores. He took a flask of brandy out of his pocket and swigged from it.

'I'll tell Bess to fill you a bath and have the kitchen make you something to eat,' I said gently. 'It's food and rest you need, not brandy.'

'I needed it to keep me awake, and now I shall need it to help me sleep.'

'You've done all you can,' I said gratefully, resting my hand on his arm as we came to the bottom of the solar stairs. 'Pray this will do the rest.' I looked down at the package. 'How much do I give to him?'

Richard tipped back his head as he took another hefty swig of brandy, held it in his mouth, swallowed. 'As much as he needs.' He wiped his mouth with the back of his hand as I waited for further instructions. 'Two spoonfuls,' he said.

'How often?'

He fastened the top of the flask. 'Give it to him morning, noon and night. In between times, too, if there's no improvement.'

The dried, powdered bark was a deep red-brown colour, like cinnamon. I tasted a few grains, spat it out in disgust. It was extraordinarily bitter. I spooned a dose into a glass of claret, sat on the bed beside Edmund and put my arm around his shoulders to lift his head and hold the cup to his mouth.

The fever did not break, so I woke him after dinner to give him another dose, and again before supper. He said his stomach and his head were hurting a little, but he seemed restful enough, so that I curled up beside him and went to sleep myself, comforted by the thought that the curative was inside him now, doing its work.

When he woke just after midnight and I asked him how he was, he complained that there was a ringing sound in his ears and rubbed at his eyes, saying everything appeared blurred.

By midday he lay with his legs drawn up to his abdomen and was moaning that his muscles felt as taut as if he was on the rack, that he badly wanted to be sick. It was as if it was some quack remedy I had fed to him. Jesuits' poison, just as the Protestants had claimed.

When Edmund vomited, I sent for Richard who had been sleeping since he arrived, over twenty-four hours ago. 'Did Dr Sydenham say it was an emetic?' I asked him.

He stood at the side of the bed in his rumpled shirt and stared down at Edmund's contorted face. He seemed unable to speak.

'Richard!'

He turned on me defensively, almost violently, his face white and sweat breaking out on his brow. He put his hands to the side of his head, raked his fingers through his hair, clutched at it. 'He said nothing. Damn it, nothing! Why would he? He was not prescribing it, only giving me what I asked for.'

'If only Dr Talbor had been there,' I said. 'Maybe his remedy does not contain the powder after all.' I sat by Edmund and put my arms around him as he writhed in pain. Sweat trickled down his brow and his heart was racing. 'I do not understand. I did not take Thomas Sydenham for a mountebank and I am sure as I can be that he is no Papist conspirator.' I glanced at Richard. 'You are certain that it was Jesuits' Powder you were given? Peruvian bark?'

'Yes, and Thomas Sydenham swore his supplier was entirely reputable,'

Richard said tersely. 'That he'd not be one to adulterate the powder with worthless substitutes.'

'But surely he would have warned you if there was even a danger of this?'

'Maybe it means it is working.' Richard's voice was oddly constricted. 'Perhaps you should give him another dose.'

'In all conscience, I cannot.' I laid the back of my hand on Edmund's pain-furrowed brow and made a swift decision. 'Fetch Dr Duckett. Edmund set more store by him than I ever have, he would want to see him. And, after all, he can do no more harm than we have done, can he?'

When the surgeon pulled back the bedclothes and drew up the sleeve of Edmund's nightshirt to bleed him, we both saw that his skin was covered in a livid purple-copper rash. Dr Duckett lifted the hem of the shirt and I gasped to see that the same rash was all over his body.

The surgeon made no comment but pressed the blade of his knife against the mottled flesh of Edmund's forearm and I watched the dark red rivulet of blood snake into a cup until it was brimful, filling the chamber with its ferrous tang. I saw my husband grow limp, but peaceful at last.

I was alone at his bedside when he awoke later, opened his eyes and cried out in great fear and distress, as if he had seen the Reaper himself over my shoulder. I immediately felt his cheek, fearing a return of the fever and delirium. But he was cold to the touch, not hot. 'What's wrong, Edmund?'

'It is so dark. Why is there no candle?'

'Of course there is a candle, darling.' I spoke calmly, quietly, as if to a child. 'Bess lit it an hour ago. Can you not see it, over there on the wash-stand?

He had turned his head at the sound of my voice, groped for my hand. 'I can't see you. Help me, Eleanor. I can't see anything.'

I stared into his eyes and saw that they were blank, flickering wildly from side to side, the pupils so dilated that the grey iris was all but gone, leaving his eyes almost totally black. He clutched at me in panic, cried pitifully for me not to leave him.

I called for Richard but he came no further than the doorway, a half-empty brandy bottle in one hand and a candlestick in the other.

'Hand me your candle,' I said, without taking my eyes off Edmund.

Richard seemed too afraid to come near the bed. I all but snatched the pewter stick off him and held the wildly flickering flame up to Edmund's face. 'Do you see it, Edmund? The light? Do you see it?'

'No.' He stared in the vague direction of the flame, as if into an abyss. 'I see nothing. Eleanor, what is happening to me?'

'I don't know. I don't know.' I looked deep into his sightless eyes, saw the wavering candle flame reflected in the large black centres, but nothing else. I was holding his hand, he was right there before me, but it seemed as if he was already a very long way away.

I did not know what to do any more and the only person I could think of who could help Edmund now was John Foskett, our curate, a pimply-faced youth still but nevertheless devout and good.

I left him alone to pray with Edmund. When he came out of the chamber to say that my husband had asked for his friend, the colour drained from Richard's face and he looked as though he had been asked to step through the gates of Hell.

'For God's sake, go to him,' I said. 'He wants to see you.'

It was not that I was unsympathetic. I knew that seeing Edmund suffer must awaken for Richard memories of the loss of other loved ones, but it was not as if I had no memories like that of my own, such searing, similar memories.

Had my father had been right all along? I wondered in amazement. Right to refuse Jesuits' Powder, right to fear it?

Richard was not with Edmund long, and then it was my turn. An hour later, Edmund died in my arms. As if lured by the peace and silence into thinking there had been an improvement in his condition, Richard came quietly into the room. When he saw, instead, the inert body laid out on the bed, I thought he was going to collapse. He clutched at the bedpost and stared at Edmund in horror and disbelief. I saw that there were tears standing in his eyes.

I should have taken him into my arms and comforted him then. We should have been a comfort to one another. But with all that had passed between us I could not bring myself even to touch him now. Those two words, *I wish*. They stood between us like crossed swords. And he seemed to know it and to feel the same way.

I brushed past his rigid shoulder as I walked slowly out of the room, walking as if in a daze down the stairs to the kitchen, to fetch a carving knife. Then I walked back to the chamber with it held down at my side in the folds of my silk skirts, like a murderess.

Richard's eyes widened almost in fear and he stepped away from me. 'What the devil are you doing?'

Lifting my cumbersome skirts, I clambered up on the bed beside Edmund. With silent tears spilling down my face, I cradled his head in my silk-draped lap and took a lock of his copper hair between my fingers. Tenderly, with utmost care, I sliced right through it with the knife. I coiled it around my finger, dragged a silver ribbon from my own head to tie around it. 'I always loved his hair,' I said. 'It was the very first thing about him that I loved . . . its brightness. I don't ever want to forget. I don't ever want it to fade.'

Richard left the room. Bess told me later that he was gone from Tickenham without even saying goodbye to me.

I barely noticed when it grew dark again. I was worn out from caring for Edmund and yet I didn't want to sleep now that I could. I didn't want to wake to a new day that Edmund would never see, to know that already, so soon, I had left him behind. I sat at my writing desk with a candle, at dead of night, and wrote out a list of tasks for the arranging of a funeral. But it was to be a very different funeral from the last one I had attended. On no account was Edmund to be buried at night. He was to be laid to rest in the morning, inside rather than outside the church, where it was always dry.

When Mary and John Burges travelled back to Tickenham after hearing the news of his death, I told Mary how much it would amuse Edmund that, even in the matter of his funeral, I stood contrary to Puritan preferences. 'I know he will not mind me doing it as I want it done.'

'It will be hard for you, to be barred from being there,' Mary said, her arm about my shoulders, as we sat on the Tudor settle by a flickering fire.

I placed my hand protectively on the mound of my belly. 'I would not risk harmful spirits reaching this baby,' I said. The precious last baby Edmund would ever give me. 'But even if I am not there, it must not be as before.'

I did not even want to think of another dark pit in that wet and misty graveyard, another coffin descending into the watery ground. Even to think of it was to feel myself sinking too, to feel darkness closing around me, finally and forever.

Mary drew me into her embrace.

'I can't believe he is gone,' I said, weeping against her plump shoulder.

I should have been used to it, the terrible finality of death. But I couldn't accept it. Even if butterflies rise from coffins and we are like them and will rise again into everlasting life, even if Edmund and I were to meet again one day in Heaven, I could not bear to think I would never, ever see him again in this world. His boots were still where he had left them by the door, still shaped to the contours of his feet. I couldn't believe he would never wear them again. His fishing pole and net were still propped in the corner. How could it be that he had used them for the very last time? He'd never again sit with them by the hump-backed bridge in the sunshine, or ride his horse, or eat his supper with me, or play with his son and see him grow.

'I just want him back,' I said. 'I want him back.'

I could not quite conform to the ideal of a courageously constant and modest widow, any more than I had been able to conform to the ideal of a modest wife. On the day of Edmund's funeral, I stood alone in my chamber at the latticed casement. As I looked down at the funeral procession, weaving between the brackish pools of floodwater, I found that my eyes were involuntarily seeking out a man who was still very much alive. Despite myself, despite everything, I was looking for Richard. It was not with any desire that I sought him, just to know that he was near. That was all I wanted, for him to be close.

Then I reeled with self-disgust at what I threatened to become: that most feared and despised of all women, the lascivious widow. A temptation and provocation to morally upstanding gentlemen, a threat to the natural order, a girl who had sampled the pleasures of the flesh and craved it still from the confines of her desolate widow's bed.

I ran down to the great hall and stood in the middle of the empty room, beneath the vaulted roof, as far away from any window as could be. I turned my head from the view of the Tickenham floodplains to the far wall where hung a faded tapestry depicting the Great Flood, the flood sent by God to cleanse the world of sinners. I wished it would take me. I wished that I could die for my sin. It did not seem right that I lived, when good, kind Edmund lay mouldering in a coffin.

I had begged forgiveness but still I had not been true to my husband in my heart and it was for this that I was being punished now. Or maybe there was no one who could punish or forgive me or hear my prayers. Maybe ague was a random executioner and there was no almighty power to intervene on our behalf. God had not saved my sister, or my mother, or my father, or my husband and I totally failed to see any divine purpose in the loss of them. It was previously impossible for me even to consider the idea that God did not exist but I found myself considering it now, dabbling with atheism, disregarding finally everything that I had ever believed in.

I rested my forehead against the stitched image of Noah's Ark and pummelled it with my fists. 'Why? Why?' Never had that question screamed at me so loud. 'Why?'

Even as I cried out, the answer insinuated itself into my head. It was my fault. It was Richard's fault. I needed someone to blame and I blamed him the most. I was dissolute and wanton, but it was he who had made me so, he who had unleashed that wantonness within me. My father was right to condemn long Cavalier curls as a dangerous incitement to lust. Edmund had died because I had acted like a whore, because I had not loved him enough, because I had broken God's sacred commandment. I had broken my wedding vows. Edmund's death was punishment. Because I had not loved him and no other as I had sworn to do.

With both hands clawed, I gripped the tapestry and tore it from its hangings, let it crumple in a great plume of dust on the stone floor. I hauled it over to the great fireplace and rolled it and kicked it on to the flames. But rather than catch light, the heavy wool snuffed out the fire in an instant. The room turned colder and darker. If He did exist, then God had forsaken me.

I raised my face to the vaulted roof and cried out into the emptiness: 'Where are you?'

'I am right here.' It was a soft-spoken and achingly familiar voice that answered me.

I spun round to the door. 'What are you doing here?'

'I have come to pay my respects to Edmund,' Richard said with a small, stiff bow.

He was dressed in a velvet suit as black as his hair, with high boots and a black feather on his hat. There were dark shadows beneath his eyes. Even lightly tanned as he always was, he looked very pale.

I had ripped holes in my black Puritan dresses after my father's funeral. Now I felt as if my heart had been ripped to shreds. But I hardened it. 'Have you no shame?' I asked him.

He hesitated. 'I can never be ashamed of loving you.'

'You have no right to love me,' I said, my voice very cold. 'You had no right to love another man's wife.'

'Nell, please listen to me.' He took a few echoing steps and they brought him closer to me, too close. 'Edmund asked me to take care of you and Forest for him.'

'Oh, God! Don't tell me that. Don't say that to me.'

'He asked me. That is all he asked of me.'

'And all I ask is that I never see you again. Not ever. Do you understand?'

His eyes raked my face. 'You do not mean that?'

'I do.'

'I came to see if there was anything I could do for you,' he said. 'Is there?'

'The only thing you can do for me is to stay away from me.'

'Edmund Ashfield was my friend,' he said slowly. 'I grieve for him just as you do, Nell. I would like very much to be a friend to you.' He glanced at the tapestry smouldering on the fire. 'You look to be in dire need of one.'

As did he. But how could I be a friend to him, when I had once wanted to be so much more? 'Do you not hear me? The last person in the world that I need is you.'

He was before me in a stride, had gripped my shoulders very tight as if he would shake me but instead pulled me roughly towards him. He held me against him for a moment and then abruptly released me.

I did not want him to. I wanted him to take me in his arms again. I wanted to beat at his chest with my balled fists and for him to hold me tighter still. I wanted to bury my face in his neck, to lay my head against the soft velvet of his coat and sob out my grief. I wanted him to kiss my tears away, and later, much later, I wanted to know that he would stroke me with warm, soft, healing hands and love me with such passion that I forgot all else.

'Stay away from me,' I rasped. 'Do not ever touch me again.'

'Sacrificing our own happiness will not bring Edmund back,' he said, bereft. 'He would not want this.'

'How can you speak of what he wanted?' I hissed, clenching my hands and digging the nails into my flesh until I drew blood. 'Don't you see? You were a false friend to him and I a faithless wife. We are to blame. We ill wished him. Something catastrophic is conjured between us when we are together. When I said I could never be your bride, you said there was one way. You asked me if I wished I was married to you instead and I said that I did wish it. We as good as welcomed the possibility of Edmund's death. You must see that we can never, ever take advantage of his death or allow ourselves one moment of pleasure because of it. We can never be together now.'

There were tears in his eyes and in mine. I let them stream unchecked down my cheeks, hot against my ice-cold face. I made myself say it. 'I will never see you again.'

Summer 1680

Mary Burges stayed in Tickenham with me awhile and then she insisted Forest and I went back with her to Hackney, with Bess in attendance, so that I could have my baby there. She had made all the necessary arrangements, securing a written certificate of my widowhood so no suspicion would befall me when I was brought to bed in childbirth away from home. I hadn't had time to ponder my new circumstances, for it even to occur to me that, without this paperwork, I was likely to be treated as barely better than a harlot, my little children as bastards.

'Bring your butterflies,' Mary suggested gently, as she and Bess helped me pack a small trunk with my own and Forest's clothes.

She might have spoken to me in an unknown language. 'Butterflies?'

'There's plenty of room for them. We can invite your friend James to visit. He still writes to you, doesn't he?'

'Yes, he still writes.' I'd not replied to his last two letters.

'I'm sure he'd like to see your collection.'

I had let Mary wrap my gowns and petticoats around the leather-bound book and deal boxes in which I'd pasted the butterflies. Not that I could ever imagine showing them to James, nor ever myself looking at them or finding joy in them again. The only reason I carried on breathing was for Edmund's children, for little Forest and the baby inside me who would never meet its father, whom Edmund would never see. I tortured myself that I was to blame. I should never have given him the Jesuits' Powder. His death felt like the greatest cross that I could ever bear. I was sure that I would weep myself as blind as he had been at the end.

Huddled inside a cloak, despite the warm weather, I took in nothing of the journey, or of Hackney itself, beyond that it was a rural, grassy little place, more like a village than an outlying parish of a great city, for all it was becoming a centre of genteel education.

I knew it no better when I'd been there several weeks.

I sat shelling peas on a stool by the open door in Mary's little white-walled kitchen, with its shining brass pans and pots of aromatic flowers, now and again pausing to throw a wooden ball at the skittles for Forest, before he exploded in one of the increasingly regular and incandescent tantrums that only his father's calm firmness had been able to control. After dinner I fetched sand from the barrel that stood in the corner of the kitchen and started to help Mary clean. But she insisted I rest and drink up my fortified wine and cordial.

'Why don't you write to James Petiver and tell him you are in Hackney?' she suggested, but I shook my head. I didn't want to see him. I didn't want to see anyone.

Before I knew it, it was time for my confinement and I retreated to the small dark birthing room beneath the eaves almost with relief. Mary and Bess were the only companions I wanted. One day Mary brought me a gift, a curious little stone within a stone set on a neck-chain.

'It's an Eaglestone,' she told me as I took it from her. 'From Africa.'

'How did you get it?'

'They're readily enough to be had in London. Here, let me put it on for you.' She leaned towards me and slipped it over my head, kissing my fore-head as she did it. 'You're supposed to wear it touching your skin when you're with child, to keep you both safe. I thought it was a pretty notion. See.' She held the little pendant in the palm of her hand. 'The two stones, one nested within the other, are like a child in the womb.'

I took it into my own hand and wanted to weep. 'Thank you, Mary. Thank you for wanting to keep me safe.'

I hated the thought that I was a burden to her, when she had enough worries of her own. She was in far more danger than was I. The Popish Plot and the subsequent wild allegations against Catholics had seen thirty-five put to death and the Catholic Duke of York exiled abroad for the alleged plot to murder the King. Anti-Papist feeling still ran dangerously high. Which is why I had not told her the precise nature of Edmund's death, could never tell her, did not even want to explore my confused, suppressed fear that it was Catholic poison which had killed him.

'I know you don't believe in amulets,' Mary said.

'I believe in them as much as I can believe in anything now.' I wrapped my fingers around the little charm and slipped it inside my cambric chemise. 'I might as well put my faith in this as in anything else. Maybe good luck or bad luck is all there is. Maybe a talisman is what I need.'

I was in bed, with barely the strength to lift my head, when Mary brought a tiny baby girl to me, all clean and pink and wrapped up in soft swaddling cloths.

'There, little one,' Mary crooned, as she placed this tranquil little stranger carefully in my arms. 'She's been waiting so very patiently to meet her mother.' Mary sat down on the edge of the bed 'We thought you'd taken leave of us, Eleanor. Do you have any recollection at all?'

I tried, shook my head. 'I remember the pains starting. Then, nothing.'

'It is probably just as well,' she said. 'The birth wasn't an easy one. You've been grievously sick.'

I gazed down into my baby's sweet face, as she made a little 'O' with her mouth. All rosy and content, she was utterly different from my first sight of Forest, bloody and naked and blue, still attached to me by the slippery pulsating cord.

'What happened?'

Mary hesitated.

'I want to know. Everything.'

'The baby came wrong,' Mary began gently. 'She was stuck so long that the midwife had to drag her out of you by her legs.' Her kind, calm voice removed only some of the horror of her words. 'You fainted from an overflow of blood just after it was over. You regained some sensible pulse and colour, but after a few days fell faint again from noxious impurities that nature should have cleaned out of you. It is a miracle you're still with us. That both of you are still with us.' She paused, looking down at the baby with adoration. 'She's the most docile, easy little thing. Hardly ever cries or complains. It's almost as if, after the violence of her delivery and the fight she had to come into the world, she wants only calmness and peace.'

'Her father wanted that too.'

'Pray he has peace now.'

'I cannot pray for anything any more. I wish I could.'

I stroked my baby's silken little cheek, shifted her slightly and felt my own flattened belly. 'She is a new life,' I whispered. 'Just like a little butterfly bursting forth from a pupa. If I could only believe in that. I owe it to her grandfather's memory to believe it.'

If I had taken more heed of his warnings, perhaps this little girl would have known a father's love as I had known it, even though I had rejected all that my father stood for. Had he been right all along? Had I been very wrong to doubt him?

'If only I could be sure that Edmund is not merely rotting in the ground but that his soul has been reborn,' I said quietly. 'If only I could be sure that he will meet his little daughter one day.'

'I pray that you find your faith again,' Mary said. 'I will always pray for you, Ma'am, and your dear girl. And for Forest.'

I had a pang of yearning to see my son. 'Where is he?'

'Busy learning to chop wood with John. Would you have me fetch him?'

'No. Leave him be,' I said. 'I'll not drag him from a boy's pleasure into a nursery. He will have precious little opportunity to do manly things, since he is adrift in a little family of women now.' The baby mewed like a kitten then so I put her to my breast. Her gums didn't hurt me as Forest's had done, her suckling no more than a gentle tug and tickle.

'Your milk will come again soon,' Mary said, standing. 'I'll tell the wet nurse we have no more need of her.'

'Thank you for caring for her so well for me.'

'I've cherished her as if she was my own.'

'She shall be named after you.'

'I'd like that.'

'Hello, my Mary,' I said when we were alone. The baby blinked her kitten-blue eyes, then looked around as if in wonder at a world still so new to her. She wrinkled her nose and it was the most delightful thing. She yawned and it was like a miracle. She fascinated me. She was my cherub, my fairy, my little princess, my companion. I was overcome with a love as profound and consuming as the one I had felt when I first saw Forest, entirely different this time, though, because Mary was of my sex. We would understand each other, would share similar experiences, similar hopes and fears. She was like me made anew.

I loosened the swaddling cloths and gave her freedom to wave her arms about. Her tiny fingers jumped open like a little frog, a starfish, like the leaves of a marsh pimpernel. They curled around my thumb and clung to me. Then the swaddling fell back from her head and I saw that she was not like me at all. She was like Edmund. She had a fluffy fuzz of the brightest copper hair. And it undid me.

I stared at the downy auburn tufts and tears streamed down my face. Edmund's daughter gazed back at me with unfocussed eyes and looked completely calm and accepting, just like her father. I held her to my face and kissed her, wetting her cheeks with my tears. I clutched her to me and rocked her, rocked myself, and told her how her father would have loved her so.

Mary let me be until a few days after I was churched, then she laid out my blue gown on the bed and sent Bess in, armed with curling tongs for my hair.

'There's someone coming to see you later,' she said as Bess stuck the tongs in the fire to heat them.

I was lounging back on the pillows, feeding the baby, but was instantly alert. 'Who?'

'James Petiver.'

'Oh.' I tried not to sound disappointed that it was not someone else, tried not even to feel it.

'I asked him to come. I hope you don't mind?' Mary seemed pleased with herself. 'He's just what you need. He has been such a good friend to you, keeping up a correspondence all this time. He's also an apothecary. One of those qualifications, or the combination of them, must surely mean he will be able to help you where the rest of us have failed.' She took the baby off me and pulled me out of bed and on to a stool. Then she picked up an ivory comb to start on my hair herself.

'I can't think what I'll find to say to him,' I said, as Bess took over and coiled a silken lock of my fresh-combed hair round the tongs. 'I fear I shall be very dull company.'

Mary watched as the rich yellow curls bounced around my shoulders. 'Sweet girl, I doubt any man could ever find you dull. But we shall let James be the judge.'

John had taken Forest to market with him and Mary had the baby with her in the schoolroom, so I was sitting alone by the fire when the maid brought James in.

He had changed so much since the first and only time I'd met him face-to-face in the Apothecaries Garden, and yet I would have known him anywhere. After so many letters had passed between us, I felt I knew him as well as I knew myself. He could have been my brother. We even looked alike, both of us fair and slight.

He was dressed in a well-cut suit of blue serge with brass buttons and a square white collar edged with lace. He had let his corn-blond hair grow longer and had tied it back with a dark blue ribbon – a practicality, I imagined, but it suited him well. In actual physical stature he was still only head and shoulders above me, but I could see instantly that in other respects he had grown from a boy to a man. He had an air of assurance he'd not had before, but was still as unaffected as ever. He took both my cold hands in his warm ones, didn't raise them to his lips and kiss them or do anything at all gallant but kept them pressed inside his and held them there as we sat down, me on the little settle and he on a stool beside me.

'It is so good to see you,' he said. This was no platitude, was not spoken out of politeness but as if he meant it from the bottom of his heart. 'I am so very sorry for your loss.'

He moved towards me slightly and then away again and I caught a scent of the herbs and lavender and other aromatic plants he worked with and turned into medicines. It was the scent of the meadows and the gardens he frequented for his trade, and it reminded me of what I'd been missing: this essence of nature, of fresh air, which emanated from his hands, his clothes, from his very being. It was somehow reflected in his indefinable eyes, flecked with hazel and green and gold, which had in them all the warmth and brightness of a sunny glade. They radiated enthusiasm, intelligence and affection.

'It is good of you to come, James.'

'I'd have come much sooner if I'd been invited.' He studied me as a botanist might study a flower, to appreciate its complexities but also to comprehend what it needed in order to blossom. 'I can't believe you've been but a few hours' walk away all these weeks.'

'I've lost all sense of time. So much has happened to me. I've become a wife and widow and a mother twice over, all in the space of two years.'

Silently, I added adulteress to that list. 'James, have you . . . have you ever used Jesuits' Powder?'

'I have too much regard for my career even to stock it at present. Why do you ask?'

I shook my head, finding I did not want to speak of Edmund's death. Having it confirmed that Jesuits' Powder was a deadly poison could change nothing. For once in my life, it seemed better not to ask, better not to know the answer.

'I should love to meet your little son and daughter,' he said. 'They must be a great comfort to you.'

There seemed no point at all in pretending, or even trying to make idle chat with him. 'They are my joy and my torment,' I said. 'I see Edmund in them, but the very thought of them makes my heart shrink because I remember his great pleasure in them. And I am so terrified of some illness or accident befalling them, of losing them too, that I am never at peace.'

James considered me. 'You are grieving,' he said gently. 'But you are also suffering from fits of the mother, I think. It's very common after giving birth to succumb to a kind of melancholy, especially when you've experienced trauma in your life. It passes, after a while. There's a physic I can give you to help.' He was still holding my hands, chafing them gently as we talked, and I felt the blood flowing in my veins again, like the sap rising in spring. 'You're in very good company as well, you know. All the great intellectuals of our time are tormented by morbid dispositions . . . Hooke, Locke, Newton.' He kept the warmth of his eyes focused on me so that I felt as if I really was a flower, opening to the warmth of the sun. 'Mistress Burges told me you'd brought your collection with you. I'd like to see it, if you would show it to me?'

I went to fetch the armful of books and cases, handed them to him with some reluctance, then sat back in my seat and watched in an agony of suspense as he turned over a page, paused to examine a specimen, then turned another, on and on, in complete silence.

He spent the longest time looking at his beloved copper-coloured butter-flies and then, mercifully, reached the end. At last he looked up. 'The quality and variety of your collection puts the rest of us to shame.'

It was so simply said, and yet it meant so very much to me.

'Thank you, James.'

'No need to thank me when I speak only the truth.'

I hadn't realised how much I had wanted his approval – almost more than I used to want my father's. And I smiled. For the first time since Edmund died, I felt a flush of joy. And with it came hope, without which I think life is unbearable. I had collected my butterflies devotedly but I hadn't thought they amounted to much. Now I wondered if I might find some meaning to life after all, might even make some lasting contribution.

James had turned back to the middle of the book. 'This insect here,' he said, pointing to a chequered red and black specimen. 'I've only ever seen one other before . . . or one very like it. Captured in Cambridgeshire.'

'Conditions in the Fens were once very similar to those where I live. I see those butterflies almost every day.' I told him then about the swallow-tails and large copper butterflies and how they seemed to have deserted the Fens when they were drained.

'That's a remarkable discovery.' James looked back at the red and black specimen. 'It would be interesting to know if it's the same with these. They're the ones you once described to me as having markings like a chessboard?'

'That's right.'

'I've a chequered dice box that looks just the same. Fritillary.'

'It should be called a Marsh Fritillary then.'

'A good name. I'll propose it at our next coffee-house meeting.'

'You can give names to butterflies, just like that?'

'A proper system of nomenclature is vital to bring order out of the chaos of the natural world. If a butterfly doesn't already have a Latin name or a common name we should give it one. You already speak of Swallowtails and Large Coppers. Let's name some more, shall we?' He spun the book back towards me, as if we were to play a board game, pointing to a butterfly with bands of bright red across its brown velvety wings.

'It reminds me of one of the flags you see on naval ships.'

'The Red Admiral?' he said.

'Red Admiral. I like it. We should call it that.'

'And this?' He pointed to one with jagged orange-brown wings, marked with black and blue. 'What would be a good name for this one, do you suppose?'

Puzzled, I leaned forward with my elbows on my knees, chin resting in my hands, to think. 'Hmmm. Not so easy.'

James reached out towards me and produced a little comb, like a conjuror at a fair might produce a coin from the sleeve of his coat. It took me a moment to realise he'd taken it from my hair. 'It looks rather like this pattern, don't you think?'

A curl flopped across my eyes. I pushed it away with my hand. 'Tortoise-shell.'

'Tortoiseshell it shall be then.'

'How do you know for sure you've found a different species, that it's not just a variation?'

'There's always much debate about species divisions. That's why we all need to keep collecting and share our findings.'

'Will other people use these names we've chosen?'

'They could still be in use hundreds of years from now.'

The notion of that amazed and cheered me, the idea that there might just be butterflies called Red Admirals and Tortoiseshells, flying around when we were long gone.

'Did I ever tell you,' I said, 'a boy once accused me of being soft in the head for chasing butterflies?'

'That doesn't surprise me in the least. You should see the strange looks I attract when folk see me out walking with a net over my shoulder, a pin-cushion round my neck, and butterflies fastened round the brim of my hat.'

I giggled. 'You pin them round the brim of your hat? What a perfect place.'

'You see, only you'd appreciate that. To the rest of the world I look an oddity indeed.'

James stayed for hours and, when he came back the next week, he arrived with a posy of flowers he'd picked from Chelsea, and a draught of physic he'd prepared for me himself.

'What is in it?' I asked.

James smiled to see a glimmer of my natural curiosity returning. 'Water pimpernel and marsh marigold, mainly.'

'Both those plants grow on Tickenham Moor,' I pondered. 'I never knew they had medicinal properties. Something else that might be lost then, if the land was converted from marsh into permanent arable land?'

'Well, for now they are plentiful enough.' He spooned out a measure of the physic for me before we had glasses of wine and slices of Mary's almond tart. Then he talked to me about his work with the paupers at St

Bartholomew's Hospital and about how he wanted to open his own apothecary shop. He talked animatedly about his group of friends who'd started meeting every Friday evening at the Temple Bar Coffee House off Fleet Street, to talk about botany and insects. 'It's the only society in the country devoted to the study of the natural world,' he said excitedly. 'We've gathered together some of the greatest minds of our day and intend to formalise our club and make it a focus for promoting botanical knowledge.'

'James, you have such an illustrious circle of friends and such a full and interesting life, I can't imagine why you'd choose to spend your precious days off with me, eating tarts in a little boarding school in Hackney.'

'Can't you?' he asked, suddenly serious.

But as the time drew nearer for his third visit, I became convinced that he'd send a message to say he couldn't come after all. I wasn't sure how I'd manage a whole week without a few hours of his company, though. The physic he gave me helped heal my body, but his presence soothed my soul. He was like a window opening out on to the world. Through his bright hazel eyes I saw, for the first time in weeks, beyond Mary's little kitchen and school, beyond my loss and my guilt and sorrow.

But he did come, and suggested that next time we should go on a butterfly hunting expedition together. 'We'll take provisions. Make a day of it.'

'Wouldn't you have a much better time with your friends?'

'I thought you were my friend.'

I couldn't have felt happier then if I'd been the staunchest royalist given an invitation to the court on the King's own birthday.

'So, where shall it be? Where would you like to go?'

I remembered the pretty names of all the places he'd mentioned in his letters. Fulham Palace Gardens. Hampton Court. Primrose Hill. The lavender fields of Mitcham. 'Oh, I don't know. I can't decide.'

He looked at me, considering. 'Let's go to Fulham Palace then,' he said. 'It's like a scene from a romance. I think you'd like it the best of anywhere.'

'What is that you are reading so avidly?' Mary asked me, looking up from the table where she was crushing almonds for marchpane.

I showed her the cover of *Philosophical Transactions*. 'It's the Journal of the Royal Society. James brought it for me. He said he thought I'd find it helpful.'

'Helpful in what way?'

'I'll show you,' I said excitedly, feeling the familiar thrill of experiment and discovery stir in me again. I put the journal down, scooped up little Mary and carried her over to the sunny leaded window. I held up my left hand towards the light, the hand upon which I still wore the bejewelled band Edmund had slipped on to my finger on our wedding day. I turned the back of my hand towards the glass and tilted it slowly, this way and that, keeping my eyes trained intently on the far wall. 'Watch very carefully,' I whispered to Edmund's little daughter.

'Whatever are you doing now?' Bess had been wiping the dishes. She put down the cloth.

'We are contemplating Isaac Newton's theory of light and colour,' I told her and Mary with a grin.

'You are an addlebrain for sure,' Bess muttered.

But at that moment I got the angle just right and a myriad dancing colours, red, orange, yellow, green, indigo, blue and violet, were splashed across the white walls of the little limewashed kitchen.

'Newton has proved that we are surrounded by colour all the time,' I said. 'Light itself is made up of a spectrum of colours.' With my thumb I stroked the band of my ring with its diamonds that were doing the job of a prism. 'So, you see, my little Mary, your father can still bring some brightness to our lives, even though he is gone from them.'

'It seems to me that it is James Petiver who has done that for you,' Mary said gently.

'Maybe. But do you see,' I said animatedly, 'Mr Newton has shown how rainbows are made?'

'Pity John didn't know that when he was preaching.' Mary looked from one tiny rainbow to another. 'How lovely to think God not only created light to banish the dark but made it so beautiful, like a true artist.'

'If experiment can reveal the components of light,' I posed tentatively, 'maybe it really can illuminate the rest of God's work. If I could only see how a butterfly is born, I could perhaps be sure that Edmund is in Heaven with my parents and my sister. I could still believe I will see them all again.'

'It's not much further now,' James said. 'Those are the gardens over there.'

We were walking along a raised path called Bishop's Walk that ran along the bank of the Thames. To the other side of us was a wide channel of still water, uncannily like one of the rhynes on Tickenham Moor. But the land behind it was nothing like the moor. It was crowded with trees, not wispy willows, but great stately trunks, with roots that spidered the ground like the veins on an old man's hand, beneath a canopy of enormous arching branches. 'The entrance is only about a quarter of a mile away,' James said.

I slid my hand into the crook of his arm and gave it a quick squeeze. 'Stop fretting about me, James. I'm not in the least tired.'

I hardly knew which way to turn my head. On one side of us was the forested garden and on the other was the river, busy with barges and tilt-boats and fleets of collier ships, the skyline punctuated with Wren's graceful spires which had arisen from the ashes of the Great Fire.

We entered the Palace Gardens under an avenue of limes and I saw then that the wide ditch was in fact a great moat which encircled the entire acreage of the grounds. It was like a scene from a myth. In front of us was a drawbridge and beyond it was the house, or palace, very old and ruinous, with battlemented towers.

'What is this place? Who lives here?'

'It's been the summer residence of the Bishops of London for centuries. The gardens are of great antiquity, have been famous for their beauty and scientific value since the reign of Queen Elizabeth. That's a tamarisk tree,' James pointed out. 'From Switzerland. Over there is a cork tree.'

With my hand still resting in the crook of his arm, he led me deeper into the strange and beautiful forest.

'The trees grew even more thickly once,' he said. 'Until one of the bishops thinned them. Legend has it that Sir Francis Bacon visited just afterwards and said that, having cut down such a cloud of trees, he must be a good man to throw light on dark places.'

'I should like to throw light on dark places.'

'Eleanor, you could do nothing but.'

I gave his arm another squeeze. 'Did I ever tell you, I was married in the same church as Francis Bacon?'

'How grand.'

'Actually, it was far from it.'

'Really?'

'"Truth requires evidence from the real world," Sir Francis said. That is such a good creed. My father had his writings in his library but never could agree that there must be evidence for everything before we can believe in it . . . even before we can believe in God.'

'Do you think we can ever see evidence of God?'

'I used to think it was all around us, in the splendour of His creation. I used to think that was the very reason we must study it, to bring us closer to Him. Or that's what my father taught me. I no longer know now which of the things he taught me are true, but I hope it is more than I have come to suspect.' I stopped and turned to face him. 'James, do you believe absolutely in metamorphosis?'

He pursed his lips. 'I am as uncertain as the next man about oft-repeated claims. Experts contradict each other. The only truly reliable approach to the study of the natural world is through one's own observation. I can't entirely believe it without the evidence of my own eyes.'

That was not what I wanted to hear at all. 'Have any of your friends at the coffee house ever seen it?'

'They are more interested in collecting and marking one species off from another than in seeing how they are born. Though it has not yet been studied properly, metamorphosis is recognised as a fact so . . .'

'So . . . what? It was recognised as fact, since the time of Aristotle, that the earth was at the centre of the universe. But now we are told that the earth in fact moves around the sun. It seems to me that the only truth we have is that we live in a chaos of superstition and experiment. How can we know where we are while natural philosophy is still vying with the old world of magic and traditional lore?

'Few now believe in unicorns as they once did, but if horned beasts are to be relegated to legend, where does that leave the poor old hippopotamus? We cannot believe Aristotle now, so does that mean we should also question the authority of the Bible? If the earth is not the centre of the universe, then where does that leave God and His creation of it? If there is a chance that a piece of rotten fruit, or a cabbage leaf, or a pile of dung can create life, where does that leave God as the ultimate creator? Where does that leave the promise of eternal life?' I ran out of breath and smiled to see James appear both stunned and speechless.

'Well,' he said at last, 'you appear to have rediscovered your curiosity. Along with your voice.'

I laughed. 'So I do.'

'What a truly remarkable person you are, and what a pity it is that you can't join our club. You've a quicker and more interesting mind than many virtuosi.'

'Why can't I join your club? Why can't I go to the coffee house with you?' I waved my hand dismissively. 'Oh, don't even bother to tell me. I already know the answer. It's only open to gentlemen.'

'I'd welcome you right away,' James said as we walked on. 'But I'm afraid we'd be a club of only two.'

'Nobody else would stay if I attended?'

'They'd be afraid a woman would hinder and corrupt the flow of their ideas, cast a malign influence over their experiments.'

I rolled my eyes in exasperation. 'You do know that is ridiculous?'

He grinned. 'I certainly have no evidence of it.'

'The Duchess of Newcastle was permitted to attend the Royal Society meeting,' I ventured.

'Just once. And she, poor lady, is considered a freak of nature, an embarrassment to her sex and her family, for her interest in science.' He tucked my hand back under his arm. 'There's something I want to show you. The conditions are perfect, so I'm sure they'll be there.'

'What will be there?'

'Wait and see. It is a surprise.'

We came to a copse of magnificent oaks with a small clearing in the middle.

'There,' James said, and looked up.

I followed his gaze into the shelter of green leaves and filtered rays of gold light.

Flickers of violet. A dozen indigo wings. Purple-black butterflies, like the drawings from the pages of the book James had made for me after I first met him.

I ran ahead a few steps into the glade. The butterflies flitted just a little higher, riding the currents of the air. I stood with face upturned to the arching branches and the sky beyond. Something about their giddy flight made it impossible for me to stand still. I turned round slowly, watching them. I held out my arms like a swaying tree, dancing in the breeze, my silk skirts swishing. The butterflies flitted higher and higher towards the tops of the trees and I was suddenly giddy.

James caught me as I almost lost my balance. As he set me back on my feet and looked into my smiling face, the light seemed to dim in his own eyes, as if he had transferred all his strength and happiness to me and had nothing left for himself. 'James, you look so sad,' I exclaimed.

'Not at all. And neither are you any more, I think.'

I shook my head. 'I don't know how you do it.'

'Do what?'

'Make me feel again how I felt as a little girl. That everything is there to be discovered. Everything is possible. That life can be good.'

'It is the study of butterflies that makes you feel that way, and having a passion, and never, ever letting go of it.'

'Thank you,' I said. 'For not allowing me to let go. For bringing me here.'

He appeared to be about to say something more, then changed his mind. 'Those purple butterflies are so shy, you've no chance of netting one unless you come prepared.'

'Which, of course, you have.'

He produced from his pocket not a flower but a small lump of meat wrapped in paper. He set this at some distance from us on the grass.

We watched. We waited. Soon enough a flicker of purple descended from above, came drifting down and settled on the carrion, to be followed by another. They fluttered their wings once or twice then folded them up, revealing an underside of shimmering purple, like shot silk.

James didn't pounce, as I was about to do. He seemed content merely to watch, to stand back respectfully and admire from a distance, to let them just be.

'Now what name would you give to them?' he whispered.

I was entranced, as if in the presence of a king all cloaked in royal purple. One was smaller than the other, and one brighter. Was one a female and one a male, one a princess and one an emperor, and if so which way around was it? Purple Emperor. Purple Princess. I'd never considered there could be butterflies that fed on meat, like human beings. They seemed to be relishing the little feast we'd brought for them.

'Do they have teeth?' I asked quietly.

'Ah, now, you'd only find that out by observing up close. Would you like to have one of them for your collection?'

'You have one already?'

'A perfect pair.'

'Did you catch them here?'

'Last spring.'

'So they're likely to be of the exact same species?'

We could study James's specimens, learn from them, we didn't have to take any more. But that didn't stop me craving one of these exquisite beauties for myself. And James knew it. He knew me too well. Without a word from me, he was already creeping towards the spot where the butterflies had alighted. He moved very slowly, as if in a dream, then at the last moment was quick as a cat with a mouse. He clapped his net around the two of them, pinched one, then the other, between his fingers, impaled them on a pin upon the brim of his hat and placed his hat back on his head, while I was still marvelling at the deftness of his fingers.

Standing in the middle of the sunny clearing, wearing a pincushion on a ribbon like a medallion, his hat adorned with purple butterflies, he looked like a very young and clever magician. He conjured two boiled eggs from his pocket and handed me one. We peeled the eggs and ate them, then he handed me his flask of whisky. 'Not a very grand meal, I am afraid.'

I took a nip and wiped my mouth with the back of my hand. 'It is the very best kind.'

As we walked back through the oaks towards the moat, I glanced at my butterflies on his hat.

'They'll be perfectly safe,' he assured me. 'I told you, a hat's the finest receptacle there is.'

'I can see it. I'm just thinking what a shame it is that I don't have that kind of a hat.'

He stopped, took it off and placed it firmly on my head. It slid down over my eyes so he adjusted it, tilting it slightly at a jaunty angle. 'Very becoming.'

'I've often thought I'd be best suited as a boy.'

'Well, I'm sincerely glad you're not one.' He gave a little cough then, as if to cover what he'd just said. 'If you were a boy, I'd have no female acquaintances at all,' he finished.

'I don't believe that for one instant.'

'Well, it is quite true.'

Surely there were plenty of girls, or one girl at least, who'd like to see his bright, clever eyes light up even more brightly with love for her, and her alone? 'You must have a sweetheart,' I questioned him curiously. 'Surely there is some pretty girl you've restored to health with your magic potions and who has lost her heart to you?'

'I wish that were so,' he said. 'But I'm afraid it has not happened.'

For a moment I thought I could almost be that girl. For James had cured me, undoubtedly he had. But my heart? It was most certainly lost long before this day. When Edmund ambled into the hall of Tickenham Court out of the rain. When I first saw Richard Glanville smiling down at me from the saddle of his black Barbary stallion, like a winter prince. In such different ways, I loved them both. I mourned Edmund still, with a grief sharpened by remorse, and I missed Richard. I missed him so much. I still met him in my dreams – sweet, tortured, passionate dreams that made me wake restlessly in the morning, with the pain of parting from him as fresh as if it had been only yesterday that I had told him never to touch me or come near me again.

I was a typical lusty widow after all, wasn't I? I saw something in James's eyes that made me think I must tread very carefully with him. It would not be fair, even for one moment, to let him think he could love me, even if he had a mind to. He was my dearest friend and I could not imagine him as anything else. I would not risk hurting him, ruining our friendship, when I needed a good friend far more than I needed another lover. My heart had been split in two. And a thing cannot be split without being broken.

I took James's hat off my head and put it firmly back on his, for all the world as if I was handing him back his heart. 'There. You look after my butterflies for me.' I lifted the pincushion that hung round his neck, let it rest in the palm of my hand. 'Why so many different sized pins?'

'If you stick a small fly with a large pin, its joints will break and it will fall to pieces.'

I looked up at him and spluttered, 'Well, if ever I marry again then, I'd best make sure my husband's yard is not too big, since I am so very small.'

He froze, mouth agape. The years fell away and he was once again the unworldly boy he'd been the first time we'd met. I collapsed with laughter. He started laughing too. We both laughed until we were bent double like a pair of crones, clutching our sides with pain, the tears rolling down our cheeks.

Autumn 1680

J ames was coming for dinner and there was something of great importance I had to ask him.

'Mary, would you take the children for me a while?'

'You know I'm glad to have them any time.' She glanced at me quickly
as she carried on with her brocading. 'But we shall be going to Mass later.
They'll have to come with us.'

I gazed down at my little daughter, asleep in my arms, and almost said
no straight away. 'I'm not sure . . .'

'Since you no longer care for any religion, what does it matter if they
attend an Anglican ceremony or a Papist one?'

Because Jesuit poison killed their father. 'I do not know. But it does.
Force of habit I suppose.'

'A father's influence runs so deep you can never be entirely free from
it, especially when that father was as commanding and powerful as yours.'
Mary stuck the needle into the brocade, set it to one side and gave me her
full attention. 'But you know, not all your ancestors were so set against
Catholics, or Cavaliers for that matter. Your uncle, who lives in Ribston
Hall in Yorkshire, is a baronet. Your mother's father, Rice Davies, is still
remembered in Tickenham for being as noble as they come. It takes ambi-
tion and a desire for grandeur to build a great house such as Ribston or
Tickenham Court, to be granted acres of land. It takes favours from the
King. Your family has the blood of brave knights running through its veins.
Who knows? Maybe even royal blood.'

Mary smiled as she saw my eyes open wide at the daring, almost traitorous thought that I, the daughter of one of Cromwell's men, could also
have royal blood. I almost felt it stirring dangerously inside me, rousing
me.

'And it's not just royal blood you may have,' she said with gravity. 'When you go back to Tickenham, you look very carefully at the wainscoting around the chimney breast in the great hall.'

I smiled. 'Is this a riddle?'

'There's a tiny chamber, a cell, built into the side of the chimney,' she said. 'There used to be a tunnel from it that led to the church, but I understand it is now blocked. It's a priest's hole,' she added with great significance. 'Where they hid Catholic priests during the Reformation. Your Catholic lineage, your children's Catholic lineage, is strong.'

'Maybe that explains my hankering for satin and gold.'

'Maybe it does.' She paused. 'So, the little ones can come to Mass then?'

'I suppose they can.'

James arrived just after Mary and John and the children had left. He brought part of his collection, in deal boxes of yellow and white and blue, because later he was going on to join his club at the Temple Bar Coffee House. And I was determined that he was going to take me with him. They might not talk so freely in front of me and I would surely never be allowed to come back. But, like Margaret Cavendish, I was going to risk all and go just the same, just once.

'Will you show these to your friends?'

James looked at me over a little square box of Blues, neatly arranged in pairs, a female beside a usually larger and more brightly coloured male. Quick as a flash, I thought of Edmund's red hair, and of Richard Glanville in green silk, and of me in drab Puritan black, fluttering towards them both. Was I a butterfly or was I a moth, fluttering irresistibly towards a bright flame that would burn me alive?

I looked at James, with his hair the colour of ripened corn and his extraordinary multi-coloured eyes. Now, why could I not have fallen in love with someone like him?

'Leonard Plukenet and Adam Buddle will be there tonight,' he said. 'They like to see my latest acquisitions, are as passionate about butterflies as you and I.'

'You could discuss the differences between the sexes?' I said leadingly.

'Maybe.'

'A one-sided debate, given the single sex of your club.'

He smiled, feigning innocence. 'We're a botanical society. We'll talk about male and female butterflies, or ants, or the reproduction of flowers, not about men and women. But still . . .'

'Still, what?'

He frowned, his finger over his lips, making a show of giving something the greatest consideration.

I giggled. 'What, James?'

'There are greater differences between men and women than between male and female butterflies, for sure. But the differences are not so great if the woman is . . . how can I say it? . . . not as voluptuous as the fashions of our age usually dictate.'

'Well, there's no need to be rude.'

'Not at all. I have no time for fashion, as is surely evident.' He lifted one of his feet, encased in outdated flat-heeled shoes. 'I think it is far more appealing for a lady to have the delicate prettiness of a butterfly.'

'Well redeemed.'

But he was still studying me, as if reflecting on a possibility. 'What differences there are could perhaps be concealed, with a little ingenuity.'

I had an inkling then of where this was leading, but didn't dare hope. Didn't dare hope that, once again, James knew me so well that he knew what I wanted or needed, almost before I knew it myself.

'There is perhaps one insurmountable difference,' he deliberated. 'The small matter of courage. It's generally accepted that a man is far braver than a woman. A man would take risks that a woman would not. A man would keep his head where a woman would lose hers at the first sign of trouble. In which case it could never be achieved.' His playful tone had turned more earnest. 'I would lose the trust and respect of my friends, all I've worked for. If they found out, I'd be a laughing stock. Would never be taken seriously again. No, it's no use. It cannot be done.'

I held my breath and leaned forward, arms pressing on my knees, peering into his face. 'What cannot be done, James?'

He expelled a long breath. 'It's no good telling you now. It'll only spoil your evening.'

'It is already spoiled,' I admitted. 'Because you are going off to your club and leaving me behind. You were thinking you could take me with you, weren't you?'

He grinned. 'Now, whatever gave you that idea?'

I grabbed his hands. 'Take me with you, James. I *am* brave, as brave as any boy. My father always told me he wished he had men of my courage marching with him for Cromwell. I will not be intimidated by anyone, I promise you. I won't fail you.'

He wavered, or pretended to waver, then sized me up. 'When we first met we were almost exactly the same size, wouldn't you say?'

I knew what he was going to suggest before he said it.

'My scheme, extraordinary as it may seem, was to take you along in disguise, dressed as a boy.'

I clapped my hands. 'James, that is the most hare-brained, madcap idea!'

'One you might have thought of yourself, I think?'

'Only far better. It's perfect. But who would I be?'

'I thought to introduce you as my assistant, my butterfly boy.'

'And what would be my name? I'd have to have a name.'

'Isaac, I thought, in homage to the great Mr Newton himself, founder of the most exclusive scientific society in Britain and the investigator of light.'

'Isaac . . . I can be Isaac. Oh, let me be Isaac. Let me do it. I will not disappoint you, I swear it.'

He had brought a parcel of clothes with him and I laughed to think how our thoughts ran in such extraordinary parallel. All the time I'd been plotting how to find a way to go with him to the coffee house, he'd been plotting how to enable me to do it, packing up his own shirts and breeches and waistcoat and boots to disguise me in.

He handed the parcel to me, but I hesitated. I realised there was still one problem and did not know how to broach it, without risking having him take it the wrong way.

'You need assistance with unfastening your gown?' he asked, very pragmatically.

I nodded. 'Bess and Mary's maid have the afternoon off. There is nobody else here, and I can't do it on my own.'

We went up to my little sloping-roofed chamber above the schoolroom and locked the door. Discreetly, James went to look out of the dormer window, hands lightly clasped behind him, his flaxen pigtail falling down the middle of his back.

I took the parcel then and laid all the items out on the bed, running my fingers lightly across them. There was something rather poignant about them. These were the clothes James had worn as a boy, when he'd been about the age he was when I first met him and was the same size as me. The shirt had been freshly laundered and carried a faint scent of lavender, but I could see where the cuffs had frayed slightly around his hands, and the cloth breeches still bore the faint creases which had formed as he had worn them, as he had walked and sat and knelt down to examine herbs and flowers and butterflies. Too small for him now. He had grown and I had not.

'I'm ready,' I said.

He made a great show of breathing deeply and gathering himself, as if he was about to do some onerous but unavoidable task. I turned my back to him so he could get at the tiny buttons and laces that held my costume together.

I expected to feel fumbling, nervous fingers, for him to take a long time over it, but instead I felt him working the tiny row of pearl buttons with the deftness with which he'd pinned a tiny butterfly. The realisation hit me and surprised me: he knows exactly what he is doing. He had done this before. This was no gauche boy who'd never undressed a woman, never seen one naked. He had done this before, with some other girl, maybe with many more than one. There was no one special, he said, but he had taken his pleasures somewhere. And there were, after all, plenty of places for a young man to take his pleasures in London, plenty of willing orange girls and pretty whores who could be had for a few pennies. Plenty of maids who'd give themselves willingly, for free, to an ambitious and clever young apothecary with warm, bright eyes, who, it was plain to see, was on the rise.

I wanted to turn round then and look at him, to see if this new realisation made him appear any different to me. I didn't feel jealous of these unknown girls at all, but the thought of James as a man, with a man's needs and urges, did make me feel strange. In the way that noises become louder in the dark when you cannot see, I was acutely aware of every movement of his fingers at my back, every slight change in pressure. I let my dress fall to the ground and felt him loosening the laces of my corset. I peeled it off, turned round and, in just my chemise, stepped out of the watery blue circle of silk.

I wondered then if I'd been entirely wrong about his past experiences. For he stood transfixed, like a boy who'd never seen a woman's body before, except in his most secret dreams, as if he couldn't tear his eyes away from me. And I, who'd been a wife and borne two children and tasted another man's ardent kisses and caresses, was acting as shy and chaste as a virgin on her wedding night.

There was no need. I was not wedded any more. I was no virgin either. I was free and ready to love another man. I did love another man. And it was not this one. My chemise slid off my shoulder. Quick as lightning, James came out of his trance and reached behind me for the shirt, holding it out to me. 'I'll wait outside while you put it on.'

When the door had softly closed behind him, I took off my under-garments. Alone and naked, I slid my arms James's shirt. The linen had worn very soft. It was so strange to think of my shoulders and elbows where James's elbows and shoulders had so often been, and it was almost as if the impression left by him, the ghost of him as a boy, was still there, slipping his arms along the entire length of mine, holding me, wrapping me in a gentle embrace. Not a lover's embrace, but the enfolding, secure and protective embrace of a brother, a twin, a part of myself. The shirt was a little too big for me and yet it felt as if it fitted as well as a hand in a glove, as well as my own skin. It still carried the faintest trace of him, the scent of herbs and fresh air that was so familiar to me. It was as if he was still in the room, standing right behind me, as if he would always be with me, no matter what.

I stepped into his breeches, smiling to myself now at the thought of which parts of his body had been in this particular garment before. I tugged the belt tight around my waist and pulled on his boots which he'd padded with straw to make them fit. I looked down at myself and laughed out loud at the picture I made, like a she-soldier from a ballad.

'It is safe to come in now,' I called.

He grinned when he saw me. 'A lad with ringlets. Well, I never.'

'Oops! I forgot.' I scooped up my hair and knotted it at the back of my head, squashing the cap on top. 'I was bound to get something wrong, since I've never been a lad before.'

James came up to me and lifted my chin, smoothed a strand of hair away and arranged the collar of my shirt. 'Hmm. You'll just about pass as my butterfly boy. A fitting name, since you're such an uncommonly pretty little fellow. We just have to hope they're all too busy with botany to pay too much attention to a dainty little lad with fair skin and golden lovelocks and the widest blue eyes. But even so they may guess our ruse. Cross-dressing is all the rage at court, I understand.'

'Would it really be so bad for you if we were found out?'

'As bad as can be,' he said lightly. 'They'd never forgive me for deceiving them. I'd likely be barred.'

I pulled the cap lower, fiddled with my cuffs. 'I can't let you take such a risk for me. I won't go.'

'You can and you shall.' He handed me a box of butterflies. 'And since you are my assistant, you'd better make yourself useful and carry one of these.'

'I'll take them both.'

James picked up the other one. 'You may be got up like a boy but I'll not forget you're a little lady underneath. I'll not burden you with too heavy a load when we've such a long way to go.'

It did not seem a long way at all. It took us well over an hour, but it was so easy and such a novelty to walk without the encumbrance of a long skirt that I practically skipped along in James's boots to the coffee house, wishing I could wear breeches and boots all the time. How lucky men were to be so unhindered. We talked as we walked. He told me how such establishments as we were about to enter were multiplying in London, how they had even attained some degree of political importance from the volume of talk which they caused. Each camp, sect or group of fashion had built a meeting place around the little bean, and he made them sound such lively, stimulating places that I couldn't wait to get there.

But I owed it to James to be as well prepared as it was possible to be.

'Tell me what it'll be like,' I said eagerly as we made our way past the mansions and beneath the swinging wooden signs of rose garlands and crossed keys. 'Tell me what to expect. How should I behave? What should I do?'

He glanced at me as I gambolled along in his breeches beside him. 'No point telling you just to be yourself, now is there? But it really doesn't matter how or who you are. A coffee house is a place for levellers, a medley of society where each man ranks and files himself as he pleases. A silly fop can converse with a worshipful justice and a reverend non-conformist with a canting mountebank. A person shows himself to be witty or eloquent and, before he knows it, he has the whole assembly abandoning their tables and flocking to his.' He patted the top of my head. 'Since you're both as witty and as eloquent as any man, you could cause a sensation.'

'I most certainly could if they guess from the lightness of my voice that I'm not a man at all. No,' I decided. 'I shall hold my tongue and not say a word. It'll be much safer. I shall be quite content just to watch and listen.'

'I do not believe you'd be capable of that.'

I grinned. 'What do they talk about?'

'Oh, there's all manner of tattle and carping.'

We passed on to the great thoroughfare of Fleet Street, past the waxwork exhibition and the church of St Dunstan's-in-the-West, where the Great Fire had stopped short. I held on to my cap as a sudden gust of wind funnelled down the street and threatened to expose my curls. We passed lawyers and countless taverns and then moved on to the goldsmiths and Temple Bar.

I almost lost my nerve when it came to going inside until James slipped his arm around my shoulders, as he might have done with any apprehensive young lad in his employ. I took a deep breath to calm myself and did just as he had told me, paid my penny and made my way with him, past the benches and tables, to the far corner of the club-room.

The air was hot and thick with a fug of pipe smoke and the strong bitter smell of coffee. Before I knew it I was sitting on a bench, pressed up against James with a steaming dish in my hand. A tall, richly dressed gentleman with a long, straight nose and glossy wig was holding forth with great verve to an attentive group on his belief, which stood opposed to most popular and much expert opinion, that fossils were actual remains of prehistoric life. He spoke in a mild Irish accent and had a very confident set to his shoulders for one so young. Most of those listening must have been twice as old as he was, but that didn't seem to perturb him in the slightest.

I leaned in towards James's ear, shielding my mouth with my hand. 'Whoever is that?'

'Hans Sloane,' he told me. 'Not yet twenty, training to be a physician. He's the most ambitious young man you're ever likely to meet. Has his sights set on becoming President of the Royal Society, no less. The older man to his right is the excellent John Ray. It's to him that both Hans and I owe our love of natural history. He is too thin and eats far too little, but has the energy and enthusiasm of a man a third his age. You'd like him. He's compiling an important global history of flora, from the specimens and descriptions Hans and I have collected for him.'

Between puffs on his clay pipe, John Ray was warning Hans Sloane not to leap to conclusions about fossils. 'To be incautious is to plunge into mere speculation and enter the borderland between science and superstition,' he said patiently. Mr Ray had a strong face, grave and enquiring, but with a touch of humour about his mouth. 'We must be ruthless in our demand for accuracy of observation and in the testing of every new discovery. New knowledge is in its infancy and we must reserve judgement until the proof is compelling.'

James glanced at me and smiled. 'A man after your own heart, in more ways than you know. He's a minister by profession, barred from the pulpit for dissent. He cannot preach, but believes he pursues his calling by studying the works of the Lord.'

For a moment I saw my father sitting in John Ray's place.

'A brilliant young naturalist friend of mine was questioning me about metamorphosis the other day,' James suddenly said to John Ray. 'I found I could not convince her that it is irrefutable.'

'Her?' Hans Sloane gave his friend a delighted, interested smile. I dipped my face to hide my hot cheeks.

'We have not yet sufficiently studied the subject and cannot venture on any rash pronouncement,' John Ray replied in more measured tones. 'I do not wish to disappoint your intriguing friend, whoever she is, but you must tell her that the time for a full answer is not yet arrived. It might take generations even of patient investigations before we reach a satisfactory conclusion. But, for what it is worth, I myself do believe in butterfly metamorphosis. We see it happen in a different way with frogs, after all.'

'What is the use of butterflies anyway?' a man called Nehemiah Grew asked.

'To delight our eyes and brighten the countryside like so many jewels,' John Ray replied. 'To contemplate their exquisite beauty and variety is to experience the truest pleasure and to witness the art of God.'

I found I was smiling at Mr Ray and he at me. I wished for all the world that I could shake off my disguise and talk openly to this wise old man.

'Tell me, young James,' John Ray enquired, 'what has been occupying you lately?'

'I have been observing the characteristic marks that distinguish day-fliers from night-fliers,' James contributed, with his typical ease and unassuming friendliness. 'I believe you are right, John. It seems to be clubbed antennae and whether or not wings are held erect or open when at rest.'

'And whether they are seen by moon or sun, of course,' Hans Sloane concluded.

'Ah, but some night-fliers are also seen by day,' James added, to much general interest. It was clear he was liked as much as he was respected amongst them all, be they young or old, sophisticate or novice. It made me feel very privileged to be with him, to call him my friend.

The talk abruptly shifted to apple pips, a handful of which Hans Sloane had produced from his pocket. Then Mr Ray talked about how his friend Willoughby had kept a tame flea on their travels in Venice. I did not catch all of what he was saying as I was distracted by the other conversations going on around me. The general level of noise in the coffee house was extraordinary, but it didn't take me long to tune my ear to the conversations of various sects, hotly debating the contents of recent pamphlets and the news in the gazettes.

James wagged his elbow at me. 'Drink up before it's cold,' he whispered to me, indicating my full dish. 'It's good for you, cleanses the brain and fortifies the body.'

'I can believe it. These people are most certainly fortified with something.'

He laughed.

'Well now, Petiver,' Hans Sloane boomed. 'Share your hilarity with the rest of us. And aren't you going to introduce us to that little fellow beside you?'

If I could have slid into obscurity beneath the table, I would have done. James cleared his throat. 'My assistant, Isaac. He helps me with my butterflies.'

'Does he indeed? And were you talking about butterflies just now?'

'He's not been in a coffee house before. He was giving me his impressions.'

Mr Sloane turned his full attention on me, as if I was the most interesting person he'd ever met. 'Well, lad, what do you make of it all?'

I felt my cheeks flame, but was thankful at least that hardly anyone else seemed to be listening.

'Come, come now, let the boy speak,' Mr Sloane said in a raised voice. 'It is, after all, the custom of the house to let every man begin his story and propose to answer another, as he thinks fit. "Speak that I may see you," does not the philosopher say? So, let us see who we have here.'

My throat dried, as I felt all eyes turn to me. But then I felt James's hand beneath the table slide across my knee, find my own hand and give it an encouraging squeeze.

'I believed I was coming to a coffee house but it seems I've stepped into a high court of justice,' I said. 'It seems that here anyone in a camlet cloak can take it upon himself to reorder the affairs of Church and State.'

Mr Sloane hooted merrily and John Ray's eyes twinkled at me kindly. 'Your little assistant is both erudite and observant,' he said. 'I'm sure he's a great asset and help to you in the observation of butterflies.'

'He is.' James still had hold of my hand under the table and pressed it a little tighter. 'I could not do without him.'

*　*　*

'You were very convincing,' James said, after the session had ended with the customary prayers and we walked back out on to Fleet Street. It was dusk and still warm. 'They were all taken in by you. Hans will probably try to poach you from me, he took you for such a bright little spark.'

'The sharpest wit would count for nothing if they knew what was, or rather was not, hidden inside my breeches.'

'Slow down,' James protested. 'Why are you walking so fast?'

'Because I'm angry. And my legs are buzzing like a beehive. My head, too, for that matter.'

He chuckled. 'Coffee does that to you, if you're not used to it. Don't be despondent, Eleanor. You did it. You outfoxed them all.'

I swung round to face him with my hands on my hips. 'And what exactly was the good of that? What happens to me now?'

'You keep on with your work.'

'It will count for nothing. None will care what I do. Just because my name is Eleanor, not Edward or some such. Because I am a woman.'

'That's not true,' James said emphatically. 'You are an outstanding naturalist and should be recognised as such.'

'Oh, James . . .'

'I mean it. Already because of you I've learned there are butterflies living only on the marshes that disappear when that marshland is destroyed. That's a valuable lesson. It shows us the importance of butterflies in telling us about the world we live in. They are like little barometers, foretelling change. If a butterfly disappears, we should take note. It could be of vital importance one day.'

We started walking again. 'Do you honestly think so?'

'Any one of those gentlemen in that coffee house would think so. Any of the great scientists of the Royal Society itself would think so. Scientists living hundreds of years from now will think so. Rarities can never be conserved unless people like you discover as much as you can about them.' We carried on in silence for a while.

When he resumed talking James told me, 'Hans has a vision of building a great institution, bigger than the Tradescants' Ark, like a giant curio cabinet, housed in its own building, where thousands of artefacts and specimens can be displayed for all to see and study. He's always telling me that he envisions my collections forming the bedrock of the insect cabinets. Think what it would be like to contribute to that great and lasting collection – the greatest natural history collection in Britain. There's no reason why yours could not be a part of it, too.'

'That would be an honour,' I conceded. 'But I honestly didn't start collecting butterflies with any mind to fame or immortality or even to science. I read that Christopher Wren and Isaac Newton were inspired to be involved in science and mathematics by the sight of a comet. For me it was the beauty and colour of a golden butterfly.'

'There's nothing wrong with being first drawn to something because you think it very beautiful,' James said quietly. 'So long as you take the time to find out and appreciate its other virtues.'

'You forget the tulip fanciers who ransomed their fortunes and ruined themselves, all for the transitory beauty of a rare flower.'

'Perhaps it was worth it. The ancients went so far as to worship butterflies for their beauty. They believed that the fire goddess followed young warriors on to the battlefield and made love to them, holding a butterfly between her lips.'

Coming from any other man this would have sounded like overt flirtation but James always seemed to be above that, his thoughts moving on the permanently higher plane of science and ideas. Our discussions had ranged over such arcane and wonderful topics in the past that we could now speak of almost anything with complete ease. But when we reached the door of the Burgeses' house, I could not help but feel relieved that our conversation had reached a natural end.

'Would you like a cup of milk before you set off back?' I didn't wait for James to answer but went straight to the jug on the table. I could hear Mary soothing one of the little ones who'd woken up, and John was no doubt in his closet, saying his prayers. I took off my hat and let down my hair, thinking it would give my kind hosts the fright of their lives if they found a strange boy in their kitchen. Not that they would be unshocked to see me with my hair cascading over a waistcoat, all the way down to a pair of brown breeches! I was about to pour the milk when I saw a letter, propped against the jug and addressed to me.

'The writing's much tidier than mine,' James said, peeping over my shoulder.

It was indeed precise, spare and bold. William Merrick's writing. I unfolded it and read. It was a short letter, but it took a disproportionately long time for me to take in the contents.

'Is everything all right, Eleanor?' James touched my arm.

I looked up at him. 'I have to return to Tickenham immediately. There's been a flood, an early flood. The rivers have burst their banks. They didn't get the cows off the moor in time and many have drowned. A boy from the village was washed away and lost his life trying to save them . . . trying to save his family's livelihood.'

James looked down at the letter, as if he would read much more than was contained within it. 'Tell me about your home, about the moor. I have travelled so little, I don't even know exactly where it is.'

I refolded the letter, tossed my hair over my shoulder and finished pouring the milk. I handed him the cup and leaned back with my hands against the table. 'It lies to the north of the Mendip Hills, near to the coast and the Bristol Channel. In summer the land is so fertile it produces the best cattle in all of England. But in winter it is wet and marshy. We call it the moor but it's really a low-lying expanse of peat, threaded with rivers. We are used to the regular onset of great autumn and winter floods that sweep in during October or November and remain until January, some- times returning throughout February and March and early-spring. You'd think it a strange spectacle to see people striding on stilts through the water, or a congregation forced to come to church in boats and carry their dead across the water to bury them. But that is how life is for us and has been for generations.' I smiled. 'I'm sorry. I'm sure you didn't want to know all that.'

'You speak about it as if you love it very much.'

'In summer there is nowhere I would rather be, and even the floods bring their own mystery and magic.'

James drank some of the milk and waited for me to go on.

'The people of Somersetshire have waged a war against water for centuries,' I said. 'I grew up hearing stories of the disastrous flood of the year sixteen hundred and seven, when a high tide met with land floods so violent that they overwhelmed everything built to withstand their force. Walls and banks were eaten though and the moor was inundated to a depth of twelve feet. The floodwaters were littered with pieces of bobbing timber and the floating corpses of dead cattle and goats. Whole villages were sunk right up to the tops of the trees, so that it appeared as if they'd been built at the bottom of the sea.'

James was listening with rapt attention, as if I was weaving a fantastical story.

'So, you see, we are used to floods,' I said. 'But nobody expects them in September. Nobody is ready for them then.'

'Isn't it too late now? What can you do? Why must you go back?'

'I am their squire now. I do not know if I shall make a very good one, but I am all they have. These people are my family, James. The women kept me company when I was having my first baby. They will look to me.'

'But what can you do?'

I threw up my hands with a small shrug. 'Have the kitchen cook up a vat of broth. Send out labourers and carts to mend any breach in the sea wall. Take a bucket and start bailing. I shall not know where I am most needed until I am there.'

'Tickenham is blessed to have you.' He plopped my hat back on top of my curls. 'You will make a most able little squire, I think.'

'I hope so. I shall do my very best.'

He handed the cup of milk to me, brought out his flask and poured a dash of whisky into it. 'If you are going to go, I shall have to give you your gift now.'

'My gift?'

He smiled. 'I do know how you like gifts. I was saving it for New Year, but you must take it home with you.' He hunted around in the pot cupboard. 'Mary has been keeping it safe for me. Now, where might she have hidden it?' He moved on to the settle, opened up the seat and peered inside. 'Ah, here it is.'

I'd been expecting more butterfly wings, but instead he produced a large and intriguing wooden box. 'James, whatever is it?'

He placed it in front of me on the table and stood back. 'Open it and see.'

I took off the lid and brought it out, recognising what it was immediately from the pictures I'd gazed at in the book my father had burnt, fearing it might carry the plague to us. I lifted it out and set it on the table, a heavy instrument with polished brass knobs and glass lenses and dials. 'A microscope.' I looked at James, but I couldn't see him all that well, since my eyes were blurred with tears. 'I've wanted one for years.'

He looked so happy, as if it was he who'd been given the most wonderful gift, not me. 'It's from Christopher Cock's workshop in Long Acre. One of the best instrument makers. By Royal Appointment.'

I put my eye against the eyepiece.

'You really need a lamp globe to help illuminate specimens properly. I was planning to bring mine over here for you to try, but you'll work out how to get a satisfactory image using sunlight.'

'I don't know what to say. How to thank you.' I looked at him, suddenly distraught. 'But, James, I don't have anything to give you in return.'

'Yes, you do,' he said. 'You can give me a promise never again to say your work has no merit.' He took my hand in his, as if binding me to a pledge. 'Promise me that that you will never, ever give up your love of butterflies, and that is all the thanks I shall ever need.'

I saw the earnestness behind his smile. It was as if he was asking me to remain faithful to our friendship, since butterflies had always been the link between us.

'I swear it.'

'I will teach you how to use the microscope properly,' he said. 'Just as soon as you return to London.'

I didn't go up to bed when James left. Instead I placed a candle as near to the microscope as I dared. It had been sold with some prepared glass slides and I slipped one under the lens, peered down the eyepiece at it, but saw nothing at all. I needed James to show me how to use it. I needed him to help me see with clarity. Maybe I would come back to London soon, but for now the summer was over. Despite repeated adjustments to the knobs and dials, all I could see before me was darkness.

Part III

Autumn 1684

Four years later

Forest and little Mary were playing with a litter of kittens by the stone fireplace in the great hall when I told them we were expecting guests. Mary jumped up and clapped her hands. 'Who?' she asked eagerly.

I couldn't answer her. It was too strange, as if time had reeled backwards. Sitting beside my daughter, I saw a ghost child in a starched white cap and dark wool dress. I heard my father tell me we were expecting guests. I saw myself jump up and clap my hands and ask who it was, just as little Mary had done.

'William Merrick,' I said, like an echo from that other time. 'And another gentleman . . . from Bristol.'

I saw little Mary's excitement drain out of her as she turned her attention back to the kittens. She didn't particularly like Mr Merrick, just as I had not liked him.

Still I had anticipated his visit eagerly that day because I was curious to meet the gentleman who was to come with him. A gentleman from Suffolk. I had looked forward to meeting him, not knowing that he was to be my husband, the father of my children, the friend of the man I had loved beyond any other.

For all that had happened to me in between, England, and especially the West Country, had not changed so very much. It was not even a safer, more secure place for my children than it had been for me as a child. We had beheaded one king then, and now here we were, a good few years on, and there had been several attempts and rumours of attempts to assassinate the new, restored one. It seemed that lessons were not so easily learned, that mistakes were made only to be repeated.

The country was rife with rumours of uprisings and plots to seize London and conspiracies to destroy the monarchy. The King's dashing illegitimate son, the Duke of Monmouth, claimed to be the rightful heir to the throne and had attempted to displace his named successor, James, King Charles's brother. The Duke had proved his popular following with a progress through our own county, through Illchester and Bath, where the children and I had gone for the waters and been caught up amongst the thousands who were there to greet him and strew his way with herbs and flowers. The handbills and broadsheets now claimed he was at the head of the plot to kill his father and he had fled to Holland, with five hundred pounds set his head, but everyone knew it was only a matter of time before he would return to the West Country and amass an army of supporters.

At least my son was too young to join them, I thought with relief, though Forest would leap at any excuse for a fight and harried me at every turn. Right now he was mercilessly pulling the kitten's tail. She had, with good reason, turned on him with a little hiss and bared her tiny pointed teeth.

'Oh, don't tease her, Forest,' I said. 'You are so cruel sometimes.'

He stuck out his lip sullenly. 'You kill butterflies.'

'So that I can study them.' That subtle difference was no doubt entirely lost on a seven year old. He was, in all honesty, probably learning something about nature by pulling a kitten's tail and watching to see how it responded. 'Don't be impertinent,' I ended half-heartedly, with too much on my mind to start another battle with him.

'Don't be angry with Forest,' Mary said sweetly, defending her brother, automatically siding with him against me as was the way with brothers and sisters. She never saw bad in anyone, was as placid and good as she had looked from the moment she was born.

In that respect at least, this situation was very different from that other day so many years ago. I had no need to echo my father and tell my own daughter to tidy her hair and clean her hands before our guests arrived, so that she looked like a little lady, not a vagabond. She was only just four years old but, bless her, she always looked and behaved like a perfect little lady, and was well loved for it by everyone.

She stuffed her hand into the pocket fastened around her waist and produced a sugared almond which she immediately offered to her brother.

'Where did you get that?' I smiled at her. 'As if I couldn't guess.'

'From Cook.'

Mistress Keene was forever slipping her titbits and treats from the kitchen 'She spoils you.' All the servants did. They adored Mary. Would do anything for her. Not that I could blame them at all. I had thought we would be the same, she and I, but we were not. She resembled Edmund physically, with her red hair and freckles, but also in her personality. She was like her father in every way, a girl who would be perfectly content with marriage to a man just like him, would look for nothing more than a quiet life of domesticity. In one part of me I was intensely glad for her, but I could not help feeling a little sorry too. Mary would be spared the pain, but she would miss out on the passion.

'Can't we go outside?' Forest challenged, in a tone I recognised as being far more like my own.

'You may go once you have greeted our visitors, so long as you promise to stay in the garden.'

'You never let us do what we want,' he exploded, scowling at me and stamping his feet in a fit of childish rage.

Swift and direct as an archer's arrow, he had found my most vulnerable point. He knew very well that the one thing I wanted for my children was for them to be as unconstrained and free as it was possible to be. 'That is not true, Forest, and well you know it.'

Further argument between us was prevented by a knock at the door. 'That must be Mr Merrick.' Or William, as he now insisted I call him.

Mary stood demurely to receive the visitors, but as soon as Bess had admitted them into the great hall and they had bowed and kissed my hand, Forest slunk straight for the door, head down in a sulk.

William was not impressed and caught him by the shoulder, but Forest threw him off so roughly that if he'd been a year or two older and stronger, he'd have run the risk of unseating our guest's expensive new periwig. The thought of which made me smile to myself. Was it any wonder my son was such a little insurgent?

'I told him he could go, William,' I said, irritated by the interference. 'Rather now through the door, than out of a window at dead of night.'

William Merrick's square jaw had slackened into jowls with age, but he was as loud and bombastic as ever. 'You are far too lenient with the little jackanapes. He'll become completely ungovernable.'

'He is only seven. And I like his spirit.'

'No good will come of spoiling that child, I tell you.'

I managed to hold my tongue. No good would come of me reminding William Merrick that he wasn't my guardian any more, had no jurisdiction over how I chose to run my household and my family. Nobody had any jurisdiction over me now. I had discovered that there was that small consolation to being a widow. To have a husband and see him die, to sleep alone and unloved in a cold bed every night for the rest of her life, was one way for a woman to be completely free. The only way for a woman to be completely free. I had nobody to hold me, nobody to kiss me and caress me, nobody to share my life with, but I was at last masterless. None in the world could call me to account, and I liked that very much.

I told Mary she might go back to the kittens once she had asked Bess to bring us some coffee.

'You've a biddable little girl there,' William conceded. 'But young Forest needs a man in his life to restore some discipline.'

'If there was a man in his life to discipline him, I'd have to be obedient to that man too,' I smiled wryly. 'No, thank you.'

'You've had no more offers?'

'I'm a wealthy widow. Naturally I have had offers.'

'From Richard Glanville again?'

Just to hear his name caused an ache of loss and emptiness in my heart. 'From him.'

There had been other suitors besides Richard, fortune hunters one and all. I barely even recalled their names, and if I had not seen them off by subtly refusing every one of their oft-repeated invitations, they soon abandoned their quest when I told them in no uncertain terms that I had no wish to wed again. Only Richard had not given up. He had tried to see me more than half a dozen times since Edmund's death. Once every six months or so he rode to Tickenham unannounced, as he had that Valentine's morning. But each time I had told Bess to send him away. I refused to speak to him. I turned him away from my door, when he'd ridden for days to see me, without even offering him the common courtesy I'd show to a beggar. I didn't trust myself to let him in, even to offer him some bread and cheese and ale to refresh him after the long ride then see him on his way again.

'I thought as much,' William said with some mirth. 'I ran into him again last week, drowning his sorrows in a bottle of rum at a dockside inn.'

I felt the prick of tears behind my eyes. I did not want to know. And yet I did. Oh, I did. 'You spoke to him?'

'He spoke to me. Begged me to tell him when last I had seen you. If you were well, if there were any other gentlemen paying you any attention. I tell you, I pitied the poor, lovesick lad. But you've got to give him credit, he's mightily tenacious. I guarantee he'll be back.'

I did not doubt it. But it would make no difference how many times he came, I would not see him. No matter how much my body burned for him and my heart pined just to hear his voice, to see his face, to touch him. This was my punishment, my penance. And it was the price I paid for my freedom. If you could call it freedom, when I was bound by the spiralling costs of this waterlogged land and with maintaining this ancient, crumbling house, bound by obligations to tenants and servants, by the constant nagging fear that my children might fall ill or drown.

'He'd not make such a bad husband, you know,' William continued. 'Richard Glanville. Nor such a bad lord for Tickenham.'

I found myself wondering then if my former guardian had helped Richard to drown his sorrows in that Bristol inn, and just what the two of them had found to talk about besides me. As if I could not guess. 'With his dying breath, my father warned me to be on my guard against unscrupulous Cavaliers,' I said viciously.

'But your father, my dear, could sometimes be a terrible bigot.'

'I will not hear him spoken of that way, sir. Do you hear me?'

'You disagree with me?'

'I do not wish to discuss my father. And I especially do not wish to discuss Richard Glanville. Not now. Not ever.'

William gave a non-committal shrug. 'As you wish.'

'All Forest needs is to be able to go outside to play and tire himself, ' I said, changing the subject back. 'He wants to fly kites and climb trees and kick his ball about on the moor. And soon it will be safe for him to do all that, won't it? Soon no more boys will lose their lives trying to save drowning cows. Soon there will be no more floods. That is, after all, why you are here.'

'Indeed.'

'I trust you have more to report this time than the last.'

'I am pleased to inform you that the necessary permissions have at long last been granted, an engineer has almost been appointed and two hundred pounds allotted to commence work. I have every confidence that a date will soon be set for the summer. My, how long we'll have waited for such a day!'

To me it felt like a lifetime. I could not help but remember how I had been cajoled into agreeing to this scheme, so that Edmund might solicit my hand, and now, before the first sod had even been dug, I was a widow of four years standing.

I woke in the darkness to the unmistakable and haunting call of a wedge of swans arriving to spend winter on the wetlands. As well as their eerie honking, I swore I could hear the beating of many great white wings.

I waited until dawn and then I went to rouse Forest and Mary from their beds.

'The swans are here,' I whispered into their intricate little ears. 'Come and see them.'

Together we stood by the window in my chamber, a child to either side of me, my arms draped around their shoulders, as we gazed out over the dawn-lit flooded moor, empty yesterday save for the mallards and a few geese, but now miraculously thronged with hundreds, almost thousands it seemed, of our serene, white winter visitors.

I was not too absorbed by the magic and mystery of their appearance to miss the exchange of glances 'twixt my son and daughter which resulted in Mary putting forth a request. 'Could we take the boat out to see them up close?' she asked tentatively.

'All right,' I acquiesced, thinking there might be few such chances left. 'So long as you both wrap up warm.'

They scampered off gleefully and Mary came back minutes later, carrying cloak, bonnet and muff. Forest had put on his thick riding coat and boots. Mary took hold of my hand and Forest's and we walked linked together.

My son wanted to row the boat and I watched him proudly as he pulled on the oars with enough strength to propel our little vessel between the majestically gliding birds.

'Beautiful, aren't they?' I said, wrapping my cloak tighter around me.

Forest's face was a picture of indifference, no sign of wonder or love for this land etched there at all, despite my best and continued efforts to instil such feelings in him.

'Have you ever wondered where the swans go in summer?' I asked both the children.

Disappointingly, my question was met with the shaking of two heads, one dark, one copper. Mary was too young, I consoled myself, and Forest too obstinate. If he did wonder, he would never admit it to me. Yet I so wanted him to love this land that would one day be his, wanted it to mean as much to him as it did to me.

'When I was a little girl, I used to wonder,' I told them. 'I used to imagine that perhaps they came with the winter and flew away again in spring because they were white and were snow birds, who took the cold away with them. It is the same ones who come back every year, though I have no idea how they find their way. I did sometimes wish I could fly away with them, wherever it was that they went, or rather that I could do the opposite of what they do, and leave Tickenham in winter to return in spring when the floods have gone. But soon the floods will be gone for good, Forest,' I said to him, wondering where the swans would go then. 'The drainage work will begin. By the time you are a grown man, it will be complete.'

This at least appeared to have spiked his interest, though for entirely the wrong reasons. 'And shall I be as rich as William Merrick?' he asked with a keenness that made me uneasy, young as he was.

As he had grown, the greedy side of Forest's nature had increasingly tended towards an unpleasant avariciousness that I did not like at all, did my utmost to discourage. 'You will only be as rich as Mr Merrick if you are as devious and ruthless as he is,' I said severely. 'Which I sincerely hope you will not be.'

'What are we to have for dinner?' he asked then. 'I'm hungry.'

'So am I,' Mary agreed.

'I hope it is not pike again,' Forest grumbled.

'I hope it's not either,' Mary echoed supportively.

Forest stuck out his tongue, pretending to gag. 'If we eat any more pike, we'll look like one.' He sucked in his cheeks and pouted his mouth, fish-like, making Mary giggle behind her hand.

'What would you like to eat then?' I asked.

'Venison,' he said. 'Like Mr Merrrick always has.'

'Hmmm. Well, when you are squire you can eat venison every day, if you like, but for now I suggest we send to the inn for a barrel of oysters. As a treat, we shall all three of us eat them by the fire.'

Forest scowled at me until I screwed up my face and scowled back comically, managing at last to make him grin.

Spring 1685

There were several occurrences in the course of the spring which proved the people of Tickenham to be as resistant to plans for drainage as ever.

First the ale barrels in the buttery were prised apart, allowing the contents to swill all over the floor. Days later, the chickens were all found dead in their coop, their necks wrung and the fresh eggs all smashed in a mess of yolk and white and shell. Then two of the pigs were butchered in the sty, their throats slit wide, splattering so much bright red blood that it resembled a slaughterhouse.

I was more angered by the needless waste than by the destruction of my property, but at least anger served to hold fear at bay, for a time. Unsurprisingly, all around me had suddenly been struck mute, deaf and blind. Nobody had seen or heard anything, it seemed. When the constable questioned them, tenants and commoners and servants all denied having even the glimmer of a suspicion as to who might have committed these vengeful crimes. Even Bess remained guiltily tight-lipped, her loyalties clearly torn in a way that disturbed me more than anything, made me more certain than ever that her own brother was behind it all. She refused to meet my eye, even when Forest told me, in her hearing, that Thomas had asked him, some while ago, if he knew what a Fen Tiger was.

'And do you?' I asked him cautiously, wondering if that was why he had taken to following me around and standing quietly at my side.

'Thomas told me they are not really tigers at all,' he said. 'But angry men.'

We were in the great hall. I sat down on the settle, and for the first time in I don't know how long, Forest let me take him on to my lap. I wrapped my arms around his strong little body and held him tight. 'Did Thomas say anything else, Forest?'

'He said the tigers were being bred in Somersetshire now. Right here, in Tickenham, and that Somersetshire Tigers are angrier even than their Fen cousins. He said they would take revenge on us for robbing the commoners of their way of life.' He twisted round to look at me. 'It's them who killed the pigs and the hens, isn't it?'

He did not deserve to hear a lie. I stroked his hair. 'I think it must be.'

'They are not done yet, are they?' he said with a heart-rending perception way beyond his years.

When William Merrick came to inspect the carnage in the pigsty he told me to show forbearance, but even he seemed to have lost much of his old brash self-assurance. He appeared almost cowed.

'I had hoped it would be different this time,' I said, as we watched two silent labourers, their pails brimming with red water, scrubbing the blood off the walls. 'I hoped the memory of that poor boy's death in the last serious floods would make a difference. What, in God's name, does it take to convince them?'

'Evidently much more than it takes to convince the investors to withdraw their funding,' William said morosely. 'Unfortunately they have heard of these recent disturbances and it has undermined their confidence in the whole project.' I had never seen my former guardian look so disconsolate. 'They will back out if there is even a whiff of more trouble. The fear is that once the work commences, the vandals will turn their attention from destroying your property to sabotaging the new sluices and walls and rhynes. Such setbacks in the Fens cost the investors dear, almost brought about their ruin. My partners had not anticipated such disastrous disturbances here.' He looked at me scathingly. As if it was my fault that I had not carried the people with me, as if to say that all would have been very different if Edmund, or indeed any other man, were here to calm, coerce and inspire solid confidence. I did not think it would have been different at all, but I would have given much to hear Edmund's unshakeable assurances that we what we were doing was right, that even the commoners would come to see that eventually. Without him, doubts assailed me again. It was my decision now, not my father's, not my guardian's, not my husband's. But having no one to tell me what to do meant there was no one to share the responsibility. My decision. And by it I should stand or fall.

'William, do you honestly believe they have no justification for what they do?'

His eyes almost popped out of their sockets. 'Justification?'

'I know there is no excuse for violence, but they see their rights being stripped away from them and what else can they do?'

'Are you actually questioning if certain circumstances make it acceptable to break the laws of this land?'

'It is not as simple as that.'

'No,' he said dryly. 'Nothing is ever simple where you are concerned. You'd find a dozen different sides to examine on a triangle.'

I laughed, glad at least that he would joke with me now. My father had liked him, I should like to find a way to like him too, and perhaps, now we were on a more equal footing, it would be possible.

We had turned and walked back inside the house. The children had gone to their beds not ten minutes before, but I heard Mary scream with terror as she sometimes did when awoken from a bad dream in the middle of the night. The scream was followed by the pounding of her bare feet on the stairs as she came running to find me in her nightshift, her thick plait of red hair flying. I caught her up in my arms and hugged her, her little arms clinging tight around my neck and her legs wrapped round my waist like a monkey's. 'Whatever's the matter, sweetheart?'

'An eel,' she sobbed. 'An eel in my bed.'

'In your bed? Are you sure?'

She nodded vigorously, her tawny eyelashes wet with tears.

'Let's go up together and see, shall we?'

In the nursery I pulled back the sheet and blankets and there it was, its slippery glistening body dark against the white linen bedding of my daughter's cot, like an evil black serpent.

For Mary's sake I made light of it, did not let her see my anger flare almost beyond control, destroying any lingering sympathy I might have had for the commoners. Damn whoever did this, I thought. Damn them all to Hell. She's just a little girl. 'It is only an eel,' I said aloud. 'It can't hurt you.'

She hid her face, having always been squeamish in a way I had never been. 'Is it . . . dead, Mama?'

It wasn't. Quite. I reached out and took hold of its slithery, twitching body. With a calmness I did not feel, I took it to the window and threw it out.

For once I was grateful that Mary did not ask the questions I would have done at her age. She did not even ask how the eel could have got into her bed. Like her father she did not dwell on things, would not dwell on who might have crept secretly into the house and up to the nursery and pushed it between her sheets. I knew better even than to think for a moment that this might be a prank of Forest's. He doted on Mary, would never have done anything that might frighten or upset her.

'We'll get the chambermaid to change the sheets in the morning,' I said hugging her close. 'You shall sleep with me tonight.'

William had left. I did not close the curtains around the bed and I kept the candle lit. I closed my eyes, but every muscle in my body remained tense, my ears alert for any sound. All I had wanted was to make our home, our little world, a better, safer place, and it seemed I had done just the opposite. And, Heaven knows, there was danger and unrest enough in this county without creating more.

Everyone said the Duke of Monmouth would sail from the continent and bring war again to the West Country any day now. His father, King Charles, had died in February and Charles's brother James had been crowned in his place, an avowed Catholic, in a country that still despised Catholicism, was still utterly opposed to a Papist on the throne. The dashing Duke was Protestant, and because of that at least half the country favoured him as King. Monmouth would move soon to take the crown of England by force. The rivers of this land would run red with blood again, as men I had known all my life rose up to fight for the grand old cause, for the battles my father had already fought and ultimately lost. I could do nothing at all to prevent that. But I had hoped at least to rid Tickenham of its lethal floods.

I sat up, pushed my hand under the pillow and reached for my notebook, knowing it was the only chance I had of finding some peace. Mary sat up too and snuggled into my side as she did when we were reading a storybook together. 'Is that your book about flufflies?' my enchanting daughter lisped, with her own endearing pronunciation that I could not bear to correct, dreading the day when she called butterflies by their proper name.

I put my arm around her, pulled the blankets up. 'It is, my little love.'
'Why do you write about them?'

'Because I like to.' But it was more than that, so much more. Because I
have to, I could have said. Because I believe it is what I am meant to do.
Because it is the only thing I can do. Because it is the only thing that really
makes me happy. Because it stops me from thinking. Because I began to
study butterflies and to write about them as a cure for longing and I am
still longing, and it is still the only cure for it that I have.

I had the time and freedom now to spend on my own observations and
catalogues and had amassed a collection of specimens and records of which
even I was proud. With Ned Tucker's help, I was cultivating a butterfly
garden near the orchard, stocked with all the plants that seemed to attract
them. But I did not write to James any more; thought it was simpler, fairer,
that way. I had sensed his deepening affection for me and knew I could
never love him like that. There was only one man I loved. Since the day I
had first seen Richard, he was all I had wanted. Even if I never saw him
again, it seemed likely that my last thoughts this side of the grave would
be of him.

I slipped a letter from inside the back cover of my observation book.
Richard had kept on writing to me, just as he kept on trying to see me. I
had consigned all his letters to the fire, except for this one. In a moment
of weakness I had opened it, read it, and once I had, could never have
destroyed it. It was a lovely letter.

My eyes drifted to the closing paragraph.

*What I once took for poverty, I now see as the greatest riches. I think I
would be content now just to be able to look at you, to talk to you, to hold
your hand, to be your friend, if only you would let me. But in a way it
makes no difference that you refuse to see me. Know that when you are
dancing, when the fields and the rivers are lit by moonlight, when the
floodwaters freeze thick enough to skate upon, I am there with you, waiting
for you. I shall always be there, Nell. I shall always be waiting.*

Belowstairs a window shattered. I sat bolt upright. I did not drop the letter
but rather my fingers tightened upon it, as if I would cling to it on a journey
through the jaws of Hell.

It was silent now. It had been raining, but the rain had stopped and there was only the occasional drip from the wooden guttering. Otherwise perfect stillness and silence. Except for the violent hammering of my own heart.

Another window smashed and Mary sprang awake. 'What was that, Mama? I heard a noise.'

I clutched her tight. 'Shush,' I told her, as reassuringly as I could.

'We know you are there,' a voice shouted from outside. 'Show yourself.'

'Who's that?' Mary squeaked.

A different voice: 'You can't hide from us.'

There were two of them then. 'Just village lads who've been drinking,' I said to my daughter. 'That's all.' I put my hand over her ear and pressed her red head against me, gathering her to me more closely, as if I could shield her from all harm with my own body.

'Come out now, if you know what's good for you.'

I recognised that voice, recognised the spite and the malice in it. Thomas Knight. Three of them then.

'Come out now or we'll burn down this house.'

I leapt out of bed as if it was already in flames. 'Stay right there,' I said to Mary as I threw a loose gown over my shift.

'Don't leave me,' she squealed, her face filled with terror.

'Go and get into bed with Forest. But do not come below stairs, do you understand?'

'They are going to set us on fire!'

I took her shoulders, looked intently into her face. 'They will do no such thing, Mary. They will not.'

If at least three, then maybe more. Maybe a whole rabble, come to protest and besiege the house just like the angry mobs that had gathered when they'd tried to drain the Fens. But there was no doubt in my mind that Thomas Knight was the instigator, and Bess would talk sense into him. I must hold them off long enough for someone to fetch her from the cottage where she lived with Ned and Sam.

I ran to the door of the room the dairymaid shared with her sister, who worked in the bakehouse. 'Wake up!'

Silence.

I lifted the latch and flung open the door. The room was empty. I flew down the dark passage to the next room where Mistress Keene slept. She wasn't there either. Everyone had gone.

My legs were shaking so much I could hardly stand. I was all alone in the house with two small children and a gang of angry men outside, threatening to burn us alive.

Another window shattered.

I ran down the stairs and grabbed my father's flintlock musket and bayonet off the wall, found the cartridge box in the buffet and ripped the twisted paper tail off one with my teeth as my father had shown me. With trembling fingers, I half-cocked the trigger, poured some of the black powder into the pan to prime it, turned the gun and emptied the rest of the charge and the lead ball down the muzzle. Then I whipped out the ramrod and rammed it down the barrel hard to force the powder and ball into place.

The gun was heavy and nearly as tall as me but as I slung it over my shoulder and headed for the door, I took courage from remembering that women during the Civil War had defended their houses against besieging enemy armies, against neighbours and friends and people with whom they had once shared meals, counting them as family. If they could do it, then so could I.

The mob that I faced was more than two dozen strong. Thomas Knight was there, Jane Jennings's husband, Matthew. There was John Hort, the eeler. Ned too, as were the Bennett boys and their father plus two other tenant farmers' lads. Two dozen against one. There might just as well have been fifty. They were armed with pitchforks, axes, pikes and scythes – those cruel and murdering weapons with their long poles and curved blades. Thomas Knight and two of the others were waving flaming torches while swigging something from a small flagon that they handed between them.

Thomas was staring at the musket. 'What's she going to do with that, d'you think?'

'I do not want to do anything with it.' I tried to keep my voice from shaking and looked directly at Ned. 'For God's sake, go home. All of you. Go back to your wives and your children and your mothers.'

'We don't want any trouble,' Ned said nonsensically.

'Then what are you doing here?'

'You've left us no option,' he half apologised. 'If we're to go on being able to afford to put bread on our tables, to feed our families . . .'

'The moor is ours,' one of the farm boys yelled ferociously. 'You've no right to take it from us.'

They all started shouting at once, each as vociferous as the next, so that I could not make out a word. They'd inched forward as one body, drawn more tightly around me. They were gesticulating angrily, pointing at me menacingly with their assorted weapons, stabbing the air between us with their pikes and pitchforks. The sound was deafening, like a crowd at a bear baiting.

'Get back,' I shouted. 'All of you.' I levelled the musket, pressed it against my shoulder, aimed the long barrel into the middle of the crowd. 'I swear I'll use it if I have to.'

They quietened, one or two even backed off.

'Come on, don't be cowards,' Mark Walker, the miller's son, sniggered. 'She's just a lass, and a small one at that. She won't know how to use it.'

I waved the gun at them, narrowed my eyes. 'Do not wager on that, Mark.'

At the edge of my vision I glimpsed someone else, the caped silhouette of a lone rider, some distance off to the right under the trees by Monk's Pool, but I had no time to wonder who he was or why he was not joining in.

'She might fire at us.' Thomas Knight stepped forward, his sharp jaw clenched, his eyes black as bile. 'I wouldn't put her to the test. She's never been quite right in the head after all, never been like other girls. And she's been without a man so long, she's forgotten what it is to be a woman.' He came up closer to me. 'That's why she's involving herself in men's business — business she doesn't understand.'

'She needs reminding of her place in the world,' John Hort sneered.

'You're the man for it, Tom,' John Bennett piped up. 'You've been itching to know what it'd be like to lie in the squire's bed. Now's your chance.'

I could smell the spirits on Thomas Knight's breath, just like I'd done in the copse on May Day when I'd had a butterfly in my hands, instead of a musket. I felt no safer for the exchange.

'Go on, Tom,' Matthew Jennings said. 'I bet she has a different taste from other girls, with her fair skin and her clean hair and her full set of teeth. You can tell she needs it. She's probably not had a man since her husband, and he died years ago.'

But the threat in Thomas's eyes was not remotely sexual but rather covetous, as if it was not my virtue he wanted from me, or such virtue as I had, but something else entirely.

I tensed my shoulders. Strands of hair had fallen loose from my night-plait and I tossed my head to flick them away from my face. He was so close that if I swung the bayonet at him it would cut his cheek, scar him for life or take out his eye. I'd never fired a musket but I couldn't fail to hit him. I did not want to shoot or stab him. He was Bess's brother and his father's favourite. It would destroy Mr Knight if anything happened to his son. Also, I saw then that Thomas bore an almost uncanny and disturbing resemblance to my own son. With his black hair and deep-set, belligerent black eyes, he had such a look of Forest that it made the idea of harming him suddenly even more abhorrent.

'We could strike a bargain,' he said. 'Like the one you made with those men from Bristol who are coming to take our commonland.'

'What is it that you want?' I said. 'Tell me what you want and I'll do my best to get it for you.'

'Aye, tell her, Thomas,' someone leered. 'Tell her that if she lets you bed her now, between clean linen sheets in the squire's own chamber, we'll do her no harm.'

'Leave her alone or I'll kill every damned one of you!'

It was a well-loved voice, a voice from my dreams, but the rider who came galloping across from Monk's Pool in a thunder of hooves was very real. He wore a long dark cloak and a scarlet plume in his hat and his right arm was raised, sword unsheathed.

Richard.

His beautiful face alight with courage, he rode his black Barbary stallion directly into the heart of the mob, wielding one sword amongst a lethal forest of pikes and pitchforks and scythes and flaming torches. John Hort turned on him, brandishing his pitchfork. The spikes glanced off the horse's flank, making it rear up, high enough to unseat even an experienced rider. But not this one. Grappling the reins in one hand, he lunged with the other. Even from the saddle of a rearing stallion, his aim was true. John Hort screamed, dropped his pitchfork, stared in shock at his assailant and then staggered off towards the church, clutching his arm. Richard sliced the sword through the air above the mob's heads. 'Who is to be next?' The ferocity in his eyes and in his voice was enough to make them scatter in all directions. Some dropped their weapons in their hurry to be away and some clung on to them, but within seconds all of them were gone.

Richard slid his sword back in its scabbard, not looking at me. A light rain had started to fall again and I felt droplets on my cheek, like tears. His cloak was studded with raindrops as if with tiny diamonds. The horse sidled, tossed its head and snorted, lifted first one hoof and then the other as if it was prancing on burning coals. Richard leaned forward and stroked its neck, making soft soothing noises to calm it. All the while he steadfastly kept his eyes averted from mine, even though he must have felt me watching him.

I'd thought every line and curve of his perfect profile was etched indelibly on to my soul. The curl of his long lashes as they lay against his cheeks, the little indentations at the corners of his kissable, childish mouth, the dark curls that fell over his smooth brow and coiled softly into his neck. But it was a ghost that I had been holding on to, a lovely but faded ghost, and here, before me now, in the moonlit rain, his beauty was almost too much for me. And yet I wanted to gaze at nothing else but the exquisite lines of his face. I could look at him for a lifetime and never have enough of looking. He was the brightest star, shining in the darkness. He was everything to me.

I should be angry with him for what he had just done, for being so rash and hot-headed. I had not invited him here, was not ready for this, should send him away as I had done all the times before. But I could not find it in my heart to be angry with him at all, did not want to send him away. I had missed him. So much. I was so glad just to see him.

His face averted, still soothing his horse, he said, 'Aren't you going to thank me for getting rid of them for you?' It was spoken with an attempt at nonchalance, at the charming confidence in which I knew him to be so proficient, but he did not quite manage to pitch it right this time.

'Thank you?' I asked half-heartedly. 'You wounded a man.'

'A warning, that's all.'

'You think they won't be back? More of them next time, and better armed.'

Now at last he turned to me, with those lovely deep blue eyes that had never lost their strange and powerful hold on my heart. 'Then I will stay and protect you.'

It was said with a touching and ardent chivalry, but at that precise moment he did not look capable of protecting anyone, looked to be in far more need of protection himself. He looked so tired, his eyelids almost too heavy for him to hold open, and any resolve I had left in me to resist him suddenly vanished.

He must have seen it since his lips came up at one side in a sweetly lopsided smile, and he was suddenly surer of himself again. He reached down and snatched the musket from my hand. 'Is it primed and loaded?'

'It is.'

He looked impressed. 'What man would care about dying if it was at the hands of such a pretty little musketeer?' He tossed the gun in the air and caught it. 'You were not intending to fire it, though?'

I smiled at him. 'I had been hoping to find a more peaceable way to reach an agreement.'

He aimed the musket into the sky, pulled the trigger and discharged it with a thunderous crack, turned to me in the drifting smoke from the exploding cartridge. 'Aye, so I saw. A whore's way.'

'You are not jealous? Of Thomas Knight?'

He slid from the saddle, propped the musket against a feeding trough. He took off his hat and hooked it over the muzzle. 'How can I not be driven half mad by jealousy, when you have kept me away from you for nearly five years?' I heard the ache of loneliness in his voice, but he seemed reluctant to step any closer to me. Did not try to touch me. Then I saw he was looking beyond me into the dark hall. 'Did all the commotion wake you, lad?' he said gently.

I spun round to see Forest, standing there in his long white nightshirt, his eyes wide with wonder. 'You stabbed him, sir,' he said, with awe in his voice. 'Did you see him, Mama? I watched from the window and saw it all. The horse up on its hind legs, kicking at the air, the flash of the sword and that man running away with blood spurting out of his arm.'

I heard Richard give a soft chuckle as I went to my son. 'Come now, Forest,' I said. 'You were too far away to see blood, and it wasn't exactly spurting.'

'It was like a real battle.'

It was a real battle. 'Well, it's over now, so you can go back to bed. Bid goodnight to Mr Glanville.'

'Goodnight, sir.'

Richard smiled at him. 'Goodnight, young fellow.'

When still he made no move, I took Forest's shoulders and spun him round, giving him a nudge in the direction of the stairs. 'Bed, Forest. Now.' I watched him go reluctantly, dragging his small bare feet, glancing back longingly into the hall where Richard had come, uninvited, to stand close behind me. 'Would you like some spiced wine?' I asked. 'There's nobody here to serve you, but I'll gladly warm some for you myself.'

He smiled. 'I'm sure it would taste all the better.'

'You can have your usual bed too, if you'd like.'

'I'll curl up by the fire with the dogs. I'd rather. It won't matter where I am. I shall not sleep.'

I do not know if he moved closer to me or I to him, but whichever way it happened, there was hardly any space between us any more.

'I do not want wine or a bed,' he said quietly. 'I just want you.' His arms were down by his sides. He made a small uncertain move to hold out his hand. I did the same. The backs of them brushed against each other. Our fingers caught, turned, entwined. I leaned my head towards his and for a moment we stood holding hands, our foreheads resting against each other. I put my arms around him and felt him shudder against me.

'If only you knew,' he murmured, 'how I have wanted to be with you.'

'I know.' I lifted my hand to the back of his head, stroked his soft curly hair. 'I know.'

My mouth found his, clung to it, as if his kiss was the very breath of life to me. And it was. All the time I had been away from him had been as one long night, a little death, and now, beneath the touch of his mouth and hands, I felt every part of me waking, softening, opening, coming back to life – a sweet, agonising fullness in my groin that was like a ripening, a bursting open. I wrapped my arms around him and clasped him to my heart, cradled his head against my shoulder, and wondered only how I had borne to be without him for so long.

He swept me into his arms and up the twisting stone stairs, my long plait falling around us both like a gilded rope that bound us together. He lay down beside me on the bed, slipped warm hands inside my shift, stroked from my breasts to my belly, moved down between my legs, and I lay quivering beneath his touch until I could stand it no longer and pulled his face down to mine to kiss him again. Then he was kissing my eyelids, my cheeks, my chin, my throat, my ears, my breasts, my stomach. He whispered my name, over and over, the name that only he had ever called me. The sweetest name, the sweetest word I had ever heard. 'Nell.'

He lifted my shift off over my head and I helped him with his shirt. I undid the laces of his breeches and slid my hand inside, and as I caressed him there, his whole body gave a spasm that filled me with a sense of power, of fulfilment. It was as if my body had been made for this and only this, had been shaped and created for the giving and receiving of this pleasure, had been made to love him and for him to love.

He unfastened my plait so that my hair spilled all over him like a golden waterfall, and let it run through his fingers. The only light in the chamber came from the hearth, and our bodies were bathed in a dim, red-gold glow. I sat back for a moment to look at him, naked on the high-canopied bed. I ran my fingers over the taut muscles of his belly and his erect penis, made him moan soft and low in the back of his throat. He reached out with both of his hands to stroke my hips, my buttocks, the insides of my thighs.

I slid out from his grasp, bent to scatter hungry kisses across his chest, biting, licking, brushing my lips against the soft little hairs that formed a denser line that led down from his navel to his groin. I kissed and licked and sucked at his nipples as if I was a kitten. I moved down that line of dark hair and kissed his hard, flat belly, and the hardness of his sex. He grasped my head in both of his hands and gave an agonised groan, pulled me closer. I could feel his heart beating so fast against mine. Then he rolled me over as a wave will roll a pebble on the shore, so he was above me once more, lying between my legs, straining against me but holding back, so that I almost cried out for him to come inside me.

But all at once he froze. He hurled himself away from me and off the bed, dragging a rug around him to cover himself. He clutched the carved bedpost and stared down at me, lying on my back, panting for breath, naked save for a pale gossamer veil of hair. But I knew it was not me he saw any more. There was a haunted expression in his eyes, a look almost of horror, and I remembered how he had clutched that same bedpost for support as he had stared down at Edmund's lifeless body.

It was so very long ago. I had spent a thousand lonely nights in this bed since then. But for the first time it occurred to me that it could be a curse rather than a blessing to be so tied to a place, to be expected to live out an entire life in one house, to be born, to be bedded and to die in the same damned great ancestral bed. It shocked me to see him seemingly so troubled now, for having loved his friend's wife, when it did not seem to have affected him so much before while Edmund was still living. I was a wife no longer but a widow now. I had spent too many nights alone.

I scrambled from the bed, quickly gathered up a pile of pillows and rugs, took them over to the fireplace. I felt him watching me as I deposited the bedding by the hearth, quickly arranged it into a little nest. I stood beside it in the warm orange glow of the flickering flames and held out my hand to him, but still he did not move. The shadows had gone from his eyes, replaced by something else entirely.

'God, Nell, you are so beautiful.'

'Come to me, then,' I said softly.

He shook his head, almost imperceptibly. 'I cannot,' he said. 'I need . . . I need . . .'

'What do you need, love?'

'More than this. Don't you understand? I need more than a romp with you every five years. I need to know that you are mine forever. All mine. Only mine.'

I waited for him to say it, to ask me. He did not. But he did come to me. 'Hold me,' he said. 'I need you to hold me.'

I lay down on the rugs and he lay beside me and I held him and stroked his hair until he went to sleep, his arms wound tight around me and his beloved dark curly head resting between my breasts.

In the morning I awoke stiff and cold and alone on the floor by a fire that was no more than a few embers.

I dressed myself and, not even pausing to fasten back my tumbled hair or put on stockings, ran downstairs. Bess was going about her daily duties as if nothing had happened. I had no time for her, for any of them. All I cared about was one person. His was the only face I wanted to see. But he was not there.

I ran out into the yard to see if his horse was in the barn but it, too, had gone.

'He left about twenty minutes ago, Ma'am. You'll probably catch him if you ride hard.' Ned carried on forking fresh straw in the stable, ashamed to look me in the face, looking instead at my bare ankles poking out from beneath my long skirts, which I was still holding up from running.

Ned was a good man. I couldn't believe he'd really meant any harm last night. He was just concerned for the future, like the rest of them. All he wanted to do was care for Bess and raise their son and have enough food to feed them all. He'd been saving for years for enough to pay for a tenancy and thought I was threatening that future. He was doing his best to make amends.

'Which way did he go, Ned, do you know?'

'Clevedon. Ladye Bay.'

Without waiting to be asked, he led my horse from the stable, but before he'd exchanged the halter for a bridle and saddled her, I led her to the mounting block, hitched up my skirts and grabbed a handful of her mane, mounting her bareback and astride like a boy. I touched my heels to her flanks and urged her into a gallop, my hair flying out behind me. I let the mare have her head, as she charged full pelt towards the rutted trackway over the ridge that led all the way from Tickenham to the coast, a distance of some four miles or so. It was a mild morning that carried a promise of summer on the faint sea breeze. It was a lovely walk on a fine day, and a short ride, but it wasn't short enough for me then, when all that mattered was getting there fast enough to find Richard.

Ladye Bay was a rocky cove, very secluded and cut deep into the craggy cliffs, with a shingle beach scattered with boulders. I'd spent hours there, with my father, alone, and then with my own children, scrambling over the rocks and upturning stones, hunting for sea anemones and ferns. I didn't take Richard for a geologist or a botanist, I just hoped little Ladye Bay had enough to occupy him for as long as it took for me to get there.

I smelled the sea and then my heart danced when I saw his horse at the top of the cliffs, tethered to a rock and contentedly nibbling grass. I left the mare there, too, and clambered down the steep winding path that led to the shore, slipping and sliding on the stones, sending them tumbling before me in my haste.

At high tide the waves crashed against the rocks with an explosion of white froth and foam, but the tide was low now and the sea was as calm as the water that lay over the moor in winter.

The small, secluded beach was deserted. I was about to turn back, assuming that for some strange reason, he must have dismounted and carried on along the costal path on foot. Then I saw something, far out in the middle of the bay, just above the surface of the grey ocean, sleek and secretive as an otter. But it was no otter, it was the head of a man, a swimmer, heading out towards the headland and the wide, open sea.

I stood with the waves lapping at my slippers and the hem of my gown, my hair whipped by the sea breeze, and watched him grow smaller. I was gripped with fear, could barely blink my eyes lest I open them again and didn't see him any more, and yet a part of me was thrilled and awed to see a man so at one with the ocean, that wildest and most untamed aspect of the whole of creation, exerting such power over lowland dwellers like me.

He had turned round and begun swimming back towards the shore with surprising speed.

When he was about ten feet away from me, he stopped swimming and stood up, waist-deep, with water streaming off his shoulders, his naked chest and his black hair. I smiled to myself with a sudden certainty that he had intended it to happen just this way. He knew I would come to look for him and had gone swimming to impress me, to demonstrate his prowess for my appreciation. He was aware, undoubtedly, of how extraordinarily beautiful he looked, striding through the breaking waves in his wet, skin-tight breeches. He walked towards me out of the water, like the most vivid early dreams I'd had of him, waking dreams that I'd had before I'd ever met him. He came to stand in front of me, his bare feet shining wet in the sand, grains of it stuck to his toes. The fine covering of dark hairs on his chest glistened with droplets of seawater.

'Will you teach me how to swim?'

He ran his fingers through his hair to shake some of the moisture from it. 'You'd faint from the cold.'

I turned my face up to his which was framed by wet black curls, his long eyelashes spiked with saltwater. 'Remember how quickly I learned to skate? I surprised you then, did I not?'

He smiled, touched my hair. 'Skating. Dancing. Swimming. Is it my role to bring excitement and danger into your quiet little life?'

'It is certainly quieter when you are not here. Safer too. But I never did want a quiet life. Or a safe one.'

'Didn't you?'

I gave a small shake of my head. 'No. I wanted my life to be like . . .'
I cast about for a way to describe what I was trying to say. 'A firework. I
wanted to live in an explosion of colour and of light.'

He smiled. 'And why are you so eager to swim?'

'I want to know what it's like. How it is done.' I had such a desire just
to touch him again, to bend my head to his chest and lick the droplets of
saltwater from his skin, to feel the tautness of the muscles in his arms,
muscles that had the strength to propel him through waves. 'I've lived all
my life in a world of sky and water. I'd like to know what it is like to fly
like a bird or a butterfly, but since that's impossible, the next best thing is
to learn to swim like a fish.'

'Did no one ever tell you it was dangerous to be too inquiring, little
Pandora?'

'They did, many times. But I chose not to listen.'

He smiled. 'You'd make a better bird than fish, I think. You are most
definitely of air and angels.'

I recognised the line from John Donne. 'I did not know you were a
poet.'

'There is much you do not know about me, Nell. Though you must
surely know that for just one of your impish smiles, I'd do anything you
asked of me.' He made a slow scan of the sea, as if considering how it was
best done. The waves made a hushing sound, sucked at my feet, impatient
to drag me in.

'Is it really so cold?'

'No woman I've ever met would last more than one minute in it.'

'One minute, you say?'

He grinned, held up a finger. 'Aye, one minute.'

It was all the encouragement I needed. In an instant I was out of my
dress, laughing and running headlong into the waves in my cambric chemise.
The first shock of the water snatched away my breath, made every muscle
in my body go rigid, made me pull myself up straight and suck in my belly.
I held my arms out of the water, bent like wings, and plunged on in until
I was up to my waist, bracing myself as each wave slammed into my body,
almost knocking me over. I let one pass and then carried on, waited for the
next onslaught, pushed through it. Already, I felt a little less cold. The saltwater felt soft as silk against my legs.

'That's far enough,' called Richard, raising his voice above the tumult of the pounding breakers, striding through them to stand in front of me. 'Where ever are you going? I did not think we were walking to Wales.'

'So what do I do?'

He cleared his throat, as if he was unsure how to begin, held his arms out in front of him. 'Push out, then round and back,' he said as he demonstrated. 'Kick with your legs at the same time.'

'Like a frog.'

'Yes, I suppose. Like a frog.'

I tried to copy him. Obviously failed.

'No. Not like that, like this.'

He took a tight hold of both my wrists and drew my arms towards him, then pushed them out firmly to the sides in an arc and more gently folded them back to the centre again, in an attitude almost of prayer. I might no longer have time for God but old habits are not so easy to abandon. I whispered a silent prayer or two right now. Don't let me make a fool of myself in front of him. Do not let me drown, or be washed out to sea either.

'Let's try,' he said. 'Shall we?'

I stretched out on the surface of the sea, my arms spread wide. I felt his hands go underneath me, palms upward, and lifted my feet off the seabed. Felt the pressure and warmth of his fingers against my belly and my chest, holding me up so that I was floating.

I tried to do as he'd shown me.

'Wider and slower,' he said. 'Keep your fingers together. Now, kick. Hard as you can.'

I tried to keep my body horizontal in the water and made a sudden lurch forward, carried in part by a wave. He took one hand away, so he was just supporting me under my belly. Then he let go completely and instantly my head sank beneath the water, my knees scraped the rocky seabed and my mouth filled with saltwater. The undertow of the wave was dragging at me. I breathed in and choked, scrambled for a footing, came up spluttering.

'You let go of me too soon,' I gasped, wiping the hair from my face.

'It takes practice.' He clearly found it all quite entertaining. 'Are you all right?'

'I am trying very hard to be dignified, even though my teeth are chattering.'

'You look as lovely as a mermaid.'

'I shall swim like a mermaid, too, before this day is done. Let's try again.'

'You are a determined little doxy, aren't you?'

I smiled, took his hand and pressed it palm-flat against my stomach. 'This time, please keep it there until I say otherwise.'

He bobbed his head, his eyes glittering. 'I am at your service, my lady. Now, spread your legs.'

I giggled. 'For you, sir, any time.' I sank down into the water, to assume a swimming posture again.

'And this time, for pity's sake, if you are about to go under, hold your breath,' he instructed.

I took my time and cleared my head before I lifted my feet off the seabed again and kicked out, once, twice. This time he let go of me one finger at a time. When I felt his hand fall away completely I took a gulp of air just before I sank. There was a rushing in my ears, then an eerie silence. I did not panic but kept on scrabbling at the water. One stroke, two. I was floating just beneath the surface, freed from the pull of the earth. I opened my eyes on to a murky blue world.

My lungs were bursting and as I tried to push up my feet went down. I broke through a wave and was back in the world again. I turned round elatedly to find Richard. 'I did it!'

'You did.'

'I can swim!'

'Almost.'

'I did not sink!'

'You did not. The sea has declared you a little witch, for sure.'

I frowned to see how close he was. 'I thought I had gone further though.'

'I came after you,' he said. 'In case you needed me to fish you out.'

He pushed through the water and stood in front of me, gently wiped the wet hair off my face and coiled a dripping strand of it around his hand. 'You shouldn't stay in too long or the cold will make your muscles stiffen and I'll have to carry you out.'

My legs felt perfectly supple. 'I think they're stiff already.'

He did not pick me up.

'Last night, would you have bedded that knave to save your house from burning?'

'No!' Then: 'What a time to ask.'

'It would not have been a loathsome sacrifice? He is desirable to you?'

'He most certainly is not!'

'You have known him a long time.'

'Yes, but in any case, I do not think he had any wish to bed me.'

'That I do not believe,' Richard said softly. 'There is not a man on this earth who would not wish it.'

'You are not exactly impartial.'

'No, I am not.' Then after a moment he said seriously, 'You need to beware of Thomas Knight, Nell. The man's trouble, a firebrand.'

'I know. I just wish I knew why. Please can we go now? I'm frozen.'

He scooped me into his arms as he had last night, my long wet hair trailing like gold seaweed. 'Swimming is not so good as skating?' he asked.

'Actually, this particular part is far better.' I rested my head against his shoulder, twined my arms up around his neck, and felt myself complete again.

When we reached the shore Richard retrieved his cloak from behind a rock, flung it round his shoulders, opened it like great black bat wings and enfolded me in it. It smelled faintly of horses and male sweat, of smoke and cologne, of him. I tucked my fingers into his armpits to warm them and gazed into his lovely eyes.

'You are very brave,' he said.

'You make me feel brave,' I told him softly. 'And terrified, all at the same time. You make me feel strong, stronger than I have ever felt before, and yet never have I felt weaker. When I am with you I want to laugh and to weep, all at the same time.'

He was smiling at me in recognition, as if at a sudden revelation that made him very happy. 'So you do love me then?'

'Yes,' I said. 'I love you.'

I was sitting by the fire, drying my hair and warming my bare toes. Richard sat in the chair at the other side of the hearth, his long legs stretched out in front of him, tall shiny boots up on the fender. There was no sound but the crackle and hiss of the apple-scented logs.

My eyes were drawn to his mouth, the slightly open pout of his kissable lips. I wanted to rise from my chair and go to him, sit at his feet and put my head in his lap, or for him to come to me so that I could stroke the black curls off his brow and bury my face in them. But I spied Forest peering round the door, seemingly almost as fascinated by this man and as desperate to be with him as I was. I sent him off to ask Bess to warm some wine for us. I felt very selfish, wanting Richard all to myself, even if all he was going to do was sit there, withdrawn and staring morosely into the fire, in a way that kept me firmly in my chair and him in his.

'What's the matter?' I asked him.

He looked up from the flames, the light of them still reflected in his eyes, but said nothing.

'What is it?' I repeated, unnerved. 'What's wrong?'

His right arm was resting on his thigh and I saw him flex his fingers then clench them. 'Five years,' he said ominously. 'You have tortured me for five years. You say you love me, and yet you let me be miserable for five whole years.'

I felt a terrible pang of remorse and did not know what to reply. I had not expected such recrimination and yet I saw that it was inevitable, a conversation we had to have at some time. 'I have been miserable too,' I told him.

'Then it was all of your own making. You have none to blame but yourself.'

'I did not think I deserved to be happy.'

His eyes flared, blazed darkly, and it was no longer the firelight that made them do so. 'Nor I?'

I gave a small shake of my head.

He turned away from me, so that I could not see his face.

'We did a bad thing, Richard. We deceived Edmund. We betrayed his trust. He did not deserve that.'

He was on his feet and in two strides was standing before me. 'You think I don't know that? Of course he didn't deserve it. He did not deserve to die either. But all I did was to love you . . . more than I have ever loved anyone else. It was utterly beyond my control. Did that warrant such unkindness to me? The cruel treatment you have shown me? You were cruel, Nell, make no mistake. Did you want me to suffer so as to make yourself feel better, is that it? Every time you sent me away, every time you spurned and humiliated me, did it make you feel that little bit more righteous? Damn it! Who are you to set yourself above God, to mete out penalties and punishment?'

I stood, squaring up to him as best I could. 'I was punishing myself.'

'Oh, aye. You Puritans are all for that, aren't you? Make life a bloody misery so your rewards in Heaven will be all the greater.' He ran his fingers though his black curls. 'So, you have decided that our penance is done now, have you, Eleanor? That I am to be your hairshirt no longer? You've decided, after all, not to wait for Heaven to claim your reward?'

I let my breath steady. 'I am Eleanor to you again, am I?' I said quietly. 'Not Nell any more?'

That seemed to penetrate his anger, dispel it. He lowered his eyes, bent his head. After a moment he let me take hold of his hand. I brought it to my lips, held it there to kiss his fingers.

'I am sorry,' I said.

He turned his face up to mine. 'All the letters I sent to you, what did you do with them?'

'I . . . I burned them.'

He made to take his hand away but I held on to it.

'Before you read them? Or afterwards?' he asked.

'Before,' I admitted, ashamed. 'All but one,' I added quickly. 'One of them I opened. And read. And once I had done, then I had to keep it. I have slept with it under my pillow ever since. Every single night.'

He gave a reluctant smile. 'Have you?'

I stroked his face. 'Please, don't let us argue any more. What's done is done. We have both suffered enough.'

He gave me an odd look. 'Tell me this. Have you ever thought it would have been more just if I had died instead of Edmund?'

'You can't ask me . . .'

'Because I have thought it. Time and again, I have thought it.'

'Stop it.'

'Edmund should be here now, instead of me. He should be here with you and his children, shouldn't he? Would you rather that? Would you rather . . .'

'No!' Then, more quietly: 'No.'

He calmed a little, as if my words vindicated him somehow. 'Shall I tell you why I did not abandon my pursuit of you years ago, the first time you refused to see me?'

'Tell me.'

'Edmund said to me once that he could see why you loved butterflies so much. Because they are proof that there is real beauty in this world. Well, you are my butterfly, Nell. Despite everything, you are the best and most beautiful thing that has ever happened to me.'

I kissed him, very gently, on his lips, then I led him back to his chair and sat on the floor at his feet, offering him my hand to hold again. For a long while we were silent, but it was a companionable silence this time rather than a tense one.

I caught Forest peeping round the door once more, though he scurried away when he knew himself discovered. 'You seem to have won a devoted admirer in my son,' I smiled at Richard. 'As it should be. You are his sponsor, after all.'

'It's not a child's admiration I seek, Nell.'

'You won mine before I even met you,' I confessed. 'When I first heard you could swim. How did you learn? Who taught you?' Despite all that he had already shared with me, I realised there was still much I did not know about him and I wanted to know it all, everything, all at once. I wanted to know every tiny detail of his life, what his hopes, his opinions, his fears were. I hardly knew where to begin. 'Where did you learn to quote poetry? And where did you learn to handle a sword so expertly? Were you ever in the militia?'

He smiled his lovely smile and I was so glad to see it again. It was like sunshine after rain. 'So many questions. Which shall I answer first? I was educated at St John's College, Cambridge, where I developed a love of music and literature, but regrettably left without gaining a degree. No, I am no militiaman. I fear I am far too undisciplined ever to be a very good soldier or scholar. But amongst those in exile were fine horsemen and swordsmen, with time on their hands, who were willing to act as riding and fencing masters to me. I was put into the saddle before I was two, was handed a sword and pistol almost before I had learned the words to ask for them. When the King lost his head and my father lost everything he had, except for me, he determined that I would never lose anything ever again, that I should learn to ride and hunt and shoot and swim too, so that when I grew to be a man I would be the best at everything, have the best of everything.'

'That sounds exhausting.' I thought it also sounded like a route to disillusionment and disappointment.

'It was certainly no boon to be thrown into a lake,' he said. 'Told to swim or drown. My first lesson in life.'

I sensed from the tone of his voice and the look in his eyes that he'd been a boy with no particular stomach for daredevilry, who had developed a taste for it only at some personal cost, learning through those hard years of exile constantly to hold his fear in check.

'That is a cruel lesson,' I said. 'One no little boy should have to learn.'

'Aren't all lessons that children have to learn rather cruel?'

'They do not have to be.'

'What d'you teach your son?'

Bess came in then with two conical glasses and the earthenware decanter of wine. She barely faltered when she saw who the extra glass was for, but by her reaction it was clear she knew this to be the same man who had unleashed his sword on the rabble last night. I found that I could not bear for her to think unkindly of Richard. It was alarming how one person could have come to mean so much to me, how my own happiness and peace of mind were so entirely bound to his, and I knew that there was nothing I would not do for him, nothing I would not do to make him happy.

'My son knows I would do anything to keep him safe,' I said, for Bess's benefit.

I don't think Richard even heard me. 'How is the man who was injured?' he asked Bess directly.

She nearly spilt the wine all over him. 'I believe he is recovering, sir.'

'Was he badly hurt?'

She cast a suspicious glance at him, but read his concern as entirely genuine and softened. 'It is just a surface wound. It will mend.'

'I am glad. Who is he? What is his name.'

'John Hort.

'And what does he do for a living?'

Bess was as surprised as was I by this depth of interest 'He's an eeler, sir.' Richard put his hand in the pocket of his breeches. 'Here.' He held out a little pile of gold coins. 'Take this to him, with my good wishes. There's enough to see he gets proper treatment and to compensate him for loss of earnings until he is fit again. Take a sovereign yourself for your trouble.'

Bess took the money willingly, as if she could not believe her good fortune. 'Thank you, sir.' She bobbed the prettiest little curtsey. 'That's very kind of you, sir.'

'That was very charitable,' I said, when she'd gone. 'I've never heard Bess call anyone "sir" so many times in such a short conversation. You've certainly won her over and no doubt will win over the entire Hort clan. Maybe even the whole village.'

'It is far better to be revered than reviled. That is another lesson I learned from my years in exile. To live too long without friendship and love is not to live at all.'

I saw that there'd been no motive behind what he'd just done beyond a simple and deep need to be loved and respected. 'You do not live here,' I pointed out quietly.

His eyes met mine. 'I shall do if you agree to marry me.'

He took my hands and stood up, raising me to my feet with him.

'I have money enough to bribe a chaplain.' He slid his open fingers into my hair, lifted the long strands of it that were still damp at the ends, but which the seawater had made more curly than ever. He rearranged it very carefully, so that it fell around my face and over my breasts. 'We could go to a Bristol church and have it done immediately. You could be my wife tonight. In a few hours we would be together.'

I caught his hand and trapped it against my cheek, turned my face into it and kissed his palm. 'You could take me and make me your wife right now,' I suggested softly. 'Once our promise is made we are as good as wedded. It is permitted and proper for us to lie with one another.'

He snatched his hand away as if I had bitten him.

'We do not need to do it in that bed,' I said, misunderstanding. 'There are . . . other places.'

'I will not lie with you, in a bed or otherwise, until you are properly mine,' he said. 'I cannot lie with Edmund's widow, with Eleanor Ashfield. I need you to be Eleanor Glanville.'

I smiled, surprised by his intensity but thinking it a quaint sentiment. 'I want to be Eleanor Glanville,' I said. 'I want it more than anything. But surely you are not serious about Bristol?'

'Either you leave with me now, or I leave alone.'

'I am being held to ransom, for a kiss?'

'If that is how you choose to see it.'

I opened my mouth to say yes, I would go with him. I would go wherever he wanted me to go, do whatever he wanted me to do. But I stopped. Other words came out. I was no serving maid who could marry as I pleased without care or consideration. I was first and foremost a landowner, guardian of an estate. 'It took months to arrange my first marriage,' I said. 'There were contracts to be drawn up and signed . . . all kinds of negotiations.'

'I don't want there to be any negotiating between us, Nell. I want us to be married like commoners and to live like kings.'

'You mean, in debauchery?'

'I mean in some luxury,' he said, ignoring my weak attempt at humour. 'That is what you've always yearned for, I think? Twenty gowns and footmen in livery and a velvet upholstered coach drawn by four horses? As my wife, I would make sure you had all that. I would make sure you had everything you ever wanted, and more besides.'

'I cannot do it like this. For my children's sake, I cannot.'

He picked up his glass and downed the contents in one gulp, his eyes flaring with mercurial light. 'First Edmund stood between us. Now it is his children. I thought there was just the two of us now, but seemingly already there are four.'

He must know as well as I did that children of a previous marriage always suffered if a widowed mother married again. 'Tickenham Court is Forest's rightful inheritance,' I said. 'The estate's wealth is my daughter's marriage portion. But if I marry you tonight and we should have children, those children would take precedence over Edmund's son and daughter. My little Ashfield children would be the ones to lose out. I love you, so much, and I want to be your wife. I want you in my bed, this night and every night, for the rest of my life. I want your face to be my first sight when I awake and the last before I sleep. I want you to get a dozen children on me. I am ready right now to give up my freedom, to give you my body and my soul and my heart, but I am not prepared to hand you my children's home, their security, their future.'

He was already walking towards the door.

'Wait! Please, wait!'

He did.

'There has to be a way.'

He looked doubtful, but he was listening.

'Let me find one. I will find one.'

'You sound very certain of it.'

'You said yourself, I am a determined little doxy. I would not marry you tonight, in any case,' I said, finding a smile for him. 'I do not want us to sneak off by ourselves to a church and then a tavern. I do not want to do it quietly, not this time. You also said to me once that if I became your wife, you'd want to celebrate before everyone, with a feast that went on for twelve days.'

I instantly regretted referring to the conversation we had had that dark Valentine's Day morning, for conjuring Edmund's ghost to stand between us again. But, oddly, Richard seemed not to be troubled by the memory of our illicit kiss, as he was evidently still so troubled by Edmund's death. I did not want to dwell on why that might be. 'Twelve days of feasting.' He smiled. 'I did say that, didn't I?'

Richard slept in the chamber he had stayed in when Edmund was alive, and this time I woke before he did. I rode back towards Clevedon to visit George Digby. I would ask him if he knew how I might make provision for my children should I take another husband. As he was a Member of Parliament, I trusted that he had some understanding of such legal matters.

Impressively attired in sumptuous tawny silk, the Earl was playing an effortless game of tennis on the Clevedon Court lawn with his tall, gangly son, but readily broke off to entertain me. Elegantly mopping his brow with scented linen, he declared he was glad of an excuse to catch his breath while he was two games ahead. 'I did at least gain one useful skill during my years in exile,' he said. 'Enforced idleness and lack of funds meant that I spent days and days playing tennis. Much cheaper than hunting, you see. And even now that I can afford to hunt all day long if I so please, I've never lost my love of the racquet.'

I smiled to myself, struck by a memory I'd thought long forgotten.

'I do count myself a great wit,' he said pleasantly. 'But I had not thought to be one at the present. Yet it seems I have inadvertently amused you.'

'My father once told me how Cavaliers enjoyed tennis so much they'd brawl and duel over the results,' I explained. 'It seems he was right about that, as about much else.'

'To be precise, the duel was over a bet of seven sovereigns on who would win the game. It was a meaure of the depth of irritability and frustration we all suffered from, the tensions of exile. So tell me,' he asked jovially as we walked past the knot garden towards the terrace, 'what else did your good father have to say about us? Besides a penchant for duelling and tennis, did he allot us any other vices?'

I hesitated.

'Come now,' Digby encouraged me. 'I am intrigued. And, I promise you, I shall not be offended at all.'

I smiled. 'Other vices? Well, let me see now. Debauchery. Drunkenness. Adultery. Fornication. Lust.' I ticked the list off on my fingers. 'General excess and moral corruption.'

'Is that why you constantly refuse that lad?' the Earl asked with a wickedly impudent gleam in his eyes. 'Is it that you fear him to be debauched and morally corrupt?' He grinned at my astonished expression. 'Oh, Richard petitioned me not a month ago to appeal to you on his behalf. I was waiting for the right opportunity to present itself.'

'It is because of him that I am here, sir.'

'Ah.'

Seated in a gold and green panelled room on plump chairs covered in striped silk, and sipping sweetened tea served in a delicate gilded china tea set, I started to explain my predicament.

'So I have no need to petition you,' the Earl interrupted. 'Young Richard has succeeded in his pursuit of you at last, and without any help. Good for him. I am glad for him – for you both.'

'I have not agreed to wed him yet,' I said quietly.

He peered at me over the rim of his cup, arched one eyebrow. 'And you will not agree if I cannot provide you with the information you need?'

'It must be a common problem,' I persisted. 'There must be a solution.'

He laughed. 'What a wonderfully optimistic approach to life you have, my dear lady.' He set down the cup with a tinkle. 'You are right, of course, that many landed gentlemen leave behind pretty widows who are still of child-bearing age, but you are wrong to think that many of those ladies are as intent on defending the position of their first born as you are. Or else, if they are, I imagine they take the standard precautions to ensure there is no issue from their second marriage. A matter of timing, I understand, either of the moon or else of a man's rod at the pinnacle of pleasure?'

I laughed, did not blush at such base talk as I would once have done, but was secretly rather shocked to hear it from the lips of so lofty a person as the Earl. Even if he had spent years in exile with our young King in waiting who presided over the most dissolute and debauched court. 'I would not deny Richard the joy of a child,' I said seriously.

'But you would deny him the joy of seeing that child inherit your estate? I do believe you would deny yourself the joy of marriage, if it came to it.' His lips curled in a knowing smile. 'It is a cool head you have on your pretty little shoulders,' he said contemplatively. 'When I watched the two of you dancing here together, some years ago, I saw only the charge of passion between you. But it seems that your passion for Tickenham Court is the stronger, hmm?'

'I do this for my children,' I said. 'Not for Tickenham Court. Not for myself.'

'But a marriage settlement will also benefit you considerably.'

'A marriage settlement?'

He grinned. 'An excellent invention and one commonly enough used now amongst the gentry. Quite simply, it is a signed agreement that preserves a wife's property rights and allows her to avoid giving up her liberty, estate, and all authority to her husband. In real terms, with such a settlement in place, Tickenham Court would remain yours after you marry, whomsoever you marry. It even remains yours to dispose of upon your death.'

I set down my own cup, feeling a stirring of happiness which I held in abeyance. For now. 'And gentlemen willingly agree to settlements that so diminish their position?'

The Earl shrugged. 'It depends on the gentleman in question, of course. On how amenable he is. But most are quite content with the arrangement.' He studied me, saw I was still unconvinced. 'Oh-ho. I do detect Major Goodricke's influence and unfavourable opinions of us still lingering in your generous and loving heart. Much as you love young Richard, you cannot help thinking of his passion for Spanish stallions and silk suits and sack, and you deduce, therefore, that he'll not be satisfied with any less than all of the coins in your coffers. Am I right? Much as you are drawn to him, you cannot help assuming that, being a Cavalier, he is therefore inclined to luxury and ease, and entirely profligate?'

'Of course not.'

But the Earl smiled almost delightedly, as if he did not mind at all my harbouring such dark opinions of all royalists, himself included.

'It is my guess that you find profligacy not so unattractive, after a life of frugal living with your Papa and Edmund Ashfield. And who would ever blame you for that, little lady? Now, I do not know your Richard nearly well enough to know if he is a wastrel or not, but I do know that life as an exile can be the most wretched existence. I know that, in all likelihood, he'd have spent his most tender years in paralysing unhappiness, endless uncertainty and much personal distress, as well as in precarious and constant need of money and a home. So I imagine he'd be more than content with regular payments from your estate, only too glad to be granted the security of an independent income. And when and if your estate reaps the rewards of drainage, his percentage will be all the more attractive. Although I imagine he might willingly forgo those extra riches to retain the good will of his neighbours. During those years as a fugitive, he'll have witnessed enough faction fighting and personal feuds to last him a lifetime, given that he strikes me as a rather overly sensitive boy, not very robust in his emotions. You are just what he needs, I think.' He raised his teacup as if in a toast. 'I vouch the lad will not refuse your terms, whatever they may be.'

When I arrived back at Tickenham Court I found Richard entertaining William Merrick in the parlour. They seemed to be on good terms but broke off their conversation as I entered and stood up.

'William,' I said, letting my former guardian kiss me, 'I was not expecting to see you again.'

'My partners were not expecting to hear that a mob had tried to burn down this house,' he said gruffly. 'As I have already told Richard, I fear we will never win them round now.'

'I don't think we should even try,' I said carefully, with a glance at Richard. 'I think we should let them take their money away for good and use it where it will be better appreciated. We'll leave the common to the commoners. And to the swans and the Swallowtails.'

'What!'

'It seems I am to spend my entire adult life sifting through my father's principles and beliefs and sorting the pearls from the pebbles,' I said. 'But I think in this he was right. It seems to me there is enough land for all to have a share. And, yes, it might be better for some who live on the wetlands, the people at least, if the land was dry all year, but until a way is found for us to have dry land and everyone to have enough of it to grow their own vegetables and cut their turfs and graze their cattle, I think it is better that we let well alone.'

William's eyes flew in appeal to Richard who looked away.

'I have said all I have to say,' I finished firmly. 'Let that be an end to it. And now I would be grateful if you would leave us, William. There are matters Richard and I need to discuss, matters of far more importance than this.'

William stormed out of the room, head down like a charging bull, nearly crashing into Bess who was entering with a tray of wine and sweetmeats.

'Did I do wrong?' I asked Richard, slipping my hand into his when we were alone.

He gave a slow shake of his head. 'It is a pity you cannot join Geroge Digby in Parliament. What a little champion you would be for the poor and the hungry and the dispossessed.' He grinned. 'Not to mention the birds and the butterflies. I cannot imagine what Merrick made of that.'

'He can make of it what he will. It is no matter.' I took Richard's other hand, held both of them. 'I found a way,' I said quietly. 'I said I would find a way for us to marry and I have.'

We moved to the chairs by the fire, where Bess had set out the drinks and food on a little table.

Of necessity, a betrothal involving a landowning family was always preceded by such negotiations as I had to have with Richard, but that did not mean I found the conversation easy. No more, seemingly, did he. He sat opposite me, very still and unsmiling, screwing his heavy ring around his finger as he listened while I explained, as tactfully as I possibly could, how the Earl of Bristol, at my behest, would have his solicitor draw up a marriage settlement that would secure Forest's position as heir to Tickenham Court, leaving it in my sole charge, whilst awarding Richard an independent and regular income from the estate once he became my husband. I thought the pair of us no different from a couple of cold-hearted traders discussing a shipment of sugar, except that the glasses of spiced wine and plate of sweetmeats remained totally untouched before us on the low table.

'Is this really what you want?' Richard asked me dully when he had heard me out.

'We could not hope to find a better solution,' I said steadily.

'No. I am sure that you could not.'

I saw that he did not like it, not at all. Why not? I felt a flicker of misgiving, turned my head away for a moment and then chided myself. It was his complicated combination of pride and insecurity which was standing in the way, that was all, wasn't it?

'Is it the money?' I challenged, my tone brittle. 'Is it not enough?'

His laugh sounded more like a cough, and there was no humour in it at all.

'George Digby suggested a sum he believed to be very generous, that would make good provision for you.' Only after I had spoken did I realise how condescending I had sounded. Oh, why was he making this so difficult? 'I am sorry. I did not mean to . . .'

'It is not the money, Nell.'

'It is that you want control of the estate then. Is that it? Because you can have it, with my blessing, if it matters so much to you.' I tried to summon a smile, tried not to think why it should matter to him. 'Believe me, I shall not stand in your way if you want to mediate in endless squabbles about boundaries and rights of pasturing, or if you want to harangue the tenants for their rents.'

'You would defend the rights of Tickenham tenants,' he said evenly. 'And the damned swans. And yet you pay scant regard to the rights of your intended husband.'

'Rights?'

'You married Edmund without a settlement,' he said abruptly. 'You gave him everything.'

'And you therefore assumed it would be the same this time? Is that why you want me?'

He looked at me as if my question were beneath contempt, beneath even warranting a reply.

'I did not even know there was such a thing as a marriage settlement when I married Edmund,' I said shakily. 'I did not have children to consider then. Surely you can see that this situation is entirely different.'

'Yes,' he said curtly. 'I do see that, all too plainly.'

His attention was diverted by something. I knew what it was before I even looked. Forest was peering round the door again, wide-eyed with guilt for being caught in the act of spying.

'Darling, you shouldn't be listening,' I said a little impatiently, wondering how long he had been there and how much he had overheard and under-stood. 'Go and find your shuttlecock and battledores and I will come and play with you in a while.'

He ignored me, bolted round the door and across the floor. I assumed he was running to me but instead he ran straight to Richard's side. Standing at his shoulder, making it utterly clear where his allegiance lay, he turned to me accusingly. 'Mr Glanville is not going to come and live with us now? He is not going to be my father?'

I looked at Richard, with the same question in my eyes and a lump in my throat. I was not the only person who loved him. Forest clearly did too. But I was doing this *for* Forest. And I could not bear for my little boy to be as distressed as I would be if Richard's answer was no.

'I want to play battledores with you, sir,' Forest implored, laying his hand appealingly on Richard's silk-clad arm. 'Mama is no good at it at all. I don't want to play with her.'

That made Richard chuckle, and when he looked at me the laughter was still in his eyes. He knew I considered myself particularly good at the game, which was not unlike catching butterflies with a trap net. He seemed genuinely heartened by Forest's rush of affection, as if it changed everything for him. Astonishingly, he brought Forest gently round to face him, so that they were on a level. He looked into my son's solemn black eyes, as if whatever he saw there would help him to reach his decision.

I sent out a silent plea: Please realise I am doing what I am only for this little boy and his sister. Please agree to it for their sake. Richard was Forest's sponsor after all. Let that count for something.

'I will come and live here, rapscallion,' Richard said gently to Forest. 'I will be glad to be your father. I will play battledores with you until you are so good at it you can never be beaten.' And in an aside to me, 'I will sign the settlement, Nell. I will sign whatever damned paper you want me to sign.'

Bess came in then to ask Forest if he would like to play leapfrog with her Sam, and he ran off, battledores forgotten for now.

'Tell me you are not angry with me, Richard,' I said.

'I am not angry with you.'

'I am sorry for what I said.'

'I can see that you are.

'You do still want me?'

For a moment that felt like a lifetime, he did not answer. 'Nell, I would want you if you were but a beggar, the daughter of beggars. If you were dressed in rags and had nothing to give me but your heart.'

I realised with a tinge of regret that I was not idealistic enough any more to believe him wholly, but it was the prettiest sentiment nonetheless, expressed in the manner of the poets he said he admired, and I felt joy bubble up inside me like the springs that bubbled up all over Tickenham land.

He pushed himself abruptly from his chair, as if shaking a great weight from his shoulders; as if he had a sudden urgent need for action, to obliterate something. He came round to my side of the table, grabbed my hand and pulled me to my feet. 'I propose that we ride at once into Bristol and hire a coach to take us to Cheapside to buy your ring,' he said with an impulsiveness that made me giggle. 'We can go to the New Exchange, too, for material for a wedding gown, and anything else we might fancy.'

We sat together in the rocking coach as we left the goldsmiths and headed for the New Exchange on the Strand, Mecca for followers of the new fashion for shopping as entertainment, a place that was filled with all that was rich and new and rare – a place that all the religious instruction I had ever received had taught me to regard as evil and corrupt as Sodom.

I could hardly wait to see it.

Even now, when we were promised to one another, Richard stood by his strange but rather touching resolution not to bed me while I still bore Edmund's name, while I was Eleanor Ashfield not Eleanor Glanville. But that did not prevent us from spending the entire journey to London touching and stroking and kissing and murmuring little words to each other, until we were both driven half to distraction. We cooled our ardour only by concentrating on discussing preparations for the wedding, planning who should come to the celebration and what amusements we would have, what fresh-killed livestock we'd need for the serving of meats roast, baked or boiled.

I wrote it all down in the paperbook I had once carried with me when I was observing butterflies, in what already seemed like a different life. I had no need of butterflies any more. I had what I had longed for. I had him right here beside me.

I had the top of the pencil in my mouth, was sucking it as I was thinking about puddings. I felt Richard watching me.

'We should make an application to the Episcopal authorities for a licence to marry at St Mary's Redcliffe in Bristol,' he declared softly. 'Queen Elizabeth herself called it the goodliest, fairest and most famous parish church in all of England. You should be a bride in no less a place.'

'But we can return to Tickenham for the feasting? And have dancing on the grass?'

'Surely. We can do whatever you want, my little Nell. We can have new silver plate for the top table, and gloves and bridal ribbons for every guest.'

'Oh, yes.' My second marriage would begin in colour and brightness and joy, and so in colour and brightness and joy it would continue. 'I have longed for a merry wedding since I was a child,' I said, tossing book and pencil aside.

He kissed me, laid his cool cheek against mine, whispered into my hair, 'Did you have such sweet dimples then? What were you like?'

I let my hand wander over his thigh, slip round to the inside of it. 'I was forever getting into trouble and doing things I shouldn't.' My hand drifted up slowly to his crotch. 'I was very curious, you see,' I whispered. 'I still am. I like to experiment.'

He closed his eyes, dropped his head on to my shoulder, shifted nearer to me as I rubbed him, felt his desire rising at my touch. When he rested back against the velvet-upholstered seat, I watched the little lines between his brows pucker now with pleasure and leaned over and put my lips against them, kissed also the grooved crescents at either side of his mouth.

'Nell,' he moaned. 'What are you trying to do to me?'

'I want to love you,' I whispered. 'I love you so much.'

'Do you?'

'Surely you know that I do?'

But he did not look sure at all.

Too soon the coach came to an abrupt halt and we were there, on the paved street in front of the arcaded façade with its expanses of plate glass, behind which were the most beautiful displays of fans and feathers and lace.

We followed the other elegantly dressed shoppers who sauntered inside into one of the sheltered long galleries. It was lined with merchants' booths, with counters and glass fronts and awnings, and shelf upon shelf of all that I had been taught to see as foreign and decadent and Popish.

Richard slipped his hand almost possessively round my waist and I felt my pulse quicken again; did not know, though, if it was with desire for him or desire for all the unimaginable and once forbidden luxury arrayed before me. I felt like a child before a table laden with cakes and sweetmeats.

'If I lived in London I should come here every day,' I said.

'Would you?' He gave me an interested smile. 'Perhaps we should live in London, then.'

'Oh, I could never leave Tickenham. But we must visit often.'

I was as delighted by the liberty of the women I saw as I was by the goods, the way they seemed free to parade publicly with their friends, to drink coffee and gossip and shop as they chose. After my experience of the closed world of scientific societies and coffee house clubs, this was a revelation.

'Are we going to just stand here gawping all day, Nell?' Richard smiled. 'Or are we going to shop?'

I carried on gawping. 'I don't know where to start. I've completely forgotten what we need.'

'It is not all about what you need, my love,' he said to me, softly suggestive. 'It is about what you want.'

'You know very well what it is that I want.'

'Besides that,' he said, his eyes crinkling. 'Besides what you already have on order for your wedding night.'

I giggled. 'You are scandalous, sir, to talk so in a public place.'

But we were not alone in our flirting. It seemed the desires of shopping were linked very closely to the desires of the flesh. Perhaps the sermon writers had a point when they associated shopping with encouraging illicit sex, even going so far as to accuse the women in this place of being little better than harlots.

The mercer's servant certainly had a tongue far freer than any I had ever heard. 'Oh, there's nothing like the feel of fine linen on your skin,' she said in seductive tones, as she caressed a bale of sheets and fluttered her eyelashes at Richard. 'Do have a feel, sir. Go on, do. 'Tis not often you get offered such a pleasure for no charge.'

'Nor from the lips of such a pretty face.' Richard returned her smile, as he ran his elegant fingers over the sheet she offered him.

'Have you touched anything finer or smoother?' she cooed.

'Only a young girl's skin,' he flirted back, clearly enjoying the repartee and obviously not unpractised in it.

'Can you imagine having anything better close to your naked skin?' she went on. 'Can you imagine anything better to lie upon or beneath?'

'Only a young girl's skin,' Richard repeated, with a chuckle.

I twined my arm very firmly around his and dragged him off up the broad avenue.

'But we need new sheets,' he protested laughingly.

'Not from the likes of her, we don't. One more second and she'd have been over the counter and ripping off your shirt, fine linen or no.'

He laughed. 'Now who is jealous?' But spoken as if it pleased him.

I slid my hand around his waist, let it rest lightly on his hip, just above the hilt of his sword. He shepherded me past a booth named Pomegranate and another shop called The Flying Horse. We bought luxurious gold silk from Naples for my gown, a bolt of burgundy wrought velvet for Richard's suit, gold lace to trim cloaks. We bought coffee, chocolate, tea, sugar and spices, and then went to a stall selling gems.

'Show me the biggest oriental pearls you have,' Richard commanded. 'The brightest and the roundest.'

He bargained with assurance and skill, drove down the price by a half and then bought them, with a small lacquered cabinet for keeping them in.

I had never seen him so at ease. 'I'd not have guessed you'd be so interested in browsing the wares of drapers and haberdashers and perfumers and silk mercers,' I said tucking my hand back inside his belt. 'You like it here as much as I do.'

He kissed my hair. 'I like buying things for you.'

'You must have something, too. What will it be?'

He chose a jewel-encrusted scabbard and silver dagger and I was sure that must be the last purchase, but he had moved on to another silver merchant. We had already bought trenchers and a sugar box, new mustard pots and salt cellars and wine pots, but he picked up an escalloped fruit dish, the kind that would be displayed on the buffet, and I felt a shadow pass over me, transitory as the shadow of the wings of a swan in flight but enough to ruin my enjoyment, because I knew, as everyone did, that plate was displayed as a symbol of status and of wealth. I understood how much it must matter to Richard, because he had seen what it did to his father to have it all plundered and stripped away. I understood, but it troubled me.

He saw that I was troubled, mistook the reason. 'Regard it as an investment,' he said. 'If we are ever in need of ready money, we can have it melted down.'

'We will have to do it immediately, if we spend any more.'

'No, we won't,' he said easily. 'The world runs on credit now. Dealers in luxuries are particularly glad to extend credit to landed gentlemen and ladies. Enjoy it now, pay for it later.'

'Why does that sound more like a warning than an opportunity?' I tried to put George Digby's comment about profligacy from my head. Failed.

Richard was looking at me strangely and I slid my eyes away and stared at the floor. 'What is it?' he asked, very low.

I raised my face to his. 'I think a beggar-girl might not do for you after all,' I tried to tease, but his eyes flared, their blue suddenly glacial.

I thought I would have to grow accustomed to this unnerving changeability of his. I would learn to notice the warning signs and triggers and find ways to avoid them and divert him, I told myself, as I had learned to divert Forest from the tantrums that erupted whenever he did not get what he wanted. Sometimes.

When John Smythe rode over from Ashton Court to see him, Richard was with Forest in the great hall, where they had both been for most of the morning. Richard had removed his small ornamental sword from his hip and was demonstrating with great patience just how to hold the hilt and draw it from the jewelled scabbard to make a lunge.

Our neighbour was a trim-bearded and very aristocratic young man who behaved as if he was twice as old as his years. He had already adopted the irascibility and pomposity of his father, Sir Hugh, who had died several years ago. In his role as Deputy Lord Lieutenant, John Smythe had come to tell us that the local militia was being put in readiness for an invasion by the Duke of Monmouth.

It should not have come as any great surprise. Talk of rebellion had been brewing since before the second King Charles died and the new King James took the throne. But why did it have to happen now, just days before my wedding?

'You will join us, of course, sir?' John Smythe said to Richard. 'Colonel Portman has sent out a call for young and able gentlemen to lead our troops.'

My eyes flew to him as my heart turned over. With a hiss of metal that reminded me poignantly of the sound of skates on ice, Richard dropped the sword into its sheath, handed the encrusted hilt back to Forest.

The boy took it in a trance, watching him as intently as was I. 'Will you go and fight, Mr Glanville?' my son asked eagerly.

The Civil War was not even a distant memory for him, no more than a thrilling adventure from the ballads that made no mention of Somerset-shire being turned into a blood-soaked battlefield, of people being starved out of their houses and those houses pillaged and burned, of children being raped and murdered before their mothers' eyes, of the inhabitants of this country being reduced to a state close to destitution from which many were only just recovering. I had been born into that time and it was still very real and raw for me. My blood felt chilled to think such hardship might return. Richard showed no outward fear except that his lovely face had gone ashen and tension was evident in every line of his body. I sank down into a chair, suddenly lacking the energy or the will to stand.

'Will you go, sir?' I had not noticed Bess come into the room, carrying an armful of my new gowns.

I glanced at her and her eyes told me everything. Ned and Thomas would be going to join the rebels. Their fathers were clubmen in the Civil War. They would see it as their duty to defend the grand old cause, the Protestant cause, just as my father would have defended it to his dying breath. He would turn in his grave to see John Smythe in his house, asking my intended husband to help lead the militia in support of a Catholic king against a Protestant pretender.

The differences between us had seemed of no account before, but never had I felt them so keenly as now, when Ned and Thomas and the other Tickenham men were probably already collecting pitchforks and scythes and rounding up their friends to rally to the cause of the Duke. The war had never been over for my father, and it seemed it was never really over for England, least of all the West Country. If Richard joined the militia, our family would be split in two. Bess and I would be on opposing sides, our men at war with one another. We would be enemies under the same roof.

Richard came over to me and sat himself down quietly on the arm of my chair. I slid my hand over to rest on his thigh, not sure if it was to comfort him or myself.

'I am to be married in a few days,' he said, finally answering the question only I had not dared to ask. 'Nothing will disrupt that, not war, nor flood, nor famine. After it is done, if the militia still needs me, I will decide what to do.'

'Very well, sir. Thank you.' With an abrupt click of his heels, John Smythe bowed and left.

Forest whipped out the little sword, sliced the air with it. 'How old d'you have to be to fight?'

'Old enough to know what you are fighting for,' Richard said.

'What are the rebels fighting for?' my son asked.

'To rid the country of King and Papists,' Richard said sardonically. 'Same as it ever was.'

I had never quite shaken off my conviction that Edmund had died of Papist poison. I could not help fearing what it would mean to have a Catholic on the throne, could not help thinking it might be better if the rebels won

334

– except that Richard would be fighting against them. If they won, he would have lost, just like his father, and I did not know how he would cope with that.

Forest came over to Richard and handed back the little sword with obvious reluctance.

'Keep it,' he said.

Forest's eyes were wide as trenchers. 'Really, sir? Can I?'

'It is too dangerous, Richard,' I said, ignoring my son's scowl. 'He is too young.'

'I was only four when my father gave me my first sword,' Richard said easily, reminding me, as if I needed reminding, of the pressure his father had put on him from such an early age, to win, always to win.

I could not be so cruel as to remind him that his father had also thrown him into a lake, to drown or to swim. I could not be so cruel as to remind him that he was not the father of my son. Though looking at them both, with their heads of black hair, Forest looked to be more Richard's child than mine.

I glanced from my husband, the son of a Cavalier, to my son, the grandson of a Roundhead major, and felt truly thankful that my father was no longer here to see them together.

'Who will win?' Forest asked, practising a parry with the sheathed sword. 'The rebels or the King?'

'Ah, now, that is always the question,' Richard said. 'Tell me, who would you stake your money on? The King with his trained infantry and mighty guns, or a disorderly rabble armed with scythes and pitchforks? Whose side would you rather be on?'

The words came to my tongue of their own volition, were out of my mouth before I could bite them back. 'You should not be so confident,' I said. 'You, of all people, should not need reminding that the first King Charles did not win. For all his battalions.'

Richard's expression darkened. 'You speak as if you would see our King and all his armies defeated too.'

'I no longer care,' I said slowly, 'whether a person be Puritan, Protestant or Papist. Just as I do not care if they be kin to Roundhead or to Cavaliers.'

'Are you quite sure of that, Nell?'

Summer 1685

My second wedding day could not have been more different from the first.

The predicted invasion had not happened and I refused to let the threat of it spoil the day.

It began with much eating and drinking, so that even before we made it to church half our party, Bess and Ned, John Hort and the Walkers and Mother Wall, were all headed for mild intoxication, everyone very loud and merry.

Richard and I travelled to Bristol in a coach with glass windows and liveried pages, the sun shining brightly all the way. I had a golden dress to match my golden curls and a necklace of sapphires and diamonds which Richard had given to me as a wedding gift.

The soaring church of St Mary Redcliffe was festooned inside with violets and roses. Precious little of the medieval stained glass had survived destruction during the Reformation and by Cromwell's army, but the very highest windows were still intact and were enough to illuminate the spacious interior with myriad colours. The sunlight filtered through them and made coloured patterns on the floor. It gleamed on the golden basin in which the guests were to cast their brightly wrapped gifts.

'Look,' I said to Richard, as we walked to the aisle over a pool of red and yellow and purple light, 'we have found the foot of a rainbow.'

He stroked back a wisp of hair that had drifted over my cheek. 'And, see, here is the gold.'

But for all the radiance around us, he appeared today as if haunted by his own private shadow. He seemed more than usually preoccupied and troubled, and I imagined it must be the promise he had made to John Smythe that was distressing him. He'd said he would join the militia, if need be, as soon as our wedding was over. I took his hand in mine, leaned into him and kissed him, to be rewarded with a gentle, transforming smile. There was a mischievous sparkle in his eyes again as he whispered to me of the wedding vow that Protestants had foresworn as pagan idolatry. 'I shall worship you with my body, Nell, forever, so long as you will always worship me with yours.'

'Oh, I will. I will.'

It was enough to irk even the mild Puritan in William Merrick who muttered that the whole event was a shameful display of pomp. And that was before he found out what was planned for later.

The bridesmaids showered us with flowers and sprinkled us with wheat as we proceeded from the church, and my smile turned to an amazed stare when I saw what was waiting to greet us on our return to Tickenham. A hundred riders on horseback had come to escort us back to the house, and all the grand families – the Smyths from Ashton Court, the Digbys from Clevedon Court and the Gorges of Wraxall – had turned out in their finest coaches.

'It is only fitting,' Richard said. 'How else should a lady and her new lord be welcomed back after their wedding?'

I turned to him. 'You knew they were planning this?'

I saw by his quiet smile that he had had more than a hand in that planning, had obviously taken it upon himself to visit all the local gentry whom my father, and even Edmund, had failed to count as friends. But clearly they were all Richard's friends now, had succumbed to his gentle, winning charm. How could they not?

The commoners and tenants were no different, seemingly. The Bennett boys came up alongside the carriage and threw flowers in at the windows, and little Alice Walker rode up with her father and handed me a bouquet of marigolds. Everyone was carrying flowers and wearing flowers and throwing garlands and posies at us all along the way.

'They were all very happy when I said that, instead of draining the land, we were planning a great feast and dole for them all,' Richard explained.

'I am sure they were.'

I insisted we stop the coach so we could get out and ride on top with the coachman for the rest of the journey, so as to have the best view of the cavalcade of drums and bagpipes and fiddlers and dancers that accompanied us, and I smiled at all the well-wishers, reached down to touch their hands.

A girl threw a rosebud and Richard reached out and snatched it from the air. He held it to his lips and looked at me over it with the most roguish, twinkling smile. 'Soon your rose will be all mine,' he whispered. 'The secret rose you keep between your legs, with petals as pink as these. I shall be like a bee, or one of your butterflies, and put my tongue into those petals.'

'Hush,' I said, flushing as hotly as a greensick girl. Just imagining him doing what he described made me almost delirious. I was glad we were in the open air, that there was a breeze to cool my skin. I was glad I had the procession to watch to distract me. It danced us back to the house and through the flower-filled rooms to the great hall and the wedding table decorated with floral rose cake.

More than a hundred guests sat down for the first sitting, to scoff breads and meats and puddings and cheeses. Fulfilling his duty as groom, Richard served me with beef and mustard, and John Foskett raised a glass and joined in, offering blessings and drinking healths. The merriment was naturally restrained while the clergyman was present and I was impatient for him to go. I was not interested in edification. I wanted mirth and fun, bawdy jests and devilish ditties. I wanted to make a May game of this wedding. I delighted in seeing cakes and ale relished, and every lusty lad with a wench at his side, all pulling at laces and loosening each other's clothes.

'There is so much kissing and flirting, I doubt many will still be maids by evening,' Richard whispered into my ear.

'It's like a wedding from the old days,' Mistress Knight came up especially to say to him, her wrinkled old face alight as if she was just a girl again. 'I never thought we'd see the likes of it again, now the gentry folk are so anxious to save their shillings.'

Richard handed her a posy from the table decoration, giving her his most adorable smile. 'What is the good of having shillings if they are not spent and scattered amongst friends?'

She beamed back at him and almost danced away with the little bouquet, as if her gnarled old legs pained her no more.

'Damn me,' I said, slipping my hand into his. 'But is there nobody my husband has not utterly charmed?'

There was one person, I realised, but I imagined that was because Richard had not even tried. Mistress Knight was seated on a bench with her husband, Arthur, and Bess and Ned, but I noted that Thomas was not with them. How he must hate me, to deny himself a feast rather than be here celebrating my wedding day, and for a moment I felt a little chill. What had I done to make him hate me so much? I shrugged. Well, it was his loss that he was missing out on today.

We had been showered with presents from everyone else. To the ones we had received in church were added more money and silverware and all manner of food or drink: swans, capons, a brace of duck, hares and fish, puddings and spices.

I took a moment to note every detail so that I should remember it always. This great hall that had seen such austerity was utterly transformed with sprigs and bouquets on every table, the feasting guests decked out in their silver buttons and scarlet stockings and with scarlet and blue bridal ribbons round their wrists and hands and hats. My children, giddy from too much sun and cider, were hiding under tables with Bess's Sam and scores of other young villagers. I did not want the day ever to end. But when it did, I consoled myself that there would be eleven more to follow just like it.

Richard had been softly caressing the inside of my wrist with little circular movements of his thumb, and now his tongue was in my ear. It tickled deliciously and I wriggled away. His arm tightened around my waist, but I came back willingly for more. He kissed me and his mouth tasted of wine. His hand strayed now under the table, found its way up under my skirts, his fingers moving slowly between my legs, stroking me, touching the secret parts of me.

'I want you, Nell,' he whispered urgently. 'I cannot wait any longer.'

The guests must have worried that if we were not soon sent to our bed we would take our marriage joys right there on the wedding table, unable to hold back from doing the act before them all. The bride cake and the posset were speedily brought forth and then everyone followed us upstairs for the public disrobing, crowding round to catch the ribbons and laces that held our clothes together. I did not even see who caught the most admired trophy, my garter. I had eyes only for Richard, for my husband. And he was looking only at me, smiling at me, that beautiful angel's smile, and there was nothing else in the world for me but him.

They all took their leave of us eventually and we tore off the rest of each other's clothes, getting into a tangle in our haste and tumbling each other naked to the bed.

Richard raised himself above me and I parted my legs for him, but for a while he seemed to want to do no more than hold himself against me as I stroked him and he gazed intently into my face. The hardness of his cock was pressing into me, stirring me, and when he began to move, very slowly, my need for him became so unbearable that my body took charge and responded to him of its own accord. I pressed back, began thrusting softly against him. I did not stop, could not stop, wanted more and more of him, just to touch and be touched, to give myself to him, give myself up to feeling. It was a letting go. Like dancing and letting the music take hold of my body, like skating on ice and not caring if I could not stop, like the wonderful weightlessness of swimming. It was beauty and bliss unbound. The sensation of his skin against mine, such soft skin, on a body that was hard and lean, took me to a world beyond any I had ever known, a world of fire and of ice, of the deepest darkness and the brightest light. Curls as black as night and eyes as bright as a summer sky . . .

'Love me,' I whispered. 'Make me yours.' And he did love me, as I had never been loved before. It was a love to be completely lost in, consumed by. It was like being split open and it was like being made whole, like receiving a blessing, like coming home.

I wept against his shoulder and cried out and clutched his hair, and when he stroked me with his warm hands it was as if the music that had played all day played on in my head, a glorious cacophony of sound. Entwined, grappling, our limbs knitted together, we were warmed as if by the hottest, brightest midsummer sun, even as dusk was falling. A bead of sweat trickled down the small cleft between my breasts and his thighs glistened as if he had just walked out of the sea.

It was all that life could be, all that it was meant to be, a sensuous explosion of touch and taste, of sight and sound and smell. The taste of his mouth, his skin. The smell of his warm perfumed curls, his sex. The sound of his moans of ecstasy. His naked body was beautiful to behold and the hardness of his cock a delight.

His hands were all over me, caressing every part of me, making my skin tingle until it was as if it was fused with his, so I could not tell where he ended and I began.

'I can't hold on any longer,' he whispered. 'I want to be inside you.' And the feel of him penetrating me at last made me cry out with the joy of being able to give myself to him completely, to give to him finally all that I had to give.

I wrapped my limbs tight around him and arched my back to draw him deeper, wanting to be closer to him still, closer, understanding only now what it meant for two bodies to become one. When I cried out for him to finish it and he finally found his relief, it was if the sun had burst inside me, the music reached a great crescendo and all the church bells were ringing, ringing, for Christmas.

We were lying in each other's arms and I was drifting in the pleasant transitory state just beyond wakefulness when Richard suddenly cried out in his sleep, words that were unintelligible but full of distress. He pushed me roughly away from him, thrashed his legs, kicking out at me as if he was fighting me off, as if in his dream I was something to be feared and meant him harm. His eyes were tightly closed, his brow furrowed, as if in pain or anguish.

I reached out to him and took hold of his shoulder, gave it a gentle shake. 'Richard.'

He turned his face into the pillow, twisted his head back again violently, as if trying to escape from something.

I shook him a little harder. 'Richard. Wake up.'

His eyes flew open, stared at me, unseeing but filled with terror, so that I knew he was not properly awake but still trapped in a nightmare world.

I stroked his hair off his face and felt that it was damp with sweat. 'I'm here,' I said. 'It's me.'

I slid my arm up under his and around his back and found that his body was running with sweat, and yet he was trembling. I held him tighter, felt the ferocious pounding of his heart through my bones.

'You had a dream,' I said. 'Do you remember what it was?'

He shook his head, his eyes suddenly guarded, so that I wondered if he did remember quite clearly but was either too ashamed or too afraid to talk about it.

'It's all right,' I murmured, kissing his brow, my mouth wet with his sweat. 'It's all right.'

Gradually his heart steadied, but he held on to me as if the fear had not left him.

When I woke on the morning of Friday 12 June, it was to a greeting from more drums and fiddles and bawdy laughter. I dressed and went below stairs to find the tables laid with food and my husband happily breaking his fast with the new guests, who were arriving from the more far-flung villages to bring their congratulations.

Good will and joy rang throughout the hall until Thomas Knight burst through the door in a state of great agitation. He climbed up on to one of the tables, trampling the flowers beneath his boots, and seized a musket from the wall. Silence fell instantly and completely, as if everyone had been turned to stone.

'This is no time for feasting,' he declared before anyone had had a chance to react. He clutched the weapon to his chest, excitement gleaming in his eyes. 'Every able man must take up his arms and make ready. I have it from a messenger. The Duke of Monmouth's fleet landed at Lyme at sunset yesterday. Hundreds are rallying to his support.'

I threw back my chair and ran outside to the orchard. Richard tried to grab my hand to stop me, but I would not be hindered. I needed air, sky, space.

Not now. It could not happen now.

The sun was still shining. The sky was a perfect summery blue and the birds were twittering. I was still newly married. But the wedding feast would not go on for twelve days. Instead of music and laughter, the air would reverberate again with the sound of cannon-fire. Instead of sharing hospitality and good cheer, neighbour would turn once again against neighbour. Blood was to be spilt once more over Somersetshire's black peat. I had wanted this marriage to begin favourably, in a blaze of colour and joy. Instead it was to begin in darkness and in battle.

Richard had his feet up on the wedding table, amidst the crushed flowers and debris of the abandoned feast. He was quaffing a cup of canary wine from a leftover flagon, his eyes strangely bright and glittering. I rested my hand on his shoulder, dropped a kiss on the top of his curly head. 'I am so sorry that marriage to me has landed you in the West Country now,' I said softly. 'If you had stayed away from me, far away from me, you might not have been embroiled in this rebellion.'

He reached back and laid his hand upon mine. Swinging his feet to the floor, he pulled me gently down into his lap. 'I could not stay away from you, Nell,' he said almost ominously. 'I had to have you, even if it meant my damnation.'

They were words he might have intended for flattery, no more than that. They meant nothing really. No. They meant something, though I did not know what. Did not in truth want to know, or even to contemplate.

He tipped the cup to my lips for me to drink, but I pushed it away. 'Will you go now? Will you go and help try to put down the rebellion?'

'You mean, will I fight for our crowned and anointed King?' With the backs of his fingers he traced the low, lace-edged neckline of my gown and smiled that lovely enquiring smile of his. 'I had a healthy regard for our second King Charles and his passion for wenching and wine, but I can't say I care as much for his brother. So maybe I should join the rebels instead, support the heroic Protestant Duke? Would you like that, little daughter of a Roundhead, my little Puritan maid? Would you like me to turn renegade for love of you?'

I flung my arms around his neck. 'All I want is for you to stay with me,' I blurted, close to tears. 'I do not want you to support anyone.'

'Then perhaps I won't.'

But I did not for a moment believe this studied indifference. He was blessedly unfettered by dogma, prayed like a perfect Anglican, but this rebellion was not just about religion, not for him. He had an unshakable allegiance to the monarchy, and the monarchy was once again under threat.

I pushed myself back so I could see his face. 'Thomas Knight and Ned and John Hort have already gone,' I said.

'Good for them.'

'They see it as their duty to fight for the cause of their fathers,' I added carefully.

'Hah! It is more that they are ready to fight for any cause, especially one led by a colourful, popular hero such as the Duke of Monmouth. Albeit that he is King Charles's bastard son, he is a very courageous and charming bastard. It's not so very hard for the political agitators to rouse a band of young hot-blooded men, ready for action and glory. They'd ride into any battle so long as it gave them a chance to wield a musket or pike and be a hero. You have a little boy. You know the games boys like to play.'

'Thomas and Ned are both older than you,' I said. I knew he was just toying with me, knew he would go and lead the militia, would be lured, like the rest of them, by the promise of action and adventure and glory. More than that, even if he would not admit it to himself, he would surely also be lured by what he could not fail to see as a chance, finally, to avenge the death of his brother and the ruin of his family fortunes.

I linked my arms around his neck, threaded my fingers into the silken black curls and kissed him, frantic little kisses, all over his face. 'I will not let you go,' I said. His eyes were so deep and so blue that I felt almost as if I could dive into them. How I wished I could. 'If you do join the militia then I am coming with you. I shall be like a camp follower in the war, the women who went to be with their husbands, facing whatever perils they faced. I will cook for you and make sure you fight on a full stomach. I will be there to tend to you if you are wounded. I will lay down my life and die on the battlefield with you, if it should come to that.'

'I would not have you put in danger,' he said. 'Not for my sake.'

'But *you* will be in danger,' I cried.

He gazed at me as if he wanted to fix the image of me in his mind, and I saw in his eyes a fatalistic acceptance of the hand that might be dealt him.

'Are you afraid, love?' I asked him.

'Of scythemen and musketeers?' He shook his head. 'No.'

'Of what then?'

'I am afraid of losing you.'

'You will not lose me. Why would you lose me?'

He did not reply.

'You are frightening me, Richard. Don't look at me that way.'

'What way?'

'As if you might never see me again.'

He stroked the stray tendrils of hair from my cheek. 'I waited so long for you, my little Nell, so long. But maybe you were right. Maybe we should not be together. Maybe we do not deserve happiness, even now. Maybe I do not deserve it.'

I took his lovely face between my hands, forced him to look at me. 'You do deserve it, Richard,' I said adamantly. 'You do. And you shall have it. I shall make you happy.'

He kissed me, almost savagely, as if to defy a fate, or a God, that might break us apart and then he left me. He swung himself up into the saddle and rode away from me and into battle.

Bess and I waited together for news, even though the men we loved were fighting on opposing sides, even though good news for one of us must mean bad for the other. We waited in the same empty rooms for the same empty, eternal days, when even the long hours of warm summer sunshine could not dispel the darkness that had fallen over Tickenham Court once again. As I tossed corn to the clucking hens, collected eggs, weeded the soggy vegetable patch, helped Sam do his father's work and feed and groom the horses, waiting for them to be requisitioned for who could say which side, I did not feel like a new wife fresh from the marriage bed. I felt like a widow still, a widow who had lost not one young husband but two.

I was helping Mary with her Latin and Bess was sweeping the floor when Florence Smythe, John's tall and elegant eldest sister, rode over with news finally, but news that brought no relief to either of us, only made the waiting even more unbearable.

'Monmouth's army is on the move,' she said. 'It is now three thousand strong. The Devon militia to the west and the Somersetshire militia to the east are converging on Axminster to prevent their advance.'

I dropped my face against little Mary's curly red hair. If it were not for her and her brother, I would have left for Axminster right then. I was sure this waiting was far worse than being at the vanguard of any fighting, no matter how brutal. But still we must wait, knowing now that a confrontation between the two armies was imminent. Still we must wait, dreading the worst.

Florence had promised she would come back as soon as she had further news, but when nearly a week had crawled by, I felt so certain something must have happened that I could wait no longer. I set out to ride to Ashton Court. A pale sun was struggling to break through the mist. As I rode through the deer park, a stag with enormous antlers appeared from out of nowhere and crossed the track in front of me, like a strange, majestic spirit.

I did not reach the mansion, but met Florence riding towards me, her cloak draped elegantly over her horse's quarters. As she reined in and we faced each other on our mounts, I saw that her eyes were brimming with tears.

'How did you know?' she said. 'I was on my way to tell you.'

I clutched the pommel of the saddle to stop myself from slipping off.

'Oh, Eleanor dear, do not be alarmed.' With a jingle of the bridle Florence leaned across to rest her hand on mine. 'It is with relief that I cry, and more than a little trepidation, not for sorrow.'

The herd of red deer over towards the ancient oak woods stopped watching us and resumed their grazing. 'It is over so quickly then? Monmouth is defeated?'

'No,' she said, tightening the reins to hold her horse steady. 'He is not. But it is over for our men. We have just heard it from the messenger. Monmouth's rebels sent cannon and musketeers to line the routes of entry into Axminster, and in the face of such determination the militia were forced to retreat. The army marched on to Chard. The militia met them again there but were routed, abandoning their weapons and uniforms by the roadside.' She laughed even as she cried. 'It was a shamefully disorderly and humiliating defeat, and my brother will be so displeased. It means the way is left open to Taunton and then for Monmouth to try for a tilt at Bristol, but at least our men can come home to us and leave it to the royal dragoons.'

I could not share her relief. 'But, Florence, where are the dragoons?'

'They are on their way. The King's Commander-In-Chief also, to inspect the city defences.'

I turned to the left, where the mist was clearing now, revealing spectacular views across the city. 'And if they do not hold? If Bristol should be taken?'

Bristol was too close. Much too close.

I did not hear the hooves of Richard's horse clatter into the yard, though I had been listening out for the sound all day, so quietly did he come back to me. He walked into the great hall as the light was failing, his riding boots caked in mud, his cloak splattered with it. Even the glinting sword buckled at his side was tarnished. There were several days' growth of dark stubble on his face, his skin was grey with weariness and his eyes looked bruised.

The instant I saw him, I checked myself from running to greet him and throwing myself into his arms, from giving him the welcome I could see he did not want, did not believe he deserved. Instead I went and took his hand and kissed it. 'My love, thank God that you are safe.'

'They have proclaimed the Duke of Monmouth King,' he said in an empty voice, as if it mattered to him very much. 'He received a rapturous welcome in Taunton and the declaration was made in the presence of a Corporation brought by swordpoint.'

'Surely they cannot do that?'

'They just did. They have hailed him the new King James.'

I saw that he found defeat almost impossible to accept. He had wanted to return to me with tales of valour, to come out on the winning side this time. And though he would never admit it, I knew he was afraid of what might happen if he did not.

'The rebel infantry are only five miles from Bristol,' he said. 'The Duke of Beaufort has said he would see the city burned, would burn it himself, rather than let it fall to traitors. A vessel in the quay, a merchantman, has already taken fire. There is nothing we can do to stop them.'

'The King's forces will stop them. They will!' I led him to the settle, pressed him to sit. Seeing that his boots were wet, I knelt by his feet and pulled them off. I went to the buffet and poured a cup of wine for him, brought the flagon over and set it on the table by the fire. He took the cup in shaking hands and drank it dry.

I knelt by him again, rested my arm on his leg and reached up to stroke his hair. 'Richard, please don't take this so hard. You did your best. You had charge of a band of ill-trained and inexperienced part-time troops, not a proper fighting unit at all.' I did not add that matters were made so much worse because they were led by gentlemen officers with no military experience. 'There is much sympathy for the rebels. It is no wonder there were desertions.'

He picked up the flagon and tried to pour from it, spilling wine over himself and the floor. I put my hand over his to steady it, poured for him.

'Tell me this, Nell,' he said then. 'Can you honestly say that in your heart you were not hoping for this? That some of your loyalty at least does not lie with the rebels? That, at the last, your Puritan blood does not run thicker than your love for me?'

347

'How can you ask . . .'

'Your loyalty to Tickenham's men then? To Bess's Ned and Thomas.'

'I cannot help hoping they will come home safe, for her sake,' I said after a moment. 'Is that so very wrong of me?'

Bess had given up on her reading and writing lessons and forgotten most of what I had taught her, but not before she had passed on the rudiments to Ned, and to Thomas, apparently. Bess said her brother had picked it up quicker than she could teach him, working most of it out for himself. She came to me now with a letter from Ned, which he had sent with a carrier, and which she wanted me to read for her.

I hesitated. 'Are you sure?'

'Just because Mr Glanville was with the militia does not make you one of them, does it? You are your father's daughter, and you know as well as I do that he would have been marching at Monmouth's shoulder.'

I gave her a look, unfolded the letter and read aloud the message from her husband. '"We have met with the King's Life Guards, bonny Bess, a hundred of them, at Keynsham. There have been injuries but do not fear, Tom and I have not taken even a scratch, such able cavalrymen we have become, but the troops of the rebel horse are scattered and Monmouth has been forced to give up his designs on Bristol. I cannot say where we are to march to now but it will not be in your direction, praise God. I pray that we are not overtaken by the King's troops and I pray that we have good weather.

'"We are all so ill shod and exhausted from toiling through deep mud under heavy rain, not that I am not well used to mud and to rain, nor mind the toil. Tom sends his wishes and I send you all my love and kisses, bonny Bessie. I hope Sam is tending the horses well for me. Keep him safe. Pray for us all."'

Richard had come silently into the hall; he wore the expression of a man who had caught his wife in the act of cuckolding him. I refused to let him make me feel guilty for having read Ned's letter. I refolded it, taking my time, and handed it back to Bess.

Richard walked away towards the parlour.

'It is people I care about, not causes,' I said, going after him and reaching for his arm. 'Can you not understand that?'

348

He poured himself some wine. 'It is which people you care about the most that I don't quite understand.'

'I care about you,' I said, almost despairingly. Why could he not believe that? Why was he still so unsure of my love for him? Why, when I loved him so very much, was it not enough? What did he need from me that he did not already have?

Damn this rebellion, I thought. Damn Monmouth. Damn the King.

I removed the wine glass from his hand, moved closer to him, so our bodies were touching. I slid my hand down between them, felt his desire.

'You want me?' I asked him.

'I always want you.'

'Come with me then,' I said softly. 'And let me show you just how much I care about you.'

It was enough to bring a smile back to his beautiful mouth. 'There is an offer I'll not refuse.'

We learned from John Smythe that Monmouth's musketeers and scythemen had finally met with a full frontal attack by the royal army of four thousand men in the hilly country just outside Philipsnorton. It was a fierce bombardment that lasted for six hours and in which over a hundred perished. Fatal injuries had included skulls being cleaved in half, scattering blood and brain, guts torn out with bayonets, and cannon-fire ripping clean through a man's body from front to back.

But Ned had written to Bess again from Bridgwater to assure her that he and Thomas were unharmed. They had spent a miserable night on the wet moors en route from Wells, where they'd quartered in the cathedral and taken lead from the roof to make bullets while awaiting a promised horde of thousands of clubmen, armed with flails and bludgeons. These reinforcements had, in the end, numbered less than two hundred.

'It does not look good for them now, does it?' Bess said, clutching Ned's letter to her.

It looked far worse when John Smythe came to report that the reprisals had already begun, that royal dragoons and horse guards had been ransacking rebel properties and had begun hanging prisoners at Pensford. When we learned that the royal army had set up an encampment outside

Westonzoyland on Sedgemoor, with all roads and bridges secured, I sent Bess home to wait with Sam and her mother.

Richard rode into Bristol for news. The first account to be had of the battle was fragmentary and scant. But because the end came on Sedgemoor, a land so like Tickenham land, because the strategic points were rhynes and bridges and flat, muddy, mist-shrouded watermeadows, I could picture it all too clearly.

Monmouth had moved his troops out of Bridgwater late in the evening of 5 July. The plan had been for the rebel infantry to launch a surprise attack at night, destroying the King's forces. In the summer fog they had marched in a silent column round Chedzoy, to form in line and advance across the deep Bussex Rhyne towards the red tents of the royal encampment. But the King's forces were alerted by a stray musket shot and set up a volley of cannon-fire that went on across the rhyne all though the night.

The rebels didn't stand a chance. The horse guards came over the Lower Plungeon river with their sabres and attacked Monmouth's men to the right, and the Oxford Blues came over the Upper Plungeon on Monmouth's left flank. By dawn the rebel army was beginning to crumble. They were pursued across the moor and cut down by horsemen on all sides, slaughtered in cornfields and ditches. It was more massacre than battle. Over a thousand were dead and three hundred taken prisoner. Monmouth himself was found asleep in a drain, dressed in the clothes of peasant. Only the star of the Order of the Garter gave away his identity.

There was no way of knowing yet if Ned and Thomas were among those wounded or captured; no way of knowing even whether they were alive or dead. We just had to wait until they and the other Tickenham men came home.

Or until they did not.

Bess did not sleep for waiting. She kept a rushlight burning at the window of her little cottage all night to guide Ned and Thomas if they should be making their weary way home, and for much of the time she sat beside the light, keeping watch for them. It was almost a superstition, I think. If she kept the light burning they could not have perished. If she let the light go out, if she turned her back on the window, she was abandoning them, abandoning hope.

She kept up her vigil even when we heard that five hundred rebels, many of them wounded, had been rounded up on Sedgemoor and herded into the parish church at Westonzoyland. She waited even when we knew that many had been hanged outside the church in chains, and when more still were hanged without trial in Bridgwater and Taunton.

She carried on waiting for Ned and Thomas to return even when the local constables were ordered to report on all those who had been absent from home during the time of the rebellion, when she knew that mancatchers were offered five shillings for every rebel they handed over. When neighbour was pitched against neighbour in a way that even we, who had been born into Civil War, would hardly have imagined possible.

Richard found me standing at the chamber window, looking out over the empty moonlit causeway, thinking of Bess doing the same. 'If you care about her and this family at all,' he said, coming to stand beside me, 'the best you can hope for is that Ned and Thomas Knight, John Hort and the rest of them, all died a hero's death in battle and never return.'

'How can you say that?' I rounded on him. 'How can you be so heartless?'

I saw him struggle to control himself. 'If they come back here they will endanger the lives of their families, or whoever harbours them under their roof or so much as offers them a crust of bread. You should not need to be reminded that gaols all across the West Country are crammed with those suspected of sympathising with the rebellion, as well as with men who were known to have been in the infantry. You know as well as I that hundreds are being exhorted to confess under pretence of pardon and then being condemned to death without trial.'

'I have known these men all my life. Ned has a son, a wife. Don't you care . . .'

He took me by my shoulders and pulled me round to face him. 'I am not heartless, Nell. Do not say that I am heartless. Just tell me this. What does Bess plan to do if her prayers and best hopes are fulfilled and Ned and Thomas do come home? How does she plan to hide them and keep them from the constables and the mancatchers?'

'I have not asked her.'

He looked deep into my eyes. 'Give me your word that if she tries to bring them here, you will not take them in?'

When I did not reply, his grip tightened on my shoulders until it hurt, until I could feel his nails digging into my flesh. 'Bailiffs are seizing the property of sympathisers as forfeiture to the Crown. I thought you loved this house, this land? Do you want to have it taken from you? Destroyed?'

'Of course not.'

'I do not want to see you reduced to living in want and in fear,' he said quietly. 'I do not want to see you hungry and cold and sick and unhappy. I do not want you to die of a broken heart in a filthy charity hospital.'

I took hold of both his hands, held them tight. His face was so care-worn that it tore at my heart. 'That is not going to happen,' I said. 'Do you hear me?'

He looked at me in silence, as if he had not heard me at all. 'Your word, Nell. Give it to me.'

I gave one small, almost imperceptible nod, doubting that I should ever be put to the test. With each day that passed it seemed less likely that we would be faced with the problem of what to do with Tickenham's rebels if they should come home.

Autumn 1685

It was nearly five weeks after the battle on Sedgemoor when I was woken in the middle of the night by Bess, standing at the side of the bed with a candle, oblivious to the hot wax that was about to spill all over her hand. 'It's Thomas,' she cried, with quiet urgency. 'You have to help me.'

Richard stirred, rolled over on to his stomach. He put out his arm as if to try to find me and his eyelids fluttered, but he did not wake. With a guilty glance at his peaceful sleeping face, I slipped quickly from the warmth of our bed, letting the hangings ripple shut behind me. I grabbed Bess's arm and pulled her with me out of the chamber, closing the door softly after us.

She was shaking, her face blotched from crying. 'He is badly wounded.' She was struggling, in her distress, to keep her voice to a whisper. 'He was shot in his side and I think his arm is broken. Ned is . . .' She broke down and sobbed.

I put my arms around her heaving shoulders. 'Bess, are you sure?'

'Tom was with him,' she rasped. 'He saw the bayonet go right through . . . Ned's chest. He still has the blood all over his shirt.' She made an effort to calm herself. 'Tom will die too, if we don't help him.'

'Where is he?'

'Below stairs. The hall. My father said we should bring Tom here. He said you would know what to do, how to treat the wounds. I've told him to wait outside. To keep a look out.'

'Good,' I said, with a glance back at the chamber door, wishing a sentry could be posted there, too, in case Richard should wake, to keep him from knowing how I was deceiving him.

Bess had propped her brother on the settle, but he was so weak and sick that he had slumped over, his eyes closed and his breathing fitful. His clothes were ragged and filthy. He had grown a thick beard and moustache, and the rest of his face was so ingrained with dirt as to render him almost unrecognisable.

Bess ran to him, crouched down on the floor beside him and stoked his mud-caked hair. She held the candle for me while I moved him as gently as I could to examine the injury.

'Someone has removed the missile and debris and tried to bandage him,' I said. 'They must have been too afraid to let him stay.'

The cloths needed changing, they were bloody and stinking and had stuck to his skin. He barely winced as I eased them away, though the pain must have been great. The wound underneath showed no sign of healing, was suppurating, still gaping and ragged and oozing fresh blood and yellow pus. I turned away and covered my mouth, trying not to retch. The pale bone of his rib was almost visible through the mess. He was so thin that the rest of his ribs were scarcely better covered.

'It needs stitching,' I said. 'Warm some water and fetch some lint and vinegar, my strongest silk thread and needle, and a large measure of Bristol Cream . . . make that for three. I'll light the fire and mix up an ointment.'

'He needs a surgeon,' Bess said.

I shook my head. 'We cannot risk it. Besides, I have more faith in my mother's remedy book than ever I have had in surgeons.'

I tipped Thomas's head back and made him drink the sherry, threw a hefty dose down my own throat then handed the glass to Bess. 'Drink,' I ordered. 'You're going to need it.' I gave Thomas a cloth to bite on, so he would not make a noise when he cried out. With Bess still holding the candle, angling it to give the best possible light, I took a deep breath and tried to stop my hands from trembling as I drew together the jagged edges of the skin as best I could. The feeling of needle going through flesh was horrible and never before had I wished I was more skilled at needlework. But I sewed as neatly as I could, suturing the wound and leaving an orifice for it to drain before rebandaging.

I turned my attention to Thomas's left arm next. It was hanging limp and was badly misshapen just above the elbow. With a glance at his half-conscious face, I put my hands to either side of the fracture and did my best to jerk it straight. There was a ghastly sensation of crunching, but if there was any sound it was masked by Thomas's scream. Bess clamped her hand over his mouth until his eyes ceased rolling in their sockets. I bound the arm to a splint of kindling wood.

'What do we do now?' Bess asked, her eyes darting towards me as we changed Thomas into one of Richard's clean shirts that she had fetched from the laundry and she trickled water between her brother's parched lips. 'Where can he go? My cottage is the first place they will look and there is nowhere for him to hide in my father's, either. Someone will see him. He will be found immediately.'

'I know what you are asking of me, Bess, and I cannot do it.'

'If you won't do it for Thomas, then do it for me, for my father and mother.'

'I am a mother too,' I reminded her. 'I am a mother of two children who need me. For their sake, I cannot risk a traitor's death.' I did not mention Richard, who had expressly forbidden me to have any contact with the rebels, who would surely see what I was doing now as traitorous to him and our marriage.

'The constable will not come knocking at this door,' Bess said.

'I cannot guarantee that. And even if he does not, there are plenty who'd betray us for a bounty of five shillings.'

'Your father would have been the first to join the Duke of Monmouth,' Bess pleaded desperately. 'He'd have gone into battle with Thomas and Ned, you know it. He might have met his death on Sedgemoor, or he might have survived and needed somewhere to hide, someone to take a risk and save him from the gallows. He would not have turned Tom away, in the most dire need, when he had been fighting for the cause. You father would have been prepared to sacrifice his own life for that cause.'

'He did sacrifice his own life for it,' I said a little harshly. 'And so left me all alone. I would not sacrifice my life so readily when there are two children depending on me.'

'Then I'll tell you why you should help Thomas.' We looked up and saw Arthur Knight standing by the doorway. 'Mistress Glanville,' he said to me quietly, 'if you turn Thomas out this night and do not help him, you are abandoning your own flesh and blood.'

'What do you mean?'

'Thomas is your half-brother.'

'That is a low trick, Arthur.'

'I swear it is no trick.'

'I'll not believe it. My father would be the last person to . . .'

'Tom is not your father's son. He is your mother's.'

'No.' I shook my head. 'No.' But it was an instinctive response, and even as I gave it, I knew that what Arthur Knight had said must be true. The disparaging comments his wife had made about my mother, my father's dying words about the base desires and carnality of women.

'It was when she was engaged to be married to your father,' Arthur Knight began clumsily. 'She had always had a . . . a fondness for me. She preferred the company of ordinary folk, had a great love for the people of this estate. She had no time for fine, false gentlemen she said, or for parties and balls. She liked to be out on the moor, chattering to me while I cut the sedges and taught her to recognise the plants and birds. We never spoke of love. We did not need to. But, of course, it could not be. And then . . . Thomas. It was kept very quiet. She went away for a while, to your father's relatives in Ribston where he set out to redeem her. He would not let her keep the baby. But my wife loved me enough to love my son, even if he was the child of another woman. Pride made her refuse any payment, though your father did offer it.'

If I'd wanted to understand why my father had been so zealous, here was one answer. He'd feared my mother's sins proved her unworthy, that she was not one of the Puritan elect, was not destined for salvation but was condemned. And I too, since I was of the female line.

After a brief silence it was Bess who asked: 'Does Tom know?'

'Yes,' I answered on Arthur Knight's behalf. 'Thomas has always known. That's why he has always despised me. That is why he told me once that I had stolen from him. Why he looks at me so covetously. He is my mother's only son. If he was not base born, Tickenham Court would be all his.'

'We didn't intend to tell him,' Arthur said hurriedly. 'But he was ill with a fever. Your mother came to the cottage then, insisted on nursing him herself day and night. It seemed certain he would die and she asked if she might tell him the truth. I think he would have guessed it anyway, from the way she was with him. Your mother loved Tom,' Arthur Knight insisted. 'She saved his life with her care. She would want you to save it now, with yours.'

I could not take it in. Did not have time to take it in now. All those years

I'd thought I had nobody, I'd had a brother living not half a mile away. A brother who hated me, who had threatened me, led a riot to my door to torch my house. Because to his mind, but for an accident of birth, it should have been his. What was now mine should all have belonged to him. But I did not have time to dwell on such thoughts. I had to act, to make a decision. 'All right,' I said hastily. 'He can stay. Just until he is stronger. Help me move him.'

His father sat beside him and hooked one of Thomas's arms around my shoulders, stood and hauled him up between us.

'Where to?' he asked.

'This way. Quickly, before anyone wakes.'

I supported Thomas's other arm, wedging my shoulder beneath his armpit. Bess took his feet and together we half lifted, half dragged him over to the great fireplace.

'Put him down here,' I said.

'Here?'

'Just do as I say.'

They did.

I lifted up the candle, ran my fingers over the wall at the side of the fireplace, dug my fingers into the crack in the wainscoting and heaved. The oak panel swung open like the small door it was, to reveal a niche cut deep into the side of the massive chimneybreast, large enough to hide one man or even two. 'It is not very comfortable,' I said. 'But it is warm and dry and, except for me and now the two of you, nobody who lives here even knows it exists.'

Bess peered inside doubtfully.

'It was constructed for just such a purpose,' I told her.

'It's a priest hole,' Arthur Knight said with wonder. 'Where they hid Catholics during the Reformation.'

'Ironic, really,' I said, 'given that Thomas is here because he tried to get rid of a Catholic king.'

'How did you know it was here?' Bess asked.

'My mother told Mary Burges and she told me to look for it, which I did, a long time ago.' I shone the candle into the low recess in the thick wall. As I crouched down and crawled in, my chest tightened with the primal fear of confinement.

357

We eased Thomas in and I made him as comfortable as I could, with a straw pallet and blankets and pillows to support his head.

'Do you think you could bear to stay with him, in case he wakes?' I said to Bess, knowing I was asking her to do something I was not at all sure I'd have been able to do myself. 'If he cries out he will endanger us all.'

Bess nodded fearfully. She squeezed herself up against the wall, took her brother's hand. Her half-brother, I reminded myself. My half-brother. It was odd to think that Thomas was as much my kin as he was Bess's. We were both his sisters, which made it feel almost as if she and I were related, were sisters, too, as I had always felt that we were.

I brought a jug of ale, a plate of bread and cheese and some custard tarts, as well as a chamber pot, a small stool and a spare candle. 'That should see you through until I can come back again tomorrow night,' I said. 'Is there anything else you want me to fetch?'

Bess shook her head then grabbed my arm as I turned to crawl back out and leave them. 'Thank you,' she murmured. 'I know what a risk you are taking for us.'

'We are all taking the most terrible risk, Bess. By sheltering a man who, in the eyes of the law, is guilty of treason, we are committing treason too. If we should be caught we will burn, or hang, or be beheaded as enemies of the crown. You do realise that?'

'What else could we do?'

I fitted the panelling into place and rested my back against it, glancing up the dark stairwell to where Richard must still be sleeping, oblivious to what I had done. Arthur Knight touched my arm as if too overcome with gratitude to speak. 'It is nearly dawn,' I said to him. 'Go home before anyone sees you here.'

I walked weakly up the stairs. Only when I sank down on the edge of the bed did I realise my legs were trembling uncontrollably. I felt sick . . . sick to my stomach and sick to my heart. I made myself take long, deep breaths, like I did when I was ill whilst carrying Forest. I realised then I had been feeling sick on and off for days, that my monthly was late. How late? I saw that my nightgown was stained with Thomas's blood and with sudden horror tore it off, bundled it up and pushed it under the bed. I climbed naked under the sheets and nestled up close to Richard, resting my cold cheek against the smooth dark hairs on his warm chest. He stirred, gathered me into his arms and turned on to his side. I felt his cock probing my belly, stiff as a cudgel. He found my hand, guided it down and I wrapped my fingers around him.

He sucked his breath in with a hiss. 'Hell's teeth, where have you been, Nell? Your fingers are icy. It's all right,' he added quickly with a smile in his voice, grabbing me as I went to withdraw my hand. 'I don't mind if you warm them on me.'

He mounted me, looked down into my eyes with love and desire, and I felt so deceitful, was so sure that he would read my deception, was so afraid of having him read it, that I averted my face.

He froze.

I turned back to him, saw his hurt. 'Richard, I need to tell you something,' I said. But he tensed, as if he suspected what it might be, and the words lodged in my throat.

At my sudden silence, he pushed himself up on his arms, pinning me beneath him, his hipbones jutting painfully into my belly. 'I am listening.'

I felt totally trapped. How could I keep such a dangerous secret from him? How could I tell him the truth when I had already broken my word to him? I could not tell him Thomas was my half-brother when I could scarce yet comprehend it myself.

'I feel sick,' I said, feebly but truthfully. 'Let me up.'

He released me, sat with me as I gulped in deep breaths, waiting until I looked to be recovered before he pressed me again. 'What is it that you need to tell me, Nell?'

I rested my hand on my belly. 'Nothing,' I said. 'It was nothing.' I could not even tell him that I thought I might be carrying his child.

'I heard at the inn last night that Monmouth has been executed at Tower Hill,' he said quietly. 'It is over now. Thank God, it is all over.'

But I knew, by the way he hurled back the covers, that he had seen, rightly, that I could not share his relief, not at all, and that he believed, wrongly, that it was because I wished the outcome had been different.

I assumed that Richard had gone for a swim. It was not the first time that he had been driven out of the warmth of our bed to the coldness of the sea, as if by unnamed demons he could only seem to banish with an early-morning dunking in the waves. I had tried not to dwell on what it was that he seemed to need to wash away after he had lain with me, what he needed to cool, to exorcise, but this time I knew all too well, and this time it did not seem to have worked. Always previously he had returned before I was even dressed. Now it was mid-morning and still he was not back.

I took Mary to fly her kite on the moor, anything to be out of that house, where my eyes constantly drifted to the panel by the fireplace in the great hall.

'Higher,' Mary kept begging. 'Higher.' And I reeled the kite out further, shielding my eyes to watch it soar into the infinite blue as still it tugged and tugged against its tether to be free. Then the wind suddenly dropped and it plummeted to the ground, landing with a crash that I felt in my very bones.

Mary ran with it and threw it back into the sky, but it was not quite windy enough to get it properly airborne again. I suggested to the children that we ride out to Ladye Bay, but I did not find Richard there as once I had done. I sat on the clifftop and watched Mary and Forest down on the beach, skimming flat pebbles across the waves. Gulls screamed, the sound harsh and desolate, and I felt the first prickle of fear. What if, in his anger, Richard had swum out too far, had not been as alert as he should have been to the currents and the undertow? I tried not to think of how he could have been dragged out to sea, his body hurled against the rocks.

I tried not to think of the treason trials that were already underway, but now that I myself was amongst the guilty, all that I had read in the gazettes over the past weeks seemed suddenly very vivid.

The trials had begun in earnest at Dorchester where three hundred and forty were brought to court accused of rebellion. They were pipemakers and yeomen, tailors and butchers and merchants, ordinary men who'd had no real craving for another revolution. To serve as the most awful warning to all would-be rebels, many of the condemned were to be taken down from the gallows before they were quite dead, to have their entrails drawn out of them and their bodies butchered. And so that none might miss out on the spectacle, these most gruesome of executions were taking place at crossroads and market places and village greens all across the West Country. Heads and limbs were being boiled in salt and tarred for preservation and public display. The streets of Somersetshire were running with blood again, and it seemed to me that even here the very air reeked of decomposing corpses.

The danger of discovery seemed greater now that the Assizes had come closer, to Wells. Of the five hundred and forty arraigned, five hundred and eighteen were accused of levying war against the King. The fortunate ones were sentenced to transportation to the plantations of Barbados and Jamaica. A hundred were to be hanged, as widely as possible, in Wells and in Bath. And at Bristol.

My eye was caught by a tawny and black butterfly and my mind latched on to it, my time-honoured salvation from sorrow and distress. The wing patterns were subtly but crucially different from the Marsh Fritillaries that frequented the moor and a Straw May Fritillary James had once drawn for me. They were redder. This one was more orange and had unusual white and black spotted tips to the forewings. There was another, just the same, just as different from all the fritillaries I had seen before, on the wing or even on paper. I swiped at it almost angrily and felled it, stowed it away in the pocket I wore fastened round my waist, called down to the children that we were going home.

I was sitting on the windowseat, watching the mist curling off the river, when Richard finally stumbled in, none too steady on his feet.

'Where have you been?' I asked him.

'Bristol,' he offered too readily, his voice slightly slurred. He unbuckled his sword, threw it down with a clatter on the table. 'The talk there is all of the treason trials. People are calling them the Bloody Assizes.'

'Please, Richard. Not now.'

He came to stand over me. 'Where are they, Nell?' he said very low.

'Who?'

'You know damn well who. Ned Tucker and Thomas Knight. Do you take me for a fool? That is what you almost told me this morning, isn't it? You know where they are, don't you?'

'No.' The lie had come to my lips of its own volition.

He said no more, nor did he move. He seemed to be waiting for me to reconsider and to say something else. When I did not, he flung the latest copy of the gazette at me, calling for Bess to bring him a bath in front of the chamber fire.

My eyes strayed to the print. Tentatively, I reached out my hand and picked up the news-sheet. What I read made me tremble so much I had to rest it on my lap in order to finish it.

Chief Justice Jeffreys and his judges are determined to show no mercy to the harbourers of fugitives. Lady Alice Lisle, widow of a man who had sat in the High Court of Justice, was accused of sheltering an escaped rebel, a dissenting minister, who had not even been tried himself. At any sign of sympathy Judge Jeffreys swore and cursed in a language no well-bred man would use at a cockfight, and he decreed that Widow Lisle should receive the only sentence possible for a woman condemned for high treason, that she was to be burned alive. Ladies of high rank tried to intercede and a plea for mercy was made by no less than the Duke of Clarendon, the King's own brother. On account of the widow's age, the sentence was commuted from burning to beheading and Lady Lisle was put to death on the scaffold in the market place at Winchester. She suffered her fate with serenity and courage.

After a while, I don't know how long, I made myself go up to Richard. He had undressed and climbed into the steaming, scented water. He was resting against the linen-draped back of the tub, arms extended along the sides, his eyes shut, dark lashes casting little shadows over his cheeks in the firelight. His black curls framed his pale face, lovely as a seraph's. I kneeled at the side of the tub, leaned over and kissed his closed lids, felt the lashes brush my lips.

He opened his eyes languorously, looked at me questioningly, sadly, and I was so near to confiding in him, so longed to confide in him. And the reason I did not quite dare was not that I did not love him enough, but that I loved him too much and the thought of losing him, of having him be angry with me and disappointed in me, was utterly intolerable.

In silence I ladled water over his head, soaped his back for him. I rubbed the tension from his shoulders with my fingers. I dried his hair with fresh linen. I acted the part of a dutiful and devoted wife, when I had so betrayed my husband that I had put both our lives in jeopardy.

Like the conspirator I was, I waited for darkness, waited until Richard was safely sleeping, and then I slid from the warmth of his arms and of our bed, creeping down the draughty stone stairwell to mix up an ointment of egg yolk, oil of roses and turpentine. I pulled back the oak panel, ducked through into the cramped little cell and tried not to gag at the smell that had tainted the confined space.

Bess was sitting on the little stool beside her brother, my brother.

'How is he?'

'Awake at least. He has taken a little bread and some cheese.'

Thomas's narrow eyes flared feral and dark in the gloom, like a wounded, cornered animal. My mother's son. I did not think I should ever be able to think of him in those terms.

'Hello, Thomas.' I knelt down beside him, carefully lifted his shirt to examine him.

His skin glistened with sweat.

'He has a fever,' Bess said.

'It is poison from the wound.'

'Shouldn't he be bled?'

I shook my head. 'From the look of him, he has already lost enough blood.'

I started to remove the bandages, but he grabbed hold of my wrist with startling strength.

I looked at him. 'I'm sorry if I hurt you.'

'Why are you helping me?' He looked at me with the black eyes of my son: Forest's eyes, proud and antagonistic and hungry. I knew now it was no coincidence that they looked so alike. This man was my son's uncle.

'I am helping you for Bess's sake. And because of what your father told me,' I said matter-of-factly. 'But don't worry,' I smiled wryly. 'I'll not expect you suddenly to start showering me with brotherly affection.' I twisted my arm free and carried on with my task. 'Now, I have to change your bandages and would advise you to hold still or it will hurt even more.'

For the first time in years I felt an urge to write to James Petiver. Though he was the very last person to boast of his abilities, I knew he was as skilled as any surgeon and many a physician. I craved his advice and reassurance, needed to know that I was treating Thomas's wound properly, doing all I could possibly do to speed his recovery and hasten the day when he was fit enough to leave Tickenham for a safer refuge.

I was at my writing table, composing the letter. There was no way of knowing if it might be intercepted and I could not risk implicating James in any way, so I was searching for a way to ask him indirectly about the treatment of deep wounds when Richard surprised me. 'Who is James?' he asked coldly, catching the salutation.

Guiltily, I whipped my arm across the letter to shield its contents from him, for all the world as if it had been a secret love letter.

'Who is he, Nell?'

I must have seemed to be behaving so oddly these past days that I did not blame him at all for being suspicious. 'James is a butterfly collector,' I said. 'I have corresponded with him for years. About butterflies,' I added unnecessarily.

'The constable is here,' he said darkly. 'Along with two lackeys armed with muskets.'

I felt as if it was I who had been wounded, so mortally that the blood was draining very quickly from my head and from my legs. At a loss as to what else to do with it, I folded the letter very small and pushed it down the tight-boned bodice of my dress. Then I walked to the door and greeted the constable, trying to appear as if I had nothing to hide, nothing at all to fear.

I knew John Piggott, a stocky, florid, self-important little man who strode about the village sticking his purple-veined nose where it was not wanted. He was clearly enjoying the even more elevated position he held with two armed men accompanying him.

'How can we help you, Mr Piggott?' I had not quite stilled the tremor in my voice.

'Routine inspection,' he said self-righteously, stepping past me, out of the steadily falling rain and into the hall, his hands clasped behind his back. He pulled himself up straight and glanced around as if to show he meant business. 'We're on the hunt for that scoundrel Thomas Knight. He's not shown up as yet in the prisons or on the death roll.' He pushed his face up closer to mine. 'Not seen him by any chance, have you, Ma'am?'

I shook my head, my mouth dry as ash. A cold bead of sweat trickled down my back. I glanced at Richard. His jaw was clenched and a muscle in his cheek began to twitch. He had not taken his eyes off me, was watching me even more closely than was the constable.

'This would be the last place Thomas Knight would come,' I managed.

'As you know, it was not so long ago that he led a mob up here and threatened to set fire to the house, while my children were asleep in their beds.'

'His sister's still your maid, though, isn't she? Wouldn't mind having a word with her, if she's about?'

'She's in the dairy. But she'll not be able to tell you any more than I have. Her brother is not here, nor has he ever been.'

'Forgive me if I don't take your word for it, madam. I'll have a look around the place, if I may?'

I stood back as they swarmed all over the house, searching every room. They threw open the doors of the court cupboard and turned over tables, pulled the tapestries off the walls and dragged drapes down from the windows. I heard their boots stamping about upstairs and sounds that indicated they were throwing up the lid of every chest, opening every garderobe, jabbing their muskets under every bed. Next they turned their attention to the new stables and the hayloft and the pigsty and chicken shed, kicking at hay bales, upending feeding troughs.

All the time Richard watched not the constable and his men but me, as if this wanton destruction of our property was nothing compared to what I had so wantonly destroyed.

Little Mary ran to me and tried to hide herself in my skirts. 'Why is the constable here, Mama?'

I stroked her hair and did not let myself think of what would happen to her if they found something now, or later, that gave me away. I did not let myself think what would happen to my children if their mother and stepfather died as traitors.

John Piggott came back to the hall, breathless and frustrated. 'Your maid broke down at mention of her brother's name. Either she is grief-stricken or guilt-stricken, but I can get no sense out of her at all. Maybe we'll pay a call on the old Knight woman and her husband again.'

'Leave them be,' I said. 'They know nothing. Have given their son up for dead.'

'Then they're right,' Mr Piggott snorted. 'He won't be able to hide forever. If he's not dead already, he'll be swinging by his neck soon enough.'

They left us amidst the upheaval. I stroked Mary's head and told her it was all over now, even though I knew it was not.

'I never realised you had such a talent for lying,' Richard said darkly.

'You were very convincing. Except that I can read your face like a page in a book. You did not convince me at all.'

Mary clung so close to me that she trod on the hem of my skirt and I could not move. Richard thrust his hand roughly down the front of my bodice, his nails scratching me, and retrieved my half-written letter to James. I tried to grab it off him but he turned his back on me, fluttered it high out of my reach as he read. When he had done, he screwed it into a tight ball, opened his fist and dropped it to the floor. 'Show me where you keep him.'

Holding Mary gently away from me, I turned and walked very calmly to the fireplace. I was almost relieved to have it done with now, for the secret to be out, but my heart was hammering so hard I was sure it would burst through my ribcage. I glanced at Richard as I dug my fingers into the wainscoting and pulled back the entrance to the priest's hole, standing aside to let him enter, just as Bess came running in to the great hall.

Richard made no sound at all, but stared down at Thomas who lay on the soiled pallet, shielding his eyes from the sudden burst of light. As if he had seen more than enough and was suffocating, Richard staggered back.

He went to the window, raised his arm and leaned against the lintel to steady himself. He balled his hand into a fist and smashed it into the rough stone above his head with a ferocity that made me flinch. 'I always knew there was something between you and that sprat,' he growled, turning to me. 'I'll bet he's enjoyed having you sneaking down to his grubby little lair to minister to him in the middle of the night. I'll bet you've both enjoyed it. Well, I shall see to it that you enjoy it no more. Or rather, John Piggott will see to it. By making sure Knight swings. If you do not want to join him, I suggest you turn him out now, so that he is far enough away from here by the time he is caught.'

I did not dare to dismiss this as an idle threat. I had never seen Richard so angry. I knew that he was hurt, desperately hurt, and was not a person to manage such emotions easily. He was liable to lash out, to do something rash that he might later regret.

He was already at the door, had banged it closed behind him.

I came to my senses, leapt to my feet, hurled the door open again. 'You are right,' I called after him. 'There *is* something between me and Thomas.'

He halted, spun round to face me.

It was still raining, a cold grey rain that was fast turning the ground outside the house into a sea of mud. His hair was already wet and he did not have a coat or cloak. I walked towards him, oblivious of the deepening puddles, soaking the hem of my silk gown.

'There always has been something between me and Thomas,' I said, having to raise my voice above the hammering of the rain. 'Only I never knew it until a few nights ago, when his father told me, in order to persuade me to give him shelter rather than turn him out as I fully intended to do. Richard, Thomas is my half-brother. My mother's illegitimate son.'

He looked at me as if he didn't believe me.

'It is perfectly true, sir,' Bess said from behind me.

'I beg you, Richard, let him go. You have no cause to be jealous of Thomas. He was born first, and born a boy, but I have Tickenham Court while he has nothing. Because of that he hates me, has always hated me.'

'But still you would beg me to spare his life?'

'He is my brother,' I said, giving weight to the word. 'He is Bess's brother.'

The rain fell like a shroud between us. The anger had gone from Richard's face. It had been replaced by . . . nothing. There was an emptiness in his eyes, a deadness, as if my deception had killed something in him.

He turned from me, towards the stables and his horse.

'It is not safe for Thomas to stay here,' I told Bess. 'Not for any of us.'

'Mr Glanville will not betray us?'

'No,' I said, my voice faltering. 'He will not. He had a brother once. He knows what it is to lose one. He will not bring about the death of yours and mine. But the constable will not give up.'

'Tom is not strong enough to ride.'

'I know he is not. You must take the cart for him to lie in. But you must leave, Bess. As soon as it is dark.'

Like smugglers with an illegal cargo, we bundled Thomas into the cart under cover of night. We laid down straw to muffle the sound of the wheels on the cobbles and wrapped rags around the horse's hooves. We used more straw and blankets to cushion the cart and make Thomas as warm and comfortable as possible.

I packed up a basket of bread and cheese, cold meat and fruit, and gave Bess all the coins I had in my pocketbook.

'Where will you go?' I asked her, as she climbed on to the seat of the cart and took up the reins.

'The same place you run to whenever you are in trouble,' she said bravely. 'To Mary and John Burges in Hackney. Nobody will ever find us there, or think to look for us even. Mary and John will help us.'

They would, even though they were Catholic and Thomas had been wounded for his hatred of them. They would help him because they were good people, who offered love and respect to every person, no matter what their creed or character. 'You take care, Bess,' I said with a glance at Thomas. I hoped he survived long enough for me to have at least some time in which to ponder our new-discovered relationship.

Once the cart had trundled out of the yard, I wasted no time in dragging the soiled pallet out of the priest hole and into the stable. I rolled up my sleeves and brought a bucket of water and a cloth. I bunched my silk skirts beneath my knees on the dirty floor and scrubbed and scrubbed at that incommodious little hole, as if I could scrub away all that had happened. It was almost daybreak when I was satisfied that all evidence of Thomas's presence there was obliterated. Almost daybreak, and still Richard had not come back. I was sure he must have gone to the inn in Bristol, taken a room there for the night. There was only one thing to do, I decided. If he was not coming home to me, I would go to him. I would beg his forgiveness, fetch him back. It was my fault and I would put it right.

The children ran out into the yard as I mounted up. Forest asked me where I was going.

'To Bristol, darling. I will not be long.'

'Are you going to see the hangings?' he asked with a hint of glee that was, I knew, prompted by his devotion to Richard, whose enemies the hanged men had been. 'I heard the servants talking,' he qualified. 'It is to be today.'

'I am not going to see the hangings, Forest.' I gave a jerk on my mare's reins, then spun her back. 'You didn't happen to hear where in Bristol, exactly?'

He shook his head.

I knew well before I reached the city walls that I had come the wrong way. A pall of death hung over the wide new streets. Bristol was the richest trading port in Britain, with the exception of London, but the usual bustle and colour of it was sadly diminished. People walked by with faces downcast and gloomy. The sledges drawing the heavy goods and the merchants in their fine coaches did not seem to be going about their business with the same zest. I rode up towards the Redcliffe Gate, towards the church where Richard and I were married. I had paid no attention then to the oddly truncated tower that had famously been struck by lightning over a hundred years ago and never rebuilt, but now it seemed like an ill-omened portent. As ill-omened as the crack in the Table of Commandments in the church where I'd married Edmund, or as Monmouth's rebellion beginning during the celebrations for my second wedding.

The ghastly structure of the gallows cast its shadow over Redcliffe Hill. Six executions had taken place, only six, a small fraction of the number being put to death all across the West. But they made a grisly display, hanging from the noose, with their tongues dark and lolling, their breeches stained with the final voiding of their bowels and bladders, their faces contorted into fixed, grotesque grimaces. A punishment as horrible as any you could find in Hell. All the more terrible because I knew it could have been me swinging from that cross beam; could still be the punishment that awaited me for what I had done.

I rode across the bridge over the Avon, saw the docks spiked with the masts of the ships that had blown into port from the Caribbean and the tropics, the scent of adventure still in their sails, and a part of me wished that I could just sail away with them. I rode on towards the elegant new houses on King Street that had been built for the merchants in the reclaimed marsh area by the quayside. Past the Merchant Venturers' Hall and opposite the almshouses was a row of half-timbered buildings with overhanging eaves and projecting gables. The last in the row was the Llandoger Trow, the inn I knew Richard had frequented on the many past occasions when he had tried to see me and I had turned him away.

With its low blackened ceiling and sawdust-strewn floor, it was a rough sort of a place behind its grand façade, a dark place where it was not difficult to imagine dark deeds being done. Mr Merrick had told me its position so close to the docks made it the haunt of slave traders and smugglers and pirates and it was easy to believe, judging by the gang of low characters sharing tankards of ale with my husband. He did not look particularly at ease amongst them, nor did he look particularly at ease with the buxom fair-haired woman who had her arm draped provocatively around his neck, but he was letting her keep it there.

I was torn between a desire to rush at her and scratch her eyes out and the need to turn away, to pretend I had not seen them together. For a moment I just watched them, unwilling and totally unable to go any closer, my mind in an agony of paralysed confusion. She was expensively but gaudily dressed in a low-cut crimson gown, her face painted and patched. For all that, she looked like me, I realised, albeit a bigger and brasher version. She was not gentry, but clearly prosperous, the widow or daughter, wife even, of a merchant or lawyer or goldsmith. One of the new moneyed class who were gaining dominance and power in England, who understood the getting and the making of money and whose collective wealth already surpassed that of the impoverished nobility. A natural choice for a man who liked to be on the winning side, I thought bitterly. Merchants and lawyers were not ruined by bad harvests and unpaid rents. They were busily building new mansions instead of borrowing to repair crumbling ones.

There were enough women occupying the inn's benches to make my arrival relatively inconspicuous. Nobody paid me much attention, beyond pinching me as I made my way over. Richard saw me but did not acknowledge me, though the girl did. She sized me up, as if measuring me against her expectations and finding me even more negligible than she had imagined. She moved away, casting me a supercilious look. 'You know where to find me if you want me,' she said seductively to Richard, trailing her fingers along his chest.

'Do you want her, Richard?' I found myself asking, forcing the question through the tightness in my throat. 'Or have you already satisfied your wanting?'

He called the landlady over to refill his pot. 'Sarah is just a friend. As you say that butterfly collector is yours. Surely you can have no objection to that?'

'James and I became friends and have remained so because we share a common interest. What interest do you share with that trollop, I wonder?'

'Gaming,' he said. 'Sarah has a great liking for cards and dicing.'

She was watching me with hatred, because I had him and she did not.

He was a man to inspire the fiercest jealousy and I was afraid of the jealousy I saw in that woman's eyes. Even if Richard did not want her, I knew beyond a shadow of a doubt that she wanted him, very much, and with the inexplicable intuition that women have for the characters of other women, I sensed she had made it, or intended to make it, nigh on impossible for him to resist her. Given half a chance she would dig her claws into him and rip us apart. She was opportunistic, scheming, not at all kind. There was a hardness, an almost chilling coldness, about her, which made me desperate to get us both far, far away from her. 'She is not your friend, Richard,' I said to him softly. 'These people are not your friends.'

He stared into his pot, swilled the ale, drank. 'It seems I have no others.'

'Oh, that is not true.' I reached out to touch the back of his hand, thinking that I had never known anyone feel things so deeply, take everything so personally. 'I am your friend. I shall always, always be your friend. I would have told you about Thomas,' I said in a low voice. 'I so wanted to tell you. I did not want to keep it from you. If only you had not become so embittered towards the rebels.'

'If only you had not risked your life and mine to save one of them.'

'You said you did not want to lose me,' I said quietly, seeking his eyes. 'Do not let this battle become ours.'

'It is you who have allowed that. It is you who harboured a traitor under our roof without telling me. Ah, but I forget. It is *your* roof, isn't it?'

I was stunned that he should bring that up now and shrank back a little from him. 'Does that still rankle with you so much?'

'It rankles that I have a wife who cares so little for my wishes and feelings.'

'If that is true, why am I here?'

'I don't know. Why are you?'

I knew that the best thing I could do was to say no more, to turn my back on him and walk away. That is just what I did. With tears streaming down my face and my heart breaking, I mounted my horse and rode back down Redcliffe Hill, past the bodies of the executed rebels, swinging from the gibbet.

So much damage had been done to this county, I feared it would never recover. So much damage had been done to my marriage, I feared it would never recover either. I still had not told Richard I was carrying his child.

As I rode out past St Mary Redcliffe, the low autumn sun appeared from behind a cloud. A butterfly fluttered beside me, the kind that James and I had named Tortoiseshells, with bright red and blue shining wings. This one, though, was faded and ragged, like most of its kind at the end of the summer. But it flitted along beside me for a while, playing on the breeze that blew in from the estuary.

For all its faded wings, it was a symbol of hope, and I was always very willing to let hope enter my heart. The butterfly reminded me that there was still brightness and beauty in the world. It reminded me how happy I had been on my wedding day, such a short time ago.

Judge Jeffreys was returning to London. The Bloody Assizes were over. These had been dark days for all who lived in Somersetshire, but maybe they were at an end. Maybe the Battle of Sedgemoor would be the last we would see fought on England's soil for a while. Maybe Richard would find a way to lay past battles to rest, and I would find a way to win back his trust.

Anything was possible. Even that my husband would come galloping after me not long after I had passed through the city gates and turned on to the open road.

I heard the distant thud of a horse's hooves behind me but hardly dared to turn round and risk disappointment. I counted to ten, closed my eyes and made a quick wish, then glanced quickly over my shoulder and laughed with delight to see him, some way off still, his cloak flying behind him, the hooves of his stallion kicking up a small cloud of dust. I had just enough time to wipe away my tears and arrange the heavy skirts of my gown and cape so that they draped more appealingly around me before he reined in alongside, the tumult causing my mount to sidle. I glanced at him out of the corner of my eye.

'Why did you not slow down, Nell?' he demanded, but good-humouredly. His dark mood had dispersed as completely as mist burned away by sunshine and he was all gentle, devastating charm again. It was very unnerving and exhilarating at the same time, like skating on melting ice. I had once lived such a dull and quiet life, but never would it be dull with him.

I gave him a sidelong smile. 'I did not slow, but you will note that nor did I urge my horse into a gallop to try and outrace you. Not that I would now,' I said meaningfully, resting a hand on my belly. 'I must ride with care these next eight months.'

There was a brief silence. 'How long have you known?' Richard asked me.

'Not long.'

'Is that why you came to fetch me back? Because you are with child?'

I cocked my head, glanced at him sideways. 'Well, it is true I would not rob another of my babies of the chance to know the man who sired them,' I said. 'Nor would I wish to rob Forest of another father, after he has already lost one.'

'I see.'

I reached out, waited for him to do the same, felt his fingers catch mine and hold on.

'More pressing than that, love,' I said, 'is the fact that I cannot be another night without you.'

He gave me his most raffish smile and after a while said, 'Do you know what we should do?'

'What's that?'

'Some more shopping, I think. If you want to make absolutely sure I come home to you every night, we must see to it that your home is as inviting and pleasing as your own little person. And at present it is still as austere as a nun's cell.'

Spring 1686

It troubled me that for some reason the news that I was carrying his child did not seem to make Richard nearly as happy as I had assumed it would. Where Edmund had anticipated the arrival of our children with real excitement, had been almost overly solicitous towards me and quietly so very proud, Richard did his utmost to ignore my pregnancy, even as my expanding belly made that increasingly impossible.

I remembered how longingly he had looked at me at Forest's baptism, how he had spoken with such yearning of the children it seemed then that we would never have. I remembered what a good father he had been to Edmund's son and could make no sense of it at all. I wondered if deep down he was still upset with me, for the way I had shunned him after Edmund's death, for deceiving him by giving shelter to Thomas Knight. Or was it something else?

He had made no further mention of shopping, and I kept quiet about it. Even in the mid stages of pregnancy, the last thing I needed was to be jolted in a coach all the way to London and back. I soon found out, though, that my husband had never intended for us to do our shopping as we had before, with an expedition to the New Exchange. His aborted foray with the militia had not been entirely unfruitful. It seemed that he'd spent most of the journey to Axminster talking to John Smythe about the new craze for bestowing money and labour on the task of beautifying mansions and gardens.

'John's sister Florence has an eye for furnishing rooms with all that is being called modern,' Richard told me as I hunted in a trunk for Forest's whipping top and little drum to pass down to the new baby. 'But she does not waste time traipsing round to different merchants. She just sends a list of what she wants to an agent in London, a cousin who has a room at the Inns of Court. He does all the buying for her and ships everything up here.'

'How convenient.' I stood and stretched, my hands supporting the small of my aching back.

Richard caught me lovingly around my waist, but when he felt its growing girth, which had necessitated the loosening of the laces of my stomacher again, he let go of me just as swiftly, as if he did not wish to be reminded. 'I spoke to Florence some time ago and she kindly added some items for us to her list,' he said. 'She is sending them over later today.'

'That's good.' I studied his face. 'Richard, you are glad we are going to have a baby?'

'Of course I am, sweetheart.' But his eyes, sliding away from the sight of me, seemed to tell a different story.

During the following weeks dozens of consignments of boxes arrived on wagons from Ashton Court, with Florence Smythe trotting over on her pretty mare to escort them, after which Richard escorted her around the house, his hand courteously upon her elbow as she pointed with her elegant, painted leather gloved fingers to one wall or corner or another, suggesting where the new looking glass might hang or where the clock and French glassware and Chinese porcelain might stand.

As I watched them together I was surprised to feel a stirring of jealousy. I knew it had to do with the fact that something was still not right between Richard and me, and that I did not know what it was or how to make it better. I found myself wondering about that woman in Bristol. Sarah. What was she to him? What had she been to him? All those years, when I had kept him from my bed and he had gone to find solace at that Bristol inn, had he comforted himself with more than just a bottle of rum? He must have done sometimes, if not with her then with someone else. And why should he not? But had he continued to see her since we were married? Had he seen her again since I had discovered them together? No. I was quite sure the answer to those questions was no. I did not listen to the voice in my head that said: *How can you trust him? His morals are not your morals. He was raised amongst Cavaliers.*

I was at least sure that Florence Smythe was no threat whatsoever. She didn't consider it even worth flirting with anyone who was not of the highest rank, much as Richard clearly sought her regard, as, of course, he had always sought everyone's, male and female, yeoman and gentleman, simply because he needed so badly to be loved.

He looked over at me now, from where he stood beside the new japanned table at the far corner of the room. Florence was chattering away to him, but I could tell he was only half listening and his smile was for me alone. I smiled back. Rationalist that I was, doubter of magic, I'd have sworn there was magic in that smile of his. Just one smile and instantly all my worries were laid to rest. Just one smile, and all was well with the world once more.

I ran my hands over a pretty toilet set, comprising a mirror and basket and candlesticks set in silver with scenes of Chinoiserie. I had always wanted to see these rooms filled with bright and pretty things. It was worth mort-gaging some of our land to have silk quilts and striped muslin curtains; worth being indebted to the Gorges of Wraxall as well as to William Merrick for a house filled with silk damask-covered armchairs and stools with tapestry cushions. I tried not to worry too much about the growing tangle of credit and mortgages within which Richard was enmeshing us. We could afford them. He said we could. As long as the rents kept rolling in and the harvests were good and the fisheries prospered. After the recent upheavals, nobody had the stomach even to mention drainage.

Florence stayed for tea served from our new silver tea service.

'John said you were considering remodelling the house and garden,' she said to my husband, sipping politely from her cup. 'You could turn your great hall into a stylish entrance lobby, and your land is positively crying out for vistas and terraces and avenues and a fountain.'

'What need have we for a fountain when for half the year we have a whole lake to look at?' I asked, a bit alarmed at the prospect of such expensive and grandiose schemes.

She shrugged and stood to leave. 'Well, be sure to let me know what else you want.'

Richard assured her that he would.

'We should have asked for more mirrors,' I said to him when she had gone. I loved the way that, even propped against the wall, waiting to be hung, they filled the rooms with light and make them look as if they went on and on. I studied my own silvery reflection, framed by gilded carving, then turned sideways and stroked the luminous folds of my saffron gown where it fell over my rounded stomach. 'I could fill the whole house with mirrors,' I added. 'If only it did not mean I should be confronted with my great belly at every turn.'

Richard came to stand behind me, slipped his arms over mine and linked our fingers. I pressed back against him, relishing the intimacy, relishing even more the fact that we were both cradling our unborn child. He looked into my reflected eyes. 'Your belly is beautiful to me, Nell,' he said.

'Is it?'

He swept aside my hair, kissed the nape of my neck. 'You are so beautiful, my Nell, it is only right that you should have beautiful things all around you.'

'These are fitting surroundings, then, in which to raise your child?'

His body tensed against mine. 'My first-born,' he said. 'Who will be born into a house we have made beautiful, a house to which he or she will have no claim.'

Now I thought I understood the problem at last. And I had already considered this. Very carefully. 'Our son or daughter will have Elmsett Manor,' I reminded him, twisting round in his arms to look at him properly. 'A Glanville child will inherit the Glanville estate, which is as it should be. You must take us to see Elmsett, just as soon as the baby is born.'

'There is nothing worth seeing,' said Richard, letting go of me. 'Nothing but a small moated manor left to rot during the Commonwealth.'

'Then we shall restore it, or have a new house built on the land.'

'I would have liked the very best for my children,' he said, a peculiar lifelessness in his eyes. 'But even my first-born must take second place.'

Summer 1687

The birth of Richard's first child, my third, was so swift and easy compared to the previous two that I found it quite exhilarating, would almost go so far as to say I enjoyed it. Perhaps it was because the baby was smaller than either of Edmund's babies had been. It was a boy, and I suggested he be named after his father, hoping it would encourage Richard to take an interest in him. Though Dickon, as he was known to avoid confusion, did not resemble his father in any way.

He looked exactly like me, flaxen haired and blue-eyed, with skin that turned honey-coloured at the first touch of the sun and was prone to a faint dusting of freckles. From the moment he was born it was clear he had my inquisitiveness too, but a gentler, more patient, altogether sweeter version of it.

It was a joy to me to encourage his interest in the world, to take him down to the moor to see the dragonflies and the otters and show him all the things I had so enjoyed being shown as a child. He was far too young as yet to comprehend how the black dots in the gelatinous spheres of frogspawn were growing tails and then legs, but I told him anyway, and it renewed my own passion for transformation. Dickon seemed to like the hatchlings best of all, the fluffy flotillas of cygnets and ducklings that glided up and down the rhynes.

My own little flock was growing rapidly. I had quickly fallen pregnant again, as half the country rejoiced in expectation of a first child being born to King James, while the other half dreaded the securing of a Catholic succession.

'The country may not be entirely united with the King in hoping for a boy but I must certainly hope you and I have another one.' Richard smiled at me as he kicked off his riding boots and pulled his shirt off over his head.

I was eating a bowl of cherries, lounging on the bolsters in my bodice and petticoat, with one hand resting on the mound of my belly. 'I am surprised you even have a preference,' I said, unable to help sounding critical. 'You barely notice poor little Dickon. I am sure he knows, young as he is, that Forest is your favourite. Why d'you want another son?'

I had not meant to sound so sharp and tensed in readiness for one of Richard's tempers. Instead, he threw himself down next to me on the bed, naked save for his breeches, and held another cherry to my lips for me to bite.

'You gave Edmund a son and then a daughter,' he said with a facetiousness that was almost worse than anger, that I did not like in him at all. 'I have followed him into your bed but I do not wish to follow in every one of his rather shambling footsteps. I should like you to give me two sons.'

I flicked his hand away crossly. 'For God's sake, Richard, why must you turn everything into a contest?' I stared up at the tester, rolled my head towards him and dared myself to say: 'You know, sometimes when you say such things, I cannot help but wonder if you only wanted me in the first place to prove that you could take me from Edmund.'

That silenced him, though he did not appear particularly surprised or shocked by my accusation. Nor did he deny it. We simply looked at each other, as if we had reached some kind of an impasse. Then he slipped his hand down inside my bodice, began to tease my nipple with his thumb. 'Not much of a contest, was it?'

I gave a gasp, jerked away from him. 'What's wrong with you? That's a horrible thing to say.' I had never seen him like this before, never heard him sound so cynical.

He tried to pull me nearer to him again but I would not let him. 'Why are you angry with me all the time, Richard? Is it still because of those years when I would not see you?'

'No.'

'Thomas Knight?'

'No.'

'What then?'

His eyes dwelt upon my face and he seemed to want to say something, struggling with himself for a moment, as if unsure of whether to speak or not, or else of how to frame the words.

'Talk to me, Richard,' I said more gently. 'Whatever it is, you can tell me.'

But he couldn't, clearly. I saw him give up almost despairingly. 'Forget what I said about Edmund, Nell. I'm sorry. Please, forget it, can't you?'

'I wish you'd say what is making you unhappy.' I faced another possibility then, asking quietly, 'Is it her? Do you want to be with her?'

'Who? What are you talking about?'

'That woman in Bristol.' I made myself say her name. 'Sarah.'

'Hell, no.' He smiled, almost with relief it seemed, as if for a brief moment, my jealousy had made him feel much better. He touched my lips. 'It's you I want, Nell. And I am not unhappy. So long as I have you, then I am quite contented.'

I smiled and frowned at the same time, because it was said with honesty and earnestness, and yet for all that he had said he was content, he looked so burdened.

'You are the most puzzling person I have ever met.'

'Am I?'

'You are.'

I let him run his fingers enticingly up my petticoat. His eyes were concentrating intently on my face, watching to see me slowly relax under his touch, as if he was determined to turn every skill he had to making me give myself up to him, as if that might make everything all right. And who was I to deny it? Maybe it could, for a while at least. My eyes slid closed and my lips parted as he worked his fingers to pleasure me, until I was lost, whimpering and writhing on a knife-edge of ecstasy and agony. He somehow knew the exact moment when I was certain I could bear no more but was also equally desperate for it never to end, and then abruptly he stopped what he was doing, began instead to torment me with his tongue until he brought me back to the summit again. It was the most exquisite kind of torture.

'Is there anything wrong with wanting to have the best and be the best?' he whispered sweetly, seductively, as he entered me.

'You are the best, love,' I sighed. 'The very best.'

He released himself inside me, as if that was all he needed to hear.

Autumn 1687

Too tired and heavy to walk down to the moor I went instead to wander in the orchard. With my pregnant belly gliding before me, I was as stately as a swan. The sunlight was ripe and golden as the apples that hung heavy on the boughs, waiting to be loaded into the wagons. After a night of heavy wind, windfalls lay scattered on the grass around the twisted, lichen encrusted trees. There was the scent of overripe fruit that was starting to decay and ferment, an over-sweet, cloying, poignant fragrance that stirred something within me. I stood resting my hands on one of the crooked boughs, and inhaled deeply, drinking in the mysterious tranquil stillness and peace of the ancient orchard.

Too soon I would be cooped up inside a dark and stuffy birthing room again. It would have been unbearable to me if it weren't for the prospect of holding another newborn baby in my arms, Richard's second, which was more than enough recompense. I hoped this one would please him more.

I watched dreamily as two Red Admiral butterflies came sailing into the orchard and settled on one of the fallen fruits, their vivid orange-banded wings fanning slowly. I thought of James Petiver, wondered what he was doing now and if he still thought of me. I decided I'd bring little Dickon to the orchard and sit him down on the grass by the fallen fruit so he could have a close view of the butterflies. It was not too early to start teaching him all that James had taught me.

Still in a dream I watched as Alice Walker, the new little cookmaid, came in through the wooden gate with a basket on her arm and started bending to collect the fallen apples at her feet. I watched her place two in her basket and then stoop to pick up a third.

'Don't,' I said, more harshly than I had intended. 'Leave them be.'

'Leave the apples on the ground, Ma'am?' She looked at me with a frown. 'But Cook needs them for baking. Mr Glanville said there would be half a dozen extra for supper.'

It was the first I had heard of it, but Richard was forever inviting people to dine without informing me, either the most illustrious of the local gentry or a hard-drinking, hard-gambling set of young men from Bristol whose company he seemed to prefer to mine nowadays.

'Take the apples from the trees,' I said to Alice. As if to demonstrate, I plucked one from the branch and took a large bite into its juicy flesh.

I had thrown the girl into a complete quandary. 'What is the matter now, Alice?'

'Cook specifically told me to collect the windfalls, Ma'am. She hates to see waste. It seems a shame to let the apples just rot.'

'Then take the best ones from the trees before they fall,' I said, mildly despairing of this mismanagement. 'The rotten ones will not be wasted. There are some little creatures that like rotten fruit all the better. If the fruit is all gone they will not come.'

She bobbed a quick curtsey. 'As you wish, Ma'am.' She put down her basket and started pulling apples indiscriminately off the tree nearest to where she stood, as if she wanted to be away before I made another alarming request. Her basket only half-filled, she scurried away as if she couldn't be gone from me quick enough.

I sighed, imagining what tall tale Alice would rush to take to Cook about the strange notions of their mistress. I took another bite of my apple, rested back against a tree and hoped they would put it down to my current condition.

The maid evidently whispered to more people than just Cook. We had a footman now, Jane Jennings's son, Will. Resplendent in his new livery of blue and gold braid, he gave me a peculiar look when he served me at dinner, almost sympathetic, as if he felt sorry for me, as if I was ill. Yet his look was wary, too, as if he was one of those who regarded insects as sinister creatures and any interest in them as somehow distasteful, if not dangerous. Richard hardly acknowledged me either, though I assumed that was at least in part due to the fact that he was so preoccupied with trying to impress our eminent guests, if they were not impressed enough already by the livery and by the great seven-branched candelabra that flickered above the sparkling silver plates and knives and spoons and the jugs of rich claret.

As well as George Digby and John Smythe, we were joined by Ferdinando Gorges of Wraxall.

At first the talk was all of William of Orange, and an open letter that had been written by him to the people of England.

'There is no question that it is a subtle bid for kingship,' George Digby pronounced. 'The man has been attempting to influence English politics for the whole of this past year. I'd not be at all surprised if he was massing an invasion force already.'

My hand went defensively to my womb. 'Please tell me we are not about to be invaded again?'

'So long as Orange chooses not to march through Somersetshire in Monmouth's trail,' John Smythe guffawed. 'I have no stomach for getting embroiled in another affray. Bet you haven't either, Glanville?'

As Richard took a hefty swig of his wine, I noted the tension in his jaw at this mention of the militia's crushing defeat at the start of the Monmouth Rebellion. 'It would be different this time,' he said steadily.

'No doubt about that,' the Earl snorted. 'If William of Orange does come to try to conquer the throne, he will bring a fleet to rival the Armada.'

The conversation turned to less serious matters, then to pure frivolity that I found very wearisome.

I nibbled at the rich feast of partridge and stuffed goose and puddings, not bothering to concentrate as the candles burned lower and the conversation became more rowdy and drunken. When Richard accidentally knocked over a bottle of fine wine and it spilt all over the gleaming new parquet floor we had barely paid for, he suggested everyone went through to the withdrawing room for cards and I rose from the table with the excuse that I needed to rest.

'I can't interest you in a game of whist?' George Digby asked blithely and with such immense charm that I was almost tempted.

'Save your breath, George,' my husband said meanly. 'Eleanor does not care for card games. It is such a regular pursuit for a lady, and my wife is anything but regular.'

'You lucky devil,' Ferdinando Gorges guffawed.

But I knew Richard had not meant to pay me a compliment. I knew that the servants had run to him with their tales and that they had irritated him. If he had been more at ease with me, did not have this perplexing need to keep picking fights with me, I knew it would not have mattered to him at all. There was a time when he would instantly have defended me. He would have dismissed it with a shrug, or applauded it even, seeing it as part of the wildness and individuality he said he had first so loved in me. But because something had soured between us, he had not taken it that way. Had taken against me instead.

Next morning, as I was rising just after sunup, Richard swayed into the room. He sat down heavily on the edge of the bed, groaning and holding his head.

I was not very sympathetic. 'You should have learned by now that too much of a good thing makes you sick.'

He dragged the drapes closed around the bed to shut out the pale morning light and climbed under the covers without even taking off his clothes, pulling the heavy blankets up tightly around him. His face was ashen and his eyes blood-shot.

I scrambled back up on to the bed, gripped by fear, knowing in that instant that no matter what our differences, he was dearer and more precious to me than ever. 'What's wrong, love? Are you not well?' I laid my hand on his forehead, terrified of what I would find, but his skin was quite cool.

He had closed his eyes and thrown one arm across them, as if the light still hurt him, dim as it was beneath the tester. 'When I do die, it will be in a debtors' jail.'

I looked at him, lying beneath the richly brocaded tester, under rich damask blankets that I had wanted almost as much as he had. 'It can't be that bad?'

'Nell, we have mortgages and debts owing to every wealthy merchant and gentleman who was supping here yesterday. I borrow from one to pay t'other and then hope to win some of it back off 'em at cards.'

'Did you win last night?' I asked in a small voice.

'No, sweetheart,' he said, deeply despondent, but in a way that made me realise he had totally forgotten our disagreement yesterday, or else considered it of no consequence now. 'I lost. It seems that, despite my best efforts, I always lose.'

Was it just anxiety over money that had been making him so irritable with me? If it was, then it was understandable. I was just glad he was sharing it with me now and strangely relieved to think that might be the whole extent of our problems, that it was not something else, something worse. Such as what? I did not want to think.

'We can sell the plate,' I suggested.

'That would barely pay for the repairs to the guttering, let alone the crack that has appeared in the west wall of the hall and all the holes in the roof.'

'Sell my jewels then. I don't need them all.'

'And have everyone pity you for having a wastrel for a husband?'

'I don't care what they think.'

'I am well aware of it.'

I did not rise to that. 'We could drain the land,' I said. 'William Merrick has always said it would bring us a great fortune.'

He blinked open his eyes and stared hard at me. 'You tried that before, remember? When you antagonised all the tenants and yeomen for miles around and they came to smoke you out.'

'So? We could try again.'

I had never seen him look so afraid. 'And what if we failed, Nell? Like they did at first in the Fens? What if this land cannot be reclaimed? We'd waste a fortune instead of making one. Lose all respect and good will. We'd lose everything.' He clung on to the damask cover as if he feared it was about to be dragged off him. 'What does any of it matter anyway? You heard what Digby said last night. The country is on the brink of revolution again. If the King does not abdicate the throne then William of Orange may demand his head. There could be another Civil War. We could lose this house to the victors if not the creditors, just as my father lost his.'

I crept back under the covers and took him in my arms. He smelt of sweat and stale wine but I stroked back his thick black curls and pressed my mouth against his forehead. 'You have me,' I said. 'Come revolution or ruin, whatever happens, whatever else we lose, we shall have each other. That is all that matters.'

He settled himself against me and eventually went to sleep. I drew the blanket over him as if he was a little boy and stayed with him until he woke. It was almost dusk when I went to fetch him a thick slice of bacon and some bread, and a glass of fresh milk to soothe his stomach.

'I am not an invalid,' he snapped ungratefully, pushing the tray away and throwing back the covers. 'Nor am I quite a peasant yet. I don't want to sup on bread and bacon like some poor farmer. I want canary wine and a supper of at least four dishes.'

I understood that where once he had been willing to let me witness his vulnerability and fear, he resented me now for having seen it, almost as if our current predicament was somehow my fault.

I tried to forget all about debts and mortgages, cosseted from the real world by the preparations for my lying-in. The gossips assembled round my candlelit bed with their chatter and their needlework and their comfits and it was just as companionable as the first time I had given birth. There was Mistress Knight, Mistress Keene, Florence Smythe and Mistress Gorges, Jane Jennings, Mistress Walker from the mill, John Hort's wife, Lucy, with her new baby son in her arms. These women, many of whom I had known all my life, were still my friends. They had seen two of my three babies born and they wished me well with my fourth. They were still at ease in my company. Until my pains grew so bad and I cried out so loud that Florence Smythe, newly delivered of a daughter herself, reached for the King James Bible I had left beside my bed.

It fell open at a particular page and two pressed golden butterfly wings came fluttering out. Jane Jennings gave a little squeal and threw back her arms as if she had seen dried toads.

'Calm yourself, woman,' Mistress Keene scolded. 'They're dead 'uns. She used to collect 'em as a child.'

'I heard tell of a witch that had a butterfly as her familiar instead of a cat,' Jane Jennings whispered. 'It flew beside her shoulder.'

'Well, them's not flying anywhere,' Mistress Keene said baldly.

But Jane was not done. 'Instead of feeding off flowers, the insect servant supped from a devil's teat on the witch's palm.'

I felt a dozen eyes scrutinise my own hands and bloated abdomen for sign of such a diabolical mark, felt a chill in my bones, and then I was lost to a surge of gripping pain that told me my baby was about to enter the world. I put my hands between my legs and felt the dome of a slippery head as I bore down and gave one final mighty push. There was heat and wetness and a tearing agony, and then there was a silence. It was shattered by the unmistakable, miraculous wail of a newborn infant.

Mother Wall told me that I had not given Richard a second son as he had wished. The pattern had been repeated. We had a daughter.

'Her name is Eleanor,' I said, suddenly wanting some unbreakable link with this house, with the past, for all I had avoided it with Forest. 'She is to be named for my mother. We shall call her Ellen.'

Jane Jennings peered at her suspiciously to see if she was properly formed but I already knew that she was perfect.

Autumn 1688

For once the sound of the steadily falling autumn rain did not dispirit me. I did not dread the coming of winter. My baby girl had mild blue eyes as soft as the mist, and her gummy smile was a little ray of sunshine that made me forget the rising floods entirely. The pitter-patter of the rain against the window was a soothing sound that only served to make the nursery seem all the more snug and warm.

The infinite nature of love astounded me. I loved my husband and my three children with my whole heart. But then along came another baby, and the amount of love I had to give expanded. I did not love any of them less for the fact that they had to share me with one more little person.

Ellen drew Richard and me closer together again too. Now that he had met her, he did not seem to mind at all that she was a girl. On the contrary, he seemed glad, was utterly enchanted by his tiny daughter. He had taken to going to sleep with her curled up on his chest, and to propping her up on plump cushions so that he could play the lute and sing to her, which was the most adorable thing to see. And to hear. Richard had a lovely singing voice, deeper than his spoken voice, very gentle. When he declared that he'd far prefer a houseful of daughters to more sons, would like me to breed a whole gaggle of girls as sweet as Ellen, I told him it would be my greatest pleasure to oblige.

'I swear that little lass grows prettier by the day.' He smiled when he strolled into the parlour and saw me cradling Ellen by a blazing fire. There were raindrops jewelling his dark cloak, and his breath, when he leaned over us to kiss us both in turn, smelled exotically of rum. He had been hunting deer at Aston Court, drinking with the Smythes and Digbys, and it had put him in a particularly bright mood. 'She is as lovely as her mother,' he said, kissing me again on my lips. 'Pretty as a princess, in fact. Or a duchess at least.'

'She is.'

He swung his cloak off his shoulders, unbuckled his sword and sprawled before the hearth at my feet. 'I have the most beautiful wife and the most beautiful baby daughter. Any man would envy me, I think.'

'Even with insurmountable debts?' I could not help but ask.

'What of them?' He gave one of the logs a kick with his boot and made the sparks fly. 'We have a loan from the Earl of Bristol, no less.'

Winter 1688

I t was the Earl himself who rode over to share the news that William of Orange had landed at Torbay in Devon. On the very anniversary of the Gunpowder Plot, he had marched on to English soil beneath a banner that proclaimed, *The Liberties of England and the Protestant Religion, I will maintain.*

William's fleet did more than rival the Armada, it was four times the size of it. Sixty thousand men and five thousand horses had sailed into the English Channel in a square formation twenty-five ships deep, so vast that it saluted Dover Castle and Calais simultaneously to demonstrate its strength. But, as George Digby returned to report, William's men did not forage or plunder or do anything to antagonise the English people, who in turn had neither rallied behind the King nor declared for William. War-weary, we all merely waited to see what turn events would take.

The first royal blood was shed in a skirmish in Somersetshire, at Wincanton, but bar that and a few anti-Catholic riots, it turned out to be a blessedly bloodless revolution that was soon ended. By the close of December, King James had fled to France, paving the way for William and Mary to be offered the throne as joint rulers.

'The real ruler now is Parliament, of course,' George Digby said with his incorrigibly merry smile as Richard poured him yet another measure of celebratory claret. 'The passing of the Bill of Rights means that never again will a King or Queen of England hold absolute power. Furthermore, it does away forever with the possibility of a Catholic monarchy.' He turned his arresting gaze from Richard to me. 'Your good father can rest in peace at last,' he said. 'Catholicism is dead forever in England.' He quaffed more wine and raised his glass in a blithe and generous toast to the neighbour who had loathed him. 'A glorious revolution indeed. So here's to

Major Goodricke. His battle is now over. He got what he wanted in the end.'

'Save that his daughter is clad in the most unpuritanical silk and sapphires and ribbons,' Richard smiled, twining one of my gold ringlets around his finger.

Over the rim of my wine goblet, in the flickering golden light of our best wax candles, I returned the mildly drunken but fond gazes of my glamorous husband and his equally glamorous friend, who were both now openly admiring me in my pearls and cerulean gown of silk brocade. I had all that I wanted too. I had all that I had ever desired, and yet it felt that something vital was still missing from my life. It lacked some purpose. It lacked that sense of adventure and discovery that had always been so necessary to me.

Stop being greedy, Eleanor, I told myself. *Do not ask for too much, or you might lose all that you already have.*

Part IV

Spring 1695

Seven years later

I looked down into my youngest son's cupped hands as we stalked through the knee-high summer growth of rushes and sedges on the moor. 'What have you found this time, Dickon?'

He stopped. I crouched down in front of him as he opened his fingers like a clamshell and I met the beady yellow eyes and pulsating throat of a small green toad. With one finger Dickon caressed its knobbly back. 'He was so far away from the river I was worried he would dry out in the heat. I am going to keep him for a while and then set him free again by Monk's Pool.'

'He will be in very good company in the nursery, what with the grass snake and the runt of the piglets and the blind hound.' I smiled fondly. 'Not to mention Snowflake.'

Dickon looked at me with his infinitely trusting pale blue eyes. 'You said she would fly away with the others when they left in the spring but she did not seem to want to go, did she, Mama?'

'No, she did not.' I stroked his sun-streaked yellow hair. 'You have obviously made her far too comfortable to want to go anywhere.'

The swan had a damaged wing and Dickon had reared her from a cygnet, feeding her from his hand. He had a talent for caring for animals that were wounded or in need of nurturing, people too, including his baby sister.

I could see Ellen now, with Mary, at the bottom of the watermeadow. In ringlets and ribbons and matching lemon gowns over white frilled petticoats, they were a beguiling sight, my two daughters, capering amidst the sunlit daisies and buttercups. Ellen was picking flowers while dancing. She danced wherever she went.

I knew that Mary was missing Forest. He had left a week ago, on a ship bound for the Low Countries where William Merrick had acquaintances. Forest was eighteen now and Flanders was said to be so like Somersetshire that I hoped he would not feel too homesick. Their agriculture techniques were far in advance of ours and it was my hope that this adventure would give Forest the perfect opportunity to learn how to manage the land he would one day inherit.

The plans to drain it had never materialised, nor would they now, or not at least in my lifetime. If I'd not put paid to those plans before Sedgemoor, I would have done it in the aftermath. It would take a long time for the West Country to recover from Monmouth's uprising and I had no desire to bring more distress to the people of Tickenham, any more than did Richard, who had taken great pains, with doles and feasts, to help them forget their losses, forget he had ever sided with the militia. It would be Forest's decision now, to drain or not to drain, and I meant him to be better informed than I or my father had ever been.

I saw Bess crossing the hump-backed stone bridge on her way back from taking a bowl of broth to her mother, old now and ill for some time.

'How is she?' Dickon inquired of my maid before I had the chance.

'Not much better, I am afraid.' She regarded him warmly, her gap-toothed smile even more pronounced as she had aged and grown stouter. 'But thank you for asking, Dickon.'

'We could take her some pottage and apple pie tomorrow,' he said. 'And some salves for the sores on her back.'

'That is very thoughtful. She'd appreciate that,' Bess told him.

'Is there anything else she needs?' I asked.

'She keeps asking for Tom.'

I took a deep breath. 'Then you must send for him, Bess. Tell him to come right away.'

'I did,' she admitted awkwardly. 'He is already here.' Then: 'Do you mind?'

'It is right that he should come back to Tickenham,' I said. 'It is his home after all.'

Since Richard had insisted we keep pace with the grandest households and hire a housekeeper and a steward, Bess had been given the official title of waiting-woman to me, but neither of us had spoken about Thomas for a long time, beyond her mentioning that he had found employment in the Billingsgate fish market. He had remained in London even after the official pardon had been issued. The rest of the men, John Hort's son and the one surviving Bennett boy, had come out of hiding, but Thomas had not returned to Tickenham and I could not pretend that I had not been relieved. Now that the reason for his hostility towards me had been brought out into the open, I feared it would be harder to face him somehow. I knew that I would never feel so at ease when I brought the children down for walks on the moor if I knew he might be there, resentful that it was not his moor we walked upon.

Bess walked with Dickon and me to the butterfly garden that her Ned had helped me plant so long ago. It was an abundant, kingly garden now, all cloaked in royal purple and gold, with thistles and purple loosestrife and the violet of the marjoram contrasting with the yellow of the marsh marigolds.

There was always a profusion of butterflies there, but this morning the combination of bright sunshine and still air had brought out a whole host of them that quite took my breath away. I halted my step. There were dozens, Large Whites, Large Coppers, Tortoiseshells, Brimstones, Fritillaries, Red Admirals, so many they were almost alarming in their great multitude. It was as if they had convened for some special purpose and we had intruded.

'A plague of butterflies,' Bess whispered with wonder.

As I took a few half-wary steps into the bright blizzard, a great swarm of them rose up in unison, an angelic ambush. I ducked and raised my hand to shield my face from the disquieting flicker and quiver of so many little wings.

The throng descended, like a handful of winged flowers, living petals thrown at a fairy bride on her wedding day, and I realised that Dickon still had not moved, was standing enraptured at the arched stone entrance to the garden. It was with a strange sweet longing for my childhood that I watched my son, as he watched the butterflies that continued to flit around like animated jewels, spangling the warm, clear air and dancing from flower to flower.

The summer had been late in coming and recently they seemed to be getting shorter every year, so short that the harvests were failing, bread was in poor supply and people were going hungry. Since the start of the new decade the winters had been colder and longer, with weeks of ice and snow and frost. So the butterflies were a particularly welcome sight. And so many, almost as if they had been biding their time, waiting for this rare warmth and sunshine, determined to make the best of it while it lasted.

'Don't you want to catch one of them?' Bess asked Dickon.

He shook his head very definitely.

'Your mother used to.'

I'd thought I had no real interest in butterflies any more, that the enchantment had left me for good, but now I was not so sure. Standing amongst this lovely cornucopia, I felt a stirring of desire for them, like a tingle in my fingertips.

Bess was watching me. 'Are you wishing you had your net, even now?'

I sat down on a stone bench in an arbour. 'Look at me.' I flicked my skirt with my ribboned slipper and made it swish. I was wearing emerald silk and there were rubies around my throat and in my ears. 'I have a closet full of silk dresses and a casket full of gems. I have a house filled with liveried footmen and japanned looking-glasses and French glassware and Chinese porcelain. What need have I to go chasing after tiny fragments of colour any more?'

If I did not exactly encourage Richard's increasing extravagance, I did not discourage it either. I had loved to hear him talk once of the elegantly proportioned Dutch merchants' houses fronting the canals in Amsterdam, the likes of which were being replicated in Bath now that we had a Dutch king. If we could not have the colonnades and domes that so impressed Richard as a destitute child, we could at least have rich interiors and replicate the grand state rooms of the Bath houses. Now we had striped muslin curtains, silk damask-covered armchairs and a glass-windowed coach in a new coach house. But they had become like bright disguises to lay over the cracks that had opened up in our marriage, like the oriental carpets we had bought to lay over the cold stone flags and the hand-painted silk paper we used to cover the fissures in the crumbling walls.

I had not found possessing such things nearly as fulfilling as I had once thought it would be, but the more Richard had, the more he seemed to want. Nothing seemed to be enough for him, as if there was a need in him that could never be met, a void that could never be filled, not even by me, least of all by me.

Dickon came to stand in front of me. 'The toad needs shade.'

'You take him on up to the house then, darling. I'll come in a while.'

He delayed, unwilling to go. 'Is my father home?'

'No. He has gone to Wraxall. '

His bony little shoulders relaxed and he set off up the path.

'I do wish the two of them could get along better,' I sighed.

'Mr Glanville always made such an effort with Forest that I can forgive him much,' Bess said, leaping to Richard's defence in a way that made me smile. 'It was a wonder to see how he was with Mr Edmund's fatherless little boy, and how Forest was with him. They still have a rare bond, don't they? It would be unusual enough for father and son to be so close, but for stepson and stepfather . . . well, you have to admit it is extraordinary.'

'It is.'

I remembered what Richard had said: *I would have liked the best for my children. But even my first-born son must take second place.* A reference to our marriage settlement. Always that. But a tiny part of me also feared it held the key to the preferential treatment Richard always showed Forest. He was the lord in waiting, the heir, when no son of Richard's ever could be.

'I agree it is a pity he does not have the same bond with his own little boy,' Bess said.

'Dickon is such a timid, sensitive child,' I said. 'And I think Richard probably was once, too, but was never allowed to be, and now he finds it difficult to accept in his own son, which only makes Dickon all the more nervous around him.'

'Well,' Bess said, 'I'll go and keep the lad company, see if he wants a glass of cider. You stay here and enjoy the sunshine. And the butterflies.'

That night I had the strangest dream. A swarm of yellow butterflies, far greater than the one that had gathered in the garden, had invaded my darkened chamber and found their way inside the bed curtains that, in my dream, were closed despite the airless summer night. In my sleep I was tormented and almost suffocated by the luminous, insistent wings. They gently battered and brushed my face, swirled before my eyes and fluttered around my head, as if to rouse me to action.

My father, like all Puritans, had set much store by dreams and what they revealed about a person's character and destiny. I did not understand what this dream meant but even when I woke it did not entirely leave me, remaining with me throughout the morning.

When Richard came to find me I had returned to the butterfly garden. He sat down on the sunny stone bench beside me, waved his hand in front of my face. 'Where are you, Nell?' he asked, with a touch of impatience. 'You seem very far away.'

I could often have said the same about him. Somehow, though I still loved him, knew he loved me, we had grown very far away from each other. How had that happened? Why?

I took his hand, brought it to my lips and kissed it. 'See? I am right here.'

The bright sunlight highlighted the slight streaks of silver in his black curls, around his temples and his ears. There was doubtless grey in my own hair too, but it did not show up so clearly against the gold. There was the faintest web of lines around his eyes too, but only when he smiled, and the blue of them had not faded. If anything the years had made him more attractive, rather than less, had added a character and dignity to his face that made it all the more compelling to me. He was still beautiful, still by turn devastatingly charming and charmingly vulnerable. He still suffered from nightmares he would never talk about, was more prone than ever to being withdrawn, more troubled than he had been before we were married. And nothing I did seemed to help him at all, so that I had practically abandoned any attempt to do so.

He was wearing ink-blue breeches and a long waistcoat but had no jacket on. I rested my cheek against the soft linen gathers of his shirtsleeves, smoothing them down lest I be smothered by the fullness of them.

'George Digby has invited me on a deer hunt,' he said. 'D'you think Dickon would like to come?'

I straightened. 'Oh, Richard, love, I don't. He would hate it.'

'You've turned the boy into a milksop,' he said harshly. 'I don't know how to talk to him.'

'Yes, you do. Talk to him as you talk to me. As you talk to the girls.'

'But he is not a girl, damn it!'

'My father treated me as if I was a boy, and I'd not have had it any other way. I was different from other girls, and Dickon is different from other boys. He does not like hunting and swordplay, any more than I liked crewelwork and embroidery. You have to respect that.'

I sensed he was on the brink of arguing with me, but he held himself back as if he did not have the stomach for another quarrel. No more did I. 'So what shall you do today?' he asked. 'If you are not to be kept busy with a needle?'

'Oh, I expect I shall find something.'

When he had kissed me goodbye, I realised that what I wanted to do was some hunting of my own. Butterfly hunting.

With mounting excitement, I went to the oak chest in the corner of our bedchamber and dug deep down, through layers of silk gowns and velvet capes, to the very bottom, to my books and boxes of specimens. I carefully took them out and laid them on the bed, going back for my observation book and all the letters I had kept from James.

I looked back over my notes and studied each butterfly, reacquainting myself with long-lost and dearly beloved friends. I reread the book James had made for me and every one of his letters, the ink faded now to a pale ochre. I devoured it all, the way I used to devour my first meal after a long fast. Then I dusted down my butterfly equipment, picked up my silk skirts and ran down on to the moor.

Dickon had carried his swan to the river and was standing at a bend, upstream from John Hort and the other fishermen and eelers, trying without success to encourage the great white bird to go for a swim. He had his stockings off and was ankle deep in the sparkling water but the bird was paddling about in the reedy shallows, its webbed feet firmly rooted to the muddy riverbed.

'Pitiful,' I grinned. 'Even I could do better.'

'You can swim, Mama?' Dickon exclaimed with surprise.

'Your father showed me how to do it a long time ago. I think, by now, I am probably an even better swimmer than he is, but for Heaven's sake, don't ever tell him I said that.'

Dickon regarded the clap net and pins and deal collecting box with cautious interest. 'You don't swim with those?'

'No,' I laughed, holding out my hand to him. 'Come with me and you'll see what these are for.'

He left his swan to splash about and scrambled out of the river, under the scornful stare of one of the fishermen. I realised with a shock that it was Thomas Knight. So he had turned to fishing now. My half-brother. The years had not been kind to him at all and his bitterness showed in a harshening of the lines of his long face, which looked almost wolfish. It was almost as if his lips and eyes had narrowed permanently for lack of joy in his life. His hair was cropped, thinning and receding. He was leaner than ever, as if resentment was eating away at his insides. He carried his damaged arm crookedly, dragging on his shoulder so that he stood slightly stooped and twisted, like a hunchback.

'Good day to you, Thomas,' I called across to him. 'Welcome back.'

He stared at me as if I was not even worthy of acknowledgement.

I walked away and Dickon ambled after me. We had gone less than a yard when a little blue wing obligingly fluttered past our noses and with a leap and a reflex swipe of the net, I had it instantly pinioned, my fingers pressing on its thorax.

Dickon was aghast. 'Why do you have to kill them?'

'To catalogue them and map the different variations and species.'

'But it is God's commandment that we must not kill.'

'We kill cattle and geese, Dickon. God would not want us to starve.'

'We do not eat butterflies,' he pointed out.

'But we do need to learn about them.'

He did not argue and I could see him mulling on that as we carried on.

I threw out my arm to stop him in his tracks when I sighted an unusually wide-banded Marsh Fritillary, feeding on the pale domed flower of a Devil's Bit scabious. I put my fingers to my lips to signal that he should keep quiet and stealthily started to creep towards it. I was about to whip out my net again, but this time it was Dickon who held me back, with a restraining hand on my arm. 'Don't, Mama, please.'

He sat on his heels and watched as the little butterfly eagerly unwound its proboscis into the flower and waved its distinctive orange-tipped antennae as it outspread its red-brown and yellow wings.

'See?' he whispered. 'It is far more interesting alive than dead.'

I let it go on feeding then flit away, just for the pleasure of seeing my son's sweet, victorious smile.

I stroked his gold hair. 'I've never shown you my collection, have I? Butterflies that are set well are just as beautiful as those basking in the sunshine. With their wings outspread, they look as if they could fly away at any moment. You'll see what I mean. And you'll see that there is a purpose to killing them, I promise.'

But Dickon was not interested in the dead butterflies, though quite perturbed by them. What interested him instead was why there was one book amongst the butterfly paraphernalia which seemed to have no connection with it whatsoever, though it had perhaps been more important to it than any other: the King James Bible. I told Dickon what his grandfather had told me, so long ago now, about butterflies being a token, a promise, and in the telling of that story I felt the same stirring of excitement that I had experienced when first I heard it. A wellspring of hope.

When Dickon had gone to bed, I sat down beside the Bible, wary almost to touch it, to open its pages after so many years. Eventually I put the candle on the stand and reached out my hand, lifting the great book into my lap. I felt the weight of it, ran my fingers over the worn leather and tooled gold lettering. I turned it on its side and let it fall open where it would. The Gospel of St John, 8, xii. The page where I had pressed the first golden butterfly. The light of the candle caught a very faint indentation in the page, the finest sparkling of bright dust.

I let my eyes rest on the words, words that had once been familiar to me as my own name but which I had let fall silent.

I read them now out loud.

'"Then spake Jesus again unto them, saying, I am the light of the world: he that followeth me shall not walk in darkness but have the light of life."'

I felt a strange peace descend on me, such as I had not felt for a very long time. I heard my father's voice, so clear he could almost have come to stand in the room. *The only light you need is the light of the Lord.*

I went to Dickon's chamber. Cadbury, the blind hound which he had found wandering, abandoned on Cadbury Camp, was curled up at the foot of the bed and gave a low growl as she heard me enter. I crouched down next to her, let her sniff my hand and fondled her ears until her tail started to thump against the floor. 'Well done, girl. You guard him well.'

I lowered myself on to the edge of the bed, reached over and stroked Dickon's golden cheek. 'You shall be my example,' I whispered to him. 'I shall study living butterflies from now on, do you hear me, my little darling? I am going to rear them, instead of killing them.'

I was going to witness the transformation, from worm, to coffin, to butterfly. From birth, to death, to resurrection.

I woke as I had woken as a child, eager and full of plans for the day. At sunrise I slid out of Richard's arms and out of bed, pulled on a simple morning gown, unfastened my hair from its plait and tied it in a knot at the back of my head. I went down to the kitchen for a wide-mouthed glass jar and was out on the moor before even the eelers were about to check their wicker traps. Only the marsh birds were awake, twittering and singing away as if they shared my anticipation, a perfect accompaniment to a glorious morning, heralding what would be another hot day. For now, it was neither too hot nor too cool, though the ground was still damp with dew, as I discovered when I got down on my hands and knees and started crawling around in the undergrowth. I paid no heed to the dark wet patches that stained my skirt, nor to the nettles which stung and scratched my hands, nor the twigs that caught in my hair. I carried on regardless, even when Thomas Knight, John Hort and the fishermen did come to take up their positions, even when I felt them watching me censoriously. What did it matter if they disapproved? What could they do?

The first worm I found had a brownish-olive body, covered with long white hairs. Hiding under the scabious, I discovered two tiny pale yellow larvae, and my search of the nettles revealed a larger worm, greenish ochre in colour, with a black head. Satisfied for now, I stood and smoothed my hand over my head and tucked a stray strand of hair behind my ears, smiling to see the scandalised stares of the fishermen, with their early-morning catch still twitching on the riverbank beside them. 'I bid you good morning, gentlemen,' I said, as if greeting the Earl of Bristol in the parlour, but bending instead to pluck another few nettle leaves to add to my supply. I giggled to myself at the picture I made: chin held high, swishing serenely through the grass in my damp-stained gown, with my jar of wriggling worms held carefully in both hands like a goblet of finest wine.

I went directly to the dovecote, a lime-coated corner of which I had decided to appropriate for my butterfly birthing room. It was sheltered and warm and, with the rows of separate openings for the birds, always well ventilated.

Over the course of the next day and night, I tended my quadruplet worms as devotedly as I had tended my four babies. It was a similar toil and done with similar willingness. I brought them fresh leaves, cleaned out their droppings, fretted over whether they were too cold or too warm, were sleeping too much or not enough, were having sufficient to eat. I kept a record of it all, but I had to record that, one by one, all the worms died.

I threw them out and swilled the jar clean in the horse trough. A good proportion must perish in the wild. I just needed a greater quantity to guarantee success.

Ellen and Dickon were keen to help me and Dickon also recruited Annie Sherburne, one of the tenant farmers' daughters, who sometimes went to feed the ducks with him. She was a tall girl with flyaway soft brown hair and the doleful eyes of a puppy. She wore a woollen dress that was thin with age and several inches too short, but which still hung off her skinny frame.

Annie proved herself a diligent little helper, young and naïve enough in the ways of the world not to be too perturbed when I took her out into the fields and beat at bushes with a long stick, or when I gave her a linen sheet and instructed her and Dickon to hold it spread out beneath the bushes to collect the worms dislodged from the branches by my thrashing.

'Will you sell them at market?' she asked as I crouched down to scoop a score of them into a jar.

I managed to keep my face straight at this natural question from a farmer's girl, for whom every crop had a market value. Why would caterpillars be any different from apples or eggs or pike, gathered in to be sold for profit? 'No, Annie,' I told her kindly. 'Nobody would want them.'

'Why d'you want 'em then?'

I stood up, the jar and its squirming contents in my hand. 'To me they are valuable because of what I can learn from them.'

'How valuable, exactly?' She leaned on the beating stick, her little face very serious. 'I told my brother Tim what I do for you and he has been collecting worms too,' she explained. 'How much would you give him for 'em?'

'Well now, how about twopence a dozen?' I suggested. 'Would he accept that as a fair price, do you think?'

She nodded vigorously.

'Good. You tell him to bring me however many he can find.'

'We need every penny we can get,' Annie said, 'with the bad harvests we've had these past two years and bread so costly. Ma says we'll soon have to choose whether to eat or have a roof over our heads, especially with two extra mouths to feed now.' She clamped her little hand over her own mouth as if to push back the words.

'What extra mouths, Annie?'

She shook her head, much afraid.

'You can tell me. I promise I shall not be angry.'

'My cousin and her baby,' she murmured. 'She was thrown out of her parish, when they found out she was with child. I know it is forbidden, but she had nowhere to go so we took her in.'

'I should hope you did. And did she have a little boy or a girl?'

'Boy.' She smiled. 'Called Harry.'

'It must be very cramped in your cottage,' I said. 'With all your sisters and brothers and grandmother.'

'There's ten of us now, Ma'am. It'll be a squeeze come winter, when it floods downstairs and we all have to live in the one room up top.'

'Tell your mother not to worry about the rent,' I said. 'She can pay half or whatever she can afford. And tell your cousin that she can have the cottage along the lane from yours, for a penny. It has been empty for I don't know how long.'

Annie's eyes were round with surprise and wonder. 'They'll never believe me.' She looked like she didn't believe her luck either.

'And how would you like to be my apprentice, Annie?'

'Oh, but my father can't pay you for an apprenticeship.'

'Why should he pay when it is you who is doing me the service? No, it is I who will pay you, Annie. A good wage. Here.' I put my hand in my pocket, took out a coin for her. I had spent too long squandering money on things I was now coming to realise mattered not at all. 'You tell your brother to bring me those worms. I might even give him sixpence if they are good ones.'

Richard had ridden out to the village, collecting rents with the steward, and as usual they had ended up in the inn, but when he waylaid me on my way back from the pantry, where I had gone for a fresh collecting jar, I saw that it had not put him in a very good humour. He caught me in his arms in a gentle enough embrace that nevertheless held me fast. 'What are you doing, Nell?' he asked sternly.

'Something that I love,' I said. 'I had forgotten how much. Please do not try to stop me.'

'Could I stop you?' he challenged. 'If I asked you to give it up, would you do it?'

I reached back and put my hands over each of his, slowly but deliberately pushing them down and away from me. 'Would you be asking, or would you be ordering?'

'Would it make a difference?'

I shook my head. 'In this instance, I think not.'

'I am your husband. You vowed to obey me. You are commanded by God to obey my orders.'

I stiffened. 'So, are you ordering me, Richard?'

'God knows, I should do,' he said. 'For the sake of local harmony, if nothing else. You need to know that Jack and Margaret Sherburne are none too comfortable about their Annie spending so much time with you, even if you do pay her for it. Her father is swayed by the wages and your rash offer of reduced rent, but Annie's mother does not want her here, not even with those extraordinary carrots dangled before her. I take it you have a plan as to how we meet our debts, by the way, if you reduce rents to a peppercorn on a whim? Perhaps in future you'd at least do me the courtesy of informing me of your decisions, even if you see no need to discuss them.'

'I'm sorry. I should have talked to you.'

'Why should you?' he said acerbically. 'It is your right to do as you wish. After all, it is your estate.'

'God in Heaven, Richard, just for once can we not come back to that? I wonder that you ever agreed to marry me, when you knew you could not have Tickenham Court as well, or were you counting on the fact that I loved you enough for the settlement to make little difference? I have never denied you money . . . never denied you anything, have I? So why can you never let it rest?'

He was staring at me very oddly and I feared I had gone too far, but I could not seem to stop. 'Is that why you favour Forest over your own son? Because he is my heir?'

I saw the warning flash in his blue eyes, like lightning in a summer sky, swift and searing, a charge of angry power that suddenly made me almost afraid of him.

'Forgive me. I should not have said that.'

'By all means.' His tone was very cold. 'It makes no difference whether you say it or not. If it is what you think.'

'I don't think. I wasn't thinking. I am just angry. Why do the Sherburnes not want Annie to work with me, for God's sake?'

'They are not the only ones who think the girl should not be doing what you've had her doing,' he said flatly.

'Collecting caterpillars and assisting with their care? What the devil is so wrong with that?'

'Have you even paused to wonder why Mistress Keene has lost her help in the kitchen and, since yesterday, there is no longer anyone to work in the brewhouse?'

Admittedly I had been rather preoccupied of late, but the matter of the kitchenmaid I did know about. 'Alice Walker was needed at the mill, wasn't she?'

'Only because her brothers didn't want her near this house. They have heard tales,' Richard said. 'They have all heard tales.'

'What kind of tales?'

'That you seek out caterpillars and keep their coffins, waiting for the worms to grow wings. They say only a witch would be concerned with such things. They say it is evil.'

I felt my spine tingle at the use of those words. 'I had hoped it was godly.'

'Shape-shifting, Nell? Use the brain God gave you! They see it as unholy, akin to attempting to breed a werewolf.'

That was not quite so preposterous as it might sound, since metamorphosis had been put forward as proof that werewolves could exist, just as it had been used to argue that alchemy was a possibility. 'This is tavern talk,' I said angrily. 'Vicious tattle. Malicious gossip. It is Thomas Knight's doing. He's not been back a month and already he's causing trouble for me. It is he who has been stirring them all up, isn't it?'

'Whipping them up more like, but then you have made it so damnably easy for him.'

'Why can't he leave me alone?' I exploded. 'Why can't they all leave me alone. I harm no one.'

'Except for yourself. Except for your reputation. And mine.'

'You did tell them it is all nonsense?' I studied his face. 'You didn't, did you? You did not speak up in defence of me at all. For pity's sake, Richard, why not?'

'I saw nothing to be gained from having them think that both of us are cracked.'

Tears pricked my eyes. I could bear being talked about, gossiped about, so long as I had his support. If he even half believed them, sided with them against me, I did not know what I would do. 'I am cracked?' I raged. 'Is that really what you think of me?'

'What I think,' he stormed, 'is that you have been writing to him again, haven't you? That is what has got you started on all this again, isn't it? You have been writing to that damned quack apothecary?'

'His name is James. And he is no quack. I have not written to him for years but rest assured, I shall,' I shouted vengefully. 'Oh, I shall. Just as soon as I have something to tell him.'

Richard snatched the glass jar out of my hand and hurled it against the wall where it shattered into shards like splinters of ice.

We stood, eyes flashing, chests heaving. Out of habit I smoothed the loose tendrils of hair off my face, and at that familiar gesture of mine I saw the anger in his eyes change to passion of a different kind. I knew that this argument would end the way most arguments between us usually did, with lovemaking, and I wanted that as much as I knew Richard did. Having him inside me was the only way I ever felt close to him any more, though even then it never seemed close enough.

He stepped nearer to me, pushed me back against the wall, his body pressing against mine. I matched his hard, angry kisses with hard and angry kisses of my own, kisses that had in them more despair than desire. I hooked one leg up around his thigh, my arm over his shoulder and my hand in his hair, to bring him nearer. His fingers were working at the fastenings of my gown, but it was taking too long for both of us.

I put my lips to his ear. 'Rip it,' I whispered. 'I want you to rip it.'

I turned round to face the wall, flattened myself against the stone and swept up my hair with my arm so he could get more easily at the row of tiny buttons down my back. I felt him give a sharp swift tug which sent them scattering like hailstones.

He stripped the gown off me and slammed into me, took me quickly and passionately up against the wall, but though the pleasure was intense, I could tell he was left as strangely dissatisfied as I.

It was no better when we did it again in bed, more slowly and lingeringly. There was something missing, always something in the way, standing between us and keeping us apart. What?

Lying in his arms afterwards, my thoughts returned to the local unrest, then ran off, as they were wont to do, on a tangent. The window was open and a faint breeze blew in, scented with river water and new-scythed grass. I drew little circles with my finger in the hairs on Richard's chest.

'Do you remember when we celebrated William and Mary coming to the throne, and George Digby said the Bill of Rights would change England for ever?'

'Aye, I remember,' Richard said. He turned over on his side so that he could see my face. He was accustomed by now to the no doubt puzzling paths my mind sometimes chose to wander and stroked strands of sweaty hair off my face with the flat of his hand, waiting for me to go on.

I propped my head up on my elbow, looked at him. 'By removing any chance of having a Papist take the throne, it has dispelled much of the hatred of Catholics, making England a safer place for them, and others too of differing faiths. In that respect England has changed indeed. Yet some things have not changed at all.'

'Where is this leading us, Nell?' Richard asked wearily.

'We may have a queen ruling jointly with her king, but nothing has changed for women like me, has it? Why should I be viewed with suspicion just because I take an interest in the world? Just because I want to do something other than household accounts?'

'I don't know, Nell.' The light suddenly went out of his eyes. 'But you are right that hatred of Catholics is not the only prejudice. There are others,' he added. 'There are plenty of others, and they can be just as malign, just as dangerous.' He rolled away from me, on to his back, threw his arm up over his eyes, almost as if he needed to blot out the sight of my face. I had not the faintest idea what he was talking about, or what I had done now to upset him.

Bess ushered my apprentice's scrawny little brother into the parlour. He was carrying a dented but perfectly polished copper pan and stood on the threshold, wary of coming any closer, as if he took me for a witch.

'You have some worms for me?' I said gently, aware that this was not a question to put him much at ease.

He nodded, gulping down his terror.

'May I see them, Tim?'

He shuffled two steps closer and held out the pan with dirty hands that stuck out from frayed shirtsleeves long outgrown.

I looked into the pan, where a few miserable looking maggots were squirming. The wrong kind of worms entirely, but an easy enough mistake to have made.

'Where did you find them?' I asked.

He swallowed hard again, tossed his head to flick the limp brown hair out of his eyes. 'In a cowpat, Ma'am.'

I smiled. Only a small boy would go digging in cowpats. 'What a good idea,' I said enthusiastically. 'I'd never have thought to look there.'

He thrust the pan at me. 'Are you going to take 'em?'

'Thank you, Tim. They will do very well.' I emptied the unpleasant contents of the pan into a pot and handed him his sixpence.

He snatched it off me and bolted for the door, almost forgetting to reclaim the pan and hardly daring to come back for it. That was something I marked well. If a small boy were so eager to be away from me that he would forsake the only means by which his mother could cook his dinner, I must be fearsome indeed.

Each morning when I went to the dovecote, there were more curled corpses to remove from the jars, until finally there was just a spotted one left, barely moving. When I came back next day, I expected it to have gone the way of the rest, though I thought at first that it had somehow just vanished. But when I looked more closely I saw something, hanging from the muslin I had fastened over the top of the jar to prevent any escape.

Dickon was rubbing Cadbury's belly when I ran to fetch him. The hound sat up and Dickon looped his arm around her neck. She turned her head and licked his face with her great pink tongue, nearly knocking him over.

'Come with me, Dickon,' I said to him. 'There's something I want to show you.'

We looked together at the small, dark, elongated shape, slightly curved, like a tiny ripening fruit, that had anchored itself to the cloth lid with a minute button of silk.

'What is it, Mama?'

'It is a little butterfly coffin. It has to be!'

I sat down at my desk and wrote to James. I asked if he had his own apothecary shop yet, and if he was still corresponding with butterfly collectors across the globe. I apologised for breaking off our correspondence, telling him I had married again, had been busy with babies, but that I had collected more butterflies since last I saw him and had cultivated a butterfly garden. And now I had reared a pupa, and it was like a small kernel of hope.

Devoted as a mourner, I took to visiting the little coffin and sitting beside it for long stretches of time, as the pigeons and doves flapped and cooed around me. I did not know how long it took for a butterfly to emerge but I would not risk missing it. I came half-dressed at dusk, and at sunrise, and in the afternoon. I watched and I waited until my limbs grew stiff from sitting so still. Over a matter of days the coffin changed, almost imperceptibly, grew paler, nearly translucent, so that I almost believed I saw the ghost of wings beneath its gossamer casing.

But then, when Annie and Dickon and I went to check on it together, we saw it changed again, blackened, shrivelled to an empty shell, one from which the life had not been expelled but had been entirely extinguished. There was to be no newborn butterfly.

'Damn it,' I said quietly.

'Why is it so important to you, Mistress Glanville?' Annie asked.

I looked from Dickon's nervous eyes into Annie's hungry ones, looked at her bony little body, tried to explain. 'The preachers have been telling us all this century that the end of the world is nigh,' I said. 'They have been preaching that the Horsemen of the Apocalypse are nearly upon us. In my short lifetime I have lived through war and plague and fire, and now it seems that if the harvests continue to fail, we are on the brink of a famine.'

Annie nodded gravely. I was telling her nothing she had not already heard from the pulpit a score of times.

'They say the comets that were seen crossing the skies before the war foretold these calamities that have befallen our age.'

She nodded again.

'Well, all I wanted, all I was hoping for, I suppose, was to see a more promising sign for once, something to hold on to in this dark time we live in.'

'A sign?' Annie said. 'From a worm, Ma'am?'

'I hoped I would see it become more than a worm.' I smiled weakly.

'That it is, Mama,' Dickon exclaimed. 'Look!'

I stepped back in revulsion. The shrivelled pupa was disintegrating before our eyes. Something was emerging from it after all. Instead of a butterfly there was a small swarm of tiny nasty pesky flies, like the ones that fed on carrion, as if to prove to me once and for all that nothing glorious ever arose from any coffin, that a tomb was a place only where rotting flesh was devoured and turned to dust.

Old habits die hard. It was still a struggle for me to discount signs and portents as nothing but superstition, hard to believe that what I had just seen meant nothing. That was why, despite instantly recognising the untidy handwriting on the package which Richard held out to me, had indeed come down to the dovecote especially to give to me, I took it from him with some foreboding, not wanting to open it right away. That it should arrive at just that moment!

'What is it?' Richard asked me suspiciously.

Our recent differences had been set aside, if not exactly resolved, which was the best I could ever hope for. Sometimes I knew why my husband was angry or withdrawn or had fallen into a dark mood, but usually I had no notion. I did know that there was no point in asking him, since he would never talk about it, but that it would pass. All I could do was try not to aggravate the situation by retaliating, try to be patient with him, which was not always easy.

I was glad to see he was now in good spirits, and did not want to risk spoiling it by having him find out that the parcel was from James Petiver.

'I think it must be a book,' I said, wondering what it was that James had enclosed with his reply to my letter. Well, whatever it was, it could wait.

I set the package aside, took Richard's arm and walked with him out on to the sunlit moor. The sky arced above us, a heavenly blue, tufted with wispy clouds that were driven along by the silkiest breeze, rustling in the willows and the long grass.

'Did you ever lie on your back and look for shapes in the clouds?' he asked me.

I smiled. 'Doesn't everyone?'

'I don't know. Do they?'

'I am sure that everyone who lives under a Somerset sky, or a Fenland one, must.'

We had been walking over an area of grass and sedge, grazed short by the cattle, but he drew me off to the side, into a patch where the grass was still thigh-high, and took off his coat and spread it out. He pulled me gently down with him, laid on his back with his arms behind his head and his legs crossed at the ankles.

I lay next to him and he unfolded one arm for me to pillow my head upon, bent it down and around my shoulder so that his hand rested lightly over my breast. We were completely hidden and it was surprisingly comfortable. The ground was soft and spongy, and the air was filled with the scent of crushed grass.

'What do you see, then?' I asked him.

'In truth, not much,' he laughed.

I watched as two white butterflies played in the air above us like living snowflakes.

'Do you know, Cabbage White butterflies have the most extraordinary and elaborate mating ritual,' I told him very softly. 'They are the most erotic little creatures on earth.'

He idly stroked my breast with his elegant fingers. 'I think *you* are the most erotic little creature on earth.'

I smiled, nestled closer to him and tilted my head closer so it rested against the side of his. 'I have watched them often,' I said. 'They chase after each other and flirt for ages, until they alight on the same flower and join their bodies. But the amazing thing is that they stay together like that and carry each other upwards into the sky. Sometimes they remain locked together for hours after their coupling, and sometimes they cannot separate at all and die still joined. They literally die of love.'

Richard lifted himself above me, looked down into my face and gave me a gentle kiss that had in it much of sorrow and regret. Or maybe that is just how I remember it because of what happened afterwards. A kiss of farewell.

It was a glorious pleasure to me to make love outside, to feel fresh air on my thighs, on my breasts, to feel the prickle of the sedges and grass beneath me and the sun on my face as our bodies moved and rocked together, the murmurs and sighs and little moans of lovemaking mingling with the calling of the marsh birds and the distant croak of a frog.

He stayed inside me a while after he was spent and then moved over so we lay side by side, still wrapped in each other's arms.

'There is much to be said for being a white butterfly,' he said, his mouth in my hair and a smile in his voice.

'If I died now,' I told him, 'I should die quite happy.'

I stroked his tumbled curls and saw that more clouds had come into the sky, not fluffy white ones for lying and gazing up at, but massing, grey, windblown clouds, that scudded much too fast ever to see shapes in. A chill had crept into the air that was almost wintry. The summer was over when it had only just begun. The world was turning back into darkness once more. But when I looked back to that time, afterwards, I had a notion that if only I had closed my eyes, the storm clouds would have rushed on over us and eventually have passed us by, and that I could have kept Richard safe in my arms forever. That we could have been like the white butterflies, two souls joined, drifting together on the warm currents of the air for all eternity.

I took James's package to the willow tree in the bend in the river, where I had read countless other letters from him. Inky rain clouds had gathered now on the horizon, were advancing towards the moor. With the sun still shining behind and around them, they cast a heavy golden-blue light.

I doubted I would finish the letter before the rain began, given that it was such a very long one, many pages long, in fact, as if James had been saving up things to tell me all these years. It was indeed a book he had enclosed with the letter, small and slim-bound, but I set that aside without so much as a glance at the title, suddenly eager only to read what James had written. He began by answering my questions. Yes, he said, he had his own shop, at the Sign of the White Cross on Aldersgate Street, and it was prospering. His customers included sea captains and ships' surgeons who still collected specimens for him from all over the world. His friend the botanist John Ray had recently recommended him for Fellowship of the Royal Society and he had been elected to Membership a month ago.

That gave me pause. I knew how much it would mean to James to be welcomed into Fellowship of the foremost scientific society of Europe. He described for me the great laboratories of Gresham College, where crucibles and furnaces were used to investigate the properties of rocks and minerals and curiosities from distant lands. He described the activities of the Royal Society so well that by the time I reached the last page of his letter, I almost felt I'd met its president, Samuel Pepys, and Isaac Newton and Edmund Halley, had listened with my own ears to the hot debates on classification, as well as to experiments in the more marginal sciences of astronomy, mathematics and physics. I felt almost as if I had witnessed for myself the dawn of science, of a new world. But I had not. When James spoke of a general feeling that England was at the centre of a worldwide scientific enterprise of lasting importance, what he really meant was London. Not Somersetshire.

And the little book he had enclosed? He said he had wanted to send it to me years ago, when first it was published, but had not done so because it would have seemed a strange thing to send to me out of the blue. It had been translated from French, he said. The author was Robert Talbor, the feverologist, who, it transpired, had sold the formula for his cure for ague to King Louis of France, on condition it not be made public until after Talbor's death. James said he remembered the interest I had once shown in Jesuits' Powder and thought I would be interested, therefore, to learn that it was indeed the secret ingredient in Talbor's mysterious miracle cure. A strong infusion of it, mixed with six drams of rose leaves and two ounces of lemon juice.

I frowned, no more than puzzled at first. If Jesuits' Powder was a miracle cure rather than a deadly Papist poison, why had Edmund died?

My brain seemed to be working very slowly and the obvious, natural explanation eluded me, hovering somewhere just out of reach, too grotesquely ugly to face. As realisation dawned, the rushing of the river faded away. The sound of the wind in the trees dimmed. In absolute silence, the book slid from my fingers. It seemed to take the longest time to fall, and when it tumbled at last into the grass, the sound of it was like a falling tree, like a breaking heart.

I sank back against the trunk of the willow, slid down it to the ground. Realisation was like a wave, crashing over my head, dragging me down. I felt ice cold, as if I had been washed away. I felt something twist and tear irrevocably inside me.

If Jesuits' Powder were a cure and not a poison then it could not have been Jesuits' Powder that I had given to Edmund. It could not have been Jesuits' Powder that Richard had brought back from London and given to me for him.

My heart had turned to lead. It felt too heavy to go on beating. The first raindrop fell on Robert Talbor's book, then on my hands, my face. The downpour came on quickly, heavily, but I could no more stand up than take flight. I did not think I would ever be able to stand up or walk again. I watched the ink on James's letter start to blur, the words begin to run. I drew up my legs away from the book, as if it was tainted. I wrapped my arms around my knees, watching the rain pimple the cover. The river began to rush but there was no break in the clouds. In what seemed like no time at all, dusk had fallen, deepened by the rain that came down now in a slanting torrent and had soaked me to my skin. I did not feel it, did not feel anything, was totally numb, wanted only to stay that way for as long as I could. I dreaded the numbness receding, as it must, giving way to a horror that would be intolerable. I rested my head against my knees, closed my eyes, wished I could sleep, sleep forever and never wake.

I did not even hear the soft thud of a horse's hooves on the damp earth. I let Richard pick me up in his arms and put me carefully into the saddle. I watched him pick up the pulpy little book and letter and put them in his pocket. I let him hold me gently all the way back over the moor to the house. He carried me into the great hall and up the stairs to the bedchamber. Bess rushed in and started fussing around me, but it was Richard who unfastened my sodden gown, pulled my wet chemise off over my head as if I was a small child. It was Richard who loosened my hair and gently dried it. I let him wipe my face, rub my arms. I let him wrap a warm blanket over me and I knew that soon, when feeling returned, I should not be able to bear for him to touch me ever again.

'Nell, in Jesus' name, what is the matter?' he said, sitting down beside me.

I turned my eyes on him dumbly, unable to reply. I wanted only to scream: What have you done? Oh, God, Richard. What have you done? Did you kill Edmund? Did you have me murder Edmund?

'It is just a turn, I'm sure,' Bess said. 'She's had too much sun to her head. We're not used to it, after all the cold.'

Richard looked cold now, and frightened, very frightened. But he would do, wouldn't he, harbouring a guilt such as that for years? No wonder that haunted, guarded look so often came into his eyes. No wonder the black moods, the nightmares, the sleeplessness. No wonder the distance between us.

I watched in a trance as he took off his shirt and untied the laces of his breeches. My eyes were drawn to the thin scar on his left thigh, remnant of an injury he told me he had sustained when, aged eight, he had engaged in swordplay with a particularly vicious Parisian boy two years older than himself. He had damaged his shoulder that time he had tried to jump his horse over the River Yeo and by the end of each day it tended to stiffen, though I knew just where to rub it to make the ache go away. I had kissed that little scar so often, stroked it with my fingers. I knew his body as intimately as I knew my own. It seemed there was not a part of it I did not know, had not caressed and kissed, but had I ever known the soul that resided in that beautiful body at all?

When he climbed into bed he reached out to take me into his arms. I flinched from his touch and straight away scrambled out of the other side. There was a flash in his eyes then, like the slash of a sword, and it was as if a mask had been cut away. He stared at me, angry and aggrieved. He said nothing, did not ask me now what was wrong. He looked as if he knew that I finally understood exactly what he had done. As if there was no further need for pretence. There was no mistaking it, he stared at me with guilt. And with hatred.

I took a torch and walked down to the moor again, found myself wandering over the river and across the Tickenham Road, up the stony track to Folly Farm, an isolated low little farmhouse, nestled in trees at the foot of Cadbury Camp. It had not been tenanted for years because it had fallen into disrepair and the funds that might have been used to repair it had been spent instead on the new coach house. The door hung on its hinges and the kitchen was empty except for a rickety table and some stools. It was dirty and dark and cold. There was a hole in the crooked lathe ceiling and a corresponding one in the thatched roof of the room above, so that it was possible to look up and see right through to chinks of starry sky. But at least, being built where the ground started to rise, it was quite dry. It was a sin that it had been left empty so long. I would see it put to rights and turned into a good home for someone.

There was half a bushel in the grate, enough to get a small fire going, and I curled up on the bare floor beside it with my cloak as a blanket. My face and my hands were warm enough, but the fire did not even air the room or do much to compensate for the broken roof. I slept with an icy chill at my back.

In the morning I went out to the well at the back of the farmhouse and washed in a bucket of cold water before going back to the house to find Bess.

She waited for me to finish sneezing before she handed me a cup of hot cider. 'Well, if you will stay out in a rainstorm, what do you expect, if you don't mind me saying?'

'Where is Richard?' I asked, wrapping my fingers around the warmth of the cup to stop them trembling.

'I take it the two of you had another falling out? Why else would you go for a midnight wander and he ride off as if the hounds of Hell were on his tail?'

They are, I wanted to tell her. Bess, they are. They have been for years. But I could not voice my fears. If I did, it made them real.

'I need to go to bed,' I said to her. But I did not know where to go. Not to the chamber I shared with Richard, nor the one he had always used when he came here as Edmund's guest. I wanted to sleep somewhere he would not think to look for me. 'I shall go to your room,' I said.

Bess looked aghast. 'In the attic, Ma'am?'

'Yes.'

I lay down on the little pallet, but I could not sleep. Thoughts flew at me haphazardly, like an ambush of arrows all fired from different angles. No judge would ever find him guilty. Even if it was Richard who had come back from London with poison, it was I who had administered it, I who put it into the claret and held it to Edmund's lips for him to drink. So easy it would have been for Richard to do it. So easy to visit an apothecary and purchase a poison instead of a cure. But why? Was it out of desperation? Out of love for me? That competitive spirit of his? Because he could not stand for Edmund to have me? Or was it purely the pursuit of wealth that had motivated him? Why else would he have been so against a marriage settlement? Why else . . .

What was I thinking? I loved him, had lived with him and shared his bed every night for ten years. Richard was not capable of murder . . . was he? The vulnerability and impulsiveness that had so enchanted me now seemed sure indications of a character that was dangerously unstable. I needed to see him. If I could only see him, only look into his eyes again,

I'd know that I'd been mistaken, horribly mistaken. I'd know it could not be true.

I heard my father's voice then, so loud he might have come to sit right beside me. *These are men who would break any trust or dare any act of treachery to satisfy their passions and appetites, who are uncontrolled by any fear of God or man . . . You will be prey to every unscrupulous Cavalier.*

'You have a visitor, Ma'am,' Bess came to tell me later, much later, when the sun was sinking in the sky again. 'Shall I tell him you are ill, or shall I help you to dress?'

'Who is it?'

'Gentleman by the name of Joseph Barnes. Asked to see the lady who collects butterflies.'

'I'll see him,' I decided, thinking that anything was preferable to lying here, with suspicion battering my head until it throbbed.

Bess helped me into my gown of moss-green silk and fastened up my hair, but as soon as she was gone I shook it loose since my head was hurting so much.

Joseph Barnes was a foppish young gentleman traveller who explained effusively that he was on the way to sample the excellent waters in Bath. 'I decided to stop at the inn in Tickenham for the night and couldn't help hearing the locals talking over their ale about the Lady of the Manor who is paying anyone who brings her worms. I went to the trouble of finding some, just for the privilege of seeing you for myself.'

'Did you?' If I'd not had so much on my mind, it would probably have unnerved me to know I was being talked about in such a way, that I was attracting such interest, but now it only added to the strange air of unreality. 'I did not realise I was locally a curiosity, sir,' I said, sneezing again. 'You'd find the caves of Cheddar Gorge far more interesting, or the cove at Ladye Bay. Even the rhynes and moors, I can assure you. They attract dragonflies and butterflies that even the Royal Society finds of interest. I am afraid I must be a great disappointment by comparison.'

He made a little bow. 'On the contrary. You are uncommonly pretty and erudite. I had imagined an old hag.'

I laughed and it sounded very odd to my ears, as if I should never laugh again. 'So where are these worms?' He did not appear to have come with any vessel at all.

He produced a highly ornamented snuffbox and opened it. Two striking little creatures wriggled most obligingly, black speckled with yellow. Despite everything, because of everything, my interest was spiked.

'I stung myself on the nettles, getting them for you,' he complained.

'Did you bring any with you?'

'Nettles, you mean?' He frowned. 'I am afraid not.'

'These are good specimens,' I said, giving one a tiny prod with my finger. 'But they will need a plentiful supply of the right foodplant. Can you show me exactly where you found them?'

He seemed glad of the chance to walk with me and set off as frisky as a young pup, bounding haphazardly from one new and thrilling scent to another.

The light was failing, the dusky blue of the vast sky streaked with palest lemon. The air was busy with gnats and, in the distance, a plover was calling. We walked over Cut Bush fields towards the Yeo, and just before the mill my fashionable companion indicated a patch of common nettles by the trackside.

'You are sure that is the plant?'

'I am quite certain.'

I thanked him, paid him sixpence and sent him on his way, then bent to pick some of the stalks. I chose the healthiest shoots and took a whole handful, tearing off the muslin trim on my gown to bind them and protect my hands from the serrated leaves. I walked back alone across the twilit moor.

Richard was standing beneath the oriel, staring not at my hair that hung down to my hips, nor at my ripped gown, but at the Gothic prickly posy I carried through the dusk. He stared as if it was of great significance, as if within its spiky leaves lay a hidden truth, an answer, as if I had come to scatter our marriage bed with stinging nettles, where once it had been scattered with bright summer flowers.

As I came closer I saw that there was something very wrong with him. He had been drinking, and his eyes were dark, so dark, against the unnatural pallor of his face, as cold and as hard as winter stars. I came on, and if I had hoped to see a man incapable of murder, I saw the opposite. I saw rage, and a naked, glittering, unadulterated hatred that made me falter and drop the nettles, afraid to go any closer. He was breathing deeply and there were beads of sweat on his brow.

He stepped up to me, raised his hand and slapped me across my cheek, so hard that my head whipped to the side and it felt as if my neck would snap. My skin stung, there was a sharp pain in my lip and the metallic taste of blood in my mouth. Before I had a chance to recover, he grabbed my arm with such force it felt as if it would be wrenched from its socket and dragged me, stumbling behind him, into the hall and up the narrow stone stairs. The clothes chest was thrown open and my boxes and observation books and an untidy pile of James's letters were heaped beside it, opened. Richard took up one of the letters, held it in front of my face, slowly ripped it in half. With one swift fluid movement he put the two halves together and tore again, let the pieces scatter to the floorboards.

He took hold of another, and started to tear.

'No!' Fury erupted inside me – uncontrolled, desperate, searing fury. I grabbed the collecting box and hit at him with it. He tore the box from me, smashed it down over my hands, cutting them and driving splinters into my skin. He snatched a specimen box and did the same with that, and with a single violent swipe of his arm he knocked the rest off the bed, sending them crashing to the floor in a flutter of broken wings and little broken furry bodies. I collapsed beside them in a flurry of silk and lace and petticoats and he brought the spurred heel of his boot down on the little wings and crushed them as if he would crush and trample my heart.

'I should have seen it before,' he said, in a guttural voice I hardly recognised as his. 'As soon as you started with this absurd fixation. Beating at trees and crawling under bushes, rambling around half dressed, like a gypsy. Talking gibberish about miracles and worms. Now you carry a gruesome bouquet of weeds, as if they were the sweetest roses. You grieve for dead maggots and pay people a small fortune to bring you live ones. You stir a pile of cow manure like a cook with the broth.'

I shook my head, shaped my mouth to deny it, but no sound came.

'Do not try to gainsay it,' he spat. 'Your word stands for naught. All that they say about you is true. It has taken me long enough to see it, but I see it now. You are not in your right mind. You must be . . . completely insane.'

* * *

422

Next to accusing me of witchcraft, lunacy was the most dangerous charge Richard could have made. The mad were creatures to inspire terror. They were bewitched, visited by Satan, possessed by demons, souls who were preyed upon by the armies of the night. Lunacy was a charge which carried with it the threat of chains and confinement, of asylums, of the loss of all rights and liberties.

It was the only charge he could have made that would enable him to overturn the marriage settlement and seize control of my estate. I did not know how easy it would be for him to accomplish, I could not even be sure that it was what he planned to do, but I did know that there were plenty of people who would support such claims.

I would fight him, fight them all with everything I had, but my first thought was to get the children away to safety. As soon as Richard had fallen into a rum-induced sleep in a chair in the parlour, I packed a trunk and went to wake the girls and Dickon.

'Hurry and put on your clothes,' I urged Ellen, setting a candle on the table and depositing a heap of gowns and stockings and breeches on the bed.

'Where are we going?' she mumbled, clutching the linen sheet over her body.

'To London,' I said, trying to make an adventure of it.

'But it's dark outside,' she complained. 'Can't we wait until morning?'

'No, sweetheart.' I pulled a petticoat over her head. 'I'm afraid we cannot. Here.' I put my hand into my pocket. 'I have brought you a treat.'

'Marchpane! In the middle of the night?'

'Why not?'

The bribe worked and I helped Ellen into her stockings, made sure Mary had her cloak. I saw the three of them out to the waiting coach, carrying Ellen in my arms, still wrapped tight in her rich-coloured blanket, with Dickon clinging anxiously to my skirts, as if he thought I might leave him behind or that someone might try to snatch him from me. The coachman folded down the iron steps and handed the girls in. The lanterns were already lit, the lights from them hazy in the mist.

Dickon suddenly turned and sprinted back to the house. I ran after him to the nursery where he began collecting up all the animals currently residing there, namely two chickens, a piglet, a toad, a pike and the swan. Together we carried them outside and set them free in a wild flurry of wings and feathers. I took the bucket and tipped the toad and the pike into Monk's Pool and Dickon came back with Cadbury at his heels.

I helped him heft her into the coach.

'You know I cannot come with you while my mother is still ill,' Bess told me as I lifted my skirts and put my foot on the first step.

'I understand.'

'Where shall I tell him you have gone?'

'Say that you do not know.'

'He is sure to guess.'

'No matter, so long as I am not here.' Here, I might have added, where thanks to our brother few were likely to question my husband too closely if he said I was not fit to manage my affairs, that I must be locked up.

The coach lurched into motion. So afraid was I of Richard waking to find us gone and coming in pursuit of us that I shouted up to the coachman to go faster. For the first few miles he drove the horses on through the night with a flailing whip. But after we had, of necessity, slowed to a steadier roll, Dickon gave my sleeve a little tug to tell me that he wanted to say something to me privately. He had not spoken one word to me since I had woken him and bundled him into the coach, but I had caught him glancing worriedly at my cut lip. He sensed my fear in a way the girls had not, knew this was no adventure. I lowered my head so he could whisper in my ear.

'Mama, are we running away from my father?'

It sounded such a despairing thing to do, I would not admit to it. And somehow it did not feel true. It did not feel as if we were running from anything, but towards it.

I turned to look down at the little head of his sleeping sister, curled in my other arm, and over to Mary who was gazing out of the window at the blue dawn-lit fields. 'No, darling,' I said to my youngest son. 'We are not running away. Look. See where the sky is turning pink. That is where we are going. We are travelling east. We are following the sun.'

'We will come back?'

'Oh, yes,' I said. 'We will come back. As soon as I have worked out what to do.'

I heard my father's voice once again . . . *Never forget you carry the stain*

of Eve's sin upon your soul . . . Never forget that Eden was lost to her because
of that sin.

Tickenham was my home, mine and my children's, and I would never
let Richard or anyone else take it from me.

I had not expected Aldersgate Street to be so grand. It was very long and
spacious, lined with innumerable inns and taverns, interspersed amongst
mansions fit for dukes and marquesses.

I had left all three children at Mary Burges's table, eating pottage and
pudding, and was glad that I had at least taken the time to change into a
gown of rose silk and creamy lace, and had tidied my hair and dabbed
rosewater on my wrists and throat.

A bell tinkled in the shop as I opened the door onto a room like none I
had ever seen before, a strange, eccentric, wonderful room. There was a
grand carved fireplace and floor and oak wainscot panelling. The far wall
was lined with tiny drawers and shelves full of beautiful glazed apothecary
jars and pill slabs. There was a dish filled with dried vipers and a crocodile
skin hung from the ceiling. Even the air was different, heavy with the exotic,
pungent scent of herbs.

James was serving a customer from behind a wide oak counter, his
corn-blond hair tied back, sleeves rolled up and a pestle and mortar at
his elbow. He did not see me when I entered, too busy measuring powder
on brass scales. 'Angelica can be used to treat any epidemic diseases, though
pray you have no use for it on your voyage, Robert,' he said as he handed
over a sachet in exchange for coins. He made notes in a ledger. Then he
looked up, saw me, and his quill stopped in mid-air. For a moment he looked
at me so oddly that I half thought he did not know who I was. Until he
smiled.

I smiled back, gestured with my hand. 'Please, do not neglect your
customer on my behalf.'

James tore his eyes away, back to the man at the counter, as if he feared
I might disappear while he was otherwise engaged. 'Robert, this is Eleanor
Glanville,' he said. 'She will be as interested as I am in the specimens you send
back from the Americas. Mistress Glanville,' he said to me, 'meet Robert
Rutherford, ship's surgeon.'

Mr Rutherford bowed.

'That is everything I think, Robert,' James said. 'Except for something to help rid you of the tetters, which I can see is still troubling you.'

The surgeon touched the back of his hand where the skin was red and flaky. 'Oh, I'm resigned to living with the itch now,' he said.

'Well, you shouldn't have to be. Try some bryony. Its leaves are good for cleansing all sores and the powder of the dried root cleanses the skin.' James handed over another sachet. 'Take both, with my compliments.'

Mr Rutherford added them to his chest. 'You are a generous man, Mr Petiver. I am much obliged to you, much obliged indeed.'

'As am I to you.' James opened a drawer behind the counter, handed over a thermometer and some quires of brown paper. 'For the plants. And here's a fresh collecting book. You have a net and bottles?'

'I do, and the printed instructions for preserving specimens which you gave to me the last time. Don't worry, sir, I know what to do now.' Rutherford grinned. 'I will be sure on this voyage to look in the stomachs of sharks for strange animals as I was unable to do last time. It'll be as if you'd been to South Carolina and Massachusetts Bay yourself when you see all that I'll bring back for you.'

'I wish you a very speedy return then,' James said as the surgeon headed for the door. 'But above all a safe one.'

'Aye, I heard how your collectors keep dying off, done in by natives and mysterious diseases or else lost at sea. Don't worry, I'll not fail you. I will be back.'

'When do you sail?'

'Next Thursday, with the tide, wind permitting. Good day to you, Mr Petiver.' He gave a nod to me as he passed on his way out. 'Good day to you too Mistress Glanville.'

James came around to the other side of the counter and took my hands. 'You have come back at last. Why has it taken you so long?'

'I honestly don't know.'

I looked for changes in him, but found none to speak of. Not even a hint of grey in his fair hair. He was just the same, lithesome and slight, with eyes that radiated warmth and boundless enthusiasm and intelligence, and were flecked with all of nature's colours. I could barely see any lines around them.

'I had not imagined your shop would be quite so extraordinary and grand,' I said. 'Even though I know you are a Member of the Royal Society and a respected man of medicine now.'

He stood back to look at me. 'You are grand and extraordinary enough yourself.' He smiled generously. 'I still do not even pretend to follow fashion, but I know enough to recognise a very fine gown and cloak when I see one.' He touched my arm, seeing that my eyes were not half so bright as my clothes, even after a little flattery. 'We cannot talk properly here,' he said. 'I'll close the shop and we'll go to the tavern and then you can tell me how everything is with you.'

We walked up Aldersgate Street towards St Botolph's church and the City gate. We passed numerous taverns on the way but James led me to the Bell Inn, a respectable establishment with wagons drawn up outside. Within it was full of gentlemen travellers, smoking clay pipes and eating oysters, beneath the low sloping ceiling. We took our pots of ale and found a quiet corner where a mongrel was curled by the fire.

'You have achieved all you set out to achieve,' I said, after he'd drawn up a stool opposite mine.

'Oh, there is always more to do, more to discover. I will never have the time to finish even a fraction of all I want to do, if I live to be seventy.'

He could well live to such a great age. He looked so full of life and vigour still.

'What has made you come back to London now, Eleanor? After all this time?'

I looked down at my hands, lightly folded in my lap, and did not know where to begin.

He touched the cut on my lip, almost healed after four days' travelling, but still visible. 'He has hurt you?'

'He did,' I admitted. 'But only once. And not badly. It is his right, after all,' I added bitterly. 'As my husband he has every authority, over my body and my conduct. If he wished to beat me, no law in this country would come to my defence. But I could bear a beating. It is not that. He says that I am mad.'

Silence fell briefly. 'It is not the first time you've had that accusation made against you, is it?' James said at length. 'I have suffered it, too, as has anyone who collects butterflies. Just last week I had a letter from a sea captain who was collecting for me in Spain when he was set upon by locals.

They accused him of sorcery and necromancy, of chasing butterflies in an attempt to commune with the spirits of the dead.'

I was shocked. 'Surely nobody really believed he was a necromancer?'

'I am afraid that the Age of Reason has not reached some parts of Spain.'

'Just as it has not reached some parts of England.' I clutched my pot of ale. 'I came to London because I am afraid of what Richard will try to do. I am afraid that he means to have me locked up so he can take possession of my estate. As my wedded husband, he could do that, couldn't he? He could lock me up and seize everything. That is what they do to the insane, isn't it?'

'It happens,' James said bluntly, and I was grateful to him for not trying to belittle my fears. 'But he would have to bring lunacy proceedings against you before he would be allowed to keep you under any restraint. He would have to petition the Lord Chancellor and convince a jury that you were incapable of managing yourself or your estate.'

'There are enough people who would support his claim.' I put down my pot and fingered the cascades of lace at the sleeves of my gown. 'James, you must have been to see the lunatics in the new Bedlam?' I whispered the question with a morbid fascination. 'Is it as terrible as they say? Are they filthy and naked and ranting, left to rattle their shackles and starve in cells that are stinking and damp and always dark?'

'Nobody is going to send you to Bedlam,' he said quietly. 'Nor anywhere like it. The asylums are for the poor.' He gave a half smile. 'Those who are wealthy and insane are committed to the care of a physician, and if they are confined, it is in a warm and comfortable room in their own country mansion. But, Eleanor, you are not mad,' he reassured me. 'You are exuberant and enthusiastic. You are passionate and obsessive. To many that may look very like madness, but you are probably the sanest person I have ever met.'

'You do not subscribe then to the notion that there are demons which prey on obsession and passion?'

'I believe that is a most convenient deterrent, put about to discourage obsession and passion, which I think a very great pity as it makes the world a far poorer place.'

I smiled to hear that. 'You are a wonderful person, James.'

'Coming from you, that is the highest praise.'

'You do not believe that all women are creatures of weak reason either?'

He let his hands fall from mine. 'I cannot speak for all women. I have known too few of them, and those I have known, I have known too vaguely. I have always been too busy.'

'That sounds a lame excuse.'

'Does it? Perhaps it is. I admit I have little faith in the state of matrimony. It does not seem to bring many people contentment. You yourself have tried it twice and it seems to me that both have led to great sorrow and pain, of one sort or another.'

'If I had not married, I would not have my children,' I said. 'If I had not married Richard, I would not have little Ellen, who is as exquisite as a doll, and Dickon, who is so clever and kind it humbles me.' I smiled. 'Oh, James, you should see how he turned the house into an ark, with all the wounded creatures he takes in. He has a talent for healing them. But I worry for him. He is so sensitive. He has never really got along with his father. I shall have to go back to Tickenham, to face Richard's accusations, but I do not want Dickon there with me.'

'How old is he?'

'Nine.'

'Is he tall? Would he pass for a couple of years older?'

'In manner, most definitely.'

'Then bring him to me and I will take him as my apprentice.'

Instantly I saw that it was a perfect solution. Since the Glanville family seat at Elmsett was ruined and there were no funds to repair it, Dickon would have to make his own way in the world. He would need a profession, and medicine would suit him more than most. I could not wish for a better master to tutor him.

'Don't worry,' James smiled. 'I will not make him bed down under the counter, like the usual sort of apprentice. He will have his own dormitory and eat his meals at my table.' His eyes met mine with rare tenderness. 'I promise to care for him as if he was my own son.'

'Thank you, James.'

'It is you who is doing me the greater service,' he said with his usual generosity. 'I need help with my work, and I know that any son of yours will be honest and quick to learn and very charming company with it.'

I felt a little pang of shameful envy that I tried very hard to quash, but could not quite. All I could think was that I should like very much to be bound as James Petiver's apprentice. I should like nothing better than to know that I would be learning from him, working side by side with him, every day for the next seven years.

Envy made me a little impatient with Dickon as I helped him sort his own possessions from the trunk and put them into a small portmanteau we had borrowed from John Burges. Dickon was as dejected as Cadbury, who trailed at his heels with her tail between her legs.

'I'll take care of her for you, I promise,' I tried to reassure him.

He turned to me then, his bottom lip trembling. 'I want to stay with you,' he said plaintively. 'Mama, why do I have to go?'

Faced with his doleful eyes, my heart completely melted. I went to him and wrapped him in my arms, a knot in my own throat. I clasped his head to my chest and pressed my lips into his hair. 'This is a great opportunity, Dickon,' I told him gently. 'You could not have a better master than James Petiver. He is a good man, a clever man, my dearest friend. You will learn so much from him. Will you try to be brave, Dickon, for me?'

He nodded.

James welcomed him with an arm about his shoulders and took him off on a tour of the premises. The back of the shop was even more bizarre and amazing than the front, like a sorcerer's laboratory, with cauldrons bubbling and steaming and liquids distilling in bottles and tubes. Outside was something equally amazing and sublime. James had established his own idyllic little physic garden.

I felt like Cadbury as I trailed behind them, up the straight grassed avenues and neat rows of herbs and medicinal plants, trying to quell the pangs of regret that only magnified with each friendly, enthusiastic word James spoke to my young son and made me wish, now more than ever, that I had been born a boy.

'You will accompany me on my rounds and become familiar with patients and diseases in a way that medical students in Oxford and Cambridge, who are restricted to academic learning, never have the chance to do,' James explained to the boy. 'There will be a few menial tasks, I'm afraid, but not too many. Most of the time you'll be learning about the mystery and craft of compounding drugs and simples, and how to recognise medicinal plants and where they grow in woods and meadows. Several times each year we shall take the Apothecary Society's state barge up the river with the other masters and apprentices and roam around the meadows of Gravesend and Twickenham, collecting plants to bring back here or take to the Company Hall for discussion.' James flicked a humorous sideways glance at me. 'Your mother was always very interested to hear about those days and the riotous suppers which usually end them.'

I glanced away, in case the envy had so magnified it had turned my blue eyes to green.

When we had completed a full circuit of the garden and were back in the shop, I knew I could delay no longer. 'I will be on my way then,' I said, going to Dickon to kiss him goodbye. His lip was trembling again. 'Don't,' I commanded softly. 'Or I will start too.'

'Mama, I will miss you.'

I stroked his cheek. 'I will miss you too, my little love.'

'Ach, stop it, the pair of you,' James said. 'You will neither of you have the chance to miss each other. Dickon, your mother is welcome here any time, she should know that. She can come to the shop every day to see you, if she wants to.' He was addressing my son, but his words were very definitely directed at me. Then he turned to face me and I knew it was a waste of time trying to conceal anything from him. My face was an open book to him. James, like Richard, read it as easily as my father used to read the Bible. He smiled as if at some private joke shared between us. 'She can be as an apprentice herself, if that is what she would like to be.'

I made myself give Dickon a day or two to settle in on his own. When I went back to the shop, I was impressed anew by its extraordinary atmosphere, part scientific, part magical. For many, the study of herbs was still allied to magic, for all that apothecaries worked side by side with physicians. Camphor vied for shelf space with brimstone, artists' dyes with substances used in alchemy. And in the midst of it all was James, standing betwixt the old world and the new.

He looked up from grinding some dried leaves and salt in the mortar and smiled to see me. 'He's in the laboratory,' he said. 'Go and see.'

Dickon was seated at a bench, wearing an apron and measuring out a jar of juice into a bowl of oil. 'It is self-heal and oil of roses,' he said. 'If you anoint the temples and forehead, it is very effectual in removing headache.'

'Always good to know.'

'And if you mix it with honey of roses, it heals ulcers in the mouth.'

'I'll try to remember,' I said.

'I cannot stop or it will spoil,' he announced busily.

'I'll not interrupt you then.' I wandered back out to the shop, feeling superfluous. 'You keep my son too well-occupied to talk to me,' I complained to James.

He put down his pestle and gave me his full attention. 'He's a capable boy. He takes notes of everything I tell him and knows the properties of the contents of a good proportion of the jars already.' I smiled with the pleasure of any mother at hearing her child praised. 'If he carries on at this rate, I'll be able to leave him in charge in a couple of months and concentrate on cataloguing my specimens.' He saw my eyes brighten for a different reason. 'I have so many sent to me now, from all over the world, that I can't keep up. I am afraid they are in the most terrible muddle. But I fear your son will be no help to me in that respect. I tried to show him some lizard specimens but he became almost distressed. Couldn't get away from them and scuttle back to the laboratory fast enough, in fact.'

I smiled. 'He does not approve of killing so much as a fly.'

'It is no matter. My collection is not to everyone's liking.'

'You know it would be very much to mine.'

He looked almost abashed. 'If I am to show it to you, it would mean going up to my rooms.'

'It may be improper, but I am a most improper person,' I smiled, linking my arm through his. 'Ask anyone in Tickenham.'

James left Dickon listening out for callers and led the way up a flight of steep, narrow stairs that ran up the outside of the shop and led to a little parlour. It smelled clean and fresh, with a hint of lavender and pencil shavings, but it was an utter mess. Clothes and books were heaped on chairs and the table, as were piles and piles of papers and letters. There were bottles of frogs, lizards, grasshoppers, and all varieties of small creatures – spiders, wasps, flies, lobsters, urchins – drowned in rum. Boxes of shells and cases of beetles, were stacked on the floor or against the walls. There was an anaconda and a rattlesnake that still looked capable of slithering across the floor. It was like being in a dreamland, being given a tantalising glimpse of a new world rich in colour, utterly different from any I had ever known or even dreamed of.

But I turned to James and pulled a face.

He read my dismay and shrugged. 'I did warn you.'

'You did,' I laughed, 'but still, I was not quite prepared. Good Lord, James, I have never seen such a jumble.'

But it was a treasure trove of a jumble, filled with promise. I raised my skirts as I would in the wet and picked my way over to the table where I lifted up a box of beetles and was met with a glimpse of a stunning butterfly beneath. It had black and white striped wings, in the sickle shape of a Swallowtail, and came from South Carolina, according to the note pinned beneath it.

'There are plenty more rare and far more beautiful even than that,' James said. He gestured helplessly around the room, scratched the back of his head. 'If only one knew where to look.'

I itched to see more but was reluctant to relegate the precious South Carolina butterfly back to its precarious pile in order to free up my hands. I might be consigning it to oblivion forever. I looked round for a more suitable place but there was none, not one clear surface.

James stepped over a tower of collecting books and came to stand beside me. 'I have tried to make some inroads.'

'You have?'

He removed the American butterfly from my grasp and set it down, turned to a cabinet behind him and opened a long shallow drawer like a tray, releasing a lovely scent of cedarwood. Contained within it was a box of butterflies, with silvery-white wings marked with brown and orange borders and striking black eyespots. 'White Peacocks from the West Indies,' he told me.

I ran my fingers over the glass. It felt like trying to reach the sky or touch the stars.

'There are butterflies in this room from all over the world,' James said tantalisingly. 'Antigua. Barbados. New York. St Christopher's Island.'

'The sea captains and ship's surgeons send them to you, just like you said they would?'

'Aye, and in greater quantities than ever I had hoped.'

433

I let my eyes linger on the captivating White Peacocks for a little longer. They were not perfect, missing a leg here or an antenna there, were ragged around the edges, but it did not seem to matter. It was heartening to know James no longer sought perfection. That he would not discard a pretty creature just for a broken wing.

'I have promised my friend John Ray that I will catalogue them, so that he can include them in his great history of insects. But I lack the time.'

'What you need, then, is a person with some experience of cataloguing. A person who has plenty of time and is badly in need of some distracting occupation.'

'And would you happen to know of such a person, by any chance?'

'Oh, I most certainly would.'

Summer 1695

There was no formal arrangement as such, but I fell into a habit of going to the Sign of the White Cross at least every other day, and for most of this time, while James and Dickon were about their apothecary business, I climbed the narrow stairs to James's rooms above the shop and tidied and organised and was happy as a bee in clover. I spent the mornings with beetles and lizards and shells; the afternoons were devoted to butterflies, which I ordered according to colour and then subdivided by size, until they were neatly graded in their cases like jewels strung on a necklace. In this room, if in no other part of my life, I had complete control. It was cathartic, putting things to rights, restoring order, squandering hours just marvelling at the glorious little beings.

If I kept myself well occupied, I managed not to think of Richard, of what he was doing all alone at Tickenham. But at night it was not so easy. It was so long since I had slept without him and I missed the comforting sound of his breathing, missed lying in his arms, missed talking to him, missed making love to him, no matter how much I told myself that that was where I had gone wrong. Had my father not warned me that the heart is seldom wise, that a woman's body is driven by base desires?

It unnerved me that Richard had made no effort to contact me in all these weeks. If I am honest, it hurt me too, and in my hurt I took his silence for proof, if I needed it, that all he had ever wanted was Tickenham Court, and that though he might be willing to let me go, he would not relinquish my estate without a fight. I knew that I must go back and fight him for it. But I could not face it, not yet. The girls were so happy being schooled by Mary, Dickon was happy with his books of herbals and anatomy. I did not know if Forest was happy. I had written to him twice in Flanders. Mary had written to him, too, but there had been no reply, and I did not doubt that he had had word from his stepfather and had taken his side, as he always had.

Sometimes, when the shop was quiet, or when I was so absorbed I worked late into the evening, James came up with two pots of warm ale to join me, or brought up a plate of cheese and bread and fruit for us to share, and I showed him particular marvels I had just unearthed.

'Look,' I said, 'this has to be my absolute favourite.'

'It is very lovely.' James smiled at my delight and looked closer at the exquisite butterfly from Surinam, with iridescent wings of green and gold and a splash of deepest crimson.

I was so proud of it that it was almost as if I had discovered it in its natural habitat, rather than in the turmoil of a little London parlour. Almost, but not quite.

'Imagine how dazzling it would be on the wing,' I said. 'How I would like to see such a sight.'

'You'll have to travel to Surinam then,' James said pragmatically.

'Wouldn't you like to?'

By way of an answer, he opened a collecting book he had brought up with him and I gasped to see the enormous Jamaican Swallowtail within. The wingspan was awesome, nearly half a foot at least, banded with luminous yellow and black. 'In his covering letter, Allen Broderick described how, because of its great size, it must hover before flowers while it feeds,' James explained. 'Of course I should like to see that for myself, but I am happy enough just to know it exists. I lack the funds to travel and cannot neglect the shop and my trade for months on end. Besides, I am not nearly adventurous enough. I far prefer to let others better suited to it do the travelling for me.' He closed the book on the Swallowtail, handing me another specimen to file. 'I have promised Edmund Bouhn this will be called Bouhn's Yellow Spotted Carolina Butterfly.'

I laughed. 'A very accurate description, since it has yellow spots, was found in Carolina and by a man named Bouhn.'

It was a strategic description too. I had learned that James was very wily in this way. Promising his collectors the kudos of having specimens named after them and seeing their names in print, was one way he spurred them on to bring back more. I had found the catalogues he printed in which he listed finds and named donors.

'I would like to have a butterfly named after me,' I said wistfully. 'I would like to be connected for all time with the most beautiful of all creatures. I would feel then that my life had some significance. That would be immortality, of a kind.'

'Of all the people in all the world to have a butterfly named after them, it should be you,' James said. 'You love them more than anyone I have ever met. You even look like one, as graceful and pretty and joyful as a little Brimstone.'

'But I have no wings. I can never travel either.' I spoke with a tug of longing that surprised me with its strength. After days spent amongst these exotic dead creatures and meeting in the shop some of the surgeons and captains bound for distant lands, I realised for the first time just how much I had always yearned to see more of the world, ever since I'd studied the names of foreign lands on my father's globe. 'I am a woman of some means, but I am just as hampered as you since ladies do not travel alone to far-off continents. And what are the chances of me discovering a new species in England? All the butterflies I see have been seen before by one of your friends. Although I did once see a Fritillary, on the cliffs, that I could have sworn had different markings from all the others.'

'But there are dozens of undiscovered butterflies still flying in English skies,' James said, in his usual tone of optimism and subtle encouragement. 'You could easily be the person to find one of them.' He looked around the now almost tidy parlour. 'After all, it can be no more taxing than trying to find anything in this room, and yet you have found just about every-thing.'

'I'm not quite finished yet.' I indicated the piles of letters still stacked against the wall. 'They should really be filed.'

James seemed to sense my reluctance to pry into his correspondence. 'You are welcome to read them, Eleanor,' he said. 'I keep no secrets from you.'

Autumn 1695

Now that I had excavated the table, James said he'd put it to use and had invited Hans Sloane to dine. 'I want Hans to meet you, and you him,' he said with a grin. 'Properly, I mean, rather than in disguise.'

'What about John Ray too?' I asked. 'Don't you want to let him have the collections for his book now?'

'Regrettably John is too old and ill to come to London any more. His legs pain him so much, he cannot even walk in his own orchard.'

'Oh.' I could not hide my disappointment. I nursed such fond memories of the kindly, wise old man. 'I was looking forward to showing him what I've done. I should enjoy being able to talk to him without worrying whether my voice sounds too high for me to pass as a boy.'

This time it was Hans Sloane who looked as if he had come in costume. I would never have recognised him if James's manservant, George, had not announced him, so regal had he become. He had served as physician to the Duke of Albermarle, Governor of Jamaica, and was now Secretary to the Royal Society and physician to King William and Queen Mary, but he looked like a duke or a king himself, as opulently dressed and as stately, with his lustrous periwig and heavily embroidered coat.

James formally introduced us.

'Ah.' Hans Sloane gave me an ebullient smile and swept a gracious bow. 'Petiver's Lady of the Butterflies. James has told me so much about you, I feel as if we have met already.'

I restrained a giggle, did not dare look at James. 'Likewise, sir.'

I heard James choke back his own mirth.

We were joined for dinner by another friend, Samuel Doody, who was as obsessive about moss and ferns as James was about insects, and also by

James's new lodger, Dr David Krieg, a Saxon physician and artist, who had come to London in the service of various noblemen and who was soon to sail again for America. Also present was Edmund Bouhn, he of Bouhn's Yellow Spotted Carolina Butterfly.

'I'm too sunburnt and windbeaten now for you to see,' Mr Bouhn said jocularly. 'But beneath this tan, I'm still jaundiced from a bout of yellow fever. I was practically the same colour as my butterfly. Though, fortunately, I was spared the pox, so I'm not spotted as well as yellow.'

Mr Bouhn seemed never to tire of talking about America and Mr Sloane never tired of talking of Jamaica and his collection of bright humming birds. I was sure I would never tire of listening to either of them. As they talked, the carriage wheels and the constant clop of hooves on the cobbles outside the parlour window faded away, so that I was transported to new and shining lands.

'You could explore the Americas all your life and never know half of them,' Mr Bouhn said, sipping his wine. 'They are so wild and so vast and so empty, so full of promise and possibilities. There are wild horses, and thousand-acre forests full of bears, rivers teeming with fish. The soil is so fertile that the flowers grow waist-high, and there are crabs on the shores almost as big as turtles. I envy you, Dr Krieg, I would return there tomorrow.'

I envied David Krieg, too, as I envied all the captains and surgeons who every day staggered into the shop on their sea legs, who made my mouth water for the taste of pineapple and pomegranates, who spoke of giant spotted cats and fish that flew and butterflies with great wings of flashing metallic blue. I could have listened to their travellers' tales all day.

'I am very fortunate,' David Krieg said. 'But I have Mr Petiver to thank for the fact I do not have to return to Germany, and can travel safe in the knowledge that my family will want for nothing while I am away.'

Everyone around the table cast warm appreciative glances at James and I had the sense that everyone here apart from myself knew exactly what Doctor Krieg meant, but I had no chance to discern more because the discussion rapidly moved on.

Hans Sloane cut a piece of the lamb. As he carved, he told us he had just spent a vast sum on the purchase of a new collection of butterflies. 'I don't suppose you're any more inclined to sell yours to me, James?'

'No, Hans,' he replied, amiable but firm. 'Not for a good while yet, at any rate.'

'But how am I to found the British Museum if my dearest friend will not even contribute?'

James poured some more wine. 'Is there no end to your quest for legacy?'

Sloane eyed him with a grin. 'You should have a mind to your own legacy, my friend. Especially since you show no sign of fathering a dynasty of little Petivers. Or are you content to go down in history as the father of British entomology, the man who made natural science popular?' He drummed his fingers on the table. 'Then again, I suppose that is not such a bad epitaph.' He gave an even heavier sigh. 'We will all of us be buried with our own dead butterflies, like the ancients were buried with their gold.'

'I think I'd rather have living ones fluttering in my tomb,' I said.

'Hmmm. That's a very pretty image, my dear,' he mused. 'Almost mystical. Like a fable.'

'I fear it is a fable that butterflies are birthed from their own little tombs,' I said. 'I reared a pupa, and all I got for my efforts were flies. But I imagine even flies deserve a place in the British Museum, sir.'

'Indeed so. Well said, my dear. Well said.'

'Why not go the whole way and call your collection the Hans Sloane Museum?' James asked.

'Too parochial.' Sloane stretched back in his chair, patted his tight paunch. 'The British Museum would always be the biggest and the best, unsurpassed.'

James laughed. 'You are an arrogant swine, Hans.'

Sloane had the grace to laugh, too. 'The cocoa importers called me arrogant when I said their therapeutic drink was not palatable to the Europeans, mixed with honey and pepper like they take it in the West Indies. But when I suggested they drink it with milk, I was hailed as a veritable genius. Now, drinking chocolate is as fashionable as drinking coffee.'

'And you have made your fortune from the commercial production of it in ingenious blocks,' James put in.

'I made a greater fortune from importing Jesuits' Powder as a remedy for tertian ague.'

'What does it look like?' I asked abruptly. 'Jesuits' Powder . . . what colour is it?'

'Dark rust-red,' Hans said. 'Like cinnamon. It is flaky. Very bitter to taste.'

I twisted my hands together. 'Is there any other substance that resembles it?'

'Undoubtedly.'

'Something poisonous?'

Sloane glanced at James. It was he who spoke. 'Jesuits' Powder is highly poisonous, Eleanor,' he said carefully. 'Given in high enough doses, it is lethal. Anything above eight drams is dangerous. The Protestants were right to fear it, in a way, though I do not believe for a moment the Catholics ever intended to use it to harm them.'

'How many drams are there in two spoonfuls?'

James frowned. 'A dozen, maybe more.'

'What are the symptoms of poisoning?'

James deferred to his friend here. 'Ringing in the ears, stomach cramps and vomiting, chaotic pulse, skin rash, blindness, headache,' Sloane told me.

'Death?'

'In some instances, yes. Not thinking of poisoning anyone, are you, Mistress Glanville?' Hans's tone was teasing, until he saw my face. 'My dear lady, are you unwell?'

I put my hand to my cheek, almost as if to remind myself of the way Richard had hit me, the violence with which he had accused me of insanity, the look of absolute and unmistakable guilt that I had seen so clearly in his eyes. It made no difference that he had given me the right medicine but the wrong dosage, did it? It changed nothing.

'Hans was much taken with you,' James said, when everyone had gone. 'It is no small thing to count as your friend and patron one of the most powerful and esteemed scientists of our day.'

It was the right thing to say, as he always did find the right thing. He sensed I wanted to talk no more of Jesuits' Powder, had always understood me implicitly, always known what I most needed, even before I knew it myself. Now he made a suggestion. 'Would you like to try to birth a butterfly again? I'll gladly help you.'

'Oh, James, there is nothing I would like more.'

He smiled. 'We can start just as soon as you finish sorting those letters.'

'And I was worried that, when they were done, I would have no more reason to be here.'

'You do not need a reason,' he said warmly. 'You should know that. But now I have given you one anyway.'

There was no sign of George coming to clear the table so I gave up waiting and went to sit on a stool with my back against the wall. I picked the top letter off the largest stack, then the next, checked date and signature, started two new piles.

James had very many devoted friends. That was plain from the sheer volume of letters he had amassed. What struck me most was the loyalty and dedication of his correspondents, the warmth with which they addressed him, and the considerable efforts and often even more considerable dangers to which they had gone, time after time, to collect specimens for him.

As I read, I found a recurring theme. Payment had been made to the English wife of ship's surgeon Robert Rutherford, and to the wife of Patrick Rattray, ship's master in Virginia, to whom James had also given free medical advice about the pox. I remembered Dr Krieg's comment over dinner, which hinted that he was only free to travel because he was certain his family would want for nothing.

There was only one explanation. With sublime generosity, James had undertaken to offer succour and support to the needy relations his many correspondents and specimen gatherers were forced to leave behind while they sailed the seas. It made no difference whether the men were in the pay of the British Navy or of merchants, James still made their dependants his responsibility. No wonder he said he could not afford to leave the shop, to go travelling himself.

It was my own personal experience that James was good and kind but I had not realised the great extent of that goodness and his kindness, had not realised that I was by no means the primary recipient of it, that others received it in equal or even greater measure. It made me wonder now if I had been wrong, all those years ago, when I had worried that he wanted there to be something more between us. It seemed that I was the very poorest judge of character.

I did not find my own letters to James amongst the piles, and wondered where they were, what had happened to them.

When the door opened at last, it startled me. It was only George, but he had not come to clear the table. 'Mr Petiver asks you to join him in the shop immediately,' he said. 'He has something he wants to show you.'

The something a beaming James had to show me was a batch of hairy green caterpillars in a chip box.

'You're not the only one who has been busy this afternoon. I took George with me to Primrose Hill and we have scoured every bed of stinging nettles.'

'And brought half of them back with you, by the look of it.' I nodded towards the bucket of spiky green plants by his feet. He had collected not just the leaves, as I had done, but dug up entire plants by their roots. While I had been discovering the depth of his kindness, he had been out all afternoon doing the kindest of things for me.

'I'm sure the key to rearing butterflies must be to recreate an environment that mimics conditions in the wild as closely as possible,' he enthused, holding out his hand to me. 'Come and see what I've done.'

I let him lead me out through the garden, to a small stone herbarium at the end of the grass path which housed a collection of dried plants, some mounted and classified and labelled, and, inevitably, a great many that were not. But because the building was reserved for plants alone there was an order to it, a certain serenity. There was tree bark stacked like driftwood in one corner, and little dishes of seeds. The plants, like orchids, that could not be pressed without losing their form, were suspended in jars of liquid on a shelf that ran all around the room and gave the little building a strangely exotic and dreamlike quality.

On a table just inside the door James had set up a large breeding cage, inside which was an earthenware pot filled with soil. Beside it were a brass barometer and thermometer. On the ground by the table was a charcoal brazier already glowing with coals.

'To regulate the temperature, now that it is autumn,' he explained. 'Pretend it is summer for as long as possible.'

'It all looks very scientific.'

'So it should. We are conducting an experiment after all.'

'It will work,' I said, my confidence soaring. 'I know it.'

James handed me a trowel. 'I thought you'd like to help with the planting and with introducing the little creatures to their new home.'

I pushed up my sleeves and worked beside him as he took each plant and bedded the roots into the crumbly soil. I watched the firm but gentle pressure of his hands against the soft dark earth, the hands of a gardener and of a scientist, of an artist and a doctor.

He sprinkled water from a can and then let me release the worms on to the leaves while he checked the instruments. 'Did you ever master how to use a microscope?' he asked me conversationally as he made a note of the readings.

I angled my hand, to encourage the last worm to wriggle off it on to the nettle, and shook my head. 'You were going to teach me, weren't you? It is my fault you never had the chance. I never came back to London.'

'You are here now.'

I smiled. 'And have distracted you from your work all afternoon. Shouldn't you get back to the shop?'

'Probably.'

'Later then,' I said.

'Later,' he echoed, catching hold of my dirty hand as if it was the fragrant, gloved hand of a duchess.

When I went back to Hackney, I generally broke in on scenes of such domestic harmony it made me feel superfluous. My Mary was either busy with her crayons or with her needle, or else reading texts that Mary Burges had set her to learn, while Ellen was regularly to be found balancing a hefty Bible on her lap in a way that would have made her grandfather proud.

This time, though, Mary was playing the flute and Ellen was dancing around the floor, in wider and wider circles. When she saw me, she stopped dancing and rushed into my arms, hugging me and crying 'Mama, Mama,' and showering me kisses.

I kissed her back then turned to Mary, seeing the despondent look in her eyes. 'Still no word from Forest?'

She shook her head. 'He used to write to me so regularly. What if something has happened to him?'

'We would have heard,' I reassured her, but utterly failed to reassure myself.

Dickon was in the laboratory, crushing dry leaves with a pestle and mortar. His forearms had grown sinewy and strong from this regular work and his fair curls flopped over his forehead, in just the way that his father's dark ones did. He looked up, gave me a confident yet very charming smile. So help me God, his father's smile.

I sat down on the bench beside him, tucking my skirts out of his way. 'Are you enjoying your work, Dickon? Do you like it here, after all?'

He paused from his compounding and set his pestle down on the table. 'I like it best when Mr Petiver takes me with him to visit patients and I help him with letting blood and drawing teeth and administering enemas and blisters.'

I wrinkled my nose. 'Strange boy.'

He grinned. 'I like it when we go to the Surgeon's Hall to watch a dissection, too.'

'Ugh! This is the person who once flinched from a dead butterfly?'

'You told me there was nothing wrong with looking at dead things, so long as you can learn from them. I want to learn all about anatomy. I want to be more than a shopkeeper and compounder of herbs,' he said very earnestly. 'I have decided that I am going to be doctor. One who attends the needs of the sick poor who cannot afford a physician.'

My heart swelled with pride, but at the same time I was fearful for him.

'Then you will be at the forefront of open warfare,' I said lightly. 'A bitter conflict that goes back to before even the Civil War, when the apothecaries declared for Parliament and the physicians for the King.' I did not want to discourage him, but neither could I bear to think of him disillusioned, his ambitions frustrated. I knew a little of what that felt like. 'You know that apothecaries who prescribe medicines independently of a physician, or give separate advice or treatment, still risk prosecution?'

'Of course I know that, Mama,' he said, as patient and condescending as if our roles were reversed, I the child and he the parent. 'I know very well that the Society of Physicians has the right to march into this shop any time it likes and destroy any substances of which it does not approve.'

I nodded. 'Very well. What does James say? Mr Petiver, I mean. Have you talked to him about this?'

'He says I am like you, determined to go my own way.'

I laughed. 'Well, I hope you are more successful at it than I have been.'

'Mr Petiver says that you are very respected. Mr Petiver says,' he began again, 'that the physicians' monopoly on medical practice cannot last forever. He says that the physicians are only too happy for us to attend emergencies at night when they don't want to be disturbed, just as they all fled from the city and left the apothecaries to treat the victims of the plague. Mr Petiver says the poor already regard us as their doctors, they respect our seven years of training. It is only right we should be allowed to attend them.'

'I cannot argue with you there. Or with Mr Petiver.'

'I met two young physicians at the coffee house yesterday,' Dickon went on eagerly. 'John Radcliffe and Richard Mead. Dr Mead has a plan to start a practice of coffee-house consultations that could set us up as general medical practitioners and pave the way for us to be given the legal right to practise. It could change medical practice in this country forever.'

I looked at his soft blue eyes, so alight with hope, ambition and plans, and I knew then that I had done right in bringing him here. James's kindness and enthusiasm was evident in every word Dickon spoke.

I could picture him returning to Somersetshire after his training, a learned professional, surrounded by dogs and cats and several swans and ducks, respected in his village as a general medical practitioner, a trusted alternative to quacks and surgeons like Dr Duckett, the first person to whom ordinary families turned when they were sick and in need.

'You were right, Mama. James Petiver is a good man. I can see why you care for him so much.'

I don't know which of our faces flushed the brightest. 'Listen to me, Dickon,' I said. 'James and I have been friends for a very long time. I love him as I would love a brother. I may not be with your father now, but you must understand that I am still his wife. I loved him more than I have ever loved any man. I have never been faithless or untrue to him.'

Dickon's boyish jaw had stiffened. 'James Petiver is more a father to me than Richard Glanville will ever be,' he said, his voice breaking with emotion. 'He is kind and good, and he guides and teaches me like a father should. It is him I wish to emulate. My father is a cruel man. I know he hit you. I despise him.' Dickon looked suddenly shy. 'Mama, James is already like a father to me. And anyone can see that he loves you and cares for you like a husband should love and care for you, like you deserve to be loved and cared for.'

I was taken aback. 'I don't know about that.'

'Well, I do.'

I had studied nature all my life, but the sheer ingenuity of creation never failed to surprise and amaze me. I had never been more surprised or amazed than I was when I visited the nettle pot in the herbarium with James and found that the worms had turned architects and builders and constructed a neat little tent out of leaves at the base of the plant. They had bound the leaves tidily together with silk and were inside it, happily wriggling and munching away.

'Well, that certainly didn't happen last time,' I said.

'Different species,' James concluded. 'Butterflies are creatures of great diversity, as we know.'

The tent structure grew as the worms grew and shed their skins. They cut through stems and pulled the whole shoot over to extend their home. And then half a dozen of them spun themselves little coffins, which hung suspended from small hooks and pads of silk inside the shelter. We had to peer inside very carefully, so as not to disturb them. The coffins, too, were quite different from the ones I had seen before, greyish and shot with shimmering gold.

'I feel I've witnessed a small miracle already,' I said. 'Even if they do not turn into butterflies.'

'They will,' James replied. 'I am sure of it.'

I was convinced by his quiet assurance, wanting it to happen more for his sake now than for mine. 'We should keep vigil,' I said. 'I'll keep watch now and then you take a turn, so we do not miss it.'

'That sounds a rather lonely way to go about it. D'you think we could perhaps time it so that our watches overlapped now and again?'

James asked me if I would like to go with him to visit John Ray and I said that nothing would please me more. I helped him fill a saddlebag with as many carefully wrapped specimen trays as would safely fit. Then, wrapped in cloaks against the autumnal breeze, we set off on horseback for the hamlet of Black Notley, near Braintree in Essex, where John Ray had grown up, the son of blacksmith, and where he still lived in a small, timber-framed Tudor house called Dewlands. It stood on a knoll and had dormer windows that looked out over a stream, the smithy and a small cluster of cottages.

We were welcomed by John's wife Margaret, twenty years his junior and formerly governess to his friend's family, who showed us into a parlour that was built around a great chimney and crowded with books, collections, and four noisy little girls with lace caps on their heads. Margaret went to fetch her husband from his study over the brewhouse and John Ray greeted James with a hug of great affection before turning to me with interest. 'Ah, Isaac, my boy,' he said with a gentle humour. 'I must say, you are suited much better to petticoats than you are to breeches.'

I let out a ripple of laughter.

'How long have you known?' James exclaimed.

'Since you never mentioned your butterfly boy again, but spoke instead, constantly, of your Lady of the Butterflies.'

'Ah.' James coughed and busied himself opening up a portmanteau and handing the trays to John Ray while his girls crowded round to see.

Seeing that poor Mr Ray was obviously wracked with pain from the sores on his legs, I helped him shift books off the comfortable but threadbare chairs so we could all sit down by the crackling fire. All the books were marked with soot from the chimney and ink stains from the children, but their father made no apology for that fact.

'You have Eleanor to thank for the cataloguing,' James said, as John Ray's eyes lingered on a tray of Blues. 'It is all her work.'

'Excellent work it is, too.' He asked his eldest daughter to take the trays to his study and bring back his manuscript.

'Insects are so numerous and the observation of all kinds of them so difficult, I think I must give the task over to more able and younger persons. But the chapter on Papilos I will endeavour to continue, if I manage to survive the winter.' He handed the sheets over to James. 'Please pardon my scribble. Some days I can scarce manage a pen.'

Even so, the writing was elegant and flowing, and it pleased me to see that the lists of butterflies were catalogued after the same fashion I had adopted, but had descriptions not just of the imagos, or adult state, but of their caterpillars and pupae too. James's name appeared many times, and I felt a surge of pride to see it, as much as if it was my own name. *Butterfly, blue. Mr Petiver found in garden near Enfield. Mr Petiver thinks it a different sex rather than species.*

Margaret Ray brought wine and, despite his pain, her husband demonstrated his phenomenal memory as he talked of his completed books: on fishes, birds, plants, flowers, the wisdom of God. He also spoke fondly of a recent visit by Dr David Krieg who had stayed two days and made several exceedingly good drawings. Then, most lovingly, he described how, now his legs had failed him, his four young daughters went out with their nets at dusk, to collect nocturnals to bring to him.

When it was almost time to go, James presented Mr Ray with the parcels of sugar and tobacco and bottle of canary wine we had brought for him. 'With my very best wishes,' James said.

'You are too generous, James. Thank you. But you do not need to bring gifts. You should know that your company, and your collections, are reward enough.'

'I'll take these to Margaret then,' James said amiably. 'She has the common sense to be appreciative.'

He went off to the kitchen, two of the girls skipping after him.

'I have a dread of loneliness,' Mr Ray said to me candidly, scooping one of his daughters up on to his lap, trying not to grimace at the pain it clearly caused him. 'I find it hard to understand why any man would choose to live alone. But I gave up urging James to find himself a wife long ago. I knew there was a secret lady who was preventing him from forming any other attachment.'

I stared at him.

'Come, you must know, surely?'

'Sir, are you saying that James . . .'

'That he loves you, my dear. Always has, for as long as I've had the pleasure of his acquaintance, and I suspect always will.'

'He has never given me any clear indication.'

'That is not his way, is it? He seeks to make others happy rather than be happy himself. He is the most selfless man I've ever met. Doles out friendship and love, and all he asks in return is . . . well, butterflies and beetles.' A wry grin. 'You are from Somersetshire, aren't you? I had the privilege of making a tour of that spectacular county in the year after the Great Fire, and of hunting out the little white pointed leaves of the water parsnip. I do so regret no longer being able to go out in the field to collect flora and fauna. But James told me in his last letter that you are as interested in breeding butterflies as in collecting them. Tell me, did the hints I passed on prove successful? Have you hatched a pupa yet?'

'Not quite yet. But it looks promising. Forgive me, I did not know you had a hand in it.'

'Well, well. I am glad to see that James isn't always quite so self-effacing. That, just once in a while, he is capable of a little ruse, in order to impress a lass.'

Did he want to impress me? Did he really?

'You have bred butterflies, too, then?' I asked our host.

'My chief concern has always been to reinterpret the Christian faith in the light of a sound knowledge of nature. Understanding transformation is a matter of the greatest importance. To study just the imago is to study but half a life. Now, did you come up against the disturbing problem of false metamorphosis, when you hatched a fly instead of a butterfly?'

'Yes!' I exclaimed. 'The first time. That is exactly what happened.'

'Ah,' he said, turning grave. 'It has blighted the hopes of all us breeders at one point or another, but we are still not much closer to knowing quite how, or why. I truly believe we are on the brink of discounting the theory of spontaneous generation, but that is the final prop, still taken by some as proof enough that lice can be created by dirty hair and an old shawl be the originator of a moth, which in my personal opinion is bunkum, used erroneously to diminish God's power and undermine our faith in Him.'

'It never undermined your faith, sir?'

'Have you ever dissected a pupa?'

'I could never bear to waste one.'

'It is no waste. The intermediate state between caterpillar and butterfly is a formless broth. Only a divine creator could organise that broth into a new creature. Only a divine creator, and one with artistic flair, I might add, could design wings of such perfect symmetry and diversity and beauty. We'll debunk spontaneous generation one of these days. We'll prove that life comes from God, not matter, if only we have enough young natural-ists, like you and James, with a love of insects.'

Margaret Ray sent us off back to London, carrying fresh bread and homemade cheese in a parcel twice as large as the ones we had given her.

'You see,' James said to me, when we dismounted under an old oak tree to eat our feast amidst a carpet of gold and crimson leaves. 'There is a gentleman who is proof, if ever you or anyone else needed it, that devotion to natural history is a sign of learning and piety rather than of insanity.'

'Oh, but our circumstances are very different, James.' I fingered a piece of bread. 'Mr Ray has published books that more than compensate for the strangeness of what he does. They have brought him respect. I am not respected in Tickenham. Here, in London, when I am with you, with John Ray or Hans Sloane, I am an entomologist, a natural philosopher, an experimenter. But in Somersetshire I am no different from your collector in Spain, alone with my net and my love of shape-changing insects that are commonly believed to represent the souls of the dead. I am a witch, a madwoman, a sorceress. A necromancer.'

James held my eyes as a sudden squall of wind shook the tree and sent a flurry of golden leaves floating down on our heads. 'So, leave Somersetshire for good,' he said simply.

I half expected him to finish by suggesting I stayed in London, with him, but he did not.

James had brought bread to toast on a fork in the brazier in the herbarium, and had skewered the first slice. There was a nip in the dusky air and we both huddled close to the heat, our toes touching. He leaned forward to put his bread in the fire and I leaned forward too, my elbows on my knees and my chin propped in my hands, to watch the bread slowly browning and crisping. He turned to me in the flickering firelight and our lips were so close we could have kissed, but he made no attempt to initiate one.

Instead he handed me my toast and I crunched a corner. 'How long do we carry on?' It had gone on for days, one week that had stretched into two, and now nearly to three.

'You have had enough already?'

I would never have enough. I did not want this time to end, but I knew

James would never be the one to suggest we gave up, and one of us had to, sooner or later. 'That is their mausoleum, I think.' I gestured at the leaf tent, willing him to contradict me. 'These worms not only build their own gilded coffins, they build a whole crypt for themselves too.'

James was shaking his head very slowly, a slight smile animating his face. 'You did not look closely enough,' he said. 'There is a change.'

'Oh, I did look closely,' I said. 'This is exactly what happened before. Days passed without movement and then the pupa distended and darkened and shrivelled to nothing at all. They have all died, I am sure of it.'

'I don't believe so.' I hadn't even dented his confidence. 'Well, we will know by morning, I should think. If it is going to happen, it will be soon. When the sun comes up, would be the most likely time. I have brought blankets so we may stay all night.'

I had not noticed them, folded neatly in a basket behind the table. I recognised them as the ones that had covered his bed. He fetched one and draped it around my shoulders. My eyes already felt gritty with tiredness and I stifled a yawn, as I clutched the blanket around me and snuggled down into it. It was not richly brocaded like the ones on the bed at Tickenham but made of simple woven wool, fragranced with the heady scent of herbs and lavender and just a touch of brimstone, the same aromas that clung to James's hair and hands and clothes. I breathed them in like balm. He brought his stool around so that he was next to me, very close. I leaned my head on to his shoulder and, after a moment, he put his arm around me.

'Sleep now,' he said, and the vibration of his voice travelled into my own body and made it hum. 'I promise you that I will not. I will wake you the moment anything starts to happen.'

I closed my eyes, my cheek against the slightly prickly cloth of his coat, his arm enfolding me. I had never felt so safe, so at peace. His body was smaller and less muscular than the bodies of the two men I had married. More like my own, in fact. It fitted around me perfectly. We were a perfect match. I felt each rhythmic rise and fall of his chest, as he breathed, until my own breathing seemed to balance with his.

'Go to sleep,' he urged again.

'I am trying.'

'You do trust me?'

'James, I have always trusted you.'

I could feel the thud of his heart, beating strongly, purposefully. I nestled closer and was overcome with a sense of profound and sweet tranquillity. I slept. I slept so deeply and so soundly that when he bent his head to my ear and whispered for me to wake up, it was impossible to believe it was dawn.

'One of the pupae is opening,' he said, as I twisted round to look into his tired but happy face.

I was fully awake and on my feet in an instant.

With one finger I carefully lifted the leaves at the front of the tent and saw that one of the little shells was indeed moving, quivering slightly. I looked at James. I rubbed my sleep-blurred eyes and looked back at the coffin. I hardly dared to breathe in case it upset the transformation process. The pupa shook more vigorously and then it split, like an egg about to hatch. An abdomen thrust forward, threadlike legs scrabbled through the opening. It was happening with such raw, astonishing speed that I was afraid to blink, in case I missed it. There was a trickle of fluid the colour of blood and then a glistening rush as the butterfly burst forth, its coffin instantly reduced to nothing now but a fragile husk, empty and abandoned.

'It is true,' I whispered in awe.

I could feel the warmth of James's smile on my face, even though I could not tear my eyes away from the butterfly to look at him. I was as entranced as I was at the birth of my own children.

'Who claimed the age of miracles is past?' he said.

The new butterfly crept out of the leaf tent and climbed tentatively up on to the stems of the plant. It rested very still then stirred. The familiar wings unfolded like fans. Dark wings, with a band of vivid orange and splashes of scarlet and the purest snowy white.

'A Red Admiral,' I whispered with wonder. It seemed extraordinary that the first butterfly we had seen being born was one we had named together, as we would have named a child.

We watched it, pumping its wings, as another butterfly emerged.

'They will be hungry,' James said, and from somewhere produced a honeycomb. 'Let's see if they will take some from you.' He took my finger and dipped it into one of the waxy cells, then made me turn it upwards and hold it out towards the butterflies, one of which fluttered up and then down on to my wrist, turned and walked with closed wings down towards the honey. One of its little feet made contact with the stickiness and it paused, did a strange stepping dance.

'It's as if it tastes with its toes,' I whispered.

It uncurled its proboscis and started to feed. Its glorious wings opened. There, perched on my finger, the butterfly that I had witnessed being born. As soon as it had had its fill it flittered off up to the rafters.

I turned to James and kissed him on his lips. 'Thank you,' I said, but it did not seem enough, not nearly enough. He had given me so much, now and over the years, had always been there, a friend to turn to, whenever I was in trouble or unhappy, always ready to enthuse and inspire, just as my father had always been. And he had never demanded anything in return, except that I did not let go of my dreams. Now, I wanted to give him something back.

In the stillness of the dawn, as the rising sun tinged the sky with peach and the air turned a pearly blue, I spread out the blanket on the earthen floor and took his hand, leading him to it. We kneeled upon it together, slowly undressing each other as the butterflies drifted down and flickered around us on their silent, velvet wings, like tiny luminous bats. James plucked at the laces of my corset and I felt the air brush my breasts, as if for the first time. We lay down, naked, and traced every line and curve of each other's bodies, until two of the Red Admirals came gliding down from the shadowy roof and landed on my belly, where James had touched me and left a trace of sweet honey. It was an awesome, exquisite sensation, to feel them walking so lightly over my skin, where it had just been caressed. James kissed me, my mouth opened for him and I felt as if all the burdens of this life were pouring out of me. Weightless, I had been lifted up on golden wings.

He ran his fingers over my back and down the insides of my arms, his touch as soft and warm as the silken touch of the morning sun, as soothing as a benediction, and I knew that, although he had never given me any hint of it, he had made love to me in his imagination a thousand times over. I stroked him and his muscles quivered like the gilded coffin before it had burst open. The beat of him within me was the firm and powerful rhythm of a Swallowtail in flight over the moors, the pulsing of the newborn Red Admiral as it slowly beat its scarlet and black wings, until they were fully open and shining and perfect. His final release was as mystical as the transformed life that had burst forth from its shell. I closed my eyes, and when I opened them, I saw that the final Red Admiral had been born and had risen from its coffin into the light.

James took me by the hand and led me through to the laboratory.

'What are we doing now?'

He pressed me down on to the bench before the microscope. 'Oh,' I said. 'I see.'

'That is just it,' he said with a smile. 'You don't see. Not properly. Not yet.'

I felt a tingle of excitement.

He scanned the cauldrons and vials and tubes in the laboratory, but seemed to find nothing suitable. 'Wait there,' he said. 'I know exactly what you should look at.'

I heard him going up the wooden stairs to his rooms, two steps at a time, and then down them again, just as fast. He had a casket in his hand. Inside were all the letters I had ever sent to him, and beneath them, wings of broken butterflies, but not just any butterflies. I was puzzled at first. One wing was tiger striped, another vivid green, another small and blue. Stupidly, I took them for the ones James had sent to me over the years and wondered how on earth they came to be here when I had left them safely hidden in my Bible. Then it dawned on me that, of course, these were not my wings, but the opposite wings of the same butterflies. Where I had a right wing, James had a left. He had broken the butterflies in two and sent me one of the wings, keeping the other for himself, as others would bite into a coin and keep half each, as a token, a love token.

'Which should it be, do you think? The exotic Brazilian or the pretty little English Blue?'

'You choose,' I said.

He selected the Blue and I watched his fingers at work as he skilfully fixed it on to a pin and slid it under the lens. He sat directly behind me on the bench, so that I was perched between his legs, with his arms around me. I rested my hands on his thighs, as he brought his head down over my shoulder, his face cheek-to-cheek with mine. He made more adjustments to the various screws, moving the butterfly up and down and from side to side.

Finally he covered my left eye with his hand. 'Look now,' he instructed.

I bent towards the lens, my eyes widened with wonder. The image was incredibly, breathtakingly clear, and yet I could not believe I was looking at a butterfly. There were ridges of tiny plated mirrors, like the scales of a fish, like a suit of the most delicate, polished armour, of an impossibly bright lapis blue.

When I eventually moved back, the rows of shining mirrors still danced before my eyes.

'Tell me exactly what you see.' I felt the breath of his words in my hair, like a soft summer breeze. 'Describe it to me, as if you were my eyes and I couldn't see it for myself.'

'I see . . .' I broke off and thought. 'I see the blue of the brightest silk and satin, of the most lustrous taffeta. Of the sky in summer and of the sea. I see the blue of ribbons and of sapphires. I see that all the riches I ever needed are right there.'

Except, said the voice in my head, for the deepest, most beautiful blue of one man's eyes.

I fed the butterflies in the herbarium every day and they soon learned that there was always honey or the juice of an overripe plum on my fingers, so that all I had to do was open the door of the little herbarium for all three of them to come sailing down to perch on my hand, my shoulder, my head, sometimes getting tangled in my long hair. I marvelled at it each time. It was the simplest, purest pleasure. They made me feel blessed, as if I had been granted a special privilege.

I heard, or sensed, James come in softly through the door at the side, to stand watching for a while.

'Don't take this wrongly, now,' he whispered. 'I am not accusing you of communing with the dead. But it is almost as if you commune with those butterflies. Almost as if you are one of them.'

I smiled up at him through my lashes. 'I am surprised you are not a great distraction to them,' I said. He had been to the Master's Day celebrations at the Apothecaries' Company Hall in Blackfriars and looked very fine and handsome in his ceremonial livery of dark blue with gold braid. 'Shut in here all their lives, the poor little things have never seen anything half so bright.'

'They have seen you.'

The butterflies flew off and I watched them go dancing upwards, not towards an open sky but a dark entrapping roof. 'I know I cannot keep them forever,' I said sadly, as protective and possessive as a new mother. 'They are a week old already. We should set them free, shouldn't we? It is not fair to keep them here.'

James did not answer but I was sure he felt as I did, that when the butterflies were gone, everything would come to an end. Their serenity, their carefree joy and simple beauty, were symbols of our brief idyll of the past few weeks, an interlude which could not last forever. In a few days it would be November. The summer had ended long ago. I had been in London for weeks, too many weeks.

'You believe Richard Glanville is responsible for your first husband's death, don't you?' he said quietly. 'You believe he poisoned him with Jesuits' Powder.'

'How did you . . . ?'

'You fear him. More than you would fear a person whose only crime was to accuse you of insanity. Edmund suffered from ague, the cure for which is the powder, and yet you asked Hans how much could kill a person.'

'I sent Richard to London for it,' I said steadily. 'I gave it to Edmund and he died, a horrible, painful death. For a long time I believed that the worst I had heard about Papist poison must be true. Then you sent me Robert Talbor's book, and I knew it was a cure after all, and so I was sure it was something else Richard had given to me. Now I know he just told me to give Edmund a dose that was too high, fatally high.'

'Eleanor, the physicians still do not know how much of the powder is most effective. Maybe it was just a mistake. And maybe it was not even his mistake. Maybe it was the mistake of the apothecary who sold it to him.'

'You do not really believe that?'

'I do not know what to believe. And neither do you, I think. You have not confronted him with this, have you?'

I shook my head. 'He would only deny it.'

'With words, perhaps. But unless he is a monster, you will know if he is telling the truth or not.'

'That is just it. I already know, James. I saw his guilt, as clear as day.'

He regarded me almost sadly. 'It is just that your heart will not accept it, will it? Because you loved him, because you love him still. And so you cannot accept the evidence of your eyes or of your head. Nor should you. Listen to me, Eleanor. There are times for weighing evidence and making reasoned deductions, and times when you should set all that aside. When you should listen to what your heart tells you, though your eyes cannot see it and your mind cannot understand. "If a man will begin with certainties, he shall end in doubts; but if he will be content to begin with doubts he shall end in certainties."'

'Francis Bacon?'

'But Sir Francis's admirable philosophy cannot be applied to love. With love it is just the opposite. There must only be certainties. Beginning with doubts is no good, no good at all.'

'But I have always doubted Richard,' I admitted. 'I could not help but love him, desire him, but I have always had my doubts about him, and now I know that I was right to doubt.'

One of the butterflies was fluttering round my head again and I raised my hand to let it settle. I walked past James with it still on my palm and pushed open the door. The sun was shining, a dying autumn sun, very soft and rich. I stood and let the butterfly feel the air on its wings before I gently tossed up my arm. I watched it flutter off, over the herb garden and away. One by one the other butterflies went soaring after the first, until all three of them were gone, over the rooftops and the trees, into the sky, which suddenly looked very small compared to Tickenham's sky.

'I have to go home, James.'

'I know that you do. Whether he is guilty or not, whether you love him or not, the law of the land says that you married him and therefore belong to him.'

'Oh, a pox on the law!'

James laughed. 'You are a glorious, lawless little person, Eleanor Glanville, and you should belong to no one. You were born to be as free as the Red Admirals. It is a tragedy that you are not.'

'But I shall not be locked up,' I said. 'If Richard still claims that I am mad, I know I have friends, powerful friends, who will refute those claims. I have you, and I have Hans Sloane and John Ray, three of the most respected natural philosophers in the country. I can depend on you, can't I?

'Always.' James put his arm around my shoulder. 'And you must keep on writing to me regularly now,' he said seriously. 'For if you do not, I shall fear something is amiss and shall come haring down to Somersetshire to rescue you. '

'I shall hold on to that thought.' I put my hand over his. 'I swear I shall never break off our correspondence again. Not for anything.'

'When will you leave?'

'After I've seen Dickon go off with you on the herbalising expedition tomorrow. He wanted to show me the state barge.'

A large and noisy group of apprentices and their masters boarded the grand apothecaries' barge that was drawn up by the steep river steps at Blackfriars, ready to take them on a last collecting trip before winter. Provisions had already been loaded on to the boat, baskets of bread and cheese and meats and a barrel of ale, and all the apprentices, dressed in their blue uniforms, carried an assortment of glass bottles and pencils and collecting books. Bright pennants and banners cracked in the stiff breeze beneath a leaden sky.

I had told Dickon that as soon as I had watched him depart, I would be leaving London to return to Tickenham, and he was so happy in his work now, and with James, that he did not mind at all. 'Have a good voyage,' I said, hugging him tight, before he climbed down to the boat. 'I hope it is a successful one.'

'I'd rather be spending my time with patients instead of plants,' he said artlessly.

'Well, keep your eyes open and . . . who knows? You might find something that'll help your patients. A plant nobody's ever found before, one that can cure cankers or start a heart again when it has stopped.'

He looked dubious. 'I am going to Twickenham, Mama, not off to the New World.'

I laughed. 'Even so.'

'I'm happy to leave all the exploration and experimentation and the making of new discoveries to the likes of you and Mr Petiver. I've no ambition to have a herb named after me, or be commemorated in the annals of the Royal Society. I'd rather just take all the knowledge that others have collected and put it to good use.'

I touched his soft cheek with the back of my hand. 'You are a good boy, Dickon. You will be a wonderful doctor.'

'Do you think so?'

'I know so. I am proud of you.'

He looked down at his polished shoes, embarrassed, as if he did not believe me. 'So long as I do not have to go and fight in a war,' he said. 'You would not be so proud of me then. I am not like your father. I am not like my father or my brother either. I would not be able to face a musket or wield a sword.'

I had not realised Richard's criticisms of him had cut so deep.

'Listen to me.' I put my hand under his chin and lifted his face to mine. 'To my mind, there is something wrong with a world that rewards women only for being modest and pretty, and men for their courage on the battle-field. I once met a fine physician who had led the cavalry but decided he would rather save lives than take them. You tell me which is the more heroic.'

'Thank you, Mama.' He kissed my cheek, smiled. 'I have the worst of fathers, but the very best of mothers.'

And yet his father, the man he had called the worst of fathers, had just such a smile, gentle and charming and utterly adorable, and I missed seeing it. I missed having him smile that smile at me, even though I feared he was a murderer.

I grabbed Dickon and hugged him tight again, so that he would not see that I was crying, and he went off, happy and excited, to join James and the others in the barge. He sat towards the back of the boat, behind the raised, crimson-damask covered chair that was reserved for the Master of the Company. He turned and lifted his hand in farewell to me as the drum started to beat a rhythm that sounded, to my ears, sombre and ominous. The rows of watermen took up their oars and started to pull out on to the swirling grey water. They were sailing with an incoming tide and the barge moved swiftly upstream and away. I stood and watched, long after Dickon had stopped waving, long after his face was just a pale shape against the grey of the river. I gripped the railing at the jetty and strained my eyes, dreading the moment when he would disappear entirely. I watched the barge grow smaller, until it was as tiny as a toy boat and the expanse of water between us seemed wider than the widest ocean.

I had the strangest presentiment that I had said goodbye to Dickon forever. That I would never see my son again.

It had turned cold. As the coach rocked through the village of Nailsea and into the mire of the Tickenham Road, ragged curtains of thick fog whipped past the windows. It was so thick as almost to obscure the other travellers on the road: the ubiquitous fishermen, a woman with a brace of duck, and a boy on a scraggy skewbald nag. I could not really see their faces and so was not particularly perturbed that they did not trouble to smile or wave or doff their caps when the coach swayed by and they caught a glimpse of my face at the window, half hidden in the dark hood of my cloak.

Down on the moor, at the edge of the floodwater, they were finishing building the Gunpowder Treason Night bonfires and I could hardly believe these would be lit in a few hours, that it was November already. In London, with James and the butterflies, winter had seemed far away still.

The ghostly figures, moving to and fro in the mist, looked almost sinister as they carried branches and armfuls of brushwood and fagots to add to the shadowy skeletons of sticks.

Maybe it was time we stopped celebrating the Gunpowder Plot. It had happened nearly a century ago, after all. Though I had loved the festivities once, when it was the only celebration Oliver Cromwell did not ban. He forbade Christmas and the May Revels, but he had encouraged this dark festival that bred hatred against Catholicism. It was a gruesome celebration though, when one thought about it, centred as it was around the burning of an effigy.

I had left my daughters in the care of Catholics, the kindest-hearted people I had ever known.

I saw the church tower dimly through the mist. To the right was the lane that led to Folly Farm, at the foot of Cadbury Camp. We were almost there now. As if she guessed my anxiety, I felt Dickon's hound trembling against my legs. In Hackney Cadbury had sensed my imminent departure and attached herself firmly to my skirts. In Dickon's absence she seemed to have transferred all her slobbering and unconditional devotion to me and I was glad that I had brought her with me, was glad of her company now. I reached down to stroke her floppy ears and let her lick my fingers.

'There, girl.' I patted her side. 'I promised Dickon I would care for you and I shall. There's no need to be afraid,' I said, thinking that her blindness was a fate almost worse than death, confining her to the terror of perpetual darkness.

The coach lumbered into the cobbled yard but nobody came out to greet me, not even the groom was there to attend to the horses. Smoke was rising from the chimneys, but otherwise the house had a strange, abandoned air about it. I was surprised that everyone seemed to have been given leave to attend the bonfire before the festivities were properly underway. It was with a sense of foreboding that I walked up to the heavy door leading into the great hall, and opened it.

Will Jennings, the footman, was coming out of the cross passage, carrying a salver of steaming roast pike.

'Where is everyone, Will?' I asked. 'Where is my husband?'

He hesitated, looked right through me, and carried on through to the parlour as if he had not heard me, as if I was a ghost. I stared after him, dumbfounded, then followed him into the parlour, Cadbury trailing at my heels. When I saw that there was nobody there, I turned and ran up the stone stairs to my chamber. The clothes chest had been removed, I noticed, and the washstand had been shifted to the opposite corner of the room. A man's shirt was tossed on the bed, not one of Richard's.

'If you're looking for him, you'll not find him here.' I spun round to see Forest, leaning lazily against the doorframe, his stockinged ankles casually crossed. 'Richard has left me in charge,' said my son, using his stepfather's given name, as if they were equals, as if the two of them were accomplices. My husband, whose claim that I was mad could enable him to wrest control of my estate, and my son, heir to that estate, who would inherit it all once I was gone.

Forest was head and shoulders taller than me now. He had grown a soft black beard and moustache. In a new tailored coat and fawn breeches, tight over his muscular thighs, he was no longer a boy. It did not seem so long ago that he was a babe-in-arms and I was sitting with him under the apple tree, whispering to him that I wanted him to grow to be a good, kind man who made me proud.

'Why are you not still in Flanders, Forest?'

'I asked Richard to pay my passage home and he did.'

'You saw no reason to tell me that you were back?'

'You should not have left him,' said my son with startling passion. 'It is not right. You are his wife. You are supposed to love him. But you don't care about him at all, do you?'

I could not help but be moved by such ardent loyalty, even while it unnerved me. I knew Forest had always been almost slavishly devoted to Richard, but until that moment I don't think I'd understood quite how much he loved him. I could not blame him for taking Richard's side now, when he had not been here to witness what had passed between us.

'Forest, please understand that I had no choice but to go. Your stepfather made . . . allegations against me, allegations that made it impossible for me to stay.'

'He said you were mad,' Forest said flatly. 'I know. And I agree with him.'

I felt as if my legs would give way beneath me and put my hand out to the bedpost, to support myself. 'How can you say that?'

'I speak only as I find.'

I turned my back on him, went to the window, pressed my hands down against the ledge and took a deep breath. 'Your real father was such a good man, Forest. I wish you could have known him.'

'Well, he is dead,' Forest spat. 'And you are as dead to me as he is. I no longer have a mother. And in future I will thank you not to come into my chamber uninvited.'

I spun back to face him, felt the blood surge into my head, pounding behind my eyes, so that I could almost see it, a haze of red. 'I am very much alive, Forest. So help me God, you do have a mother. This is my chamber, my house, and so it will remain until I die. Unless you are willing to murder me, there is nothing at all that you or your stepfather can do about it.'

'Oh, isn't there?' He pushed himself into an upright position and his face hardened in a cunning and steely resolve.

'I could ride to Bristol right now and draw up a will to disinherit you,' I warned.

'You could.' His tone indicated I would be wasting my time. He smirked, unperturbed, as if he knew something that I did not, as if nothing I did could make any difference, as if nothing I did could stop them.

'Where is he, Forest? Where is Richard?'

His smile was full of malice. 'You will know soon enough where he is.'

The kitchen was a hive of activity, everyone busy in preparation for the great bonfire feast. Pots bubbled on the fire above which hung rabbits, ducks, geese and fish, waiting to go into them. The vast room was warm with aromatic steam. On the long table there were puddings and pies, bowls of sugar and spices, and great slabs of butter. Trenchers were already set out with roast pike and trout and baked eels. The maids chattered gaily as they chopped piles of apples and rolled pastry, scurrying to and fro from oven to table while Mistress Keene shouted instructions above the din.

They all stopped when they saw me, frozen like a tableau.

'I'd like a plate of bread and cheese,' I ordered. 'And some warmed ale.'

For a moment nobody moved, and then they all resumed their tasks and their chatter as if I had not spoken. Nobody even acknowledged my demand. Only Mistress Keene looked at me, still standing waiting. She wiped her liver-spotted hands on her apron, grabbed a loaf of bread and came bustling round the table. She thrust it at me as if I was a beggar.

'You should go,' she mumbled aside. 'While you still can.'

She had already turned away but I grabbed her arm. 'What do you mean?'

'I didn't do it,' she said, looking back at me with pity in her eyes. 'I might not approve of some of your ways but I'd not betray myself, for one thing.' She glanced furtively round the kitchen, as if to check who was listening to what she was saying to me. They all were, though trying to pretend they were not, eyes down, ears pricked. 'Only a fool would sign something when they could not read what was written above. How would I know if it was even close to what I said? They could have writ down any answer and asked me to sign it as gospel truth, I would not know any different.'

'What are you talking about?'

She shook her head, took up her wooden spoon and went back to her post.

I snatched a quarter round of cheese and a flagon of cider, like a thief in my own kitchen. As I ate and drank I walked down to where the flat-bottomed boat was tied up by the hump-backed bridge. Cadbury seemed determined to come with me so I guided her aboard. I rowed between the drowned trees and reed beds with her sitting upright in the bow, her nose high and sniffing the air, ears flicking back and forth to the noisy honking of the swans and the geese and the eerie cries of the marsh birds.

Bess was stirring a pot over the fire in her cottage, splashing about in half an inch of silt and water that had seeped in under the door as the floods had risen. She looked thinner, her once lustrous hair hung lank and her apron was grimy. I had always relied on her to be sharp and direct but she would not look at me now.

She laid three wooden bowls and spoons on the table. One for herself. One for Sam. The other was for Thomas, I presumed. There was no fourth bowl for her mother.

'She died a month ago,' Bess volunteered.

'I did not know.'

'How could you? You were not here.' There was recrimination in her voice, as if she thought I had stayed away too long. It seemed that I had, but I was beginning to wish I had not come back at all.

'She will be much missed.'

Bess went back to her stirring. The broth was thin and pale and did not smell good. 'Thomas and Sam are both out at the bonfire, but they'll be back soon and in need of something to warm them.'

'Bess, tell me what is going on.'

She seemed reluctant. 'Mr Glanville left Forest in charge and, as you have no doubt seen for yourself, he's acting like the squire already and having a high time of it.'

'And Richard?' I asked. 'Where is he? Do you know?'

She glanced up at me from her stirring. 'No. But I do know this – he's not been moping for you. He's had someone to warm his bed for him at night.'

I felt my stomach clench. 'Who? What do you mean?'

'Sarah Gideon. Floozy from Bristol. Near as damn it moved herself into the big house as soon as you were gone.'

It was as if an icicle had been driven like a spear into my heart, dripping cold ice into my blood. Sarah. The woman in the red dress, from the Llandroger Trow. From so many years ago. In how many ways had he betrayed me? Had our marriage been a complete sham?

I was sure I did not want Richard any more, that he was a villain, a murderer. But if I no longer wanted him, why did the images that rushed into my head cause me such agony? Why did the thought of that woman in bed with him make me want to be sick? Why did the thought of him touching her, of her touching him, make me want to weep, to scream, to kill them both? Why did the thought of him kissing her, of her kissing him, make me feel as if my heart was being ripped out of me? Why did the image of him making love to her make me feel that the world was an ugly, ugly place and that life was hardly worth living any more? Above all, why did the thought that he might actually care for her fill me with the most terrible emptiness and loneliness and despair?

'Is she with him now?'

Bess shrugged. 'She left for Elmsett about two days ago. Good riddance to her, I say. Don't like her much. Nobody does.' She flashed me one of her bold looks, her face red and moist from the steam coming off the pot. 'They'd not oblige the likes of her. They'd not even do it for Mr Glanville, much as they liked him before all this turned him sour. They do it for Thomas.'

I frowned. 'Do what for Thomas?'

'She's been visiting us all with a man who makes us swear an oath. They have a sheet of vellum with a list of questions on it. She goes through the questions one by one, writes down the answers that people give her. Writes and writes and writes, every single word we say. Then she has us put our name to it.'

'What are the questions about?'

'You.'

'Me?'

'Yes, lamb,' Bess said. 'You.'

'Richard's mistress is collecting sworn affidavits against me?'

'If that's what they are called, then yes.'

'But why?' I was sure Sarah Gideon hated me, but what did she hope to achieve by gathering testimonies against me? It seemed a lot of trouble to go to just for spite.

Bess stirred more vigorously. 'God's blood, don't tell me I need to spell it out for you.'

'It seems that you do, Bess.'

'Your husband and his harpy want to prove you are of unsound mind and take charge of your estate. Thomas helps them and in return will get the share he's always felt he was owed.'

My head was hurting, felt dulled, as if I had suffered a blow to it, or drunk too much wine. 'Why do they need him to . . . help them?'

'Some folk here oblige because it makes 'em feel important or because they have some axe of their own to grind with you, but a lot are afraid of putting their name to what they cannot understand. But they do it for Thomas. They trust him. They will do whatever he asks them.'

'And what exactly does Thomas ask them to do?'

'Answer the questions just how she wants 'em answered. Give her what she wants to hear.'

'What does she want to hear?'

The stirring slowed and Bess rested the handle of the spoon against the side of the pan. 'She wants to know all about your butterflies. About how you chase after them and what you do with them.'

'What do people tell her? Let me guess now. Communing with the dead? Witchcraft? Shape-shifting?'

Bess looked scornfully at the dog trailing at my heels. 'They say you care more for butterflies, and even for a blind bitch, than for your own children. They say only a madwoman would prize butterflies as if they were jewels, would take more interest in the hunting of them than of fish or fowl to fill the larder shelves. They say that you'd rather pay servants to lay sheets beneath bushes on the moor than on beds, and that you pay more for worms than most would pay for a round of Cheddar.'

'What did you tell her, Bess?'

'I refused to talk to her. Got the sharp end of Thomas's tongue for it too.'

'Thank you.'

She shrugged. 'Makes no difference what I say or don't say. Add a few whispers together and they're as loud as a shout. And there always were plenty of whispers about you.'

It was almost dark. Down on the moor people were gathering round the great beast that was already turning slowly on a spit over the cooking flames. Soon they would be lighting the bonfires. I found my feet taking me down towards the crowd, towards these people who had been my friends once, but had now spoken out against me.

I stopped short when the stuffed effigy of the Pope began to be slow marched to its pyre across the dark, flat wasteland, accompanied by the menacing beat of a drum. I pulled my hood up and walked the rest of the way to the edge of the crowd, as all eyes watched the effigy hoisted on top of the bonfire. The fire itself was being set alight with flaming torches. The flames caught and flared and leapt triumphantly higher. Dark figures moved around it like spectres, their faces phantasmagorical in the flames. I looked to find my half-brother amongst them, but could not see him.

As I moved through the midst of the crowd, I felt hostility like a knife in my back. Mistress Keene, Mistress Jennings, Mistress Bennett and Mistress Hort: these women had known me since I was a child, had been with me in the birthing chamber when my own children were born. They and their families had served at the house or worked the land for generations. They were my family, and yet they treated me now as an outcast.

They had always been mildly disapproving of me, mistrusting and misunderstanding me because I did not conform to their image of what a lady should be, but now Sarah Gideon and Thomas had taken that mistrust and bent it to their own ends. Had legitimised it, magnified it, given it full rein. And Richard? Had he helped to turn them against me, where once he had rescued me?

There was the same tension in the air as there had been when the mob had come to the house and threatened to burn it. Every member of this crowd now treated me with the same enmity that Thomas had always shown. Contempt had spread like a canker, infected them all like a plague. They were glancing towards me, hissing and whispering. As I passed through the crowd, they moved back, gave me ground. Alice Walker hurled an apple, someone else threw an onion. It was surprising how much it hurt when I was hit between my shoulders, on my arm. I ignored it. I did not bow my head in shame. I did not lower my eyes. I kept on walking. I ignored the catcalling boys and cursing drunkards. I ignored the fingers clawing my cloak, pulling my hair.

Then a great cheer went up and all attention was diverted back to the fire. The flames had reached the effigy of the Pope and caught its stuffed feet. I watched them lick up the straw legs, catch a hand and devour an arm.

I looked around for Forest, but caught the eye of little Annie Sherburne. She gave me a timid smile that meant more than I'd probably ever be able to tell her. She was holding her little brother's hand and in her other arm she cradled a baby. When I smiled back at her, she came over to me.

'Is this Harry, your cousin's child?' I asked her.

She nodded. 'He is almost walking now.'

The heat of the fire was so searing it made my eyes water. Annie directed her gaze towards the back of the crowd, to her mother and a girl I took for the mother of the infant. I received weak smiles from both women.

'I'm glad to see not everyone hates me, Annie.'

'Oh, but we could never hate you, Mistress Glanville,' the girl said earnestly. 'Not when you have been so kind to us.' She lowered her eyes then as her father came to stand by her side.

'Good day to you, Mistress Glanville,' he said with gruff courtesy.

'Good day to you too, Jack.'

'I'd have you know, I did not want to talk to that woman,' he muttered. 'But I was left with no choice.' Jack Sherburne was a large man with a rugged, weathered face, but his eyes were honest and kind though he kept them averted from me, looking directly ahead as he spoke, to make it look as if he was not really speaking to me at all. His expression was strained. 'Your son said the rent would be tripled if we did not cooperate.'

'She made me talk, too,' Annie said and I felt her grave young eyes entreating me to forgive her. 'All I said was that I helped you collect worms and to feed them and care for them. There's no harm in that, is there?'

'No, Annie,' I said. 'There is no harm in it at all.'

I noticed there was a man weaving his way through the crowd. Dressed in a wool coat and cap, he appeared to be looking for someone, with some urgency.

'I told her how good-humoured and well pleased you always were when we were working with the butterflies,' Annie said enthusiastically. 'And how I liked collecting the worms, and how you paid me very well for it.'

Her father spoke again. 'I made a point of saying how generous you have been to us. How you gave a home to my sister and her little one when she had nowhere else to go. That must count for something.'

I did not doubt that it would only count against me: that I paid good money for butterflies and worms, but failed to collect proper rents. I thanked them both, all the same. 'Do you know what others have said?'

Jack Sherburne was a good Anglican. He would not want to repeat slander.

The man who was searching the crowd had stopped to speak to someone who was pointing in my direction. 'Please, Jack. I have to hear it.'

'They all agree that you do not live according to your station,' he continued gravely. 'That you wander around on the moor half-dressed. That you are so busy with your worms, you do not keep enough food in the house and have to send out to the public brewhouse instead of brewing yourself as a gentlewoman should. They say you beat your maid with a holly stick when the worms died, which we all know is the foulest lie. But you know how it is,' he added apologetically. 'Once this kind of story gets a hold, it runs rife and twisted as bindweed.'

With some cultivation, most certainly. I saw Thomas now, standing by the spit roast, surveying the scene almost proprietorially. Someone who was integrated into this community, had lived amongst the commoners all his life so that he was accepted by them, someone who had led a near riot and carried everyone with him; someone who still nursed his own vendetta against me, his own grievance. Thomas Knight, who had put words into these people's mouths and incited them to speak against me. Thomas Knight, whose life I had saved at risk of my own. Whose life I had begged Richard to spare.

Annie's little brother turned his face into his sister's wool skirt. 'Can we go now, Annie, please? I don't like this part.'

I saw that Thomas was bending low, trying to tie the top of a writhing hessian sack. I knew, from years of attending these occasions, that the sack contained a litter of kittens.

I listened to the crackle and hiss of the fire. I watched the flames reflected on the floodwater like a river of molten gold. Little sparks and embers shot up into the black sky and looked, briefly, so like golden butterflies that I wondered if I really was losing my grip on sanity. Thomas raised his arm high, the pathetic wriggling hessian sack clenched in his fist. As the effigy of the Pope toppled from his fiery throne, Thomas swung his arm and hurled the sack with all his might on to the flames, just so that the drama of the occasion could be enhanced by the terrible, desperate screaming of the kittens as they were burned alive. I had seen this standard but most gruesome Gunpowder Treason Night ceremony performed many times before, but never had it repulsed me as much as it did now.

The man in the cap had seen me and was hurrying over. Only when he swept off his hat did I see that it was James's manservant, George. My heart lifted for a moment, so pleased was I just to see a friendly face, one associated with happier times. His eyes were red-rimmed with tiredness, the lines of his face ingrained with dust as if he had ridden hard all day.

'Whatever are you doing here, George?' I asked.

'Looking for you, Ma'am. I have been looking for you all over.' He held out a letter. 'Mr Petiver said I was to give it to nobody but you and that I was to stay with you until you had read it.'

The seriousness of his tone alarmed me. 'Has something happened?'

'Please.' He nodded towards the letter.

I broke the seal and unfolded the paper with trembling fingers. It was quite different from the letters James had sent me in the past, only a few short, hastily scribbled lines which I could just make out in the lantern which Annie held up for me.

I turned to George. 'You were there?' My voice was very quiet. 'You saw what took place?'

A short nod. 'A gentleman came to the shop,' he said carefully. 'Dark hair, blue eyes, drunk as a sailor. He demanded to see you, and when I swore you'd gone, it was young Mr Glanville he wanted. When my master told him your son was not available either he vaulted over the counter and took hold of Mr Petiver by the throat, accusing him of . . . well, I won't repeat the exact words . . . taking liberties with you. I tell you, I thought my master was done for. But your son heard the scuffle and came out of the laboratory. When he saw who it was that had come looking for him he turned as white as a winding sheet, but he was very brave. He bade the man leave go of Mr Petiver and that he did, though his hand stayed on the hilt of his sword. Your boy did not try to make a run for it,' George said finally. 'But I cannot tell you he went willingly.'

James's letter was almost screwed up in my hand, I was gripping it so tightly. 'What does my husband want?'

'That I do not know.'

'He must have said something? What did he say? What does he want with my son?' Dickon was Richard's son too, I reminded myself, trying to take heart from this. It was Forest who was the heir to my estate. There was nothing to be gained from harming Dickon. 'He could not hurt him,' I said, more as a question than a statement of fact. 'He would not hurt his own son.'

There was a brief silence. 'Is there anything at all that I can do for you?' George asked finally.

I shook my head. 'Only go directly back to London and tell James that I am grateful for his offer to come to me but that he must not. It would only make matters worse. Tell him to stay where he is, in case Dickon comes back, or is still in London and needs his help. And, George, tell him . . . tell him to be careful.'

He hesitated. 'What will you do, Mistress Glanville?'

'I shall find them. I shall find my son.'

I ran all the way back over the marshy moor, my cloak streaming from my shoulders, my lungs bursting and the muscles in the backs of my calves as hot as irons by the time I reached the stables. There was no sign of the coachman and I doubted he'd do my bidding now, even if I could find him.

I took a dagger from the armoury to defend myself from vagabonds and highwaymen; filled a pouch with some of my jewels, so that I could sell them. Stowing both hurriedly in my pocket, I ran down to the stable, to my mare Kestrel's stall. I slipped the bridle over her head, threw on the saddle, tightened the girth, then led her out to the mounting block where I swung myself up on to her back. I clicked to signal her to walk and felt her strong muscles roll beneath me as we clattered out of the yard.

It would have been wise to wait until morning, to set out on my journey in the light rather than in the dark, but I could not wait. I did not know the way to Suffolk except that it lay east, and that first I must therefore pass through Bristol and on into Gloucestershire. I had a dwindling purse of money which I had brought back with me from London. Together with the jewels, I reckoned it would be enough. It would have to be enough. The mist thinned as I rode out of Tickenham, but the smoke of countless bonfires made it look as if drifting patches of it still lingered. The air was heavy with the pungent smell of burning. There were great bonfires still flaring bright as beacons on village greens and at street corners, and rows of much smaller fires outside the doors of little hovels and cottages. The sporadic explosion of fireworks sounded like the rumble of distant cannon-fire, as if all England was at war again, except that everywhere there was revelry and merrymaking. The festivities meant that people were abroad late into the night, drinking and carousing and throwing crackers and squibs, so that the dark roads at least were far from deserted.

I rode on. It grew quieter as I travelled through Bristol and out on to the Tetbury Road towards Cirencester. But the mired, rutted lanes and byways of Somersetshire had given way to firmer, drier ground which made the going easier and quicker. I could not think of stopping. I could not rest my head not knowing where Dickon was resting his.

The mare plodded through the night and her steady gait made me drowsy even though I tried to stay alert to the many dangers of the road, especially for a woman travelling alone. I could not get out of my mind the last time I had seen Dickon, when he had told me that he had the best of mothers and the worst of fathers and then waved goodbye. He had always been afraid of his father, but I hoped he trusted me enough to know that I would be coming to get him.

I rode on. Dawn broke cold and windy. I was so tired I nearly fell asleep in the saddle and woke only when I almost slipped off it. I stopped at an inn to breakfast, saddle-sore and exhausted, but hoping that the wheaten bread and butter would revive me a little. I found another inn to spend the night in then continued on through the rolling Cotswolds towards Stow and the steep little road through Burford, each secluded village made desolate and almost apocalyptical-seeming by the smouldering heaps of cinders that marked the places where the bonfires had been. There was a keen wind. It blew the grey ash into the air, like a storm of dirty snowflakes.

Kestrel and I both rested again at an inn on the outskirts of the Roman town of Cirencester, now a flourishing wool town with a large and bustling market square that drew people in from many miles around. I was sure that there would be somebody there who could tell me the way to Suffolk. I asked two stallholders, but in the end it was a cloth merchant who said that I should head towards Oxford and thence to the large village of Aylesbury. He knew the way well, since it was a centre for lace-making and he had traded there. 'You should reach Oxford by nightfall with the wind behind you,' he said.

I rode on. Oxford was a very pleasant place, with its twilit towers and spires and noble high street that was surprisingly clean, well-paved and of great length. I rested again, slept little, and next came to the village green at Aylesbury. I stopped to eat at a humble inn where a woman served me with mutton that had been stewing for much too long, but was at least piping hot. She insisted on talking to me, but I was so fatigued I could barely make my lips move. She told me proudly that her husband and son were both craftsmen. I told her, just as proudly, that my son was an apothecary, but was going to be a doctor to the poor.

'Send him this way,' she said with a chuckle, and I did not tell her that he had probably already passed through Aylesbury.

I came to Cambridge then, Cromwell's country, where Richard had gone to college and developed his love of music and literature. Where once had fluttered Fritillaries and Large Coppers and Swallowtails. It reminded me of home, surrounded as it was by willows. It lay in a valley, with marsh and bog and fen all around it. The buildings were indifferent and the streets narrow, badly paved and dirty, but I felt more comfortable there than in almost any other place I had stayed on this interminable journey. When I asked the inn-keeper for directions to Suffolk he agreed to let his son guide me partway, in the morning, for a shilling.

The boy did not say much as he trotted alongside me on a little mule, except to caution me that Sudbury was a grim town on the river River Stour, very populous and very poor. But I was still ill prepared for the strange hinterland I found myself travelling through, a place of ramshackle dwellings and narrow filthy lanes. Great gangs of urchin children ran around barefoot, their pinched faces pockmarked and their feet red-raw in the November frost. A little beggar boy ran up to us, weeping sores on his hands and around his mouth, and I tossed him a coin when he told me his sister and his mother were both dead of the bloody flux.

'How far to Elmsett?' I asked, desperate to be away from these harrowing sights that filled me with nothing but apprehension.

He frowned. 'Don't know it. But Ipswich is only about ten miles away.'

My guide and I parted company and I rode on to Ipswich alone. It was as different from Sudbury as could be, a large seaport on the banks of the River Orwell, with prosperous houses, and streets that were clean and broad and paved with small stones and led down to the waterfront. More houses huddled alongside the extensive docks that were crowded with tall-masted ships being loaded and offloaded with timber and iron, corn and wool. Masters, mates, boatswains and carpenters milled about. I stopped half a dozen of them, but they were either arriving from Newcastle or Scandinavia or else embarking for the Low Countries. They had never heard of Elmsett either.

I rode up into the town centre with its abundance of medieval churches and an inn called the White Horse, right at its heart.

There was an old grey-bearded man behind the bar who looked more like a sea captain than any man at the harbour had done. 'Can you tell me how to get to Elmsett, sir?' I felt like a person from a ballad or myth, doomed to keep on travelling, repeating this one question, searching for somewhere that did not exist, that I would never find.

'Eight miles north-west of here,' he said. 'Look out for the elm trees and the ancient church above the valley.'

I saw the small flint church in stark outline against the colourless November sky. It stood on a hill above valley sides that were cloaked with a forest of autumnal elms. I rode past a farm and a mill and came to a small village green, with a large tree under which the smithy had his forge. A farmer was waiting to have his horse shod and the blacksmith was at work with his anvil and hammer on a glowing horseshoe. I asked the farmer the way to Elmsett Manor, for what I hoped was the last time.

He shielded his eyes to look up at me in the saddle, my gown and riding cloak clearly of good quality but dusty and dishevelled.

'I take it you've come to see young Mr Glanville.' He winked aside to the blacksmith, as if to hint that I was just one in a line of loose, but well bred, young women who had come looking for Richard Glanville in the wilds of Suffolk. 'You're too late, I'm afraid. He was here, but he left about a day or so ago.'

My spirits plummeted. 'Are you sure?'

He nodded. 'Just his father there now.'

I had not even known that Richard's father was still living.

The blacksmith said that Elmsett Manor lay not a quarter of a mile away, at the edge of the wood and I continued on with a heavy heart, but with a little flicker of curiosity, too, to meet this man about whom I had heard so much, and none of it very favourable.

I passed through fields and meadows left uncultivated and run to seed badly. Withered leaves drifted down from the eponymous elms as I rode beneath them, ducking to avoid low branches, the horse's hooves muffled by the dead foliage on the ground. This would be a strange and melancholy place even in summer when these most funereal of trees were in full leaf.

I came upon Elmsett Manor unexpectedly, a small gabled building of silver-grey flint. The house was situated well back in the trees, half-hidden by them and encircled by a little moat, silvery also under the white sky. One wing had crumbled away, left roofless and entirely derelict. The rest looked to be in very poor repair but that only added to its romantic air, made it even more like a place in a story, somewhere a fairy princess, rather than a young apprentice boy, might have been held captive.

An elderly man was sitting on a stone bench beside the moat, a worn blanket over his knees. He was holding a fishing net. The drawbridge was down and I crossed over it, the horse's hooves making a hollow sound on the damp and rotten planks that sagged alarmingly as we passed over.

The man looked up. He did not acknowledge me but lifted the blanket, folded it, rose and came towards me. He had thick hair which would once have been very dark but was now as silvery as the water in the moat. His eyes had the shape of Richard's, but were brown not blue. He must have been in his early-sixties, tall and slender still, very striking.

I slid down from the saddle and hooked the bridle over a gatepost. 'Mr Glanville?'

'I am,' the man replied.

'And I am Eleanor Glanville, Richard's wife.'

'I have been expecting you.'

'Where is my son Dickon, sir? Have you seen him?'

'Yes, I have seen him.'

'Is he well? Is he safe?'

'I believe so. Please.' He held out his hand to me. 'You look very tired. Won't you come inside and share some supper with me?'

There was a time when it would have delighted me to be in a place so connected with Richard's past, and to meet his father. I could not equate this courtly gentleman at all with the embittered, uncaring man who had so mercilessly pushed his son to succeed, had thrown him in a lake, to drown or else swim. Either Richard had lied to me, as seemed entirely likely, or time had brought about a mellowing in his father.

I was shown through to a dilapidated parlour. Despite the dark and decayed furnishings, the faded tapestries that failed to cover the evidence of peeling, badly damp-stained walls, Elmsett Manor was not quite how I had imagined it either, not totally ruined. Only two or three rooms seemed to be habitable, but with sufficient funds to lavish on its restoration, it could be beautiful again.

We sat at a small worn table and were served with baked trout that Richard's father ate in the old way, with a spoon, a knife and his fingers.

'Do you know where they have gone?' I asked him.

'They headed up the coast. To a place called Whitby, in the North Riding of Yorkshire.'

'Yorkshire? So far away? Why?'

Richard's father rested his spoon on the edge of the plate. 'None of this is Richard's doing,' he said. 'You must believe that.'

'I am afraid I find it rather hard.'

'It was jealousy that drove him to take the boy.'

'Jealousy?'

There was a stiffening of the lines of his face, a flicker of anger in his eyes that was strangely familiar to me. 'You bound your boy, my son's boy, as apprentice to your lover.'

I lowered my eyes, suffering a stab of remorse. It seemed pointless to argue that James and I had become lovers only after Dickon's apprenticeship had begun.

'They knew this was the first place you'd come looking for them,' Richard's father said. 'Your boy is refusing to cooperate. They took him to Yorkshire to give them more time to convince him.'

'Convince him of what? What do they want from him?'

'Sarah Gideon is the widow of an attorney,' Mr Glanville explained. 'She has a devious, grasping nature and a good knowledge of the law — a formidable mix. They are putting pressure on your son to sign affidavits against you, testifying to your unsuitable way of life, your state of mind, your unhealthy interest in butterflies.'

'Don't they have enough against me already?'

'The boy's testimony will count for much. He acted as your assistant, I understand.' He picked up his spoon again. 'I believe they have taken a lodging near the harbour, above an inn.'

'Why would you tell me that?' I asked, instantly suspicious. 'Why help me to find them when you and I are strangers to one another?'

'I do not condone this,' he said quietly. 'And your son is my grandson.'

'Then why did you let him go?' I burst out. 'Why did you not find a way to help him?'

He looked at me as if to say that I knew the answer already. A man in his sixties was no match for the unstable, violent man my husband had become. 'I helped your boy every day, in the only way I could. I contrived to get pen and ink to him. He wrote a letter to you but Richard discovered it and it seemed to cause him some distress. I am afraid he destroyed it.'

'Do you know what it said?'

'Your son said only that you could trust him as he trusted you, and that he did not believe the many wounding things his father said about you.' He looked down at his plate. 'I secretly took him food, even though that woman vowed to have me thrown out of my own home if she discovered one morsel of bread had passed the boy's lips.'

I pushed my own plate away in horror. 'She means to starve Dickon?'

'Oh, she threatens much.'

'What else has she threatened?'

'She has told your lad that if he does not sign the documents he will starve to death, or else be sold as a slave to the plantation owners in the New World . . . threats as ludicrous and empty as they are vicious.'

'But Dickon does not know that!' I shouted. 'He will believe her.'

'Richard would not see harm done . . .'

'Then why does he not stop her? Why is he doing this? Does he hate me so very much?'

Mr Glanville lowered his eyes, did not answer that. 'Richard is not himself. He is drinking too much, not sleeping enough.' His father ran his hand over his face. 'He has always been highly changeable. I am afraid I was a very poor father to him. He was a child who desperately needed warmth, affection, a confidant. Above all else he needed loving approval, but I was able to give him none. Had nothing left to give.' His eyes were full of regretful tears. 'If ever a boy needed a mother's love, it was that little lad.'

I held up my hand to silence him and walked distractedly to the other side of the room. There was a mottled mirror hanging on the wall and for a moment it was not my face I saw but Richard's, as he had looked when I had first fallen in love with him. Youthful, beautiful, troubled. Memories flooded me. His angelic smile, gentle and uncertain, when I held him in my arms after he fell from his horse. The need and the loneliness I had sensed in him when he had danced with me. The passion and the intensity of that first kiss. I wanted to weep then. I felt a dragging in my heart that was like compassion, like love, and a need to protect and comfort that somehow transcended all that was happening now, made it seem completely unreal, almost irrelevant. I suffered a moment of deceptive lucidity during which I was quite certain that Richard had not murdered Edmund, that somehow I had brought all this upon myself. But the moment passed and reality intruded like a blow to my heart.

I blinked. His image in the mirror was replaced by my own and I thought the dilapidated surroundings suited me very well. With violet smudges under my eyes, dirt on my cheeks, my dress filthy and torn and straggles of hair hanging loose and uncombed about my shoulders, I no longer looked like a lady who would live in a fine mansion. I looked like a vagabond, a gypsy who wandered from place to place, who had no belongings and no fixed abode, and I found that I would not mind that at all.

'I believe Richard has convinced himself this is all for my benefit,' his father was saying. 'We were estranged, you see, for many years. I did not even know he had married or that I had two grandchildren. I think he feels guilty for that now, wants to make some kind of recompense. He saw how distraught I was to see this house in ruins when we returned from exile. He knew how important it is to me, to this family, and I think he hoped to find a way to enable me to see it restored before I die.'

My heart hardened. 'He has it in mind to abandon Tickenham Court, doesn't he? Plans to sell it off to the drainage speculators and use the profit to rebuild Elmsett?'

It would not matter to Richard if the commoners were bent on destruction and vandalism, would not matter if he was loathed and spurned in Tickenham, if he no longer lived there, if he had already taken the money and fled.

I was not a gypsy. There *was* somewhere that I belonged. I belonged at

Tickenham Court. I was Eleanor Glanville of Tickenham Court. I had sworn to my father that I would protect it from unscrupulous Cavaliers and so far I had made a very sorry job of it, but I would do my best to put that right, just as soon as I had found my son.

Whitby was many, many miles away from Elmsett, too many miles, but the route was straightforward at least. All I had to do was go north towards the Fens and the great estuary of The Wash and then follow the east coastline all the rest of the way.

I rode first towards Stowmarket where I had to cross a tributary of the River Gipping to the south of the town. It was deep and fast-flowing and Kestrel shied and sidled when I tried to urge her to walk into the water. She would not be persuaded and I had to dismount and lead her in. When the water was up to my waist I climbed back into the saddle and leaned forward, my arms wrapped around her neck, as her hooves slipped on the smooth rounded stones on the riverbed and she bucked and stumbled.

We made it through with no mishap but my skirts were still dripping wet and I was shivering when we reached the market town of Bury St Edmunds, a place famed for its beautiful situation and wholesome air, with a ruined abbey haunting the town centre. The monks had long since gone, replaced by gentry and people of fashion who thronged the fair to buy toys and trinkets. There was a time when I would have loved nothing better than to stop and join them, to browse and to shop. But I found I had nothing in common with such people any more. I felt very distant from them now, could not have made polite conversation if my life depended upon it.

Just as dusk was falling I arrived in Thetford, another market town with another ruined priory and buildings of flint. I stopped at the Bell Inn and was served with a supper of sprats and given a bed with sheets grimy and infested with lice. I spent the night itching and scratching, and continued itching as I rode on again to King's Lynn, the port on the east bank of the River Great Ouse, the vast-mouthed river that carried the outfall of all the waterways which drained the Fens.

King's Lynn had a Guildhall with a flint-chequered façade, fine medieval merchants' houses on cobbled lanes, a new customs house overlooking the harbour and quay, where grain and butter, hides and wool, were loaded on to ships bound for the Netherlands. But for all its ancient grandeur, it felt like a town on the margin, a final outpost of civilisation at the edge of the flat lowland of the Fens and the vast three-sided bay that was The Wash.

I fed Kestrel a bag of oats and rode out into the wilderness. A bleaker, more inhospitable place I had never seen nor dared to imagine. The wildness and vast desolation of The Wash made the marshland of Tickenham seem tame in comparison. It was raining, a cold, windswept rain that poured down from banks of leaden clouds and was carried horizontally over the expanses of saltmarshes and shifting sandbanks.

The tide was far out, exposing the ridges of sand and mud and sheets of shallow water cut with deep channels as far as the eye could see. There were dense flocks of wetland birds, oystercatchers and terns, geese and ducks and waders and their forlorn cries added to the utter desolation and strangeness of this place. A few souls braved its treacherous wastes, hunting for shrimps and cockles, but their presence did not make the place seem any less lonely. So caked were they in mud, from head to toe, they scarcely resembled human beings at all.

The flat lowland was such a quagmire that Kestrel sank up to her shanks so I had to dismount to urge her on, slipping and sliding from one clump of higher ground to another. Time after time, I went into bog up to my knees. I was accustomed to Somersetshire bog and marsh but this was different, a sucking, viscous, frightening mud. I hauled myself clear with difficulty. My boots were so heavy and caked that it felt as if I had rocks tied to my feet. I had mud up to the tops of my legs, over my hands and splattered on my face. My skirt and cloak were slick with it and wet from the rain, and my hair was plastered to my head. I grunted with effort and frustration and despair. But not once did I consider turning back.

I rode on, the rain stinging my face like biting insects, trying not to think that Dickon had been made to travel through this God-forsaken place, without even a good dinner in his belly to warm him. And mud might be the least of the dangers facing him.

I rode on to the rickety bridge that crossed the River Nene and thence to the River Welland, which was shallow enough for me to wash myself. I rode on to the River Witham, and thence into Lincolnshire.

I had run out of money, but parted with a pearl necklace for a straw pallet to sleep on, a bowl of burnt porridge, and cold water to wash in. I felt as if I had been travelling forever and yet I was only halfway there, with over a hundred miles left to go. I awoke feeling feverish. My head throbbed and every bone and muscle in my body ached. I hardly knew where or even who I was any more.

I held on grimly to Kestrel's reins with my chapped hands and clung to the image of the boy I was pursuing. I had chased butterflies over fields and ditches, and I would follow my son to the ends of the earth, if need be. He would always be my baby, no matter how big he grew. Since the day he was born, every small hurt or minor distress he suffered had been as a thorn upon my soul. I would suffer any danger or discomfort, any accusation or slur, any number of locks and chains, to know that he was safe. I would willingly trade my life for his, if it came to it.

The roads and days merged, each new town, each new inn, much like all the rest. All I could do was keep going, one step at a time, one mile at a time, counting down the landmarks. I saw the medieval city of Lincoln with the castle atop its steep hill, the half-timbered Tudor houses and Gothic bridge and the magnificent cathedral, its central tower like a finger of stone pointing to Heaven. My way lay in a different direction entirely, north to Driffield in the Wolds where there were trout streams to cross, and further north still, along a straight Roman road to the fortified town of Malton with its shallow ford over the Derwent.

I passed the alum works and saw the Gothic pillars and arches of Whitby Abbey, standing high on a headland above the German Ocean with the black North York Moors behind it. I could barely believe I had journeyed so far to come to such a place. A little fishing port with white houses, closely and irregularly built on narrow cobbled streets. A cold, wet, windswept place of slanting sunbeams.

There were two inns on the harbourside, only one with lodgings above. It was more a tavern really, looking like a smugglers' den.

The landlady was a wrinkled old woman who smelt of fish. What teeth she had left were blackened stumps and she spoke in a north country accent that was almost incomprehensible. Yet she looked at me most disapprovingly, warily even, as if it was I who was to be mistrusted. She kept me outside the door of her apartment, only opening it partway and peering round it as she informed me that a man and boy and woman who fitted the descriptions I gave her had lodged with her, but had left on Monday.

'What day is it now?' I had lost all track of time.

'Tuesday.'

I had come all this way and again I had missed him, by just one day. I collapsed at the top of the dingy stairwell and wept with fatigue and despair.

The woman took pity on me when I sobbed and told her that Dickon was my son. She helped me down to the tavern where she sat me in a corner and brought me a dish of smoked herrings in cream.

'These were your boy's favourite,' she encouraged. 'He could gobble up two whole platefuls in one sitting. Surely you can manage a few bites?'

'He was having enough to eat?' I asked. 'He was not too thin?'

She looked at me as if my concerns were foolish. 'As I say, he was never full up, like all young lads, but he certainly wasn't starving to death. It's you who's too thin, madam, if you don't mind my saying.'

I took a bite. The fish melted in my mouth, was delicious. I had not realised how hungry I was.

'Did he seem unhappy or frightened in any way?'

'Cheerful, more like.'

'Cheerful?'

'Aye. Especially the last night they were here, and he stayed up drinking brandy and talking with his father until past midnight.'

'Did you hear what they talked about?'

'Some of it.' She helped herself to a swig of ale from my pot. 'Doctoring mostly. His father was promising to set him up with his own examining rooms.'

I should have been relieved that Dickon was not in bad straits. But it distressed me to think that he was so easily won over, with what were surely false bribes and promises. I despised myself for being disappointed to hear that he seemed at ease now in his father's company, that they were companionable, making plans together. Then it occurred to me that Richard, or Sarah Gideon, or both of them were entirely capable of bribing this woman to feed me such a story.

'Was there no animosity at all between the two of them?' I tested.

'Only over the papers.'

'What papers?'

'Some papers Mr Glanville seemed keen for the boy to sign. Couldn't help but notice,' she apologised for her nosiness. 'His father pushed them at him that night, before the talk about medicine. The lad pushed them back. Mr Glanville refolded them and put them in his pocket, said that they would keep for another day.'

I should not have doubted him. Dickon was just playing along, still refusing to sign anything, stalling until I came to rescue him, as he knew I would.

'Do you have any idea where they might be now?' I asked, hoping to God her inquisitiveness extended that far.

She tapped the side of her nose with her forefinger. 'I could hazard a guess that they are on their way to Newington Green.'

'Near London.' She might as well have said Mexico, the great distance it seemed to me then. 'What makes you think they have gone there?'

'Mistress Gideon asked me to post a letter for her. Then, lo and behold, a letter comes back and the next day they set off. My bet is she was writing to a relative of hers to ask if they could pay a visit. I think I can just about remember the address . . .'

I would always be a few miles, a few hours, behind them. They had not covered their trail very well, but they did not need to. So long as they kept on moving from place to place, I would never catch them. But I would die before I ceased trying.

I parted with my last necklace in Lincoln and bought a brown wool dress from a secondhand clothes seller. It was too big for me and undoubtedly had lice living in the seams, but I had lice a-plenty already and at least it was thick and warm and not in rags and tatters like my own gown.

I stayed at the same inn in Kings Lynn that I had before but the landlord did not recognise me. Instead of giving me the best room that was reserved for quality folk, I was allotted a pallet under the eaves.

It took me two weeks to reach Newington Green and find the small cottage owned by a shady character whose name was Street. He denied all knowledge of Sarah Gideon or of Richard Glanville until I gave him every last penny I had, whereupon he told me that they had gone to Mitcham.

'Mitcham?'

'It is the Montpellier of England, don't you know? Surrounded by fields of lavender and camomile and peppermint for the London perfumiers.'

'But why have they gone there?'

'There are many fine, fine houses. John Donne lived there, and Sir Walter Raleigh.'

'Please, sir. I have no more money to give you.'

'Sarah had an appointment with a French tailor, to be measured for her wedding gown.' He closed the door in my face.

I filched a pie from a market stall and spent the night beneath a tree, shivering myself to sleep, with my fingers wrapped tightly around the dagger. I was in fear of my life now. I was searching for Richard and yet I was in terror of him finding me first – finding me and taking his sword to my throat. Or else of Sarah Gideon doing the job for him.

She was no longer content to be his mistress, she wanted to be his wife, and Richard was evidently prepared to overlook entirely the fact that he already had one. It would no longer be enough just to prove I was mad and lock me away. They were not prepared to wait until eventually nobody even remembered I existed. Sarah had gone to Mitcham to have her wedding gown made. They wanted me out of the way immediately, altogether, forever.

James had written to me of Mitcham, so long ago it seemed like a dream. He'd described swathes of violet flowers that exuded the most soothing fragrance and attracted clouds of white butterflies. There was no lavender now. The bare fields were brown instead of purple. There were no white butterflies. It seemed there was no beauty left in the world, no hope.

I rode over the common to the Manor of Mitcham Cannons. If Mitcham were anything like Tickenham, whoever resided there would be aware of any visitors to the village. The benevolent gentleman who opened the door took me for a beggarwoman and invited me in for bread and cheese and to warm myself by the fire. He never even had the chance to tell me his name. My own name caused too much of a stir.

'I am Eleanor Glanville of Tickenham Court in Somersetshire,' I said, my voice croaking from disuse. 'I am looking for my son. He is travelling with my husband, Richard Glanville, and a woman. I was told they were in Mitcham.'

The man stared at me aghast and I thought I knew why. I was still clutching the dagger beneath my tattered riding cloak, and wearing the old brown dress that hung off my shoulders and trailed past my feet. My boots had holes in them and my hair hung in snarls around my dirty face. I had been travelling so long that I had quite forgotten how to be still. I paced back and forth, chewing on bread that I held in fingers that were cracked and bleeding from the cold. I must look like a madwoman. I felt like one.

'He told you I was mad, sir?'

My benefactor shook his head very slowly. 'No, Ma'am. He did not tell me you were mad. He told me that you were dead.'

I stopped pacing. 'Dead?'

'It was my understanding that Richard Glanville's wife died of ague, some months ago.'

How cruel. It was the cruellest mockery, to claim that I had died of the disease that had killed the rest of my family, the disease I had feared all of my life.

'Dead?' I repeated, pacing again. I took five steps forward, came up against the wall and turned, took five steps back. 'Dead of ague?'

'They obviously feared it might be called into question. While his betrothed was having her wedding gown fitted, Glanville had an appointment with a solicitor, to have an affidavit drawn up to present to the clergyman who was to conduct their wedding. It stated that he was free to marry since his first wife was no longer living and he was a widower.'

Five steps forward, five steps back. 'Who signed it? Who signed the affidavit?'

'They planned for the boy to sign, Glanville's son.'

'Did he do it?'

'Apparently he came down with some affliction and was unable.'

'He is my son too,' I said. 'And he is a good boy. He would not perjure himself to enable his father to commit bigamy. He would not swear before God that I am dead when he knows it for a lie.'

'Then you should take great care, madam,' the gentleman said. 'Maybe your boy will leave them no option but to turn the lie into truth.'

'Where are they now?'

'They were on their way to Somersetshire.'

The liveried footman who opened the door of William Merrick's grand square-fronted residence on King Street in Bristol took one look at me and would have closed it on me immediately, had I not anticipated his reaction and stuck my foot in the way.

486

'Please tell your master Mistress Glanville is here to see him,' I said, and obviously managed to convey enough of my old authority to make him reconsider.

I was eventually taken through to the silk-papered drawing room where I sat and waited on an over-stuffed chair. The luxury all about me was in such contrast to my recent travails that it was almost offensive.

Mr Merrick strode in, checked himself when he saw me, bowed and raised my hand to his lips but did not kiss it, as if fearing to contract a disease. 'Eleanor. It has been some time. I heard from Forest that you were . . . travelling.'

I had no time to waste on pleasantries. 'You know why?'

He took the time to sit down properly, waited for me to do the same. 'I know that after you abandoned your husband, he sought to find consolation in drink and also in the arms of another woman. She happens to be a conniving little minx named Sarah Gideon, widow of an attorney, who is no doubt using your husband's drunkenness and misery to further her own ends.'

'He met her at the Llandroger Trow, didn't he? I saw her with him, a long time ago.'

'She and her now deceased husband both frequented that particular tavern, yes. I do believe she always had a fondness for your husband, as most women seem to.'

'She and Richard, with the help of Thomas Knight, have collected affidavits against me, to prove that I am mad, so that they can assume control of my estate. Now it seems that is no longer enough for them and they are bent on passing me off as dead – or on seeing to it that I really am, for all I know.'

William shook his head from side to side in weary dismay. 'Your father believed I would advise you wisely and I trust that I have always done so, when you have allowed me. But I am afraid that I am at a loss as to how to advise you in your current predicament. This is outside the scope of my experience. I am an enterprising businessman. Richard Glanville, it would appear, is naught but a cynical adventurer, as ruthless and corrupt as any buccaneer. And now he is unstable and a drunkard with it, and under the influence of a manipulative harlot!'

'I did not come here seeking your advice, William,' I said. 'I wish only to write a new will, to supercede the existing one drawn up for me by

George Digby's attorney along with our marriage settlement.' I did not explain that the Earl of Bristol was so similar to Richard in his affiliations and background that I had not wanted to risk going back to him or his attorney. 'I wish you to witness it, William, and ensure it is placed in the hands of your own solicitor.'

He looked vaguely uncomfortable.

'You can do that for me?' I pressed him.

He gave a brief nod, showed me to a rosewood writing desk by the window, handed me a sheet of vellum and a quill.

My hands were shaking as I dipped the pen in the ink and began to write. The scratching of the nib on the paper was the only sound in the room. I wrote three lines and then signed my name. 'There. It is done.'

'So quickly?'

I vacated the chair, dipped the nib again, handed Mr Merrick the pen for him to sign as witness.

He did not take it, but bent his head over the paper as he read what I had written. He stiffened, straightened slightly and looked at me askance, as if he doubted I knew what I was doing. He was clearly reluctant to put his name to the document.

'It is my right, is it not, under the terms of my marriage settlement, to see my estate and possessions disposed of exactly as I see fit?'

'Indeed so, but . . .'

'Then it is my wish to leave everything to my uncle, Henry Goodricke, Fourth Baronet of Ribston, my late Aunt Elizabeth's son. He was taught to love Tickenham by my mother so it is fitting that I entrust her estate to his care. Everything but a few pounds, which I bequeath to each of my children and to Mary and John Burges.'

'You would disinherit your eldest son?'

'I have no choice,' I said. 'Forest is in collusion with his stepfather, and as things stand has everything to gain by my death. But I do not do this only in order to safeguard my life, I must also safeguard the future of Tickenham Court, as I swore to do. If I leave it to Forest, I am as good as leaving it to Richard and his mistress. No, if I am one day to face my father in Heaven, I cannot have that on my conscience.' I pushed the pen at William. 'Please. Sign it.'

He vacillated. He took the pen reluctantly, but still he did not put it to the paper. He had the look of a person upon whom it had suddenly dawned that they were in the company of someone not wholly sane.

I gripped the back of a chair. 'You do not think I am capable of making a will? You do not think I am of sound mind?'

His laughter was almost nervous. 'Now that you mention it, I confess I am in some agreement with your commoners. As you know, I have long thought that nobody wholly in possession of their wits would go in pursuit of butterflies.'

My hand went for the dagger I still kept in my pocket and I pulled it out. With my other hand I grabbed William Merrick's wrist. 'Sign, Goddamn it!'

He looked so terrified that I laughed, which only frightened him more, as if he feared I was a cackling loon. But whatever he thought of me, he did not dare refuse me. I stood over him while he wrote his name and then I made him fetch the footman to be second witness, and since the boy did not know how to write, he signed with a thick, dark cross.

'What is your name?' I asked the boy.

'Richard,' he said.

It almost winded me. 'Well, Richard,' I said gently, folding the paper and handing to him, 'take this for me, now, to your master's solicitor.'

He nodded, and with a glance at my former guardian who, funnily enough, did not contradict my instruction, he turned and ran out of the room.

The sun disappeared behind dense cloud and a fine rain spat in my face. Then the rain eased and mist rolled in, low and thick as a grey sea. When I breathed, it looked as if mist came out of my mouth, as if it had finally penetrated me, body and soul.

I waited to feel Kestrel's hooves sink beneath me into the mud. My mind reeled back, so that I could have sworn I was on the east coast again, and that soon I would see the great tidal mudflats and hear the lonely cries of wading birds. But the mist cleared and it was the flooded moors of Tickenham which spread out all around me, shimmering in a winter sunset. There must have been prolonged and torrential rain while I had been away for the water had come up, high enough to inundate most of Cut Bush field, deep enough to drown the causeway completely. It was gushing and lapping now at the road as if to wash me away.

I saw a man standing alone further down the road, at the point where the track veered off to the left up to Tickenham Court and the rectory. My heart gave a jolt. It was not Richard. It was not Dickon. But it was someone I knew instantly, even from a distance, from his profile, from the angle of his shoulders and the way he stood, keen and watchful, perfectly at peace amidst the swans and the geese.

James.

I was sure it was not really him, that he was not really here, that I was as stark raving mad as they said I was, but he turned towards the road, as if he had been watching out for me, waiting for me. He started to walk towards me, and suddenly I knew that I wasn't imagining it at all, and it did not matter that I was dirty and worn out with tiredness, that my hands shook and that the servants he had met had inevitably warned him that I was completely insane. All that mattered was that he was here.

I rode towards him, tumbled from my horse and splashed on unsteady legs across the flooded road, into his arms. If he was shocked by my appearance, he did not show it at all. All that showed in his eyes was the deepest sympathy and concern.

'I am too late,' I said. 'Dickon is not here, is he? I cannot find him, James.' My breath caught on a sob, and if he had not been holding me up I would have fallen in the mud at his feet. 'I have searched all over the country and I cannot find him.'

He smoothed my windswept hair away from my pale, dirt-streaked cheeks. 'Dickon is here,' he said quietly. 'He is quite safe. But you cannot go to him.'

'I must.' I tried to break away from his embrace but he held me fast. 'James, I must see him.'

'It was Thomas Knight who sent for me,' James explained steadily. 'It seems he had an attack of conscience, on account of the fact that he owes his life to you. He wrote to me, warning that you must not go back to the house, not stay here. Thomas is convinced that they mean to have you declared insane so that it will appear as if you have taken your own life. He says they plan to shut you away where you can never be found. Sarah Gideon is determined to become Sarah Glanville before the month is out.'

'Is she here? Is she in my house, with my sons, my husband?'

He took a deep breath, reluctant to confirm it. 'She is.'

I tethered Kestrel safely to a tree, turned, waded ankle-deep through the floodwater, scaring a pair of mallards into hasty, clattering flight as I retrieved the rowing boat James had brought with him. When he saw there was no arguing with me or stopping me, he climbed aboard too. We each took up an oar.

The flooded expanse of the moor offered no place at all to hide, no opportunity to reach the house in any degree of secrecy. She'd have been able to see us approaching from far away, and she was there, waiting for us in the great hall, alone.

She looked almost no different from the way she had before, only even more showy and extravagantly dressed, in vermillion silk and dripping garnets as red as her painted lips.

She took in my dirty face and hands, my ragged hair and filthy rags, and she looked well pleased. She offered me the most self-satisfied smirk, and then said condescendingly, and with astonishing gall: 'I bid you welcome to Tickenham Court.'

I stared at her smug, over-painted face and it was as if all the distress I'd kept bottled up over the ordeal of the past weeks was suddenly chan-nelled, had to find release. Unthinking, I did to her what Richard had done to me. I slapped her. Hard. Across her face. 'That was for Dickon,' I said, in a voice so calm and yet so wrathful that it did not sound like my own.

It had not wiped the smile off Sarah's face, only widened it, sharpened it, and I realised that my appearance and actions only served to confirm her accusations of insanity. I was proving them right, playing into her hands. I was my own worst enemy. But I did not care any more. I did not care. In fact, it was almost liberating to be considered mad. I could do whatever I liked. 'Where is he? Where is Dickon?'

She removed her hand from her cheek, which I was pleased to see was now much redder than the other one, despite the ridiculous amount of powder she was wearing. I was quite prepared to pull out the dagger that had so alarmed William Merrick if I did not receive a satisfactory answer from her. 'D'you hear me, you bitch? I want my son.'

'Well, you cannot have him, I am afraid,' she said, a touch flustered now. 'He is out.'

I did not believe her. 'Out?'

'He's gone to a tenant's cottage. A child there is running a fever. He insisted on taking some medicine and staying with the boy until the fever has broken.'

That was so like Dickon that I did not doubt now that she was telling the truth, but there had to be more to the story.

'You let him go?' I asked. 'You broke him then, in the end? He has done . . . what you wanted him to do?'

I saw instantly that it was not so. 'His brother has accompanied him,' she said. 'To mind him, and bring him back.'

Tears sprang into my eyes. *Well done, Dickon. And you said you were not brave.*

'Where is my husband?'

'He is sleeping.'

For some inexplicable reason, that threw me. There was an intimacy in those three words, a familiarity. *He is sleeping.* I knew, so well, how Richard looked when he was asleep. So many times I had watched over him after he'd suffered a nightmare. In the early days of our marriage, it was my greatest pleasure just to lie beside him and watch him. I knew the way his hair curled on the pillow, and his eyelashes fluttered when he was dreaming. I knew how his lips slightly parted. I knew that he preferred to sleep on his stomach, with his arm thrown up over his head, or on his right side, and that sometimes he would curl up his legs and his arms like a little boy. I knew the sound his breath made.

What did it matter to me? I never wanted to sleep beside him again.

'Wake him,' I commanded.

She did not move.

'Wake him, I said. Or I shall.'

She backed herself against the door, palms pressed to the wood, barring my way, as if for some reason she wanted to keep us apart, was determined to prevent me from going to Richard. 'I cannot.'

'Why not?'

'He's drunk.'

I looked at the floor, at the ceiling, back at her. 'So. He is a drunkard, a debtor, a would-be bigamist and a murderer. The pair of you are very well suited.'

She frowned. 'Murder?' She shook her head, gave a short laugh. 'Who said anything about murder? You think he means to kill you? Oh, no. Far better for us just to lock you away and throw away the key than run the risk of being tried for murder. He did say that for you, though, death would be far kinder than confinement.'

I was sorely tempted to tell her then how Richard had already murdered his own friend, but I did not want to drag poor Edmund into this, did not want to involve him in any way in the sordid mess that my life had become. Besides, there seemed a strong chance Sarah Gideon would commend such behaviour in any case.

'You were always so set on having my husband, weren't you? Why? Why him? Why have you gone to all this trouble?' I asked her.

In the moment's pause before she answered, as my eyes met hers, I knew that she had never truly loved Richard. Or if she thought she did, then it was the self-seeking kind of love, that looked only for what was to be gained. And I told myself that they were indeed well suited, were well deserving of one another, for Richard had loved me no better, had he?

Considering the way she had systematically set about turning my friends and neighbours against me and destroying my life, I'd assumed Sarah must hate me. But I realised now that, just as she was incapable of real love, so she must be incapable of hatred also. She did not hate me but was altogether indifferent to my feelings, as I imagined she was indifferent to the feelings of everyone but herself. Which made her the most dangerous kind of person. She was driven not by love or hatred but by pure self-interest. Maybe Richard was just the same. Maybe they had been planning this for years.

'Why do I want him?' she repeated with a snigger. 'Are you blind? He is a beautiful man. A gentleman.' She fingered one of her jewelled rings. 'He and I share an appreciation of beautiful things.'

'Then it is a wonder what he sees in you.'

Behind me, I heard James give a quietly congratulatory chuckle.

Sarah narrowed her eyes at me. 'He said you had a sharp tongue at times. 'Tis a pity your mind's not so sharp.'

I did not want to hear what Richard had said to her about me.

'I expect it must be difficult for you,' she went on. 'Seeing me here, in your house. Knowing it is I now who share your handsome husband's bed at night.' She stroked her stomach. 'Knowing I am to bear his child.'

I stared at her.

'That's right,' she said. 'I am carrying Richard Glanville's baby.'

'That is a lie,' I said, very quietly. But how could I be certain?

How could Richard? But even if it was true that she was with child, it might not be his . . . Still, why did it matter to me now? I had said it myself: Richard Glanville was a drunkard and a debtor, a bigamist and a murderer. I did not want him any more. In fact, I never wanted to see him again. The pair of them were in this together, were equally to blame. My husband had colluded and conspired with this woman to abduct his own son, to blackmail him, to accuse me of unspeakable things.

'May you rot in Hell,' I told her.

'Oh, I don't doubt that I shall. But I think it will be a much more interesting place in which to spend eternity than Heaven, don't you?'

Her total remorselessness was chilling, and it served somehow to confirm my worst suspicions of Richard, to suddenly take away all the pain of losing him. The man I had thought him would find no comfort in this woman's arms, would want nothing to do with her kind. A man who had murdered his friend and sought to swindle his wife and child out of their inheritance, however . . .

'You could not win him back, you know,' said Sarah. 'No matter how hard you tried. You never did know how to satisfy him, did you? How to give him what he needed? I pity him, wedded to a lunatic for so long, shackled to such an unsuitable wife. If he is a drunk and a debtor and a bigamist, then have you ever considered that it is *you* who have made him so?'

I didn't understand what she meant, nor why that stung me, but it did. James saw it and grabbed hold of my arm. 'She is not worth it, Eleanor.'

There was a noise outside, footsteps in the cross passage, voices. It was Will Jennings together with John Hort, both carrying muskets taken from my father's armoury. 'Everything all right, ma'am?' Will asked.

I experienced a moment's relief at seeing them, was about to reassure him that all was under control, until I realised he was not addressing me but Sarah.

'I suggest you leave now,' she said icily. 'While you still can.'

James gave an insistent tug on my arm, but I stood rooted to the spot. I stared her down, glad to see that for the first time she looked almost

afraid, despite the armed men waiting to do her bidding. I hoped in that
moment that I looked truly and totally insane. I hoped that I looked like a
madwoman, a witch, a sorceress, a necromancer. I hoped my eyes blazed
with a wild and terrifying vengeful light that would haunt her for the rest
of her days.

For added effect, I gathered a gob of spittle in my mouth and hurled it
at her face. As I let James lead me quietly out of the great hall, I looked
back at her over my shoulder, kept on staring at her as I watched her dab
it off with a lace-edged cloth.

Then the great oak door closed between us with a resounding clang. I
was standing in the familiar muddy, misty yard, outside my own door, on
my own land, and feeling utterly lost.

James was looking at me with what appeared to be unequivocal approval.
God bless him. What other man would approve of my behaviour just now?
'I told you I should have been born a boy,' I said, not sure now whether I
wanted to laugh or cry. 'Ladies do not curse and spit, do they? I hadn't
been planning a tap-room brawl, I assure you.'

'You gave her no more than she deserved,' James said. 'And you got
what you came for too, didn't you?' he added gently. 'You did not see
Dickon but I think that is probably just as well. It would only distress him.
You know he is well, and happy enough. He is being allowed to do what
he loves. And when you are no longer a threat to their plans, they will no
longer be a threat to his. Even if that harpy has a child, now or at some
point in the future, and is determined for it to inherit your husband's estate
instead of Dickon, as she surely will be, they will be doing the boy a great
service. He is not destined to be a squire but a country doctor. Running an
estate would only get in the way of his doctoring, and that's all the boy
wants to do.'

I nodded. 'But what do I do now, James?'

'Come with me,' he said, as if that would solve everything, and I almost
believed it could. 'Show me that little cove where you saw the unusual
Fritillary.'

As we rowed away, I looked back towards the house, rearing starkly
against the apricot and saffron sky. The last rays of the low winter sun lit
the traceried windows of the hall, but instead of making it look welcoming,
it looked forbidding.

James handed me his flask of whisky and, when I had thrown a warming slug of it down my throat, produced two hard-boiled eggs from his pocket, the staple diet for all his expeditions.

'Whisky and eggs,' I said, my lips cracking as they tried to form the unfamiliar shape of a smile. 'I feel better already.'

James looked appreciatively around him at the swans and wild geese and the submerged trees, the arc of the sky.

'Living beneath such a sky,' he said, 'it is no wonder you have such a love for all that's in it, for creatures with wings.'

'My father always did tell me my mind should never be on earthly things.'

'How could it be, in such a place as this? You said it was magical at this time of year, but it is more wild and beautiful even than I had imagined.'

All I wanted for now was to ride away from it, with James, to the coast. When we came at last to the edge of the water we mounted Kestrel and started towards the ancient ridge that led to Clevedon.

He made me talk of other things. Of the Royal Society, Hans Sloane and John Ray.

'How is John?'

'No better, sadly. David Krieg went to stay with him recently and prescribed some new physic for his legs. You do remember David, the Saxon physician?' James asked with an odd significance I did not even try to understand.

'Of course I remember him.'

'He is sailing from Bristol for Virginia in a few days,' James said, as if this news should be of the greatest importance to me.

'Is he?' I said, not much interested.

'He is in a fever of excitement to be there and take up his paintbrush. He has promised to bring back for me some more of the black and white sickle-winged specimens and the yellow spotted ones. You remember those, too?'

'I do.' The memory of magnificent butterflies fluttered and gleamed in my mind, sparks of beauty and promise where for so long there had only been despair.

'The New World,' James said, as a skein of wild geese called overhead and he lifted his eyes to watch them. 'It is there waiting, for those who are not daunted by wide rivers and endless skies, those who are brave enough to take their own path across wild open plains.'

I must have had an inkling then of where he was leading me, but I was so weary I could not think, could not resist. I was flotsam, carried along on a tide. I'd have let him take me anywhere, could have ridden with him beneath Somersetshire's vast sky forever. But too soon the track came to an end and there we were, with Ladye Bay below us and a sea crested with white. We dismounted and James took me to him and we stood in a gentle embrace on the rugged, windy cliff. We watched the winter sun sink lower in the sky and lay a shining path over the sea that led all the way to the far horizon.

'Remember the Red Admirals,' James said, so quietly, I was not sure if he had spoken at all or if it was only a whisper on the wind. 'Remember how you wanted so much to keep them. But you knew that if they were kept shut up in the dark, they might as well never have been born.'

Instinctively, my arms tightened around his back. 'Do not say any more.'

'I don't need to say it. You know it yourself. You know what you have to do, what you are meant to do. A husband does not need the law of coverture to take from his wife all that she has, all that she is. He does not need to lock her in an asylum to rob her of her freedom, of her very essence. We live in a society which expects a wife to be a helpmeet, prepared to suppress any interests or passions of her own, in order to devote every waking hour to tending to her husband's needs and wishes, finding complete contentment in ordering his household. And that is not you.'

I drew away a little so that I could see his face. 'But have you never wanted someone to do that for you, James?'

'What I want, what I have always wanted, is to see you become all that you can be. It is because I love you that I let you go. You were not made to be confined, Eleanor, not in any way. When you were sitting at the table in my parlour, which you tidied so diligently, when you were reading the travellers' tales from sea captains and ships' surgeons, when you heard them talk over the shop counter of their voyages and listened to David Krieg's talk of America at dinner, when you saw the wonderful creatures they brought back with them from distant lands and seas, can you tell me honestly you did not wish yourself far, far away from London and from my little shop?'

497

'No! Yes! Sometimes.'

The golden path across the sea widened as the sun dipped lower, to the rim of the world. It was so solid and so bright, it seemed you could step out on to it.

'I am no explorer, as you know,' James said. 'Nonetheless, I have been doing some exploring today. There's a little cave in this cliff, with a ledge inside it, always dry. A woman could go into that cave and it would be like a cocoon. She could shed her silk gown, and if she found something waiting for her on that ledge, she could come out again as a butterfly boy, as Isaac. And if her discarded silk gown were found by the seashore, all would believe she had gone from this world. And then she would be free, forever.'

The golden track across the sea shimmered enticingly as I stared at it. 'Come with me,' I said.

'Who would there be to receive all those specimens and letters?'

'They are only letters.'

'But I have made them my life's work. And you should not belittle their importance. You and I have said a hundred times more words to each other in letters than we have ever spoken face to face. It will be no different, wherever you are. I shall go on hearing your voice in the words you write to me, as though you are right there beside me. Your letters have sustained me through all the years I have loved you. I hear your smile, when you write something amusing. I touch the page your hand has touched as it formed those words, and I feel you are as close to me as you are now.'

'Your letters sustained me too,' I admitted. 'They were always my escape and sanctuary.'

He reached into his coat and took out his observation book and a pencil, handing them both to me. 'Now you must write to someone else. Now you must escape for good and find a new sanctuary.'

Eventually I took the book and the pencil, found a blank page, scratched out a few shaky lines. For Dickon. But for his father's eyes. I tore out the page and folded it, gave the book and the pencil back to James. 'I don't want her to get her hands on it.'

'I will go back to the house and send him to you.' James did not put the observation book in his pocket again immediately. 'It is a pity it is not summer,' he added. 'This is where you saw your mysterious little Fritillary, isn't it? We could have looked for one together.'

'I have one already,' I said. 'Pressed in the Bible, in my chamber. Take it.'

'If it turns out to be a new species, it will be named for you, and you will be remembered in butterfly books for all time.'

'It is you who should be remembered.'

'I am content to catalogue the finds of others, and for them to form the bedrock of a great museum to the natural world.'

'If I am remembered, I think it is more likely to be as the lady whose relations tried to prove she was mad, on the grounds that nobody in their right mind would go in pursuit of butterflies.'

He smiled. 'No matter. Nobody reading about you in years to come will think it at all strange to love butterflies and to want to learn more about them.'

'You taught me all I needed to know,' I said. 'About butterflies and about so much more. Always remember that those weeks with the Red Admirals were the most peaceful days and nights of my life.'

'Like the Red Admirals themselves. Beautiful and short-lived, and all the more lovely for it.' He reached inside his coat to put his book away and drew out something else. A pistol. He placed it in my hand. 'I have spoken to Richard Glanville,' he said. 'He is not like her at all. I do not think for one moment that he would do you harm, but just in case I am wrong.'

I curled my fingers round the cold dead weight of the gun and felt a knot in my throat. 'I can't say goodbye to you.'

He kissed me, a warm, open, loving kiss. 'Does that feel like goodbye?'

It did not.

'Will you think about what I have said?'

'I will.' But I could not watch him ride away.

If James had looked back as he left me, he would have seen me standing alone on the edge of the cliff, staring out to sea with the wind blowing my skirts back against my legs, whipping my tangled mane of hair back from my face.

I closed my eyes and prayed for deliverance.

The faces of all four of my children came in turn to my mind. Mary kissing a pink rose. Ellen with her rosary. Dickon trying to teach his pet swan to swim. Forest rowing a boat out on the floodwater. I lingered on each one and practised saying farewell. Then I saw my first family, my father and mother and my little sister, their faces so clear again they could have been standing right there before me, beckoning me to join them.

I thought then of Edmund, of Richard and of James. My father told me that the three stages of the lifecycle of a butterfly symbolised the three states of being. Life and death and resurrection. And yet I felt I had gone through three stages already. Three men I had loved, three very different men. My life with Edmund an uncomplicated and pleasant routine of day-to-day living, of eating, sleeping, raising a family, which for the most part had made me content: might have continued to content me had not Richard stirred up in me a maelstrom of wild emotion and dark intensity, like the miraculous transforming soup inside a pupa, potent and intoxicating and giving of life. And then James had loved me. His love had given me wings at last and would set me truly free, if I could only let it.

A pair of gulls glided beneath me. If I held out my arms and jumped, I was sure I would not fall but fly.

When Richard found me, I had been standing on the clifftop so long I felt as if I was a statue, a carved masthead on a galleon, proud and strong and forward facing. I sensed his presence behind me and slowly turned to him. I still did not know if I was going to leave this life behind, leave Tickenham forever, but just the possibility made me feel unfettered, strangely powerful.

In the gathering twilight, I saw that the past months had taken a far worse toll on him even than they had on me. He looked ill, was unkempt, unshaven. He wore no cloak, no coat even, just a shirt that was badly crumpled, the lace coming unstitched. His eyes looked bruised. And yet those beautiful eyes, like his whole being, still blazed with raw emotion. His gaze never left my face.

'How could you, Richard?'

He seemed unable to answer, to utter a single word. He just went on staring fixedly at me, as if he would climb inside my skull. He wore both dagger and sword at his hip and I held the pistol at my side. My finger instinctively tightened around the trigger. He saw me do it. He saw everything.

'How could you?' I repeated.

At last he found his voice, but only to echo what I had asked. 'How could you?'

'What did I do?'

There was the longest silence. 'You did not . . . trust me.'

This answer was so utterly unexpected that for a moment it stunned me, so that I did not move when he stepped up to me, did not register what was happening until I saw that he had raised his hand, as if he would strike me again or push me over the cliff. But he did not hit me, he did not push me, he touched my cheek, as if he needed confirmation that I was actually there. 'You did not trust me,' he whispered again. 'Why did you not trust me, Nell? "Love always trusts." Is that not what Paul said to the Corinthians? But you did not trust. You have always been so ready to think the very worst of me.'

I wanted to deny it. Could not.

'You never could hide your thoughts from me and it was always there, on your face and in your eyes. Mistrust. I pretended not to see it, learned to ignore it, hoping it would go away. But every time I saw it, every time you turned away from me, it was like a dagger piercing my side, twisting. When I saw the horror and fear in your face after I carried you in from the rain, and when I read that book Petiver had sent to you about Jesuits' Powder, I knew that you believed I had willingly brought about Edmund's death. That I was capable of murder. You believed me wicked enough to have killed my friend. They said you were mad and I wanted to believe them. I *had* to believe them, don't you see? I accused you of madness. Wanted to hear everyone else accuse you of madness in the most powerful terms. I wanted them all to sign their name to declarations against you. I needed to convince myself that you knew not what you did, that you had lost your wits. How else could I bear it?'

He spoke very quietly, very calmly. His words carried neither reproach nor recrimination, but were all the harder to bear for that, and there was in his voice and his eyes a mesmerising quality which meant I could not look away, could barely blink. Could only stare at him with mounting horror.

'From what James Petiver has told me, I take it you now know that it *was* Jesuits' Powder I brought back from London. But you still suspected me, didn't you? You thought I purposely gave you the wrong information about how to administer it? I did not. Nor was I negligent or careless with the instructions, Nell. I never had any. You forget that there was much fear surrounding the powder then. I was served by an apprentice who was so afraid of being accused of Jesuit sympathies he wanted to rush me out of the shop faster than you could say "Hail Mary". He did not trouble to mention dosage, and when you asked me, I did not have the heart to tell you that I had no idea. I could not bear to disappoint you. I so wanted to prove myself worthy of the trust you had placed in me, that I had seen blazing in your eyes when I left for London, that I had seen so very seldom. And never saw again.'

Tears stung my eyes. I could not shape a single thought, nor shape my mouth to speak. I was aware only of sensations of the most agonising pain.

'I rode without rest,' he said. 'I was so tired, it was as if I was drunk, and I spoke without thinking, did not believe it mattered so much anyway. Prescriptions are usually so arbitrary, aren't they? One physician tells you one dose and another tells you something quite different. I made the most terrible, terrible mistake and it is that which has haunted me ever since, that which has given me nightmares. You did see guilt in my eyes, oh, yes, every time I lay with you and felt a moment's happiness in your arms, I suffered the most insufferable guilt, but I loved you so much I'd rather have suffered it a million times over than be without you. You chose to believe I was guilty of murder, not of a mistake. You say you loved me, but that that is not love, is it? You loved only despite your better judgement. You never for a moment loved me unreservedly. And I needed that, Nell. It was all I ever wanted.'

'Richard, I . . .'

But he was not ready to let me speak. 'Every time we argued about the marriage settlement, I saw doubt and mistrust in your eyes. Every time. That is why I kept raising it. I hoped your reaction would change, but even after a decade of being married to me, you still half took me for a fortune hunter. That should not have mattered to me so much, when so many marriages are founded on fortune hunting, but it did matter to me. Why did it not occur to you that I resisted that settlement from the start, that it always hurt me, only because I needed some proof, something to hold on to, something to show me that you loved me above all else? I know you did it for Edmund's children, but I could not help but think that you loved the land and that house more than you loved me. That you loved Edmund more than you loved me. It seemed to me that you gave everything to him so readily, your estate, all of your trust. I wanted you to give to me what you had given to him. There is nothing I would not have done for you, nothing I would not have given to you. I would have died for you, Nell. That is how you know if you love a person, I think. If you would give your life for them. I would have given my life for you. But you gave me so little.

'The only time I laid a hand on you, you thought I had finally revealed myself as the ruthless villain you had always half suspected me to be. But I had read your treasured letters from James Petiver, and I saw, even if you did not, that he loved you, that for years he had loved you. He shared your passion for butterflies, the mainstay of your life, and it was as if you spoke to each other in a different language, a language I could not under-stand. You entered a world with him in which I had no place. If you had trusted me and loved me as I wanted you to, that would not have mattered. But you did not trust me and so I could not trust you. I doubted your love for me and so his presence in your life, your affection for him and his for you, was torture to me. I hated James Petiver, hated him, because he loved you and because it was he who sent you that book . . . the book that damned me in your eyes.'

I watched, appalled, as a single tear slid down his face. He wiped it away impatiently with his sleeve like a child and went on. 'I thought that in some way I could atone for what I had done to Edmund, by being a good father to his son. That is why I worked so hard at winning Forest's trust. Because I wanted to be a father to him, since he had no other. But even that disturbed you, didn't it? You distrusted my motives.'

'Why did you not say something?' I cried. 'Why did you keep all this to yourself?'

'What could I say? What would it have changed?' His face was wet with tears now and he let them fall unchecked. 'Half of the time I did not even know how I felt. It is astonishing, the capacity we have for denial, to practise deception upon ourselves, to block out a truth that is too painful to bear.'

I moved closer to him and he did not move away. He let me put my arms around him and his own arms went around my back, his fingers clutching at me. He turned his face into my neck and I felt the wetness of his tears and the scratch of stubble against my skin.

I stroked his tangled windblown curls and he made a sound, half moan, half whimper, and his shoulders shuddered.

'Hush,' I said, holding him tighter, kissing him and sobbing into his hair. 'Hush.'

I did not need a court to judge me. This felt like my own Day of Judgement. I had thought myself so enlightened. And it was as if only now had a mirror been held up to my face and I saw that I had been as blind as Dickon's hound, as blind as Edmund when he died.

It was not only Edmund who had been poisoned, it was me, and it was a far more dangerous, invidious poison I had taken than Jesuits' Powder.

Oh, yes, I had been bent on questioning my father's every belief: in eternal life, in metamorphosis, resistance to land reclamation, hatred of Papists. But I had clung in the pit of my being to his most ardent contempt for the men who had been his enemies in the Civil War, the men he believed to be untrustworthy, depraved and dissolute, morally corrupt. The things he'd hated and feared most because my mother had broken her most sacred vows to him and committed adultery with a sedge-cutter. So deep had that inherited mistrust been rooted within me, I had never entirely overcome it. *Reserve judgement until the truth is compelling*, wasn't that what John Ray had once said? Yet that was not what I had done.

There was a certain justice in my current predicament, I realised. Thomas Knight had used as his weapon against me the widespread prejudice against women who did not behave as was expected of them. But I was guilty of a far worse prejudice against my own husband. I had been reared on hatred and had allowed the vestiges of that hatred to taint my judgement of the man I loved and who had so loved me.

Richard drew away from me. 'When you left me I went to get drunk in Bristol,' he said. 'I have no recollection of it. I do not know how long I was there, or how much I drank, or how I ended up in her bed.'

'You don't need to explain any more.'

'Sarah told me she wanted to be my wife, to have my child. She wants it to inherit Elmsett, as if I had never had another wife, as if you had never been. And I wanted that too, Nell, I wanted it. I wanted to obliterate you. I did not care what she did,' he finished. 'I was beyond caring about anything.'

'And you hated me,' I said softly. 'You wanted vengeance, you wanted to hurt me, as I had hurt you. You wanted to betray me, as I had betrayed you.'

He did not answer, did not need to. That is the danger of loving too deeply. The capacity to hate just as deeply is always there. The light and the dark.

'Can you ever forgive me?' I asked.

'I love you,' he said starkly. 'I can forgive you anything.'

'I love you too,' I sobbed, stroking his face. 'I never stopped loving you. You need to know that. Even when I feared what you had done, what you would do to me, even when I saw that you hated me – I still loved you.'

He gave a little smile and it lacerated me. 'Can you forgive *me*, Nell? I need you to forgive me.'

'What is there to forgive?' He had taken a cold-hearted, scheming jezebel into his bed, but only after I had turned him out of mine. He had taken our son, but only after I had already taken him from his father and placed him in the care of a man who was my lover. He had accused me of madness, and what was it but a kind of madness, not to trust the man who had given me so much love? What was it but madness to accuse, of the worst possible crime, the man whose smile had always lit up my heart with its gentle charm and beauty? 'There is nothing to forgive,' I said. 'Nothing.'

But how could we even begin to find our way back from here, how could we ever find a way forward? There was too much against us. I did not see how it was possible. And yet how could I go, how could I begin anew, as James had suggested, without the person I loved most in all the world? How could I ever leave him now? How could I go on living, without ever seeing that lovely smile, without ever looking into his beautiful eyes? How could I kiss him goodbye and know it was the last kiss?

How could I stay?

I let go of him. I turned my back and walked away down the narrow rocky path to the bay. I carried on down the beach and, at the water's edge, I waited for him. The tide was coming in, crashing against the headland, as low grey clouds scudded above us. The encroaching waves hissed on the shingle, like the whispers of conspirators.

He wrapped his arms around himself, his hands tucked under his armpits.

'On his deathbed my father warned me to protect Tickenham Court against unscrupulous Cavaliers,' I said. 'And it was those that words that stayed with me, shaped the way I saw you, saw everything. And because of that I no longer want Tickenham Court, no part of it. The very thought of it sickens me now. I cannot be Eleanor Glanville of Tickenham Court any more. But there is only one way for me to be free, truly free.' Only now did I hold out the letter.

When he reached out and took it, I saw that his hand was trembling.

'If I had known what you have just told me, I might not have written it,' I said. 'But I think, in a way, it is as well that I did. I've told Dickon to sign the affidavits that say I am mad. Or that he may sign one that says I am dead. I told him he cannot be accused of perjury, whatever he says about me. If he swears that I am dead he will be committing no sin. I shall be dead – dead to this world and gone to a new and better one.' I let my cloak slip to the ground and shrugged off my second-hand woollen dress. I bundled them both up and handed them to Richard. 'Put them on the rocks for me. Where they will easily be found when they come to search for me. It will be all the proof they need. They think I am mad, and this is what the mad do.'

'But, Nell, you can swim,' he said desperately. 'I taught you how to swim.'

'You did,' I smiled. 'You taught me well. And Dickon knows it. James too. Nobody else. I am asking you to guard my secret for me, Richard. You wanted me to trust you and I am putting all of my trust in you now.' I put the clothes on the pebbles by his feet. 'Will you do this for me. Will you do as I ask?'

'Do not ask it of me!' He lurched for me and grabbed my hands and somehow we both collapsed on our knees in the lapping water, were pulled down with each other. I sank beside him in the wet sand and took him in my arms, held him tight, and we clutched at each other, rocking together to the rocking of the waves.

'Please, Nell, I beg you. Don't go. Stay with me.'

He stroked my face, kissed it as I kissed his, both wet with tears.

'I have to go,' I wept. 'I have to.'

'Where?'

'I don't know yet. I shall only know it when I find it.'

'I will come to you,' he said. 'Let me come. Wherever it is.'

'You need a home,' I said gently. 'You cannot to back to wandering. Whereas I . . . I think I need to wander.'

'Then so do I. All the years I was in exile, I dreamed of coming home. I thought that home was a manor house, surrounded by watermeadows and filled with beautiful things that I would never have to lose or leave. But Elmsett is not home. Tickenham Court is not home. You are home for me, Nell. Only you. Wherever you are is where I want to be. I told you once I'd love you if you had nothing to give me but your heart. I swear I will ask nothing from you but that. There would be no secrets between us now, nothing that we cannot share. Believe me, trust me, as you have never trusted me before. Send for me and I will come. Wherever it is that you are going.'

I did not tell him that it could not be. I gifted him hope. I gifted it to myself. For is not hope the most precious gift there is?

Virginia: Summer 1700

Five Years Later

So, James, we go on with our letters, just as we began. This is a new beginning for me, in a new world. It has taken me many months and much hardship and subterfuge to reach it, but now I am here. In God's own country.

My clothes were found on the rocks, where Richard left them, and he and Dickon and you are the only ones who knew I exchanged them for the shirt and breeches you had left for me, with your uncanny foresight, even before I came back to Tickenham. With the moonlight making a silver path on the black sea just like the golden one the sun had made earlier, I walked as a lad to Bristol and found David Krieg. Later, with him, I boarded the ship bound for America.

It was such a typically thoughtful suggestion of yours that the little orange and black butterfly be named the Glanville Fritillary. I like to think that Richard's name will live on, too, that he and I are bound together for all time, that we shall soar forever on those bright lovely wings.

It is only love that prevails in the end, and there are so many different kinds of love, aren't there? And one of the most precious of all must be a mother's love, of which Richard was deprived, a love that is unconditional and eternally forgiving.

I can forgive Forest entirely for what he has done. Of course I forgive him. There is surely nothing a child could do to a mother that she could not find it in her heart to forgive utterly.

I always knew that my will would never stand and that he would use my alleged madness to try to have it overthrown. I knew that the girls would take direction from their older brother, would be swayed by him, as they always were. I wanted them all to be free, as I am now free, but they were, of course, perfectly free to choose differently. And if Forest had accepted my last wishes, there would not have been the grand spectacle of the court case. How I should have liked to have been there to see that for myself!

All those affidavits presented against me, signed by the people of Tickenham, accusing me of committing the very great sin of beating bushes with sticks for worms, wandering the moors at dawn with my clothing in disarray, and surely the greatest crime of all, having to send out to the inn for ale, because I did not brew my own as a gentlewoman should!

I am glad I was so vilified. Had I not been, then the great Hans Sloane and John Ray would not have been subpoenaed to come to the Assizes in Exeter and defend me, to testify that entomology is a sane and sober science, and that I was a great entomologist. It does not matter that even their testimony was not enough to prove my sanity, to prove that it is a valid occupation to observe butterflies. It was enough for me. I was so astonished and touched to know those gentlemen regarded me so highly. It is just a pity that recognition often comes only after death.

I am glad that I saved Thomas Knight's life, for he has given me mine.

If I had not been so maligned, I should not be here.

Awake thou that sleepest and arise from the dead, and Christ shall give thee light.

James, I have awoken and I am bathed in light. I find I am in the most wondrous place. There are bright, fragrant flowers of unspeakable beauty, and lush green grass, and mighty forests and ravines, and in the distance a range of mountains that look almost blue. The people of this land are adorned with beads and with the bright feathers of wild birds. The air is scented with honeysuckle and it is alive with butterflies, so many butterflies, with iridescent wings as wide as my hand.

Instead of white swans, there are pink birds living on this land's swamps. Imagine that! There are crimson birds, and birds with brilliant green wings and blue heads. And they are always singing. Here, the sun is always shining, even in the autumn when the leaves burn with scarlet and gold of such vividness it is a sight to behold. And I hope that, through my eyes, you too can see this magnificent New World you say you are not brave enough to see for yourself.

The old one is dead to me, as I am dead to it. Eleanor Glanville is dead. Water claimed me in the end, as seems fitting. I have no burial place. My coffin was the dark and stinking hold of that ship, my shroud a pair of boy's nankeen breeches and a shirt, the clothes of Isaac, the butterfly boy, bound for America to help the good Dr Krieg, to devote every waking moment to collecting specimens for you. Sleeping below deck every night, swaddled in a hammock, my mind turned, naturally, to caterpillars awaiting metamorphosis.

I left the grey English waters behind and sailed to an ocean that glowed with phosphorescence, that was alive with schools of jellyfish, where dolphins swam beside the ship and great whales broke through the waves. The water claimed me, but only so that I could be liberated, baptised, so that I could throw off suffering and pain and enter a bright new world. Like a butterfly, I once gorged on material things; I was entombed; and then I took flight and am transformed.

Now I am free to watch butterflies every day, to do what I was put upon this earth to do. My life here is very simple. I live off the land and what you pay me for the specimens I send to you, which will form the bedrock of that great museum, as beautiful a shrine to our friendship as ever there could be.

I am reborn, just as my father always told me I would be. I know now that all that he taught me, on that count, was good and true. And secure in that knowledge, we have nothing at all to fear.

Because if I have learned anything at all, it is this: there is always, always hope, even when it seems that all hope is lost.

So please tell Dickon that he may let his father know that my name now is Hannah. It is a good Puritan name, but I did not choose it for that. I chose it for my own reason. It means, 'The grace of God'.

Historical Note

Lady of the Butterflies is based on fact. The Glanville Fritillary is named after Eleanor Glanville, who is now recognised as a distinguished pioneer entomologist. According to her biographer, she 'gained happiness from natural history in the midst of great fear and sorrow'. When her relatives, led by her son Forest, brought lunacy proceedings to set aside her will, on the grounds that 'no one who was not deprived of their senses would go in pursuit of butterflies', it became a *cause célèbre*.

Eleanor's escape to America is my own flight of fancy. Her true final resting place remains a mystery, as does that of Richard Glanville. Amongst James Petiver's many correspondents there was an unknown girl from Virginia, named Hannah, and a 'butterfly boy'.

James Petiver (1663–1718) was the first person to give butterflies English names, many of which – Brimstone, Admiral, Argus, Tortoiseshell – are still used to this day, and it is with his catalogues and preserved specimens that the documented history of butterflies begins. After his death, his collections were purchased by Sir Hans Sloane and formed the foundation of the British Museum, later the Natural History Museum, where some of his correspondence with Eleanor and the folios in which he pasted specimens are preserved. It is recorded fact that Eleanor's son Richard was James Petiver's apprentice and that he was abducted from Aldersgate Street by his father, though I have brought the period of his apprenticeship and abduction forward a few years, for the sake of narrative drive.

After overturning Eleanor's will, Forest sold the Manor and Lordship of Tickenham. He apparently lived on at various houses in the parish and died unmarried at the age of forty-four, leaving no will. None of those who left testimonies had anything good to say about him. His half-brother Richard (Dickon) Glanville married and settled near the Somerset village of Wedmore and was one of the first general practitioners. I understand his descendants still live in Wedmore. Eleanor's daughters seemed wary of marriage after their mother's experience of it. Mary Ashfield died a spinster in 1730, and of Ellen Glanville it is known only that she was living unmarried in Rome in 1733. Counter to accusations presented against Eleanor at the Assizes, her son Richard went on lasting record as saying that he had, 'the best of mothers and the worst of fathers'.

The disease commonly known as ague in the seventeenth century, and which claimed so many lives in the Fens and Somerset Levels, was eventually identified as malaria. Peruvian bark, so called Jesuits' Powder, is the source of quinine. The actual cause of Edmund's death is not, however, recorded, and though Eleanor did have a servant called Bess Knight, I gave her an illegitimate half-brother for the sake of plot.

The Tickenham, Nailsea and Kenn Moors were not properly drained until the last years of the eighteenth century, but fenland was one of the earliest habitats lost to butterflies. The progressive draining that was begun in England in the seventeenth century left less than three per cent of fenland still remaining by the twentieth. This destruction resulted in the first known butterfly extinction, that of the Large Copper, which was last seen in 1851. The Swallowtail survives now only in the Norfolk Broads. Of Britain's butterflies today, 71 per cent are now declining and 45 per cent of species are threatened, mainly due to loss of habitat. The Glanville Fritillary is classified as rare, but is still to be found on the Isle of Wight. I am reliably informed that Natural England has plans to reintroduce it to Sandy Bay at Weston-Super-Mare, a few miles from Eleanor's ancestral home.

During the course of writing this novel, Britain was hit by repeated and devastating floods, caused in part, according to leading environmentalists, by the loss of wetland floodplains. In 2007, the study of butterflies was formally accepted by the Government as an important environmental barometer.

I don't think anybody would see a love of butterflies as a sign of lunacy now, and Eleanor's story is particularly pertinent at a time when Butterfly Conservation is urging people to leave legacies to the charity in their own wills, to help save Britain's declining butterflies. They have never needed support more than now and I am certain that if Eleanor was alive today she would be leaving a legacy to this cause. I like to think that in telling her story and working with Butterfly Conservation to raise awareness of the plight of Britain's butterflies, I am helping her to do just that. In a way it makes up for what her relatives did to her all those centuries ago! For general enquiries about leaving a legacy to Butterfly Conservation, or to find out more about its work, contact Butterfly Conservation on telephone 01929 400209, email info@butterfly-conservation.org or see www.butterfly-conservation.org.

Acknowledgements

I referred to many books whilst researching the various aspects of this novel.

For details of Eleanor's life, and for suggesting the title of this book, I am indebted to *The Making of a Manor: The Story of Tickenham Court* by Denys Forrest (Moonraker Press, 1975). Further biographical material on Eleanor is taken from *Elizabeth Glanville, an Early Entomologist*, by Ronald Sterne Wilkinson (Entomologists' Gazette vol. 17), *The Life of a Distinguised Woman Naturalist, Eleanor Glanville* by W. S. Bristowe (Entomologists' Gazette vol. 18) and *Mrs Glanville and her Fritilliary* by P. B. M. Allan (Entomologists' Record vol. LXIII). Details of James Petiver's life and career are taken from *James Petiver, Promoter of Natural Science* by Raymond Phineas Stearns (Proceedings of the American Antiquarian Society, October 1952). Michael A. Salmon's *The Aurelian Legacy: British Butterflies and their Collectors* (Harley Books, 2000) contains invaluable advice on early butterfly collecting and collectors, while more timeless information about butterflies is to be found in *Butterflies*, Dick Vane-Wright (Natural History Museum, 2003), *The Millennium Atlas of Butterflies in Britain and Ireland* (Oxford University Press, 2001) and *Breeding Butterflies and Moths: A Practical Handbook*, by Ekkehard Friedrick (Harley Books, 1986). *The Spirit of Butterflies: Myth, Magic and Art* by Maraleen Manos-Jones (Harry N. Abrams, 2000), *The Pursuit of Butterflies and Moths: An Anthology* by Patrick Matthews (Chatto and Windus, 1957) and *Butterfly Cooing Like a Dove* by Miriam Rothschild (Doubleday, 1991), go a long way to capturing the magic of butterflies.

For details of life in seventeenth century England, I relied very heavily upon David Cressy's *Birth, Marriage and Death: Ritual, Religion and the Life-Cycle in Tudor and Stuart England* (Oxford University Press, 1997),

The Weaker Vessel: Woman's Lot in Seventeenth-Century England by Antonia Fraser (Phoenix Press, 2002) and *Ingenious Pursuits: Building the Scientific Revolution* by Lisa Jardine (Anchor Books, 2000). Also of great assistance was *The World of the Country House in Seventeenth-Century England* by J.T. Cliffe (Yale University Press, 1999), Liza Picard's *Restoration London: Everyday Life in London 1660-1670* (Phoenix, 1997), *Bonfires and Bells*, David Cressy (Weidenfeld and Nicolson, 1989), *Women and Property in Early Modern England*, Amy Louise Erickson (Routledge, 1993), *Mind-Forg'd Manacles: A History of Madness in England from the Restoration to the Regency* by Roy Porter (Athlone Press Ltd., 1987), and *The Cavaliers in Exile, 1640–1660* by Geoffrey Smith, (Palgrave Macmillan). For the history of malaria I referred to *The Miraculous Fever-Tree* by Fiammetta Rocco (HarperCollins, 2004).

Her Own Life: Autobiographical Writings by Seventeenth-Century English-women (Routledge, 1992) helped me find Eleanor's voice and some of her vocabulary, while *The Somerset Levels*, Robin and Romey Williams (Ex Libris Press, 1996) and *The Natural History of the Somerset Levels* by Bernard Storer (Dovecote Press, 1972) helped me describe her home. Michael William's *The Draining of the Somerset Levels* (Cambridge University Press, 1970) and *The Monmouth Rebellion: A Guide to the Rebellion and Bloody Assizes*, by Robert Dunning (Dovecote Press, 1984) were also invaluable resources.

I had almost finished writing *Lady of the Butterflies* when I discovered two books, one old and one newly published, which provided me with fresh inspiration and information on the quest to understand metamorphosis: *John Ray, Naturalist: His Life and Works* by Charles E. Raven (Cambridge University Press, 1950) and the wonderful *Chrysalis: Maria Sibylla Merian and the Secrets of Metamorphosis* by Kim Todd (I. B. Tauris & Co, 2007), the latter of which is the fascinating biography of a seventeenth century butterfly collector and artist who was obsessed with butterfly life-cycles and travelled to the New World on an expedition to study them.

My great thanks go to Stewart Plant, who gave me access to Eleanor's lovely home and the now well-drained moors around it, as well as providing insight into what it is like to grow up and live at Tickenham Court. Thanks also to Dave Goodyear of the Natural History Museum and the researchers at the Guildhall Museum.

For endless encouragement and patience my thanks as always to Tim, as well as to Daniel, James, Gabriel and Kezia (who was born at the same time as the idea for this book). Also to Jane Gridley. A big thank you to Broo Doherty for her belief and support, and to Rosie de Courcy and all at Preface. Lastly, to David, for being my inspiration.